The Devil's Fortune

Praise for *Summer's Squall*

"The author obviously did a lot of research for the book and it showed, not in boring lists of facts, but in the way the book was fleshed out. In addition, the descriptions were beautifully done, not telling but showing the beauty of the area."

Among the Reads Review

"Good character development, plot, surprises, thought provoking with excellent descriptions of the Colorado mountain country."

Amazon Reviewer

Praise for the Award-Winning, Chincoteague Island Books: *Island of Miracles* and *Island of Promise*

"A beautiful account of the love and the healing support of community!"

Chandi Owen, Author

"This is the kind of story that makes me long to run away from my perfectly fine life for the sole purpose of stumbling upon something magical."

Alex Jacobs, Author, The Dreamer

Praise for Award-Winning, *Whispering Vines*

"The heartbreaking, endearing, charming, and romantic scenes will surely inveigle you to keep reading."

Serious Reading Book Review

"Schisler's writing is a verbal masterpiece of art."

Alex Jacobs, Author, The Dreamer

"Amy Schisler's Whispering Vines is well styled, fast paced, and engaging, the perfect recipe for an excellent book."

Judith Reveal, Author, Editor, Reviewer

Also Available by Amy Schisler

Suspense Novels
A Place to Call Home
Picture Me
Summer's Squall

Contemporary Fiction
Whispering Vines

Chincoteague Island Trilogy
Island of Miracles
Island of Promise
Island of Hope (coming 2019)

Children's Books
Crabbing With Granddad
The Greatest Gift

Collaborations
Stations of the Cross Meditations for Moms (with Anne Kennedy, Susan Anthony, Chandi Owen, and Wendy Clark)

The Devil's Fortune

By Amy Schisler

Chesapeake Sunrise Publishing
Bozman, Maryland

ISBN: 978-1-7322242-2-3

Published by:
Chesapeake Sunrise Publishing
Amy Schisler
Bozman, MD
2019

To my husband, Ken, my biggest supporter and a fan of pirates. I love you.

The human heart has hidden treasures, in secret kept, in silence sealed; The thoughts, the hopes, the dreams, the pleasures, Whose charms were broken if revealed.
-Charlotte Bronte

PART ONE

ST. CLEMENTS MANOR
The Maryland Colony South
June 10, 1725

Anne Bonny stood on the shoreline and watched the ship sail away under the light of the moon. One of the most notorious women in the world, she was now abandoned in a strange land, left to fend for herself. She cursed the captain of the ship as she turned to look at the house overlooking the river. She was surprised he had only dumped her on the beach instead of making his way up to the house. She was sure, from the looks of the house, that there were many riches inside. She put her hand to her bosom to ensure that she still possessed her own small bag of riches.

The red-brick structure, topped with dormer windows and three tall brick chimneys, looked empty, perched on the shores of the Wicomico River. Judging by its size, architectural design, and brick exterior, Anne surmised that the house was probably built by one of the colony's wealthier landowners, perhaps a Calvert or a Slye. Anne knew that both families had lost their heralded roles in the colony, but they owned property in these parts at one time. She and her crew knew the names of all of the landholders in the colonies though they weren't always apprised of the latest news about the families or their estates. A life on a ship wasn't ideal to knowing the latest society gossip. Of course, Anne didn't care about gossip, unless it was gossip about where people kept their valuables. She once heard that Blackbeard had his sights set on raiding the Slye estate and absconding with their treasure, but he had died several years back without ever making it this far upriver.

Turning back to the shore, Anne gazed across the river out to the great Potomac and beyond to the Virginia shoreline. Unlike many women of the time, she knew the geography well. Raised on a ship and taught to navigate as well as any man, Anne had plundered and pillaged with the best of them. Only now, on this lonely shore, did she realize what that life of adventure had cost her. At only twenty-eight, there would be no future for her; that was certain. She could find refuge for a night or two in the stately, brick house, but there was nowhere for her to hide. Her picture was posted in towns from the Caribbean to Massachusetts, and though some thought she was dead, others would be out for her blood. She looked at the house. She had never seen so many windows on a house before. A palace, yes, but not an ordinary house. The sight made her wonder once again who the inhabitants were.

Anne cradled her protruding stomach. The journey from her jail cell in Cuba had been a long one, and she was quite far along now. Her last bairn had saved her from the gallows, and she was due to be hanged as soon as he was born. She just narrowly escaped her fate when a mate helped free her from her cell and hastened her to the dock. She fled to the nearest ship and hid below decks, but the captain, as fierce a pirate as her Jack had been, discovered her and demanded payment. Having no virtue left to protect, she gave him the only payment she could afford, and he gave her another nine months of misery.

This time, however, the bairn would not be able to save her from execution, should she be caught, for the time had come for her crying out. Another pain gripped her as she stood on the shore; it was time to head inside. She knew that other women in her condition had help when their time came. The last time she delivered a bairn, in her jail cell, her dear friend, Mary, had been with her; and she in turn was there to help young Mary. There would be no help for Anne when this bairn arrived. Neither Mary nor her child had survived Mary's crying out. There was little chance that Anne would survive hers, but she was determined to hold on, for the sake of this child, the one stolen from her after his birth in the jail cell the previous year, and the one she abandoned in Cuba, though those children surely knew nothing about her.

Anne tested all of the doors until she found one unlocked, obviously the main door used by the family as it was around the back of the house, near where the family's carriage would be parked. The night breeze rushed past her, ushering her into the small entryway. A carpeted runner ran from the back door to the front door, alongside a staircase, painted butter yellow. Anne went toward the front of the house where two rooms sat on each side of her. To her left, Anne saw a cozy red-paneled room, with a deep, wood-framed fireplace, recently used but cold and dark now. The room contained a sofa and comfortable looking chairs, bookcases lined with leather-bound tomes, and lacy curtains at the windows. A spinning wheel sat in a corner next to a chair with a hand-embroidered pillow. Turning to the room on her right, Anne saw the long, smooth table, a wooden bowl of cherries in the center, and long matching benches tucked under it. A grand, glass-doored hutch sat on one cream-colored wall, laden with dishes, and another wood-framed fireplace vied for attention on the far wall.

Anne quietly moved through the room toward the open door at the other end. Beyond a small corridor, she found the cooking kitchen. The large, brick fireplace held an arm, upon which a kettle hung above nested logs. A heavy cast-iron pot sat on small but sturdy feet in the bottom of the fireplace. Beside the hearth, sat a small baking oven, and Anne could imagine the smell of freshly baked bread drifting from the kitchen toward the main house. A pump was perched above a dry sink, and utensils hung from the ceiling and the walls.

Most of what she would need, she could find in here—water, a basin, a knife, perhaps some small rags. She would also need blankets and a soft bed—things that a house of this means was sure to provide. First, though, she needed a hiding place. If she and the bairn survived the night, which was doubtful, they would need the coinage and gems she had managed to pilfer from the ship she stowed away upon. The captain was none too happy when he learned of her presence, after her escape from the jail, and was even more annoyed when her condition became known, even though he was complicit in her current predicament. He threatened to turn her in, but that would mean coming into contact with the authorities himself. He would rather abandon her and his own offspring to die on the shoreline than turn her over to her captors. Some thought there was a code for such matters, for abandoning a pirate in need, but Anne knew that was not the case. There was no honor among thieves and no code among pirates. Every ship's captain made up his own rules, and those could change with the wind.

Stepping carefully in and out of the rooms, Anne listened for a change in the sound of her footsteps. Her breathing was becoming labored, and the pains increased, but she refused to lose focus. Finally, she found a soft spot in the floor. She pried up the board as a spasm took hold, forcing a shrill and guttural scream to escape from her throat, nay, from her very soul. She loosened the ties on her bodice and pulled the leather pouch from its hiding place. She laid the bag inside the hold beneath the board and hastily popped the board back into place before she found her way to a grand feather bed, the likes of which she had never lain.

It was there that she and the bairn were found the following morning, one dead, and the other miraculously alive.

June 10, 1725

Robert McMillan and his two young children returned to the manor, weary and worn. Robert's sister, Cora, was alive, thank the good Lord, but they had to bury one of her twins. He ran his fingers through his thick black hair as he entered the brick house from the back door near the carriage path. He had to check on the hogs, having left them for the past two days, and he hoped they were well. He hadn't had time to think about his own home and land when his sister and her husband, John, needed him so.

"Papa." Young Crystin tugged on his sleeve as he reached into the small under-stair closet for the boots he wore in the yard.

"Papa," Crystin insisted. "I think she's dead."

"Crystin, child," he sighed as he turned toward the four-year-old. "It was the boy who died. Your girl cousin is doing fine."

"No, papa, the lady. I think she's dead. And her baby, too." Crystin pointed up the stairs.

The hairs stood on the back of Robert's neck. Had someone come into the house while they were gone?

"Papa, please, come see," Crystin tugged, and Robert followed her up the stairs to his bedroom.

"Mercy me," Robert exclaimed when he saw the woman and child in his marital bed.

"Crystin, get out," he asserted as he drew closer to the blood-stained bed.

"But Papa, is she—"

"Crystin," he roared before blinking his eyes and swallowing his temper and his fear. He turned to the little girl. Her eyes were wide, and tears threatened to spill down her chubby cheeks. "Dear child, go find your brother. Tell him to ride to the Boyds' farm and ask them to fetch Dr. Stern."

"I want mama," the little girl said, tears sliding down her cheeks.

"Mama is taking care of Aunt Cora. Now, Crystin, go find your brother, Evan. Now."

"Yes, papa," she whispered before scooting out of the room.

Robert rolled up his sleeves and wiped his brow. He found a pulse on the woman, but he didn't check the child. The baby boy was a pale, bluish color, his cord still attached to his little body. He was tiny, early perhaps, and appeared to not have taken a breath. He returned his attention to the woman. She was with fever but breathing, albeit shallow. He hoped the doctor would arrive with haste.

*****

"Ye has more color today." A woman with the familiar Irish brogue entered the room with a tray of broth and a cup of whiskey. It was all Anne had been allowed to eat or drink for the past two days, since giving her son the name, Jack, and allowing permission for him to be buried out back.

"The doctor says yer to git up and move around a bit this morning."

The thought of getting out of the plush feather bed made Anne's head swim. She was sure it was because she wasn't accustomed to being on land, though she supposed it could also be due to the birthing and loss of blood. She closed her eyes and inhaled the scent of the seawater that floated in on the breeze.

Opening her eyes, she looked toward the lace curtains that fluttered at the open window. The soft, pink quilt lay at the foot of the bed, tossed aside during Anne's feverish night. Cross-stitched samplers hung between the windows and over the bed. Closets flanked the fireplace where the night fire still smoldered in the warmth of the sunny morning.

"As soon as yer better, the master has given orders for ye to be taken to 'is brother's house. Miss Cora hasn't been able to make enough milk to feed the young'n, and yer milk should still be aplenty." The woman prattled on as she helped Anne sit up and take the tray.

Anne shook her head as she tried to understand the woman's ramblings. She was going to nurse another woman's bairn? What did they think she was? A nanny goat?

"And Miss Beth is ready to come home. She won't be sharin' her bed with the likes of ye." She huffed to show her distaste for the woman in her master's bed. "Miss Cora is awful sick," the woman continued on, taking the quilt and shaking it with fervor out the window as if to rid it of any pests that Anne may have brought in with her. "She's been in bed e'er since she lost her bairn. O' course, the little girl survived, but that don't seem to be o' any comfort to Miss Cora. She wants both bairns. A shame, 'tis. Her little Jenny is as sweet as a sunrise."

"Excuse me, but who is Cora?"

The woman stopped adjusting the covers around Anne and stood up, her eyes widening with surprise. "Why, she's Master Robert's sister, o' course. She lost her bairn the day before, er, well, the day ye arrived. Out o' her mind with grief, she is, and she's got the other bairn to feed."

"What makes anyone think I'm willing to feed the bairn?"

The woman frowned as she looked down at Anne. "Well, it doesn't much matter if ye is willing or not. Master Robert says ye will do it, or the magistrate will take ye away to the gallows."

So, they know, Anne thought. *If I refuse to tend to the woman and her child, they will hang me for piracy.* She closed her eyes and took a deep breath. She thought about the satchel under the floorboards. Had they discovered it? She didn't know. She'd have to do what they said and nurse the bairn and listen for any talk about her satchel. She'd do what she must and bide her time until she could get back into the house and claim what was hers. Then she'd find a way to board another ship. Once she had her strength back, she'd be as fit as any man, and she'd do whatever it took to be captain of her own ship again.

August 1729

Anne heaved the wash from the baskets and piled it into the tub. She muttered to herself as she worked.

"Washn' and cookin' and lookin' after that spoilt child. What kind of life is this?" she grumbled. "I should be on the high seas, commanding a ship and giving orders instead of taking them." She huffed and tried to blow the fiery red hair from her eyes, but the tendrils stuck to the perspiration on her forehead. "It's hotter than tarnation in this heaven-forsaken place," she complained as she pushed her hair back with her wet, soapy hand and began scrubbing the clothes in the tub.

"Mither, what are you saying?" little Jenny asked, using the Gaelic word. It was Anne who had taught Jenny the word for a woman who parents a child, among other Gaelic words, phrases, and songs.

Anne took a deep breath and looked at the child. She couldn't help but smile. Yes, the lass was spoilt, and Anne had a hand in that, she supposed. Her Jack had been laid in the ground, but this living child had suckled at her breast. Jenny was the only reason Anne hadn't slit the throats of everyone else in the house and fled on the first ship that came into port. She supposed she had mellowed in the past few years, but she loved the little girl as if she were her own, nay, more than she had ever loved her own.

"I'm just singing a song from home, lassie."

"Can you sing it to me?" the child begged, her eyes sparking with delight.

Anne laughed. "Ye ken the words as well as I do, Lassie. Let's hear ye."

The little girl laughed and launched into the most recent song Anne had taught her.

Beidh aonach amárach i gContae an Chláir.
Beidh aonach amárach i gContae an Chláir.
Beidh aonach amárach i gContae an Chláir.
Cé mhaith dom é, ní bheidh mé ann.

'S a mháithrín, an ligfidh tú chun aonaigh mé?
'S a mháithrín, an ligfidh tú chun aonaigh mé?
'S a mháithrín, an ligfidh tú chun aonaigh mé?
'S a mhuirnín ó ná héiligh é.

The children's song washed over Anne as she scrubbed the clothes on the washboard, rinsed them, and hung them to dry. The little girl's tinny voice could scarcely hold a tune, but the sound and the story of a girl asking her mother if she could go to the fair, contented Anne. It reminded her of home, a home many years gone, from which she was taken as a little girl by her father. For years, Anne was dressed as a boy and called Andy. She married her husband, James Bonny, just to spite her father, and little good it did her. Her father's dislike for pirates and mistrust of James had them both kicked out of the house.

Anne thought about her husband and about the second man she had taken off with. Calico Jack, as he was known, was a fierce and vengeful man, but he held Anne's heart in his palm like a fistful of jewels. She even abandoned their first-born son to a woman in Cuba so that she could rejoin her lover on the sea.

Anne shook her head. What was she thinking? To give up her child only to lose the next two—one to the jailer and the other to the angels. Raised in Ireland as a good Catholic girl, she knew better than to do the things she had done, but she did them anyway, and she had nothing to show for it. A missing child, an unbaptized bairn, a bairn in the ground, and now the sentence of spending her days as a nursemaid and laundress. If only she could get back into the manor house. If only she could find the satchel she left behind before her time of crying out came, and the bairn was taken home to God. If only she could take the bag, find a ship, and sail to Cuba. She'd have to leave Jenny behind, but she could reclaim everything that was rightfully hers.

July 1730

Anne tried to hide her belly as she served tea to the Mistress of the house. Never the same since the day she lost the bairn, Cora just stared out the window. Not that Anne knew how she was before. She'd only known the after. There were good days—days Cora played with Jenny, read to her, even smiled at the little girl. Then there were the rest of the days—the days she wouldn't eat, wouldn't dress, wouldn't even get out of bed. Today wasn't so bad. At least she'd dressed and come down to the dining room, but her mind was still in her bed, or in the grave with the bairn where it seemed to be most of the time. At first, the doctor had said that it was birthing sickness, that some women got that after their crying out. However, Mistress Cora never got well again, and Anne didn't think she ever would.

Anne had gained a new understanding for the love a mother could have for a child. Anne had not been there for any of her children. Not the boy she abandoned in Cuba to run off with Jack, not the bairn she birthed in jail, and not the child who died in her arms. Alas, Jenny had given her the gift of a child's love, and, this time, she vowed that things would be different. This time, she would keep this bairn and shower it with love, the way Jenny had showed her she could.

"Anne," Cora said quietly.

"Yes'm?"

"You can leave me now."

Anne nodded and left the room. Neither woman looked at each other, and Anne wondered if Cora knew. What had she expected? As soon as the bairns were born, and Cora could get out of bed, she had moved from the master bedroom. She hadn't been back since. Anne knew this to be a fact. And poor Master John. He was a healthy, virile man. Why should he be punished for something he hadn't caused?

Anne stopped in the entry and stood in front of the piece of furniture with the low cabinet, a mirror on front, meant to let a woman know if her ankles were showing. She smoothed her hand over her belly. No, Master John shouldn't have to suffer because of the disposition of his wife. And Anne shouldn't have to suffer the curse of never being a mother.

Anne thought about the child within her. She knew that the Master would never claim him, but he would see that the child was taken care of. And as soon as the time was right, Anne would find a way to take the child and run. She just needed to get back into the manor house and claim what was rightly hers, and now her child's.

June 1732

"Don't ye go near that fire," Anne scolded Sean as he toddled away from her. She was boiling water for the wash while trying to keep an eye on her son. She wiped her brow with her apron, but it did little to stop the sweat from running down her face.

She longed for the deck of a ship, the wind in her hair, the open seas, and the endless sky. She loathed the work she did, the restrictive clothes she was forced to wear, taking orders, and being summoned to the bed of a man who cared only about his needs and not her own.

As she stared off into the trees, she heard the rattling of a carriage. She turned to see Master Robert coming into the yard. He climbed down from the driver's seat, nodded her way, and went into the house. She had overheard that he was remarrying, his young wife having succumbed to smallpox the prior winter. He had three young children, two boys and a girl, to care for, and he was going to need a wife to help around the manor. Aileen, the woman who cared for Anne those years ago, wasn't as young as she once was, and she needed help looking after the young'uns.

A door slammed, and Anne inclined her ear toward the raised voices.

"I need her," Master John said. "What will Cora do without her help?"

"It's about time Cora woke up and started taking care of herself," Robert told his brother-in-law. "You've let her wallow for much too long. It's not healthy for my sister or my niece for that matter. She needs to be a wife and a mother again. Maybe if you'd taken her back to your bed instead of…" He looked toward Anne.

"Watch your tongue," John warned. "You've no right to accuse me of anything."

"There's no accusation. Everyone knows who the father of her child is. And it's a disgrace to my sister that you've taken a pirate wench to your bed."

Anne's heart thudded. It was the first time anyone had referred to her past since she came to help Mistress Cora. She knew that her likeness was once posted on the docks all along the seaboard, but she didn't know if any of the McMillans had seen them or if any were still hanging there. Was she being sent to prison? Was the magistrate on his way here at this moment? And why now? She had been living with Master John and Mistress Cora for six years now. Why turn her over to the magistrate now?

Anne wrung her hands as she looked at her child. What would become of Sean? Was she to lose this child, too? The only one she ever wanted?

"Anne," Robert called. "Go, pack your things. And the boy's."

"Where are we going?" she asked contritely.

"Home," Robert said. "Now, hurry."

"Home?" Anne inquired, picking up Sean.

"Yes, home. To the manor. Now, get moving," Robert snapped at her.

"What rights have you got to take my servant?" John asked.

"She showed up at my house those years ago. I gave her to you when Cora needed her. Now, I'm staking my claim on her."

Anne hurried into the house to get her things. She was going back to the manor! She was going to be able to find her hidden satchel and leave this place. Anne felt real hope for the first time since the day she stood on the shoreline, watching the ship sail away.

*****

Each day, Anne noticed things about the house that she hadn't that first time she was there. Being in labor tended to narrow one's focus. Now that she was living in the house, Anne was intrigued by the architecture. Though no expert on anything that stood on dry land, even Anne was able to recognize that the house was unique. The foundation, which included the brick portico in the front, was a perfect square. The two rooms at either end were also perfect squares. The outside of the house formed a collection of perfect rectangles with the height of the brick walls equaling the height of the pitched roof. This all made River Terrace truly a sight to behold.

Having lived on a ship for most of her life, Anne had always been fascinated by houses and noticed things about them. She knew enough to know that this house was unique. Aside from the geometrical architecture, she knew that the brickwork was unlike most other brickwork of the time. The chimneys were stacks of small, narrow bricks rather than the more popular large bricks that formed elaborate, and often times, ostentatious chimneys of other houses she had seen throughout the colonies. Even the bricks that made up the exterior walls were distinctive. They were laid out in narrow rows, alternating red hues, so that the house resembled a chess board with narrow dark and light red bricks.

Anne found herself in a constant state of amazement each time she discovered something new about the house and its tenants.

"How long have you lived here, Master Robert?" she asked one night at dinner. Unlike at Willow Grove, Anne took her meals with the family at River Terrace.

"Other than when I was at school, since I was a lad," he answered. "My father built the house and the barn after we were granted the land."

"Did he build it himself?"

Robert chewed his cornbread, and Anne waited for his answer. She could see his tongue probing his upper gums as though a kernel of corn had found its way between his teeth. He smacked his lips and wiped his mouth with his napkin. "I don't believe so. I remember another man being here a lot at the time, but we lived in a small log house over yonder." He pointed toward the back corner of the lot. "And we, John and I, weren't allowed to be near the work as it was being done. We were quite young. Why do you ask?"

"Aye, I've traveled up and down the colonies a great many times, and I've never seen a house quite like this. It's a character in itself."

"Aye, 'tis. My father was quite a learned man. He studied in Florence and Paris and was very interested in architecture."

"But he was a doctor, aye?"

Robert nodded. "Aye, he was a doctor in England and then here."

"And you never wanted to be a doctor?"

Robert lifted a brow and regarded her for a moment, his chicken leg perched in front of his mouth. "I thought about it, but finance was more interesting to me."

"But you're a farmer. Why farm when you could be a banker?"

"I was a banker." A dark cloud entered his eyes. "Until Beth passed and Aileen became infirmed and unable to tend to the children."

"Oh, yes," she said meekly. "I had forgotten that you worked in the town before…"

Anne looked around the house, not as grand as Versailles, which she remembered seeing once shortly after it was built; though for the colonies, the house was more than simple.

"Did your mother decorate the house?" she asked, changing the subject back to a more agreeable one. She thought of the expensive lace and velvet cushions that adorned the parlor and the expertly made quilts and rugs in the bedrooms. Not her bedroom off the kitchen, of course, though even that was nicer than she imagined it would be.

"Some of it. Beth made it her own, God rest her soul."

"May I be excused, father?" Evan said. "I have studies to do."

"Aye," Robert answered. "You've got to keep up your schoolwork so that you can go to William and Mary next year."

"Yes, father." Evan took his dishes to the kitchen and returned to the room. "May I use your desk, father?"

"Aye. It's yours for the rest of the night." Robert smiled, and Anne found herself smiling at the man who studied at Eton and graduated from King's College but returned to his home in the colonies. She admired how much he loved his simple farmer's life, his family, and his grand but somehow simple house.

December 29, 1733

"When you brought me, I was of the mind that you were betrothed," Anne said as she removed Robert's shirt.

"You were of the wrong mind." He unbuttoned his breeches. "I couldn't replace Beth with any woman, and I didn't want to."

"And now you have me." Anne helped him lower to the bed and removing his boots.

"Aye." He caught her face in his hand and forced her gaze to his. "But I will not be tricked. Leave me to undress myself and go fetch me a whiskey."

"Can you manage?" she asked, standing and taking his shirt, folding it over the nearby chair.

"I can manage. I might be half-frozen and weak with fever, but I don't need the likes of you warming me."

"Hmmp." she shook her head and headed toward the door. "'Tis not likely I'd make a fool of myself over you."

"My brother-in-law was a different story, aye?" He slid his breeches to the floor and rolled under the covers.

Anne stood still in the doorway. Without looking back, she said in a low voice, "It was your brother-in-law who took me to his bed. I didn't ask for his hairy hands to be on my body nor for his seed to enter my womb."

"No, though you didn't fight back either, and I reckon you could have killed him in his sleep if you had wanted to."

"I could have killed him while he was awake if I had wanted to," she said calmly before going down the stairs.

Strange woman, he thought as he stared up at the ceiling. *Hard worker, kind to the children, never shirks her daily chores. But she has a wary look about the eye, and I've often caught her gazing out on the water as if she's waiting for a ship to come take her away. If the day comes, will she take her boy with her? What else will she take from me when she goes?"*

He didn't like where his thoughts went after that, so he closed his eyes and summoned sleep. When she returned with the hot stones that she slid under his mattress, he kept his eyes shut and forced his breathing steady. He would not defile his wife's memory by allowing himself the pleasure of a pirate woman, but it was the pirate woman's face that he saw in his mind as he drifted off to sleep.

December 30, 1733

The fever took hold during the night, causing Robert to toss and turn, throwing the covers off before pulling them back over himself again. His dreams were filled with memories of Beth, her smile, her laugh, her gentle ways and soothing voice. He awoke, drenched with sweat, after his subconscious mind saw Anne raising a knife to his beautiful bride. His mind, though dense with fever, was no longer clouded by uncertainty. Anne was no more than a witch who cast a spell over him, and he would not give into her wanton ways.

When the morning dawn pierced the shadows of his room, Robert felt a little better. He could hear Anne moving about the rooms below and wondered what she was doing so early.

Did she ever sleep?

He eased himself to the side of the bed. Sitting up, he placed his feet on the floor and took several deep breaths, trying to stop the dizziness that washed over him. The chair, onto which he had tossed his breeches, was just out of his reach. He mustered the strength to stagger toward it and grasped the pants, pulling them to him in an urgent attempt to stay upright. Collapsing back onto the bed, he hastily dressed. He could not afford to lose another day's work, and the boys were too young to take on all of his chores.

"What the devil do you think you're doing?" Anne roared as she entered the room with the same tray with which dearly departed Aileen had brought Anne her meals when she lain in the bed with fever some seven years past. The maidservant had succumbed to smallpox in the fall, and he thanked God each day that his children had not gotten it themselves.

"I have work to do," Robert feebly answered, the fever-induced headache still nagging his brow.

Anne placed the tray on the dressing table and stood in front of him, her hands on her hips. "Master Robert, you need to stay in that bed for at least another day. I will send Evan and young James up, and you can recite a list of chores to them, but you will stay in that bed."

"They're too young to do everything properly," he argued but was suddenly too fatigued to stand.

"Properly or not, they can do them. And Evan is near fourteen now, practically a man. And he's nearly as tall and strong as you are."

"Papa." Evan stood in the doorway. "I can do your chores. I know exactly what to do, and I can tell James. We'll get it all done."

Too weary to protest, Robert simply nodded and retreated under the covers. Anne was right. He hadn't noticed how old Evan had gotten, though he was almost a man indeed. He could handle the chores for a day or two.

December 30, 1735

Two years, Robert thought as he looked at the ceiling. *For two years, I've battled fever, stomach upset, pain, loss of feeling in my limbs, and sometimes the inability to walk. If only Dr. Stern knew what ails me.*

"How are you getting along today, Robert?" Anne asked from the doorway.

"Not very well, I'm afraid. How are the boys doing today?"

"Oh, they've got everything under control. The hogs and horses have been fed. The chickens are happy. We got five eggs today, so breakfast will be a good one."

Five measly eggs. Robert closed his eyes. *My family practically starves while I lay in bed.*

"And the stores? Do we still have enough food for the winter?"

"Aye, Robert, we have more than enough. With the work you were able to do and all that the boys did this past harvest, we had a very good year. You know that."

Robert wrinkled his brow as he thought about the previous harvest. Did they have a good year? His thoughts were often jumbled, and he was never certain that his memory was serving him correctly.

"And Crystin? Where is she?"

"Robert, don't you remember? Crystin is here, managing the farm. She's a smart lass, she is. She keeps things running in fine order when Evan is away."

"Away? Where is Evan?"

Anne shook her head and looked at Robert with pity. It was a look he despised but could do little about. "Robert, Evan is home now, for Christmas, but he will return to William and Mary after the New Year. He is sixteen now. Do you not remember?"

Oh, yes, that's right. Evan attends college now. Maybe we aren't starving. Maybe things aren't as bad as they seem.

Robert nodded and closed his eyes, assured that all was well.

"Will you be getting up this day?" Anne asked.

"Shortly," Robert replied though he wasn't sure his legs would hold him this morning.

"Very well. I will start your breakfast."

Robert waited until Anne left the room and then managed the effort to drag his legs to the side of the bed. He sat up and took a deep breath before reaching for his cane. Hauling himself from the bed, he used the cane to make his way to the window. His gaze went to the water, and his heart skipped a beat.

Riding the waves, and heading toward his shoreline, was a ship with a black flag. The flag depicted crossed bones over a heart. It was an ominous sight and one that Robert was sure hadn't been seen in the Tidewater region for nearly twenty years. How had that ship gotten past both the Virginia and Maryland patrols?

Summoning the strength, Robert made his way to the chair that held his breeches, sat down, and got dressed. What would they say when they found Anne living in his house? What would she do? She had remained loyal to his family for so long. Would she turn on them now?

*****

Anne spied the ship from the window above the water pump. Her heart leapt at the sight. Would she finally be free?

Free from what? A warm home, plentiful food, happy and loving children? Her dear Robert?

Her mind raced as her thoughts collided. This was what she had prayed for, wasn't it? It had been quite some time since she prayed to return to the sea. Her life at River Terrace was not easy, but it was pleasant. And though he didn't know it, and probably never would, she was in love with Robert McMillan, with his whole brood.

She watched as the ship dropped anchor. A rowboat was lowered to the water just as the outside door to the kitchen flew open.

"Anne, pirates," Evan breathed.

"Aye, I see them. Go fetch your brothers and sister and take them to the cellar."

"No," he protested. "I am the man of the house now. You will take them to the cellar. I'll stay here."

Anne saw the fear in his eyes even as he straightened his spine and tried to look like the man he was becoming.

"Evan, go fetch the others quickly. We don't have time to squabble. I might," she faltered and looked away. "I might know how to reason with them."

Evan looked at her for a moment before turning to go. He hesitated and looked back. "It's true then, aye? You were one of them?"

"There's no time for prattle. Go, now."

Evan nodded and hastily went to fetch the others. Anne watched the men climb from the boat onto the shore as she listened to the children hurrying into the cellar. She breathed deeply, wringing her hands, and tried to think of what she would say and do.

"Are you going with them?" Robert asked quietly from the doorway. Anne turned to face him.

"My life is here now. I do not wish to go…" She let the sentence trail off as she looked away.

"But they might insist," he finished the sentence for her.

"The children are in the cellar. Perhaps you—"

"Don't. I'm not hiding in my own house."

Anne nodded before reaching for the guns above the fireplace. She handed the rifle to Robert and kept the pistol for herself.

"This one is for distance. It would be better if I held the—"

"No," Anne said. "You keep back. I will talk to them." She hid the pistol under her apron and opened the door. Squaring her shoulders, she went out into morning sunlight to meet the visitors.

*****

Robert's weak and trembling legs betrayed him and gave out as he watched her walk out the door. He cursed as he grabbed the nearby butcher's block and tried to steady himself. The rifle fell to the floor. Grasping his way across the room from the butcher's block to the pump, he watched through the window. He held up his spyglass to get a better look.

He was intrigued by the looks of the men. Some wore hats while others wore kerchiefs around their bald heads. Some were covered with tattoos, and a few had piercings in their ears. They all wore leather boots and carried weapons at their sides.

Anne stopped and called out to them. He couldn't hear what she said, but the men halted. There was an exchange of words taking place, and Robert wished he knew what was being said. After a few moments, Anne nodded and turned toward the house. The men followed. What was going on?

*****

Anne led the men toward the house and prayed that he didn't know. Did he? Could he? She had aged ten years, and in the time since, she had borne two children and helped in the raising of four others. Her skin was the pale color of her youth, not the ruddy, sun-kissed complexion of her wild years. The thing he surely could not see was the softening of her heart. Did it show in her eyes? Were they not the same as they had been back when he was one of her crew? She walked in front of them, careful not to look back at Mad Matthias Hawkins.

When Anne opened the door to the kitchen, Robert and the rifle were gone. She hastened to the broth she had begun brewing for the mid-day meal.

"I've got broth cooking. You could use that on a cold day like this." She stood tall, hoping she looked defiant, and refused to look at the men as she ladled the broth into a wooden bowl.

"Surely, you're not alone in this house." The man pulled a lock of her red hair from her kerchief and lifted it to his nose.

"Aye, for the morning. My master and his family will be home for the noon meal." She hoped that would dissuade them from staying.

"Your master, you say," another man said. "Not your husband."

"No, my husband is dead." As she spoke, she felt the cold stare of Mad Matthias.

"Aye, he is," Matthias said. "More than a decade now."

Anne froze, her hand suspended above the pot. She felt the tension in the room rise but held fast in her spot, refusing to turn around or acknowledge him. With a shaky hand, she ladled more broth into the bowl.

"And who might that husband be?"

"'Twas Calico Jack himself," Matthias said. "Me ole cap'n."

Hot broth splashed on her dress as Anne's arm was grabbed, spinning her around. The bowl fell to the floor, spilling broth on the smooth stones.

"Anne Bonny," the man smiled, his missing front tooth giving him a menacing, lop-sided grin. "Well, well. By all accounts you're supposed to be dead."

"Not by all accounts." Matthias took an apple from a hanging basket and biting into it. "I heard she made off with a heavy sack of gold before jumping ship and swimming to the mainland, disappearing into the cliffs."

Not quite, but too close for comfort, she thought.

"That's ridiculous," Anne retorted. "Do you think I'd be serving broth and tying nappies on bairns if I had a sack of gold."

The man with the missing tooth looked around the kitchen and laughed. "Nice try, but a sack of gold would be more than enough to build this fine house and furnish it with these nice things. Perhaps you were caught, and the family forced you to go to work for them instead of sending you to the gallows."

The hair on the back of her neck stood as she thought about how close he was to the truth.

"There was no sack of gold." She pulled her arm from his grip. "This house was here long before I was abandoned on the shoreline." The pistol in her apron felt cold and heavy, and she knew that she couldn't take six men by herself. Where had Robert gone?

"Cap'n Brown," a man called from the main house. "Lookie what I got here."

Anne's gaze followed the voice, though she couldn't see where he was or what he had. The captain gave her a hungry look before turning and heading down the corridor. Anne followed, trying to figure out how many men she could take down on her own.

She gasped when she reached the room where they took their meals. Robert was lying on the floor, his eyes closed, his breathing labored. The rifle was at his side. No wonder he hadn't come to her aid. His sickness had overcome him.

"Your master and his family are out for the morning, you say?" Matthias said with a sneer.

"He must have come back early. He is very sick. You can see that. He has bouts of delirium and fainting spells. He's of no use or harm to you." She resisted the urge to go to Robert's side.

"And what about the rest of the family?" Matthias looked around. He stepped over Robert and went to the sitting room. He returned with a schoolbook in one hand and a wooden horse in the other. “There are certainly more. Where are they?”

“Gone, I told you,” Anne said, remembering the fierceness she once possessed. “They’re out until noon. You can be gone before they come back if you eat your broth and leave.”

“And why would we leave?” the captain asked. He waved his arms around the room. “You have all of the comforts we could want right here. This man,” he nudged Robert with his boot, “is of no danger to us. Certainly, a wife and children would offer no harm. I think we should stay here for a time, wait until the thaw, perhaps. We might find the wife and children to our liking, just as I find you to my liking.” His wagged his tongue at her, and his eyes danced as he teased her, testing her reaction.

“When the family returns, they will have men with them. Lots of men. Master Robert needs help, and the men are coming to tend to his land.”

“What tending could there be in the cold of winter? There is nothing in the fields.”

“There are animals—”

“Which would have been cared for at dawn. No, I don’t think there is anyone coming with them. *If* they are coming at all. Perhaps…” the captain looked around. “Perhaps they are all here now, hiding somewhere.”

Anne felt her blood run cold.

“Find them,” he ordered his men. He took hold of her arm, yanking her so hard that the pistol fell from her waistline. “What have we here?” He bent to the ground and retrieved the weapon. “Were you going to use this on us while we sat at your family table and slurped our broth?”

Anne held her chin firm, refusing to look away or back down. Sensing her indignation, the captain raised the pistol and brandished it against the side of her head. Anne fell to the ground, her head exploding in pain.

"Search the house. Find the rest of them. And take whatever you want. There is sure to be fine jewelry here and money. Gather it up along with whatever food can be taken onto the ship."

The men dispersed as Anne's world turned black. The last thing she saw, as her vision blurred, was Robert's lifeless body, lying next to hers.

PART TWO

CHAPTER ONE

The wipers were completely ineffective as the storm doused the windshield with sheets of rain. Courtney strained to see into the dark night, but the glare from the streetlights only made the visibility worse. It was the kind of rain that made it impossible to see and nearly impossible to steer. The pelting drops pounded her windshield with thundering force, seeming to come sideways rather than from the sky above. Everything was shrouded by dark clouds, the glow of twilight absent from the sky.

Courtney could just barely make out the red glow of the stoplight ahead. As she neared the intersection, the light turned green, and Courtney continued down the Baltimore street, hoping to get to her apartment before the streets flooded, as they were apt to do when the rain was this heavy.

As Courtney entered the intersection, she never had time to process the bright headlights beaming through the passenger side window before the sound of crunching metal and shattering glass accompanied the impact that rolled the car over and over, onto its side, and into a utility pole.

July, One Year Later

The clouds gave way to sunshine as Courtney reached for her sunglasses. She gripped the steering wheel with one hand as she slid the expensive Oakleys, a necessity these days to help prevent headaches, onto her nose and quickly placed her other hand back on the wheel. She was aware of every car on the road, every traffic pattern, even every squirrel that might dart into her path. Being the survivor of an accident that, by all accounts, should have taken her life, made Courtney hyper aware each time she got behind the wheel.

Courtney passed by soybean plants, tall green and yellow stalks of corn, and huge, sweet-smelling leaves of tobacco. Though she never smoked, Courtney would forever love the smell of fresh tobacco leaves. It never failed to take her back in time to when she would ride on the back of her grandfather's tractor as he and his team gathered the previously hand-cut stalks, already drying in the sun, and then speared them and lay them into rows on the trailer bed for hanging in the barn to completely dry. She opened the windows to fill her senses with the memory of that idyllic time. Tobacco fields were few and far between now, and Courtney wanted to soak in the scent while she could.

She meandered down the winding, country roads, listening to a local radio station that seemed to play no singers younger than the George Jones and Tammy Wynette generation. The tunes added to her nostalgia as she envisioned her parents singing and dancing in her tiny, childhood living room. Courtney let the memories flood her mind as she drove. It seemed more than fitting to relive her childhood as she neared the house where she spent many summers in her younger years, in fact, the happiest times in her life.

St. Mary's County, in Southern Maryland, was a place that, in many ways, still resembled its colonial roots. Chesapeake Bay tributaries carved the county into dozens of water-surrounded towns and flowing fields of corn, tobacco, and soybeans. Its many waterways made the county the perfect place for the bustling naval base that was built during World War II and still employed most of the county's workforce. The area surrounding the base continued to expand, in the years since its creation, into housing developments, shopping malls, and restaurants. However, the rest of the county remained the proverbial land that time forgot, where Friday nights meant high school football, and most of the men worked in the fields or on the water, a place where one could find open spaces filled with peace and quiet.

Turning off the main road, really nothing more than a narrow, country road itself, Courtney continued another couple miles to the gravel driveway in front of the old, white, one-story farmhouse that sat in the heart of the town of Bushwood. Set close to the road, the house had a small front yard, with a circular drive lined by straggly-looking forsythia bushes, and a backyard that had been parceled down to an acre. The adjoining acreage displayed perfectly aligned rows of corn, no longer a part of the original farm and no longer fields of tobacco.

Courtney turned off the car and gazed through the windshield at the sagging house with its peeling paint, beveled porch, and missing shutters. She sighed as she remembered what the house had looked like back when her grandfather had been alive. While everyone in the family tried to pitch in to help her grandmother, it was clear that the house that Granddad had built, almost fifty years prior, was not standing up to the test of time.

Breathing in deeply and mustering the courage to see if the inside was as badly neglected as the outside, Courtney opened the door and climbed out of her SUV. Though she cringed every time she filled the Ford Explorer with gas, she vowed to never again own a small car. Feeling safe while on the road was not just a matter of choice for Courtney; it was a primal need.

Over the past year, Courtney's world had changed dramatically. Having survived the accident, though in critical condition, she remained hooked up to monitors and in a medically-induced coma for several weeks. When removed from the coma-inducing medicine, she continued to be sedated for many days before the doctors decided to allow her to fully awaken. Once awake, her head still ached, and her motor skills were slow. Miraculously, there didn't seem to be any permanent damage to her brain. Though her mother might argue otherwise as the first thing Courtney did, once awake, was break off her five-year engagement to the perfect-in-almost-every-way Spencer Carlton.

Months later, a long scar, not yet hidden by her hair as it slowly grew out, travelled down the side of Courtney's face, from her scalp to her earlobe, cutting dangerously close to her left eye. The shattered windshield sent a long shard of glass into her face at the same time the air bag pounded into her body and caused the massive concussion. In what the first responders and hospital medical team all deemed a miracle, the crash left Courtney almost unscathed except for the scar and head trauma. The blow to her head took away the ability to walk and do other simple tasks, but hours of physical and occupational therapy helped her recover her motor skills in time. The driver of the other car, a man who had no business being on his cell phone in that weather, had been almost as lucky, but his spinal injuries were going to take much longer to heal. Courtney almost felt sorry for his family when the judge ruled on her behalf and awarded her over a million dollars for his negligence.

Courtney walked up the few short steps onto her grandmother's porch and remembered how she would take them in one long, running jump as a child. She opened the door and immediately felt the calming effect that this house always had on her. She was home.

"Gram, I'm here," Courtney called. The smell of tomatoes filled the house, beckoning her to follow it to the kitchen. There she found her grandmother standing in front of the stove, stirring a large pot of boiling tomatoes.

"Courtney!" Her brown eyes sparkled as they took in her granddaughter. "You're finally here. Come give me a hug. I can't leave the stove just yet."

Courtney embraced her soft, slightly round grandmother and peered over the older woman's shoulder to inhale the heavenly scent.

"Canning tomatoes?"

"Yes, the best batch Ben and I have had in years."

Courtney's grandmother always spoke as if her husband of forty-nine years was still in the house. Courtney supposed that, in many ways, he still was.

"You can put your bag in your room. I put fresh sheets on the bed this morning and opened the windows to air it out."

"Thanks, Gram." Courtney gave her grandmother a kiss on the cheek.

She went behind the kitchen and through the pantry of the cookie-cutter house. When Ben added the pantry and bathroom, many years after building the house itself, he installed two doors, one on each side of the bathroom, connecting the necessary room to both ends of the house. Courtney made a stop in the little room, decorated with pink rugs and matching shower and window curtains. When she was finished, she exited the door on the opposite side and went to the room that had been her mother's as a child. The bedroom was the room that Courtney had claimed for herself when she began spending her summers in the country as a young girl. In some ways, it felt more like her own room than the one in the house where she grew up. This was where she could truly relax, where there were no expectations, no need to be the brainchild who was always pushed to excel more than others, no need to stay up all night studying for the exam she already knew she would ace, nobody making fun of her for her cheery outlook and plain-Jane looks. In this room, she was simply Courtney McMillan, beloved granddaughter.

After a thorough assessment of the room, that assured her it was just as she remembered it, Courtney headed to the car to get her suitcase. She looked at the other rooms as she passed through them. Despite the condition of the outside, the inside was as neat and cozy as it had always been. Throw pillows dotted all of the beds, chairs, and sofa. Knick-knacks brightened the shelves and tabletops, and photo albums were piled all around the house—photography had been one of her grandfather's favorite past-times.

Stealing herself against the blistering heat, Courtney hauled her suitcase out of the SUV, heaved it up the steps, and rolled it into the house and down the hall. She wasted no time but went right to unpacking, laying the clothes neatly in the tissue paper lined drawers or hanging them in the closet. She breathed slowly and deeply as she worked, willing the eternal pounding in her head to not grow fiercer.

She didn't know how long she would be living in the house, though until her own place was habitable, this would be home. She looked forward to sharing the house with her grandmother once again and wished for the thousandth time that her grandfather was still there with them.

Courtney picked up the photograph that sat on the dresser. She wore a white dress and veil as she stood in front of her mother's lilac bushes. Her grandparents were on each side of her. They all smiled as her mother took the picture, creating a lasting memory of her First Communion. The little girl in the photo had no idea that, someday, her grandfather would be gone, and she would be living with her aging grandmother at the age of thirty, wondering what she was going to do with the rest of her life. Courtney shifted her gaze from the rugged, copper-skinned man on her right to the beautiful, raven-haired woman to her left.

Lilian Helen Gibson was seventeen when she met Benjamin Eugene Russell. She was a coat check girl at a local club, and Ben, four years her senior, was a regular attendee with his friends. He used to tease that he knew the first time he ever handed her his hat and coat that she would someday be his bride. Lily, on the other hand, was coy each time they met, not letting on that she was the least bit interested. It drove Ben crazy and made him all the more determined to make her his own. It wasn't until after they were engaged that she told him the truth—that Lily was head over heels for Ben from the moment she laid eyes on him. She wasn't allowed to date until she turned eighteen, and her father would have ended the relationship before it began had he known that this 'older man' was interested in his daughter, so she hid her feelings from everyone, including Ben.

Courtney thought about the story as she gazed at the image of her grandmother. Though she was now soft around the middle and trying hard to conceal her grey hair with her at-home dye, there were still traces of that beautiful girl who stole Ben's heart. Lily had dark brown eyes that twinkled when she laughed, and a smile that could light up the darkest night. She was strong and resilient and was afraid of nothing. And though she didn't go to college, she was one of the most intelligent women Courtney had ever known. She had the kind of smarts you couldn't learn in school, and Courtney was determined to soak in all the knowledge she could while she had the chance. Courtney had a truly impressive IQ, but her grandmother had all the intelligence Courtney needed in mind and heart. In short, her grandmother was everything Courtney had ever wanted to be.

"All settled?" Her grandmother asked from the doorway.

"Settled for now," Courtney answered, placing the picture back on the dresser and smiling at her grandmother. "I have no idea how long I'll need to stay. There's so much work to be done on the house, and how long the permits will take is anybody's guess. I hope you don't mind."

"Oh, nonsense. This is your home, but you and your brothers don't get down here as much as I wish." Lily frowned, and a cloud passed over her features before she brightened and smiled warmly at Courtney. “It’s so good to have you here, especially after we all thought…”

Courtney went to her grandmother and took her hands. “Don’t worry, Gram. I had no intention of leaving you all.”

“Well, I’m glad to hear that.” Lily blinked back a tear. “Because I have no intention of going anywhere any time soon. Now, are you hungry? I’ve made your favorite—chicken salad with chips and a fresh bowl of peaches.”

“I’m starving.” Courtney wrapped her arm around Lily and leading her toward the kitchen.

*****

Courtney pulled up in front of the house, not knowing whether to laugh or cry. She had always been fascinated by the colonial-era house and used to fantasize about living there. She spent her childhood hearing the stories about hidden pirates’ treasure and secret passages. Her excitement about owning and restoring the house had been building for weeks now, and she could hardly believe she sat there, staring at the building that was now deeded in her name. That building was in a deep state of disrepair, with a sagging porch and leaning chimney, and bright-white honeysuckle vines covering everything—the house, the barn, and the few unidentified bushes that sat beside the house. There were stray green shingles littering the yard, and the red trim around the windows and door was chipped and peeling, but the house was all hers. She turned off the vehicle's engine and climbed out.

Courtney walked through the tall grass, noticing abandoned gardens and what was left of an old well, and she smiled as she thought back to all the times she tossed a penny inside the opening while closing her eyes and making her wish. Be careful what you wish for, she thought as she stopped and gazed at the house.

The oldest part of the house was perfectly symmetrical, with a red door in the middle, flanked by two windows on each side, each filled with old wavy panes that would most certainly cost a fortune to replace if broken. The green roof held five, evenly spaced dormer windows. A wooden porch, which had seen better days, bordered the front of the house. It looked strange to Courtney, and it took her a minute to realize it had not existed when she was a child. To the left of the main part of the house, sat the addition, built with brown cedar siding that both flattered and contrasted the whitened red brick of the old section. It had red-trimmed windows that matched the older windows. There were four windows that ran across the front of the brown siding. A built-out section in the center of the wall held a tall red-brick chimney.

Carefully maneuvering her way around the rotten boards on the ugly, added-on porch, and thinking that it had to go –fast, Courtney put the key in the dead bolt and turned it. As she pushed the door open, the pent-up heat rushed at her along with the stench of mold and mildew. Feeling sweat pool along her neck, she wished that she had kept the short hairstyle her mother gave her in the hospital when she was in the coma. Courtney had since let her brown hair grow longer than it had been since she graduated with her master's degree because it helped cover the scar on her face. Today, however, she wasn't worried about the scar. Her hair was pulled back from her face with a headband. Still, sweat ran in streaks down her cheeks, and she hadn't even begun working yet.

Feeling the slow pulse of a headache creeping into the left side of her temple, Courtney propped the door open and reached into the purse that hung at her side. She opened the prescription bottle of migraine medicine and popped one pill into the back of her mouth. She swallowed it and felt the hard pill push its way down her dry throat. She prayed that the tap water in the old kitchen pipes worked and was good enough to drink and kicked herself for not bringing water with her when she left her grandmother's house.

There were no ceiling lights in the small foyer, though the whitewashed walls reflected the sun coming in through the naked windows. She wondered if white was the original color and thought, probably not. The small bit of information she knew about the house told her that the original Colonial-era owners were quite wealthy. Colored paint, most likely red or yellow, perhaps even cream, would have been used to show off their wealth.

Courtney went farther into the house and looked around. Though the carpet would need to be pulled up—hopefully revealing the original hardwood floors—and the walls would need to be painted, the room wasn't nearly as bad as she feared. The foyer held a staircase that led to the two bedrooms that looked out over the Wicomico River. The paint on the staircase was chipping badly, revealing several layers. Picking at the paint with her fingernail, Courtney spied a bit of yellow at the bottom.

I knew it, she thought with a triumphant smile as she wondered what else she could discover about the house.

Courtney peered into the room on the right and tried to imagine what it had once looked like. It was no longer the stately room she was sure it had once been. The paneled walls were stained, the white almost a grey. One of the windows was cracked, and the chandelier that once hung from the ceiling was missing, the wires exposed and capped off. The original chandelier would have held candles, and Courtney wondered how much light the room was able to capture through the windows.

Courtney headed to the other side of the house and ran her hands along the chair rail that lined the foyer as she passed through. She stood in the room to the left of the stairs and looked at the chipping white paint on the windowsills—lead paint, no doubt. The room smelled heavily of mildew, and Courtney wondered again about what they would find under the carpeting. She hoped that the wood wasn't damaged.

Hoping to find the newer part of the house in a better condition, Courtney made her way to the somewhat modern kitchen. It was part of the addition that had been built over the original footprint of the colonial kitchen. She sighed as she surveyed the holes where the appliances had been ripped out, the rusty sink, and the cabinet doors that dangled from the broken hinges. So, this is where the real work begins, she thought. Courtney had known that there would be no appliances in the house, though she had hoped that the kitchen would be in better condition. Of course, it hadn't been a kitchen in the beginning. That would have been a separate building, sparing the house if a fire were to break out in the great cooking fireplace, or so she thought that's what she had been taught in history class at one time. Courtney looked around and wondered if she should leave the kitchen as it was or move the appliances and counters as she renovated. She blew out a breath and shook her head. There were so many decisions to be made. She made her way through the kitchen to the giant master suite before going back to the kitchen for a drink of water.

The house and the land had belonged to her father's family, generations past, when the entire town had been one massive estate given to a distant ancestor by Lord Baltimore in the early colonial days. Over the years, the house had changed hands many times, often sitting empty and uncared for. An addition was added on at some point in time, but she didn't know when. When Courtney heard, from one of her cousins, that the house was being sold, she jumped at the chance to own it, sight unseen. Though her cousin, Sami, warned her that she would be getting in over her head, Courtney made an offer, a pathetically low one, that the owner quickly accepted. Looking around now, she wondered if her offer was exceedingly high.

She crossed the room and turned on the tap, letting it run for several seconds, watching as the brown, dirt-infused liquid turned yellow and then clear. She cupped her hands and filled them with the cool water. She sipped just a taste and closed her eyes. The water tasted as crisp and clear as a freshwater stream. Just like in her grandmother's house, the tap water was delicious, cold and fresh as it flowed from the artesian well in the yard. Courtney filled her hands again and greedily drank the soothing liquid that more than quenched her thirst.

Courtney decided she had no time to lose, with the amount of work before her, and so she moved through the house, trying to open the windows. The ones that weren't stuck refused to stay open, and she was forced to go outside and search for sticks to prop them up. The open windows did little to assuage the heat. Courtney almost burst into tears there and then, but she took a deep breath, squared her shoulders, and resumed her trek through the house, opening all the doors and praying for a passing storm to tamper the heat and humidity. Once the house was completely open, a slight breeze blew in off the river. Satisfied that she had done all she could, Courtney went to her car to rummage for something to put water in. Surely, there would be an empty water bottle, travel cup, or drive-through cup somewhere in the car. Thankfully, she found a McDonald's cup under the passenger seat.

It took almost two hours, many trips to the sink to satisfy her thirst, and several trips out into the hot sun, but Courtney managed to haul all of the discarded trash and cabinets to the garbage dumpster that had been delivered before she arrived. The room looked worse than when she had first begun. She probably should have waited for the contractor before she dived into ripping the cabinets apart, but she couldn't stand the way they hung here and there, making the kitchen look like a Jack-O-Lantern with a crooked smile, holes where teeth should have been, and dangling bicuspids and incisors. Again, she wondered if she should completely renovate the addition and move everything around. As she stared out the kitchen window at the river outside, she realized that the designer of this part of the house knew what he or she was doing—what a view that was. And the view from the adjoining master suite was even better. She had already decided that she would add floor-to-ceiling windows and French doors to the suite that would open out to the waterfront.

Courtney took a deep breath and surveyed her work. She looked forward to the arrival, later in the week, of the historical architect. He would know what she should do with this room and the others. She bit her lip and wondered how far over her head she was. Clearly, her family was right. She had no idea what she was doing. The undertaking before her was daunting, to say the least. The last couple to own the house had practically gone broke before giving up and putting the house on the market. Though, by the looks of things, they hadn't gotten very far in making any improvements, and Courtney wondered how they had spent all their money. Feeling defeated, and not sure what more to do without expert advice, Courtney went back through the house, closing doors and windows.

After she locked the house, Courtney slowly climbed into her Explorer and drove the half mile back to her grandmother's. She turned onto the long driveway that led to the back of the house, leaving the circular drive in front for people just stopping in for a quick visit or delivery. Her grandmother had recently discovered Amazon, and she and the UPS driver were becoming fast friends.

When Courtney reached the end of the driveway that curled around back, she noticed an unfamiliar truck parked beside her grandmother's garage.

"Gram?" she called as she entered the back door. The most delicious scent drifted through the air, but Courtney couldn't quite place it. She wasn't the chef in the family and lived mostly on bowls of cereal and carryout specials.

"In here," Lily's voice called from the bathroom.

Courtney made her way through the long, added-on pantry/laundry room behind the kitchen. She heard her grandmother's voice and that of a man. Something about the voice was familiar, but she didn't know who it belonged to.

"Gram?" Courtney said tentatively when she reached the doorway.

Lily poked her head around the shower curtain that encircled the bathtub. The showerhead had been added shortly before her grandfather's death, so there was no traditional shower stall or walled-in tub.

"Hey, sweetheart, you remember Gavin, don't you?"

"Hey, Court," a voice called from inside the shower.

Going on the assumption that her childhood friend was fully clothed behind the curtain, Courtney reached for the pink vinyl and pulled it aside.

Gavin Slade was lying on his back in the tub, his long legs bent, one eye closed, and the other eye peering up into the faucet.

"What on earth are you doing?" Courtney asked.

"I can't get the stopper to work," Lily told her. "I asked Gavin to take a look. He's good at fixing all kinds of things. I don't know what I'd do without him."

Lily smiled lovingly at the man she had practically raised, the son of a much younger woman who lived across the street. Lily was Gavin's babysitter, from the time he was born until he was in high school, and she loved him as much as her own four children.

"I think I've got it fixed." Gavin maneuvered up from his awkward position in the tub, wrench in hand. "Let's give it a try."

He stepped out of the tub and pulled up on the little knob atop the faucet. He turned on the water, and all three watched as it pooled in the tub. An onlooker might have thought they were anticipating the eruption of a geyser that would burst into the air at any moment.

"You did it," Lily shouted. "Thank you! Can I pay you back with dinner?"

Gavin looked at Courtney. "It's an arrangement we have. I pretend that she's taking me away from an important job or some pressing matter, and she pretends that I need to be repaid somehow."

Courtney saw the twinkle in her grandmother's eyes and knew that Lily treasured these moments—a little company, dinner made for someone in need, a light conversation—the things that a person missed when most of their family and friends were no longer alive.

"Far be it from me to stand in the way of your make-believe ritual," Courtney said. "Besides, Gavin and I haven't seen each other in years."

Lily clapped her hands. "Yippee! I'll go check on the pot pie."

"Gram, it's almost one hundred degrees outside. Are we really having pot pie?"

"It's Gavin's favorite. I started making it as soon as he said he would stop by."

Gavin shrugged and held out his hands as if in surrender.

Courtney rolled her eyes and grinned before a sour taste rose into her throat. Remembering what she looked like at the moment, she gazed down at her dirt-covered clothes and reached for her hair. Tendrils of her dark waves had escaped from the headband, but her scar was still exposed. She blushed as she covered her face with her hand and looked away.

"Um, maybe I could shower and change first?" she asked timidly.

"It's all yours." Gavin smiled as if he didn't even notice the scar, or as if they were still kids playing a game of canasta at Lily's kitchen table. He picked up his toolbox and brushed past her, and Courtney caught a whiff of his aftershave and smiled. She was pretty sure it was exactly the same aftershave he wore back in high school.

She heard Gavin tell Gram that he was going to put his tools in the truck as she closed the door to the bathroom. She hurried through the door on the other side and retrieved clothes before going back for a quick shower. As she rinsed her hair, she thought back to the night, fifteen years prior, when she and Gavin kissed under the weeping willow tree in her grandmother's backyard. They were so young and innocent, trying out their newfound feelings for each other after being the best of friends since birth. She smiled as she recalled the way he gently lifted her face toward his. He had undergone a growth spurt that summer, putting him almost a full foot above her. Their summer romance didn't last beyond her return home in the fall, though she never forgot about him or the kiss. She knew very little about Gavin now except for the reports from her grandmother. He had moved to the other side of the country after his graduation, and Courtney had never seen or heard from him again. Shortly before the accident, her grandmother reported that he had moved back home to help his mother take care of the family farm when his father was hospitalized. She wasn't sure if he had stayed or had returned after his father's death.

Courtney let the shower spray cool water onto her face as she tried to remember anything else her grandmother had told her, but so many of her memories and conversations had been lost from those weeks before and after the accident. She could recall nothing that her grandmother told her about Gavin's present circumstances. It would be fun to catch up, see what he'd been up to with his life, perhaps meet his wife and kids. She hoped they weren't overly sociable, though, as she had way too much work to do to attend backyard barbecues and pool parties.

Gavin's laugh filled Lily's kitchen as Courtney walked in, freshly showered and feeling more civilized. She had left her hair to hang down over her scar and nervously ran her fingers through the locks as she walked into the room. Gavin and Lily were sitting at the table, each with a mug of beer in front of them.

"Gram," Courtney admonished her grandmother. "What are you drinking?"

"Courtney, you know darn well that a beer isn't going to hurt me. I've been drinking a beer on hot afternoons practically my entire life, and I'm not going to stop now."

"Gram, your pacemaker—"

"Has nothing to do with anything. The doctor says I can have a drink, and I'm going to have a drink." As if to prove her point, Lily picked up the frosty mug and took a large gulp. She smacked her lips as she put the mug back on the table.

Courtney turned to Gavin. He laughed. "Don't look at me. We've been drinking beer together since I turned eighteen. It was never my idea."

"Eighteen?" Courtney repeated.

"Yes, eighteen." Lily's tone and frown showed that she was clearly exasperated. "If he's old enough to fight, he's old enough to drink."

"Wait. He's never even been in the military." She turned back to Gavin. "Have you?"

"No, but I was a Boy Scout. Does that count?"

"Don't you go getting all high and mighty on us." Lily tried to suppress a smile. She was genuinely enjoying this little tit for tat. "I know who got to taste test all of your grandfather's wines all summer those many years ago. How old were you when he started making his own wine? Twelve?"

Courtney felt the heat rise to her cheeks and bit her lips together. She looked at the two of them, their eyes sparkling and the alcohol causing their cheeks to turn rosy.

"Well," Courtney said as she walked back into the pantry. "I guess if you can't beat 'em, join 'em." She pulled a bottle of wine from what was left of her grandfather's reserve and popped off the plastic cork. She returned to the kitchen and took a wine glass from the cabinet.

"Court," Gavin began, but Lily held up her hand and winked.

Courtney eyed them and wondered what was going on as she poured the wine and took a sip. She sputtered as wine squirted across the room. Lily erupted with laughter.

"What the heck?"

Lily slapped her thigh as Gavin spoke. "Yeah, it's pretty awful stuff."

"Awful? What were we all thinking? It's horrible!" She wet a paper towel and wiped the wine that dripped from her chin. "We actually drank that?"

"Well," Lily said. "It wasn't *that* bad when he first made it, but it's been sitting for a long time."

"Why haven't you thrown it out?" Courtney asked as she cleaned the floor and cabinet face with a sponge.

Lily's expression fell. "Because Ben made it. It was the last batch he ever bottled."

Courtney sighed and looked at her grandmother. Oh, how she loved that woman.

"Is there any more beer?" she asked with a smile.

CHAPTER TWO

Courtney worked in the heat and humidity, the only comfort provided by the fan she had brought from Lily's. She wasn't sure if the pounding she heard was in her head or at one of the doors. She paused in her assault on the rotten floorboards in the small powder room under the stairs and listened for the sound. The tiny bathroom was barely usable, and Courtney couldn't help but wonder who thought it was a good idea to put it there. The knocking continued, and Courtney wiped the sweat from her brow as she stepped over the hole in the floor to see who was at the front door. She wasn't expecting anyone, but thought perhaps her cousin, Sami, might be coming by to see what she'd gotten herself into.

When Courtney opened the front door, a young woman was standing on the porch, holding a basket of homemade muffins; a little red-haired girl was hiding behind her legs.

"I hope I'm not bothering you. Maddy and I just baked muffins, and we thought you might like some."

Courtney smiled and accepted the generous gift. "I would love some. Thank you." She hesitated, trying to decide if it was impolite to take them and say goodbye so she could get back to work. Her grandmother would be mortified by her rudeness. "Would you like to come in? I'm not really ready for entertaining…"

"Oh, no, thank you. I'd love to come by and see your progress as you get settled, but I don't want to interrupt you now. I just wanted to welcome you to town. My name's Hannah. We live across the street." She gestured to the little rancher across the road. "Maddy and I are going for a morning bike ride. I figured I'd drop off the muffins on our way out."

"It's really nice to meet you, Hannah. I'm Courtney. Thank you so much for the muffins."

"You're welcome. I'm so glad you're fixing up this old house and moving in. The local kids have kind of taken it over as a party house, and I'm sick of the noise and the comings and goings at all hours of the night. I hope it won't be too much work for you though. I heard that you aren't married."

Courtney remembered what it was like in the small town. Everyone was either related or a recent newcomer, and, as in all small towns, they all knew everything about everybody. As a child, she couldn't go anywhere without hearing, "You must be Lily and Ben's granddaughter, Courtney, down from the city."

Courtney nodded and forced a smile. "That's correct. I, um, I'm not married." She decided not to go into the gory details about how a near-death experience had made her realize that she was not actually in love with Spencer. He was a great guy, the perfect guy by all accounts, but the longer they were together, the less she had been able to picture them in the future, rocking in their chairs on the front porch. Work consumed him, and she didn't want that. After waking up, and seeing him holding vigil by her bedside, she immediately felt love and guilt at the same time. What did it say about her that the first thought she had when she opened her eyes was that she was grateful for his attention but had no desire to see him? She knew that she had to tell him the truth as soon as she had the strength. He had been hurt and even angry, but she was sure that he would understand in time.

Courtney, lost in thought, suddenly realized that Hannah was staring at her, smiling politely while waiting for Courtney to say more.

"I'm sorry. I've just got a lot on my mind these days." Courtney offered a half-hearted smile. "The house needs so much work." She sighed and gestured toward the interior.

"I'm sure. It was empty for a long time. I'm told that the couple who lived here was really sweet but had a hard time with the renovation. I guess it was much more work than they imagined. And then there were the incidents…" Hannah looked away.

"Incidents?" Courtney asked.

"Oh, I'm sure they won't start up again. If they ever really happened. I mean…it was kind of crazy." Hannah shuffled her feet uncomfortably. "I think the Suttons were just old and in over their heads. They were never really, um, comfortable here. Too much work, I suppose."

"I bet," Courtney said though she felt like she was missing something. "It's quite a house, pretty unusual compared to the others in the area. Did they have any specific problems with the house that I should be worried about?"

"Not that I know of," Hannah said without meeting Courtney's eyes. "I'm sure everything will be fine. It's a great old house. It's been here longer than anyone can remember. My parents grew up here, and they said there are all kinds of legends surrounding the house. They say that pirates used to anchor their ships at the dock. Some say that the original owners of the house were pirates, and others say they were pirate sympathizers or shrewd businessmen who bought the pirates' treasure and sold it on the black market. I think all the legends and stories might have freaked the old couple out a bit."

A laugh escaped from Courtney's throat as she pictured one of her father's stately ancestors doing business with pirates.

"Is that so? Well, I'll let you know if I find any chests of gold hidden in the attic."

Hannah laughed but eyed Courtney with suspicion. Courtney hoped that she hadn't insulted the woman who seemed to offer nothing but sheer kindness and kinship.

"Well, thanks again for the muffins. I promise to invite you over when I'm ready for guests."

The congenial smile was back as Hannah nodded and waved her hand. "That sounds delightful."

As Courtney turned her head, she heard the small gasp from Maddy and noticed the look, both horrified and curious, that briefly passed over Hannah's face. Reaching up to her face, Courtney gently pulled some hair out of her headband to cover her scar.

"It was nice meeting you, Hannah. And you, too, Maddy." Courtney made sure that her smile and tone were genuine as she looked from mother to daughter, though she felt exposed, as if she were standing naked in the doorway. "I really hope you come back to see the progress from time to time, but don't expect too much. It's going to be a long process."

"We'd love to come back," Hannah said, sounding sincere. "Come on, Maddy. Let's leave Courtney to her work."

After saying goodbye, she watched Hannah lift Maddy into the toddler seat mounted on the back of her blue, ten-speed bike. Maddy continued to stare at Courtney until her mother turned the bike in the direction of the pier at the end of the road where Courtney's cousin owned a country store. It was close enough to walk, and Courtney vowed to make it a point to walk down there as much as possible once she was settled.

She took the basket into the kitchen and placed it on the counter, wondering if Hannah and Sami were friends.

"Mmm," she murmured as she savored the warm blueberry muffin. "This is so much better than the peanut butter and jelly sandwich I brought with me." She pushed away the discomfort about her scar and the questions she was left with from the conversation.

An hour later, there was again knocking at the door. Sighing, Courtney called out, "I'm coming," and made her way toward the door, lugging a load of boards with her.

"Can you open the door, please?" Courtney called to the visitor.

The door gently swung open, and a man stuck his face inside the foyer. "Courtney?" He gazed into the room and jumped as his eyes settled on her. "Sorry. Let me get those for you."

Eyeing his dark suit, Courtney felt guilty about enlisting his help.

"Oh, I've got them," she said.

"Nonsense." He set down his briefcase and took the boards from her.

"The dumpster's around the side of the house." She felt guilty as she followed him onto the porch. "Watch where you step. A lot of the boards are missing or rotten."

She watched him maneuver the porch, walk briskly down the steps, and disappear around the corner. She waited until he returned. He wiped the dust off his suit and removed his sunglasses as he reached the door.

"Thank you," she said. "I have to get a drink. It's as hot as blazes in here. Can I get you something?"

"No, thanks," he said following her. "The outside of the house is spectacular, but those honeysuckle vines have got to go." He stopped in between the foyer and the kitchen and looked around.

"Yeah. I haven't gotten to them yet." She continued walking toward the kitchen. All thoughts were on water and her migraine pills.

She filled her bottle with water and took a long drink. She retrieved the pills from her purse and tossed two into the back of her throat before taking another long drink. The man was gone from the dining room, as she had already labeled it, but she found him in the foyer. He was bent over, looking into the small room under the stairs. Courtney swallowed hard as she watched him stare into the earth beneath. He might have been the most handsome man she had ever seen, and it suddenly occurred to her that she had been so hot and preoccupied that she had not even bothered to find out who he was.

"I'm glad you're ripping this out," he frowned, gesturing toward the hole in the floor. "What a horrible idea—to put a bathroom here. It throws off the perfect balance of the whole entry way."

"Oh, I didn't realize that." She looked around the space before turning to face him. "I just wanted to get rid of the rotten boards. Where are my manners? I'm

Courtney. And you are?" She reached for his hand and noticed the strange color of his eyes. They were the same shade of blue as the starry background of the American Flag, a deep, dark blue that she had never seen in someone's eyes.

He took her outstretched hand and shook it, holding it a bit too long. Courtney wondered if he was taking in her scar, and she instinctively pulled her hand away and reached up to pull her hair onto her face. When she looked back up into his deep blue eyes, she expected to see the usual—curiosity, horror, or pity. Instead, she saw warmth and friendliness.

"Jason Mills. Nice to meet you."

"The historical architect." She felt the heat rise to her cheeks. She hadn't intended to be so dirty and sweaty for their first meeting. "I didn't expect to see you until tomorrow. Did I get the date wrong?"

"No, no, I am scheduled to come tomorrow, but I was down in St. Mary's City, on another site, and finished early. I thought I'd come take a look and see what we've got to work with." He looked around and whistled. "Wow! This place is going to require a heck of a lot of work. Are you prepared for that?"

"Are you asking if I can afford it or if I understand how long it's going to take to complete?"

Jason smiled. "Both." He looked around. "This house is remarkable. Just look at how many windows there are and all in casements! The original owners must have been quite wealthy. I could tell as soon as I drove up and saw all these beautiful, symmetrical windows that it has quite a story to tell."

"A story? What do you mean by that?" Courtney was intrigued.

"Just look at the geometry of the place. Perfect squares and rectangles everywhere. And the brickwork is exquisite for a house of its era, almost unseen anywhere else in architecture from the early 1700s. The cruck roof alone is unlike anything I expected to find. Such things were unheard of in North America." He turned to face her. "This house, the brickwork, the roof, even the paneling…" He walked into the room to the right of the foyer and reached out to touch the wall. "The walls must be twelve feet high. Amazing." He ran his hand along the wall as if it were a golden calf to be worshiped and revered.

"I wasn't sure what to expect on the inside, but I knew from the outside that this house was a living, breathing remnant of the past, and perhaps the only house like it still standing today." He turned toward the far wall. "Just look at this paneling," he marveled as he stood back and faced the wall. "My God, it's exquisite. I can't believe these panels could possibly be originals, but…" His voice trailed off as he walked toward the far wall. He ran his hands along the symmetrical squares and rectangles that came together to form the paneled wall. "I think they might be. And hand-carved, too. Except this one." He tapped on the rectangle that formed the bottom middle part of the wall. "It's a different wood and made by a machine. Look at the difference in the hue. There's an almost unperceivable difference in paint color, and the cut of the wood is definitely not the same, but so close." Courtney knew he was talking to himself and not to her, and she was mesmerized by this man and the effect that the house had on him. Could he be right? Was this truly an anomaly—a house unlike any others in the country?

Jason stood back and turned toward Courtney as if just realizing she was still there. "I'm certain there's a fireplace behind this board." He knocked on the middle panel. "Listen," he said before knocking on the panel to the right of it. "Hear the difference?"

She did, and she nodded as she walked closer.

"It's hollow in here, and…" He ran to the open window and stuck his head outside, twisting his body to look up to the roof of the house. "There's a leaning chimney above. Is there a fireplace upstairs?" Though he asked Courtney the question, he was already moving from the room, rushing toward the staircase in the adjoining hall. Courtney turned and hastened to keep up with him.

When they reached the room above, he stopped in the doorway and stared at the plaster wall in front of them, a frown on his face. Two doors stood on each side of the wall, though there was solid plaster in between with a rectangular discoloration that showed where a large picture hung for many years.

"I'm sure I'm right." He absent-mindedly rubbed his chin. He went to the wall and began knocking on the plaster as he had done on the panels below.

"Yep, hollow in the middle." He was triumphant as he stood back and surveyed the wall. "They're going to be stunning once you uncover them." He stopped and looked at Courtney. "You are going to uncover them, right?"

She swallowed and blinked a few times before finding the words. "I, I guess so. I mean, I do want to return the house to its original state as much as possible."

She thought about what Hannah said. "Are you sure it's a fireplace and not a secret passage?"

Jason nodded, his blue eyes sparkling. "Most definitely. Do you have any idea who built the original house?" he asked, changing the subject and heading out of the room. He stuck his head into the room across the hall and bounded back down the stairs. Courtney raced to keep up.

"Um, I'm not sure," she said as she followed him down the stairs. "The land was owned by my father's family in Colonial times. I don't know when the house was built or by whom. The property has been out of our hands for over a hundred years."

"I'd love to find out who designed it, but I'm not sure that it's possible." He turned and looked at her. "You must return this house to how it once was. It's going to be remarkable—a house that will be studied and talked about for generations to come."

Courtney wasn't sure how she felt about that—excitement, yes, but apprehension as well. Would she be able to do the house justice? It seemed like such a daunting task.

Jason went to the opposite side of the house and walked through the doorway to the other first floor room. He entered and then turned abruptly toward Courtney. "Have you checked to see what you're allowed to do with the house? As far as what the county historical codes will allow?"

Courtney swallowed. "Um, I'm not sure. I mean, I didn't realize I had to do that. I guess I assumed that was your job."

"Yes, of course." Jason made a clicking noise in the back of his throat as he continued to surmise the house. He walked around the room, knocking here and there, assessing the windows, and lifting the carpeting. He peered up at the beams in the ceiling.

"I'll check into the codes and see what I can find out about previous renovations. I'd like to start dating the bricks and the wood. I bet these walls are two feet thick. What a find." He exhaled and smiled broadly, his eyes sparkling like dark blue sapphires. "It's going to be quite a project."

Courtney still wasn't sure she was up to this, but from the look on his face, the renovation was a project that Jason was quite pleased to be a part of.

*****

"Jason says I need to have someone from the county historical department come out and tell me what can and can't be done to the house, and that we need to date the bricks, the wood, and the foundation. He says that the house could be the only one like it in the country, the world even!" Courtney let out a long breath and took a bite of her roll. "Gram, I'm so overwhelmed."

"Now, honey, don't you worry. It sounds like this Jason knows what to do. I'm sure everything will come together in a jiffy." Lily poured herself another glass of iced tea and refilled Courtney's.

"I don't know, Gram. I rushed into this without knowing what I was getting into. I lived in the same house my entire life before going to school and getting an apartment. Whenever anything goes wrong, I just call the super, and he takes care of it. I've never even used a drill. What do I know about fixing up a house?"

"You've hired the best construction company in the county. You'll have no problems getting it fixed up once you have the plans finalized."

"I hope you're right. He's sending someone down tomorrow to take a look at the house. I told him that I have no idea when I'll be able to start, but his guy is going to figure out what permits I need. That is, if the historical society lets me do anything." She put her elbows on the table and held her head in her hands. "Oh, what have I done?"

"Have some more steak," Lily coaxed. "Everything looks brighter on a full stomach."

Courtney smiled at her grandmother's logic. "I'm not so sure about that." She shook her head and suppressed a chuckle.

*****

"Hello," the familiar voice called. "Anyone home?"

Courtney entered the small entrance hall with a smile on her face. "Hey, Gavin. Are you coming by to laugh at the grand predicament I've gotten myself into?"

"Actually, I came to take a look around, get some measurements, and help you make some decisions."

Courtney was confused, but then understanding dawned on her. "Gram called you. I'm sorry about that. She shouldn't have. I'm expecting someone from the construction company any minute. I'm sure he'll be able to help pull me from my pit of despair."

Gavin gave her a quizzical look. "Um, Court, didn't you know?" He pointed to the truck in the driveway. For the first time, she read the writing on the driver's side door.

"You work for Collin's Construction? I thought you had a degree from somewhere out west. Math or something." She was thoroughly perplexed. "Why didn't you say anything at dinner the other night?"

"It was Engineering, and I figured you already knew. The house never really came up in the conversation other than your buying it and hoping it all goes well. I figured you didn't want me to talk about work at dinner. Anyway, I'm working for Mitch while mom and I figure out what she's going to do with the farm. Then it's back to my real job. It's been kind of fun actually, doing construction, wiring, and general fixer-upper stuff. I get to experiment with things I've wanted to try but have only designed on paper and handed off to someone else. It's like seeing my world from the space shuttle instead of just inside of NASA's control center."

Courtney smiled at his analogy though she was still confused. "But Gram called you a handyman. I thought she meant you were *her* handyman."

Gavin laughed. "I guess I am her handyman, but I'm really just keeping busy. I'm trying to convince mom to sell the farm and move out to Portland with me."

"What about your family? Will she move in with you?"

Gavin pressed his lips together and shook his head. "Mom is my family. We're all we've got. That's why I want her to come live with me. She can't run the farm by herself, and she's gotten several really nice offers on the land. She just doesn't want to leave dad."

Gavin's eyes clouded over, and Courtney knew he was remembering his father, a man she had truly loved. He always knew how to make people laugh. Unfortunately, he had a long, losing battle with cancer. He was buried in the same cemetery as her grandfather.

"I wondered why you didn't mention a wife or kids at dinner the other night. I didn't want to pry." For reasons unknown, Courtney felt herself blushing.

"When you said you were here temporarily, I assumed you were in a hurry to get back to them."

Gavin shook his head. "No, but I left this town for a reason. It was too small for me. There wasn't enough opportunity or potential for a successful future. And now, working on the water and farming are dying. This county's going to see big changes real soon. More housing developments are going to crop up as the naval base expands, and more shopping centers, movie theaters, and other commercial businesses are going to move in. The old-timers are going to be pushed out, and a lot of people will be very unhappy."

"Wait. Wouldn't that make this the ideal place for you? Lots of engineering possibilities?"

"Only if I work on the base, and I'm not interested in designing ships or airplanes. The rest of the stuff is all the same construction, nothing new or innovative." He shook his head. "Despite the few things I've handled or played around with for Mitch, there's nothing here for me."

Something in Courtney's chest constricted at the words—a sharp pain she couldn't identify. She blinked and wondered why it even mattered to her whether Gavin stayed or went back west. Gram would certainly miss his mother, but she was at the point in life where she was used to saying goodbye. Remembering that Gavin was on the clock, and refusing to think further about his leaving, Courtney took Gavin by the arm and led him into the large addition that contained the master suite and the kitchen.

"Well, I've got something for you to work on. How about helping me decide whether to keep this room as it is or change it up? Maybe move the fixtures to a different wall? Or leave them where they are so I can see the river when I'm at the sink? What do you think?"

Gavin walked around the room, taking in the gaping holes in the wall and the missing cabinets. He spent several minutes inspecting the walls and the floor; Courtney watched as he became someone she didn't know. Though the truth was, she didn't know him, not anymore. Their friendly conversation over dinner, mostly reminiscing about the past, hadn't revealed anything to her. She had learned more about him in the past fifteen minutes than she had that other evening. She realized that she had been seeing him as her childhood friend and playmate, but now, she saw a total stranger.

He was tall and quite muscular, not at all what she would have imagined for someone who sat at a desk all day, working with figures and drawings. His piercing, blue eyes were the color of the June sky, and his dirty-blonde hair was cropped short, so unlike the longhaired boy she once knew. His hands were large and strong, and she could picture them holding a power tool, not a pencil. What exactly did an engineer do anyway? She tried to think back to her job as a financial advisor. Had she ever actually talked to or worked with an engineer? She didn't think so. And weren't there about a dozen different kinds of engineers? What kind was he?

As she watched Gavin take measurements and jot things down in a notebook, she wondered if she had ever really known him at all. In her mind, he remained the fifteen-year-old boy she had last seen before heading home at the end of the summer before her sophomore year. She hadn't returned to the town either of the following summers except for short weekend visits. Work and preparation for college had gotten in the way, and her childhood friendship and first kiss had faded into the past. Perhaps it was best to keep it that way.

Gavin, who was kneeling on the floor in the corner of the room, paused in his work and looked up at Courtney. "So, why isn't your fiancé helping you make these decisions? Shouldn't he have a say?"

"I guess Gram didn't mention that I'm no longer engaged." She bit her lip and looked away. It was not her favorite topic.

"Nope. I'm sorry, Court. I know you were together a long time."

"It's okay. After the accident…" She reached up and began to trace her scar with her finger, gazing out of the window over the sink. "I decided I didn't want to marry Spencer." She turned back toward Gavin. "He's a great guy, truly he is. And maybe he'd have made a wonderful husband, just not mine. I didn't want the life that we would have had together, and it would have been unfair to him if I had kept him from finding someone else."

"So, I guess we're both kind of back to where we started," Gavin said with a sarcastic chuckle.

"I guess so." Courtney was unsure as to how to answer that. "And we've both got a lot on our plate, so I'll let you get back to work."

"Hey Court," he called as she opened the front door.

"Yeah?"

"Take a look at all those vines when you go outside. They're going to wreak havoc on the house and barn. You need to get rid of them."

"I know, I know." She let out a deep sigh. As soon as it was cooler, the honeysuckle would be a top priority.

Leaving Gavin to concentrate on his work, Courtney went outside to do what she had come to love doing the most when she felt overwhelmed or confused or just needed a reminder as to why she was here. She stood outside the house and gazed up at the dormer windows, the green shingles, the leaning chimney. She turned toward the water and tried to imagine what her ancestors saw the first time they stepped foot on this land. She thought about how beautiful the house and the yard were going to look once the work was finished.

Courtney took a few moments each day to think about how much this all meant to her, though today, the sense of peace and calm that she usually felt was missing. She was keenly aware of the summer heat, and the humidity nearly took her breath away and caused both her head and heart to pound uncontrollably. And she realized there was something else that made her heart beat so rapidly, and it wasn't being with Gavin.

A feeling of uncertainty washed over her, and suddenly, as she stood facing the water, a shiver overcame her. She looked around for the source of the ominous feeling but couldn't quite place the foreboding she experienced. It was then, for just an instant, that Courtney felt as though she was being watched.

*****

"The past is always intriguing, especially when it comes to that old house," the docent said to Courtney as they walked to the archives in the back of the museum.

The historical society seemed to be in no hurry to send someone out to survey River Terrace, as Courtney's house was known to the locals. Lily suggested that Courtney use the waiting time wisely and do her own research on the property. As it was once part of St. Clement's Manor, Courtney drove to the small St. Clement's Island Museum to see what information they had on the history of the property.

"I've heard some of the legends about pirates and treasure and secret passages," Courtney told Marcia, a woman in her fifties with greying hair and sparkling green eyes.

"Yes, those stories have been around for years, since long before your mother and I were born, but nobody ever put much stock in them."

"You know my mother?" Courtney asked.

Marcia smiled, "The prettiest girl to ever graduate from St Joseph's School. We all thought so. She was a couple years ahead of me, but we all knew who she was. All the boys hoped she would change her mind about your daddy, but she waited for him to serve his time in the military, and they married as soon as he got home. Lucky girl, she was, to have found such a handsome man and a life near the city."

Courtney thought about what Gavin said a few days prior about the small town with few opportunities. Funny, she had never seen it that way. To her, this area was truly the happiest place on earth.

"Here are the papers you're interested in. They're mostly farm journals, ledgers, property documents. I'm not sure they will answer any of your questions, though I'm happy to make copies of anything that helps. You'll need to wear these," Marcia added, handing Courtney a pair of white gloves.

Courtney thanked Marcia and began perusing the documents after putting on the gloves. Many were notebooks, barely held together, with formal handwriting in the kind of bright blue ink that came from a pot and quill rather than a plastic pen. She gingerly turned the pages, careful not to harm them, and read over some of the entries. One journal had a name on the inside cover—Robert McMillan, obviously a relative of hers.

December 14, 1724 – acquired two hogs, three pounds each.

Did that mean they weighed three pounds or cost three pounds? Courtney wasn't sure. She read on.

January 7, 1725 – Blizzard. Lost one mule and three chickens to the cold.

February 3, 1725 – The river is frozen all the way across. No ships can make it through. Supplies running low. Down to two sacks of flour and one sack of cornmeal. Only three jars of beans left.

Courtney skimmed the pages until she saw an entry that looked interesting.

April 10, 1725 – Came home from burying my sister's child to find a woman and child in our bed. The woman's child, God rest his soul, did not live through his birth. A hard sight after the funeral of my own kin. The woman is near death herself. Sent for Dr. Stern, but there is not much to be done save to nourish the woman and wait.

April 11, 1725 – Anne is her name, and she has more color today. The child was given a Christian burial and named Jack, for the woman's husband, though no ring is on her hand, and she refuses to say where the husband is. If she is strong enough tomorrow, she will be taken to John's house to nurse little Jenny, Cora's remaining child. Cora does not have the strength after burying the twin. The magistrate suspects Anne was left here by a pirate's ship that was seen mooring in our harbor while we were away. A close eye will be kept on her lest she try to abscond with the silver.

Courtney wondered about the woman and child. Who was she, and where had she come from? Could this be one of the sources of the pirate legends? She took a picture of the entries with her phone and slowly flipped forward, page-by-page, running her finger down the text, but she found no other references to Anne nor to the child she presumably nursed. The journal continued with musings and recordings, recounting farm life for a period of four more years, before it ended abruptly just after Christmas in 1730. Courtney searched through the stack of papers but couldn't find any more of Robert McMillan's writings. *How odd*, she thought. Marcia was right, River Terrace's past was intriguing, indeed.

*****

When Courtney's stomach began to growl, she looked at her watch and sighed. The morning had slipped away as she perused the many farm journals—though no others written by Robert—copies of land records, and other documents that had been donated or collected by the museum over the years. One of the most interesting documents was the manifest from the Ark and the Dove, the ships that landed on what is now St. Clement's Island, in 1634. The surnames of the passengers and the crew were more than familiar to Courtney. Almost all of them belonged to the long line of her ancestors who populated the area.

Carefully placing all of the documents back into their proper folders, Courtney began to think about the threads of the past, woven through time, creating a tapestry of family histories that was yet to be completed. How did those many colorful threads tie together? What picture did they weave? What secrets did they conceal? She longed to be more connected with her family's past. She knew so much about her mother's family, thanks to Lily, but so little about her father's family other than what was historical record. Her grandmother died when she was just a baby, and her grandfather talked very little about the past when he was alive. She didn't even know what her paternal grandmother looked like. Did they have the same features? The same personality? What was *her* family like? Were they farmers, watermen, bakers, blacksmiths, or merchants? In the early 1700s, her family had obviously owned the manor, but what about all of the generations in between?

Taking a deep breath, Courtney stood and arched her back. Miraculously, her head felt fine, no throbbing from the dim lighting in the archive room or the hours staring at the faint, old documents. She went to the door and motioned to Marcia.

"All done for today?" Marcia asked as she approached Courtney.

"Yes, thank you. I took lots of pictures, without flash of course, but I still have so many questions.

Unfortunately, I don't know that I'm going to find any answers here. Maybe not anywhere."

Marcia laid her hand on Courtney's shoulder in a caring gesture. Her eyes conveyed her empathy.

"Sometimes the past is better left in the past. You never know what skeletons you may dig up when you try to unearth things long past buried."

A shiver ran down Courtney's spine. Was Marcia speaking from her own experience, what she had witnessed of others who came looking for answers, or to something in the McMillan family past?

"Thanks," Courtney mumbled as she hurried from the room. She walked briskly through the little museum and out into the blazing heat of the summer day. Once outside, she gazed across the water to the lighthouse that stood on St. Clement's Island. Her family once owned the lighthouse, too, years after the colonial times. She believed it may have been in the late 1800s, but she wasn't sure. She had always been fascinated by the old white house with the beacon in the center of its roof. To think that her family had actually lived there was a source of pride for Courtney and all of her family. She hoped that some day soon, River Terrace would boast the beauty and charm to which the lighthouse had been restored. Courtney was certain that it was her mission to make that happen.

CHAPTER THREE

Courtney's phone sounded before eight in the morning as she and Lily were hanging the wash on the line. Her grandmother had already showered, dressed, washed clothes, dusted the house, and made breakfast. Courtney felt guilty that she had slept until 8:00, so she finished her pancakes, smothered with homemade peach syrup, and volunteered to help with the laundry. She reached into her pocket and stared at the number on the buzzing phone. It was a local number, though one she did not recognize.

"Hello." She hoped she had good enough service for them to hear each other.

"Courtney? It's Jason Mills, the architect."

"Oh, hi, Jason." She felt a flutter of excitement in her stomach. Were they ready to begin? "Do you have news about the permits and the historical society?"

"I do. Can we meet for lunch?"

"Sure. How about my cousin's store? She has a great lunch counter." She gave him directions to the waterfront country store just a couple hundred yards from River Terrace.

"Great. I'll see you around 11:30 if that's okay."

"Perfect." Courtney said goodbye and disconnected the call.

"Good news?" Lily asked.

"I hope so," Courtney responded, picking up her t-shirt, shaking it out, and reaching for a clothespin on the line. "He didn't sound like it was bad news…" *Did he? If all was a go, wouldn't he have just said so? Were they meeting in person so that he could let her down easy?*

"Courtney," her grandmother called her back from her thoughts. "You have that look about you. I'm sure everything is fine."

Courtney shook her head and smiled. "You know me so well."

"You're a chip off the old block. Your mother used to get that same look every time I asked her how a test went. She would say she aced it, and then that look would come over her, and I knew she was second-guessing every answer she had written down."

"I guess we McMillan women can't hide anything from you."

"That's because you're not just McMillans. You're Russells and Gibsons, too. And I know a thing about the Russells and the Gibsons."

Courtney frowned. "What about the McMillans? I've realized that there is so much about them that I don't know."

Lily pursed her lips. "Well, I only know what your daddy told me, and it's not much. His momma and daddy were good people—solid, nurturing, hard-working, church-going folk. I guess that's all we really needed to know. Unfortunately, they both died when you were young."

Inhaling deeply, Courtney blinked and nodded. "I don't know much more than that myself. Maybe we could invite mom and dad down to visit this weekend, and I could ask dad for more information. Would that be okay?"

"Okay? To have two more mouths to feed, another bed to make, more noise in the house, and people underfoot?" Lily beamed. "Why nothing would make me happier."

*****

"Oh my gosh, remember when you fell off the pier, and Gavin jumped in with his clothes on, and we all followed?" Sami laughed as she recounted yet another scene from their childhood.

"And the time we all had chiggers from head to toe after spending the afternoon picking blackberries from Gram's forbidden bushes behind the barn?" Courtney wiped the tears from her eyes that accompanied her non-stop laughter. She and Sami spent most of their summers together trying to stay out of trouble. Lily's sister-in-law, Sissie, was Sami's grandmother, and the two families were almost inseparable, especially the cousins.

"Your grandmother was so angry with us," Sami said. "She said that we ruined her plans to make jam and hoped we'd all have stomachaches that night."

"I would rather have had a stomachache than those darn chigger bites." Courtney shook her head, her ankles itching just from the memory.

"Well, would you look there, what has the wind blown into town?" Sami asked as the bell over the door chimed. "Is *that* the architect?" Sami's eyes widened as she watched the stranger look around the small store and deli. "Mmm-mmm. Wow." She blew out a breath and fanned her face.

"Shh," Courtney gave her cousin a warning look as she stood and waved to Jason.

"Good to see you again, Courtney." Jason reached to shake her hand.

"You, too, Jason." She gestured toward Sami. "This is my cousin, Sami. She runs the store."

Jason took Sami's hand. "It's a pleasure to meet you." He looked around the store, filled with fishing poles, bait, lures, and life jackets, as well as grocery staples. "This place is legendary around this part of the county."

"It's been here a long time," Sami nodded. "My great-great-grandparents opened the store just after the Great Depression. Nobody thought it would last, yet here we are, nearly a hundred years later."

"And still selling the same things," Courtney said. "And I mean *exactly* the same things." She and Sami laughed at the old joke as Jason raised an eyebrow in question. When they were younger, it always seemed like some of the items on the store's shelves had been there longer than the cousins had been alive.

"Well, I'll let you two have your meeting. Can I get you a soft crab sandwich, or maybe a crab cake?" Sami asked Jason.

"A soft crab sandwich sounds perfect," he replied. "And a Coca Cola, please."

"Courtney?" Sami asked her cousin.

"Surprise me," Courtney replied before turning to Jason. "You'll love the soft crab. It's amazing."

"I'm sure I will." Jason looked around once more. "Truthfully, I'm amazed this place is still in business. Your cousin must be up to her ears in debt."

Courtney bristled at the comment, though, inwardly, she admitted that she had always wondered the same thing. The truth was, Sami loved this place. She would never let it go even if it cost her everything.

"The place is doing just fine." Courtney went on the defensive. "Sami's a genius at marketing and bringing people in."

Jason surveyed the empty stools and the many boats that sat idle along the pier outside the window. "Uh-huh. Looks that way."

Courtney's face turned red. "Do you have news for me or not?"

Jason's features softened, and he touched Courtney's arm. She tried to ignore the tingling feeling that raced from his fingers to her stomach.

"I'm sorry. I didn't mean to hurt or upset you. It's my line of work. Sometimes I see things as nothing more than houses or old buildings from the past. I forget that people are involved and that they have feelings and attachments."

"Don't you have any attachments?" Courtney asked, then blushed, growing ever more aware of the light caress of Jason's fingers and the absence of a ring. She pulled her arm away and looked toward the kitchen, wishing Sami would make a reappearance. She looked back at Jason and offered a smile as she absent-mindedly reached up to pull a strand of hair over her scar. "Now I'm sorry. That didn't come out right, and it's none of my business."

"I'm an open book, Courtney." He grinned. "What you see is what you get."

Courtney wondered if there was an underlying meaning to his words. Was that his way of telling her that he's single? Was he coming on to her? It certainly felt like it. In this modern day and age, she knew she should be offended, but she wasn't. She swallowed as she looked into his eyes, trying to decipher his meaning.

"Here you go." Sami set a plate down on the counter in front of Jason. She added a plate in front of Courtney with a crab cake, no bread, just as she liked it. "Your gram's recipe," Sami winked. Courtney looked at the plates, piled high with French fries and homemade coleslaw.

"Thanks, Sami," Courtney smiled. Sami nodded with a smile and walked away, leaving the two to their lunch.

After a few bites, Jason turned back to Courtney. "So, about your house."

Wiping her mouth with her napkin, Courtney nodded. "Good news or bad news?"

"Both, actually." He took a sip of his Coke. "You can tear down the newer part if you want, but I wouldn't. It's not original, but I'm sure it's from the 19th Century, so it's quite old and historic in and of itself. You have to build on the original foundation and leaving that intact allows you to maintain the space without violating the footprint. You can build up, but not out any farther."

"Okay. I'm not interested in building up." She thought for a moment. "And the newer part is pretty big with rough-ins for a washer and dryer." Courtney thought about all of the HGTV fixer-upper shows she had watched from her hospital bed. "Do you think I could renovate the master bathroom, maybe add a jacuzzi?"

Jason nodded as he thought about the prospect. "That's not a question for me. You'll have to ask your contractor. As far as the historical integrity of the house, that won't matter. Upgrades are done to old houses all the time. It's the outside and the things like the paneling, windows, ceiling beams, floors, those kinds of things that we want to keep as original as we can."

"Sounds good." Courtney took a long drink of water. "If I'm going to do this, I'm going to do it right. I want to scour yard sales and flea markets for things to bring out the original beauty of the house. I bet there's a gold mine waiting to be discovered in Gram's attic alone." Her mind raced with possibilities.

Jason smiled. "Sounds like you have a plan, but there's a lot of work to be done before you begin decorating. You should keep as much of the original wood and brick as possible. And we should see if the floors can be refinished without ruining them. I'd like to take a closer at them actually. I'm not sure if the floors that are under the carpeting are even the original ones. From the quick peek I took, they didn't seem as worn as I would have thought for floors that were put down in the 1600s."

"To be honest, I can't say that I noticed. I'm not sure I'd be able to tell if they were old or new, or at least newer."

"You'll be able to tell. The original floors would be rougher with more knots and holes. Floors weren't meant to be aesthetic back then, just functional." He took another bite of his sandwich and wiped his mouth with his napkin. "Let me do a little more research on the house, and then I'll begin drawing up some plans. I can probably get them to you in a couple weeks, but I'm going to want to see the house again, probably more than once, before I'm at a point where I'd want to share them with you. And I want to confirm that the original floors exist under the newer floors. That's going to take some testing. I'll have to remove a small piece and take it with me."

"Okay. In the meantime, can I go ahead and begin tearing things out? Like the panels where the fireplaces might be?"

"Probably, but I think I should take one more look before you start. I'd like to see the panels again, and the stone and brick, take some pictures, and get a closer look at the wooden beams. I think some of those are the originals, and I'd like to see what kind of condition they're in."

"Absolutely," Courtney agreed. "When do you want to come by?"

Jason picked up his sandwich and looked over top of it toward Courtney, posed to take a bite. "How about as soon as I finish this delicious sandwich?"

Courtney grinned. "Works for me." She was more than happy to have his opinion on when and how to get started, and she was happy for an excuse to not say goodbye just yet.

"Not so fast." Sami placed a piece of coconut cake in front of each of them. "You can't leave without having dessert."

"Sami, you're killing me," Courtney told her with a roll of her eyes. "Did Aunt Sissie make this?"

Sami grinned, her eyes twinkling. "Uh, yeah." She turned toward Jason. "My grandmother's coconut cake is the best cake you will ever eat in your life. I guarantee it."

"Then I don't see how I can turn it down." Jason flashed Sami a million-dollar smile, and Courtney's stomach flipped. She was going to have a hard time working so closely with him. His sex appeal was through the roof. Courtney just hoped that the cost of what he had planned for the house wasn't through the roof as well.

*****

"Gram, your Internet has the slowest connection I've ever used." Courtney was trying to peruse Pinterest for kitchen ideas, but the connection was slower than a possum crossing the road.

"Well, we don't use it for much. We've got the cheapest tier they offer." Lily was stretched on the couch, *Wheel of Fortune* playing on the television. Courtney sat in what she always thought of as 'Granddad's chair.' She was trying to load pages on her laptop and wondered if Lily would always speak in terms of 'we' rather than 'I' when it came to the house.

"I'm going to have to call and get them to switch us to a faster connection. Don't worry, I'll pay for the extra."

"That's fine, dear. You do what you have to do to get your plans together."

"Thanks. Hey, do you know anyone who does mold removal? Gavin says I may have a real problem in the cellar and that I should call a professional. He thinks the insulation should be replaced and the whole area treated. I didn't even know that professional mold removing was a thing."

"Hmmm," Lily thought for a moment. "We never had a cellar or anything, so I never had to worry about that. You might want to Google it. That's the right term, right?"

Courtney laughed. "Yeah, it is. I'll Google it." She looked up a mold contractor, read the reviews on Yelp, and sent him an email. She was scrolling through the page, willing the images to load faster, when she saw a notification appear in the corner of the screen. She clicked on the box, and her email program opened. "Mom and Dad are definitely coming this weekend," she told her grandmother. "Dad wants to know if we can get crabs."

"You'll have to call your cousin, Jim, and see if he can spare a bushel. Crabs have been running slow this week, but he could probably save some for you."

"I'll text him," Courtney said, reaching for her phone. "Should we invite Gavin and Jan? I'm sure Mom and Dad would love to see them."

"That would be nice. Jan is so good to me. I like to do something for her every now and then."

Gavin's mom was about twenty years younger than Lily, but the two of them did everything together and had for as long as Courtney could remember. She knew that her parents would want Jan and Gavin included.

After texting Jim, Courtney sent a text to Gavin. He answered almost immediately.

Mom's a yes, but I've got plans. Rain check?

Plans? Courtney frowned. Of course he had plans. He was back home after a long time away, and no doubt he had a lot of friends to catch up with. Oh well, it's not a big deal, she thought as she texted him back. For some reason, it felt like a big deal. Just then, Courtney received a text from Sami, as if her cousin could read minds and wanted to remind Courtney that there were more fish in the sea.

Hey, how did it go with Jason? Any news on the house? Is he single?

Courtney smiled and shook her head as she answered the text. Though she knew their relationship was professional, she couldn't stop her thoughts from wandering toward Jason. Would he like to join them for crabs? Or would that be weird?

As if on cue, Courtney's phone buzzed, and she wondered if Jason had telepathically known she was thinking about him. Her stomach lurched a little when she read the screen.

Hey, sweetheart. Just thought I'd check in to see how things are going. I miss you.

Spencer. Courtney smiled. She missed him, too, though she was pretty sure she didn't miss him in quite the same way that he missed her. She missed his companionship, his sense of humor, his kindness and generosity, his old-fashioned courtesy, and the way he worked so hard to get ahead. The last characteristic was exactly the reason she broke up with him. He loved her deeply. She knew that. And she wished, more than anything, that she could return the depth of his love. In truth, they wanted different things in life, and she was no longer willing to compromise.

Hi Spencer. All is good here. Working hard on the house.

I'd love to come down and see it sometime.

Now, that would be a problem. She didn't want to give him any false hope.

We'll see. It has a long way to go. It's been a long day, so I'm going to head to bed. Thanks for checking in.

She stared at the screen for about thirty seconds. The message had been read, but he hadn't replied. Good, she thought. Maybe he was finally starting to move on.

Courtney sighed. She hated hurting Spencer, but she really didn't have time to be thinking about any men. She had work to do. Checking her browser, she was grateful to see that the images had finally loaded. There was no time in her life for dating or even thoughts about dating, not Spencer, not Jason, and not Gavin. She had work to do, and the workload was going to increase dramatically over the coming weeks.

*****

"So, you know where and how we're able to begin?" Gavin asked, looking around and realizing for the first time just how much work this was going to be.

"Yes, Jason marked everything he thinks is original—the wooden beams and wall pieces, most of the paneling. He needs to run some tests, but he seems to think the previous restorers kept as much as they could. He wants to date everything for sure, so he took some small pieces with him. I'm not sure how that works." She crinkled her nose, and Gavin recognized the girl he knew years ago. "Somehow, he'll be able to determine if they're original, and if not, what time period they're from. He says we can date each section of the house and everything in it. Oh, and I got a hold of a mold expert. Unfortunately, he can't get here for a while. He's booked until fall, and there doesn't seem to be anyone else in the area."

"Okay, we'll just stay out of the cellar until then. You're leaving the kitchen how it is and updating it, right?"

"Uh-huh," she answered absent-mindedly as she stared into the dark upstairs of the house.

Gavin went to her side and gazed up. "What are you thinking?"

Courtney inhaled and let the breath out in one long stream. "There are two rooms upstairs with the small landing between them. Do you think it's possible to add a bathroom?"

"Let's go up and check it out, but let me lead. I'm not sure how safe this staircase is."

He saw Courtney shoot him a defiant look, but she didn't protest, and he didn't acknowledge it. He took the steps slowly, carefully testing each one before putting his weight on it. Courtney rolled her eyes, but he ignored her. The staircase was remarkably strong. Some of the railing uprights were missing, though, otherwise, the whole thing was in great shape. It was made of good, strong oak, and was surely standing the test of time.

Gavin went into the bedroom to the right. It was about nine by thirteen, give or take. The wall on the far end, from floor to ceiling, was plastered, with doors on each side of the wall. Closets, perhaps, built on each side of the fireplace. He was certain Jason was right about the missing fireplaces both here and below. It made sense for the time that the house was built, architecturally and thermally. Plus, there was a chimney on the outer wall.

"Jason said it's okay to remove the paneling where the fireplaces are, right?" he asked

"Yeah." Courtney followed him toward the wall. "Are you sure you can do that without harming the rest of the wall?"

It was Gavin's turn to roll his eyes. He didn't bother answering but went instead to the wall and ran his hand across the panels, knocking here and there as he presumed Jason had.

"Hold on," he said. "I'll be right back."

Gavin ran down the stairs, grabbed a hammer and saw from his pile of tools, and took the flight two at a time, no longer worried about its sturdiness.

"Stand back." He reached into his tool apron and retrieved a pair of goggles. It took several hard blows, but Gavin managed to break through the wall with the hammer. He tore off the goggles and began ripping the paneling from the wall. "Come see," he motioned to Courtney.

"Oh my gosh," she whispered. "It *is* a fireplace, and not completely closed in, just covered up with the paneling." She looked at Gavin. "That's amazing."

"I wonder if there's a matching one on the other side."

Gavin hurried from the room and crossed the landing to the other room. It was larger, about nine by sixteen. There was a matching paneled wall on the opposite side. Without waiting for a word from Courtney, Gavin replaced his goggles and began assaulting the panel as he had done in the other room. Just as before, the wood gave way to a covered-up fireplace.

"I'm confused," Courtney said. "There's nothing in the room below except an old woodstove with a pipe."

"Think again. There's a hearth behind the woodstove, larger than need be. I'm betting there's a fireplace in the wall behind it just like the one in the other room."

"Can we go check it out?"

Gavin nodded as he followed her but stopped just short of the landing.

"Hey, Court, what about the bathroom?"

She stopped at the top of the stairs and looked around. "What do you think?"

"I think we could take some of the length off this bedroom and enclose a small bathroom." He walked onto the landing and faced the wall to the right of the bedroom door. "There's a bathroom under the stairs, right?"

Courtney nodded but frowned. "There is, but Jason says I should rip it out and return the space to its original configuration as an under-the-stairs closet. I guess that presents a problem, huh?"

"Well, if we keep it, we can tap into those pipes. If you rip it out, then it would be an issue. And I hate to disappoint you, but Jason might tell you that a bathroom in the old section is a bad idea, not consistent with the times, and all that."

"Mmm," Courtney sighed. "You're probably right. Can you come back to that later?"

"Sure. No need to decide now."

They went downstairs and into the room to the right of the stairs. He tilted his head as he looked at the bricks that he was sure hid a fireplace.

"We're not going to figure it out today." Gavin pointed toward the brick wall. "It's going to take some work to remove the woodstove and get it out of the way. And then we have bricks to work with and not just wood or plaster. It's going to take time to remove the right ones without damaging the whole wall. But…" he walked toward the added-on part of the house and stood in the doorway, looking from one room to the other. "I think we could install a fireplace that is open on both sides, giving you one in this room and in the kitchen. It would give the kitchen a modern feel, but we could retain the look of the original fireplace in here."

Courtney moved to Gavin's side, and he became keenly aware of her.

"I love the idea," Courtney breathed, and Gavin liked that she appreciated what he saw and approved of it. "Do you think, structurally, we can do it?" She smelled like a mixture of sweat and flowers. Her hair was a mess, with strands sticking out of her short ponytail in every direction, and she had dirt smudged on her cheek, just below her scar. Something tugged at his gut, and he swallowed hard. Several moments went by before Gavin realized he hadn't answered her.

"Gavin?" Courtney turned toward him.

"Um, oh, sure, I think we can." He shifted uncomfortably and took a step back to survey the wall. "Just thinking through the logistics of how best to tackle it."

For the first time since he was fifteen years old, Gavin felt his world turning upside down because of Courtney McMillan.

"It's hot in here. I need some air," he said before turning and heading outside.

What the heck are you doing, Gavin? She left you once and never looked back. This time, you'll be the one leaving. Keep it that way.

*****

"There will be a fireplace on both sides of the house like there was in the original building. Actually, four of them, two up and two down. And the kitchen will be kept in the newer part but will have a fifth fireplace that is part of the existing one in the older part of the house, one of those you can see through on both sides. Oh, and Gavin said we can possibly install an upstairs bathroom, though we have to see what Jason thinks because it wouldn't be historically accurate." Courtney didn't stop to take a breath as she told Lily about the plans for the house over breakfast. "I plan to create a first-floor master bedroom and bathroom in the newer section, along with a laundry closet, but we haven't even looked at that part of the house yet. Even though it's newer, it's a mess. Gavin says the wiring is a fire just waiting to happen. Structurally, it's sound and doesn't need as much attention as the older part, so I guess we've just ignored it because we know there's not as much preliminary stuff to be done in there, except in the kitchen of course."

"Courtney," Lily seized an opportunity to speak when her granddaughter took a sip of her coffee. "Slow down. I can barely keep up. And five fireplaces? Isn't that overkill?"

Courtney grinned. "I'm sorry, Gram. I'm just so excited. I won't actually use all five. I'll probably decorate them. You know, with flower arrangements or some fancy fireplace antique something or other. I mean, I could use them." She frowned. "If I have guests, or a family someday, we might need them for heat. I don't know if we can add heat. Or air. But if I have kids, a fire would be dangerous…" Courtney shook her head and blinked.

"Too much to think about right now. Anyway, Gavin and I have already started knocking out the paneling that hid the fireplaces, and Jason is working on some sketches as he researches the history of the house. I can close my eyes and envision it." She closed her eyes and inhaled deeply, imagining her Pinterest images as actual rooms in the house.

"Don't count your chickens before they hatch," her grandmother warned. "You never know what problems you or Gavin or this Jason might run into. That house is four-hundred years old. It may have things wrong with it that you haven't dreamed of encountering."

"I know," Courtney sighed as her grandmother's words brought her back to reality. "I can't help it. I've been intrigued by that house for as long as I can remember. I want it to be perfect."

"Well, perfect takes time, and patience, and perseverance. Don't let your excitement cause you to rush things that should be taken slowly and methodically."

"You're right," Courtney agreed. She dragged her last bite of scrapple through a puddle of syrup as she thought about what she was going to work on today. Taking a bite of her favorite breakfast meat, she looked back at Lily. "Gram, do you think I'm crazy? To be spending the settlement money this way?"

"Well, how else would you have spent it?" Lily asked as she walked into the next room and opened a drawer in the long buffet. "Now, where did I put that?" she murmured to herself.

"I don't know. There isn't anything else I want. I've already invested a good chunk for later, and I'm not one to travel much, especially alone. I want to do something concrete with the money and have something to show for it."

Lily slammed the drawer with a huff.

"What are you looking for?"

"Just an article I remember saving. I'll find it. I'll just call on Saint Anthony to help. Anyway," she returned to the kitchen and laid her hand on Courtney's shoulder. "If your heart is telling you that this is the right thing to do, then it is. I've always been a big believer in listening to your heart. Pray about it, and God will put the answer in your heart."

Courtney smiled up at her grandmother. The woman had no idea how much she had influenced Courtney over the years with her faith-filled advice, her quiet confidence, and her joyful heart. One of the reasons she wanted to buy the house down the road was so that she could be there for her grandmother the way her grandmother had always been there for her.

"Well, I guess I'll be heading out." Courtney patted her grandmother's hand and stood from the table. "Gavin and I are meeting Jason at the house to hear his ideas and see what he's discovered about its history."

"I hope you're keeping a journal of your progress," Lily suggested as she began gathering the breakfast dishes. "You're going to want your children to have the answers that you're working so hard to find."

Courtney tilted her head and hummed as she thought about it. "That's a great idea, Gram. I honestly hadn't thought about it, but you're right. I should be documenting everything that we find and do." She went to her grandmother, wrapped her arms around the older woman, and kissed her cheek. "What would I do without you?"

"You'd be just fine," Lily said quietly, and for a moment, Courtney felt an inexplicable lump in her throat. She gave her grandmother a squeeze.

"I'll see you later." Courtney blinked away her tears. She had already lost her grandfather, and not having her grandmother around was not something that Courtney wanted to consider.

*****

Sweat ran down Courtney's back as she went through the house, opening windows. One of the first questions she wanted to ask Jason was whether she was allowed to install air conditioning and central heat. She hadn't thought about it before this morning, and she hoped Gavin would have an idea as to how that could be done, if at all. She could always use window units for air, but they would ruin the look of the house.

At the top of the stairs, she stopped abruptly before heading back to the first floor. Had she heard something? The hair on the back of her neck stood as she strained to hear movement.

Glancing at her watch, she shook her head. Too soon for either of the men to arrive. She came early to do a walk-through, open the house, and make sure she didn't have any other questions to add to her ever-growing list. Jason and Gavin weren't due for another hour.

As she put her foot on the top step, an eruption of gooseflesh ran up her arm, and she froze. There it was again—the faint sound of someone walking through the house. Boots. It definitely sounded like boots, and not the work boots that Gavin wore. She swallowed as she gathered her courage to call out.

"Hello," she called. "Is somebody down there?"

She had been told that teenagers sometimes used the house as a place to hide out and drink or get high, vices she had never understood. Surely, they wouldn't take the risk of doing that now that the house had been sold and was being renovated, would they? Not during the day anyway.

"Hello," she called again. Perhaps it was her imagination. She listened intently but didn't hear anything. She made her way down the stairs slowly, leaning over the railing to see better as if she were a spy on a cloak and dagger mission. There was a strange smell in the air, something she hadn't noticed when she was down there just a few minutes before. What was it? She shook her head as the phantom smell dissipated. Smoke? The kind from her grandfather's pipe, she thought. No, impossible.

"You fool," she said to herself. "You're letting your imagination get away from you." She took a deep breath to clear her head. She was just being silly, remembering too many of the old ghost stories that she heard when she was a little girl.

As she wandered into the next room, she suddenly felt the same thing she felt when she was outside a few days earlier. She had the eeriest sensation that she was being watched.

*****

A chorus of humming filled the large room as the generator and fans stirred the warm air into something of a deceptive breeze. It was nearly impossible to escape the humidity, and Gavin didn't feel like the fans he set up made a difference in the room, not a big one anyway. He'd taken a break from working on the wiring to listen to what Jason had to say.

"The carpet has got to go," Jason said as he did a close inspection of the floorboards that were visible where part of the carpet had been torn away from the molding. "We're going to want to remove all of it and see what's underneath as soon as possible."

"How do we know there's anything decent underneath?" Courtney asked though they all knew that the old, worn, and stained carpets had to go whether the floors underneath were good or not.

"Well, hopefully there aren't any rotten boards anywhere. And the floors that are under the carpet are not only in good shape but are the original flooring. I've walked the whole length of the house trying to feel for anything that might be bad. There are a few questionable spots, but, for the most part, it seems to be pretty solid. We won't know for sure, though, until we rip out everything and get a good look from one end of the house to the other. Whatever we find, I promise to help you achieve authenticity." Jason laid his hand on her shoulder and smiled, but something in Gavin's gut twisted at the sight, and he had a hard time believing it was sincere. There was something about the guy that bugged him.

Gavin stood up from the stooped position where he assessed the flooring and watched the two of them. Courtney smiled at Jason, a sweet, trusting smile, and Gavin's gut twisted even more. Courtney was his oldest friend. They'd been friends since birth. Sure, they'd lost touch over the years, but still, he felt protective of her. And then there was…

"Gavin? Hello?" Courtney realized he'd tuned them out, lost in the memory of a stolen kiss under a weeping willow tree.

"I'm sorry, what did you ask me?"

"Your thoughts on ripping up the carpet to see what's underneath."

"Oh," Gavin scratched the day's-old growth on his chin. "I'm not a fan of starting with the floors. There's a lot to do on the walls, like finding the fireplaces, taking off the old paint, securing anything lose on the stairs, replacing the railing, taking out the woodstove, remodeling the kitchen, and a million other things we haven't even thought of yet. All of those should be done before we ever even think about ripping up the floors. They should be dead last as far as the renovation."

Gavin thought he detected a look of annoyance cross Jason's features, but Jason was quick to nod and stand to face Gavin.

"You're right, of course. There are many other things that need to be done before we worry about the floors. I'm just letting you know that it needs to be done. I think we should start a list of what needs to be done, like the things you just said, and determine the order."

Gavin eyed Jason for a moment before slowly nodding his head in agreement. "Sure, that sounds like a good plan. Luckily, Courtney and I have already started one."

The two men stood still and looked at each other, a palpable intensity between them, like two wolves circling a shared prey. Gavin refused to look away, though he knew it was childish, and he wondered what it was about Jason that set his teeth on edge. The guy seemed like a decent, hard-working, well-educated man. He was friendly, kind to Courtney, and only wanted what was best for her and for her future home. He needed to give the guy a break, but it was hard to tame his inner wolf. Finally, it was Courtney who broke the standoff.

"Okay, then, let's get started. Where do we begin?" She looked from one man to the other, waiting for a response. After a moment, Jason turned toward her.

"I'd like to run some more tests on the walls to see if we can determine the age of the paint. We already know, from the tests I did last week, that the wood is original, or at least from the right time period. I propose we remove the existing paint and see how many layers there are over the original wood. We can see what the original colors were throughout the house. We also need to determine what we keep and what we remove as far as the panels. If there's space in the walls between the panels and brick, I think it would be nice to add shelves seated in the walls on each side of the fireplace. That's probably how it was originally set up."

"Oh, I like that idea." Courtney's eyes lit up.

"Easily done." Gavin looked at the panels. "And there are already closets in those walls upstairs, so there's a good chance there's space. Do you need to keep that middle panel for your testing, or can I go ahead and finish removing it?"

"Go ahead. We've already determined that it's not part of the original," Jason responded. "And if it was, you've already damaged these and the panels upstairs." He scowled as he looked at the hole Gavin had ripped in the paneling.

Gavin ignored the words and the tone. "Okay, I'll get started on that as soon as I finish the wiring. The faster we know everything is safe, the faster we can get the electric company to turn the power on. I can't do much without my tools."

"Makes sense," Jason agreed. "I definitely need more light in here."

"Then, I'll get moving." Gavin turned to go outside to get the necessary tools. As he walked from the house, he heard Courtney say, "Jason, I'm so happy you're on this project with us. I can't imagine how I would ever know how to go about this without you."

Gavin hurried from the room before he could hear Jason's response.

"Oh, Jason, I'm so happy you're here by my side," Gavin mimicked as he walked out into the heat and humidity of the Mid-Atlantic day. Maybe those fans were helping after all, he thought. Anything was better than the still, heavy air that clung to him as soon as he exited the house. Though that little voice in his head told him that not all of the heat he was feeling was caused by the weather.

CHAPTER FOUR

"You look so good," Jodie said as she hugged her daughter. "Best you've looked since…" Jodie bit her lip and gazed at Courtney as she released her hold.

"Thanks, Mom." Courtney turned toward her father.

"Come here." Her father had tears in his eyes when he reached for her. Courtney had become accustom to seeing her father cry. He'd had a hard time shutting off the waterworks ever since the accident. She imagined being told that your daughter was probably going to die and then living through the miracle of her recovery would do that to a person.

Once the round of hugging was completed, Courtney reached for her mother's bag and carried it into the house.

"Gram has a queen-sized bed in the back bedroom now, so we're putting you and Dad in there. I hope you don't mind."

"Of course not," Jodie told her. "Whatever is easiest."

Courtney continued on, bag in hand, but noticed her mother had stopped in the doorway to look at a picture on the wall. It was of Courtney's grandfather, standing proud and tall on one of the many boats that he had built. This particular one was a special order by the Governor of the State of Maryland. Her grandfather was awfully proud of that boat.

"He was so proud of that boat," Jodie said wistfully as if reading Courtney's mind.

Courtney dropped her mother's overnight bag and draped her arms around her mother's shoulders. She gazed at the photo. "Not as proud as he was of you." Courtney rested her head against her mother's.

"Or of you," Jodie added with a sigh. She turned toward her daughter. "So, tell me what's going on with the house. What's the latest?"

"Oh, mom, it's going to be wonderful, but it's not going to be easy. Let me take your bag to your room, and then I'll tell you all about it over lunch." They headed toward the back of the house until Jodie paused at the kitchen door and took Courtney by the sleeve.

"I heard from Spencer the other day." Jodie's tone was tentative.

"Oh, really? And how's he doing?" Courtney asked, trying to mask the irritation she felt. Her mother refused to give up on them getting back together.

"Not too well. He misses you. He asked if we'd seen you lately and how you were doing."

"Well, that was nice of him." Courtney pulled her arm from her mother's grasp. "I'll be back," she grumbled, taking the bag into the nearby added-on bedroom. She took a deep breath, headed back to the kitchen, and went straight to the cabinet for a wine glass. She had a feeling she was going to need a drink. "Red or white?"

"Red, but have you taken your migraine medicine recently?"

"If you mean today, then no, I have not. I'm good to have a glass of wine."

"Okay. So," Jodie began. "As I was saying, Spencer said he'd love to see the house."

Courtney sighed. She should have known her mother wouldn't drop it. "Mom, he's already asked. I told him that it's not ready yet."

"That you're not ready yet."

As she uncorked the wine, Courtney took a deep breath and swallowed. "Mom, it's over between Spencer and me. You know that. Why can't you let it go?" She turned toward her mother and handed her a glass of Merlot.

"Spencer is just so right for you. He's handsome, intelligent, hard-working."

"He's hard-working all right." Courtney shot a knowing look at her mother.

"Now, Courtney, you can't fault him for trying to provide for you and your future family. And now that you have your settlement, you don't need to feel like you'd be—"

"I'd be what? Unable to provide as much as he could? Living off of his partner salary? Mom, I had a good job. I made a more than decent salary. I didn't need Spencer's money. And I didn't need the long hours he put in and all the times I spent waiting for him. I needed *him*. Or so I thought. But the truth is, I needed me. I need to be my own person."

"And being with Spencer didn't allow you to do that? He never demanded that you be anything but you. He loves you for who you are."

"I get that mom, and a part of me will always love Spencer, but I realized I don't want to marry him. I don't want that life. Please understand that."

"What's going on in here?" Courtney's father asked, coming into the kitchen.

"Nothing. Same as always. Here." She handed him the glass of wine. "I don't think I should have this after all. I need to check on Gram. I'll be back."

Courtney walked past them and out to the side porch where Lily had been hiding. She could hear her mother complaining to her father as she closed the door behind her. "She's so stubborn. I don't know why she's doing this."

"How's it going?" Lily asked, looking up from her favorite sun-bathed chair on the airy porch.

"I'm sure you heard." Courtney leaned against one of the beams.

"Give her some time. She'll come around. You and Spencer were together for so long that it just seemed natural to her. She's at as much a loss as you are right now. You're both trying to find you."

Courtney shook her head. "I'm right here, Gram. Nobody needs to find me."

"Are you so sure about that?"

Courtney looked at Lily. No, she wasn't sure of anything at the moment.

*****

"Oh, Courtney." Jodie stood in the room and turned to take it all in. Courtney knew what she saw—the gaping hole in the wall that was a barely recognizable fireplace, the cracked and peeling paint, the expensive window with the hairline fracture running through the pane, and the hole in the ceiling where once hung a chandelier. Jodie's brow shifted downward, her mouth turned inward, and her lips whitened as she pressed them together between her teeth.

"I know." Courtney read the look on her mother's face. She could feel the pounding beginning to take hold in her head. "I warned you that it won't be easy. It's a lot of work."

"A lot of work?" Jodie repeated. "Courtney Jane, it's a money pit. It's going to take you years to pull this together. Why would you saddle yourself with this now? At your age? Alone?"

"Mom, we've gone over this—"

"Look, I get it. You needed a fresh start, a job away from the city, a life without a reminder of the day you almost..." She choked back the emotion that Courtney heard in her voice.

"Mom, it's not that. I'm okay with what happened. I was bored with my job. I hated living in the city. I needed a change. And Gram's not getting any younger. It's good for her that I'm—"

"Don't you dare," Jodie turned on her daughter. "Don't you dare use my mother as an excuse to have this early mid-life crisis of yours."

"I'm not using her as an excuse," Courtney bit back. "And it's not a crisis. This is for me. It's what I want to do."

"You want to throw away six years of school, your degree and your MBA for, for this?" She threw her arms up in the air and looked at Courtney with pleading eyes.

"Mom, I've wanted this my whole life. I got that degree and the MBA, and the stuffy job, because I had no idea what I wanted to do with my life. Now, I do."

"Courtney," Jodie sighed with exasperation. "That makes no sense. This isn't a calling. It's, it's a nightmare!"

Courtney took a deep breath, closed her eyes, and slowly exhaled. "Mom, I understand your being upset. I really do. And I know that this isn't my calling. I will get a job. I will find something I enjoy and make a living at it; but, for now, this is what I need."

Jodie's look told Courtney that her mother wouldn't pretend to understand, but maybe she would give up the fight, for the time being, and let her daughter do what she had to do.

"If you two are finished in here, let's head to Sami's," Courtney's father, Rick, said from the doorway. "I'm starving, and it's hot as Hades in here."

"It is, and both Jason and Gavin vetoed central air." Courtney mumbled more to herself than to her parents. "Anyway, mom, lunch?" Courtney asked tentatively.

"Fine. Let's go eat." Jodie shook her head as she headed toward the entry hall. "But we're buying," she added. "You're going to blow through that settlement money in six months' time. Mark my words."

Courtney bit her lip. It wasn't exactly a show of support, but she knew her mother recognized her resignation. Nothing was going to change Courtney's mind.

"By the way," Rick beagn as Courtney locked the front door. He gestured toward the vines covering the side of the house. "You've got to do something about all this—"

"Honeysuckle." Courtney sighed. "I know."

*****

"I'm really not sure what to tell you," Rick said after dinner that night as they sat around the crowded table. Gavin's mother had left, and they were all fully satiated by the bushel of steamed crabs. There was enough left over for Jodie and Rick to take some home with them the next afternoon, and Courtney felt content with the meal and the conversation. Jan was a gem, and they all enjoyed spending time with her and listening to her share stories about the people around town. She got out much more than Lily did, and she knew everything about everybody. But now, they were trying to figure out what they knew about the McMillan family history, and that was something Jan would have known nothing about.

Rick continued. “My parents never shared much family history with me. We know we owned the manor, and that, at some point, the state took that away, after the Revolution, maybe when Catholicism was outlawed in the state. I’m not sure”

“I still don’t know how that happened,” Courtney said. “Maryland was founded as a free-religion colony. Our ancestors came here to set up a Catholic settlement. Lord Baltimore and all of the Calverts were Catholic. What happened?”

“Fear, jealousy, greed.” Her father buttered a roll as he spoke. “As newcomers came to the state, they feared that the Catholics had too much power. They were afraid of the Pope, not understanding his place in the Church. They thought he would grow strong politically and make everyone who lived here become Catholic. And it didn’t help that the majority of wealthy landowners, like the Calverts and our family at the time, were Catholic.”

“But didn’t they see that they were doing exactly what they feared the Catholics would do to them?”

“Maybe some did, but others were raised to believe that Papists, as they called us, were heathens, worshipping idols and corrupting the teachings of Christ."

"But that wasn't true." Courtney shook her head.

"Yes, but there are still those who believe that today," her mother interjected. "So, we haven't come very far, have we?"

Courtney sighed and shook her head. "Okay, but what about our family?"

"Well," Rick continued. Placing his elbows on the table, he made a steeple with his fingers and pressed them against his chin. "At some point, the only land we had left was the lighthouse on the island. My great-great Uncle Jerome sold it, and then it eventually was sold to the state park service."

"And we have all of Jerome's journals, the letters he kept, and the documentation about the sale, but what about before that? What about River Terrace? When did we lose that?"

Rick rubbed his chin and thought about it. "I honestly don't know, princess. I would tell you if I did."

"Oh! That reminds me." Lily jumped from her seat and left the room.

Jodie watched her go, turned toward Courtney, and raised her brow, but Courtney just shrugged.

"Okay, what about the records at the museum?" Jodie asked, letting Lily's behavior go. "Mom said you had done some research in their archives."

"I did, but it didn't give me anything concrete. It looks like I'm going to have to dig deeper, search county land records, maybe even drive up to Annapolis and go through the state charter and other historical documents."

They all sat in silence for a moment before Courtney remembered the journal. "Hold on. I want to show you all something."

Courtney went to the back bedroom and retrieved her laptop where she had downloaded the pictures she had on her phone. When she returned, Lily was back at the table, an old yellow newspaper clipping in her hand.

"What's that?" Courtney asked.

"Saint Anthony came through again. This is an article I kept from a while back. I ran across it when you first told me you were buying River Terrace, and I put it aside for you." Lily blushed. "But I forgot where I put it. I finally found it this morning."

"Is it about the house?" Courtney leaned over to see the fragile paper. A photograph of the house was placed at the top of the story.

"It is. You don't have to read it now, though it does talk a bit about your family being the original owners. Most of the article is about the Suttons and how they were trying to restore it. Of course, we know that didn't happen."

"Hold onto it," Courtney told her. "I'll take a look later, but don't forget where you put it." She smiled at her grandmother before turning back to her father. "I came across these pages in an old journal. Do you know who Robert McMillan was?" she asked, showing her father the computer screen.

He read through the entries and shook his head. "Sorry, but no. I mean, I know he was the original owner, but I don't know anything else. Why do you ask?" he asked, handing the laptop back to her.

"Robert's the man mentioned in the article," Lily said. "As the first owner of the house."

"Is that all it says?" Courtney asked.

"Yes." Lily perused the text. "Just that the house was built in the late 1600s by Robert McMillan who lived there until his death." She frowned. "It says, 'Robert McMillan Senior.' And there's no death date. I don't know if the one you came across is him or Robert Junior." She took off the paperclip that held the second page and scanned it. "There's nothing else, I'm afraid."

"That's okay." Courtney placed the laptop on the table and went back to her seat across from her father. "I don't know why, but for some reason, I just feel like he's important." She shrugged. "I mean, other than him building the house. Or his son, maybe. Anyway, it was just a feeling I had."

"You know what you need to do," Jodie said, all traces of her earlier disappointment gone. "You need to contact cousin Clarissa. She knows everything there is to know about the family history. She can probably answer a lot of your questions."

"Do you think she'd come down here, or should I go up to Bethesda?" Courtney liked the idea of talking to her father's cousin, though she didn't like the thought of making the three-hour journey to the northern DC suburbs.

Rick shook his head. "I don't think it would be fair to ask her to come all the way down here."

"Nonsense," Jodie said. "Clarissa is always looking for an excuse to come down here. She may live north of DC, but Southern Maryland will always be her home."

*****

"Gram, did you see here that the Suttons thought that River Terrace was haunted?"

"Oh, people have been saying that for years."

Lily was watching a Hallmark movie as Courtney sat in the old recliner and read the article. Her parents had left after Mass that morning, and Courtney resisted the urge to spend the afternoon at the house. She and Lily picked blackberries instead. Lily was planning on making jam that week, and Courtney enjoyed spending the afternoon helping her pick the berries. The heat wave had broken, and for the first time since she arrived, Courtney didn't feel like her clothes were glued to her body. She still had no complaints about spending the afternoon in the air conditioning and tried to use the respite to learn something from the article Lily found.

"Listen to this." She read the snippet out loud.

"Their neighbors in the quiet town of Bushwood think they're crazy. And they might be to put up with ghosts in their living room, snakes in the closet, and a rotten floor that collapsed one evening, sending the kitchen table into the ground underneath. One morning, they awoke to find snow in their bed from a crack in the roof they didn't know existed."

"Uh oh," Courtney looked up. "Gavin found a bad spot in an upstairs bedroom and said he was afraid there might be a leak. I wonder if they never got around to fixing it."

"Better have him check it out," Lily told her.

Courtney nodded. "I will. Listen,

"Renee Sutton said, 'We were told that the house was haunted when we first moved in, and everyone told us we'd never stay, but we've been here six months already, and we love it.' The Suttons moved into the house in October of 1990, just over a year ago, and they say they plan to stay.

"They couldn't have loved it that much. They left it suddenly and in horrible condition." She continued,

"The Suttons don't know whose spirits continue to inhabit the house, though they are hoping to find ways to live amicably. 'Sometimes we hear someone walking through the parlor with heavy boots on, and we can smell his pipe tobacco,' Renee Sutton said. Once, the couple returned home to find all of the furniture turned upside-down. The doors lock and unlock on their own, and the windows will sometimes slam shut. 'It's always an adventure around here,' Renee laughed.

"I don't know that I'd be laughing," Courtney said, remembering the sound of boots and the smell of tobacco she experienced.

"Have you encountered anything ghostly so far?" Lily asked.

Courtney bit her lips together and shook her head. "No overturned furniture or locked doors." She chuckled uneasily, thinking perhaps it was better not to share the incident with Lily.

"Well, maybe the ghosts have crossed over to the other side."

"You don't really believe in that kind of stuff, do you, Gram?"

"I'm open to the possibility." She shrugged. "Who knows."

Who knows, indeed. Courtney shivered and finished the article. She was sure there had to be a reasonable explanation. She just didn't know what it could be…

*****

Courtney, Lily, and Clarissa laughed their way through dinner. Clarissa, a red-haired woman in her sixties, tall, thin, and quite amusing, regaled them with stories about her childhood with her cousins, including Courtney's father. She told tales about relatives long gone and about some of the more well-known characters in the county.

"Lily, you sure know how to make a body feel welcome." Clarissa finished her glass of sweet tea before continuing. "This lemon meringue pie is the best I've ever tasted."

"Well, you can thank the morning baker at the local market for that," Lily said. "Courtney can tell you, I don't bake."

"Now, you didn't have to tell me that," Clarissa told her. "I would have bragged to all of the family about how wonderful your pie is."

"Everyone in the county knows that it was Ben's sisters who did all the prize-winning baking."

"But nobody can fry chicken the way Gram does," Courtney interceded. "Talk about prize-winning."

"I'll have to come back for that."

"Consider yourself invited," Lily said with a smile. "Just show up on any Sunday afternoon."

"I might just do that." Clarissa turned to Courtney. "For now, I guess we should get down to business. What is it you want to know, Courtney?"

"How much do you know about the history of River Terrace?"

Clarissa sat back and took a deep breath as she gazed across the room. She blinked a few times, shifting her jaw back and forth. Courtney watched her and wondered if her distant cousin was starting to forget all that she knew about the family history.

"Well, honestly," Clarissa began, "not much. I know a lot about the island and its owners, including my great-grandparents, but that was back during the war, the Civil War, and up through the 1940s. I know the lineage that dates back to the house, though I don't know that anyone knows specifics about the family, other than what's written in the journals."

"You know about the journals?" Courtney asked.

"I sure do know about them. I donated Robert Junior's to the museum."

Courtney sat up straighter. "Really? I had no idea. Were there more? His journal from the 1720s ended rather abruptly."

"Ah, yes, that was Robert McMillan Jr. He owned the manor house then."

"Yes." Courtney's anticipation caused her heart to beat a little faster. "Do you know what happened to him?"

"Well, he died, obviously, but the circumstances are a little, well, sketchy, I guess you'd say."

"Sketchy? What do you mean?" Courtney had no idea why the man interested her so much or what bearing it had on the house. Ever since she read the entry about the stranger and her baby and the loss of the twin, she couldn't help but wonder what happened to everyone involved. And the fact that the journal ended so suddenly had left her curiosity piqued.

"He was sick for a while. Based on what we know from his brother's journal—"

"Hold on, his brother had a journal?"

"Yes, his brother John. Though those journals aren't down here. They're at Pratt Library in Baltimore in their Maryland collection. His family moved there soon after Robert's death."

"Okay." Courtney thought a trip to Baltimore was in her near future. "So, about Robert's death…"

"Yes, as I was saying, according to John, Robert was sick for a very long time. He seemed to have periods of near-paralysis, loss of feeling in his hands and feet, mental confusion, and was often in pain."

"Polio?" Courtney asked.

Clarissa shook her head. "No, in those days, it would have wiped out the entire family, and there probably would have been documentation of an epidemic. Using the information we have, what we know about diseases of that time, and modern medical information, it's believed he suffered from a thiamine deficiency."

"Thiamine?"

"It's a basic vitamin deficiency, almost unheard of in that extreme today, but common in Colonial days."

"Okay, so he died of a vitamin deficiency. Why is that sketchy?"

"It wasn't the deficiency that killed him. I don't really remember all of the details, though according to John's writings, his brother was killed by pirates. As many around here know, there have always been rumors, legends really, about a pirate uprising of some sort around that time."

"Pirates?" Lily said. "Hogwash. Why would there be pirates in Bushwood or anywhere in the Wicomico River for that matter?"

"Oh, there were plenty of pirates in these waters back in the sixteen and seventeen-hundreds. The Bay and all of its rivers, including the Patuxent, Potomac, and our own Wicomico, were prime locations for pirates for nearly 200 years. The Potomac, which feeds the Wicomico, was the main route to Alexandria and eventually DC where the merchants awaited imported goods. The New World, with its distance from Europe and its untapped resources and treasures, was a great target for pirates. Dutch raiders preyed on the towns along the Bay and rivers throughout the 1600s; some of them were sanctioned by the Dutch government, and others were simply privateers.

"In the late 1600s, a band of pirates went up and down the Chesapeake, plundering their way in and out of the rivers from the head of the Bay all the way down to the Atlantic. They eventually made their way clear up to Rhode Island where they were captured. During the 1600s, the pirates were welcomed by the Tidewater colonists, who found them quite amenable to fair trade and bartering. This was illegal, but the colonists could often get goods from the pirates less expensively than they could from the English merchant ships."

Clarissa stopped and poured herself another glass of tea from the glass pitcher on the table, added two heaping spoonsful of sugar, stirred it, and took a long drink. Setting her glass back on the table, she took a deep breath and continued. "After a very successful series of pirate raids in the late 1600s, Maryland and

Virginia stepped up their defenses and placed militia watchers along the coast and patrol ships, the beginning of the navy, in the water. But pirates found holes in the militia posts and continued to raid and plunder, taking whatever they needed from guns to cattle."

"Cattle?" Courtney asked. "They actually stole cattle and took them onboard?"

"Oh, yes. One of the main things they took, when they raided the islands and coastal towns along the Bay, was food. It's a long journey from the Caribbean, where most of the pirates had their bases, and by the time they reached the Chesapeake, they were starving. Islands, like Smith and Tangier Islands on the Eastern Shore, were easy pickings for pirates, giving them sustenance to continue their sojourn up the Bay. And the stories that traveled up and down the Maryland and Virginia coastlines kept the colonists and the government officials in a constant state of fear. It was in the early 1700s, during the golden age of piracy, that the waters in and around the Chesapeake saw the most action from pirates."

Courtney shook her head, feeling the need to clear it from the bombardment of information. "How do you know all of this?"

"I've spent my entire life learning the history of the region. It's so much more fun and fascinating than most people realize."

"I'll say," Courtney agreed. "I can hardly keep up with you, and I still want to know more."

"Why don't you two head into the living room, and I'll get the dishes taken care of," Lily told them.

"Nonsense." Clarissa stood and began clearing the table. "If I eat, I clean. No arguments."

They worked together to clear the table and wash the dishes. Each took a turn in the single bathroom before rejoining in the living room and making themselves comfortable.

"By the early 1700s," Clarissa continued, "piracy in the Caribbean had reached new heights, and the colonists no longer supported the plunderers. It didn't take long for the pirates to begin targeting the merchant vessels heading to the colonies. One of the premier shipping routes was up the Bay to the Baltimore Harbor. With so many rivers and tributaries shooting off from the Chesapeake, there were many places for ships to hide and lots of small, coastline villages to plunder. That's when Blackbeard made his way up to the Tidewater."

"Wait." Courtney held up her hand. "Blackbeard? As in the character from the Disney pirate movies?"

"The one and the same." Clarissa's eyes twinkled.

"Hold on, isn't he just a myth, a composite of all of the old pirate tales and legends rolled into one?"

"Not at all," Clarissa insisted. "Blackbeard was considered the fiercest and most feared pirate of the time from the West Indies to the Colonies. He was more formidable than Disney could ever dream him into being. According to most accounts, other than a few raids in the lower part of the Bay, he was captured and executed before he was able to get this far north. However, there are some texts that claim he may have visited River Terrace."

"Really?" Courtney asked, hardly able to believe it could be true.

"Maybe. I once read something that stated it as a fact. It was around 1720, I believe, though there's not much evidence to support it. Whether he was here or not, the next several years were particularly heavy with pirate activity."

"1725," Courtney said, sitting up on the couch and clutching a pillow in her lap. "That's the date in the journal when Robert McMillan found the woman and her stillborn child in his bed."

"Anne," Clarissa supplied. "Not much is known about her other than her name, but I always wondered…"

Courtney felt the hairs stand on the back of her neck as she watched the thoughts play across Clarissa's features. "You always wondered what?"

"There were a few female pirates during that golden age. One was Anne Bonny, the most notorious of the women pirates. She was Irish, from good stock, but fell in love with a pirate. There was more than one pirate who tickled her fancy, according to the legends. Anyway, historical accounts differ as to whatever happened to Anne. She was arrested and sentenced to death but was found to be pregnant. Her execution was postponed until after she gave birth, but there are no records of her ever having been put to death. Some accounts say she was indeed hanged. Others say she mysteriously disappeared, perhaps rescued by her band of pirates. Still, others say she escaped only to be found and hanged somewhere else."

"So, we really don't know for sure?" Courtney asked.

"We really don't. All we know is that she had the baby in prison in 1720, escaped, and disappeared."

"And may have turned up here in 1725, again pregnant," Courtney supplied.

Clarissa shrugged. "Perhaps. It may seem far-fetched, but you know what they say, truth is stranger than fiction." Clarissa yawned, and Courtney knew it had been a long day for her older cousin.

"Let's call it a night," Courtney said.

"Agreed. I'm anxious to see that house of yours, and I'm an early riser."

"Then I'll see you in the morning, Clarissa. And thank you. This has truly been an enlightening evening."

Despite not really learning anything more about her father's family or about the history of the house, Courtney felt renewed hope that she was destined to restore the house to its original glory. Her family may have lost the manor many years ago, but she was determined to be the one to bring it back to life and to discover all of its secrets.

*****

After an early breakfast, Courtney drove Clarissa to River Terrace. The morning sun beamed down on the grey rooftop, and the wavy-glass windows reflected the light, giving the house an eerie glow.

"It's just as I remember it. Only, it looks like it's seen better days."

Courtney looked from what was remaining of the sagging porch, which Gavin had started to strip away, to the leaning chimney. The house had most definitely seen better days.

"It does need quite a lot of work," Courtney admitted. "The plan is to return it to its original state as much as possible with modern upgrades. And to modernize the addition where the kitchen and master suite is. Some of that has been done in the kitchen, but even that is outdated. The master suite was never finished, though I have a vision that I hope to bring to fruition."

Clarissa nodded. "That would be nice. And I like that you're taking the house back to how it was. I like it when old homes are returned to their original glory. It's a shame to tear them down and completely forget about the past."

"I agree. I've loved this house forever, and I hate that it hasn't always been given the love it deserves."

"Houses are a lot like people, Courtney. We can dress them up, show them off, buy them fancy things, and keep them looking nice, but without love and attention, they simply fall apart and become lifeless. We all need love and attention."

"Have you been talking to my mother?" Courtney asked. "She's so worried that I will spend all of my time and energy on this instead of on finding a significant other and starting a family. She's still really angry that I broke up with Spencer."

"There's something to be said for finding that significant other." Clarissa turned toward Courtney. "I lost my James years ago, but I wouldn't trade that time in my life for anything in the world. We all need someone to talk to, to lean on, to build a life with, to share hopes and dreams with. Look at your grandparents. Theirs was one of the most beautiful and fulfilling relationships of all time. We would all be blessed to find what they had."

Courtney bit her lips. She knew Clarissa was right, but, so far, she hadn't found that one person with whom she could see herself sharing her hopes and dreams with or building a life together, including Spencer. She wasn't sure there was a person for her out there who would see the world the way she did. Almost dying had changed her in many ways, and she didn't think anyone else could or would understand that.

She offered Clarissa a faint smile and shrugged. "Well, I guess for now, I'll have to settle for building the house of my dreams. We'll have to see about the rest. Shall we go in?"

"Sure, sweetie. Let's go see this house of yours."

They exited the car and walked up to the front door, maneuvering their way around the partially dismantled porch.

"Be careful. Gavin put in temporary steps, but he needs to finish clearing out the porch before he builds permanent ones."

"The house looks better already without that ugly porch. It hid the brickwork and the beautiful old windows."

"Jason says the same thing." Courtney unlocked the door.

"Who's Jason?"

Before she could answer, Courtney let out a gasp as she turned on the overhead light. "Oh my gosh, who did this?" she cried.

Gavin's makeshift workbench had been overturned, his tools scattered around the small entryway. Across the wall along the staircase, red paint dripped from the words that had been hastily scrawled with a paintbrush – *Leave my house alone.*

"Oh my," Clarissa breathed as she and Courtney stood and looked at the message.

Courtney brushed away the tears as her initial alarm turned into anger. "How dare they. How dare someone come in here and vandalize *my* house. Who would do this? Who would claim that this is their house? I'm the owner. It's my name on the deed."

Clarissa reached out and touched Courtney's shoulder. "I think we should call the sheriff."

Courtney shook her head. "I don't know what to do." She sighed, trying to control her anger and think rationally. "Maybe it was just a group of kids playing a prank."

"Even so, they broke into your house, and they messed with Gavin's tools. What if they broke something? He will need to replace it, and he'll need a police report for his insurance. And you need to send a message to whomever did this that they won't get away with doing it again."

"I guess you're right," Courtney sighed, reaching into her back pocket for her phone. "I just hope they don't come back."

"What the heck?" Gavin's voice rang from the doorway.

Courtney held up her hand. "Yes, I'd like to report a break-in." She relayed the information to the sheriff's department as she watched Gavin assess the damage to his tools. "I'm so sorry, Gavin," she said after disconnecting the call. "Is anything broken?"

"It doesn't look like it." Gavin surveyed the mess on the floor before shifting his gaze to the wall. "What's that supposed to mean?" He gestured toward the paint.

"I have no idea." Courtney's anger returned. She balled her hands into fists, what was left of her fingernails biting into her palms. "If it's a warning of some sort, then it's not going to work. Who the heck do they think they are, telling me to get out of my own house?" She huffed, flexing her fingers before placing her fingertips on each side of her temple and taking a deep breath, exhaling into her hands. She looked up and shook her head.

"You're Gavin," Clarissa said, reaching her hand toward Gavin. "I haven't seen you since you were a child. I'm Courtney's cousin, Clarissa."

"It's nice to meet you ma'am." Gavin took her hand as Courtney willed herself to calm down before a migraine could creep in. She could already feel the pressure building.

"There's no ma'am here. It's just Clarissa."

"Yes, ma'am, I mean Clarissa," Gavin smiled. He turned back to Courtney. "Was the house locked when you got here?"

"Yes, locked and empty. Though we haven't gotten any farther than this. Maybe I should check the other doors or see if there's more damage anywhere." She leaned back and peered into the next room.

Gavin shook his head. "Actually, I think we should go outside, leave this the way it is, and not touch anything. The police won't want us disturbing the scene."

"Gavin, you sound like we're at the scene of a murder." Courtney looked around the room and shivered at the thought.

"It might not be a murder, but it's still a crime scene. Come on," he gestured toward the door with his head. "Let's get out of here. We can walk around the outside of the house and see if anything looks strange."

Glancing around once more at the room, Courtney sighed and let Gavin usher them out of the house. He closed the door behind him and wiped his brow. Courtney noticed that he was already sweating, and the heat of the day had barely settled in.

"By the time we get back in and open the windows, it's going to be sweltering in there." She was feeling the weight of a lost day.

"We'll manage. Come on." Gavin gently tugged on her arm. "Let's take a walk around the house and check things out."

Courtney nodded but turned to her cousin. "Clarissa, do you want me to run you back up the road before the sheriff gets here? It might be a while before I can take you back to Gram's."

"Do you think he'll need to talk to me?"

Courtney thought about it and shrugged. "I don't know, but he can always stop at the house when we're done here."

"Well, it is dreadfully hot out here." Clarissa looked up at the clear sky.

"Come on, then, I'll take you back. Gavin, do you mind?"

"Not at all. I'm going to take a look around back."

"Thanks." Courtney sighed. "I don't know what I'd do without you." She meant it, she realized as she walked toward her Explorer. Gavin had been there for her for as long as she could remember, with the exception of the past fifteen years, though that was as much her fault as anyone's. She hadn't reached out to him, hadn't really given him more than a passing thought now and then. Now she regretted losing touch, but she hoped they could keep in touch once he went back to Portland. The thought both comforted and unnerved her at the same time.

"He's a keeper," Clarissa said as she closed the Explorer door. "I can tell these things."

Courtney smiled. "He is. Someday, he's going to make some girl very happy."

"But not you?" Clarissa asked.

Courtney shook her head. "That ship has sailed." She thought wistfully about the kiss so many years ago.

"We thought, maybe, when we were younger, that there was something there, but neither of us made any attempt to act on it. I guess it wasn't meant to be."

"Yet here you both are, thrust together, older and wiser."

Courtney turned toward her cousin, a woman who had lived a long, full life. "It's a nice thought, Clarissa, but I don't think Gavin is the least bit interested in me. As I said, that ship has sailed."

"Ships often sail—sometimes all the way around the world—but they always find their way back to their home port and the comfort of the familiar harbor."

Smiling, Courtney turned the car toward her grandmother's house. She knew that Clarissa meant well, and she liked the analogy, but she knew that Gavin thought of her as a friend, as Lily's granddaughter, and as a client. There was nothing else there. Besides, now that she was seeing her own dreams come to realization, she could never be the reason he gave up on his dreams. He'd made it clear that Bushwood was not where he saw his future, and by extension, that included her. Which was just fine with Courtney. She couldn't understand why everyone was trying to push her into a relationship. Her mother with Spencer. Sami with Jason. Now Clarissa with Gavin. Couldn't anyone see that she was not looking for a man? Suddenly, her grandmother's words came back to her, and Courtney wondered if she really *was* looking for herself.

*****

It was all Courtney could do not to cry as she scrubbed the paint off the wall. Gavin had tried to talk her out of it. They were going to paint over it at some point anyway, but she couldn't stand the sight of the words.

"There's nothing they can do, is there?" she asked, taking a break from her work to look at Gavin when he walked inside to get a drink.

"It doesn't sound like it," he admitted. "But they've got it on record in case something else happens. If the person is ever caught, it's to your benefit to have it documented."

"I know." She blew out her breath in frustration. "I just wish I knew why they did it."

"You heard him." Gavin wiped his brow with the tail of his shirt. "Most likely kids, probably drinking or getting high, looking for some kind of outlet. They're probably ticked that you bought the place, and they won't be able to sneak in here and party anymore."

"I know, and it makes sense, except that…"

"What?" he asked, going forward and leaning against the banister, his arm draped over the newel post.

"Well, if it was kids partying, then why didn't we see evidence of that? I mean, I wasn't much of a drinker in school, but I did go to my fair share of parties. Kids don't clean up after themselves, especially if they're at someone's house that they don't care about. Where are the beer cans? The cigarette butts? What about the paint can? Don't you think they would have just left it rather than take it home?"

Gavin took a breath and rubbed his chin with the hand that had been dangling from the post. "Hmmm, those are good questions. Let me see." His face took on a pensive look as he glanced up at the ceiling before moving his eyes back to hers. "Okay, first of all, they probably took the can of paint from their own garage, so they had to put it back before their dad noticed it was gone. Second, kids don't smoke cigarettes these days. They juul. There could be cartridges laying in the grass that we missed."

"But there aren't any beer cans, and there aren't any cartridges, or whatever they are, inside the house. But…" She bit her lips and took a breath, releasing it as a thought occurred to her. "What does a juul smell like?"

Gavin shrugged. "I don't know. I think they come in different flavors, so they might all smell different. Why?" His brow creased with concern.

"It's probably nothing." Courtney waved her hand in front of her and shook her head. "Most likely my imagination, but one day last week, I got here really early to open the house and get it cooled down. While I was upstairs, I was sure that I heard someone walking through the house, someone with heavy boots on. Heeled boots, not work boots. I called, but nobody answered. When I got downstairs, I caught the whiff of something, tobacco smoke of some kind, like from a pipe. It was faint and very quick, but for just a moment, I smelled it and thought of my grandfather." She caught her bottom lip between her teeth. "Does that sound crazy?"

Gavin shook his head. "Before this morning, I might have told you that you're letting all of the old ghost stories and legends get the best of you, but after this," he gestured toward the paint, "it's possible that somebody was hiding in the house when you arrived. They may have made a run for it while you were upstairs. And if they were smoking something, you might have caught the lingering scent."

Gooseflesh ran up Courtney's arms as she thought about Gavin's scenario. "Someone may have been hiding in the house while I was upstairs?"

Gavin shrugged. "Who knows. It's possible."

Courtney dropped the rag into the bucket of soapy water and walked down the steps.

"I'll be back," she told Gavin.

"Where are you going?"

"To pay a visit to a neighbor," she called as she went out the front door.

*****

"What a pleasant surprise," Hannah said as she welcomed Courtney inside. "I hope everything's okay. I saw the sheriff's car at the house earlier. Can I get you a glass of tea?" She walked toward the back of the house and gestured for Courtney to follow.

"That would be heavenly, thanks." Courtney trailed her into the kitchen. The house was adorable with bright colors and artsy pictures on the walls. Hannah noticed Maddy playing with a doll in the living room. The little girl looked up and smiled but went back to feeding her baby. "It was just some kids messing with stuff. I was actually wondering if you'd seen or heard anything."

Hannah poured two glasses of tea and held up the sugar bowl.

"No thanks."

"Let's sit," Hannah suggested, gesturing to a tiny sunroom off the kitchen.

"How sweet," Courtney said, looking at the little room. "It's so pretty and cozy."

"I love it out here," Hannah told her as Maddy toddled into the room and sat on the floor in the middle of the sunlit room. "It's my favorite part of the house."

"I can see why," Courtney told her, settling onto a white wicker loveseat plush with blue and green floral pillows. She took a sip of her tea before placing it on a coaster on the mosaic table in front of her. "So, did you by any chance notice anything last night?"

Hannah shook her head, a look of pity on her face. "I'm sorry, but no. Maddy wasn't feeling well last night. Earaches, you know." Hannah smiled at Maddy, and Courtney nodded as though she did know. "I'm afraid that, when she's upset, I don't pay attention to anything else. Once I got her to quiet down and fall asleep, I was wiped out. I fell asleep as soon as my head hit the pillow. And with the house closed up, and the AC and fans running, well, you know…"

Courtney nodded. "Yeah, I understand. I just don't know how somebody was able to get into the house. Everything was locked up tight this morning. There were no signs that anyone forced the doors or windows open. I just don't get it." She took a long drink of her tea and enjoyed the feel of the cool liquid as it slid down her throat. She hadn't realized just how hot and thirsty she was until that moment.

"I know this sounds crazy, but…well, never mind." Hannah shook her head and looked away.

"No, go ahead. What is it?" Courtney leaned forward in her seat.

"Well, I'm not saying that I believe any of this nonsense, though there have always been rumors. I mean, they can't be true, but even the kids have said…" She raked her bottom lip through her teeth and ran her fingers through her long, red hair.

"Have said what?" Courtney asked, growing more curious and a little impatient.

"They've said that, sometimes, strange things happen in the house, like sounds and smells. I don't know, crazy stuff that doesn't make sense. I'm sure they were making it up. Now that I've actually said it out loud, it's laughable."

Courtney wasn't laughing. "What kinds of sounds and smells?" she asked, her heart beginning to pound. The familiar ache began to creep into the side of her temple.

"I'm not sure." Hannah thought for a moment, blinking as though she was trying to picture something. "Footsteps, I think?"

"And the smell?" Courtney was on the edge of her seat.

Hannah shook her head. "I don't know. I'm not sure if I ever heard what it was exactly, but I'm sure you have nothing to worry about. I mean, you don't actually believe in that kind of stuff, do you? Legends and folklore and tales of pirate ghosts? I mean, the old couple who lived there years ago always said there were. Oh, forget it. It's all nonsense." Hannah looked worried, and Courtney felt the need to put her at ease, forcing herself to laugh and wave the notion away before taking another long drink.

"Of course it is. How ridiculous. Like you, I've heard those old stories about the house my entire life. I guess that, for a moment, I just let it all get to me. It's kind of unnerving to know that somebody was able to break into my house." Still, the article about the ghosts that the Suttons encountered lingered in her mind.

"I'm sure it is." Hannah's eyes were wide with sympathy. "I can't imagine what that must feel like."

She looked toward Maddy. "I'd be scared to death if someone broke in here. I'm not sure Maddy and I could stay if that happened. I'd always be on edge."

"What about your husband?"

Hannah lifted her shoulders and smiled shyly. "Just me and Maddy. A night of pleasure my junior year that ended up with a pink stripe on a white stick." She blushed. "My parents kicked me out, and the father wanted nothing to do with us. So, I went to one of those shelters for unwed mothers, and, after Maddy was born, I moved in here with my grandfather. He passed away about a year ago." She looked away, her eyes moist with unshed tears.

Courtney thought of her own grandfather, and her heart constricted. "I'm so sorry. I had no idea. I know how hard that must have been for you."

Hannah just nodded, pressing her lips together and blinking several times. "He was the only family we had. I keep hoping my parents will come around, but they didn't even attend the funeral." She sniffed. "They were very angry with Pop Pop for taking us in."

"What did they want you to do?"

She shrugged. "They wanted me to give her up so that I could go to college. I earned my GED at the shelter, and I've been taking a few online classes, but they wanted me to be a doctor or a lawyer or something. They thought I was throwing my life away. They still do," she said quietly.

"Oh, Hannah, I'm so, so sorry. Maybe they'll change their minds." She looked at Maddy and smiled. "I mean, who could stay away from that beautiful little face?" Maddy giggled and rocked the baby doll in her arms.

"Maybe they will. Maybe they won't. Anyway, Maddy and I are doing just fine on our own."

"What do you do? I mean, jobwise?" Courtney asked, hoping she wasn't being too nosy.

"I take classes mostly. Pop Pop left me enough money to get by without having to work for a while. He wanted me to use it to live on for as long as I could so that I could get my degree. I'm majoring in business though I have no idea what I'm going to do with it. I really want to have my own business someday, but it's kind of a pipe dream."

"I'm sure you can do it. And it's great that you're able to go to school and not have to worry about money, at least for a while."

"It won't last long, but, hopefully, I can finish my courses. I've only got one more semester to go."

"That's great, Hannah. Your grandfather would be very proud of you."

"He would," Hannah agreed, smiling at Courtney. "And he'd really love the changes I've made to the house, the paint and bright colors. He really let it get run-down after Mom Mom died. Maddy and I have tried to make it our own." She smiled as she looked at her little girl. "I spend more time on Pinterest than I should, but it's the only creative outlet I have these days."

"You've done a great job decorating, and I've loved our chat." Courtney stood, "I hate to go, but I guess I should get back. Thanks for the tea."

"Anytime," Hannah told her. "I'd love to do this more often. It's hard to make friends when you spend all your time inside on the computer and can't have a social life, not that I mind," she added quickly as she gazed at Maddy.

"We'll definitely do this again," Courtney agreed. "Soon. Today, though, I've got a lot to do, and I'm sure you're busy, so I'll see myself out."

"Sounds good, Courtney. Don't be a stranger."

"I won't," Courtney promised, and she meant it. She was impressed by Hannah's resilience and determination. She hoped they could get to know each other better. They could both use a friend. "One more question," Courtney asked, pausing in the doorway. "Did you know the Suttons?"

"The couple who owned the house? Not technically. They lived here in the nineties, and I was born in 1998. I think they abandoned the house the year after I was born. I may have met them, but who remembers anything from when they were one? Why do you ask?"

Courtney shrugged. "Just wondering, I guess. I read an article about them that my grandmother kept for some reason. The house has been sitting, uninhabited, for twenty years. I wonder why they never tried to sell it before."

Hannah shook her head. "No clue. Maybe they hoped to come back and finish someday."

"You've never seen them around since they left?"

"Nope. Not sure that they ever came back."

"Huh. Oh well. I guess it's another River Terrace mystery."

"You could try to contact them. They can't be that hard to find these days."

"Maybe I will." Courtney wondered what she would say to them—*Hey, I'm the idiot who bought your house. Is it really haunted?*

Courtney said goodbye and walked back across the road, surveying the house as she drew near. She knew that all the talk about ghosts and pirates was meaningless, but she had a strange sense of foreboding as she looked up at one of the windows on the second floor. Once again, she was unable to shake the feeling that she was being watched.

CHAPTER FIVE

Courtney and Jason sat at a small table in Sami's store, looking at the plans that he had put together.

"These look nice." Courtney's skin tingled at the proximity of his face to hers as they leaned over the blueprints.

"It really leaves the entire house as it is, minus the porch, but highlights the architectural features of the original design. And I have great news." Jason sat back and showed his big, sexy smile. "We can install both heat and AC in the addition. You'll have to use window units and baseboard heat in the rest of the house, which you should probably keep closed off as much as you can, but it's better than nothing."

"It sure is." Courtney gave a sigh of relief. "What else?" She leaned back over the drawings, eager to hear more.

Jason pointed to an area on the specs. "This would be your master suite. I was able to put in the jacuzzi you wanted as well as the laundry closet between the bedroom and the kitchen."

"I like this." She tapped her finger on a room across from the laundry closet. "What are these?"

"I wanted to talk to you about that. It's a bathroom. To replace the one under the stairs." He pointed to the space where the current bathroom was. "Having a bathroom here really takes away from the integrity of the house. As you know, it's way too small and barely functional. The floor is rotten, and the pipes are old and contain lead. A nice coat closet would be a better use of the space and is probably what was originally there."

Courtney sat back and took a breath. "I know. You've mentioned that before. You're right, though I was really hoping to find a way to keep that one and add one upstairs."

Jason shook his head. "I get it, but I'm not backing down on this. As I've said, it takes away from the integrity of the house, and replacing those pipes and making the bathroom more functional would be very costly. Besides, the couple that renovated the house before removed the doorway that was here." He pointed to the wall at the back of the entryway beside the bathroom. "After we talked about it before, I took some pictures to study the space." He took a few enlarged photographs from his briefcase and laid them on the table. "If you look at the brickwork on the backside of the house, you can see where they walled it up to make room for the bathroom. See how it makes the entryway look awkward and too small? The space should be opened back up and the door replaced. I bet we could find a door from that time period, or have one made, at a reasonable price. The bricks could be taken out, and the back of the house would then be restored to the way it's supposed to be."

Courtney nodded silently as she looked from the photographs to the plans and thought about what Jason was saying. The cost of the upstairs bathroom could be shifted to the restoration of the entryway and to reverting the back of the house to its original design. She'd like that, but her heart ached at the reality that she had to let go of the notion of an upstairs bathroom. She sighed.

"I really liked the idea of the second-floor bathroom."

Jason sat back and looked at her. "I get it. In modern designs, that would be essential, but in colonial times, there wouldn't have been any bathroom at all inside the house. Having one in your master suite and the one between the bedroom and the kitchen would keep the original part of the house more historically accurate. You've got a huge addition with way more space than you could possibly need for a bedroom and kitchen. You should make better use of that space, and let the older part speak to its history."

"I know you're right," she said reluctantly. "What about a wall of windows on the back of the addition, facing the water? Can I do that?"

It was Jason's turn to sigh. "You could, but, again, it would really take away from the historical integrity of the house. We can modernize the inside all you want, though you're going to want the addition, at least on the outside, to look as much a part of the Colonial era as you can. It's all about the historical—"

"Integrity of the house," Courtney cut him off. She looked back down at the plans and clicked her tongue. "Okay, I get it. We'll add the second bathroom to the addition, take out the one under the stairs, and replace the door."

Jason reached for her hand. "I'm sorry, Courtney. I don't mean to spoil your plans."

Courtney looked down at her hand in his. A swarm of butterflies took flight in her stomach. "Um, it's fine," she managed to say through the lump in her throat, heat rising into her cheeks. "I do want to do what's best for the house." She slowly raised her eyes to meet his and saw compassion in his gaze. He squeezed her hand before letting go, and she immediately felt the heat leave her fingers. She pulled her hand into her lap and clasped it with her other hand. "So, uh, what's the next step?"

"Have Gavin take out the bathroom and all of the pipes and fittings. Restore the original wall and measure out the placement of the door based on the exterior changes to the bricks. I'll see if I can locate a door through my contacts." He began rolling up the blueprints, all business, oblivious to the swarm of insects in her gut.

"Will do. The porch is already gone, and the new steps are in place. You know, you're right." She nodded as she thought about the exterior design of the house. "What I think of as the front of the house was clearly meant to be the back of the house. It doesn't make sense that there isn't a door on the other side. The exterior on that side, with the posts and the beautiful roof that extends out, clearly tell us that the front of the house is what faced the water."

"Yes, that was pretty standard for waterfront homes at the time. Most visitors arrived by boat, so the front of the house was waterfront. As I said before, where your driveway is would have been the back of the house, only meant to be seen by people arriving on horseback, heading to the stables, or by delivery coaches, using the servant's entrance."

"The more I think about it, the more I know you're right. And that's why I hired you to begin with, right?" She looked up at him as he stood.

"I'm glad we agree on this. I think the day you hired me might turn out to be the luckiest day of my life," he said with a broad smile.

The heat returned to Courtney's cheeks, and the butterflies in her stomach began performing aerial dives. She couldn't find any words to say what she was thinking because she wasn't exactly sure of what that was. She couldn't read Jason, his expressions, or his actions. Was he interested in her or just in her house? She swallowed and stood.

"I think this arrangement is going to be great for both of us."

Jason stared at her for a moment, and Courtney thought she saw a question in his eyes. Was he hoping she would say more, something unrelated to their business relationship? She couldn't figure out what was going on between them. Before she had time to think about the implications of anything more than a professional relationship between them, Jason nodded his head toward her and leaned down to pick up his briefcase.

"I'll be in touch. About the door," he hastily added.

"Sounds good." Courtney breathed a sigh of relief. She couldn't place her finger on whatever feelings there were between them, and she wasn't sure she wanted to take the time to figure them out. He was a man of mystery, her grandmother would say, and she had more than her share of mysteries to deal with already.

*****

Gavin looked at Courtney and swallowed. She looked upset, and alarm bells sounded in his brain as he thought about the break-in and the possibility of someone being in the house. “What’s wrong?”

“Nothing. Just a change in plans.” She explained the changes, and he watched her carefully as she spoke.

“Okay,” he said slowly, not sure that was the actual issue that was bothering her. “That’s not surprising. Jason already told you the bathrooms were a bad idea, and I agree with him. Is that what you’re upset about?”

“I was at first,” she told him, pulling back her hair into a ponytail. It had grown out significantly in the past few weeks, and she seemed less self-conscious, often pulling the hair back, off her face, no longer worrying about letting strands hang down to cover the scar. “But I get what he’s saying. I’m okay with it now.”

“Then what’s bothering you? Something is. I can see it.”

Courtney looked at him in amazement, her eyes wide, her mouth slightly open. “What, how… why would you say that?”

“Court, it’s me. I’ve known you forever. We were born three days apart and spent half our lifetime as friends. I can tell when there’s something wrong.”

“We haven’t seen each other or talked or anything in fifteen years, how could you…” her voice trailed off as she gazed at him like he was a puzzle in which all of the pieces were the shades of the same color.

“Don’t worry about how I know, just tell me what’s going on.” Gavin’s patience was growing thin, and his concern was deepening.

“I don’t know exactly.” She looked away. “It’s Jason. I mean, it’s the way he acts, the things he says.” She bit her bottom lip the way he’d seen her do many times when something was on her mind, a problem she couldn't solve. Her discomfort made the alarm bells go off again.

"Court, did he do something? Inappropriate, I mean?"

She shook her head and blinked before turning her gaze back to him. "Not really, I mean, no, not at all. It's just...I feel like I'm getting mixed signals from him. I can't tell if his interest is strictly in the house, or if he's..." She bit her lip again, and Gavin's stomach dropped.

"You think he's interested in you?" Gavin asked, a little more vehemently than he'd intended. Courtney bristled.

"Well, he might be," she retorted, anger clouding her hazel eyes. "Does that surprise you?"

"No, that's not what I meant." Gavin put his hands up to ward off her accusatory stare. "I was just trying to make sure I understood what you were saying. Of course, it wouldn't surprise me. I mean, you're great. You're pretty, smart, ambitious, hard-working." Gavin stopped when he noticed her grin.

"And?" she teased. "Is that all?"

"And..." He thought of the line in Hamlet about protesting too much. "I can see why he might be interested in you. That's all. You'd make a good pair," he said, though that wasn't what he was thinking at all. What he was thinking was that he'd like to knock Jason's cocky grin off his face the next time he saw him.

Courtney stared at Gavin, obviously trying to read his thoughts. "Well, whether he is or isn't, I haven't got the time or the inclination to start any kind of relationship right now. The only commitment I have time for, at this point, is this house, and it's going to take all of the time and attention I've got to give."

"Sounds about right, and I've got a lot to do before I head back west."

Leaving any further conversation unsaid, Gavin headed toward the kitchen to get a bottle of water from the cooler. He had no idea what had come over him. He was leaving as soon as he could get his mother to sell the farm. He needed to get this job done before then so that he could get on with his real life. If Jason and Courtney had feelings for each other, that was none of his concern.

Except that it was his concern. He cared about Courtney. They had been in each other's lives for a long time despite the years apart. He didn't want to see her get hurt, and he wasn't sure that Jason was the right man for her.

He guzzled the entire bottle in one drink, crushed the plastic bottle, replaced the cap, and threw it into a nearby trashcan. He tried to put all thoughts of Courtney and Jason out of his mind as he gazed out the window toward the water. Unfortunately, memories of himself and Courtney jumping off the dock and into the cool river, her infectious laugh, and that vulnerable look in her eyes were flooding his senses.

*****

"Oh, Jason, it's perfect." Courtney she ran her hand over the smooth wood. The new back door was almost identical to the original front door. "How did you get such a close match?"

Jason shrugged as if it was nothing, but his wide grin gave away his pleasure at being able to supply such a find. "I took a picture, made a few calls, sent a few emails. It was nothing."

Courtney couldn't stop beaming. "It's not nothing. It's exactly the right door, the right wood, the right stain. I just can't believe you were able to get it."

"Honestly, that's what we do—my colleagues and me. It's like a game to us, a giant puzzle that we all get to work on together to assemble all the pieces. Though I must admit, they're all quite jealous of my involvement with River Terrace. As soon as we confirmed that there is no other house like it anywhere in the country, probably the world, they all wanted in. Finding you the door was just the beginning. Whatever you need, they're all chomping at the bit to provide."

"Jason, I could just kiss you right now," Courtney blurted out. She felt the heat rise to her cheeks, and she looked away, squeezing her eyes shut. "Oh, geez, I'm sorry. I meant…"

She imagined Jason leaning the door against the wall and moving closer to her, taking her chin between his fingers, and lifting her face up toward his.

Courtney's heart began to race, and she swallowed, unable to take her gaze from his.

"Court?" Gavin called from the kitchen. "Have you seen my hammer?"

Courtney jumped, instinctively raised her hand to pull her hair over her scar, and tore her gaze from Jason. Her face was red hot, and she hoped Jason had no idea what she had been thinking. His head was cocked to one side, his grip still firmly on the door, as he looked inquiringly at her.

"I'd better go help him find the hammer." She scurried around Jason before he could stop her.

As she headed through the future dining room, she silently admonished herself. What was she thinking? Jason was working for her, and despite all the help he was providing, she barely knew him. She heaved a breath and shook her head. Men were so much more trouble than they were worth. She'd have to keep reminding herself that, about both of the men she was working with, before she did something she'd regret

*****

A week later, the bathroom was completely gone, the original wall was back in place, and the new door was installed. Courtney, Gavin, and Jason stood in one of the upstairs bedrooms, staring at an opening in the sheetrock.

"It's not good," Gavin told them. "The leak is pretty bad. The wood is rotten, and the roof is likely to cave in if we don't stop everything and fix it."

"You're going to need a whole crew in here to shore-up that wall, raise the roof, and straighten the chimney without causing further damage," Jason said.

Courtney felt her heart plummet as she looked at the rotting boards inside the wall.

"I was afraid this might be what we'd find, but it's even worse than I suspected" Gavin said. "It's why I've been putting it off ever since Courtney told me there might be a leak and I took a quick peak. I should have torn into the wall more, but I kept working on other things first with the hope that we could wait until farther into the fall, when the attic is not so hot, but we can't wait any longer. That storm last night was pretty bad. Another one like it, and some of these boards are going to go."

Jason nodded. "I think so, too. Can we get up into the attic and see how bad things look from that angle?"

"Yeah, let's do that. Court, can you stay here in case we need any tools or anything?"

Courtney looked at Gavin. She couldn't decide if he was asking her because he might actually need her to retrieve something for him or because he didn't want her climbing up into the attic. Shrugging, she gave in.

"Sure, I'll stand nearby. Let me know if you need me to do anything."

She watched as the men hoisted themselves up through the ceiling doorway in the landing. She could hear their voices as they surveyed the damage done by years of rain and snow. They were up there for several minutes before she heard them making their way back toward the opening.

"Gavin, help me with this," Jason suddenly said, his voice rising with excitement.

"What is it?" she called. "What did you find?" Was it good or bad? She strained to see up into the room, but she couldn't see anything without climbing up the ladder. She reached for the rung when she heard Jason again.

"How many are there?"

"A dozen at least."

"A dozen what?" she called with impatience.

"Do you think these will work to replace the ones in the wall?"

"I think so," Gavin replied. "But I need to see them in better light. They could be rotting or have termites or any number of things. From here, they look pretty good, so we'll have to see."

"Courtney," Jason called, "we're going to lower some boards down to you. Can you grab them?"

"Sure, I'm ready. Go ahead."

She reached for the first board as they eased it down the ladder. Ten more followed, eleven in all. They took up a whole section of the small landing. Jason descended the ladder with a wide grin on his face.

"I can't be sure, but from the looks of these, and from what I've seen of the boards inside the wall, these might be original boards from the building of the house."

"What?" Courtney was shocked. "How can that be?"

"They've been up in the attic, undisturbed. Though it gets hot up there, and plenty humid, these boards were off in a corner away from the leak in the roof and with enough air around them to keep them from holding moisture."

"That's incredible." She was unable to fully grasp how it could be possible that these boards were over 300 years old.

"It is, but it's not unusual. The builders would have kept them in case they needed them. If the attic was rarely used, they could have easily stayed hidden in the dark corner for all these years."

"How did you ever see them?" she asked.

"That bulb gives just enough light to see into the corners, and as I looked around for other breaches in the roof or walls, something didn't seem right to me. The floor was too high over there." He gestured toward an area above them. "I wanted to see why, and there they were."

"And you're going to use them to fix the wall and the roof in there?" She pointed to the room where the leak was.

"If I'm right, and these are originals, and they're in as good a shape as they seem to be, then, yes, we're going to use them. And," he began picking up the boards and studying them, one by one. "If I can think of a way to use one of them somewhere in the interior of the house, we should…as a way to show off the find. Maybe as a mantel or something."

Courtney nodded. "Okay, let me think about it, too."

"What do you want to do with them for now?" Gavin asked.

"Let's take them into the other room so that they're already there if we decide we can use them. I'll take one with me so that I can run some tests on it," Jason said.

"Won't you need to test all of them in case there are termites or something?" Courtney asked. The thought sent up a chill up her spine.

Jason shook his head. "No, I can test one. They were all piled together, so if one is unusable, there's a good chance they all are, and vice versa. Once I've run the tests and determined the age, I'll carefully inspect each individual board, just in case."

They worked together to move the boards into the adjoining room. When they were done, Courtney was drenched with sweat.

"I think I'll take a quick break. I need to cool down."

"Me, too." Gavin attempted to wipe the sweat off his face with his dirty, sweaty arm.

"I'm going to take this board and head out," Jason told them. "I should be able to tell by the cuts in the wood approximately when the beam was made. If it was cut by a pit saw, it's almost certain to be from the sixteen-hundreds, though a gash saw could mean it's from any time in the sixteen, seventeen, or eighteen-hundreds. That means we'd have to carbon-date it. That isn't always accurate, but we can get close enough to determine the approximate age."

"How long will it take?" Courtney asked.

"Just a few days," Jason said. "Though it could be rather costly," he added with hesitation.

"So, what else is new?" Courtney gave a sigh. "Every time I turn around, something else is going to be 'rather costly.' It's no wonder my mother told me I'm going to eat through all my money in less than six months. I can't imagine what it's going to cost to fix the roof."

"And the chimney," he added. "We should do both at the same time."

"Thanks for the reminder." Courtney sighed.

"Look, I've got a guy I've worked with many times over the years. He's good, and he owes me a favor. Let me see if he can give me a good price."

"Oh, Jason, that would be great. I would so appreciate anything you can do to help keep the costs down." Courtney suddenly felt Gavin's gaze boring into her.

"I've got to go," Gavin said. "I'm going to see how quickly I can get a team of guys in here." He pushed his way between Courtney and Jason and hurried down the stairs.

"Sometimes, I get the feeling he doesn't like me." Jason frowned as he watched the outside door slam shut.

"I'm sure that's not true. He's got a lot on his mind these days. Family stuff. Not to mention the ceiling and the storm damage. That's really going to slow him down, and he'll have to bring in a crew to help fix it. It's a lot to think about," she rambled, feeling the need to defend Gavin even though she understood why Jason felt that way. Gavin had made it clear to Courtney that he didn't care for Jason. She just couldn't figure out why.

*****

It took two weeks, but Jason was able to confirm the wood was indeed as old as the house, and Gavin was able to pull together a crew. Courtney prayed every night that there would not be another tremendous storm, and, so far, they'd been lucky, but by the looks of the week-long forecast, that would soon change.

After carefully considering the best way to tackle the project, the work crew, along with Jason and Gavin, met at seven in the morning to get started. They hoped to get the hardest part of the work done before the late August sun made it to the highest point in the sky and began baking them all in the oven that served as an attic.

From the front yard, or what would have once been considered the back yard, Courtney watched, holding her breath, as the roof was raised and held into place with temporary supports. She could hear the men as they called out to one another. Jason was beside her, and she could tell that he was itching to be part of the action taking place inside. Shielding her eyes with her hand, Courtney looked up, amazed at the sight before her.

The sagging roof was secured and put back into its proper place. The wall was reinforced, and the chimney was straightened. It boggled her mind that all of that could be done without the deconstruction of the entire side of the house. The only thing that was destroyed was the mass of vines blanketing that side of the house, and Courtney was glad that there would be fewer of them for her to cut down on her own.

"How do they do that?"

"It's pretty remarkable, isn't it?" Jason said with as much awe in his voice as Courtney felt. "I just hope they don't damage that roof. It's the only documented one to be found anywhere in the United States."

"What makes it so unique?"

"Well, it's a cruck roof, as you know." Jason spoke but never took his eyes off of the work going on in front of them. "The rafter support system comes from ancient Europe. It uses massive oak timbers to support the roof and distribute its weight down through the outside walls. This raises the front and back walls on the second floor by two feet, allowing the gabled roof to equal the first-floor exterior walls in height. It's quite genius and an architectural marvel."

"So, the original builder or architect knew something that most other builders of his time might not have. By using ancient building methods, he created something that probably would not have been seen in any other new construction anywhere else in the world."

"Correct. He was an architectural and engineering genius. He had to know that he was building something that was going to be a marvel to later generations."

"In that case, I'm so happy that Gavin is the one overseeing this. He's a genius himself when it comes to engineering." She felt Jason stiffen. "And you, of course, as the premier architect that you are. I'm so lucky to have you both as part of my team."

"Yeah, about the team part…"

"What?" Courtney's eyes widened. "You're not backing out, are you? Are you taking another job?"

"No, no, not that," Jason assured her, taking his eyes off of the house for the first time. "I'm just wondering if Gavin is really the right guy for this job. I mean, he seems to be a one-man show. I thought there would be a whole team of people working on this. It's going to take so much longer than necessary with only one construction worker. I can recommend another company if one guy is the best these guys can do."

"Whoa." Courtney felt her defenses go on high alert. "First of all, Gavin is *not* a construction worker. He's a highly skilled engineer. I'm darn lucky to have him on this at all. I was the one who told Mitch that I couldn't afford a big crew and that I wanted someone who could work quickly and efficiently without extra labor costs. Gavin and I have been friends our entire lives. I trust him. He knows what he's doing. And if he needs an extra crew, he'll bring in whomever he needs to get the job done." She pointed to the second story. "Case in point."

Jason took a step back, his arms raised defensively. "Courtney, I'm really sorry. I didn't mean to upset you. I've worked on many projects like this, and I just thought that it might be best if we had more hands on deck. It has nothing to do with Gavin."

Courtney eyed him with suspicion. She wasn't so sure about that. "Again, if and when we need more people, Gavin will get them. I've never trusted anyone more, and I know he will do what's right by me. End of subject." She hoped she wouldn't anger Jason to the point of quitting. He really was the best around, and she needed him to be part of this. Replacing Gavin was out of the question.

Jason hesitated for a moment. “Okay, I get it. I won’t bring it up again. Just keep in mind, this is going to take years to complete, and from what I understand, Gavin isn’t planning on being around for that long. I hope you know what you’re doing. Making a decision like this based on a childhood friendship and emotional attachment isn’t always the best way to go about things. I hope you don’t regret it.”

Courtney returned her gaze to the upper floor. She could see Gavin through the window. She was certain she was right, but Jason had a point. How long would Gavin be willing to stick around to see this through? He’d made no secret of the fact that he was heading west as soon as his mother was ready to leave. What if she suddenly decided she wanted to go? Would he abandon Courtney and all of their, her, dreams? She shook the thought away. She’d take it one day at a time and pray that they finished the house before he had to make that decision.

*****

Saturday provided a much-needed break from the heat and exhaustion of renovating the house, but after sleeping until nine and enjoying a lazy morning helping Lily with her weekly house cleaning, Courtney found herself back at River Terrace. She stood in front of the new wall and ran her hand over the drywall. It was hard to believe that the roof could be raised, the beams replaced, the chimney straightened and secured, and the wall rehung in just a day. Sure, the spackling on the plaster needed to finish drying, and the wall would need to be painted, but the enormity of what the men had been able to accomplish in just one day both pleased and amazed her.

Courtney stood back and gazed at the wall. She ran her eyes along the perfectly seamed joints and let them wander across the closet door to the fireplace that now opened up into the room. She smiled, envisioning what the room would look like when they were finished. It would have cream-colored walls and lacy curtains with—

Suddenly, the door slammed behind her, causing Courtney to jump and grab her chest.

"Why on earth?" She headed to the door.

Courtney tried to open the door, but the knob would not turn. Annoyed that it wasn't working, she tried to twist harder, but nothing happened.

"That's just great," she muttered, examining the knob. It was old, more than one-hundred years old if she had to guess. There was no button or turning lock, just a keyhole that required a key on either side to lock or unlock it.

Then, how could it have possibly locked?

The article she read about the previous owners came to mind. They believed the house was haunted.

"Ridiculous," she said out loud. "But if they knew there was a problem with the locks, why didn't they replace them?" She sighed as she tried to turn the knob once more.

Realizing she was not going to be able to open it without a key, Courtney took the house key from her pocket and tried it in the lock, but it didn't work. She looked around for something she might be able to use to jimmy the lock. All of the tools that were used previously that week had been packed up and moved downstairs. The room was empty. Courtney reached into her back pocket to retrieve her phone, but she found nothing except a stray string and some lint.

"Oh, no," she groaned, picturing her phone laying in the console of her SUV.

Frustrated, she went to the window and pushed it open. A wave of heat hit her in the face as she thrust her head through the opening and peered down at the awning that framed the waterfront side of the house. The awning and the posts that held it up were over 300 hundred years old. Would they hold her? And if they did, could she manage the approximately fourteen-foot drop without hurting herself? She thought of her prolonged hospital stay and decided it wasn't worth the risk.

Releasing an aggravated breath, she pulled herself back inside and lowered the window. She walked to the opposite side and opened a window that overlooked the driveway. Her SUV was too far away for her to jump down onto the roof, and there wasn't anybody walking down the road. There was little chance she'd be able to get the attention of a passing driver, but, perhaps, if Hannah was outside, she could get her attention.

Courtney strained to see across the street, but there was no movement inside or outside Hannah's house. Was she even home? Her car was there, but there wasn't any way to see if her bike was parked in the carport.

Closing the window, Courtney sagged against the wall and slid down to the floor. Certainly, Lily would come looking for her at some point. They had agreed to go to the Saturday evening Mass at Holy Angels rather than the Sunday morning service. When she didn't show up to get ready, Lily would know something was wrong. Courtney looked at her watch and groaned. It was only 1:00. It was going to be a long afternoon.

She laid her head back against the cool drywall and closed her eyes. A sound from downstairs caused her to bolt upright, straining her ears. Could Gavin have stopped by? Hannah? She stood and went to the door.

"Hello?" she called out. "Is someone down there?"

She listened, her ear against the door, but didn't hear any response. Assuming the noise was her imagination, she stood and sighed.

There it was again.

Her heart began to pound as she heard the thud of heavy boots walking on the floor below.

Pounding on the door, Courtney yelled as loudly as she could. "Help! I'm locked in a room upstairs. Please come get me out."

The sound of shattering glass interrupted her calls, and Courtney held her breath as she took in the sudden silence. The sounds of the boots moving back across the room faded as Courtney suppressed a tear. Biting back a frustrated scream, she dropped back to the floor and cradled her head in her hands to stave off the pounding in her brain that echoed her fists on the door.

What had broken? There was no glass anywhere in the house other than the windows. She raised her head and looked toward the ceiling.

"Why?" she pleaded as a tear rolled down her cheek. "Why is this happening? How did the door lock? What just happened downstairs? What am I supposed to do next?" she asked in desperation. She closed her eyes and shook her head.

"Dear God, please help me. Please guide me. Please let me know what I'm meant to be doing here. I'm so lost. I thought this house was the answer. I thought this would bring me peace." She looked back up at the blank ceiling. "If not this, then what am I supposed to be doing? What am I meant to do with my life?"

When no answer came, not that she expected any, Courtney laid down on the floor and curled herself up into a ball. She was still there an hour later when more sounds from below woke her up.

*****

Gavin took in the site of the shattered green glass in front of the hearth. Where had that come from? He bent down and gently fingered a pointy shard. It was thick and smooth. He put it back and ran his gaze across the scattered pieces before his eyes locked on a round tube-like piece. He picked it up and examined it. It was the neck of a bottle. Wine? Liquor? He sniffed it, but he didn't detect any odor. He shook his head and stood.

"Courtney?" he called. "Where are you?"

When no answer came, his heart began to thud. Was she hurt? Had she encountered someone in the house again?

He began running through the downstairs, calling her name. There was no sign of anyone in the room across the hall, nor in any of the rooms of the new addition. He was heading back toward the foyer when he heard her.

"Gavin, is that you? Help me! I'm locked in!"

Gavin took the stairs, two at a time, and went straight to the closed door.

"Court, I'm here. Are you okay?"

"I'm fine," she called, and he thought she sounded like she was crying.

"Are you hurt?"

"No, no I'm okay. Just please get me out of here."

He looked around for a key before coming to his senses and remembering that he was in an unfinished, unfurnished house. He ran his hand along the top of the door just in case. Nothing.

"Do you have a key somewhere in the house?"

"I, I don't think so. I've never seen one anywhere."

He ran his fingers along the top of the door to the other room. Nothing there either. He exhaled as he ran his hand through his hair. It had grown out quite a bit since he'd been home. He really needed to get it cut. Bringing his mind back into focus, he went over to the locked door.

"Court, I'm going to find something I can use to get the door unlocked. I'll be right back."

"Please, hurry. I'm getting claustrophobic in here, and my head is killing me."

"I'll hurry. Hang tight."

Racing back down the stairs, Gavin grabbed his entire toolbox and hauled it up the steps. Opening it, he examined the screwdrivers and drill bits and thought through what might work best. He tried a couple different tools, but nothing worked. Inspecting the hinges, he said to Courtney, "I have an idea. Back away from the door."

"You're not going to chop it down, are you?"

"Of course not, but I need to use a hammer, and I don't want the sound to bother your head."

"Okay," she answered through the door. "My head is already pounding. My medicine's in the car."

"It will just take a minute," Gavin assured her as he held the screwdriver to the bottom of one of the pins in the hinge. He hit it with his hammer, but it didn't budge. Banging harder, the screwdriver slipped, and he hit his finger with the hammer.

"Ouch!" He shook his hand vigorously and held it out to examine his throbbing finger.

"Are you okay?" Courtney called.

"Yeah. Hold on." He blew on his thumb as if that might stop the pain and put the screwdriver back in place. He hit it hard with the hammer, and the pin began to give. He continued hammering until the pin popped up and out of the hinge, clanging as it fell and hit the floor. "Two more to go," he called to Courtney.

When he finally yanked the door from the jamb, nearly breaking the lock as it tore from the doorplate, his heart was racing in his chest. He leaned the door against the wall as Courtney barreled into him, almost knocking him over.

Her arms went around his middle, and her head buried into his chest. "Oh, Gavin, thank you. Thank you."

He put his arms around her and held her close, his face against her hair. He closed his eyes and took in the scent of flowers. Once both of them were breathing normally again, Gavin released Courtney and nudged her back a step so that he could face her.

"What happened?"

"I don't know. I was checking out the new wall, and, suddenly, the door slammed shut. I tried to open it, but it was locked. I left my phone in my car and couldn't come up with any safe way to get out of here."

"Was the bottle already broken when you got here?"

"Bottle?" Courtney looked at him with a raised brow. "What bottle?"

"There's a broken liquor bottle that's been smashed on the hearth in one of the rooms below."

"The glass! That's what it was." She breathed a sigh of relief. "I was afraid it was a window being smashed."

"You heard it? You were up here when it happened?" Gavin looked around as if there was someone hiding nearby. He felt a lump in his throat. Someone was in the house with Courtney. Had they locked her in that room?

"I heard someone walking—the same boots as before, I think. I called out for them to let me out, but then I heard the glass shatter. I kept yelling, but they walked to the other side of the house and that was it."

"How long ago was that?"

Courtney looked at her watch and shook her head. "I don't know. An hour? Maybe two? I think I fell asleep."

Gavin grabbed her hand and pulled her down the stairs after him. "Stay here," he told her as he left her in the foyer and headed toward the kitchen. He didn't think she'd actually listen, but she stayed put while he searched the house. When he returned, she was sitting on the bottom step.

"I didn't see anyone when I got here, but I wanted to check again." He held his hand out to her and helped her up. "We need to get you back to Lily's. She's a nervous wreck."

"She called you?" she asked as they exited the house.

Gavin watched Courtney try to lock the door with the key that she retrieved from her pocket, but her hands were shaking. He gently took the key from her hand and locked the door. "Yeah, when you didn't answer your phone. We both tried to call you, and then

I told her I'd come down and make sure everything was okay."

Just then, his own phone began singing in his pocket. He took it out and smiled at the display. "Speaking of…" He handed the phone to Courtney.

"Gram. Yes, I'm okay. Yeah, Gavin found me. Yes, yes, I'm really fine. I know. I'm sorry, it was in my car. I know. I'll explain everything when I get home. Yes, right now. Love you, too." She handed Gavin the phone. "She's worried. I'd better get home and tell her what happened."

"I'll go with you." He expected her to protest, but she just nodded.

Gavin and Courtney went to their respective vehicles, but Courtney stopped by the door and turned toward him. "Gavin? What do we tell her?"

"What do you mean?"

"I mean, what do we tell her happened? I'm not even sure myself. Was someone there? Did they lock me in? Did I lock myself in somehow? Where did the bottle come from?"

Gavin thought about it for a moment. "I think we should tell her as little as possible. You locked yourself in somehow and didn't have any way to get out or to call for help. Let's not worry her."

"I agree." She opened her door. "And Gavin?"

"Yeah?" he asked looking over the hood of his truck.

"Thanks again." She smiled, and his heart skipped a beat.

"No problem." He swallowed the lump in his throat, unwilling to meet her gaze. He climbed into the truck, closed the door, and started the engine. Instead of putting the truck in reverse, he stared at his whitening knuckles as he gripped the steering wheel. The thought of something happening to her caused his chest to constrict. Despite all of the promises to himself that he was not going to get involved with Courtney, he felt himself being pulled toward her like a magnet to steel. Even after fifteen years, she still had that effect on him. Now, what the heck was he going to do about it?

CHAPTER SIX

Courtney sat at the wooden table in the climate-controlled room at the Pratt Library and picked up the top book on the pile. John McMillan's journal was in remarkably good shape, better than his brother's. It was made of worn, brown leather and bound with leather bindings that reminded her of the laces on the shoes she wore with her school uniform once upon a time. She carefully opened the book and read the date of the year that it entailed—1720. She skimmed the pages but found nothing about River Terrace except a brief mention about John and Cora's wedding there. After they were married, they built Willow Grove.

Perusing a few more books, Courtney eventually found the year, 1725, and the first mention of Anne. John firmly believed she was the wife of a pirate, but he didn't associate her with James Bonny or indicate that he thought she was the infamous Anne Bonny. After talking to Clarissa, Courtney had done some internet searches on Anne Bonny, and it did seem that she and the Anne from River Terrace could have been one in the same; though most sources presumed that she died in childbirth or shortly thereafter, probably in prison, there was no actual documentation of her death.

John detailed the discovery of Anne and her baby and how Robert had suggested she be brought to Willow Grove to nurse Jenny. John lamented over the grief of his wife, and it was clear that he loved her deeply. As Courtney read on, his feelings may have ebbed over time. He grew impatient with Cora, whom Courtney thought was clearly suffering from post-partum depression that must have grown into a debilitating depression from which she took years to recover. An odd entry from 1729 made Courtney wonder even more about John and Cora's marriage.

Dear God, forgive me. The babe looks so like Jenny looked when she was birthed. How will I ever deny him? Cora will know in an instant.

What baby? Seemingly not Cora's. Courtney flipped a few pages until she came upon another entry. The journal, which began as a daily estate accounting, like Robert's, was progressing into more of a personal diary, deeply personal. John had a guilty conscience, and it appeared that he used the journals as his means of confession.

Sean has his mother's red hair but the McMillan eyes and mouth. Robert has stopped speaking to me though I have not told him, nor anyone, of my transgression, not even Father O'Leary.

Were John and Anne in love, or was their affair nothing more than a satisfying of their carnal needs? Nowhere did John ever mention her name or any feelings about her, but, somehow, Courtney knew she was the mother. Perhaps it was the reference to her red hair. Courtney continued to turn the pages, her eyes scanning for more information.

June 17, 1732 – Robert has taken Anne and Sean away, claiming her as his servant. He can have her. She has brought me nothing but misery and shame. But Sean, how I will miss seeing him every day.

There were no more references to Anne for several years, though John often mentioned seeing Sean, missing him, or wondering how he was doing. Apparently, the rift between the two brothers was not easily mended. Had Robert taken Anne as his mistress? Did he raise Sean as his own? Courtney skimmed the writings until she reached December 31, 1735.

The snow fell heavily last night. It took the better part of the day to dig out. Robert has been ill for some time now, and though I will never forgive the man for taking my son, he is my brother, and he has taken good care of the lad. I will venture out in the morn to see if Robert and his children are faring well after the storm.

January 1, 1735 – May God forgive an unforgiving man. I spent years loathing my own kin, my own brother, and now I am shamed more than I ever have been. My heart is heavy with grief. For how many days did Robert lay on the floor in his own excrement and blood? Crystin thinks perhaps two full days, but time cannot be measured in a dark cellar. I will forever be indebted to my nephew and niece who harbored my son from the band of pirates that killed their father and disappeared with Anne. Crystin tells a frightful tale of a pirate discovering their hiding place in the cellar but not seeing the children as they huddled in the dark corner. The children held their breath, Crystin's hands over the mouths of James and Sean to keep their crying from being heard, Evan's shaking hand as it held a butcher knife, their only defense. For years, Robert feared a pirate invasion, and he was well prepared. The tunnel, hidden behind the winter preserves, contained jars of food, jugs of ale, and warm bedding. When the children heard the pirates in the house, they retreated to the hidden cavern. There, they remained, resisting the urge to reveal themselves when they heard the shot that, unbeknownst to them, killed their father. Not until they heard my voice, did they come out from hiding. Dirty, cold, and mildly inebriated from the ale, they told the tale of seeing the ship with the flag of crossed bones, enter their harbor. Evan was told to keep his kin safe, and, thank the good Lord, he did just that. Though he wanted to confront the pirates, he heeded his sister's pleas and remained with the young'uns. Tonight, they will sleep, warm and safe, in my house.

Courtney blinked as she read the passage again. A secret tunnel? A hidden cavern in the cellar? Her heart raced. Were they still there? And what happened to the children? And to Anne? She desperately wanted answers. These were her own kin, and she felt as if she had grown up with them as surely as she had grown up with Gavin and Sami.

January 2, 1735 – Sean's cries for his mother are almost too much to bear. Though Cora tries to comfort him, he will not be consoled. Young James, the same tender age as Sean, cries for his father, but Evan remains stoic. Crystin tries desperately to soothe the young'uns and to coax Evan from his turmoil, though his shame will not relent. I know too well how that feels, but I am a man, and Evan is not much more than a boy. I cannot let him go on for years, like Cora did, unable to forgive himself for something he could not have prevented. I must push back my own guilt at the broken relationship with my brother, God rest his soul. We must find a way to lead each other back to the light of life and away from the darkness of death and shame. I fear that we will need to leave our beloved home and start anew. The children cannot live with the constant reminders of their loss.

Courtney skimmed through the final years that John detailed in his journal. The family moved to Baltimore, as Clarissa said. The younger children seemed to get better. They started school and, it seemed, gained back their childhood exuberance. Crystin married and started a family of her own. There was not much mentioned of her once she moved out of the family home. Evan, it seemed, never recovered. Courtney wiped away a tear as she read about the poor boy's battle with depression and his eventual death. John didn't give any details, but it appeared to have been tragic and possibly self-inflicted. John must have died a few years after the move, for the journals stopped not long after Evan's death. Or perhaps his own grief made it too difficult to continue documenting the tragic news of his shrinking family. Nowhere could Courtney find any other information about Crystin, James, or Sean, who was eventually given the McMillan name, according to John's family tree in the worn, leather-bound Bible, preserved with the rest of the documents. It did not list the name of Sean's mother.

*****

"Be careful with the paneling," Jason said, looking over her shoulders.

Courtney sat back on her heels, removed her dust mask, and eyed the work she had done so far, stripping the layers of paint from the wall around the fireplace with an electric sander set to a gentle but effective setting. "I'm being careful. How does it look?"

Jason had stopped by to see how things were progressing. He'd taken quite an active interest in the house and was prone to stopping by nearly every day. Courtney wondered if he had any other clients, but she never asked. She enjoyed his frequent visits.

"It looks good. Before long, the walls will look just as they did when they were first erected." His eyes had a far-away look as though he could see back in time to what the paneling had originally looked like.

"Gavin and I plan to have everything stripped by the end of the week. The bottom layer seems to be red, just as you suspected."

Jason looked pleased. "It was an educated guess. The wealthier the family, the more regal the paint."

Standing, Courtney gazed at the paneling. "I think red will look wonderful in here. It will really give depth to the room."

"And opulence. That was the goal. People never talked about money in those days. They just showed off how much they had."

Courtney laughed. "I'm not sure things have changed all that much."

"You might be right about that." Jason looked toward her with a smile. Her stomach flipped, and Courtney wondered how a man could get so under her skin the way Jason did. One minute, he had her back up in defense, and the next, her stomach was filled with butterflies.

"Hey, Courtney." His voice was quiet. "I know that Gavin isn't planning on doing the floors any time soon, but I was wondering…" Jason looked behind him as if to make sure Gavin was still hard at work on the paneling in the other room. "I'm dying to know what's underneath this carpet—oak, pine, old, new? How would you feel if I start taking up some of the carpeting in the foyer, starting where we left off by where the bathroom was beneath the stairwell? The bathroom was put in during a recent renovation, and the flooring over there was replaced at that time, but I'm betting that the further out we go, the more likely we'll find old wood."

"Um, I'm not sure." Courtney felt uncomfortable. "I mean, I'd love to know about the floors, too, but Gavin was pretty insistent that they had to be done last."

"You know, he's absolutely right, and we should wait to finish them. But what could it hurt to at least start taking a peek here and there? And that area is out of the way. I'm only talking about a small area, and just removing a board or two, for testing purposes. Then we could start removing more of the carpeting, moving out slowly as you all finish each room, doing a little at a time instead of waiting and tackling the whole floor at once. What do you think?"

"I don't know. I think I should see what Gavin says."

A cloud passed over Jason's face, but his expression quickly cleared, and he smiled at Courtney—the same smile that caused the butterflies to take flight. "Yeah, that's fine. I've got to go. Just let me know, okay? I can come back any time to work on it myself. That way, I'm not stopping you or Gavin from your work. I know how important it is to stay on task. We want everything to go smoothly so that you can have the masterpiece you deserve." He smiled at her.

Courtney smiled back. "Okay, Jason. I'll ask Gavin what he thinks. I'll text you and let you know, all right?"

"Sounds great," he said, though he didn't move. His eyes lingered on hers for a moment before his gaze dropped to her lips and back up to her eyes. Courtney felt her insides melt, and, without thinking, the tip of her tongue peeked out to wet her lips. She thought she saw a spark in his eyes, and she began to lean toward him.

"Ahem."

Courtney jumped and looked toward the doorway.

"How's it going in here?" Gavin asked, his mask hanging around his neck, his arms folded across his chest, jaw set, and blue eyes flashing with emotion. Was it anger?

"It's going great. Jason was just wondering—"

"How things are progressing," Jason quickly interjected. "Everything looks great." He walked toward the doorway. "I've got to head back to the office, but it was nice seeing you both. I'll stop back in tomorrow."

He nodded his head at Gavin as he passed by. Courtney watched the men eye each other.

"Hey," she said casually. "How's it going in there?" She echoed his words and swallowed the lump in her throat. Why did she feel so guilty?

"Isn't his office a little out of the way for him to drop by here all the time? Doesn't he have work to do?" Gavin walked toward Courtney with his gaze on the paneling. "I'm almost done. And you? Looks like you got distracted."

"He came here to ask me a question." Courtney's jaw twitched with irritation. She looked at the man standing next to her. "Where do you get off saying I got *distracted*? What the heck is that supposed to mean?"

Gavin turned toward her. His eyes met hers and held them for what seemed like an eternity. If Jason caused her to feel butterflies in her stomach, then Gavin stirred up a whole flock of geese, large ones, with enormous flapping wings. Courtney caught her breath as she watched the play of emotions in his eyes. She saw his jaw tense again, the muscle tick up slightly. Her heart began to pound as they continued their standoff.

Suddenly, Gavin blinked and turned. "We've got a lot of work to do." He walked away. "Don't let me hold you up."

"Wait a minute, I'm not finished," Courtney called.

"Well, I am," Gavin yelled back in a huff.

Courtney's blood began to boil as she watched him leave. She yelled back to him, "Jason wants to know if he can work on the flo—"

"No," Gavin barked from the next room. "We'll start working on the floor when I say we start working on the floor. Period."

Courtney felt heat riding a wave up the back of her neck. She considered going after him, but then what? She didn't want to fight with him, and he had told Jason he wasn't ready to begin on the floors several times already.

She tried to think about something other than Jason or Gavin, and, for the thousandth time since leaving Baltimore a few days prior, she wondered about Anne and Robert. What did they feel for each other? Did they sit in this room, gazing into each other's eyes, or did she spend all of those years just waiting for the pirate ship to return and take her away? Courtney guessed she would never know. Just as it seemed she would never know exactly what was going through Gavin's mind.

*****

"On one hand, I feel like things are coming together quickly. On the other, it's taking forever," Courtney lamented to Hannah. They were having lunch at a little dining table in the corner of the sunroom while Maddy slept.

"I can't imagine the amount of work it must be. And, honestly, I'm dying to see it."

"Come over any time. I'm usually there, and I'm always happy to take a break. This chicken salad is great by the way. It's my favorite lunch."

"Mine, too. I don't often have anyone to make it for."

"Invite me over for more any time you feel like making a batch." Courtney savored another bite. "My gram makes it sometimes, but my Aunt Grace made the best chicken salad ever. I think because she always made it for me with a big helping of love."

"I remember her. She was a really special lady. She lived next door to your grandmother, right?"

"She did. I miss her."

"It's so sad when we have to say goodbye." Hannah frowned. "Let's talk about happier topics. What exciting things have you uncovered in the house?"

"Not much." Courtney popped a grape into her mouth. "Though the history of the house is fascinating. It was built in colonial times and designed by some unknown architectural genius who used all kinds of special building features not seen anywhere else here in America. There's some really unique feature with the roof that I don't quite understand, but Jason is in love with the fact that he 'discovered' it."

"Who's Jason?"

"He's the historical architect I hired to help us do the renovation the right way. He insists that we do everything we can to bring the house back to the original showplace that it was when it was built. And I'm all for that, but it's exhausting having to check with him and the historical society every time I want to make the smallest change. And he and Gavin are so stubborn about what I can and can't do alone. Like, there's apparently some kind of secret tunnel or cave beyond the cellar, and they won't even let me go down and check it out. It's driving me crazy!"

Hannah set her glass of iced tea down on the table and looked at Courtney with wide eyes. "A secret cave? And you haven't been down there to see what's in it?"

Courtney shook her head and once again felt the frustration she'd felt for days, ever since she read John's journal and rushed home to tell Gavin about it. "They keep saying that the cellar isn't safe because of mold. The removal guy is coming in a couple weeks. It took forever for him to fit me into his schedule, and they say I can't go down there until he's done."

"To heck with that! It's your house."

"I know, but I get that they're looking out for me. And after the door locking incident, I'm a little leery of being in the house alone, so I haven't tried to sneak down there when they aren't there."

"Door locking incident?" Hannah raised her brow. "Do tell." She motioned for Courtney to continue.

Courtney shrugged. "It was nothing, really, just an ancient lock that wouldn't work. Unfortunately, I was on the other side of the door when it decided to stop unlocking."

"You were locked in somewhere?" Hannah's mouth was open wide.

"I was. In one of the upstairs bedrooms. And I was alone and had left my phone in the car. Gram was worried sick when I didn't answer."

"I bet. You never know what could go wrong in an old house like that. Were you scared?"

"Not really, at least not at first, but…" she shifted in her seat. "After a while, I thought I heard someone downstairs, and then an antique rum bottle was shattered, and I didn't know what the sound was, and—"

"Hold on, an antique rum bottle? What's that all about?"

"I have no idea," Courtney sighed. "Gavin took it to some friend of his who is a collector of antique liquor bottles. Who knew there was such a thing? Anyway, he said it was from the early 1700s and was quite rare and precious. How it got into the house, and who smashed it, we have no idea. It makes no sense that somebody would bring it in with them and just break it."

"Unless it's someone who has been carrying it around with him for the past three-hundred years." Hannah spoke in a spooky Halloween voice.

Courtney frowned and shook her head. "Nonsense. I don't believe any of those old stories. Besides, whoever heard of a ghost who carries a bottle around with him? Would that even be possible?" She clicked her tongue and blew out a breath. "Listen to me. I can't believe I even asked that. The whole premise is ridiculous."

"You don't think it's a poltergeist, do you? Aren't they attached to buildings or places and like to break things?"

"I don't know anything about poltergeists except for that old movie. My brothers and I watched it once. Scared the heck out of me. But, no, I don't think that's it."

"Then what do you think happened?"

"I think, and Gavin agrees, that the door locked accidentally. One or more of the local kids was probably fooling around in the house, not realizing I was there, and things got out of hand. What other explanation could there be?"

Hannah thought it over for a moment. "If you say so. I can keep an eye on things if you want. When you're not there, I mean."

"That would be great. Thank you."

"No problem. I just hope they don't do anything worse."

"You and me both," Courtney agreed, happy to have Hannah there as both a lookout and a friend. They might be ten years apart, but they had fallen into a comfortable friendship that Courtney appreciated. It was nice to have another female besides Gram and Sami to talk to.

*****

Courtney held her breath as she waited for Gavin's head to appear back in the darkened opening of the cellar doors. She had finally convinced him to let her take a peek, promising they wouldn't stay down there for long. She just wanted to see the area for herself. He reluctantly agreed but insisted that they both wear dust masks to limit the amount of mold, and possibly asbestos, that they were breathing.

"Come on down," he called, and Courtney could barely contain her excitement as she put on her mask and lowered herself down the rickety old stairs. Gavin was at the bottom and helped her make the last step onto the uneven ground. "Be careful. There are a lot of holes and uneven places in the dirt. And broken shelves with nails in them. Broken glass, too. It looks like the Suttons never got as far as fixing this up at all."

Courtney blinked, trying to adjust her eyes to the darkness. "There's no light?"

"Not that I can find. I can install one, but, for now, turn on your flashlight."

Gavin's phone flashlight was already on, and Courtney illuminated hers. They waved the lights around the dark, damp space.

Courtney tried not to gag. "It smells terrible in here. Even with the mask on."

"Yeah, that's the mold. It's above the insulation."

"What's down here?" she asked, trying to see into the far reaches of the space.

"Like I said, lots of broken glass, fallen shelving, some old pegs for hanging root vegetables, I would guess. Not sure what else they would've been used for."

"Did you check out the entire thing?"

"If you're asking if I found the hidden tunnel, the answer is no. I only checked the sturdiness of the beams when I came down those weeks back. I didn't want to breathe the air for too long. When does your mold crew get here?"

"The week after next, first thing Monday morning."

"Then take five minutes to poke around, and then we're out of here. You can wait two weeks to explore further."

"You're no fun," she said, though she could already feel the stench having an effect on her and knew she needed to get to her migraine medicine soon. "Can we follow along the walls and see if they lead anywhere?"

"We can try, but there are a lot of shelves, and—Darn!"

"What?" Courtney asked, bumping into him.

"I just hit my knee on a shelf. Be careful here. It's sticking out, and there's a huge nail in it."

"Did it cut you?"

"I think so, but it's okay. I've had a tetanus shot."

"Um, a tetanus shot? Hmm." Courtney bit her lip.

"You haven't had one, I'm guessing." His tone was one of disapproval.

"I don't know. When would I have had one?"

"As a kid and then updated as needed as an adult. I guess you never needed one for work."

"Not in a high-rise financial institution in the middle of a city, no."

Gavin reached back and took hold of her hand. "Then be extra careful. And go get one before next week. I'm thinking we should clear all this stuff out before the mold guys get here, and I don't want you getting cut and getting a life-threatening infection."

Courtney nodded, realizing he couldn't see her, but unable to answer as his hand gripped hers. It had been fifteen years since her hand had so easily slipped into his. The feeling was a jolt to her system.

Gavin moved a few more feet before stopping. "Court, I think we need to go back up. The air is heavy with who knows what, and there's a lot of broken stuff piled up everywhere. It's just not safe. Let's come back down one day next week with an actual plan as to how we're going to deal with all this. *After* you've had your shot."

As much as she hated to stop their exploration, she knew he was right. "Yeah, I can feel my head starting to—" she reached up and rubbed the side of her temple where her brain behind the scar was beginning to ache.

"Are you okay?" Gavin asked, squeezing her hand.

"Yeah, I, I think so. My head just…"

Tugging on her hand, he pulled her toward the sunlight in the doorway. "Come on, we're out of here. I'll get some guys to come out one day next week and help me clean this out. I don't want you back down here until the mold is gone and the insulation has been replaced." He helped her to the ladder and waited at the bottom until she eased herself out into the daylight. She pulled the mask from her face and sucked in the air, the sweet smell of honeysuckle tickling her nose. There was a nice breeze as September ushered in slightly cooler days. The temperatures were expected to climb again by the weekend, though, for now, the warm air and gentle breeze was just what Courtney needed.

Gavin followed Courtney out of the cellar and lowered the doors. He turned to face her and removed his mask. "Court, don't get any ideas about going back down there on your own."

She held up her hand. "Don't worry. I'm not going back down there until those mold guys give me the all-clear." She took a deep breath and exhaled. "I've got to get my medicine," she said, but she didn't move. She suddenly felt dizzy and reached out to grab hold of Gavin's arm to steady herself. She blinked several times and breathed in and out.

Gavin grasped her arms and held her steady. "Court, are you okay?"

She nodded, looking at the ground as she tried to stave off the feeling that she was going to pass out. As she gained her composure, she noticed the rip in his jeans and the blood that was soaking through below his knee.

"Gavin, you're really hurt." She forgot her momentary dizziness.

Without letting go of her, Gavin looked down at his leg. "Yeah, but it's fine. I'm more worried about you."

"I'm fine, but we need to get you checked out. You may need stitches." She tried to free herself from his grip, but he wouldn't let go.

"I know. I'll get it taken care of, but I want to know what just happened to you."

"I don't know." She looked up at him. "I just got really dizzy. Must have been the mold."

Gavin looked at her with concern. "Are you sure? Maybe we should get you checked out."

Shaking her head, Courtney let herself relax in his hold. "I think I'm okay now. I'll just go take a pill, and that should help."

Gavin continued to hold onto one of her arms as she walked to her car.

"Court, how many of those things do you take?" he asked as he watched her pop a pill into her mouth and wash it down with a drink from a bottle of water in her console.

She shrugged. "I don't know, one or two a day. Not every day. Only when I feel a headache coming on."

Gavin took the bottle from her and read the label. "This has all kinds of side effects."

"I haven't had any. It says, 'may cause.' So far, I'm good."

"And you don't take it more than twice a day, right?"

"Right. I know the rules. I also don't take it with alcohol, and I get my blood pressure checked regularly."

"How regularly? When was the last time you had it checked?"

"Um, well, I went to the doctor just before I came down here."

"As in, two months ago," Gavin stated.

"Yeah, I guess so. Has it been that long?" Courtney bit her lip.

"Yeah, it's been that long. This says, drowsiness, dizziness, nausea, dry mouth, and tingling of the hands and feet. Does it affect blood pressure, too?"

"Well, it can. I mean, it has been known to raise blood pressure, so I'm supposed to have it checked." As she said the words, she knew she hadn't followed through on them. It had been more than two months since she'd been checked. The doctor gave her strict instructions to stop at any drug store or clinic on a weekly basis to have her pressure taken, but Courtney hadn't really thought about it in weeks.

"Let's go." He pulled her toward his truck as he pushed her door closed.

"Where are we going?"

"To the urgent care in Leonardtown. I won't make you go to the hospital, but you're getting checked out."

"Gavin." She tried to hold her ground, but he continued to move, and she stumbled toward him. Gavin turned and caught her, putting their faces within inches of each other. Courtney felt breathless. “I’m okay, really. I feel fine now.”

“Yeah, and you have a history of strokes in your family, and you’re on medicine that raises your blood pressure. We’re not taking a chance.”

Courtney gazed into his eyes, so close she imagined she would feel his eyelashes brush against her if he blinked. She swallowed as she recognized worry in his creased brow and tight lips. “Okay,” she whispered. “But please don’t call Gram.”

He regarded her for a moment before nodding. “All right. We’ll get you checked out and make sure everything is okay, and then we’ll decide what to tell Lily.”

“And Gavin,” she said before either of them looked away.

“Yes?” His voice was low as he stared into her eyes.

“You’re getting your leg checked out, too.”

He blinked once and backed up, letting go of her and raising his hands in defeat. “Fair enough. Let’s go.”

*****

“Ten stiches?” Lily asked before spearing a piece of fresh, steamed broccoli with her fork. “How long was the cut?”

“Long, and he was acting like it was a little scratch. I couldn’t believe it when I finally saw it. Men. They’re so stupid sometimes.”

“Well, I’m not sure how smart it was to be doing all you’re doing in that old house without a tetanus shot.” Lily frowned at Courtney.

“Okay, guilty as charged.” Courtney had told Lily about Gavin’s cut and about her getting the shot, but she had left out the parts about the dizziness and the blood pressure scare. Her vitals were all good, and the doctor agreed that the smell and the abundance of mold could have made her dizzy, especially with the head trauma she had sustained. She was more sensitive to sights, sounds, and smells than the average person and probably would be for the rest of her life. The doctor consulted Courtney's neurologist, and both agreed that she should not go back into the cellar until it was cleared and that she should cut back on the amount of time she spent working on the house. She hadn't told Lily that either. No need to worry her.

"I think I'm going to go up and stay with Clarissa for a few days. She has some boxes of family documents that she hasn't donated to the museum. She wanted to go through them first. Do you mind?"

"Mind? Of course not. You're not a child anymore. It's not like you're down here spending the summer with me while your parents are at work. You can come and go as you please."

"I just hate to leave you here alone."

"Who says I'm alone? Jan is across the street, Sami is down the road, and Ben is here. He will always be here."

Courtney smiled and looked lovingly at her grandmother. "I suppose you're right about that." What she would give to someday have a love like that. Clarissa was right. Lily and Ben had a storybook romance, one that Courtney hoped to replicate someday. An image of Gavin came to her mind and was quickly replaced by an image of Jason. Could one of them be the man of her dreams? Shouldn't she know that by now? She bit her lip and wondered if either, or neither, was right for her. Spencer's image pushed both of the others from her mind, and she shook her head to clear her thoughts.

"What's that look about?" Lily asked.

"Gram, how did you know that Granddad was the one? Was it really love at first sight?"

"Oh, heavens no. I thought he was nice-looking, and I counted the days until we could date, but it was not love at first sight. Despite the romance novels and chick flicks, love takes time. You need to get to know each other, learn about what makes each person unique, understand how they fit into your life. I once heard a quote by the author, Erich Segal, that I've never forgotten. It went something like, 'True love is quiet. If you hear bells, you need your ears checked'."

Courtney laughed. "I'll have to remember that."

"No, you won't. Because one morning, you will wake up and say to yourself, 'Ah, there it is.' And in the peaceful quiet of the morning, you will finally hear the bells and realize that they were there all along."

"What's that mean?"

"That sometimes love doesn't hit you between the eyes. It seeps into your soul like the scent of the lilac, slowly floating in on the breeze and taking over your senses without you even realizing it until you suddenly smell its aroma so intensely that you can taste the sweetness on your tongue."

"Gram, I never knew you were such a poet."

"Not a poet, my dear, just a girl who spent the better part of her life deeply in love."

Later that night, Courtney searched Google for information about Erich Segal and his quote about love.

True love comes quietly, without banners or flashing lights. If you hear bells, get your ears checked.

Hmm, she thought, maybe Gram and Segal were right. After all, Gram had the love of a lifetime, and Segal supposedly penned one of the greatest romance novels ever written which evidentially had been made into an Oscar-award winning movie, one of the highest grossing films of all time. She went to her movie account and searched for *Love Story*. Maybe she'd see if Clarissa wanted to watch the classic with her. She could use a good love story to take her mind off the house, the hidden tunnel, and Anne the pirate. Unfortunately, it probably wouldn't take her mind off of Gavin or Jason or even Spencer, much to her dismay.

CHAPTER SEVEN

A box of tissues sat on the couch between Courtney and Clarissa. Both women wiped their cheeks and blew their noses.

"I had forgotten what a great movie that is. How beautiful the story is," Clarissa sniffed.

"I've never seen it before." Courtney sniffed, not trying to hold back her tears. "It was won…wonderful,"

"Oh, that Ryan O'Neal. What a looker he was."

"Was? Is he dead?"

"I'm honestly not sure. Which I suppose means that he may still be good looking. Probably better looking. Why does that happen? Men get better looking with age, and women just get old."

Courtney laughed. "I don't know about that, Clarissa. You still look pretty good to me."

"Well, that's because I'm not old. And I always get my beauty sleep." She rose from the couch. "I'll see you in the morning."

"Good night, and thanks for letting me stay here for a few days."

"Always happy to have company, especially family."

Courtney watched her cousin retreat down the hall and pulled out her laptop and did a Google search. Yep, still alive and still good looking. She smiled and thought about the movie. Right up until she died, Oliver and Jenny loved each other deeply, giving up dreams, money, even family to be with each other. What was that like? Had Anne done that? Had she given up the swashbuckling, adventurous life of a pirate to be with Robert? Unfortunately, it looked like the world would never know.

*****

"I wonder if we should be wearing gloves. These are so old and fragile."

Clarissa sat up straight in the high-backed kitchen chair and looked at the documents on the table. "Maybe we should be. I never thought about it."

"Look at this old picture." Courtney held up a sepia portrait of a family, dressed in fancy clothes with dour looks on their faces.

Clarissa took the photo and turned it over. She squinted to read the faded writing on the back. "That's my great-great grandfather and his wife and children." She handed the photo back to Courtney.

"Why do they look so unhappy?"

"Nobody smiled in pictures back then. I think it was superstitious or something like that."

"Weird. It just makes them look like they were miserable."

"Maybe they were. Hard to know. They've all been gone for so long. I didn't know them at all. Well, I knew the little boy on the right. That's my great-grandfather. He died when I was in high school. We had our grandparents and great-grandparents around for much longer back then, what with people marrying and having babies younger."

Courtney put the photo back in the pile and dug through the box.

"Oh, look," she cried. "It's a picture of River Terrace. Who are these people?" She handed the photo to Clarissa.

Peering at the picture through her reading glasses, Clarissa made a face. She turned the picture over and shook her head. "I have no idea."

"They must be family, right? Why else would we have it?"

"I guess so. This boy looks familiar."

Courtney stood and went behind her cousin to get a closer look. "Hey, he looks like Patrick when he was younger."

"You're right, he does. He could be your brother, without a doubt."

"So, they must be family."

"Must be, but I have no idea who they are."

"Is there a date on the back?"

Clarissa shook her head. "If there was, it's gone now. The whole picture is starting to disappear."

"Like in Back to the Future," Courtney said. Clarissa stared blankly at her. "When Marty couldn't get back to the future, his older brother and sister started fading from the photograph in his wallet."

"Not quite the same." Clarissa handed her back the picture.

"I guess not." Courtney sighed. "Too bad we don't know who they are."

"Not that it would tell us anything."

"Well, it would tell us that our family had a connection to the house at some other point in time."

"Could be that John held onto the house when he left the area. These could be descendants of his. You could probably find the deed to the house from this time period. Judging by their clothes, this was the mid 1800s."

"They had photographs back then?"

"They did, but rarely would a family have had a portrait taken, especially at their home. They had to be quite wealthy. And probably of some prominence."

"Clarissa, would you mind if I take this back with me? I'd like to show it to the curator at the museum and see if he knows anything about it or about the family."

"Sure, but let's put it in a plastic bag with some cardboard behind it. That should protect it."

After some more searching, they put the contents of the boxes back in the closet in Clarissa's spare room and went to make dinner.

"I'm sorry there wasn't more. Maybe that picture will bring you some answers." Clarissa talked while pan-searing a couple of chicken breasts.

"Maybe, but answers to what?" Courtney asked as she helped Clarissa with the food preparation. She finished chopping a carrot into a bowl of spinach and reached for a cucumber. "I'm not even sure what I'm looking for. I have the house. Nothing about it or my family history is going to make a difference. I really have no idea what I'm searching for." She stopped and faced Clarissa, the cucumber in one hand and a paring knife in the other. "Why do I have this nagging sense that the house is trying to tell me something? That there is something about it or about myself that I'm supposed to discover?"

"I'm afraid I can't answer that, Courtney. I can only offer that you're at a crossroads in your life. You've turned thirty, and you're still single. You broke off a five-year engagement. You survived a near-death experience, spent months in the hospital and then in rehab. You decided your job wasn't the right job for you. I think you're searching for *you*, Courtney. Not for a house or a history or even a husband. I think you're trying to figure out who *you* are. Perhaps you're searching in all the wrong places."

Courtney stood, facing her cousin, with a lump in her throat. The realization hit her that Lily was right. And so was Clarissa. Courtney had experienced all of those things. She had no idea what she wanted in life. She hated her career, her life in the city, and the future she would have had with Spencer. She wanted something different. Something more. The problem was that she had no idea what that something was. And more, how? More exciting? More money? More connections? None of that felt right. She didn't know what she wanted or who she was. And she didn't know where or how to find the answers.

She turned back to the salad that she was making and began to wonder if she had made a huge mistake. Many in fact. Maybe she should have stayed with Spencer, gone back to her job, and started planning her wedding.

No, that wasn't right either. She shook her head as she turned back toward her cousin.

"I just don't know what I want. *Who* I want. What I want to do. It's all so darned confusing."

"You'll figure it out, Courtney. You just need to find yourself first. The rest will fall into place."

"Find myself how?" she pleaded. "Where? You said it yourself, I'm thirty years old. Why haven't I 'found myself' yet?"

"Again, perhaps you've been looking in all the wrong places."

"Then where the heck am I supposed to be looking?" She tried to reign in her temper. She shouldn't have raised her voice toward Clarissa. But her cousin just shrugged, a secretive smile on her lips.

"Only you can answer that, Courtney. And you will. When the time is right. Pray about it. The answers will come."

Courtney resisted the urge to roll her eyes. Why was that her family's answer to everything? She'd been praying her entire life, and, so far, it hadn't gotten her anywhere.

*****

Dropping her bag by the front door, Courtney turned back and wrestled her recently-made key from the decades-old knob in the kitchen door.

"Gram," she called, wondering why the house was so quiet. She double-checked the time on her watch—1:00. Shouldn't her grandmother have the television on for her daily dose of *Days of Our Lives*?

"Gram, I'm home."

A tingling chill ran down Courtney's spine as she hastened toward the living room. It was empty. She looked in the bedroom. Nothing there. Feeling almost frantic, Courtney went to the bathroom, but the door wouldn't open. Shoving it a bit harder, she looked inside the room and gasped when she saw the legs sprawled on the floor.

"Gram, open the door! Gram, get up!"

Courtney ran back through her grandmother's bedroom, tore through the living room and dining room, and raced through the kitchen. She rounded the doorway to the long pantry and hurled herself at the other bathroom door. It opened instantly, and Courtney had to grab the sink in front of her to keep from stumbling on top of Lily. Her instincts, from many years as a Girl Scout, kicked in; and Courtney knew just what to do. Dropping to the floor, she felt for a pulse.

"Thank God, thank you, God. Gram, I'm here. I'm here. It's going to be okay." She checked Lily's breathing as she reached into her back pocket for her phone. "Yes, I have an emergency." She proceeded to tell the operator about Lily and gave her the address.

Within ten minutes, the ambulance arrived, but Lily was still unconscious.

"Do you think she fell and hit her head?" Courtney asked.

"We won't know until we get her checked out, ma'am. Give us some room, please."

Courtney backed away. The adrenaline that pumped through her system kept her from crying or breaking down.

"Courtney!"

She heard the yell from the kitchen.

"Gavin, back here!" She sucked in a deep breath, relieved to have someone else there with her besides the paramedics. Gavin reached her side as the paramedics loaded Lily onto a board and lifted her to the stretcher they had wheeled into the nearest bedroom.

"What—?"

"I don't know." She shook her head. "I came home and found her here. She's breathing, but she won't wake up."

"Are you coming with us?" the EMT asked.

Without saying anything to Gavin, Courtney followed the paramedics through the opposite door.

"I'll follow you," Gavin called before turning the other way to go out to his truck. Courtney didn't acknowledge him as she followed Lily to the ambulance.

It was an hour before the doctor came through the emergency room doors. By that time, the room was filled with McMillans. Using Courtney's phone, Gavin had called Rick and Jodie. They called Courtney's brother, Patrick, and his wife Marie. They rushed down from the hardware store as quickly as they could, and Courtney's youngest brother, Jimmy, was on his way. They all stood as the doctor made his way to them.

"She's stable."

"What happened?" Jodie asked.

"We're certain that she fell and hit her head on the tub. There's a mild contusion on the back of her head." He reached up and placed his hand on the back of his own head, whether on purpose or subconsciously, Courtney didn't know. "We're going to run some tests and try to determine if the fall was the cause of the blackout or vice versa."

"Is she conscious now?" Patrick asked.

Courtney knew the answer by the look on the doctor's face. He shook his head. "No, and we don't know why. As soon as she has the CAT scan, we'll let you know if we see anything."

"Can we see her?"

"Not yet. They're getting ready to take her down to X-ray. I, or one of my staff, will be back out when we know something or if she wakes up." They watched him retreat back through the double doors.

"If? He said, 'if she wakes up.'" Jodie sunk back into a chair.

"I don't think he meant it like that." Rick sat beside his wife and put his arms around her.

Jan rushed through the door and ran to Gavin as soon as she spotted him. She hugged him and then Courtney. "What's the news?"

"There isn't any. She's being taken for a CAT scan. She's still unconscious." Courtney could hardly finish her sentence; the word unconscious was barely louder than a whisper.

"Can I get you anything?" Gavin asked.

Nobody answered, but Courtney looked into his blue eyes, hoping to find solace and strength. What she saw was only a reflection of her own worries and fears.

Gavin took her hand and gently tugged. "Let's go for a walk. We can bring back drinks for everyone. They're going to need caffeine when the fatigue from the worry kicks in."

Courtney nodded and let him lead her down the hall toward the cafeteria.

"It's all my fault. I shouldn't have left."

Gavin stopped and pulled her to face him. "Don't be ridiculous. She's lived by herself for a long time now. This could have happened with or without you there."

"But I would have found her sooner if I hadn't been at Clarissa's."

"When did you last talk to her?"

"This morning. I called to tell her I was on the way home."

"Then being at Clarissa's made no difference. If you had been here, you would have been at the house, or the museum, or Hannah's or Sami's. You wouldn't have been home until late this afternoon. You actually got home earlier than you normally would have. Isn't that true?"

"I, I guess so." Courtney's tears began to flow. She had managed to keep it together for so long, but now, she couldn't stop herself from crying.

Gavin pulled her to him and wrapped his arms around her. "Sh, it's okay. She's going to be fine."

"How do you know that?" she asked, looking up at him.

"She's a tough old bird. She'll wake up, and then she'll be telling the doctors and nurses how to do their jobs."

Courtney smiled. That was true. Lily might not have a single degree to her credit, but she could organize and run anything, and she'd be trying to run the hospital before long.

Gavin placed his finger on her chin and tilted her face up toward his. "She's going to be okay. I promise."

Courtney nodded and said a prayer that he was right. She didn't know if it would do any good, but she sure was going to give it a try.

*****

"Is this the best my taxpayer dollars can afford? It's not a nightgown. It's a thin piece of cloth with a string around the top." Lily pulled the covers up over her hospital gown. "And what is this that they're trying to feed me? There's not a piece of meat in this whole bowl. It's just a bowl of broth. I should go down to that kitchen and show them how to make a proper soup."

"Mom, don't be ridiculous. You can't get out of bed, and you can't have anything else to eat until the doctor says so. They're still running tests."

"I don't need tests. I need to be home. I've got things to do."

"Like what?" Jodie asked.

"Like picking the apples and making applesauce before the blackbirds ruin the whole lot."

"Gram, I can go home and pick the apples. Don't worry," Courtney assured her.

"How will you know how to make the applesauce?"

"I'll figure it out. I'm sure I can find your recipe."

"It's in the box on the cart under the microwave. Don't you go getting one off Google. Mine is the best. And don't alter it. It's perfect just the way it is. My grandmother devised that recipe, and it doesn't need changing."

"Well, aren't we feisty today?" a nurse said from the doorway. She moved the tray out of the way and onto the counter, so she could check Lily's vitals.

"I don't like hospitals," Lily told her, and Courtney remembered the long hours Lily spent sitting by Ben's bedside just down the hall. She imagined that Lily spent a fair amount of time sitting by Courtney's own bed at Maryland Shock Trauma as well.

"As soon as they figure out what happened, you can go home," Patrick said. "And you can fix your applesauce." He leaned down and loudly whispered, "Court's not much of a cook, you know."

"Hey, I can cook," Courtney protested.

"Yeah, grilled cheese," her brother teased.

"Well, look who's talking." Marie playfully punched her husband. "If you're such an expert, you can make dinner tonight." Courtney heard the nurse laugh as she finished her check and left the room.

"There's only one chef in this family," Jimmy said from the doorway. "The rest of you can stay out of the kitchen." He entered the room, wearing a crisp, white smock over a pair of navy pants, and went to his grandmother. He leaned down and kissed her on the cheek. "Hey grandma, how are you feeling?"

"Like I was hit in the head with a bathtub. And hungry. What did you bring me? You smell like garlic and tomatoes."

Courtney was glad to see the twinkle in her eyes as she looked up at Jimmy.

He shook his head. "Sorry, grandma, but they wouldn't let me smuggle anything in to you. I tried, but the aroma of sage and oregano coming from the stew pot gave me away, and it was confiscated. It's probably being sold on the black market as we speak. My cooking brings a high price, you know."

"Oh, Jimmy, you do make me smile."

He made everyone smile. It was his specialty. Everyone loved Jimmy. He loved to make people laugh, but, more than that, he loved to make people eat. And he did it well. His restaurant was one of the most popular ones in DC, and he often catered to such customers as foreign dignitaries and Supreme Court Justices.

"So, just a concussion?" Jimmy asked.

"They think so," Jodie said. "We're still waiting on all the test results, but it looks like Mom just tripped on the bathroom rug and went down hard, hitting the tub on her way to the floor."

"Thank Heaven that a concussion is all that happened," Jimmy said. "It could have been much worse."

"It certainly could have," Jodie agreed.

Courtney's phone buzzed. She looked down and saw a text from Gavin.

If it's a bad time, just say so, but I need you to come to the house at some point today.

"Do y'all mind if I duck out to make a call?"

"No, go ahead. Now that I'm here, Grandma won't want to pay attention to anyone else."

"Thanks a lot, Jimmy." Courtney bent to kiss her grandmother. "I may need to run to the house for a bit. Gavin has a question about something. Is that okay?"

"Sure, honey. Don't worry about coming back. I hope to be home by bedtime."

Courtney looked at her mother and raised her brow. Jodie just shook her head.

"Okay, Gram. I'll see you soon. I love you."

"I love you, too, Courtney. Don't worry. I'll be home before you know it."

Courtney hoped that was true.

*****

"There's good news and bad news," Gavin told Courtney when they met in the driveway.

"Great, more bad news. I guess you should give me the good news first." She swung the car door shut and walked around to where Gavin was standing in the yard. He saw the dark circles under her eyes

"How's Lily?"

"She's okay. Getting feisty and ready to go home. I guess those are good signs."

"And they still think it was simply a fall?"

"Looks that way. All of the tests came back negative, but she does have a concussion. Turns out it's the first one she's ever had. The doctor said it was a miracle, at her age, that she actually woke up." Courtney's eyes misted over. "I don't know what I would have done if I had lost her." She held her lips together tightly, and Gavin watched as the blood drained from them, turning them white.

"Hey," he said, putting his arms around her. "She's fine. A bump on the head. She's not going anywhere."

"I hope you're right." She buried her head in his chest, and he couldn't help but think that she felt so right against his beating heart. Pushing the thought aside, he gently nudged her away so that they were facing each other, but he held onto her arms.

"I am. She may be old, but she's young at heart."

Courtney nodded and gave him a weak smile. "So, what's the good news?"

"Follow me." They walked around to the back of the house where he picked up two dust masks that were lying on top of the cellar doors. He pulled open the doors. "We're not staying for long, but I thought you'd like to see what I found."

Her eyes widened, and she broke out into a dazzling smile. "A tunnel? A cave? What is it?"

"You'll see." He stepped through the doors and onto the ladder. "I'll go first."

Gavin descended into the cellar and reached up to help Courtney ease her way down. He and three other men had worked all week, while Courtney was away and then at the hospital, to clear out the insulation, the broken shelves, and all of the other objects in the cellar. The space was almost empty. He pulled the string on a lightbulb hanging from a beam above them.

"You installed a light," Courtney excalimed before frowning. "Is that the good news surprise?"

Gavin laughed and shook his head. "No, silly, but I hope you're pleased that there's a light down here now."

"I am absolutely pleased."

"Good, come on." He turned and led her through the cellar. "You can see that there's lots of space. Eventually, I can put in new shelves, and you can use it for storage. It's sealed up pretty well and should stay dry. After the experts are here next week, it should be even better. I checked, and they not only deal with mold removal but with full cellar and crawl-space upgrading. They're going to make sure you can keep out the dampness in the future. And I'm going to replace the ladder with a nice set of stairs, just to be safe."

"That's awesome. It smells better already."

"It does, but the mold is still here, so don't take off the mask."

Courtney nodded. "What else?"

"I found all kinds of cool bottles and jars that you might want to incorporate into your decorating. I put them in the barn for now with all of the other stuff we're saving as we go along."

"Oh, I can't wait to go through them."

"I'm sure. I bet you also can't wait to see this." He took her arm and pulled her toward a dark area at the back of the cellar. He reached up to pull another string which turned on a bulb that illuminated an opening in the cellar wall.

Courtney sucked in her breath, her mouth and eyes opened wide. "It's the tunnel," she breathed.

"I wouldn't call it a tunnel exactly, but yeah. It's a narrow path to another room."

"Can I see it?"

"Yes, but you'll need your flashlight. I'll try to install some kind of light eventually, but there's nothing in there now."

Gavin lit up his phone and led the way through the narrow space and into a room that measured about six by six feet.

"This is where they stayed for at least two full days." Courtney could hardly fathom how it must have been for the children. "Oh my gosh, I can't imagine how frightened they must have felt."

"I'm sure they were. It would have been pitch black, and, at that time of year, freezing cold. Honestly, it's a miracle they survived."

Courtney shook her head and looked at Gavin. "They were just children. How horrible it must have been."

"Come on," he tugged on her hand. "We've been down here long enough. There's nothing more to see. Let's go."

When they climbed out into the sunlight, Gavin had to blink a few times to adjust his eyes. He closed the cellar and turned toward Courtney. Instead of excitement at the find, he saw sadness.

"What's wrong?" He lifted his hands to her shoulders.

"It's just so sad. They lost their mother. Their father was shot by pirates. Then they had to leave their home after almost freezing to death all that time in the pitch blackness. It just makes me really grateful for what I have but so sad for all they went through."

Gavin tilted her chin up. "But they survived, and it sounds like they ended up having a pretty good life from what you learned."

"Except for Evan." She pouted her lip slightly, and Gavin wondered what it would be like to kiss her all these years later. He knew better than to go there, especially when she was feeling so vulnerable, so he dropped his hands from her shoulders.

"Not everyone can go through all that and remain unscathed. At least the others got past it."

"I guess so. Can I go look at the stuff in the barn?"

"In a minute. I think we should talk about the bad news."

*****

"All of them?" Courtney asked, staring at the closed doors in the newer section of the house.

"All of them—the bedroom, master bathroom, and both upstairs bedrooms. And no way to open them except to take them off the hinges like I did before."

"How odd. I hate to do it, but I guess we're going to have to get all new knobs. And these old ones are so pretty." She frowned and shook her head in disbelief. How, or more to the point, why did the doors lock? Or was the real question, who?

"You can get some real nice replicas. And they'll have keys," Gavin told her.

"Well, I guess if that's the extent of the bad news, I can live with replacing the knobs." She turned to look at Gavin and, seeing the look on his face, rolled her eyes. "It's not the end of the bad news," she stated.

"Afraid not. Come on." He walked to the room at the other side of the house that they had begun referring to as 'the parlor.' Courtney followed. "Remember the broken window we nailed shut so that the glass would remain intact?"

"Yes." Courtney elongated the word, afraid of what was coming next.

"When I got here this morning, the window was open, wide open. And the nails are completely gone. Nowhere to be found. And the window is shattered."

"No, you've got to be kidding." She closed her eyes and let out a long sigh. "Why on earth? How did that happen?" she asked, raising her gaze to meet Gavin's.

"I don't know, but didn't that article you read to me say that things happened like that all the time when the Suttons lived here?"

"Yeah, but…" She turned and looked at Gavin. "Don't tell me that you're beginning to believe in ghosts?"

"I'm not, but somebody sure wants us to believe that something spooky is going on."

He had a point. Real or not, there were definitely ghosts in the house. And she was going to figure out who they were and what they wanted.

*****

"This is the most amazing cake I've ever seen." Courtney swiped a bit of green frosting from the mermaid's tale. She licked her finger and relished the sweet taste of sugar and vanilla. "I can't believe you planned this all by yourself."

"I love doing stuff like this," Hannah said. "I just hope she appreciates it when she's older and doesn't cry to have a cake from the Giant Food bakery."

"She wouldn't dare." Courtney watched the group of three-year-olds playing with their baby dolls.

"Do you think it's too much? To have an elaborate birthday party for a three-year-old?"

"Who cares? I mean, as long as you admit that the party is really for us. The real fun is putting it together, don't you think?"

Hannah laughed. "I agree. I've always wanted to be a mom just so I could design Halloween costumes and throw lavish birthday parties."

"I know exactly what you mean. My mom and I once put together so many weddings that we often kidded about going into the business ourselves."

"Why didn't you?"

Courtney shrugged. "I guess the real world, and a real job, came calling."

"If I had enough money to not worry about paying the bills, this is exactly what I would do for the rest of my life."

"Throw 'Little Mermaid' parties for three-year-olds?"

"Not just that." Hannah readjusted a giant clamshell hanging from the dining room chandelier. "I would throw all kinds of parties for all ages. It would be my dream job to do nothing but plan fun events for other people."

"How cool." Courtney meant it. Hannah was truly in her element when it came to putting together parties, designing cakes, and decorating like a Pinterest queen. She hoped that maybe, someday, Hannah could see her dream come true.

Sighing, Courtney watched the other moms from Maddy's playgroup. She wasn't one of them, and she felt awkward being the only non-mom at the party. She admitted to herself that she was pretty envious of their lives. Sure, she was the one getting to conjure Pinterest magic into a showcase house, but they were the ones who used every day magic to turn their houses into homes.

"Hey, thanks for the invite, but I should be getting back to the hospital."

"I understand. I'm glad Lily's feeling better." Hannah reached for a knife to cut the cake. "Are you sure you don't want to take a piece home? The last thing I need is leftover birthday cake."

Courtney laughed. "Same here, but thanks for the offer. And thanks for keeping an eye on the house."

"No problem. I'm really sorry about the window. I wish I had seen or heard something."

"You've had your hands full getting ready for today. I'm sure we'll catch them soon."

"I'm sure," Hannah agreed, trying to offer an encouraging smile. She was becoming such a good friend. Courtney just wished she had seen someone or something that would help them solve this mystery.

CHAPTER EIGHT

Hey, it's me. How's it going down there? I hope you're doing well. I miss you. 🩶

A heart. Spencer actually added a heart. In the five years they were together, Courtney couldn't ever remember him using an emoji of any kind. She looked at her watch. It was nine in the morning. Since when did he text at nine in the morning? When did he text any time before leaving work for the day? Usually it was at night, and it was almost always to say that he was running late again or that he had to see a client and had to cancel dinner.

All is good here. How's work?

She figured she should keep it casual. And work was his favorite subject. To her surprise, he answered immediately. That was happening a lot lately. 'A lot' being the half a dozen times he'd texted her over the past few months. That might actually have been a record, now that she thought about it.

Work is okay. Too much of it. I feel like I need a break. Can I come down next weekend? I'd love to see the house.

Courtney blinked as she reread the message. Was this a joke? Clearly, these messages were not from

Spencer. Had someone taken his phone to play a joke on them both?

"What's up?" Jodie asked.

"Spencer. He's actually talking about taking a few days off from work. I mean, he said 'weekend,' so not actual work days, but still…" She looked at her mother. "When does Spencer ever take off from work?"

"What did he say?" she asked as she poured milk into a bowl of Special K.

"That he wants to come down next weekend to see the house. Did you tell him about Gram?"

"Not a word. I promise. He must just want to see you." Jodie took a seat across from Courtney at the table.

"No, he said, 'the house'."

Jodie waved her spoon in the air as she chewed. Swallowing, she said, "He means you. He might have said 'house,' but he wants to see you."

Exhaling, Courtney looked back down at the messages on her phone. "I know." She looked up at her mother. "What do I say?"

"What do you want to say?"

It was the first time Jodie hadn't tried to push her own opinion about Spencer off on Courtney.

"I, I don't know. I mean, I guess it would be nice to see him. As long as he doesn't get the wrong message."

"Why don't you say that you're really busy, but you could spare an hour or so to show him around. That ought to teach him what it feels like."

Who was this woman? Was Courtney actually talking to her mother? The woman who thought Spencer walked on water?

"You think Spencer needs to be taught a lesson?"

"Well, honey, maybe if he hadn't been so glued to his desk, you wouldn't have broken off the engagement. I may have been upset about it, but I'm not blind. And in the past month or so, I've come to realize that you would have been miserable being married to a high-profile attorney. You want different things, a different kind of life. Maybe Spencer isn't the right person for you, but if he is, maybe he's realizing the same thing."

Courtney sat back in the chair and thought about what her mother said. She still wasn't sure that she and Spencer were right for each other, though the idea of seeing him was actually kind of nice. It would be good to see him again and to show off the work they'd done so far.

"Well, then, I guess I'll tell him exactly that. If he thinks it's worth his time to come all the way down here for an hour or so, then that's his decision." She didn't honestly expect him to come, but she texted him anyway.

"What do you know?" She was amazed a moment later as she stared at the thumbs up emoji on the screen.

"He's coming?" Jodie asked.

"He says he is. I'll believe it when I see it." She picked up her bowl and put it in the dishwasher. "Give Gram my love." she leaned down and kissed her mother on the cheek.

"I will. I think she'll be able to come home today. I'll let you know."

"Sounds good. Just send me an emoji."

"What?" Jodie said with a confused chuckle.

"Never mind. I'll talk to you later."

Courtney brushed her teeth, grabbed her purse, and headed outside to her car. There was a lot she wanted to get accomplished today, especially if Spencer was actually going to show up in a few short days.

*****

Courtney sorted through the pile in the barn. There were antique canning jars, apothecary jars, and liquor bottles. There were several jugs that most likely held beer.

"What's this?" She spied a piece of faded calico beneath the pile, tugged on the material, and pulled an entire doll out from beneath the glass. "Oh!" she gasped in surprise. The doll had a soft body and a china head. She was amazed that the entire head was still intact. There wasn't even a scratch on the white face.

Gently turning the doll in her hands, Courtney looked for anything that would identify it, but found nothing. Even without any markings of ownership, she was certain that it had belonged to Crystin. Though she would have been a teenager by the time they hid in the cellar, it would have made sense that she wandered down there from time to time when she was a child. Perhaps, she took it with her that day as a comfort item. Courtney had a stuffed elephant that she took to college with her.

Cradling the doll in her arms, Courtney felt a real connection to the child who once played with it. She would box up the glass bottles and jugs and decide later what to do with them, but the doll was definitely going to go in one of the bedrooms. Maybe, someday, it would sit on a shelf in Courtney's daughter's room.

*****

"What about installing cameras?" Courtney asked Gavin. She had finished going through the pile in the barn and had been thinking about the intruder. As soon as she saw that Gavin was taking a break for lunch, she approached him. He had been so busy earlier, stripping the hideous wallpaper in the master bedroom, she hadn't wanted to disturb him. He sat on the front steps and spread out his lunch before taking a long drink of water. Courtney sat down on the lowest step.

"To catch whoever is coming in?" he asked before taking a bite of his sandwich.

"Yes. I can go buy a few, one for each door."

"Waste of money."

"Why" she asked, feeling a bit annoyed. She thought it was a good idea.

"Too easy to get around being filmed. And for the right quality, you'd have to spend a good chunk of change. Those outdoor cameras that people use to catch deer and stuff are too grainy. You'd never be able to identify anyone."

"I guess I could stay here one night—"

"No way." He shook his head. "That's not going to happen."

"Gavin, I'm not afraid of ghosts. I want to catch whoever is doing these things."

"I get it, and, so far, it's been pretty harmless stuff, but I don't want you here if someone decides to take it up a notch. And your grandmother would have a fit."

Courtney frowned. "You're right about that. I don't want to upset her when she's just getting home."

"Let's just continue to keep track of it. If it's just some kids playing pranks, they'll get tired of the game pretty soon. Especially if we don't let them know it bothers us."

He had a point there.

Courtney began fidgeting with a tall blade of grass.

"So, Spencer might come down this weekend. To see the house," she added, glancing up at Gavin.

His brow went up in surprise. "Really? I didn't think he was still in the picture."

"He's not. We text now and then. Small stuff. He's been asking for a couple months if he could come take a look, and I figured, why not? To be honest, I doubt he shows."

"Did he do that a lot? Not show up for stuff?" He took a drink of water but kept his eyes on her over the bottle.

"No, not to that extent. He always let me know he had to cancel."

"But he cancelled a lot." Gavin bit into a large, green apple.

"Yeah, he canceled a lot. I mean, I understand. He was trying to make partner, and he did. It was quite an accomplishment at his age."

"But it meant a lot of extra hours."

"It did. I was okay with it. I worked a lot of extra hours, too, but after the accident…" She turned her attention back to the blade of grass.

"You realized life is short."

Courtney sighed and looked back at Gavin. "Yeah, I did. When I woke up, and he was there by my bedside, the first thing I thought of was, 'wow, it took me almost dying for him to take the day off from work.' I know that's not fair, but it's what I thought. I told everyone that I had just had a revelation that he wasn't the one, but what I actually realized was that I wasn't the one. Some other woman might be perfectly happy sitting home while he climbed the legal ladder, but not me. I wanted someone who would want to do the things I wanted to do and not work all the time."

"And what is it that you want to do, Court?" he asked quietly.

Courtney reached up and played with a loose strand of hair, dropped it, and fingered her scar. She thought about Gavin's question for several moments before taking a deep breath and letting it out.

"Honestly? I have no idea. Which makes it even worse that I broke things off. I mean, it wasn't as if I had a list of things that I was dying to jump out of the bed and do. Heck, at that point, I wasn't even sure I could walk. I just, I don't know, I just didn't think I wanted to live the life I, we, had been living."

Gavin took the last bite of his apple and tossed it into his lunch bag as he chewed. "Well, one thing's for sure." He stood and reached for her hand, pulling her up. "You've got a lot to concentrate on while you figure it out."

"You ain't kidding about that." She laughed at his words. "You ain't kidding."

"How about, for now, you give me a hand with this wallpaper? I'm almost done. Once it's all gone, we can start prepping all the walls. Next week, it's going to be painting time."

Courtney's heart leapt. "It's about time," she said, following him into the house.

*****

"I'm really impressed, CJ." Spencer used his pet name for her as he took in the room. "This house is going to be quite spectacular when it's all done."

"You should have seen it before. It was a mess."

Spencer looked around the kitchen and chuckled. "It *was* a mess?"

Courtney surveyed the room from his point of view. There were no appliances or cabinets. Pipes and wires hung in odd places around the walls. The linoleum flooring needed to be replaced or ripped out altogether, depending upon what she decided. She was thinking of a brick or stone floor to make it look more like a colonial kitchen though the appliances and cabinets would all be modern. There was a gaping hole in the wall that looked through the fireplace and into the room on the other side. Courtney couldn't help but laugh.

"Okay, okay, it's still a mess, though honestly, it's so much better than it was. We've made a tremendous amount of progress."

"Who's 'we'," he asked, turning toward Courtney.

"Me, Gavin, and Jason, the historical architect, though Jason doesn't actually do any of the work. He just consults."

"Gavin. Isn't he the kid you were friends with when you were younger?"

Courtney chuckled. "Yeah, but he's not a kid anymore. He's an engineer."

Spencer sent her a questioning look. "An engineer? What's he doing renovating a house?"

"Long story. He's just keeping busy while he helps his mom with the farm. His dad died not too long ago, remember?"

Spencer nodded. "Oh, yeah. You came to the funeral."

"And you had to work." Courtney regretted the words immediately. "I'm sorry, Spence. I didn't mean anything by that."

He turned toward her and reached for her hand. "It's okay, CJ, and you're right. I had to work; or, I guess, I chose to work. I seemed to do that a lot when we were together, and I'm sorry. It wasn't fair to you."

Courtney tried to pull her hand away, but he held it tighter. "Spencer, let's not talk about that right now. Let me show you the rest of the house."

"You can, but, please, hear me out first."

Courtney caught her breath and nodded. "Okay, you came all the way down here, so it's only fair that I listen to what you have to say."

"CJ, I messed up. I could have lost you that night, well, technically, I did lose you; but I mean, I could have lost you in every way possible. I know that made you do a lot of thinking, and it did the same for me. I know that I took you for granted. I expected you to sit home and wait for me, but I was never willing to stop working and be with you. I missed funerals and weddings and even just days of being lazy with you. I was an idiot, and I see that now. Courtney, I guess what I'm trying to say is that I still love you. I'm asking for another chance to make things right."

"Spence—" He placed his finger on her lips and shushed her.

"Don't answer me now. Just think about it. Take your time. I'm not going anywhere."

Courtney let out a breath and looked down at her feet. She didn't know what to say. She swallowed and looked back up at Spencer with a forced smile. "I'll think about it."

Spencer's face broke into a wide grin, and Courtney saw the young undergrad she fell in love with. "That's all I'm asking. Thank you. Now, how about showing me the rest of the house?"

*****

"Spencer, I'm so glad you stayed for dinner." Jodie passed the basket of rolls. "How are things at work?"

Spencer glanced at Courtney before answering. "Work is good. Busy, but I'm taking a step back for a bit. Now that I'm a partner, and we've got a whole new crew of kids who just passed the Bar, I can delegate a good deal of my work to others. I plan on cutting back my hours substantially and hope to be able to maintain a normal nine-to-five work day."

"How wonderful." Jodie sent an *I told you so* look at Courtney.

"That would be nice." Lily eyed Courtney's steak as she sipped her chicken noodle soup. She was back home and back on a regular diet, but the doctor said she should slowly ease back into solid foods.

"I'm sure it's not that easy," Courtney told them. "Paring down your hours. Won't you have to oversee the new hires to make sure they're doing their jobs?" She stabbed a juicy piece of pink steak with her fork, dipped it in A-1 sauce, and plucked it into her mouth.

"Sure, I'll have to make sure they're working, but that won't be too bad. I'm looking forward to having a normal life." He watched Courtney as he said the words, and she felt her heartbeat increase. Was he serious?

"How are you parents, Spencer?" Rick asked, and Courtney was happy for the change of subject.

Throughout the rest of the meal, she found herself watching Spencer, seeing him in a new light. No, not a new light, the old light. His laugh, his relaxed expression, his casual demeanor—they all belonged to the Spencer she used to know. Did that mean that he really existed somewhere inside the workaholic he had become? And if that old Spencer had reemerged, for how long would he stay?

*****

"How's Spencer?" Gavin asked as he and Courtney walked to their cars after Sunday Mass.

"He's good."

Gavin suspected there was more that she wasn't saying.

"Good, huh? Good, as in, he's settling into life without you? Or good, as in he'll be back for another visit?"

When she didn't meet his gaze, he knew the answer. Instead of telling him what had happened the day before, she just shrugged.

"Oh, I don't know. He says he'll be back to see how things are going, but we'll see. He's got his work to do, and I've got the house to worry about. Maybe we'll have time for him to make another visit, maybe not."

Her noncommittal attitude struck a chord in Gavin, and he wasn't sure he liked the casualness of her answer. She definitely wasn't pushing Spencer away like she had been. So, what did that mean for her future? Was she going to go back to Baltimore or stay and finish the house? And what would she do when it was finished?

"I'll see you tomorrow, okay?" Her parents and Lily headed toward them.

"Yeah. I'll be there when the mold crew arrives at eight."

Courtney smiled. "Sounds good. See you then."

As he watched her get into the car with her family, he couldn't help but wonder if he had lost his chance. Again.

*****

"Everything looks really great," Jason said after Courtney took him through the house.

"It's really coming together, isn't it?" she asked. "I can hardly believe it's the same house."

"You're doing a great job, and so is Gavin." Courtney noticed the surprise in his tone.

"I told you he was the right man for the job. So, what's the big news you have for me?"

"Come out to the barn with me."

"The barn?" Courtney repeated. "What for?"

"It's a surprise. Trust me." He looked into her eyes.

Courtney surveyed what she saw in those dark blue orbs and knew that she did trust him despite Gavin's misgivings.

They walked back through the upstairs bedroom that was ready for painting and past the other bedroom, similarly finished with a fixed ceiling, new sheetrock, oak-stained fireplace trim, mantle, and closet doors, and new door knobs as well. They descended the stairs, and Courtney smiled as she ran her hand along the recently sanded railing. The steps had also been sanded and were ready to be refinished. The new chair rail in the foyer would be painted along with the railing, the trim, and the doors. The beige color she chose was called, Treasure Trove, which she found so appropriate for a house with a pirate history. The walls would shine with Ray of the Sun yellow.

Courtney felt energized as they passed the two rooms on each side of the foyer. The one to the right, the parlor, was going to be stunning. It boasted a fireplace, surrounded by the original paneling, and three wavy glass windows, one recently replaced for a ridiculous sum. The bookcases, seated deep into the walls on both sides of the fireplaces, were going to show off the many trinkets and treasures they had found during the past few months—old keys, broken pottery, iron tools, buttons and beads, wooden checkers and a hand-carved chess rook, and even an old shoe. The room would be painted Chili Pepper red. Courtney envisioned Oriental rugs throughout all of the rooms and the foyer and had been scouring local auctions and flea markets with Sami. So far, she had bought two large rugs and one floor runner for the foyer with the perfect yellow flowers to match the paint.

As they reached the front door, she could hear Gavin's music playing in the kitchen. He was almost done installing the new glass-enclosed fireplace that would allow views of the dining room through the brick-framed fireplace that was now flanked by a mantel made of one of the beams found in the attic. The appliances would not be delivered for another few weeks, once the painting was complete. Once they were installed, the floors would be restored. The floors would take some time. Stripping, sanding, staining, and varnishing would make those the most time-consuming and stunning of the projects. A brick floor would be installed in the kitchen, and Courtney couldn't wait to see the difference that would make in the look and feel of the room. Jason, in addition to whatever news he was delivering, had come down to help begin the pulling up of the carpeting.

As they walked across the yard, Courtney inhaled deeply. The smell of honeysuckle, once one of her favorite scents, now assaulted her every time she walked outside. Since the weather had become more agreeable, she was going to begin tearing the vines from the bricks on the house and the wooden slats on the barn. Despite the now-sickening smell and the obnoxious way it had taken over everything, she was going to miss it.

"How much time have you spent exploring in here?" Jason asked as they entered the old barn.

"None. I've been collecting the things we find in the house and storing them over there." She gestured to the assortment of boxes in the corner. "But other than that, I haven't given it a thought." She looked around at the beams and tresses. "How old do you think it is?"

"Well, to be honest, I assumed it was built much more recently than the house, but I wanted to be sure, so I did some poking around." He walked to the ladder that led to the loft above them. "Did you know that Catholicism, with the exception of a total of forty years, was illegal in Maryland until after the Revolutionary War?"

"I did." Courtney thought back to her conversation with her father.

"And that Maryland, and specifically St. Mary's County were founded by Catholics?"

Courtney nodded. "Mmm-hmm."

"And I assume you know that your family was among the founders and have been Catholic ever since."

"I do, but I don't understand what this has to do with the barn."

"You will," he assured her. "One more question. Did you know that, during the period when it was illegal, many Catholics celebrated Mass in their homes, often creating secret chapels?"

"I'm sure I learned that somewhere…" Courtney had no idea where this was going, but Jason seemed to be getting more and more excited as he went on.

"Follow me." He turned toward the ladder and began his climb into the loft. He continued speaking as he ascended. "It turns out that this barn was built sometime in the early seventeen-hundreds. I was able to find some documentation about it in some of my books on the history of Maryland barns, but the books said nothing about the barn's clandestine history."

"I don't understand." Courtney pulled herself up into the loft from the last rung of the ladder.

"Okay." Jason opened his arms to the long, narrow loft before them. "Look around this space. Take a good look. Use your imagination and tell me what you see."

Courtney looked from one side to the other, though all she saw was a dirty old hayloft. She shook her head. "I'm sorry. I just don't get it."

"Let me help you with the vision. First, look at the floor. What do you see?"

Courtney walked farther into the loft and inspected the floor. On each side of the room, there were marks in the floor, evenly spaced, making nice, neat rows, one after the other, the length of the room. "There was something here. Some kind of planks bolted to the floor."

"Not planks, but, yes, there were rows of something bolted to the floor. Now look up. What do you see at the far end of the room?"

"The floor raises. How odd." She walked closer. "And there's a… wait, what is it?" She walked up onto the raised floor and went to the back wall where a hole had been cut into the wall. On one side, there were holes where, perhaps, a door had been attached. Understanding dawned on her, and she turned back to Jason.

He was grinning widely as he saw the recognition on her face. "Well?"

"It's an altar and a hole where the tabernacle was." Her heart beat faster with every word.

Jason nodded. "This was a chapel." He pointed to the floor. "There were pews here." He went to one of the side walls and pointed to something. "Come see," he waved to Courtney.

It was faint, and she almost couldn't make out the images, but she knew exactly what it was. "It's one of the Stations of the Cross." She was amazed by what she saw. "Are there more?" Before Jason could answer she walked a few feet and stopped, examining the wall. "There are more. Oh my gosh. They're all painted right on the walls." She raced around the room. "Station Five, Station Six. Oh my gosh!"

"I know." Jason was obviously as excited as she was. "Up until now, historians assumed that the only church in the area at the time was Sacred Heart, near where Willow Grove was, but they were wrong. That *was* the first church in Bushwood; but, for a while, the most *important* one was right here at River Terrace."

"This is incredible. This barn and its chapel are almost as old as the house, then. How on earth has the barn stood all these years? How is it still in this good of shape? I can't believe it."

"A miracle?" he asked with a smile.

"A miracle," she repeated. "What else could it be?"

CHAPTER NINE

Courtney and Gavin stood beside each other, looking down at the broken cellar door.

"And you're sure it wasn't done by the wind?" Courtney asked.

"What wind? There wasn't any last night. Not even a breeze. Someone did this."

"Why?"

"My best guess is that it wasn't done on purpose. I think they were startled by something and let the door slam shut. The doors are old. It's not surprising that it broke, only that it didn't happen sooner."

"Gavin, why would someone be down there?"

He shrugged. "Why all the other times? What are they trying to accomplish? And why is this time different?"

Courtney furrowed her brow and looked at him. "Different? How? Because they didn't mess anything up or leave the doors locked and the windows open?"

"Precisely. They left no visible signs that they were here. We would never have known if not for the broken door."

"Maybe they were scared away before they could get in this time. Maybe whoever it is wanted to do something but didn't get a chance. You're sure nothing in the cellar was disturbed?"

"There was nothing to disturb. It's empty."

"Yes, but they could have broken the bulbs or brought something in like with the rum bottle."

"Exactly. But there's nothing out of the ordinary."

"Hmm…" Courtney stared at the door and tried to come up with some kind of explanation. "I just can't imagine what they're trying to do or find."

"Me neither." He puffed out his cheeks and released a loud breath. "None of it makes sense."

"Well, I guess we'll just have to replace the door and hope it doesn't happen again."

"Yeah, but we're running out of time. Every time I have to stop and fix something or redo something I've already done, it adds time, and I'm…" He looked away, and Courtney saw the truth in his eyes, felt it in her heart.

"You're leaving."

Gavin squeezed his lips together and nodded without meeting her gaze.

"When?"

"First of the year. Mom's ready. We're not going to sell the farm just yet, but she's ready to go."

A tear formed in the corner of Courtney's eye, but she blinked it away. "Okay," she sighed. "Then let's get this done." She smiled at Gavin, trying to reassure him that it was okay that he was leaving town. Leaving her.

"Court," he began, his eyes meeting hers. "If there's a reason I should stay, I mean, if you need me here…"

Smiling, Courtney shook her head. "No, Gavin, you need to go. You've done so well for yourself out west. I've seen the articles about the work you've done, the engineering wonders you've proposed in the green building industry. You act like what you do is no big deal, but you've won awards—"

"My company, not me," he corrected her.

"No," she emphatically shook her head. "You. You won those awards for your company. You were right when you told me that what you do isn't being done here. For a while, I thought, maybe, you could change that, make those things happen here, but what you're doing out there, it's amazing. Perhaps, someday, this area will be ready for those kinds of innovative ideas, but it's not yet."

Gavin's smile stretched from ear to ear. "You really do get it."

"I do, Gavin. I hope that, someday, I will find my own green building engineering ventures. So to speak." She laughed, and she saw the tension in his shoulders release. "This," she gestured to the house "is certainly *not* what you're meant to be doing. Someday, I'll tell people that the famous Gavin Bernard renovated my house, and they won't believe me because the rest of your work is so, so… you know."

"You're pretty special, Court, you know that?"

"I don't know about that, but I do know that I've really enjoyed the time we've spent together these past few months. I'd hate for another fifteen years to go by before we do it again."

"I can't argue with that. Come on." He took her by the hand. "Let's see what engineering wonders we can do to this house today."

"Speaking of engineering wonders and green buildings, I have something in mind that I think will be right up your alley."

*****

It was trivia night at Sami's. Courtney put together a team, consisting of herself, Gavin, Hannah, and even Jason. She was shocked when he accepted, but she was pleased that he was joining them.

Perhaps with Gavin leaving, I can see where things might be heading with Jason.

She felt a twinge of guilt as she thought about Spencer, whom she had been texting and talking to regularly lately. They used to love trivia night at their favorite downtown bar. That was when they were graduate students, before they were engaged, and before Spencer became married to his job. She doubted he would have come down had she called him. Rolling her eyes, she dismissed the thought. Trivia Night? On a Thursday? Who was she kidding?

The truth was, they'd been having a lot of nice talks lately. And Spencer kept saying he'd love to see the latest progress on the house. He hadn't said he missed her again, and other than the day he admitted he still loved her, he hadn't proposed they get back together, but Courtney wondered what it all meant.

"A pitcher of beer?" Sami asked after hugging Courtney and saying hello to the rest of the group at the table.

"That would be perfect," Courtney said.

"I can't remember the last time I went out with friends." Hannah grinned broadly. "Or the last time I had a beer."

"I'm so glad you could come," Courtney told her.

"I'm so glad your grandmother was willing to stay with Maddy. She seems to be doing much better since her fall."

"You can't keep Lily Russell down," Gavin said.

"That's for sure." Courtney watched other parties arrive for the contest. She was happy for Sami that so many people were there.

"I think I'll get something different." stood from his seat and headed to the bar.

Gavin raised his brow. "Beer not good enough for him?"

"Oh, stop it." Courtney swatted his arm. "He can have whatever he wants."

Gavin shot her a questioning look, but she rolled her eyes and ignored his assumption.

The beer flowed, and the conversation was easy, punctuated throughout the night with trivia questions, ranging in degrees of difficulty. Several times, Jason excused himself to get another drink or order food.

"What's up with Jason?" Courtney said when he suddenly decided he was dying to try the crabmeat nachos. "He could just ask Molly. She's been checking on us all night."

"I think your architect has more on his mind tonight than trivia and food." Hannah gestured to the corner of the counter which had been converted into a full bar for the evening.

Jason was leaning against the bar, a wide grin on his face. Sami leaned in from the other side with just as wide a grin and a sparkle in her eye that Courtney hadn't seen before.

"Well, I'll be…I had no idea." She shook her head as Gavin turned around to check out the scene. "I knew she thought he was good-looking, but—"

"Good-looking?" Hannah shook her head. "Honey, good-looking is the understatement of the year when it comes to him. If I didn't have Maddy, mmm, mmm, mmm, what I wouldn't do to him."

Courtney laughed and then looked seriously at Hannah. “Maddy shouldn’t stop you from pursuing a man. You’re young. You’re entitled to go out on a date.”

“And watch him bolt for the door as soon as he learns I have a toddler? No, thank you. I’m doing just fine without a good-looking man, or any man, by my side. Besides, look who’s talking. You’re so wrapped up in that house that you never go out. You’re there all the time.”

“I’m out tonight,” Courtney said with satisfaction.

“Yep, you’re out tonight. For the first time. And how long have you been in town?”

“Oh, stop. I didn’t know anyone before.”

“You knew Gavin. Right, Gavin? You could have gone out with him.”

Courtney picked up on the mischievous look in Hannah’s eye and shook her head. “Nice try, Hannah, but Gavin and I are just friends.”

“Not ‘just’ friends.” Gavin reached across the table and took her hand. “The best of friends.” He smiled, and Courtney saw the same glimmer in his eyes that she had seen many times when they were growing up. Maybe the romantic vibes she had felt over the past few months had amounted to nothing, but their friendship was one of the best things to happen to her in a long time.

*****

“I can’t believe we’re waiting for Patrick to arrive with the appliances. I didn’t think this day would ever come.”

Courtney and Gavin stood at the kitchen window and watched for her brother to arrive. He didn't ordinarily make deliveries himself, but he hadn't seen the house since their grandmother's fall, and he was excited to see the progress.

"He's here," Courtney cried. She dashed from the kitchen and ran out the front door. "There's a door to the kitchen if you drive around to the other side of the house." She motioned to Patrick as to where to go.

She followed on foot and bit her lip as she anxiously waited for him to walk to the back door of the delivery van. They hugged, and Courtney thanked him for coming all the way down to the house, a good hour from his store.

"Hey Courtney." Chris, one of Patrick's employees called to her. "I hear you've gotten yourself into quite the project."

She grinned. "Yeah, I guess you could put it that way."

"Lead the way," Patrick told her, opening the door and climbing into the back of the van. "Just stay back while we get the stove out."

Courtney agreed as Gavin appeared at her side. "Need help?"

"No, thanks. We've got it. Just get the kitchen door for us."

Within a couple hours, the appliances were in place.

"You've got the gas company coming out tomorrow, right?" Patrick asked.

"I do, and you're sure you've got everything else hooked up right?"

Patrick rolled his eyes. "Seriously? Do you think I don't know what I'm doing?"

"Of course not, but you are the owner of the store, not the delivery crew."

"Have you seen everything I've done on my own house?"

"Okay, okay, I'm sorry! I'm just making sure."

Patrick shook his head and looked at Gavin and Chris who were both grinning at the exchange. "Sisters," he said in exasperation.

After Courtney gave Patrick and Chris a tour of the house, and they said their goodbyes, she stood in the kitchen and looked at the new refrigerator, stove, and dishwasher. She felt like she could cry joyful tears. Once the gas was hooked up and turned on, she would be able to move in. Obviously, she would need furniture, and she wasn't planning on moving in right away, but she could do so whenever she chose. She wanted to take her time choosing pieces for the house, both the old and new parts, and she wanted to spend more time with Lily, so she was in no hurry.

*****

Courtney gazed at the flooring in the parlor. The carpeting was gone, and the floors, though old, scuffed, and in desperate need of refinishing, had been verified as original to the house. She could hardly believe that she was standing on the same boards where her ancestors, pirates, and even the infamous Anne Bonny once walked. She was overwhelmed with a feeling of connection to the past.

As she looked at the floor, she felt a buzz in her back pocket and reached for her phone.

Are you busy this weekend? I'd love to come see the house. Maybe take you out to dinner?

Courtney stared at her phone. Another weekend of not working at the firm? What had gotten into him?

"What's going on?" Gavin asked from behind her. Courtney jumped and clutched her phone to her chest, catching her breath.

"You scared me."

"Sorry. You looked pretty serious. Everything okay?"

She bit her lip and furrowed her brow.

"I guess so. I mean, yes, everything's okay. It's just…"

"What?" He put his hands on her shoulders. "Tell me." He was so caring, so gentle. They shared a real connection and always had, but Courtney now realized that was all they shared. That, many years of memories, and a great love for Lily.

"This." She held up her phone.

Gavin read the message and took a deep breath.

"Court, we've known each other for a long time, and I've loved you my entire life."

At her widened eyes, he smiled and shook his head. "As a sister, then as a potential girlfriend, and now…" He looked away, and she watched as his thoughts played across his features. "For the past few months, I've wondered. I've even hoped. Even thought of asking you to go to Portland with me, but the truth is…" he sighed.

"We're not right for each other, Court. You're the sister I never had, and I will always love you, but you don't love me. Not in the way that I'd want you to. And that's okay." He lifted his hand to her face and gently laid his finger on her scar. "You've been through something that few people will ever experience, and I don't want to diminish that. You're living your life, following your dreams, figuring out where you belong, and, though it's new for you, and on a whole different level than most people, it's something I've already done. I know what I want, where I want to have it, and how I want to achieve it. Growing up, you always had it together, and I was always trying to catch up. Now, you're the one trying to find your way, and I can't do that for you."

He paused and took a deep breath. "But what I can do is tell you that I think you already know what you want. Or, at least, who you want. Pondering a future with me, which I know you did." He raised his brow and grinned at her.

Courtney nodded and smiled. "I did."

"Well thinking about that, and flirting with Jason, they might have helped you move farther along on this road you're traveling, but they were just detours. Your heart is already taken and has been for a long time. I didn't see it at first, or I didn't want to. You were determined to move on, and I wanted you to. You weren't the only one pondering our future together." She laughed, and he continued. "But lately, I see the look in your eye when you mention his name. I saw your excitement as you prepared for his visit. You might not be ready to try again, and he might not have truly changed. And that's something you need to give a lot of thought to, but if you decide to give it another try, I'm betting he'll come running."

Courtney inhaled and looked down at her phone as she released her breath. "I just don't know what to believe. When we first started dating, and when we got engaged, everything was so perfect. Yes, our graduate classes came first, but we always made time for each other. After he passed the bar, though, things changed. He changed. He was so thirsty for something I couldn't give. He became consumed with work, with becoming a partner, with living the life of a high-powered attorney. At the same time, I was miserable in my job. I hated finance, hated crunching numbers all day and staring at a computer screen, looking outside on a beautiful day and knowing I couldn't take just five minutes to enjoy it. The accident gave me an excuse to get out. Out of everything. It allowed me to tell everyone I wasn't taking anything for granted and not being taken for granted. I had no idea what I was going to do with my life, but the second Sami told me that this house was for sale, I knew it was a sign. I was sure that, once I got here, everything would fall into place. And here you were, just like always, making me laugh and think about the future. I was sure you were part of the sign."

"And Jason?"

She shrugged and let out an amused chuckle. "Oh, I don't know. A devastatingly handsome man to sweep me off my feet? In spite of the scar."

"Who cares about the scar. You need to stop worrying about that. Oh, and, Court? Jason's in love with the house, not you."

She laughed. "Yeah, I know. I think he might have thought, for a time, that it was the other way around, but he seems to have found another interested party these days."

"They're really seeing other?"

"They are. Sami's actually closing early tonight and making a romantic dinner for two."

"Good for them."

"I agree. Anyway, I think I've realized that I was using the house as a means of escape. I was running away, but I didn't know from what."

"And now?"

She caught her bottom lip in her teeth. "Now, I'm still not sure. I really do love it here, and I know that this could be home, but what good is a home with nobody to share it with? And where does Spencer fit in? He can't live here even if he does love me. He's worked so hard to get to where he is."

"Have you asked him?"

"Asked him? To take me back? I'm not sure that's even what I want."

"No, have you asked him what he wants? Is he happy being a partner? He says he misses you and that he wants to give it another try. Does that mean he's truly willing to change?"

Courtney shook her head. "I don't know, Gavin. I really don't. And I can't very well ask him if I don't know what I want the answer to be myself."

"Then just give it time. See what happens. There's no need to rush anything. My mother has always told me that everything happens in God's time. No matter how much we try to speed things up, sometimes, God just wants us to slow down."

"That reminds me of one of my mother's favorite sayings, 'we plan, God laughs.' She says that, no matter what we think we should be doing, we will eventually end up doing what God wants us to do."

"I think there's a lot of wisdom in that," Gavin said.

Sighing, Courtney looked around at the room one more time.

"I guess I'll invite Spencer down for the weekend and see what he thinks about the house. I'm not sure it's going to go anywhere, but as long as he's making the effort, I can at least try to meet him halfway."

Gavin put his arm around her shoulders. "And see where God's plan takes you."

"Yep, we'll see where He takes both of us." She leaned her head against him and wondered how she was going to manage when he was gone.

*****

"This is the most incredible find ever." Spencer surveyed the space as he and Courtney stood in the loft of the barn.

Laughing at his childlike enthusiasm, Courtney shook her head. She hadn't seen him like this in years. "Oh, I think many archaeologists would disagree with that."

"Okay, maybe it's not King Tut's Tomb, but, seriously, it's a pretty spectacular discovery."

"It is," she agreed. "And Gavin has some great ideas as to how to renovate the whole barn using green building techniques. Now, if only I knew what to do with it."

"Hmm, that's a good question. You certainly don't want to destroy or demolish it, nut there aren't many modern uses for a church in a loft. Though I seem to remember hearing something about a famous church in an attic. It's in Europe somewhere. Belgium, maybe? France? I'm not sure. But people go from all over the world to visit it. I think it was a secret chapel. Maybe during the war?" He bit the inside of his cheek like she'd seen him do so many times when he was stumped about something or when studying for a particularly difficult exam.

"Huh, I'll have to look into that." She looked around the space. "Even still, what on earth would I do with it?"

Spencer suddenly snapped his fingers. "Amsterdam! I'm pretty sure that's where the chapel in the attic is."

"I will definitely look it up, but what about *this* chapel in the attic? I don't know what on earth it means. Why is it here? What am I supposed to do now that I've discovered it? Tear it out? Redo it? For what?"

"I don't know, but you've always been a believer that there's a reason for everything. There must be a reason why it's here on the property you bought."

Courtney blinked as she gazed at Spencer. He was right. She used to say that all the time. She had completely forgotten about that. But now…the accident, the house being for sale, working with Gavin and Jason, the things they'd found, the chapel…were they all part of a bigger meaning? Had she been looking at everything as individual pieces instead of parts of a whole? Was there a reason that all of these things had happened in her life within the space of two years?

"CJ? Are you okay?"

She turned toward Spencer and saw something in his eyes that she hadn't seen in a long time—concern, care, and love.

"Yeah, just thinking." She forced a smile. What was she supposed to be doing? And what role, if any, did he play in it? Maybe it was time to take her mother, her grandmother, and Gavin's advice and pray about it. It seemed so silly, but maybe, just maybe, it would help somehow.

"Come on, I'm hungry. Let's go back to Gram's and get ready for dinner."

"Sounds good." Spencer took her hand as they walked toward the ladder.

Courtney fought the urge to pull away, and, within seconds, the old feelings returned. The ones she used to get when Spencer held her hand. Back when things were new and exciting.

Letting go of her, Spencer made his way down the ladder and then waited at the bottom to help her down. As her feet hit the floor, his hands went to her waist to steady her. She turned slowly until they were face to face.

"Spencer, I—" she began quietly. He touched his finger to her lips.

"Don't say anything," he whispered. "Let's just enjoy the evening together."

She nodded and swallowed as she tried to decipher her own feelings.

They walked outside and toward his car. Spencer stopped next to the passenger side door and looked around at the large property, the colonial house, the mysterious barn.

"You know, CJ, I think I might have an idea."

She turned to look at him and raised her brow.

"Remember after we graduated, when your brother, your best friend, and your cousin were all getting married around the same time? You and your mom became the family wedding planners. You had so much fun putting the weddings together. In fact, I'm not sure I've ever seen you so happy. Anyway, for that whole year, you kept talking about how much you loved helping people with their weddings and you wished you could do that all the time. I never really understood why you didn't give it any serious thought."

"Well, I guess because I had just earned an MBA and landed a great job in the city. It felt silly to want to give that up to do something so, so…"

"Frivolous?"

Courtney frowned. Hearing him describe it like that made her heart sink. Maybe he hadn't changed. They'd had a five-year engagement because he was never interested in discussing the actual wedding. He just didn't understand how important that day was in a girl's life. "Yeah, I guess so." She knew her tone gave away her feelings. She reached for the door handle, but he grabbed her hand.

"CJ, is it frivolous if it brings you joy and contentment? Or if it brings someone else joy? Weren't you always telling me that what made you happy was seeing others happy?"

Courtney blinked and slowly shook her head. "Who are you?" she breathed.

Spencer smiled. "I'm the man who fell in love with a girl about ten years ago and let her get away because I didn't understand what she meant by that—the truth about happiness comes from seeing and making others happy. I lost sight of what it means to want happiness for others. To share in their joy. To celebrate their triumphs. You did that for me. All the way. Law school, the bar exam, the job, the partnership. You were always my biggest cheerleader, and I took you for granted."

"Spencer, you—"

"Don't. Don't try to make excuses for me. It's true. For now, I want you to think about yourself. What would make you happy? If you could live the rest of your life doing just one thing, what would it be?"

She turned from his gaze and took in the sight before her. There was a beautiful house that had the potential of attracting house enthusiasts and history buffs for miles. There was a giant barn, with a chapel in the loft, and enough room on the first floor to be renovated into anything she wanted it to be. The yard, now bare without the honeysuckle vines, provided a magnificent landscape just waiting to be discovered. She broke out into a wide smile as she pictured what all of it could be.

"Spencer, I always knew you were smart, but you just might be a genius."

CHAPTER TEN

Courtney stood in the northern bedroom, contemplating how she would fill the room. The painting was finished, and the floors were being restored, first the upstairs and then the downstairs. She had managed to find an antique bed, made of cherry wood, with beautiful hand-carved posts on each corner. It would be splendid against the eastern-facing wall. She frowned as she thought about having to bring firewood up the stairs each time she had an overnight guest, but that wouldn't be that often. She could handle it.

Envisioning the bed, adorned with one of the hand-crocheted coverlets that belonged to her great-great grandmother, Courtney smiled. The china doll would be the perfect accent piece. She bit her lip to contain her enthusiasm. The minute she was given the okay to move the bed into the house, she was going to set it up and place the doll on the pillow. There wouldn't be any other furnishings, but those things would come in time.

Sighing with contentment, Courtney went across the landing to the room with the southern exposure. The afternoon sun shone through the windows, giving the room a warm, cozy glow in spite of the chilly November air. So far, she had no furniture to put in this room, but she knew that she and Sami would find the perfect pieces on their Saturday morning yard sale excursions. It would take time, but she was in no rush. The newer part of the house would be inhabitable soon, and she hoped to move in before Christmas. She had several months or more to get everything in shape before the barn would be ready and the property could be opened to the public.

Descending the stairs, Courtney listened as Gavin chatted with the men who were helping him with the floors. Replacing bad boards, and sanding, staining, and varnishing the wood was a pain-staking process, and Courtney was glad that Gavin had brought in two more men to help with the work. She knew he wanted to have his mother's house packed up by the end of the year, and she didn't want their work on River Terrace to hold up his plans.

The sun's rays pushed through the grey clouds as Courtney walked outside and headed toward the barn. They wouldn't begin working on it until after the new year. Gavin spent hours drawing up the plans and devising features that would allow the barn to maintain its historical assets while using green technology to create the venue of the future. Though he would be overseeing the project from Portland, he promised to make monthly trips back east to keep abreast of the work. This could prove to be the engineering and architectural design that could catapult him to the top of his field.

The box of treasures, as they had come to call it, was still in the corner of the barn. Everything in it would be moved into the house before work began on the building. Gently moving aside pottery, apothecary and liquor bottles, and the myriad of buttons that they had saved, Courtney reached for the doll. She took the doll outside into the sunlight. The air was cold, but the sun felt good as it beat down on her black, quilted jacket. She held up the doll and assessed its condition. The doll's head was perfect, though the stained and torn dress would need to be replaced. Courtney lifted the doll's skirt to see what kind of shape the body was in. She frowned when she saw the open seam, and it occurred to her that the doll felt too limp. She must have lost her stuffing through the opening. Moving a bit of the soft material aside, Courtney gasped at the shiny, green glint that caught the light.

Reaching inside the doll's body, she delicately pinched the stone between her fingers and retrieved the large stone from the cavity of the body. She placed the doll under her arm and held the green gem up to the light, so she could get a better look at the cut. It was stunning and quite large for its kind. She was no expert on jewels, though she had worked in a jewelry store for a year in college, and she knew how to tell if a stone was real.

"Whatcha got?" Gavin asked, walking toward the barn.

"You're not going to believe this, but I think I found a genuine emerald." She continued to hold up the gem, and he joined her in assessing it as it glistened in the golden rays.

"Are you sure it's real?" He sounded dubious.

"I think so." She looked from the stone to Gavin. "I worked at a second-hand jewelry store my sophomore year, and I learned how to tell the real stuff from the fakes. This has all the markings of a real, priceless stone. And I mean priceless. I've never seen an emerald this big. I can't begin to imagine how many carats it is."

"Where did you find it?"

She reached under her arm and pulled out the china doll. "Inside the body. That can't have been an accident. The seam was carefully undone, not ripped or torn, and the stuffing was removed to make room for it, and others, I bet. Almost all of the stuffing is missing from the body."

Gavin took the doll and inspected it. "I don't see any others."

"I didn't either, but I can't imagine that this was the only one. Where do you think it came from?"

Gavin shrugged. "Who knows. It could have been in there for a couple hundred years. As far as we know, that part of the cellar remained a secret for almost the entire existence of the house."

"Why hide it in the doll?"

"No clue, but didn't your cousin tell you that there were pirates in the house on more than one occasion? Maybe they were hiding it from them."

"She said there might have been, and my research confirmed it. John McMillan said that pirates killed his brother, Robert. And they all suspected that Anne was a pirate, or, at the very least, sailed with them."

"She's the woman who lived here, right? The one Clarissa thinks was some famous female pirate?"

Courtney nodded. "Yes, though there's no proof of it and no historical records put her here during that period, but I believe she was, in fact, Anne Bonny, female pirate. By most accounts, she died a few years before, in the Caribbean, but I think she was here. I can feel it." Her eyes widened as she looked at Gavin. "Do you think this might have been part of a pirate's treasure?"

"I have no idea, but if Clarissa is right, and pirates made their way up here from the Caribbean, it's possible."

"Very possible. Cartagena, Colombia, is the emerald capital of the world."

"Isn't that in South America?" One side of Gavin's mouth rose as he raised a brow and gave Courtney a questioning look.

"Yes, but it's in the Caribbean. Didn't you ever see *Romancing the Stone* with Michael Douglass and Kathleen Turner?"

Gavin shook his head. "Never heard of it."

"It's an old movie from the 80s. One of my mom's favorites. Anyway, it takes place in Cartagena. It's in South America, but it was a mecca for Caribbean pirates. It has a historic downtown that's surrounded by a wall and has lots of pirate charm. I went there once with my dad when I was a senior in high school. He had to go there on business, and I was the lucky child who got to tag along since I was the last one at home." She smiled at the memory of drinking her first margarita as they listened to a Latino guitar player outside of the Church of St. Peter Claver. "Anyway, the country is famous for their emeralds."

"Among other things. I can't believe your mom let you go there alone with your dad."

"I wasn't alone. My dad's sister went, too, as my chaperone. But I did all the speaking since she didn't know a word of Spanish. And she let me try all the cocktails I wanted to. It was great fun." She smiled mischievously, remembering the fun she and her Aunt Chrissy had.

"Except for the cartel hanging around."

Courtney shook her head in dismissal. "Not at all. The United States helped Colombia get rid of the cartel back in the 90s. It's one of the safest places in the world now."

"I find that hard to believe."

"Suit yourself. I'd go back in a heartbeat." Shrugging off his doubts, she held the emerald back up to the light. "Wherever this came from, it has to be worth a fortune. I can't believe nobody came looking for it over the years."

"Maybe nobody knows it exists," Gavin offered.

"They must not. If I had known about it, I would have moved heaven and earth to find it."

They stood in the warmth of the sun, oblivious to the cold and unaware of the other pair of eyes that caught the glint of the emerald Courtney held above her head.

*****

The kitchen floors gleamed in the morning light as Courtney, Gavin, and Jason met to go over the progress.

"I brought you something." Jason handed Gavin and Courtney each a Krispy Kreme doughnut. Famous throughout the state for their secret recipe and fresh-baked goodness, the best way to eat them was hot out of the bakery oven.

Courtney's eyes lit up. "I haven't had one of these in years." She took the confection and smacked her lips. "And it's still warm. Oh my gosh."

"I usually resist the urge to stop by there in the mornings, but I just had this feeling that today is going to be a good day, so I figured, why not?"

"I'd forgotten how good these things are." Gavin nearly ate his entire doughnut in one bite.

"There are more where those came from." Jason held up the box.

"Don't tempt me," Courtney said as she savored her treat. She was also savoring the truce that had been established between the two men. With Jason dating Sami, and Gavin heading west, both men had been getting along like long-lost friends, eager to share details about their lives and future plans. Their comradery made everything go more smoothly, and Courtney was more than grateful for the change.

"So, how's the floor coming?" Jason asked, looking down and surveying the room.

"Great." Gavin reached for another doughnut. "The kitchen is complete. We had no issues at all. We may have to replace some boards in the older section, but that shouldn't slow us down."

Jason nodded. "Any surprises? Find anything… unusual?"

Courtney looked at Gavin and shrugged. "Not that I know of. Gav?"

"Not really. Anything in particular you were worried about?"

Jason lifted his shoulders. "No, but it's an old house. There's no telling what you might find as you go along." He shifted his gaze toward the older section of the house. "Have you checked all the loose or broken boards in there?" He jerked his head toward the other rooms.

"Not yet. We're doing that today," Gavin told him, and Courtney wondered what was going on. Jason seemed a bit off, like he knew something he didn't want to share.

"Mind if I stick around for a bit?"

"Sure," Gavin said. "Are you overseeing or helping? You're kind of overdressed for crawling around on the floor." He motioned to Jason's khaki pants, dress coat, and tie.

"I can change if you need help," he offered.

Courtney watched the exchange, and a strange feeling crept up her back. Jason had helped with many things, but he'd never gotten on the floor to do the dirty work. What was he up to?

"Hey, Jason, before we all start looking at the plans and assessing our progress, can you come upstairs for a minute? I have a question I need to ask you about one of the rooms. I mean, since you seem to have some time to help out some more."

She thought she saw a look of annoyance flash across Jason's face before he smiled at her and nodded. "Sure, I can do that." He looked back at Gavin, and Courtney wondered again what was going on between them.

"Do you want me to come, too?" Gavin asked, returning Jason's critical look.

"No, that's fine," Courtney assured him. "We'll be right back, and then we can all go over whatever we need to talk about. Come on, Jason, let's start upstairs. I have some questions about the north bedroom."

She led the way up the stairs, trying to figure out if his odd demeanor was just her imagination. When they reached the room, she thought about all of the strange things that had happened in the house and decided it was time to lay all her cards on the table.

"Look, Jason, I need to know something." She put her hands on her hips and looked him in the eyes.

"Go ahead," he said with some hesitancy.

"Why did you take this job?"

For a moment, he looked taken aback. He shook his head a little and blinked before saying anything. "What do you mean?"

"I mean, what drew you to this house, this project?" She folded her arms across her chest and cocked her head to the side as she waited for his answer. She wasn't sure what she wanted or expected him to say, but so many things began to come back to her as she stood looking at him—his obsession with the floors, his aggression toward Gavin's plans for each stage of the renovation, and all the surprise visits he made each time they were taking apart different areas of the house.

"What person in my shoes wouldn't want to be a part of this?"

"Meaning what?" she asked, narrowing her eyes in suspicion.

"Courtney, is something wrong? Have I done something to make you want to get rid of me? Are you upset that I'm seeing Sami?"

She took a deep breath and released it before returning her hands to her hips. "I want to know the truth, Jason. What aren't you telling me? Maybe you did take this job for all the right reasons, but there's something else going on here. You act like, like, I don't know, like you think you may stumble onto a pirate's chest hidden under the floorboards or in the walls."

As soon as the words left her mouth, she saw the shift in his stance and the way he quickly glanced away while licking his lips. She had hit on something. "You don't honestly believe in all those pirate's treasure legends, do you?" An image of the emerald, safely tucked inside the safe in Lily's house, flashed through her mind.

Jason looked away before puffing air through his cheeks and closing his eyes. When he faced her again, his face was awash with guilt.

"You did. You thought you might find some kind of valuable treasure inside the house. Is that why you took the job? Why you've been showing up when you didn't need to? What were you planning on doing? Taking the loot and running off with it behind our backs?"

Jason put up his hands in front of him. "No, no, nothing like that." He sighed. "Please, let me explain."

She refolded her arms across her chest and thrust out her chin. "Go ahead. I'm waiting."

He ran his hand through his hair, causing the perfectly-combed bangs to become a bit disheveled. She hated that it made him look even sexier. She was angry with him, and the look only distracted her.

"Look, that first day I left here after meeting you, I thought for sure I had met the love of my life—not you, the house." His cheeks flamed, and he pressed his lips together. "Maybe a little bit you. I mean, I was so caught up in everything. You were amazing—beautiful, kind, smart, a bit shy and awkward about…" He pointed toward her scar, and she resisted the urge to reach for it. "Anyway, I'd never met anyone like you. You were willing to take on this whole thing," he gestured around him, "without having a clue how you were going to do it. I was impressed and intrigued. But the house, man, that was the real kicker. I'd never even dreamed of stumbling onto something so special. I knew immediately that we had a real architectural and historical treasure in our hands. And I'm not talking about pirate's loot."

She remembered how he had been on the first day—the excitement in his eyes and voice, how he had reacted to the bricks, the paneling, the roof, the hidden fireplaces. He truly was in awe of the house and all the history it held inside its walls. She began to loosen her stance just a bit.

"I started thinking more and more about the history of the house and the area. Like you, I was dying to know more. As you know, I began researching, digging deeper and deeper into the historical accounts but also the legends and stories. I started thinking that, perhaps, there might be some truth to them. I mean, think about it, we already have an amazing and unprecedented historical find in the house itself. What if there was more, a hidden treasure, a chest of Spanish doubloons, a bag of stolen gems? We'd not only have made architectural history, but geological, cultural, and who knows what else?"

"And what would you have done if you had found something? Would you have even told us about it?" she asked, not trying to hide the hurt and accusation in her voice. She had trusted him, and he had been holding out on them.

"Of course I would have, but I didn't want you to think I was a fool. I mean, what were the chances that pirates really left something here or that, if they had, nobody had found it over the years? I knew I was letting my imagination get away with me, but I couldn't help it. The more I thought about it, the more excited I got, and the more I hoped there really would be something to find."

Jason stopped speaking and looked at Courtney, obviously waiting for her to say something. She heard voices downstairs and knew that Mitch and Stew had already arrived and would be anxious to get back to work on the floors in the original dining room. Gavin was probably irritated that she and Jason had been gone for so long. He'd have to stop working on the floors in order to meet with them.

She thought about all of the loose boards, the box of things they had found in the walls, and the emerald that was inside the china doll. She debated whether or not to say anything to Jason about it.

"What's going on with Sami?"

His raised brow and slightly opened mouth told her that the change in topic took him by surprise.

He answered slowly. "Well, we like each other."

"And what does that mean?" she asked. "Is it going anywhere?" She knew it was none of her business, but if things were getting serious, it would lend itself to his credibility. He couldn't very well continue seeing her cousin if he was lying to her.

"I'm not sure. I'd like to keep seeing her. I think she could be the one." He smiled awkwardly, his face reddening, and Courtney believed him.

"You're honestly not dating her just so that you can stick around once your work is done and continue searching for some real or imagined treasure?"

He grimaced, sincerely wounded by her question. "I wouldn't do that to her." He met Courtney's gaze. "Nor to you." It was his turn to cross his arms in front of him. "Look. Courtney, I screwed up. I should have leveled with you, but I haven't done anything illegal or dishonest. I'm not the one who keeps breaking in here if that's what you're thinking." The thought had crossed her mind. "I've worked hard to help you with this house and to discover its history. I've always been up front with you about everything I've discovered, and I would have continued to be so, even if it was the treasure of Blackbeard himself that I uncovered. If you can't see that I'm a good guy, a hard worker, honest—"

She held up her hands to stop him. "Okay, okay. I'm sorry. You're right. You've been a real blessing since day one, and I appreciate everything you've done." She shook her head. "I just don't like that you were keeping something from me. And it could have been a big something."

"Or a nothing at all." he held his empty hands out in front of him. "I wasn't going to say anything unless we actually found something. Why bring it up if there was nothing there to begin with? All of my credibility would have been called into question."

He had a point there. It was the same reason she hadn't told anyone that she was seriously wondering if the house actually was haunted. Still…she was sure that the emerald was worth a lot. Should she tell him, or should she wait until she had it appraised and insured? No, she wasn't ready to tell anyone else about the gem. Only Gavin and Lily knew what was hidden in the safe, and Courtney felt it best to keep it that way for now.

"Look, Jason, I don't know if pirates really hid anything here or not. I don't know if Anne Bonny, or whoever she was, had any treasure, or if any of the families who lived in this house ever socked their gold and valuables away in the walls or floors. What I do know is that this house is a treasure, and it wouldn't be worth nearly as much as it's going to be if it weren't for your help and guidance. The barn alone is one of the most incredible finds of our time, not to mention the boards we found in the attic, the uncovered fireplaces, and the cruck roof. I owe all of that to you."

"Does that mean we can let this go? Be friends and colleagues and continue making this house and barn and property into a real historical showplace?"

She smiled at the eagerness in his voice and the pleading in his eyes. Despite his transgression, she really did like Jason, and she did trust him.

"Yes." She held her hand out to him. "Friends, colleagues, and, perhaps, family someday?" She raised her eyebrow and smiled.

"You never know." He took her hand. "I'm sure going to try my best to head in that direction."

*****

Courtney tapped her fingers on the table. The aromas of marinara sauce and garlic bread filled the kitchen. Lily's house felt warm and cozy, but Courtney wasn't able to relax. She couldn't stop thinking about Jason's admission that he'd been treasure hunting, or, at least treasure hoping. And she was keenly aware that every day that passed was a day closer to Gavin leaving. Then there was Spencer and her growing feelings for him. Despite her insistence that she was over him, she found herself looking forward to his texts, calls, and visits.

"What's wrong, sweetie?" Lily asked as she set the plate of spaghetti on the table in front of Courtney.

"I don't know," she replied. "Nothing specific. I guess everything is just hitting me at once."

"What's hitting you? Your life looks pretty good from where I sit." Lily took her seat, and they paused to say grace.

"It's just that, well, once the floors are done, everything changes."

The lines and creases on Lily's forehead deepened as she looked at her granddaughter. "What does that mean?"

Courtney blew on her forkful of noodles and sauce. After she chewed and swallowed, she looked at Lily. "I guess I'm a little overwhelmed. I can't wait to get the okay from the health department to move into the house, but I don't want to leave you." She reached across and laid her hand over Lily's.

Lily picked up her hand, tossing Courtney's aside, and waved it in the air. "Oh phooey. I'll be just fine."

Courtney laughed. "I know you'll be fine, but what about me?"

"You? Why, you're the strongest woman I know. Why wouldn't you be fine?"

Courtney's heart melted. All her life, she had loved, admired, and tried to emulate Lily. All she wanted was to be just like her grandmother with her smarts and strength.

"Gram, that's what I've always said about you." Courtney felt herself tearing up. "I'm going to miss you so much."

"Miss me? You're only moving a mile down the road. I'll probably see you more once you move than I do now. Most days, you're gone at the crack of dawn and home after dark."

Courtney knew her grandmother was right and that she was trying to make her feel better, but Courtney also saw the tears glimmering in Lily's eyes.

"You do have a point there. But there's Gavin, and Jason and Sami, and the barn and what it all means for my future—"

"Sweetheart, slow down. Let's take everything one point at a time. What about Gavin?"

"Gavin's leaving right after Christmas. How can I live in Bushwood without Gavin here?"

"Courtney, you lived for years in Baltimore while he was in Oregon. Besides, it's not like you're dating. Or is there something I've missed?"

Lily raised her brow and leveled an inquiring gaze on her granddaughter. Courtney sighed.

"No, we're not dating, and we're not going to, but in my mind, Gavin and Bushwood are synonymous. I don't know how to live here without him."

"Did you know that he was going to be home when you bought the house?"

"No, but still…"

"Nonsense. You and Gavin will stay in touch, and he'll be back to oversee the barn renovation."

"I know, I know." Courtney took a bite of her garlic bread. "I'm just used to him being here."

"Well, you'll just have to get past that. People grow up and move on. You can't expect them to stay where you want them to just so that you can maintain what you perceive as the status quo." She took a sip of her tea while holding up her index finger to signal that she wasn't finished. "Now, what about Jason and Sami? How have they upset your personal apple cart?"

Courtney was beginning to feel a bit selfish but was honest with her grandmother. "Nothing, I guess. They seem happy, but I'm afraid it will throw off the whole dynamic between us."

Lily's fork stopped midway to her mouth. "You're jealous."

Courtney blinked. "I'm what? I'm not jealous. Why would you say that?" Her stomach lurched as she went from feeling selfish to feeling like she had been punched in the gut. Was she really jealous of her cousin?

"Why else would you have a problem with Sami and Jason? You've liked him from the start. He's a good guy. And handsome as the devil. Sami deserves that."

"She does. She really does." Courtney smiled, forcing herself, for the first time, to view the situation from outside of her own motives and fears.

"What about Spencer?"

Courtney swirled the pasta around her fork, refusing to meet Lily's gaze. Her stomach churned again as she thought about Spencer. She shrugged sheepishly. "I don't know."

"He's coming this weekend." It was not a question. Courtney had told Lily earlier that Spencer wanted to see the house again. "Seems like he's showing a lot of interest in a house he'll never live in."

Courtney raked her fork through her food, having lost the desire to eat after the revelations of their conversation. "Well, I guess he's not just interested in the house." Her eyes were downcast, refusing to meet Lily's gaze.

"Well, you don't say?" Lily's words dripped with sarcasm.

"Gram," Courtney looked at her grandmother. "It's not. We're not—"

"Whatever 'it' is or you two are doesn't matter right now. What matters is what may be. Let him come. Let things happen. There's no rush, and there's no judgment. Pray about it, and let God do the rest."

Courtney sat back in her chair and rested her fork on the plate. "Really? That's your advice? To 'pray about it'? That's supposed to make all of these feelings and worries go away? Because you may be surprised to learn that that's exactly what I've been doing, and it's not working. I've been praying day and night that God will shed some light on what I'm supposed to be doing and feeling but, so far, nothing. I've gotten no answers, no signs at all. Am I supposed to just sit around and wait forever, praying that, someday, I'll understand something I should have figured out long ago?"

"Of course not, but does feeling this way and worrying about everything make anything better?"

Courtney pressed her lips together. "I guess not."

"Then why do it? Let God worry about it. Whatever his plan is, it's going to happen whether you worry about it or not. See where he takes you. Just let him know that you're willing to let him be in charge. You'll be amazed at how much easier life is when you don't have to be the one in the driver's seat."

Courtney smiled. "Like that Carrie Underwood song?"

"Just like it. Let him take the wheel. Just go along for the ride and enjoy the scenery. Even if you have to take a detour now and then, it will be worth the trip."

Laughing, Courtney reached for her fork. "Gram, your faith is inspiring. I'll do my best to give it a try. I just hope I'm not on a dead-end street."

"So what if you are? We live on a dead-end street, and if you ask me, there's no prettier view than the one at the end of this road where the river meets the horizon, and the setting sun lights the water on fire. Sometimes, the dead-end street is the best one on the block."

Courtney smiled. She had never thought of things from that perspective before, but letting someone else take the wheel sounded heavenly, especially for someone who had almost died when she was in the driver's seat. Perhaps the miraculous outcome of her accident had been the result of someone else stepping in and taking the wheel just when she needed it most.

CHAPTER ELEVEN

"What do you think?" Courtney wasn't sure why she was nervous. His opinion shouldn't matter that much, but it did.

Spencer took in the master bedroom with the double walk-in closets and large windows facing the water. Though Jason was against making too many structural changes, she had insisted that Gavin double the size of the windows in her room.

"The view is amazing. He peered into the sky and seemed to be making some kind of mental calculation. "They face the west?"

"That's right. The sunset is spectacular." She thought about her conversation with Lily from the other night and smiled. This was one pretty great dead-end road.

"I bet. Even better is that you don't have to worry about covering the windows with anything to block the sunrise. You can have the view and still sleep late on the weekends."

Courtney couldn't stop the scoff that left her lips. "Since when do you know anything about sleeping in?"

Spencer turned to face her, a strange look in his eyes. Was it hurt? "I would love to sleep in on the weekends. In fact, I'm thinking of making it a new habit."

She felt the tiniest flutter in her stomach. "Really?" she said quietly. "What about the partnership?"

"I'm not sure it's all it's cracked up to be." He shrugged. "To be perfectly honest, I'd rather have what we had, back before I passed the bar, before life spun out of control." He took a small, hesitant step toward her. "In fact, I'm pretty envious of Jackie's life."

"How is Jackie doing? I miss her."

"She's the same pain-in-the-neck sister she always was, but with the baby… I don't know." He shrugged and took another small step. The butterfly flapped its wings a little harder. "She's pretty darn happy these days. Her life, it just looks really awesome."

Courtney felt a bit let down. "So, you're really just interested in moving on to the next stage, huh? You've got the dream job, and the dream family is what is expected next." That's all it was. Just a case of the grass is always greener.

Taking one more step, Spencer reached for Courtney's hand. "No, I'm interested in moving onto the next stage *with you.* You have no idea what it's been like this past year." He shook his head, and Courtney thought she saw moisture in his eyes. He met her gaze and squeezed her hand. "CJ, I don't sleep, I can't eat, I can't focus at work. I go through the day like a robot, doing what I have to do to fill my quota of billable hours, but all I can think about is how much I want to be home with you. I hate going back to my place because you're not there, and there's no chance of you stopping by. When things got rough between us, before the accident, there were nights I was relieved that I got home too late for you to come over. I was exhausted, burning the candle at both ends just to make partner. I couldn't think about a future or a family or even you. All that mattered was moving up the ladder. Then, once I got there, you almost died, and I spent every night by your bed, wondering why I hadn't made as much effort to see you when you were still alive. I was so far gone with grief over everything that, in my mind, you were already dead."

Courtney swallowed the lump in her throat. His words hurt so much. She wanted to pull her hand away and run from him, but he held her in an iron grip as he continued.

"I was so angry with myself for not working as hard on us as I worked on my job. I knew it was over even before you woke up. I knew that God was telling me that I'd blown it."

She had never heard him talk about God. It wasn't anything they'd ever discussed. She always assumed he didn't even believe. In anything, really.

"When you woke up and told me it was over, I just accepted it. I threw myself into work, positive that it would make everything better, but it didn't." He released her hand and went back to the window. She massaged the feeling back into her fingers. "Remember that church on the corner that you sometimes went to on Sundays?"

She nodded, unable to speak, not sure of where he was going. The thought that he couldn't see her acknowledge him didn't even cross her mind as she watched him from behind. He absent-mindedly ran his hand through his air, and she smiled as she recalled all the times he did that when he was lost in thought.

"One day, several months ago, I found myself standing in front of the altar." He gazed out the window. Her heart began to pick up its pace. This was a man she did not know. When he turned around, she didn't even recognize him anymore. His expression was one she had never seen before.

"I've been going back ever since." He couldn't have surprised her more if he had told her he was moving to Ethiopia. "I've been taking some classes, talking to a priest."

"Spencer, I—"

"Please, let me finish."

She nodded and found herself looking for some place to sit. Her legs felt like Jello. She hadn't purchased any furniture for the room, and the wall seemed too far away. She was afraid to move, afraid that her legs would collapse if she shifted her weight in any way. Who was this man?

"For a while, I thought that you were the problem. You didn't understand how hard I'd worked for this. You were pressuring me." He held up his hand. "You weren't. I know. But I needed someone to blame. I was so unhappy, and you were the easiest target. It took a while, but eventually I saw that I was my own worst enemy. I drove myself to work harder, longer, better, and I drove you away."

"Spence, it wasn't just you. I made mistakes, too." It was the first time she had admitted it—to him or to herself.

"Maybe so." He shook his head. "But our breakup was on me. Totally on me. And you know it."

This time, he took the steps swiftly and confidently. He took both of her hands in his and looked her in the eye. "I know I screwed up, and I know you don't trust me, but I know that what we had was real. I've prayed and prayed, and every answer is the same. Everywhere I go, I see you. I see reminders of you, of us, of the life we had and could have still. Every prayer ends with the thought of you. I've tried to move on, I've tried telling God that there must be another answer, but there isn't. The answer is you, and it always has been."

She didn't have time to think about, to anticipate in the least, what happened next. It was so natural, so right. His arms were around her waist, and hers instinctively went around his neck. When they came together, she felt what she had never felt inside of the house that was supposed to solve all her problems. She felt like she had finally come home.

*****

Courtney, Spencer, and Lily attended Mass together the next morning. When it came time to receive Communion, Spencer walked behind Courtney and bowed his head for a blessing. He had told her the prior evening that he was going to formally enter the Church at Easter. The knowledge still shocked her, but she was convinced that it was what he truly wanted. He had found God, and he had found himself. More astonishing to her was that, with his suggestion about the barn, his revelation about his feelings, and a kiss that must have been laced with magic, he might even have helped her find herself.

When they said goodbye that afternoon, Courtney cried. They were tears of both joy and happiness.

"I'll be back on Wednesday," Spencer promised.

Courtney just nodded. She was experiencing too many emotions to speak. She gave him one more hug and then watched him get into his car and close the door. He smiled and waved through the glass before driving away.

She wasn't sure how long she stood there after his car was no longer in sight, Eventually, she heard the screen door open.

"It's freezing out here. The weatherman says it's going to be the coldest Thanksgiving on record. Come in here before you end up too sick to enjoy it."

Smiling, Courtney went into the house. She stopped just inside the door and turned to envelop Lily in a hug.

"What's that for?"

"For reminding me to be open to what might come. And for encouraging me to pray."

Lily held her granddaughter in her arms. "Did you receive an answer?" she asked.

"Maybe." Courtney laughed through more tears. "Whatever the answer is, I know that it's going to lead to something wonderful."

At that moment, her cell phone buzzed in her back pocket.

"It's Gavin." Courtney frowned at the phone. She slid the button and lifted the phone to her ear. "Gavin? What's up?"

"Court, I need you to come to the house. It's important."

"Is everything okay?" Panic began to set in. He sounded upset. What had happened?

"Just get here." He disconnected, leaving Courtney to stare at the screen.

"What's the matter," Lily asked, reaching for her hand.

Courtney shook her head. "I don't know, but it's bad. I've got to go."

"Do you want me to come?"

"No, I'll call you." Courtney grabbed her coat from the hook behind the door and raced to her car. She tried calling Gavin as she sped to the house, but he didn't pick up. She careened into the driveway and slammed on her brakes beside his truck. She quickly headed to the house only to stop short when she heard him call her name from the barn. She changed directions and headed toward his voice. Twilight was just about over, and the last light of the day gave itself over to the instant dark of the late-November night. She could feel the dampness of the late-fall evening settling in. Though it was only November, the air was thick and smelled like snow.

The inside of the barn was dark, but Gavin met her at the door, his hand firmly gripped around Hannah's arm.

"What the—? Hannah, Gavin, what's going on here?" She looked from one to the other. Gavin's brown eyes looked frozen, hard as ice. His jaw was set, and she could feel anger emanating from his body. Hannah's eyes were red and puffy. She had been crying and refused to look at Courtney. "Hey, I asked you a question. What is going on?"

"Are you going to tell her, or am I?" Gavin's voice as cold as steel.

"I, I…" Hannah shook her head as she stared at the ground.

Gavin loudly exhaled and released her arm as he pushed her into a sitting position on the cold, hard ground.

"She's the one," he spat angrily. "It was her all along."

"I don't understand. What are you talking about?"

Gavin turned on the heavy-duty flashlight in his hand and shined the beam into the dark building. The boxes had been emptied onto the ground. Broken bottles littered the space along with the buttons, old coins, and all the other small treasures they had found during the renovation.

"What happened?" Courtney asked just as the realization dawned on her. She turned to Hannah. "You did this? You dumped out my things and destroyed my property?"

When Hannah turned her gaze toward Courtney, sparks of anger filled her eyes and penetrated the darkness. "Your things? Your property? I've got just as much right to them as you have."

"Again, what are you talking about? I'm the one who bought the house and the barn and everything in them. What right do you have to them?"

"I have just as much claim to this land as you do. Maybe even more. Your family sold the land and everything on it. My family has waited hundreds of years to be able to claim what was rightfully ours. And you took it right out from under us."

"Hannah, I've had enough of this. What the heck are you talking about?"

"I saw it!" Hannah yelled. "I saw the emerald. You have the treasure, and it belongs to me."

Courtney shook her head. What was going on? Her mind raced to figure it out, but her jumbled thoughts and torn emotions only made her head ache. Hannah was her friend. She was supposed to be watching over the house, helping to take care of it. Why had she done this? What on earth was she talking about?

"Hannah, I don't understand," Courtney pleaded. "What treasure? And how is it yours?"

"It was my family's treasure, hidden long ago under the floorboards of the house." She thrust her head toward the house.

"Hannah, there was no treasure under the floorboards. That was all just a legend. And what do you mean 'your family'?"

"I saw it. You were holding it in your hand," Hannah insisted.

"The emerald," Courtney said.

"It's mine, and I want it, along with all of the other gems and coins."

"Hannah." Courtney sighed. "There are no other gems, no coins, no hidden treasure."

"You're lying! You found it, and I want it back."

Courtney realized she was shivering and could no longer feel her feet or her hands. She looked at Gavin.

"Can we go inside the house? Maybe start a fire?"

"There's no wood, Court, remember?"

"I have to get back to Maddy." Hannah sat up straighter. "I only meant to be gone for a few minutes. She fell asleep watching a movie, but it's not bedtime yet. She's probably scared to death."

"Yeah, well you should have thought about that before you came over here to destroy Courtney's things." Gavin's voice was full of contempt.

"Please," she pleaded with Courtney. "I'll explain everything. Just let me check on Maddy."

Courtney didn't know if it was a trick or not. She no longer trusted anything Hannah said, but she knew that Hannah loved that little girl, and Courtney didn't want anything to happen to an innocent child.

"Let's go." Courtney reached for Hannah's hand. "But don't even think of doing anything stupid."

Hannah didn't answer, and Courtney gripped her hand like a vice.

"Are you sure this is a good idea?" Gavin asked, following them across the yard. "I think we should call the police."

"Let's see what she has to say." Courtney hoped she didn't regret the decision.

They could hear Maddy's cries before they reached the front steps. Hannah tried to pull away from Courtney, but Courtney refused to let go. She let Gavin move in front of them and open the door. The little girl, her face bright red and wet with tears, ran across the room and threw herself into her mother's arms. Courtney let her hand go so that Hannah could go to her daughter. Courtney stood in the doorway taking in the scene of the mother and child. Could this young woman, not much more than a child herself, really have been the one breaking into the house these past few months?

It took a good fifteen minutes for Hannah to calm Maddy. Gavin paced the small living room as Courtney stood by, unsure of what to do with herself.

"I guess we should sit," Hannah said. Courtney couldn't gauge her mood. She didn't seem angry any longer but gone was the friendly façade she had worn for all of Courtney's previous visits.

"I guess so," Gavin said, taking the large armchair by the cold fireplace.

"Can you please start from the beginning?" Courtney asked, rubbing her hands together for warmth. Her toes were beginning to tingle, but she still felt cold. She thought that, perhaps, it wasn't a physical chill that had gripped her.

Hannah started to sit in the loveseat but stopped. She went to a bookshelf and took down a worn, leather book. She stared at the book for a moment before turning and walking over to where Courtney sat on the couch. Hannah handed the book to her without saying a word.

Courtney gently opened the book. There was no name or introduction, only a blank sheet. She turned the page and saw the penmanship of a child, long, loose, and ragged. She began reading silently.

Uncle John said I should write down my thoughts and feelings. I dunno want to. I dunno kin what to write. I miss me mother. I dunno kin why she left with the pirates. She tol me that she was a proper lady now. She did no want that life. I wish I kinned why she left.

"I don't understand." Based on the little Courtney knew from watching *Outlander*, the writing seemed a mixture of English and Gaelic. *Who wrote this?*

She wrestled with the text until comprehension began to dawn on her. The baby. Anne's baby. Was it possible? Was this journal his?

"It was written by Sean McMillan. Passed down to his children, and to theirs, and so on, until it came to me."

Courtney blinked as she stared at Hannah. "You?" The word came out in a breath, barely a spoken word at all.

"Yes, me. My great, great, great-whatever was Sean McMillan, son of a pirate but also son of a McMillan.

Courtney looked back down at the page. "It says, 'Uncle John,'"

Hannah nodded. "Later, he writes that his uncle confessed to being his father. Sean inherited Willow Grove and moved back there as an adult. It's long gone now," she said bitterly.

"But River Terrace still stands." Courtney was confused.

Hannah made a face of disgust and sniffed. "It does."

"So, we're...cousins?"

"I guess," Hannah shrugged. "In some twisted mangrove tree kind of way. Certainly not a traditional family tree." Courtney could almost taste the bitterness of Hannah's words.

"I still don't understand. Why not just tell me? Why spray paint on the walls? Smash the bottle?" She sat up straighter and widened her eyes. "And lock me in the room. It was you, wasn't it?"

Hannah curled her lip, and her nostrils flared. "Yes, it was me, but no matter what I did, you wouldn't leave."

"I don't get it. That house stood empty for years. You had lots of opportunities to search it. Why did you wait until now?"

"I didn't. I searched high and low. I spent hours and hours looking for the treasure. I couldn't find it, but when you bought the house, and you started ripping it apart, taking out the new and stripping it down to the old, I knew the treasure would finally be found. It has to be somewhere that was hidden by carpeting or new boards and paneling. It would finally be uncovered."

Courtney shook her head. "None of this makes sense. First, what makes you think there's even a treasure to be found? Second, if there was a treasure, how do you know it wasn't found years ago?"

Hannah shook her head. "Don't you see? It's all in there." She motioned to the journal. "Sean wrote that Anne told him stories about her days as a pirate. He wrote them all down. She told him how she had escaped prison and stole away on the ship that brought her here. He described how she was discovered, how the night before they abandoned her, she took a whole sack of gems and coins and hid it in her dress. They left her here to die. Can you imagine?"

Courtney shook her head.

"But she didn't die. And she was caught and forced to become a nursemaid to Jenny who was to be Sean's sister. She became John's mistress, and they had Sean. Then Robert McMillan, John's brother, claimed her after his wife died, and he took her and Sean to live with him here at River Terrace. Sean wrote about living here and how much he loved it. Unlike his real father, Robert treated him like a son, and Sean looked up to him. It wasn't until Robert died and Anne disappeared that Sean was reunited with his father. He didn't know the truth until he was older, after his father was dead. After he inherited the estate, Crystin, who he referred to as his sister, told him the truth—that they were really cousins and not siblings. He was devastated to learn the truth. He never knew that the man who raised him was his father. He always thought his father might be a pirate because he was too young to follow the timeline of Anne's stories and their lives here in Bushwood, or St. Clement's Manor, as it was known then."

"Hold on." Courtney felt lost in all of the information, her head was beginning to pound. "What does any of this have to do with a treasure under the floor?"

Hannah sighed. "Anne told Sean about it. It was part of her story. She told him that, someday, after she died, he was to find it and use it to educate himself. She wanted him to be the man that Robert should have been, the man that he was before he got sick and before he was killed. She admired Robert, perhaps even loved him, and wanted Sean to be like him, not like his father, a man who never even acknowledged him as his own."

"Okay, I get it, but what about my second question, how do you know the treasure wasn't found long ago?"

"Well, Sean never found it. Turn to the back of the journal."

Though almost the entire journal read as both a diary and a storybook, with the writing changing and maturing as the writer grew and matured, the back was a detailed log of a hundreds-year search.

"You see, every family member who ever owned the journal carefully documented the search for the treasure. It has never been found."

Courtney was astonished as she read the ledger. Over the course of more than three hundred years, a careful accounting had been kept of all of the treasure hunts. Some were done by family members who lived in the house, others by descendants who broke into the house as Hannah had. It was a laundry list of crimes committed and futile searches. Every person came up empty-handed.

"This says that Sean began looking for the treasure after he and Crystin returned to the manor as adults. Couldn't it have disappeared before then? Perhaps Anne herself took it with her when she left with the pirates."

"No," Hannah vehemently protested. "She insisted that the treasure belonged to Sean. She would never have taken it."

Courtney stared at the young woman she had come to regard as a friend. Hannah's fiery red hair flowed like burning lava down her back. Her fierce green eyes sparkled in the light. Courtney could almost picture her as a pirate and thought to herself, this is what Anne Bonny looked like at that age when she was queen of the high seas. Hannah possessed the same hair and eyes that John described in his own journals. Not only had Sean's writings been passed down to generation after generation, so had his genes.

"Okay." Courtney felt herself giving in to some of Hannah's long-held beliefs. "So, the treasure has never been found as far as your documentation shows. What makes you so sure that I have it or that it's still in the house?"

"I saw the emerald," Hannah said with a triumphant smile. "I know that you found it in the house."

Courtney laughed. "One emerald. Not a whole bag of gems. One. There is nothing else to be found."

Hannah shook her head and shot up from the couch, glaring at Courtney.

"I don't believe you. You're lying. You know where the rest is."

Courtney swallowed and cast a sidelong glance at Gavin who had remained still and quiet throughout the conversation. He made a subtle motion with his phone, and Courtney gave a quick nod before shifting her attention back to Hannah. Still seething and breathing fire, Hannah failed to notice the exchange. She was clearly on the verge of becoming hysterical, perhaps even dangerous.

"Hannah, you've got to get this through your head. There was one emerald. I found it inside a china doll. Was that ever mentioned in the writings?"

Hannah straightened her back and blinked. "A doll? What doll? Where was it?"

"Inside the secret cavern behind the cellar. Which you seemed so surprised to hear about when I told you that day."

"I was surprised. Sean never mentioned it. In fact, he rarely wrote about those few days at all."

"Traumatized, no doubt." Courtney's gaze flickered to Maddy. What would happen to her? Would she be traumatized, as well, if she lost her own mother? Trying not to think about it, Courtney looked at Hannah. "Why didn't you tell me? Why not level with me and work together to find it. Or at the very least, tell me we're related?"

"Because I don't know you. Just because we both have McMillan blood doesn't mean I can trust you."

Courtney almost laughed at the irony of Hannah's statement. She didn't know what else to say or what to think. Her temple was throbbing, and she knew that she needed to get to her medicine before her head began to explode in pain. She needed time to think this through, and she couldn't do that if she was fighting a migraine. She closed her eyes and brought her hands to her face. The pounding grew louder and harder. She felt sick to her stomach. The pain was so intense…

"Court, are you okay?" Gavin spoke for the first time since they had arrived. His voice sounded far away.

"I think…" but she couldn't think. Hannah was her cousin, her friend, her confidant, and now her nemesis. It didn't make sense. Courtney reached for the coffee table as a wave a dizziness came over her. She heard Gavin from a great distance calling her name, but the room became black.

*****

When Courtney opened her eyes, she felt as if she was awakening from a very long sleep. The room was dark, and she heard the sounds of beeping machines and faint voices in the hall. Spencer was holding her hand, and she squeezed her eyes tight, trying to focus. Nothing was clear. Her head was shrouded in a fog; pain coursed through her temple. Bits and pieces of memories scrolled through her mind. The hard, pelting rain. The green light ahead. Headlights to her left, glaring through the window. The sound of smashing metal and shattering glass.

She shook her head and was met with pain. In her mind, she saw Lily's smile, Lily in a similar bed, Gavin, Clarissa, and Sami. The faces of Hannah and Jason were so clear. She could almost remember their voices. The dream had seemed so real…

"CJ," Spencer whispered. "Can you hear me?"

"Is she awake?" That voice. It was so familiar.

"She's coming to," Spencer said.

"I'll get the doctor," the other voice said. Who was it?

"Courtney, honey, can you hear me? Sweetheart, don't leave me again. Please open your eyes."

Courtney swallowed and opened her eyes. There was Spencer. She groaned, either in pain or misery that she was going to have to break his heart, she did not know which. No, wait. The memory of telling him goodbye was so vivid. As was the house, the glint of an emerald, the scrawl in a journal, no several journals. She looked at Spencer and tried to speak, but her throat was so dry.

"Shh, now, don't say anything." His voice was calm and soothing. "You've had a traumatic experience, and you hit your head pretty hard."

She tried to lift her hand, but it was weighed down by the covers. Using all her strength, she fought to free it and lift it to her face. The scar—it was there. Not stitches, or a scar that was deep and puckered. An old scar that had healed.

"Does your head hurt, honey? Do you want some pain medicine?"

She felt more than saw the door open, a chilly gust of air surrounded her.

"Well, well, we're awake, are we?" A stranger in a white coat leaned over her. He shined a light in her eyes and gently touched a place on her temple, near the scar. The pain shot through her skull. "You've got quite a bump there. I hear you have a tendency to hit your head on hard objects." He smiled, but Courtney didn't find him funny.

"I," she gathered her thoughts. "What happened?"

"Apparently, you passed out. Hit your head pretty hard on an antique marble table. Your friends couldn't wake you up, and with your history, they were afraid you might have done some real damage. They were smart to bring you here. We did a CAT scan. Everything looks fine."

"How," she swallowed what little spit she could muster, trying to moisten her throat. "How long was I…"

"Asleep? About sixteen hours. A long time for a bump on the head. Probably some lingering effects of the previous head trauma. All tests are negative. I'd like to keep you for another twenty-four hours, but I've consulted your neurologist, and we both think you'll be fine."

It wasn't a dream. She looked to Spencer and saw Gavin standing beside him. "Lily?"

"She's on her way," Gavin answered. "We made her go home last night. She fought us, but Spencer assured her he wasn't going anywhere."

"How did you—?"

"Lily called me right after Gavin called her. I was about halfway back to Baltimore, but I turned around and got here as fast as I could."

"Your parents are on the way. I told them not to come until this morning," Gavin told her.

"We're all staying at Lily's. I was taking off Wednesday to head back down anyway, so it only made sense to call in for today and tomorrow, too." Spencer smiled and squeezed her hand. "Don't ask me to go. I won't leave you again. Seeing you like this, it brings back…" he swallowed and blinked away a tear. "Anyway, don't get any ideas that you're better off without me. We're not going down that road again."

"It's a dead-end street," Courtney said quietly.

"It's what?" Spencer asked.

"Nothing," she smiled as she looked at him. "I'm just enjoying the view."

"Um, doc, is she okay?" Gavin asked.

The doctor looked from Courtney to Spencer. "She may be a little confused for a while, but she should be fine."

Courtney closed her eyes as sleep overtook her. She may be confused, but her thoughts about Spencer were clear. She recalled Lily's words about the dead-end road and Clarrisa's words about a ship always returning to its home port. She had a lot to sort out, but she was beginning to see the way home and feel the calm seas that were ushering her right into a safe harbor.

*****

"So, she's home?" Courtney asked as she was wheeled down the hall of the hospital. She felt perfectly fine, but, as the nurse said, rules were rules.

Gavin held the glass door open for the nurse to push the chair outside. "Yeah. My friend, Sam, is representing her. He says it's up to you whether or not to press charges."

"What do you think?" she asked as Spencer pulled the car up to the curb.

"I don't know, Court. It's your call. She's pretty messed up, but she hasn't had a great life. I'm not making excuses for her, but is it worth going to court and ruining her and Maddy's lives?"

"Ready?" Spencer asked, opening the passenger door. "Hey, Gavin. What's going on?"

"Just came by to let Court know that Hannah's home. I'm heading to the store for mom. She needs more boxes, and the produce department is saving them for her."

"We'll see you Thursday at noon?" Spencer asked.

"Wouldn't miss it," Gavin called as he waved goodbye and headed to his truck.

Spencer helped Courtney into the car and closed the door once she was settled inside. She watched him hurry around to the driver's side and smiled at him when he climbed into his seat. He reached over and took her hand, a gesture she welcomed.

They drove in silence for a few minutes. Courtney thought about Hannah and how she should handle the situation. Spencer squeezed her hand.

"Lots on your mind, huh?"

She let out a breath. "Yeah. I honestly don't know what to do. I mean, she didn't really hurt anything. And I get why she was angry."

"CJ, seriously? Put yourself in her shoes. Is that how you would've handled things?"

She shook her head, knowing he was right. "Of course not, but what good would it do to press charges?"

"She should at least pay for the damages."

"How? I feel like I'd be adding insult to injury."

"It's not your fault that she's had a bad lot in life or that her family never found the supposed treasure."

"No, but I did find the emerald. I haven't taken it to the jeweler yet, but maybe I should do that next week."

"Courtney, are you thinking of giving it to her? Let me remind you that it is, by all rights, yours. She has no legal claim to that or anything else that you might find."

"Calm down, Spence. I don't need a lesson in legalities at the moment. I know it belongs to me legally. What I don't know is if it truly belongs to me, I mean in the grand scheme of things. Or that it shouldn't at least be shared by both of us."

"So, what are you thinking?"

"I'm not sure, but there must be a way to make things right. A way that doesn't let her off the hook but doesn't make her suffer any more than she already has."

"I wish I knew how to help you."

"Being here helps." Courtney looked over at him with a smile.

"I can do that." He picked up her hand and kissing her knuckles. "In fact, I'm looking forward to doing that for a long, long time."

*****

"A toast." Rick lifted his glass. "To many future Thanksgivings at River Terrace."

"Here, here." Patrick raised his glass.

"Whoa, wait a minute. Who says I'm taking this on from now on?" Courtney protested even as she clinked her glass with Jodie's.

"Why not? You've got more than enough space for all of us in that dining room of yours," Jimmy said. "And I'll even do the cooking for us. That way we won't die."

"Hey, that's not nice," Courtney said through everyone's laughter.

"I kind of like having you all here for Thanksgiving," Lily said. "It's been a long time since we celebrated a holiday here."

"It has been, Mom," Jodie agreed. "That's why we all agreed when Courtney suggested it. It brings back a lot of memories."

"It sure does. We miss having you all here," Lily said, and Courtney knew that the 'we' included Ben. "I just wish your brothers and sister could be here."

"They're here in spirit, mom." Jodie reached over and covered her mother's hand with her own. "They have their own families to spend the holiday with."

"How about this?" Courtney offered. "Next year, the entire clan can celebrate Thanksgiving at River Terrace."

"I love it," Lily said.

"And my offer to do the cooking still stands," said Jimmy. "If you make your stuffing, Grandma. And Mom makes her mashed potatoes. And Marie makes her—"

"Wait, what are you going to be cooking?" Patrick asked him.

"The turkey of course."

"So much for you cooking the meal." Courtney gave her brother a friendly push.

"When do you move in?" Marie asked Courtney.

"Hopefully, the first week in December," Courtney answered, hardly able to believe it herself. "The county should issue the occupancy permit next week. Gavin says everything is ready."

"Gavin, you've done a remarkable job on the house." Jodie reached for the tea pitcher. "I have to admit, I never thought it would happen, especially so fast."

"Believe me, it's far from done, but thanks for the compliment. The older part of the house has some work left, but it's mostly stuff that Court can handle. And then there's the work on the barn. That's going to take the better part of a year. We've decided not to attempt to start on it until late spring."

"We thought it would be best to wait until we know the weather will be good," Courtney added. "Can someone please pass the sweet potatoes?"

"Will you have heat this winter?" Lily asked.

"The newer part has heat. The older part has fireplaces, and we're putting in new baseboard heating.

That won't be finished for a while," Courtney explained. "Mitch has someone new coming in to take over for Gavin, and I really like him. Gavin says he knows what he's doing."

"Jan." Jodie addressed Gavin's mother. "Tell us about your plans for life in Portland."

Attention turned to Jan as she talked about her plans. Courtney noticed how Jan glowed with pride when she talked about Gavin's work in Portland and how much she enjoyed the times she visited him. The wine and conversation flowed throughout the meal and late into the afternoon. When Courtney felt a dull headache beginning to form, she quietly slipped outside. She sat on the front porch swing, hugging herself to stay warm despite the coat she wore. She looked at the stars and thought about all that had transpired over the past two years.

When she heard the door creak, she didn't have to look to know who was coming out. She smiled as Gavin approached the swing. They sat in silence, his feet gently pushing them back and forth.

"Just like old times, huh?" he said.

"Feels that way, except…"

"Except not?"

Courtney laughed quietly. "Yeah, except not."

Gavin took her hand. "Spencer's a good guy. He loves you."

"I know he does." She looked down at their joined hands. "I love him, too." She turned toward Gavin and saw her happiness reflected in his eyes.

"I know, and I'm glad. He's right for you, Court, in a way that I never could be."

"Oh, but you're right for me, too. You're the best friend I ever had, the only person, other than family, that I've known my entire life. I don't ever want to lose this." She squeezed his hand.

"You won't. I've already let Spencer know that I'll be back, and if he ever hurts you, he'll have me to answer to."

She laid her head on his shoulder. "I could never have gotten through the summer or fall without you. The house, Lily's fall, Hannah's exploits. I'll never forget everything you've done for me."

"I sure hope not. Someday, I hope to make use of that barn of yours."

"It's a deal. Only…"

Gavin looked at Courtney. "Only what?"

"You don't get to bring anyone to my barn until I've met and approved of her first."

Gavin laughed. "We'll see, Court, we'll see."

When the door creaked again, Gavin let go of her hand and stood.

"I thought you might be cold out here." Spencer held up a blanket.

"She's all yours," Gavin said. "Take care of her."

"You know I will," Spencer replied. Gavin nodded and left the two of them alone on the porch.

Spencer spread half the blanket around Courtney's shoulders and pulled the other half over his own shoulders as he sat next to her on the swing. They huddled together under the blanket.

"You sure can see a lot of stars out here," he remarked after a few minutes.

"You sure can. Gavin, Sami, and I spent quite a few nights, laying in the back yard, making wishes on those stars."

He slipped his arm between the blanket and her shoulders and pulled her close. “And how did that work out for you? The star wishing?”

“I think I finally figured out which wishes really mattered and how to make them come true. How about you? Ever wish on any stars?”

“Not that I remember, but I’m pretty sure I don’t have to. Like you said, I finally figured out how to make my wishes come true.”

*****

“Did you say 3.4 million?” Courtney asked, barely able to say the words.

“I said, about 3.4 million. Truthfully, though, it’s only worth what someone will pay for it.”

“And how does one find someone to pay that much for an emerald?”

The jeweler removed his monocle and blinked. “Usually at an auction house. The more well-known ones like Christie’s or Sotheby’s could attract that type of clientele.”

By the time Courtney thanked him and climbed into her SUV, her head was spinning. The emerald was a twelve-carat, unflawed gem. Courtney felt like a target just having it in her possession. No wonder Hannah’s family spent three hundred years trying to find it. What on earth was she going to do with it?

Every night for a week, thoughts of the multi-million-dollar stone flooded her dreams. Courtney had no idea what to do with it. She decided to take her grandmother’s advice and pray about it. It worked for her as far as sorting out her feelings for Spencer. She figured it might work for this, too.

Then, it happened. She awoke from a dream in which everything was made so clear, she wondered why she hadn't thought of it earlier. She knew exactly what to do with the emerald, the money it would bring, and her predicament with Hannah.

*****

On Christmas Eve, the entire family attended Mass at their home parish outside of Washington, D.C. Courtney wondered what Hannah would think when she received the special delivery on Christmas Day. The check from Harry Winston would help Hannah continue her education, send Maddy to any college she could get into when the time came, and even buy them a new house if they wanted one. If Hannah invested wisely, the money would take care of them for the rest of their lives. That was, after she paid her debt to Courtney, but it wasn't money Courtney was after. It was knowledge.

For Courtney, the money would pay for the entire renovation of the barn and all of Gavin's flights back and forth to oversee the project. It would also ensure that she could take her time finishing the house and furnishing it with the best antiques money could buy.

The newspapers would report about the sale of the emerald and its historical context. Jason was beside himself at being able to provide most of the background information for the articles. He was the primary historian on the house, its architecture, its cultural and historical importance, and its renovation. He would be flooded with job offers, but he assured Courtney that no job would ever bring him the joy that

River Terrace had brought. Not to mention its leading him to the love of his life.

Courtney felt so blessed as she lit a candle on her way out of Mass. She was heading into the new year as a home owner, a soon-to-be business owner, and, so far, a content girlfriend. She was surrounded by the people she loved most in the world. A year ago, she was learning how to live again. Now, she was living the life she always dreamed she could have. Lily was right, God's perfect plan would happen. You just had to trust in his timing, and let it be.

<u>EPILOGUE</u>

1750

The doll was heavy, but Crystin didn't know where else to hide them. She had carefully opened the seams, pulled out the stuffing, and filled the doll's body with what her father had called, "The Devil's Fortune." Before moving the empty shelves to expose the hidden cavern, she looked behind to make sure nobody had followed her into the cellar. Polly was her favorite doll when she was a little girl, but she had only begotten boys, and they had only begotten boys. She kept it for many years in the hope that she would be able to pass it on, but alas, that was not to be. Instead, her favorite doll would be the caretaker of the gems until Crystin found a way to finally put the curse to rest.

Robert McMillan had gone to his grave believing that the satchel he had found under the loose floorboard, shortly after Anne's mysterious arrival, was the root of all of their turmoil. Crystin had not put much stock in that belief, but after many years of watching her family suffer, she understood why her father had felt that way. First, her mother died, then Robert become ill. Their home was invaded by pirates, and her father was killed. Soon after, the guilt and torment drove Evan to take his own life. After fleeing to Baltimore and leaving the treasure hidden in the attic, Jenny married and died in childbirth. James suffered from the effects of smallpox and never saw his sons grow into the fine young men they had become. Crystin's husband died young, leaving her with three small children. And her cousin, Sean, watched his home, Willow Grove, burn to the ground. No, she no longer doubted that the gems and gold coins, most likely stained with the blood of innocent men, had brought these curses upon them. Only God could relieve her family of the torment they caused. Thus far, He had not seen fit to do so.

Crystin hid the doll in an empty pickling barrel and left it in the farthest corner of the cavern. She carefully pushed the shelves back into place and refilled them with the few jars she had managed to scrape together after the hurricane devastated their crops.

Climbing up from the cellar, Crystin silently prayed that the Lord would grant them forgiveness and allow her grandchildren to find the peace that had eluded their family for the past twenty-five years.

As she rounded the house, she caught sight of the barn. Her father had such high hopes for the barn, an ostentatious sight, too large for their harvest and the few animals they owned before the loss of crops caused her to have them slaughtered for food and money. Robert had hoped to build a tobacco empire on this land, but he was taken from them before his dream could be put into action. Crystin had no idea what to do with the monstrosity now. It mocked her each time she looked its way. The empty building was one more symbol of all they had lost. Perhaps she would tear it down and be rid of its ridicule once and for all.

The sound of a wagon drew her attention, and she rounded the house to find Father McConnell stepping down from his seat.

"Good morning, Father. What brings you out this way on this fine day?"

"Aye, Crystin, if only it was a fine day."

"Father, what is it?" She asked, hurrying to his side.

"The authorities have shut down Sacred Heart. Her doors are chained, and I have been forbidden from opening them."

"What about tomorrow's Mass?"

"There will be no more Masses. Many have come here, seeking a better life, and though our parish has been blessed with growth, there is no place large enough to hold us in secret. I fear that our faith will be stamped out of the colony. And on top of that, the men who brought their families here to build churches will need to move on to another colony where their labors are appreciated. I'm delivering the bad news to everyone in the parish."

Out of the corner of her eye, Crystin saw the barn, the enormous, empty barn, with a loft as long as the barn itself. She thought of the gems and gold coins and what they could do to help her community. Would God then forgive her family and lift the curse?

"Father, would you have time for a bit of coffee and a scone? I have an idea that just might save our parish and my family."

June 10 - Present day

Lily and Courtney stood inside the elevator as it rose to the second story. Courtney held her breath as the doors opened and felt Lily's sharp intake of breath as the chapel was revealed. The afternoon sunlight beamed through the high, round windows, casting a honey-colored glow on the wooden pews. The pews glistened so brightly, they appeared to be wet with dew.

A deep-maroon carpet ran up the aisle between the two rows of seating and spread itself up the three steps and across the altar. The gold-leaf tabernacle was dazzling in the light, giving the appearance that the rays surrounding the dove were extensions of the golden beams of sunlight dancing around the room. Along the walls, the Stations of the Cross came alive with bright colors, thanks to art students from the local college who restored the once-faded paintings.

Swags of lily of the valley and white roses hung on the sides of the pews. Sprays of the same white flowers, coupled with stems of lilacs, decorated the altar. A white runner, rolled up and ready, would be laid on the carpet before the bride made her way to the altar.

"Oh, Courtney," Lily whispered. "It's magnificent."

"It is, isn't it?" Courtney beamed with pride.

"I'm so early. I feel funny seeing everything before the family does."

"Nonsense, you are family."

"You know what I mean," Lily said as she slowly made her way toward the front.

"Is this good?" Courtney asked when they reached the third row.

"Yes, this is perfect." Lily looked around. "Do they still do the bride's side and the groom's side?"

"They do. Why wouldn't they?"

"Well, you know how things are these days. Traditions don't mean much to most young people."

"Gram, they mean everything to me. You know that."

Courtney's phone buzzed, and she hastily pecked out a reply. "I've got to go. The bride is here. You going to be okay up here by yourself?"

"Who says I'm by myself?" She gestured to the tabernacle where the blessed Communion hosts were stored.

Courtney gave her grandmother a kiss on the cheek and hurried down the steps, feeling too much excitement to use the elevator. As she neared the bottom, her heart caught in her chest at the sight of the man in the doorway.

"You're early." She and Spencer embraced, and he kissed her in a way that, on that day, should be reserved for the bride.

"I missed you."

Courtney laughed. "I just saw you an hour ago."

"An hour was too long."

"The bride's here, so I have to run. How'd the meeting go?" she asked as they walked toward the limo where one bride and four of the five bridesmaids tumbled out into the yard, carrying garment bags, shoes, and makeup cases.

"Perfectly. I start in two weeks."

Courtney stopped and hugged him. "Congratulations. Now, you're sure that you won't be bored practicing down here in the slow-paced country? It's a far cry from the hustle and bustle of the big city."

"It's exactly the pace I want." He grabbed her for another quick kiss before shooing her off toward the bridal party.

Two hours later, Courtney bit back tears as she gazed at the beautiful bride.

"Don't you dare start that, Courtney Jane. My makeup is perfect, and I don't have time to redo it."

"I can't help it. You look amazing. And happy. You look so happy."

"You look pretty amazing, too. Spencer isn't going to be able to keep his hands off of you."

"Well, he'd better because I don't have time to redo my makeup either. I don't know why I let you talk me into being in this wedding and running it at the same time."

"Don't worry. I'm sure Hannah has everything under control."

"I know she does. She's a great partner."

Sami shook her head. "I still can't believe, after everything she did—"

"It's long past," Courtney interrupted. "Let bygones be bygones. Heaven knows I've made my share of mistakes."

"I suppose we both have."

Courtney's phone began vibrating on the marble-topped antique dressing table. She picked it up and smiled.

"The groom is in place. Ready?"

"You bet." Sami radiated love and excitement. She was most certainly ready.

The bridesmaids moved as a group from the room in the barn. A bridal chamber had been created on one side of the newly installed elevator. The chamber housed a bathroom, a changing room, and a large room with antique dressing tables and a wall of mirrors. On the other side of the elevator, was a smaller room for the groomsmen. Streamers hung from the barn ceiling and stretched across the grand ballroom, once a home to livestock and, years later, drying tobacco leaves. Today, the room rivaled any banquet hall and was fit for a queen. All of the lights, the music, and even the elevator were powered by solar energy.

A commercial kitchen filled the back of the building where a world-class chef was preparing the meal. Jimmy would run up the stairs just in time to see the vows before heading back to work. Every feature in the kitchen, from the sink to the ovens to the dishwasher, worked on solar energy, and all food waste was recycled into compost. The compost fertilized the gardens where all of the fruits and vegetables were grown. Gavin and Courtney had thought of every possibility to make River Terrace green as well as self-sufficient.

At the back of the chapel, Courtney gave Sami one last hug before Courtney began her walk down the aisle. She beamed at Spencer who stood with Gavin and the other groomsmen. She turned and smiled at her parents and brothers as she passed their pews. She winked at Lily and at Aunt Sissie, the matriarch of the family, looking regal and misty-eyed as she awaited her granddaughter's entrance. Courtney then turned her focus to the groom, anticipating his expression when he would see Sami for the first time in her wedding dress. Courtney knew the exact moment Sami came into view. Jason's smile stretched from ear to ear, and his eyes filled with love and adoration.

Later that night, Courtney and Spencer sat on the outdoor swing, staring at the stars. The June warmth was a far cry from the November chill they had felt the last time they sat on a swing and gazed at the heavens.

"I still can't get over all of the stars you can see from here," Spencer said.

"I know," Courtney agreed. "They're just amazing."

"Look at that one." Spencer shifted his weight on the swing. "It's so big and bright. It sparkles like a diamond."

"Where?" Courtney asked, straining to see the particularly bright star he referred to.

"Not up there. Down here."

Courtney felt the swing lighten as she turned toward Spencer. He knelt on the ground, holding a box out in front of him. Nestled in velvet sat a two-carat diamond that radiated light like the stars themselves. She swallowed as she looked from the ring to Spencer's gaze.

"Courtney Jane McMillan, I know we did this once already, but I wasn't ready then to make a real commitment to you, to us. Please tell me you'll give me the chance to do it right this time."

Courtney looked back down at the ring. It was right this time. She knew it. Still, something inside of her made her hesitate. She was so sure, the first time Spencer asked, that their life was going to be perfect. Then they had let so many other things get in their way. Then Courtney nearly died, and then she bought the house. Gavin re-entered her life, and she met Jason. She feared they might lose Lily. Then they discovered the chapel, and everything began to fall into place. And it was Spencer who helped her figure it all out.

She took a deep breath, but before she could answer, she heard cries from across the yard.

"Hurry up and say yes," Lily called. "I want to be around for the wedding."

"And we've got a plane to catch," Gavin called, his mother by his side.

"What are you waiting for?" Sami said, captured in Jason's loving embrace.

Courtney shook her head and laughed. "Did everyone know about this but me?" she asked Spencer.

"I needed moral support." He grinned, and Courtney's heart melted a little more.

"Well, I guess I can't let them down." She stood and reached for his hand.

Spencer stood and pulled her to him. "Is that a 'yes'?"

"It's a yes."

They kissed under the light of the moon as the shadow of a ship sailed across the gentle waves behind them, just as it did on that same night, nearly three hundred years before. A woman stood on the deck as the ghost ship steered toward the harbor.

Most people venture out into the world, but the lucky ones, like Courtney, are able to return to the safety and comfort of their home ports. Some of them, at the end of a dead-end road.

Historical Notes and Acknowledgments

My mother's cousin, Patti, was a big fan of my writing, but she often pulled me aside and said, "I wish you would write a ghost story for me." I always smiled and said, "Someday," not sure that I ever would. This past year, we unexpectedly lost our dear cousin, and I found myself longing to, somehow, incorporate a "ghost" into one of my novels in honor of Patti. Though the "ghost" in this novel turned out to be very much alive, trying to make others believe that the house was haunted, I couldn't help but honor Patti's wish by having Anne Bonny sail into the harbor on a ghost ship at the end of the novel. Perhaps she had been there the entire time, searching for the gems or waiting to see if they were finally put to good use. I like to think that would have made Patti smile.

Anne Bonny was born sometime around 1697, but the date of her death is unknown. She was an Irish lass who fell in love with a pirate, James Bonny, and was disowned by her father, sentencing her to a life on the high seas. When Anne's husband turned on his fellow pirates and began spying on them for the Governor of the Bahamas, Anne became angry and began "socializing" with other pirates. She ran off with pirate, Calico Jack Rackham. The two of them, along with Anne's friend, Mary Read, stole the ship, *William*, and succeeded in becoming quite accomplished pirates. Only the crew knew that Anne and Mary were women as it was unlawful for women to sail as crew on pirate or merchant ships. When Anne's pregnancy began to show, she was forced to leave the ship until after the child's birth. In order to return to the ship, and her life of piracy, Anne abandoned the child in Cuba. When Anne, Mary, and Calico Jack were captured, in October 1720, Anne and Mary were given stays of execution because they were both found to be with child. Mary died in childbirth while in prison, but Anne and her child survived. What happened to Anne beyond that is cause for speculation. She was never seen or heard from again. Some accounts say she returned to her father, others to her first husband. Still other accounts say she died in prison, changed her name and returned to piracy, or married and enjoyed a happy family life in the colonies. Whatever happened to Anne can only be left to the imagination. All of the information contained in the book about pirates was historically accurate.

On March 25, 1634, the Ark and the Dove landed at St. Clement's Island in the Maryland colony. The passengers on the Ark and the Dove, Catholics from England and Wales, sought life in the new land where they could practice religious freedom, as Catholicism had been outlawed in England, Wales, and Scotland by the British Crown. Some of my ancestors were on those ships and settled in what is today St. Mary's County, Maryland. Passenger, Father Andrew White, celebrated the first Catholic Mass in the New World, and the colonists erected a large cross on the island to memorialize the event. Governor Ritchie dedicated a new forty-foot cross in 1934 to commemorate the 300th anniversary of the founding of the state of Maryland. My grandfather, Eugene Benjamin Morgan, was one of the carpenters who built that cross, which still stands on the island today, several years before he met the love of his life, Mary Lillian Gibson.

From 1850 until the early 1900s, my father's family, father, Joseph McWilliams, son, Jerome, and daughter, Josephine, owned and lived on what was then called Blackistone Island. The men saw to the daily business of the island, and the women operated the lighthouse. The name of the island has since been reverted to its original name, St. Clement's Island. In the early 2000s, a foundation was established to restore the lighthouse on the island and turned it into a museum, an extension of the St. Clement's Island Museum that sits on the mainland. The lighthouse opened to the public in 2008. Pages from our Uncle Jerome's journal can be seen at the St. Clement's Island Museum.

Lord Baltimore granted the Sly family the land that was known as St. Clement's Manor and now encompasses most of modern-day Bushwood, Maryland. While the nobles who arrived in the area were Catholic, many of the workers were Protestant and soon outnumbered their Catholic neighbors. Following the example of Britain, Catholicism was outlawed in the colony off and on between 1649 and 1692 when the Maryland Toleration Act was passed. The Act was repealed in 1694, and Catholicism was once again outlawed until 1776. During this time, many Catholics were forced to practice their religion in secret, often turning attics and other hidden rooms into chapels.

Ocean Hall, built in 1703, sits on the shores of the Wicomico River in Bushwood, Maryland. Captain Gerard Sly built the house. He never owned slaves and died without the riches of his brother, Robert, builder and owner of Bushwood Manor, the finest home in the county. Current owners, Dr. James Boyd and his wife, Jennifer, spent ten years renovating the house in order to restore its Colonial charm and beauty. With the aid of a historical architect, they were able to identify and keep the original wall panels, restore the covered-over fireplaces, use siding found for the addition, move the dormers to their correct places (replacing one that was missing), maintain the original brick, and reinforce the cruck roof—the only known one of its kind in the Americas. More architectural finds were uncovered under the foundation than in any other historic house in Maryland. Though the present-day barn was moved to the property, a chapel was built inside the house and held forty people. While there was no hidden treasure, the house did contain many items such as keys, buttons, toys, pottery, shoes, and other pieces of past lives. Jamie and Jennifer, on my tour of the house, assured me that there were no secret rooms or hidden passageways; however, I knew from the start that River Terrace would indeed contain all of the purported legends and rumors from my childhood.

Thank you, Jamie and Jennifer, for spending a day with me and giving me a tour of your magnificent home. I loved hearing about the history of the house and seeing the fruits of the renovation.

For Further Reading:

A General History of the Robberies and Murders of the most notorious Pyrates Captain Charles Johnson (1724) – reissued with notes and introduction by David Cordingly (2010)

"The Fact and Fiction of Cork Pirate Captain Anne Bonny," *The Irish Examiner*, 31 August 2018

History of St. Mary's County, Maryland, 1634-1990, Regina Combs Hammett (1991)

Ocean Hall, Discovery of An American Classic, Dr. James Carroll Boyd, M.D. (2011)

Pirates on the Chesapeake, Donald G.Shomette (1985)

Shipwrecks on the Chesapeake, Donald G.Shomette (1982)

"St. Clement's Island, Witness to American History," Blessing of the Fleet Program, Optimist Club of the 7th District of Maryland (1995)

Beidh Aonach Amárach *(There's a Fair Tomorrow)*
An Irish Children's Song

Beidh aonach amárach i gContae an Chláir.
Beidh aonach amárach i gContae an Chláir.
Beidh aonach amárach i gContae an Chláir.
Cé mhaith dom é, ní bheidh mé ann.
Curfá:
'S a mháithrín, an ligfidh tú chun aonaigh m
'S a mháithrín, an ligfidh tú chun aonaigh m
'S a mháithrín, an ligfidh tú chun aonaigh m
'S a mhuirnín ó ná héiligh é.
Níl tú a deich nó a haon déag fós.
Níl tú a deich nó a haon déag fós.
Níl tú a deich nó a haon déag fós.
Nuair a bheidh tú trí déag beidh tú mór.
Curfá
Táim-se i ngrá le gréasaí bróg…
Mur' bhfaigh mé é ní bheidh mé beo.
Curfá
B'fhearr liom féin mo ghréasaí bróg…
Ná oifigeach airm faoi lásaí óir.
Curfá
Is a mháithrín an ligfidh tú chun aonaigh mé…
Is a mhuirnín óg ná healaí é
Curfá
Beidh aonach amárach in gContae an Chláir
Cén mhaith domh é ní bheidh mé ann
Curfá
Tá 'níon bheag agam is tá sí óg…
Is tá sí i ngrá leis an ghreasaí bróg
Curfá
'S iomaí bean a phós go h-óg…
Is a mhair go socair lena greasaí bróg
Curfá
Níl tú ach deich nó aon deag fós…
Nuair a bheas tú trí deag beidh tú mór
Curfá
B'fhearr liom féin mo ghreasaí bróg…
Ná fir na n'arm faoina lascú óir
Curfá

There's a fair tomorrow in the County Clare.
There's a fair tomorrow in the County Clare.
There's a fair tomorrow in the County Clare.
But what's the use I won't be there.
Chorus:
Oh mother, won't you let me go to the fair?
Oh mother, won't you let me go to the fair?
Oh mother, won't you let me go to the fair?
My fondest child, Oh please don't ask.
You're not even ten or eleven years old.
You're not even ten or eleven years old.
You're not even ten or eleven years old.
When you're thirteen I'll let you go.
Chorus
I'm in love with the cobbler man…
If I don't get him, I can't live on.
Chorus
The cobbler is the man I like the best…
I prefer him to an officer with golden braid.
Chorus
Oh mother, won't you let me go to the fair?...
My fondest child, Oh please don't ask.
Chorus
There's a fair tomorrow in the County Clare…
Why should I care, I won't be there.
Chorus
I've a little daughter and she's very young…
And she's in love with a cobbling man
Chorus
There is many a maid who married young…
And lived in peace with her cobbling man
Chorus
You are not ten or eleven yet…
When you're thirteen you'll be more mature.
Chorus
I'd rather have my cobbling man…
Than an army officer with his gold bands
Chorus

About the Author

Amy Schisler has been writing all of her life as an author and freelance writer. Her first children's book, *Crabbing With Granddad*, is an autobiographical work about spending a day harvesting the Maryland Blue Crab.

Her debut novel, *A Place to Call Home*, was released in 2014. A second edition was published in March of 2015. *Picture Me, A Mystery*, published in 2015, was the winner of a 2016 Illumination Award. Amy's critically acclaimed novel, *Whispering Vines*, published in 2016, was awarded an Illumination Award as well as the LYRA for the best ebook romance of 2016. *Island of Miracles* (2017) was the winner of an Illumination Award and a 2018 Catholic Press Award for best inspirational work of fiction. Amy released her children's book, *The Greatest Gift*, as well as her novel, *Summer's Squall,* in 2017. Amy's novel, *Island of Promise,* the second book in the *Chincoteague Island Trilogy*, is the recipient of the Oklahoma Romance Writer's Best Inspirational Fiction Book of 2018. All of Amy's books may be purchased in bookstores as well as online on all major print and ebook sites.

Amy, who grew up in Southern Maryland, graduated from the University of Maryland with a master's degree in Library and Information Science. A former librarian and teacher, she now lives on the Eastern Shore of Maryland with her husband, three daughters, and two dogs. She is the author of a weekly blog which has over a thousand followers around the world. Her topics range from current events to her daily life.

Follow Amy at:

http://amyschislerauthor.com

http://facebook.com/amyschislerauthor

Book Club Discussion Questions

Warning – These contain spoilers!

1. Anne Bonny was a real pirate who wreaked havoc on the seas in the early 1700s. Historians can only guess as to her fate since her death was never recorded. What do you imagine happened to her? Do you think that someone like her truly could be redeemed?

2. Learning about one's family history can be fascinating. Have you ever looked into your family history? Were there secrets there that you wish you hadn't known?

3. Courtney's accident was the catalyst she needed to make changes in her life. Have you ever been given the gift of being able to start over? Did you take the chance? How was your life changed as a result? Are you happy with your choice?

4. Have you ever had a childhood dream that you saw come to fruition? What was it, and how were you able to make it happen?

5. Many people are nostalgic about unrequited or first love. Who was your first love or the "one that got away"? If you were single, and fate brought you back together, would you give it another try?

6. Courtney, understandably, was leery of going back to Spencer. Do you believe he really "saw the light" and changed for the better? Can people change? What signs were there that he truly had, or had not, become a better person? What would you have done if you had been in Courtney's shoes?

7. Crystin's father, Robert, believed the pirate's gems were the cause of his family's bad luck. Rather than spend the gems, he hid them, believing them to be "stained with blood." Do you believe in bad luck? Do you believe that something done or had in the past can be the reason for such luck? Like Crystin, would you seize the opportunity to use the supposed object of bad luck for something good in the hopes of changing your luck?

8. Imagine finding an amazing historical find in your house or on your property. Would you preserve it? Modernize it? Sell it? How would you rationalize your decision?

9. Courtney chose to forgive Hannah and welcome her into family business rather than press charges against her for all that she did. How would you have felt in Courtney's situation? How would you have handled it?

10. Do you believe in ghosts? Do you believe that spirits from the past are still among us as we live our daily lives? Why or why not?

CPSIA information can be obtained
at www.ICGtesting.com
Printed in the USA
LVHW012128070120
642793LV00004B/650

9 781732 224223

Rare Vascular Plants of Alberta

Rare Vascular Plants of Alberta

BY THE ALBERTA NATIVE PLANT COUNCIL

Edited by
LINDA KERSHAW
JOYCE GOULD
DEREK JOHNSON
JANE LANCASTER

Principal Contributors
ALBERTA NATURAL HERITAGE INFORMATION CENTRE
CHERYL BRADLEY
BONNIE SMITH
ANNE WEERSTRA

University of Alberta Press

Natural Resources Canada / Ressources naturelles Canada
Canadian Forest Service / Service canadien des forêts

Published by

The University of Alberta Press and
Ring House 2
Edmonton, Alberta T6G 2E1

The Canadian Forest Service
Northern Forestry Centre
5320–122 Street
Edmonton, Alberta T6H 3S5

Printed in Canada 5 4 3 2 1

Canadian Cataloguing in Publication Data

Main entry under title:

Rare vascular plants of Alberta

Includes bibliographical references and index.
ISBN 0-88864-319-5

1. Rare plants—Alberta. I. Kershaw, Linda J., 1951-
QK86.C2R37 2001 581.68'097123 C00-910171-3

∞ Printed on acid-free paper.
Colour scanning and prepress by Elite Lithographers Co. Ltd., Edmonton, Alberta.
Printed and bound in Canada by Kromar Printing Ltd., Winnipeg, Manitoba.
Book design by Carol Dragich.
Proofreading by Jill Fallis.

The University of Alberta Press acknowledges the financial support of the Government of Canada through the Book Publishing Industry Development Program for its publishing activities. The Press also gratefully acknowledges the support received for its program from the Canada Council for the Arts.

Canada

Contents

Kershaw, L.; Gould, J.; Johnson, D.; Lancaster, J. 2001. *Rare vascular plants of Alberta*. Univ. Alberta Press, Edmonton, Alberta and Nat. Resour. Can., Can. For. Serv., North. For. Cent., Edmonton, Alberta.

This book describes about 485 species of rare native vascular plants found in the province of Alberta. Species descriptions are divided into four main sections based on growth form (woody plants, broad-leaved herbs, grass-like plants, and ferns and fern allies). Common, scientific and family names are included for all primary entries. A general description of each plant is followed by descriptions of habitat and maps showing the distribution of most species in both Alberta and North America. Each species description is concluded with notes on synonymy, descriptions of related or similar-looking plants, etymology of the scientific names and, for some species, medicinal or aboriginal uses of the plants. The appendices include keys to some of the more difficult-to-identify genera, listing of the species by natural region, species new to Alberta, species previously considered rare for the province but not included here, and species classified as rare in Canada. An illustrated glossary, a reference list, and an index conclude the book.

This book has been several years in the making, and many people have contributed to its compilation and production. The Alberta Native Plant Council (ANPC) has been interested in rare plants since its inception in 1987 and has always supported the idea of producing a book about these species.

Alberta Environmental Protection has supported the project from the beginning, through the Recreation and Protected Areas Program and later the Alberta Natural Heritage Information Centre (ANHIC), initially headed by Peter Lee and then by Dan Chambers. Staff at, and contributors to, ANHIC have provided a great deal of assistance to the production of this book. They include Peter Achuff, Lorna Allen, Dana Bush, Patsy Cotterill, Kathi De, Joyce Gould, Graham Griffiths, Coral Grove, Roxy Hastings, Miranda Hoekstra, Julie Hrapko, Duke Hunter, Derek Johnson, Linda Kershaw, Jane Lancaster, Mike Luchanski, Karen Mann, Marge Meijer, Gavin More, Bill Richards, John Rintoul, Christy Sarafinchin, Cindy Verbeek, Dragomir Vujnovic, Cliff Wallis, Kathleen Wilkinson and Joan Williams. Joyce Gould has played a key role in providing information from the ANHIC database for this guide.

The ANPC was able to contribute to the ANHIC database by hiring summer students in 1993 (Kim Krause), 1995 (Ksenija Vujnovic) and 1996 (Heather Mansell) to help with the huge job of entering rare plant information. This work was funded in part by the Summer Career Placement Program of Human Resources Development Canada.

We thank the Canadian Forest Service, the co-publishers of this book for their efforts. In particular, the editorial and production assistance of Brenda Laishley (with assistance from Denise Leroy in editing the reference list) and the manpower and logistical support provided by Derek Johnson and Dan MacIsaac.

Many specimens were examined in different herbaria as information was collected for the database. A special thank-you to the staff who facilitated access to specimens for this essential work: Brij Kohli (University of Alberta Herbarium), Mike Luchanski and Roxy Hastings (Provincial Museum of Alberta Herbarium), C.C. Chinnappa and Bonnie Smith (University of Calgary Herbarium), Derek Johnson (Northern Forestry Centre Herbarium, Edmonton), Walter Willms and Harriet Douwes (University of Lethbridge Herbarium), William Cody and Paul Catling (Agriculture Canada

JG

Athyrium alpestre

Tanacetum bipinnatum

Herbarium, Ottawa), George Argus, Mike Shchepanek and Albert Dugal (National Museum Herbarium, Ottawa) and Warren Wagner (University of Michigan Herbarium). The assistance of staff in the collection of information from the herbaria at various national and provincial parks is also greatly appreciated.

Many volunteers came forward to collect information for different groups of plants. This was coordinated by Linda Kershaw, and contributors included Peter Achuff, Cheryl Bradley, Debra Brown, Dana Bush, Adrien Corbiere, Patsy Cotterill, Dave Ealey, Gina Fryer, Joyce Gould, Graham Griffiths, Julie Hrapko, Derek Johnson, Linda Kershaw, Jane Lancaster, Dan MacIsaac, Debra Nicholson, Bill Richards, Art Schwarz, Bonnie Smith, Joan Williams and Kathleen Wilkinson.

Several ANPC members helped to produce the Guidelines for Rare Plant Surveys. This project was coordinated by Jane Lancaster, with contributions from Lorna Allen, Joyce Gould, Anne Weerstra, Kathleen Wilkinson and Joan Williams.

When the bulk of the data had been collected, work began on writing the species accounts for the book. This was coordinated by Linda Kershaw, with Cheryl Bradley, Joyce Gould, Derek Johnson, Linda Kershaw, Cindy Verbeek and Anne Weerstra writing text for different species. Peter Achuff, Joyce Gould, Derek Johnson, Linda Kershaw and Cliff Wallis wrote the text for the introduction, Linda Kershaw wrote and illustrated the glossary, Coral Grove compiled the appendices (these were updated and revised by Derek Johnson and Marie Paton), and Elisabeth Beaubien compiled the Alberta phenological information. Linda Kershaw edited the text, and it was then reviewed by Adolf Ceska, Bill Crins, Vern Harms, Derek Johnson and John Packer. Bruce Ford and John Hudson also reviewed the sedges.

As the ANHIC database became more complete, it was possible to use its information to generate maps electronically, and the Alberta distribution maps in the book were generously provided by ANHIC. A special thank-you to Joyce Gould, Duke Hunter, John Rintoul and Dragomir Vujnovic for their work. Another group, working in the Biota of North America Program (BONAP) at the University of North Carolina, studies plant distributions across the continent, and they kindly provided us with North American maps for our rare species. Our thanks to

John Kartesz and Amy Farstad for their help. The production of current maps is a complicated process, requiring intensive research and the accumulation of large amounts of information. Without the support of ANHIC and BONAP, we could not have included these important elements in the book.

The collection of photographs and illustrations continued throughout the project. Jane Lancaster coordinated the collection of photographs and illustrations, with some help from Linda Kershaw and Ruth Johnson. Original illustrations by John Maywood and Joan Williams were provided by ANHIC and commissioned by the ANPC. Previously published illustrations in the book are used, with kind permission, from the University of Washington Press, the New York Botanical Garden, the Royal British Columbia Museum, Stanford University Press, the National Museum of Canada, William Wagner and Bill Merilees. Illustration sources are listed on pp. 481–82. Photographers who donated slides for use in the book include Peter Achuff, Lorna Allen, Ralph Bird, Terry Clayton, Bill Crins, Teresa Dolman, Joseph Duft, Joyce Gould, Dierdrie and Graham Griffiths, Bonnie Heidel, Julie Hrapko, Derek Johnson, John Joy, Linda Kershaw, Tulli Kerststetter, Fred Korbut, Jane Lancaster, Archie Landals, Peter Lee, Peter Lesica, William Merilees, Bob Moseley, Sandra Myers, Jim Pojar, John Rintoul, Steve Shelly, Kathy Tannas, Jim Vanderhorst, Warren Wagner Jr., Cliff Wallis, Cleve Wershler and Steve Wirt. ANHIC, the Devonian Botanic Garden, Lone Pine Publishing, the Montana Natural Heritage Program, the Recreation and Protected Areas Division of Alberta Environmental Protection, and Waterton Lakes National Park also contributed photographs. Photo sources are listed on page 482.

JG
Erigeron trifidus

Fund-raising and financial management have been necessary throughout the life of the project. Our thanks to ANPC treasurers Dave Downing, Joyce Gould and Dan MacIsaac; intrepid secretary Lorna Allen; and the people who helped with applications for funding, Dana Bush, Derek Johnson, Linda Kershaw, Gavin More and Margaret Zielinski. The Canadian Forest Service provided substantial financial support toward the completion of this book. Several other groups have provided financial support over the years for the rare plants project. The Federation of Alberta Naturalists provided a generous grant in 1993, which has supported most aspects of the project since its

DJ
Carex pseudocyperus

inception. We also received grants and donations from the Alberta Sports, Recreation, Parks and Wildlife Foundation to place copies of the book in public and high school libraries, Canada Trust Friends of the Environment, Canadian 88 Energy Corporation, Gulf Canada, Quadra Environmental Services, Axys Environmental Consulting, the Red Deer River Naturalists and several private supporters.

The search for a publisher also required the energies of dedicated workers. Thanks to Elisabeth Beaubien, Joyce Gould, Derek Johnson, Linda Kershaw, Dan MacIsaac and Carla Zelmer for their efforts in this. Thank you to our co-publishers, the University of Alberta Press and the Canadian Forest Service. Glenn Rollans, Carol Dragich and Leslie Vermeer at the University of Alberta Press, and Brenda Laishley at the Canadian Forest Service transformed our manuscript, photos, drawings and maps into this beautiful book.

Most of the work for this guide has been done by dedicated volunteers, and more than 100 individuals and organizations have been involved in the rare plants project since its beginning. We hope that this book will help Albertans to learn more about our rare vascular plants, and that it will play a part in conserving the rich diversity of species and habitats in this province.

—Linda Kershaw, Joyce Gould,
Derek Johnson and Jane Lancaster

The word 'rare' sparks the imagination. To many people, it suggests mystery, adventure and great value. If something is rare, it is precious—perhaps even priceless. Rare things may be difficult to find, but are cherished when discovered.

Many rare plants and animals can be discovered in Alberta's wild and not-so-wild places. Some are big and beautiful, but more often the discovery and appreciation of rare wild things depend on your ability to go slowly and look closely.

This book is for anyone interested in learning more about rare plants in Alberta. Teachers, students and natural history enthusiasts can use it to learn more about the wide variety of rare plants in Alberta. Land-use planners, foresters, environmental consultants and researchers can determine which rare species to expect in different habitats or regions, and how to identify these plants during fieldwork.

PL

Montia linearis

Rare Plants in Alberta

Approximately 30 percent (about 485 species) of Alberta's native vascular plants are classified as rare in the province. Similarly, recent work on bryophytes has shown that approximately 25 percent of the moss flora is rare (Vitt and Belland 1996). Of the rare vascular species, approximately 268 (55 percent) are restricted to an area of less than 3 percent of the province, and less than 10 percent of the province supports approximately 153 (31 percent) of Alberta's rare plants. The Waterton–Crowsnest area in southwestern Alberta has by far the highest concentration of rare vascular plants in the province. Other areas with large numbers of rare species include the northern Rocky Mountains (Jasper National Park, Cardinal Divide and north) and parts of extreme southeastern Alberta.

Many factors determine the distribution of rare species. Some rare Alberta species may have developed or persisted as isolated populations. The flora of Alberta is young. Much of this province was covered by a massive ice sheet 15,000 to 16,000 years ago. Most species that survived glaciation moved south in advance of the ice sheet, and when the ice sheet finally retreated, they moved north again. However, some species were able to persist in small areas (refugia) that were not covered by ice. Refugia have been identified along the Front Range of the Rocky Mountains and in the Cypress Hills. It is difficult to determine which species survived in these areas and how important these populations were to re-colonization, but genetic research may eventually provide some of this information.

JG

Adenocaulon bicolor

DG

Carex pseudocyperus

As new areas are explored, new species are discovered. In fact, 31 species of vascular plants that are new to Alberta have been discovered since the publication of the second edition of the *Flora of Alberta* (Moss 1983). These species are listed in Appendix Three. Many recently discovered species—and many rare species in general—are small, ephemeral plants that either grow inconspicuously for most of the year or grow in rarely visited habitats (high on mountains or in the middle of ponds, for example). As more of these sites are studied, more plants are located, and we may learn that some species are not as rare as we now think they are. Other species are new to the flora because of recent taxonomic revisions. These species are also listed in Appendix Three. For example, western false-asphodel (*Triantha occidentalis* ssp. *brevistyla* and ssp. *montana*, p. 44) has recently been reclassified as a species separate from sticky false asphodel (*Triantha glutinosa*) (Packer 1993), and Siberian polypody (*Polypodium sibiricum*) has been split from rock polypody (*Polypodium virginianum*, p. 370) (Haufler et al. 1991).

Plants may be rare because of one or more factors in a myriad of variables that affect geographic range, habitat specificity and population size (Rabinowitz 1981). Changes in both biotic (living) and abiotic (non-living) factors affect plant populations. Biotic changes might involve the introduction of aggressive non-native species that out-compete local native plants. Abiotic changes may include alteration of drainage patterns or fluctuations in climate. Both direct and indirect effects can contribute to species rarity. For example, changes in nearby habitats may have no obvious, direct impact on a rare species, but if they result in the loss of the insects that pollinate the plant's flowers, they can have a devastating, though less obvious, effect.

Many human activities can contribute to species' rarity. Agricultural and urban expansion, roads, mining, oil and gas development, long-term fire suppression, global warming and stabilization of sand dunes and surface water levels are all examples of human activities that could cause some plants to become rare. Plant populations may also decline as a result of over-collecting. In some cultures, a plant may be considered valuable, and therefore a target for collection, simply because it is rare. A recent study in the United States found that up to ten percent of the rare species in that country were rare because of collecting (Schemske et al. 1994). Fortunately, over-collecting does not yet appear to be a serious problem in Alberta, but it does introduce some important questions about the use and sharing of rare species information.

LA

Spergularia salina

Types of Rare Plants

Most of Alberta's rare vascular plants are 'peripherals'—that is, species at the edge of their geographic range. The North American distribution maps featured with each species account show which species are widespread outside of Alberta. Increasing evidence suggests that peripheral populations are often genetically different from those at the centre of a species' range. This genetic diversity can be important in enabling a species to adapt to change. Soapweed (*Yucca glauca*) and western blue flag (*Iris missouriensis*) are examples of peripheral species.

Species that are restricted to a particular geographic area are called 'endemics.' Alberta and its immediate region have only a few local endemics. For example, dwarf alpine poppy (*Papaver pygmaeum*) is known only from northern Montana, southeastern British Columbia and southwestern Alberta. Some very dynamic habitats, such as the Athabasca sand dunes, support rapidly evolving taxa. For example, sand-dune chickweed (*Stellaria arenicola*) evolved recently from the common species long-stalked chickweed (*Stellaria longipes*) (Purdy et al. 1994).

Some rare Alberta species are 'disjuncts'—that is, populations separated from the main range of their species by 500 km or more. Wood anemone (*Anemone quinquefolia*) is a good example of an Alberta disjunct. Here, it is known only from near Nordegg, and the nearest population to this is in east-central Saskatchewan.

DJ

Papaver radicatum

A few of Alberta's rare vascular plants have widespread distributions within North America but are uncommon wherever they are found. Bog adder's-mouth (*Malaxis paludosa*) is an example of this type of rare plant.

To monitor and manage rare species successfully, we must understand both the biology of the species and the reasons for its rarity. For example, genetically variable (plastic) plants, such as those found in some peripheral populations, may be able to adapt to new environments, whereas plants with less variability (e.g., some disjunct or endemic populations) may be unable to survive seemingly minor changes in their specific habitats.

PL

Draba macounii

Lists of Rare Plants

In 1978, Argus and White produced the first publication on rare Alberta plants: *The Rare Vascular Plants of Alberta*. This listed 350 species (approximately 20 percent of the known vascular flora) as rare, and defined a rare plant as 'one with a small population size within the province or territory.' In 1984, Packer and Bradley published *A Checklist of the Rare Vascular Plants in Alberta*, which included 360 species. They considered a species rare if it had been collected in five or fewer localities in the province. Argus and Pryer (1990) used these lists, and similar publications from other jurisdictions, to assess rarity on a national basis in *Rare Vascular Plants in Canada*. This nation-wide list classified 125 Alberta species (about 7 percent of the province's vascular flora) as nationally rare.

Lists of rare species are constantly being revised and updated. Additional collections may show that a plant is too common or widespread to be classified as rare. Taxonomic revisions may result in the 'lumping' of two or more species, which together are too widespread to be considered rare. Field surveys and re-identification of plant collections may show that a plant was misidentified and that a species was thus falsely reported.

There are many differences between the list of rare species included in this book and lists from other publications. Appendix Four (Taxa previously reported as rare for Alberta but not included in this book) and Appendix Five (Species reported from or expected to occur in Alberta but not yet verified) address some of these discrepancies.

In 1996, Alberta joined the Nature Conservancy network of Conservation Data Centres (known as Natural Heritage Programs in the United States). Each centre or program assesses species rarity using number of occurrences and population size as the main criteria. Status is assessed using the following system of classification.

The Nature Conservancy Element Ranks

Species (and sometimes other taxa such as varieties and subspecies) are ranked using the following numbers and letters. Each number or letter is preceded by either a G for global rank or S for subnational (provincial or state) rank.

1 — 5 or fewer occurrences and with low population size

2 — 6–20 occurrences or with low population size

3 — 21–100 occurrences

4 — apparently secure, >100 occurrences

5 — abundant and demonstrably secure, >100 occurrences

F — falsely reported

H — known historically, may be rediscovered

P — potentially present, expected in the province or state but not yet discovered

Q — questionable taxonomic rank

R — reported but without documentation for either accepting or rejecting the report

U — status uncertain, more information needed

X — apparently extinct or extirpated, not expected to be rediscovered

? — no information available, or the number of occurrences estimated

LK

Sagina nivalis

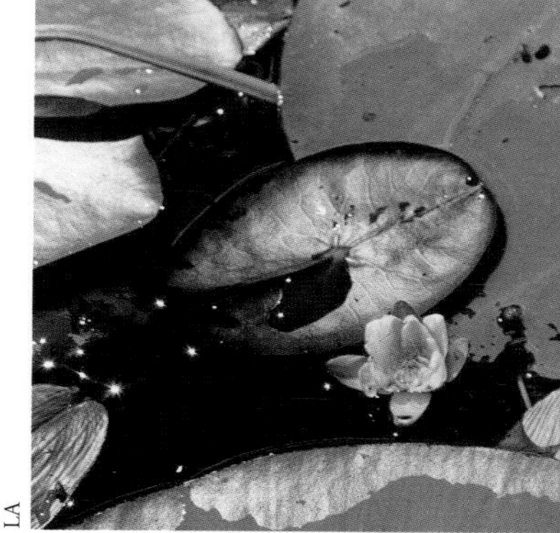

LA

Nymphaea leibergii

Because each conservation data centre uses the same criteria to determine rarity, results can be pooled to assess status at subnational, national and global levels. Many of Alberta's rare vascular plants are considered globally abundant and are common in adjacent provinces and states. For example, soapweed (*Yucca glauca*) is ranked S1 in Alberta, because it is known from fewer than six locations, and because these are the only Canadian sites, it is ranked N1 in Canada. However, soapweed is common from Montana south, and therefore it has a global ranking of G5. The populations in this province are important components of the flora and overall biodiversity of both Alberta and Canada, and are worthy of conservation.

This guide includes taxa that have a ranking of S1 to S3, species that are reported from or otherwise expected in the province, and species that are considered extirpated from the province. The numbers of taxa in each group are as follows: S1, 211 species; S1?, 2 species; S1S2, 25 species; S2, 186 species; S2?, 1 species; S2S3. 13 species; S3, 26 species; SH, 4 species; SRF, 4 species; SU, 14 species; SX, 1 species;

DJ

Diphasiastrum sitchense

S?, 1 species. Appendix Two lists all of the rare species included in this book, the natural regions in which they are found and their provincial ranking.

Conservation of Rare Plants

Biological variation (biodiversity) can be viewed at many different levels, from broad landscapes to specific habitats, local communities and even the genetic variation within a single species. Variability within a species is usually assessed on the basis of differences in form, but unseen changes in genetic make-up from one plant to the next are equally important. It is essential to consider diversity at all levels to conserve Alberta's natural biodiversity.

Management activities have traditionally focussed on individual species, but other levels of biodiversity (e.g., landscape, community and habitat) are increasingly being taken into consideration. No species lives in isolation. Most rare plants reflect the presence of rare habitats, where other organisms may be equally or even more threatened. The distribution of small plants and animals in Alberta is largely unknown. We cannot monitor, let alone understand the specific requirements of, every species. However, the recognition of rare species may help to identify threatened habitats that should be given special attention. Conservation of habitat through good land-stewardship is the most effective and efficient way to ensure the long-term protection of species.

Legislation and policy at both federal and provincial levels can provide protection for plants. At the provincial level, Alberta's endangered species are now included in an amendment to the Wildlife Act. The minister responsible for the act may designate a plant to an endangered species list. If designated, a plant would enjoy protection under the endangered classification of this act. The Endangered Species Conservation Committee and Scientific Subcommittee have been established to evaluate the status of species that may be at risk in Alberta, to list those that are threatened or endangered, and to advise the Alberta minister of environmental protection on appropriate legal designation and protection in the Wildlife Act. The committees will also facilitate the planning and implementation of recovery programs for species at risk. Other legislation that may be used to protect plants include the Historical Resources Act, Public Lands Act, Provincial Parks Act, National Parks Act and Wilderness Areas, Ecological Reserves and Natural

Areas Act. There is no federal endangered species legislation at this time.

Several plants that are rare in Alberta have been listed as vulnerable, threatened or endangered by the Committee on the Status of Endangered Wildlife in Canada (COSEWIC). COSEWIC has representatives from the federal and provincial governments and from selected non-government organizations. This committee determines the national status of plants and animals in Canada on the basis of scientific data summarized in a status report. Such information is invaluable for the management of sites and species, but the listing of a species by COSEWIC has no tie to legislation.

JG
Brasenia schreberi

Rare Plant Surveys

Rare plant surveys document the occurrence of rare species in a given area, both through literature and through field surveys. The first step in conducting a rare plant survey is to gather existing rare plant information for the area. Lists of rare species that are known to occur in specific regions are available from the Alberta Natural Heritage Information Centre (ANHIC). Other sources of information—such as local naturalists, distribution maps and published reports—should also be reviewed to determine rare species potentially in the area. Flowering and fruiting dates and ecological information pertaining to these species should be collected wherever possible to assist in determining appropriate timing for the survey and potentially significant habitats that may require more intensive study; herbarium labels, published literature and local naturalists are valuable sources for this type of information. If significant habitats in the study area are known, these should be located on aerial photographs and topographic maps. Interpretation of photos and maps may also identify other potentially significant habitats.

LA
Romanzoffia sitchensis

Rare plant field surveys should be conducted in a full range of habitats at several times of year (spanning the growing season). Ideally, sites should be surveyed over a number of growing seasons to take biological and climatic fluctuations into consideration. For example, some species do not produce stems or leaves, let alone flowers, in dry years, so they are difficult to find and identify during droughts. Other factors, such as grazing and insect predation, can reduce vigour and visibility in some years but not in others. Lack of discovery does not necessarily mean that a species is absent.

JG

Cypripedium acaule

Both 'random' and 'directed' surveys (including intensive hands-and-knees ground surveys in potential significant habitats) can be done, but most field time should be devoted to directed surveys. Random surveys are generally used to determine the rare-plant potential of major habitat types. They typically involve inspecting all species within a randomly selected, 1-m wide, 250- to 500-m straight-line transect across a habitat type. The spacing of these transects depends on the density of the vegetation cover, the visibility through it and the size of the plants in it. Directed surveys are tailored to the habitat being surveyed. They use a meandering pattern to sample specific microhabitats in habitats with high rare-plant potential. In some wetlands, this may involve seeking out small hummocks and areas of standing water or exposed mud, while in others it may focus on the interface between the wetland and the adjacent woodland. Hands-and-knees ground surveys are used along random and directed survey routes in high-potential microhabitats. They involve close examination of ground cover and parting the vegetation to inspect all plants, including small, less conspicuous species.

When we document rare species, the location, habitat, plant community, aspect, slope, relative abundance, soil type, texture, drainage and date should be recorded as precisely as possible. Any additional information on phenology, vigour, size or age classes, and factors affecting the plants such as moisture conditions, competition, insect pests, current land use, grazing pressure and other threats should also be recorded if possible. A map showing the detailed location and extent of the population is extremely valuable for relocating the population. A photograph of the plant and its distinguishing characteristics is an essential part of this documentation. Collection of rare plants is discouraged but may be necessary in order to confirm the identification of plants in some of the more difficult groups. A specimen should be taken only when more than twenty individual plants can be seen at the site *and* the proper permit has been obtained (where applicable). Collections should always be filed in a recognized herbarium (e.g., University of Alberta Herbarium, University of Calgary Herbarium or Canadian Forest Service Herbarium) so that they are available for study by others. In some cases, it may be necessary to bring a taxonomic expert into the field to confirm an identification.

ANHIC collects information related to the location, phenology, population size and biology of rare and uncommon species. It also tracks changes in species status (e.g., new sites) and taxonomy (e.g., name changes as a result of reclassification). New sightings should be always reported to ANHIC. A Rare Native Plant Report Form (Appendix Seven) should be completed and submitted whenever a rare plant is sighted. This information will then be added to the central data bank and used to update species status and distribution. The latest rare species list (known as the tracking list) is available from ANHIC, care of Alberta Environmental Protection (Second Floor, 9820–106 Street, Edmonton, Alberta T5K 2C6, 780-427-5209).

Two publications from the California Native Plant Society (Nelson 1984, 1987) discuss how to carry out rare plant surveys, and the Alberta Native Plant Council (ANPC) has also produced a set of guidelines (ANPC 1997). These publications provide more detailed descriptions of rare plant surveys.

JP

Ranunculus occidentalis

How You Can Help

There are many ways that we can contribute to the conservation of rare plants in Alberta. A valuable first step is to learn more about these unusual species and their habitats, and to share this information with others. This increases our appreciation of Alberta's wild plants and encourages the land-stewardship practices that accommodate the conservation of rare species. We can often accomplish more as a group than we could on our own, and it can be fun to share ideas and experiences with others. Groups such as the ANPC and the Federation of Alberta Naturalists play important roles in the conservation of biodiversity in Alberta. Their activities often increase public awareness of threatened species and habitats. They also share an appreciation of the beauty and importance of natural systems through talks, papers, field trips and books.

JG

Arabis lemmonii

About the ANPC

The ANPC is an active group of volunteers striving to promote knowledge of Alberta's native plants and to conserve these plants and their habitats. Members include people from all walks of life: from naturalists, gardeners and students to teachers, ecologists and botanists. There are four main action committees. The Education and Information Committee organizes field trips, courses and speakers' programs. The Rare Species Committee gathers information on rare Alberta species and, most recently, has compiled

DJ

Pedicularis flammea

this book. The Reclamation and Horticulture Committee sets out guidelines for collecting and planting native species, provides information on reclamation and produces lists of suppliers of native seed and nursery stock. The Conservation Action Committee increases public awareness and approaches industry and government agencies regarding pressing environmental issues, provides stewardship for protected areas, and monitors habitats affected by development. If you would like more information about our group, write to us.

Alberta Native Plant Council
Box 52099, Garneau Postal Outlet
Edmonton, Alberta T6G 2T5

Natural Regions of Alberta

Alberta is a large, diverse province. It encompasses 662,948 km^2, from the Northwest Territories in the north (60°N) to the United States in the south (49°N), and from the heights of the Continental Divide in the Rocky Mountains in the west to the rolling prairies and boreal forest in the east. This broad area encompasses six natural regions and twenty subregions, each with a distinctive combination of physical features (climate, geology, soils, hydrology) and biological features (plant and animal species, vegetation communities). A vast patchwork of habitats supports approximately 1,800 species of vascular plants, 600 species of mosses and 650 species of lichens, along with untold numbers of fungi.

The distinguishing features of each natural region and subregion are described below, along with notes about some of the rare plants. Many rare species occur in more than one natural region. Appendix Two provides a complete list of rare species and their natural regions.

Canadian Shield Natural Region

The Canadian Shield extends into the far northeastern corner of Alberta and contains two quite different subregions. The Kazan Upland Subregion, north of Lake Athabasca, is characterized by exposed, glaciated Canadian Shield bedrock. The Athabasca Plain Subregion includes part of the north shore of Lake Athabasca and an area south of Lake Athabasca where shallow glacial outwash deposits cover Canadian Shield bedrock.

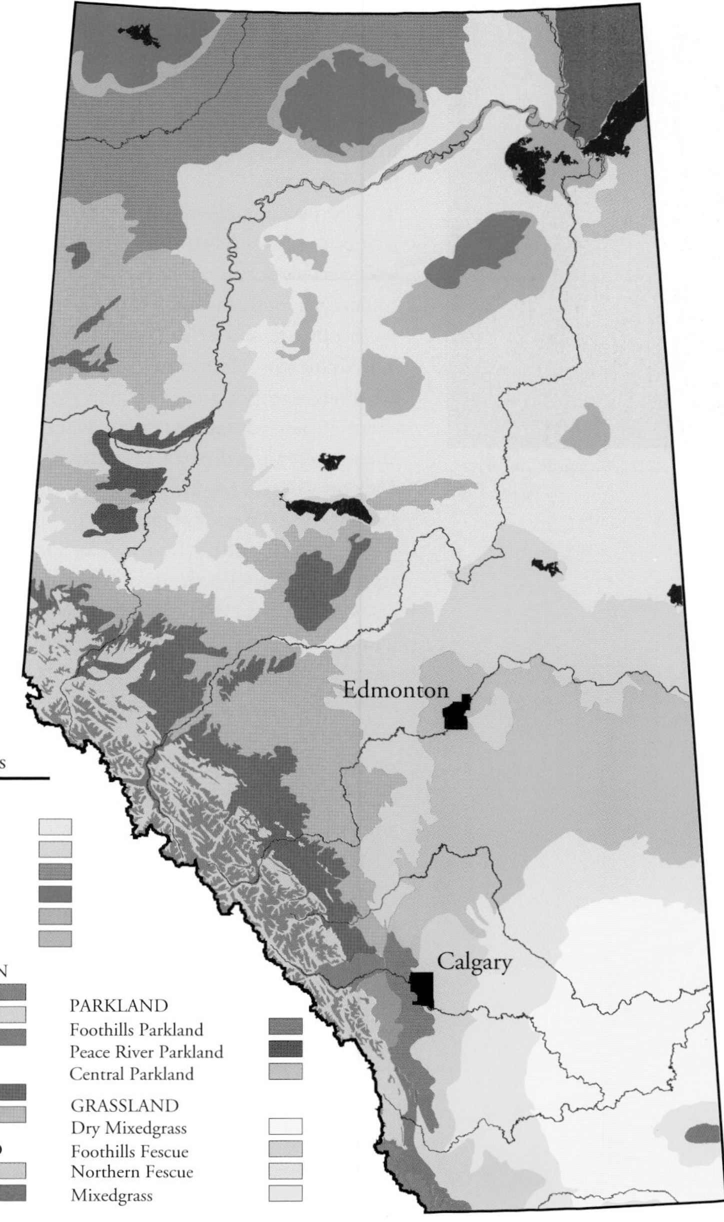

Natural Subregions

BOREAL FOREST
Central Mixedwood
Dry Mixedwood
Wetland Mixedwood
Sub-Arctic
Peace River Lowlands
Boreal Highlands

ROCKY MOUNTAIN
Alpine
Subalpine
Montane

FOOTHILLS
Upper Foothills
Lower Foothills

CANADIAN SHIELD
Athabasca Plain
Kazan Upland

PARKLAND
Foothills Parkland
Peace River Parkland
Central Parkland

GRASSLAND
Dry Mixedgrass
Foothills Fescue
Northern Fescue
Mixedgrass

AL

Kazan Upland Subregion at Wylie Lake

Kazan Upland Subregion

Extensive outcrops of acidic bedrock and scattered patches of glacial deposits determine the vegetation pattern in this area. Much of the rolling terrain has either exposed bedrock or too little weathered material over the bedrock to qualify as soil. Organic soils and permafrost occur in low, wet areas.

The upland vegetation is a mosaic of barren rock, open jack pine (*Pinus banksiana*) forests on sand plains and rocky hills, and black spruce (*Picea mariana*) stands in wet peatlands (muskegs). Jack pine forests are most widespread, especially in the northeast, and often contain aspen (*Populus tremuloides*). The understorey on sandy sites is quite simple, and lichens are often as important as vascular plants. The forests of rocky sites typically contain jack pine, black spruce and white birch (*Betula papyrifera*), with saskatoon (*Amelanchier alnifolia*), common bearberry (*Arctostaphylos uva-ursi*), three-toothed saxifrage (*Saxifraga tricuspidata*), pasture sagewort (*Artemisia frigida*) and reindeer lichen (*Cladina mitis*) in the understorey. On deeper soils, forests of jack pine, white birch and black spruce have more diverse understoreys, with green alder (*Alnus viridis* ssp. *crispa*), bog cranberry (*Vaccinium vitis-idaea*), common bearberry, common blueberry (*Vaccinium myrtilloides*), lesser rattlesnake plantain (*Goodyera repens*), crowberry (*Empetrum nigrum*), bunchberry (*Cornus canadensis*), common Labrador tea (*Ledum groenlandicum*), reindeer lichens (*Cladina mitis, C. rangiferina* and *C. stellaris*) and snow lichen (*Cetraria nivalis*).

Low areas support peatlands. These are mainly acidic, mineral-poor bogs dominated by black spruce, common Labrador tea, reindeer lichens and peat mosses (*Sphagnum* spp.). Fens (mineral-rich peatlands) are rare because of the acidic bedrock and soils.

Athabasca Plain Subregion

This broad, flat subregion is covered predominantly by water- and wind-deposited materials in the eastern part and by glacial deposits in the west. Most deposits are derived from Athabasca sandstone, and there are extensive sandy beaches along Lake Athabasca. Distinctive landscape features include large areas of kame deposits and active dunes. The kames, at over 60 m in height, are among the largest in the world, and the active dune system is the largest in Alberta.

Flag Person
Fort Saskatwan
780-998-2266

1856

604 691 0250
Alison

Extensive jack pine forests cover the sandy uplands, sometimes co-dominant with white spruce (*Picea glauca*). Typical understorey species include common bearberry and reindeer lichens on dry sites, and common blueberry and feathermosses (stair-step moss [*Hylocomium splendens*] and Schreber's moss [*Pleurozium schreberi*]) on moister sites. Open, 'park-like' white spruce forests occur along the shore of Lake Athabasca.

Peatlands range from dry bogs, dominated by black spruce, common Labrador tea and reindeer lichens, to wetter peatlands with black spruce, tamarack (*Larix laricina*), common Labrador tea and peat mosses. Shrubby peatlands typically contain common Labrador tea, northern laurel (*Kalmia polifolia*), water sedge (*Carex aquatilis*), reed grasses (*Calamagrostis* spp.) and peat mosses.

PLe

Dunes in the Athabasca Plain

Rare Plants

About 30 rare species (6 percent of Alberta's rare vascular plants) occur in the Canadian Shield Natural Region; of these, 7 are restricted to this region in Alberta. Several grow on sand dunes along Lake Athabasca and farther south in the Athabasca Plain Subregion. These include American dune grass (*Leymus mollis*), Indian tansy (*Tanacetum bipinnatum* ssp. *huronense*) and sand-dune chickweed (*Stellaria arenicola*). Other notable species from this region include horned bladderwort (*Utricularia cornuta*), Greenland wood-rush (*Luzula groenlandica*) and stemless lady's-slipper (*Cypripedium acaule*).

Boreal Forest Natural Region

The Boreal Forest constitutes the largest natural region in Alberta. It covers broad lowland plains and discontinuous hill systems where the bedrock is deeply buried by glacial deposits or, along major rivers, by fluvial deposits. This vast, diverse region is divided into six subregions—Dry Mixedwood, Central Mixedwood, Wetland Mixedwood, Boreal Highlands, Peace River Lowlands, and Subarctic—distinguished by differences in vegetation, geology and landform, but many of the changes from one subregion to the next are gradual and subtle.

SM

Dry Mixedwood habitat at Heart River

PLe

Wetland Mixedwood habitat at McClelland Lake

Dry Mixedwood, Central Mixedwood, Wetland Mixedwood and Boreal Highlands Subregions

These four subregions have similar vegetation. Aspen (*Populus tremuloides*) is widespread, in both pure and mixed stands, and balsam poplar (*Populus balsamifera*) often grows with aspen in moister areas. With time, white spruce (*Picea glauca*) or balsam fir (*Abies balsamea*) gradually replace the aspen and balsam poplar, but frequent fires seldom permit this progression. Pure deciduous stands are common in the southern part of the Dry Mixedwood Subregion, and mixed stands of aspen and white spruce are widespread farther north.

Mixedwood forests contain a mosaic of deciduous and coniferous stands, with species typical of each. The diverse understoreys of upland aspen forests commonly include low-bush cranberry (*Viburnum edule*), beaked hazelnut (*Corylus cornuta*), prickly rose (*Rosa acicularis*), red-osier dogwood (*Cornus sericea*), bluejoint (*Calamagrostis canadensis*), wild sarsaparilla (*Aralia nudicaulis*), dewberry (*Rubus pubescens*), cream-coloured vetchling (*Lathyrus ochroleucus*), common pink wintergreen (*Pyrola asarifolia*) and twinflower (*Linnaea borealis*). Both balsam poplar and white birch (*Betula papyrifera*) also grow in these forests. Spruce and spruce-fir forests are not common, and they generally have a less diverse understorey with large patches or carpets of feathermosses including stair-step moss (*Hylocomium splendens*), Schreber's moss (*Pleurozium schreberi*) and knight's plume moss (*Ptilium crista-castrensis*).

Dry, sandy sites usually support open jack pine (*Pinus banksiana*) forests with a prominent carpet of lichens. Common understorey species include common bearberry (*Arctostaphylos uva-ursi*), common blueberry (*Vaccinium myrtilloides*), bog cranberry (*Vaccinium vitis-idaea*) and prickly rose.

Peatlands occur throughout the six subregions, but they are most extensive in the Wetland Mixedwood Subregion. Peatland complexes typically contain both mineral-poor, acidic bogs—dominated by black spruce (*Picea mariana*), common Labrador tea (*Ledum groenlandicum*) and peat mosses (*Sphagnum* spp.)—and mineral-rich fens—featuring tamarack (*Larix laricina*), dwarf birches (*Betula* spp.), sedges (*Carex* spp.), tufted moss (*Aulacomnium palustre*), golden moss (*Tomenthypnum nitens*) and brown mosses (*Drepanocladus* spp.).

Climate and vegetation vary slightly from one subregion to the next. The Dry Mixedwood Subregion has a drier, warmer climate than the other Boreal Forest subregions. Its vegetation is transitional between the Central Parkland (Parkland Natural Region) and Central Mixedwood subregions, with pure aspen forests being more common and peatlands (muskegs) being less extensive. The Central Mixedwood Subregion has a slightly cooler, moister climate than the Dry Mixedwood Subregion. Mixedwood and white spruce forest and peatlands are more common than in the Dry Mixedwood Subregion, and white birch is widespread, forming nearly pure stands in some areas. The Wetland Mixedwood Subregion is characterized by a greater proportion of wetlands, including peatlands, willow-sedge complexes (on mineral soil) and upland black spruce forests. Permafrost occurs in many peatlands in this relatively flat, moist, cool region. The Boreal Highlands Subregion includes rolling uplands and steep slopes on hill masses and plateaus in the Central Mixedwood and Wetland Mixedwood subregions. It has a relatively cool, moist climate (especially during the summer), and permafrost is common. Balsam poplar, white spruce and black spruce are more common than in the mixedwood subregions, with coniferous forests covering much of the landscape.

CWa

Boreal Highlands habitat in the Cameron Hills

Peace River Lowlands Subregion

This subregion encompasses terraces and deltas along the lower Peace, Birch and Athabasca rivers, including the Peace-Athabasca Delta, which is one of the largest freshwater deltas in the world. Fluvial processes and landforms are most important in this area.

White spruce forests with large trees (16–23 m tall) are characteristic of moist to wet river terraces, but little remains of these very productive forests, because of heavy logging. Drier upland sites typically support jack pine forests with understoreys of green alder (*Alnus viridis* ssp. *crispa*), bog cranberry, reindeer lichen (*Cladina* spp.) and feathermosses. Mixedwood forests of aspen, balsam poplar and white spruce occupy mesic upland sites. Non-forested communities include a complex mosaic of aquatic, shoreline, meadow, shrub and marsh vegetation, maintained in large part by periodic erosion and deposition of river sediments, especially in the Peace-Athabasca Delta area.

AL

Peace River Lowlands habitat

The Caribou Mountains in the Subarctic Subregion

Subarctic Subregion

The Subarctic Subregion occurs on the Birch Mountains, Caribou Mountains and Cameron Hills, all of which are erosional remnants rising above the surrounding plain as flat-topped hills. Peat deposits and permafrost are widespread, with occasional deposits of glacial till. The climate is cold, and the 45-day frost-free period is about half that of the mixedwood subregions. Open black spruce forest dominates the landscape, with an understorey of common Labrador tea, northern Labrador tea (*Ledum palustre*), cloudberry (*Rubus chamaemorus*), bog cranberry, peat mosses and reindeer lichens. Fires have resulted in large areas of heath shrub and lichen vegetation with scattered, young black spruce. Upland sites with mineral soil typically support black spruce, white spruce–aspen and white spruce–white birch forests. Stands of black spruce with lodgepole pine (*Pinus contorta*) (jack pine in the Birch Mountains) also occur in small areas with warmer, drier sites.

Rare Plants

More than 110 rare species (about 25 percent of Alberta's rare vascular plants) occur in the Boreal Forest Natural Region, and about 20 of these are found in this natural region only. Several species in the Subarctic Subregion have their main range to the north; these include Russian ground-cone (*Boschniakia rossica*), bog bilberry (*Vaccinium uliginosum*), polar grass (*Arctagrostis arundinacea*) and purple rattle (*Pedicularis sudetica*). Another group of rare boreal species is associated with saline or alkaline soils, such as those of the 'Salt Plains' in northern Wood Buffalo National Park; these include sea-side plantain (*Plantago maritima*) and mouse-ear cress (*Arabidopsis salsuginea*). These habitats also contain disjunct populations of species that are common in southern Alberta, such as green needle grass (*Stipa viridula*), needle-and-thread (*Stipa comata*), wild bergamot (*Monarda fistulosa*), purple reed grass (*Calamagrostis purpurascens*) and prairie sagewort (*Artemisia ludoviciana*). Other notable rare plants in this region include white adder's-mouth (*Malaxis monophylla* var. *brachypoda*), bog adder's-mouth (*Malaxis paludosa*), pitcher-plant (*Sarracenia purpurea*), northern slender ladies'-tresses (*Spiranthes lacera*) and water lobelia (*Lobelia dortmanna*).

Rocky Mountain Natural Region

The Rocky Mountain Natural Region is part of a major geological uplift that trends along the western part of Alberta forming the Continental Divide. It is distinguished from the Foothills Natural Region by its geology. The Rocky Mountain Natural Region has upthrust and folded carbonate and quartzitic bedrock, whereas the Foothills Natural Region has mostly deformed sandstone and shale. This is the most rugged natural region in Alberta, and it ranges from about 10 km wide near Waterton Lakes National Park to more than 100 km wide in its central portion. Elevations rise from 1,000 to 1,500 m in the east to 3,700 m along the Continental Divide in the west. The three subregions—Montane, Subalpine and Alpine—reflect environmental differences associated with changes in altitude.

RJ

Montane habitat on the Kootenay Plains

Montane Subregion

South of the Porcupine Hills, this subregion occurs mostly on ridges that extend out from the foothills, but to the north, the Montane Subregion is found mostly along major river valleys, with small, disjunct areas at Ya-Ha-Tinda on the Red Deer River and in the Cypress Hills. Elevations range from 1,000 to 1,350 m in Jasper National Park to more than 1,600 m along the east slopes south of Calgary. Chinooks keep this region intermittently snow-free in the winter. The landscape is covered by a mosaic of open forests and grasslands.

Characteristic montane trees include Douglas-fir (*Pseudotsuga menziesii*), limber pine (*Pinus flexilis*) and white spruce (*Picea glauca*). Typical understorey plants in Douglas-fir forests include pine reed grass (*Calamagrostis rubescens*), hairy wild rye (*Leymus innovatus*), low northern sedge (*Carex concinnoides*), common bearberry (*Arctostaphylos uva-ursi*), junipers (*Juniperus* spp.) and snowberry (*Symphoricarpos albus*). Distinctive species in the Waterton Lakes National Park area include creeping mahonia (*Berberis repens*), mallow-leaved ninebark (*Physocarpus malvaceus*), mountain maple (*Acer glabrum*), purple clematis (*Clematis occidentalis*) and bluebunch wheat grass (*Elymus spicatus*).

Limber pine forms open stands on rock outcrops and eroding slopes. Common understorey species include common bearberry, junipers, bluebunch wheat grass, bluebunch fescue (*Festuca idahoensis*), northern bedstraw (*Galium boreale*), field mouse-ear chickweed (*Cerastium arvense*), crested beardtongue (*Penstemon eriantherus*) and scorpion-

LA

Typical Subalpine habitat

weed (*Phacelia* spp.). Grasslands are typically dominated by bluebunch wheat grass, fescue grasses (*Festuca* spp.) and oat grasses (*Danthonia* spp.) with a variety of forbs. Lodgepole pine (*Pinus contorta*) forests cover many upland areas and are similar to those of the adjacent Subalpine Subregion. White spruce forests occur on mesic sites, especially along stream terraces, and aspen (*Populus tremuloides*) forests typically occupy fluvial fans and terraces.

Subalpine Subregion

This cool, moist subregion lies between the Montane and Alpine subregions in the south (at 1,600 to 2,300 m) and the Upper Foothills (Foothills Natural Region) and Alpine subregions in the north (at 1,350 to 2,000 m). Below-freezing temperatures occur in all months, the frost-free period is usually less than 30 days, and winter precipitation is higher than in any other part of Alberta.

The Subalpine Subregion consists of two portions: the Lower Subalpine, characterized by closed forests of lodgepole pine, Engelmann spruce (*Picea engelmannii*) and subalpine fir (*Abies bifolia*), and the Upper Subalpine, characterized by intermixed open and closed forests. Engelmann spruce–subalpine fir forests typically occur on higher, moister sites. Pure Engelmann spruce is characteristic of high-elevation stands. At lower elevations, spruce trees (often white spruce–Engelmann spruce hybrids) are more common, and burned areas are covered by extensive lodgepole pine forests.

Forests in the Waterton Lakes National Park area support many species that do not occur farther north. These include bear grass (*Xerophyllum tenax*), thimbleberry (*Rubus parviflorus*), mountain wood-rush (*Luzula piperi*), yellow angelica (*Angelica dawsonii*) and mountain-lover (*Pachystima myrsinites*).

Upper Subalpine open forests are transitional to the treeless Alpine Subregion above. Dominant trees include Engelmann spruce, subalpine fir, whitebark pine (*Pinus albicaulis*) and, south of Bow Pass, subalpine larch (*Larix lyallii*). Some forests contain dwarf shrubs that also grow in the Alpine Subregion, including red heather (*Phyllodoce empetriformis*), yellow heather (*Phyllodoce glanduliflora*), white mountain-heather (*Cassiope mertensiana*), grouseberry (*Vaccinium scoparium*) and rock willow (*Salix vestita*).

High-elevation grasslands are mostly found on steep, south- and west-facing slopes in the Front Ranges. Dominant species include hairy wild rye (*Leymus innovatus*), June grass (*Koeleria macrantha*) and common bearberry.

PA

Typical Alpine habitat at Pipestone Pass

Alpine Subregion

The Alpine Subregion includes all areas above treeline, including vegetated slopes, rock fields, snow fields and glaciers; there are extensive areas of unvegetated bedrock. This is the coldest subregion in Alberta, with essentially no frost-free period. Alpine vegetation typically forms a fine-scaled mosaic, in which minor variations in microclimate can produce marked changes in species composition. Significant factors include aspect, wind exposure, time of snow melt, soil moisture and snow depth.

Deep, late-melting snow beds are occupied by black alpine sedge (*Carex nigricans*) communities. Moderate snow-bed communities typically support dwarf-shrub heath tundra, which is dominated by heathers (*Phyllodoce* spp.), mountain-heathers (*Cassiope* spp.) and grouseberry. Common species in shallow snow areas on ridge tops and other exposed sites include white mountain avens (*Dryas octopetala*), snow willow (*Salix reticulata*), moss campion (*Silene acaulis*) and bog-sedge (*Kobresia myosuroides*). Diverse, colourful herb meadows blanket moist sites below melting snowbanks and along streams. Communities at the highest elevations consist mainly of lichens on rocks and shallow soil.

Some floristic differences are apparent south of Crowsnest Pass. Mountain-heathers are absent, heathers are less common than farther north, and bear grass meadows occupy some low-elevation sites.

Rare Plants

More than 300 rare species (about 65 percent of Alberta's rare vascular plants) occur in the Rocky Mountain Natural Region; of these, about 140 are restricted in Alberta to this natural region. More than 25 species grow in the Alpine Subregion and are connected by a series of high-altitude habitats to the Arctic tundra to the north. These 'arctic-alpine' plants include alpine harebell (*Campanula uniflora*), alpine bitter cress (*Cardamine bellidifolia*), seven sedge species (*Carex glacialis, C. haydeniana, C. incurviformis* var. *incurviformis, C. lachenalii, C. misandra, C. petricosa* and *C. podocarpa*), alpine mouse-ear chickweed (*Cerastium beeringianum*), alpine gentian (*Gentiana glauca*), alpine alumroot (*Heuchera glabra*), alpine sweetgrass (*Anthoxanthum monticola*), koenigia (*Koenigia islandica*), arctic lousewort (*Pedicularis langsdorfii*), woolly lousewort (*Pedicularis lanata*), hairy cinquefoil (*Potentilla villosa*) and snow buttercup (*Ranunculus nivalis*).

AL

Lower Foothills habitat at Running Lake

The mountains of southwestern Alberta, especially in the Waterton Lakes National Park and Castle River areas, contain many species that are not found farther north in Alberta. These include Jones' columbine (*Aquilegia jonesii*), big sagebrush (*Artemisia tridentata*), large-flowered brickellia (*Brickellia grandiflora*), mountain hollyhock (*Iliamna rivularis*), bitter-root (*Lewisia rediviva*), dwarf bitter-root (*Lewisia pygmaea*), biscuit-root (*Lomatium cous*), Brewer's monkeyflower (*Mimulus breweri*), small yellow monkey-flower (*Mimulus floribundus*), dwarf alpine poppy (*Papaver pygmaeum*), Lewis' mock-orange (*Philadelphus lewisii*), mallow-leaved ninebark (*Physocarpus malvaceus*), pink meadowsweet (*Spiraea splendens*), western yew (*Taxus brevifolia*) and western wakerobin (*Trillium ovatum*). This area is also a continental 'hot spot' for rare species of grape fern (*Botrychium* spp.), with eight species currently known from this area, including the Waterton moonwort (*Botrychium* x *watertonense*), which is endemic to Waterton Lakes National Park. Front-range fleabane (*Erigeron lackschewitzii*) and mountain dwarf primrose (*Douglasia montana*) are found in Canada only in Waterton Lakes National Park.

Another group of rare mountain species extends into western Alberta from moister areas in BC. These include oval-leaved blueberry (*Vaccinium ovalifolium*), spreading stonecrop (*Sedum divergens*), western red cedar (*Thuja plicata*), western hemlock (*Tsuga heterophylla*) and western larch (*Larix occidentalis*).

Foothills Natural Region

The Foothills Natural Region is transitional between the Rocky Mountains and Boreal Forest natural regions. It consists of two subregions: Lower Foothills and Upper Foothills.

Lower Foothills Subregion

The Lower Foothills Subregion includes rolling hills created by deformed bedrock along the edge of the Rocky Mountains and flat-topped erosional remnants, such as the Swan Hills. Although it is cooler in summer than the adjacent, lower Boreal Forest subregions, it is warmer in winter because it is less affected by cold arctic air masses. Mixed forests of white spruce (*Picea glauca*), black spruce (*Picea mariana*), lodgepole pine (*Pinus contorta*), balsam fir (*Abies balsamea*), aspen (*Populus tremuloides*), white birch (*Betula papyrifera*) and balsam poplar (*Populus balsamifera*) dominate, with lodgepole pine stands indicating the lower boundary (adjacent to the Boreal Forest) and the nearly pure coniferous forests (without aspen, balsam poplar or birch) of the Upper Foothills indicating the upper boundary. Hybrids of lodgepole pine, a mountain species, and jack pine (*Pinus banksiana*), a boreal species, occur along the eastern boundary and at lower elevations.

Lodgepole pine forests dominate in the upland, especially after fire, with common understorey species including Canada buffaloberry (*Shepherdia canadensis*), white meadowsweet (*Spiraea betulifolia*), junipers (*Juniperus* spp.), common bearberry (*Arctostaphylos uva-ursi*) and common blueberry (*Vaccinium myrtilloides*). On more mesic sites, white spruce and aspen are more frequent and understoreys are more diverse, including prickly rose (*Rosa acicularis*), common Labrador tea (*Ledum groenlandicum*), bunchberry (*Cornus canadensis*), twinflower (*Linnaea borealis*), common fireweed (*Epilobium angustifolium*), bog cranberry (*Vaccinium vitis-idaea*) and feathermosses (stair-step moss [*Hylocomium splendens*], Schreber's moss [*Pleurozium schreberi*] and knight's plume moss [*Ptilium crista-castrensis*]).

Black spruce forests occupy wet organic soils (muskegs) and some moist upland sites, with typical understorey species including common Labrador tea, dwarf birch (*Betula* spp.), bracted honeysuckle (*Lonicera involucrata*), horsetails (*Equisetum* spp.), bishop's-cap (*Mitella nuda*), twinflower, peat mosses (*Sphagnum* spp.), tufted moss (*Aulacomnium palustre*) and golden moss (*Tomenthypnum nitens*). Fens, both patterned and unpatterned, are common, with dwarf birch, common Labrador tea, willow (*Salix* spp.), sedges (*Carex* spp.), buck-bean (*Menyanthes trifoliata*), rough hair grass (*Agrostis scabra*), tufted moss, golden moss, peat mosses, and scattered black spruce and tamarack (*Larix laricina*).

AL

Upper Foothills habitat at Switzer Provincial Park

Upper Foothills Subregion

The subregion generally lies between the Lower Foothills and Subalpine (Rocky Mountain Natural Region) subregions on strongly rolling hills along the eastern edge of the Rocky Mountains and in the Swan Hills and Clear Hills. It has the highest summer precipitation in Alberta. Its winters are colder than those of the Lower Foothills Subregion, but are similarly less affected by cold Arctic air masses.

Upland forests of the Upper Foothills Subregion are dominated by white spruce, black spruce, lodgepole pine and, occasionally, subalpine fir (*Abies bifolia*). Hybrids between white spruce and Engelmann spruce (*Picea glauca–*

CWa

Central Parkland habitat at Rumsey

P. engelmannii) and between subalpine fir and balsam fir (*Abies bifolia–A. balsamea*) are sometimes found. The understorey resembles that of a lodgepole pine forest, with a well-developed carpet of feathermosses (stair-step moss, Schreber's moss and knight's plume moss) in older stands.

Black spruce dominates wet sites with organic or mineral soils. Typical understorey species include common Labrador tea, dwarf birch, bracted honeysuckle, horsetails, bishop's cap, twinflower, peat mosses, tufted moss and golden moss.

Rare Plants

Roughly 80 rare species (about 18 percent of Alberta's rare vascular plants) occur in the Foothills Natural Region. Only four of these (wood anemone [*Anemone quinquefolia*], northern oak fern [*Gymnocarpium jessoense*], western white lettuce [*Prenanthes alata*] and small twisted-stalk [*Streptopus streptopoides*]) are restricted in Alberta to this natural region, reflecting the transitional nature of the Foothills Natural Region. Many of its rare species also occur in the Rocky Mountain and Boreal Forest natural regions. Some rare species of interest include goldthread (*Coptis trifolia*), northern beech fern (*Phegopteris connectilis*) and rose mandarin (*Streptopus roseus*).

Parkland Natural Region

The Parkland Natural Region (with the exception of the Peace River Parkland Subregion) forms a broad transition between the grasslands of the plains and the coniferous forests of the Boreal Forest and Rocky Mountain natural regions. This region is found only in the prairie provinces of Canada, except for a few small tongues that extend into the northern United States. Its three subregions—Central Parkland, Foothills Parkland and Peace River Parkland—are distinguished by location, soil and vegetation.

Central Parkland Subregion

This subregion gradually changes from grassland with groves of aspen (*Populus tremuloides*) in the south, to aspen parkland, to closed aspen forest in the north. True aspen parkland, with continuous aspen forest broken by grassland openings, is now rare as a result of agricultural clearing. The two major forest types—aspen and balsam poplar (*Populus balsamifera*) stands—have dense, species-rich understoreys. Snowberry (*Symphoricarpos albus*), saskatoon (*Amelanchier alnifolia*), beaked hazelnut (*Corylus cornuta*), choke cherry (*Prunus virginiana*), bunchberry (*Cornus canadensis*), wild lily-of-the-valley (*Maianthemum canadense*) and purple oat grass (*Schizachne purpurascens*) are typical of aspen stands, whereas red-osier dogwood (*Cornus sericea*), pussy willow (*Salix discolor*), northern gooseberry (*Ribes oxyacanthoides*), green alder (*Alnus viridis* ssp. *crispa*), bracted honeysuckle (*Lonicera involucrata*), tall lungwort (*Mertensia paniculata*), palmate-leaved coltsfoot (*Petasites palmatus*), bishop's-cap (*Mitella nuda*) and red baneberry (*Actaea rubra*) are characteristic of the moister balsam poplar stands.

CWa

Foothills Parkland habitat at the Palmer Ranch

The grassland vegetation of the 'parks' is essentially the same as that of the Northern Fescue Subregion (Grasslands Natural Region). Plains rough fescue (*Festuca hallii*) dominates most sites, with western porcupine grass (*Stipa curtiseta*) important on south-facing slopes and saline soils, along with June grass (*Koeleria macrantha*) and western wheat grass (*Elymus smithii*).

Shrub communities of buckbrush (*Symphoricarpos occidentalis*), wild roses (*Rosa* spp.), choke cherry, pin cherry (*Prunus pensylvanica*), saskatoon and silverberry (*Elaeagnus commutata*) are more extensive in northern sections, often extending out from the forest in belts.

Foothills Parkland Subregion

This narrow (1–5 km wide) transitional band between the Grasslands and Rocky Mountain natural regions lies along the eastern edge of the southern foothills. It is very diverse, with rougher topography than the Central Parkland Subregion and rapid changes in elevation and climate over short distances. Its northern boundary (near Calgary) is the northern limit for many distinctive southwestern species, including lupines (*Lupinus* spp.), oat grasses (*Danthonia* spp.) and bluebunch fescue (*Festuca idahoensis*).

The grasslands of this subregion are similar to those of the Foothills Fescue Subregion (Grasslands Natural Region): fescue–oat grass communities with many forb and grass species. The aspen forests resemble those of the Central Parkland Subregion, but several Central Parkland species (e.g., beaked hazelnut, high-bush cranberry [*Viburnum opulus* ssp. *trilobum*], wild sarsaparilla [*Aralia nudicaulis*], bunchberry and wild lily-of-the-valley) are absent, and some plants (e.g., yellow angelica [*Angelica dawsonii*]) are restricted to southwestern Alberta. Glacier lily (*Erythronium grandiflorum*) blankets much of the forest floor in southwestern sectors in early to mid May.

JR

Peace River Parkland habitat at Silver Valley

Peace River Parkland Subregion

This northern subregion has relatively short, cool summers, long, cold winters, high precipitation, less wind and lower evaporation than other Parkland subregions. The till deposits of the uplands are covered by forests similar to those of the surrounding mixedwood subregions of the Boreal Forest, dominated by aspen and white spruce (*Picea glauca*), with some balsam poplar (especially on wetter sites). Grassland soils are mostly saline (forest soils are not), and this is an important factor in maintaining these grasslands, with fire, and possibly climate, playing a secondary role. The upland grasslands are dominated by sedges (*Carex* spp.), timber oat grass (*Danthonia intermedia*), western porcupine grass, slender wheat grass (*Elymus trachycaulus*), inland bluegrass (*Poa interior*), three-flowered avens (*Geum triflorum*) and low goldenrod (*Solidago missouriensis*). On steep, south-facing slopes, western porcupine grass, sedges, and pasture sagewort (*Artemisia frigida*) dominate. Other common species include Columbia needle grass (*Stipa columbiana*), June grass, green needle grass (*Stipa viridula*), bastard toadflax (*Comandra umbellata*) and mountain goldenrod (*Solidago spathulata*). Several species that usually grow farther south or west are found here. These include brittle prickly-pear (*Opuntia fragilis*), Richardson needle grass (*Stipa richardsonii*), Columbia needle grass, Drummond's thistle (*Cirsium drummondii*) and low goldenrod.

Rare Plants

More than 100 rare species (about 20 percent of Alberta's rare vascular plants) occur in the Parkland Natural Region; most of these are also found in the Boreal Forest, Grasslands or Rocky Mountain natural regions, but 10 are restricted in Alberta to this transitional region. These include few-flowered aster (*Aster pauciflorus*), field grape fern (*Botrychium campestre*), sand millet (*Panicum wilcoxianum*), marsh gentian (*Gentiana fremontii*) and few-flowered salt-meadow grass (*Torreyochloa pallida*). Several rare plants are found only in southwestern Alberta, in the Foothills Parkland Subregion and, in some cases, also in the adjacent mountains. These include Geyer's wild onion (*Allium geyeri*), alpine foxtail (*Alopecurus alpinus*), blue camas (*Camassia quamash*), intermediate hawk's-beard (*Crepis intermedia*), mountain lady's-slipper (*Cypripedium montanum*), small-flowered rockstar (*Lithophragma parviflorum*), linear-leaved montia (*Montia linearis*) and small baby-blue-eyes (*Nemophila breviflora*).

Grasslands Natural Region

This southern natural region is flat to gently rolling with a few hill systems. Most of the bedrock is covered with thick glacial till, with many areas of fine-textured materials associated with glacial lake basins. Deep river valleys, carved into bedrock, contain badlands with many coulees and ravines. The four subregions—Dry Mixedgrass, Mixedgrass, Northern Fescue and Foothills Fescue—are distinguished by their climate, soil and vegetation.

JG

Dry Mixedgrass habitat at Milk River

Dry Mixedgrass Subregion

This is the most extensive grassland subregion. It has the warmest, driest climate in Alberta, with the lowest summer precipitation and little snow cover. The characteristic soils are Brown Chernozems.

Mixedgrass regions have both short and mid-height grasses. Mid-height grasses (needle grasses [*Stipa* spp.]), western wheat grass [*Elymus smithii*] and June grass [*Koeleria macrantha*]) and a short grass (blue grama [*Bouteloua gracilis*]) are most common. Northern wheat grass (*Elymus dasystachyus*) and western porcupine grass (*Stipa curtiseta*) are characteristic of moister sites. Communities of needle-and-thread (*Stipa comata*) and blue grama are widespread, but western wheat grass and northern wheat grass are also important on hummocky moraines. Sand dunes are usually dominated by needle-and-thread, sand grass (*Calamovilfa longifolia*), June grass and low shrubs such as silver sagebrush (*Artemisia cana*), silverberry (*Elaeagnus commutata*), buck-brush (*Symphoricarpos occidentalis*) and prickly rose (*Rosa acicularis*).

CWa

Mixedgrass habitat at the Turin Dunes

Mixedgrass Subregion

This subregion has slightly moister, cooler summers than the Dry Mixedgrass Subregion, and its characteristic soils are Dark Brown and Brown Chernozems. Vegetation is similar to that of the Dry Mixedgrass Subregion, but communities generally produce about 25 percent more biomass and have a greater abundance of species that favour cooler and moister sites (e.g., western porcupine grass and northern wheat grass). Fine-textured soils in glacial lake basins are usually covered by communities of northern wheat grass and June grass, and blue grama is more common on drier, exposed sites. Extensive narrow-leaf cottonwood (*Populus angustifolia*) forests grow on terraces of the Oldman, Belly, Waterton and St. Mary's rivers.

Northern Fescue habitat at the Hand Hills

NORTHERN FESCUE SUBREGION

This narrow belt of grassland is characterized by gently rolling terrain with Dark Brown and Black Chernozems. The climate is transitional between the Mixedgrass and Central Parkland (Parkland Natural Region) subregions.

Plains rough fescue (*Festuca hallii*) dominates, but June grass, western porcupine grass, northern wheat grass and Hooker's oat grass (*Helictotrichon hookeri*) are also important. Common forbs include prairie crocus (*Anemone patens*), prairie sagewort (*Artemisia ludoviciana*), field mouse-ear chickweed (*Cerastium arvense*), wild blue flax (*Linum lewisii*), smooth fleabane (*Erigeron glabellus*), northern bedstraw (*Galium boreale*), harebell (*Campanula rotundifolia*) and three-flowered avens (*Geum triflorum*). In sand-dune areas, rough fescue grasslands have scattered silverberry shrubs or thickets of rose and buckbrush.

FOOTHILLS FESCUE SUBREGION

This is the highest (up to 1,400 m), most western grassland subregion, forming a narrow band between the Mixedgrass and Foothills Parkland (Parkland Natural Region) subregions, with disjunct sites in the Cypress Hills and on the Milk River Ridge. Chinooks are frequent, so winters are relatively mild, but there is relatively high snowfall in late winter and early spring. The soils are predominantly Dark Brown and Black Chernozems.

Foothills rough fescue (*Festuca campestris*), bluebunch fescue (*Festuca idahoensis*), Parry's oat grass (*Danthonia parryi*) and timber oat grass (*Danthonia intermedia*) dominate, but June grass, northern wheat grass, western porcupine grass, Columbia needle grass (*Stipa columbiana*), early bluegrass (*Poa cusickii*) and Hooker's oat grass are also common. Forbs are more common and more diverse here than in the Northern Fescue Subregion and typically include sticky purple geranium (*Geranium viscosissimum*), prairie crocus, woolly gromwell (*Lithospermum ruderale*), golden bean (*Thermopsis rhombifolia*), prairie sagewort, low larkspur (*Delphinium bicolor*), heart-leaved buttercup (*Ranunculus cardiophyllus*), shooting stars (*Dodecatheon* spp.) and western wild parsley (*Lomatium triternatum*). Balsamroot (*Balsamorhiza sagittata*) is characteristic of the region near the foothills but is absent from the Cypress Hills. Many species grow in the Foothills Fescue Subregion but not in the Northern Fescue Subregion, including Parry's oat grass, bluebunch fescue, Columbia needle grass, sticky purple geranium, silky perennial lupine (*Lupinus sericeus*), kittentails (*Besseya wyomingensis*), western wild parsley, American thorough-wax (*Bupleurum americanum*), squawroot (*Perideridia gairdneri*), woolly gromwell and Williams' conimitella (*Conimitella williamsii*).

Rare Plants

Almost 125 rare species (about 27 percent of Alberta's rare vascular plant species) occur in the Grasslands Natural Region; about 55 of them are restricted in Alberta to this region. Most rare plants in the Grasslands Natural Region are at the northern or western edge of their range, extending into Alberta from widespread populations in Saskatchewan and the United States.

About half of the rare species in this subregion grow in grasslands. Many others occupy more specialized habitats. Water hyssop (*Bacopa rotundifolia*), smooth boisduvalia (*Boisduvalia glabella*), chaffweed (*Anagallis minima*), downingia (*Downingia laeta*), hairy pepperwort (*Marsilea vestita*) and woollyheads (*Psilocarphus elatior*) grow in pools and on the edges of sloughs. Shadscale (*Atriplex canescens*), spatula-leaved heliotrope (*Heliotropium curassavicum*), scratch grass (*Muhlenbergia asperifolia*), Moquin's sea-blite (*Suaeda moquinii*) and poison suckleya (*Suckleya suckleyana*) grow on alkaline or saline soils. Sand verbena (*Tripterocalyx micranthus*), smooth narrow-leaved goosefoot (*Chenopodium subglabrum*), bur ragweed (*Ambrosia acanthicarpa*) and western spiderwort (*Tradescantia occidentalis*) are typical of sandy habitats, whereas Watson's goosefoot (*Chenopodium watsonii*), small cryptanthe (*Cryptantha minima*), nodding umbrella-plant (*Eriogonum cernuum*) and greenthread (*Thelesperma subnudum*) are found in badlands and on other eroding slopes.

CWa

Foothills Fescue habitat just east of the Porcupine Hills

LA

Hydrophyllum capitatum

About the Species Accounts

This guide includes all of the vascular plant species that are currently recognized as rare in Alberta. The species accounts are divided into four major sections on the basis of growth form: woody plants (trees and shrubs), herbs (most non-woody plants), grass-like plants (grasses, sedges, rushes), and ferns and fern allies (horsetails, ferns). The coloured bars at the top of each page identify these sections. Within each section, plants are organized by family, with similar families grouped together, and within each family similar genera and species appear together. Each species account is organized as follows.

LK
Ranunculus uncinatus

Names

Common and scientific names (with the scientific authority) appear at the top of the account; the family name is displayed beside the colour bar. Most common names are taken from the master list published by Alberta Environmental Protection in 1993, whereas scientific names generally follow the *Flora of Alberta* (Moss 1983) except where there have been recent taxonomic revisions. *Flora of North America* (Flora of North America Editorial Committee 1993, 1997, in press) and *A Synonomized Checklist of the Vascular Flora of the United States, Canada and Greenland* (Kartesz 1994) are the main sources of information for such revisions. This guide includes rare vascular plant species only. Rare subspecies, varieties, forms and hybrids are not covered. However, a variety or subspecies name may be noted with the species name, if it is the only one found in Alberta.

Descriptions

Many books and papers provided information on different species, but five floras were the main sources used in composing the plant descriptions. These were *Flora of Alberta* (Moss 1983), *Budd's Flora of the Canadian Prairie Provinces* (Looman and Best 1979), *Vascular Plants of the Pacific Northwest* (Hitchcock et al. 1955–69), *Vascular Plants of Continental Northwest Territories, Canada* (Porsild and Cody 1980) and *Flora of the Yukon Territory* (Cody 1996).

DJ
Plantago maritima

Whenever possible, plants are described in everyday language, with few technical terms (e.g., 'caespitose' and 'glabrous' have been replaced with 'tufted' and 'hairless'). In some cases, technical terms are included in brackets after a replacement word or phrase; e.g., 'awn' has been replaced with 'bristle (awn)' and 'panicle' with 'branched cluster (panicle).' Terms that are not easily replaced are retained in the descriptions but are also included in the illustrated glossary (see pp. 425–50).

Diagnostic features vary from group to group and from species to species. For example, leaf size and shape may be important in one group, whereas seed characteristics may be diagnostic in another. These key characteristics are highlighted with bold text. Some plants can change dramatically with changes in their environment. For example, a species may have loose clusters of large, spreading leaves in moist, shady sites, and compact clusters of much smaller leaves when growing on exposed ridges. The size ranges included in the descriptions should help to identify the degree of variability that can be expected. Sizes observed for Alberta plants are presented in normal text, but if larger or smaller sizes have been recorded from areas outside the province, these are presented in braces before or after the Alberta range. For example, if leaves on Alberta plants are 5–10 cm long, but the same species' leaves are 2–8 cm in Alaska and 5–15 cm in Washington, leaf length will appear as 5–10 {2–15} cm.

The first descriptive section, 'Plants,' describes the plant as a whole: its longevity (annual, biennial, perennial), size, colour, branching, hairiness and rooting structure. The next section, 'Leaves,' describes the leaves: their arrangement (alternate, opposite, whorled), shape, size, texture, colour, edges and stalks. The third section, 'Flowers,' encompasses the greatest variety of structures and varies the most from one group of plants to another. In most woody plants and herbs, it focusses on individual flowers, but in the aster family, 'Flowerheads' (rather than single florets) are described; in grass-like plants, 'Flower Clusters' are described; and in the ferns and fern allies, 'Spore Clusters' are described. These descriptions include the colour, shape, size and hairiness of flowers and flower parts, and the size, shape and arrangement of flower clusters.

JG

Viola pallens

The 'Flowers' section ends with the flowering period, which indicates when to look for flowers and, by extension, when you are likely to find fruits. Alberta information is provided whenever possible, but most of these data pertain to other regions, such as the Pacific Northwest and the Rocky Mountains. Flowering dates based solely on published information for regions outside Alberta are presented in braces. For example, if plants have been observed blooming only in July in Alberta but are reported to bloom from May to July in the United States and from July to August in Alaska, the flowering period appears as July {May–August}. However, it is important to remember that this information is only a general guide. Phenology can vary from year to year and from site to site. Spring may arrive early one year and late the next. In years with ideal conditions, plants may flower profusely, but during droughts or unusually short summers, the same plants may not bloom at all. Similarly, plants might bloom in June on sheltered, south-facing hillsides at low elevations and in August on exposed alpine slopes.

The fourth and final descriptive section, 'Fruits' (or 'Cones'), describes the type, colour, shape, size and texture of the fruits and seeds. A description of their arrangement may follow, but only if this is notably different from that of the flower clusters.

LA
Erigeron radicatus

Each species account is accompanied by a line drawing to illustrate the habit (the appearance of the whole plant) and small details that may help with identification. Whenever possible, a colour photograph is also included. If available, the order of the illustrative material is as follows: photograph(s) of primary species, Alberta and North American distribution maps of primary species, line drawing(s) of primary species, photograph(s) of secondary species, line drawing(s) of secondary species, Alberta distribution map of secondary species. If no photographs were available, line drawings are substituted in their place.

Habitat

A description of the general habitat for the species follows the plant description. Alberta information is presented first, but if the species has been found in different habitats outside the province, this information is included at the end of the section as habitats 'elsewhere.' The habitat notes may help you to determine whether you are looking at the plant described. For example, if the habitat is described as 'dry, rocky, exposed ridges' and you are in a moist, shady forest, chances are that you are looking at a different species. However, once again, the notes are only a general guide.

JL
Aristida purpurea

Distribution

Two maps showing species distributions are presented: one for Alberta and one for North America. The records from Alberta are plotted using two symbols indicating the time period during which the collection was made, as follows: ◦ (open circles) prior to 1950 and • (closed circles) 1950 to the present. If more than one collection exists for a given locality, only the most recent collection is mapped. Not all species have an Alberta distribution map; in some cases, the information supplied with the collection was not specific enough to be able to locate a dot on a map. The Alberta Natural Heritage Information Centre provided the Alberta maps in 1998–99. They are meant to help you to compare the location of your find with other records from the province. Perhaps you will discover that you have found a new location for a plant, or perhaps the Alberta distribution will suggest that you have misidentified your specimen. John Kartesz at the University of North Carolina provided the North American distribution maps (unless otherwise noted). If the species has been found in a state, province or territory but is not considered rare there, that political

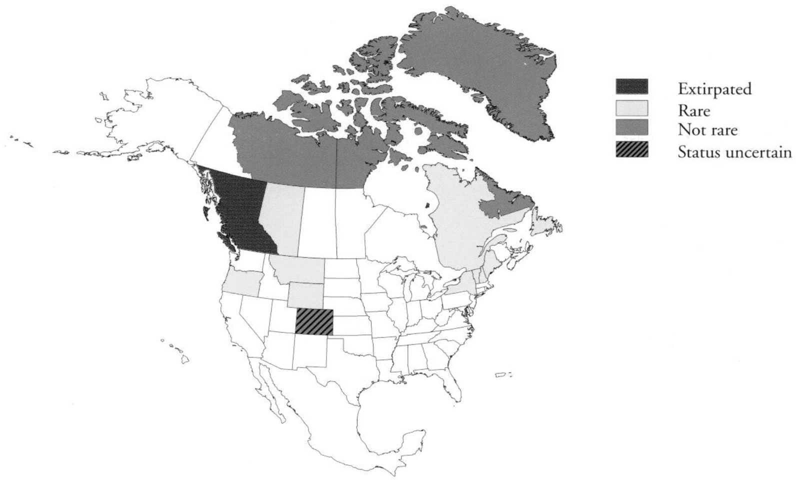

jurisdiction is shaded green. If the species has been found in a state province or territory and is considered rare there, that political jurisdiction is shaded yellow. If the species has been extirpated (no longer occurs) in that state, province or territory, that political jurisdiction is shaded red. Diagonal lines indicate that the status shown for the species in that particular political jurisdiction is uncertain. The North American maps are very helpful in identifying widespread species that are rare in Canada only because their ranges extend just across the Alberta border from the north, south, east or west.

Notes

This section encompasses a wide range of topics, including synonyms, other rare species, similar or related common species, ethnobotanical information, natural history notes and etymology (name derivation). The type and amount of information available varies greatly with the species.

The notes often begin with other names for the species (synonyms) that have appeared recently in published papers and floras. Plant names often change as more is discovered about the relationships between different groups. Two species may be lumped into one, two varieties may be recognized as separate species, or two species may be reclassified in separate genera. Many groups have been revised recently, several in association with work on the *Flora of North America*, and these revisions have been

Leymus mollis

incorporated into the text. For example, when the name in the *Flora of Alberta* is different from that in the *Flora of North America*, the *Flora of North America* name appears at the top of the account and the *Flora of Alberta* name appears in the notes section.

The 'Notes' section sometimes includes descriptions of similar or related plants that are also rare in Alberta. These descriptions are not as detailed as those presented for the primary species. Instead, they focus on key characteristics that can be used to distinguish the species from their close relatives. Each description is followed by a general outline of the species' habitat and flowering period, and is accompanied by illustrations and distribution maps. The 'Notes' section may also include information about common plants that could be confused with the rare species, highlighting the characteristics that distinguish the two.

In some cases, information about historical uses (aboriginal and/or European), edibility, toxicity, natural history and plant lore is also presented, but the type and amount of information available for rare species is usually limited. Information about historical uses of plants comes from areas outside Alberta, where the species is common. It is presented to give the reader a better sense of our rich natural heritage and is *not* meant to encourage the gathering of rare plants in Alberta.

Rare Vascular Plants

of Alberta

Trees & Shrubs

WESTERN RED CEDAR

Thuja plicata Donn *ex* D. Don
CEDAR FAMILY (CUPRESSACEAE)

LK

Plants: Coniferous trees to 40 {75} m tall; **trunks straight, vertically lined, grey, buttressed at base,** 1–3 {5} m in diameter; **branches spreading to hanging** but upturned at tips; crown cone-shaped when young, irregular with age; bark thin, cinnamon to greyish, fissured, easily peeled off in long, fibrous strips.

Leaves: Opposite, evergreen, **scale-like,** 3 {1–6} mm long, pointed, overlapping, **shiny yellowish green,** aromatic; arranged in 4 rows with upper–lower pair **flattened** and side pair **folded, in flat, fan-like sprays.**

LA

Cones: Male and female cones on same tree in clusters at branch tips; pollen (male) cones reddish, almost round, 2 {1–3} mm long; seed (female) cones narrowly egg-shaped, 8–12 {14} mm long, with **6–8 dry, brown scales;** seeds reddish brown, with 2 membranous wings; {April–May}.

Habitat: Rich, moist to wet (often saturated) foothill and montane slopes.

Notes: Aboriginal peoples twisted, wove and plaited the long, soft strings of inner bark to make a wide range of items, including baskets, blankets, clothing, ropes and mats. The trunks were used to make dugout canoes and rafts, and frames for birch-bark canoes. Fine roots were split, peeled and used to make water-tight baskets for cooking. Larger roots were formed into coils which were alternately bound together in pairs using the split roots. Bark was woven into baskets where air could circulate around stored berries, or whole sheets were formed into containers. The light, easily worked wood splits easily and resists decay. It was used by many tribes to make cradle boards, bowls, roofing, siding and a variety of implements. Today, it is widely used for siding, roofing, panelling, doors, patio furniture, chests and caskets. Western red cedar has been heavily logged for its lumber, and it is disappearing from parts of its range where trees are not replanted. • Western red cedar is very shade tolerant, but it has a low resistance to drought and frost. It indicates relatively wet regions in the Rockies. In BC, this tree can reach over 1,000 years of age. • The specific epithet *plicata* means 'folded,' in reference to the flattened, overlapping leaves.

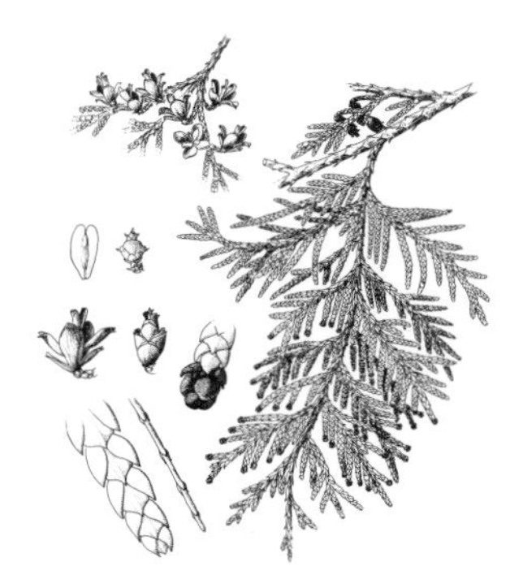

DJ

JG

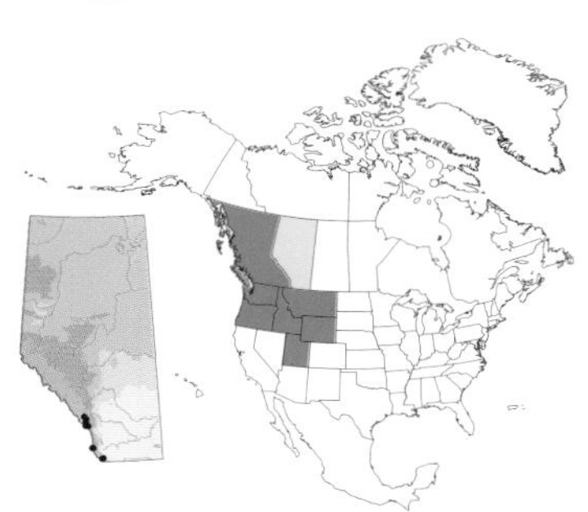

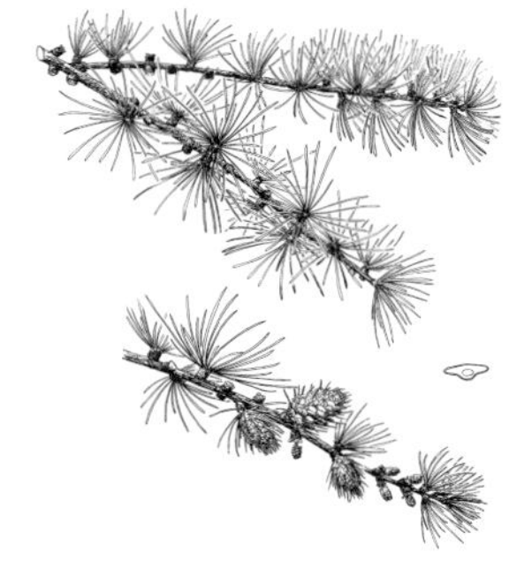

WESTERN LARCH

Larix occidentalis Nutt.
PINE FAMILY (PINACEAE)

Plants: Slender coniferous trees, usually 25–50 m tall; trunks straight, usually 1–1.3 {2} m in diameter; **branches short, well spaced with sparse leaves**; twigs orange-brown, hairy at first, but usually hairless by the end of the first year; **bark cinnamon-brown**, becoming 10–15 cm thick, deeply furrowed with **large, flaky scales**; crown short and cone-shaped.

Leaves: Tufts of 15–30 soft, **deciduous needles on stubby twigs**, 2.5–5 cm long, pale yellow-green in spring and summer, bright yellow in fall, shed for winter.

Cones: Male and female cones on same tree; pollen (male) cones yellow, about 1 cm long; seed (female) cones brown, egg-shaped, **2–3 cm long**, with **3-pointed bracts** projecting beyond the scales, borne on curved stalks; cone **scales wider than they are long**, smooth-edged, **woolly below when young**; seeds reddish brown, 3 mm long, with a 6-mm wing; {May–June}, mature in a single season.

Habitat: Moist to dry, often gravelly or sandy sites in upper foothill and montane zones; elsewhere, often with ponderosa pine and Douglas-fir.

Notes: Some tribes hollowed out cavities in western larch trunks and allowed the sweet syrup to accumulate. This sugary liquid could be concentrated by evaporation to make it even sweeter, but some warned that eating too much 'cleans you out.' The sweet inner bark was eaten in spring, and lumps of pitch were chewed like gum year-round. The sap and gum contain galatin, a natural sugar with a flavour like slightly bitter honey. Dried larch gum was also ground and used as baking powder. • The wood was used for making bowls, and rotted logs were collected for smoking buckskins. Today, it is often used in heavy construction, and it also makes good firewood. Arabino galatin, a water-soluble gum, is extracted from the bark for use in paint, ink and medicines. • Mature western larch trees have thick bark and few lower limbs, and as a result they are able to survive low-intensity fires, sometimes living 700 to 900 years. Larch seeds germinate readily and young trees grow rapidly on fire-blackened soils, but fire suppression and selective cutting have reduced populations in many areas.

WESTERN WHITE PINE, SILVER PINE

Pinus monticola Dougl. *ex* D. Don.
PINE FAMILY (PINACEAE)

JG

Plants: Evergreen trees usually less than 30 m tall, but sometimes up to 50 m; trunks straight, 1 m or more in diameter; young bark silvery-grey, thin, smooth; mature bark greyish, furrowed, with small, rectangular, flaky scales, cinnamon-brown under the outer scales; **branches symmetrical, arranged in circles** (whorled); relatively wind-firm, with spreading, shallow roots and a few deep roots; crowns symmetrical, cone-shaped, short-branched.

Leaves: Bundles of 5 very slender, flexible evergreen needles, {3} **5–10 cm long,** blue-green with whitish lines, blunt or slightly pointed (not sharp-pointed), **finely toothed** along the edges.

Cones: Male and female cones on same tree; pollen (male) cones yellow, scarcely 1 cm long, clustered; **seed** (female) **cones yellow-brown** (green to yellowish or purplish when young), **cylindrical, slightly curved, 10–25 cm long,** 6–9 cm thick, pitchy, **hanging on stalks** at upper branch tips; cone scales thin, spreading, deep red to chocolate-brown at the base, blunt at the yellowish brown tips, lacking prickles; seeds reddish brown, 7–10 mm long, with a large, narrow wing 2–3 times as long as the seed, widest above the middle and pointed at the tip; {May–June}, mature in the fall of the second year.

Habitat: Open rocky slopes in the mountains; elsewhere, on moist, north-facing mountain slopes, in mixed forest or pure stands.

Notes: Other 5-needle pines in Alberta have smooth-edged needles about 12.5 cm long and egg-shaped, short-stalked cones with thick scales. • This species was named by David Douglas in 1825, during his exploration of the west coast of North America. • The bark was boiled to make medicinal teas for treating stomach disorders and purifying the blood. • Western white pine trees are very susceptible to white pine blister rust, a fungus that was introduced from Europe. • Western white pine requires more than 500 mm of precipitation annually and a precipitation/evaporation ratio of greater than 1. Low relative humidity and rainfall are doubtless limiting factors in Alberta. • The wood is easily worked and is good for carving and construction.

LK

LK

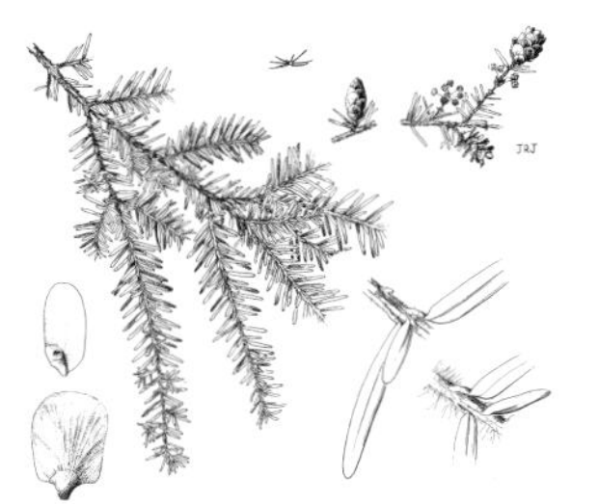

WESTERN HEMLOCK

Tsuga heterophylla (Raf.) Sarg.
PINE FAMILY (PINACEAE)

Plants: Coniferous evergreen trees, usually 30–50 m tall, sometimes taller; buds 2.5–3.5 mm long; trunks straight, up to 1 {2} m in diameter; branches slender, down-swept, appearing feathery; crown open, narrowly cone-shaped, with a **flexible, nodding tip**; bark yellowish brown and finely hairy when young, becoming dark greyish brown with age and developing deep furrows and flat ridges; **inner bark dark orange with purple streaks.**

Leaves: Flat evergreen **needles, 5–20** {30} **mm long**, of **unequal lengths**, blunt-tipped, shiny yellowish green above, whitish beneath with 2 broad bands of stomata, borne on small stubs, **held at right angles to branches in 2 opposite rows.**

Cones: Male and female cones on same tree; pollen (male) cones 3–4 mm long, yellowish; seed (female) cones oblong to **egg-shaped, 15–25** {10–30} **mm long, hanging**, purplish green when young, light brown when mature; scales thin, wavy-edged; mature in a single year and shed intact.

Habitat: Moist, shady montane forests; elsewhere, at lower elevations in moist woodlands mixed with hardwoods.

Notes: Western hemlock is very shade tolerant. • The boughs were used for bedding and as a disinfectant and deodorizer. The wood is hard and strong, with an even grain and colour. It is widely used to make doors, windows, staircases, mouldings, cupboards and floors. It also provides construction lumber, pilings, poles, railway ties, pulp, and alpha cellulose for making paper, cellophane and rayon. • This attractive, feathery tree is a popular ornamental, and several cultivars have been developed. • Western hemlock is also known as Pacific hemlock and west coast hemlock. The generic name *Tsuga* is a Japanese name that has been adopted as a scientific 'Latin' name. The specific epithet *heterophylla,* from the Latin *hetero* (variable) and *phyllum* (leaf), refers to the variably sized needles.

WESTERN YEW

Taxus brevifolia Nutt.
YEW FAMILY (TAXACEAE)

Plants: Evergreen shrubs or small trees, 10–15 m tall; trunks often twisted; **bark thin, scaly, red-brown or purplish**, sloughing off to expose rose-coloured underbark; branches spreading or drooping; **young twigs** dark green or olive-green, **hairless**.

Leaves: Flat, needle-like, 1–2 cm long, 1–2 mm wide, shiny, dark green on upper surface, yellowish green beneath, **tipped with a tiny spine**; arranged spirally along the branches but **twisted into 2 opposite rows**, giving the branches a flattened appearance.

Flowers: Male (staminate) and female (pistillate), from leaf axils, usually on separate trees; male cones inconspicuous, tiny (2 mm wide), tipped by a yellow lobed cluster of stamen-like structures on a short stalk; female cones with single ovules in green, cup-like structures on short, scale-covered stalks; {April–June}.

Fruits: Red, fleshy, cupped 'berries' 4–5 mm broad, with single hard seeds; seeds brown or dark blue, egg-shaped, 5–6 mm long.

Habitat: Moist woods, under the canopy of larger conifers.

Notes: The seeds, bark and leaves are **highly poisonous**, containing taxine, a potent alkaloid. • Yew bark is the source of the drug taxol, used to treat ovarian and breast cancers. • The flexible, strong wood was used by native people to make bows, canoe paddles, clubs, combs, shovels, harpoons, sewing needles, fish hooks, knives, spoons and snowshoe frames. The berries were sometimes eaten in small quantities as a contraceptive. • At high elevations, western yew is reduced to a low, spreading shrub. It does not form pure stands in forests. • The berries are eaten by a wide variety of birds, and the needles are browsed by moose in winter. • *Taxus* is from the Greek name for yews, which was perhaps derived from *taxon* (a bow), a common use for yew wood in earlier times. *Brevifolia* is Latin for 'short-leaved.'

WM

JG

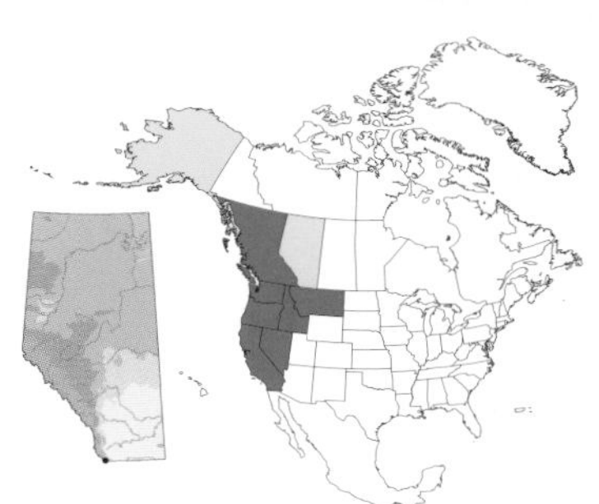

ES

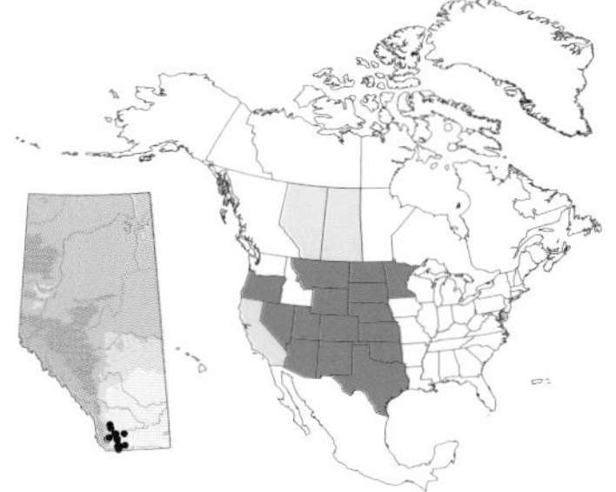

NARROW-LEAVED COTTONWOOD

Populus angustifolia James
WILLOW FAMILY (SALICACEAE)

Plants: Slender **deciduous** trees, up to 12 {20} m tall; branches directed upward; twigs orange-brown; **buds sticky, aromatic**, hairless, covered by **several scales**; crown nearly cone-shaped; bark whitish green to yellowish green, smooth when young, slightly furrowed with low ridges on lower trunk when mature.

Leaves: Alternate, narrowly to broadly lance-shaped, **3–5 times as long as they are wide**, 5–8 {4–11} cm long, **gradually tapered to a pointed tip**, wedge-shaped to rounded at base, finely round-toothed; **stalks** slightly flattened or channelled on the upper side and rounded beneath, **short**, up to ⅓ as long as the blade.

Flowers: Tiny, in the axils of conspicuously fringed scales that are soon dropped, forming long, slender, **loosely hanging clusters** (catkins); male and female catkins on separate trees; male (staminate) catkins 2–3 cm long, with about 12–18 stamens per flower; **female** (pistillate) **catkins 4–10 cm long**; {April} May.

Fruits: Narrowly egg-shaped, wrinkled capsules, hairless, 5–6 mm long, on 1–2 mm stalks, in **hanging catkins**, splitting into 2 parts when mature; seeds minute, with a tuft of soft, white hairs at tip, often dispersed in **large fluffy masses**.

Habitat: River valleys and streambanks.

Notes: Typical narrow-leaved cottonwood is seldom found in Alberta, because it hybridizes readily with black cottonwood (*Populus balsamifera* L. ssp. *trichocarpa* (T. & G. *ex* Hook.) Brayshaw), balsam poplar (*Populus balsamifera* L. ssp. *balsamifera*) and plains cottonwood (*Populus deltoides* Marsh), producing hybrids that resemble both parents and that are difficult to identify. Its bright white branches and twigs distinguish it from other trees during winter. • At first glance, this small, slender tree looks more like a large willow (*Salix* spp.) than a cottonwood, but willows have only a single scale covering each bud, their male flowers have few (often 2) anthers, and their female catkins tend to be shorter, rarely hanging. • Cottonwood trees produce millions of tiny, fragile seeds with fluffy tufts of hairs that carry them on the wind.

Raup's willow

Salix raupii Argus
WILLOW FAMILY (SALICACEAE)

Plants: **Erect shrubs, 1–2 m tall; branches hairless,** glossy, chestnut-brown when young, greyish brown with flaky bark by the third year.

Leaves: Alternate; **blades widest at or above the middle, 3.2–5.8 cm long, 1.2–1.9 cm wide,** blunt to pointed at tip, rounded to pointed at base, **lacking teeth or with inconspicuous, rounded teeth, hairless** (sometimes with hairs at the edges when young), **bluish grey with a thin, waxy coat on the lower surface; stalks yellowish,** 5–9 mm long, hairless; stipules narrow, 1–3 mm long.

Flowers: Tiny, in the axils of **pale lemon-yellow to bicoloured** (yellow with pink or brownish tips), 1.6–2.5 mm long, **scale-like bracts,** forming dense, elongating clusters (catkins), with male and female flowers on separate plants; male (staminate) catkins 2.5–3.5 cm long, on leafy branchlets 8–12 mm long; female (pistillate) catkins 2–3.5 cm long, on leafy branchlets 5–18 mm long; **styles 0.6–0.8 mm long,** stigmas 0.4 mm long; **in spring, with the leaves.**

Fruits: **Greenish brown capsules, hairless** or with 2 longitudinal bands of short, fine hairs, **4.4–8 mm long, on short, hairy stalks.**

Habitat: Lush mountain meadows and willow fens.

Notes: This species is critically imperilled due to extreme rarity in all parts of its range. • Raup's willow is very similar to extreme variants of Barclay's willow (*Salix barclayi* Anderss.) and Farr's willow (*Salix farriae* Ball). Barclay's willow is distinguished by its soft-hairy branches, distinctly toothed leaves, long stipules (up to 2 cm long) and hairy floral bracts. The young leaves of Farr's willow often have white and reddish hairs on the midvein; the capsules tend to be smaller (4–5 mm) and the bracts darker (brown to tawny) than those of Raup's willow. Raup's willow may also be confused with bog willow (*Salix pedicellaris* Pursh), but bog willow is easily distinguished by its firmer, narrower leaves, which are bluish grey with a thin, waxy coating on both surfaces, and by its shorter styles and stigmas (0.1–0.2 mm).

JG

JG

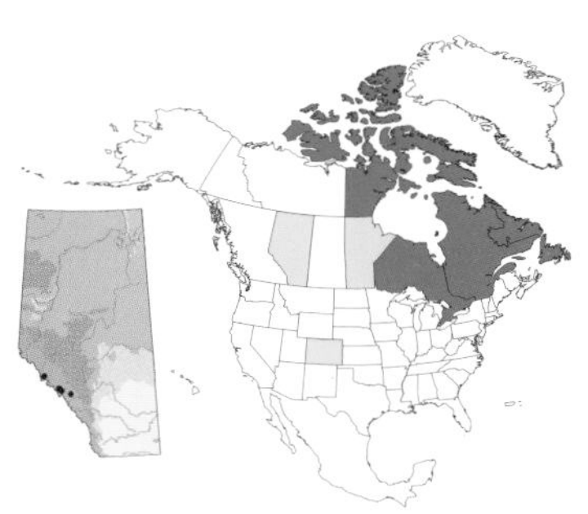

WOOLLY WILLOW, LIME WILLOW

Salix lanata L. ssp. *calcicola* (Fern. & Wieg.) Hult.
WILLOW FAMILY (SALICACEAE)

Plants: Erect, low shrubs, up to 50 cm tall; branches stout, gnarled, reddish brown, **covered with long, soft hairs when young**, slightly hairy when mature.

Leaves: Alternate; **blades broadly elliptic to egg-shaped**, widest at or below the middle, 2–5 cm long, 1.5–3.5 cm wide, abruptly pointed at the tip, usually rounded at the base, smooth or with fine, gland-tipped teeth along the edges, sparsely long-hairy to almost hairless, bluish grey with a thin, waxy coat on the lower surface and with a broad, conspicuous midvein; stalks short; **stipules prominent**, rounded or sometimes long-tapering, dotted **with tiny glands** on edges and upper surface, **persisting** after the growing season; **overwintering buds large** and rounded, with long, soft hairs.

Flowers: Tiny, on very short stalks in the axils of dark, scale-like bracts with long, soft hairs, forming dense, elongating clusters (catkins), with male and female flowers on separate plants; **female** (pistillate) **catkins stout, 5–6 cm long, stalkless**; styles up to 2.5 mm long; in spring, before the leaves.

Fruits: Hairless, reddish brown capsules, 7–9 mm long.

Habitat: Calcareous riverbanks, floodplains and meadows.

Notes: This species has also been called *Salix calcicola* Fern. & Wieg. • The specific epithet *lanata*, from the Latin *lana* (wool), refers to the woolly leaves; *calcicola* refers to the calcareous habitat.

ALASKA WILLOW, FELT-LEAVED WILLOW

Salix alaxensis (Anderss.) Coville ssp. *alaxensis*
WILLOW FAMILY (SALICACEAE)

LK

Plants: Gnarled to erect, deciduous shrubs or small trees, 1–3.7 {9} m tall; branches reddish brown, sometimes with persistent greyish hairs, conspicuously white-woolly or grey-woolly when young.

Leaves: Alternate, **elliptic to egg-shaped**, widest above middle, 4–10 cm long, 2–2.5 cm wide, pointed at tip, narrowly wedge-shaped at base, dull green and sparsely hairy above, **densely white-woolly beneath**; edges rolled under, toothless or glandular and wavy; stalks 3–15 mm long, yellowish, sometimes enlarged around the bud, with 2 persistent, linear bracts (stipules) at the base.

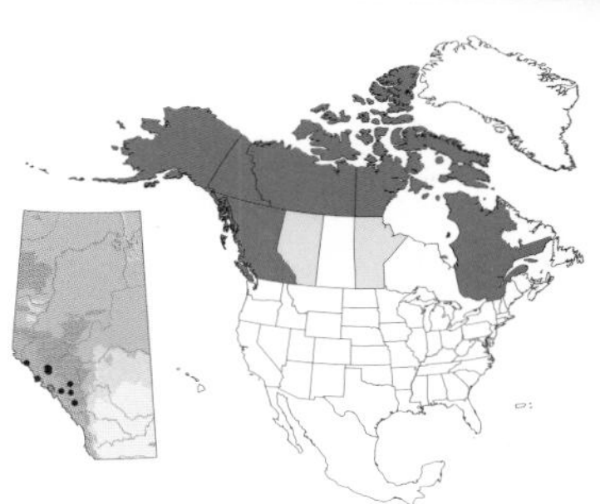

Flowers: Tiny, in the axils of dark brown to black, silky-hairy scales, forming **dense, stalkless clusters** (catkins), with male and female on separate plants; male (staminate) catkins about 4 cm long, with 2 anthers per flower; female (pistillate) catkins 6–10 {12} cm long, with green, hairy pistils; {May} June, before the leaves.

Fruits: Sparsely hairy capsules, 4–5 mm long, with stalks less than 1 mm long; seeds minute, tipped with a tuft of silky hairs that allows them to be carried by the wind.

Habitat: Alpine slopes; elsewhere, on gravel bars and river terraces, on glacial moraines and in young forests.

Notes: Changeable willow (*Salix commutata* Bebb) is another rare Alberta willow. It is smaller (0.2–2 m tall) than Alaska willow, but its twigs are often densely white-woolly. Changeable willow is most easily identified by its leaves, which have rounded teeth along their edges, green lower surfaces (not coated with a whitish bloom, as is the case with most willows), and silky to woolly hairs on both sides (especially when young). It forms thickets in subalpine areas and produces nearly hairless, tawny, 3.5–7 cm long female catkins in July {August–September}, with or following leaf growth. • Hoary willow (*Salix candida* Fluegge *ex* Willd.) is a much more common, more widespread species that also has white, woolly hairs on its lower leaf surfaces. Hoary willow is distinguished by its narrower (0.5–1.5 cm wide) leaves and its leafy-stalked catkins which appear with the leaves.

S. COMMUTATA

JP

JP

SITKA WILLOW

Salix sitchensis Sanson *ex* Bong.
WILLOW FAMILY (SALICACEAE)

Plants: Shrubs or small trees, 1–6 m tall, sometimes lying on the ground in exposed areas but otherwise erect; branches **brittle**, smooth, dark reddish brown and **densely velvety-hairy when young**, becoming grey, furrowed and scaly with age.

Leaves: Alternate; blades elliptic to narrowly egg-shaped, generally widest toward the tip, 4–9 {18} cm long, 1.5–3.5 {6} cm wide, short-pointed or rounded at the tip, tapered to a narrow base, toothed; upper surface green, with greyish, flat-lying hairs; **lower surface pale and satiny, with silky hairs** and evident veins; stalks yellowish, velvety, 5–15 {20} mm long; stipules variable, small and soon shed or well developed, leaf-like and persistent.

Flowers: Tiny, in the axils of brown, dark-tipped, scale-like bracts with long, soft hairs; forming dense, elongating clusters (catkins), with male and female flowers on separate plants; male (staminate) catkins 2.5–5 cm long, 1–1.5 cm thick on 2–10 {20} mm long leafy stalks, **single stamen** per floret; **female** (pistillate) **catkins 3–9 cm long** when mature, on **short, leafy stalks**; styles 0.4–0.8 {0.3–1.2} mm long, stigmas 0.1–0.3 mm long; May, usually as the leaves appear (rarely before).

Fruits: Tawny, **silky-hairy capsules**, {1} 3–5.5 mm long, on short (0.5–1.4 mm long) stalks.

Habitat: Alluvial soil on the Athabasca River flood plain.

Notes: The common, widespread species Scouler's willow (*Salix scouleriana* Barr. *ex* Hook.) has a hairy form that resembles Sitka willow, but its styles are shorter (0.2–0.6 mm), its stigmas are longer (0.2–1 mm), its leaves have a bluish grey, thin, waxy coating on their lower surface, and its twigs are not brittle. • The satiny sheen on the lower surface of the leaves is diagnostic of Sitka willow in Alaska. • The wood has been used by native people in drying fish, because its smoke does not have a bad odour. The pounded bark has been applied to heal wounds. • *Sitchensis* means 'of Sitka,' Alaska, near which it was collected by Karl Heinrich Mertens in 1827.

STOLONIFEROUS WILLOW

Salix stolonifera Coville
WILLOW FAMILY (SALICACEAE)

JP

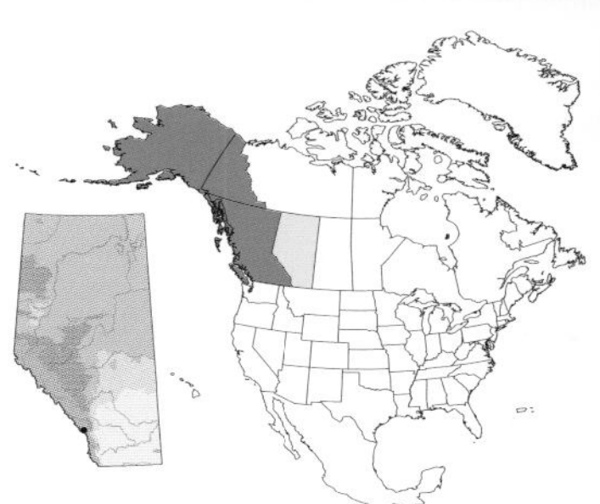

Plants: Dwarf shrubs; branches rooting at joints (nodes), trailing on the ground or spreading underground, reddish brown, hairless and glossy, sometimes with a waxy, bluish grey coating.

Leaves: Alternate; **blades broad**, widest at or above the middle, **1–2.5 cm long, 0.5–2 cm wide**, rounded at the tip, pointed to rounded at the base, usually without teeth, **hairless or sparsely hairy**, green on the upper surface, bluish grey with a thin, **waxy coating on the lower surface**; stalks slender; stipules tiny.

Flowers: Tiny, in the axils of dark brown, sparsely hairy, scale-like bracts, forming dense, elongating clusters (catkins), with male and female flowers on separate plants; **female** (pistillate) **catkins 1.5–4 cm long on long** (1–6 cm), **leafy branchlets**; styles about 0.8–1.4 mm long; in spring, when the leaves appear.

Fruits: Smooth, essentially hairless capsules, usually **reddish purple** (sometimes greenish or whitish) **when young**, becoming brown with age, 5–7 mm long, short-stalked.

Habitat: Wet hummocks at alpine elevations.

Notes: This species hybridizes with arctic willow (*Salix arctica* Pallas) and Barclay's willow (*Salix barclayi* Anderss.) in BC. Arctic willow is distinguished by its silky-woolly pistils, and Barclay's willow is usually a larger (1–3 m tall), erect shrub with longer (3–7 cm long) leaves and catkins (4–7 cm long) and obvious stipules. • Snow willow (*Salix reticulata* L.) is another dwarf willow, but it has shorter pistils (4–5 mm long) and styles (0.2–0.3 mm long), and its leaves have distinctive netted veins. • Smooth willow (*Salix glauca* L.) is occasionally of a dwarf stature, but its pistils have long, soft or woolly hairs, its bracts have short, wavy hairs, and its branchlets are hairy. • *Stolonifera* is Latin for 'bearing stolons,' referring to the horizontal, rooting stems (stolons) of this species.

CWa

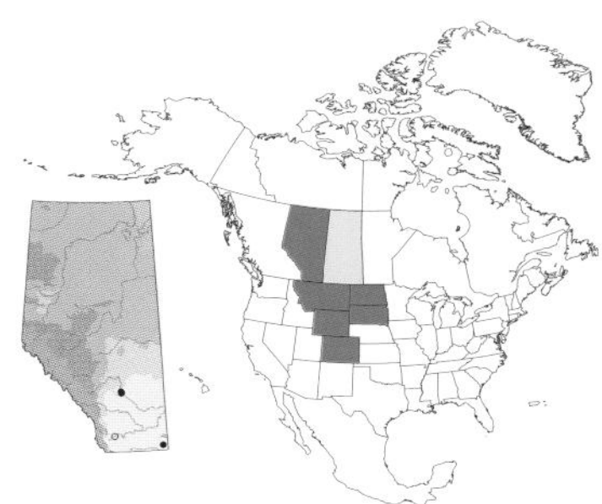

SHADSCALE, SALTBUSH

Atriplex canescens (Pursh) Nutt. var. *aptera* (A. Nels.) C.L. Hitchc.
GOOSEFOOT FAMILY (CHENOPODIACEAE)

Plants: Low, somewhat rounded **shrubs**, 10–40 cm tall; branches numerous, spreading, white-scaly when young, eventually smooth and shedding outer layers of bark.

Leaves: Alternate, or the lower ones opposite; **blades** variable, elliptic to spatula-shaped or linear, 1–5 cm long, **greyish** with a covering of fine, **bran-like particles, veins in a netted pattern visible under magnification** (kranz-type venation), toothless; stalks short or absent.

Flowers: Small, lacking petals, with male and female flowers on separate plants; male (staminate) flowers tawny (sometimes reddish-tinged), with a {3} 5-parted calyx densely covered in fine scales, numerous, borne in many narrow, elongated, dense (sometimes interrupted) clusters (spikes) that usually form leafy, branched clusters (panicles); female (pistillate) flowers lacking a calyx, but with a fused **pair of bracts completely enclosing the ovary**, 4–6 {8} mm long in flower (up to 20 {25} mm long in fruit), **prominently 4-winged**, the wings broader than the body, wavy-edged to irregularly toothed, few to many flowers in less congested spikes and panicles; {June–August}.

Fruits: Single, vertical seeds, 1.5–2.5 mm long, enclosed by enlarged, winged bracts.

Habitat: Saline flats, sometimes on sandy soil.

Notes: This variety has been considered a species, *Atriplex aptera* A. Nels., by some taxonomists. • Shadscale is a valuable browse species for wildlife and livestock in arid regions; however, it is **mildly poisonous.** It can tolerate high concentrations of salt, and because of this it is being studied for revegetation of disturbed sites in dry areas. Shadscale is known to form mycorrhizal relationships with soil fungi.

LEWIS' MOCK-ORANGE

Philadelphus lewisii Pursh
HYDRANGEA FAMILY (HYDRANGEACEAE)

CWa

Plants: Erect, deciduous shrubs, 1–3 m tall; **branches opposite**, loose, spreading, with brown, flaky bark; twigs reddish and hairless.

Leaves: Opposite, broadly lance-shaped, 2–6 {7} cm long, with **3–5 main veins** from the base, **slightly rough** to touch, hairless to somewhat hairy (especially on lower side of veins), **fringed** with short, curved hairs, short-stalked.

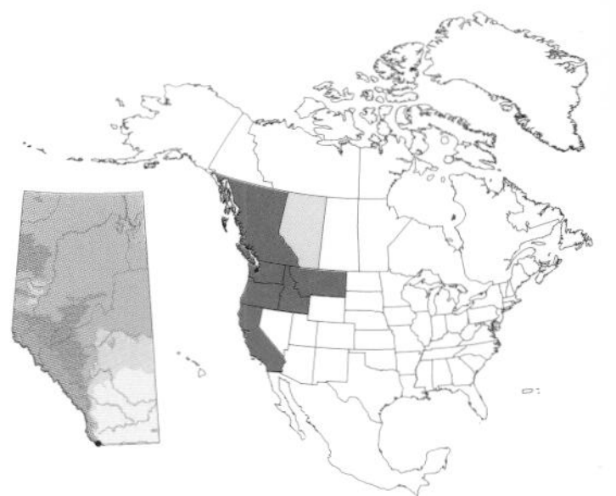

Flowers: White, about 3 cm across, cross-shaped, with both male and female parts (perfect); sepals fused to ovary for most of their length; 4 or 5 broad, rounded or notched, spreading petals surround a cluster of 25–40 bright yellow stamens and 4 styles; 3–11 flowers in **showy, fragrant clusters** (racemes) at branch tips; {May} July–August.

Fruits: Woody, oval capsules, 6–10 mm long, splitting into 4 parts (valves), with many tiny, rod-shaped seeds.

Habitat: Well-drained sites in montane forests; elsewhere, on rocky hillsides with sagebrush or ponderosa pine.

Notes: Lewis' mock-orange is the state flower of Idaho. • The stiff, hard wood has been used to make combs, knitting needles, rims for birch-bark baskets and cradle hoods. Dried, powdered leaves or charcoal from burned branches was mixed with pitch or bear grease to make salves for treating sores and swellings. Branches were boiled to make a medicinal tea for treating sore chests and for washing or soaking eczema and bleeding hemorrhoids. • Mock-orange leaves were mashed and used as soap. • Deer and elk browse on the branches of Lewis' mock-orange, but it is not a preferred food. • The specific epithet *lewisii* honours Captain Meriwether Lewis, of the Lewis and Clark Expedition, who first collected this plant in Idaho.

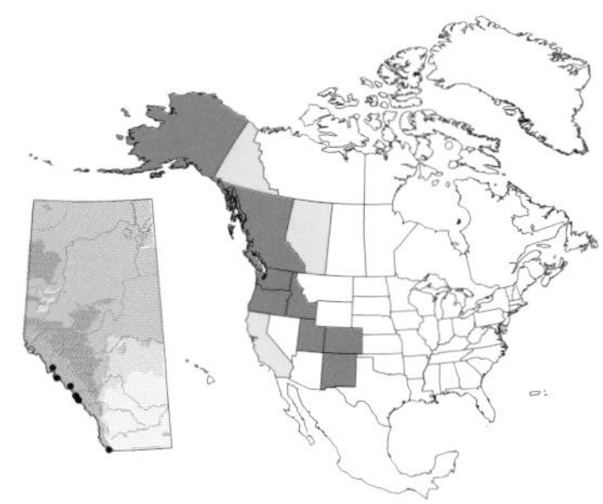

MOUNTAIN CURRANT, TRAILING BLACK CURRANT

Ribes laxiflorum Pursh
CURRANT FAMILY (GROSSULARIACEAE)

Plants: Sprawling shrubs up to 1 m tall; branches usually **spreading** or running along the ground, grey or brown, without prickles (unarmed).

Leaves: Alternate, maple-leaf-shaped, with a **strong odour** when crushed; blades 6–8 cm long and 7–10 {2.5–12} cm wide, heart-shaped at base and tipped with **5–7 toothed, triangular lobes**, hairless on the upper surface, light green and slightly hairy with small, yellow glands near base on the lower surface; stalks 5–7.5 cm long.

Flowers: Red to purple, saucer-shaped, about 6–8 mm across, with both male and female parts (5 stamens; 2 styles); 5 triangular, 3–4 mm long petals; 5 egg-shaped to rounded, {2.5} 3–4 mm long, **hairy sepals, glandular-hairy on the ovary and stalk**; {6} 10–20 flowers in erect elongated clusters (racemes) 10–14 cm long; {May} June, as the leaves expand.

Fruits: Purplish black berries with a whitish, waxy covering (bloom), **short-stalked** (less than 0.5 mm long), **glandular-hairy**, {8} 12–15 mm in diameter, unpleasant-smelling when crushed; {late July–early August}.

Habitat: Moist subalpine woods; elsewhere, also in disturbed areas such as open meadows and logged areas.

Notes: A much more common species, skunk currant (*Ribes glandulosum* Grauer), resembles mountain currant and also grows in moist woods and openings. It is distinguished by its red fruit, which is covered with long-stalked glands (1.2 mm long), and by its shorter (2–2.5 mm), essentially hairless sepals. • The generic name *Ribes* comes from the Arabic or Persian *ribas* (acid-tasting), in reference to the acidic fruit of many species. *Laxiflorum* means 'with loose flowers,' in reference to the open flower clusters.

DEVIL'S CLUB

Oplopanax horridus (Sm.) T. & G. *ex* Miq. var. *horridus*
GINSENG FAMILY (ARALIACEAE)

Plants: **Strong-smelling, spiny, coarse** deciduous shrubs, 1–3 m tall; stems erect to sprawling, thick, **armed with many long spines**, crooked, **seldom branched**, often entangled.

Leaves: Alternate, **broadly maple-leaf-shaped with 5–7 toothed lobes, 10–30 {40} cm wide**, prickly on the ribs beneath, **spreading on long, bristly stalks near stem tips.**

Flowers: **Greenish white**, 5–6 mm long, with both male and female parts (5 stamens; 2 styles), with 5 petals and 5 sepals, nearly stalkless, in dense heads (umbels) forming **10–30 cm long, branched, pyramid-shaped clusters** (panicles) at stem tips; {May} June–August.

Fruits: **Bright red, slightly flattened, berry-like drupes**, 4–5 {6} mm long, 2-seeded, in **showy clusters.**

Habitat: Moist to wet, shady sites.

Notes: The berries are **not edible**, but the young, fleshy stems have been eaten. • Some people have an **allergic reaction** to the spines of these plants. The spines break off easily and can cause infections when they remain embedded in the skin. • The wood has a distinctive, sweet smell. The aromatic roots were mixed with tobacco and smoked to relieve headaches. • The stems have been used medicinally. Dried pieces, scraped free of prickles, were steeped in boiling water to make medicinal teas for treating flu and other illnesses, relieving stomach troubles, improving appetite and aiding weight gain. Stem sections were boiled to make a tonic and blood purifier with laxative effects. Root tea was used to treat diabetes. Dried stems were burned and the ashes were mixed with grease to make a salve for healing swellings and running sores. • These large, attractive plants are sometimes grown as ornamentals in gardens, but they grow slowly, and gardeners must be careful to avoid their dangerous spines. • The generic name *Oplopanax* was derived from the Greek *hoplon* (weapon) and *panax* (ginseng), a closely related, large-leaved plant.

LA

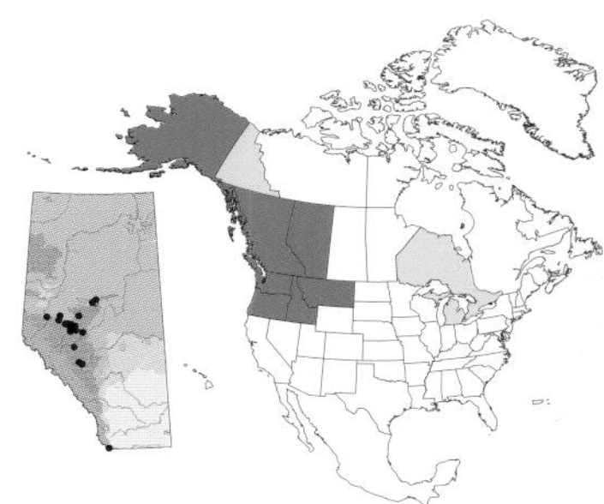

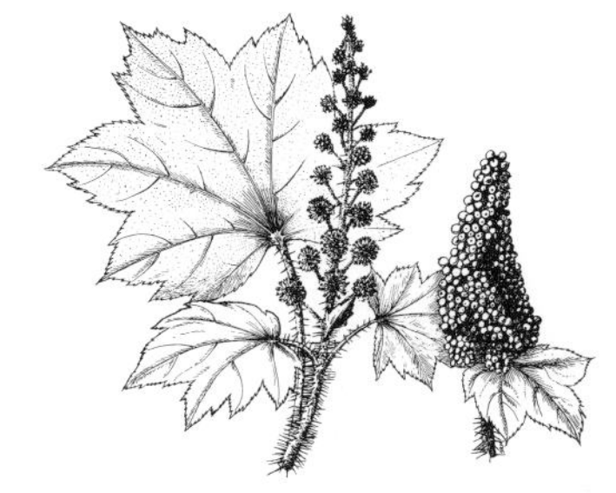

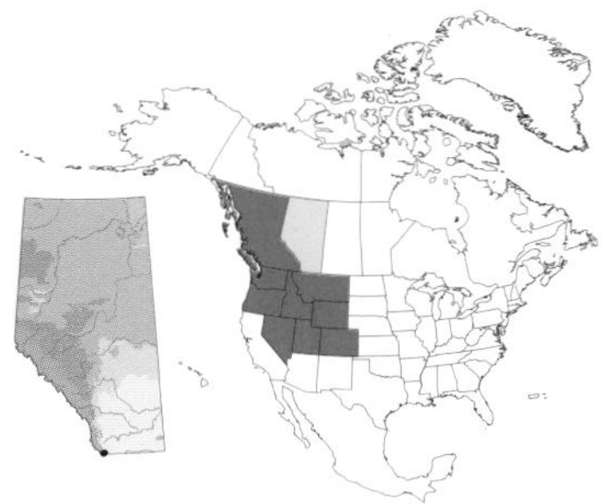

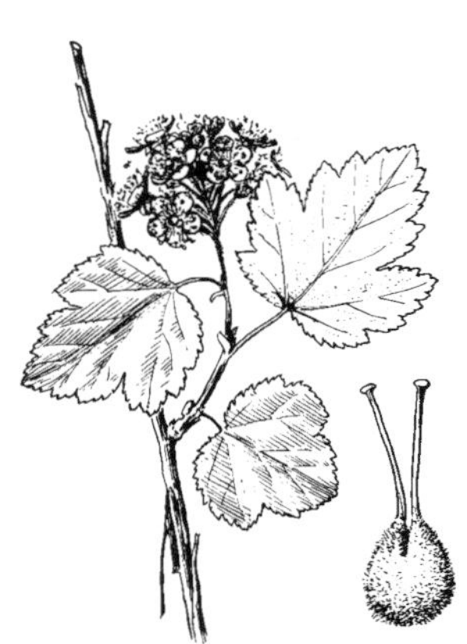

MALLOW-LEAVED NINEBARK

Physocarpus malvaceus (Greene) Kuntze
ROSE FAMILY (ROSACEAE)

Plants: Deciduous shrubs, {0.5} 1–2 m tall, with **star-shaped hairs**; branches arching, with **brown bark shredding** in strips.

Leaves: Alternate, **somewhat maple-leaf-shaped**, 3–5 lobed, about **2–6 cm long** and wide, edged with round teeth, **strongly veined, shiny and dark green above**, paler beneath, hairless or with branched hairs.

Flowers: White, saucer-shaped, about 1 cm across, with both male and female parts (many stamens; 2 styles), with 5 rounded petals and 5 persistent sepals, several, in rounded clusters (corymbs) with star-shaped and woolly hairs, borne at branch tips; {June} July–August.

Fruits: Reddish, **egg-shaped pairs of flattened, keeled, pod-like fruits** (follicles), with erect styles, joined on lower half, **fuzzy**, about 5 mm long, usually containing 2 seeds per pod.

Habitat: Dry, open or lightly wooded montane slopes and ravines; also in canyon bottoms and thickets south of Alberta.

Notes: The Okanagan used mallow-leaved ninebark as a good-luck charm to protect their hunting equipment. • Mallow-leaved ninebark makes an attractive garden addition. It is best grown from cuttings. Seeds should be sown in the autumn, but they are slow to become established. • The common name 'ninebark' was given to these shrubs because they were believed to have 9 layers of shredding bark. The generic name *Physocarpus* was taken from the Greek *physa* (bladder) and *carpos* (fruit), because of the inflated pods of most species.

PINK MEADOWSWEET

Spiraea splendens Baumann *ex* K. Koch var. *splendens*
ROSE FAMILY (ROSACEAE)

Plants: **Slender shrubs**, 0.5–1.5 m high with ascending, densely clustered, reddish brown branches.

Leaves: **Alternate**, short-stalked, simple; blades **egg-shaped or elliptic**, 1.5–4 cm long, **rounded at both ends, toothed toward the tip**, bright green above, paler beneath, essentially hairless.

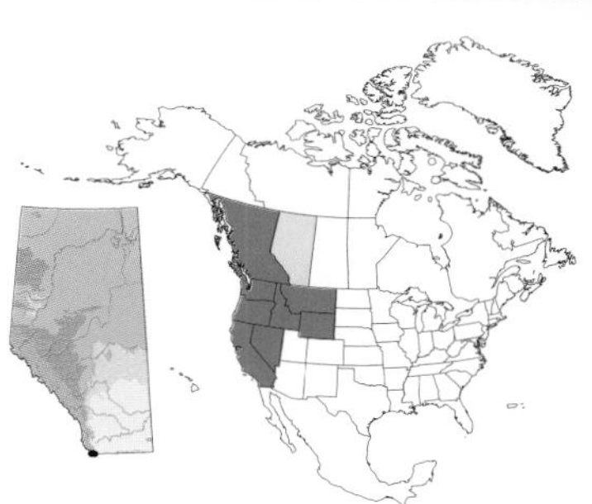

Flowers: **Pink or rose-coloured, sweet-scented**, with both male and female parts (15–many stamens; 5 styles); **5 petals 1.5–2 mm long**; 5 sepals, egg-shaped, blunt-tipped; many flowers in **dense, flat-topped clusters 2–5 cm across**; {June–August}.

Fruits: Pod-like fruits that split open down 1 side (follicles), firm, shiny, **2.5–3 mm long, in erect groups of 4 or 5**, each usually containing 4 narrow, tapered seeds.

Habitat: Moist woods, wet meadows and boggy areas near timberline.

Notes: This species has also been called *Spiraea densiflora* Nutt. *ex* T. & G. • White meadowsweet (*Spiraea betulifolia* Pallas) is a much more common species. It also has flat-topped flower clusters, but its flowers are white and its leaves are larger (2–8 cm long) with larger teeth (2 mm vs. 1 mm or less). • The generic name *Spiraea* is from the Greek *speiraira*, a plant used in wreaths and garlands. Some garden varieties of *Spiraea* are called 'bridal-wreath.'

JG

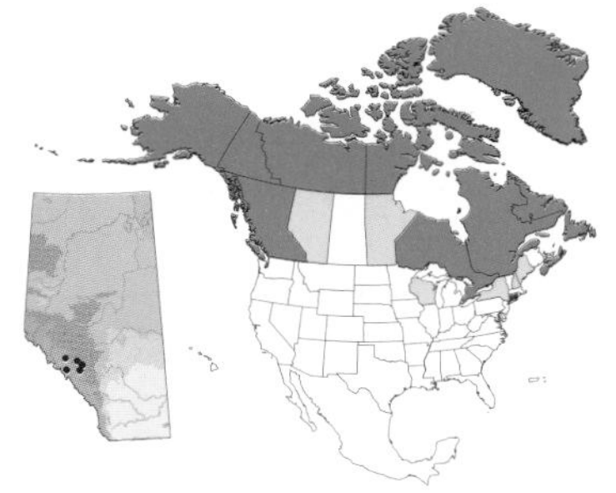

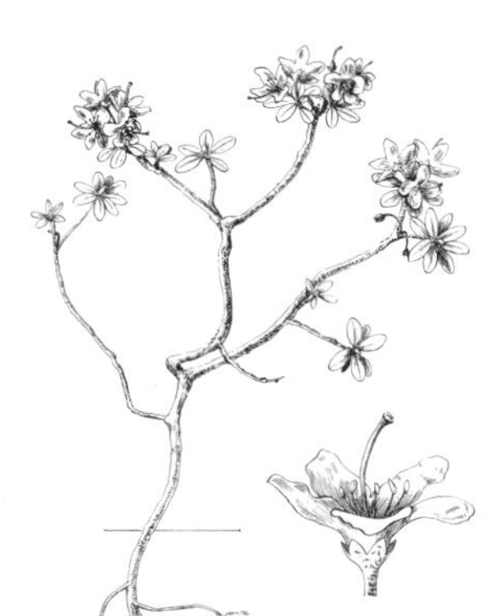

LAPLAND ROSE-BAY

Rhododendron lapponicum (L.) Wahl.
HEATH FAMILY (ERICACEAE)

Plants: Small shrubs, matted and 5–25 cm tall or bushy and up to 80 cm tall (in protected sites); twigs densely covered with tiny, brown, bran-like scales.

Leaves: **Alternate**, elliptic to oblong, widest above the middle, blunt-tipped, 6–18 {5–20} mm long, **persisting for more than a single growing season**, thick and **leathery**, **brownish beneath with dense, rusty-brown scales**, greenish above with scattered scales, short-stalked; buds scaly and conspicuous.

Flowers: **Deep rose-purple**, very fragrant, broadly cupped, 1–2 cm across, 8–12 mm long, with 5 spreading lobes, slightly bilaterally symmetric (zygomorphic), with both male and female parts (5–10 stamens; 1 style); calyx 0.5–1.5 mm long, with 5 tiny, triangular lobes, fringed with hairs; 5–10 stamens, projecting from the mouth of the flower on hairless filaments; stalks 6–10 mm long, scurfy; 3–6 flowers **in flat-topped clusters** (umbel-like) at the branch tips; June.

Fruits: Capsules, 4–8 mm long, scurfy, splitting lengthwise into 5 parts; seeds tiny and edged with small wings; June {July–August}.

Habitat: Moist alpine slopes and upper subalpine sites near timberline; elsewhere, on dry, rocky tundra and heathlands and occasionally in woodlands.

Notes: The only other species of this genus that is native to Alberta, white-flowered rhododendron (*Rhododendron albiflorum* Hook.), is easily distinguished by its thin, pale-green, deciduous leaves and its white flowers, which are borne in small (1–3-flowered) clusters from leaf axils along the branches. • Some sources report that the leaves and flowers of Lapland rose-bay have been used to make tea, but all rhododendrons are **poisonous**, as is the honey made from their nectar, so these plants should be treated as **toxic**. • Many beautiful rhododendrons are cultivated around the world in flower gardens. • The generic name *Rhododendron* was derived from the Greek *rhodon* (rose) and *dendron* (tree). The specific epithet *lapponicum* means 'of Lapland.'

OVAL-LEAVED BLUEBERRY

Vaccinium ovalifolium J.E. Smith
HEATH FAMILY (ERICACEAE)

Plants: Spreading, diffusely **branched, deciduous shrubs,** 20–60 cm tall (sometimes to 100 cm); **twigs angled,** hairless, yellowish green, often reddish, greyish with age.

Leaves: Alternate; blades elliptic to oblong-oval, blunt-tipped, 2–4 {5} cm long, **hairless, thin, greyish green** with a thin, waxy coating on the lower surface, **essentially toothless** (sometimes slightly wavy or very finely toothed below the middle); stalks 1–2 mm long.

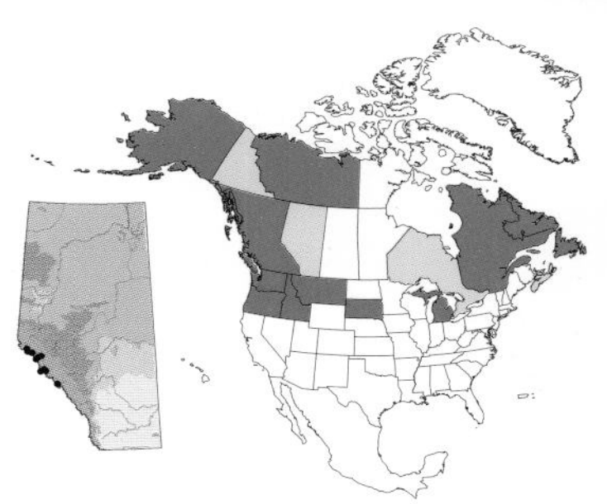

Flowers: Pinkish, urn-shaped, with 5 petal lobes, about 7–9 mm long, usually **longer than they are wide** and broadest below the middle, with both male and female parts (10 stamens; 1 style); stamens with short, hairless filaments (shorter than the anthers) and large anthers tipped with a pair of slender tubes and bearing 2 spreading bristles (awns); styles usually included within the flower; **borne singly** from leaf axils on 1–5 mm long stalks; {May–July}, before the leaves are half expanded.

Fruits: Hanging, **blackish blue berries with a whitish, waxy covering** (bloom), 6–9 mm wide; **stalks strongly bent downward, not enlarged immediately below the berry,** 1–5 mm long; {July–September}.

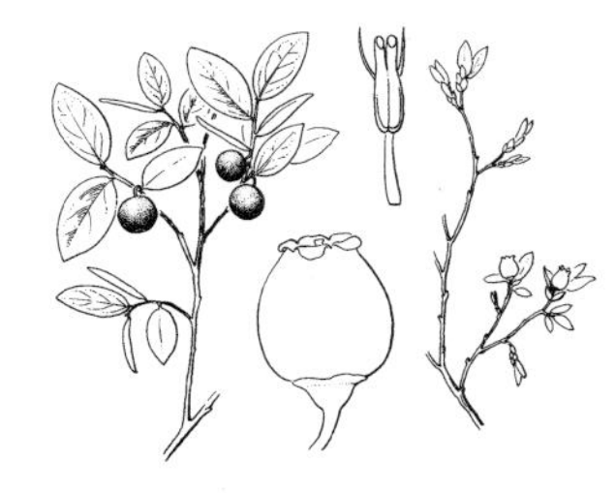

Habitat: Moist subalpine thickets and woods; elsewhere, on peaty soils and in coastal forests.

Notes: This species has also been called tall huckleberry, oval-leaved huckleberry and blue bilberry. • Low bilberry (*Vaccinium myrtillus* L.) and tall bilberry (*Vaccinium membranaceum* Dougl. *ex* Hook.) are 2 common species that are also nearly hairless and that have angled twigs and scattered bluish black berries. They are easily distinguished from oval-leaved blueberry by their finely toothed, pointed leaves. • Another rare Alberta species, bog bilberry (*Vaccinium uliginosum* L.), has rounded (not clearly angled) reddish or brownish twigs and firm, dull green, toothless leaves with rounded tips and wedge-shaped bases. Its flowers are commonly tipped with 4 (rather than 5) petal lobes and contain 8 (rather than 10) stamens. Bog bilberry grows in bogs and on alpine slopes, and is reported to bloom from May to July. • The fruit of both species is edible and delicious.

V. ULIGINOSUM

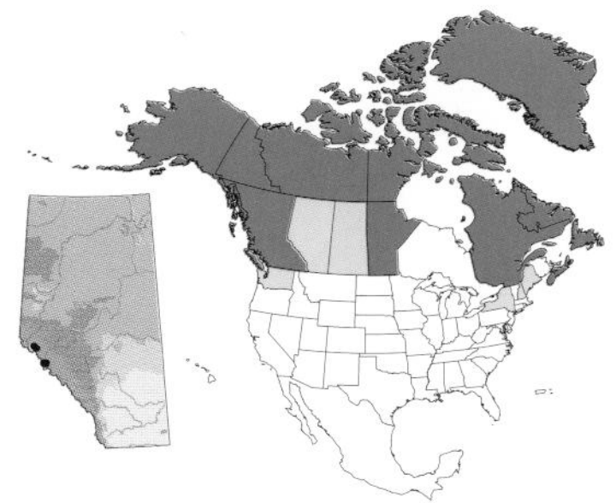

ALPINE AZALEA

Loiseleuria procumbens (L.) Desv.
HEATH FAMILY (ERICACEAE)

Plants: Dwarf evergreen shrubs about 5–6 cm tall; stems much branched, tufted, spreading on the ground (prostrate), up to 30 cm long, mat-forming.

Leaves: **Opposite, evergreen**, narrowly elliptic to oblong, **2–8 mm long**, leathery, hairless on the upper surface, short-hairy beneath, rolled under along the edges, borne on short stalks that partly clasp the stem.

Flowers: **Pink** or sometimes whitish, **3–4** {5} **mm long**, with both male and female parts (5 stamens; 1 style), with **5 spreading petals** that are fused together at the base; **5 sepals**, red, hairless, 1.5–2.5 mm long; **5 stamens**; 2–6 flowers in small, flat-topped clusters (corymbs) at the branch tips; June–July {August}.

Fruits: Egg-shaped capsules, 3–5 mm long, containing many seeds in 2 or 3 compartments; July–August.

Habitat: Moist alpine meadows and rocky subalpine slopes; elsewhere, in dry, stony heathlands.

Notes: The generic name *Loiseleuria* commemorates Jean Louis Auguste Loiseleur-Deslongchamps, a French botanist who lived 1774–1849. The specific epithet *procumbens* (to fall forward or bend over) refers to the prostrate growth form of this small shrub.

BIG SAGEBRUSH

Artemisia tridentata Nutt.
ASTER FAMILY (ASTERACEAE [COMPOSITAE])

Plants: Greyish, wintergreen shrubs, **aromatic**, much branched, erect, {0.5} 1–2 m tall; bark greyish and shredding on older branches, densely silvery-hairy on young twigs.

Leaves: Alternate, **narrowly wedge-shaped, 3-toothed at tip** and tapered to base, 1–2 cm long, densely silvery-hairy.

Flowerheads: Small yellow or brownish heads, 2–3 mm across, of 5–8 disc florets, with both male and female parts (perfect); involucres 3–5 mm high; numerous, in **long, narrow, branched clusters** (panicles) 1.5–7 cm wide; August–September {July–October}.

Fruits: Sparsely hairy, seed-like fruits (achenes), not tipped with a tuft of hairs (pappus).

Habitat: Dry, open sites from the plains to near timberline, locally abundant, often covering many hectares.

Notes: Although they can be quite bitter, the seeds of several sagebrushes were used for food, and those of big sagebrush were considered the best. They were eaten raw or dried, often ground into meal and cooked. • Sagebrush leaves were boiled to make a tea for treating colds and pneumonia and aiding in childbirth. It was said to act like Epsom salts and to cure indigestion and flatulence, and the Navajo drank it before long hikes and athletic contests to cleanse the body. In the sweat bath, moistened branches are sometimes thrown onto hot rocks, and the resulting vapours are grimly inhaled until the participants are nearly prostrate. • The leaves were burned as a fumigant or smudge, and leafy branches were bound together to make brooms. The shredding bark was woven into mats, bags and cloaks. The wood was burned when no other fuel was available. • Livestock do not like to eat big sagebrush, and overgrazing of grasslands can result in dramatic increases in the abundance of this shrub.

LA

DJ

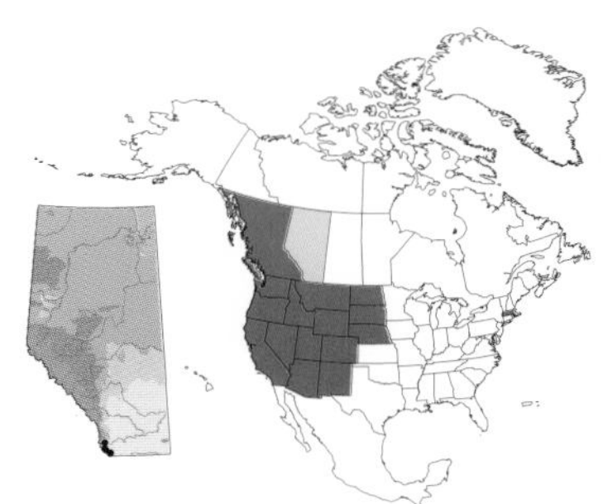

Monocots

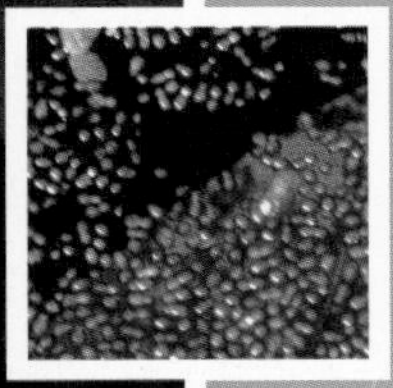

GLOBE BUR-REED

Sparganium glomeratum (Beurling *ex* Laest.) L.M. Neuman
BUR-REED FAMILY (SPARGANIACEAE)

Plants: Aquatic perennial herbs; stems slender, erect or floating, up to 2.5 m long; from fibrous roots and creeping buried stems (rhizomes).

Leaves: In 2 vertical rows on the stems, **ribbon-like, 3–10 mm wide, mostly floating** on the surface of the water, stalkless, slightly expanded at the base and sheathing the stem.

Flowers: Tiny, male or female (unisexual); female flowers with 3–6 sepals (no petals) and 1 ovary; numerous flowers in dense, round male or female heads, **crowded, with 1 {2} male head(s) above 3–5 female heads**, held above the water on erect stalks; July {August}.

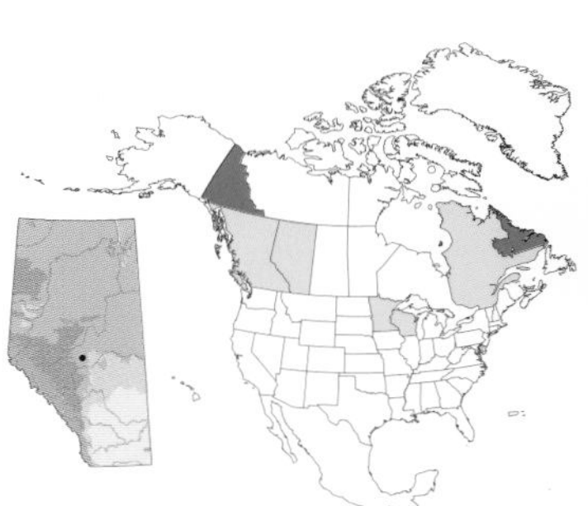

Fruits: Dry, dull brown, nut-like 'seeds' (achenes), **ellipsoid, 4–5 mm long, tipped with a straight beak about 1–1.5 mm long**, forming dense, 1–1.5 cm, **bur-like heads**; mid to late summer.

Habitat: Cool lakes, ponds and slow streams; often in water 1–2 m deep; possibly introduced.

Notes: Another rare Alberta species, floating-leaved bur-reed (*Sparganium fluctuans* (Engelm. *ex* Morong) B.L. Robins.), grows in ponds and flowers in July and August. It is similar to globe bur-reed, but its cross-veins form a distinct pattern on the lower surface of the leaves, it has branched flower clusters with 2 or more male heads per branch (rather than solitary), and its achenes are tipped with stout, flat, strongly curved (not straight) beaks. • Many shorebirds and waterfowl, including common snipes, rails, black ducks, wood ducks, mallards and coots, eat these nut-like fruits. Muskrats feed on the leaves.

S. FLUCTUANS

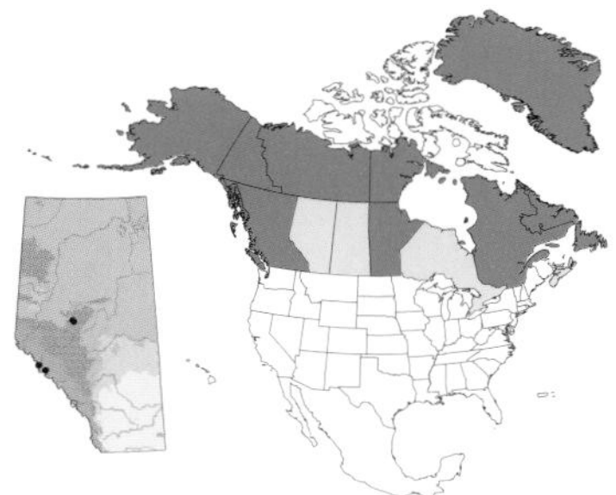

NORTHERN BUR-REED

Sparganium hyperboreum Beurling *ex* Laest.
BUR-REED FAMILY (SPARGANIACEAE)

Plants: Slender **aquatic perennial** herbs; stems weak, submerged or floating, 10–30 cm long; from fibrous roots and creeping buried stems (rhizomes).

Leaves: In 2 vertical rows on the stems, ribbon-like, 10–30 {50} cm long and **1–5 mm wide, opaque, often yellowish**, mostly floating on the surface of the water, stalkless, sheathing the stem.

Flowers: Tiny, male or female (unisexual); female flowers with 3–6 scale-like sepals (no petals) and 1 ovary; numerous flowers in dense, round male or female heads, arranged in **small, unbranched clusters** with a **single, stalkless male head** at the tip (touching the uppermost female head) and **2–4 female heads below**, held above the water on erect stalks; July–August.

Fruits: Dry, **nut-like, ribbed** 'seeds' (achenes), **spindle-shaped to club-shaped, 4–5 mm long**, tipped with a **short point** up to 0.5 mm long, forming dense, 10 {5–13} mm wide, bur-like heads.

Habitat: Alpine lakes, in shallow water up to 50 cm deep; elsewhere, widespread at lower elevations across boreal North America and Eurasia.

Notes: The thick roots of some bur-reeds have been collected, cooked and eaten, but they are usually too small and scattered to warrant gathering. It is generally unwise to gather the roots of aquatic plants for food, because wetlands can be very sensitive to disturbance. In addition, poisonous plants commonly share these environments, and their roots could be confused with those of edible species.

SLENDER NAIAD, SLENDER WATER-NYMPH

Najas flexilis (Willd.) Rostk. & Schmidt
WATER-NYMPH FAMILY (NAJADACEAE)

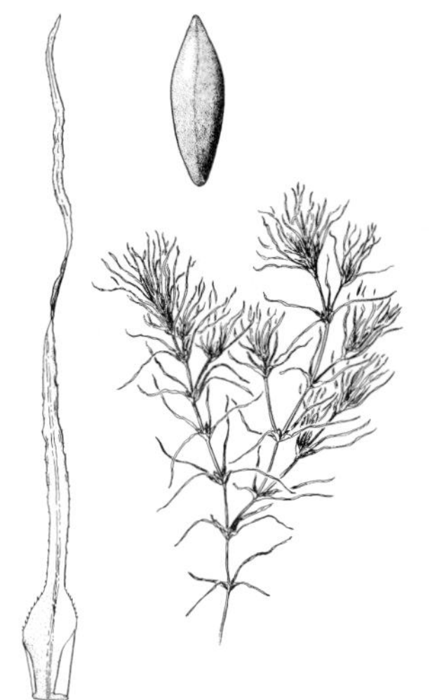

Plants: **Delicate**, pale green, aquatic annual herbs; stems **submerged**, about 1 mm thick (or less), 30–60 {10–150} cm long, with **many alternate branches** giving the plants a **tufted** appearance.

Leaves: **Crowded at stem tips in sub-opposite pairs**, 1–3 cm long, 0.5–1 mm wide but with **enlarged, clasping bases** and slender, tapered tips, edged with tiny, sharp teeth.

Flowers: **Tiny, male or female** (unisexual), **stalkless**; male flower with 1 stamen in a membranous sheath; female flowers with a single, exposed pistil (not enclosed); flowers **solitary** (sometimes with 1 male and 1 female together) in the axils of the lower pair of leaves; {April–June} July–August.

Fruits: **Membranous-walled** 'seeds' (achenes), **3–4 mm long**, tipped with a slender, 1–2 mm long style, containing pale brown, shiny, 3 mm long seeds.

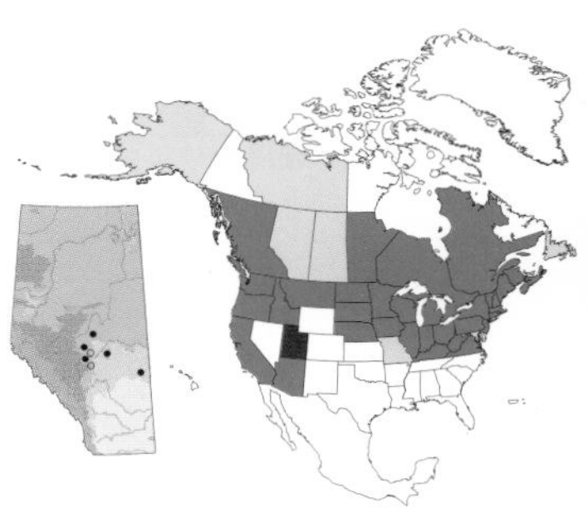

Habitat: Ponds and streams; elsewhere, in clear, shallow to deep, fresh or brackish water.

Notes: Slender naiad is usually an annual plant, reproducing by seed each year. In some cases, however, the base of the plant may survive over winter and produce new plants from shoots the following spring. • This is a true aquatic plant. Its tiny flowers are pollinated underwater. • When abundant, slender naiad is an important food for waterfowl, which eat all parts of the plants. • The generic name *Najas* is taken from the Greek *naias* (a water nymph). The specific epithet *flexilis* means 'pliant.'

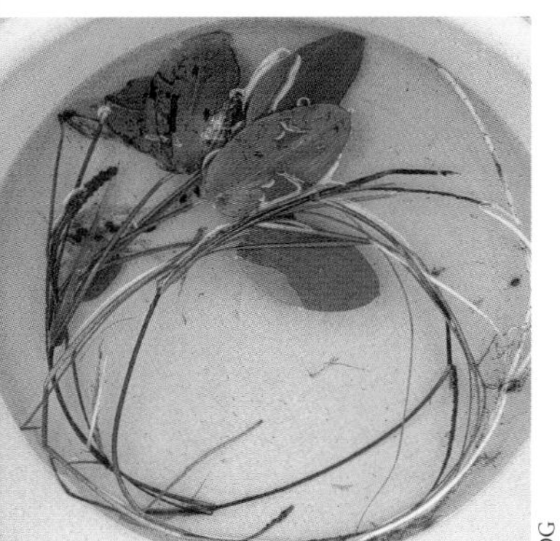
DG

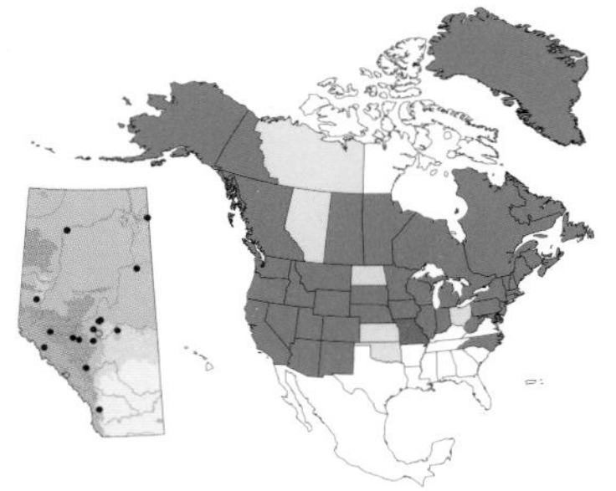

FLOATING-LEAVED PONDWEED

Potamogeton natans L.
PONDWEED FAMILY (POTAMOGETONACEAE)

Plants: **Aquatic perennial** herbs; **stems submerged, 1.5 m long**, 1–2 mm thick, with few branches; from extensive, slender underground stems (rhizomes), often with overwintering tubers.

Leaves: Alternate, **leathery, of 2 kinds; floating leaves flat, egg-shaped to elliptic**, 4–9 {10} cm long, rounded to heart-shaped at the base, 13–37-nerved, with stalks longer than blades; **submerged leaves linear**, 10–20 cm long, 0.8–2 mm wide, obscurely 3–5-nerved; **stipules free from rest of leaf**, 4–10 cm long, stiff, **fibrous.**

Flowers: **Greenish, inconspicuous**, with 4 minute petals (tepals); **many**, in 10–12 whorls, forming dense **spikes** {1} **2–5 cm long and about 1 cm thick, held above water** on long (4–14 cm) stalks; June–July {August–September}.

Fruits: **Greenish, shiny, short-beaked 'seeds' (achenes)** 3–5 mm long, slightly fleshy at first, dry and hard when mature.

Habitat: Still or slow-moving, shallow water.

Notes: The thickened, buried rhizomes of these plants are a source of starch for both humans and animals. • The generic name *Potamogeton* was derived from the Greek *potamos* (a river) and *geiton* (a neighbour), in reference to the habitats of many species. The specific epithet *natans* means 'floating,' a reference to the leathery floating leaves of this species.

BLUNT-LEAVED PONDWEED

Potamogeton obtusifolius Mert. & W.D.J. Koch
POND WEED FAMILY (POTAMOGETONACEAE)

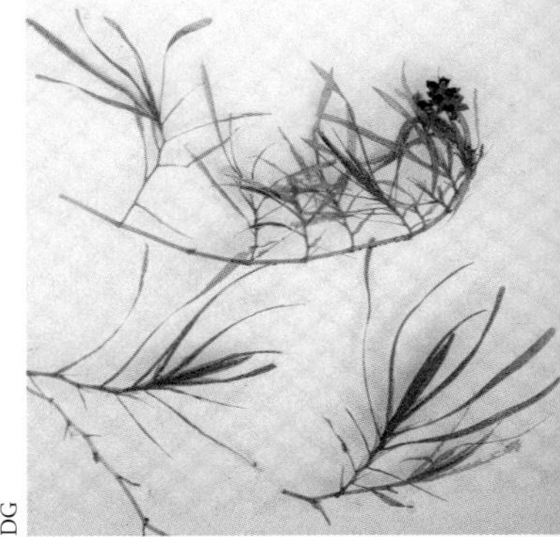

DG

Plants: Green or often reddish, **submerged aquatic perennial** herbs; stems slightly zigzagged, 50–100 cm long, slender, with pairs of conspicuous glands at each joint, much branched; from slender underground stems (rhizomes); producing winter buds.

Leaves: Alternate, translucent, all broadly **linear**, 3–9 {10} cm long, **2–3** {1–4} **mm wide**, usually **3-nerved** (sometimes 5-nerved), with 2–4 rows of white air channels (lacunae) bordering the midvein; **stipules 1–2 cm long, open** (not sheathing), translucent, eventually shredding into fibres from the tips.

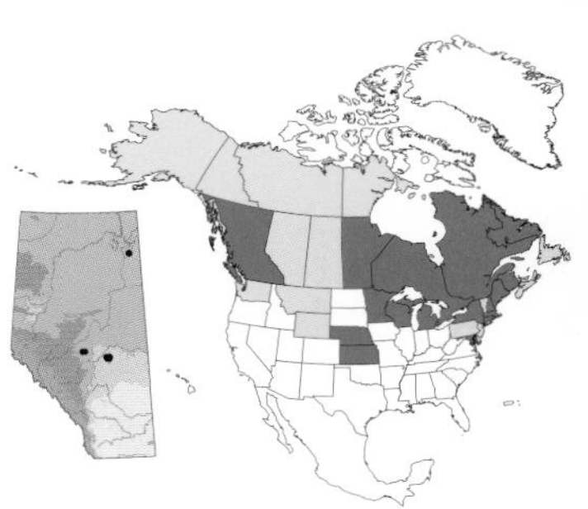

Flowers: Greenish, inconspicuous, with 4 minute petals (tepals); **many**, in dense whorls, forming egg-shaped to cylindrical **spikes 8–17** {20} **mm long, held above water** on short (1–4 cm long), stout stalks; {July–September}.

Fruits: Rounded or slightly flattened, dry 'seeds' (achenes) **2.5–4 mm long**, often tipped with a short (up to 0.7 mm) beak.

Habitat: Shallow lakes and ponds, often growing in organic sediment.

Notes: Another rare species, leafy pondweed (*Potamogeton foliosus* Raf.), is very similar to blunt-leaved pondweed, but its leaves are slightly narrower (usually less than 1.5 mm wide), its stems have no glands at their joints, and its fruits are smaller (2–3 mm long), with a sharp, wavy ridge along the back. Leafy pondweed grows in shallow, standing water, and it is reported to bloom from July to September. • These aquatic species often overwinter by producing dense, leafy winter buds at the tips of their branches. These are dropped in the autumn and sink to the bottom of the water, where they lie in the mud through the winter. In spring, the buds sprout and grow into new plants.

P. FOLIOSUS

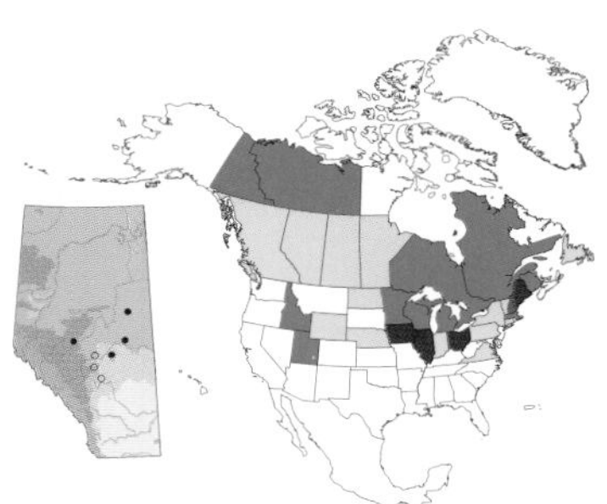

LINEAR-LEAVED PONDWEED

Potamogeton strictifolius A. Bennett
PONDWEED FAMILY (POTAMOGETONACEAE)

Plants: Olive-green to brownish, **submerged aquatic perennial** herbs; stems leafy, 50–100 cm long, very slender, slightly flattened, rather sparingly branched toward the top, sometimes with paired glands at the joints (nodes); from slender underground stems (rhizomes); producing slender winter buds on non-flowering branch tips.

Leaves: Alternate, crowded, **stiff** with firm, down-rolled edges, all **linear**, 2–6 cm long, **0.5–2.5 mm wide**, tapered to a slender point, **3** {5}**-nerved** but the side nerves faint; **stipules 1–2 cm long**, often overlapping and thus covering the stem, **white, strongly ribbed**, soon shredding into fibres.

Flowers: Greenish, inconspicuous, with 4 minute petals (tepals); **many**, in 3 or 4 well-spaced whorls or pairs, forming slender **spikes 1–1.5 cm long, held above water** on very slender stalks 1–9 cm long; {July–September}.

Fruits: Dry 'seeds' (achenes) **2–3 mm long**, sometimes with a very low ridge (keel) along the back.

Habitat: Shallow lakes and ponds.

Notes: Linear-leaved pondweed is distinguished from other slender-leaved pondweeds by its stiff, 3-nerved leaves and its whitish, strongly fibrous stipules.

WHITE-STEMMED PONDWEED

Potamogeton praelongus Wulfen
PONDWEED FAMILY (POTAMOGETONACEAE)

Plants: Large, **submerged aquatic perennial** herbs; stems whitish to olive-green, 2–3 {6} m long and 2–3 mm thick, zigzagged, freely branched near the top; from stout (2–6 mm thick), white underground stems (rhizomes) with rusty spots; producing winter buds.

Leaves: Alternate, shiny, all **oblong to lance-shaped,** tapering gradually to round, somewhat hooded tips, stalkless, rounded and slightly clasping at the base, 10–30 {7–35} cm long, {1} **2–3 cm wide**, with **3–5 main nerves** and several fainter veins; **stipules whitish, 2–8** {10} **cm long, conspicuous and persistent**, free of the leaf blades and **open** (not sheathing).

Flowers: Greenish, **inconspicuous**, with 4 minute petals (tepals); **many**, in 6–12 dense whorls, forming **spikes 3–4** {2.5–5} **cm long, held above water** on stout, 10–30 {50} cm long stalks; {May–June} July–August.

Fruits: Dry 'seeds' (achenes) **4–5** {7} **mm long**, egg-shaped, widest above middle, tipped with a thick, short (0.5–1 mm long) beak, prominently ridged down the back.

Habitat: Deep, clear water in lakes and ponds; in water up to 6 m deep.

Notes: In the autumn, these plants produce winter buds beneath conspicuous white sheaths, in the form of short, densely leafy branches. These buds begin to grow at an amazing rate the following spring. In southern BC, some plants can reach up to 5 m in length by the first week of May. • Pondweeds are very important to the ecology of many lakes and ponds. Their seeds are a favourite and important food of many wild birds, and most parts of the plants are eaten by waterfowl, shore birds, marsh birds, muskrats, beaver and deer. Most species provide food, shelter and shade for fish and small aquatic organisms. They are especially important in providing habitat for many insects that, in turn, are eaten by fish.

LK

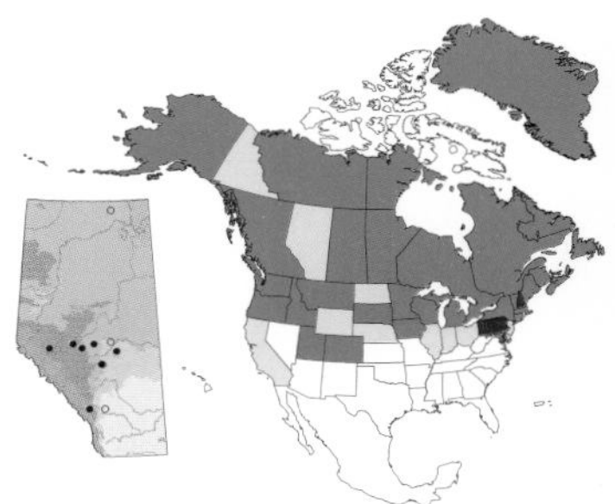

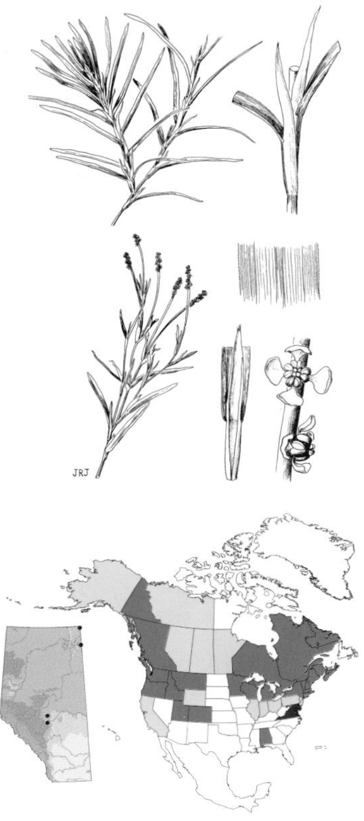

Robbins' pondweed

Potamogeton robbinsii Oakes
PONDWEED FAMILY (POTAMOGETONACEAE)

Plants: Leafy, submerged aquatic perennial herbs; stems stout, round, 0.5–3 m long, freely branched, creeping on mud and rooting at lower joints; from underground stems (rhizomes); producing winter buds.

Leaves: Alternate, **crowded, in 2 opposite vertical rows**, widely **spreading**, dark brownish green, all **linear to lance-shaped**, pointed at the tip, stalkless and somewhat clasping at the base, 2–8 {12} cm long, **3–5** {8} **mm wide**, edged with **fine, sharp, white teeth, with 20–35 fine nerves** (or more); **stipules** pale, with their bases **joined to the leaf blades in a** {5} **10–15 mm long sheath**, shredding into white fibres, which often cover the stem between the leaves.

Flowers: Greenish, **inconspicuous**, with 4 minute petals (tepals); **many**, densely whorled, with about 4 whorls per spike and **several 7–20 mm long spikes** per branched cluster, **held above water** on flat, stiff, 3–5 {7} cm long stalks; {August–September}.

Fruits: Blackish 'seeds' (achenes) **3–4 mm long**, egg-shaped, widest above middle, tipped with an inconspicuous beak, sharply ridged down the back.

Habitat: Shallow to deep (1–3 m), quiet water in lakes and ponds, usually growing on organic material or muck.

Notes: Robbins' pondweed rarely produces mature seed. Instead, it reproduces vegetatively by growing from stem (stolon) tips and joints and by producing coarse, leafy winter buds. • Pondweed seeds can be carried for thousands of miles by migrating waterfowl. These birds not only carry the seeds for great distances and deposit them in favourable habitats, but they also improve the seeds' ability to germinate. In fact, germination of the seeds of at least one species proved possible only after the seeds had passed through a bird's digestive tract or been exposed to similar conditions.

WIDGEON-GRASS

Ruppia cirrhosa (Petagna) Grande
DITCH-GRASS FAMILY (RUPPIACEAE)

Plants: Submerged aquatic perennial **herbs; stems slender, forked**, up to 80 cm long; from elongated underground stems (rhizomes) and runners (stolons).

Leaves: Alternate, spreading, in 2 vertical rows (ranks), **thread-like**, 5–20 cm long, scarcely 0.5 mm wide; basal appendages (stipules) 5–15 mm long, **sheathing the stem** and with the tips sometimes free for 1–2 mm, thin and translucent along the edges.

Flowers: Tiny, lacking obvious sepals and petals, consisting of 2 stamens and 4 ovaries; borne in small, stalked, **spike-like** structures with 2 flowers at the tip, from the sheaths of the uppermost leaves, the thick stalk (spadix) elongating to carry the flowers to the surface of the water; July {August}.

Fruits: Egg-shaped or pear-shaped, somewhat fleshy, **drupe-like achenes**, 3–4 mm long, borne **on slender stalks in flat-topped** (umbel-like) **clusters at the tips of slender, 3–50 cm long, coiled stalks** (elongated spadixes) from upper leaf axils.

Habitat: Saline and alkaline lakes, ponds and ditches; elsewhere, in brackish or salt water along the coast, rarely in fresh water.

Notes: This species has also been called *Ruppia maritima* L. and *R. occidentalis* S. Wats. • Some taxonomists include widgeon-grass in the pondweed family (Potamogetonaceae). Although the unique clusters of flowers and fruits on their long, coiled stalks are unmistakable, non-flowering plants can scarcely be distinguished from some of the narrow-leaved pondweeds, especially sago pondweed (*Potamogeton pectinatus* L.), which is widespread in Alberta. • Widgeon-grass flowers are usually pollinated at the water surface by floating pollen, but some straight-stalked flowers are pollinated underwater. This is a highly variable species, with many forms. • The generic name *Ruppia* commemorates Heinrich Bernhard Ruppius (1688–1719), a German botanist who wrote *Flora Jenensis*. The specific epithet *cirrhosa* means 'tendrilled,' referring to the long, coiled flower stalks.

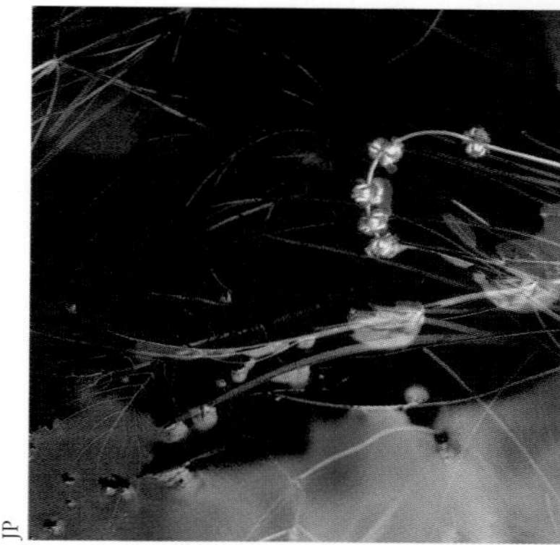
JP

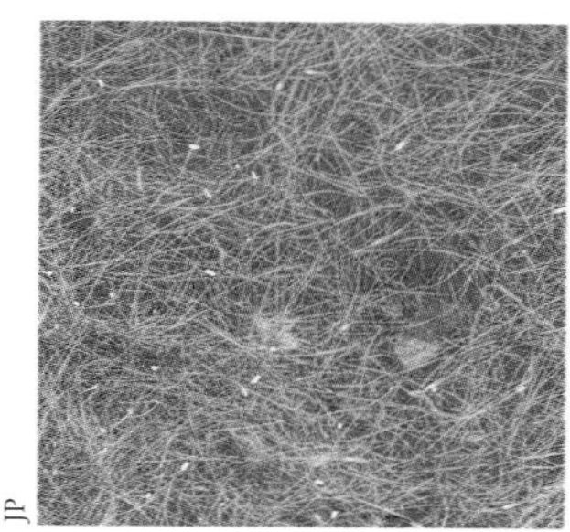
JP

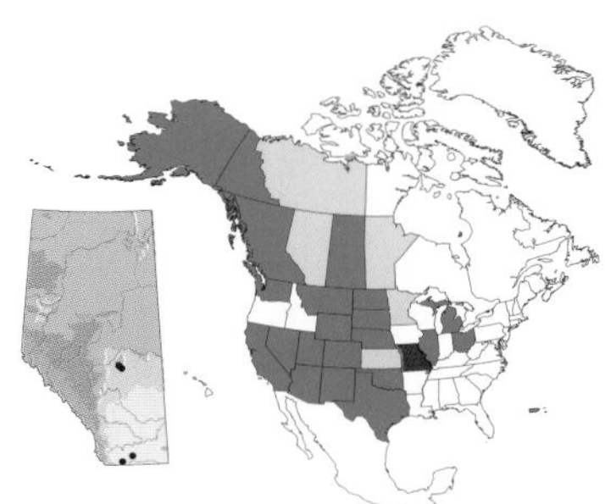

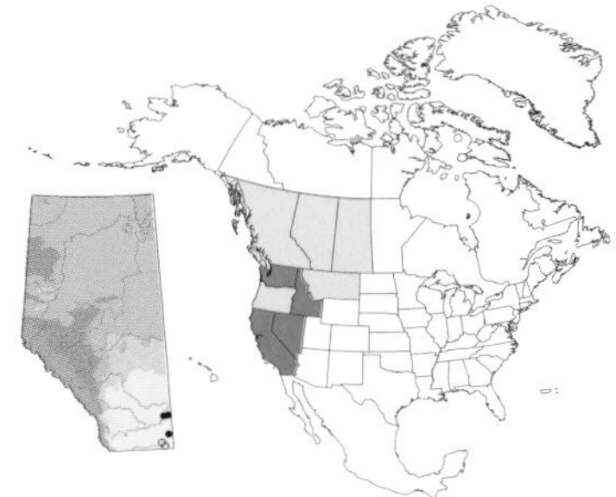

FLOWERING-QUILLWORT

Lilaea scilloides (Poir.) Hauman
ARROW-GRASS FAMILY (JUNCAGINACEAE)

Plants: Small, densely tufted, **semi-aquatic annual herbs;** stems very short, essentially absent; from fibrous roots.

Leaves: Basal, rush-like, cylindrical (terete), linear to awl-shaped, {3} 8–35 cm long, 1–4 mm thick, soft, with dry, translucent, sheathing bases.

Flowers: Tiny, lacking petals and sepals, each with **1 stalkless stamen or 1 carpel (or both); flowers in 2 types** of clusters; **solitary female flowers enclosed in the leaf bases,** each with a 3-sided carpel tipped by a thread-like style up to 10 cm long and ending in a head-like stigma; **small, 0.5–4 cm long spikes on slender, leafless stalks** 5–20 {3–25} cm long, each spike with female flowers at the base and male flowers at the tip; male flowers in the axils of 2–3 mm long bracts but these are soon dropped; female flowers tipped with short, stout styles; July {June–August}.

Fruits: Erect, dry, single-seeded, {3} 4–6 mm long, ribbed, those in the stalked spikes **flattened and 2-winged,** those of the lower flowers in the leaf sheaths, **3-sided and tipped with 3 small horns.**

Habitat: Slough edges and mud flats; elsewhere, in sloughs and dry creek beds, shallow water and tidal flats.

Notes: This species has also been called *Lilaea subulata* Humb. & Bonpl. and has been placed in the flowering-quillwort family (Lilaeaceae). • Flowering-quillwort usually grows in shallow water, where the stigmas of the lower female flowers and the spikes of mixed flowers float on the surface or are held above the water. They are also often stranded in mud at the edges of receding ponds. The non-flowering plants might be mistaken for quillworts (*Isoetes* spp., pp. 352–53) at first glance, but they are truly stalkless, without the bulbous stocks found at the bases of quillwort plants. • The genus *Lilaea* was named in honour of Alire Raffeneau Delile (1778–1850), a French authority on the flora of north Africa and Asia Minor. The specific epithet *scilloides* refers to the similarity between the leaves of flowering-quillwort and those of a squill (*Scilla* sp.), a member of the lily family (Liliaceae).

BROAD-LEAVED ARROWHEAD, SWAMP POTATO, WAPATO

Sagittaria latifolia Willd.
WATER-PLANTAIN FAMILY (ALISMATACEAE)

LA

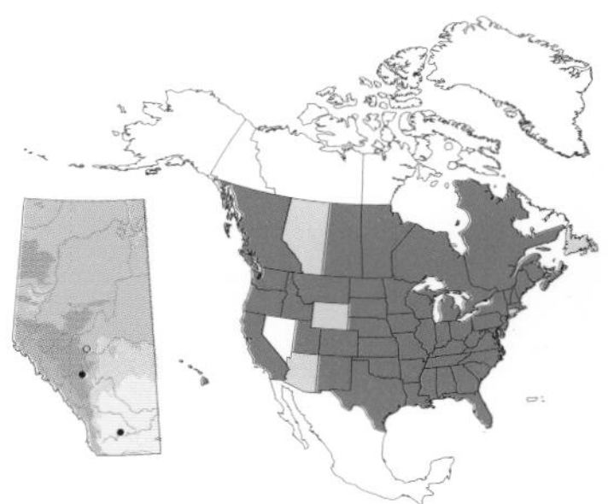

Plants: **Emergent** perennial herbs; stems 30–60 {20–80} cm tall; from slender underground stems (rhizomes) that often end in **tubers.**

Leaves: Of two types; emergent leaves **arrowhead-shaped** with the **basal lobes equal to or shorter than the upper part of the blade,** up to 25 cm long, on long, angled stalks; submerged leaves (when present) thin and ribbon-like, about 4–10 mm wide.

Flowers: **White, 2–4 cm wide,** each with **3 petals,** 3 small, green sepals, male or female (unisexual), from the axil of a blunt-tipped, **egg-shaped bract 5–10** {15} **mm long;** flowers arranged in **2–8 whorls of 3,** usually with male flowers above female flowers on the same plant (sometimes with male or female plants), in 20–50 {90} cm long clusters; August {July–September}.

Fruits: Dry, **egg-shaped** 'seeds' (achenes), 2.3–3.5 {5} mm long, with 0.5–1.5 mm long **beaks projecting horizontally** from their tips, flattened, broadly winged, **in round, dense heads** that are **usually over 1.5 cm in diameter;** mid to late summer.

Habitat: Ponds, lakes and ditches.

Notes: This species has also been called *Sagittaria sagittifolia* L. var. *latifolia* Muhl. • Arum-leaved arrowhead (*Sagittaria cuneata* Sheld.) is a widespread species that resembles broad-leaved arrowhead, but it is generally a smaller plant (20–40 cm tall) with smaller (less than 1.5 cm) heads of smaller (2–2.5 mm long) achenes bearing small (less than 0.5 mm), erect (not horizontal) beaks. The bracts in its flower clusters are lance-shaped and slender-pointed. • The leaf shape of broad-leaved arrowhead varies with changes in water level and other environmental factors, but it is less 'plastic' than that of arum-leaved arrowhead. • The seeds and tubers (especially the tubers) are valuable food for waterfowl and marsh birds. Muskrats and porcupines eat the leaves and tubers. • Many native peoples used the large, chestnut-sized tubers for food. Swamp potatoes were roasted and eaten, or were cooked and dried for later use.

TWO-LEAVED WATERWEED, LONG-SHEATHED WATERWEED

Elodea bifoliata St. John
WATERWEED FAMILY (HYDROCHARITACEAE)

Plants: Aquatic perennial herbs, **submerged**, with only the flowers reaching above the water; stems slender, sparingly branched in 2s; with roots anchored in mud or free floating.

Leaves: Opposite and well spaced on the lower stem, occasionally more crowded on the upper stem, linear, blunt-tipped (rarely pointed), 1–2 {4} mm wide, edged with fine, sharp teeth; **larger leaves** {17} **20–26 mm long.**

Flowers: Inconspicuous, either male or female on each plant, each surrounded by an enlarged bract (spathe) and consisting of **3 sepals, 3 petals** and the reproductive organs **at the tip of a slender, stalk-like tube** (hypanthium) **that holds the flower at or above the water surface; male** (staminate) **flowers** with a 2–15 mm long spathe, a 4–30 cm long hypanthium tube, 3 broad, 3.5–5 mm long and 2–2.5 mm wide sepals, 3 slender, white, 5 mm long and 0.5 mm wide petals, 3 sterile stamens (staminodia) and 6 fertile stamens with 3.1–4.5 mm long anthers; **female** (pistillate) **flowers** with a **3–7 cm long spathe,** a 15–40 cm long (or longer) hypanthium tube, 3 white, spoon-shaped, 4 mm long and 1.3 mm wide petals, 3 sepals about 3 mm long and 1.3 mm wide, and a single, inferior, 3–4 mm long ovary tipped with 3 stigmas 1–2 mm long; solitary flowers in leaf axils; July–August {September}.

Fruits: Capsules, about 10 mm long, containing 6 seeds, each 5–6 mm long.

Habitat: Sloughs, ponds and lakes, in quiet or running water.

E. CANADENSIS

Notes: This species has also been called *Elodea longivaginata* St. John, and it was called *Elodea canadensis* Michx. in the first edition of the *Flora of Alberta*. • Canada waterweed (*Elodea canadensis* Michx.) has not yet been found in Alberta, but it grows in BC, Montana and eastern Saskatchewan, so it may be discovered here eventually. Canada waterweed is distinguished by its shorter (rarely over 15 mm long) leaves, which are mostly crowded and borne in whorls of 3 (rather than in pairs). It grows in similar habitats and is reported to flower from July to September.

WATERMEAL, COLUMBIAN DUCKMEAL

Wolffia columbiana Karsten
DUCKWEED FAMILY (LEMNACEAE)

Plants: **Tiny aquatic plants**, consisting of a **round to egg-shaped body** (thallus) about **1 mm long**, **floating low in the water** with the centre of the upper side exposed above the surface of the water, greenish, without white dots on the rounded upper surface, **lacking roots**; pores (stomata) few (usually fewer than 10); can be found from June to early October.

Leaves: None.

Flowers: Tiny, inconspicuous, either male or female, with 1 of each sex on the upper surface of the plant; male flowers with 1 stamen; female flowers with 1 ovary; **none** yet found in Alberta, apparently reproducing only by budding here.

Fruits: Single, tiny, thin-walled 'seeds' (utricles); not yet found in Alberta.

Habitat: Beaver ponds in hummocky moraines; elsewhere, in moderately to extremely nutrient-rich ponds.

Notes: This species has also been called *Wolffia arhiza* Wimm. • Watermeal is readily carried on the feet and feathers of waterfowl and doubtless reached Alberta in this way. However, these plants are so tiny and inconspicuous that they are easily overlooked. They are often discovered by phycologists studying water samples under a microscope. • Watermeal overwinters at the bottom of ponds as young bulblets (turions). In northern parts of its range, it reproduces largely or entirely by budding (asexual reproduction, without flowers), so some Alberta populations could be clones of single plants. It can form virtual monocultures or can grow intermixed with similar small floating plants, such as northern duckmeal (*Wolffia borealis* (Engelm. *ex* Hegelm.) Landolt), common duckweed (*Lemna turionifera* Landolt, also called *Lemna minor* L.) and larger duckweed (*Spirodela polyrhiza* (L.) Schleiden). • The stabilization of water levels as a result of beaver activity is very beneficial to watermeal. Stable water levels and sufficient depth of water to ensure that the pond does not freeze to the bottom in winter are essential for survival, because these plants cannot survive drying or prolonged freezing. • Like northern duckmeal, watermeal provides superior feeding for dabbling ducks in the autumn.

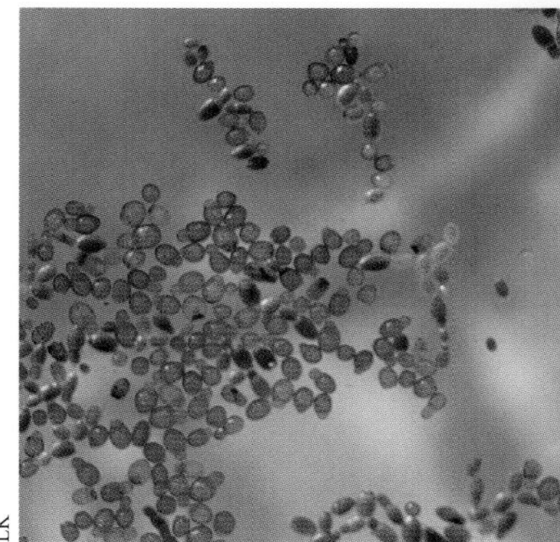

LK

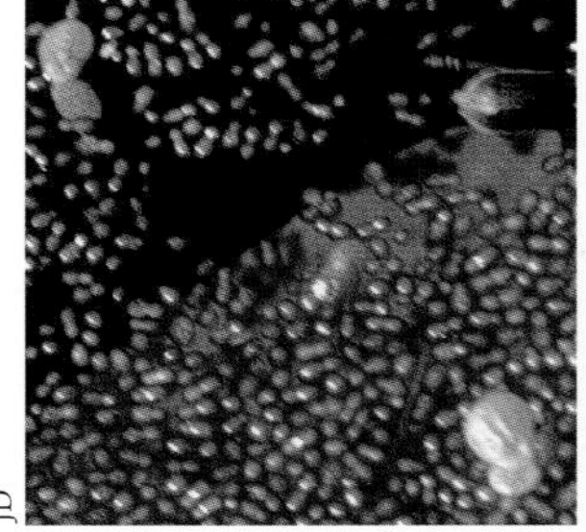

JD

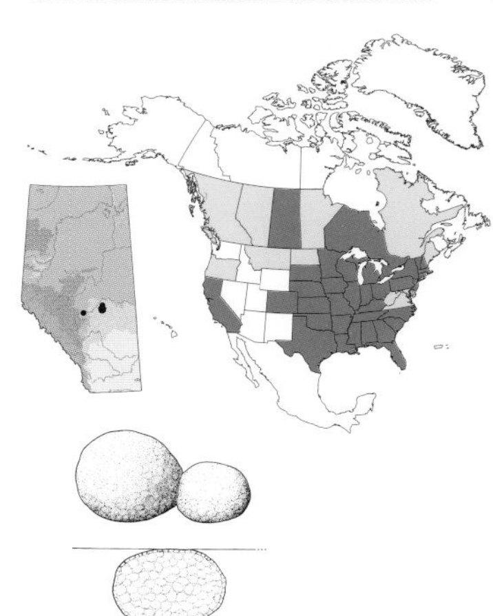

LEMNA TURIONIFERA

LA

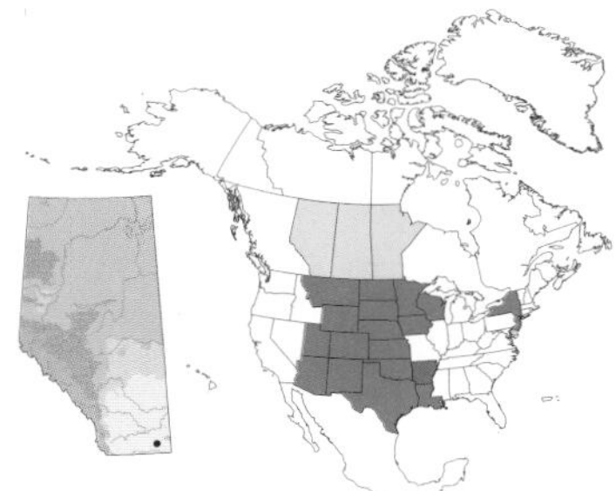

WESTERN SPIDERWORT

Tradescantia occidentalis (Britt.) Smyth var. *occidentalis*
SPIDERWORT FAMILY (COMMELINACEAE)

Plants: Blue-green perennial herbs; stem erect, smooth, almost succulent, greyish with a waxy coat (glaucous), 10–50 {60} cm tall, branched, with 2–5 joints (nodes); roots thickened.

Leaves: Alternate, **linear to narrowly lance-shaped, parallel-veined**, often folded lengthwise or with edges rolled inward, 10–30 cm long and 4–12 mm wide, **with loose, inflated sheaths**; sheaths 2–4 times the width of the blade, hairless, prominently parallel-veined.

Flowers: Blue, sometimes purplish or rose-coloured, with **3 petals and 3 sepals**; **petals egg-shaped, 7–15 mm long**; sepals green with purplish edges, glandular-hairy, elliptic, sharp-pointed, 6–12 mm long; **6 stamens**, with bearded stalks (filaments); stigmas single, head-like (capitate), at the tip of a very thin style; few to many flowers on 1–2 cm long, glandular-hairy stalks in **spreading, flat-topped clusters** (cymes) at branch tips or from upper joints (nodes) **above 2 leaf-like, 5–15 cm long, strongly sheathing bracts**; June {July}.

Fruits: Oblong capsules with 3 cavities, each containing 1 or 2 seeds, splitting lengthwise along 3 lines; seeds ridged and pitted, grey; late July–August.

Habitat: Sand dunes, sandy plains and dry grassland.

Notes: Often only a single flower in each cluster opens each day and lasts only a few hours. • The generic name *Tradescantia* commemorates John Tradescant Sr., an English horticulturist who lived ca. 1580–1638. The specific epithet *occidentalis* is Latin for 'western.' The common name 'spiderwort' refers to sticky threads that can be pulled from the broken stem tips; these were likened to the strands of a spider's web. The suffix 'wort' comes from the Old English for 'plant.'

Geyer's Wild Onion

Allium geyeri S. Wats.
LILY FAMILY (LILIACEAE)

LA

Plants: Slender perennial herbs with an onion-like aroma; single stems, {10} 20–50 cm tall; from egg-shaped (or more elongate) bulbs, usually clustered, with whitish inner layers, outer layers persisting as fibrous, **rather coarse meshed netting** (reticula) **enclosing 1 or more bulbs.**

Leaves: Alternate on lower stem, usually **3 or more, narrow, channelled**, concave-convex in cross section, 1–5 mm broad, with bases sheathing the stem.

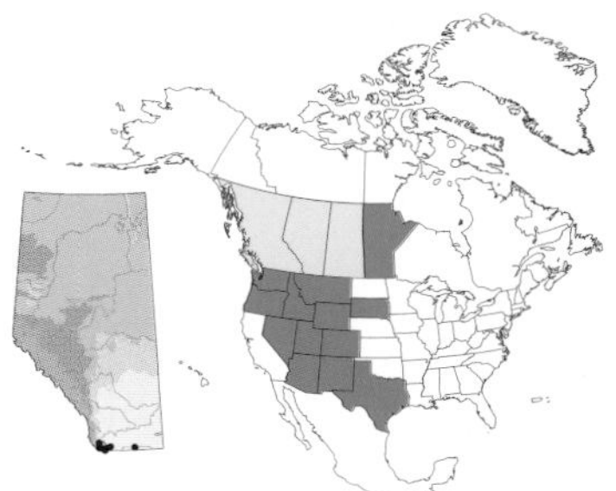

Flowers: Pink, rarely white, with **6 tepals** (3 petals and 3 sepals), **often replaced with small, pointed, bulb-like structures** (bulbils); tepals 6–8 {4–10} mm long, egg-shaped to lance-shaped, with **erect**, blunt to long-tapered tips, often obscurely toothed along the edges and with tiny bumps (papillae) on the midrib, becoming thickened along the midrib and permanently covering the capsule; stigma head-like (capitate), sometimes with 3 obscure lobes; **10–25** (sometimes more) **flowers in erect, flat-topped clusters** (umbels) with 2–3 bracts at the base; bracts egg-shaped to lance-shaped with slender-pointed tips, mostly 1-nerved; stalks (pedicels) often less than twice as long as the tepals; {May} June–July.

VAR. *GEYERI* VAR. *TENERUM*

Fruits: Egg-shaped capsules tipped with 6 inconspicuous, rounded knobs, on rigid and stiffly spreading stalks; seeds black, shiny, **honeycombed on the surface, with a tiny blister** (pustule) **in each hollow**.

Habitat: Wet meadows and streambanks.

Notes: In Alberta, there are 2 varieties of this species, var. *geyeri*, which has only normal flowers, and var. *tenerum* M.E. Jones (also called *Allium rubrum* Osterh. and *Allium rydbergii* Macbr.), which has most flowers replaced with slender-pointed, egg-shaped bulbils. • This species could be confused with other wild onions. Nodding onion (*Allium cernuum* Roth) has nodding flowers and lacks fibrous bulb coats. Prairie onion (*Allium textile* Nels. & Macbr.) has netted outer bulb layers, but its plants usually have only 2 leaves per stem and its tepals are usually white and spreading. The honeycombed seeds also lack tiny blisters. • All onions are edible, and many species (e.g., scallions, garlic, leeks and chives) are cultivated.

WESTERN FALSE-ASPHODEL

Triantha occidentalis (S. Wats.) Gates
LILY FAMILY (LILIACEAE)

Plants: Slender perennial herbs, **sticky with more or less cylindrical, glandular hairs; stems leafless** or with 1–3 leaves near the base, glandular or glandular-hairy, especially near the top, erect, 10–80 cm tall; from short underground stems (rhizomes).

Leaves: Basal, **linear**, up to 50 cm long and 8 mm wide.

Flowers: White or greenish, 3–7 mm long, with **6 tepals** (3 petals and 3 slightly shorter and wider sepals), 6 stamens and 3 styles; 3–45 flowers, usually in 3s in the axils of **deeply 3-lobed bractlets**, forming dense, round or egg-shaped **spikes** or sometimes open or interrupted clusters **1–8 cm long**; {June–August}.

Fruits: Egg-shaped to broadly ellipsoid **capsules**, 4–9 mm long, clearly longer than the persistent tepals at the base, **papery, 3-cavitied; seeds** about 1 mm long, covered **with an inflated, white, net-like envelope** and tipped with a tail-like appendage at one or both ends (rarely lacking).

Habitat: Wet, calcareous sites.

Notes: Some taxonomists have called this species *Tofieldia occidentalis* S. Wats., while others have included it in *Tofieldia glutinosa* (Michx.) Pers., where it comprised 3 subspecies, ssp. *montana* Hitchc., ssp. *brevistyla* Hitchc. and ssp. *occidentalis* Hitchc. Two subspecies have been found in Alberta. *Triantha occidentalis* ssp. *brevistyla* (C.L. Hitchc.) Packer has seeds with a strongly inflated netted envelope about 1–2 times as long as it is wide, and its stems are covered with a mixture of stubby glands (½–2 times longer than wide) and stout, cylindrical hairs (2–4 times longer than wide). *Triantha occidentalis* ssp. *montana* (C.L. Hitchc.) Packer has less swollen seed envelopes (3–4 times longer than wide), and its stems have coarse, cylindrical hairs (4–6 times longer than wide) and no stubby glands. • Western false-asphodel could be confused with the more common species, sticky false-asphodel (*Triantha glutinosa* (Michx.) Baker). Sticky false-asphodel is distinguished by the predominance of conical or dome-shaped glands (dubbed 'haycocks') on its stems and by the scarcely lobed bractlets beneath its flowers. Its seeds do not have a loose, white, netted envelope.

BLUE CAMAS

Camassia quamash (Pursh) Greene var. *quamash*
LILY FAMILY (LILIACEAE)

Plants: Perennial herbs; stems {20} 30–60 cm tall, leafless; from **egg-shaped bulbs** 1–3 cm thick, covered with brown or black scales.

Leaves: **Basal, grass-like**, linear, 6–15 mm wide, 20–40 cm long.

Flowers: **Pale to deep blue or violet, star-shaped**, about 4–5 cm across, with **6 linear, 3–9-nerved petals** (tepals); stamens 6, with anthers attached at the middle to thread-like filaments; stigmas 3-lobed, on thread-like styles; many flowers in showy clusters 5–30 cm long; May–July.

Fruits: Ellipsoid, 3-sided capsules, {12} 15–18 mm long, containing shiny black seeds.

Habitat: Moist to wet meadows.

Notes: Camas was a prized root crop in many areas, and tribes fought for the right to collect in certain meadows. Its role was likened to that of cereal plants in Europe. Settlers and explorers used it less, because large quantities caused vomiting and diarrhea in the uninitiated and, as Father Nicholas Point observed, 'very disagreeable effects for those who do not like strong odours or the sound that accompanies them.' • Girls competed in the annual camas harvest to show their worth as future wives. One young woman was reported to have collected and prepared 60 42-litre sacks of camas roots. Men were excluded from the harvest because they would bring 'bad luck,' and if a woman burned any bulbs, some of her relatives would soon die. The roots were roasted, pounded, made into cakes, eaten raw or stone-boiled, but most were cooked and dried. The bulbs were baked in pits with hot stones for several days, and when they were done, they were dark brown, with a glue-like consistency and a sweet taste, like that of molasses. They were then mashed together and made into cakes which were sun-dried for storage. During the cooking process, insulin (an indigestible sugar) breaks down to fructose; cooked, dried bulbs are 43 percent fructose by weight. Camas was the principal sweetening agent of many tribes before the introduction of sugar. Cooked, dried bulbs kept indefinitely. David Thompson reported eating 36-year-old bulbs that still had good flavour.

CWa

DJ

ROSE MANDARIN

Streptopus roseus Michx.
LILY FAMILY (LILIACEAE)

Plants: Perennial herbs; stems simple or occasionally branched, 15–50 cm tall, **with a sparse fringe of hairs at each joint** (node) opposite the leaf base; from extensive underground stems (rhizomes).

Leaves: Alternate; blades **egg-shaped**, pointed at the tip, 3–10 cm long, 1–5 cm wide, stalkless, **smooth-edged or fringed with several-celled hairs**.

Flowers: Rose-coloured with white tips, or white to greenish yellow and streaked or spotted **with reddish purple, bell-shaped, 6–10 mm long**, with 6 petal-like segments (tepals) curving outward at their tips; stalks 5–20 mm long, curved but not bent, sparsely coarse-hairy; flowers **single** (sometimes 2) **in leaf axils**; June–July.

Fruits: Round, **red berries**, 5–6 mm across, several-seeded.

Habitat: Moist, coniferous woods and streambanks.

Notes: Small twisted-stalk (*Streptopus streptopoides* (Ledeb.) Frye & Rigg) is another species of moist, coniferous woods that is rare in Alberta. It differs from rose mandarin in having saucer-shaped flowers, with petal-like segments that curve outward from their bases (rather than from their tips), and its leaves are shorter (3–5 cm long) with single-celled, translucent teeth crowded along the edges. The flowers of small twisted-stalk are rose to reddish brown with yellowish green tips, and they are reported to appear in June or July. • The common twisted-stalk in Alberta, clasping-leaved twisted-stalk (*Streptopus amplexifolius* (L.) DC.), has larger plants (50–100 cm tall) with greenish white flowers on kinked or bent stalks, and its leaf joints (nodes) are hairless. • Native people believed that twisted-stalk berries were good food for grizzly bears but not for humans. • *Streptopus* is derived from the Greek *streptos* (twisted) and *pous* (foot), referring to the bent or twisted flower stalks. The specific epithet *roseus* is Latin for 'rose-coloured,' a reference to the flowers.

S. STREPTOPOIDES

JP

WESTERN WAKEROBIN

Trillium ovatum Pursh
LILY FAMILY (LILIACEAE)

LA

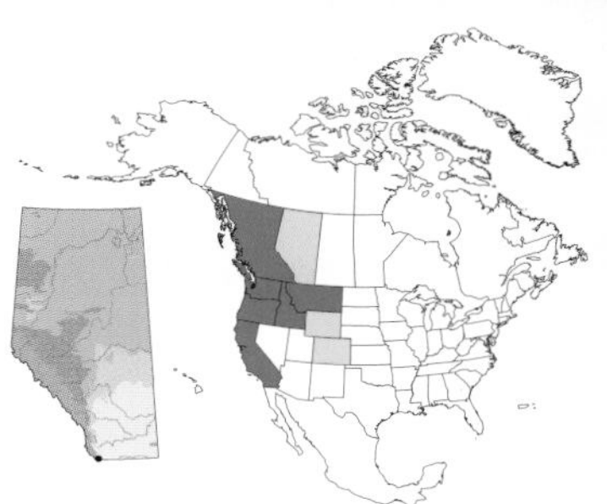

Plants: Low, hairless perennial herbs; stems stout, erect, {10} 20–40 cm tall; from stout, short, fleshy rootstocks (rhizomes).

Leaves: In a whorl of 3 (sometimes 4 or 5) **at the stem tip**, stalkless, 6–12 {5–15} cm long, 4–8 cm wide, **broadly egg-shaped,** tapered to a short, slender point.

Flowers: White (pink to purplish with age), **about 6–9 cm across,** with **3 broad, white petals alternating with 3 small, green sepals**; single, erect, on a long (4–5 cm) stalk from the centre of the leaf whorl; May–June {March–July}.

Fruits: Yellowish green, berry-like capsules, oval, slightly winged; seeds numerous, shed in a sticky mass.

Habitat: Moist to wet, shady mountain woods and thickets.

Notes: Some tribes used these thick rhizomes to help mothers during childbirth—hence another common name, 'birthroot.' The leaves have been eaten as cooked greens. • Trillium seeds each have a small, oil-rich body that attracts ants. The ants carry the seeds to their nests, where they eat the oil-rich part or feed it to their young, and discard the rest. This is a very effective way to disperse seeds, and North American forests contain many 'ant plants' (plants whose seeds contain oil bodies), including wild ginger (*Asarum* spp.), bleeding hearts (*Dicentra* spp.) and many violets (*Viola* spp.), as well as trilliums. • The generic name *Trillium*, from the Latin *tri* (three), refers to the 3 leaves, 3 petals, 3 sepals and 3 stigmas of these plants. The flowers bloom in the spring, just as the robins return or 'wake up' from their winter absence—hence the name 'wakerobin.'

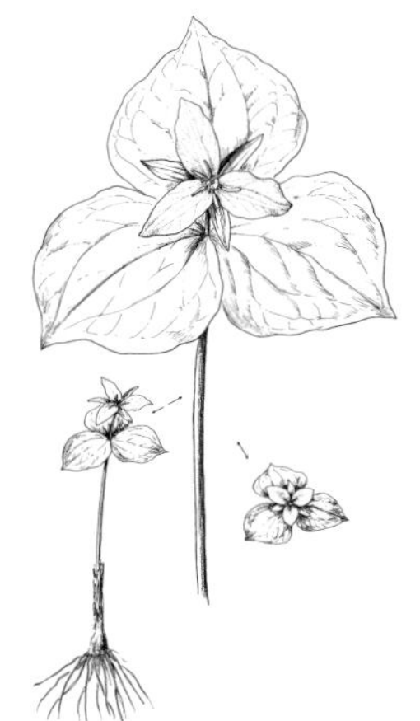

CWa

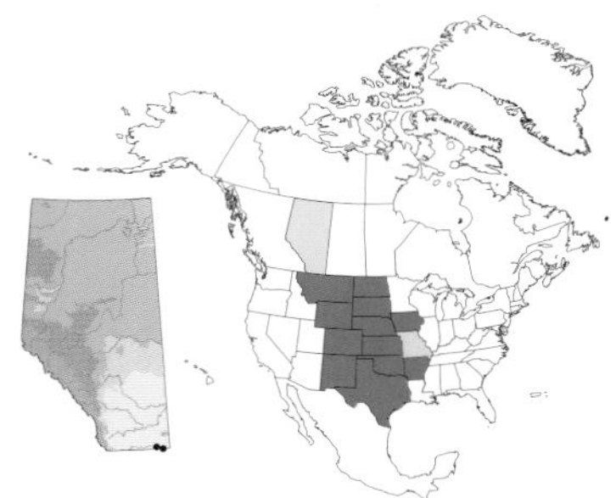

SOAPWEED

Yucca glauca Nutt. *ex* Fraser
AGAVE FAMILY (AGAVACEAE)

Plants: Coarse, evergreen perennial herbs; flowering stems erect, 50–100 {150} cm tall; from 1 or more short, woody root crowns.

Leaves: Basal, densely tufted, stiff, linear, stiffly sharp-pointed, 20–40 {60} cm long; edges rolled inward, whitish, with a few frayed fibres.

Flowers: Cream-coloured to greenish white, showy, bell-shaped, 3–5 cm long and wide, with 6 leathery, egg-shaped petals (tepals); many **nodding** flowers **in long clusters** (racemes); {May–July}.

Fruits: Hardened, oblong capsules, 5–7 cm long, with many thin, flat, black seeds.

Habitat: Dry, open grassland slopes and coulees.

Notes: Soapweed has sometimes been included in the lily family (Liliaceae). • The flower petals were eaten raw in salads and the young seed pods were roasted in ashes and eaten. Ripe fruits were split in half, their seeds and fibre were scraped out, and the remaining pulp was then baked and eaten. • The fibrous leaves were split and used as all-purpose ties, but they were not twisted or plaited to make cord or rope. • The Navajo pounded the roots with rocks to remove bark and soften them, then vigorously stirred the softened mass of fibres in warm water to whip up suds. This was used as soap to wash wool, clothing, hair and the body. It was also said to reduce dandruff and baldness. • Soapweed and a small, white, night-flying moth (the yucca moth, *Pronuba*) depend on one another for survival. The flowers open fully only at night, when they are visited by a female yucca moth. She takes a ball of pollen and flies to another flower, where she eats through the ovary wall and deposits an egg inside. She then climbs to the stigma, deposits the pollen from the first flower and moves to the anthers to collect a second ball of pollen before flying to the next plant. By fertilizing the flowers, she assures the development of seeds, which will provide both food for her young when the eggs hatch and new plants for future generations of moths. Ripe yucca pods almost always have a tiny hole, where the grub ate its way out.

WESTERN BLUE FLAG

Iris missouriensis Nutt.
IRIS FAMILY (IRIDACEAE)

Plants: Perennial herbs; stems **clumped, about 20–50 cm tall**; from **thick, spreading underground stems (rhizomes).**

Leaves: Mainly basal, linear, **sword-shaped**, 20–40 {50} cm long, 5–10 mm wide.

Flowers: Pale to deep blue, sometimes pale with purple lines, about **6–7 cm across**, with **3 backward-curved, purple-lined sepals, 3 erect, narrower and paler petals and 3 flattened, petal-like style-branches**; 2–4 flowers on stout, leafless stalks up to 6 cm long; {May} June–July.

Fruits: Erect capsules, 3–5 cm long.

Habitat: Open, moist to wet (at least in spring) meadows and streambanks.

Notes: Western blue flag roots are **poisonous**, and they should never be taken internally. People gathering edible rootstocks in wetlands, such as those of cattails (*Typha* spp.) or sweetflag (*Acorus americanus* (Raf.) Raf., previously called *A. calamus* L.), must be careful not to confuse them with blue flag rhizomes. Iris rootstocks are odourless and unpleasant-tasting, whereas those of cattails are odourless and bland, and those of sweetflag are pleasantly aromatic. • Historically, small amounts of blue flag roots were taken to induce vomiting and cleanse the system. Blue flag was an official drug in the US *National Formulary* until 1947 for the treatment of syphilis, as an alternative to the use of bismuth, arsenic, mercury and so on, but its effectiveness was questionable. The fresh roots were also said to be effective in treating *Staphylococcus* sores, when applied as a poultice.

CWa

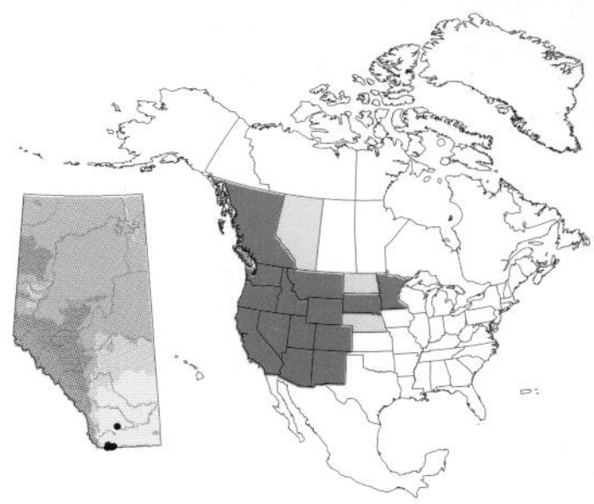

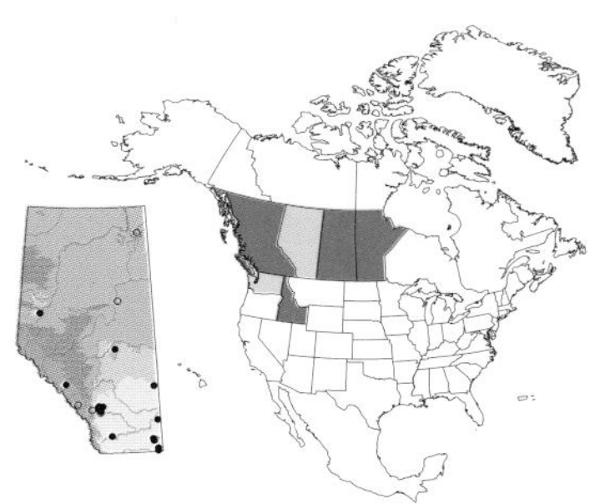

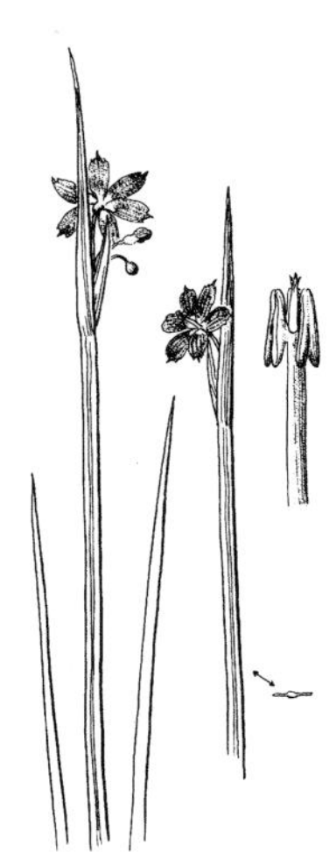

PALE BLUE-EYED GRASS

Sisyrinchium septentrionale Bicknell
IRIS FAMILY (IRIDACEAE)

Plants: Slender, tufted perennial herbs; stems 2-edged, flattened, 10–20 cm tall, 1–2 mm wide; from short underground stems (rhizomes) and fibrous roots.

Leaves: Alternate, near stem base, attached edgewise to the stem (like iris leaves) in 2 vertical rows, linear, grass-like, **1–2 mm wide**.

Flowers: Pale violet-blue to almost white, delicate, about 8 mm long, with 6 spreading tepals; **tepals blunt or tapered to slender points**; flowers in small clusters from the axils of 2 erect bracts, with **flower stalks usually shorter than the inner bract**; outer bract 2.5–4 cm long; {April} May–July.

Fruits: Rounded capsules, 3–4 mm high, containing many black seeds.

Habitat: Moist meadows and grassy streambanks.

Notes: This species was called *Sisyrinchium sarmentosum* Suksd. *ex* Green in the first edition of the *Flora of Alberta*, but that name now applies to a distinct species. • Common blue-eyed grass (*Sisyrinchium montanum* Greene) is widespread in Alberta. It is very similar to pale blue-eyed grass, but its leaves are generally wider (up to 4 mm wide), its flower stalks are longer (longer than the inner bract), and its tepals are either notched or abruptly bristle-pointed. Some taxonomists have included both of these species in *Sisyrinchium angustifolium* Mill., but that name now applies to an eastern species. • The generic name *Sisyrinchium* was given to an iris-like plant by the Greek philosopher Theophrastus (ca. 372–c. 287 BC) and was later adopted by Linnaeus. The specific epithet *septentrionale* is Latin for 'northern' or 'of northern regions.'

STEMLESS LADY'S-SLIPPER

Cypripedium acaule Ait.
ORCHID FAMILY (ORCHIDACEAE)

LA

Plants: Perennial herbs, 10–30 {60} cm tall; stems **single, erect, leafless**, hairy; from short underground stems (rhizomes) and coarse, thick roots.

Leaves: **Basal**, **2**, nearly opposite, narrowly **oblong or egg-shaped**, 10–28 cm long, 5–15 cm wide, stalkless, strongly **pleated**, sparsely hairy, bright green.

Flowers: Deep to pale pink, showy, with **yellow-green to purplish brown, 3–5 cm long, lance-shaped sepals** (3) **and side petals** (2) above a hanging, inflated, **3–6 cm long, pouch-like lip** that is usually **pink** (occasionally white) with purple veins and **deeply grooved** down the middle; **solitary**; late June–July.

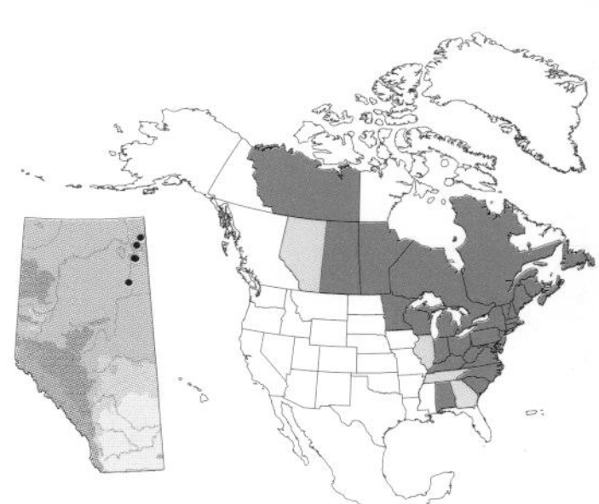

Fruits: Erect capsules, widest at the middle, 3 cm long, 1 cm wide, strongly ribbed, containing thousands of tiny seeds.

Habitat: Wetlands, woods and sand dunes; elsewhere, in habitats with sterile, acidic soil and light shade, including sand ridges, jack pine woods and sphagnum bogs.

Notes: Stemless lady's-slipper is also known as pink lady's-slipper and moccasin-flower. It is the only lady's-slipper in Alberta that has only basal leaves (none on the flowering stalk) and a pink, deeply grooved lip petal. • The hairy plants **can cause a rash** in sensitive individuals. • Stemless lady's-slipper has been used by native peoples as a sedative. • Pollination is carried out primarily by bees, which enter the lip through a slit at the upper end and exit through an opening at the base of the pouch. These beautiful flower pouches can also conceal danger: they often harbour predators such as crab spiders. • Colonies of stemless lady's-slipper produce few seed capsules. This is due in part to the mechanism of pollination. Bees are initially attracted to the flowers by smell and colour, but they soon discover that the flowers contain no nectar or available pollen and avoid these flowers. Each capsule contains tens of thousands of seeds, and this high seed set helps to offset the small number of mature capsules. • Picking and trampling can limit population size, especially if the flower that is killed is one of the few to set seed. • Stemless lady's-slipper is the provincial floral emblem of Prince Edward Island.

LA

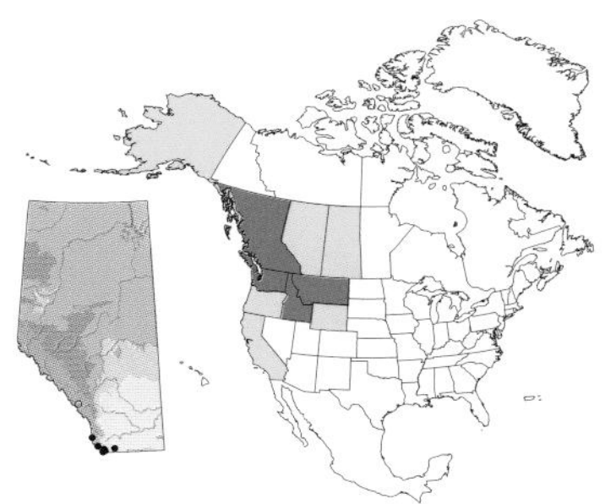

MOUNTAIN LADY'S-SLIPPER

Cypripedium montanum Dougl. *ex* Lindl.
ORCHID FAMILY (ORCHIDACEAE)

Plants: Glandular-hairy perennial herbs; **stems leafy**, 20–50 {70} cm tall; from short underground stems (rhizomes) and coarse, thick roots.

Leaves: Alternate, 4–6, egg-shaped to broadly lance-shaped, 5–16 cm long, 3–8 cm wide, with many parallel veins, stalkless, sheathing at the base.

Flowers: White and purple or purplish green, showy, sweet-scented, about 8–10 cm across, with **3 greenish brown to brownish purple**, lance-shaped **sepals** (3–6 cm long, 1–1.5 cm wide), **2 narrowly lance-shaped, twisted, brownish purplish petals** (4–7 cm long, 3–6 mm wide) spreading to the sides, and a **broad, white, pouched lower lip petal**, tinged and veined with pink or purple near the base and spotted with purple on the inside (2–3 cm long, 1.3–1.7 mm deep and wide), also with an **egg-shaped, purple-dotted, yellow** lobe (staminode) at the mouth of the pouch; flowers usually **in pairs** but sometimes single or 3 per plant; June–August.

Fruits: Oblong capsules, 2–3 cm long, 1 cm wide, erect or ascending, containing many tiny seeds.

Habitat: Moist open places in the mountains at elevations below 1,700 m.

Notes: Mountain lady's-slipper most closely resembles yellow lady's-slipper (*Cypripedium calceolus* L.), but yellow lady's-slipper has single, bright-yellow flowers with a triangular staminode at the mouth. The only other lady's-slipper in Alberta with a white pouch is sparrow's-egg lady's-slipper (*Cypripedium passerinum* Richards.), and that species has much smaller flowers with short (1–1.5 cm long), egg-shaped sepals. • Orchids, and especially members of the genus *Cypripedium*, are ancient erotic and sexual symbols. The common name 'orchid' and the scientific names *Orchis* and Orchidaceae all stem from the Greek *orchis* (testicle). The generic name *Cypripedium* is derived from the Latin *Cypris* (Venus, the goddess of love and beauty) and *podion* (small foot). This refers to the delicate, slipper-like pouches of these beautiful flowers. The specific epithet *montanum* means 'of the mountains.'

BROAD-LIPPED TWAYBLADE

Listera convallarioides (Sw.) Nutt.
ORCHID FAMILY (ORCHIDACEAE)

WM

Plants: **Delicate** perennial herbs 8–20 {35} cm tall; stems slender, glandular-hairy on upper parts; from fibrous roots.

Leaves: Opposite (or nearly so), **1 pair near the middle of the stem, broadly egg-shaped** to almost round, blunt or abruptly pointed, 3–5 {2–8} cm long, hairless.

Flowers: **Yellowish green**, with 3 lance-shaped to linear, **4–5 mm long sepals** and 2 slightly smaller petals, all **bent backward above a broad lower lip petal**; lip wedge-shaped, 8–10 {13} **mm long, fringed** with fine hairs, **notched at the tip**, narrowed abruptly to a **slender basal section** (claw) and usually with 2 small teeth near the base, **projecting** outward almost **horizontally**; stalks slender, 4–8 {10} mm long; 5–25 flowers in slender, elongated clusters (racemes); {June} July–September.

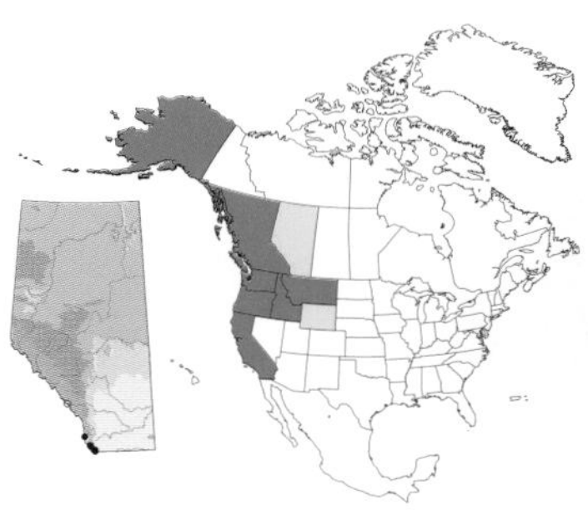

Fruits: Many-seeded, oval capsules, usually slightly glandular.

Habitat: Boggy woods and meadows; elsewhere, in deep woods, on streambanks and by lakes.

Notes: This species has also been called *Ophrys convallarioides* (Sw.) Wight. • Broad-lipped twayblade might be confused with another rare species, western twayblade (*Listera caurina* Piper, also called *Ophrys caurina* (Piper) Rydb.), but the flowers of western twayblade have a smaller (4–6 mm long) lower lip with 2 prominent teeth at their base and without the fringing hairs and slender claws found in broad-lipped twayblade. Its ovaries and capsules are also hairless. Western twayblade grows in moist woods and flowers from June to July {August}. • Charles Darwin studied the fascinating pollination mechanisms of twayblades. These tiny flowers shoot their pollen out in a sticky drop of fluid that glues the pollinia to visiting insects. • The name 'twayblade' originated from the archaic word *tway* (two), in reference to the 2 leaf blades on these delicate plants. *Listera* honours Dr. Martin Lister, an English naturalist who lived 1638–1711.

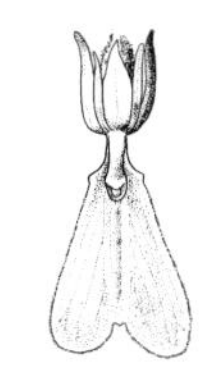

L. CAURINA

TC

JRJ

TT

BOG ADDER'S-MOUTH

Malaxis paludosa (L.) Sw.
ORCHID FAMILY (ORCHIDACEAE)

Plants: Slender perennial herbs; **stems** erect, 5–15 {4–20} cm tall; from a swollen 'bulb' (corm).

Leaves: Alternate, near the stem base, **2–5**, broadly lance-shaped, blunt-tipped, 5–12 mm long, 3–10 mm wide, stalkless, sheathing the stem, **often producing small bulbils in their axils.**

Flowers: Yellowish green or pale green, inconspicuous, **1–1.5 mm long** and less than half as wide, **rotated 180°** and therefore with the lip petal pointing upward; **sepals broadly lance-shaped, 2 pointing upward and 1 pointed downward (like a lip)**; petals about as long as the sepals, with **2 slender side petals and a broader, green-striped lip petal pointing upward** (erect); 15–30 flowers in very slender, loose, elongated clusters (racemes); {June–August}.

Fruits: Erect capsules, 4 mm long, 2 mm wide, splitting into 3 parts to release many tiny seeds.

Habitat: Mossy ground (usually on peat moss [*Sphagnum* spp.]) in bogs and fens.

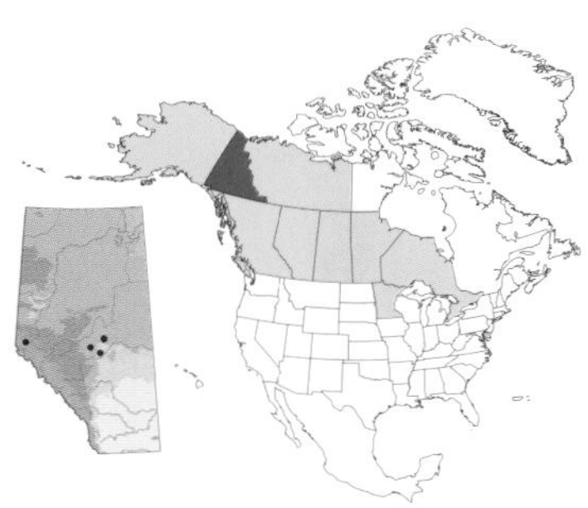

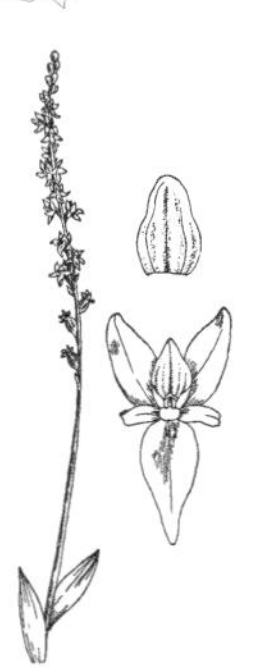

Notes: This species has also been called *Ophrys paludosa* L. and *Hammarbya paludosa* (L.) Kuntze. • The genus *Malaxis* can be distinguished from other orchids by its swollen stem bases. The 2 members of this genus that occur in Alberta both have leaves near the stem base. This feature can be used to distinguish them from other tiny orchids such as the twayblades (*Listera* spp.). • White adder's-mouth (*Malaxis monophylla* (L.) Sw. var. *brachypoda* (A. Gray) Morris & Ames, also known as *Malaxis brachypoda* (A. Gray) Fern.) is also rare in Alberta. It has a single leaf (rarely 2), and the lip petal has 2 small lobes (auricles) at its base and points downwards. White adder's-mouth typically grows in slightly drier, less acidic habitats such as damp woods, thickets and the drier parts of bogs and fens. It is reported to flower from mid June to August. • Bog adder's-mouth is thought to be one of the rarest orchids in North America, but because of its small size and inconspicuous colour, it may often be overlooked. • Both adder's-mouths are pollinated by small insects.

M. MONOPHYLLA var. *BRACHYPODA*

JG

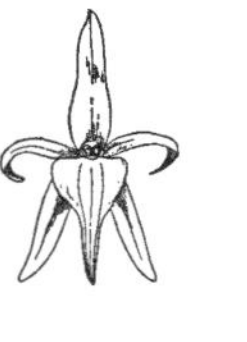

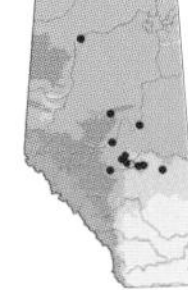

SLENDER BOG ORCHID

Platanthera stricta Lindl.
ORCHID FAMILY (ORCHIDACEAE)

JP

Plants: Slender, hairless perennial herbs; stems erect, 20–50 {110} cm tall; from clusters of fleshy, swollen roots.

Leaves: Alternate, several, oblong to lance-shaped, often widest above the middle, 4–12 {3–18} cm long, slightly less than 3 times as long as they are wide, stalkless, clasping or sheathing the stem; the lowermost 2 or 3 leaves reduced to bladeless sheaths.

Flowers: Green, sometimes tinged with purple or brown, odourless or with a faint fragrance, about 1 cm long, somewhat 2-lipped, with 3 sepals, 3 petals and a hollow basal appendage (spur); sepals and petals 3–7 mm long, with the egg-shaped upper sepal and 2 upper petals curved together in a hood, and the 2 narrower side sepals flanking the slender lip petal; **spur pouch-shaped,** often purplish, **½–⅔ as long as the lip petal** and often hidden beneath it; many stalkless flowers **in loose, narrow, elongating clusters** (spike-like racemes) ⅓–½ as long as the stem; late June–August.

Fruits: Many-seeded capsules about 1 cm long.

Habitat: Wet meadows and forests.

Notes: This species has also been called *Habenaria saccata* Greene. • The bog orchids are recognized by their small, slender-lipped flowers, each with a hollow spur projecting back from the base, and by their numerous leaves (although some species have only 1–3 basal leaves). Slender bog orchid might be confused with northern green bog orchid (*Platanthera hyperborea* (L.) Lindl., also called *Habenaria hyperborea* (L.) R. Br.), but northern green bog orchid has slender, cylindrical spurs that are 5–8 mm long (as long as the lip petal). Its flower clusters also tend to be much more densely flowered.

JG

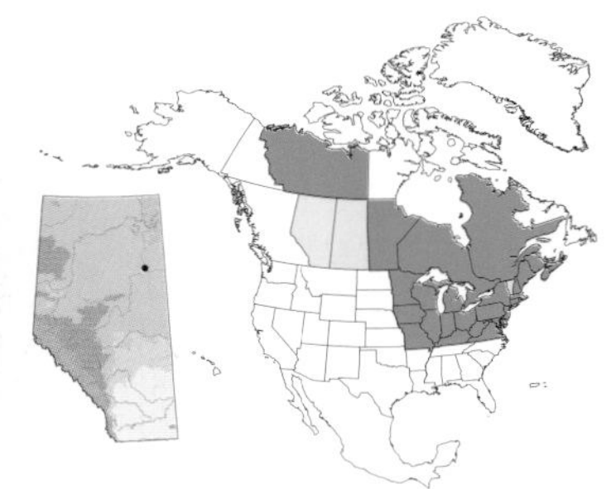

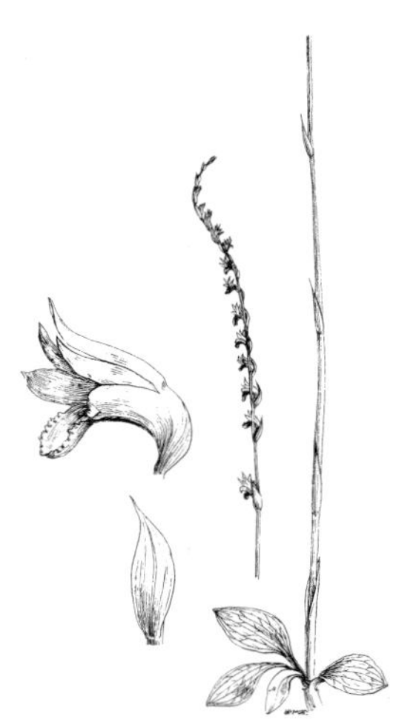

NORTHERN SLENDER LADIES'-TRESSES

Spiranthes lacera (Raf.) Raf. var. *lacera*
ORCHID FAMILY (ORCHIDACEAE)

Plants: Slender perennial herbs; stems erect, 20–80 cm tall; from clusters of 2–several fleshy, tuberous roots.

Leaves: In a **basal rosette** of {2} 3–5, light green, shiny, **oval to elliptic**, 1–4 {5.5} cm long, 1–2 cm wide, short-stalked, usually wilted or withered by flowering time.

Flowers: Crystalline white, fragrant, {2.5} 3.5–5.5 mm long, somewhat 2-lipped; sepals 4–5 mm long, with the egg-shaped upper sepal joined to the 2 side petals, and the 2 narrower side sepals flanking the lower lip; petals 4–5 {6} mm long, the 2 upper petals linear and blunt-tipped, and the lower **lip** petal wider (oblong, 2–3 mm wide), fringed at the tip, and marked **with a** distinctive **green spot** at the centre; 13–25 {9–35} flowers in a single, vertical, spiralling row, forming a **slender spike**, often with the **lowermost flowers separated**; mid July {August}.

Fruits: Egg-shaped capsules, 3–5 mm long and 2 mm wide.

Habitat: Dry, rocky, open woods and grassy areas in or near jack pine–lichen forest, often with common blueberry (*Vaccinium myrtilloides* Michx.).

Notes: This species has erroneously been called *Spiranthes gracilis* (Bigel.) Beck. • Hooded ladies'-tresses (*Spiranthes romanzoffiana* Cham.) is the only other ladies'-tresses in Alberta. It has narrower, linear leaves, its lip petal does not have a green spot, and its flowers form compact spikes with several vertically spiralling rows of flowers. Where they occur together, these species produce hybrids known as *Spiranthes* x *simpsonii*. • Northern slender ladies'-tresses grows for 3–5 years before it begins flowering. It can spread rapidly once it invades an area, and colonies are known to persist for several decades. It was first reported for Alberta in the early 1990s, where it is known only from the northeastern corner of the province. • Northern slender ladies'-tresses is pollinated by several species of small bees. • The generic name *Spiranthes* was taken from the Greek *speira* (coiled) and *anthos* (flower), in reference to the spiralling rows of flowers. The specific epithet *lacera* means 'lashed or torn,' a reference to the ragged edge of the lip petal. The common name 'ladies'-tresses' probably stemmed from the resemblance of the twisted flower spike to a braid of hair.

Dicots

NODDING UMBRELLA-PLANT

Eriogonum cernuum Nutt.
BUCKWHEAT FAMILY (POLYGONACEAE)

CWa

Plants: Slender annual herbs, 10–40 cm tall; stems freely branched, usually divided in 3s (trichotomous) near the base and in 2s (dichotomous) on the upper parts, **slender**, hairless or somewhat woolly near the base; from slender taproots.

Leaves: **Basal**, spreading; blades **round to oval**, 1–2 cm wide, densely **white-woolly beneath**, usually greenish and slightly woolly on the upper surface; stalks shorter to longer than the blades, **lacking stipules**.

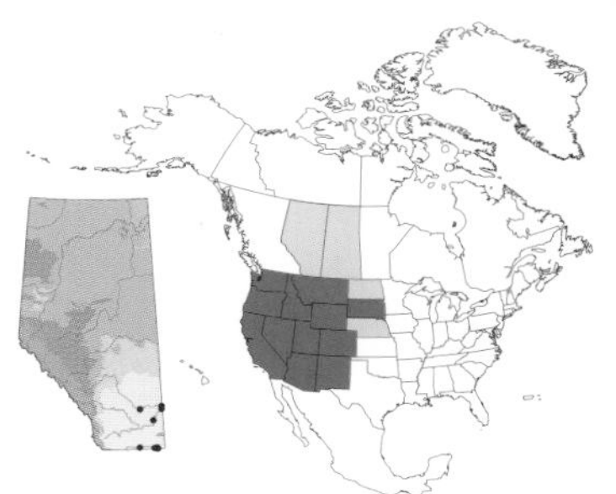

Flowers: **White to pink**, cone-shaped, **about 2 mm across** and 2 mm long, with **3 broad, wavy-edged lobes** (sepals) notched at the tip, **alternating with 3 narrower lobes** (petals); 3 styles and 3 stigmas; **9 stamens**, ¾ as long as the sepals and petals; borne on short stalks in **several-flowered, flat-topped** (umbel-like) **heads from hairless, 5-lobed cones** of fused bracts (involucres) about 1.5–2 mm long, these heads borne singly **on slender branches about 5–15 mm long** that are often **bent sharply downward** in open, freely branched clusters (cyme-like); {June} July–September.

Fruits: Dry, **3-sided,** seed-like fruits (achenes), enclosed in the calyx.

Habitat: In coarse-grained sand in badlands, on dry valley rims and slopes, and on active (though usually partially stabilized) sand dunes; elsewhere, on sandy desert hills.

Notes: The total population of nodding umbrella-plant in Alberta is estimated at fewer than 10,000 plants. A few small populations are found in Dinosaur and Writing-on-Stone provincial parks, but none of the larger populations are yet protected formally. With dune stabilization, other species will eventually crowd out some populations. • Umbrella-plants (*Eriogonum* spp.) are an important source of nectar for bees, and the honey produced from these flowers is said to be of excellent quality. • The specific epithet *cernuum* means 'nodding,' in reference to the nodding flower clusters.

SILVER-PLANT

Eriogonum ovalifolium Nutt. var. *ovalifolium*
BUCKWHEAT FAMILY (POLYGONACEAE)

Plants: Tufted, white-woolly and silky-hairy perennial herbs; stems **5–15 cm tall**, leafless; often **forming mats** from densely branched, woody root crowns.

Leaves: Basal, many, **egg-shaped to round**, widest at or above the middle, **about 1 cm long**, densely white-woolly, stalked.

Flowers: Creamy to pale yellow, pink-tinged with age, hairless, 4 mm long, with 3 oval to round outer tepals and 3 spatula-shaped inner tepals; on small, slender stalks in hairy, cup-like involucres which are **stalkless and form a dense head-like cluster** (umbel) above a whorl of very small involucral bracts; June–July {May–August}.

Fruits: 3-sided, seed-like fruits (achenes).

Habitat: Dry, open, often rocky sites.

Notes: Another species that may occur in Alberta, few-flowered umbrella-plant (*Eriogonum pauciflorum* Pursh, also called *Eriogonum multiceps* Nees), is a low (usually less than 20 cm tall), tufted, perennial plant with small clusters of whitish or pale-pink flowers at the tips of slender stems. However, it has slender, lance-shaped leaves and the outer surface of its flowers is covered with long hairs. Few-flowered umbrella-plant grows on eroded banks and rocky ridges in prairie badlands. It flowers in July {August}. • Silver-plants can do well in sunny rock gardens, but they are often difficult to grow. They are best propagated from seed. • Prospectors and miners believed that this species indicated the presence of silver ore, so they called it 'silver plant.' • The generic name *Eriogonum* was derived from the Greek *erio* (woolly) and *gony* (knee or joint), in reference to the woolly stems and jointed flower stalks of many species.

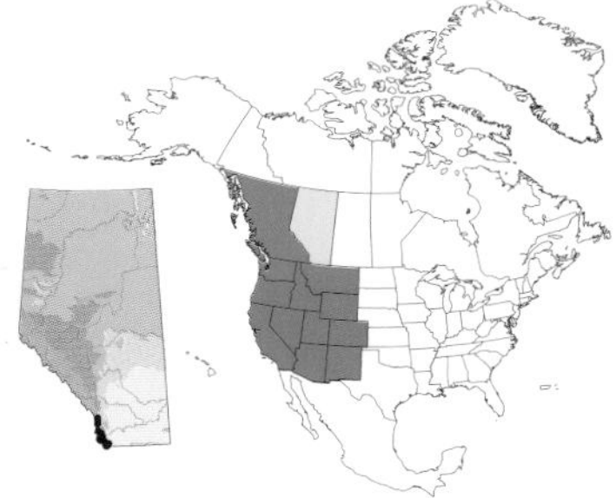

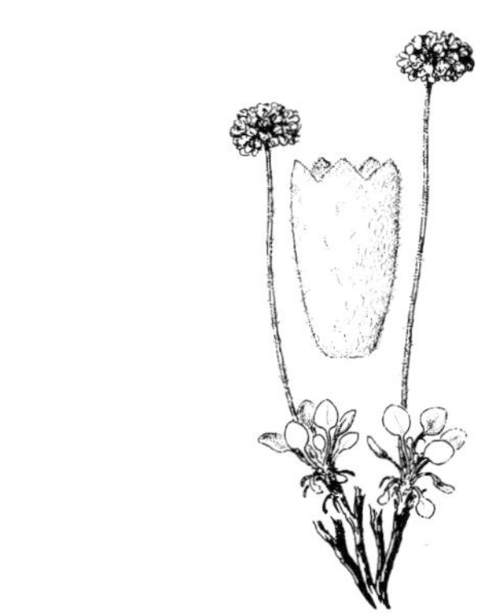

E. PAUCIFLORUM

KOENIGIA

Koenigia islandica L.
BUCKWHEAT FAMILY (POLYGONACEAE)

Plants: Tiny, hairless annual herbs; stems slender, simple or branched, 1–4 {15} **cm tall, often reddish**; from slender taproots.

Leaves: Alternate or opposite, somewhat **fleshy**, broadly elliptic to lance-shaped, widest above the middle, **2–5** {9} **mm long**, 1.5–3 mm wide, with translucent, **sheathing stipules** (ochreae).

Flowers: Green, sometimes whitish or reddish, inconspicuous, **1–1.4 mm long**, with 3 sepals and no petals; few to several in small, flat-topped clusters (umbels) immediately above 2–4 leaf-like bracts; July–August.

Fruits: Hairless, **3-sided**, seed-like fruits (achenes), enclosed by the sepals.

Habitat: Moist silt or mud in alpine areas; elsewhere, by snow beds and on wet moss.

Notes: Koenigia is found all around the world; in western North America, its range extends from Alaska to Colorado, but its tiny plants are easily overlooked. It is classified as rare in the continental Northwest Territories, British Columbia, Alberta, Manitoba, Ontario and Colorado. Most annual species penetrate only short distances into the Arctic from the south. However, koenigia is found far to the north, reaching Devon Island in the Canadian Arctic Archipelago, both coasts of Greenland, and Peary Land. It seems unlikely that it ever grows as a biennial. All viable seeds sprout promptly in their first spring, even though a partial delay of germination beyond the first year would be an effective safeguard against disastrous summers. This tiny plant is usually confined to wet sites in areas with irregular topography, where evaporation keeps plant temperatures below the lethal level in summer, and where variations in relief both ensure dynamic warming of the air and allow stratification of the air close to the surface.

LK

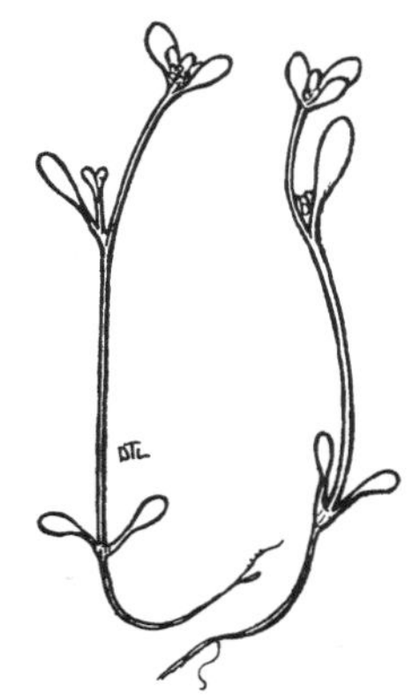

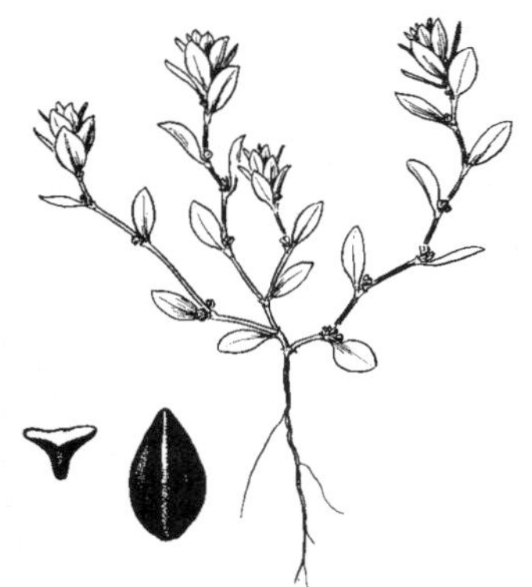

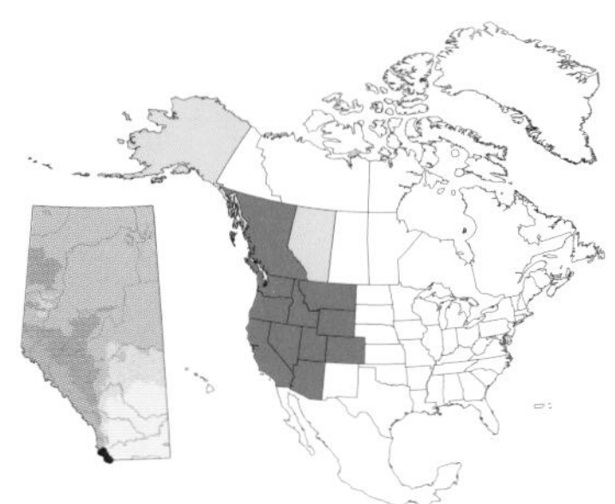

LEAST KNOTWEED

Polygonum minimum S. Wats.
BUCKWHEAT FAMILY (POLYGONACEAE)

Plants: **Dwarf annual** herbs, **3–15** {25} **cm tall**; stems **wiry**, less than 1 mm thick, leafy, usually **branched** at the base and **ascending**, sometimes unbranched and erect, often zigzagged, round or slightly angled, with rough lines of bran-like particles; from shallow taproots.

Leaves: **Alternate**, usually crowded and only slightly smaller on the upper stem and concealing the flowers; **blades jointed** at the base, **oblong-elliptic to egg-shaped**, blunt-tipped or slightly pointed, **5–15** {20} **mm long**, some usually at least ½ as wide as long; stalks short or absent; sheathing stipules (ochreae) usually 2-lobed, becoming **torn** along the edge.

Flowers: **Greenish with white or pinkish** (not yellow) **edges**, cone-shaped, usually **less than 2.5 mm long**, cut about ⅔ of the way to the base into **5 broad lobes**; **3 stigmas**, nearly stalkless; **in groups of 2–3** {1–4} **on erect, 1–2 mm long stalks from leaf axils**, from the tip of the stem almost to the base; July–August {September}.

Fruits: **Dry, shiny, dark brown or nearly black** seed-like fruits (achenes) **with 3 concave sides**, 2–2.5 mm long, only slightly longer than the petal lobes, **erect** or nearly so.

Habitat: Dry ground in alpine to subalpine zones, rarely below 1,100 m elevation; elsewhere, on sandy soil and rock outcrops.

Notes: Least knotweed plants may flower when they are only 2–3 cm tall. Leaf production continues gradually throughout the lifespan of the plant and declines only slightly during fruit development. After a leaf has expanded, a flower develops in its axil. In this way, sexual reproduction continues throughout the life of the plant, and flowers and fruits at all stages of development can be found on a single plant. Drought delays reproduction and slows seed production, but least knotweed has greater drought tolerance than most other annuals in these habitats. • The generic name *Polygonum* was taken from the Greek *poly* (many) and *gony* (knee or joint), in reference to the many swollen joints of some species.

WHITE-MARGINED KNOTWEED

Polygonum polygaloides Meissn. ssp. *confertiflorum* (Nutt. *ex* Piper) Hickman
BUCKWHEAT FAMILY (POLYGONACEAE)

CWa

Plants: Small, hairless annual herbs, 3–15 {2–25} cm tall; stems **erect or ascending**, unbranched or branched in 2s, usually sharply angled; from slender taproots.

Leaves: Alternate, linear to **linear–lance-shaped, 1–3** {0.5–4} **cm long** and about 1–2 mm wide, with obscure side veins, jointed at the base above 4–7 {2–8} mm long, **short-sheathing stipules** that are **deeply cut into slender lobes.**

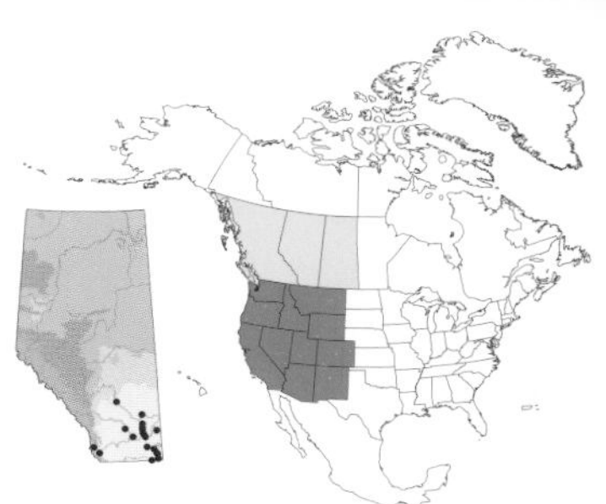

Flowers: Greenish with white or pinkish edges, broadly **cone-shaped, 2–2.5** {3.5} **mm long** and wide, **cut over ⅔ of the way to the base** into **5 oblong to lance-shaped lobes**, the outer 3 clearly broader and longer than the inner 2; usually **8** (sometimes 3) **fertile stamens; 3 styles,** about 0.3 mm long; numerous, almost stalkless, erect or spreading, in small clusters of {1} 2–4 **in the axils of crowded, linear, leaf-like bracts** that are less than 3 times as long as the flowers, forming **dense spikes** about 1 cm long and ⅓–⅔ as wide **at stem tips**; June {May–August}.

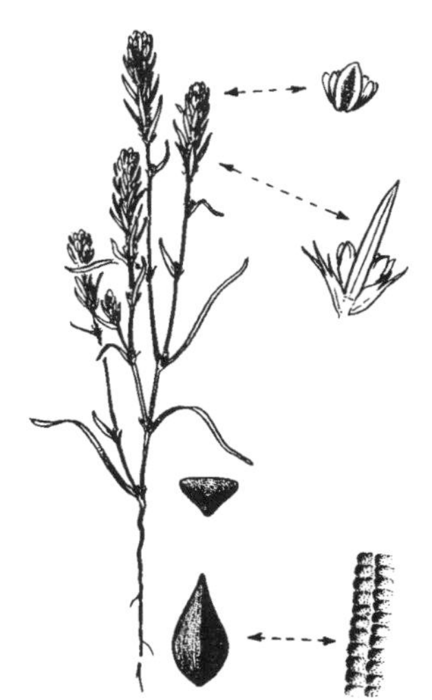

Fruits: Dry, **3-sided,** seed-like fruits (achenes), 1.5–2 mm long, greenish yellow to brown, shining and almost smooth, to (commonly) **dull blackish and prominently ribbed** (often on the same plant).

Habitat: Moist meadows and flats; elsewhere, in damp silty or gravelly areas, in seasonally wet sites (e.g., vernal pools).

Notes: This species has also been called *Polygonum watsonii* Small, *P. imbricatum* Nutt., *P. kelloggii* Greene var. *confertiflorum* (Nutt. *ex* Piper) Dorn and *P. confertiflorum* Nutt. *ex* Piper. • This is a complex species, which includes several taxa that were once recognized as separate species. *Polygonum polygaloides* and *P. watsonii* were distinguished from *P. confertiflorum* and *P. kelloggii* primarily on the basis of the number of fertile stamens (8 in the former 2 species and 3 in the latter 2) and by their shorter bracts, which lack white edges.

ALPINE SHEEP SORREL, MOUNTAIN SHEEP SORREL

Rumex paucifolius Nutt. *ex* Wats.
BUCKWHEAT FAMILY (POLYGONACEAE)

Plants: **Hairless** perennial herbs; stems loosely tufted, 1–few, slender, 20–60 {15–70} cm tall, unbranched below the flower cluster; from short underground stems (rhizomes) on thick taproots.

Leaves: Several, basal and {1} 2–3 alternate on the stem, **lance-shaped or elliptic** (never arrowhead-shaped), **tapered to a blunt tip and a wedge-shaped base,** 4–10 {13} cm long and about 2.5 cm wide; stalks long on basal leaves, but gradually shorter and eventually absent on upper leaves, **sheathing the stem with fused, membranous stipules** at their bases.

Flowers: **Greenish**, usually **red-tinged**, with **male and female flowers on separate plants** (dioecious), cupped, about 2–3 mm long and wide, with **3 spreading to erect, lance-shaped outer lobes** (never bent sharply backward) and **3 rounded inner lobes**; **3 stigmas**; stalks very slender, clearly jointed near the base; numerous, in branched clusters (panicles) with many vertical branches, the whole cluster often as long as the stem; {June–July} August.

Fruits: **Smooth, 3-sided,** seed-like fruits (achenes), about 1.5 mm long, with 3 sharp angles, enclosed by **3 reddish, veiny, round to heart-shaped flaps** (valves) {2.5} **3–4 mm long**, nodding on slender stalks at least as long as the valves; valves veined, rarely with a tiny (never large and conspicuous) bump (callosity, tubercle) near the base.

Habitat: Moist meadows from montane to alpine elevations.

Notes: Many dock and sorrel species (*Rumex* spp.) are eaten as vegetables, but most are high in oxalic acid, which can be toxic in large amounts. Alpine sheep sorrel is said to be one of the more acid-tasting species. • Although alpine sheep sorrel is widely distributed, its populations are usually very local and sporadic. It is easily distinguished from other dioecious docks by its tapered leaf bases and upward-curved sepals at the base of its flowers and fruits. Other species have pointed lobes at the base of their leaf blades and their 3 small outer sepals are bent sharply backward. • These plants are pollinated by wind, so they produce large amounts of pollen. Dock plants are notorious among allergy sufferers as a source of irritation. For example, green sorrel (*Rumex acetosa* L.) can produce about 4 million pollen grains per plant.

WEDGESCALE, SALTBUSH

Atriplex truncata (Torr.) A. Gray
GOOSEFOOT FAMILY (CHENOPODIACEAE)

Plants: Annual herbs; stems erect, 15–40 {100} cm tall, often with many **ascending branches**; from slender taproots.

Leaves: Alternate, or the lower opposite; blades broadly oval to triangular, with wedge-shaped to heart-shaped bases, 10–25 {40} mm long, nerveless, **covered with fine, grey granules** (sometimes few on the upper surface), **veins in a netted pattern visible under magnification** (kranz-type venation), **toothless**, though sometimes wavy-edged; stalks short or absent.

Flowers: Small, **inconspicuous**, without petals, either male or female but with flowers of both sexes on the same plant; male (staminate) flowers with a 5-parted calyx; female (pistillate) flowers lacking a calyx, but with a pair of **triangular bracts 2–2.5 {3.5} mm long** with broad tips and tapered bases, usually **tipped with 3 shallow teeth**, usually **smooth** (sometimes with 1 or 2 obscure bumps (tubercles) on the sides); in compact, head-like clusters in leaf axils and at the branch tips; {June–July} August.

Fruits: Dry seeds, about 1.5 mm long, enclosed by the united, enlarged bracts.

Habitat: Alkaline flats and disturbed areas.

Notes: This species is very similar to Powell's saltbush (*Atriplex powellii* S. Wats.), also considered rare. Powell's saltbush has oblong flowers and fruit bracts (widest above the middle) with a flattened lobe at the tip and small bumps on the sides. Its leaves are prominently 3-nerved. Powell's saltbush also resembles silver saltbush (*Atriplex argentea* Nutt.), a common species, but the latter has teeth all along the edges of the flower or fruit bracts and much larger, toothed leaves. Powell's saltbush is a species of alkaline flats and badlands that flowers from {July} August to September. • Also rare in Alberta is four-wing saltbush (*Atriplex canescens* (Pursh) Nutt.). Four-wing saltbush is a shrub, 10–40 {200} cm tall, with spreading, woody branches. This widely distributed, highly variable complex grows on saline flats and flowers {June to September}. It is distinguished from Alberta's other shrubby *Atriplex*, salt sage (*Atriplex nuttallii* S. Wats. in the *Flora of Alberta*), by the 4 conspicuous, longitudinal, wavy-edged to irregularly toothed wings on the bracts enclosing its seeds.

JL

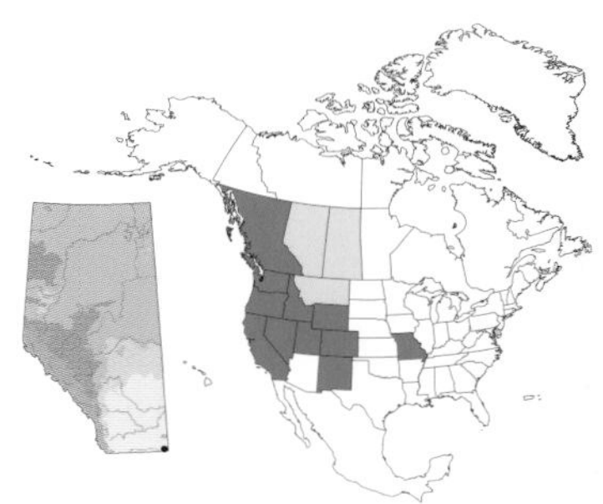

A. POWELLII

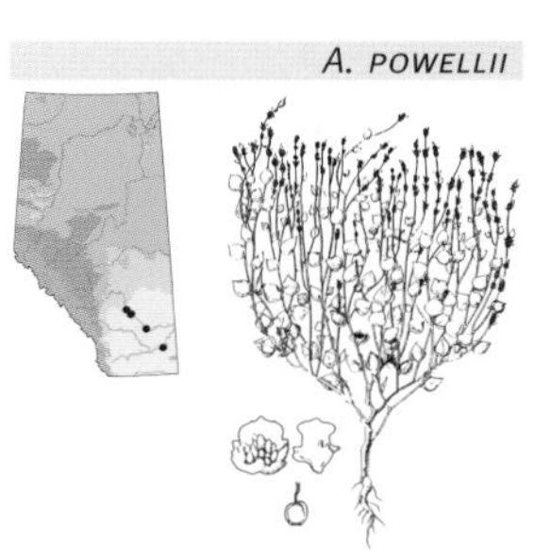

NARROW-LEAVED GOOSEFOOT

Chenopodium leptophyllum (Nutt. *ex* Moq.) Nutt. *ex* S. Wats.

GOOSEFOOT FAMILY (CHENOPODIACEAE)

Plants: Greyish green to whitish annual herbs **covered with fine granules** (farinose); **stems erect** or nearly so, up to 40 {80} cm tall; from slender taproots.

Leaves: Alternate; **blades** linear to lance-shaped, up to 30 mm long and **less than 15 mm wide, 1-veined from the base**, not toothed, sometimes with 1 or 2 lobes above the base, fleshy; stalks short.

Flowers: Small, **lacking petals**, with both male and female parts; **calyx split** almost to the base **into 5 lobes with a sharp ridge down the back** of each, remaining attached to the mature fruit; numerous, in loose to dense head-like clusters, widely spaced on a single stem or on several branches; {May} June–August.

Fruits: Thin-walled, single-seeded nutlets, **covered by the calyx lobes when mature, mostly horizontal**, lens-shaped, **0.9–1.1 mm long** and 0.9–1.1 mm wide, black, with a slightly wrinkled seed coat.

Habitat: Open, slightly disturbed, sandy areas; elsewhere, in sandy blowouts under deciduous vegetation and on shale cliffs.

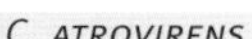

C. ATROVIRENS

Notes: Another rare Alberta species, dark-green goosefoot (*Chenopodium atrovirens* Rydb., also called *Chenopodium fremontii* S. Wats. var. *atrovirens* (Rydb.) Fosberg), also has moderately to densely mealy plants with slender leaves (less than 15 mm wide and 1–5 times longer than wide) and horizontal, lens-shaped seeds (rarely vertical). However, its calyx lobes are much smaller, and they do not cover the mature seeds. Dark-green goosefoot grows in open, disturbed areas, usually at higher elevations, and is reported to flower from June to September. It could be confused with a more common species, meadow goosefoot (*Chenopodium pratericola* Rydb.), but meadow goosefoot is more erect, with flowerheads in elongated clusters. Its leaves have 1 or 2 lobes or teeth above the base and its calyx closely covers the mature fruit. Meadow goosefoot grows along the edges of sloughs and in open, disturbed, moist alkaline areas in the parklands and prairies.• The seeds of narrow-leaved goosefoot were used for food, mixed with cornmeal and salt. Raw or cooked plants were also eaten.

SMOOTH NARROW-LEAVED GOOSEFOOT

Chenopodium subglabrum (S. Wats.) A. Nels.
GOOSEFOOT FAMILY (CHENOPODIACEAE)

Plants: Erect or semi-erect annual herbs; stems light green, 10–50 {60} cm tall, with **many ascending branches,** smooth or sparsely mealy (farinose) on the upper parts; from slender taproots.

Leaves: Alternate; **blades** fleshy, linear, 1–5 cm long, **1–4 mm wide, 1-veined,** greenish, only **lightly mealy**; stalks slender.

Flowers: Small, lacking petals, with both male and female parts in the same flower; **flowers in dense, head-like clusters, widely spaced on 1 stem or on several branches;** calyx lobes egg-shaped, sharp-pointed, broadest above the middle, with a sharp ridge down the back, remaining attached to the fruit; July {May–August}.

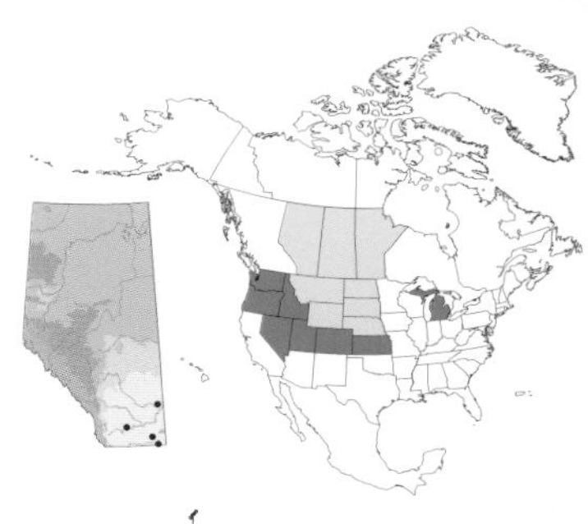

Fruits: Thin-walled, single-seeded nutlets, **covered by the calyx lobes when mature** but eventually falling free, **mostly horizontal,** lens-shaped, **1.3–1.6 mm long** and 1.2–1.4 mm wide, black, shiny.

Habitat: Sand dunes.

Notes: Another rare Alberta species, dried goosefoot (*Chenopodium dessicatum* A. Nels.), is similar to smooth narrow-leaved goosefoot, but dried goosefoot is branched from the base, which gives its plants a spreading appearance. Dried goosefoot grows on undisturbed saline soils and flowers in {May–July} August. • Both of these species are very similar to narrow-leaved goosefoot (p. 66), and some taxonomists included all 3 in the same species. Smooth narrow-leaved goosefoot has 1-veined, green, slightly mealy leaves and larger (1.5 mm) seeds that eventually fall free; narrow-leaved goosefoot has 1-veined, greyish, densely mealy leaves and smaller (1 mm) seeds that remain firmly attached to the outer wall of the fruit; dried goosefoot has 3-veined, greyish, densely mealy leaves and smaller (1 mm) seeds that eventually fall free. • The generic name comes from the Greek *chen* (goose) and *podos* (foot) because of the shape of the leaves of some species.

C. DESSICATUM

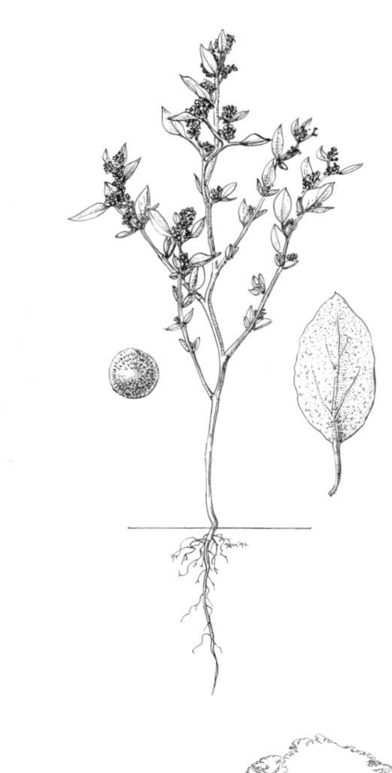

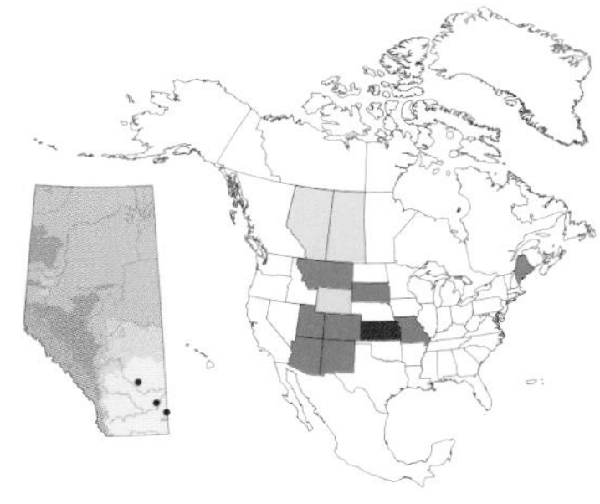

WATSON'S GOOSEFOOT

Chenopodium watsonii A. Nels.
GOOSEFOOT FAMILY (CHENOPODIACEAE)

Plants: **Foul-smelling** annual herbs; **stems angular**, erect or ascending, **2–15 cm tall**, freely branched, covered with fine granules (farinose); from slender taproots.

Leaves: Alternate, **broadly diamond-shaped to egg-shaped**, blunt-tipped, **wedge-shaped at the base**, 15–35 mm long, **more than 15 mm wide**, thick, **densely mealy** (farinose) **on both surfaces**, toothless.

Flowers: Small, lacking petals, with both male and female parts; 5 calyx lobes, egg-shaped or oblong, densely farinose; numerous, in large heads (glomerules), closely to widely spaced along leafy upper branches, forming branched, spike-like clusters (paniculate spikes); {June–September}.

Fruits: Thin-walled, single-seeded nutlets, **covered by the calyx lobes when mature, mostly horizontal**, lens-shaped, 1–1.3 mm long, 0.9–1.3 mm wide, with a **coarsely wrinkled seed coat.**

Habitat: Open areas, mainly in badlands.

Notes: Another species reported for Alberta, hoary goosefoot (*Chenopodium incanum* (S. Wats.) Heller, also called *Chenopodium fremontii* S. Wats. var. *incanum* S. Wats.), resembles Watson's goosefoot in having leaves 10–30 mm long that are diamond-shaped to round and densely covered with granules (though sometimes smooth above). It also has very similar flower clusters, though sometimes these lack leaves. However, hoary goosefoot is a larger plant (to 50 cm tall) and it lacks angular stems; it is not ill-smelling, and its seeds fall free of the calyx rather than remaining attached to it. It grows on dry plains, hillsides and open, sandy ground, and is reported to flower from June to September.

C. INCANUM

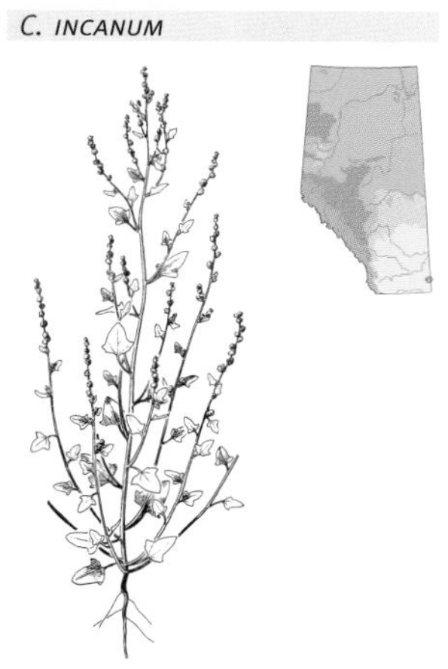

Moquin's sea-blite

Suaeda moquinii (Torr.) Greene
GOOSEFOOT FAMILY (CHENOPODIACEAE)

Plants: **Perennial herbs**; stems erect to ascending, 20–70 cm tall, **hairless or short hairy**, branched; from a woody base and stout taproot.

Leaves: **Alternate, crowded**; blades **fleshy, very narrow, flat to almost cylindrical**, 1–2 cm long, **narrow at the base.**

Flowers: **Small**, without petals; **5 sepals**, fused at the base, **fleshy, of approximately equal lengths, rounded on the back**; 1–3 in the axils of upper leaves, stalkless, each usually with 2 small, translucent bracts; {June} July.

Fruits: **Black nutlets, 1.5–2 mm wide**, smooth or slightly net-veined, usually horizontal, enclosed by the sepals.

Habitat: Moist saline or alkaline soil.

Notes: This species has also been called *Suaeda intermedia* S. Wats. • Western sea-blite (*Suaeda calceoliformis* (Hook.) Moq., also called *Suaeda depressa* (Pursh) S. Wats.), an annual species, is much more common in Alberta. Its sepals are unequal in length, with hood-like tips and a lengthwise ridge on the back (like the keel of a boat). Its leaves are 1–4 cm long and they have enlarged (rather than wedge-shaped) bases. The plants are usually green, but they can become almost black at maturity.

CWa

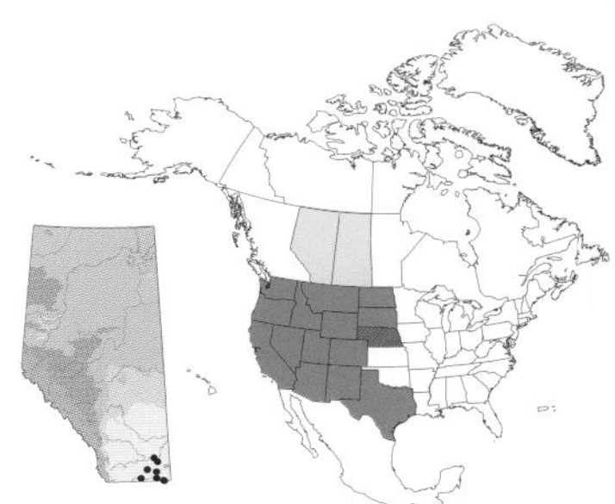

JL

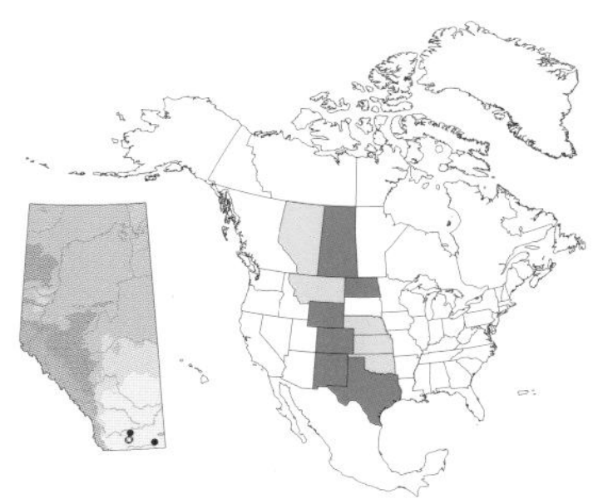

POISON SUCKLEYA

Suckleya suckleyana (Torr.) Rydb.
GOOSEFOOT FAMILY (CHENOPODIACEAE)

Plants: Low, somewhat **fleshy annual herbs**; stems reddish, hairless or with a few small scales, {10} 20–40 cm long, **spreading near the ground, with ascending branches;** from taproots.

Leaves: Alternate, essentially hairless; **blades round to broadly diamond-sided, tapered to a wedge-shaped base,** 1–3 cm wide, wavy-toothed along the upper edge; stalks equal to or longer than the blades.

Flowers: Small, **inconspicuous**, lacking petals, **male or female** (unisexual), but with both sexes on the same plant (monoecious); male flowers with a 3- or 4-lobed calyx and 3–4 stamens, in leaf axils toward stem tips; **female flowers** lacking sepals but **with 2 small, stiff bracts** that enlarge in fruit, in leaf axils **below the male flowers;** June {July–August}.

Fruits: Small, thin-walled and single-seeded (utricles), 5–6 mm long, abruptly pointed at tip, enclosed by a **flattened pair of 5–6 mm wide bracts with toothed wings and notched tips.**

Habitat: Moist, saline lake shores; elsewhere, along streams.

Notes: These plants contain hydrocyanic acid, which makes them **toxic to livestock**—hence the name 'poison suckleya.' They are reported to have caused the poisoning and death of cattle.

CALIFORNIAN AMARANTH

Amaranthus californicus (Moq.) S. Wats.
AMARANTH FAMILY (AMARANTHACEAE)

Plants: Low, **mat-forming annual** herbs, green to reddish purple; stems freely **branched**, up to 30 cm long, prostrate; from weak, slender taproots.

Leaves: Alternate; **blades** elliptic to egg-shaped, usually widest above middle, **5–15 mm long**, with wavy, somewhat thickened edges; stalks very slender, 5–15 mm long.

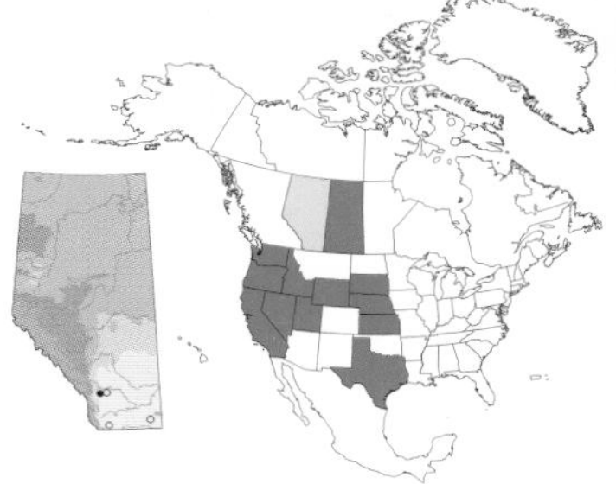

Flowers: Male or female (unisexual) but with both sexes on the same plant (monoecious), **small** and inconspicuous, with **2 lance-shaped, 1–1.5 mm long bracts**, no petals, and **0 or 1** (female flowers) **or 3** (male flowers) **pointed sepals**; in small clusters in leaf axils; {July–October}.

Fruits: Ovoid, single-seeded capsules with 2 or 3 beaks, opening by a cap at the tip (circumscissile); **seeds round, lens-shaped, about 0.7 mm wide.**

Habitat: Moist, often disturbed ground on lake shores and roadsides; elsewhere, on moist alkaline flats.

Notes: This species may have been introduced to Alberta. • Many species of *Amaranthus* around the world have been used as pot herbs, but others are reported to be **toxic to livestock** and have caused the poisoning and deaths of pigs and cattle. • The generic name *Amaranthus* was taken from the Greek *amarantos* (unfading), in reference to the long-lasting flowers, which keep their appearance after they have been picked and dried. Some poets used amaranth as a symbol of immortality, and in ancient Greece it was used to decorate tombs and images of the gods.

LA

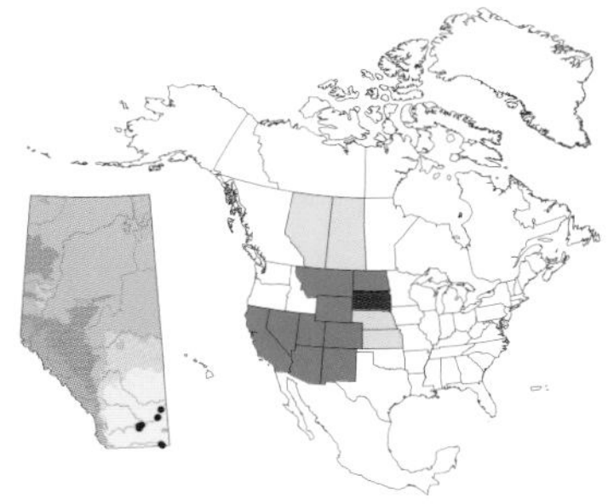

SAND VERBENA

Tripterocalyx micranthus (Torr.) Hook.
FOUR O'CLOCK FAMILY (NYCTAGINACEAE)

Plants: **Annual herbs**, lying on the ground; **stems brittle, trailing but** with **tips pointing upward**, up to 60 cm long, almost hairless or with short glandular hairs.

Leaves: **Opposite** pairs; blades elliptic to egg-shaped, widest at or below the middle, 2–6 cm long, 1–3 cm wide; stalks usually slightly shorter than the blades.

Flowers: **Greenish white, tubular**, tipped with 5 wide-spreading lobes, 10–12 mm long, 3–5 mm across at tip, lacking petals but with **5 glandular-hairy, petal-like sepals**; in **flat-topped clusters** (umbels) with a whorl of small (5–10 mm long), lance-shaped bracts at the base, clusters on stalks shorter than the leaves and growing from leaf axils; {May–July}.

Fruits: Dry, seed-like fruits (achenes) enclosed in **2 or 3 wide, papery, conspicuously veined wings**, 20 {15–28} **mm long**.

Habitat: Sandy ground, usually on hard-packed level ground, but also on active, south-, west- and east-facing slopes of dunes and dune ridge tops.

Notes: This species has also been called *Abronia micrantha* Torr. • The encroachment of vegetation on active sand-dune areas is reducing the suitable habitat of this species. • Sand verbena superficially resembles wild begonia (*Rumex venosus* Pursh), but wild begonia is a perennial plant with running, elongated underground stems (rhizomes) and stout (not brittle), erect stems; its flowers are borne in leafy, branched clusters (panicles) at the stem tips. • Young sand verbena plants sometimes resemble members of the goosefoot family (Chenopodiaceae) in shape, colour and mealiness (of the underside of the leaves). • Several *Abronia* species have been grown in borders, rockeries and baskets. They make colourful displays in gardens and as cutflowers. Bougainvillea, a cultivated showy vine, is also in the four o'clock family. • The wings on these fruits aid dispersal by the gusty winds of sand-dune fields. • The four o'clock family is so named because the flowers tend to open in the late afternoon. The Greek word *nyx* means 'night,' a reference to the late opening of the flowers. *Micranthus* means 'small-flowered.'

BITTER-ROOT

Lewisia rediviva Pursh
PURSLANE FAMILY (PORTULACACEAE)

LA

Plants: Low perennial herbs; stems leafless, 1–3 cm tall, with a whorl of **5–7 slender, leaf-like bracts**; from deep, **fleshy taproots**.

Leaves: Basal, **1–5 cm long**, club-shaped, **fleshy** and **nearly cylindrical**.

Flowers: Deep to light rose-pink (sometimes whitish) with a yellow or orange centre, **4–6 cm across**, with **12–18** lance-shaped **petals** and **6–9** pinkish, egg-shaped **sepals**, on long, slender stalks jointed just above the whorl of bracts; solitary; {April–June} July–August.

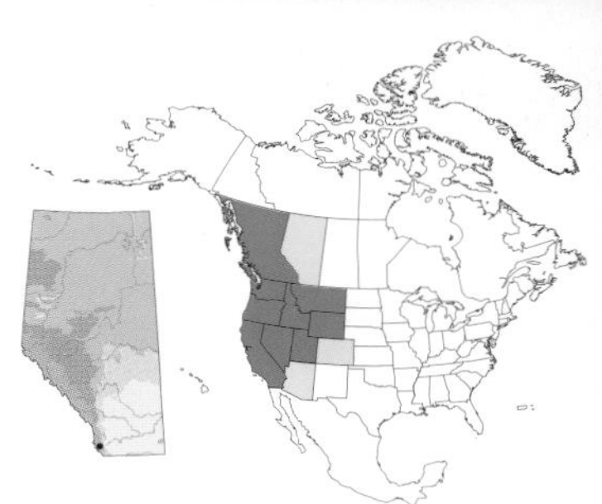

Fruits: Egg-shaped capsules with 6–20 dark, shiny seeds.

Habitat: Dry, open, montane sites; elsewhere, on desert flats.

Notes: Dwarf bitter-root (*Lewisia pygmaea* (A. Gray) B.L. Robins. ssp. *pygmaea*) is another rare Alberta species. It resembles bitter-root, but it has longer (5–15 cm), flatter leaves and smaller flowers (about 1.5–2 cm across) with 6–8 petals and only 2 sepals. Dwarf bitter-root grows on dry, rocky, alpine slopes and is reported to flower from late May to August. • These roots were one of the most important crops of the Flathead and Kutenai. Europeans found them too bitter, but native peoples considered them a treat. They were collected early in the spring, because their brownish black covering was most easily removed before the plants flowered. Roots were peeled and washed, then boiled until soft or dried for 1–2 days for storage. The inner core or 'heart' was removed to reduce bitterness, and storage for 1–2 years was also said to help. The cooked roots were eaten alone, mixed with sweeter foods such as berries and camas roots, or added to stews, soups and gravies as a thickener. • It took a woman 3–4 days to fill a 23-kg bag with these small roots, but this was enough to sustain a person through winter.

L. PYGMAEA

JG

JP

SMALL-LEAVED MONTIA, SMALL-LEAVED SPRING BEAUTY

Montia parvifolia (Moc. *ex* DC.) Greene
PURSLANE FAMILY (PORTULACACEAE)

Plants: Succulent **perennial** herbs, **often producing bulblets** in leaf axils; stems several, very slender, 5–20 {25} cm long, erect or spreading at the base; from **short, thick root crowns** and **slender underground stems** (rhizomes), often forming patches from spreading, runner-like (stoloniferous) stems.

Leaves: Mainly basal, but also alternate on the stems, several, thick and **fleshy**; blades 1.5–3 {6} cm long, varying from **spoon-shaped** and 2–3 mm wide **to almost round** and 2 cm wide; stalks usually as long as the blades or longer; **stem leaves** gradually **reduced** to bracts on the upper stem.

Flowers: Rose-coloured or white with pink veins, rather showy, funnel-shaped to broadly cupped, about 1.5–2 cm across, with **5 spreading, 6–10** {15} **mm long petals** and **2 unequal sepals**, 1.5–3 mm long; **6–10 stamens**; nearly erect in the axils of small bracts, usually 3–8, in elongating clusters (racemes); July {May–August}.

Fruits: Capsules, almost entirely covered by the persistent calyxes, splitting into 3 segments (valves) to release 2 {1–3} black, shiny, 1–1.5 mm long seeds covered with tiny bumps.

Habitat: Moist montane to alpine slopes and ledges, preferring sites that are moist in early summer and dry later; elsewhere, on lake shores, seepage areas and mossy streambanks.

Notes: This species has also been called *Claytonia parvifolia* Moc. • Linear-leaved montia (*Montia linearis* (Dougl. *ex* Hook.) Greene), also known as slender-leaved spring beauty, is also rare in Alberta. It is an annual species with fibrous roots and its stems are branched near the base. Its leaves are thin, linear and alternate on the stem, and it has white, nodding flowers. Linear-leaved montia flowers from May to July on moist to dry, open sites on sandy plains and hills at lower elevations. It also grows in disturbed habitats and in open woodlands. This is the most common, widespread species of the genus. • When a capsule opens, its 3 sections curl inward and downward. This presses the seeds firmly against one another and eventually throws them outward, up to 2 m from the plant.

M. LINEARIS

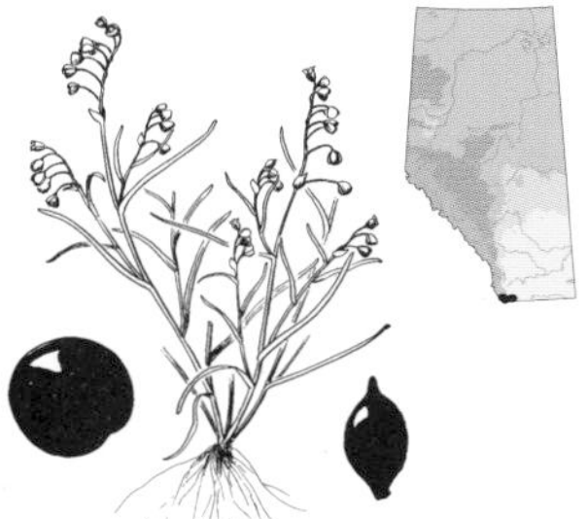

LOW SANDWORT

Arenaria longipedunculata Hult.
PINK FAMILY (CARYOPHYLLACEAE)

DJ

Plants: **Low, tufted or loosely matted perennial** herbs; stems short, **2–4 cm high**; from thread-like, underground, light-coloured runners (stolons).

Leaves: Opposite in **1 or 2 pairs**, overlapping, lance-shaped to egg-shaped (**about twice as long as they are wide**), blunt or somewhat pointed, slightly fringed near the base, **2–6 mm long.**

Flowers: White, inconspicuous, about 3–5 mm long, with 5 petals and 5 sepals; **petals rounded or shallowly notched** at the tip, equal to the sepals; sepals egg-shaped, blunt or slightly pointed, hairless or with short glandular hairs, indistinctly 3-nerved; **10 stamens**; **3 styles**; **solitary**, on erect, 1–2 cm long, finely hairy stalks with 1 pair of pointed, egg-shaped bracts below the middle.

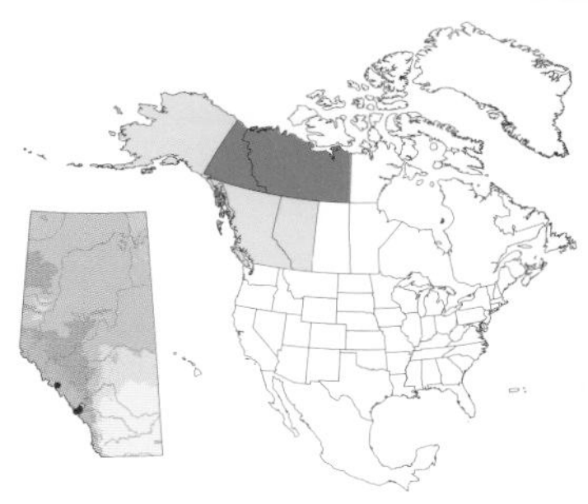

Fruits: Egg-shaped capsules, slightly longer than the sepals, **splitting open from the tip into 6 tooth-like segments**; seeds several, brown, round, shiny, slightly wrinkled, 0.7–0.8 mm long.

Habitat: Moist gravelly areas at higher elevations; elsewhere, in wet, often mossy, places along rivers and streams and in tundra, on moist calcareous or serpentine gravel and in moist rock crevices.

Notes: This species has also been included in *Arenaria humifusa* Wahl. and called *Arenaria cylindricarpa* Fern. • In sheltered and shaded situations, low sandwort may grow taller and produce flowers and capsules that are raised well above the plant mat. This form has been called *Arenaria pedunculata* Hult. • *Arenaria* species are very similar to *Minuartia* species. The two genera are distinguished mainly by their capsules, which split into 3 parts in *Minuartia* (1 segment per style) and into 6 parts in *Arenaria* (2 segments per style) • The generic name *Arenaria* is from the Latin *arena* (sand) because of the sandy habitats of some species. The specific epithet *longipedunculata* refers to the long flowering stalks (peduncles).

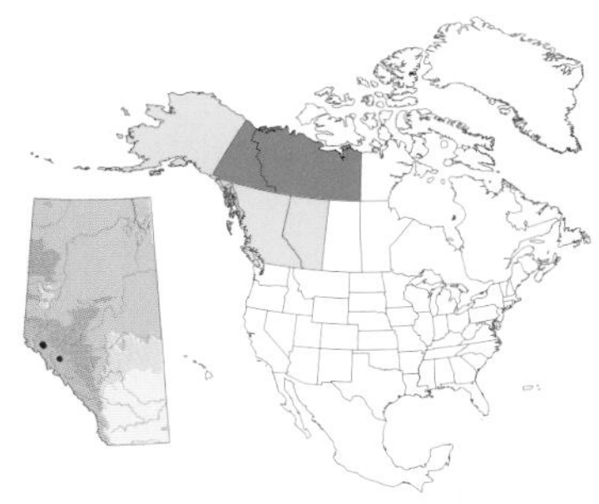

PURPLE ALPINE SANDWORT

Minuartia elegans (Cham. & Schlecht.) Schischkin
PINK FAMILY (CARYOPHYLLACEAE)

Plants: Loosely tufted, often purplish, **hairless** perennial herbs **about 2–4 cm tall**; stems numerous, from a branched root crown, forming tufts up to 30 cm in diameter.

Leaves: Opposite and in compact clusters (fascicles) in the axils of the main leaves, linear, blunt-tipped, **3–10 mm long, 1-nerved or** appearing **nerveless**.

Flowers: White, saucer-shaped, about 5–6 mm across, with **5 petals** and **5 sepals**; petals oblong to egg-shaped, widest above the middle, blunt or shallowly notched at the tip, no longer than the calyx, rarely absent; **sepals separate, purple**, **3–3.5** {2–4} **mm long, broadly lance-shaped**, pointed at the tip, slightly ridged down the back (keeled), weakly **3-nerved**; 10 stamens; 3 styles; solitary, on **1–4 cm long stalks** at the stem tips; July–August.

Fruits: Ovoid or oblong **capsules, 2–4 mm long, splitting open from the tip into 3 tooth-like segments** to release tiny, minutely bumpy or spiny, kidney-shaped seeds.

Habitat: Moist, gravelly alpine slopes; elsewhere, on dry, turfy, gravelly or sandy calcareous barrens.

Notes: This species has also been called *Arenaria rossii* (R. Br. *ex* Richards.) Graebn. ssp. *elegans* (Cham. & Schlecht.) Maguire and *Minuartia rossii* R. Br. var. *elegans* (Cham. & Schlecht.) Hult. • This species is a member of the *Minuartia rossii* complex, which includes *Minuartia rossii, M. austromontana* and *M. elegans.* These 3 species have distinct geographical distributions. Ross' sandwort (*Minuartia rossii* (R. Br.) Graebn.) is a high-arctic to alpine species that has not yet been found in Alberta. Green alpine sandwort (*Minuartia austromontana* Wolf & Packer) is the most common species in Alberta, where it grows in the Rockies. It is distinguished from purple alpine sandwort by its green, linear to lance-shaped sepals and its usual lack of petals. Its leaves are awl-shaped and fleshy, and its plants are densely tufted. • The generic name *Minuartia* commemorates Juan Minuart (1693–1768) of Barcelona. The specific epithet *elegans* means 'elegant.'

KNOTTED PEARLWORT

Sagina nodosa (L.) Fenzl ssp. *borealis* Crow
PINK FAMILY (CARYOPHYLLACEAE)

DJ

Plants: Slender, **tufted** perennial herbs; **stems** ascending to loosely spreading to lying on the ground, **5–25 cm long, thread-like**, hairless or hairy at the joints; from branched root crowns.

Leaves: Opposite on the stem and basal (but not in rosettes), linear, 1.5–3 cm long on the lower stem, **1–2 mm long and forming dense clusters** (fascicles) in leaf axils **on the upper stem**, giving the plant a knotted appearance.

Flowers: White, showy, saucer-shaped, about 6–10 mm across, with **5 petals** and **5 sepals** (sometimes 4 petals and 4 sepals); **petals** separate, **rounded or shallowly notched** at the tip, **3–5 mm long; sepals separate**, often purple-tipped, elliptic, 2–3 mm long, hairless or with gland-tipped hairs at the base; **8 or 10 stamens; 4 or 5 styles**; single, at branch tips; July {August–September}.

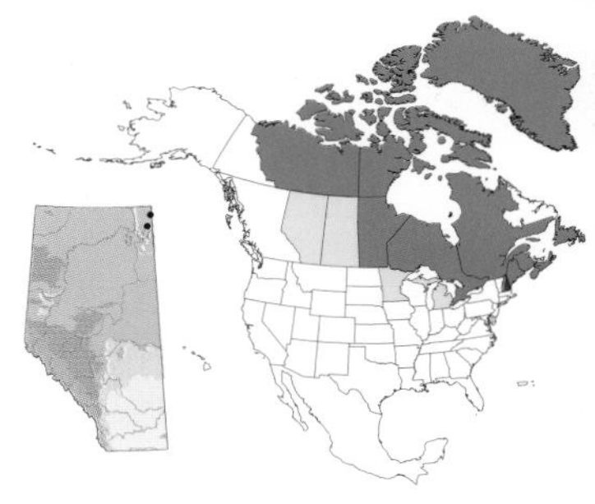

Fruits: Capsules, 3–4 mm long, with sepals pressed to the outer surface, **splitting into 4 or 5 thick segments** (valves) to release **many** dark brown to black, smooth to distinctly pebbled, egg-shaped to kidney-shaped **seeds** 0.5 mm long.

Habitat: Moist rocky, gravelly, sandy or peaty places, especially on shores; elsewhere, on damp sand in dune slacks, on dry sand on the lee side of fixed dunes and on salty ledges along the coast.

Notes: Snow pearlwort (*Sagina nivalis* (Lindbl.) Fries, also known as *Sagina intermedia* Fenzl) is a similar plant reported to occur in Alberta. It is distinguished by its smaller (less than 5 mm wide) flowers with fewer (mostly 4), shorter (about as long as the sepals) petals. It forms low (1–5 cm tall), compact cushions without leaf clusters in the upper leaf axils. Snow pearlwort grows in moist, gravelly alpine areas. • Spreading pearlwort (*Sagina decumbens* (Ell.) T. & G.) is an annual species without basal leaf clusters. It has small, 5-petalled flowers with purple-edged sepals, and its capsules split only halfway to the base. Spreading pearlwort is reported from Alberta and grows on sandy, alpine sites. • Double-flowered forms of knotted pearlwort are sometimes used as a filler in rock terraces and walls, and as a ground cover, but the plants do not withstand traffic as well as grass, and they are apt to invade nearby areas and become a troublesome weed.

S. DECUMBENS

S. NIVALIS

ALPINE BLADDER CATCHFLY

Silene involucrata (Cham. & Schlecht.) Bocquet ssp. *involucrata*
PINK FAMILY (CARYOPHYLLACEAE)

Plants: Perennial herbs, often purplish; stems single, erect, 5–35 cm tall, covered with long, **purple-banded, gland-tipped hairs** in the upper parts; from branched crowns of taproots.

Leaves: Mainly basal, lance-shaped, widest toward the tip, stalkless, 1.5–5.5 cm long, 2–8 mm wide, fringed with hairs; stem leaves in 1–3 pairs, narrower.

Flowers: Erect, single (sometimes 2 or 3); **5 petals, white to pinkish, broadly 2-lobed** at the tip and **projecting** {2} 3–7 mm **past the sepals**, narrowed abruptly to a slender base; 5 **sepals**, hairy, **united to form a 1–2 cm long bell or urn with 10 purple nerves**; 5 (sometimes 4) styles; July.

Fruits: Erect capsules, opening at the tip by 4 or 5 (sometimes 8–10) teeth; seeds kidney-shaped to round, edged with a narrow, flattened section (wing), 1–1.5 mm long.

Habitat: Gravelly and turfy alpine slopes; elsewhere, dry sites in meadows and on rock outcrops, river terraces and floodplains in arctic tundra.

Notes: This species has also been called *Silene furcata* Raf., *Lychnis furcata* (Raf.) Fern., *Lychnis affinis* J. Vahl and *Melandrium affine* J. Vahl. Its Alberta population is isolated (disjunct) from the widespread northern populations. • Nodding cockle (*Silene uralensis* (Rupr.) Bocq. ssp. *attenuata* (Farr) McNeill, also called *Lychnis apetala* L. and *Melandrium apetalum* (L.) Fenzl.) is a more widespread, small species of rocky alpine slopes. However, its flowers nod, and their purplish petals are usually shorter than (and therefore contained within) its urn-shaped calyxes. • Alpine bladder catchfly often grows near animal dens. • The derivation of *Silene* is uncertain. It is either from the Greek *sialon* (saliva), referring to the sticky bands on the stem, or from *seilenos*, a type of woodland deity or satyr.

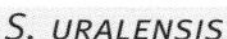
S. URALENSIS

LK

SALT-MARSH SAND SPURRY

Spergularia salina J. & K. Presl var. *salina*
PINK FAMILY (CARYOPHYLLACEAE)

Plants: Small **annual herbs**, more or less glandular-hairy; **stems 5–20 cm long**, much branched, widely spreading or lying on ground; from slender taproots.

Leaves: Opposite; blades **somewhat fleshy**, slender to thread-like, **cylindrical**, 1–2.5 cm long, 0.6–1.5 mm wide, sharply pointed at the tip, bearing **triangular, membranous stipules** up to 4 mm long at the base.

Flowers: White or pinkish, with 5 small petals (shorter than the sepals) and 5 sepals 2.5–5 mm long; **usually 3 styles**; numerous, in loose, spreading clusters (cymes); May–August.

Fruits: Egg-shaped capsules, 3.5–6 mm long, usually splitting to the base into **3 parts**, containing smooth, **brown or reddish seeds** 0.5–0.9 mm long.

Habitat: Brackish or saline mud and sands.

Notes: This species has also been called *Spergularia marina* (L.) Griseb. var. *leiosperma* (Kindb.) Ghrke. • Two-stamened sand spurry (*Spergularia diandra* (Guss.) Boiss.) has been introduced to Alberta from Europe. It has narrower leaves (0.5–1 mm wide), round capsules and black, 0.4–0.5 mm long seeds. • Salt-marsh sand spurry appears to be native to Alberta, but there are both native and non-native populations elsewhere. In southern Ontario, introduced populations are spreading along highways in response to the accumulation of salt used for melting ice in winter. • The generic name is derived from *Spergula*, a similar genus. *Spergula* was derived from the Latin *spargo* (to scatter), in reference to the wide scattering of the seeds.

LA

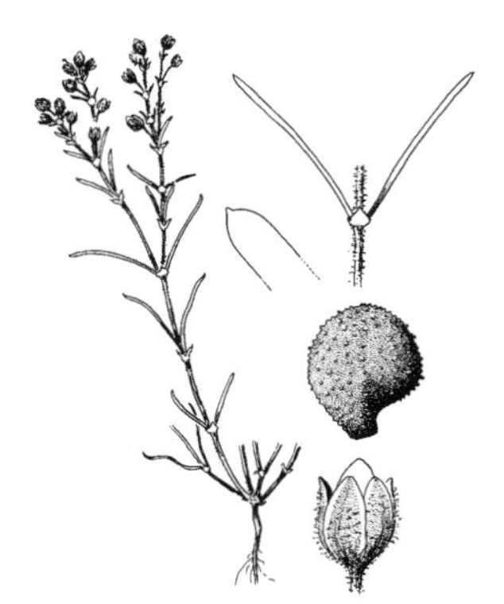

LA

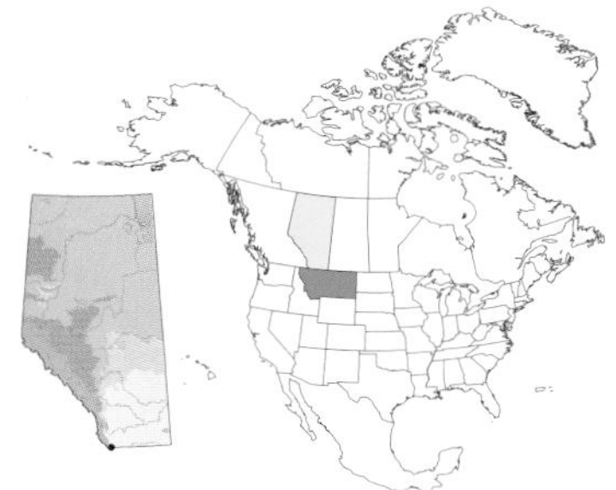

S. NITENS

AMERICAN CHICKWEED

Stellaria americana (Porter *ex* B.L. Robins.) Standl.
PINK FAMILY (CARYOPHYLLACEAE)

Plants: Delicate perennial herbs; stems slender, **sticky-hairy**, leafy, 10–20 cm long, lying on the ground; forming **loose mats** from elongated underground stems (rhizomes).

Leaves: Opposite, sticky, stalkless; blades **egg-shaped**, 1–3 cm long, usually blunt-tipped.

Flowers: White, with **5 deeply notched petals** 1½–2 times as long as the sepals; 5 sepals, blunt-tipped, 3–4 mm long, with glands; styles commonly 3; few, in branching, leafy clusters (cymes); {July} August.

Fruits: Elliptic capsules, shorter than the sepals, splitting lengthwise into 6 sections, several- to many-seeded.

Habitat: Rocky slopes, usually at high elevations.

Notes: Shining chickweed (*Stellaria nitens* Nutt.) is a delicate annual species with thread-like stems up to 20 cm tall. Its leaves are mainly on the lower half of the stem, and its flowers are borne in large, open clusters with membranous (not leaf-like) bracts. Shining chickweed has been reported to occur in Alberta. It grows on gravelly sites or grassy slopes in prairies and along streams, and is reported to flower from April to June. • Chickens and other poultry are said to like the seeds of these plants, hence the name 'chickweed.' The generic name *Stellaria* was derived from the Latin *stella* (star), in reference to the shape of the flower. *Americana* means 'of America.'

MEADOW CHICKWEED

Stellaria obtusa Engelm.
PINK FAMILY (CARYOPHYLLACEAE)

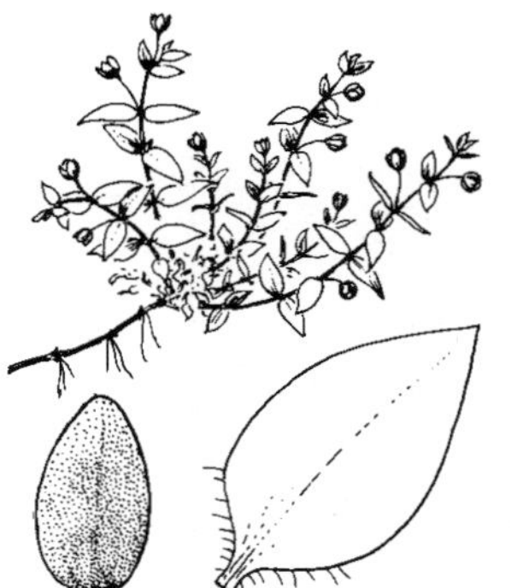

Plants: Delicate, hairless perennial herbs; stems numerous, branched, lying on the ground, 5–15 cm long; forming **loose mats.**

Leaves: Opposite, stalkless; blades **egg-shaped, 4–8 mm long**, pointed at the tip, **fringed** with hairs along lower edges.

Flowers: Petals usually absent, 5, white and tiny when present; 4 or 5 **sepals**, sometimes fused at the base, 2–3 mm long, **blunt-tipped**; styles commonly 3; **single, in leaf axils**; {June–July}.

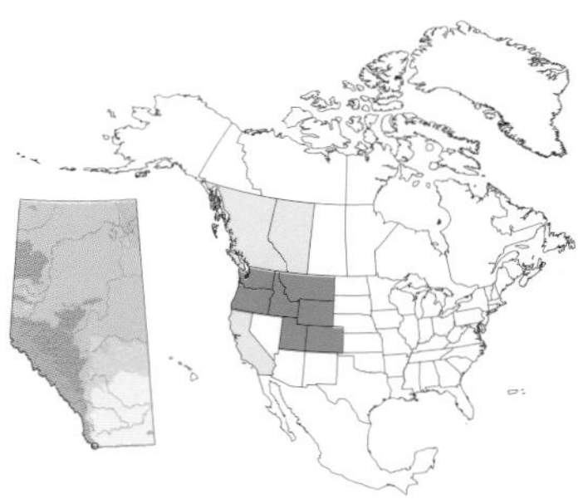

Fruits: Broadly **egg-shaped capsules**, blunt-tipped, longer than the sepals, splitting lengthwise into 6 sections, containing several to many wrinkled seeds.

Habitat: Damp meadows, on lake shores and stream sides.

Notes: Wavy-leaved chickweed (*Stellaria crispa* Cham. & Schlecht.) is a similar species that is also rare in Alberta. It too has single flowers in the leaf axils with either no or tiny petals, but its sepals are longer (3–4 mm long) and pointed and they have dry, translucent edges. Its leaves are usually hairless and often longer than those of meadow chickweed (up to 3 cm long), and they tend to have wavy edges—hence the specific epithet *crispa*, which is Latin for 'curled.' Wavy-leaved chickweed flowers in June and July in moist woods and clearings. • The blunt-tipped sepals of meadow chickweed give rise to its specific epithet *obtusa*, which means 'blunt' in Latin.

S. CRISPA

JG

UMBELLATE CHICKWEED

Stellaria umbellata Turcz. *ex* Kar. & Kir.
PINK FAMILY (CARYOPHYLLACEAE)

Plants: Delicate perennial herbs; stems slender, erect to ascending, **10–30 cm tall**; from creeping underground stems (rhizomes).

Leaves: Opposite, stalkless; blades **narrowly lance-shaped to elliptic**, 5–20 mm long, hairless or fringed with hairs on the lower edges.

Flowers: Green to whitish, lacking petals or with 5 tiny, white petals; sepals usually 5, 2–3 mm long, with dry, translucent edges; styles commonly 3; numerous, in upper leaf axils above **dry, translucent bracts**, and in open, spreading clusters (cymes) with branches eventually bent backward; {July–August}.

Fruits: Egg-shaped capsules, 4–5 mm long, splitting lengthwise into 6 teeth, containing several to many slightly wrinkled seeds.

Habitat: Moist woods, meadows and banks from subalpine to alpine elevations.

Notes: Another rare Alberta species, sand-dune chickweed (*Stellaria arenicola* Raup), also has whitish, translucent bracts in its flower clusters, but unlike umbellate chickweed, it has showy flowers on erect or ascending stalks and its petals are usually longer than their sepals. Each petal is deeply cut into 2 slender lobes, so at first glance, these flowers seem to have 10 linear petals. Sand-dune chickweed is very similar to the much more common species long-stalked chickweed (*Stellaria longipes* Goldie), but sand-dune chickweed has straw-coloured capsules that open by 6 teeth at the tip which are bent sharply back. Long-stalked chickweed usually has purplish black capsules with erect teeth. Sand-dune chickweed grows on the shifting sand of sand dunes, and flowers in July and August. • The specific epithet *umbellata*, from the Latin *umbella* (parasol), refers to the loose, umbrella-shaped flower clusters.

S. ARENICOLA

JG

PYGMY WATER-LILY

Nymphaea leibergii Morong
WATER-LILY FAMILY (NYMPHAEACEAE)

Plants: **Aquatic** perennial herbs; leaf and flower stalks arising from the tip of unbranched, cylindrical, erect, **thick, fleshy underground stems** (rhizomes).

Leaves: Usually **floating, broadly heart-shaped**, with a deep, **V-shaped hollow** at the base between 2 pointed lobes, **5–12 {3–19} cm long, 3–7 {2–15} cm wide**, with 7–13 main veins, green on the upper surface, often deep purplish beneath; stalks hairless, long, slender.

Flowers: **White, without fragrance**, broadly cupped, **3–4 {7.5} cm across**, with **8–15 white, purple-veined petals** in whorls of 4 and **4 greenish sepals**, all about **2–3 cm long**; stigmatic disc with upcurved, tapered or slightly boat-shaped **appendages 0.6–1.5 mm long around the edges**, yellow or purplish-tipped; 20–40 stamens, yellow, sometimes purplish-tipped; **solitary, floating**, attached to buried stems by a long stalk; August {June–September}.

Fruits: Round, leathery, berry-like capsules, about 1 cm wide, containing egg-shaped, 2–3 mm long seeds, each tipped with a small appendage that becomes sticky when wet.

Habitat: Quiet streams, ponds and lakes, usually in deep water; elsewhere, in water 25–200 cm deep.

Notes: This species has also been called *Nymphaea tetragona* Georgi ssp. *leibergii* (Morong) Porsild. • Small white water-lily (*Nymphaea tetragona* Georgi) is similar to pygmy water-lily, and these 2 rare taxa have often been included in the same species. Small white water-lily has stigmatic discs edged with larger (usually over 3 mm long) appendages, and its sepals have prominent lines of attachment that leave a tetragonal pattern on the receptacle. Small white water-lily grows in ponds, lakes and quiet streams, and is reported to flower throughout the summer. • Water-shield (*Brasenia schreberi* J.F. Gmelin), a member of the water-shield family (Cabombaceae), occurs in northeastern Alberta. It is easily recognized by its floating, elliptic, 5–10 cm long leaves, with long, slimy stalks attached at the centre of the blade and covered with a thick gelatinous sheath. Its small, inconspicuous flowers are reported to appear in late July to September. The leathery, 1- or 2-seeded pods do not split open. Water-shield grows in shallow, calm or slow-moving water.

JD

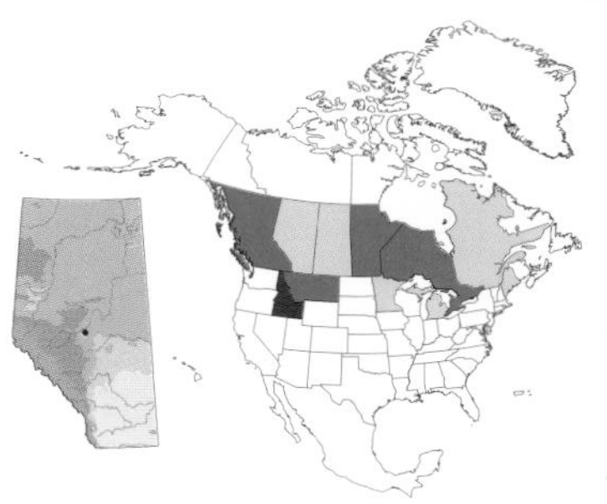

N. TETRAGONA

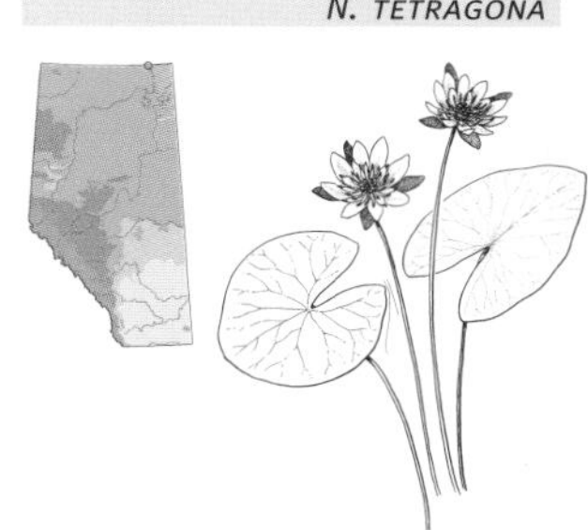

BRASENIA SCHREBERI

DJ

DJ

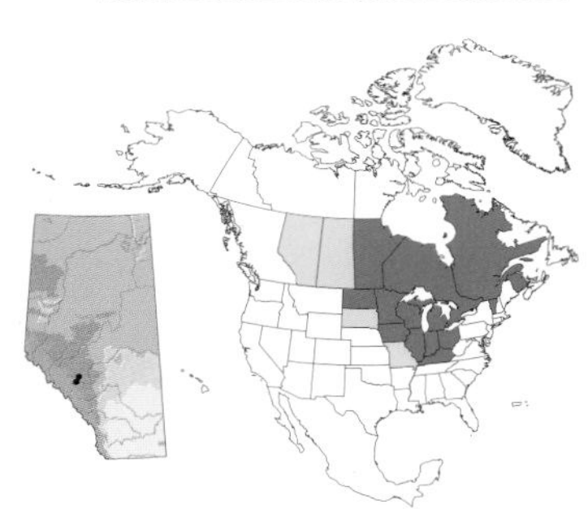

WOOD ANEMONE

Anemone quinquefolia L. var. *bifolia* Farw.
BUTTERCUP FAMILY (RANUNCULACEAE)

Plants: Delicate perennial herbs, 10–20 {5–30} cm tall; stems slightly hairy; growing from crisp, slender (1–4 mm thick), white, elongated underground stems (rhizomes).

Leaves: Basal leaves single or absent, long-stalked, divided into 3–5 leaflets, coarsely and unevenly toothed or deeply and irregularly cut, with the terminal leaflet diamond-shaped to lance-shaped and 1–4.5 cm long; **stem leaves** (involucral bracts) **usually 3, in a circle** (whorl) below the flower, stalked, divided into 3–5 leaflets; leaflets lance-shaped to egg-shaped and widest above middle, tapered to a wedge-shaped base, deeply and irregularly cut and lobed.

Flowers: White to pinkish or purplish-tinged, with 5 {4–6} **petal-like sepals** 1–2 {0.6–2.5} cm long; no petals; 30–60 stamens; conspicuous, **single**, on slender stalks with long, soft, spreading hairs; {April–June} July.

Fruits: Dry, seed-like fruits (achenes), 3–4 {2.5–4.5} mm long, spindle-shaped (fusiform) with a stiff, curved to straight, 0.5–2 mm long tip, densely covered with short, stiff hairs, numerous, in dense, round, head-like clusters on 1–6 cm long stalks.

Habitat: Moist woods in the main foothills; elsewhere, in thickets, on open hillsides, in aspen and mixed woods, in clearings, and on sandy stream sides and riverbanks.

Notes: This variety also encompasses *Anemone nemorosa* L. var. *bifolia* (Farw.) B. Boivin and *A. quinquefolia* L. var. *interior* Fern. • All anemones contain acrid, poisonous compounds that **may irritate the skin.** They **should never be eaten.** • The word *Anemone* is commonly assumed to be derived from the Greek word *anemos*, which means 'wind,' probably in reference to the exposed, windy places where many of these plants grow. Many species are early bloomers, and it was once believed that their flowers opened at the command of the first mild breezes of spring.

GOLDTHREAD

Coptis trifolia (L.) Salisb.
BUTTERCUP FAMILY (RANUNCULACEAE)

Plants: Small perennial herbs; flowering stems slender, {4} 5–15 cm tall; from thread-like, **bright yellow or orange underground stems** (rhizomes).

Leaves: Basal, evergreen, shiny, on slender 1.5–12 cm long stalks, divided into **3 leaflets**; leaflets short-stalked or stalkless, egg-shaped, 7–20 mm long, wedge-shaped at base, broadly 3-lobed and sharply toothed at the tip.

Flowers: White with a yellowish base, **10–16 mm across**, with 5–7 elliptic to spoon-shaped sepals and 5–7 inconspicuous petals; **petals reduced** to small, fleshy, club-shaped structures (staminodia) tipped with nectar; single, erect; July {May–August}.

Fruits: Pod-like, splitting open along 1 side (follicles), **7–12 mm long** (including a prominent, 2–4 mm long beak), **on long stalks** (equal to or longer than the follicle), in a spreading **whorled cluster of** {3} **4–7 at the stem tip**; seeds 1–1.5 mm across, shiny, black.

Habitat: Damp, mossy woods; elsewhere, in muskeg, willow scrub and tundra.

Notes: Goldthread has been used in preparations to combat alcoholism, because it is said to relieve the craving for alcohol. The roots are very astringent, and they were either chewed or boiled to make medicinal teas for treating sore throats, canker sores and other mouth irritations—hence another common name, 'canker-root.' It was also used as an eyewash and as a topical anesthetic on the gums of teething children. Goldthread was listed in the *US Pharmacopoeia* from 1820 to 1882, and at the turn of the century 500 g of the root fetched about a dollar. Today, these attractive, shade-tolerant plants are sometimes grown as ground cover in wooded areas. • The generic name *Coptis* was taken from the Greek *kopto* (to cut), in reference to the deeply cut leaves. The common name 'goldthread' refers to the long, slender, yellow underground stems.

RB

LK

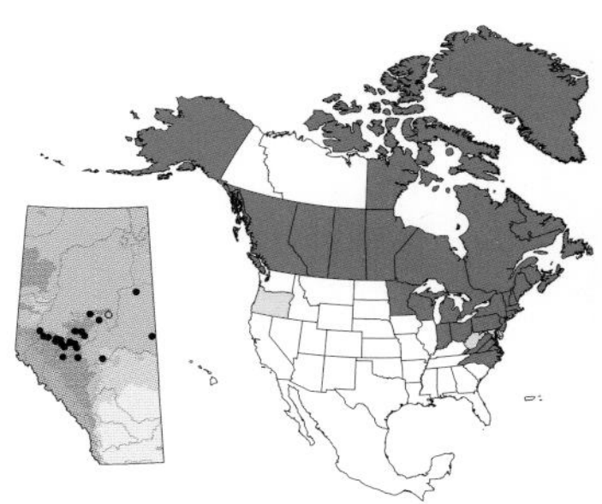

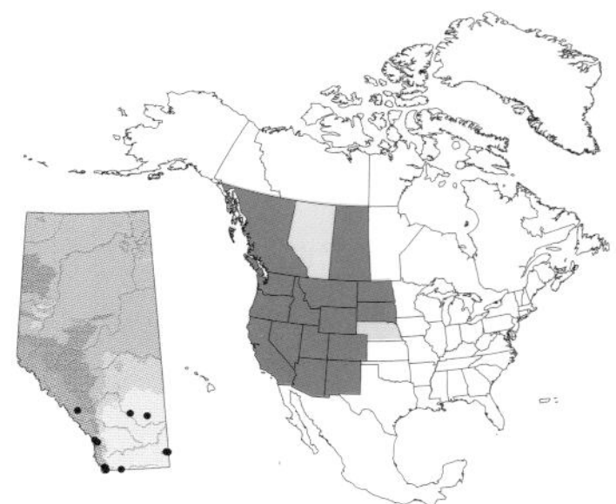

R. OCCIDENTALIS

EARLY BUTTERCUP

Ranunculus glaberrimus Hook.
BUTTERCUP FAMILY (RANUNCULACEAE)

Plants: Rather fleshy, **hairless** perennial herbs with acrid juice, usually less than 10 cm tall; stems usually several, **erect to lying on the ground, 4–18** {20} **cm long**; from clusters of thick, fleshy roots.

Leaves: Mainly basal; basal leaves nearly round to narrowly egg-shaped, often widest above the middle, rounded at the base or tapered to long, slender stalks, smooth, wavy or toothed along the edges, sometimes 3-lobed; stem leaves similar to the basal leaves but short-stalked.

Flowers: Yellow (sometimes white with age), **saucer-shaped, 10–25 mm across**, with **5** {6–8} **separate petals** and **5 sepals**; petals 6–15 mm long, broad and conspicuous, each with a nectar-producing pit at the base; **sepals** 5–8 mm long, usually tinged with purple, with or without hairs, soon shed; 40–80 stamens; 1–6 on long stalks (up to 10 cm long), in open clusters (corymbs); {March} May–June.

Fruits: Finely hairy 'seeds' (achenes), 1.5–2 mm long, widest toward the short (0.5–0.8 mm), straight beak; 75–100 {30–150} borne on round receptacles in large (1–2 cm wide), round heads.

Habitat: Grassland and meadows in the prairies; elsewhere, in ponderosa pine woodland and sagebrush desert.

Notes: Western buttercup (*Ranunculus occidentalis* Nutt. var. *brevistylis* Greene) is also rare in Alberta. It is a larger plant (stems 20–70 cm long) with hairy, deeply cut, 3–5-lobed and toothed basal leaves. Its showy yellow flowers are about 1.5–2 cm wide, and its flattened achenes are edged with a distinct, narrow wing and tipped with a long, nearly straight beak (hooked at the tip only). Western buttercup grows in moist alpine and subalpine meadows, and is reported to flower from April to June. • The generic name *Ranunculus* was derived from the Greek *rana* (a little frog), in reference to the aquatic habit of many species.

ALPINE BUTTERCUP

Ranunculus gelidus Karel. & Kiril. ssp. *grayi* (Britt.) Hult.
BUTTERCUP FAMILY (RANUNCULACEAE)

JP

Plants: Small, tufted, grey-green perennial herbs, 5–12 {2–22} cm tall, essentially **hairless; stems** usually several, simple or forked in 2s, with a cluster of small leaves at or somewhat below the middle, **often arched** when in fruit; forming small, firmly rooted tussocks from short, branched crowns on slender, 0.5–1 mm thick roots.

Leaves: Basal, simple; **blades heart-shaped** to kidney-shaped, 5–15 {18} mm long and **8–20** {30} **mm wide, twice deeply cut in 3s** into blunt, egg-shaped to lance-shaped lobes widest above the middle; stalks curved, white, 1–6 {8} cm long; stem leaves stalkless or short-stalked.

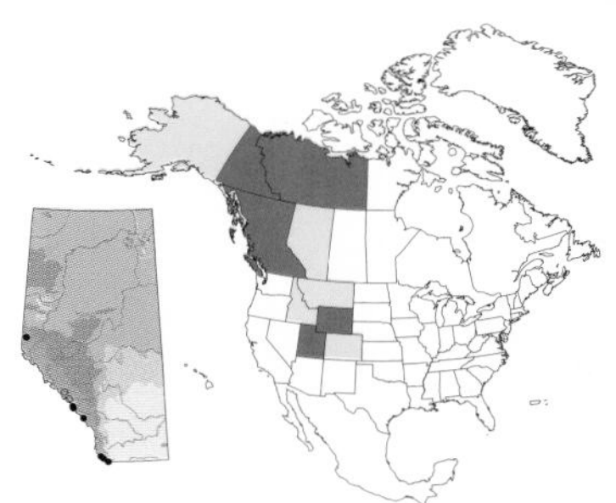

Flowers: Pale yellow, often purplish-tinged, with 5 sepals and 5 petals; sepals 2.5–4.5 {5} mm long, soon bent backward and then shed; petals 3.5–5 {3–6} mm long; stalks 3–7 cm long; 1–3 {5}; {June} July–September.

Fruits: Plump, hairless, lens-shaped, seed-like fruits (achenes), **2–2.5 mm long**, with a slender, curved or hooked, 0.5 {0.4–0.8} mm beak; borne in **cylindrical heads, 5–9** {4–13} **mm long** and 4–6 mm wide.

Habitat: Dry, rocky alpine slopes; elsewhere, on moist, gravelly alpine slopes.

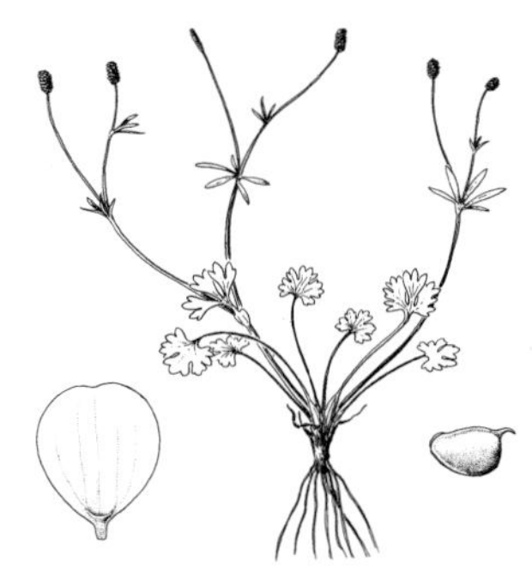

Notes: This species includes *Ranunculus karelinii* Czern., *R. grayi* Britt. and *R. verecundus* B.L. Robins. *Ranunculus verecundus* was previously separated on the basis of its larger size (10–20 cm tall) and smaller achenes (1–1.5 mm long), but these characteristics appear to vary over the range of the species. • Alpine buttercup is very similar to mountain buttercup (*Ranunculus eschscholtzii* Schlecht.), but the basal leaves of mountain buttercup are usually folded, the petals are often much larger, and the achenes have a slender, straight beak. • Alpine buttercup could be confused with dwarf buttercup (*Ranunculus pygmaeus* Wahl.), but dwarf buttercup has erect stems when in fruit and its achenes are only about 1 mm long. • Another rare Alberta buttercup, hairy buttercup (*Ranunculus uncinatus* D. Don), is similar to alpine buttercup, but it is a larger (20–60 cm tall) plant of moist, shady woodlands at lower elevations, and its achenes have prominent, 1–2 mm long, hooked beaks. Hairy buttercup is reported to bloom from April to July.

R. UNCINATUS

LK

DJ

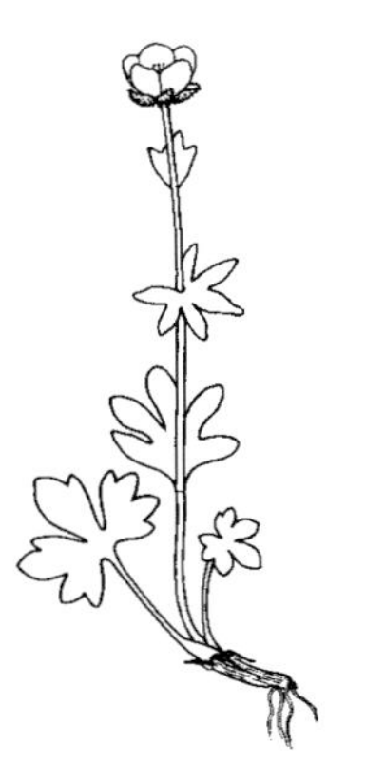

SNOW BUTTERCUP

Ranunculus nivalis L.
BUTTERCUP FAMILY (RANUNCULACEAE)

Plants: Tufted perennial herbs with acrid juice, **hairless or with sparse brown hairs**; stems slender, unbranched, **erect, 3–15 {30} cm tall** (elongating in fruit), few to several; from fibrous roots.

Leaves: Basal, with {1} **2 or 3 on stem; basal leaves** kidney-shaped, 1–2 cm long and usually wider, squared or notched at the base, **3-lobed**, with the side lobes often shallowly cut, borne on 1–5 cm long stalks; **stem leaves similar** but often larger and more deeply lobed and with undivided side lobes, squared to broadly wedge-shaped at the base, usually stalkless.

Flowers: Deep yellow, saucer-shaped, 15–25 mm across, with **5 separate petals** and **5 sepals**; petals 9–12 mm long, broad and conspicuous, each with a nectar-producing dot or pit at the base; **sepals** 5–9 mm long, **densely brownish black-hairy on the back**; stamens usually numerous; solitary; June–July.

Fruits: Plump seed-like fruits (achenes), 1.5–2 mm long, **without winged edges**, tipped with a straight, firm, slender beak 1–1.5 mm long, borne on essentially hairless receptacles, in 5–15 mm long, **egg-shaped to cylindrical heads.**

Habitat: Moist **alpine** slopes, often near melting snow beds and by streams.

Notes: Snow buttercup might be confused with the common species mountain buttercup (*Ranunculus eschscholtzii* Schlecht.), but mountain buttercup flowers have pale-yellow hairs on their sepals. • The specific epithet *nivalis* is Latin for 'snowy,' in reference to the snow-bed communities where this species is often found.

JONES' COLUMBINE

Aquilegia jonesii Parry
BUTTERCUP FAMILY (RANUNCULACEAE)

LA

Plants: Dwarf perennial herbs, finely hairy and more or less glandular (even on flowers), 5–12 {3.5–20} cm tall; from short, branched underground stems (rhizomes).

Leaves: Basal, crowded, finely hairy, greyish with a thin, waxy coating (glaucous) on both surfaces; **blades rarely over 1 cm long**; 1 or 2 times divided in 3s; leaflets crowded, deeply cut into 3 or 4 oblong to rounded lobes; stalks slender, 3–8 {1–12} cm long.

Flowers: Blue or purplish, showy, facing upward (erect), with 5 sepals and 5 petals; **sepals deep blue or purple, petal-like**, oblong–lance-shaped to broadly elliptic, **15–22** {25} **mm long; petals often whitish**, expanded at the tip into a **rounded blade about 6–8** {13} **mm long**, each prolonged backward at the base as a **stout, straight, blue tube** (spur) **8–10** {5–15} **mm long; single**, on erect stalks about 2–5 cm long; July {June–August}.

Fruits: Erect groups of **5 pod-like fruits that split open along inner side** (follicles), 15–20 {12–25} mm long, tipped with an 8–12 mm long beak, hairless, greyish with a thin, waxy coat; seeds black.

Habitat: Alpine scree slopes; elsewhere, in subalpine and alpine areas on limestone talus slopes and in rock crevices.

Notes: The nectar-producing spurs on these flowers attract long-tongued pollinators, such as moths, capable of reaching the fragrant nectar stored at the spur tips. • The generic name *Aquilegia* was derived from the Latin *aquila* (eagle) because the spurs on the petals were thought to resemble the talons of an eagle. The common name 'columbine' comes from the Latin *columbina* (dove-like) because the spreading sepals and arched spurs were thought to resemble a circle of 5 doves drinking from a central dish. This resemblance is more obvious in species with nodding flowers and curved spurs, where the spurs point upward and inward.

DJ

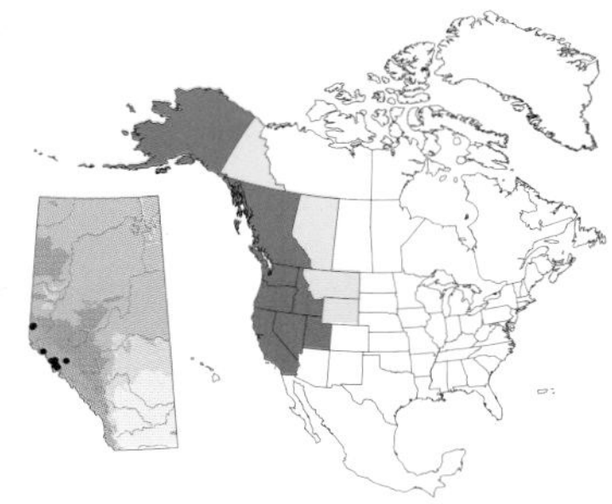

SITKA COLUMBINE

Aquilegia formosa Fisch. *ex* DC. var. *formosa*
BUTTERCUP FAMILY (RANUNCULACEAE)

Plants: Stout perennial herbs, {15} **30–100 cm tall**; stems freely branched, hairless to copiously hairy or glandular-hairy; from short, branched underground stems (rhizomes).

Leaves: Mainly basal, long-stalked; blades **thin, usually tinged bluish** with a thin, waxy coating (glaucous), **twice divided in 3s** (biternate); **leaflets deeply lobed** or coarsely blunt-toothed, **15–50** {68} **mm long.**

Flowers: Red and yellow, usually nodding, showy, with 5 petals and 5 sepals; **petals** expanded at the tip into **a yellowish, 3–5** {6} **mm long, egg-shaped blade** (widest above the middle), each prolonged back from the base in a **straight, 13–21 mm long, reddish tube** (spur) **with a bulbous, nectar-producing tip; sepals pale to deep red, petal-like**, spreading or bent back (reflexed), 14–26 mm long, longer than the blades of the petals; **stamens numerous, projecting** well past the petals; few to several, **nodding** to hanging on slender stalks in elongating clusters (racemes); June–July {May–August}.

Fruits: Erect groups of 5 pod-like fruits that open on the inner side (follicles), shaggy with soft hairs or glandular-hairy, **15–25** {29} **mm long**, spreading at the tip, with firm, slender beaks 9–12 mm long; seeds black.

Habitat: Open woods and rocky slopes from lowlands to timberline; elsewhere, in moist sites on partly shaded roadsides and in woods, subalpine meadows and thickets.

Notes: This species has also been called *Aquilegia canadensis* L. var. *formosa* (Fisch.) S. Wats. and *Aquilegia columbiana* Rydb. Other common names include western columbine and crimson columbine. • Sitka columbine is similar to, and often hybridizes with, yellow columbine (*Aquilegia flavescens* S. Wats.), but yellow columbine is a smaller (20–75 cm tall) plant, with wholly yellow flowers, and it usually grows at higher elevations (in alpine areas), although the ranges of these 2 species do overlap to some extent. • In Europe, where columbines were used medicinally, children sometimes died from overdoses of the seeds. In North America, some native peoples rubbed columbine seeds in their hair to control lice. • Sitka columbine is easily grown and maintains itself from seed. Its beautiful flowers attract hummingbirds and butterflies.

DWARF ALPINE POPPY

Papaver pygmaeum Rydb.
POPPY FAMILY (PAPAVERACEAE)

Plants: Loosely **tufted perennial** herbs with milky sap; flowering stems leafless, 5–6 {3–12} cm tall, with spreading yellowish (sometimes purple-mottled) hairs; from taproots.

Leaves: Basal, many, blue-green on both surfaces, 2–5 cm long, hairless on upper surface but often with stiff, flat-lying hairs on the lower surface and on the stalks; blades broadly egg-shaped, much shorter than their stalks, 1–1.5 cm long, deeply cut into **pinnate lobes**; stalks to ⅔ of the leaf length.

Flowers: Yellow, or orange with a yellow spot at the centre (usually drying pinkish), **cupped, 1–2 cm across,** with **4 or more large, thin petals**; 4 or 5 stigmas in a convex disc; buds oval, nodding, with 2 dark-hairy sepals; solitary; July–August.

Fruits: Erect, **egg-shaped to cone-shaped capsules**, 2–2½ times longer than wide, widest at the tip, 1–1.5 cm long, tipped with a disc-like stigma with 4 or 5 rays, conspicuously stiff-hairy with yellow, bulbous-based bristles.

Habitat: Alpine scree slopes and ridges.

Notes: This species has also been called *Papaver alpinum* L., *Papaver nudicaule* L. ssp. *radicatum* (Rottb.) Fedde var. *pseudocorydalifolium* and *Papaver radicatum* Rottb. var. *pygmaeum* (Rydb.) S.L. Welsh. • Poppy flowers do not produce nectar, and most species are self-pollinating, but they are visited by many insects in search of pollen. The expanded, star-shaped stigma provides a good landing platform for visiting insects. The parabolic shape of the flowers focusses radiation on the stigma, increasing temperatures there by an average of 5.9°C, and thus increasing the rate at which pollen grains develop once they have landed. In calm, sunny weather, these flowers constantly face the sun. On exposed sites, flowers may open while they are still touching the basal rosette of leaves, keeping them within the warmest layer of air, near the ground. As the seeds develop, the stalks elongate. Eventually, the seeds are dispersed by the 'censer mechanism,' in which the long, elastic stalks swing to and fro in the wind, shaking out thousands of tiny seeds through small holes at the top of the capsule (like a salt-shaker).

JG

WLNP

JL

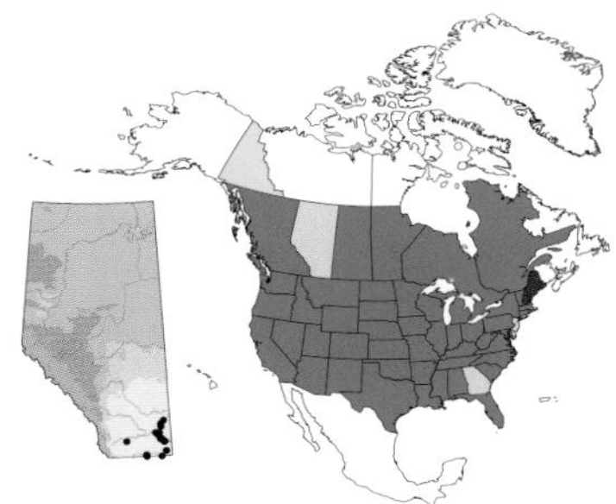

American pellitory

Parietaria pensylvanica Muhl. *ex* Willd.
NETTLE FAMILY (URTICACEAE)

Plants: Slender, **finely hairy annual herbs, sprawling to erect;** stems branched or unbranched, 5–50 {4–60} cm long, sparsely to densely hairy; from slender taproots.

Leaves: Alternate, spreading; blades **narrowly egg-shaped or elliptic, 1–8** {9} **cm long,** 3-veined, toothless; **stalks slender,** ⅙–⅓ as long as the blades; lower leaves soon withered.

Flowers: Green to brownish, inconspicuous, 1.5–2 mm long, with **4 calyx lobes** and **no petals, either male or female;** 4 stamens; **1 ovary, stigma and style;** nestled in a tuft of several linear, 2–4 mm long bracts on a short stalk, forming small clusters of intermixed male and female flowers in leaf axils on the upper half of the stem; {May–July}.

Fruits: Shiny, light reddish brown seed-like fruits (achenes), 0.9–1.2 mm long.

Habitat: Shady, gravelly sites, often in disturbed areas; elsewhere, in heavy woods and on shaded banks, on talus slopes and ledges, and around hot springs.

Notes: American pellitory is rather different from its close relatives the nettles (*Urtica* spp.), which have stinging hairs and opposite leaves. • Extracts of the European species pellitory-of-the-wall (*Parietaria officinalis* L.) were highly valued as a remedy for gravel, dropsy, stone of the bladder and other urinary complaints. • The generic name *Parietaria* was derived from the Latin *paries* (a wall) because the European plants of this genus were commonly found growing from crannies in old walls.

CLAMMYWEED

Polanisia dodecandra (L.) DC. ssp. *trachysperma* (T. & G.) Iltis
CAPER FAMILY (CAPPARIDACEAE)

CWa

Plants: Clammy, foul-smelling, sticky-hairy annual herbs; stems 10–80 cm tall, usually freely branched; from weak taproots.

Leaves: Alternate, divided into **3 narrowly to broadly lance-shaped leaflets** 1–4 cm long and often widest above the middle; stalks 1–4 cm long.

Flowers: Yellowish white, about 1 cm across, with **4 showy petals, 4 small sepals** and 5–16 conspicuous stamens; petals {7} 8–12 mm long, tipped with broad, notched lobes abruptly narrowed to a slender, purplish, stalk-like base (claw); sepals purplish-tinged, lance-shaped, 3–4 mm long, soon shed; **stamens purplish**, unequal in length, **projecting to 1 side** of the flower on thread-like filaments 10–20 mm long; ovaries superior, solitary, with styles 4–6 mm long; few to several, on slender, ascending, 10–22 mm long stalks in elongated clusters (racemes); {June} July.

Fruits: Erect, **swollen, veiny, pod-like capsules, with gland-tipped hairs**, cylindrical or slightly flattened, narrowly oblong to elliptic, {2.5} 3–5 cm long, stalkless or nearly so but narrowed to a stalk-like base 1–3 mm long, splitting in 2 to release many slightly roughened seeds.

Habitat: Gravelly or sandy soil, often on disturbed or eroding sites; elsewhere, in sagebrush scrub, in gravel pits, along railways and on sandy stream beds, shores, plains and foothills, often in desert 'washes.'

Notes: This species has also been called *Polanisia trachysperma* T. & G. • At one Alberta site, clammyweed is found growing on a sparsely vegetated sand-dune blowout. • Probably fewer than 10,000 plants grow in Alberta. It is possible that more clammyweed plants in Alberta are growing on man-made disturbances than in natural habitats. Encroachment of vegetation onto active blowouts could eliminate some populations, but at present most Alberta populations appear stable. Over the long term, other plants eventually crowd out clammyweed. • The subspecies *dodecandra* is also reported from Alberta. It grows in the Cypress Hills in Saskatchewan.

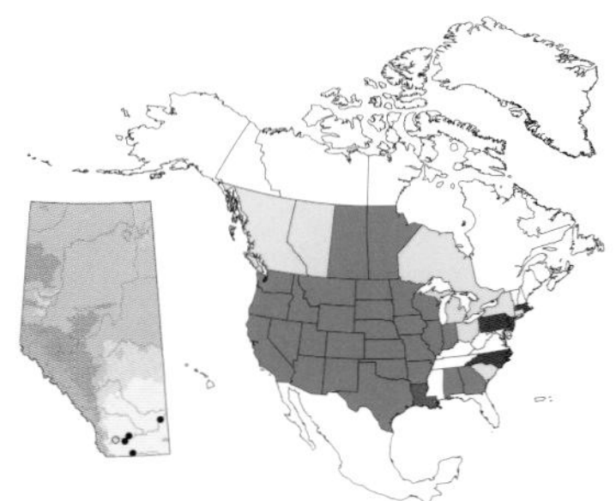

CREEPING WHITLOW-GRASS

Draba reptans (Lam.) Fern.
MUSTARD FAMILY (BRASSICACEAE [CRUCIFERAE])

Plants: Delicate **annual** herbs; stems thread-like, erect, {2} 5–20 cm tall, simple or branched at the base, with bristly hairs near the base, hairless above; from branched root crowns.

Leaves: Mostly in basal rosettes, spatula-shaped to broadly egg-shaped and widest above the middle, 1–3 cm long, 2–10 mm wide, **not toothed**, fringed with simple hairs, bristly with coarse, simple and **long-stalked branched hairs** on both surfaces, the **upper surface with once-forked hairs** and the lower surface with repeatedly branched (dendritic) or forked hairs; **1–3 stem leaves**, crowded near the base.

Flowers: White, about 5 mm across, with **4 sepals and 4 petals; petals yellow, with a shallow notch at the tip**, 3–4 {2–5} mm long; **sepals** 1.5–2.5 mm long with simple hairs; **6 stamens; style 0–0.15 mm long**; branch flowers distinctly smaller, often lacking petals; 3–12 flowers on hairless, spreading to ascending **stalks 2–7 mm long**, in **elongating, rather flat-topped clusters** (subumbellate racemes); April {March–May}.

Fruits: Slightly curved, **linear to narrowly oblong pods** (siliques), **5–20** {22} **mm long**, 1–2 mm wide, **about 6 times as long as they are wide**, hairless or with stiff, unbranched hairs, splitting in 2 to release 15–80 small (0.5–0.8 mm long) seeds.

Habitat: Sparsely vegetated, exposed, sandy or gravelly sites, especially in naturally disturbed areas, in grassland at low elevations; elsewhere, in dry forests and on dry beach strands and limestone outcrops or pavements.

Notes: Creeping whitlow-grass is inconspicuous and easily overlooked. Cultivation of sandy areas poses a potential threat, and one population on the Milk River is near a proposed dam site. Stabilization of dunes by other vegetation could also eliminate some sites. It is unclear whether dunes in native grassland were kept active by periodic drought, fire, grazing or a combination of these factors. • The generic name *Draba* was taken from the Greek *drabe* (acrid or biting), in reference to the bitter sap of many mustard species. Dioscorides first used this name for some unknown member of the mustard family, and it was later applied to this genus. The specific epithet *reptans* means 'creeping.'

AUSTRIAN WHITLOW-GRASS

Draba fladnizensis Wulfen
MUSTARD FAMILY (BRASSICACEAE [CRUCIFERAE])

BM

Plants: **Tufted perennial** herbs; **stems erect, 1–9** {15} **cm tall**, unbranched, usually **hairless**, sometimes with mostly simple hairs near the base, rarely hairy throughout; from simple or branched root crowns.

Leaves: Mainly in basal tufts, lance-shaped, widest above the middle, 3–10 {25} mm long, 1–2 mm wide, toothless, with a prominent midrib, **hairless or sparsely covered with long, unbranched hairs** on both surfaces and fringed with straight hairs; **stem leaves usually absent**, but **1 or 2**, small, toothless or minutely toothed leaves are sometimes present.

Flowers: **White**, about 4 mm across, with **4 petals, 4 sepals** and **6 fertile stamens** (2+4); petals 2–3 mm long; sepals 1–1.5 mm long, with simple hairs; **styles 0.1–0.2 mm long**, evident to nearly obsolete; 3–12, on straight, erect or ascending stalks in elongating clusters (racemes); July {August}.

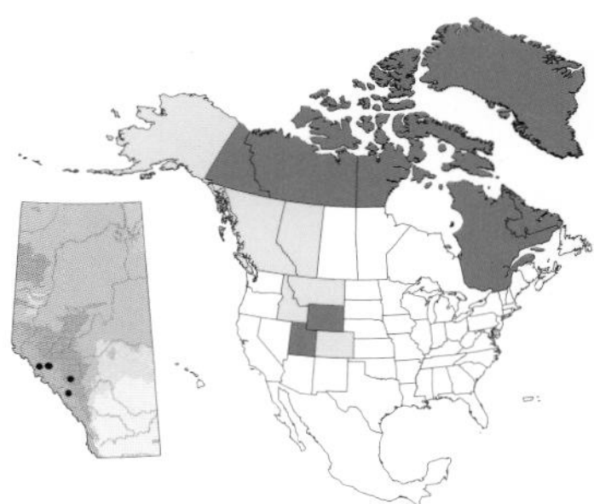

Fruits: **Oblong–egg-shaped to lance-shaped pods** (siliques), 3–6 {9} mm long, 1.5–2 mm wide, **mostly hairless** (sometimes with a few simple or forked hairs), containing many small, 0.7–0.9 mm long seeds.

Habitat: Alpine gravel and scree slopes; elsewhere, on turfy tundra and in cold ravines and subalpine fir forests.

Notes: Dense-leaved whitlow-grass (*Draba densifolia* Nutt.) is a similar species that is also rare in Alberta. It is distinguished by its yellow flowers and densely hairy stems and siliques. Its pollen is not fertile. Dense-leaved whitlow-grass grows on alpine ridges and scree slopes and flowers in {June–July} August. The small plants often expand through offsets, and some clumps cover about 1 m^2. The Alberta populations are apparently very local but stable. • The specific epithet *densifolia* means 'densely leaved.'

D. DENSIFOLIA

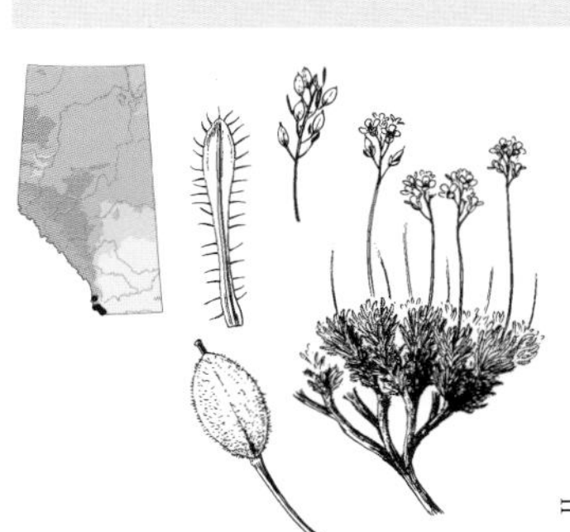

JJ

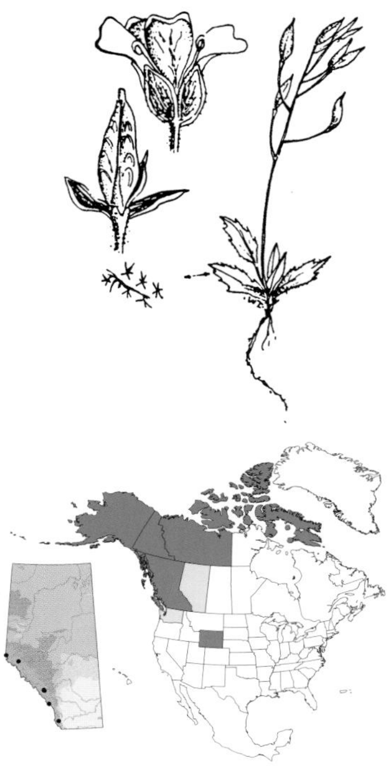

LONG-STALKED WHITLOW-GRASS

Draba longipes Raup
MUSTARD FAMILY (BRASSICACEAE [CRUCIFERAE])

Plants: Low, **loosely tufted perennial** herbs; **stems slender, erect** or somewhat spreading, 10–15 {25} cm tall, branched, with sparse simple, forked or star-shaped hairs (sometimes hairless); from **branched root crowns.**

Leaves: Mainly in loose basal tufts, lance-shaped, widest above the middle, toothless or finely toothed, **1.5–3 cm long**, 1–5 mm wide, with **sparse, 4-branched hairs on both surfaces** (sometimes hairless on the upper surface) and simple or branched hairs along the edges; **stem leaves 1–3** {0–5}, about as wide as the basal leaves.

Flowers: White to creamy-white or yellowish, about 5 mm across, with **4 petals, 4 sepals** and 6 (4+2) stamens; petals 4–5 mm long; sepals 2.5–3 mm long, hairless or with a few simple hairs; **styles 0.6–0.9** {0.5–1} **mm long**; {2} 3–15, on slender, spreading stalks 5–15 mm long, in rather flat-topped (but soon elongating) clusters (racemes); {June} July–August.

Fruits: Narrowly egg-shaped to linear–lance-shaped pods (siliques), 4–13 {3–15} mm long, 2–3 mm wide, **hairless**, containing many seeds about 1 mm long.

Habitat: Moist banks and ledges in alpine areas, often by snow beds; elsewhere, in ravines, near streams and springs, and on gravelly beaches and open grassy slopes.

D. MACOUNII

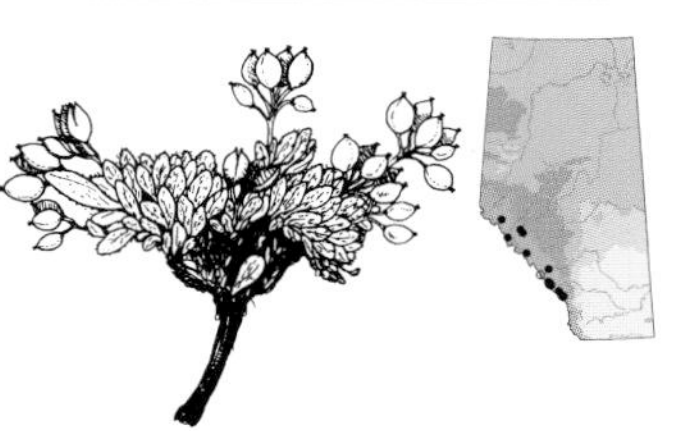

Notes: A yellow-flowered species, Kananaskis whitlow-grass (*Draba kananaskis* Mulligan), endemic to Alberta and Alaska, has recently been included by some taxonomists in long-stalked whitlow-grass. It was distinguished from long-stalked whitlow-grass by its yellow (rather than white) flowers and its short-stalked (rather than stalkless) leaf hairs. Kananaskis whitlow-grass grows on dry alpine slopes at elevations around 2,200 m and flowers in July. It is normally a self-fertilized species. • Macoun's whitlow-grass (*Draba macounii* O.E. Schulz) is another rare Alberta species. It is recognized by its yellow flowers on short (1–8 cm), leafless stems; its short-stalked, hairless, elliptic to egg-shaped pods (siliques); and its densely tufted basal leaves with predominantly cross-shaped hairs. Macoun's whitlow-grass is found on alpine slopes, where it flowers in July.

D. KANANASKIS

WINDY WHITLOW-GRASS

Draba ventosa A. Gray
MUSTARD FAMILY (BRASSICACEAE [CRUCIFERAE])

PL

Plants: Small, **tufted perennial** herbs, **silvery-green with a tangle of branched hairs; stems erect, 0.5–4 {6} cm tall, leafless**, branched, greyish with many fine, simple hairs and forked hairs; from loosely branched root crowns.

Leaves: Basal, numerous, linear to egg-shaped and widest above the middle, tapered to a wedge-shaped base, **4–14 mm long**, 1.5–2 {2.4} mm wide, with a prominent midrib, densely covered with **long-stalked, star-shaped hairs on both surfaces**, also fringed with simple hairs; withered leaves persisting for several years (marcescent).

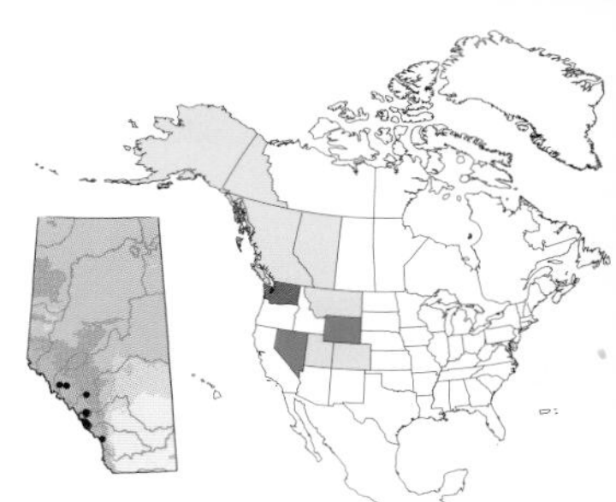

Flowers: Yellow, about 5 mm across, with **4 petals, 4 sepals** and 6 (2+4) stamens; **petals** 2–4 {5} mm long; **sepals** 2–3 mm long, hairy; **styles 0.5–1 mm long**; 3–10 {20}, in short, condensed clusters that elongate in fruit (racemes); July–August.

Fruits: Flattened, **broadly oval to egg-shaped pods** (siliques) rounded at the tip, **4–5** {2.5–5.5} **mm wide, 3–8 mm long,** on spreading stalks of about the same length, **densely covered with soft, long-stalked, repeatedly branched** (dendritic) **hairs**, containing 10–16 seeds 1.5–2 mm long.

Habitat: Alpine ridges and scree slopes; elsewhere, in alpine tundra and at the base of cliffs.

Notes: These plants are agamospermous, that is to say, they produce seeds asexually (without fertilization). The resulting offspring are genetically identical to their parent. • Whitlow-grasses require sunny locations on open, gritty soil. Soils rich in lime are usually preferred. They are usually propagated by dividing plants, but they can also be grown from seed in the fall or spring.

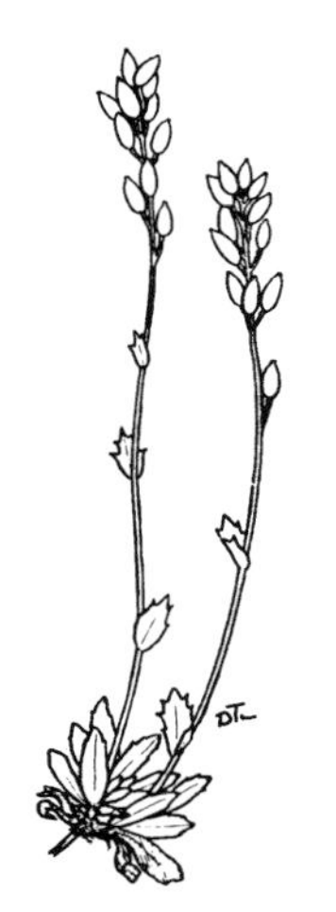

SMOOTH WHITLOW-GRASS

Draba glabella Pursh
MUSTARD FAMILY (BRASSICACEAE [CRUCIFERAE])

Plants: Tufted or loosely matted perennial herbs, 10–30 {40} **cm tall**; stems simple or freely branched, erect, hairy with few to many **soft, star-shaped hairs** (sometimes hairless on the upper stem); from simple or extensively branched, woody root crowns.

Leaves: Mostly in dense basal clusters, lance-shaped, widest above middle and tapered to slender stalks, 5–50 mm long, 3–18 mm wide, toothless or with a few small, scattered teeth, sparingly to densely covered with **short-stalked, star-shaped hairs with** {7} **9 or more rays; stem leaves** 2–7 {1–10}, lance-shaped, 5–40 mm long, 2–18 mm wide, **usually toothed**, with simple and branched hairs above and below.

Flowers: White or cream-coloured, with **4 sepals and 4 petals**; sepals 2–3 mm long, with simple and 2-forked, flat-lying hairs; petals {3.5} 4–6 mm long; **styles 0.2–0.5 mm long**; 5–20 {30}, on ascending stalks in elongating clusters (racemes); {May–July}.

Fruits: Narrowly lance-shaped pods (siliques), 7–14 {6–15} **mm long**, 2–4 mm wide, **often twisted**, hairless or hairy; **lowest stalks** 3–12 mm long, **shorter than or equal to the pod**; seeds 0.7–1.3 mm long.

Habitat: Moist banks and ledges at alpine elevations; elsewhere, on rocky, sandy or gravelly shores, on rocky, grassy tundra, and on slaty and calcareous cliffs.

Notes: Smooth whitlow-grass could be confused with a more common species, northern whitlow-grass (*Draba borealis* DC.), but northern whitlow-grass has mostly cross-shaped hairs on its leaves and its styles are longer (up to 1 mm long). • Smooth whitlow-grass is strongly nitrophilous (nitrogen-loving). It is often found growing in areas enriched by animal dung. • The specific epithet *glabella* is from the Latin *glaber* (smooth or hairless), perhaps in reference to the hairless pods.

NORTHERN BLADDERPOD

Lesquerella arctica (Wormskj. *ex* Hornem.) S. Wats. var. *purshii* Wats.
MUSTARD FAMILY (BRASSICACEAE [CRUCIFERAE])

JG

Plants: Low **perennial** herbs, **silvery with dense stalkless or short-stalked, star-shaped hairs**; stems single to several, erect to spreading or lying on the ground, 5–25 {30} cm long; from woody crowns on stout taproots.

Leaves: In prominent basal rosettes, 2–6 {1–15} cm long, egg-shaped to lance-shaped, widest above the middle, **not toothed**, tapered to short stalks; stem leaves narrower, 5–15 {30} mm long, essentially stalkless, **not clasping**.

LK

Flowers: Yellow, about 1 cm across, with **4 petals, 4 sepals** and 6 stamens (2+4); **petals 4–7 mm long**, egg-shaped, widest above the middle; **sepals** oblong; **styles generally 1–2.5 mm long**; few to several, in loose, elongated clusters (racemes); June–July {May–August}.

Fruits: Rounded, usually inflated pods (siliques), **4–6** {9} **mm long**, hairless or sparsely covered with tiny, stalkless, star-shaped hairs and containing 5–7 {4–8} plump seeds per cavity (locule), **erect**, on **straight or slightly curved**, 5–20 {40} mm long **stalks**.

Habitat: Dry, sandy or calcareous slopes and ridges, often in alpine areas; elsewhere, on rocky, gravelly or clay soils on river flats.

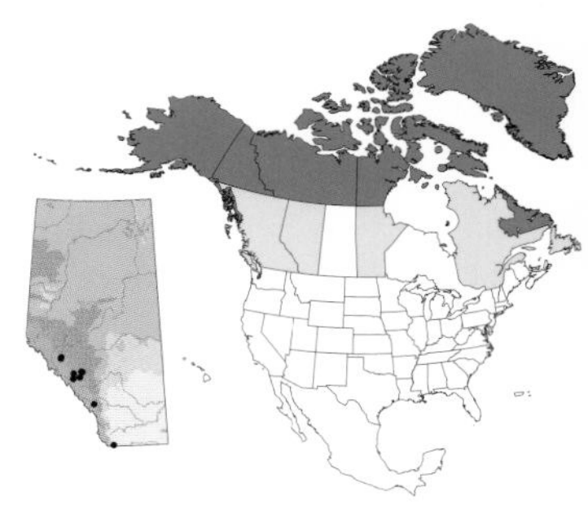

Notes: The generic name *Lesquerella* commemorates Leo Lesquereux, an American bryologist who lived 1805–89. The specific epithet *arctica* means 'of the northern or polar regions.'

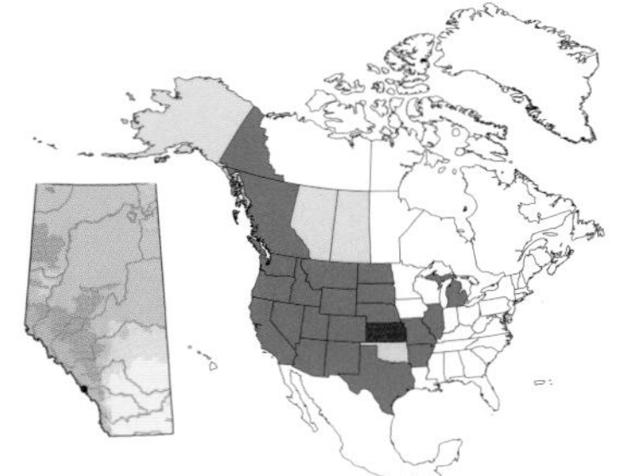

BLUNT-LEAVED YELLOW CRESS

Rorippa curvipes E.L. Greene
MUSTARD FAMILY (BRASSICACEAE [CRUCIFERAE])

Plants: Low, somewhat tufted **annual** or biennial herbs, usually less than 10 cm tall; stems slender, hairless, 10–50 cm long, erect to spreading on the ground, usually branched (beginning near the base), single or several; from taproots.

Leaves: Basal and alternate on the stem, with **scattered, simple hairs** on the upper surface, hairless beneath; blades 4–13 cm long, 0.5–3 cm wide, regularly pinnately divided and angularly toothed; stalks short or absent; **stem leaves** somewhat smaller, oblong to spatula-shaped, sometimes slightly clasping the stem.

Flowers: Yellow, about 2–3 mm across, with **4 petals and 4 sepals; petals** oblong to spatula-shaped, about 1 mm long, 0.2–1 mm wide, **shorter than the sepals**; sepals 1.5 mm long, spreading; stamens usually 6; styles 0.2–1 {1.3} mm long; several to many, erect to nodding, on **short stalks** (2–5.1 {1.6–8} mm long), in elongating clusters (racemes) at stem tips or from leaf axils; {May–September}.

Fruits: Hairless, straight or curved, **egg-shaped to short-cylindrical pods** (siliques) **constricted near the middle**, 2–5 {1.4–8.7} mm long, splitting in 2 to release 10–80 brown, heart-shaped seeds over 0.5 mm long; borne on short stalks half as long as the pods.

Habitat: Moist ground, including mud flats, shores, roadsides, stream beds and wet meadows.

Notes: Two varieties have been found in Alberta: var. *truncata* (Jepson) Rollins (which has also been called *Rorippa truncata* (Jeps.) Stuckey) and var. *curvipes*. Variety *curvipes* has egg-shaped to pear-shaped pods that taper to a pointed or rather blunt tip and that are usually less than twice as long as they are wide at maturity. Variety *truncata* has short, cylindrical pods that have a squared tip and are more than twice as long as they are wide when mature. • Slender yellow cress (*Rorippa tenerrima* E. Greene) is a similar species that is also rare in Alberta. It is distinguished from blunt-leaved yellow cress by its siliques, which are rough with tiny, nipple-shaped bumps (papillae) and which taper to a cone-shaped tip without narrowing at the centre. It flowers in September {May–August} in moist, usually sandy, often alkaline sites.

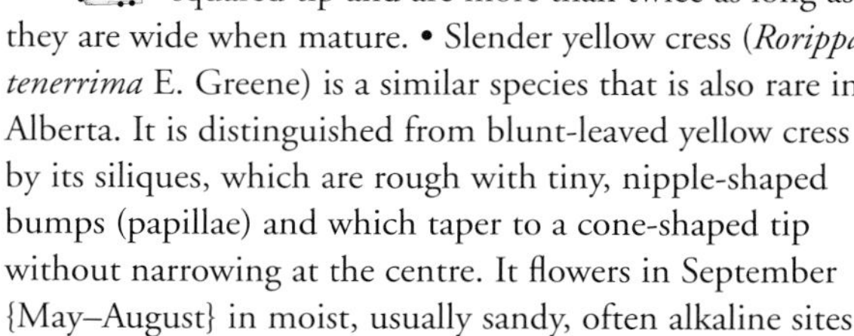

R. TENERRIMA

SPREADING YELLOW CRESS

Rorippa sinuata (Nutt. *ex* T. & G.) A.S. Hitchc.
MUSTARD FAMILY (BRASSICACEAE [CRUCIFERAE])

Plants: Perennial herbs, essentially hairless, but the stems, lower leaf surfaces and pods often sparsely to densely **dotted with small, hemispheric, air-filled sacs** (modified hairs); stems 10–40 {50} cm long, ascending or spreading on the ground, branched from the base; from slender, creeping underground stems (rhizomes).

Leaves: Basal and alternate on the stem, lance-shaped, widest above the middle, 2–7 {1.6–8.5} cm long, **deeply pinnately cut** into **blunt lobes, with or without short teeth; upper leaves** stalkless, often **clasping** the stem with small basal lobes (auricles), only **slightly smaller** than those below.

Flowers: Light yellow, about **4 mm across**, with **4 sepals and 4 petals**; sepals inconspicuous, much shorter than the petals; petals oblong to narrowly spatula-shaped, 4 {2.5–6} mm long, styles stout, about 1–2 mm long, tapered gradually from base to tip; pointing upward or curved downward on slender stalks 5–9 mm long; several to many, in branched, elongating clusters (racemes); June {April–July}.

Fruits: Linear-oblong to lance-shaped, cylindrical pods (siliques), {5} **7–15 mm long**, {1.5} 2 mm wide, straight or slightly arched, often somewhat wrinkled, hairless, narrowed abruptly to a slender **beak 1–3 mm long**; stalks 3.5–15 mm long, slightly curved to S-shaped; seeds in 2 vertical rows, angular, heart-shaped, about 40–80 per pod.

Habitat: Shores, stream flats, ditches and roadsides; elsewhere, in woods, vacant fields, and wet lowlands, often in alkaline areas.

Notes: Spreading yellow cress could be confused with the introduced species creeping yellow cress (*Rorippa sylvestris* (L.) Besser), but the leaves of creeping yellow cress have pointed lobes that are clearly toothed, and each pod is tipped with a short (up to 1 mm long) beak.

BH

BH

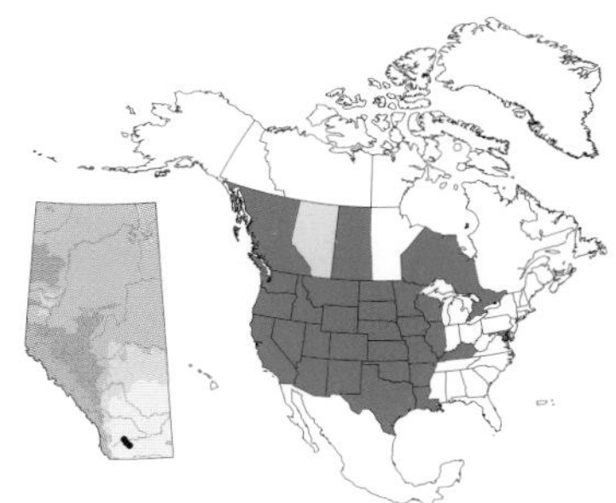

DJ

DJ

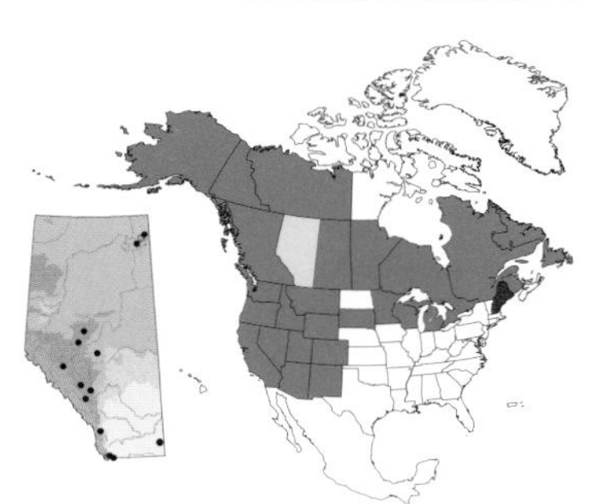

American winter cress

Barbarea orthoceras Ledeb.
MUSTARD FAMILY (BRASSICACEAE [CRUCIFERAE])

Plants: Hairless to sparsely hairy biennial herbs (sometimes perennial); stems erect, 20–50 {10–60} cm tall, **often purplish near the base**, angled, usually single, hairless and freely branched; from woody crowns on taproots.

Leaves: In a **basal rosette** (first year), up to 12 cm long, pinnately divided, with a large terminal lobe and 2–8 small side lobes, long-stalked; **stem leaves** (second year) **alternate**, similar to basal leaves but smaller upward on the stem and with clasping bases.

Flowers: Pale yellow, with **4 sepals and 4 petals**; **petals** spatula-shaped, **2.5–5 mm long**; several to many, in elongating, often branched clusters (racemes); {March–May} June–early August.

Fruits: Narrow, slightly flattened or somewhat **4-angled pods** (siliques), straight or slightly curved, **2–4** {1.5–5} **cm long**, 1.5–2.5 mm wide, tipped **with a short** (0.3–1 {2} mm), **beak-like style**, pointing upward on 2–3 mm long, **thick** (up to 1 mm wide) **club-shaped stalks**; seeds flat, brownish, minutely pitted, in a single row.

Habitat: Streambanks, wet meadows and moist woods; elsewhere, on sand bars and rocky cliffs.

Notes: In Alaska and northeast Asia, where this species is common, young plants and buds are eaten raw or cooked. Raw plants have a radish-like flavour and are said to be high in vitamin C. • The genus *Barbarea* was named for St. Barbara, a Christian martyr of the 4th century AD who refused to renounce her belief in God. The protection of St. Barbara was usually invoked against lightning and fire, so she became the patron saint of military architects, artillery men and miners (people who work with gunpowder).

MOUSE-EAR CRESS

Arabidopsis salsuginea (Pallas) N. Busch
MUSTARD FAMILY (BRASSICACEAE [CRUCIFERAE])

CWa

Plants: Small **annual** (or biennial) herbs, **hairless, blue-green** with a thin, waxy coating (glaucous); stems erect, **5–15 {20} cm tall**, usually **branched** above and near the base; from slender taproots.

Leaves: Alternate (sometimes also with a sparse basal rosette of stalked, egg-shaped leaves), oblong to lance-shaped, blunt-tipped, 3–20 mm long, 1–4 {10} mm wide; **without teeth**, stalkless, **clasping the stem with small basal lobes** (auricles).

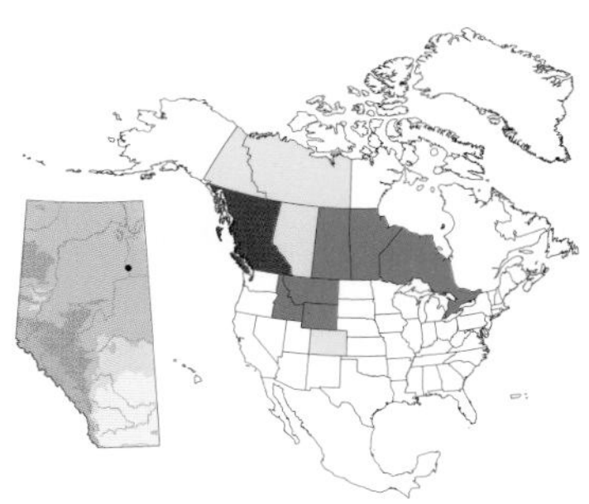

Flowers: White, about 3 mm across, with **4 petals, 4 sepals** and 6 (4+2) stamens; petals spatula-shaped to egg-shaped, widest above the middle, 2–3 {3.5} mm long; **sepals yellowish to pinkish with translucent edges, 1.5–2 mm long, soon shed**; styles 0.1–0.2 mm long; several to many, on straight, slender, spreading stalks 1–9 mm long, in dense, elongating clusters (racemes) without bracts; {late April–June}.

Fruits: Linear, almost cylindrical pods (siliques), 7–16 {20} mm long, 0.8–0.9 mm wide, straight or slightly curved, nearly erect, containing a single row of plump, oblong seeds about 0.6 mm long.

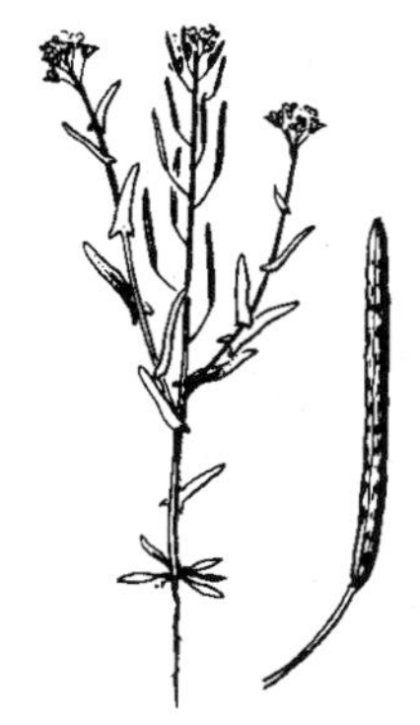

Habitat: Flat, moist saline ground by springs and lakes; elsewhere, in open, sandy alkaline soils in dry lakes and in salt plains and meadows.

Notes: This species has also been called *Thellungiella salsuginea* (Pallas) O.E. Schulz. • This species has a broad range but is seldom collected. One reason for this spotty distribution might be its dependence on saline habitats, which are often isolated from one another in arid regions. • The specific epithet *salsuginea* means 'of salt marshes.'

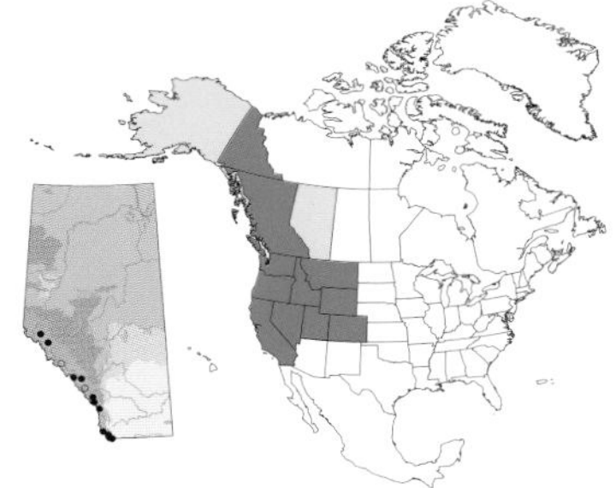

Lemmon's rock cress

Arabis lemmonii S. Wats.
MUSTARD FAMILY (BRASSICACEAE [CRUCIFERAE])

Plants: Slender, tufted perennial herbs, **greyish with tiny repeatedly branched** (dendritic) **hairs** (at least on the lower parts); stems few to many, unbranched, 5–20 {40} cm tall; from branched root crowns.

Leaves: Basal leaves broadly spatula-shaped, blunt-tipped, 1–2 cm long, sometimes edged with a few teeth, **felted with tiny hairs; stem leaves** oblong to lance-shaped, 4–10 {15} mm long, stalkless, **with basal lobes** (auricles) **slightly clasping** the stem.

Flowers: Pink to purple, with **4 sepals and 4 petals**; sepals 2–3 {3.5} mm long, blunt-tipped, often pink or purple-tinged; petals 4–6 mm long, spatula-shaped; styles very short; few to several, on 2–5 mm long stalks in elongating clusters (racemes); July–August.

Fruits: Hairless, straight or slightly curved, **linear pods** (siliques), 2–5 cm long, **2–3.5 mm wide, evidently flattened**, pointing upward to nodding (**usually horizontal**), containing a single row of round, narrowly winged seeds about 1 mm wide.

Habitat: Alpine slopes, often on unstable ground.

Notes: Lemmon's rock cress might be mistaken for the more common species Lyall's rock cress (*Arabis lyallii* S. Wats.), but the leaves of Lyall's rock cress are usually fleshy and hairless, never greyish and felty.

HALIMOLOBOS

Halimolobos virgata (Nutt.) O.E. Schulz
MUSTARD FAMILY (BRASSICACEAE [CRUCIFERAE])

Plants: Biennial (sometimes annual or perennial) herbs; stems usually single (sometimes several), 10–40 cm tall, erect or ascending, freely branched (sometimes unbranched), greyish with long straight, simple or forked hairs mixed with short, branched hairs; from simple root crowns.

Leaves: Mainly in a basal rosette but also alternate on the stem, **densely covered with repeatedly branched** (dendritic) **hairs**; basal leaves {2} 3–6 cm long, 5–10 {15} mm wide, egg-shaped to lance-shaped, widest above the middle, **wavy-toothed** (sometimes minutely so), tapered to stalks; **stem leaves** smaller (1.5–4 cm long), shorter-stalked upward on the stem, the upper leaves stalkless and **clasping with small basal lobes** (auricles).

Flowers: White with pinkish veins, about 5 mm across, with **4 petals and 4 sepals; petals** spatula-shaped, 3–4 mm long; sepals 2–3 mm long, often purplish, with relatively large, spreading hairs; 6 stamens; styles 0.2–0.5 mm long; numerous, on slender, ascending, 7–11 {5–12} mm long stalks, in loose, elongating clusters (racemes); May–July.

Fruits: Erect (or nearly so), hairless, **cylindrical** (or slightly 4-sided), **linear pods** (siliques), {1.5} **2–4 cm long and 1 mm wide**, strongly nerved; seeds many, crowded in 2 irregular rows, about 1 mm long.

Habitat: Dry prairies; elsewhere, on bushy hillsides, moist meadows and alkali flats; sometimes becoming weedy.

Notes: Halimolobos could easily be mistaken for a rock cress (*Arabis* sp.), but rock cresses have clearly flattened pods, whereas the pods of halimolobos are cylindrical.

JL

BH

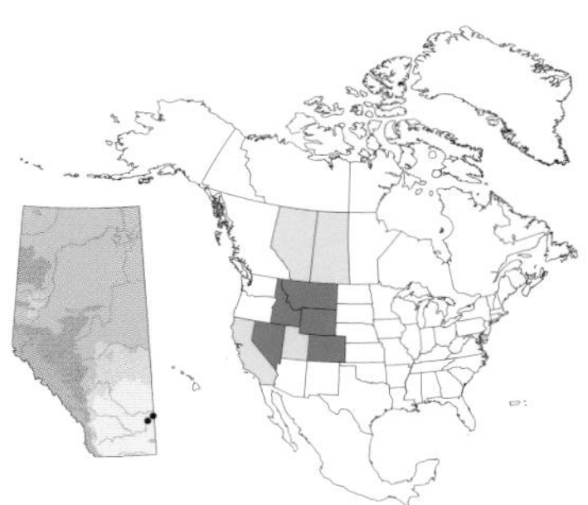

LK

LK

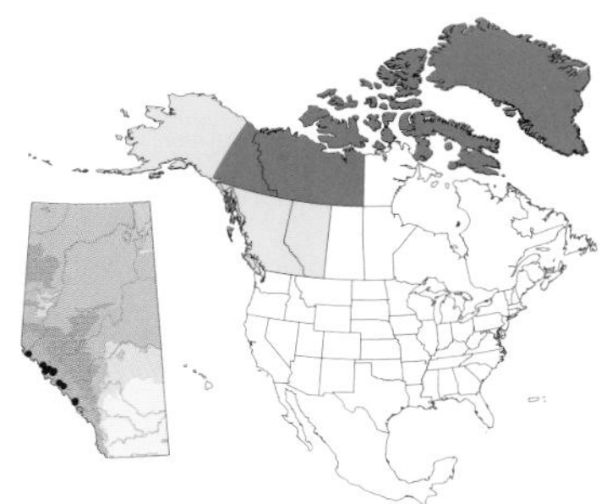

PURPLE ALPINE ROCKET, PURPLE ROCKET

Erysimum pallasii (Pursh) Fern.
MUSTARD FAMILY (BRASSICACEAE [CRUCIFERAE])

Plants: Biennial or short-lived perennial herbs with **parallel, flat-lying hairs** that are attached at their middle, **low and tufted in flower, 10–20 {3–35} cm tall in fruit;** from swollen, unbranched (rarely branched) crowns on stout taproots.

Leaves: Many, in a prominent **basal rosette, linear to narrowly lance-shaped** and widest above the middle, 5–7 cm long, toothless or wavy-toothed, tapered to a slender stalk; old leaf bases persistent (marcescent).

Flowers: Fragrant, showy, bright purple, 2–4 cm across, with **4 sepals** and **4 petals;** sepals oblong, 5–8 {10} mm long, purplish, with translucent edges; petals 10–16 {20} mm long, slender at the base, abruptly flaring to a broad lobe at the tip; styles 1–3 mm long; **50 or more, in compact, short-stalked clusters** (racemes) often nestled among the basal leaves, these clusters greatly elongating in fruit; {July}.

Fruits: Erect to spreading-ascending, **flattened, linear pods** (siliques) {3} **4–10 cm long,** 2 {3} mm wide, slightly curved, purplish; lower stalks 7–12 {5–20} mm long; seeds pale brown, oval to oblong, 2 mm long.

Habitat: On shale in alpine areas; elsewhere, on clay banks and sandy, gravelly or rocky slopes. Also noted as a dung-loving calciphile often found near animal burrows, below bird cliffs and around settlements.

Notes: These plants can spend 1 to several years in the rosette stage before flowering and dying. Their long seed pods are well-adapted to the gradual release of seeds. As the pods dry, their sides gradually curve away from the supporting frame or membrane, separating from the top, bottom or occasionally both ends. In this way, a considerable period elapses between the release of the first and last seeds. Released seeds often stick to animal fur, and these plants are often found around ground squirrel burrows and fox or wolf dens.

ALPINE BRAYA, PURPLE-LEAVED BRAYA

Braya purpurascens (R. Br.) Bunge *ex* Ledeb.
MUSTARD FAMILY (BRASSICACEAE [CRUCIFERAE])

LK

Plants: Low, tufted perennial (rarely biennial) herbs; stems **5–15** {3.5–20} **cm tall**, single to many, leafless, slightly to densely hairy with simple to 3-branched hairs; from simple or branched woody crowns on thick taproots.

Leaves: Basal, tufted, somewhat **fleshy**, green to deep purple, spoon-shaped to narrowly lance-shaped, widest toward the blunt tip, 1–3 {0.6–6} cm long, fringed with hairs, nearly hairless to somewhat hairy on the surfaces, **essentially toothless.**

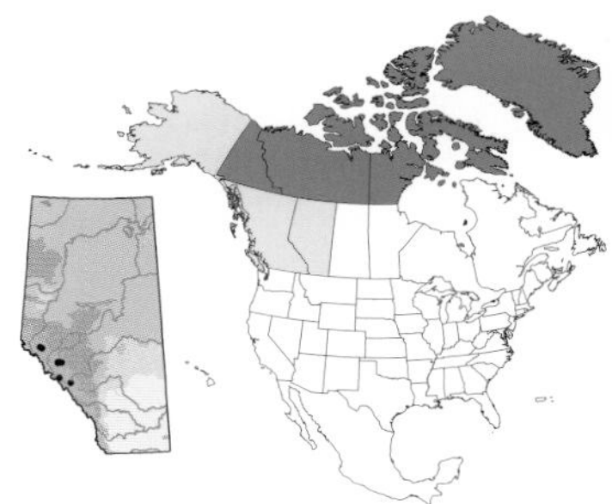

Flowers: White or purple-tinged, with **4 petals and 4 sepals**; petals 3–4 {4.5} mm long, broad-tipped, tapered to a slender base; sepals purple, egg-shaped, 1.5–2.5 {3.7} mm long; stamens 6 (2+4); stigmas head-like; several, in head-like clusters elongating in fruit (racemes); June–August.

Fruits: Plump, straight pods (siliques), about 10 mm long and 2–3 mm wide, broadly elliptic to lance-shaped or oblong-cylindrical, **sometimes constricted between seeds** (torulose), minutely hairy, tipped with a stout, 1 {0.5–2} mm long style, erect to spreading on 2–8 mm long stalks; seeds in 2 rows.

Habitat: Calcareous alpine scree slopes; elsewhere, in alpine meadows, on moist clay, sand and gravel barrens and on seashores.

Notes: This species includes *Braya americana* (Hook) Fern. It has also been called *Braya glabella* Richards. • The only other braya species formally reported from Alberta, leafy braya (*Braya humilis* (C.A. Mey.) Robins.), has leafy stems and longer (10–30 mm), narrowly cylindrical, clearly torulose pods. Leafy braya is more common and grows in areas from open woods and gravel bars to alpine slopes.

LK

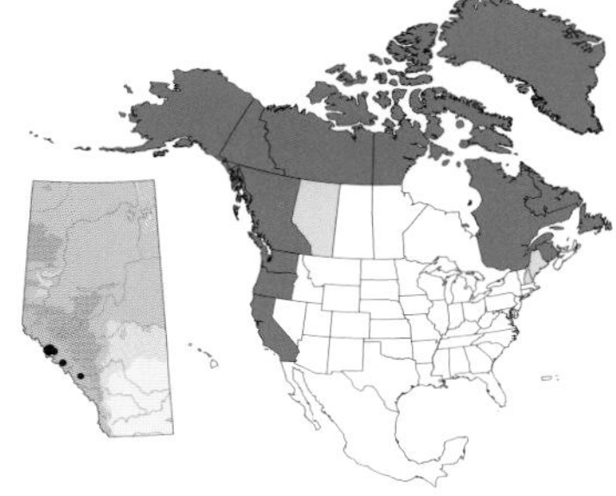

ALPINE BITTER CRESS

Cardamine bellidifolia L.
MUSTARD FAMILY (BRASSICACEAE [CRUCIFERAE])

Plants: Tiny, hairless perennial herbs; stems several, **tufted**, {2} 3–10 cm tall, essentially leafless; from simple to many-branched root crowns on vertical taproots.

Leaves: In basal rosettes; blades thin, **egg-shaped or elliptic**, 5–15 mm long, without teeth or with 2–4 vague teeth; stalks slender, 2–4 times as long as the blades.

Flowers: White, about 5 mm across, with **4 sepals and 4 petals**; petals **3–4** {5} **mm long**; 1–5, in short, flat-topped clusters (subumbellate racemes), elongating in fruit; July–August.

Fruits: Linear pods (siliques) **2–4 cm long**, flattened, tipped with a short (1–3 mm long) persistent style, **opening elastically from the base**, held **erect** on 4–10 mm long stalks; seeds in a single row, without wings.

Habitat: Moist alpine banks and ledges; elsewhere, moist gravelly or rocky sites in subalpine to alpine zones.

Notes: Alpine bitter cress might be confused with some of the small white-flowered whitlow-grasses (*Draba* spp.) or with alpine braya (*Braya purpurascens* (R. Br.) Bunge *ex* Ledeb., p. 107), but those species have smaller (usually less than 1 cm long) pods and their plants are usually at least somewhat hairy. • As the seed pods dry, the sides gradually curl away from the supporting membrane, separating from the top, bottom or occasionally both ends. A considerable amount of time can elapse between the release of the first and last seeds. Under severe climatic conditions, seeds may not be released until the following spring. • Alpine bitter cress is a good example of a species with genetically dwarfed races. Most plants in alpine sites are barely distinguishable from those of high-arctic populations. However, when grown under warmer, temperate conditions, plants from alpine populations are tall and have large, irregular leaves, whereas those from high-arctic regions remain as small as plants on the more desirable sites at 80–82° N, and have small, regular leaves. Alpine plants have retained the ability to produce more robust plants and larger amounts of seed when occasional warm summers occur, but arctic plants never produce flowers far from the ground.

SMALL BITTER CRESS

Cardamine parviflora L.
MUSTARD FAMILY (BRASSICACEAE [CRUCIFERAE])

Plants: Slender, **hairless** annual or biennial herbs; **stems leafy**, usually solitary, 10–30 {40} cm tall, simple to freely branched; from weak fibrous roots.

Leaves: Alternate on the stem, sometimes also clustered near the base, **pinnately divided** into **3–6 pairs** of **linear to spoon-shaped or oblong** leaflets and tipped with a larger, linear-oblong to somewhat lance-shaped leaflet that is widest above the middle, usually toothless; **leaflet bases not extending along the central stalk** (rachis).

Flowers: White, about **2–3 mm across**, with **4 petals** and **4 sepals**; petals 1.5–3 mm long; 6 stamens, the outer 2 attached lower down than the inner 4; numerous, on spreading stalks in **elongating clusters** (racemes); {March–May} July.

Fruits: Linear, 0.8–1 mm wide, **1–3 cm long pods** (siliques) tipped with a **0.5–0.7** {0.2–1} **mm long style**, usually flattened, essentially nerveless, **opening elastically from the base**, pointed upward; stalks 5–8 {4–10} mm long; **seeds in a single row**, wingless, 0.7–0.9 mm long.

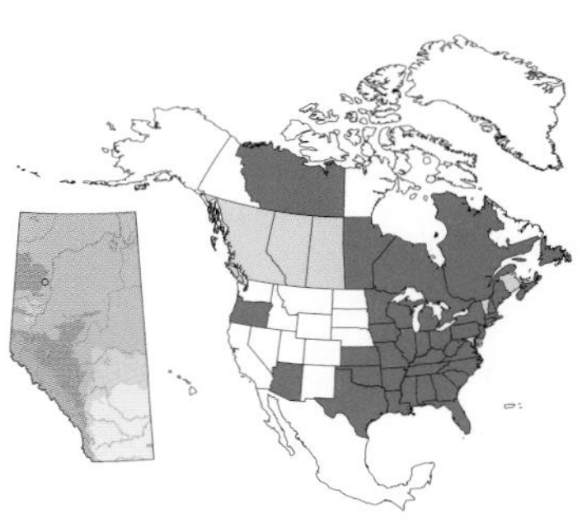

Habitat: Sandy ground and dry, open, mixed woodland; elsewhere, in seepage areas and on rocky outcrops, rocky or sandy shores, solifluction soil and scree slopes.

Notes: Mountain bitter cress (*Cardamine umbellata* Greene, also known as *Cardamine oligosperma* Nutt. *ex* Torr. & A. Gray var. *kamtschatica* (Regel) Detling) is another rare Alberta species of moist mountain sites. Most of its leaves are in a rosette at the base of the stem, and their leaflets are relatively wide, ranging from egg-shaped to round or kidney-shaped. Its flowers are slightly larger than those of small bitter cress (3–4 mm long vs. 1.5–3 mm long) and are borne in short (1–2 cm long), open clusters from July to September. • Small bitter cress might be confused with Pennsylvanian bitter cress (*Cardamine pensylvanica* Muhl. *ex* Willd.), but Pennsylvanian bitter cress is usually taller (10–50 cm) with less-branched stems that are hairy at the base. The bases of the leaflets extend down along the central stalk, the uppermost leaflet is much broader (elliptic to kidney-shaped) and the styles at the tips of the seed pods are more conspicuous (0.5–1.5 mm long).

C. UMBELLATA

JP

LK

DJ

JG

MEADOW BITTER CRESS, CUCKOO FLOWER

Cardamine pratensis L.
MUSTARD FAMILY (BRASSICACEAE [CRUCIFERAE])

Plants: Slender, hairless (sometimes sparsely hairy) perennial herbs; stems erect, leafy, 20–40 {8–50} cm tall; from short underground stems (rhizomes).

Leaves: In a basal tuft and alternate on the stem; lower leaves **pinnately divided** into 5–17 small, stalked, toothless or obscurely toothed leaflets; basal leaves long-stalked, with round to lance-shaped leaflets; upper leaves stalkless, with lance-shaped to linear leaflets.

Flowers: White to pinkish or purplish, with **4 petals** and **4 sepals**; petals showy, **8–13** {15} **mm long**, egg-shaped, widest above the middle; sepals erect, ⅓ as long as the petals; 6 stamens, the outer 2 attached lower down than the inner 4; styles up to 1 mm long; several to many, on spreading-ascending stalks in elongating clusters (racemes); {May} June–July.

Fruits: Straight, linear pods (siliques) 20–30 {15–40} mm long and about 1.5 mm wide, tipped with a persistent style (beak) 1–2 mm long, usually flattened, nerveless or nearly so, opening elastically from the base; lowest stalks 12–18 mm long; seeds in a single row, wingless.

Habitat: Moist meadows and swamps; elsewhere, in calcareous shallow water, springs and swampy woods, calcareous meadows and thickets, wet places and along creeks.

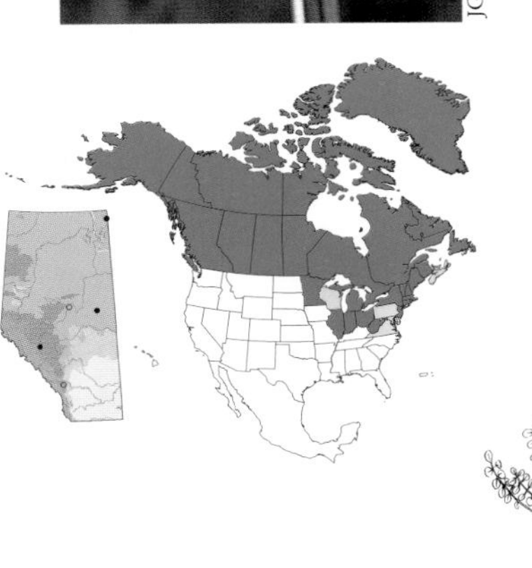

Notes: Other common names for this plant include lady's-smock and mayflower. • Meadow bitter cress is a highly variable boreal species. It often reproduces vegetatively by young plantlets that grow from the bases of its leaflets. • *Cardamine* is derived from an ancient Greek name, *kardamon*, used by Dioscorides for some cruciferous plant. The specific epithet *pratensis* means 'of meadows.'

OBLONG-LEAVED SUNDEW, ENGLISH SUNDEW, GREAT SUNDEW

Drosera anglica Huds.
SUNDEW FAMILY (DROSERACEAE)

DJ

Plants: **Small**, often **reddish, insectivorous** perennial herbs; flowering stems erect, leafless, 6–25 cm tall; from winter resting buds.

Leaves: In a **basal rosette**, covered with reddish, **tentacle-like, gland-tipped hairs; blades egg-shaped to elongate–spatula-shaped**, broadest above middle, 1–3 {3.5} cm long, 3–4 mm wide; stalks 2–6 {7} cm long, with 5 mm long, fringed stipules at base.

Flowers: White, with 4–8 equal petals; petals spatula-shaped, about 6 mm long; sepals oblong, 5–6 mm long; 1–9, in uncoiling clusters (scorpioid cymes); June–August.

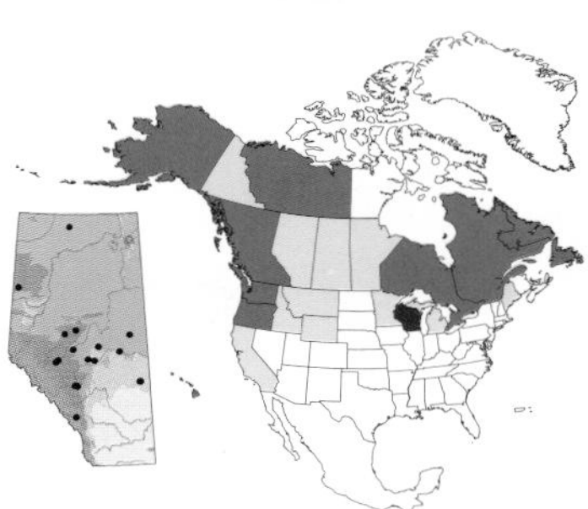

Fruits: Capsules, covered with microscopic bumps (tubercles), containing many black, **spindle-shaped, 1–1.5 mm long seeds**.

Habitat: Peaty, usually calcareous sites in swamps and fens, where the water-table is at or just below the surface; elsewhere, also on lakeshores.

Notes: This species has also been called *Drosera longifolia* L. • The edges and upper surfaces of the leaves are covered with stalked, tentacle-like, gland-tipped hairs that secrete a drop of mucilage at their tips. When an insect (usually a midge or another small fly) alights on the surface of the leaf, it becomes stuck on 1 or more of these glands, and nearby tentacles bend inward to entrap the prey. This bending is actually the result of rapid growth along 1 side of the stalk, but it can occur in less than a minute. The more the insect struggles, the more tentacles are activated. An insect may be totally entrapped within 20 minutes, but digestion can take a week. Once digestion has been completed, the tentacles unfurl, poised to entrap another victim. The nitrogen obtained from insects and other prey enables sundews to live in environments that are nitrogen-poor. Small flies, fungus gnats and gall-wasps are the main pollinators of sundew flowers. • The specific epithet *anglica* is Latin for 'English' and was given because this plant was first described from England.

JG

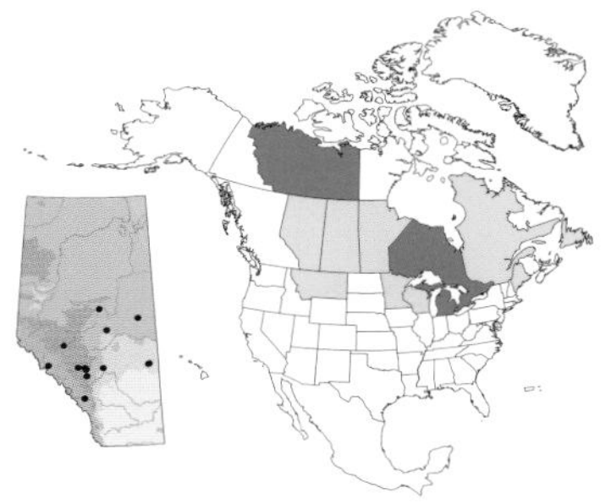

SLENDER-LEAVED SUNDEW, LINEAR-LEAVED SUNDEW

Drosera linearis Goldie
SUNDEW FAMILY (DROSERACEAE)

Plants: **Small**, often **reddish, insectivorous** perennial herbs; flowering stems erect, leafless, 6–13 cm tall; from winter resting buds.

Leaves: In a **basal rosette**, covered with **reddish, tentacle-like, gland-tipped hairs; blades linear**, 2–5 {6} cm long, about 2 mm wide; stalks with small, fringed stipules at base.

Flowers: White, with 4–8 equal petals; petals egg-shaped, broadest above middle, about 6 mm long; sepals oblong, 5–6 mm long; 1–4, in uncoiling clusters (scorpioid cymes); July {June–August}.

Fruits: Capsules, covered with microscopic bumps (tubercles), containing many black, **oblong to egg-shaped, 0.5–0.8 mm long seeds.**

Habitat: Bogs, often in marly sites; requires alkaline conditions for growth; elsewhere, also on wet, calcareous shores.

Notes: Sundew tea was used in the past for respiratory ailments. Extracts were also said to cure pimples, corns and warts. • The generic name *Drosera* was derived from the Greek *droseros* (dewy), in reference to the dew-like drops of liquid on the leaves. The specific epithet *linearis* refers to the slender, linear leaves.

PITCHER-PLANT

Sarracenia purpurea L. ssp. *purpurea*
PITCHER-PLANT FAMILY (SARRACENIACEAE)

Plants: Tufted, **insectivorous** perennial herbs; flowering stems leafless, 20–40 cm tall; from stout underground stems (rhizomes).

Leaves: In a **basal rosette, 10–20 {30} cm long**, curved tubes (pitchers) with a **broad wing** on the inner side **and a hood-like flap** over the opening at the top, green to yellowish **green with red or purple veins**, usually containing water; inner surface with **stiff, downward-pointing hairs** near the top, smooth and slippery near the base.

Flowers: Deep reddish purple, 5–7 cm wide, nodding, with a **broad, umbrella-shaped style** surrounded by 5 large, incurved petals and 5 broad sepals; **solitary**, on a long leafless stalk from the centre of the leaf rosette; July.

Fruit: Capsules with 5 cavities, containing many seeds.

Habitat: Wetlands, usually with sphagnum moss (*Sphagnum* spp.).

Notes: Other common names for this unusual plant include side-saddle flower, Indian pipe and frog's trousers. • Young leaves are flat and develop into a pitcher only after they have reached full length. • Pitcher-plants are insectivorous, supplementing their diet with nutrients from animal protein. This helps them to grow in environments where some nutrients are in poor supply. Insects are attracted by the brightly coloured leaves and nectar. Within the pitchers, downward-pointing hairs and a slippery surface direct the insects into the leaf cavity and then prevent escape. The insects drown in the pool of water at the bottom of the tube and are digested by acids and enzymes secreted by the plant. However, some insects, for example the larvae of some species of mosquitoes, are known to live in the leaves of pitcher-plants. • These unusual flowers are pollinated by insects, primarily bumblebees and honey-bees. • The pitcher-plant is the floral emblem of Newfoundland. • The generic name *Sarracenia* commemorates Dr. Michel Sarrasin de l'Etang, an 18th-century physician to the French court who collected some of the first specimens of Canadian plants. The specific epithet *purpurea* means 'purple,' a reference to the purple flowers.

DJ

DJ

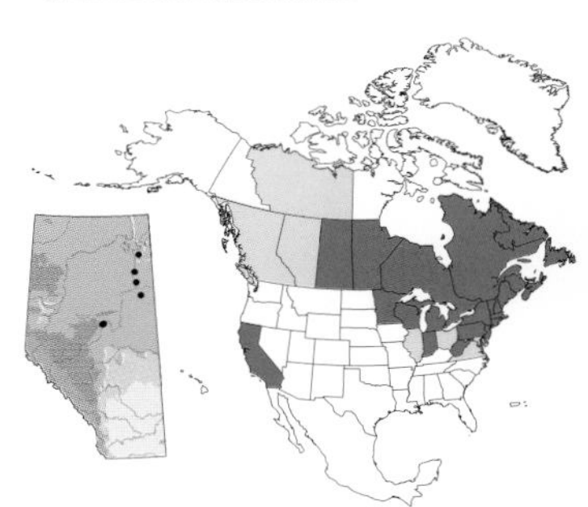

JP

JP

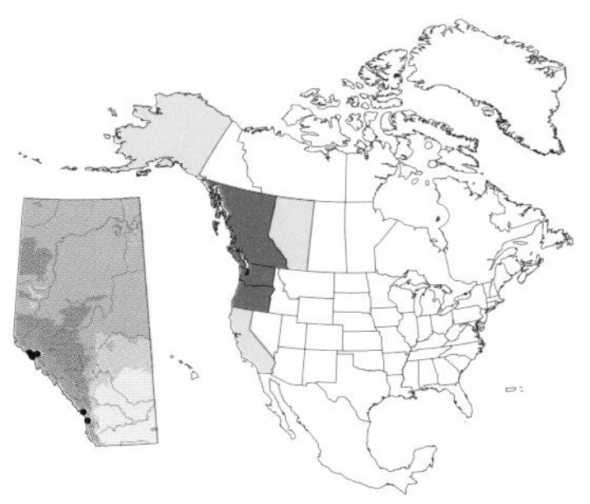

SPREADING STONECROP

Sedum divergens S. Wats.
STONECROP FAMILY (CRASSULACEAE)

Plants: Succulent, mat-forming perennial herbs; stems lying on the ground, rooting at joints (nodes) and producing erect non-flowering and flowering branches about 5–15 cm tall.

Leaves: Opposite (or nearly so) along stems, fleshy (succulent), stalkless, hairless, 4–10 mm long, **oval or egg-shaped** (widest above the middle) **to round**, narrower on flowering branches.

Flowers: Yellow, with 4 or 5 petals and sepals; petals longer than the sepals, tipped with a tiny point; sepals triangular, joined at the base; 3–15, in loose to dense, spreading clusters (cymes); {July} August–September.

Fruits: Pod-like fruits that open along one side (follicles), 4 or 5 per flower in star-like clusters, joined at the base for 1.5–2 mm and with tips pointing outward.

Habitat: Moist alpine or subalpine ridges, rocky ledges, crevices and talus slopes.

Notes: Other stonecrops that occur in Alberta have much narrower, alternate leaves. The most common, lance-leaved stonecrop (*Sedum lanceolatum* Torr.), has erect follicles and stems that grow in clumps. Narrow-petalled stonecrop (*Sedum stenopetalum* Pursh) is found only in southwestern Alberta. Its leaves are flattened, becoming brown or dry and translucent, and small bulbs replace some of the flowers. • *Sedum* is an ancient Latin name supposedly derived from *sedeo* (to sit), in reference to the squatty habit of the plants. The specific epithet *divergens* means 'spreading widely,' in reference to the fruits.

SPIDERPLANT

Saxifraga flagellaris Willd. ssp. *setigera* (Pursh) Tolm.
SAXIFRAGE FAMILY (SAXIFRAGACEAE)

Plants: Perennial herbs; stems **3–20 cm tall**, glandular-hairy; from slender underground stems (rhizomes) and also many slender, **arching or trailing stems** (stolons) **up to 10 cm long and sprouting at tips.**

Leaves: Mainly in basal rosettes, egg-shaped to lance-shaped, widest above middle, **spine-tipped, 5–10 {15} mm long, fringed** with stiff white hairs; stem leaves several, gradually smaller upward, hairless above, glandular-hairy beneath.

Flowers: Bright yellow, about **1–1.5 cm across**, with 5 petals and 5 sepals; petals spreading, egg-shaped, widest above middle, pink-spotted near the base; **sepals purple** and **glandular**, in a bell-shaped calyx with lobes 2–5 mm long; 1–3 {5}; July {August}.

Fruits: Pairs of erect pod-like fruits (follicles), {4} **5–10 mm long, often bright red** with 2 spreading tips.

Habitat: Moist, turfy, limestone slopes and ridges in alpine areas; elsewhere, on streambanks and gravelly to rocky slopes at high to low elevations.

Notes: This species has also been called *Saxifraga setigera* Pursh. • Yellow mountain saxifrage (*Saxifraga aizoides* L.) is another small, yellow-flowered saxifrage, but its plants lack stolons and its linear leaves are succulent, hairless, and borne mainly on the stems (rather than in basal rosettes). • Spiderplant is very decorative in gardens, but it can be difficult to grow. Plants are usually propagated by rooting rosettes at the tips of stolons and then severing from the parent plants once their roots are well established. • Spiderplant has been classified as rare in BC and Alberta, and it is protected by law in New Mexico. • *Saxifraga* is from the Latin *saxum* (rock) and *frangere* (break). This may refer to the tendency of saxifrage plants to grow between rocks, or to the historical use of the plants to treat kidney stones.

JG

LK

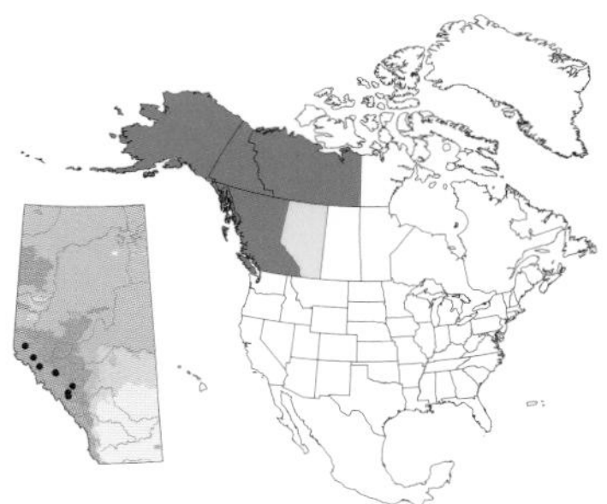

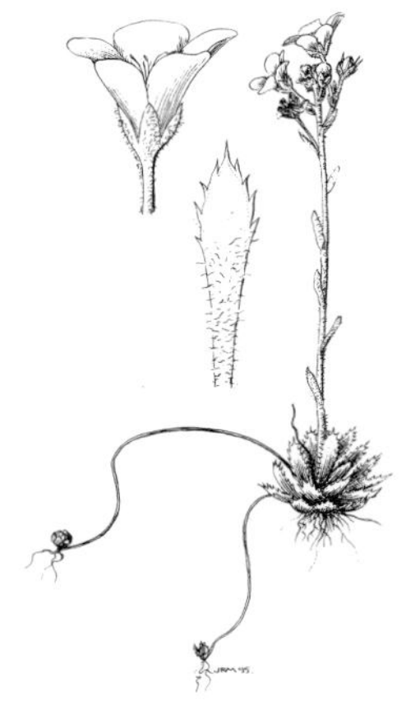

LK

ALPINE SAXIFRAGE

Saxifraga nivalis L.
SAXIFRAGE FAMILY (SAXIFRAGACEAE)

Plants: Perennial herbs, 4–15 {22} cm tall; stems (flowering stalks) single, erect, with silky, gland-tipped hairs, often **purplish**; from short, thick underground stems (rhizomes).

Leaves: In a **basal rosette**, thick, green and hairless on upper surface, **purple on lower surface**, usually with coarse, rusty-coloured hairs along edges; blades 1–3 cm long, round to egg-shaped, tipped with 9–20 coarse, rounded teeth, tapering to broad stalks about as long as the blade.

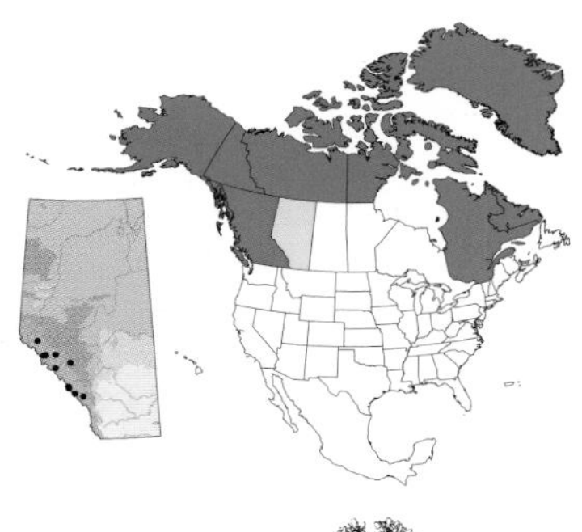

Flowers: Reddish-tinged, with 5 petals and 5 sepals; petals 3 mm long, greenish white, purplish or reddish on the back, slightly longer than the sepals; sepals purplish; stalks very short, glandular-hairy; 3–12, in **compact, branched clusters** (cymes); July {August}.

Fruits: Pod-like fruits that split open down 1 side (follicles), **purplish, 5–6** {7} **mm long**, egg-shaped, 2 per flower, joined at base and with tips curved outward.

Habitat: Moist alpine slopes, ridges and rock crevices.

Notes: Oregon saxifrage (*Saxifraga oregana* J.T. Howell var. *montanensis* (Small) C.L. Hitchc.) is found on alpine slopes in the Crowsnest Pass. It is a much larger plant, 15–120 cm tall, with narrow basal leaves that are 6–20 cm long and widest toward the tip. The fragrant, greenish white flowers are numerous in branched clusters (panicles) with white-hairy stalks. The petals are often unequal in size or with some absent. This species flowers from June to early July. • Rhomboid-leaved saxifrage (*Saxifraga occidentalis* S. Wats.) is a common species that has longer leaves (more than 2 cm long) that lack the purple lower surface, and its flower clusters are more open, flat-topped and spreading. • Red-stemmed saxifrage (*Saxifraga lyallii* Engler) often has purplish stems, but it grows to 30 cm tall and has open flower clusters and fan-shaped leaves. • Another rare saxifrage has been reported to occur in Alberta, but its presence has not been verified. Yellowstone saxifrage (*Saxifraga subapetala* (E. Nels.) Rydb.) is very similar to Oregon saxifrage, and some taxonomists consider it a variety of the same species (*Saxifraga oregana* J.T. Howell var. *subapetala* (E. Nels.) C.L. Hitchc.). It is usually distinguished by its slightly smaller (5–7 mm wide), greenish-tinged flowers in narrow, elongating flower

S. SUBAPETALA

PL

clusters (rather than pyramidal panicles) on sparsely hairy or glandular stalks (rather than on conspicuously long-hairy stalks). • Saxifrages have been used in the treatment of scurvy. The fresh leaves are high in vitamins A and C, and they have been used in salads. Several species are cultivated as ornamentals. • The specific epithet *nivalis* was derived from the Latin *nivea* (snow).

S. OREGANA

STREAM SAXIFRAGE

Saxifraga odontoloma Piper
SAXIFRAGE FAMILY (SAXIFRAGACEAE)

LA

Plants: Perennial herbs; stems erect, 10–75 cm tall, hairless near base, glandular toward tips; from elongated underground stems (rhizomes).

Leaves: **Basal**; blades **round**, 2.5–10 cm wide, **heart-shaped at the base** and **toothed all along the edges**, hairless or sparsely hairy; **stalks 1–3 times longer than the blades.**

Flowers: White with 2 yellow or green basal spots at the base of each petal, with 5 petals and 5 sepals; petals 2–5 mm long, broad at tip, **abruptly narrowed to a slender base**; sepals 1.8–2.8 mm long, hairless or glandular-hairy along the edges only; in open, branched clusters (panicles) with spreading to erect, glandular-hairy branches, the hairs often reddish purple; July {June–August}.

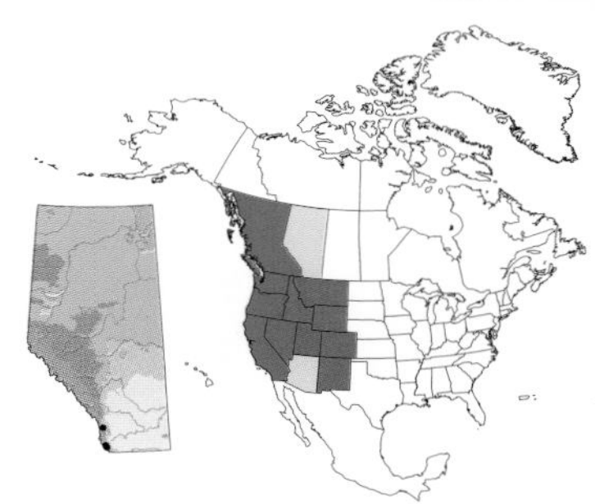

Fruits: Pod-like fruits that split open down 1 side (follicles), usually **purplish, 5–9 mm long**, 2 (sometimes 3 or 4) per flower, fused for ⅓–⅗ of their length and with **firm, slightly spreading tips.**

Habitat: Shady mountain streambanks and wet cliff faces.

Notes: Cordate-leaved saxifrage (*Saxifraga nelsoniana* D. Don ssp. *porsildiana* (Calder & Savile) Hult.) is also rare in Alberta. It is distinguished from stream saxifrage by its narrower (slender to broadly elliptic), often pinkish petals, which taper gradually and lack spots at their bases. It grows in moist rocky sites and along streams in alpine areas. • Alaska saxifrage (*Saxifraga ferruginea* Graham) is another rare Alberta species with open, branched flower

clusters (panicles). However, it has much narrower (spatula-shaped) leaves that taper gradually to wedge-shaped bases. Its flowers have 3 broad and 2 narrow petals, and small bulblets usually replace some blooms. Alaska saxifrage grows on moist, often rocky, alpine sites, and blooms in {June} July and August. • Red-stemmed saxifrage (*Saxifraga lyallii* Engler) is a common species whose fan-shaped leaves are toothed only above the middle and have stalks about as long as their blades. • There is some controversy about whether the Alberta plants are hybrids with red-stemmed saxifrage or the true stream saxifrage. • The specific epithet *odontoloma* is from the Greek *odonto* (tooth) and *loma* (fringe, border), presumably referring to the toothed edges of the leaf.

S. NELSONIANA

LA

LA

S. FERRUGINEA

LA

HEUCHERA-LIKE BOYKINIA, TELESONIX

Boykinia heucheriformis (Rydb.) Rosendahl
SAXIFRAGE FAMILY (SAXIFRAGACEAE)

Plants: Perennial herbs; stems 5–20 cm tall, with **glandular hairs**; from thick, scaly, elongated underground stems (rhizomes).

Leaves: Mostly basal; blades **kidney-shaped to round**, 1–6 cm wide, with shallow, rounded or pointed lobes edged with rounded teeth, bearing stalkless glands; **stem leaves** alternate, **fan-shaped**, short-stalked or stalkless.

Flowers: Reddish purple to deep pink; 5 petals, widest toward their tips, equal to or slightly longer than the sepals; 5 sepals, fused at base, 9–13 mm long; 10 stamens; 5–25, in **short, leafy, branched clusters** (panicles), somewhat nodding to 1 side; June–August.

Fruits: Capsules, **split** about halfway to base **into 2 firm, slightly spreading points**; seeds brown, shiny, 1–2 mm long.

Habitat: Rocky outcrops and talus slopes (often limestone) in alpine areas. Alberta populations are disjunct and restricted to glacial refugia.

Notes: This species has also been called *Telesonix jamesii* (Torr.) Raf. and *Telesonix heucheriformis* Rydb. • These plants are eaten by elk and deer. • The generic name *Boykinia* commemorates Samuel Boykin (1786–1848), an American banker, physician and naturalist who lived in Georgia. The specific epithet *heucheriformis* means 'like (in the form of) *Heuchera*,' a similar genus in the saxifrage family.

DJ

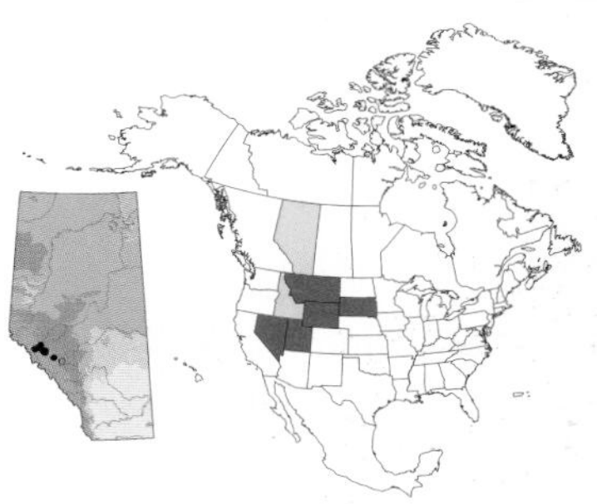

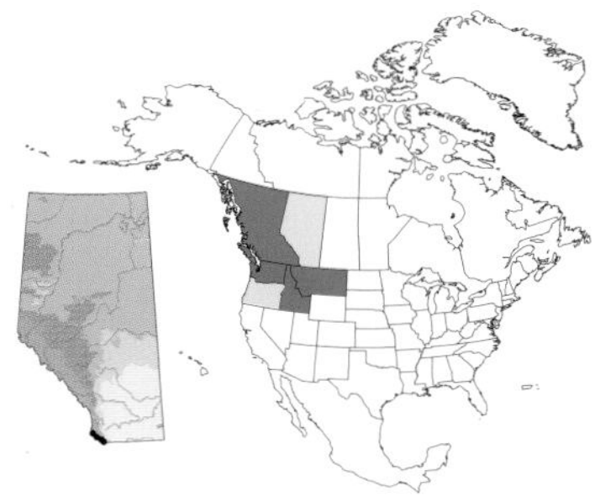

BLUE SUKSDORFIA

Suksdorfia violacea A. Gray
SAXIFRAGE FAMILY (SAXIFRAGACEAE)

Plants: Delicate perennial herbs, 10–20 cm tall, lightly **hairy and glandular** on lower parts, becoming more densely so in upper portions; from elongated underground stems (rhizomes) bearing **small bulbs.**

Leaves: Basal (1–3) and alternate (2–5); blades **kidney-shaped, 1–2.5 cm wide** with **5–7 shallow, slightly toothed lobes**, more or less short-hairy; lower leaves long-stalked; stem leaves with large, **deeply cut stipules at base,** becoming smaller, wedge-shaped and almost stalkless upward, with 2–4 teeth at the tip.

Flowers: Light violet (rarely white); **5 petals 5–9 mm long, erect**, narrowed abruptly to a whitish or yellow base; **calyxes narrowly cone-shaped**, 2–3 mm long, with **5 narrowly lance-shaped, erect lobes**; 2–10, borne on 2 or 3 erect branches in elongated, loose, branched clusters (corymbs); May–July.

Fruits: Capsules, 4–6 mm long, with warty, brownish seeds about 0.5 mm long.

Habitat: Among wet rocks along mountain streams and in damp, mossy areas.

Notes: White suksdorfia (*Suksdorfia ranunculifolia* (Hook.) Engl.) is also rare in Alberta, known only from wet rock faces and crevices in Waterton Lakes National Park. It differs from blue suksdorfia in having 5 or 6 basal leaves with 3–10 cm long stalks and round, 2–4 cm wide blades that are deeply cut into 3 wedge-shaped lobes with irregular, rounded teeth. The middle stem leaves have expanded bases that clasp the stem. Its flower clusters are nearly flat-topped with short branches bearing several flowers. The flowers have smaller (2.5–6 mm long), spreading petals that are white (often purplish at the base). The calyxes are broadly bell-shaped, with 5 broadly triangular spreading lobes, and the stamens are attached to a thick disc that is not found in blue suksdorfia flowers. White suksdorfia flowers from June to July. • The distribution of these species may be correlated with the extension of ice during the last glaciation (i.e., they occur beyond the maximum extent of the glaciers).

S. RANUNCULIFOLIA

ALPINE ALUMROOT

Heuchera glabra Willd. *ex* R. & S.
SAXIFRAGE FAMILY (SAXIFRAGACEAE)

WM

Plants: Slender perennial herbs; flowering stems single to several, 10–60 cm tall, hairless near the base but **conspicuously glandular and hairy** on the upper parts; from **well-developed, scaly, horizontal to ascending underground stems** (rhizomes).

Leaves: Mainly basal; blades 2–9 cm long, 1.5–4 {9} cm wide, **somewhat maple-leaf-like**, broadly heart-shaped, notched at the base and tipped with {3} **5–7 shallow, irregularly sharp-toothed lobes, essentially hairless**, sometimes with small gland-tipped hairs on the lower surface or with a few tiny, stiff hairs on the upper surface when young; 1 or 2 stem leaves, usually more or less bract-like; **stalks long and slender with 2 broad lobes** (stipules) at the base.

Flowers: White, cone-shaped, about 5 mm long, with **5 slender petals**; petals 2–4 times as long as the sepals, with spoon-shaped blades, ¼–½ as long as their slender stalks (claws); **calyxes cone-shaped**, squared at the base, 2–3 {1.5–3.5} **mm long, glandular-hairy**, cut less than halfway to the base into 5 egg-shaped to oblong lobes; **5 stamens, projecting from the flower**, equal to or slightly longer than the petals; pistils with 2 stalkless, head-like stigmas, each at the tip of a hollow, spreading point (beak); numerous, in the axils of small bracts on thread-like branches in **open, branched clusters** (panicles); July–August {June–September}.

Fruits: Oval capsules tipped with 2 firm, spreading points (beaks), protruding from the calyx, 5–6 {9} mm long, **splitting open between the beaks**; seeds brown, somewhat crescent-shaped, 0.7–0.8 mm long and ⅓–¼ as wide, with rows of tiny spines; August.

Habitat: Moist alpine scree slopes; elsewhere, on damp, shady rocks and riverbanks (such as spray zones near waterfalls), rocky meadows and slopes, and grassy hillsides.

Notes: Other common names for this species include alpine heuchera, smooth alumroot, smooth heuchera and mountain saxifrage. • Alumroot plants are commonly used as mordants—substances to make dyes colourfast. • The powdered roots were used to stop bleeding and heal wounds and sores. Root tea was taken as a tonic or as a treatment for diarrhea or stomach flu, and it was also gargled.

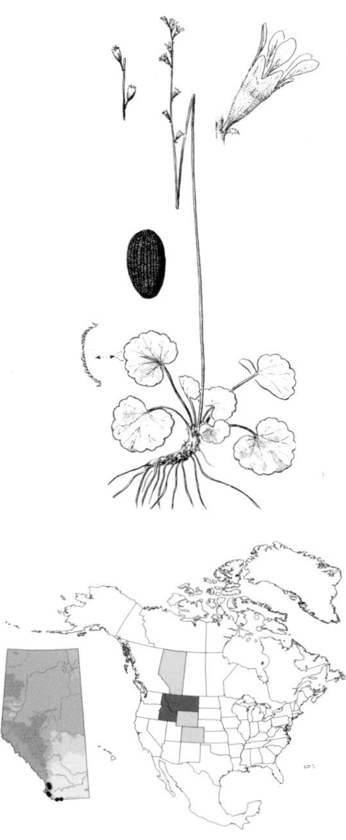

Williams' Conimitella

Conimitella williamsii (D.C. Eaton) Rydb.
SAXIFRAGE FAMILY (SAXIFRAGACEAE)

Plants: Slender perennial herbs; flowering stems leafless, 20–40 {60} cm tall, with fine gland-tipped hairs; from short, ascending underground stems (rhizomes).

Leaves: Basal; blades **round to kidney-shaped,** 1–4 cm wide, leathery, usually purplish on the lower surface, edged with broad, rounded, double teeth and **stiff hairs;** stalks slender, 1.5–6 {1–10} cm long.

Flowers: White, cone-shaped, with **5 small, slender petals;** petals 4–5 mm long, with a blunt, broadened, lance-shaped blade at the tip of a slender base (claw); **calyxes cone-shaped, 4–6 mm long** (up to 9 mm long in fruit), tipped with 5 spreading, egg-shaped lobes about 1 mm long, attached to the ovary for ⅓–½ of its length; 5 stamens, opposite the sepals, with filaments about the same length as the anthers; pistils with 2 stalkless, head-like stigmas, each at the tip of a hollow point; 5–10 {12}, on 1–5 mm long stalks in the axils of slender bracts, forming loose, finely glandular-hairy, elongating clusters (racemes); June.

Fruits: Capsules, enveloped almost entirely by the enlarged calyxes, splitting open along the inner (ventral) **side of the 2 small, hollow points at the tips;** seeds numerous, black, slightly roughened, about 1 mm long.

Habitat: Open montane slopes; elsewhere, in rich montane forests and on moist cliffs and rocky slopes, often on limestone.

Notes: The leaves of Williams' conimitella resemble those of alumroots (*Heuchera* spp.) and bishop's-caps (*Mitella* spp.), but the conimitella leaves are broader (more kidney-shaped) and their edges are fringed with stiff hairs. When bishop's-caps are in bloom, they are easily identified by the feathery petals of their flowers. • The generic name *Conimitella* was derived from the Latin *conos* (cone) and *mitella* (bishop's cap), in reference to the cone-shaped flowers of these *Mitella*-like plants. The specific epithet *williamsii* commemorates R.S. Williams (1859–1945), a Montana botanist who built the first cabin where Great Falls, Montana now stands and who was the last rider for the Pony Express.

SMALL-FLOWERED ROCKSTAR

Lithophragma parviflorum (Hook.) Nutt. *ex* T. & G.
SAXIFRAGE FAMILY (SAXIFRAGACEAE)

LA

Plants: Perennial herbs; stems **glandular-hairy, 10–30 cm tall**, often rough to touch; from thin underground stems (rhizomes) with scattered, rice-like bulblets.

Leaves: Mainly **basal**, 1–3 cm long, palmately divided into **3–5 wedge-shaped sections that are once or twice 3-lobed or 3-toothed**, sparsely white-hairy, long-stalked; stem leaves smaller and stalkless upward.

Flowers: White to pinkish or purplish, broadly funnel-shaped or star-like, 5-sided, 12–15 mm wide, with **5 spreading petals** and 5 small calyx lobes; petals **4–10 mm long, deeply 3–5-lobed at the tip** (appearing as if 15 or 25 slender petals), abruptly narrowed to a slender base; 3–9 {11}, in elongating clusters (racemes); {April} May–July.

Fruits: Capsules, splitting open along 3 lines.

Habitat: Moist montane meadows and open woods; elsewhere, often in dry grassland or sagebrush desert.

Notes: Smooth rockstar (*Lithophragma glabrum* Nutt., also called *Lithophragma bulbifera* Rydb.) is another rare Alberta plant. It has nearly hairless leaves, and it often produces small bulblets in the axils of its lower leaves. Smooth rockstar also has fewer (2–5) flowers in more head-like clusters, and its stems are covered with purple-tipped hairs. It grows on dry plains and montane slopes, and flowers in July and August. • Rockstar is sometimes called 'fringe-cup.' The generic name *Lithophragma* was derived from the Greek *lithos* (stone) and *phragma* (wall) because these plants usually grow on rocky slopes.

L. GLABRUM

LK

LA

LK

FRINGE-CUPS

Tellima grandiflora (Pursh) Dougl. *ex* Lindl.
SAXIFRAGE FAMILY (SAXIFRAGACEAE)

Plants: Perennial herbs; stems 40–80 cm tall, unbranched, **stiff-hairy on the lower portion**, **glandular** and less hairy upward; from short underground stems (rhizomes).

Leaves: Basal and alternate; blades **heart-shaped to kidney-shaped, 3–10 cm wide**, sparsely stiff-hairy, shallowly 5–7-lobed (sometimes 3-lobed), with irregular, broad, pointed teeth; **basal leaf stalks 5–20 cm long, very hairy**; 1–3 stem leaves, smaller upward.

Flowers: Greenish yellow when young, reddish with age, short-stalked, **fragrant**; **5 petals, fringed** with 5–10 thread-like segments at tips; **calyx greenish, glandular**, 5–8 mm long (longer when fruit appears), with 5 erect, triangular lobes; 10–35, in **narrow, elongated, branched clusters** (panicles); {April–July}.

Fruits: Egg-shaped capsules, approximately 10 mm long, **with 2 spreading beaks**; seeds brown with rows of tiny bumps.

Habitat: Rocky seeps and rich, moist soil.

Notes: The leaves of fringe-cups resemble those of sugar-scoop (*Tiarella unifoliata* Hook.) and certain species of bishop's-cap (*Mitella* spp.) and alumroot (*Heuchera* spp.). However, the flowers of these other species are smaller and not fragrant, and their petals are not tipped with the characteristic fringe. • Fringe-cups was first discovered in Alberta in 1986, in the South Castle River valley. • The Skagit pounded and boiled fringe-cups to make a tea used for any kind of sickness, especially for lack of appetite. It is also said to have been eaten by woodland elves to improve night vision. • Fringe-cups thrives in sites that are high in nitrogen. Its seeds readily germinate and take root, resulting in new, vigorous plants that often crowd out the mother plant. • *Tellima* is an anagram of *Mitella*, the genus under which this plant was first described. *Grandiflora* is derived from Latin meaning 'large-flowered.' The common name 'fringe-cups' refers to the highly divided petals which form a fringe around each flower.

SMALL NORTHERN GRASS-OF-PARNASSUS

Parnassia parviflora DC.
GRASS-OF-PARNASSUS FAMILY (PARNASSIACEAE)

Plants: Slender, hairless perennial herbs; stems 5–30 cm tall, with a single, 7–16 mm long, **narrowly egg-shaped leaf** (bract) **usually borne below the middle** and **not clasping** the stem; from short, erect to ascending underground stems (rhizomes).

Leaves: Basal (except for a small, single stem leaf), slender-stalked; **blades 1–2** {2.5} **cm** long, elliptic to egg-shaped, **tapered to base**.

Flowers: White with greenish or yellowish veins, with 5 petals, 5 sepals and 5 clusters of specialized, gland-tipped structures (staminodia); petals 5–7-veined, oblong to elliptic, 5–9 {4–10} mm long; sepals usually only slightly shorter than the petals; staminodia slender, borne **in clusters of 5–7** {9} **at the tip of small, oblong scales;** single; July–August {September}.

Fruits: Blunt-tipped, ovoid capsules, 7–11 mm long.

Habitat: Bogs and streambanks; elsewhere, in wet meadows.

Notes: This species is sometimes considered a small-flowered variant of northern grass-of-Parnassus (*Parnassia palustris* L.), and these 2 species often appear to merge through *P. palustris* var. *montanensis* (Fern. & Rydb.) C.L. Hitchc., which is almost exactly intermediate in its characteristics. Northern grass-of-Parnassus is usually distinguished by its heart-shaped basal leaves, its clasping stem leaf and its large clusters of 7–15 staminodia. • The white, saucer-shaped flowers are designed to attract flies. The glistening glands at the tips of the staminodia appear to be drops of pure nectar, but they are really false nectaries designed to lure insects to the flowers. When nectar-seeking visitors land at the staminodia, they either touch the stigma (fertilizing the flower) or brush against the stamens (picking up pollen to carry to the next flower). Usually they are so strongly attracted to the false nectaries that they do not even bother eating the pollen on the stamens. The anthers mature first, and later, when the 2-pronged stigma opens, most of the flower's own pollen is gone. This reduces the chances of self-fertilization.

Macoun's cinquefoil

Potentilla macounii Rydb.
ROSE FAMILY (ROSACEAE)

Plants: Low, spreading perennial herbs; stems ascending or spreading on the ground, 4–12 {20} cm long and usually less than half as tall; usually few to several; from stout, sparingly branched root crowns on taproots.

Leaves: Mainly in a basal tuft, but also with 1 or 2 alternate leaves on the stem; blades **pinnately divided into 7–9** {5–11} **leaflets**; leaflets about 1 cm long, **cut to the midrib into linear to lance-shaped lobes** about 1 mm wide, **usually greyish with a mixture of flat-lying, stiff hairs and woolly hairs on the upper surface, densely white-woolly beneath** and with overlying straight hairs; stalks with a pair of lance-shaped, 3–10 mm long lobes (stipules) at the base.

Flowers: Yellow, saucer-shaped, 10–15 mm across, with 5 shallowly notched, egg-shaped petals twice as long as the cupped, **silky-hairy calyx**, which has 5 lance-shaped, 3–6 mm long lobes (sepals) alternating with 5 smaller lobes (bractlets); 2–5, in open clusters (cymes); {June–August}.

Fruits: Smooth seed-like fruits (achenes), about 1.5 mm long, with slender, thread-like styles attached below the tip, in compact clusters surrounded by persistent calyxes.

Habitat: Dry rocky slopes on the eastern slopes of the Rocky Mountains.

Notes: This species has also been called *Potentilla concinna* Richards. var. *macounii* (Rydb.) C.L. Hitchc. and var. *divisa* Rydb. • Macoun's cinquefoil could be confused with the more common species sheep cinquefoil (*Potentilla ovina* Macoun), but the leaves of sheep cinquefoil lack woolly hairs (tomentum) on their lower surfaces. • Another small, rare cinquefoil has been discovered in Alberta. Colorado cinquefoil (*Potentilla subjuga* Rydb., also called *Potentilla rubripes* Rydb. and *Potentilla concinna* Richards. var. *rubripes* (Rydb.) C.L. Hitchc.) is very similar to Macoun's cinquefoil, and some taxonomists consider both species to be varieties of *Potentilla concinna*. Colorado cinquefoil is distinguished by its greenish, stiff-hairy upper leaf surfaces (rather than greyish and woolly). It grows on mountain slopes from Alberta to Colorado and flowers in spring and early summer.

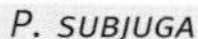

P. SUBJUGA

BRANCHED CINQUEFOIL, STAGHORN CINQUEFOIL

Potentilla multifida L.
ROSE FAMILY (ROSACEAE)

Plants: Densely tufted perennial herbs; stems erect or spreading, 10–20 {40} cm tall, sparsely to densely covered with spreading hairs; from stout, rather woody root crowns.

Leaves: Basal and alternate on the stem, 5–10 cm long; blades **pinnately divided into 5–7 leaflets that are deeply cut into parallel, linear lobes** about 1–1.5 mm wide and arranged **like teeth on a comb** (pectinate), **rolled under along the edges**, green and sparsely covered with flat-lying, stiff hairs on the upper surface, densely **white-woolly beneath**, and silky-hairy on the midribs; stalks either shorter than or much longer than the blade, with a pair of toothless lobes (stipules) at the base.

Flowers: Yellow, saucer-shaped, 6–10 mm across, with 5 egg-shaped petals above an **equally long or slightly longer, silky-hairy, bell-shaped calyx** with 5 triangular to egg-shaped, 3–5 mm long lobes (sepals) alternating with 5 linear lobes (bractlets); 3–15, in open clusters (cymes); July.

Fruits: Dry seed-like fruits (achenes), about 1.2 mm long, with slender, thread-like styles, in compact clusters surrounded by persistent calyxes.

Habitat: Gravel bars and open slopes; elsewhere, on scree slopes and open gravelly or sandy ground, often near streams and lakes or on roadsides.

Notes: This species has also been called *Potentilla virgulata* A. Nels. and *Potentilla bimundorum* Sojak. • Branched cinquefoil could be mistaken for the much more common species prairie cinquefoil (*Potentilla pensylvanica* L.), but the stipules of the upper stem leaves of prairie cinquefoil are toothed (at least near the base) and its stems are usually much taller (20–50 cm tall). • The generic name *Potentilla* is from the Latin *potens* (powerful), in reference to the strong (mainly astringent) medicinal properties of these plants. The specific epithet *multifida* was taken from the Latin *multi* (many) and *fidus* (split), in reference to the many slender lobes of the leaflets.

DJ

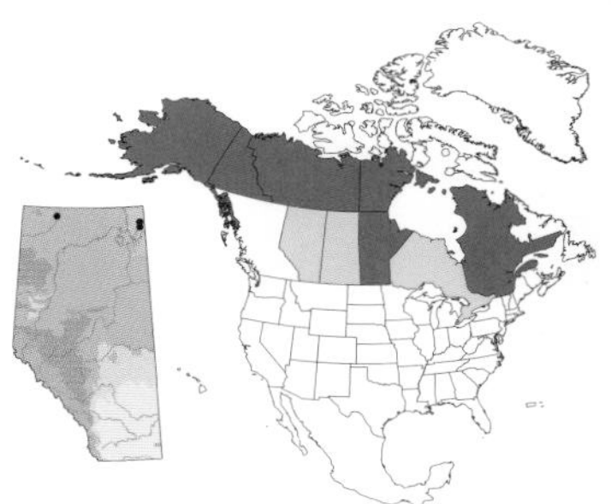

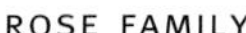

JG

SMOOTH-LEAVED CINQUEFOIL, FEATHER-LEAVED CINQUEFOIL

Potentilla multisecta (S. Wats.) Rydb.
ROSE FAMILY (ROSACEAE)

Plants: Sparsely hairy perennial herbs, stems **5–20 cm tall**, with a mixture of short, spreading and long, flat-lying hairs; from a thick, branched root crown.

Leaves: Mostly basal, hairless to sparsely hairy on the upper surface, densely hairy on the veins beneath, **3–4 cm long, pinnately** (rarely palmately) **divided into 5–9 leaflets**; leaflets 5–15 mm long, **deeply cut** (to the midrib) **into slender** (0.5–2 mm wide), **linear or oblong segments**; stalks as long as blades; stem leaves alternate.

Flowers: Yellow, 1–1.5 cm across, with **5 sepals and 5 smaller, alternating bractlets** below 5 petals; sepals lance-shaped, 3–5 mm long; petals 5–8 mm long; **2–10**, in spreading clusters (cymes); June {July–August}.

Fruits: Dry seed-like fruits (achenes), about 1 mm long.

Habitat: Dry alpine slopes.

Notes: *Potentilla multisecta* is often treated as a variety of mountain cinquefoil (*Potentilla diversifolia* Lehm.), and it may be an alpine ecotype of that species. However, the leaflets of mountain cinquefoil are borne close together, in an almost palmate arrangement (not clearly pinnate), and they are toothed or shallowly lobed (not cut almost to the midrib). • Smooth-leaved cinquefoil could be confused with prairie cinquefoil (*Potentilla pensylvanica* L.), but that is a larger (20–50 cm tall) species of dry prairies and open slopes. • Smooth-leaved cinquefoil often grows with sheep cinquefoil (*Potentilla ovina* Macoun), and in several ways it appears transitional to that species. • The specific epithet *multisecta*, from the Latin *multus* (many) and *sectus* (to cut), refers to the finely divided (feather-like) leaves of this species.

BUSHY CINQUEFOIL

Potentilla paradoxa Nutt.
ROSE FAMILY (ROSACEAE)

Plants: Annual, biennial or short-lived perennial **herbs**; stems **leafy**, spreading to ascending, 20–50 {90} cm long, unbranched or branched, hairless near the base but often stiff-hairy on the upper parts; from simple or branched root crowns on taproots.

Leaves: **Alternate, pinnately divided into 2–4 {5} pairs of leaflets** (upper leaves sometimes with 3 leaflets), **almost hairless**; leaflets 1–3 cm long, oblong to egg-shaped and widest above the middle, tapered to a wedge-shaped base, edged with **blunt teeth**; stalks short, with a pair of well-developed lobes (stipules) at the base.

Flowers: **Yellow, saucer-shaped, 5–7 {9} mm across**, with 5 bractlets, 5 sepals and 5 petals **all about 3–4 mm long**; petals egg-shaped, widest above the middle; sepals stiff-hairy, triangular to egg-shaped, widest above the middle; stamens 20 (sometimes 10–15), often with sterile (abortive) anthers; ovaries numerous, **tipped with an equally long style** that is somewhat **thickened** at the base; **in diffusely branched, leafy, open clusters** (cymes), often bearing flowers over the upper half of the plant; {June–July}.

Fruits: Smooth, dry seed-like fruits (achenes), about 1.2 mm long, **with a corky, wedge-shaped thickening nearly (or equally) as large as the achene on the inner side**, sometimes with obscure, wavy, lengthwise ridges, in compact clusters surrounded by persistent calyxes.

Habitat: Moist flats and sandy lake shores and riverbanks; elsewhere, in damp meadows and prairies.

Notes: Drummond's cinquefoil (*Potentilla drummondii* Lehm. ssp. *drummondii*, sometimes classified as var. *drummondii*) is another rare Alberta cinquefoil, with open clusters of yellow flowers and with sparsely hairy, pinnately divided leaves whose leaflets are lobed only halfway to the middle (or less). It is distinguished from bushy cinquefoil by its few (0–2 rather than many) stem leaves, which are almost palmately divided (rather than clearly pinnately divided) and which are edged with sharp teeth (rather than rounded lobes). Drummond's cinquefoil tends to have showier flowers (10–20 mm across vs. 5–7 mm), with petals that are much longer than the sepals. It grows in moist meadows in subalpine and alpine areas, and flowers

JL

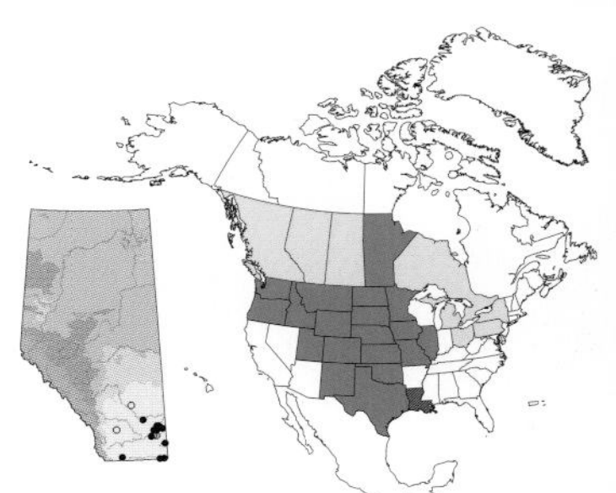

P. DRUMMONDII ssp. *DRUMMONDII*

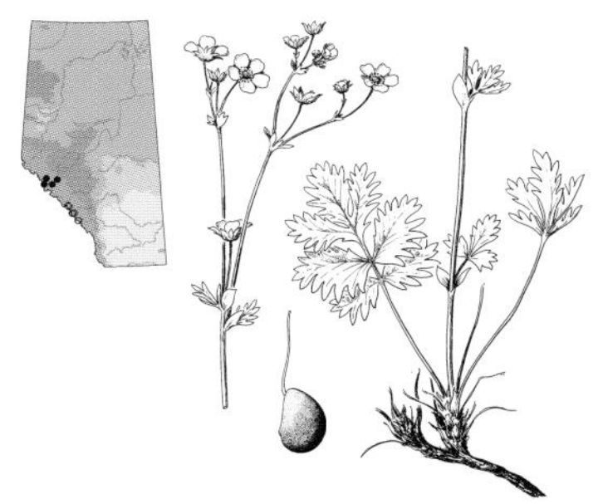

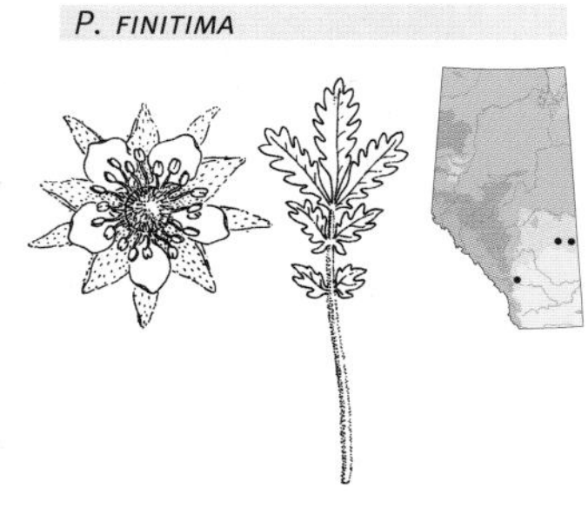

in July {June–August}. • Another rare species in Alberta, sandhills cinquefoil (*Potentilla finitima* Kohli & Packer, also called *Potentilla lasiodonta* Rydb. and *P. pensylvanica* L. var. *arida* B. Boivin), is distinguished from the other 2 species by leaves that are densely woolly-hairy below and by bractlets that are much longer than, and at least as wide as, the sepals.

JL

LOW CINQUEFOIL

Potentilla plattensis Nutt.
ROSE FAMILY (ROSACEAE)

Plants: **Low, spreading perennial herbs**, with **fat, tapered, flat-lying, white hairs**; stems single to several, slender, branched, usually ascending or spreading on the ground, 10–20 {30} cm long; from thick, rather woody root crowns on taproots.

Leaves: Mostly basal, numerous, **pinnately divided into 7–15 {17} light green, 5–8 mm long leaflets** that are **deeply cut** (almost to the midrib) into oblong to almost linear lobes, stiff-hairy to nearly hairless and **similarly green on both surfaces**.

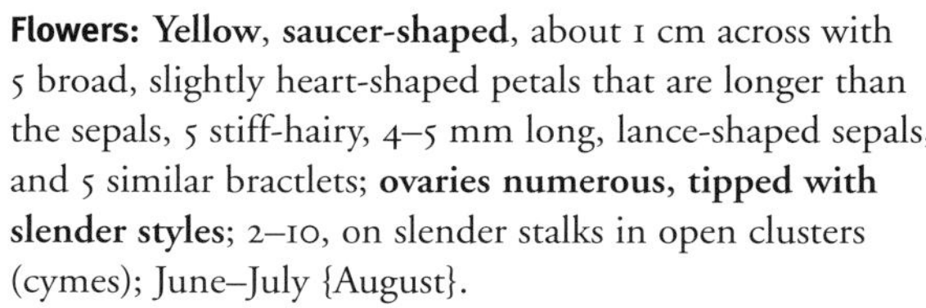

Flowers: **Yellow, saucer-shaped**, about 1 cm across with 5 broad, slightly heart-shaped petals that are longer than the sepals, 5 stiff-hairy, 4–5 mm long, lance-shaped sepals, and 5 similar bractlets; **ovaries numerous, tipped with slender styles**; 2–10, on slender stalks in open clusters (cymes); June–July {August}.

Fruits: Dry seed-like fruits (achenes), numerous, in compact clusters surrounded by persistent calyxes.

Habitat: Coulees and dry flats in prairie grassland; elsewhere, on moist to dry meadows and hillsides.

Notes: Low cinquefoil is distinguished from other *Potentilla* species in Alberta by its low-spreading stems, thick, white, flat-lying hairs and leaves with 7–15 pinnate leaflets that are green on both surfaces.

HAIRY CINQUEFOIL

Potentilla villosa Pallas *ex* Pursh
ROSE FAMILY (ROSACEAE)

LA

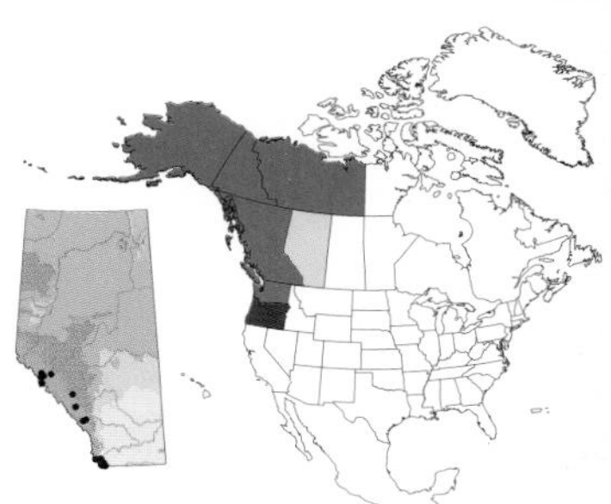

Plants: Tufted perennial herbs with **long, soft, greyish hairs,** but may be **silky-hairy throughout**; stems **8–12** {2–20} **cm tall, often branched** and curved or bent above the middle, with woolly hairs overlain by spreading hairs; from a stout, branched root crown on thick, ascending underground stems (rhizomes).

Leaves: Basal and alternate, **divided into 3 rather leathery, brownish to olive-green leaflets**, sparsely **silky-hairy on the upper surface, white-woolly with overlying silky hairs and usually prominently veined beneath**; leaflets mostly 0.5–2 cm long, egg-shaped, widest above the middle, wedge-shaped at the base, irregularly cut ⅓–⅔ of the way to the midrib into blunt lobes; 1–3 stem leaves, short-stalked; stalks mostly as long as or longer than the blades, with conspicuous toothless lobes (stipules) about 1 cm long at the base.

Flowers: Yellow, saucer-shaped, 10–15 mm across, with **5 showy, heart-shaped, 5–8 mm long petals** above a **densely silky-hairy, 7–11 mm long calyx** with 5 triangular, 3–5 {6} mm long lobes (sepals) alternating with 5 elliptic bractlets of similar size or slightly narrower; stamens usually 20; pistils numerous with slightly warty, thick-based styles attached just below the tip and about as long as the fruit; 2 {1–5}, in rather open, spreading clusters (cymes) with conspicuous, leafy bracts; June–August {September}.

Fruits: Dry seed-like fruits (achenes), smooth or with a netted pattern, {1} 1.7–2 mm long, numerous, in compact, head-like clusters.

Habitat: Alpine slopes and ridges; elsewhere, on rocky slopes and ridges, coastal bluffs and arctic tundra, rare inland.

Notes: This species has also been called *Potentilla nivea* L. var. *villosa* (Pallas *ex* Pursh) Regel & Tiling and *Potentilla villosula* Jurtz. • Two common, small alpine cinquefoils could be mistaken for hairy cinquefoil. Snow cinquefoil (*Potentilla nivea* L.) is very similar, but its plants have only cobwebby or woolly hairs, never long, silky hairs like those found on hairy cinquefoil. One-flowered cinquefoil (*Potentilla uniflora* Ledeb.) is usually a smaller (4–8 cm tall) plant with unbranched stems that bear larger (15–20 mm wide), single flowers. The veins on its lower leaf surfaces are hidden beneath dense, woolly hairs. • Hooker's cinquefoil

P. HOOKERIANA

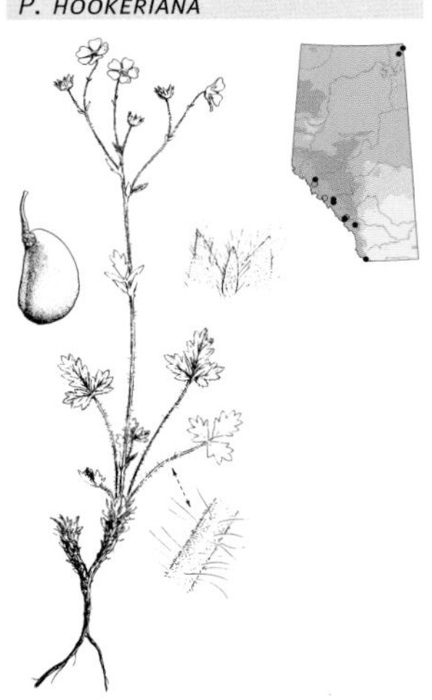

(*Potentilla hookeriana* Lehm.) is another small, rare Alberta cinquefoil, with yellow flowers and with leaves divided into 3 leaflets (trifoliate) that are densely woolly on their lower surface. It is distinguished from hairy cinquefoil by its larger flower clusters (usually more than 3 flowers) and by the absence of woolly hairs on its leaf stalks. Hooker's cinquefoil grows on dry, rocky alpine slopes, and flowers in {June} July and August. • Hairy cinquefoil is most common and widespread along the coast. Relative humidity could be a limiting factor in interior sites. • The specific epithet *villosa* is Latin for 'shaggy' or 'hairy,' in reference to the long, soft hairs of these plants.

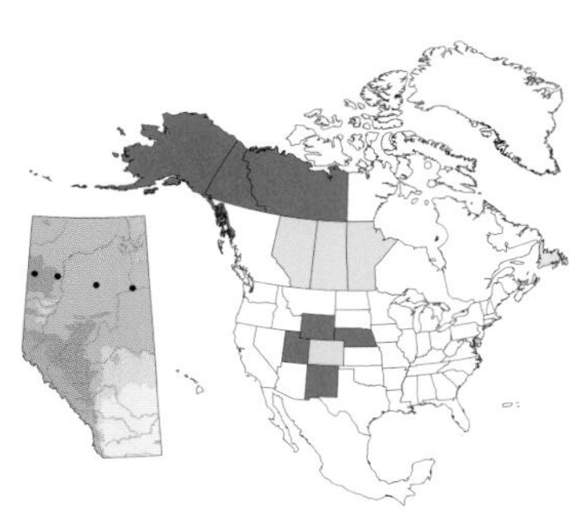

Bodin's milk vetch

Astragalus bodinii Sheldon
PEA FAMILY (FABACEAE [LEGUMINOSAE])

Plants: Mat-forming perennial herbs; stems numerous, very slender, spreading on the ground, 10–30 {60} cm long; from central taproots.

Leaves: Alternate, pinnately divided into 7–15 {19} leaflets; leaflets lance-shaped to oblong, 4–12 {2–19} mm long, hairless on the upper surface, with scattered, stiff, flat-lying hairs beneath.

Flowers: Pink to bluish purple, pea-like, 7–10 {11} mm long; calyxes tipped with 5 awl-shaped lobes 1.2–2.4 mm long, black-hairy and white-hairy; few, in loose, elongating clusters (racemes) on slender stalks up to 25 cm long; July.

Fruits: Erect, black-hairy pods, **short-stalked** (stalks less than 2 mm long, within the calyx), 5–7 {10} mm long, obliquely egg-shaped to oblong-ellipsoid, abruptly sharp-pointed, single-cavitied.

Habitat: Moist meadows and gravel banks; elsewhere, in thickets and invading disturbed ground along roads.

Notes: This species has also been called *Astragalus yukonis* M.E. Jones. • A more common species, alpine milk vetch (*Astragalus alpinus* L.), is very similar to Bodin's milk vetch, but it has larger (3–4 mm vs. 2.5 mm long) calyxes and its black-hairy pods hang on slender, 3–4 mm long stalks (within the calyxes).

LOW MILK VETCH

Astragalus lotiflorus Hook.
PEA FAMILY (FABACEAE [LEGUMINOSAE])

CWa

Plants: **Low, tufted** perennial herbs usually less than 10 cm tall, more or less **silvery with straight, parallel, flat-lying hairs** attached by the middle; stems branched, erect or spreading, {1} 2–10 cm long; from deep taproots.

Leaves: Basal, **5–10 cm long**; pinnately divided into {3} **5–15 leaflets**; leaflets oblong to elliptic, 5–15 {20} mm long, **½–⅕ as wide as they are long, pointed**; with a pair of lance-shaped, 2–5 mm long appendages (stipules) at the base of each stalk.

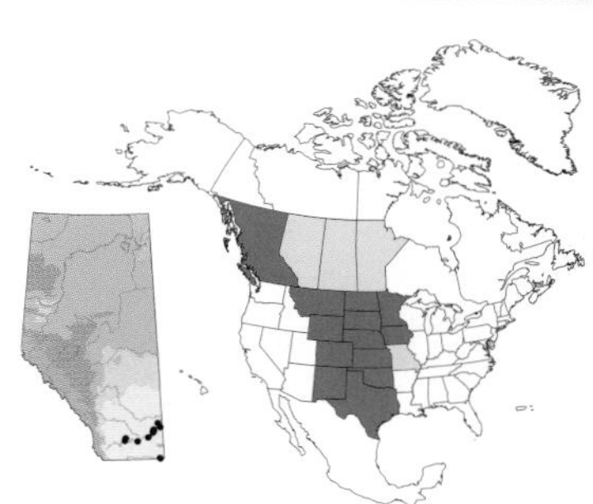

Flowers: **Yellowish white**, sometimes purplish-tinged, **7–10 mm long**, usually long and narrow, with the upper petal (banner) equal to or longer than the lower and side petals (keel and wings); calyx white-hairy, tipped with long, slender teeth; 10 stamens, 9 united, 1 free (diadelphous); 2–12, on short (1 mm) stalks in compact clusters that elongate in fruit (racemes), **often nestled among the leaves or barely taller than them**, sometimes on elongated stems up to 8 cm tall; May {June}.

Fruits: Densely hairy, rather leathery pods, inflated but slightly flattened from top to bottom, somewhat crescent-shaped, 1–2 {2.5} cm long, 6–8 mm wide, tipped with a long, firm, pointed tip (beak), stalkless (within the calyx), single-celled, covered with an interwoven mixture of woolly and stiff flattened hairs.

Habitat: Dry slopes and prairie, sandy-gravelly dune slacks in active blowout areas; elsewhere, on gravelly or sandy hillsides, pebbly or sandy lakeshores, clay, loam, silt or gravelly soil.

Notes: Pursh's milk vetch (*Astragalus purshii* Dougl. *ex* Hook. var. *purshii*) is a similar species that is also rare in Alberta. Its leaflets are only about twice as long as they are wide, with rounded tips, its hairs are attached by their bases, and its flowers are 20–30 mm long. Pursh's milk vetch grows in dry prairies in Alberta; elsewhere, it is also found in mixed grasslands and on sand plains. It is reported to flower from

A. PURSHII

JL

April to June. • Although there is a considerable amount of potential habitat in the Little Rolling Hills, low milk vetch has not been found there to date. Cultivation of native grasslands on sandier soils is probably the greatest threat to this species. Encroachment of other plants (e.g., Russian thistle [*Salsola kali* L.]) on active dune blowouts may also be a problem. It is not clear whether dunes in native grassland were kept active by periodic drought, fire, grazing or a combination of those factors. • Low milk vetch sometimes produces small, closed, self-fertilized (cleistogamous) flowers near the surface of the ground.

JG

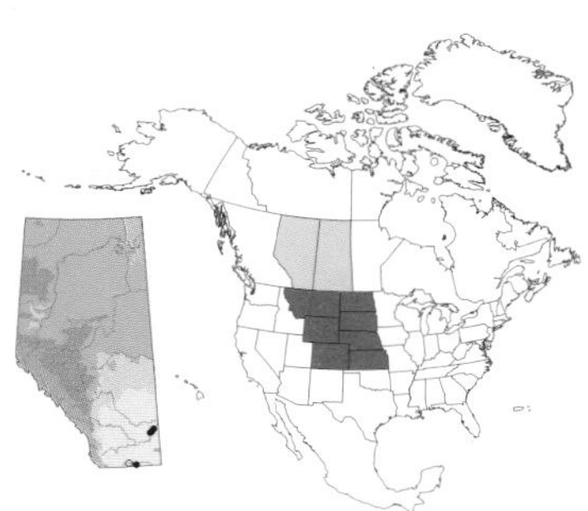

PRICKLY MILK VETCH

Astragalus kentrophyta A. Gray var. *kentrophyta*
PEA FAMILY (FABACEAE [LEGUMINOSAE])

Plants: Prostrate perennial herbs, 5–10 cm tall, with **flat-lying, parallel hairs attached by the middle**; stems spreading on the ground, branched, 10–40 cm long; forming **mats** up to 50 cm across, from strong taproots.

Leaves: Alternate, silky with flat-lying hairs, pinnately divided into **5–7 stiff, linear to lance-shaped leaflets 5–12 mm long, each tipped with a sharp spine.**

Flowers: Yellowish white, often **tinged with purple, 4–6** {7} **mm long, pea-like**; upper petal (banner) arched back; flowers **solitary or 2–4**, in small clusters (racemes) **from leaf axils**, on stalks shorter than the leaves; June–July {August–September}.

Fruits: Greyish-hairy, elliptic pods, {3} 4–7 mm long, stalkless, not splitting open.

Habitat: Dry prairies, in hard-packed or gravelly sand in blowout areas and on exposed, eroding soils, often along trails; elsewhere, in low foothills and on sand dunes.

Notes: The needle-like leaves of prickly milk vetch help to minimize water loss in the hot, dry environments where this plant thrives; its long, strong taproots anchor it in shifting sands and reach deep for water in sandy soils. These plants are known to grow in association with mycorrhizal fungi. • Dam construction could flood some populations of this species along the North Milk River.

HARE-FOOTED LOCOWEED

Oxytropis lagopus Nutt. var. *conjugens* Barneby
PEA FAMILY (FABACEAE [LEGUMINOSAE])

CWa

Plants: Silvery, silky-hairy perennial herbs, densely tufted, often cushion-like, **stemless** except for leafless, hairy flowering stalks; from taproots with branched crowns.

Leaves: Basal, ascending, covered in long silvery hairs, 3–11 cm long, **pinnately divided into 5–17 leaflets; leaflets opposite** or offset, egg-shaped to elliptic, 3–15 mm long, toothless, with edges raised or rolled inward; stalks with a pair of silky-hairy, membranous lobes (stipules) at the base (sometimes almost hairless with age).

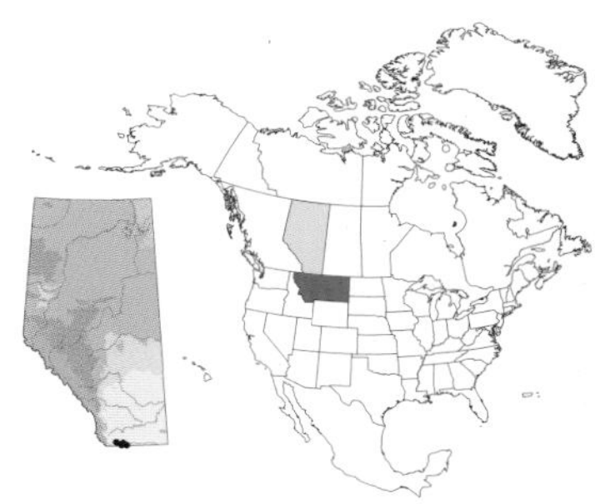

Flowers: Pink-purple or blue-purple, pea-like, 13–16 {20} mm long, with the lower 2 petals joined in a sharp-pointed keel 11–14 mm long; **calyxes** 8–11 mm long, with dense, spreading, silky, white hairs concealing the surface, **swollen to inflated when the flowers open;** 5–18 {20}, in the axils of **dark, shaggy-hairy bracts**, forming head-like to oblong, elongating clusters (racemes) 2–4 cm long on erect to arching or low-spreading stalks 2–13 cm long; late May–early June.

Fruits: Erect or spreading, papery or almost membranous **pods**, oblong to egg-shaped, covered **with spreading, silky hairs, broadly heart-shaped in cross-section**, 6–15 mm long, 4–7 mm wide, tipped with a short beak, projecting from the calyx, short-stalked (within the calyx).

Habitat: Sandy or grassy knolls and hillsides; elsewhere, on sagebrush plains.

Notes: Hare-footed locoweed might be confused with some of the smaller milk vetches (*Astragalus* spp.). These 2 genera are most easily separated by the keels of their flowers, which are blunt-tipped in milk vetches and sharply pointed in locoweeds (*Oxytropis* spp.). Milk vetches usually have leaves with stems, whereas most locoweeds are stemless, with all of their leaves arising from a root crown. • Cultivation has eliminated many sites where hare-footed locoweed may have grown, but the steepness of most remaining areas makes further cultivation difficult. Because of the abundance of gravel in suitable habitats, gravel operations now pose the largest single threat. Effects of grazing require further study, although sites are mostly inaccessible to cattle due to the steepness of the hills on which they are found.

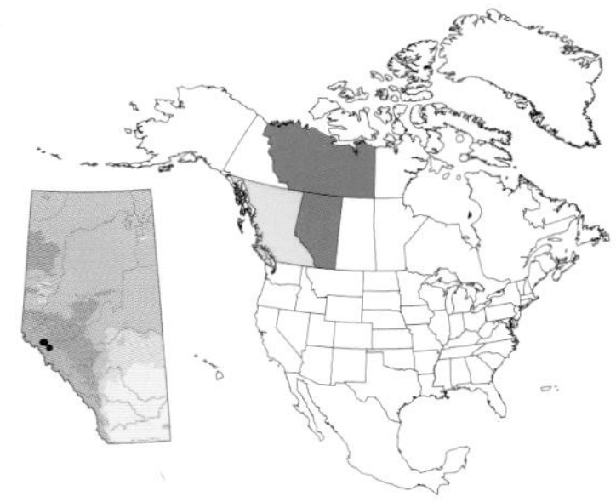

PURPLE MOUNTAIN LOCOWEED

Oxytropis jordalii Porsild var. *jordalii*
PEA FAMILY (FABACEAE [LEGUMINOSAE])

Plants: Low perennial herbs; **flowering stems leafless**, green to purplish green, 10–15 cm tall; from branched root crowns.

Leaves: Mainly basal, {4} 6–14 cm long, **pinnately divided into 9–25 leaflets** and with 2 lobes (stipules) at the base of the stalk; leaflets narrowly lance-shaped to oblong-elliptic, curved inward; stipules edged with club-like 'hairs,' otherwise hairless or with soft, spreading hairs.

Flowers: Pink or purple, pea-shaped, 11–14 mm long; keel 10–12 mm long; calyx bell-shaped, 5–7 mm long, with a mixture of black and pale hairs; **6–12**, in compact, head-like clusters that elongate when mature (racemes); June–August.

Fruits: Papery pods, oblong to egg-shaped, 8–15 mm long, thinly covered with mixed black and white hairs, **stalkless or short-stalked** (within the calyx).

Habitat: Alpine and subalpine meadows and dry ridges.

Notes: This species has been reported incorrectly for Alberta. Alberta plants identified as this species are referrable to *Oxytropis campestris* (L.) DC. var. *davisii* Welsh. • This species was named in honour of Louis Henrik Jordal (1919–52), a Norwegian collector who worked in Alaska and was a graduate student in Michigan and an author. • Many species of *Oxytropis* are **poisonous to livestock**, causing a form of insanity called 'locoism' and eventually death. To be lethal, large amounts must be eaten over a long period of time, but these plants are habit-forming, so this often happens. Late yellow locoweed (*Oxytropis monticola* A. Gray), a close relative, probably causes more livestock deaths than all other locoweeds combined. • The generic name *Oxytropis* was taken from the Greek *oxus* (sharp) and *tropis* (keel), in reference to the sharply pointed keels of the flowers.

SILVERLEAF PSORALEA

Psoralea argophylla Pursh
PEA FAMILY (FABACEAE [LEGUMINOSAE])

Plants: Silvery-hairy perennial herbs dotted with tiny glands; stems erect, 30–60 cm tall, freely wide-branched; from creeping underground stems (rhizomes).

Leaves: Alternate, densely silvery-hairy, mostly **divided into 3 leaflets** but lower leaves sometimes with 5; **leaflets** egg-shaped and widest above the middle to elliptic, **2–4 {5} cm long, 5–15 {20} mm wide**, toothless; stalks slightly longer or shorter than the blades, with a pair of slender lobes (stipules) 3–8 mm long at the base.

Flowers: Purple or deep blue, pea-like, 7–10 mm long, with the broad upper petal (banner) and 2 slender side petals (wings) all extending forward past the 2 incurved lower petals (keels); **calyxes** silvery with dense, silky hairs, the 2 mm long tube tipped with 4 slender, 2–3 mm long teeth above a lower 6 mm long tooth; several, in 1–3 well-spaced whorls of 2–4 flowers each, forming spike-like clusters 2–5 cm long, at branch tips; June–July.

Fruits: Silky-hairy, egg-shaped **pods**, about 8 mm long, tipped with a short, straight beak, thick, single-seeded, not splitting open, enclosed in a persistent calyx up to 1 cm long.

Habitat: Prairie grassland; elsewhere, on eastern slopes of the Rocky Mountains.

Notes: Silverleaf psoralea lacks the large tuberous roots of its well-known, edible relative, Indian breadroot (*Psoralea esculenta* Pursh). However, it was used by some tribes to make a medicinal wash for cleaning wounds. This plant is very common across the prairies.

JL

DJ

ARCTIC LUPINE

Lupinus arcticus S. Wats. ssp. *subalpinus* (Piper & B.L. Robins.) D. Dunn
PEA FAMILY (FABACEAE [LEGUMINOSAE])

Plants: Loosely tufted perennial herbs; stems ascending to erect, 30–50 {13–60} cm tall, few to several; from branched root crowns.

Leaves: Mainly basal, palmately divided into 5–9 leaflets; leaflets narrowly elliptic to lance-shaped, often widest above the middle, pointed, 1.3–9 cm long, 4–19 mm wide, hairless on the upper surface, with sparse, stiff, flat-lying hairs beneath; stalks long, mostly 6–21 cm long.

Flowers: Bluish purple (rarely white), **pea-like,** 15–20 mm long; upper petal (banner) bent back from slightly below the middle; numerous, in whorls, in loose (sometimes dense), elongated clusters (racemes) 4–14 cm long on 4–10 cm long stalks; August.

Fruits: Yellowish, silky-hairy pods, 2–4 cm long, containing 5–8 seeds.

Habitat: Open, grassy sites in tundra, heath and woodland in northwest North America.

Notes: *Lupinus* is a large and taxonomically difficult genus, with about 100 species in North America. Many hybridize, producing a wide range of intergrading forms and varieties. Lupines can be very 'plastic'—their size and appearance may vary greatly with different environmental conditions—and this can also make identification difficult. • The generic name *Lupinus* was taken from the Latin *lupus* (wolf) because these plants usually grew on poor land, where they were believed to rob soil of nourishment, like a wolf in the fold. In reality, lupines benefit the soil. They have nitrogen-fixing bacteria in nodules on their roots which allow them to survive on poor sites, and when the plants die and decompose, they add their accumulated nitrogen to the soil.

Wyeth's lupine

Lupinus wyethii S. Wats.
PEA FAMILY (FABACEAE [LEGUMINOSAE])

Plants: Tufted **perennial herbs**, covered with short, stiff, flat-lying, yellow hairs; flowering **stems unbranched, 40–50** {20–60} **cm tall, solid** (or only slightly hollow).

Leaves: Basal and alternate, numerous, **palmately divided into 9–11** {8–13} **leaflets; leaflets narrow**, 2–4 cm long, 2–6 mm wide, widest above the middle, abruptly narrowed to a sharp point, **yellow-hairy on both surfaces**; stalks 3–6 times as long as the blades on lower leaves but much shorter on upper leaves.

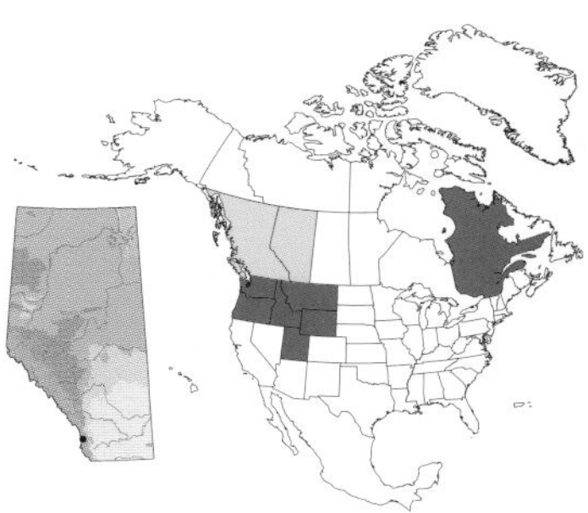

Flowers: Deep violet or purple, pea-like, 11–16 mm long; upper petal (banner) often reddish, yellowish or white-centred, **hairless, strongly bent backward**; 2 side petals (wings) hairless, curved forward and touching at the tips; 2 lower petals joined in a fringed, sickle-shaped keel with a beak-like tip; **calyx** silky-hairy, deeply **2-lipped**, the upper lip 2-toothed, **cut less than ⅓ of its length**, the lower unlobed; **10 stamens, fused** together **to form a tube** (monadelphous), with larger and smaller anthers alternating; numerous, **scattered or in whorls, forming 15–25 cm long**, elongating **clusters** (racemes) on erect stalks, well above the leaves; {July–August}.

Fruits: Flattened, hairy **pods**, 2.5–4 cm long, splitting in half lengthwise to release 4–8 greyish, mottled seeds.

Habitat: Roadside in subalpine forest and larch–whitebark pine forest; elsewhere, from sagebrush plains and valleys to montane forests to open ridges in the mountains.

Notes: Wyeth's lupine could be confused with least lupine (*Lupinus minimus* Dougl. *ex* Hook., p. 140), but least lupine is generally a smaller (10–40 cm tall), more densely hairy plant with smaller (10–12 mm long) flowers and more deeply cut upper lips on its calyxes. • Another rare species reported for Alberta, large-leaved lupine (*Lupinus polyphyllus* Lindl.), has taller (about 50–100 cm), hollow stems and larger (4–10 cm long) leaflets that are hairless on their upper surface. It grows in moist woods, on shorelines and in meadows; it is reported to flower from mid June to early September.

L. POLYPHYLLUS

DJ

LA

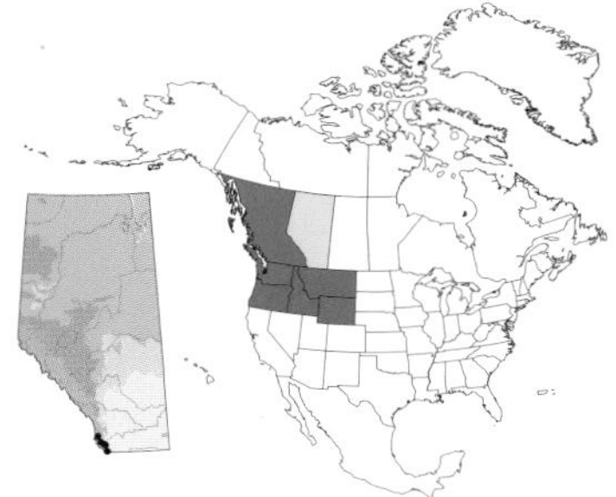

LEAST LUPINE

Lupinus minimus Dougl. *ex* Hook.
PEA FAMILY (FABACEAE [LEGUMINOSAE])

Plants: Tufted, **densely silky-hairy perennial herbs; flowering stems** 10–40 cm tall, clearly **taller than the leaves.**

Leaves: Mainly **basal** and **less than 10 cm**, plus **1–3 alternate on the stem, palmately divided into 6–8** {5–10} **leaflets**; leaflets 1.5–2.5 {1–4} cm long, lance-shaped, widest above the middle, abruptly narrowed to a sharp point, often folded in half lengthwise, densely silky-hairy on both surfaces; stalks 6–12 cm long.

Flowers: Blue, occasionally silvery-brown, **pea-like**, about **10 mm long**, with a **broad, rounded upper petal** (banner), **hairless**, strongly **bent backward** near the middle; 2 side petals (wings) curved forward and touching at the tips; 2 lower petals joined in a fringed, sickle-shaped keel with a sharp, beak-like tip; calyx deeply 2-lipped, the upper lip 2-toothed, the lower 3-lobed or unlobed; **10 stamens, fused** together **to form a tube** (monadelphous), with larger and smaller anthers alternating; several to many, **in whorls forming dense, 2–15 cm long**, elongating **clusters** (racemes) on erect, 3–10 cm long stalks; June {July–August}.

Fruits: Flattened, hairy **pods**, 2–3 cm long, splitting in half lengthwise to release 4–6 seeds.

Habitat: River flats and open gravelly areas to alpine elevations.

Notes: This species could be confused with alpine lupine (*Lupinus lepidus* Dougl. *ex* Lindl.). These 2 species are very similar, but alpine lupine is often matted and its leaves are usually over 10 cm in height, with 4 or more leaves commonly on the stem. The upper petal of its flowers is also elliptic to oblong-elliptic rather than round. Alpine lupine grows on river flats and gravelly habitats from grasslands at low elevations to alpine areas in the mountains. It is reported to flower from March to June.

Carolina Wild Geranium

Geranium carolinianum L.
GERANIUM FAMILY (GERANIACEAE)

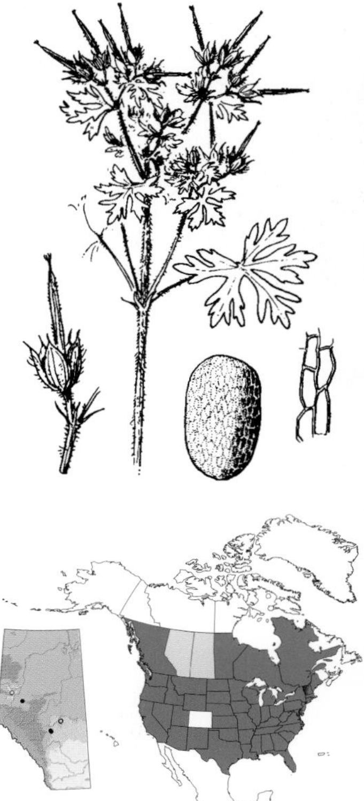

Plants: Bushy **annual** herbs, 10–50 {70} cm tall; stems usually erect, **freely branched**, with long, soft hairs that are spreading or pointing downward; without rootstocks or branched bases.

Leaves: Alternate, broadly heart-shaped to rounded, 2–7 cm wide, **cut** ⅓–½ to the base **into 5–7 radiating** (palmate), sharply toothed and lobed **segments** with wedge-shaped bases.

Flowers: Rose-purple, saucer-shaped, with 5 broad, **2–8 mm long petals**; petals rounded or with a notched tip; **sepals broadly egg-shaped**, about as long as the petals, tipped with a 1–1.5 mm long bristle, ribbed with 5 silky-hairy nerves; 10 (rarely 5) fertile stamens, in 2 unequal sets; styles joined with the elongated receptacle to form a slender **column** tipped with a short **beak 1–1.5 mm long; stalks shorter than the calyxes**, covered with tiny, downward-pointing hairs; few, in crowded, flat-topped clusters (corymbs); {April–July}.

Fruits: Hairy, awl-shaped capsules (columns) 10–15 mm long, **tipped with a 1–1.5 mm long beak** (to 2.5 mm including the free stigmas), splitting open from the base upward into 5 segments that recoil when dry and fling out the seeds (like a slingshot), borne on **stalks** that are **shorter than or slightly longer than the calyxes**, containing rounded seeds with a faint netted pattern of about 50 rows of small square or rounded hollows.

Habitat: Clearings and disturbed sites; elsewhere, on granite outcrops and in dry, rocky woods, often on sandy soil.

Notes: Western plants of this species have also been called *Geranium sphaerospermum* Fern. or *Geranium carolinianum* L. var. *sphaerospermum* (Fern.) Breitung. • Carolina wild geranium might be confused with the common weedy species Bicknell's geranium (*Geranium bicknellii* Britt.), but the fruits of Bicknell's geranium are borne on longer stalks (much longer than the calyxes) and the fruits are about 2 cm long, with 3–5 mm long beaks. • The sticky, glandular hairs and stiff, downward-pointing hairs on the upper stems and calyxes help to deter insects from climbing up to steal nectar from the flowers.

LK

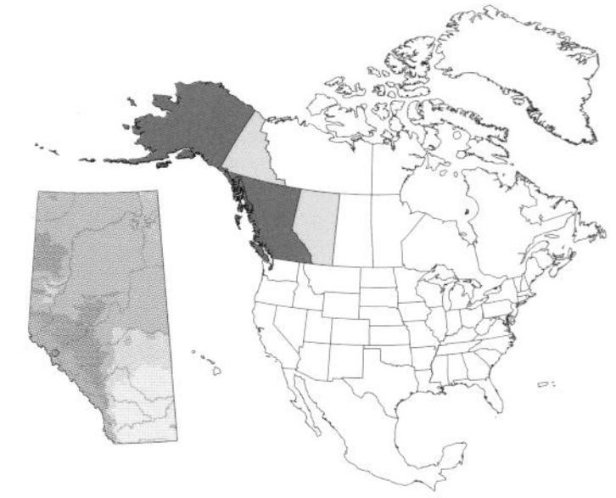

WOOLLY GERANIUM

Geranium erianthum DC.
GERANIUM FAMILY (GERANIACEAE)

Plants: Perennial herbs; stems erect or ascending, 20–80 cm tall, with downward-pointing hairs; from thick, scaly, branched underground stems (rhizomes).

Leaves: Few, alternate, 1 or 2 near the base and 1 or 2 on the stem, **wider than they are long**, usually **3–10 cm long** from the hollow between 2 lowest lobes (sinus) to the tip, **cut almost to the base into** {3} **5–7 radiating** (palmate), sharply toothed and lobed **segments**, sometimes with the edges of the 2 lowest segments overlapping, **uniformly hairy on the lower surface**, long-stalked, but stalkless on the upper stem.

Flowers: Rose to blue or violet (rarely white), very showy, saucer-shaped, with 5 broad petals; **petals 16–20 mm long, fringed near the base and soft-hairy on the lower half of the upper surface; sepals 8–12 mm long, bristle-tipped,** glandular-hairy; 10 stamens (rarely 5), in 2 unequal sets; styles joined with the elongated receptacle to form a slender, beak-like column; 2–several, on slender stalks from leaf axils, **usually not as tall as the leaves**; {June–August}.

Fruits: Cylindrical capsules tapered to **long, slender beaks,** 25–32 mm long (including the 6–9 mm long beak), splitting open from the base upward into 5 segments that recoil when dry and fling out the seeds (like a slingshot).

Habitat: Moist open woods and meadows in prairie, montane and subalpine zones; elsewhere, in willow thickets and rich meadows, from forests to above timberline.

Notes: This species has also been called *Geranium pratense* L. var. *erianthum* (DC.) Boivin. • Woolly geranium might be confused with the common species sticky purple geranium (*Geranium viscosissimum* Fisch. & Mey.), but the undersides of the leaves of sticky purple geranium are hairy only along the veins, and the flowers are much more conspicuous, clearly overtopping the leaves. • The generic name *Geranium*, from the Greek *geranos* (crane), refers to the long, slender beak of the fruits, which was thought to resemble the bill of a crane. The specific epithet *erianthum*, from the Greek *eryon* (wool) and *anthos* (flower), refers to the woolly anthers of the flowers.

FRINGED MILKWORT

Polygala paucifolia Willd.
MILKWORT FAMILY (POLYGALACEAE)

Plants: Perennial herbs, 1–14 cm tall; stems hairless, **branched toward the tip**; from slender runners (stolons).

Leaves: Alternate, **crowded near stem tip**, short-stalked or stalkless; blades **egg-shaped to oval**, pointed, **1–5 cm long**, 1–2 cm wide; lower stem leaves small to scale-like.

Flowers: Pink to rose-purple, 10–20 mm long, pea-like, with **3 petals (middle petal with a fringed crest** about 6 mm long) and 5 sepals (3 small sepals 3–6 mm long and **2 large, petal-like sepals** 10–17 mm long); 1–4, at stem tips; May–early July.

Fruits: Egg-shaped, 2-seeded capsules, 6–7 mm long, splitting open lengthwise; seeds about 3.5 mm long, egg-shaped, tipped with a small, whitish 2-lobed appendage.

Habitat: Moist coniferous or mixed woods.

Notes: Fringed milkwort produces 2 types of flowers. If the showy pink, springtime flowers (chasmogamous) are not fertilized, the plants produce small, inconspicuous flowers (cleistogamous) on short side stems near the ground surface. These self-fertilize without opening and produce seed for the following year. The leaves of fringed milkwort continue to grow to the end of the growing season. • The generic name *Polygala* was derived from the Greek *poly* (much or many) and *gala* (milk), in reference to the milky secretions of some plants of this genus, and the belief that a diet high in milkwort would increase the milk production of both domestic cows and nursing mothers. The small number of leaves of fringed milkwort is reflected in the specific epithet *paucifolia*, which means 'few-leaved.' Some people call this the 'Snoopy flower,' because it resembles a tiny, dancing Snoopy (of *Peanuts* cartoon fame).

LA

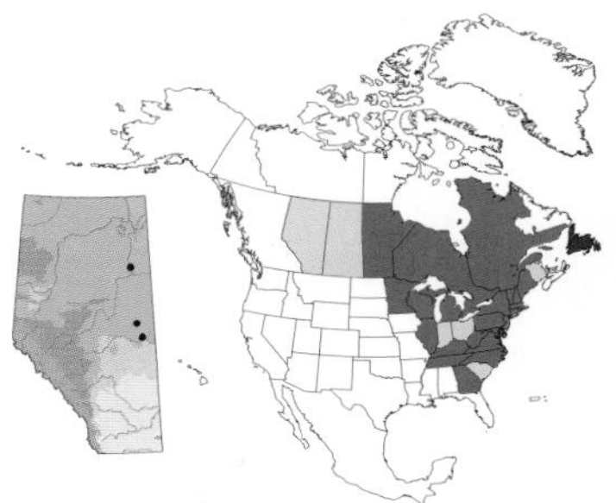

CWa

JG

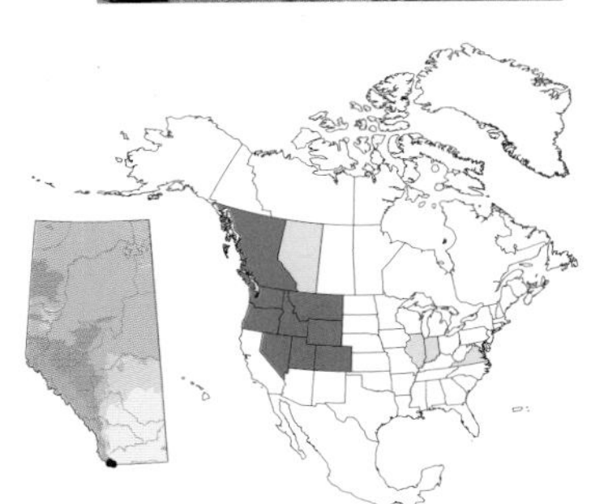

MOUNTAIN HOLLYHOCK

Iliamna rivularis (Dougl. *ex* Hook.) Greene
MALLOW FAMILY (MALVACEAE)

Plants: Stout perennial herbs with **sparse, star-shaped hairs**; stems leafy, 0.5–2 m tall; from underground stems (rhizomes).

Leaves: Alternate, **maple-leaf-shaped**, 5–15 cm wide with {3} 4–7 triangular lobes, coarsely round-toothed.

Flowers: Rose-purple to pink or nearly white, cup-shaped, about 3–4 cm across, with 5 broad petals each about 2 cm long; **sepals 3–5 mm long**, blunt-tipped, above 3 slender bracts; **on short** (less than 1 cm), **stout stalks;** stamen with filaments fused into a tube tipped with a cluster of separate anthers; styles slender, tipped with head-like stigmas; in long, loose clusters (racemes); July {August–September}.

Fruits: Hairy, oblong, wedge-shaped segments (carpels) about 8 mm long, arranged like wedges on a wheel of cheese, splitting to release 2–4 seeds.

Habitat: Moist foothill and montane slopes and meadows, often along roads and streams.

Notes: This species has also been called *Sphaeralcea rivularis* (Dougl. *ex* Hook.) Torr. *ex* Gray. • These showy flowers look like miniature garden hollyhocks. Their fruits break into sections, like the segments of an orange, and these are easily collected and planted in a garden. But be forewarned: some people find that the stiff hairs **irritate their skin**. • In some areas, mountain hollyhock is the first species to appear after a forest fire.

WESTERN ST. JOHN'S-WORT

Hypericum scouleri Hook.
ST. JOHN'S-WORT FAMILY (CLUSIACEAE [HYPERICACEAE])

CWa

Plants: Perennial herbs, 20–40 {10–80} cm tall; stems many, erect, hairless, with reddish buds; from spreading, horizontal underground stems (rhizomes).

Leaves: Opposite, oblong to egg-shaped, blunt-tipped, **1–3 cm long, black-dotted along edges**, stalkless, slightly clasping.

Flowers: Bright yellow, about 2–2.5 cm across, with **5 broad petals edged with black dots or teeth** and 5 black-dotted sepals ½ as long as the petals; **75–100 stamens** gathered in 3 bundles; few, in leafy, open clusters (cymes); late July–early August.

Fruits: Membranous capsules, 6–9 mm long, slightly 3-lobed, containing yellowish, net-veined seeds up to 1 mm long.

Habitat: Moist slopes, ledges and shores in alpine and subalpine areas.

Notes: This species has also been called *Hypericum formosum* H.B.K. var. *scouleri* (Hook.) C.L. Hitchc. • Large St. John's-wort (*Hypericum majus* (Gray) Britt.), another rare Alberta plant, is an annual species with small, inconspicuous flowers in which the petals and sepals are both about 4–5 mm long and the petals have no black dots. Its leaves are blunt-tipped, and they have 5–7 strong, parallel nerves. It grows on wet sites in the plains, foothills and boreal forest, and flowers from late June to September. • Two compounds found in St. John's-wort plants (hypericin and pseudohypericin) have been found to be potent antiviral agents with no serious side-effects, so St. John's-wort is being studied for use in the treatment of AIDS. Hypericin, extracted from the dark dots on the leaves and flowers, is used as an antidepressant.

H. MAJUS

JH

ES

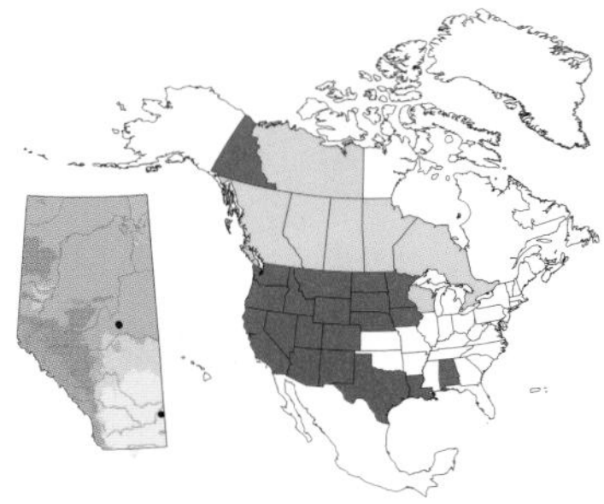

THREE-STAMENED WATERWORT, MUD CRUD

Elatine triandra Schk.
WATERWORT FAMILY (ELATINACEAE)

Plants: Small, tufted, **semi-aquatic** annual herbs; stems slender, spreading on the ground, rooting at the joints, sending up erect 2–15 cm tall branches; **often forming mats.**

Leaves: Opposite, essentially toothless, hairless, **linear to spatula-shaped, 3–8 mm long**, squared or notched at the tip, tapered to short stalks at the base.

Flowers: Very small and inconspicuous, about 2 mm long, with {2} 3 sepals and {2} 3 petals attached at base of a single ovary; 3 stamens; **solitary, in leaf axils**; {early summer–fall}.

Fruits: Membranous, **2- or 3-celled capsules, splitting lengthwise along the partitions** to release many straight or slightly curved, cylindrical seeds, honeycombed with 8–10 lengthwise rows of 9–25 {27} angular pits.

Habitat: Shallow water and mud flats, mostly by ponds and slow-moving streams.

Notes: Some taxonomists divide this species into 3 varieties: var. *americana* (Pursh) Fassett, var. *brachysperma* (A. Gray) Fassett (sometimes called *Elatine brachysperma* A. Gray) and var. *triandra*. The last 2 varieties have been found in Alberta. • Ducks enjoy eating these tender semi-aquatic plants. • The origin of the generic name *Elatine* is unclear. Some say it was derived from the Greek *elatino* (fir-like), and others report that it is the ancient name of some obscure herb. The specific epithet *triandra* comes from the Greek *tri* (three) and *andros* (male), referring to the 3 stamens in the tiny flowers.

MACLOSKEY'S VIOLET, NORTHERN WHITE VIOLET

Viola pallens (Banks *ex* DC.) Brainerd
VIOLET FAMILY (VIOLACEAE)

JS

Plants: Small perennial herbs, usually 3–6 cm tall; **stems absent**, leaves and flower stalks all growing from the base of the plant; with slender, **creeping underground stems** (rhizomes) and white, **thread-like runners** (stolons).

Leaves: Basal, broadly heart-shaped, longer than they are wide, **1–3 cm long**, rounded or blunt-pointed, **hairless**, edged with indistinct to prominent, rounded teeth; stipules thin, lance-shaped, with tiny glandular teeth; stalks 2–4 cm long.

LA

Flowers: 5-petalled, **white** (even on the back) **with purple lines** (pencilling) on the 3 lower petals, bilaterally symmetric, 5–14 mm long; **side petals usually with a few short hairs** at the base, lowest petal projecting back from its base in a short, fairly prominent spur; solitary, nodding, on leafless stalks, usually taller than the leaves; May–July {August}.

Fruits: Rounded to cylindrical, **hairless capsules**, greenish, splitting into 3 parts; seeds numerous, black at maturity, with a small swelling near the base, 1–1.3 mm long, ejected by force.

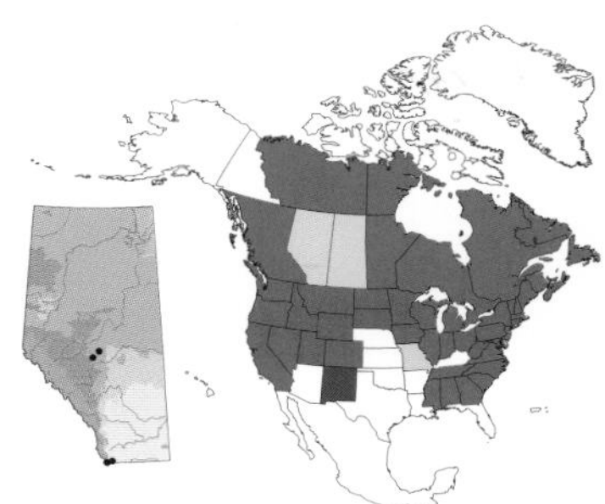

Habitat: Wet ground in moist woods; elsewhere, most common in coniferous stands and bogs; often on sphagnum hummocks, but also in swamps and wet thickets, hollows, crevices and meadows.

Notes: This taxon is often treated as a subspecies of *Viola macloskeyi* Lloyd (*Flora of Alberta* [Moss 1983]). True *Viola macloskeyi* is known only from Oregon and California. • Kidney-leaved violet (*Viola renifolia* A. Gray) could be confused with Macloskey's violet, but its plants do not have stolons, its side petals always lack hairs, and its leaves are often hairy and larger (2–6 cm wide). • Macloskey's violet is also very similar to marsh violet (*Viola palustris* L.), but marsh violet usually has blue to violet-coloured petals, and its leaves are usually wider (2.5–3.5 cm wide) and heart-shaped to kidney-shaped. • Another rare Alberta species, broad-leaved yellow prairie violet (*Viola praemorsa* Dougl. *ex* Lindl. ssp. *linguifolia* (Nutt.) M.S. Baker & J.C. Klausen *ex* M.E. Peck, also called *Viola nuttallii* Pursh var. *linguifolia* (Nutt.) Jepson), has yellow flowers, and its slender, narrowly

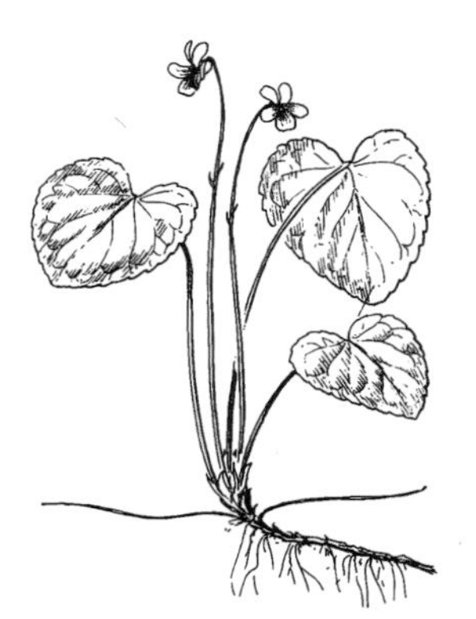

V. PRAEMORSA

LA

egg-shaped to lance-shaped leaves have wedge-shaped bases that taper to their stalks (rather unusual for a violet). It grows in dry, open forests at low elevations and flowers in July. It is distinguished from the common yellow prairie violet (*Viola nuttallii* Pursh) by its long-hairy, slightly broader blades (usually less than 3 times as long as wide), which have rounded tips. The leaf blades of common yellow prairie violet are usually at least 3 times as long as they are wide, and they have pointed tips. • Violets produce 2 kinds of flowers. The showy flowers that we recognize as violets appear in the spring. Their nectar-filled spurs and delicately lined petals attract insects, which carry pollen from one bloom to the next. Normally only a small percentage of these flowers are pollinated, so most plants produce inconspicuous (cleistogamous) flowers in the summer. These flowers have small (or no) petals, and they never open, but most produce seed through self-fertilization within the closed calyx.

CROWFOOT VIOLET

Viola pedatifida G. Don
VIOLET FAMILY (VIOLACEAE)

Plants: Low perennial herbs; **stems absent**, leaves and flower stalks all growing from base of plant; with **short, vertical underground stems** (rhizomes) up to 5 mm thick.

Leaves: Basal, **palmately divided into 3 parts and each part cut into 2–4 linear lobes**, usually **wedge-shaped at the base**, up to 10 cm wide, hairy to nearly hairless, edged with tiny hairs.

Flowers: Showy, **bright violet**, bilaterally symmetric, **1–2 cm long**, with 5 showy petals and 5 persistent, lobed sepals; 3 lower petals hairy (bearded) at base; lowest petal projecting back from its base in a short, fairly prominent spur; **solitary, nodding**, on leafless stalks from rhizomes, taller than the leaves; {April} May–June.

Fruits: Yellowish grey, hairless capsules, 10–15 mm long; seeds numerous, 2 mm long, light brown, with a small swelling near the base, ejected by force.

Habitat: Dry gravelly hills and exposed banks in prairie grassland.

Notes: Some violets disperse their seeds explosively. The walls of the drying capsules build up pressure as they fold inward, and eventually the seeds are catapulted into the air. Some violet seeds have swellings or 'oil bodies,' which attract ants. The ants often carry the seeds some distance before eating the oil body.

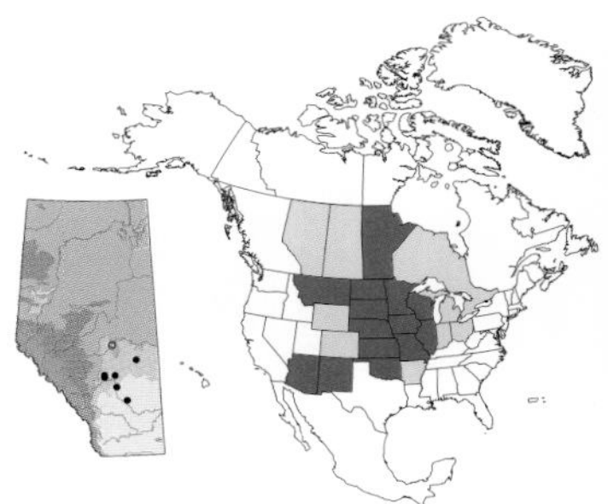

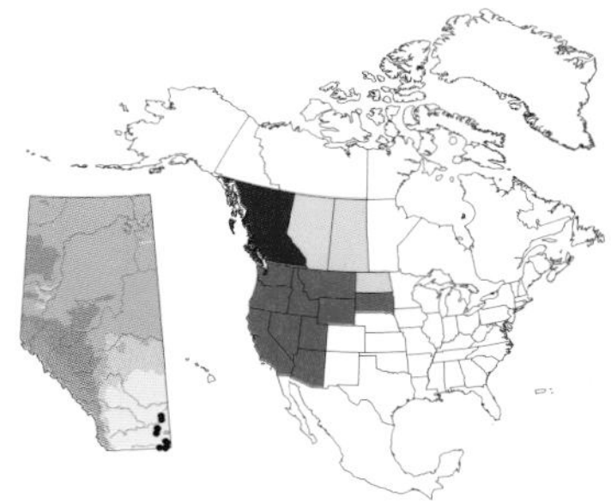

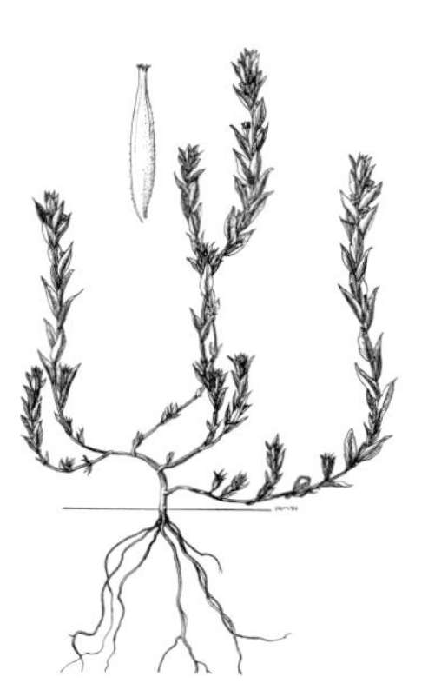

SMOOTH BOISDUVALIA

Boisduvalia glabella (Nutt.) Walp.
EVENING-PRIMROSE FAMILY (ONAGRACEAE)

Plants: **Low-growing annual** herbs, pale greenish, hairless or with sparse, flat-lying hairs; stems spreading and lying on the ground, 10–30 cm long, usually **branched from near the base**; from slender taproots.

Leaves: Alternate, numerous and fairly evenly spaced; blades **lance-shaped, 10–15** {5–18} **mm long**, 3–6 mm wide, **edged with small teeth** or toothless, stalkless.

Flowers: Pinkish or purplish red, **inconspicuous**, with **4 sepals, 4 petals and 8 stamens on a receptacle** (hypanthium) **at the tip of an elongating, stalk-like ovary**; sepals erect; petals 2–4 mm long, deeply 2-lobed; styles single; **anthers erect, attached near their base**; single in upper leaf axils, crowded near the stem tips, forming elongating, leafy clusters (racemes); {June–July}.

Fruits: Slender, 4-ribbed capsules, 6–8 mm long, 1–1.5 mm wide, slightly curved and pointed, finely hairy, with **4 cavities** each containing 6–14 seeds; **seeds** about 1 mm long, brownish, hairy but **lacking a tuft of hairs** (not comose); mid to late August.

Habitat: Mud flats, especially on alkaline clays, in the prairies; elsewhere, on dried streambanks and slough bottoms and in moist depressions or mud flats.

Notes: Some taxonomists now classify this species as *Epilobium pygmaeum* (Speg.) P. Hoch & Raven. • The generic name *Boisduvalia* commemorates Jean Alphonse Boisduval (1801–79), a French naturalist and author of a flora of France.

SHRUBBY EVENING-PRIMROSE

Calylophus serrulatus (Nutt.) Raven
EVENING-PRIMROSE FAMILY (ONAGRACEAE)

JL

Plants: Erect perennial sub-shrubs, sparsely hairy to pale grey with dense, fine, flat-lying hairs; stems slender, 10–50 {60} cm tall, usually **many-branched from the base**, leafy; from branched, **somewhat woody root crowns.**

Leaves: Alternate, with **bunches of small leaves in the axils of larger leaves**; blades linear to oblong or spatula-shaped, {1} 2–5 cm long, 3–10 mm wide, edged with few to many fine sharp teeth, sometimes toothless.

Flowers: Yellow, with **4 sepals, 4 petals and 8 stamens on a funnel-shaped, 4-angled, 6–15 mm long receptacle** (hypanthium) **at the tip of an elongating, stalk-like ovary; sepals separate**, spreading or **bent backward**, ridged lengthwise on the back; petals 8–25 mm long, edged with fine, rounded teeth; stamens scarcely ½ as long as the petals, with **anthers attached near their middle**; styles shorter than the stamens, tipped with a shallowly 4-lobed, disc-shaped stigma; stalkless in upper leaf axils, forming elongating clusters (racemes); {May} June–July.

Fruits: Slender capsules, 15–25 {30} mm long, greyish white with fine hairs, splitting lengthwise into **4 compartments; seeds numerous, lacking a tuft of hairs** (not comose).

Habitat: Sandy prairies and dunes; elsewhere, in moist depressions in grasslands, gravel flats, disturbed sites and dry fields.

Notes: This species has also been called *Oenothera serrulata* Nutt.

CWa

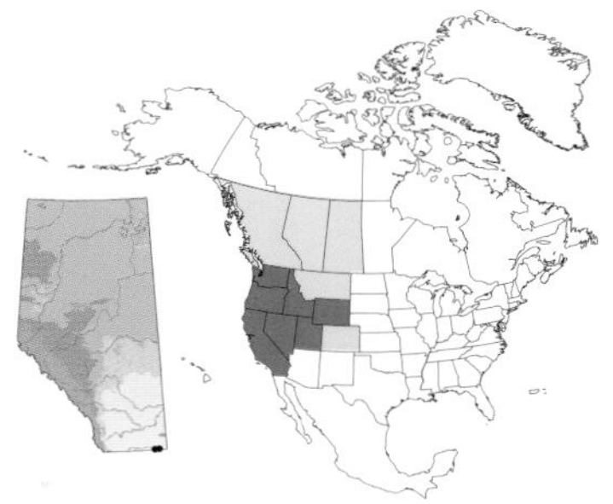

UPLAND EVENING-PRIMROSE

Camissonia andina (Nutt.) Raven
EVENING-PRIMROSE FAMILY (ONAGRACEAE)

Plants: Small **annual herbs**, often wider than they are tall, **greyish** with fine, close hairs; **stems slender, 3–10 {15} cm long, branched** from near the base, **ascending and leafy near the tips**, spreading and essentially leafless near the base; from weak taproots.

Leaves: Alternate; blades **linear to narrowly lance-shaped** and widest above the middle, {5} 10–30 mm long, 0.5–2 mm wide, toothless; stalks short.

Flowers: Lemon-yellow, tiny and inconspicuous, with **4 petals, 4 sepals and 8 stamens on a receptacle** (hypanthium) **less than 2 cm long at the tip of an elongating, stalk-like ovary**, stalkless; **sepals bent backward**; petals 1–1.5 mm long, egg-shaped; stamens short, with oval **anthers, 0.5 mm long and attached near their middle**; stigma head-like, projecting past the petals on an elongated style; single in the upper leaf axils, forming narrow, crowded, leafy clusters (spikes); May {June–July}.

Fruits: Spindle-shaped, 4-sided **capsules**, thickened at the base, 6 {4–8} mm long, greyish white with fine hairs, splitting lengthwise into **4 compartments** to release many **seeds without tufts of hairs** (not comose).

Habitat: Dry prairie slopes, flats and depressions, on moist sandy soil; elsewhere, on exposed sandy soil, in moist swales on south-facing hillsides, and in sagebrush areas.

Notes: This species has also been called *Oenothera andina* Nutt. • Upland evening-primrose cannot tolerate heavy grazing; however, minor disturbance from moderate grazing may be needed to provide a suitable seedbed of exposed soil. • A Washington variety, var. *hilgardii* (Greene) Munz (sometimes called *Camissonia hilgardii* (Greene) Raven), has much larger flowers, with petals up to 4.5 mm long.

TARAXIA, SHORT-FLOWERED EVENING-PRIMROSE

Camissonia breviflora (Torr. & Gray) Raven
EVENING-PRIMROSE FAMILY (ONAGRACEAE)

PL

Plants: Low, tufted **perennial** herbs, **5–10 cm tall**, more or less densely covered with fine, close hairs, **without flowering stems; from long taproots.**

Leaves: In a basal rosette; blades lance-shaped, often widest above the middle, **5–10** {3–15} **cm long** and 5–15 mm wide, deeply cut into many **pinnate lobes**; stalks slender, ½–⅔ as long as the blades.

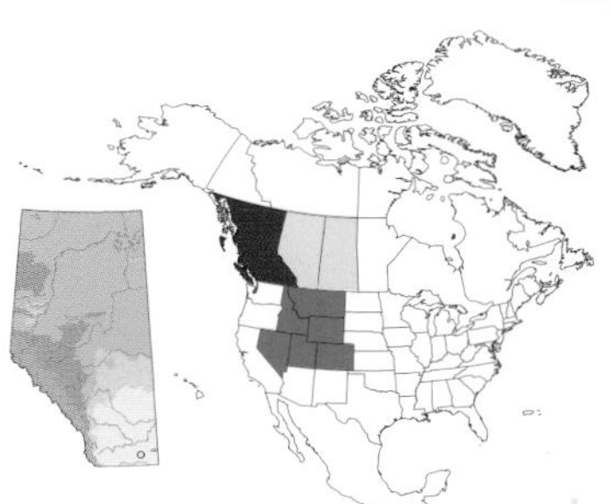

Flowers: Yellow (not purplish with age), cupped, about 1 cm across, with **4 sepals, 4 petals and 8 stamens on a flared, 10–25 mm long receptacle** (hypanthium) **at the tip of an elongating, stalk-like ovary; sepals bent backward; petals 5–8** {10} **mm long**; stamens unequal, the longer 4 slightly more than ½ as long as the petals; style about the same length as the petals, tipped with a **round, slightly lobed stigma**; few to several, **nestled among the leaves**, arising **from the root crown**; {June} July.

Fruits: Hairy, leathery, **narrowly egg-shaped to oblong to spindle-shaped capsules** tapered toward the tip, 4-sided, **15** {10–25} **mm long**, roughened with many rounded bumps, **splitting lengthwise into 4 compartments; seeds numerous, lacking a tuft of hairs** (not comose); May–July.

Habitat: Clay flats, including dry slough bottoms and alkaline shores; elsewhere, in dry meadows and on streambanks.

Notes: This species has also been called *Oenothera breviflora* T. & G. and *Taraxia breviflora* (T. & G.) Nutt. • Another rare Alberta species, low yellow evening-primrose (*Oenothera flava* (A. Nels.) Garrett), is similar to taraxia but is distinguished by its stigma, which has 4 linear, 3 mm long lobes, and by its larger, 12–18 {10–20} mm long petals. The flowers of low yellow evening-primrose turn purple with age, and the 2–3 cm long capsules are winged on all 4 angles. It grows on clay flats and slough edges and is reported to flower in July and August. • Low yellow evening-primrose could be confused with the common butte-primrose (*Oenothera caespitosa* Nutt.), but butte-primrose has white (pink with age) petals that are more than 2 cm long, and its capsules are not winged.

OENOTHERA FLAVA

CWa

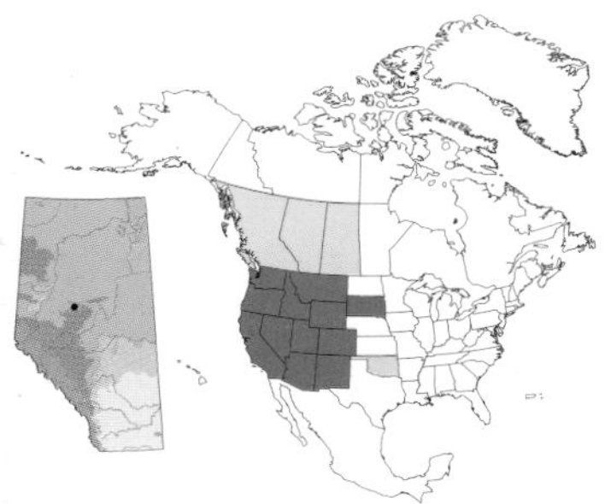

E. SAXIMONTANUM

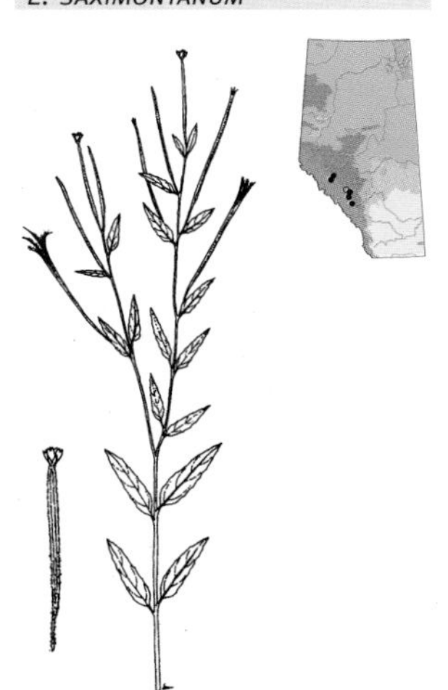

Hall's willowherb

Epilobium halleanum Hausskn.
EVENING-PRIMROSE FAMILY (ONAGRACEAE)

Plants: Slender perennial herbs; **stems erect, 2–60 cm tall,** usually simple, with **lines of stiff hairs running down from the leaf bases,** usually with stiff and glandular hairs on upper parts; from slender underground runners (rhizomes) with **clusters of small, round, compact bulbs** (turions) near the stem base.

Leaves: Opposite; blades lance-shaped, 5–47 mm long, 3–14 mm wide, edged with short, stiff hairs but otherwise mostly hairless, toothless or edged with small, conspicuous teeth; **stalks present,** sometimes short.

Flowers: White, often fading to pink, with **4 sepals, 4 petals and 8 stamens on a receptacle** (hypanthium) about 2 mm long at the tip of an elongating, stalk-like ovary; sepals green, 1.2–2.8 mm long, hairless or sparsely glandular-hairy; petals 1.6–5.5 mm long, notched; stamens of 2 lengths, with anthers 0.3–0.9 mm long; ovary 10–14 mm long, usually densely covered with glandular and low, stiff hairs (rarely hairless); styles 0.8–5 mm long tipped with a **club-shaped stigma;** few to several, on slender stalks in elongating clusters (racemes), nodding in bud; July.

Fruits: Slender capsules, 24–60 mm long, hairless to hairy (not glandular), **on stalks 8–38 mm long,** splitting lengthwise into 4 compartments; **seeds** numerous, narrowly egg-shaped, **1.1–1.6 mm long, less than 0.8 mm wide,** rough **with tiny bumps** (papillae), tipped with a **3–6 mm long tuft of white hairs** (coma), which **easily breaks away;** July.

Habitat: Moist ground; elsewhere, in moist coniferous forests.

Notes: This species has also been included in *Epilobium glandulosum* Lehm. var. *macounii* (Trel.) C.L. Hitchc.
• Hall's willowherb is similar to another rare species, Rocky Mountain willowherb (*Epilobium saximontanum* Hausskn.), which differs by having stalkless, clasping leaves that are often wider (4–24 mm) than those of Hall's willowherb. The underground bulbs (turions) of Rocky Mountain willowherb are longer and fleshier than those of Hall's willowherb, the capsules are stalkless (rather than stalked), and the seeds have a conspicuous collar (inconspicuous on seeds of Hall's willowherb). Rocky Mountain willowherb

grows in moist montane and subalpine meadows and on streambanks; it flowers in July and August. • Another small willowherb has falsely been reported to occur in Alberta. Oregon willowherb (*Epilobium oreganum* Greene, also called *Epilobium exaltatum* Drew) is very similar to Rocky Mountain willowherb, and some taxonomists consider both species part of the same variety (*Epilobium ciliatum* Lehm. var. *glandulosum* (Lehm.) Hoch & Raven). It is distinguished by its thicker (almost as wide as long) flower tube and spreading (rather than almost erect) sepals, and by the many spreading branches on its slender stems. It grows in similar moist sites and flowers in July and August. • The generic name *Epilobium* comes from the Greek *epi* (upon) and *lob* (pod), in reference to the pod-like fruit that develops from the base of the fading flower.

SLENDER-FRUITED WILLOWHERB

Epilobium leptocarpum Hausskn.
EVENING-PRIMROSE FAMILY (ONAGRACEAE)

Plants: Delicate perennial herbs, often loosely clumped, **upper leaf axils sometimes with bud-like growths** (gemmae), which fall off and grow into new plants; stems erect to ascending, 8–30 cm tall, branched, hairless except for **lines of stiff hairs running down from the leaf bases;** from slender underground runners (rhizomes) with **small, round bulbs** (turions) underground and at the base of the stem.

Leaves: Opposite; blades narrowly lance-shaped to elliptic, 8–40 mm long, 4–13 mm wide, sparsely hairy along the edges but otherwise hairless, **toothed toward the tip;** stalks winged and 3–5 mm long on lower leaves, absent on upper leaves.

Flowers: White (fading to pink), with **4 sepals, 4 petals and 8 stamens on a receptacle** (hypanthium) **at the tip of an elongating, stalk-like ovary;** sepals lance-shaped, 2.9–4 mm long, with straight, stiff, flat-lying hairs; petals 4–6.5 mm long, notched; stamens of 2 sizes with anthers 0.4–0.8 mm long; ovaries 12–19 mm long, densely covered with straight, stiff hairs; styles 3.2–3.8 mm long, tipped

E. GLABERRIMUM

with a **broadly club-shaped stigma**; several, in nodding to somewhat erect, elongated clusters (racemes); July–August.

Fruits: Slender capsules, 25–55 mm long, 1–2 mm wide, sparsely hairy, split lengthwise to reveal 4 compartments; **seeds numerous, 0.8–1.2 mm long, rough with tiny bumps** (papillae), tipped with a **persistent tuft of tawny, reddish, 3–6 mm long hairs** (coma); {August}.

Habitat: Moist, open, stony slopes.

Notes: This species has also been included in *Epilobium glandulosum* Lehm. var. *macounii* (Trel.) C.L. Hitchc. • Another rare species, pale willowherb (*Epilobium glaberrimum* Barbey ssp. *fastigiatum* (Nutt.) Hoch & Raven, also called *Epilobium platyphyllum* Rydb., *Epilobium fastigiatum* Nutt. var. *glaberrimum* (Barbey) Piper and *Epilobium affine* Bong. var. *fastigiatum* Nutt.), has hairless stems, often with a greyish, waxy appearance (glaucous), and stalkless leaves. Its flowers are pink to rose-purple, and its seeds are 0.8–1 mm long with distinct rows of small bumps (papillae). Pale willowherb grows on rocky mountain slopes and streambanks and in moist forests and meadows. It flowers in {July} August and produces fruit in August and September. • A species of subalpine scree slopes, wonderful willowherb (*Epilobium mirabile* Trel., also called *Epilobium clavatum* Trel. var. *glareosum* (G.N. Jones) Munz) has also been reported from Alberta. It is distinguished from pale willowherb by its white flowers, densely close-hairy stems and larger (1.7–2.2 mm long) seeds, which are covered with netted veins.

E. MIRABILE

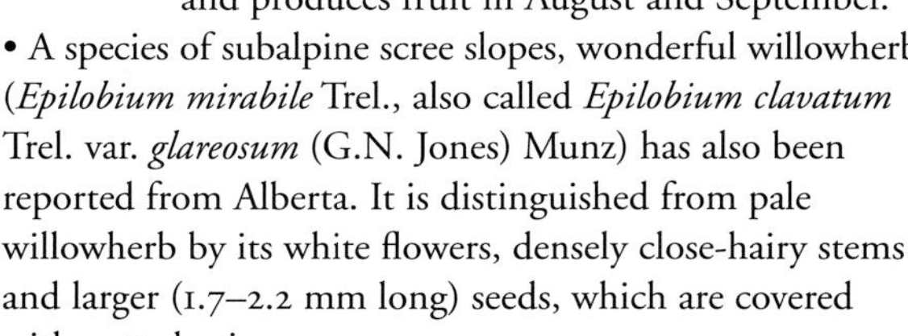

CLUB WILLOWHERB

Epilobium clavatum Trel.
EVENING-PRIMROSE FAMILY (ONAGRACEAE)

Plants: Clumped perennial herbs; **stems ascending, 5–22 cm tall, with lines of stiff, flat-lying hairs running down the stem from the leaf bases**, also with stiff and glandular hairs on the upper stems; forming large clumps from **scaly underground stems** (rhizomes) that send out **numerous wiry shoots and suckers** (soboles).

Leaves: Opposite; blades egg-shaped to elliptic, **12–28 mm long**, 6–16 mm wide, hairless or with sparse hairs on the midrib and edges, **toothless** (sometimes finely toothed); stalks 0–3 mm long.

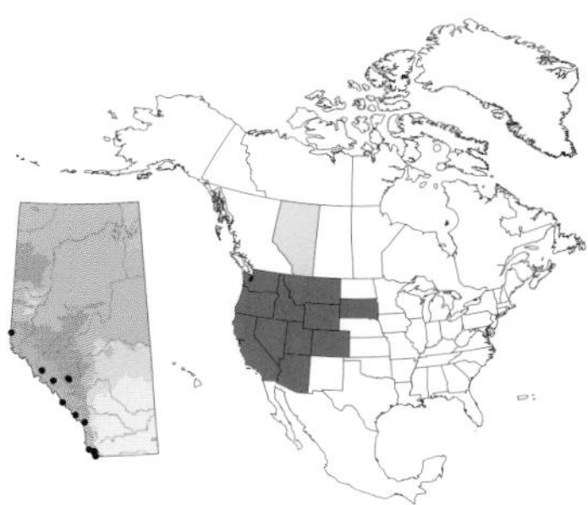

Flowers: Pink to rose-purple, with **4 sepals, 4 petals and 8 stamens on a receptacle** (hypanthium) **at the tip of an elongating, stalk-like ovary**; sepals 2.5–4.2 mm long, hairless or sparsely glandular-hairy; petals 36–60 mm long, notched; stamens of 2 sizes, with anthers 0.4–0.9 mm long; ovaries 8–20 mm long; styles 1.4–3.2 mm long, tipped with a narrowly club-shaped to head-like stigma; few, in **erect, usually glandular-hairy, elongating clusters** (racemes); July–August {June–September}.

Fruits: Club-shaped capsules, 2–4 cm long, hairless or sparsely hairy, splitting lengthwise into 4 compartments; **seeds** numerous, narrowly egg-shaped, widest above the middle, **1.3–2 mm long**, net-veined or rough with tiny bumps (papillae), tipped with a **5–15 mm long tuft of white hairs** (coma) which **breaks away easily**.

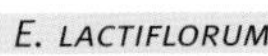
E. LACTIFLORUM

Habitat: Moist alpine slopes.

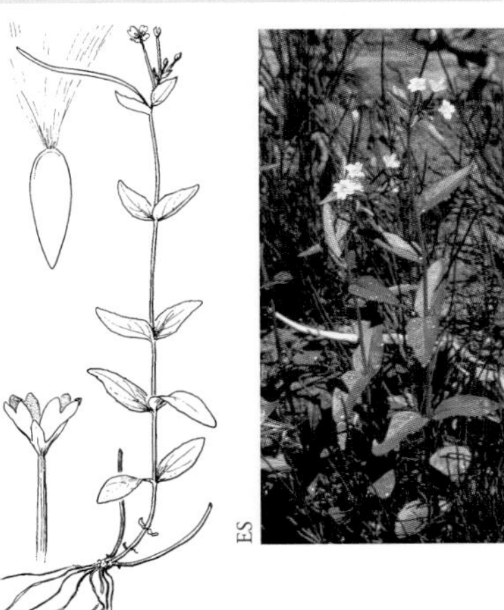
ES

Notes: A similar species, white willowherb (*Epilobium lactiflorum* Hausskn.), is also rare in Alberta. White willowherb is a larger plant, with taller (15–50 cm) stems, larger (20–55 mm long), toothed leaf blades, and longer (5–10 cm) capsules. As its name suggests, it has white flowers, though these are occasionally pink-tinged or marked with red veins. White willowherb grows at slightly lower elevations, on moist montane and subalpine slopes, and flowers from June to August.

JH

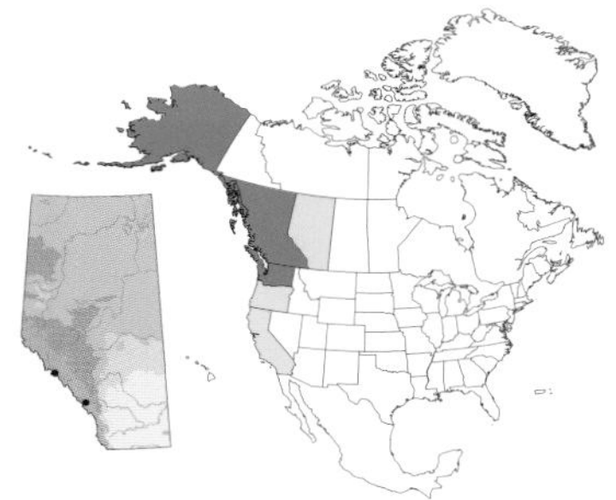

YELLOW WILLOWHERB

Epilobium luteum Pursh

EVENING-PRIMROSE FAMILY (ONAGRACEAE)

Plants: Robust perennial herbs; stems erect, several, sometimes branched above, 15–75 cm tall, with **lines of hairs running down from the leaf bases**; from scaly, underground runners (rhizomes) that send out numerous wiry shoots and suckers (soboles); occasionally with condensed bulbs (turions) at the stem base.

Leaves: Mostly opposite; blades egg-shaped (sometimes elliptic), 25–78 mm long, 12–35 mm wide, edged with fine, translucent teeth, hairless except for sparse, straight hairs on the midrib and edges; stalks short or absent.

Flowers: Yellow or cream-coloured, with **4 sepals, 4 petals and 8 stamens on a 1–2 mm tall, cupped receptacle** (hypanthium) **at the tip of an elongating, stalk-like ovary**; sepals narrowly lance-shaped, 10–12 {8–13} mm long, densely covered with glands; petals 12–22 mm long, heart-shaped with shallowly notched tips; stamens of 2 lengths, with anthers 22–30 mm long; ovaries 20–35 mm long, densely covered with glands; **styles erect**, 15–22 mm long, **extending beyond the petals, tipped with a broadly 4-lobed stigma**; 2–10, on 5–30 mm long stalks, borne singly in upper leaf axils, forming elongating clusters (racemes), nodding in bud; {July} August–September.

Fruits: Erect, linear capsules, 35–75 mm long, splitting lengthwise into **4 compartments**; **seeds** numerous, **1–1.2 mm long**, tapered to a long, slender point, net-veined, tipped **with a persistent, reddish tuft of 6.5–8 mm long hairs** (coma); {July} August–September.

Habitat: Moist woods and streambanks in the mountains.

Notes: This is the only willowherb in Alberta that has yellow flowers. The specific epithet *luteum* means 'yellow.'

LOW WILLOWHERB, GROUNDSMOKE

Gayophytum racemosum Nutt. *ex* T. & G.
EVENING-PRIMROSE FAMILY (ONAGRACEAE)

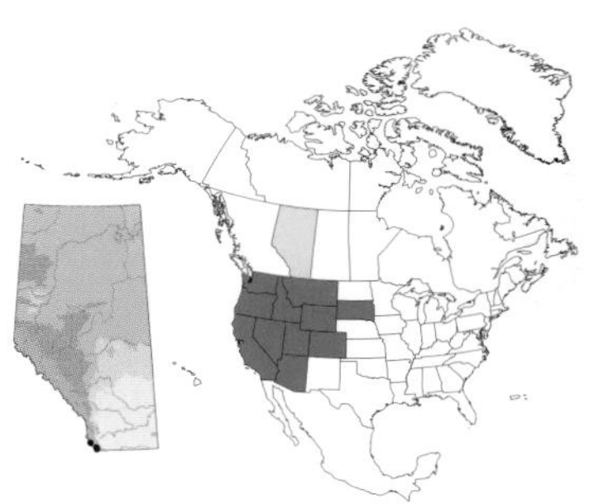

Plants: Small, slender **annual** herbs; stems erect, 10–30 {5–40} cm tall, hairless or sparsely hairy, usually **freely branched mostly from near the base**, appearing very leafy above; from weak taproots.

Leaves: **Alternate** (the lower sometimes opposite); **blades linear to narrowly lance-shaped** and widest above the middle, 1–3 cm long, only gradually reduced in size up the stem, usually hairless (sometimes sparsely hairy), stalkless or short-stalked.

Flowers: **White**, sometimes reddish, **tiny** and inconspicuous; with **4 sepals, 4 petals and 8 stamens at the tip of an elongating, stalk-like ovary**; sepals bent backward, hairless or sparsely hairy, soon shed; petals about 1 mm long; stamens of 2 types, those opposite the petals shorter and sterile; ovaries hairless or sparsely hairy, tipped with a rounded stigma; borne singly in upper leaf axils, crowded, forming narrow, elongating clusters (racemes); {June–August}.

Fruits: Erect, slender, hairless **capsules** 8–14 {7–15} mm long, essentially stalkless, **splitting lengthwise into 2 compartments**; few **seeds** (fewer than 10 per cavity), about 1 mm long, **lacking a tuft of hairs** (not comose).

Habitat: Disturbed ground on open montane slopes; elsewhere, on sandy or gravelly soil and snow beds at foothill to alpine elevations.

Notes: This species has also been called *Gayophytum helleri* Rydb. var. *glabrum* Munz. • The generic name is a combination of the name J. Gay (author of a flora of Chile) and the Greek *phyton* (plant)—hence 'Gay's plant.'

JP

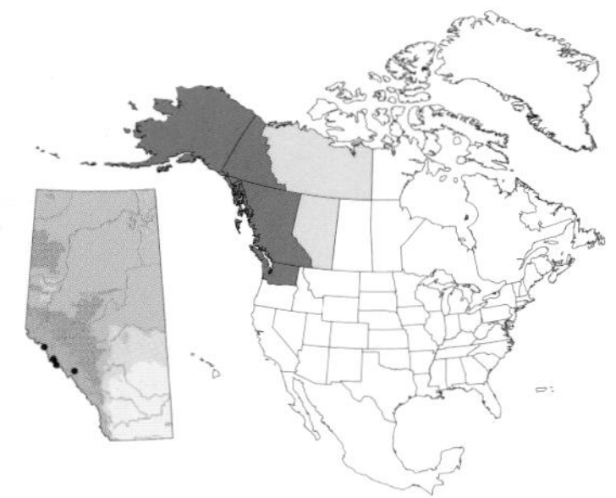

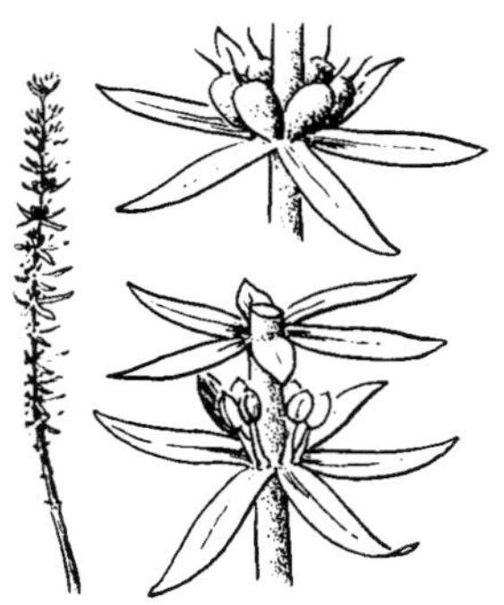

MOUNTAIN MARE'S-TAIL

Hippuris montana Ledeb.
MARE'S-TAIL FAMILY (HIPPURIDACEAE)

Plants: **Aquatic or amphibious** perennial herbs, hairless, with delicate, unbranched stems **1–10 cm tall, 0.2–0.5 mm thick**; from slender, creeping underground stems (rhizomes).

Leaves: Linear, pointed, **5–10 mm long**, 0.5–1 mm wide, stalkless, **in whorls of 5–8**, not toothed, lobed or divided.

Flowers: Green, stalkless; **tiny, lacking petals**, with 1 short-stalked anther and 1 ovary about 1 mm long and bearing a thread-like style, **usually male or female** and with female flowers above male flowers (sometimes with both male and female parts); **single in upper leaf axils**, thus forming whorls; July–August {September}.

Fruits: Single-seeded, nut-like, not splitting open.

Habitat: Moist open sites along streams and on mossy banks.

Notes: Mountain mare's-tail could be confused with common mare's-tail (*Hippuris vulgaris* L.), but common mare's-tail is a larger plant, with leaves over 1 mm wide and 1 cm long and stems more than 1 mm thick. Most of its flowers have both male and female parts. Mare's-tails also resemble horsetails (*Equisetum* spp.), but horsetails have hollow, jointed stems, and they reproduce by spores rather than flowers and seeds. • Hippuridaceae is a small family, consisting of a single genus, and some taxonomists include it in the closely related family Haloragidaceae (the water-milfoil family). The generic name *Hippuris* was derived from the Greek *hippos* (horse) and *oura* (tail).

BISCUIT-ROOT

Lomatium cous (S. Wats.) Coult. & Rose
CARROT FAMILY (APIACEAE [UMBELLIFERAE])

Plants: Delicate, essentially **hairless** perennial herbs; flowering stalks **usually leafless, 5–35 cm tall; from thick, round to elongated taproots.**

Leaves: Basal, sometimes with 1 stem leaf, parsley-like, **deeply cut 3 or more times** into narrowly elliptic to lance-shaped segments.

Flowers: Yellow, small, with 5 petals, 5 stamens and 1 **hairless ovary** tipped with 2 styles; many tiny flowers on 1–3 mm long stalks in dense, **round clusters** (umbellets), each cluster above a whorl of small (2–5 mm long), broad-tipped, egg-shaped, elliptic or lance-shaped bracts and borne at the tip of a slender stalk; 5–20 unequal (1.5–10 cm long) stalks (rays) forming an umbrella-shaped cluster (umbel); May {April–July}.

Fruits: Broadly elliptic pairs of flattened seed-like fruits (schizocarps), 5–12 mm long and 3–5 mm wide, with 5 prominent ribs (sometimes with alternating smaller ribs), edged with a broad **wing almost as wide as the body**, splitting apart when mature and usually hanging from the tip of the central stalk (carpophore), hairless or granular-roughened.

Habitat: Dry, open, rocky slopes and flats in the montane zone; elsewhere, on dry hillsides, often with sagebrush, in the foothills and mountains.

Notes: This species has also been called *Lomatium montanum* Coult. & Rose. • All *Lomatium* species are edible. The large, starchy roots were cooked or dried and ground into flour for making bread, cakes and biscuits—hence the name 'biscuit-root.' The roots and meal were important trade items among some tribes. Large, flat cakes of meal were carried on long journeys for food. The leaves add a strong parsley taste to salads. • The generic name *Lomatium* was taken from the Greek *loma* (a border), in reference to the flattened edges (wings) on the fruits.

CWa

LA

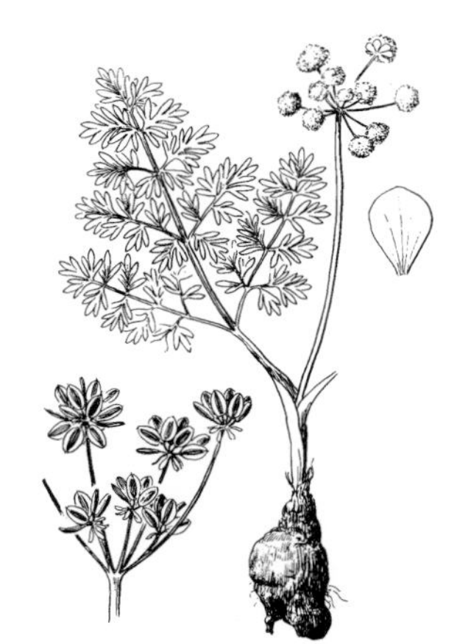

JP

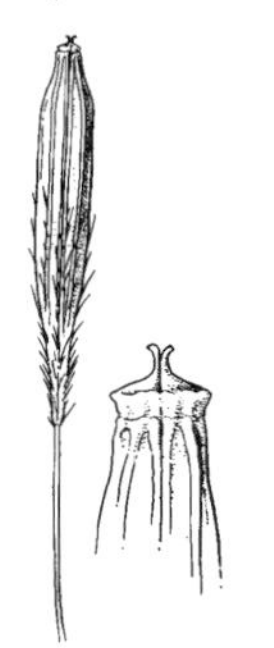

PURPLE SWEET CICELY

Osmorhiza purpurea (Coult. & Rose) Suksd.
CARROT FAMILY (APIACEAE [UMBELLIFERAE])

Plants: Slender perennial herbs; stems 20–60 cm tall, rather leafy, hairy or hairless; from **thick, aromatic roots.**

Leaves: Basal and **alternate on the stem,** 1–3 times divided in 3s; leaflets lance-shaped, 2–6 cm long, sharply toothed or lobed; lower leaves stalked, upper leaves nearly stalkless.

Flowers: Purple or pinkish, sometimes greenish white, small, with 5 petals, 5 stamens and a broad, thickened disc with 2 styles each less than 0.5 mm long; few, on erect or widely spreading stalks in small, **umbrella-shaped clusters** (umbellets), these clusters borne on slender stalks (rays) in larger umbrella-shaped clusters (umbels); bracts at the base of the umbellets very small, often absent; {June} July.

Fruits: Bristly-hairy, club-shaped pairs of seed-like fruits (mericarps), **8–13 mm long, tipped with a small, thick, 2-styled disc** (stylopodium) that is **0.5–2 mm high** and **wider than it is long,** prominently 5-ribbed (sometimes with alternating smaller ribs), splitting apart from the base when mature and usually hanging from the tip of the central stalk (carpophore).

Habitat: Moist coniferous woods and slopes in montane and subalpine regions; elsewhere, in meadows, on streambanks and in redwood forests.

Notes: This species has also been called *Osmorhiza chilensis* Hook. & Arn. var. *purpurea* (Coult. & Rose) Boivin. • Purple sweet cicely is easily confused with spreading sweet cicely (*Osmorhiza depauperata* Philippi) and blunt-fruited sweet cicely (*Osmorhiza berteroi* DC., also called *Osmorhiza chilensis* Hook. & Arn.), with which it is thought to hybridize. However, both of these species have hairy leaves. Blunt-fruited sweet cicely usually has white or greenish (sometimes purple) flowers, and its 12–22 mm long fruits are narrowed (constricted) below the relatively narrow (longer than wide) tip. Spreading sweet cicely has pink-purplish flowers and wide-spreading or reflexed rays tipped with club-shaped fruits that curve abruptly to broad-pointed tips. These more common species grow in moist woods to middle elevations in the mountains. • Smooth sweet cicely (*Osmorhiza longistylis* (Torr.) DC.) is also rare in Alberta. Unlike purple sweet cicely, it has persistent bracts

O. LONGISTYLIS

DJ

at the base of the small flower clusters, whitish flowers, longer styles (2–3 mm) and longer fruits (18–22 mm). Like purple sweet cicely, its fruits are bristly-hairy and taper into long, slender tails. Smooth sweet cicely grows at lower elevations, in moist woods in the parkland and prairies, rather than in mountain forests as does purple sweet cicely. It flowers in June. • The roots have a licorice-like odour when crushed. Several tribes enjoyed their delicate sweet flavour and ate them steamed, boiled or in stews.

O. LONGISTYLIS

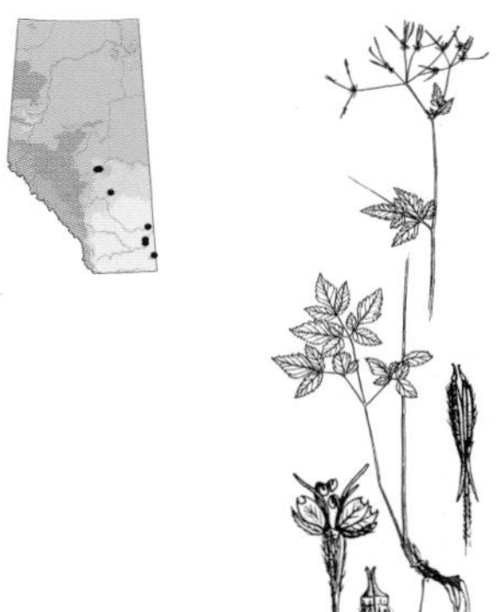

ARCTIC WINTERGREEN

Pyrola grandiflora Radius
WINTERGREEN FAMILY (PYROLACEAE)

JG

Plants: Low, evergreen perennial **herbs**, hairless; stems 5–15 {25} cm tall; from slender, creeping underground stems (rhizomes).

Leaves: Basal, **firm** and leathery, shiny green on the upper surface, often reddish beneath; blades 2–4 {1–4.5} cm long, **oval to round**, thickened at edges, with obscure, rounded teeth or toothless; stalks 1–8 cm long, longer than or equal to their blades.

Flowers: Creamy or greenish white, often pinkish-tinged, about **1.5–2 cm across**, with 5 showy, 5–10 {12} mm long, spreading, rounded petals, 5 smaller, {2} 3–4 mm long sepals, small (at most 2.3 mm long) lemon-yellow anthers and a **long, curved style** with a collar below the tip; 4–11, on 2–8 mm long stalks in elongated clusters (racemes); July {June–August}.

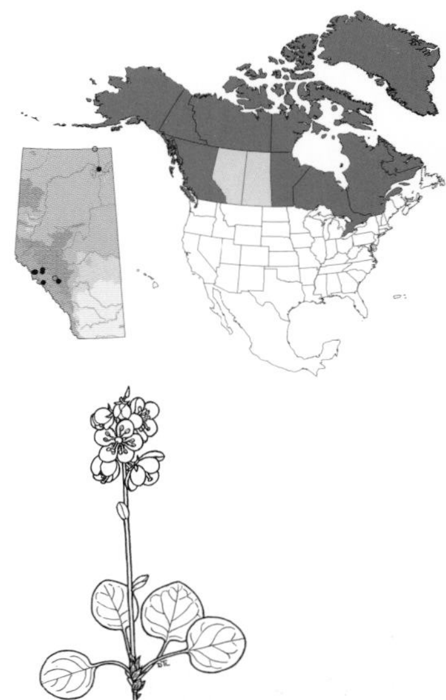

Fruits: Round capsules, splitting open from base to tip; segments edged with cobwebby hairs at first; seeds numerous, tiny, with a loose, fleshy seed coat.

Habitat: Alpine slopes; elsewhere, in woods and heathlands.

Notes: The leaves of arctic wintergreen are very similar to those of common pink wintergreen (*Pyrola asarifolia* Michx.), but common pink wintergreen has smaller (5–7 mm long), pink petals, smaller (2–3 mm long) sepals and large (up to 3.5 mm long), reddish purple anthers.

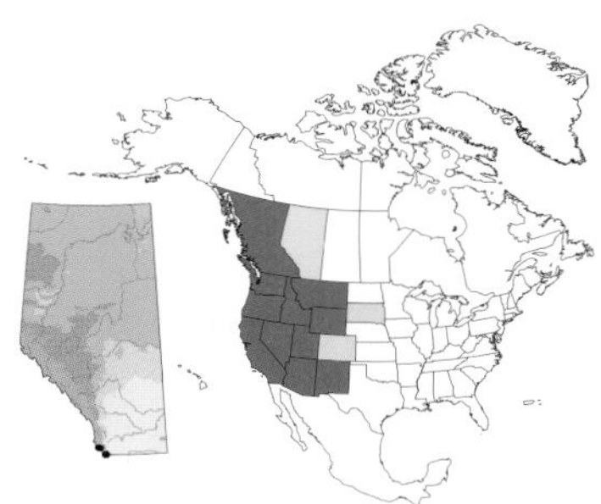

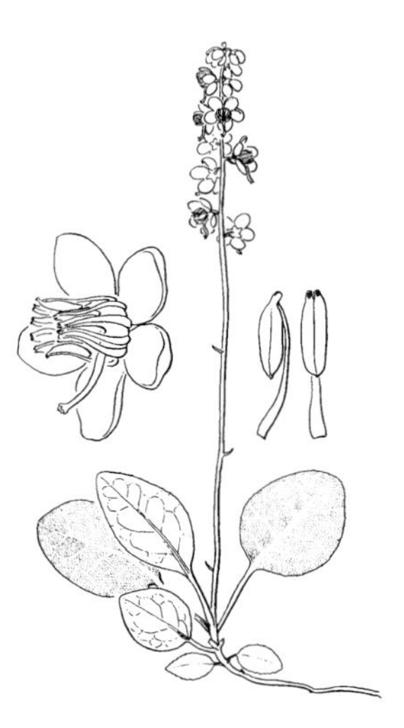

WHITE-VEINED WINTERGREEN

Pyrola picta J.E. Smith
WINTERGREEN FAMILY (PYROLACEAE)

Plants: Low, evergreen perennial herbs, hairless; stems reddish brown, 10–20 {25} cm tall; from slender, creeping underground stems (rhizomes).

Leaves: Basal, **firm** and leathery, **deep green, mottled with white or grey** along the larger veins on the upper surface, usually somewhat purplish on lower surfaces; blades 1–6 cm long, **narrowly to broadly egg-shaped**, commonly **pointed** at the tip and tapered at the base, thickened at edges, with small teeth or toothless, longer than or equal to their stalks.

Flowers: Yellowish to greenish white (or purplish), mostly **nodding**, about **1 cm across**, with 5 showy, spreading, rounded petals, 5 small (1.5 mm long), fused, reddish sepals and a **long** (5 mm), **curved style**; several, on spreading, 4–8 mm long stalks in elongated clusters (racemes); {June} July–August.

Fruits: Round capsules, splitting open from base to tip; segments edged with cobwebby hairs at first; seeds numerous, tiny, with a loose, fleshy seed coat.

Habitat: Moist to dry, coniferous forests.

Notes: This species is easily distinguished from other wintergreens by the whitish mottling along its leaf veins. The leaves could be confused with those of rattlesnake-plantain (*Goodyera* spp.), but the leaves of that orchid are narrower and softer (not leathery). • The generic name *Pyrola* was taken from the Latin *pyrus* (pear) because the leaves of some species are often pear-shaped. The specific epithet *picta* means 'brightly marked or painted'—a reference to the white veins on the leaves. • Although these plants have green leaves and are capable of producing food by photosynthesis, they also take nutrients from decaying plant material using specialized fungi (mycorrhizae) that are intimately associated with their roots.

PINE-SAP

Monotropa hypopitys L.
Indian pipe family (Monotropaceae)

CWa

Plants: **Fleshy**, saprophytic herbs, **waxy white, yellowish white or pinkish**, lacking green pigment, often drying black, commonly fragrant; stems stout, unbranched, 10–30 cm tall, often clustered, usually more or less **downy**; from dense masses of matted roots.

Leaves: Alternate, **scale-like**, smooth-edged or somewhat fringed, 1–1.5 cm long on upper stem, thicker and smaller toward stem base.

Flowers: Waxy white to yellowish or pinkish, **urn-shaped, 10–14 mm long**, with 2–5 (usually 4) lance-shaped sepals and **4 or 5 overlapping petals; petals 10–12 mm long, scale-like**, somewhat **pouched** at the base, **fuzzy** on 1 or both sides; uppermost flowers largest; few to many, short-stalked, in dense, elongating clusters (racemes), **nodding at first but soon erect**; {May–June} July.

Fruits: **Erect**, egg-shaped to round **capsules**, 5–8 mm long, opening from tip by 4 lengthwise slits; seeds numerous, tiny.

Habitat: Rich, shady coniferous forests, on humus.

Notes: This species has also been called *Hypopitys monotropa* Crantz. It is found around the world in the northern hemisphere. • Pine-sap resembles the more common species Indian pipe (*Monotropa uniflora* L.), but Indian pipe is white (rarely pinkish) and its stems are tipped with single nodding flowers. • In colour and texture, the nodding flowers of pine-sap resemble congealed pine resin, and these plants often grow under pines, so it was believed that they 'sapped' the strength of these trees. This may be true, to some extent. The roots of pine-sap share mycorrhizal fungi with some trees, and nutrients from the conifers may pass to the pine-sap via the fungi. The interrelationships between mycorrhizal fungi, pine-sap and trees are complex, and studies suggest that substances from the fungi help trees to fight some diseases. • The generic name comes from the Greek *monos* (one) and *tropos* (direction), referring to the flowers which are turned to 1 side. The specific epithet *hypopitys* was derived from the Greek *hypo* (beneath) and *pitys* (pine tree), referring to habitat.

DJ

CWa

PINE-DROPS

Pterospora andromedea Nutt.
Indian pipe family (Monotropaceae)

Plants: Fleshy, clammy-fuzzy herbs, covered with glandular hairs, purplish or reddish brown to pinkish, lacking green pigment; stems erect, unbranched, 20–80 {90} cm tall, stout (often more than 2 cm wide at the base), remaining as fibrous dried stalks for at least 1 year; from dense masses of mycorrhizal roots.

Leaves: Numerous, alternate, **scale-like**, lance-shaped, 1–3.5 cm long, thick, crowded near the stem base.

Flowers: Pale yellowish, urn-shaped, {5} 6–8 mm long, hairless, with 5 short, spreading lobes at tip and 5 **glandular-hairy, reddish brown sepals** at base, **nodding**, on glandular-hairy stalks about 1 cm long, from the axils of slender bracts; numerous, in **erect, elongating clusters** (racemes) **10–30 cm long** (usually equal to the rest of the stem); {June} July–September.

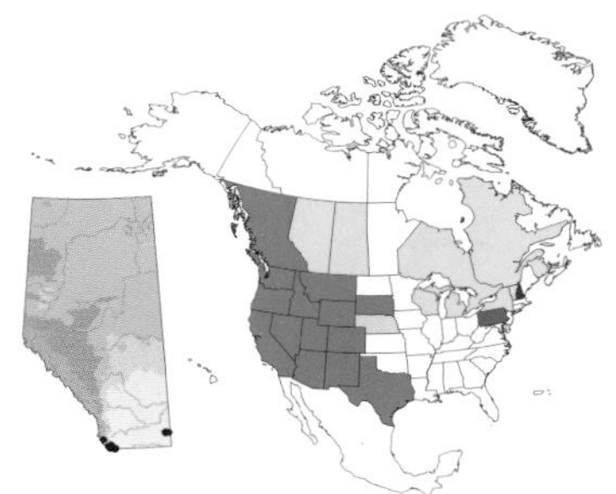

Fruits: Nodding, round, **pincushion-like capsules**, 8–12 mm broad, purplish red; seeds numerous, tiny, tipped with a broad, netted wing many times longer than the egg-shaped seed.

Habitat: Dry coniferous woods, on deep humus.

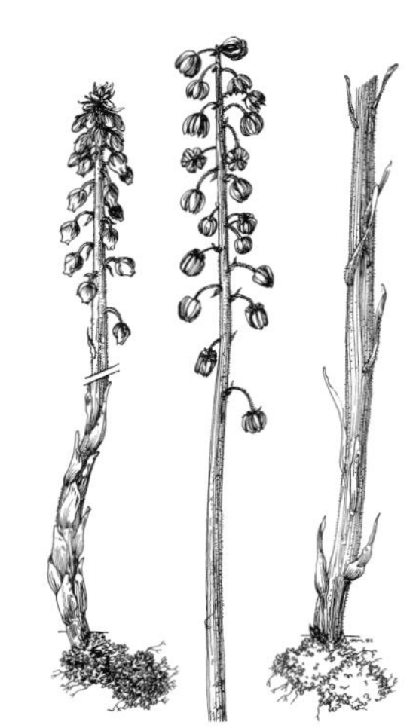

Notes: Pine-drops was once thought to be a parasite, feeding on the roots of coniferous trees. It was later classified as a saprophyte, believed to derive its food from dead organic matter on the forest floor through a symbiotic association with soil fungi (mycorrhizae). It is now thought to be a parasite of fungi that feed on the roots of coniferous trees. Because of this dependence on soil fungi, it is extremely sensitive to disturbance. • Some tribes pounded the stems and fruits of these plants to make a medicinal tea for treating bleeding from the lungs. The dry powder was used as a snuff for nosebleeds. Europeans used pine-drops as a sedative and to stimulate perspiration. • The generic name *Pterospora* was derived from the Greek *pteros* (a wing) and *sporos* (seed), alluding to the lovely translucent wing borne by each seed. The specific epithet *andromedea* alludes to the resemblance of these flowers to those of the genus *Andromeda*. The plants grow under pines and their flowers resemble drops of resin—hence the common name 'pine-drops.'

GREENLAND PRIMROSE

Primula egaliksensis Wormskj.
PRIMROSE FAMILY (PRIMULACEAE)

DJ

Plants: Tiny perennial herbs; flowering stalks leafless, usually {5} 6–18 cm high.

Leaves: In a basal rosette, thin, 1.5–5.5 cm long (including stalks); blades egg-shaped to spatula-shaped, often widest above middle, flat or wavy along the edges; **stalks often as long as the blades or longer.**

Flowers: Violet or deep lilac (sometimes white) with a yellow eye, 5–9 mm across, with 5 petals fused in a slender, 6–8 mm long tube (longer than the sepals) but each ending in a broad (1.6–4 mm wide), abruptly spreading, notched lobe (limb); sepals 4–9 mm long, fused into a tube at the base, cut about ¼–½ of the way to the base into 5 lobes, fringed with **gland-tipped hairs**; 5 stamens, not extending past the mouth of the corolla; styles thread-like (filiform), with head-like (capitate) stigmas; 1–6, in a flat-topped cluster (umbel) above a whorl (involucre) of lance-shaped, 3–6 mm long bracts with enlarged, cupped bases; June–July {August}.

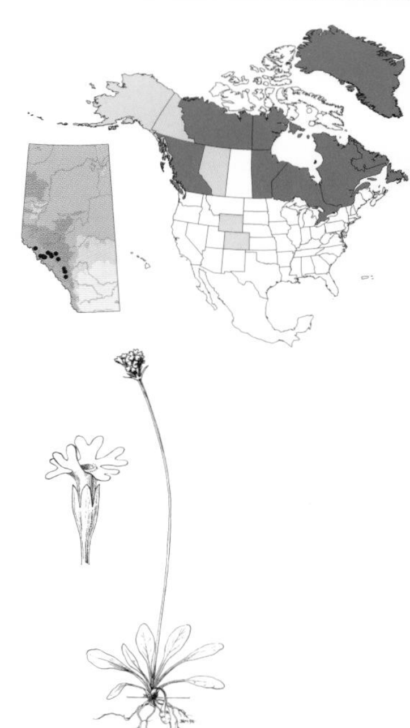

Fruits: Slender, cylindrical capsules, 2–3 times as long as the sepals, splitting into 5 parts at the tapered tip; seeds pale, smooth.

Habitat: Marshy ground, wet meadows and shores in alpine and subalpine areas; elsewhere, in wet meadows and on wet, calcareous lakeshores and riverbanks.

Notes: Erect primrose (*Primula stricta* Hornem.) is another slender primrose that is also rare in Alberta. It is a larger plant (10–30 cm tall) with round-toothed leaves, and its showy lilac flowers, 8–12 mm wide, appear in June and July. Erect primrose grows on moist alpine slopes and in wet areas in the boreal forest. It prefers saline soil. • The generic name *Primula* was derived from the Latin *primus* (early or first) because many species flower early in spring.

P. STRICTA

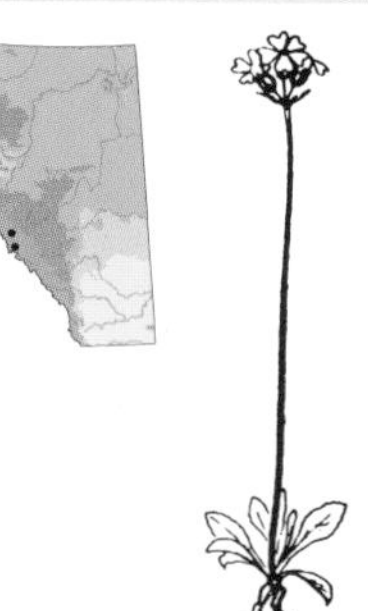

JL

JL

JL

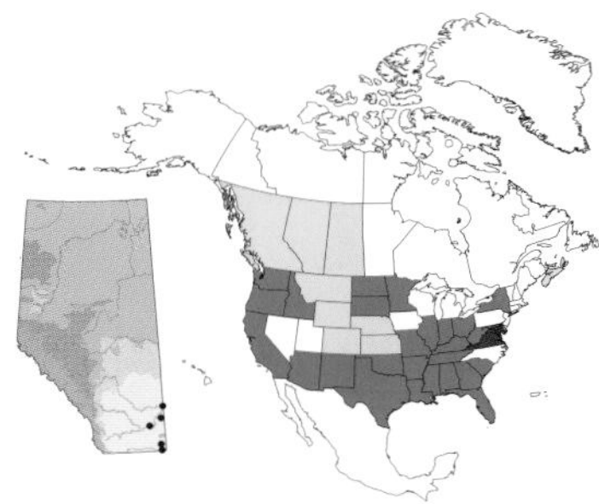

CHAFFWEED, FALSE PIMPERNEL

Anagallis minima (L.) Krause
PRIMROSE FAMILY (PRIMULACEAE)

Plants: Small, **hairless annual** herbs, **2–10 cm tall**; branches erect or with bases spreading on the ground and tips ascending, often rooting at the joints.

Leaves: **Alternate**, oblong, spoon-shaped or egg-shaped and widest above the middle, 4–8 {10} mm long; almost stalkless, with the lower edges extending down the stem.

Flowers: Greenish, **inconspicuous, about 2 mm long**, with 4 sepals and 4 petal lobes; corolla white or pinkish, scarcely half as long as the sepals, with 4 spreading lobes at the tip of a broad tube, withered and persistent on the capsule lid; sepals narrowly lance-shaped, 2–3 mm long, edged with small sharp teeth; 4 stamens opposite the corolla lobes; solitary in leaf axils on short (1 mm long) stalks; {May–July} August.

Fruits: **Rounded capsules about 2 mm long**, splitting in 2 just above the middle, **shedding the top as a lid and leaving the cupped lower ½ on the plant**; seeds brown, pitted.

Habitat: Moist soil and mud by ponds; elsewhere, occasionally in flooded areas and in damp places along paths in woods, usually in acid soils.

Notes: This species has also been called *Centunculus minimus* L. • The generic name *Anagallis* was the ancient Greek name for pimpernel. The specific epithet *minima* means 'small.'

MOUNTAIN DWARF PRIMROSE, MOUNTAIN DOUGLASIA

Douglasia montana A. Gray
PRIMROSE FAMILY (PRIMULACEAE)

Plants: Low, **cushion-forming or matted** herbs, about 3 cm tall; **stems slender, branched, slightly woody**, spreading, tipped with tufts of short leaves; flowering stems erect, leafless; from persistent **root crowns** and underground stems (rhizomes).

Leaves: Crowded **at branch tips** in **compact rosettes**, linear to lance-shaped, about **4 {8} mm long**, fringed with tiny, stiff hairs that are rough to the touch.

Flowers: Purple, lilac or bright pink, 6–8 mm long and about 1 cm across, with **5 showy corolla lobes and 5 slender-pointed calyx lobes**; corolla with erect or spreading, oblong to egg-shaped lobes about 4 {5} mm long at the tip of a narrow tube, also bearing 5 small ridges around the mouth of the tube; calyx reddish, hairy or hairless, equal to or slightly longer than the corolla tube, cut about halfway to the base into 5 ridged lobes; stamens opposite the corolla lobes and contained in the flower tube; styles thread-like; single (sometimes 2), on 1–4 leafless, 5–25 mm long, hairy stalks from the centres of the leaf rosettes, usually with 1 or 2 bracts at the base of the flower; {June–July} August.

Fruits: Capsules, slightly longer than the calyx tube, containing 1 or 2 brown, finely pitted seeds.

Habitat: Dry alpine slopes; elsewhere, in dry places from foothills to mountain tops.

Notes: Mountain dwarf primrose is superficially similar to the common plant moss phlox (*Phlox hoodii* Richards.), but moss phlox has paired hairy leaves, hairy sepals, nearly stalkless flowers and broader, more rounded petals. • Mountain dwarf primrose grows with white dryad (*Dryas octopetala* L.) on a single alpine summit in Waterton Lakes National Park. It is extremely rare, with a population of about 10,000 plants at this single site. • The genus *Douglasia* was named in honour of David Douglas (1798–1834), a famous early botanical explorer in the northwest. The specific epithet *montana* means 'of the mountains.'

JL

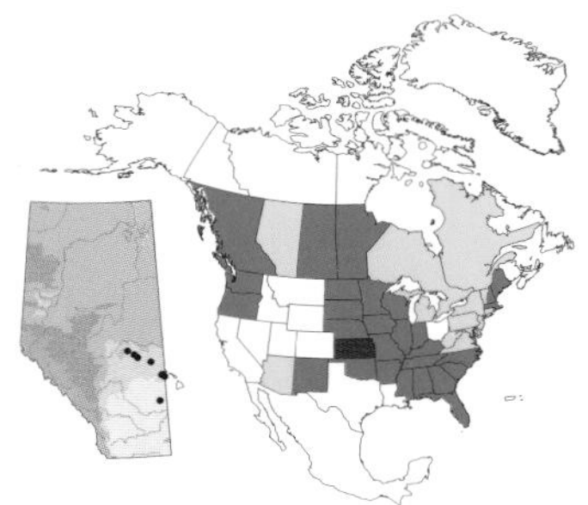

LANCE-LEAVED LOOSESTRIFE

Lysimachia hybrida Michx.
PRIMROSE FAMILY (PRIMULACEAE)

Plants: Erect perennial herbs; stems leafy, 40–100 cm tall, almost hairless; from **short** (never extensive) **underground stems** (rhizomes).

Leaves: Opposite or whorled, linear to **lance-shaped, gradually tapered to both ends**, 3–10 cm long, **1–3 cm wide**, rough-edged but rarely fringed with hairs; **leaf stalks hairless or inconspicuously fringed**, the lower stalks **10–30 mm long.**

Flowers: Bright yellow, about **15 mm across**, with 5 {6} **broadly egg-shaped, flat-spreading petal lobes** at the tip of a short, inconspicuous tube; each lobe usually tipped with a short, stiff point and edged with fine, irregular teeth; **calyxes deeply cut into 5** {6} **firm, pointed segments**; 5 stamens, alternating with tiny sterile stamens; styles slender; **single, on thread-like stalks in upper leaf axils**, often appearing in whorls; July {June–August}.

Fruits: Round or egg-shaped capsules, splitting open lengthwise into 5 parts.

Habitat: Moist meadows and shores; elsewhere, in thickets, dry to moist open woods, and swamps.

Notes: This species has also been called *Lysimachia lanceolata* Walt. ssp. *hybrida* (Michx.) J.D. Ray, *Steironema lanceolatum* (Walt.) A. Gray var. *hybridum* (Michx.) A. Gray and *Steironema hybridum* (Michx.) Raf. • Fringed loosestrife (*Lysimachia ciliata* L.) is a similar, much more common species distinguished by its more extensive, elongated underground stems (rhizomes) and broader (3–6 cm wide), egg-shaped to lance-shaped leaves, with shorter (5–20 mm) stalks that are conspicuously fringed with hairs. The flowers of fringed loosestrife are also larger, with lobes about 1 cm long. • The generic name *Lysimachia* honours King Lysimachus, a Macedonian general who ruled Thrace 323–281 BC. Some sources report that it was taken from the Greek *lysis* (a losing or ending) and *mache* (strife). There was an ancient belief that these plants would calm savage beasts and that a piece hung from the yokes of oxen would be enough to appease any strife or unruliness. Loosestrife does appear to repel gnats and flies, so this might help to keep bothersome pests away from the faces of such beasts of burden.

NORTHERN FRINGED GENTIAN, RAUP'S FRINGED GENTIAN

Gentianopsis detonsa (Rottb.) Ma ssp. *raupii* (Porsild) A. Löve & D. Löve
GENTIAN FAMILY (GENTIANACEAE)

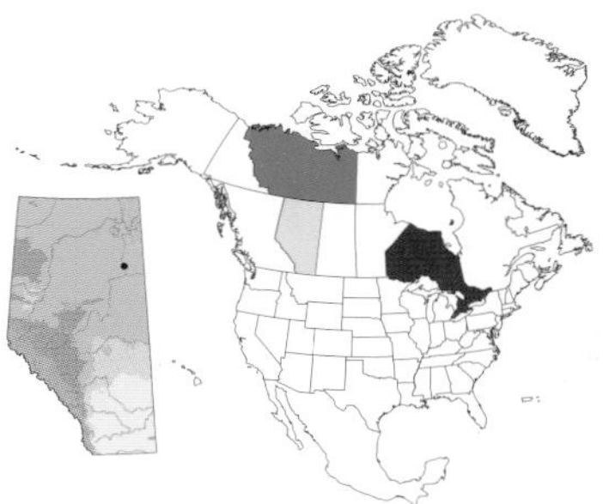

Plants: Hairless **annual or biennial** herbs; stems erect, 5–40 {60} cm tall, branched in the upper sections, **often purplish.**

Leaves: Basal (often in rosettes) and **opposite** on the stem; basal leaves **egg-shaped to spoon-shaped,** 5–35 {60} mm long; stem leaves widest at or above the middle, 15–65 mm long, 1–7 mm wide; **uppermost leaves blunt-tipped.**

Flowers: Blue (rarely whitish), **broadly goblet-shaped, 1–4 cm long,** 0.8–1.5 cm wide, with a corolla tube cut about halfway to the base into **4 elongate, rounded lobes fringed with slender teeth; 4 calyx lobes, smooth or wrinkled** but without tiny bumps (papillae), **not prominently ridged,** glossy and purplish at the centre, thin and translucent along the edges; 1–few, on erect, long stalks; late June–early August.

Fruits: Cylindrical capsules, as long as the persistent flower tube, containing many small, dark seeds; {August}.

Habitat: Wet meadows and saline flats.

Notes: This species has also been called *Gentianella detonsa* (Rottb.) G. Don ssp. *raupii* (Porsild) J. Gillett and *Gentiana detonsa* Rottb. • Northern fringed gentian resembles the common fringed gentian (*Gentianopsis crinita* (Froel.) Ma), but the calyxes of fringed gentian have tiny bumps (papillae, visible only with magnification) at their bases and on the dull green or purplish ridges (keels) of at least 2 of their lobes. The upper leaves of fringed gentian are pointed rather than blunt. • Subspecies *raupii* is the only subspecies in Alberta. In Canada, it is found only in the Mackenzie Basin drainage and the Hudson Bay areas. • The specific epithet *detonsa* was taken from the Latin *de* (concerning) and *tonsus* (shaven). The subspecies name *raupii* honours H.M. Raup, an American botanist born in 1901, who spent considerable time in the Northwest Territories.

PL

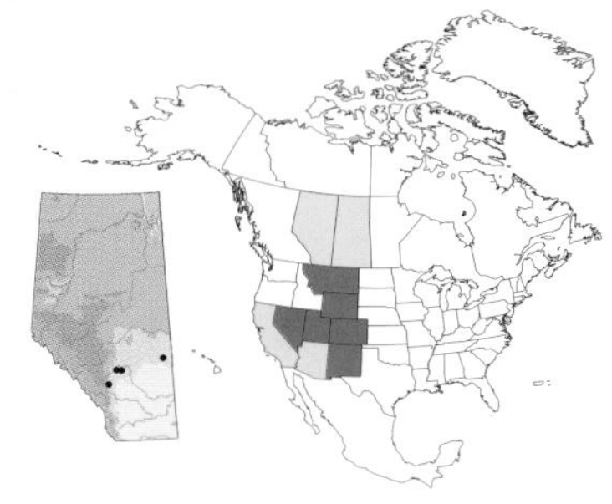

MARSH GENTIAN, LOWLY GENTIAN

Gentiana fremontii Torr.
GENTIAN FAMILY (GENTIANACEAE)

Plants: Low biennial herbs, 1–10 cm high; stems lying on the ground to erect-ascending, branched at base; from weak, slender roots.

Leaves: In basal rosettes and opposite on the stem, pale green with **broad, white edges**; basal leaves round to egg-shaped, 2–13 mm long, 1.5–1.8 mm wide; stem leaves pressed to the stem, **scarcely bent backward**, not toothed, oblong to lance-shaped, less than 6 mm long, with **bases of pairs fused into a sheath ¼–½ as long as the blades.**

Flowers: Greenish purple to **whitish**, tubular, 7–10 {15} mm long, tipped with 5 lobes; calyx tubes, 4–8 {12} mm long, cut less than ¼ of the way to the base into 4 or 5 faintly ridged lobes; solitary, erect; June {July–August}.

Fruits: Slender, papery capsules, splitting in half to release many small seeds; August.

Habitat: Moist grassy meadows; elsewhere, in moist sandy areas and meadows.

Notes: This species has also been called *Gentiana aquatica auct., non* L. • Marsh gentian is similar to moss gentian (*Gentiana prostrata* Haenke *ex* Jacq.), and many floras (including the second edition of *Flora of Alberta*) include it in that species. The leaves and sepals of moss gentian do not have wide, white edges, the stem leaves are bent backward and the basal and stem leaves are very similar in shape and size. Moss gentian grows in alpine areas. • The generic name *Gentiana* refers to Gentius, king of Illyria (an ancient region along the east coast of the Adriatic Sea) in the second century BC, who was said to have discovered the medicinal properties of *Gentiana lutea*. The specific epithet *fremontii* honours Major-General John Charles Fremont (1813–90), a plant collector of the western US.

ALPINE GENTIAN, GLAUCOUS GENTIAN, PALE GENTIAN

Gentiana glauca Pallas
GENTIAN FAMILY (GENTIANACEAE)

DJ

Plants: Small, somewhat **fleshy perennial** herbs, often **bluish green** with a thin, waxy coating (glaucous); stems **erect, 3–10** {2–15} **cm tall**; from creeping underground stems (rhizomes).

Leaves: In **basal rosettes** (winter rosettes present) and in **2 or 3** {4} **pairs on the stem**, shiny, bluish green; basal leaves oval, widest at or above the middle, 1 {0.5–2} cm long, 1 cm wide; stem leaves oval, widest at or below the middle, 0.5–1.5 cm long.

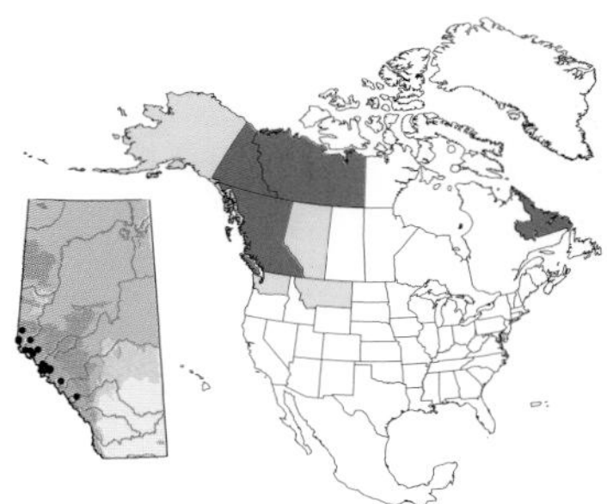

Flowers: Dark to greenish blue, tubular, 12–18 {10–20} **mm long**, tipped with **5 small** (about 2.5 mm long), blunt-tipped, broadly triangular to **egg-shaped, 3-veined lobes, alternating with 5 vertical folds** (pleats); calyx 5–7 mm long, green or purplish, tubular, tipped with 5 lance-shaped, blunt or pointed, unequal lobes, about ½ the length of the tube; **5 stamens**, contained within the corolla tube; 3–5 {7}, stalkless, in closely crowded clusters (cymes), sometimes with short-stalked lower flowers in upper leaf axils; June–August {September}.

Fruits: Erect capsules projecting slightly from the mouth of the persistent flower tube, containing many flattened, net-veined seeds.

Habitat: Moist subalpine and alpine meadows and slopes.

Notes: The compact basal rosettes of leaves and clusters of small, blue-green flowers distinguish this species from other gentians in Alberta. • The tubular flowers of the gentians are adapted for pollination by bumblebees. • The specific epithet *glauca* refers to the blue-green (glaucous) plants and flowers.

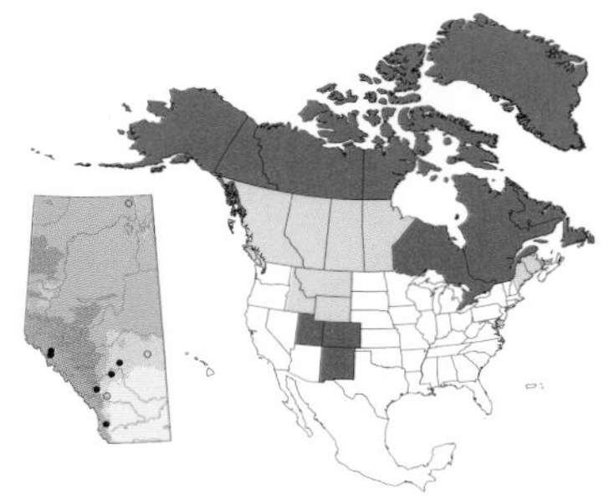

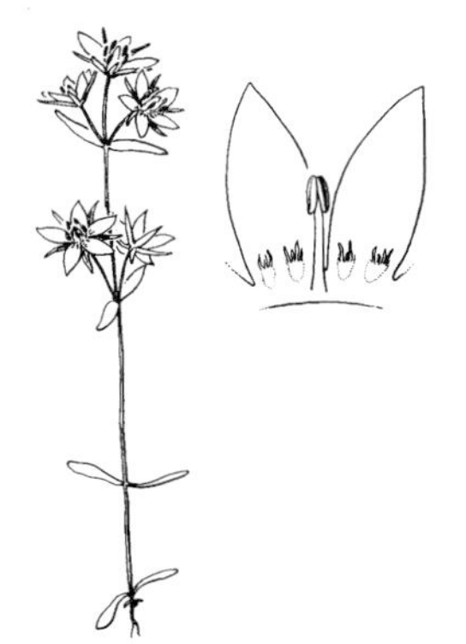

MARSH FELWORT

Lomatogonium rotatum (L.) Fries *ex* Nyman
GENTIAN FAMILY (GENTIANACEAE)

Plants: Slender **annual** herbs; stems erect, 10–35 {5–45} cm tall, unbranched or with strongly upward-pointing branches; from poorly developed taproots.

Leaves: Basal and opposite; lower leaves spatula-shaped, soon withered; middle and upper leaves **opposite**, mostly **linear to lance-shaped, 1–3** {0.5–5} **cm long**, 0.1–0.3 cm wide, slender-pointed, stalkless.

Flowers: White or bluish with purple veins, saucer-shaped, about 2 cm across, with **4 or 5 lobes widely spreading** at the tip of a **very short tube**; each lobe 10–12 {6–15} mm long, 8–20 mm wide, with 2 small, fringed scales at the base; calyxes with 4 or 5 slender lobes with prominent midveins, alternating with and equal to or longer than the petals; stamens 0.5 cm long, with flattened filaments, attached to the base of the petals; ovaries to 1 cm long, with 2 **stigmas** attached to the surface and **extending down the sides** as fine lines; few, on slender stalks from upper leaf axils, in elongated clusters (raceme-like); {late July} August–early September.

Fruits: Oblong to egg-shaped capsules, up to 1.5 cm long, splitting open from the tip, the segments curving strongly back; seeds light to dark brown, longer than they are wide, 0.5–0.75 mm long; late August–early September.

Habitat: Wet meadows and flats, often on saline soils.

Notes: A common relative, felwort (*Gentianella amarella* (L.) Börner), sometimes resembles marsh felwort, but felwort has many blue, funnel-shaped flowers that are borne in the axils of the leaves over much of the stem. • Marsh felwort has spread rapidly across North America since deglaciation. • The generic name *Lomatogonium* was derived from the Greek *lomato* (fringed) and *gone* (a seed), a reference to the stigma, which runs in lines down the side of the ovary. The specific epithet *rotatum* is from the Latin *rotatus* (wheel-shaped), in reference to the broad, almost flat, round flowers.

GREEN MILKWEED

Asclepias viridiflora Raf.
MILKWEED FAMILY (ASCLEPIADACEAE)

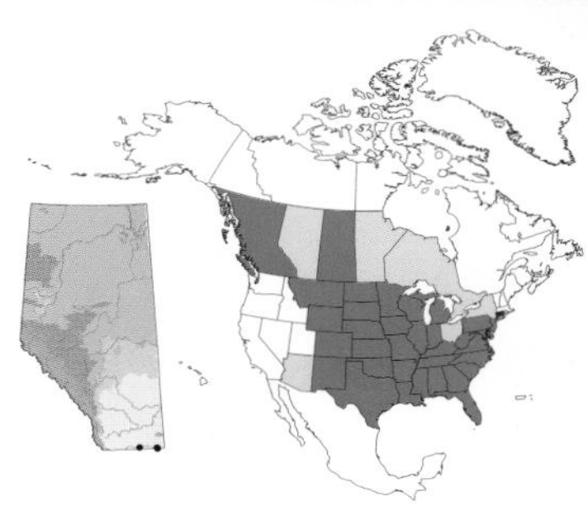

Plants: Perennial herbs with white, **milky juice** (latex) and tiny, downy hairs; stems 20–60 {120} cm long, often sprawling at the base; from deep taproots.

Leaves: Opposite or alternate, 2–8 {10} cm long, egg-shaped to oblong–lance-shaped, leathery with age, wavy-edged.

Flowers: Pale green and purple, about 1 cm long, with **5 greenish white, spreading to down-turned petal lobes around a projecting tube of fused stamens tipped with a broad, purplish, 5-hooded structure lacking horns** (corona); sepals persistent but inconspicuous; stalks hairy, short; numerous, in dense, round clusters (umbels) at stem tips and in leaf axils; {June–July}.

Fruits: Pairs of soft, spindle-shaped, pod-like fruits that split open down 1 side (follicles), finely hairy but otherwise smooth (not bumpy), stalked; seeds broad, flat, tipped with a tuft of long, white, silky hairs.

Habitat: Dry hillsides, often on sandy soil.

Notes: Green milkweed is very similar to low milkweed (*Asclepias ovalifolia* Dcne., p. 176). Both are relatively small species (usually less than 60 cm tall) with downy pods that lack the numerous small bumps found on the fruits of many other milkweed species. Both have greenish white flowers, but in low milkweed the tips of the 5 horns on each flower are curved inward, whereas in green milkweed these points are straight. • At the slightest damage, these plants ooze quantities of milky sap, which **contains toxic alkaloids**. Some cases of **livestock poisoning** have been attributed to milkweeds, but some insects eat milkweed with impunity, and many have developed the ability to incorporate alkaloids from the plants into their own bodies. This makes them poisonous and less tasty to predators. • Milkweed flowers produce large amounts of fragrant nectar, and their pollen grains stick together in masses called pollinia. When an insect lands, its feet slip into little slits on the sides of the flower and catch on wire-like filaments with a mass of pollen on each end. When the insect pulls its foot out, it carries tiny saddlebags of pollen. Sometimes an insect cannot free its foot and is trapped on the flower.

LA

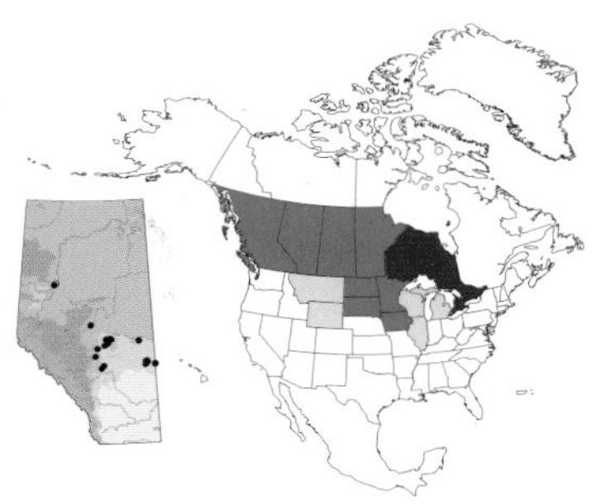

LOW MILKWEED

Asclepias ovalifolia Dcne.
MILKWEED FAMILY (ASCLEPIADACEAE)

Plants: Downy perennial herbs with white, **milky juice** (latex); stems {15} 20–60 cm tall; from deep taproots.

Leaves: Mostly opposite, 3–7 {8} cm long, egg-shaped to lance-shaped, rounded or slightly pointed at the tip, tapered to a short stalk at the base.

Flowers: Greenish white (sometimes purplish tinged), less than 1 cm long, with **5 spreading to down-turned petal lobes around a projecting tube of fused stamens tipped with a broad yellowish, 5-hooded structure with 5 incurved horns** (corona); sepals persistent but inconspicuous; stalks long and slender; 10–18, in loose, round clusters (umbels); June–August.

Fruits: Hanging pairs of soft, stalked, **spindle-shaped, pod-like fruits** that split open down 1 side (follicles), downy-hairy but otherwise smooth (not bumpy); seeds broad, flat, tipped with a tuft of long, white, silky hairs.

Habitat: Open woods and slopes; elsewhere, in moist prairie.

Notes: The young shoots, unopened flower buds and immature seed pods of several milkweed species were eaten raw or cooked in soups and stews. The **poisonous alkaloids** are destroyed by heat. It has been suggested that milkweed has a tenderizing effect on meat. Milkweed seeds have also been used for food occasionally. • The Cheyenne collected the dried juice from milkweed stems and chewed it like gum. The juice was also used to temporarily brand livestock because it stained the hides on animals for several months. The fibrous older milkweed plants were sometimes used to make string and rope.

COMMON DODDER

Cuscuta gronovii Willd.
MORNING-GLORY FAMILY (CONVOLVULACEAE)

WJC

Plants: **Leafless, parasitic annual herbs**; stems rather coarse, **orange or yellow**, often **climbing high, twining** around other plants and drawing nutrients from them by means of **suckers**; producing aerial roots but not rooted in the ground when mature.

Leaves: Reduced to tiny scales.

Flowers: **Whitish**, 2.5–3 {2–4} mm long, **bell-shaped**, tipped **with 4 or 5 blunt, broadly egg-shaped lobes** that are shorter than the tube, bearing **copiously fringed scales in the throat,** which are much shorter than the tube; calyx short, with rounded lobes; stigmas head-like; stalks short or absent; several, in **dense, head-like clusters** (cymes); August {July–October}.

WJC

Fruits: **Ovoid capsules**, 3–6 mm long, tipped with styles about half as long as the capsule, **not splitting open**, containing 2–4 seeds, each 2–3 mm long.

Habitat: Growing on a variety of coarse plants (usually shrubs) in moist, shady areas.

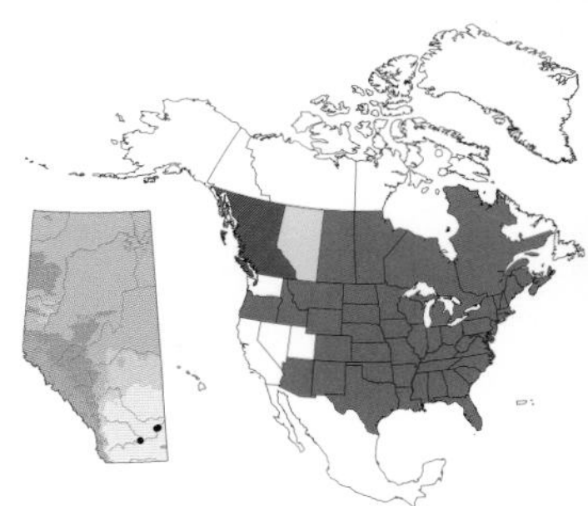

Notes: This is a difficult genus to identify because species are often differentiated on the basis of microscopic flower characteristics. • When a dodder seed germinates, it produces roots and a slowly rotating shoot. This shoot wraps around the first plant it contacts and soon fastens itself to the host using aerial roots and suckers. Once the shoot has joined with a suitable host, the roots and lower stems wither and decay. Dodders lack chlorophyll and are unable to produce food through photosynthesis, so they depend entirely on their host for sustenance. Their stems produce specialized suckers that penetrate the host tissue and draw out nutrients. Most plants produce many flowers and abundant seed as the season progresses, ensuring continuation of the cycle the following year.

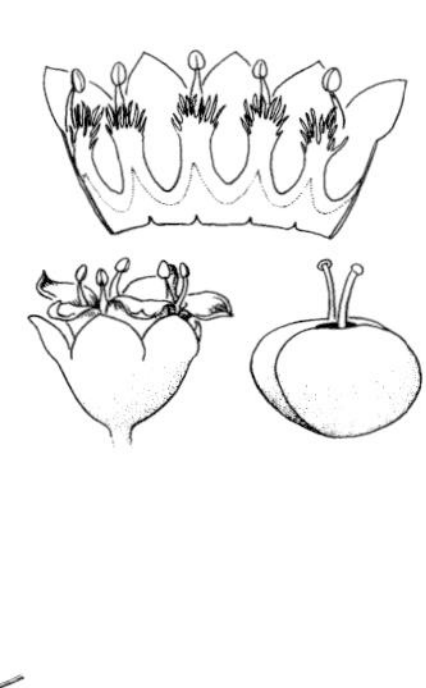

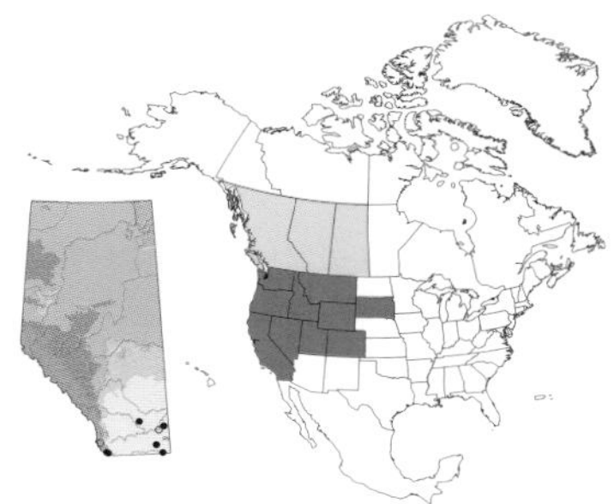

NORTHERN LINANTHUS

Linanthus septentrionalis H.L. Mason
PHLOX FAMILY (POLEMONIACEAE)

Plants: Slender **annual** herbs; stems erect, **freely branched,** 5–30 cm tall; from taproots.

Leaves: Opposite, palmately divided into 5–7 thread-like segments, 5–20 mm long, hairless or with short hairs, stalkless.

Flowers: **White, pale blue** or **lavender, funnel-shaped, 2–5** {6} **mm long** and wide, with 5 broad, spreading lobes at the tip of a **short tube with a ring of hairs at the mouth; calyx tubular,** ½–⅔ as long as the petals, **tipped with 5 equal, triangular lobes** with slender points, dry and translucent below the hollows (sinuses); styles projecting from the flowers, tipped with a 3-lobed stigma; **single, on slender, spreading stalks from upper leaf axils,** forming spreading, branched clusters (cyme-like panicles); late May–June {July}.

Fruits: Capsules, with **2–4** {8} **seeds in each of 3 cavities.**

Habitat: Dry hillsides and plains; elsewhere, in forest openings and dry meadows.

Notes: This species has also been called *Linanthus harknessii* (Curran) Greene var. *septentrionalis* (Mason) Jepson & V. Bailey. • Linanthus seeds become gummy when wet. • The generic name *Linanthus* was taken from the Greek *linon* (flax) and *anthos* (a flower) because these blooms were thought to resemble tiny flax flowers. The specific epithet *septentrionalis* is Latin for 'northern.'

SLENDER PHLOX

Phlox gracilis (Hook.) Greene ssp. *gracilis*
PHLOX FAMILY (POLEMONIACEAE)

Plants: **Slender annual** herbs, not tufted; stems single, erect, rarely spreading on the ground, 10–40 cm tall, usually **branched and with fine glandular hairs** (at least on the upper stem); from weak taproots.

Leaves: **Mainly opposite, toothless**, elliptic to oblong, 2–5 cm long; **upper leaves lance-shaped to linear, alternate.**

Flowers: **Pink or lavender, trumpet-shaped**, {9} 10–14 mm long, with **5 spreading lobes** at the tip of a **slender, 8–12 mm long, yellowish tube; calyx glandular-hairy**, 5–6 mm long, cut about halfway to the base into **5 slender lobes**, not enlarging in fruit, eventually **ruptured by the growing capsule; 5 stamens**; stigmas 3-lobed; single and stalkless or in pairs (1 stalkless and 1 stalked), borne in the axils of alternate leaf-like bracts, forming branched, cyme-like clusters; {March–May} June.

Fruits: Capsules, splitting open along 3 vertical lines.

Habitat: Dry to moist open ground; elsewhere, in thickets and bottomlands.

Notes: This species has also been called *Microsteris gracilis* (Hook.) Greene. • The generic name *Phlox* was taken from the Greek *phlox* (flame) in reference to the brightly coloured flowers of some species. The specific epithet *gracilis* is Latin for 'slender' or 'graceful.'

PL

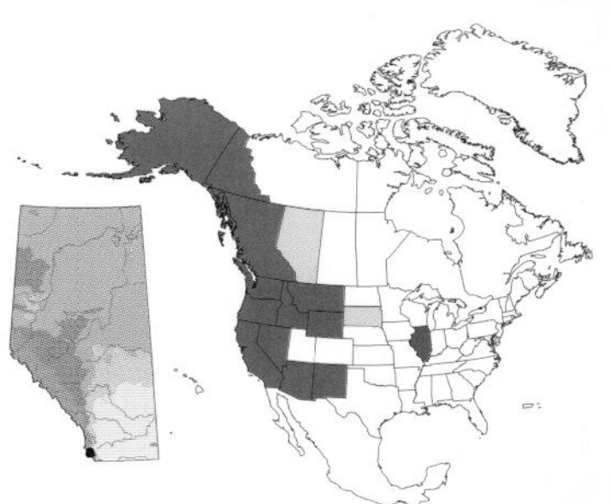

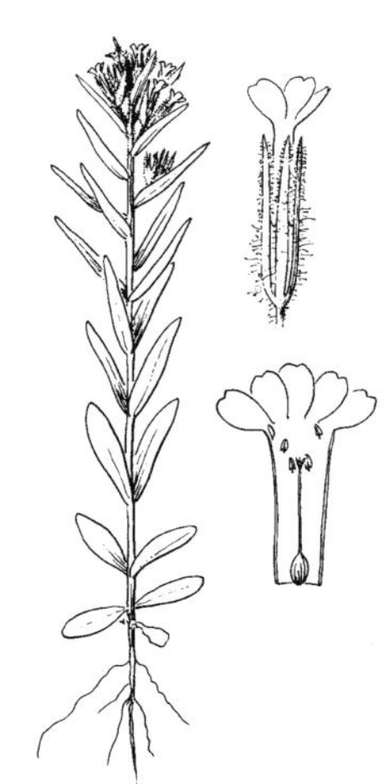

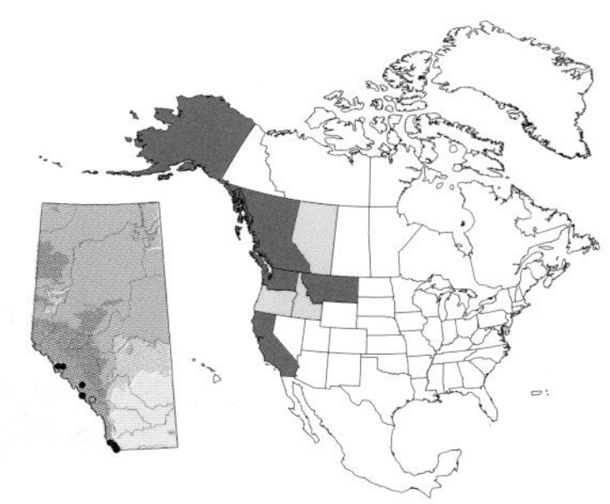

Sitka romanzoffia, mistmaiden, cliff romanzoffia, Sitka mistmaiden

Romanzoffia sitchensis Bong.
WATERLEAF FAMILY (HYDROPHYLLACEAE)

Plants: **Delicate perennial** herbs, usually almost hairless; stems slender, 10–30 cm tall, with a **bulbous base**; from underground stems (rhizomes).

Leaves: Mainly basal, **round to kidney-shaped, shallowly 5–7-lobed to coarsely toothed**, 1–3 {4} cm wide, rather fleshy, long-stalked.

Flowers: **White or cream-coloured with a golden eye**, broadly funnel-shaped, 7–10 **mm across**, with 5 broad petal lobes and 5 small, slender, hairless sepals; few to several, in **loose, uncoiling clusters** (raceme-like cymes); {June} July–August.

Fruits: Oblong, 2-chambered capsules with many seeds.

Habitat: Moist, rocky slopes, cliffs and ledges, in subalpine to alpine zones, often in spray zones near waterfalls; elsewhere, in wet places in the montane zone.

Notes: This little plant could be mistaken for a saxifrage (*Saxifraga* spp.) at first glance, but its flowers have broad, 5-lobed funnels (rather than separate petals) and form 1-sided, uncoiling clusters (rather than branched, panicle-like clusters). The capsules of Sitka romanzoffia are oblong and blunt-tipped, rather than 2-beaked. • The generic name *Romanzoffia* commemorates Nikolai Rumiantzev, Count Romanzoff (1754–1826), a Russian patron of botany who sponsored Kotzebue's expedition to the Pacific Northwest coast.

WATERPOD

Ellisia nyctelea L.
WATERLEAF FAMILY (HYDROPHYLLACEAE)

Plants: Delicate, more or less hairy annual herbs; stems {5} 10–40 cm tall, **usually freely branched**, sometimes unbranched.

Leaves: Opposite on lower stem, alternate above, 2–6 {10} cm long, **deeply pinnately cut** into 7–13 lance-shaped or oblong lobes; **stalks fringed** with stiff hairs.

Flowers: Whitish, often tinged blue, 6–12 mm across, **narrowly bell-shaped**, with tiny appendages in the throat, equal to or slightly longer than the calyx; calyx cut almost to the base into 5 lobes 3–5 mm long; stalks usually less than 1 cm long; **single, from leaf axils**; May–June {July}.

Fruits: Round, bristly-hairy capsules about 6 mm in diameter, **above 5 large** (usually about 1 cm long), **net-veined, wide-spreading sepals**, on long (up to 5 cm) stalks, splitting into 2 parts to release 4 round, 2.5–3 mm long, net-veined seeds.

Habitat: Moist shady woods and streambanks; elsewhere, on lake edges.

Notes: The generic name *Ellisia* commemorates the English botanist John Ellis, who lived 1710–76.

CWa

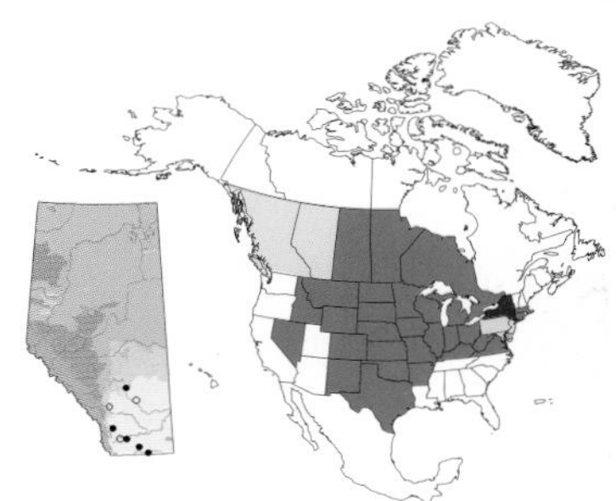

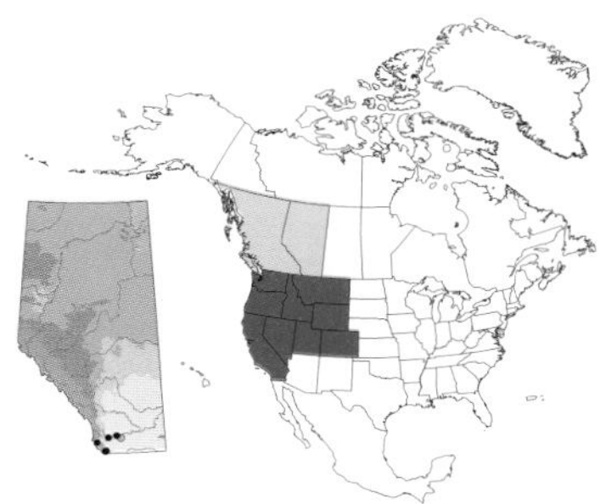

SMALL BABY-BLUE-EYES

Nemophila breviflora A. Gray
WATERLEAF FAMILY (HYDROPHYLLACEAE)

Plants: **Delicate annual** herbs; stems weak, usually ascending or loosely erect, sometimes spreading on the ground, 10–20 {30} cm long, generally branched, angled, with tiny, downward-pointing prickles; from weak taproots.

Leaves: Mostly alternate, egg-shaped in outline, **pinnately divided into 3–5 oblong to lance-shaped, pointed lobes** up to 2 cm long and 7 mm wide, thin, with coarse, stiff, often flat-lying hairs, conspicuously **fringed** with hairs (especially on the stalk).

Flowers: **White or purplish**, **cupped**, with a **5-lobed, 2 mm long corolla** and a longer, **deeply 5-lobed calyx**; calyxes **fringed with long, stiff hairs** and bearing a slender, 1–2 mm long, backward-bent lobe (auricle) in each of the 3–5 mm deep hollows (sinuses) between the lobes (sepals), growing with age to equal or surpass the capsule; **5 stamens**, shorter than the sepals; styles 0.5–1 mm long; **single, short-stalked**, from leaf axils or stem tips; {April–May} June–July.

Fruits: **Rounded capsules**, 3–5 mm long, **spreading or nodding on 5–15 mm long stalks**, cupped in the persistent calyxes, splitting in 2 to release a **single seed** tipped with an appendage that is soon shed.

Habitat: Moist montane woods and open slopes, in protected places, usually aspen groves, from foothills to moderate elevations in the mountains; elsewhere, in shrub thickets and coniferous woods, often on moist shale.

Notes: The appendage at the tip of the seed attracts ants, which feed on it. The ants also carry the seeds to their nests, thus helping to disperse and plant the seeds. • The generic name *Nemophila* was taken from the Greek *nemos* (a grove) and *philein* (to love) in reference to the wooded habitat of some species. The specific epithet *breviflora* means 'with short flowers.'

LINEAR-LEAVED SCORPIONWEED

Phacelia linearis (Pursh) Holzinger
WATERLEAF FAMILY (HYDROPHYLLACEAE)

JG

Plants: Slender **annual** herbs, hairy with tiny and bristly hairs; stems erect, 10–40 {50} cm tall, unbranched to freely branched; from weak taproots.

Leaves: Alternate, **linear to lance-shaped, 2–6** {1.5–11} **cm long**, 1.5–12 mm wide (excluding the lobes), **undivided or some deeply cut** into 3–7 linear to lance-shaped lobes, mostly stalkless; lower leaves soon withered.

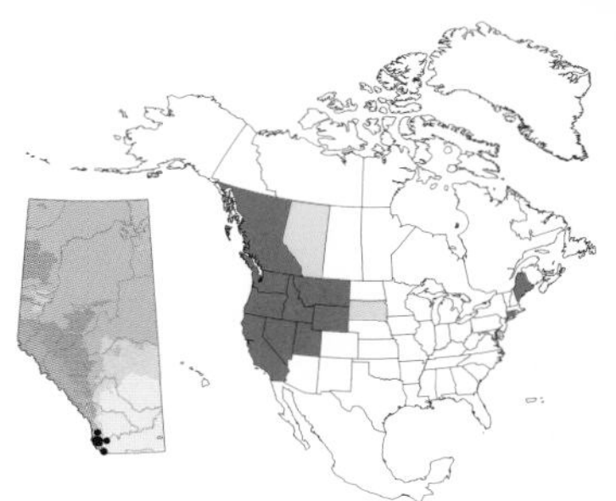

Flowers: Bright blue to blue-lavender (rarely white), **broadly bell-shaped**, showy, about 1 cm long, 8–18 mm across, with **5 broad petal lobes**, 5 linear, bristly fringed sepals, and **5 hairless stamens extending only slightly past petals**; several, in **compact clusters** (scorpioid cymes) **that uncoil as the flowers develop** and elongate in fruit; {April–May} June–July.

Fruits: Capsules containing about 6–15 black, oblong, coarsely pitted seeds.

Habitat: Dry, open slopes and plains.

Notes: Many phacelias make excellent ornamental plants in rock gardens. They are best grown from seed. • The common name 'scorpionweed' likens the coiled branches of the flower cluster to the tail of a scorpion. The generic name *Phacelia* was derived from the Greek *phakelos* (a fascicle or bundle), in reference to the dense flower clusters of some species.

LA

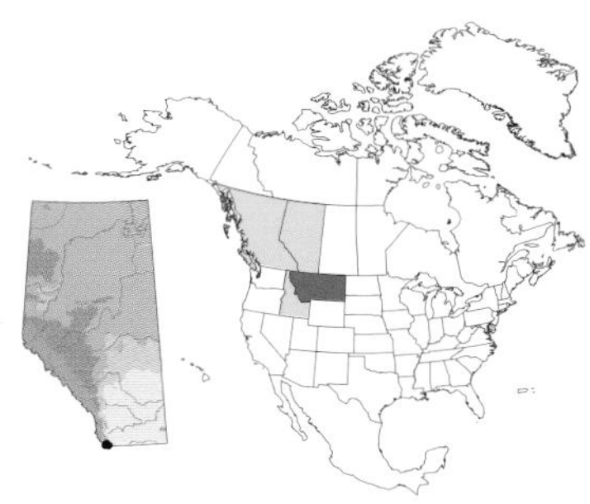

LYALL'S SCORPIONWEED

Phacelia lyallii (A. Gray) Rydb.
WATERLEAF FAMILY (HYDROPHYLLACEAE)

Plants: Dwarf **perennial** herbs; stems 10–20 {25} cm tall, sparsely hairy on the upper parts; from stout, branched crowns on taproots.

Leaves: Mainly basal but also alternate on the stem, **lance-shaped**, widest above the middle, **5–10 cm long**, up to 3 cm wide, **coarsely pinnately divided** into many oblong or lance-shaped lobes, with scattered hairs, sometimes glandular-hairy.

Flowers: Deep blue to bluish purple, bell-shaped, 8 {5–9} cm long and wide, with **5 petal lobes**, 5 slender, stiff-hairy sepals and **5 long, slender stamens 1½–2½ times as long as the petals** and projecting from the mouth of the flower, numerous, in **short, dense clusters that uncoil** as the flowers develop and elongate in fruit (scorpioid cymes); July–August.

Fruits: Capsules containing about 8–18 oblong, densely pitted seeds.

Habitat: Rocky alpine slopes, on talus and in rock crevices.

Notes: Lyall's scorpionweed is closely related to the more common species silky scorpionweed (*Phacelia sericea* (Graham) A. Gray) and was once considered a variety of that species. However, silky scorpionweed has more finely divided leaves (cut almost to the midrib into slender, linear segments) and longer (up to 20 cm long), spike-like flower clusters, and its stamens are 3 times as long as their corollas.

LARGE-FLOWERED LUNGWORT, LONG-FLOWERED BLUEBELLS

Mertensia longiflora Greene
BORAGE FAMILY (BORAGINACEAE)

TD

Plants: **Bluish green** perennial herbs, **10–30 cm tall**; stems erect or ascending, **hairless**, solitary or in clusters of 2–5; from **short, dark tuberous roots**, shallow and easily detached.

Leaves: **Alternate, few**; blades **elliptic to egg-shaped, usually widest above the middle**, blunt-tipped, **lacking distinct side veins**, 2–8 {10} cm long, **mostly 1½–4 times as long as wide**, hairless or stiff-hairy, sometimes fringed with hairs (ciliate), stalked on the lower stem to stalkless on the upper stem; **lower leaves soon withered**.

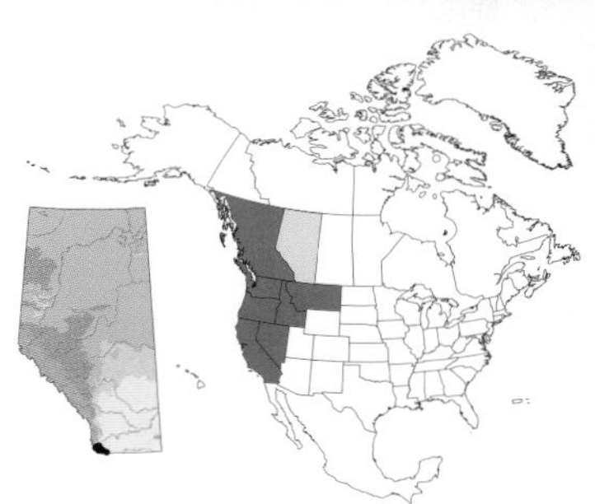

Flowers: **Blue** (occasionally white), **15–20 mm long**, with 5 rounded lobes at the tip of a long **tube 2–3 times as long as the flared upper part** (throat and limb), smooth inside; calyx hairless, 3–6 mm long, deeply cut into 5 lance-shaped lobes; stamens with broad, flat, 1.5–3 mm long filaments; styles extending past the anthers but included in or projecting slightly from the flower; numerous, **in compact, nodding clusters, elongating in fruit** (raceme-like), often with small flowering branches in the axils of nearby leaves; {April} May–June.

Fruits: Clusters of 4 small, erect nutlets, somewhat ridged, attached above the base to a convex receptacle.

Habitat: Open woods, moist slopes and meadows; elsewhere, on mesic, basaltic or sandy soils with sagebrush or ponderosa pine and along subalpine streams.

Notes: The common lungwort in Alberta, tall lungwort (*Mertensia paniculata* (Ait.) G. Don), has taller (usually 40–80 cm) plants with hairy stems, and its leaves have strong side veins. • Lance-leaved lungwort (*Mertensia lanceolata* (Pursh) A. DC., also known as prairie lungwort) is a similar species that is also rare in Alberta. Some taxonomists include *M. lanceolata* in *M. longiflora*. These species are often difficult to distinguish, and both grow on slopes in the mountains in southwestern Alberta. However, lance-leaved lungwort has narrower (mostly

M. LANCEOLATA

JG

oblong to lance-shaped) stem leaves, and the corolla tubes of its flowers are only slightly, if at all, longer than the throat and limb. It flowers from {May} June to July. • Most first-year plants produce only basal leaves. • The generic name *Mertensia* commemorates F.C. Mertens (1764–1831), a German botanist.

CWa

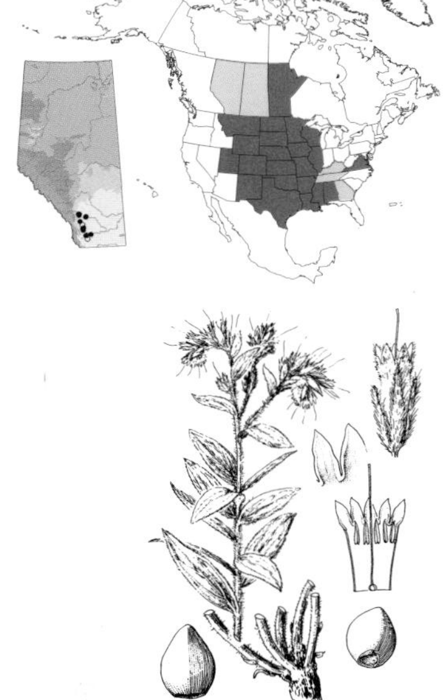

WESTERN FALSE GROMWELL

Onosmodium molle Michx. var. *occidentale* (Mack.) I.M. Johnston
BORAGE FAMILY (BORAGINACEAE)

Plants: Large, **loosely rough-hairy perennial herbs** with stiff, flat-lying and spreading hairs; **stems several, stout,** {30} 40–80 cm tall, branched above; from woody roots.

Leaves: Alternate, egg-shaped to broadly lance-shaped, 4–6 {3–8} cm long, with **5–7 prominent veins**, toothless, stalkless; lower leaves soon withered.

Flowers: Dull **yellowish white or greenish, tubular,** {10} **12–20 mm long**, tipped with 5 small (2–4 mm long), **erect, triangular lobes**; calyx 7–12 mm long, with 5 slender, densely stiff-hairy lobes; numerous, in leafy clusters with **dense, 1-sided, uncoiling branches** (scorpioid racemes or spikes); June–July.

Fruits: Shiny white or brownish nutlets, 2.5–3.5 {5} mm long, smooth or with a few scattered pits.

Habitat: Gravelly banks and dry, open woods.

Notes: This variety has also been called *Onosmodium occidentale* Mack. • People are reported to have been **poisoned** after drinking herbal teas containing this plant. • The generic name *Onosmodium* was taken from *Onosma*, a similar Eurasian genus. The specific epithet *molle* means 'soft,' perhaps in reference to the soft appearance of these hairy plants.

SMALL CRYPTANTHE, TINY CRYPTANTHE

Cryptantha minima Rydb.
BORAGE FAMILY (BORAGINACEAE)

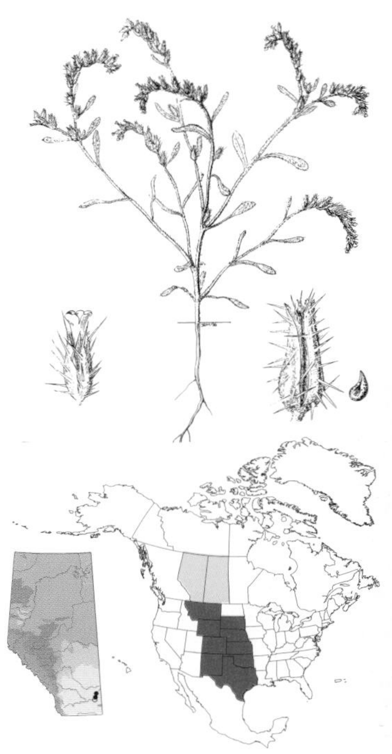

Plants: Dwarf **annual herbs, 10–20 cm tall** in flower; stems branched, erect, bristly-hairy.

Leaves: Mostly **alternate, spatula-shaped, 5–15 mm long** and 2–3 mm wide, gradually becoming smaller higher up the stem.

Flowers: White, tiny, 2.5–3 mm long and a little over 1 mm across; **calyxes 2–2.5 mm long** in flower, enlarging to about 5 mm long in fruit, eventually shed, **covered with long, bristly hairs**; numerous, **in the axils of small bracts** on 1 side of slender, uncoiling branches, forming spreading clusters (cymes); {May–June}.

Fruits: Small clusters of 4 whitish nutlets of different shapes (heteromorphic), 1 smooth, 1.6–2 mm long and about 1.2 mm wide, the other 3 covered with tiny bumps, 1.2–1.5 mm long and 0.7–0.9 mm wide.

Habitat: Dry, eroded prairie slopes.

Notes: Another species that may occur in Alberta, slender cryptanthe (*Cryptantha affinis* (A. Gray) Greene), differs from small cryptanthe in having somewhat larger plants, 2–3 cm long linear to oblong leaves, slightly larger flowers and 4 nearly identical, egg-shaped nutlets. It is also reported to flower slightly later, in June and July. • A more common Alberta species, Fendler's cryptanthe (*Cryptantha fendleri* (A. Gray) Greene), produces clusters of 4 smooth, lance-shaped nutlets. It grows on sandy soil and dunes and blooms from May to July {August}. It is locally abundant in Alberta, but its populations seem to fluctuate greatly with changes in moisture conditions. It also requires eroding surfaces, so stabilization of dunes is a threat to some populations. • The generic name *Cryptantha* was taken from the Greek *krypto* (to hide) and *anthos* (flower) because several species have flowers that never open and appear hidden. The specific epithet *minima* is Latin for 'very small or least.'

C. FENDLERI

PL

C. AFFINIS

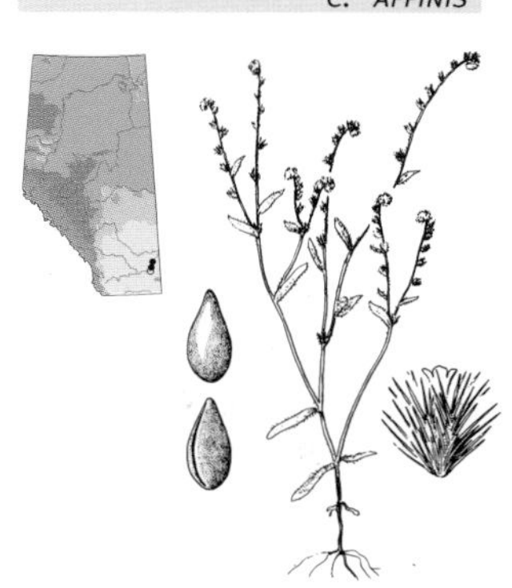

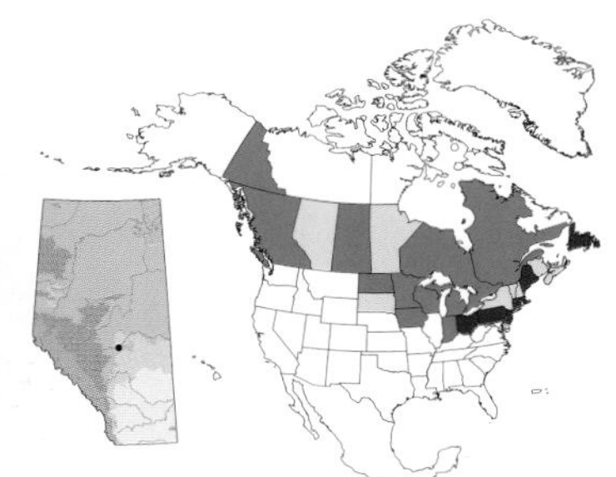

HOUND'S-TONGUE, WILD COMFREY

Cynoglossum virginianum L. var. *boreale* (Fern.) Cooperrider
BORAGE FAMILY (BORAGINACEAE)

Plants: Coarse-hairy perennial herbs; stems erect, unbranched, leafy, 40–80 cm tall; from taproots.

Leaves: Basal and alternate, with **many stiff, flat-lying hairs**; lower leaves tapered to long, slender stalks; upper leaves smaller, stalkless and clasping; blades elliptic, 7–20 cm long, 2–7 cm wide.

Flowers: Blue (sometimes white), **funnel-shaped**, with 5 spreading lobes at the tip of a short tube, {5} **6–8 mm across**; sepals {1} 2–3 mm long; numerous, in **leafless clusters** with 3–several **elongating, 1-sided**, spreading **branches** (false racemes); {June–July}.

Fruits: Clusters of **4 nutlets** {3.5} 4–5 mm long, covered with short, **barbed prickles**, borne on 5–15 mm long, down-turned stalks.

Habitat: Dry woods; elsewhere, sometimes in moist woods.

Notes: This species has also been included in *Cynoglossum boreale* Fern. • A somewhat similar plant, fringed stickseed (*Hackelia ciliata* (Dougl. *ex* Lehm.) I.M. Johnston), has larger (8–12 mm wide) blue flowers in more compact clusters and leaves that do not clasp the stem. Fringed stickseed is best identified by its nutlets, which are edged with broad prickles that are joined for at least ⅓–½ of their length and that curve upward to form a shallow cup. It grows on dry, open slopes, often in sagebrush and pine woodlands, and has been reported to occur in Alberta. It flowers from May to June. • The hooked spines on the nutlets catch on the fur, feathers or clothing of passers-by, effectively dispersing the seeds to new sites. • There have been **reports of deaths of horses** after feeding on hay containing the related species common hound's-tongue (*Cynoglossum officinale* L.), and cattle grazing on pasture with hound's-tongue are said to have been poisoned. It is also said to be **mildly poisonous to people**, and **the stiff hairs on its fuzzy leaves can irritate sensitive skin**. • According to early herbalists, a poultice of bruised hound's-tongue leaves was the only treatment needed to cure lesions from the bites of mad dogs. Hair loss from high fevers could also be controlled by massaging a salve, made from bruised leaves and swine's grease, into the scalp. • The bruised fresh roots of hound's-tongue have a heavy, unpleasant odour that was said to repel insects and rodents. • The rough surface of the nutlets, or possibly of the leaves of some species, was thought to resemble the surface of a dog's tongue—hence the common name 'hound's-tongue' and the generic name *Cynoglossum*, from the Greek *cynos* (dog) and *glossa* (tongue).

SPATULATE-LEAVED HELIOTROPE

Heliotropium curassavicum L.
BORAGE FAMILY (BORAGINACEAE)

Plants: Low, succulent, short-lived, **hairless** perennial herbs (usually annual elsewhere); stems with **spreading bases** (often on the ground) and ascending tips, 10–40 cm long, usually **coated with a whitish bloom** (glaucous); from weak, slender roots.

Leaves: Alternate, **fleshy, lance-shaped to spatula-shaped**, widest above middle, 2–4 {6} cm long, short-stalked, toothless; basal leaves reduced to scales.

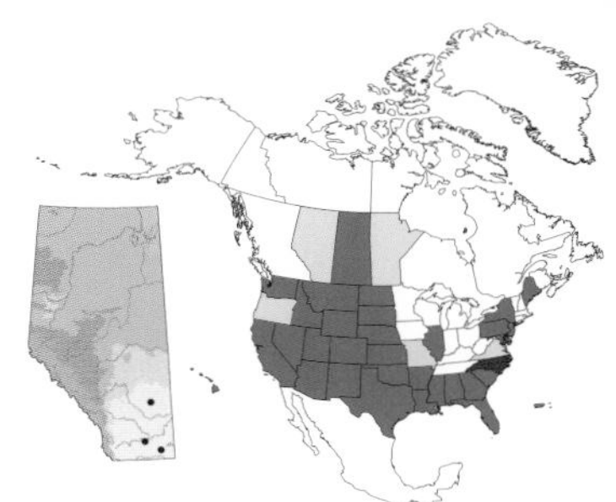

Flowers: White (sometimes faintly bluish) **with a yellow eye**, 6–8 {5–9} mm across with 5 widely spreading lobes at the tip of a short tube; calyx 2–3 mm long; numerous, in branched clusters with **short, densely flowered, 1-sided, uncoiling branches** (scorpioid spikes) on **leafless stalks** up to 6 {10} cm long; June–July {August–September}.

Fruits: Clusters of **4 nutlets** 1.5–2 mm long, tardily splitting apart.

Habitat: Saline flats, often on dried lake beds; elsewhere, most common along the seacoast and in salt marshes.

Notes: The generic name *Heliotropium* was taken from the Greek *helios* (the sun) and *tropos* (to turn) because some species were said to open in the morning facing east and to gradually turn to the west, following the sun as the day progresses. Then, during the night, the same flower was said to turn east again to meet the rising sun the following morning. The specific epithet *curassavicum* means 'of Curaçao' (in the Caribbean Sea).

DJ

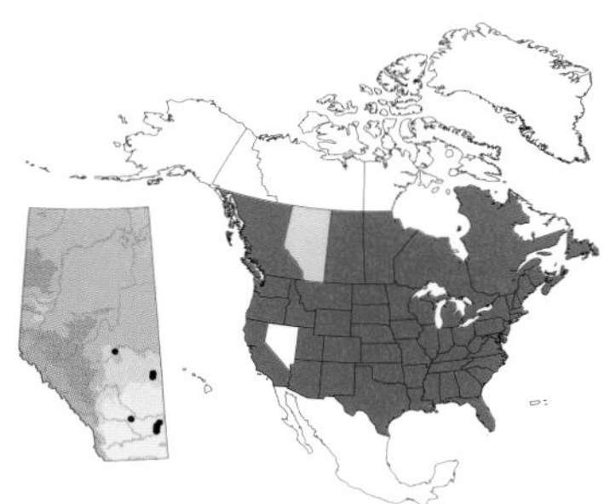

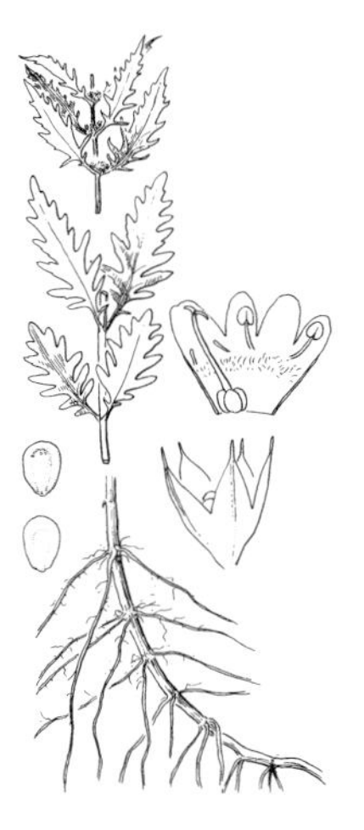

American water-horehound

Lycopus americanus Muhl. *ex* W.C. Barton
MINT FAMILY (LAMIACEAE [LABIATAE])

Plants: Slender perennial herbs; stems erect, 20–80 cm tall, 4-sided, nearly hairless (hairy at the joints); from trailing runners (stolons) and slender underground stems (rhizomes).

Leaves: Opposite, spreading horizontally, lance-shaped, gradually tapered at the tip, abruptly narrowed at the base, 2–7 {8} cm long, **deeply pinnately cut**, short-stalked; upper leaves smaller, toothed to toothless.

Flowers: Bluish white, about 3 mm across, with 4 petals (lobes) at the tip of a short tube, hairy within; sepals fused into a cupped **calyx tipped with 4 equal, slender-pointed lobes**; numerous, **in dense whorls from upper leaf axils**; July {June–August}.

Fruits: Nutlets, 3-sided, **1–1.5 mm long**, 0.8–0.9 {1.2} mm wide, with a thickened, corky ridge along the side angles and across the tip, shorter than the calyx lobes.

Habitat: Marshy sites and moist, low ground along streams.

Notes: American water-horehound might be confused with a mint (*Mentha* spp.), but water-horehounds do not have the characteristic minty aroma. • Plants of this genus are called water-horehounds because they grow in wet, marshy environments and resemble true horehound (*Marrubium vulgare* L.), a European mint that is also a common introduced weed in much of North America. • The generic name *Lycopus* was taken from the Greek *lycos* (wolf) and *pous* (foot) as a translation of the French common name for these plants, *patte du loup*.

FALSE DRAGONHEAD

Physostegia ledinghamii (Boivin) Cantino
MINT FAMILY (LAMIACEAE [LABIATAE])

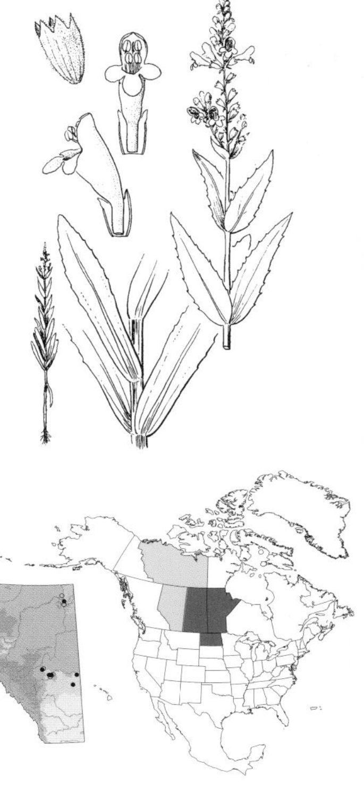

Plants: Perennial herbs, hairless or with very fine hairs; stems 4-sided, erect, 30–90 {20–100} cm tall, unbranched or branched at the base of the flower cluster; from an underground stem (rhizome) or rhizome-like base with fibrous roots.

Leaves: Opposite, 3–10 cm long, 5–20 mm wide, **elliptic–lance-shaped to linear-oblong**, pointed, **stalkless**, edged with **blunt or hooked teeth** (sometimes almost toothless); lower leaves soon withered.

Flowers: Rose-pink to lavender-purple, showy, **8–16 mm long, funnel-shaped**, enlarged at the mouth and tipped with an **erect, hooded upper lip** and a **spreading, 3-lobed lower lip; calyx** somewhat inflated, 4–6 mm long, 5-toothed, 10-nerved, **with short, fine, gland-tipped hairs**; 4 stamens, under the upper lip; several to many, almost stalkless, in the axils of **small, egg-shaped bracts**, in **elongated, spike-like clusters** (racemes) at the stem tip and sometimes also from the axils of upper leaves; {July–September}.

Fruits: Smooth, ovoid nutlets.

Habitat: Moist woods and streambanks; elsewhere, on lake shores and in marshes.

Notes: This species was once included with *Physostegia parviflora* Nutt. *ex* A. Gray, *Physostegia virginiana* (L.) Benth. var. *ledinghamii* Boivin and *Dracocephalum nuttallii* Britt. It is not synonymous with *Dracocephalum parviflorum* Nutt. (also known as *Moldavica parviflora* (Nutt.) Britton), which is American dragonhead.

CWa

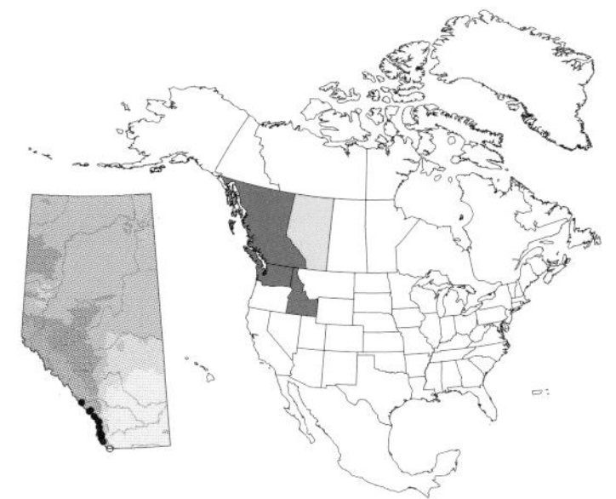

SHRUBBY BEARDTONGUE, SHRUBBY PENSTEMON

Penstemon fruticosus (Pursh) Greene var. *scouleri* (Lindl.) Cronq.
FIGWORT FAMILY (SCROPHULARIACEAE)

Plants: Low, bushy semi-shrub, {5} 10–40 cm tall; stems freely branched, often reddish and brittle, glandular-hairy near top, forming **dense clumps from a woody base.**

Leaves: Opposite and in basal clusters, narrowly **lance-shaped**, 2–5 {6} cm long (much smaller upward on flowering stems), **dark green and hairless above**, saw-toothed to nearly toothless.

Flowers: Bluish lavender to pale purple, 3.5–4.5 {3–5} **cm long, tubular, 2-lipped**, long-white-hairy on lower lip; calyx with dense, glandular hairs on slender, pointed lobes; anthers long-woolly; borne **in pairs in short clusters** (racemes) at branch tips; June–July {August}.

Fruits: Capsules, 8–12 mm long.

Habitat: Dry, rocky slopes and open woods in subalpine and alpine zones.

Notes: Shrubby beardtongue could be confused with elliptic-leaved beardtongue (*Penstemon ellipticus* Coult. & Fisher), a low (5–15 cm tall), mat-forming (rather than bushy) species with broader (elliptic to egg-shaped) leaves. • The leaves and flowers of shrubby beardtongue were added to cooking pits with wild onions (*Allium* spp.) and the roots of arrow-leaved balsamroot (*Balsamorhiza sagittata* (Pursh) Nutt.). • The stems, flowers and leaves were soaked or boiled to make an eyewash and a bath for relieving rheumatism. The boiled tea was taken to relieve sore backs, ulcers and kidney problems and to 'clean out your insides.' It was also used as a wash for treating arthritis, aches and sores (on both humans and horses). • Bees and hummingbirds pollinate these long, tubular flowers. • The generic name *Penstemon* was derived from the Latin *pente* (five) and *stemon* (thread), referring to the 5 (4 fertile plus 1 sterile) stamens of these flowers. Penstemons are called beardtongues because of their bearded sterile stamen.

WATER SPEEDWELL

Veronica catenata Pennell
FIGWORT FAMILY (SCROPHULARIACEAE)

Plants: **Semi-aquatic** perennial herbs; stems stout, **succulent, hairless** or with a few fine, glandular hairs in the flower cluster, more or less erect, 40–80 {20–100} cm tall, with ascending branches; from creeping underground stems (rhizomes) with fibrous roots.

Leaves: **Opposite, narrowly elliptic to oblong**, 2–7 {10} cm long, {2.5} 3–5 times as long as wide, toothless or sharply toothed, stalkless, **clasping** the stem.

Flowers: **White to pink or pale bluish**, about 5 mm across, with a short, inconspicuous tube tipped with **4 broad, nearly equal, widely spreading lobes** and with 2 stamens projecting from the centre; **calyxes** deeply cut into **4 lobes**, highly variable; numerous, on slender 3–8 mm long stalks in loose, elongating, 4–12 cm long, branched clusters (racemes) **from upper leaf axils**, essentially hairless; July {June–September}.

Fruits: Slightly heart-shaped capsules, 2.5–4 mm long, mostly wider than high, shallowly notched at the tip, borne on slender, widely spreading stalks; seeds numerous, up to 0.5 mm long.

Habitat: Marshy, muddy or gravelly ground and shallow water, by ponds and streams and in ditches; elsewhere, by springs and spring-fed streams.

Notes: This species includes *Veronica comosa* Richt. var. *glaberrima* (Pennell) Boivin and *Veronica salina auct. non* Schur. It is sometimes included in *Veronica anagallis-aquatica* L. • Water speedwell might be confused with marsh speedwell (*Veronica scutellata* L.), but marsh speedwell has linear leaves that do not clasp the stem with their bases. • Another Alberta speedwell, thyme-leaved speedwell (*Veronica serpyllifolia* L. var. *humifusa* (Dickson) Vahl), has slightly smaller (5–8 mm wide) flowers in elongated clusters at the stem tips only (not from leaf axils). Its lower leaves are stalked and its capsules are deeply notched and covered with glandular hairs. Thyme-leaved speedwell blooms in June

V. SERPYLLIFOLIA

DJ

{May–August}. It grows on moist, montane slopes in Alberta and in moist meadows and roadside ditches elsewhere. • The generic name *Veronica* comes from the Latin *vera iconica* (true likeness). The flowers of some species were said to bear markings similar to those that were left on the cloth used by St. Veronica to wipe the face of Jesus as he carried the cross.

JD

JD

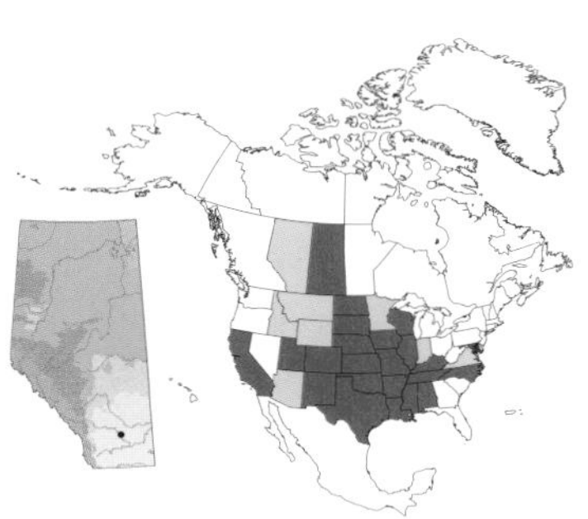

WATER HYSSOP

Bacopa rotundifolia (Michx.) Wettst.
FIGWORT FAMILY (SCROPHULARIACEAE)

Plants: Succulent, aquatic perennial herbs; stems branched, 10–40 cm long, floating, bearing spreading hairs at the tips; from fibrous roots.

Leaves: Opposite, hairless, with several **nerves in a finger-like pattern**, nearly round to broadly egg-shaped and widest above the middle, 1–3 cm long, stalkless.

Flowers: White with a yellow centre, about **5–10 mm across**, tubular–bell-shaped with **5 equal, spreading lobes at the tip of a tube**; upper lobes external in bud, lobes equal to or a little less than tube in length; 5 sepals, separate, 3–5 mm long, dissimilar, the upper one nearly round, the others much narrower; **4 fertile stamens**; borne singly **on stout, 5–20 mm long stalks from leaf axils**; {June–September}.

Fruits: Capsules, splitting open lengthwise, containing many seeds.

Habitat: Mud-bottomed pools.

Notes: The generic name *Bacopa* is the Latin form of an aboriginal name that was used for a plant of this genus by natives of French Guiana.

FIELD TOADFLAX, BLUE TOADFLAX

Nuttallanthus canadensis (L.) D.A. Sutton
FIGWORT FAMILY (SCROPHULARIACEAE)

Plants: Slender, bluish green annual or winter annual herbs, essentially hairless, 10–60 cm tall, with **a single to several erect**, unbranched, sparsely leafy **stems** and also a **spreading rosette of short, low-lying stems** with ascending tips; from short taproots.

Leaves: Mostly **paired or in 3s on lower stems**, mostly **alternate on upper erect stems, linear**, 1–3.5 cm long and 1–2.5 mm wide on erect stems, shorter and wider on low-lying stems.

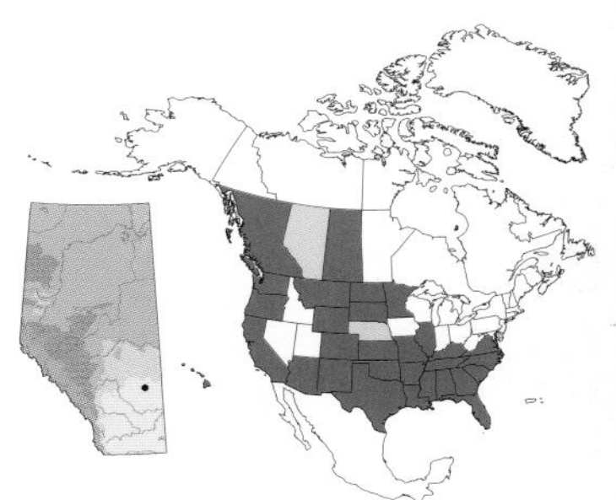

Flowers: Light blue, funnel-shaped, with a small, 2-lobed upper lip, a **broad, paler, 3-lobed lower lip** and a **slender tube** (spur) extending down and **curved forward** from the base, 8–12 mm long (excluding the 2–9 mm long spur); lower lip paler, scarcely raised; several, in leafless, elongating clusters (racemes); {April–June}.

Fruits: Broadly ellipsoid capsules, 2.5–4 mm long, with many angled seeds.

Habitat: Moist, sandy sites.

Notes: This species has also been called *Linaria canadensis* (L.) Dum.-Cours.

CWa

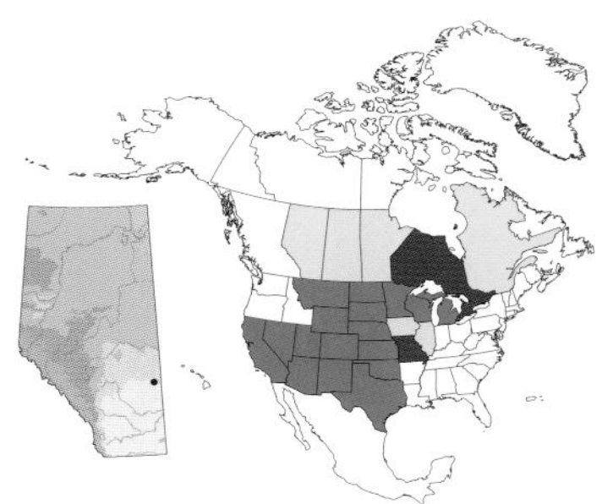

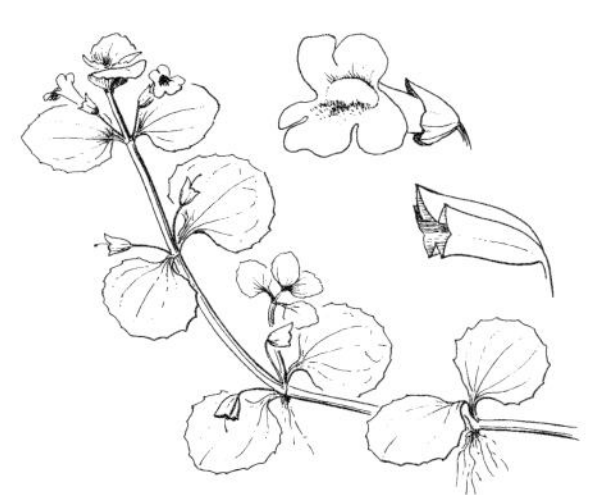

SMOOTH MONKEYFLOWER

Mimulus glabratus Kunth
FIGWORT FAMILY (SCROPHULARIACEAE)

Plants: Low, diffusely spreading perennial herbs; stems weak, hairless or inconspicuously hairy, **creeping or floating**, often **rooting at the joints** (nodes), 5–60 cm long, leafy; from underground stems (rhizomes).

Leaves: Opposite, broadly egg-shaped to **round** to somewhat kidney-shaped, 1–4 cm long, **veiny**, with 3–7 finger-like (palmate) nerves, toothless or edged with small, irregular teeth, **nearly stalkless**.

Flowers: Bright yellow, sparingly (if at all) red-spotted, {10} **15–25 mm long, tubular**, with an **open throat and 2 broad lips**, the upper lip 2-lobed and the lower lip fuzzy and 3-lobed; **calyx** 5-angled, 5-toothed, irregular, **with a large upper tooth** and short, blunt side and lower teeth, **inflated in fruit**, 5–12 mm long; **4 anther-bearing stamens**; few, long-stalked, in the axils of upper leaves; {May–August}.

Fruits: Many-seeded capsules, inside inflated calyxes.

Habitat: Wet places, often in water and around springs.

Notes: Smooth monkeyflower might be confused with yellow monkeyflower (*Mimulus guttatus* DC., p. 197), but yellow monkeyflower is a larger, more erect plant with larger flowers (25–45 mm long) and larger mature calyxes (12–17 mm long). • Small yellow monkeyflower (*Mimulus floribundus* Dougl. *ex* Lindl.) is another rare Alberta species. It is a small (5–25 cm tall), usually sticky-hairy annual plant with small (7–15 mm long), only slightly 2-lipped flowers, which have sharply angled calyxes with 5 nearly equal teeth. Small yellow monkeyflower grows on moist banks in montane areas, and it flowers in July {May–October}. • The generic name *Mimulus* was derived from the Latin *mimus* (a mimic or actor) because these flowers were thought to resemble small, grinning faces.

M. FLORIBUNDUS

LA

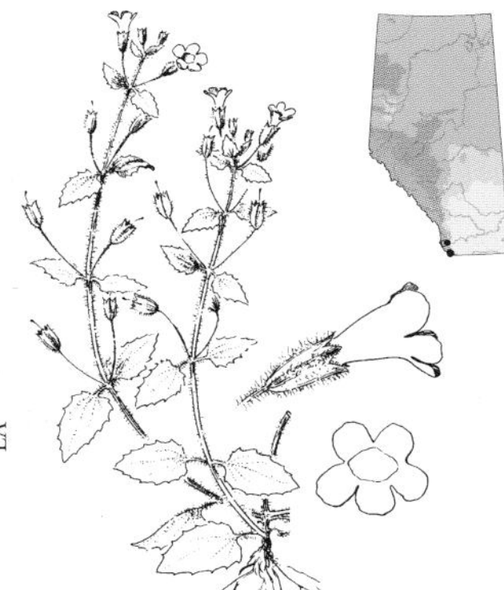

YELLOW MONKEYFLOWER

Mimulus guttatus DC.
FIGWORT FAMILY (SCROPHULARIACEAE)

TD

Plants: Highly variable annual or perennial herbs; stems stout and erect or weak and trailing, 20–60 {5–80} cm tall, often rooting at joints (nodes); from fibrous roots (annual) or stolons (perennial).

Leaves: **Opposite, oval** or egg-shaped, widest above the middle, 1–5 cm long, **coarsely and unevenly wavy-toothed, 3–7-veined**; lower leaves stalked; upper leaves stalkless and clasping.

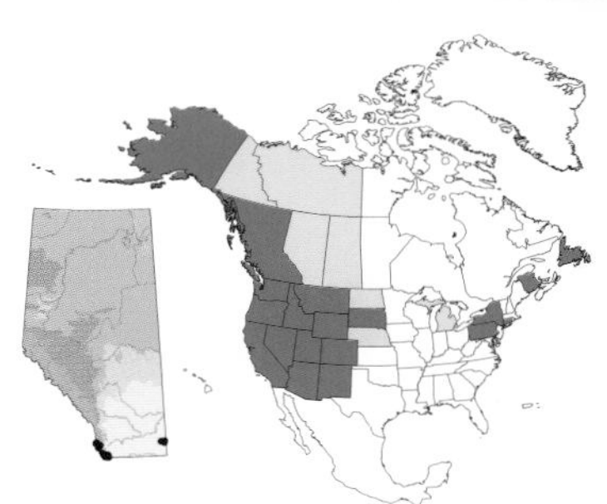

Flowers: **Bright yellow, snapdragon-like**, trumpet-shaped and 2-lipped, {1} 2–4 cm long but usually less than 2 cm when few in number, slender-stalked; lower lip larger than upper, **hairy and spotted with crimson** or reddish brown; sepals quite unequal, fused, 1–2 cm long; few to several (usually more than 5), in loose clusters (racemes) on slender stalks; {April–June} July–August.

Fruits: Broadly oblong capsules, 1–2 cm long, contained **in inflated 'balloons' of fused sepals.**

Habitat: Wet meadows, springs and streambanks.

Notes: Large mountain monkeyflower (*Mimulus tilingii* Regel) is also rare in Alberta. It is very similar to yellow monkeyflower (some taxonomists include these taxa in the same species), but its plants are low-growing (less than 20 cm tall) with many sod-forming underground stems (rhizomes) (sometimes with stolons too), and its flowers are few (usually 1–5) and large (2–4 cm long). It grows in wet alpine sites, where it flowers in August {July–September}. • Yellow monkeyflower plants were eaten raw or cooked by native peoples and early settlers in the Rocky Mountains, but they are bitter when raw. The stems and leaves were also applied to burns and wounds as poultices, to speed healing and stop bleeding. • The 2 rounded lobes of the stigma are initially widespread, but when they are brushed by a pollen-laden insect, they immediately fold together (like the pages of a book), holding the pollen firmly. This prevents self-pollination when the same insect backs out of the flower.

M. TILINGII

PL

PA

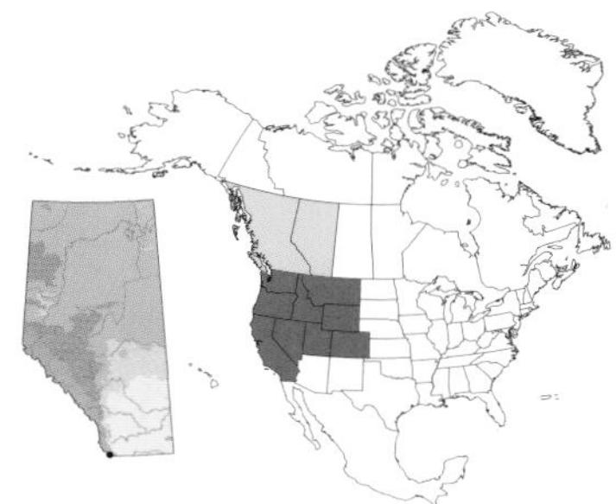

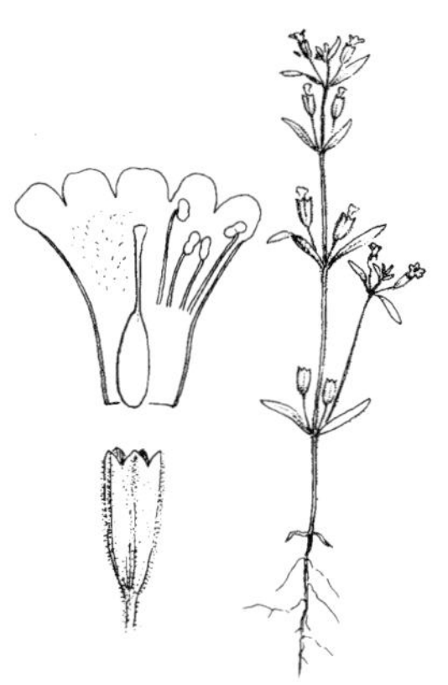

BREWER'S MONKEYFLOWER

Mimulus breweri (Greene) Coville
FIGWORT FAMILY (SCROPHULARIACEAE)

Plants: Delicate, often reddish annual herbs with copious glandular hairs; stems slender, **less than 15 cm tall**, unbranched or sparingly branched; from weak taproots.

Leaves: Opposite, long and narrow, 1–2 cm long, 1–4 mm wide, faintly 3-nerved, entire, stalkless.

Flowers: Red to purple, often with **yellow markings in the throat**; funnel-shaped, **5–10 mm long**, somewhat 2-lipped, with 5 small, nearly equal petal lobes at the tip of a slender tube; calyx tube glandular-hairy, tipped with 5 short, nearly equal teeth; {June–August}.

Fruits: Small, ascending capsules, splitting in half to release numerous seeds.

Habitat: Moist slopes and meadows; elsewhere, on moderately dry slopes.

Notes: Red monkeyflower (*Mimulus lewisii* Pursh) is the only other red-flowered monkeyflower that occurs in Alberta. It is a 30–70 cm tall perennial with large (3–5 cm long) flowers and grows in wet places in the mountains. • Brewer's monkeyflower was first discovered in Alberta in 1997 and is known only from Waterton Lakes National Park. • The specific epithet *breweri* commemorates W.H. Brewer, an American naturalist who lived 1828–1910.

LEAFY LOUSEWORT, SICKLETOP LOUSEWORT

Pedicularis racemosa Dougl. *ex* Hook.
FIGWORT FAMILY (SCROPHULARIACEAE)

Plants: Perennial herbs, essentially hairless; stems 15–50 cm tall, **unbranched**, clumped; from fibrous roots.

Leaves: Alternate, **lance-shaped to linear**, 3–8 cm long, largest near middle of stem, **coarsely round-toothed**, often reddish.

Flowers: White, sometimes tinged pink, 12–15 mm long, 2-lipped, with a **broad, 3-lobed lower lip and an arching upper lip tapered to a sickle-shaped, down-curved beak;** calyx 2-lobed; few flowers, from leaf axils and in long, loose clusters (racemes); {June} July–August.

Fruits: Smooth, flattened, curved capsules.

Habitat: Dry, open subalpine slopes; elsewhere, in coniferous montane stands and on alpine slopes.

Notes: A more common species, coil-beaked lousewort (*Pedicularis contorta* Benth. *ex* Hook.), is very similar to leafy lousewort, but its calyx is 5-lobed and its leaves are deeply cut into narrow, toothed leaflets, giving them a fern-like appearance. • Large-flowered lousewort (*Pedicularis capitata* J.E. Adams) is a small (5–15 cm tall) species with compact, head-like clusters of relatively large (25–30 mm long), white to faintly pinkish flowers with broad, square-tipped (beakless) hoods. Its small leaves are finely pinnately divided (rather fern-like), and its flowering stems are usually leafless. Large-flowered lousewort is also rare in Alberta, where it grows on calcareous alpine slopes and flowers from June to August. • Louseworts are said to be edible in an emergency, raw or cooked, but they contain enough glycosides to **cause severe illness** if they are eaten in quantity. • The generic name *Pedicularis* from the Latin *pedis* (a louse), and the common name lousewort both come from the early belief that animals that ate these plants were more likely to be infested with lice. Most animals do not eat these plants, and therefore it is more likely that such livestock were grazing in poor pastures, where they were more likely to become weakened and louse-ridden.

WM

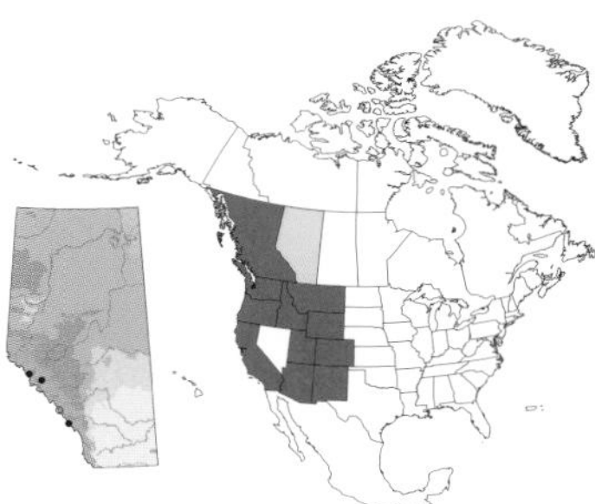

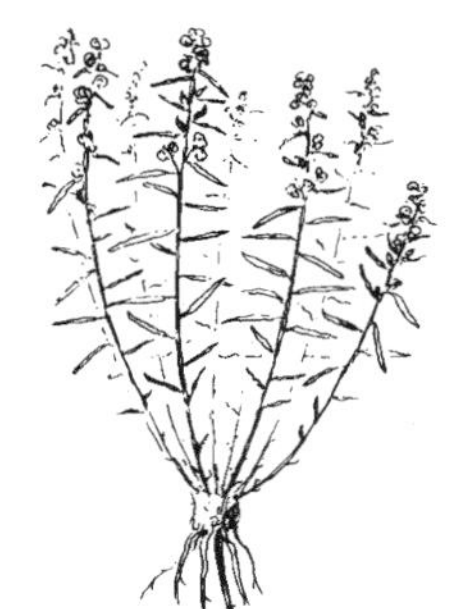

P. CAPITATA

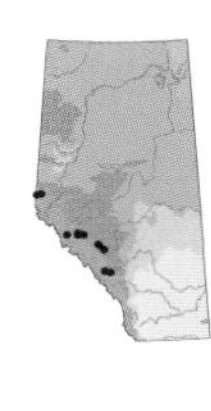

JG

DJ

P. LANGSDORFII

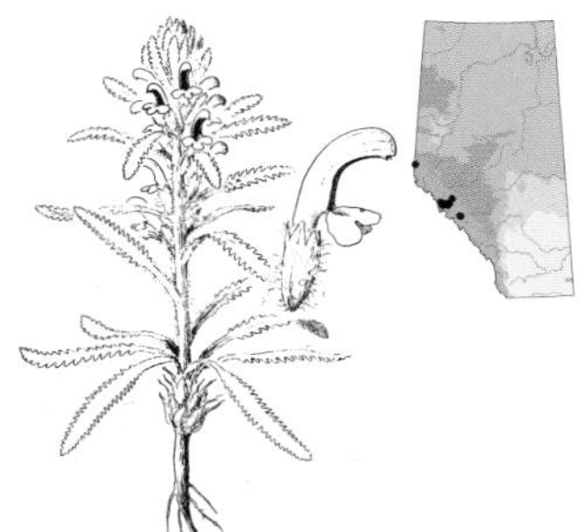

PURPLE RATTLE

Pedicularis sudetica Willd. ssp. *interioides* Hult.
FIGWORT FAMILY (SCROPHULARIACEAE)

Plants: **Slender** perennial herbs, **hairless to sparsely soft-hairy**; stems erect, unbranched, {5} 10–40 cm tall, with 0–2 {3} small leaves, single or in small clumps; from **short, branched** underground stems (rhizomes).

Leaves: Mainly basal, linear to lance-shaped, **feather-like, pinnately divided** into narrow, toothed lobes, long-stalked.

Flowers: **Rose-pink to crimson-purple**, showy, **15–24 mm long**, strongly 2-lipped, with a **slender, purple, arched, 6–13 mm long upper lip** (galea) **tipped with 2 tiny, slender teeth** above a pink or spotted, **broad, 3-lobed lower lip**; calyxes 8–12 mm long, tipped with 5 slender, pointed lobes, woolly to hairless; **numerous, in woolly to soft-hairy spikes**, compact and head-like at first but elongating in fruit, often with 1 or 2 leafy bracts at the base; July {August}.

Fruits: Slightly flattened, **oblong capsules**, 9–14 mm long, tipped with a **short point**, containing many rough-textured seeds.

Habitat: Fens; elsewhere, in wet, calcareous tundra and on lakeshores.

Notes: Two other rare species, arctic lousewort (*Pedicularis langsdorfii* Fisch. *ex* Stev. ssp. *arctica* (R. Br.) Pennell, also called *Pedicularis arctica* R. Br.) and woolly lousewort (*Pedicularis lanata* Cham. & Schlecht., p. 201), have leafy stems and stout, yellowish taproots (rather than rhizomes). • Louseworts have typical bee-pollinated flowers, and their range coincides with that of bumblebees. All louseworts are partial parasites, capable of producing their own food, but also of stealing nutrients from their neighbours through sucker-like attachments on their roots. Once this relationship is established, the plants are very difficult to transplant.

WOOLLY LOUSEWORT

Pedicularis lanata Cham. & Schlecht.
FIGWORT FAMILY (SCROPHULARIACEAE)

Plants: **Stout, woolly** perennial herbs; stems erect, unbranched, 5–15 {40} cm tall, usually densely white-woolly and leafy; from **bright lemon-yellow taproots.**

Leaves: Alternate, **crowded**, linear to lance-shaped, feather-like, **pinnately divided** into narrow, toothed lobes.

Flowers: **Rose-pink to lavender** (rarely white), showy, faintly scented, **18–20** {15–25} **mm long**, strongly 2-lipped, with a narrow, **straight or slightly arched, 3–5** {8} **mm long upper lip** (galea) above a **broad, 2–5 mm long, 3-lobed lower lip**; calyx 4–5 mm long, tipped with 5 pointed, triangular lobes 0.5–1 mm long; **numerous, in dense, copiously woolly, elongating spikes**; June–July.

Fruits: Slightly flattened, pointed, egg-shaped capsules, 8–13 mm long; seeds large, with loose, ashy-grey, honeycombed seed coats.

Habitat: Rocky alpine slopes; elsewhere, in moist, stony tundra.

Notes: Woolly lousewort might be confused with another rare Alberta species, arctic lousewort (*Pedicularis langsdorfii* Fisch. *ex* Stev. ssp. *arctica* (R. Br.) Pennell, also called *Pedicularis arctica* R. Br., p. 200), but arctic lousewort is much less woolly (often almost hairless) and the upper lip of its flower is tipped with 2 slender teeth which are not found on woolly lousewort flowers. Arctic lousewort grows on moist alpine slopes and flowers in July {June–August}. • Purple rattle (*Pedicularis sudetica* Willd., p. 200) has flowers very similar to those of woolly lousewort, but its stems are hairless and almost leafless. • Northern native peoples ate the shoots and young flowering stems raw, cooked or mixed in fat and stored. The roots have been likened to carrots, and they were eaten raw, roasted or boiled. Children enjoyed sucking nectar from the base of the long flower tubes. • Some tribes used the roots as a tobacco substitute or boiled them to make a yellow dye.

JG

LA

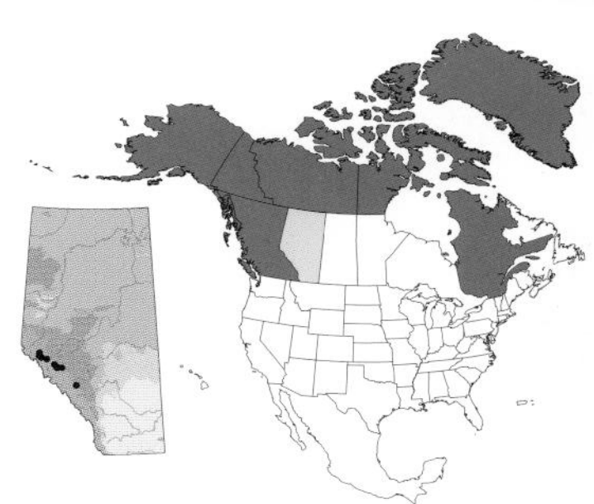

P. LANGSDORFII

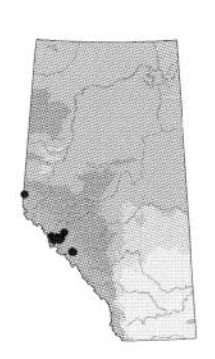

LA

CWa

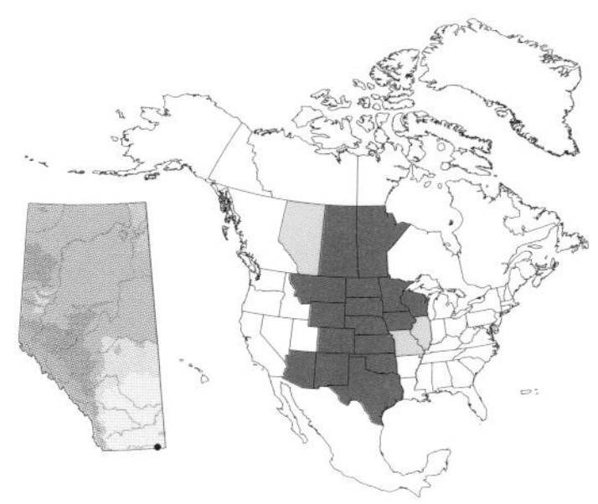

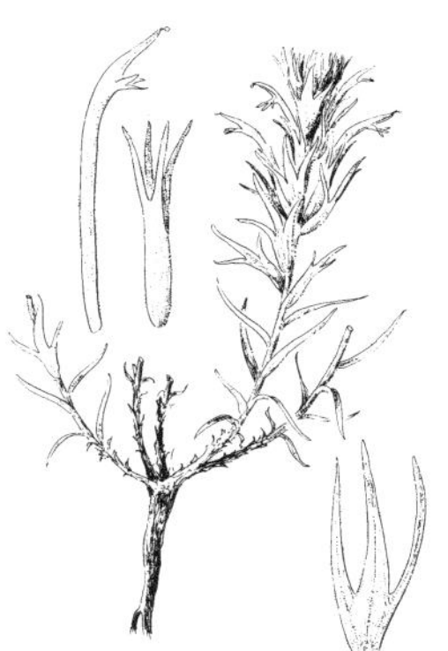

DOWNY PAINTBRUSH, DOWNY PAINTED-CUP

Castilleja sessiliflora Pursh
FIGWORT FAMILY (SCROPHULARIACEAE)

Plants: Loosely clumped perennial herbs, **ashy-grey with silky and woolly hairs**; stems erect or ascending, 10–40 cm tall, sometimes branched near the base; from branched root crowns.

Leaves: Alternate, 2–4 cm long, linear and undivided on the lower stem, **broader and tipped with 3–5 slender, spreading lobes on the upper stem**, densely covered with short, often woolly hairs.

Flowers: Pale yellow, sometimes pinkish or purplish, {4} **4.5–5.5 cm long**, projecting well past the bracts, with a **long, arched tube tipped with a 1 cm long upper lip** (galea) **and a prominent, 3-lobed lower lip** 3–5 mm long, covered with tiny, often gland-tipped hairs; calyx yellowish, minutely glandular-hairy, tubular, 2.5–4 cm long, tipped with 4 slender, almost equal lobes 5–15 mm long; bracts leafy, green, mostly cut to below the middle into 3 slender lobes, short-hairy or woolly; **4 stamens**, enclosed in the upper lip; styles slender, usually protruding from the tip of the upper lip; numerous, in the axils of bracts in dense spikes that elongate in fruit; June {May–July}.

Fruits: Capsules, splitting open lengthwise, containing many seeds with netted veins; {May–July}.

Habitat: Dry mixed prairie grasslands, on dry, sandy soils.

Notes: Downy paintbrush resembles stiff yellow paintbrush (*Castilleja lutescens* (Greenm.) Rydb., included in *Castilleja septentrionalis* Lindl. in the first edition of the *Flora of Alberta*, but not a synonym of that species), but stiff yellow paintbrush has straighter (not arched), shorter (less than 2 cm) flower tubes, branched stems, spreading leaves and short, stiff hairs. It grows on grassy slopes in Alberta (also in open coniferous woods elsewhere) and is reported to bloom from May to August.

PALE GREENISH PAINTBRUSH

Castilleja pallida (L.) Spreng. ssp. *caudata* Pennell
FIGWORT FAMILY (SCROPHULARIACEAE)

Plants: Slender perennial herbs; stems 20–40 cm tall, single or in small clumps, hairless or sometimes finely hairy on the upper parts and rather coarsely hairy in the flower cluster; from short, weak taproots.

Leaves: Alternate, **narrowly lance-shaped** (not lobed), 3–9 cm long, hairless on the upper surface, finely hairy beneath; upper leaves up to 1 cm wide at the base, **tapered to slender tails** at the tip.

Flowers: **Yellowish to yellowish green**, slender, **tubular, 16–26 mm long, 2-lipped, almost hidden in the axils of showy greenish to yellowish bracts**; bracts simple (rarely cut into 3–5 slender lobes at the tip); **calyx tubular**, 4-lobed, **cut at least halfway to the base** on the sides; **corolla tubular**, slightly longer than the calyx, with a slender, greenish, **3.5–8 mm long upper lip** and a broad, toothed, yellowish lower lip about ⅓ as long as the upper lip; 5–12, in elongating clusters (racemes); June–July.

Fruits: Capsules, 7–10 mm long, splitting lengthwise; seeds numerous, wedge-shaped, 1.5–2 mm long, with coarse, netted ridges.

Habitat: Moist tundra, lakeshores; in Alaska, on stream-banks, terraces and bars, and in woods and thickets.

Notes: Pale greenish paintbrush might be confused with stiff yellow paintbrush (*Castilleja lutescens* (Greenm.) Rydb., included in *Castilleja septentrionalis* Lindl. in the first edition of the *Flora of Alberta*, but not a synonym of that species), but the flower clusters of stiff yellow paintbrush have 3–7-lobed bracts and the leaves are very slender (linear), densely short-hairy to short-bristly and rough to the touch. • Paintbrush plants commonly join roots with neighbouring plants to absorb nutrients.

DJ

SZ

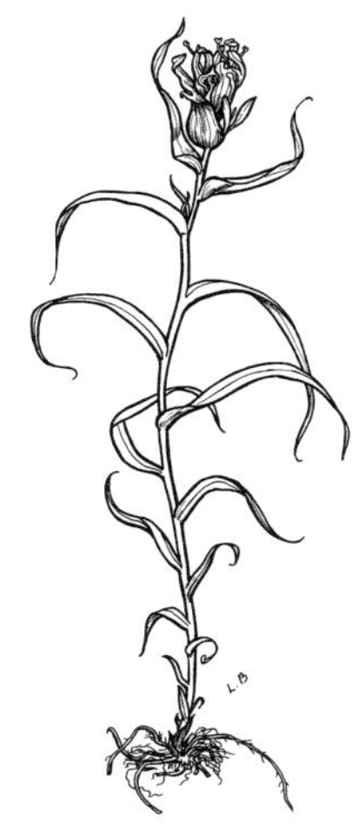

DJ

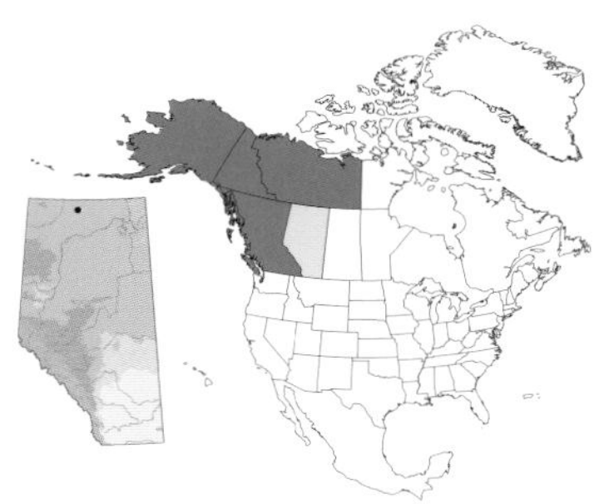

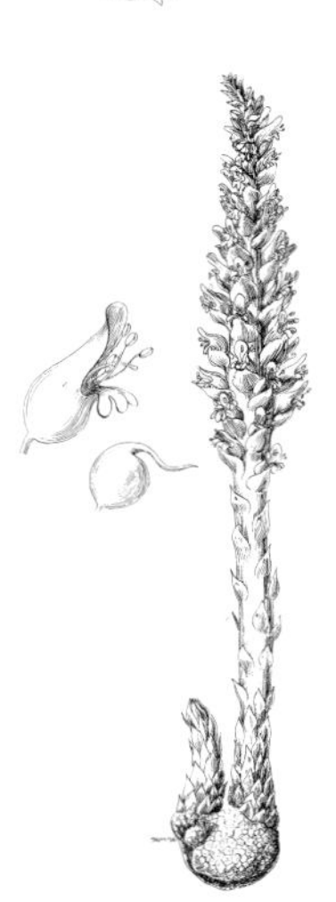

Russian ground-cone

Boschniakia rossica (Cham. & Schlecht.) Fedtsch.
BROOMRAPE FAMILY (OROBANCHACEAE)

Plants: Fleshy, **brown, cone-like parasitic herbs,** hairless (or nearly so); stems 10–40 cm tall, 4–15 mm thick, usually yellowish or purplish, single or few together; from 15–25 mm thick, **tuber-like underground stems** (rhizomes).

Leaves: Alternate, overlapping, **yellowish to purplish or brown, scale-like,** 3–10 mm long, triangular to egg-shaped, smooth to fringed along edges.

Flowers: Brownish red to purplish, 8–13 {15} **mm long,** with 5 lobes forming **2 unequal fringed lips,** stalkless, in the axils of fringed bracts; calyxes 3–6 mm long, irregularly lobed, fringed with short hairs; numerous, in **dense spike-like clusters** (racemes) **6–25 cm long;** {June} July.

Fruits: Capsules, 6–7 mm long, splitting open irregularly; seeds very small (0.001 mg) and numerous (over 300,000 per plant).

Habitat: Beside, and parasitic on, green alder in open, wooded or shrubby areas.

Notes: Russian ground-cone lacks chlorophyll and cannot produce food through photosynthesis. Instead, it parasitizes green alder shrubs, drawing all of its nutrients from their roots. The tiny seeds are swept into cracks in the soil, where they grow quickly, in search of a host plant. If they are lucky enough to come into contact with an alder root, they join with it and begin to develop a tuber and eventually a cone-like flowering stalk. The drain of reserves from year to year makes the end of the host root die off at an early age, so established tubers are usually attached to root tips. Plants may grow underground for 4–5 years before sending up a flower spike. • The tubers are often eaten by bears.

ONE-FLOWERED CANCER-ROOT

Orobanche uniflora L.
BROOMRAPE FAMILY (OROBANCHACEAE)

Plants: Delicate parasitic herbs; 1–3 flowering stalks per plant, slender, **5–10** {3–20} **cm tall**, covered with fine, glandular hairs; from **soft, 1–5 cm long underground stems.**

Leaves: Inconspicuous, scale-like, alternate near base, lance-shaped, up to 10 mm long.

Flowers: Purplish to yellowish white, 15–25 {35} **mm long, 2-lipped**, with rounded, minutely fringed lobes at the tip of a curved tube; calyx 4–12 mm long, with 5 slender, tapered lobes; single, on erect, slender stalks; {April–May} June–August.

Fruits: Capsules, splitting lengthwise when mature.

Habitat: Moist woods, with stonecrops (*Sedum* spp.), saxifrages (*Saxifraga* spp.), species of the aster family (Asteraceae) and other vascular plants; elsewhere, in open, moist to dry sites or woods.

Notes: Another rare Alberta species, Louisiana broomrape (*Orobanche ludoviciana* Nutt.), produces dense, 10–25 cm tall spikes of purplish (sometimes yellowish), stalkless flowers. These sticky, glandular-hairy plants are parasitic on sageworts (*Artemisia* spp.) and other members of the aster family (Asteraceae) in the prairies, and they flower in July–August {September}. • Broomrapes lack chlorophyll and cannot produce their own food through photosynthesis. Instead, they join to the roots of host plants, which supply all of their nutrients. • The generic name *Orobanche* was taken from the Greek *orobos* (a clinging plant) and *ancho* (to strangle), in reference to the parasitic roots of these plants.

JL

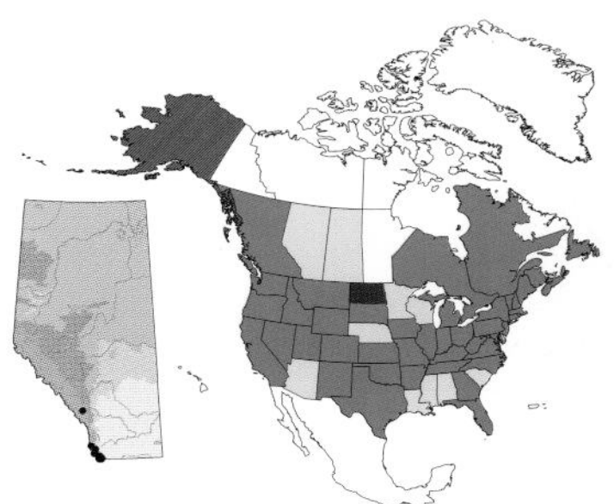

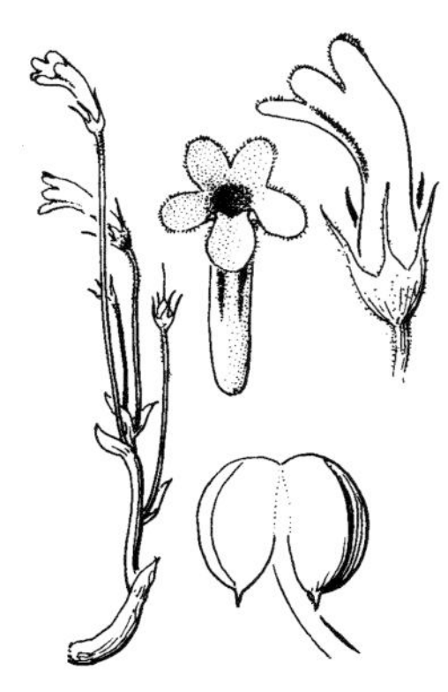

O. LUDOVICIANA

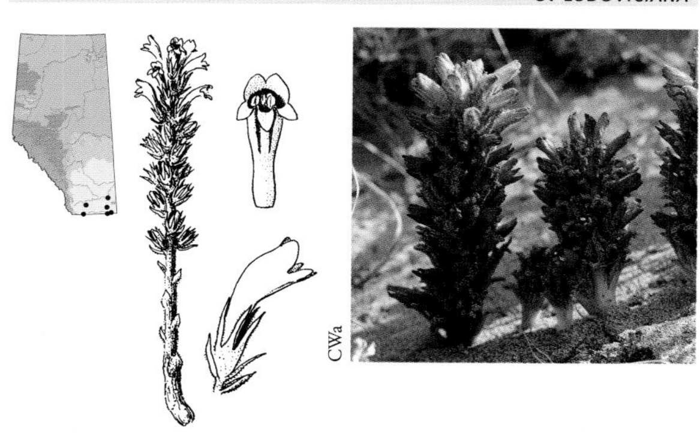

CWa

SMALL BUTTERWORT, HAIRY BUTTERWORT

Pinguicula villosa L.
BLADDERWORT FAMILY (LENTIBULARIACEAE)

Plants: Small, insectivorous perennial herbs; flowering stems **2–5 cm tall**, with long, soft hairs near the base and **glandular hairs above**; forms winter buds.

Leaves: Basal, egg-shaped to elliptic, up to 1 cm long, **fleshy**, upper surface covered with **greasy-slimy glands, yellowish green, rolled upward** along the edges.

Flowers: Purple to bluish violet, violet-like, **7–8** {6–10} **mm long** (including spur), funnel-shaped, with a 2-lobed upper lip and a broad, 3-lobed lower lip at the mouth and a straight, nectar-producing spur extending back from the base; calyxes with a 3-lobed upper lip and a 2-lobed lower lip; **single**, nodding on erect, slender stalks; mid June–July.

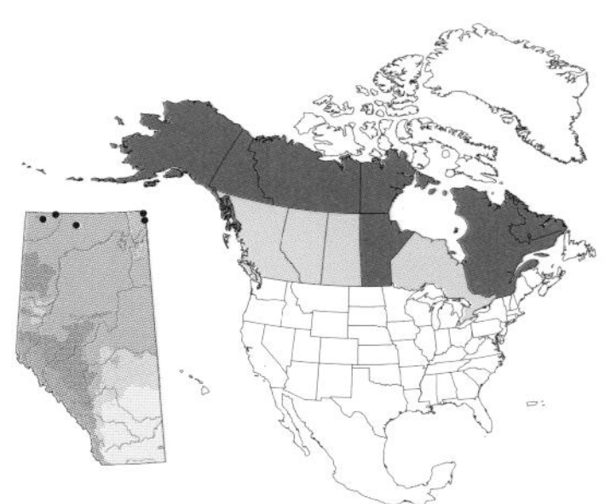

Fruits: Erect, round capsules, 3–5 mm long, splitting into 2 parts, containing many small seeds.

Habitat: Sphagnum hummocks in peatlands.

Notes: There is only 1 other species of butterwort in Alberta, common butterwort (*Pinguicula vulgaris* L.). Common butterwort is easily distinguished by its hairless flowering stalks and larger (15–20 mm long) flowers. • Butterwort leaves are greasy to the touch because of the droplets of mucilage produced by stalked glands on the upper surface. When small insects land on the leaf, they are restricted by this glue-like substance, and their movement results in the production of more mucilage. This leads to the eventual death of the trapped insect by suffocation and its digestion by acid and enzymes that are also secreted by the leaves. The leaves also change shape to entrap their prey. Their edges roll over the prey, and the surface becomes dished to hold secreted liquids. These changes are slow (inward rolling of leaves can take as long as 2 days), but they help to cover the insect in glands and fluids while preventing it from being washed off the leaf during periods of rain. • The common name 'butterwort' and the scientific name *Pinguicula,* from the Latin *pinguis* (fat), both refer to the greasy or 'buttery' feel of the leaves. The specific epithet *villosa* is Latin for 'hairy' or 'shaggy,' in reference to the hairy flowering stalks.

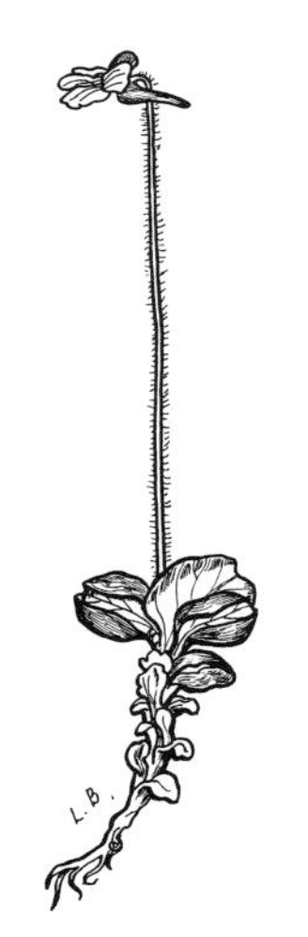

HORNED BLADDERWORT

Utricularia cornuta Michx.
BLADDERWORT FAMILY (LENTIBULARIACEAE)

DJ

Plants: **Semi-aquatic** perennial herbs; **stems mainly underground**, root-like, delicate, finely branched, bearing specialized leaves; **flowering stems erect**, above ground, **10–25** {3–30} **cm tall**, leafless, straight, wiry.

Leaves: Alternate, **thread-like**, small, **with tiny bladders** (specialized leaflets) along the edges, mostly **underground** so seldom seen.

Flowers: **Bright yellow**, fragrant, **15–20 mm long** and wide, with an egg-shaped upper lip (widest toward the tip), a **large, protruding, helmet-shaped lower lip** at the mouth, and a **slender, 10–12 mm long spur** projecting back and down from the base; calyx 2-lipped, much smaller than the corolla; 1–3 {6}, short-stalked, each in the axil of 3 small bractlets, forming small, elongating clusters (racemes); June–July {August}.

Fruits: Capsules covered by persistent, beaked calyxes.

Habitat: Poor fens, muddy shores and calcareous wetlands.

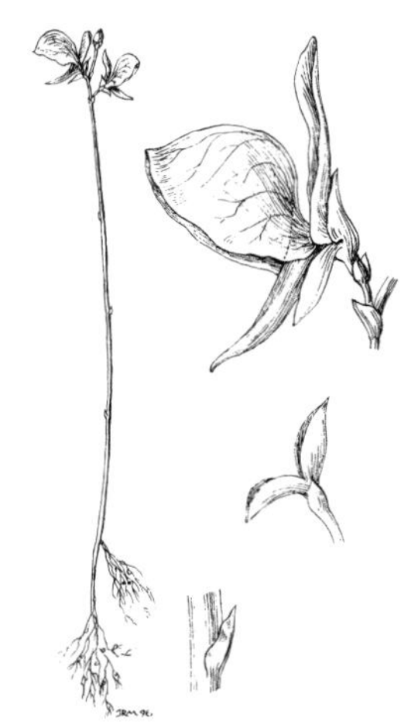

Notes: Horned bladderwort is seldom seen, except when in flower. Its inconspicuous leaves, buried in the moist soil, and its yellow, long-spurred flowers distinguish it from other Alberta species. • Bladderworts are carnivorous plants. They obtain nutrients by trapping and digesting tiny animals. The small bladders have a trapdoor, surrounded by stiff hairs. When a small invertebrate brushes against these sensitive hairs, the trapdoor springs open and water rushes in, carrying the prey with it. Once the bladder is full, the door closes, and digestive enzymes and acids are secreted, beginning the process of digestion. As the prey is broken down, specialized cells absorb water from the bladder, sending nutrients to the plant. This process takes about 30–120 minutes. When it is completed, a partial vacuum is recreated in the bladder, and the trap is reset. • In the east, horned bladderwort has been observed growing in water with a pH of 5.6–6.9. • The generic name *Utricularia* comes from the Latin *utriculus* (a small bottle), in reference to the tiny bladders, which trap small aquatic animals. The specific epithet *cornuta* is Latin for 'horned,' a reference to the stiff spur at the base of each flower.

CWa

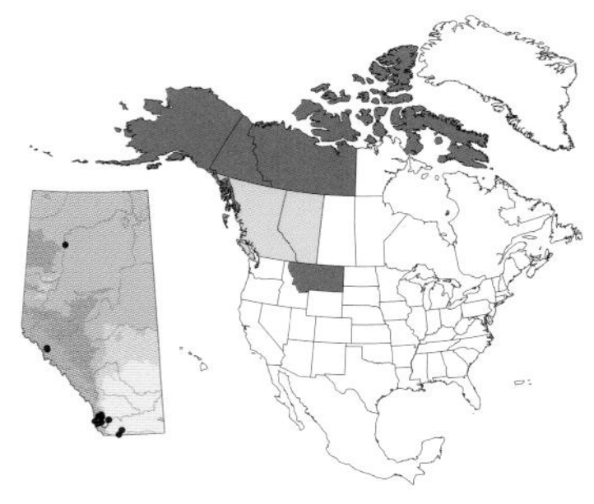

WESTERN RIBGRASS

Plantago canescens J.E. Adams
PLANTAIN FAMILY (PLANTAGINACEAE)

Plants: Tufted perennial herbs, soft-hairy with **segmented** (jointed) **hairs**; flowering **stems leafless, woolly-hairy**, 10–15 {8–30} cm tall, longer than the leaves; from stout crowns on thick, elongated taproots.

Leaves: In **basal clusters, lance-shaped** (sometimes oblong to linear), 5–15 {25} cm long, 3–5 nerved, toothless or irregularly toothed.

Flowers: White or greenish, inconspicuous, **about 2 mm long**, with 4 spreading, 2 mm long, minutely fringed lobes, stalkless, in the axils of broadly egg-shaped, 2 mm long, scale-like bracts with translucent edges; stamens sometimes conspicuous, up to 7 mm long; numerous, in **dense, 3** (to 12) **cm long spikes**, elongating in fruit, lower flowers sometimes more widely spaced; June.

Fruits: Oblong capsules, splitting horizontally below the middle (circumscissile), freeing a blunt, **cupped lid** and releasing 2–4 black, finely pitted seeds, each 1–1.5 mm long.

Habitat: Grassy and gravelly slopes, on non-alkaline soil; elsewhere, on steep open slopes, riverbanks, eskers and scree slopes.

Notes: This species has also been called *Plantago septata* Morris *ex* Rydb. • Western ribgrass could be confused with the more common species saline plantain (*Plantago eriopoda* Torr.), but saline plantain has wider leaves, yellowish brown or reddish wool on its root crowns (around the leaf bases) and sparingly hairy stems and leaves. • The seed coat of most plantains is high in mucilage, and it swells and becomes slimy when wetted. Plantain seeds have been used for many years as a bulk laxative, and the clear, sticky gum they exude has been used in the manufacture of lotions and hair-wave products.

SEASIDE PLANTAIN

Plantago maritima L.
PLANTAIN FAMILY (PLANTAGINACEAE)

Plants: Perennial herbs, essentially hairless; **stems** (flowering stalks) **leafless**, 5–25 cm tall, usually slightly taller than the leaves; from **long, thick taproots** with branched crowns.

Leaves: **Basal, fleshy, linear to lance-shaped**, up to 22 cm long and 1.5 cm wide, with **3–5** (sometimes 6 or 7) **parallel nerves**, smooth-edged or with a few small teeth.

Flowers: **White or greenish**, with **4 dry, translucent**, 1–1.5 mm long, **spreading lobes** at the tip of a **hairy tube**; calyx with 4 lobes rounded on the back, all alike or 2 long and 2 short, fringed with hairs; bracts broadly egg-shaped, 1.5–6 mm long, about as long as the sepals; numerous, in **1–10 cm long spikes**; June {July–August}.

Fruits: Egg-shaped or cone-shaped **membranous capsules**, with the **top coming off like a lid** (circumscissile); seeds 1.5–3 mm long; seed coat mucilaginous when wet.

Habitat: Saline marshes and alkaline soil.

Notes: Linear-leaved plantain (*Plantago elongata* Pursh) grows on alkaline prairie. It is a smaller (up to 8 cm tall) annual plant, with very slender leaves (about 1 mm wide). • Plantain and *Plantago* were derived from the Latin *planta*, or 'sole of the foot,' because the leaves were thought to resemble a footprint. Common plantain (*Plantago major* L.) was sometimes called 'white man's foot,' because it seemed to follow the white man wherever he settled. • The specific epithet *maritima* is Latin for 'of the sea,' because this species is often found in coastal areas.

LA

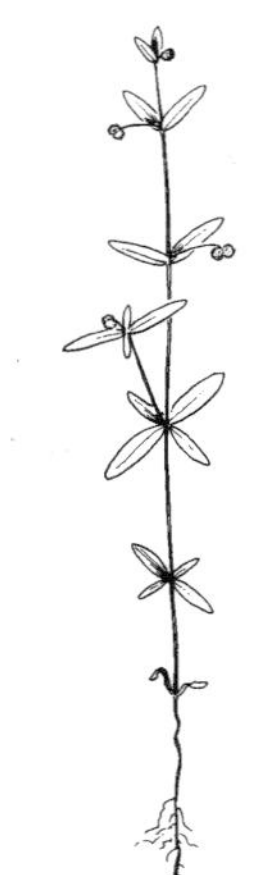

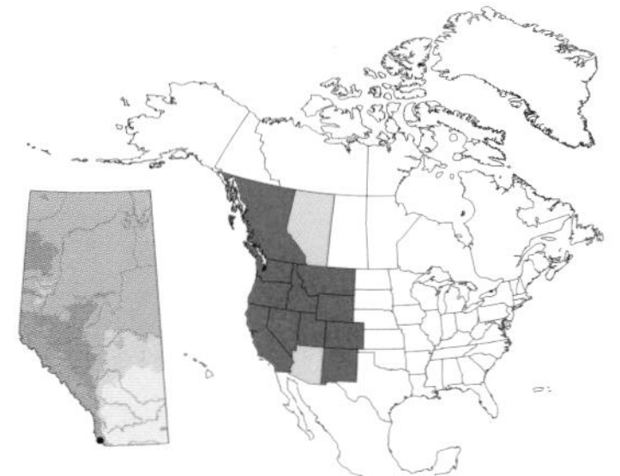

THIN-LEAVED BEDSTRAW

Galium bifolium S. Wats.
MADDER FAMILY (RUBIACEAE)

Plants: Slender, **hairless annual herbs**, 5–20 cm tall; stems mostly erect, unbranched or moderately branched, usually 4-sided; from short, weak taproots.

Leaves: Opposite (upper leaves) **and in circles** (whorls) **of** 4 (lower leaves) that often have **1 pair smaller than the other**, linear to elliptic or a little wider, **blunt-tipped or slightly pointed, mostly 1–2** {2.5} **cm long**, toothless.

Flowers: White, inconspicuous, **tiny, 3-lobed, soon shed**; calyx essentially absent; 4 stamens (rarely 3); 2 styles; solitary, short-stalked in leaf axils, erect at first, but eventually widely spreading on stalks up to 3 cm; {May–August}.

Fruits: Nodding pairs of round, 1-seeded **nutlets 2.5–3.5 mm long, bristly with short, hooked hairs.**

Habitat: Dry, open areas, often on disturbed sites; elsewhere, in moist meadows and open coniferous forests.

Notes: The 2 other small bedstraws in Alberta that have leaves in whorls of 4—small bedstraw (*Galium trifidum* L.) and Labrador bedstraw (*Galium labradoricum* Wieg.)—are both perennial species with creeping rhizomes and hairless fruits. • The generic name *Galium* was derived from the Greek *gala* (milk) because a common European species, *Galium verum* L., was used to curdle milk. The specific epithet *bifolium,* from the Latin *bi* (two) and *folium* (leaf), refers to the paired leaves on the upper stem.

LONG-LEAVED BLUETS

Hedyotis longifolia (Gaertn.) Hook.
MADDER FAMILY (RUBIACEAE)

Plants: Delicate, **tufted perennial herbs**; stems numerous, 10–25 cm tall, usually 4-sided, hairless and purplish, unbranched or branched in upper parts; from branched root crowns.

Leaves: Opposite, linear to narrowly oblong, 1–3 cm long, tapered to a stalkless base with **2 small, whitish or purplish appendages** (stipules), 1-nerved, smooth or minutely roughened along the edges.

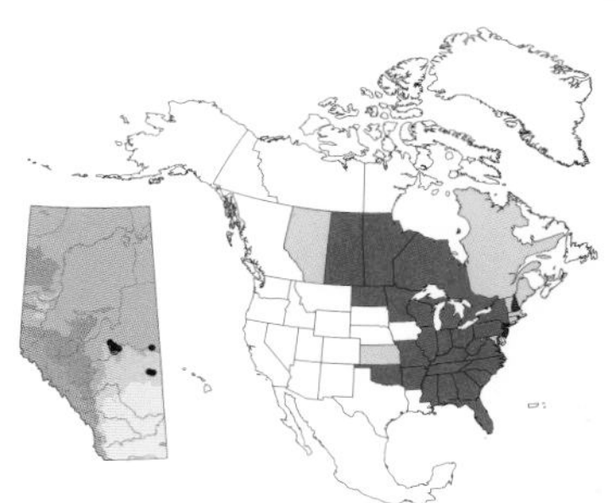

Flowers: Purplish to pink or white, {3–5} **6–9 mm long, funnel-shaped**, tipped **with 4 spreading lobes**, hairy within the tube; **calyx persistent, with 4 awl-shaped, 1–2** {2.5} **mm long lobes**, often extending past the tip of the mature capsule; 4 stamens, often projecting out past the petals; numerous, in crowded or loose, leafy, spreading clusters (cymes); June–July {May–September}.

Fruits: Ovoid capsules, splitting open across the tip to release small, pitted seeds.

Habitat: Sandy soil in open woods and on dunes; elsewhere, in grasslands.

Notes: This species has also been called *Houstonia longifolia* Gaertn. • These flowers are dimorphous—that is, they have 2 forms. In one case, the style is short and hidden in the corolla tube, while the stamens project out from the mouth of the flower; in the other case, the styles project from the flowers and the stamens are contained within. Pollen from long-stamened flowers is usually transferred to the stigmas of long-styled flowers, and pollen from short-stamened flowers usually pollinates short-styled flowers. This is one way the flowers can reduce the chance of self-pollination and therefore increase the exchange of genes among local populations.

JG

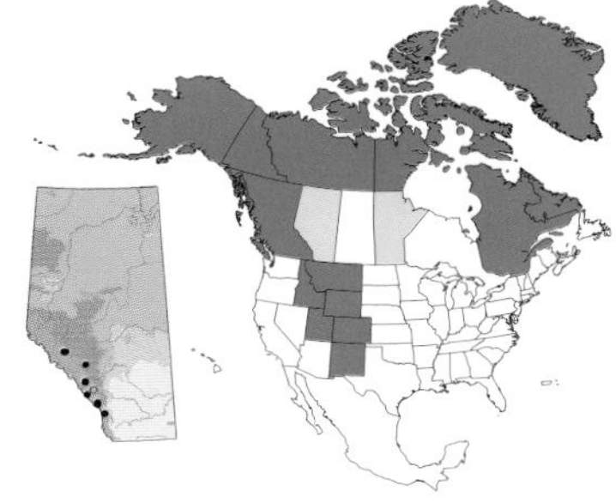

ALPINE HAREBELL, ARCTIC HAREBELL, ARCTIC BELLFLOWER

Campanula uniflora L.
BLUEBELL FAMILY (CAMPANULACEAE)

Plants: Small, hairless perennial herbs; stems solitary or few, usually **less than 10 cm tall** (elsewhere, up to 30 cm); from taproots.

Leaves: Alternate, simple; lower leaves spatula-shaped, 2–3 cm long, **toothless**; upper leaves linear.

Flowers: Pale blue, funnel-shaped, with 5 fused petals, **5–10 mm long**, 4–8 mm wide; **5 sepals, hairy, slender**, joined at base; 5 stamens, attached at the base of the corolla; 3 stigmas; **solitary**, nodding when young, erect when mature; July {August}.

Fruits: Erect, hairy capsules, 1 cm long, containing many smooth seeds.

Habitat: Exposed, stony alpine slopes; elsewhere, on calcareous cliffs and scree slopes and in moderately moist to dry meadows and ridges in the montane, subalpine and alpine zones.

Notes: Alaska harebell (*Campanula lasiocarpa* Cham.) is the only other *Campanula* species in Alberta with solitary flowers. It is easily distinguished by its toothed leaves, broader (bell-shaped) flowers and toothed calyx lobes.
• The generic name *Campanula* is derived from the Latin *campana* (bell), in reference to the shape of the flower. The specific epithet *uniflora* means 'one-flowered.'

DOWNINGIA

Downingia laeta (Greene) Greene
LOBELIA FAMILY (LOBELIACEAE)

TC

Plants: **Small, hairless annual** herbs; stems 5–20 cm tall, slender, with or without branches, erect or spreading and ascending, sometimes rooting at the joints; from fibrous roots.

Leaves: **Alternate**, lance-shaped, 5–20 mm long, toothless, stalkless; lower leaves smaller, narrower and soon shed.

Flowers: **White to light blue or purplish** with white or yellow markings, inconspicuous, bearing **5 petal lobes and 5 leaf-like sepals at the tip of a long, slender, stalk-like tube** (an elongated, inferior ovary); **corolla 4–7** {8} **mm long, slightly 2-sided, with 5 similar lobes** at the tip of a short tube; **sepals** 4–7 {3–8} mm long, **linear** to linear-elliptic, joined only slightly at the base; **5 stamens, fused into a tube** around the style at the centre of the flower and tipped with 2 bristles; stalkless (though ovaries may resemble stalks) in the axils of leaf-like bracts, forming elongating clusters (racemes) at the stem tip; {June} July–August.

Fruits: **Slender, pod-like capsules**, 2–4.5 cm long, 1–2 mm thick, containing many seeds.

Habitat: Shallow water and banks near ponds; elsewhere, in wet meadows.

Notes: With its long, stalk-like ovaries tipped with small, inconspicuous petals, downingia might be mistaken, at first glance, for one of the small willowherbs (*Epilobium* spp.). However, small willowherbs have opposite leaves and their flowers have 4 equal, separate petals.

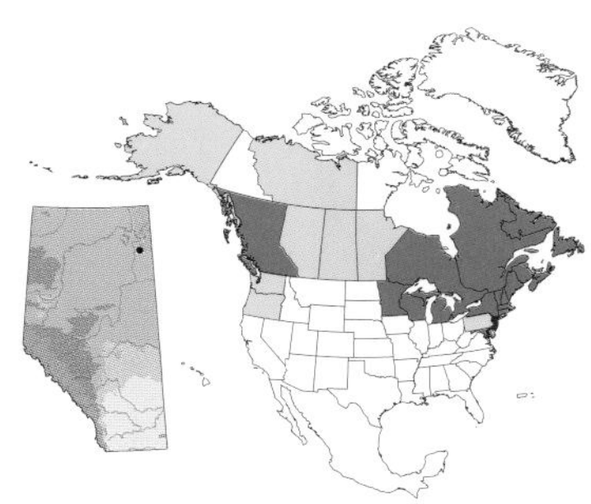

WATER LOBELIA

Lobelia dortmanna L.
LOBELIA FAMILY (LOBELIACEAE)

Plants: Emergent aquatic perennial herbs: hairless; stems 10–100 cm tall, slender, hollow, essentially leafless; from fibrous roots.

Leaves: In a **basal rosette, submerged**, fleshy, **tubular, 2–8 cm long**, somewhat curved; stem leaves reduced to a few thin scales.

Flowers: Lilac to pale blue or white, showy, 10–20 mm long, with a broad, **deeply 3-lobed lower lip** and **2 linear, backward-curved upper lobes** at the tip of a **slender tube** that is **split almost to the base** along its upper surface; calyx about 5 mm long, tipped with 5 blunt lobes; 5 stamens, forming a tube around the style inside the flower tube, with some or all anthers hairy at the tip; few, in elongating clusters (racemes) on slender, leafless stems; July {June–August}.

Fruits: Nodding, oblong **capsules, 5–10 mm long**, 3–5 mm wide, with **2 chambers** (locules), splitting open from the tip to release many rough seeds less than 1 mm long.

Habitat: Shallow water near the edges of ponds, lakes and on sandy shores; elsewhere, also on gravelly, silty or muddy bottoms, sometimes deeply submersed but with flower stalks above water.

Notes: Water lobelia often grows with quillworts (*Isoetes* spp.), and the sterile rosettes of these plants might be confused at first glance. However, quillwort leaves have broad, flattened bases and grow from thick, corm-like stems. • Another rare Alberta species, spiked lobelia (*Lobelia spicata* Lam.), is a terrestrial plant that grows on dry to moist sandy soil on the prairie. It is easily distinguished by its leafy stems, broad, lance-shaped to egg-shaped leaves and many flowers in slender, almost spike-like clusters. • The generic name *Lobelia* commemorates Matthias de L'Obel, a Belgian botanist who lived 1538–1616.

L. SPICATA

BUR RAGWEED

Ambrosia acanthicarpa Hook.
ASTER FAMILY (ASTERACEAE [COMPOSITAE])

Plants: Erect annual herbs; stems 20–60 {10–80} cm tall, leafy, much branched, with stiff, white hairs; from slender taproots.

Leaves: Alternate, numerous, 2–8 cm long, once or twice deeply pinnately divided into slender lobes, mostly stiff-hairy on both surfaces (sometimes hairless on the upper side) and stalked (upper leaves sometimes stalkless).

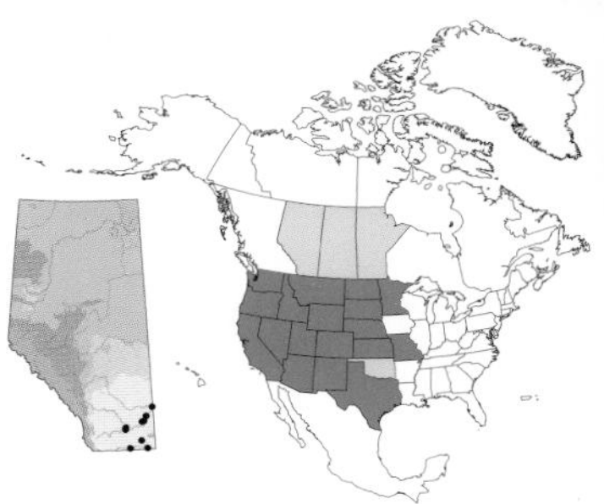

Flowerheads: Yellowish, either **male or female**, but with **both sexes on the same plant** (monoecious), including **disc florets only** with **inconspicuous** (sometimes absent) **petals**; male (staminate) flowerheads 2–4 mm wide, several-flowered, with involucres of fused oval bracts, borne in long, nodding, leafless clusters (racemes) at stem tips; female (pistillate) flowerheads about 7–8 mm long, single-flowered, the developing seed (pistil) enclosed by an **involucre** of fused bracts armed **with 8–15 spreading, straight spines**, solitary or clustered in the upper leaf axils; July {August–October}.

Fruits: Dry seed-like fruits (achenes) without bristles (pappus) at the tip, **enclosed in a ridged, bur-like, spiny involucre.**

Habitat: Sand dunes; elsewhere, in open, usually sandy places.

Notes: This species has also been called *Franseria acanthicarpa* (Hook.) Coville. It can be distinguished from other ragweeds (*Ambrosia* spp.) by its involucres, which have several rows of spines rather than just 1. • The specific epithet *acanthicarpa* comes from *Acanthus* (a subtropical genus of plants with seeds enclosed in spiny bracts) and *carpa* (fruit), hence 'fruit like *Acanthus*.' • The pollen of ragweeds (*Ambrosia artemisiifolia* L., *Ambrosia trifida* L. and *Ambrosia psilostachya* DC.) is a common cause of hay fever.

LA

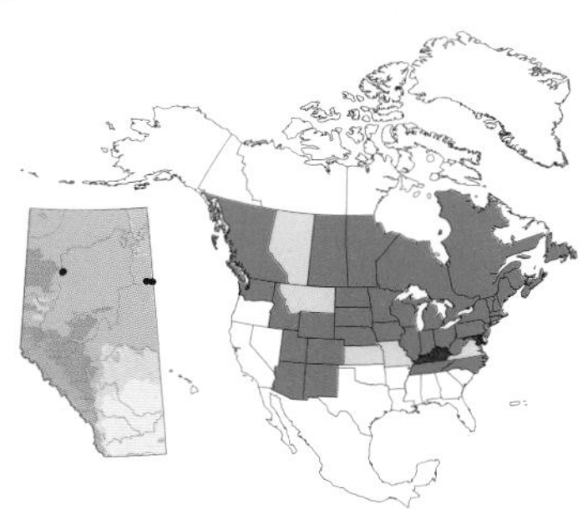

SPOTTED JOE-PYE WEED

Eupatorium maculatum L.
ASTER FAMILY (ASTERACEAE [COMPOSITAE])

Plants: Robust perennial herbs; stems stout, erect, 60–150 cm tall, **purple or purple-spotted**; from fibrous roots.

Leaves: In **whorls of 3–6**, lance-shaped to egg-shaped, 6–20 cm long, 2–7 cm wide, sharply pointed at the tip, coarsely sharp-toothed, stalked.

Flowerheads: Pink to purple, with **disc florets only**; involucres 6–9 mm high, often pinkish, in overlapping rows of bracts; numerous, in showy, **flat-topped clusters** (corymbs) **15–20 cm across**; August {July–September}.

Fruits: Gland-dotted seed-like fruits (achenes), 3–4.5 mm long, tipped with a tuft of white, hair-like bristles (pappus).

Habitat: Wet to moist meadows and open woods.

Notes: This species has also been included in *Eupatorium purpureum* L. or called *Eupatorium bruneri* A. Gray. • The Navajo boiled this plant to make a tea for treating arrow wounds. • Joe Pye was a famous medicine man who is said to have used this plant in New England to induce sweating and thereby break fevers during a typhus outbreak. The generic name *Eupatorium* commemorates Eupator Mithridates, a first-century king of Pontus, who was said to have used a plant of this genus as an antidote for poison.

LARGE-FLOWERED BRICKELLIA

Brickellia grandiflora (Hook.) Nutt.
ASTER FAMILY (ASTERACEAE [COMPOSITAE])

Plants: **Perennial** herbs; stems 20–80 cm tall, minutely hairy, often branched above, somewhat woody at the base; from long, thick, spindle-shaped roots.

Leaves: Mostly alternate, but sometimes opposite, usually somewhat hairy, faintly dotted with glands; blades **triangular to egg-shaped or lance-shaped**, 2–10 {12} cm long and 1–6 cm wide, notched to broadly wedge-shaped at the base, coarsely toothed; stalks 0.3–7 cm long.

Flowerheads: **Cream-coloured to greenish yellow**, 8–12 mm wide and high, with 5-lobed **disc florets only**; involucres 7–11 mm high, with several overlapping rows of **striped bracts**, the outer bracts **hairy** with slender, elongated tips; receptacles flat, without hairs or scales (naked); **florets with both male and female parts**; few to several, **nodding**, in spreading clusters (panicle-like cymes); July–September.

Fruits: Seed-like, 10-ribbed fruits (achenes), about 5 mm long, thickened at the base, **tipped with a tuft of white, hair-like bristles** (pappus).

Habitat: Eroded slopes and rocky banks.

Notes: Large-flowered brickellia may be confused with another rare species, purple rattlesnakeroot (*Prenanthes sagittata* (A. Gray) A. Nels.), but rattlesnakeroot has milky juice and winged leaf stalks. Its flowerheads have hairless involucres without stripes and are borne in narrow, elongated clusters. Purple rattlesnakeroot grows in moist, often shaded sites. • The generic name *Brickellia* honours John Brickell (1749–1809), a physician and botanist who lived in Savannah, Georgia. The specific epithet *grandiflora*, from the Latin *grandis* (large) and *floreo* (flower), refers to the large flowerheads.

PRENANTHES SAGITTATA

TD

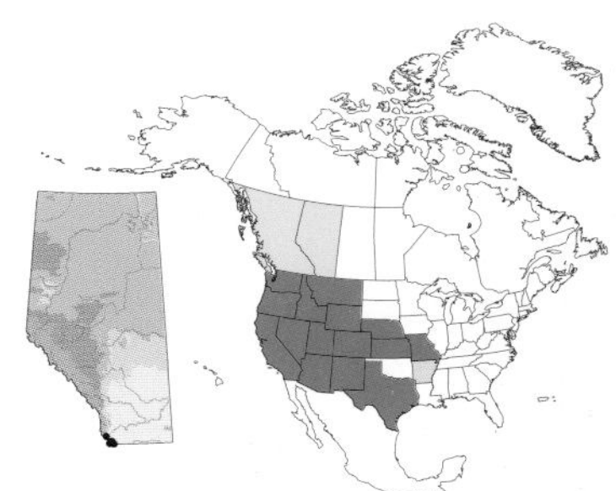

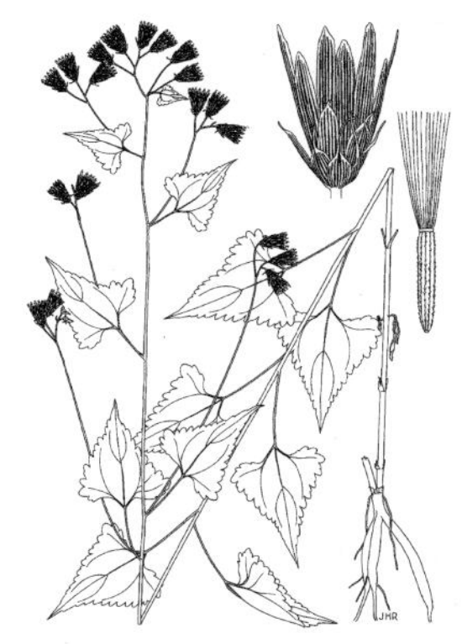

TD

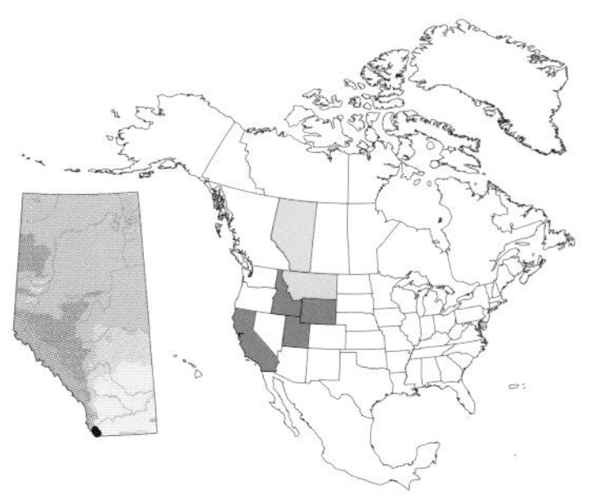

ALPINE TOWNSENDIA

Townsendia condensata Parry *ex* A. Gray
ASTER FAMILY (ASTERACEAE [COMPOSITAE])

Plants: Low, **cushion-like** perennial herbs **without flowering stems**; from taproots.

Leaves: In rather erect, basal clusters, 1.2–3.5 cm long, 2–4 mm wide, **spatula-shaped**, with long, white hairs; blades short, without teeth, abruptly narrowed to long stalks.

Flowerheads: White, pink or lavender, about 4–5 cm across, with numerous 8–16 mm long ray florets around a 1–4 cm wide, yellow button of disc florets; involucres 8–18 mm high, **densely woolly**, bracts overlapping, lance-shaped to linear, pointed, with whitish, translucent edges fringed with soft hairs; receptacles flat, without hairs or scales (naked); ray florets with female parts only; disc florets with both male and female parts; **single to few, stalkless, nestled among the leaves**, early June–early August.

Fruits: Flattened, 2-nerved seed-like fruits (achenes), 3–4.4 mm long, covered with forked or barbed hairs, tipped with a **tuft of rough, hair-like bristles** (on disc florets) **or a crown of small scales** (on ray florets).

Habitat: Exposed shale ridges in alpine areas.

Notes: Another rare species, low townsendia (*Townsendia exscapa* (Richards.) Porter), is distinguished from alpine townsendia by its slightly hairy (not densely woolly) involucral bracts and its linear to lance-shaped (rather than spatula-shaped) leaves. Low townsendia grows on dry hillsides and prairies rather than on alpine ridges, and flowers in May. • The generic name *Townsendia* commemorates David Townsend (1787–1858), an amateur botanist of West Chester, Pennsylvania. The specific epithet *condensata* means 'compressed,' in reference to the compact, cushion-like plants.

T. EXSCAPA

JL

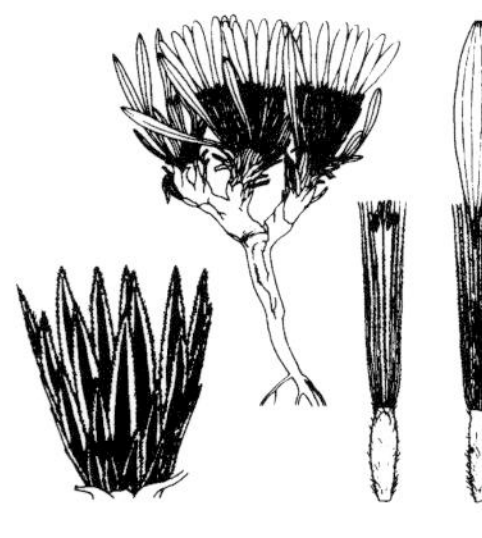

FEW-FLOWERED ASTER

Aster pauciflorus Nutt.
ASTER FAMILY (ASTERACEAE [COMPOSITAE])

Plants: Perennial herbs; **stems** {10} 20–50 cm tall, **hairless near the base**, branched and glandular near the top; from slender underground stems (rhizomes).

Leaves: Alternate, much smaller upward on the stem; **lower leaves** linear to lance-shaped, widest above the middle, **4–8 cm long and 2–3 mm wide**, rather fleshy, **hairless**, without teeth, stalked; upper leaves linear, stalkless.

Flowerheads: Blue or whitish, 15–25 mm across, **usually with more than 15, 4–6 mm long ray florets** around a yellow cluster of 5-lobed disc florets; involucres **rather fleshy, hairless, glandular**, 5–8 mm high, with **unequal** linear to lance-shaped **bracts in 2 or 3 loose, overlapping rows**; ray florets with female parts only; disc florets with both male and female parts; styles with flattened branches more than 0.5 mm long and hairy appendages; **few**, borne singly on spreading branches in open, somewhat rounded to flat-topped clusters; July–August.

Fruits: Several-nerved seed-like fruits (achenes), **tipped with a tuft of hair-like bristles** (pappus).

Habitat: Alkaline flats; elsewhere, also in salt marshes.

Notes: Another rare species, meadow aster (*Aster campestris* Nutt.), resembles few-flowered aster, but it is found in dry, open areas, often on alkaline soil, at low to moderate elevations in the mountains. Meadow aster has finely hairy stems and numerous purplish flowerheads with rays up to 12 mm long. Its leaves are {2} 3–5 cm long, about 5 mm wide and only slightly smaller on the upper stem. Meadow aster flowers in July and August. • The specific epithet *pauciflorus* means 'few-flowered'; *campestris* means 'of the fields.'

A. CAMPESTRIS

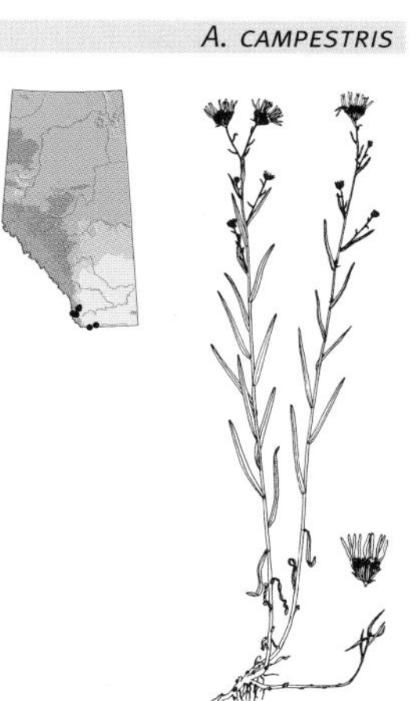

JL

RB

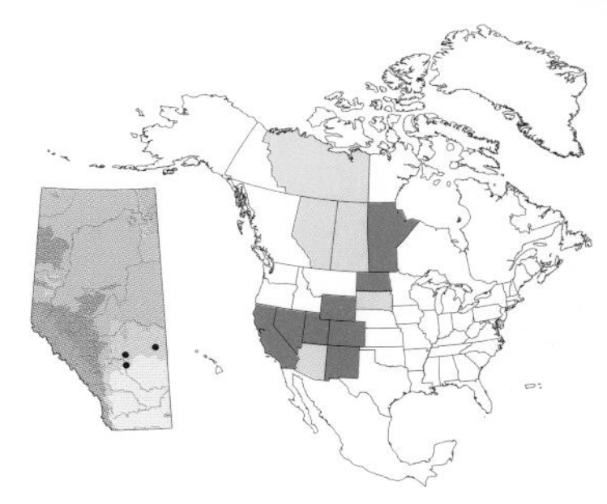

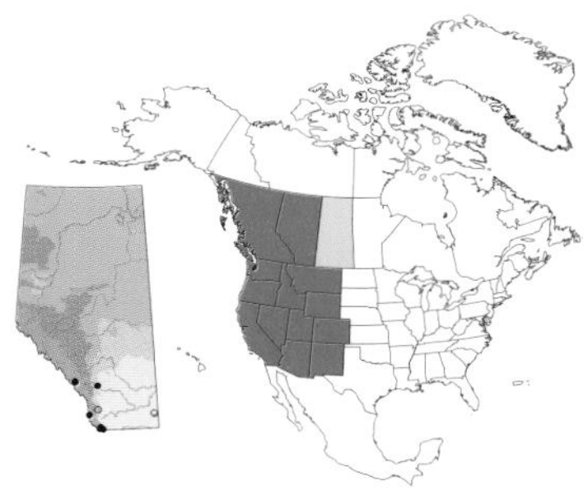

Eaton's aster

Aster eatonii (A. Gray) J.T. Howell
ASTER FAMILY (ASTERACEAE [COMPOSITAE])

Plants: Perennial herbs; stems 30–80 {100} cm tall, often reddish, minutely hairy on the upper parts; from creeping underground stems (rhizomes).

Leaves: **Alternate**, linear to lance-shaped, 6–12 {5–15} cm long, 4–20 mm wide (usually **7–13 times as long as wide**), hairless or rough with short, stiff hairs, usually **toothless and stalkless**.

Flowerheads: **White or pink**, with 20–40 **ray florets 5–12 mm long** around a **yellow button of disc florets**; involucres 5–9 {4.5–10} mm high; **involucral bracts leafy** or completely green (at least some of the outer bracts), loosely overlapping or curved outward; numerous, in **long, narrow, leafy clusters** (raceme-like); {July} August–September.

Fruits: Dry, hairy seed-like fruits (achenes), tipped with a tuft of **white, hair-like bristles** (pappus).

Habitat: Moist montane woodland and streambanks.

Notes: Eaton's aster often hybridizes with leafy-bracted aster (*Aster subspicatus* Nees). These species are very similar, but leafy-bracted aster has only a single to few flowerheads, and its lower leaves are usually stalked and sharply toothed. • Another rare annual aster reported to occur in Alberta, tansy-leaved aster (*Machaeranthera tanacetifolia* (Kunth) Nees., also called *Aster tanacetifolius* Kunth), is easily identified by its taproot and finely dissected, almost feathery leaves in combination with large (about 3 cm wide) blue to bluish purple flowerheads with yellow centres. It grows on dry, open plains and hillsides, and is reported to flower in July and August. • The generic name *Aster* was taken from the Greek *astron* (star), in reference to the star-like appearance of these radiate flowerheads.

MACHAERANTHERA TANACETIFOLIA

FLAT-TOPPED WHITE ASTER

Aster umbellatus Mill.
ASTER FAMILY (ASTERACEAE [COMPOSITAE])

Plants: Perennial herbs; stems 30–200 cm tall, finely hairy, leafy near the top; from creeping underground stems (rhizomes).

Leaves: Alternate, 5–15 cm long, lance-shaped to egg-shaped or elliptic, gradually narrowed to the base and to the tip, smooth or rough to the touch on the upper surface, finely hairy beneath, toothless, short-stalked to almost stalkless.

Flowerheads: **White**, about 12–20 mm across, with 4–7 wide-spreading, 4–8 mm long ray florets around a yellow cluster of 5-lobed disc florets; receptacles without hairs or scales (naked); involucres hairy, 3–5 mm high, with few, pointed bracts pressed together and ascending; ray florets with female parts only; disc florets with male and female parts; styles with flattened branches more than 0.5 mm long and hairy appendages; **numerous, in flat-topped clusters** (corymbs); July–September.

Fruits: Several-nerved seed-like fruits (achenes), **more or less hairy**, tipped with a tuft of **hair-like bristles** (pappus) in **2 rows**, the **outer row tiny** (less than 1 mm long), the **inner row** longer, stiff, and **often thick-tipped**.

Habitat: Moist woodlands and swampy sites; elsewhere, in moist thickets and meadows.

Notes: This species has an interesting distribution. It is generally an eastern species, with populations in Saskatchewan limited to the east-central region (Duck Mountain and the Porcupine Hills), so the Alberta populations are rather disjunct from the main range. • The specific epithet *umbellatus* comes from the Latin *umbella* (a parasol), in reference to the flat-topped, umbrella-shaped flower clusters.

LA

DJ

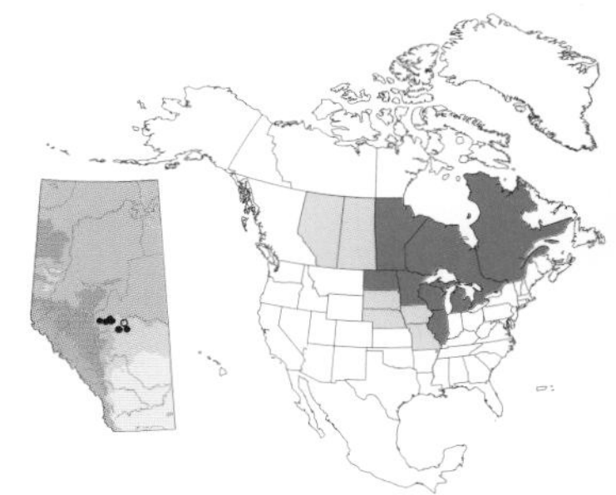

LK

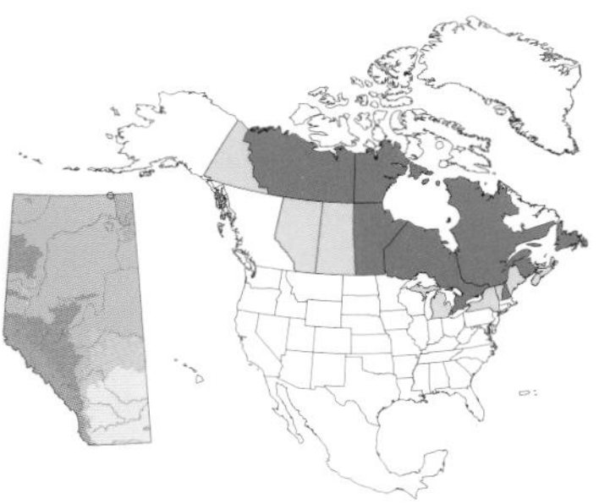

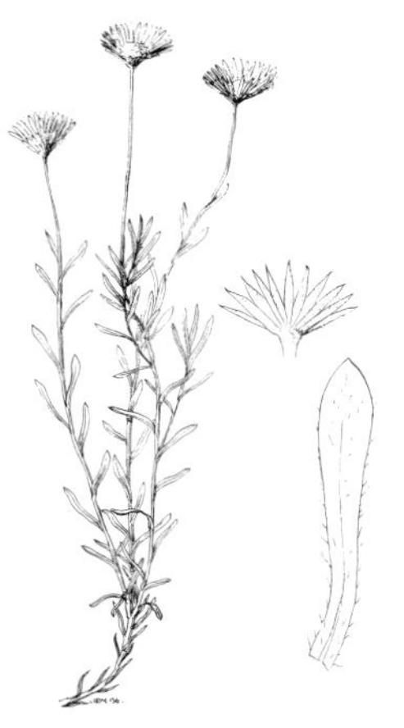

WILD DAISY FLEABANE

Erigeron hyssopifolius Michx.
ASTER FAMILY (ASTERACEAE [COMPOSITAE])

Plants: Tufted perennial herbs; stems slender, leafy, mostly **10–30 cm tall**, sparsely hairy or nearly hairless, branched, often with **short, leafy shoots in leaf axils**; from a short, branched woody base with many fibrous roots.

Leaves: Alternate, numerous, **crowded** (overlapping on the stem), **largest at mid-stem, linear or linear–lance-shaped**, 2–3 cm long and **1–3 mm wide**, thin, soft, nearly hairless but with scattered hairs along the edges, not toothed, stalkless or short-stalked.

Flowerheads: White, sometimes pink or purplish, about 1.5 cm across, with 20–50 small (**4–8 mm long**, about 1.5 mm wide) ray florets around a button of yellow disc florets; involucres 4–6 mm high, the **bracts equal**, **thin**, soft, pointed, **with a few somewhat sticky hairs**; receptacles flat, without hairs or scales (naked); 1–5, on long, mostly leafless stalks; July–August.

Fruits: Hairy, nerved seed-like fruits (achenes), tipped with a **tuft of yellowish, hair-like bristles** (pappus).

Habitat: Shores, banks and ledges; elsewhere, on calcareous ledges, talus and gravelly shores, in fens and in wet openings in coniferous forests.

Notes: The specific epithet *hyssopifolius* means 'with leaves like hyssop.' Hyssop (*Hyssopus officinalis* L.) is a Eurasian mint species that has toothless, lance-shaped leaves less than 3 cm long and that produces leafy shoots in the leaf axils, very similar to those of wild daisy fleabane.

TRIFID-LEAVED FLEABANE, THREE-FORKED FLEABANE

Erigeron trifidus Hook.
ASTER FAMILY (ASTERACEAE [COMPOSITAE])

JG

Plants: Small, **densely tufted** perennial herbs; flowering stems 4–8 {3–10} cm tall, leafless (sometimes with a small bract near the middle), densely glandular-hairy and usually with long, spreading, many-celled hairs, often white-woolly below the flowerhead; from compact, many-branched crowns on taproots.

Leaves: Basal; blades lance-shaped to narrowly egg-shaped or oblong, **1–2** {3} **cm long**, usually **tipped with 3** (sometimes 2) lance-shaped to oblong **lobes**, each 3–5 {8} mm long and **more than 1 mm wide**, sparsely glandular-hairy on both surfaces and fringed with stiff hairs, abruptly narrowed to a 1–2 mm wide 'stalk' (basal segment).

Flowerheads: White (sometimes pinkish), drying purple, about 1–1.2 cm across, with 20–30 {40}, linear to spatula-shaped, 10–15 mm long ray florets around a yellow button of disc florets; involucres 8–10 mm high, glandular-hairy, crimson or crimson-tipped, with 25–30 narrowly lance-shaped, 5–12 mm long, **equal bracts**; receptacles flat, without hairs or scales (naked); solitary; {May–July}.

Fruits: Densely hairy, 2-nerved seed-like fruits (achenes), 2–2.5 mm long, tipped with a **tuft of 15–20 hair-like bristles** (pappus) 3–4 mm long.

Habitat: Alpine slopes.

Notes: Trifid-leaved fleabane produces seed asexually and probably originated as a hybrid between *Erigeron compositus* Pursh and *Erigeron lanatus* Hook. • The specific epithet *trifidus* means 'split into 3 parts,' in reference to the 3-lobed leaves.

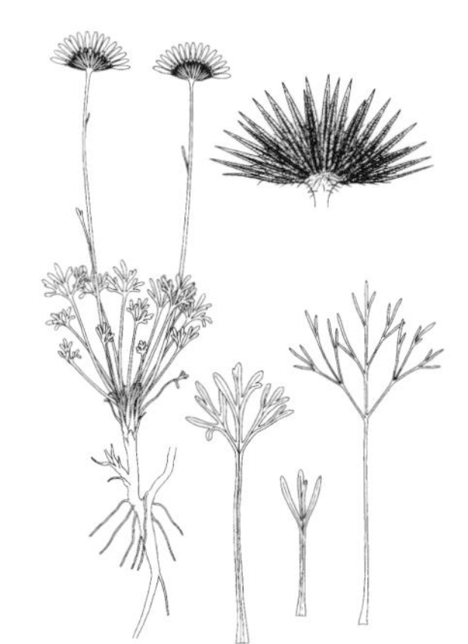

TK

FRONT-RANGE FLEABANE

Erigeron lackschewitzii Nesom and Weber
ASTER FAMILY (ASTERACEAE [COMPOSITAE])

Plants: Perennial herbs; stems with **long, soft hairs, without glands**; from long, thick taproots.

Leaves: Basal and alternate on the stem; basal leaves linear to broadly lance-shaped, not toothed; 5–10 stem leaves.

Flowerheads: Blue, with **30–68 ray florets; involucral bracts woolly with interwoven hairs** that often have thin, purple 'bands' (cross-walls); **solitary**, on woolly stalks.

Fruits: Dry seed-like fruits (achenes), 1.5–2.5 mm long, tipped with a tuft of 15–24 hair-like bristles (pappus).

Habitat: Gravelly slopes in *Dryas*-dominated tundra; elsewhere, in exposed mountain sites on limestone and dolomite rock.

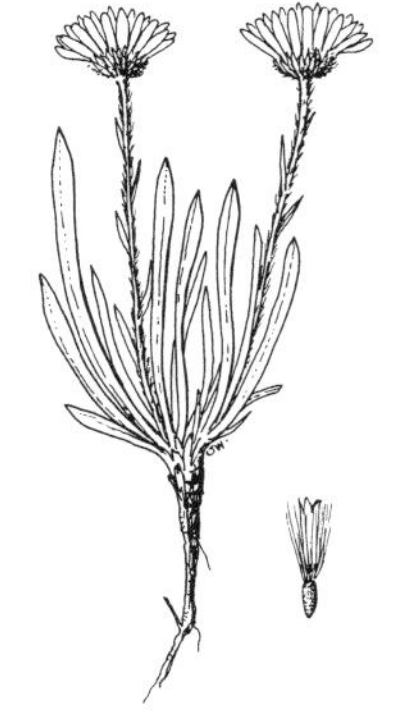

Notes: Another rare Alberta species, yellow alpine fleabane (*Erigeron ochroleucus* Nutt.), closely resembles front-range fleabane. It is distinguished by its smaller (3–3.5 {2.5–3.8} mm long) disc corollas, its 4–8 mm high flowerheads with 40–80 {30–88} ray florets and its smaller (1.1–1.5 mm long) achenes. Yellow alpine fleabane grows in dry exposed areas, primarily in the montane zone, and flowers from June to August. Two varieties are recognized, var. *ochroleucus* and var. *scribneri* (Canby) Cronq., the latter being a shorter, more slender form. • These small fleabanes might be confused with the more common species large-flowered fleabane (*Erigeron grandiflorus* Hook.). However, the lower leaves of large-flowered fleabane are broadly lance-shaped or spatula-shaped with rounded tips, the flowering involucres are 8–10 mm tall with conspicuous glandular hairs and the flowerheads have 100–125 ray florets. Large-flowered fleabane grows on alpine slopes. • Front-range fleabane is endemic to southwestern Alberta and Montana. It is a species that has evolved only recently and appears to have been derived from yellow alpine fleabane. • The specific epithet *lackschewitzii* honours Klaus Lackschewitz (1911–95), the Montana botanist who first collected this species. The common name refers to the range of this species, in the front ranges of the Rocky Mountains.

E. OCHROLEUCUS

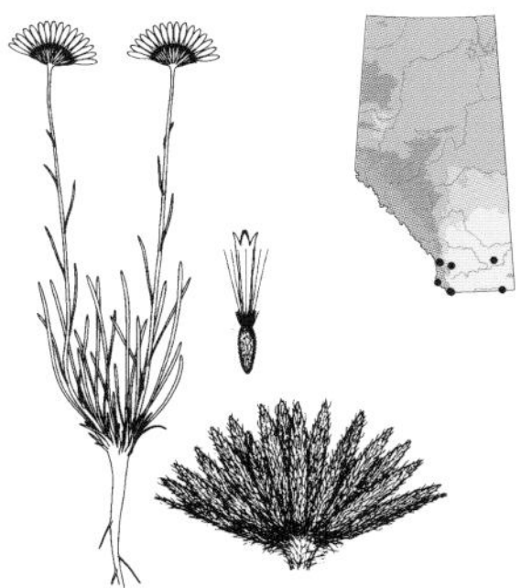

PALE ALPINE FLEABANE

Erigeron pallens Cronq.
ASTER FAMILY (ASTERACEAE [COMPOSITAE])

JG

Plants: **Small, loosely matted** perennial herbs, sparsely to moderately **sticky-glandular and hairy** with long, multi-celled hairs, some hairs with thin, purplish black bands (cross-walls); flowering **stalks leafless**, 2–3 {6} cm tall; from slender-**branched, woody bases** and underground stems (rhizomes).

Leaves: Basal; blades **spatula-shaped to lance-shaped, widest above the middle, some tipped with 3 rounded lobes**, up to 2.5 cm long and 4 mm wide.

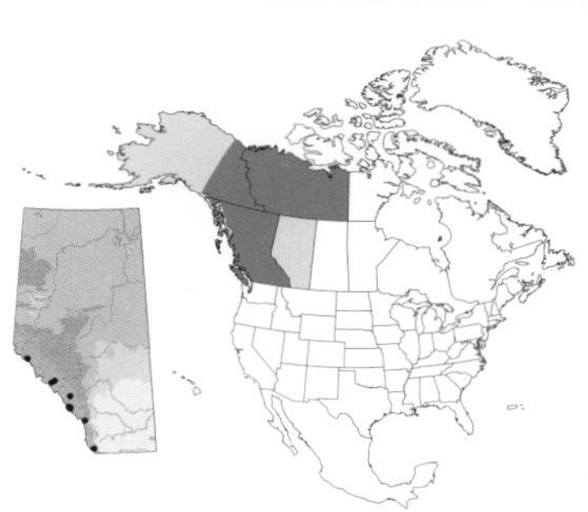

Flowerheads: **White or pinkish to purplish, about 1.5–2 cm across**, with 50–60 {90} small (4–5 mm long and 0.5–0.9 mm wide) ray florets around a yellow button of 3.5–5 mm long disc florets; involucres 6–8 mm high, green or sometimes purplish, with few thin bracts, woolly and sticky, with long, flattened, gland-tipped hairs; receptacles flat, without hairs or scales (naked); **solitary**; June–early August.

Fruits: Short-hairy, 2-nerved seed-like fruits (achenes), tipped with a **tuft of yellowish white, hair-like bristles** (pappus) in 2 rows, the inner row with 35–40 bristles, longer than the corolla, and the outer row with short, inconspicuous bristles.

Habitat: Rocky slopes in alpine areas; elsewhere, in sandy or gravelly areas including riverbanks.

Notes: This species has also been called *Erigeron purpuratus* Greene ssp. *pallens* (Cronq.) G. Douglas. • The specific epithet *pallens* is from the Latin *pallere* (to become pale), perhaps referring to the pale colour of the flowerheads.

JL

JG

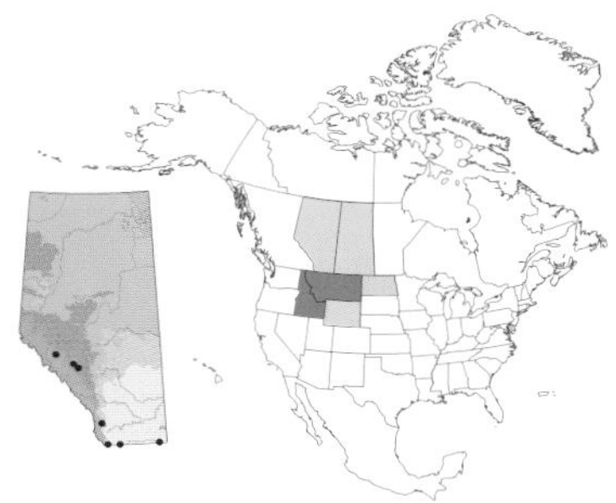

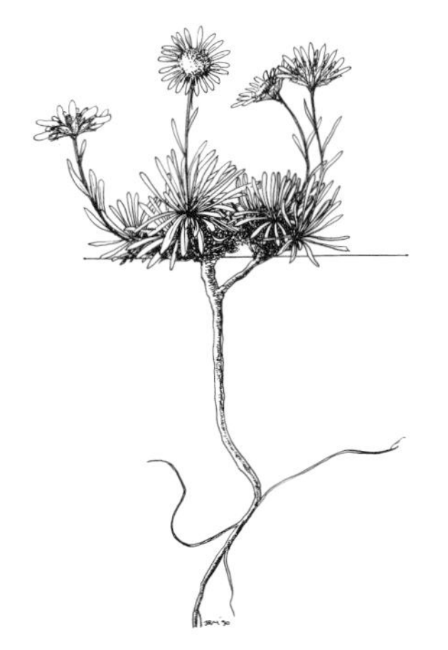

DWARF FLEABANE

Erigeron radicatus Hook.
ASTER FAMILY (ASTERACEAE [COMPOSITAE])

Plants: Small perennial herbs; flowering **stems erect, 3–5** {10} **cm tall**, with coarse or soft hairs (especially near the top), almost leafless; from **branched root crowns** on taproots.

Leaves: Basal, sometimes also with 2 or 3 small, linear stem leaves; **basal leaves slender, lance-shaped, widest above the middle, 1–2** {3.5} **cm long** and 2.5 mm wide, fringed with hairs, hairless or finely hairy on the surfaces, **lacking teeth.**

Flowerheads: White, 1–2 cm across, with 20–50 small (**5–8 mm long** and 2 mm wide) **ray florets** around a yellow button of 2.3–3 mm long disc florets; involucres about 5 mm high and 7–10 mm wide, greenish, glandular-sticky, **with short, soft hairs**, and **equal,** narrowly lance-shaped to oblong **bracts**; receptacles flat, without hairs or scales (naked); **solitary**; late May–July.

Fruits: Ribbed seed-like fruits (achenes), **tipped with 6–12 fragile bristles** and some short, narrow, outer scales (together making up the pappus).

Habitat: Dry, open ridges, rocky slopes, hilltops and grasslands, in sites considered to have escaped Wisconsinan glaciation.

Notes: The total Alberta population of dwarf fleabane is estimated at 1,000 plants and the Canadian population at 5,000 plants. Populations of this species are very local and infrequent and therefore easily eradicated by disturbance. However, populations commonly are found in sites that are difficult to access. • Another rare species, yellow alpine fleabane (*Erigeron ochroleucus* Nutt., see p. 224), resembles dwarf fleabane, but yellow alpine fleabane is tufted (rather than branched at the base) and its leaves are larger (more than 2 cm long) with enlarged, translucent, whitish or purplish bases. Its flowering stems have evident leaves and its involucral bracts are relatively broad and dark yellowish green and sometimes have a brown midrib and purple tips. The ray florets can be blue or purple, as well as white, and up to 12 mm long and the disc florets are 2.8–4.3 mm long. Its achenes have as many as 20 pappus bristles, and their outer bristles are larger than those of dwarf fleabane. Yellow alpine fleabane grows on dry, open slopes and flowers from June to August.

SPREADING FLEABANE

Erigeron divergens T. & G.
ASTER FAMILY (ASTERACEAE [COMPOSITAE])

Plants: Biennial or perennial herbs; **stems leafy, 10–40 cm tall** (sometimes to 70 cm), often **freely branched**, with spreading hairs and glands; from taproots.

Leaves: Basal and alternate, gradually smaller upward on the stems, numerous, covered with **spreading white hairs on both surfaces**; basal leaves lance-shaped, widest above the middle, or spatula-shaped, 1–4 cm long and 1–3 mm wide, **without teeth**, stalked, withered and shed first; stem leaves linear, **toothless**, stalkless or short-stalked.

Flowerheads: Blue, pink or white (drying pink or purplish), about 2 cm across, with 75–150 slender, 5–6 {10} mm long, 0.5–1.2 mm wide ray florets around a 7–11 mm wide yellow button of 2–3 mm long disc florets; involucres **hairy and glandular**, 4–5 mm high, made up of narrow, greenish, equal or overlapping bracts, with thin, **translucent edges and tips**; receptacles flat, without hairs or scales (naked); **several to many**, in branched, open clusters; {May–July}.

Fruits: Seed-like fruits (achenes), 2–4-nerved, tipped with **5–12 fragile bristles and several short, narrow outer scales** (together constituting the pappus).

Habitat: Dry, open areas at lower elevations in the mountains.

Notes: This species has also been called *Erigeron divaricatus* Nutt. • The generic name *Erigeron* was taken from the Greek *eri* (early) and *geron* (old man), probably referring to the early flowering and fruiting of most fleabanes. The specific epithet *divergens,* from the Latin *dis* (apart) and *verger* (to turn), refers to the spreading hairs that cover these plants.

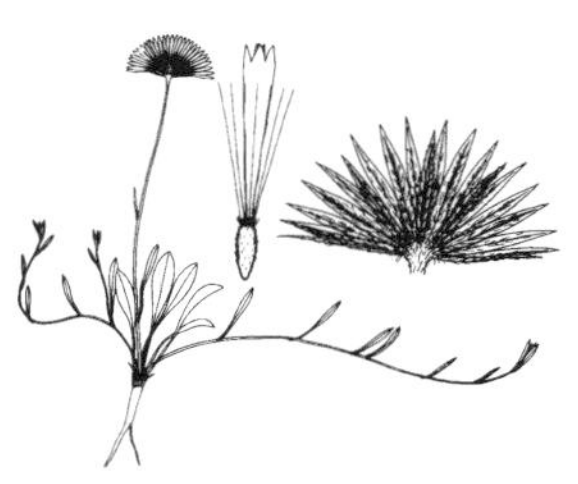

CREEPING FLEABANE

Erigeron flagellaris A. Gray
ASTER FAMILY (ASTERACEAE [COMPOSITAE])

Plants: Biennial or short-lived perennial herbs; stems 5–40 cm tall, hairy; **erect** (flowering) **to trailing and rooting at the tips** (vegetative runners); from taproots.

Leaves: Basal and alternate on stems; basal leaves lance-shaped, widest above the middle, without teeth, stalked; stem leaves few, small, linear to narrowly lance-shaped and widest above the middle.

Flowerheads: White (sometimes pink or blue), with many 5–10 mm long, 1 mm wide ray florets around a yellow button of 2.5–3.5 mm long disc florets; involucres with short, spreading hairs and small glands, 3.5–5 mm high, **the bracts greenish with translucent edges and tips**; receptacles flat, without hairs or scales (naked); solitary; June–August.

Fruits: Nerved seed-like fruits (achenes), **tipped with 10–15 bristles and several short, narrow outer scales** (together comprising the pappus).

Habitat: Dry, open woods, lakeshores and disturbed or poorly vegetated areas; elsewhere, in sagebrush meadows, disturbed grasslands and rocky streambanks.

Notes: The specific epithet *flagellaris* is from the Latin *flagellare* (to whip), referring to the whip-like, trailing stems.

WOOLLYHEADS

Psilocarphus elatior A. Gray
ASTER FAMILY (ASTERACEAE [COMPOSITAE])

CWa

Plants: **Small, loosely greyish-woolly annual** herbs; **stems** erect or spreading at the base, {1} 3–15 cm tall, branched; from weak taproots.

Leaves: **Opposite** (mostly), **linear to linear-oblong**, 5–18 {35} mm long, **without teeth**, **stalkless**; uppermost leaves surrounding the flowerheads.

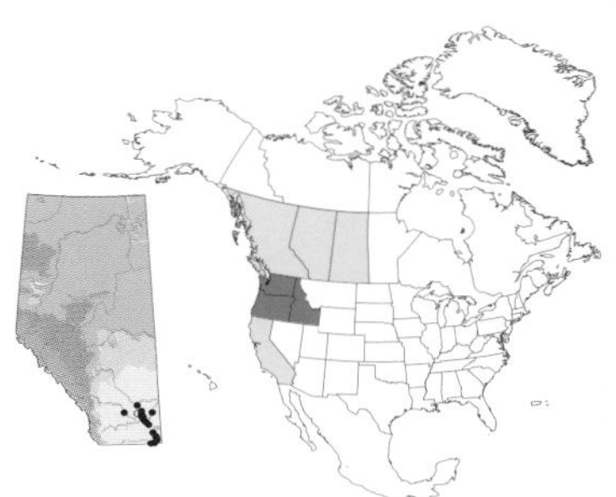

Flowerheads: **White**, round, 4–8 mm wide, with 2 types of **disc florets**; outer florets numerous, **thread-like**, loosely **enveloped by a small** (about 3 mm long), **sac-like, woolly bract with a small translucent appendage just below the tip**, with female parts only; central florets few, tubular, without a bract, with only the male parts functioning; **true involucres absent**; **receptacles round**; numerous, in **compact clusters** at branch tips and in branch axils; May {June–July}.

Fruits: Oblong seed-like fruits (achenes), 1-1.7 mm long, brown, smooth, **without bristles** (pappus) **at the tip**, loose in a woolly, bladder-like bract.

Habitat: Dried beds of pools from spring runoff.

Notes: This species has also been called *Psilocarphus oregonus* Nutt. var. *elatior* A. Gray. • The generic name *Psilocarphus* comes from the Greek *psilos* (bare) and *karphos* (chaff), in reference to the small, translucent appendage near the tip of each female flower bract.

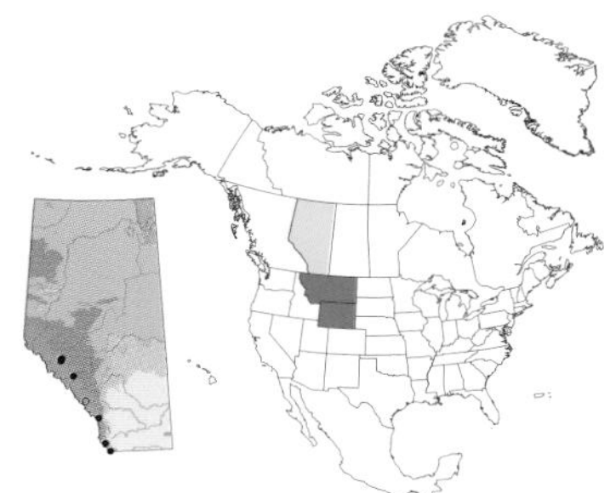

AROMATIC EVERLASTING

Antennaria aromatica Evert
ASTER FAMILY (ASTERACEAE [COMPOSITAE])

Plants: Mat-forming perennial herbs with a **citronella-like odour** (when fresh); flowering stems 2–6 cm tall, **woolly and glandular**; from **short trailing stems or runners** (stolons) and branched, woody root crowns.

Leaves: Mostly in flattened, basal rosettes, but also alternate on the stems, densely woolly and glandular on both surfaces; **basal leaves** 5–10 mm long and 3–8 mm wide, **spatula-shaped**, tapered to a wedge-shaped base and tipped with a short, sharp point; **stem leaves small**, linear to lance-shaped, widest above the middle, 3–7 mm long and 0.5–2 mm wide, the uppermost often with brown, translucent tips; withered leaves persistent (marcescent).

Flowerheads: Green or brownish, 8–20 mm wide, including **disc florets only, male or female**, with sexes **on separate plants** (dioecious); receptacles without hairs or scales (naked); female flowerheads with thread-like florets, 2-lobed styles and 5–7 mm high involucres; male flowerheads with tubular florets, undivided styles and 4–6 mm high involucres; **involucral bracts** loosely woolly, usually glandular and light green or light brown at the base, becoming **translucent brown or green** toward the blunt or pointed, irregularly cut tips; 2–5, in fairly compact clusters; July–early August.

Fruits: Dry seed-like fruits (achenes), 1.5–2 mm long, tipped with a tuft of hair-like bristles (pappus) that are joined at the base and **shed as a unit**.

Habitat: Limestone talus from treeline to alpine regions, in areas that were not covered by ice during the Wisconsinan glaciation.

Notes: This species has also been called *Antennaria pulvinata* Greene. • It appears that aromatic everlasting has not migrated very far since the last glaciation. • The specific epithet *aromatica* refers to the fragrant living plants.

CORYMBOSE EVERLASTING

Antennaria corymbosa E. Nels.
ASTER FAMILY (ASTERACEAE [COMPOSITAE])

Plants: Thinly woolly perennial herbs; flowering stems erect, slender, 10–30 cm tall; forming loose mats from **leafy trailing stems or runners** (stolons).

Leaves: Mostly in flat basal rosettes, but also alternate on the flowering stems; **basal leaves** 2–4 cm long, **narrowly lance-shaped**, widest above the middle, tapered to a narrow base, **greyish and thinly woolly on both surfaces; stem leaves small**, linear.

Flowerheads: Whitish with **dark spots**, about 4 mm across, with disc florets only, male or female, with sexes on separate plants; receptacles without hairs or scales (naked); involucres 4–5 mm high, their **bracts woolly at the base** and with a **dark brown or blackish spot below the whitish tip**; male flowerheads with tubular florets and undivided styles; female flowerheads with thread-like florets and 2-lobed styles; several, on short stalks in **compact, flat-topped clusters**; {June–July} August.

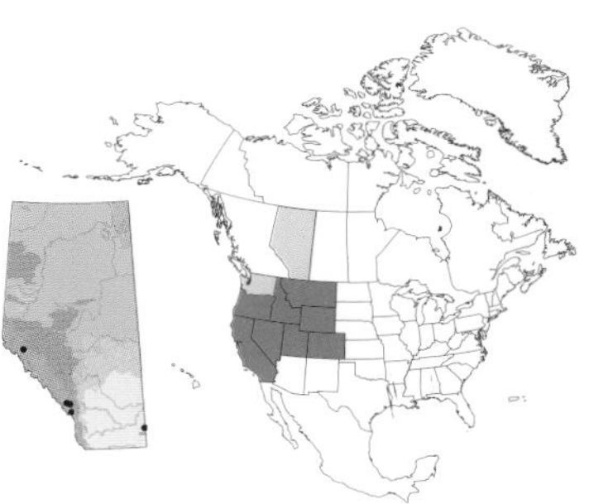

Fruits: Dry seed-like fruits (achenes), tipped with a tuft of hair-like bristles (pappus) that are joined at the base and **shed as a unit.**

Habitat: Moist open woods and meadows; elsewhere, in moist or wet subalpine and alpine meadows.

Notes: Corymbose everlasting is similar to another rare species, one-headed everlasting (*Antennaria monocephala* D.C. Eaton), but one-headed everlasting has only a single flowerhead per stem, its involucral bracts have blackish tips and its leaves are green and hairless (or sparsely hairy) on their upper surface. One-headed everlasting grows on alpine slopes and ledges, and flowers in July and August. • The specific epithet *corymbosa* refers to the arrangement of the flowerheads in flat-topped, corymb-like clusters.

A. MONOCEPHALA

LK

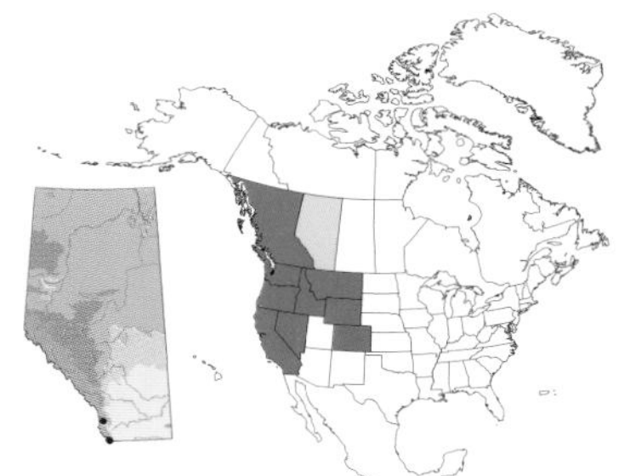

SILVERY EVERLASTING

Antennaria luzuloides T. & G.
ASTER FAMILY (ASTERACEAE [COMPOSITAE])

Plants: Clumped perennial herbs; flowering stems erect, 10–50 {70} cm tall, clustered, grey-woolly; from branched, rather woody root crowns.

Leaves: Basal and alternate on the stems; **basal leaves erect**, narrowly **lance-shaped**, widest above the middle, 3–8 cm long and 2–8 mm wide, usually with **conspicuous nerves**, thinly woolly, tapered to a short stalk; **stem leaves well developed**, mostly **linear**, gradually smaller upward.

Flowerheads: Greenish brown with whitish-tipped bracts, about 5 mm across, with disc florets only, male or female with sexes on separate plants; receptacles without hairs or scales (naked); **involucres 4–5 mm high, mostly hairless to the base**, with pale greenish brown, whitish-tipped, **translucent** bracts; male flowerheads with tubular florets and undivided styles; female flowerheads with thread-like florets and 2-lobed styles; several to many, in **compact, often flat-topped clusters**; {May–June} July.

Fruits: Dry seed-like fruits (achenes), tipped with a tuft of hair-like bristles (pappus) that are joined at the base and **shed as a unit**.

Habitat: Gravelly slopes and open places at low to moderate elevations in the mountains.

Notes: The generic name *Antennaria* refers to the fancied resemblance of the thick pappus hairs in the male florets of some species to the antennae of some insects. In silvery everlasting, these hairs are strongly club-shaped, flattened at their tips and more or less minutely toothed.

COMMON CUDWEED, TALL CUDWEED

Gnaphalium microcephalum Nutt.
ASTER FAMILY (ASTERACEAE [COMPOSITAE])

WM

Plants: **Tufted**, short-lived **perennial** herbs, **white-woolly;** stems several, clumped, erect, 20–70 cm tall, unbranched or moderately branched; from woody **taproots.**

Leaves: Basal and alternate on stems, **numerous, mostly linear** (lower leaves sometimes lance-shaped and widest above the middle), 3–10 cm long and 2–10 mm wide, stalkless, with smooth (toothless) **edges** that sometimes **extend slightly down the stem as wings.**

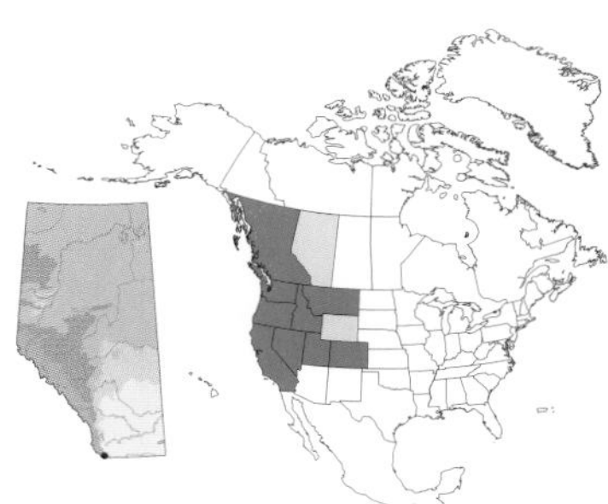

Flowerheads: Yellow or whitish, about 6 mm high, **with disc florets only; involucres 4–7 mm high**, with many **translucent white to tan bracts**, woolly only at the base (if at all); receptacles flat, without hairs or scales (naked); **outer florets** very slender, with **female** parts only; **central florets** with **both male and female** parts; numerous, on short stalks in small, compact heads forming open clusters; August {July–September}.

Fruits: Hairless, nerveless seed-like fruits (achenes), **with a tuft of hair-like bristles** (pappus) that is **soon shed.**

Habitat: Dry, open sites; elsewhere, on burned sites and streambanks, and around hot springs.

Notes: This species has also been called *Gnaphalium thermale* E. Nels. • Common cudweed resembles another rare species, clammy cudweed (*Gnaphalium viscosum* Kunth), but clammy cudweed has single stems and glandular stem and upper leaf surfaces. Clammy cudweed grows in open woods and flowers from July to September. • The cudweeds (*Gnaphalium* spp.) may be confused with pearly everlasting (*Anaphalis margaritacea* (L.) Benth. & Hook. f. *ex* C.B. Clarke), but the leaves of pearly everlasting have dark green upper surfaces and their edges do not run down the stem. Its plants spread by means of underground stems (rhizomes), and its pappus bristles remain attached to the seeds. • The cudweeds also resemble some species of everlasting (*Antennaria* spp.), but everlasting has male and female flowerheads on separate plants and lacks extended leaf edges.

G. VISCOSUM

WJC

COMMON BEGGARTICKS, TALL BEGGARTICKS

Bidens frondosa L.
ASTER FAMILY (ASTERACEAE [COMPOSITAE])

Plants: **Annual** herbs; stems {20} 30–150 cm tall, usually reddish, furrowed, hairless or sparsely hairy, branched toward the top; from weak, slender roots.

Leaves: **Opposite, numerous**, finely hairy or (usually) hairless, 5–10 cm long; **blades pinnately divided into 3–5** lance-shaped, coarsely toothed **leaflets** up to 10 cm long and 3 cm wide, **the tip leaflet** (and sometimes lower leaflets) **stalked**; leaf stalks slender, 1–6 cm long.

Flowerheads: **Orange** (sometimes pale yellow), bell-shaped to bowl-shaped, 12–20 mm across, with **0–8 inconspicuous** (less than 3.5 mm long) **ray florets** around a cluster of 5-lobed disc florets; **involucral bracts in 2 distinct overlapping rows**, with 4–8 {16} green, leafy, fringed, **10–20 mm long outer bracts** around the broader, translucent (at least in part), 7–9 mm long inner bracts; **receptacle surface with dry scales**; disc florets with both male and female parts; several, in open, branched clusters; {June–October}.

Fruits: Flat seed-like fruits (achenes), {5} 6–12 mm long, strongly 1-nerved on each face, brown or blackish, **tipped with 2 stiff, barbed bristles** (awns).

Habitat: Moist ground and ditches; elsewhere, in wet or occasionally rather dry waste places.

Notes: The generic name *Bidens*, from the Latin *bi* (two) and *dens* (tooth), refers to the 2 barbed bristles at the tip of each achene. The specific epithet *frondosa* is Latin for 'leafy.'

COMMON TICKSEED

Coreopsis tinctoria Nutt.
ASTER FAMILY (ASTERACEAE [COMPOSITAE])

JL

Plants: Erect, hairless **annual** herbs; stems slender, branched, 40–100 {30–120} cm tall; from fibrous roots.

Leaves: Usually opposite, fairly scattered, 5–10 cm long, once or twice pinnately divided into slender lobes, short-stalked to almost stalkless.

Flowerheads: Orange-yellow, about **2.5 cm across**, with 8 {6–10} **ray florets around a dark, red-purplish button of fertile disc florets**; ray florets 8–12 mm long, often reddish brown or purplish at the base, lacking stamens and pistils; involucres 7 {6–10} mm high and 10–15 mm wide, with **2 unequal rows of bracts**, all somewhat **joined at the base**; outer bracts slender, about 2 mm long; inner bracts egg-shaped, 5–8 mm long, orange or brown with translucent edges; several to many, **on long, slender stalks** in branched, open clusters; July {June–September}.

Fruits: Black, oblong to wedge-shaped seed-like fruits (achenes), **flattened** parallel to the outer bracts, **1–4 mm long**, curved inward, tipped **with or without 2 tiny bristles** (pappus).

Habitat: Clay flats and slough edges; elsewhere, in irrigation ditches.

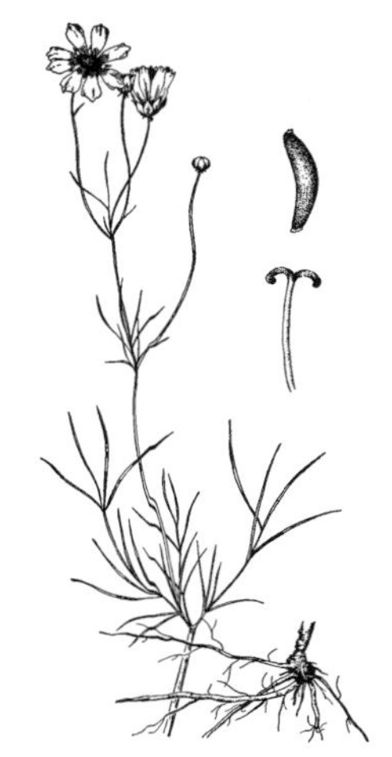

Notes: This showy wildflower is often grown in flower gardens, and it frequently escapes to grow in the wild. It can occur very sporadically, growing abundantly one year and then disappearing for several seasons. • The common name 'tickseed' refers to the small, dark achenes, which were thought to resemble tiny insects.

GREENTHREAD, TICKSEED

Thelesperma subnudum A. Gray var. *marginatum* (Rydb.) T.E. Melchert *ex* Cronq.
ASTER FAMILY (ASTERACEAE [COMPOSITAE])

Plants: Essentially hairless perennial herbs; stems usually single, 10–20 cm tall; from creeping underground stems (rhizomes).

Leaves: Opposite (sometimes alternate on the upper stem), mostly crowded near the stem base; **lower leaves irregularly pinnately divided into slender**, 1.5–5 cm long and {1} 1.5–3 mm wide **lobes**; upper leaves linear, gradually reduced to bracts on the upper stem.

Flowerheads: Yellow, about 1 cm across, with **disc florets only; involucres 6–9 mm high**, with 2 overlapping rows of bracts, the outer bracts leafy and 2.5–5 mm long, **the inner bracts larger**, translucent, fused together for the lower ⅓–⅔; **receptacles** flat, covered **with thin scales**; florets with both male and female parts; 1–3, on 7–10 cm long stalks from upper leaf axils; {May–June}.

Fruits: Flattened, linear–oblong seed-like fruits (achenes), hairless but sometimes covered with tiny bumps (papillae), tipped with **2 inconspicuous** (sometimes absent), **barbed bristles** (awns).

Habitat: Dry eroded hills, on sandy soil; elsewhere, in mixed grasslands dominated by western wheatgrass (*Elymus smithii* (Rydb.) Gould).

Notes: This species has also been called *Thelesperma marginatum* Rydb. • The generic name *Thelesperma* comes from the Greek *thele* (nipple) and *sperma* (seed), referring to the tiny, nipple-like bumps on the seeds of some species.

PICRADENIOPSIS

Picradeniopsis oppositifolia (Nutt.) Rydb. *ex* Britt.
ASTER FAMILY (ASTERACEAE [COMPOSITAE])

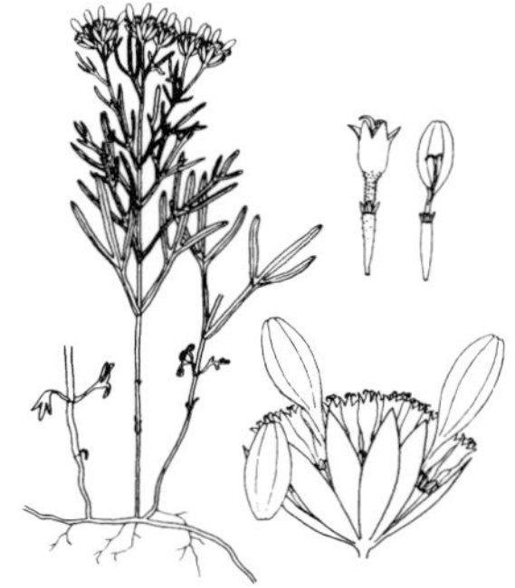

Plants: **Tufted perennial** herbs, **greyish with fine, flat-lying hairs**; stems leafy, erect, 10–20 {50} cm tall, **usually freely branched** from near the more or less woody base (sometimes unbranched); from tough, slender, creeping underground stems (rhizomes).

Leaves: **Opposite** (sometimes a few alternate), **numerous**, 1–4 cm long, with **tiny, pitted glands**; blades once or twice palmately divided into 3 {5} linear segments; stalks short.

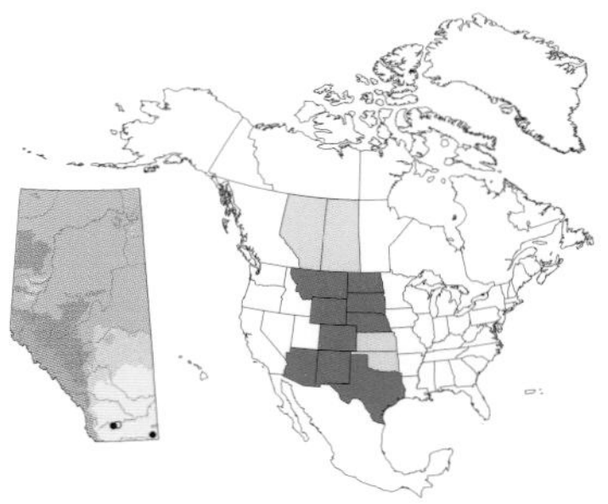

Flowerheads: **Yellow**, 7–10 {12} mm across, with **few** (5 or 6), **inconspicuous** (2–4 {5} mm long) **ray florets** around a dense cluster of disc florets; involucres finely greyish-hairy, 5–7 mm high, with **2 overlapping rows of bracts**, the outer bracts ridged lengthwise, the inner bracts with thin, almost translucent edges; receptacles flat, without hairs or scales (naked); ray florets with female parts only; **disc florets glandular** on the lower part of their tubes, with both male and female parts; several, borne at the tips of upper branches, forming flat-topped clusters; July {August–September}.

Fruits: Slender, 4-sided seed-like fruits (achenes), 4 mm long, glandular, **tipped with a few blunt, translucent scales** (pappus).

Habitat: Badlands and roadsides; elsewhere, as a rather persistent weed in cultivated land and on saline flats and dry plains.

Notes: This species has also been called *Bahia oppositifolia* (Nutt.) A. Gray. • The specific epithet *oppositifolia* refers to the opposite leaves.

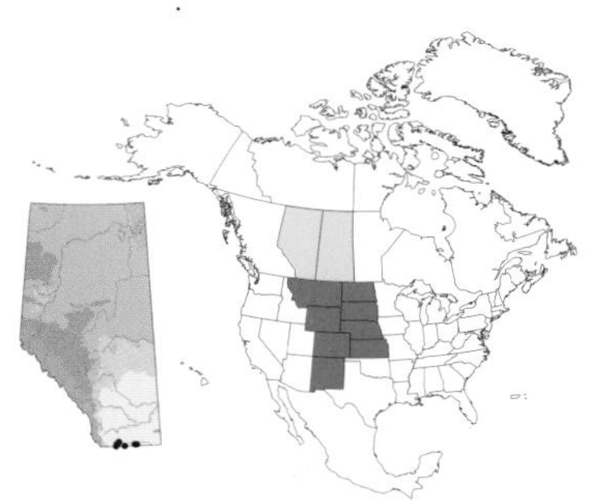

TUFTED HYMENOPAPPUS

Hymenopappus filifolius Hook. var. *polycephalus* (Osterh.) B.L. Turner
ASTER FAMILY (ASTERACEAE [COMPOSITAE])

Plants: Perennial herbs; stems 20–40 {10–90} cm tall, few to several, almost hairless or sparsely covered with soft, woolly tufts; from stout, woody root crowns on deep, woody taproots.

Leaves: Mostly basal, but also alternate on the stem, 2–7 cm long; **blades once or twice pinnately divided into linear or thread-like segments**, covered with soft, white, woolly hair when young, almost hairless and purplish with age, stalked (lower leaves) to stalkless (upper leaves); stem leaves few and smaller.

Flowerheads: Yellowish, 12–20 mm across, with tubular **disc florets only**; involucres 5–7 mm high, their **bracts** pressed together, with broad, blunt, **yellowish**, **translucent** tips; receptacles small, without hairs or scales (naked); florets with both male and female parts; several to many, in open, flat-topped clusters (corymbs); May–August.

Fruits: Silky-hairy seed-like fruits (achenes), **4- or 5-sided, widest toward the tip**, 15–20 nerved, tipped **with a crown of tiny scales** (pappus) less than 1 mm long.

Habitat: Dry gravelly or sandy sites on valley slopes and at the edges of coulees and badlands.

Notes: This species has also been called *Hymenopappus polycephalus* Osterh. • The generic name *Hymenopappus* comes from the Greek *hymen* (membrane) and *pappos* (old man), in reference to the translucent scales and greyish, silky hairs (like those of an old man) on the fruits. The specific epithet *filifolius*, from the Latin *filum* (thread) and *folium* (leaf), refers to the thread-like segments of the leaves; *polycephalus*, from the Greek *polys* (many) and *kephale* (the head), refers to the many flowerheads.

Indian tansy

Tanacetum bipinnatum (L.) Schultz-Bip. ssp. *huronense* (Nutt.) Breitung
ASTER FAMILY (ASTERACEAE [COMPOSITAE])

Plants: Perennial herbs; stems 10–80 cm tall, **with long, soft hairs** (at least when young); from slender, elongated underground stems (rhizomes).

Leaves: Alternate, 2 or 3 times pinnately divided into small leaflets with pointed lobes, **5–20 cm long**, 2–8 cm wide, stalkless or short-stalked, covered with long, soft hairs.

Flowerheads: Yellow, with a **few small ray florets** around a **1–2 cm wide button of disc florets**; involucral bracts overlapping, dry, translucent at the tips and on the edges; **1–15, in flat-topped clusters**; May–July.

Fruits: Dry seed-like fruits (achenes), angled or ribbed, commonly with glands, **lacking bristles at the tip** but sometimes with a small crown of short scales.

Habitat: Sandy or gravelly shores, sand dunes and gravel bars.

Notes: This species has also been called *Tanacetum huronense* Nutt. var. *bifarium* Fern. and *Chrysanthemum bipinnatum* L. var. *huronense* (Nutt.) Hult. • Common tansy (*Tanacetum vulgare* L.) is Alberta's only other tansy species. It is an introduced species that is stouter and larger than Indian tansy, with stems 40–180 cm tall. The leaves of common tansy are hairless and dotted with tiny pits, and the flowerheads are more numerous (20–200) and smaller (5–10 mm wide). Common tansy is a noxious weed.

DJ

LA

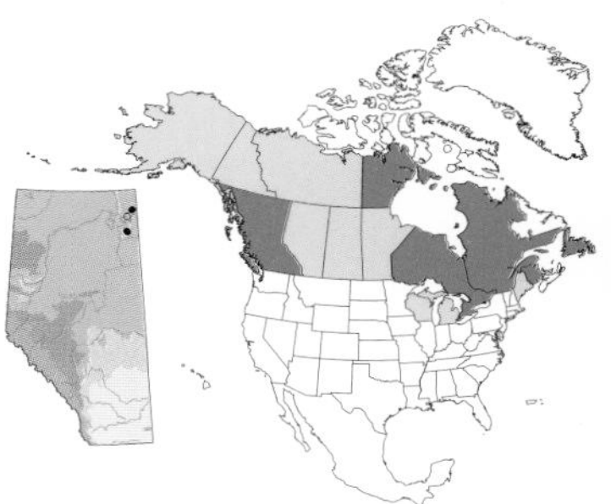

FORKED WORMWOOD

Artemisia furcata Bieb. var. *furcata*
ASTER FAMILY (ASTERACEAE [COMPOSITAE])

Plants: Perennial, usually aromatic **herbs; stems mostly 10–20** {5–30} **cm tall**, greyish white with fine, silky hairs; from branched root crowns and short, stout underground stems (rhizomes).

Leaves: Mostly basal, but also alternate on the stem, **greyish on both surfaces** with flat-lying, silky hairs; **basal leaves** 2–5 {1–12} cm long, **once or twice palmately divided into 3 or 5 slender** (about 1 mm wide), linear to narrowly elliptic **segments**, long-stalked; stem leaves few, sometimes not divided, short-stalked or stalkless.

Flowerheads: Yellow, 6–10 mm across, with 5-lobed, glandular and sometimes hairy disc florets; involucral bracts overlapping, 3–6 mm long, egg-shaped to elliptic, with **broad, brownish black, translucent edges**, irregularly cut or fringed tips, and woolly outer surfaces; receptacles without hairs or scales (naked); outer florets with female parts only; **central florets with both male and female parts**; about 5–12, stalked or stalkless, **in narrow, elongated clusters** (racemes or spikes); {July} August–September.

Fruits: Sparsely long-hairy seed-like fruits (achenes) without bristles (pappus) at the tip.

Habitat: Rocky **alpine** slopes; elsewhere, on ledges and rocky or sandy slopes at low to high elevations.

Notes: This species has also been called *Artemisia trifurcata* Steph. *ex* Sprengel and *Artemisia hyperborea* Rydb. • The generic name *Artemisia* honours Artemis, the Greek goddess of the moon, wild animals and hunting. The specific epithet *furcata*, from the Latin *furca* (fork), refers to the divided (forked) leaves.

HERRIOT'S SAGEWORT, MOUNTAIN SAGEWORT

Artemisia tilesii Ledeb. ssp. *elatior* (T. & G.) Hult.
ASTER FAMILY (ASTERACEAE [COMPOSITAE])

LK

Plants: Erect, **aromatic** perennial herbs; stems usually finely **woolly**, 60–120 {15–150} cm tall; from woody root crowns, strong underground stems (rhizomes) and fibrous roots.

Leaves: **Alternate**, elliptic to lance-shaped, sometimes widest above middle, {2} 5–20 cm long, highly variable, **toothless to sharply toothed or pinnately lobed**, green and almost hairless on the upper surface, **densely white-woolly beneath**.

Flowerheads: **Yellowish**, sometimes tinged reddish, small, with **20–40 disc florets**; involucres {3} **4–5 mm high**, **woolly**, with blunt-tipped, often dark-edged bracts; numerous, short-stalked or stalkless, in erect, **elongating, branched clusters** (panicles); July–October.

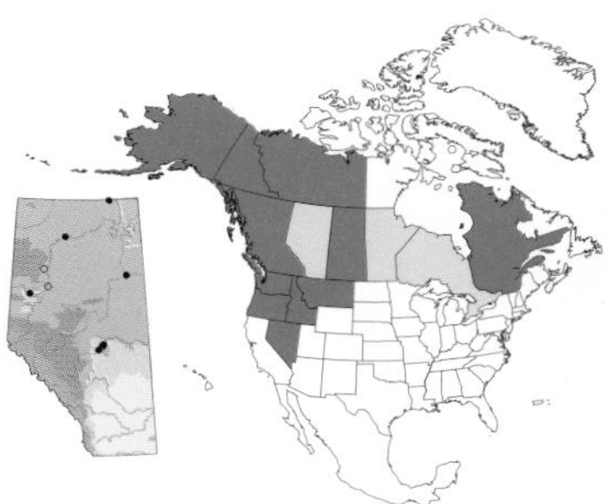

Fruits: Dry, **hairless** seed-like fruits (achenes), **without bristles** (pappus) at the tip.

Habitat: Open woods and river flats; elsewhere, on open, rocky or gravelly alpine slopes or in heathlands.

Notes: This species has also been called *Artemisia herriotii* Rydb. • This aromatic plant was widely used as a medicine by native peoples. It was brewed to make medicinal teas for treating infections, fevers, cancer, rheumatism, tuberculosis, stomach aches, sprains, sore limbs, athlete's foot, itching, earaches, toothaches, chest ailments and colds. Modern herbalists give the tea to treat colds, constipation, kidney problems and internal bleeding. It is also used as a gargle for sore throats and applied to sore eyes and cuts. Raw leaves are chewed to relieve colds, flu, fever, headaches and ulcers, and they are also recommended as a mosquito repellent. Boiled leaves have been used as poultices on arthritic joints, and they were sometimes mixed with dog food as a supplement.

LONG-LEAVED ARNICA

Arnica longifolia D.C. Eat.
ASTER FAMILY (ASTERACEAE [COMPOSITAE])

Plants: Densely tufted perennial herbs; flowering stems several, erect, 30–60 cm tall, hairy, with smaller, sterile, leafy stems from the thickened base; forming large patches from **branched root crowns and short, stout underground stems** (rhizomes).

Leaves: Opposite, in **5–7 pairs**, largest near mid-stem; blades narrowly lance-shaped to elliptic, gradually tapered to a pointed tip, 5–12 cm long and 1–2 cm wide, somewhat rough to the touch (finely stiff-hairy) and often slightly sticky (finely glandular-hairy), **toothless**; stalks short (lower leaves) to absent (upper leaves), often joining at the base to encircle the stem.

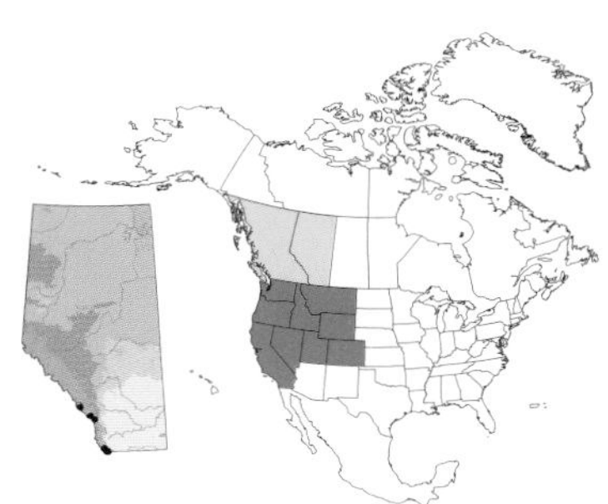

Flowerheads: Yellow or orange, bell-shaped, about 2 cm across, with 8–11 {13} ray florets around a dense cluster of disc florets; involucres **evenly glandular-hairy**, 7–10 mm high, with mostly equal, **sharp-pointed bracts**; receptacles without hairs or scales (naked); ray florets 1–2 cm long, with female parts only; disc florets 5-lobed, with both male and female parts; single to several, in open, branched clusters; July–August {September}.

Fruits: Slender, 5–10-nerved seed-like fruits (achenes), glandular-hairy, tipped with a tuft of **finely barbed, straw-coloured, hair-like bristles** (pappus).

Habitat: Open, rocky subalpine slopes and cliffs; elsewhere, on well-drained soil or rock by springs and seeps and along cliffs and riverbanks at moderate to high elevations in the mountains.

A. AMPLEXICAULIS

JP

Notes: Another rare species, stem-clasping arnica (*Arnica amplexicaulis* Nutt.), resembles long-leaved arnica but has toothed leaves, longer underground stems (usually) and fewer stems that are seldom, if at all, tufted. Its flowerheads have pale-yellow rays, the leaves can be up to 6 cm wide and the pappus bristles are light brown and somewhat feathery. Stem-clasping arnica grows in moist woods and along streambanks (usually at lower elevations than long-leaved arnica); it flowers in July and August.

NODDING ARNICA

Arnica parryi A. Gray
ASTER FAMILY (ASTERACEAE [COMPOSITAE])

Plants: Perennial herbs; stems solitary, 20–50 {60} cm tall, usually silky-woolly near the base, glandular (at least on the upper parts); from slender underground stems (rhizomes).

Leaves: **Opposite**, basal and **in 2 or 3 {4} pairs on the stem**, much smaller upward on the stem; blades lance-shaped to egg-shaped, 5–20 cm long and 1.5–6 cm wide, toothless or finely toothed, more or less glandular and silky-hairy, tapered to a short stalk (lower leaves) or sometimes stalkless (upper leaves).

Flowerheads: **Yellow**, bell-shaped (sometimes narrowly so), about 1–2 cm across, **with disc florets only**; involucres mostly 10–14 mm high, glandular and finely hairy, with almost equal, sharply pointed bracts; receptacles without hairs or scales (naked); **florets** 5-lobed, **with both male and female parts**; several, often **nodding in bud**, in open, branched clusters; July–August.

Fruits: Slender, 5–10-nerved seed-like fruits (achenes), hairless, hairy or glandular, tipped with a tuft of **straw-coloured to light brown, barbed to almost feathery bristles** (pappus).

Habitat: Open woods at lower elevations in the mountains; elsewhere, on grassy hillsides and scree slopes in the foothills and at moderate elevations in the mountains.

Notes: This is the only *Arnica* in Alberta that lacks ray florets.

WM

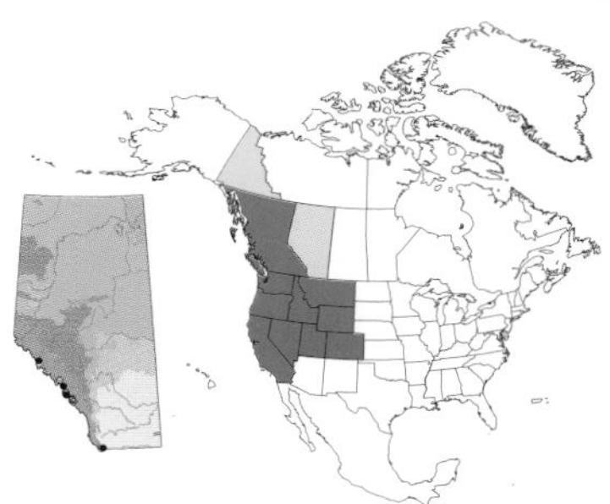

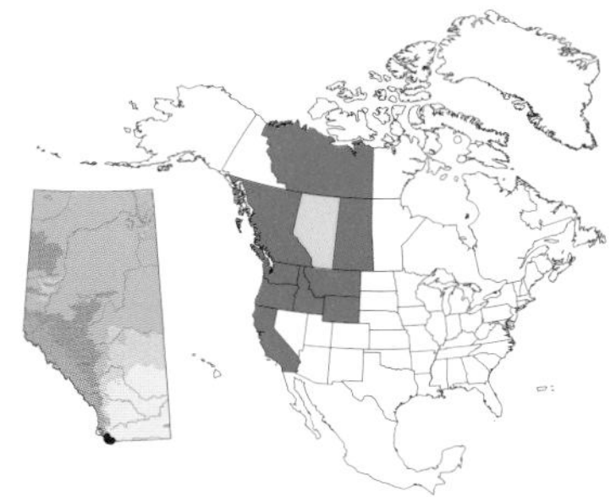

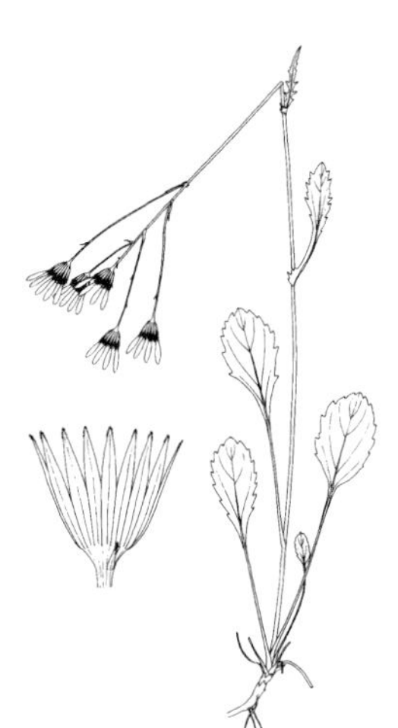

ALPINE MEADOW BUTTERWEED

Packera subnuda D.K. Trock & T.M. Barkley
ASTER FAMILY (ASTERACEAE [COMPOSITAE])

Plants: Small, **hairless perennial** herbs; **stems** usually single and **5–15** {30} **cm tall**; from creeping underground stems (rhizomes) with fibrous roots.

Leaves: Basal and alternate on the stems; basal leaves **2–4** {6} **cm long**, with **broadly egg-shaped to round blades** that are much shorter than their stalks, edged with rounded teeth or more or less toothless; 2 or 3 stem leaves, smaller upward on the stem, lance-shaped, often widest above the middle, pinnately lobed.

Flowerheads: Yellow, 2–3 cm wide, with few, 7–14 mm long ray florets around an 8–15 mm wide button of many disc florets; **involucres** {5} 6–8 mm high, **green or crimson, not black-tipped**, with **equal**, linear **bracts**; receptacles without hairs or scales (naked); ray florets with female parts only; disc florets with both male and female parts; solitary (sometimes 2); {June–September}.

Fruits: Seed-like fruits (achenes), 5–10-ribbed, tipped with a **tuft of soft, white, hair-like bristles** (pappus).

Habitat: Moist meadows in alpine and subalpine zones; elsewhere, in forest clearings.

Notes: This species has also been called *Packera buekii* D.K. Trock and T.M. Barkley, *P. cymbalarioides* (Buek) Weber & Löve and *Senecio cymbalarioides* Buek. It is *not* synonymous with *Senecio cymbalarioides* (T. & G.) Nutt. *non* Buek or *Senecio streptanthifolius* Greene. • Alpine meadow butterweed is distinguished from other small, hairless butterweeds (*Senecio* spp.) in Alberta by its single flowerheads. It is most similar to arctic butterweed (*Packera cymbalaria* (Pursh) W.A. Weber & A. Löve, previously called *Senecio cymbalaria* Pursh, *Senecio conterminus* Greenm. and *Senecio resedifolius* Less.), but alpine meadow butterweed has stems arising from a slender, creeping rhizome and its plants are either hairless or with permanent woolly hairs only in and near the leaf axils or at the base of the head. Arctic butterweed, on the other hand, has stems that arise from a short, branching, horizontal to ascending root crown, and its plants are usually hairless when mature but they are often lightly cobwebby-woolly, especially on the lower half of the plant. Arctic butterweed also grows in slightly different habitats, preferring dry, rocky alpine or subalpine sites. • Another rare, single-headed species, large-flowered ragwort (*Senecio megacephalus* Nutt.), is distinguished by its larger plants (20–50 cm tall) with narrower and longer lower leaves (10–20 cm long) and larger flowerheads (3–5 cm wide). It grows on rocky alpine and subalpine slopes in a few localities in the Waterton area. • The generic name *Packera* honours Dr. John Packer (1929–), a professor of botany at the University of Alberta who produced the second edition of the *Flora of Alberta* (Moss 1983).

SENECIO MEGACEPHALUS

AMERICAN SAW-WORT

Saussurea americana D.C. Eat.
ASTER FAMILY (ASTERACEAE [COMPOSITAE])

PL

Plants: Perennial herbs, **cobwebby-hairy** (at least when young); stems stout, 30–100 cm tall, unbranched except in the flower clusters; from short, stout underground stems (rhizomes).

Leaves: Alternate, numerous; blades **narrowly triangular**, up to 15 cm long and 8 cm wide, progressively smaller upward on the stem (becoming lance-shaped), sharply toothed, bright green on upper surface, **cobwebby-hairy beneath**; stalks up to 3 cm long (lower leaves) to absent (upper leaves).

Flowerheads: Purple, with **disc florets only**, 10–14 mm high; florets with both male and female parts, 11–12 mm long, 5-lobed; bracts hairy, green with dark edges; outer bracts broad; inner bracts narrow, 7–8 mm long, progressively longer than outer bracts; numerous, short-stalked, in **crowded, erect, sometimes flat-topped clusters**; {July–August} September.

Fruits: Light brown, hairless seed-like fruits (achenes), 4–6 mm long, longer than wide, tipped with 2 rows of bristles (pappus); outer bristles short, hair-like, soon shed; **inner bristles feathery**, joined at the base, shed together.

Habitat: Moist open slopes and meadows.

Notes: Brook ragwort (*Senecio triangularis* Hook.) has similar large, triangular, toothed leaves but its flowers are yellow.

LA

LA

BH

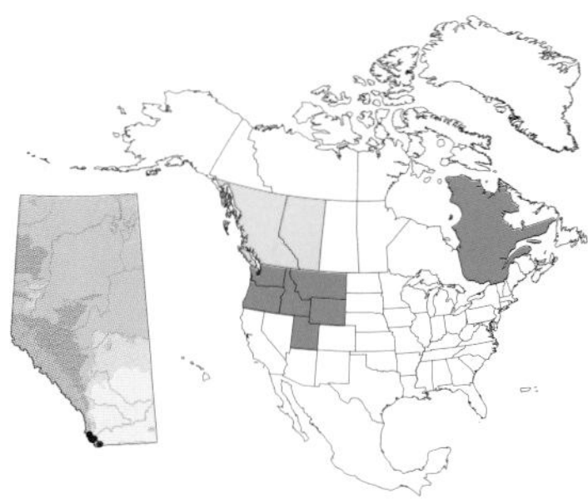

ELK THISTLE

Cirsium scariosum Nutt.
ASTER FAMILY (ASTERACEAE [COMPOSITAE])

Plants: Erect, **spiny biennial** herbs; stems 30–80 cm tall, fleshy, ribbed, hairy, mostly unbranched; from taproots.

Leaves: Alternate, gradually smaller toward the top of the stem, stalkless, **with spiny edges**; lower leaves narrowly egg-shaped (wider above the middle), tapering at the base, **hairless on the upper surface**, woolly beneath, **lobed only slightly to halfway to the midrib**; upper leaves narrowly elliptic to linear, shallowly lobed.

Flowerheads: White to pink or reddish purple, with **disc florets only; involucres 2–3 cm high, without cobwebby hairs or glands**, the inner bracts often longer than the outer; outer bracts broadly lance-shaped, 2.5–5 mm wide at the base and tipped with a slender spine 2–4 mm long; **receptacle densely bristly**; disc florets with both male and female parts, 5 **lobes of the corolla elongated**, styles with a thickened, hairy ring, anthers 6–10 mm long; 5–15, short-stalked, clustered at the stem tip and sometimes in upper leaf axils; June–September.

Fruits: Oblong, somewhat flattened seed-like fruits (achenes), 5.5–6.5 mm long, hairless, brown with a narrow, yellowish band at the top, tipped with a **tuft of feathery bristles** (pappus) 4–5 mm long, **shorter than the corolla.**

Habitat: Moist meadows, streambanks, open woodlands and slopes from low to high elevations.

Notes: Some taxonomists have included this species with *Cirsium hookerianum* Nutt. and others with *Cirsium foliosum* (Hook.) DC. It has also been called *Cnicus scariosus* (Nutt.) A. Gray and *Carduus scariosus* (Nutt.) Heller. The taxonomy is still problematic. • The generic name *Cirsium* is from the Greek *kirsos* (a swollen vein), for which thistles, called *kirsion*, were a reputed remedy.

RUSH-PINK

Stephanomeria runcinata Nutt.
ASTER FAMILY (ASTERACEAE [COMPOSITAE])

Plants: **Perennial herbs** with **milky juice**; stems slender, **10–20 cm tall, freely branched**; from taproots.

Leaves: Alternate, **linear to narrowly lance-shaped, 1–7 cm long**, 4–15 mm wide, with **sharp, backward-pointing teeth**, stalkless; upper leaves smaller and toothless.

Flowerheads: **Pink or white**, 10–15 mm long, **tubular**, usually **5-flowered**, with **ray florets only**; florets with both male and female parts; involucres 9–12 mm high, with 5 main bracts; **numerous**, at branch tips; June–July.

Fruits: **Pitted or bumpy** seed-like fruits (achenes), about 5 mm long, tipped with a tuft of white, **feathery bristles** (pappus).

Habitat: Dry hills and plains, often on eroded sites.

Notes: Skeletonweeds (*Lygodesmia* spp.) resemble rush-pink, but none of their leaves are toothed and the pappus bristles at the tips of their achenes are hair-like (not feathery). • Major modifications to waterways pose the greatest threat to the survival of this species in Alberta. • Although it is an attractive plant, rush-pink is not useful for horticultural applications because it prefers rather extreme climatic and habitat conditions. • The generic name *Stephanomeria* is derived from the Greek *stephanus* (a crown or wreath) and *mereia* (a division). The specific epithet *runcinata* is Latin for 'a large saw,' referring to the downward-pointing, saw-like teeth of the leaves.

JG

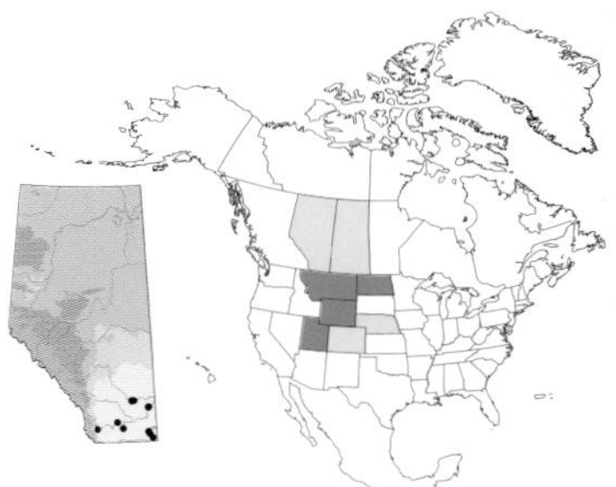

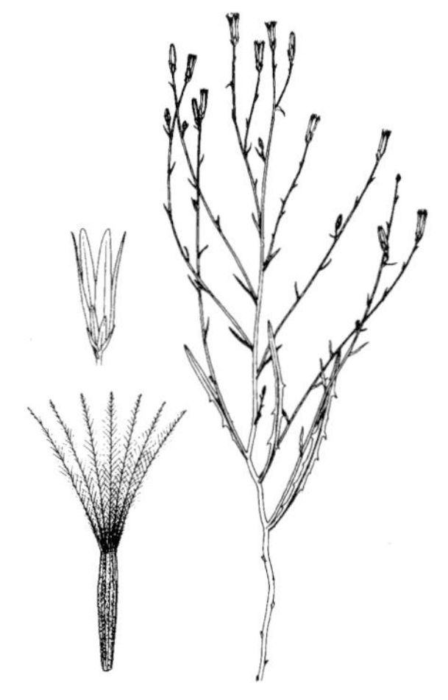

CWa

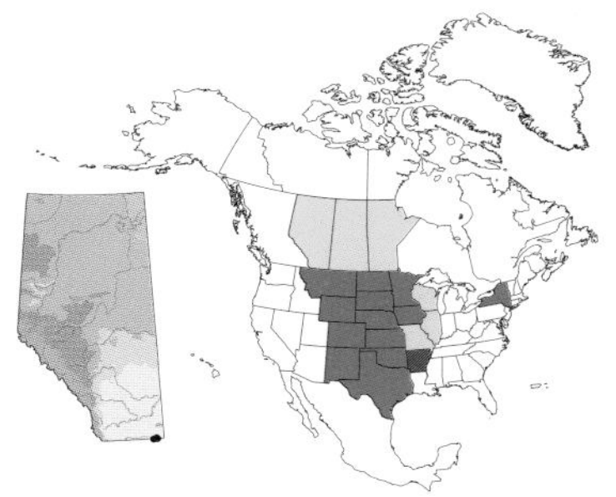

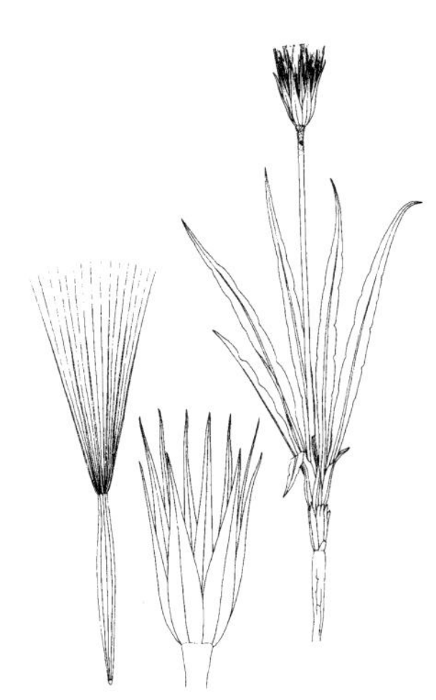

PRAIRIE FALSE DANDELION

Nothocalais cuspidata (Pursh) Greene
ASTER FAMILY (ASTERACEAE [COMPOSITAE])

Plants: Perennial herbs **with milky juice; stems single, leafless**, erect, {5} 10–30 cm tall, hairless or with woolly hairs on the upper parts; from stout taproots.

Leaves: Basal, several, 7–30 cm long and 3–20 mm wide, **linear**, tapered to a slender point; **fringed with long, soft hairs; edges** toothless, usually **irregularly curled** and crinkled.

Flowerheads: Yellow, about 2 cm high and wide, **with ray florets only**; florets with both male and female parts; involucres 17–25 mm high, often speckled, with **almost equal** (slightly overlapping), lance-shaped to linear, often long-tapered **bracts; solitary**; {April–June}.

Fruits: Dry seed-like fruits (achenes), 8–10 mm long, gradually tapered to both ends, **tipped with a tuft of hair-like bristles** (pappus) **mixed with slender, needle-like scales** (not much wider than the hairs).

Habitat: Prairies; elsewhere, in dry, open places, often on gravelly soil and in parkland.

Notes: This species has also been called *Microseris cuspidata* (Pursh) Schultz-Bip. and *Agoseris cuspidata* (Pursh) Raf. • The specific epithet *cuspidata* (pointed) refers to the long, slender points on the tapered bracts and leaves. • Prairie false dandelion could be confused with the common yellow false dandelion (*Agoseris glauca* (Pursh) Raf.), but that species does not have long, white hairs on its leaf edges and does not have slender scales in the pappus (at the tip of its achenes).

ANNUAL SKELETONWEED

Shinneroseris rostrata (A. Gray) S. Tomb
ASTER FAMILY (ASTERACEAE [COMPOSITAE])

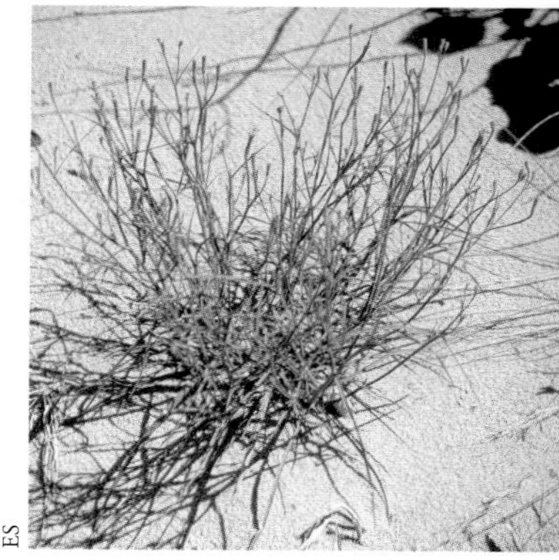
ES

Plants: **Annual** herbs with **white milky juice; stems stiff, slender**, erect or spreading, 30–60 {10–100} cm tall, striped, hairless and **often nearly leafless**, with **strongly ascending branches**; from tough, thin taproots.

Leaves: Alternate, **5–20 cm long** on lower stems (smaller and awl-shaped on the upper stems), narrowly linear, sharp-tipped, 3-nerved, stalkless.

Flowerheads: **Pink or rose**, about 12 mm across, with 7–9 {6–10} **ray florets**; florets with both male and female parts; **involucres cylindrical, 10–16 mm high**, with 7–9 main bracts and a few small basal ones; receptacles flat, without hairs or scales (naked); numerous, at the tips of short, scaly branches in elongated clusters toward the main branch tips (racemes); August {July–September}.

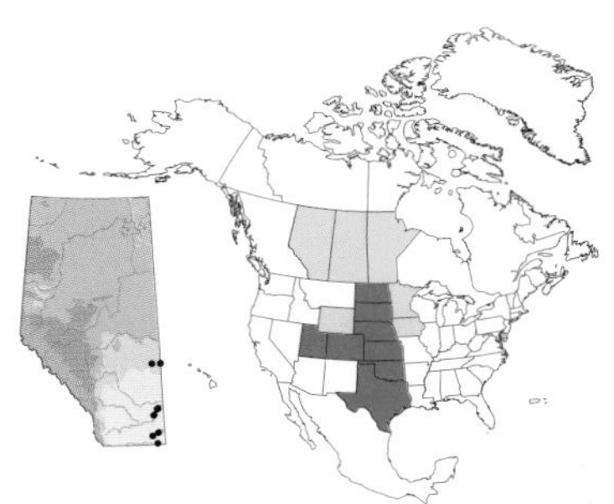

Fruits: Slender, spindle-shaped seed-like fruits (achenes), 8–10 mm long, 4–8-ribbed, tipped with a **tuft of whitish, soft, hair-like bristles** (pappus).

Habitat: Sandy banks and dunes, where there is considerable loose sand; elsewhere, in canyons and on sandy plains.

Notes: This species has also been called *Lygodesmia rostrata* A. Gray. • Annual skeletonweed is sometimes confused with common skeletonweed (*Lygodesmia juncea* (Pursh) D. Don), a much more widespread perennial plant that has creeping underground stems (rhizomes), yellowish milky juice and smaller (seldom over 5 mm long), usually scale-like leaves.

LA

CWa

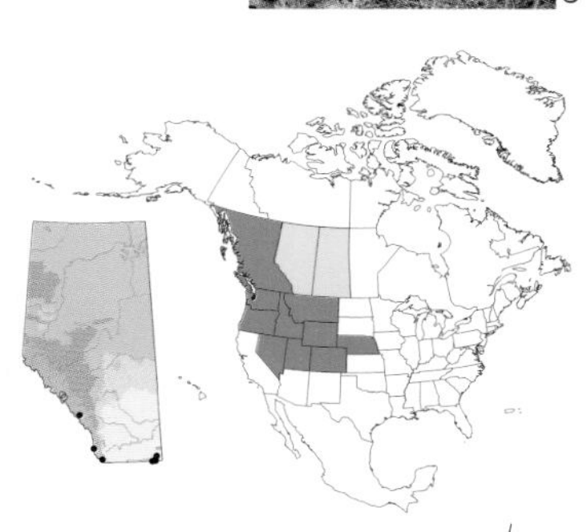

SLENDER HAWK'S-BEARD

Crepis atribarba Heller
ASTER FAMILY (ASTERACEAE [COMPOSITAE])

Plants: **Perennial** herbs with milky juice; 1 or 2 stems, **15–70 cm tall**; from branched, somewhat woody root crowns on **taproots**.

Leaves: Mostly basal, but also alternate on the stem; **lower leaves** 10–35 cm long, pinnately cut into **linear to narrowly lance-shaped segments**, hairless to woolly, mostly **without teeth**; upper stem leaves much shorter, linear, toothless.

Flowerheads: **Yellow**, with about 10–35 {40} **ray florets**; involucres grey-woolly, sometimes with bristly, black hairs, **lacking glands**, 8–14 {15} mm high and 3–5 mm wide, with **2 overlapping rows of bracts**, the 5–10 outer bracts less than half as long as the 8–10 inner bracts; florets 10–18 mm long, with both male and female parts; 3–30, in open, branched, almost leafless clusters; {May} June–July.

Fruits: **Cylindrical**, 10–20-ribbed seed-like fruits (achenes), gradually tapered to a slender point, **usually greenish**, tipped with a tuft of **whitish, hair-like bristles** (pappus).

Habitat: Dry, open, grassy slopes at moderate elevations in the mountains.

Notes: This species has also been called *Crepis exilis* Osterh. and *Crepis occidentalis* Nutt. var. *gracilis* DC., and has been misspelled *Crepis atrabarba* Heller. • Small-flowered hawk's-beard (*Crepis occidentalis* Nutt.) is also

C. OCCIDENTALIS

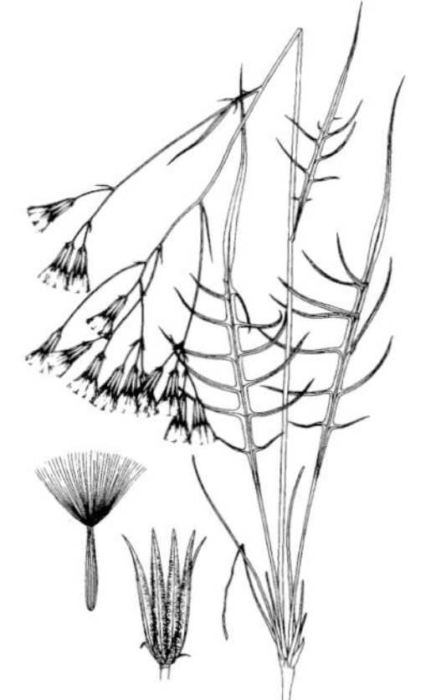

CWa

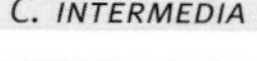

rare in Alberta. It is distinguished from slender hawk's-beard by its broader (5–10 mm wide), glandular-hairy involucres, its smaller plants (mostly less than 35 cm tall) and its brownish seeds. The lower leaves of small-flowered hawk's-beard may have broader segments that are less deeply lobed and toothed. It grows on dry, eroding slopes in the prairies and flowers in May and June {July}. • Another rare species, intermediate hawk's-beard (*Crepis intermedia* A. Gray), is intermediate in form between slender hawk's-beard and small-flowered hawk's-beard. Like slender hawk's-beard, it lacks gland-tipped hairs and has involucres less than 5 mm wide, but like small-flowered hawk's-beard, it has brownish (or yellowish) seeds and its leaf segments are usually toothed. Intermediate hawk's-beard grows in dry, open areas and flowers in {May–July} August. • The generic name *Crepis* was originally used by the Roman naturalist Pliny (AD 23–79) to refer to another plant. It was taken from the Greek *krepis* (a boot or sandal).

C. INTERMEDIA

CWa

WESTERN WHITE LETTUCE, WING-LEAVED RATTLESNAKEROOT

Prenanthes alata (Hook.) D. Dietr.
ASTER FAMILY (ASTERACEAE [COMPOSITAE])

Plants: **Perennial** herbs with **milky juice**; stems single, leafy, erect, 30–70 {15–80} cm tall, hairy near the tip; from slightly thickened roots.

Leaves: Alternate, several; blades **arrowhead-shaped or heart-shaped** (lower and middle leaves) to oblong or lance-shaped (upper leaves), up to 12 cm long and 11 cm wide, hairless, thin, with or without irregular teeth; stalks with narrow, flattened sections (wings) along the edges.

Flowerheads: **White**, about 1 cm across, **with 10–15 ray florets only**; involucres 10–13 mm high, with **about 8, sparsely glandular-hairy bracts**; ray florets with both male and female parts; few to several, long-stalked, from upper

JP

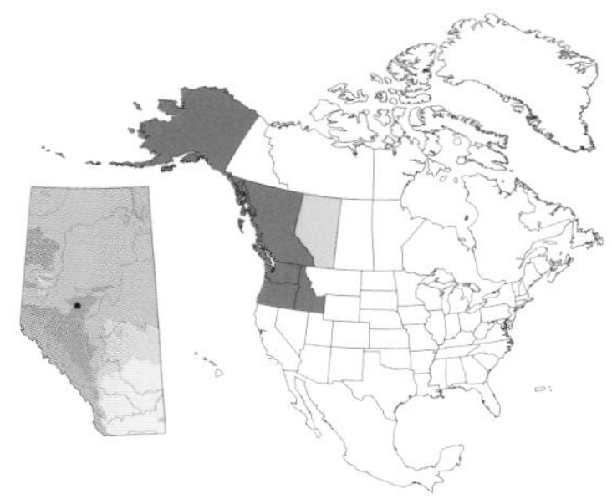

leaf axils, **forming broad, branched, flat-topped clusters** (corymbs), with long side branches spreading or **nodding in fruit**; August {July–September}.

Fruits: Ribbed, cylindrical seed-like fruits (achenes), tipped with a **tuft of dirty-white, hair-like bristles** (pappus).

Habitat: Edges of moist woods and thickets; elsewhere, on streambanks and in other moist, often shaded places.

Notes: This species has also been called *Prenanthes hastata* Jones. • Another rare Alberta species, purple rattlesnakeroot (*Prenanthes sagittata* (A. Gray) A. Nels.), also called arrow-leaved rattlesnakeroot, resembles western white lettuce but is distinguished by its narrow, elongated cluster of ascending (not nodding) flowerheads (though these may become spreading when in fruit). It flowers in July and August. The ranges of the 2 species are widely separated. Purple rattlesnakeroot grows in moist montane and foothills woodlands and thickets in extreme southwestern Alberta, whereas western white lettuce is a west coast species with a widely disjunct population in the Swan Hills. • These 2 plants could be confused with yet another rare species, large-flowered brickellia (*Brickellia grandiflora* (Hook.) Nutt., p. 217), but brickellia does not have milky juice or winged leaf stalks, and it has more distinctly toothed leaves and striped involucral bracts. • The generic name *Prenanthes,* from the Greek *prenes* (drooping) and *anthe* (blossom), refers to the nodding mature flowerheads. The specific epithet *alata* means 'winged,' referring to the flattened edges of the leaf stalks.

P. SAGITTATA

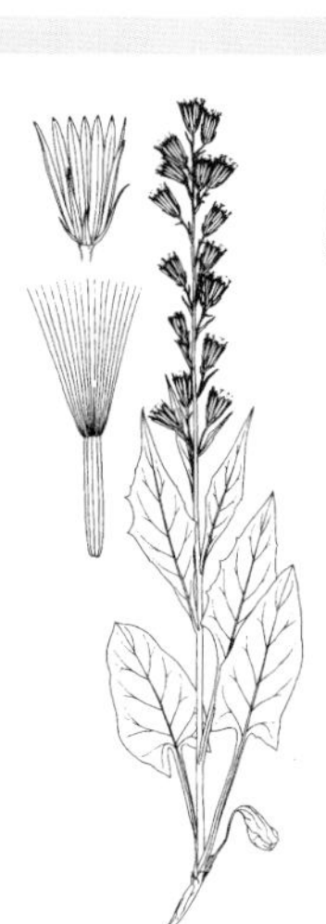

WOOLLY HAWKWEED

Hieracium cynoglossoides Arv.-Touv. *ex* A. Gray
ASTER FAMILY (ASTERACEAE [COMPOSITAE])

Plants: Perennial herbs with **milky juice, bristly with long, spreading, white or yellowish hairs**, sometimes **also with star-shaped hairs**; stems single, erect, 20–100 cm tall, covered with long, white or yellowish bristles; from **short underground stems** (rhizomes).

Leaves: Alternate, mainly on the lower ⅓ of the stem, {5} 8–20 cm long, **linear to lance-shaped**, tapered to winged stalks, toothless or with indistinct small teeth; upper leaves much smaller, stalkless.

Flowerheads: Yellow, about **1 cm across** with 15–50 ray florets 7–14 mm long; florets with both male and female parts; involucres 7–12 mm high, with **1 row of bracts** covered **with long, dark-based, white or yellowish bristles**, sometimes with short, black, gland-tipped hairs; several, in flat-topped, often compact clusters (corymbs); {June} July–September.

Fruits: Slender, ribbed seed-like fruits (achenes), tapered to the base, blunt and with a tuft of **white, hair-like bristles** (pappus) at the tip.

Habitat: Open woods and montane slopes.

Notes: This species includes *Hieracium albertinum* Farr. • Hawkweeds are often difficult to identify. Many can produce large amounts of seed without fertilization, and when this happens each of the offspring is genetically identical to the parent. A single successful plant can produce large populations of identical offspring, each capable of reproducing and spreading to other areas. Hundreds of species (microspecies) have been identified in this genus. • The genus name *Hieracium* was taken from the Greek *hieros* (hawk). The ancient Romans (e.g., Pliny, AD 23–79) believed that hawks used these plants to maintain their excellent vision, and consequently hawkweeds were also used to make salves and drops for improving human eyesight.

ES

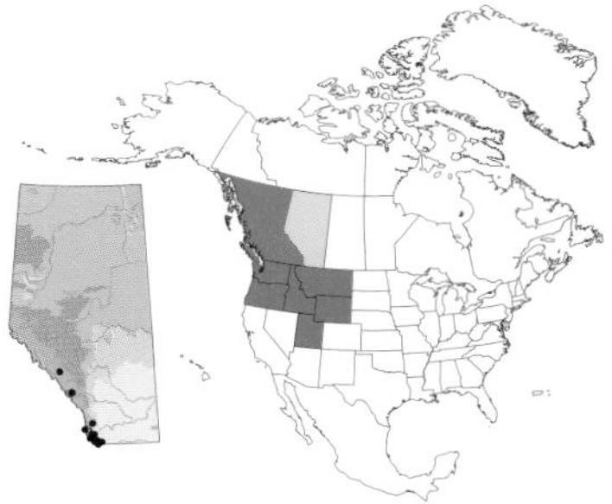

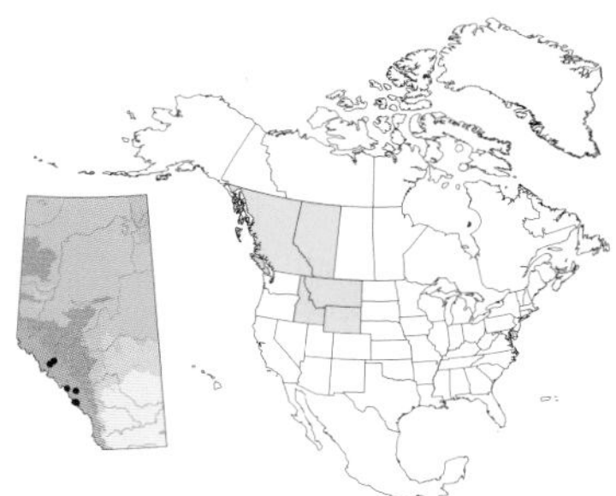

PINK FALSE DANDELION

Agoseris lackschewitzii D. Henderson & R. Moseley
ASTER FAMILY (ASTERACEAE [COMPOSITAE])

Plants: Perennial herbs **with milky juice**; 1–3 flowering stems, leafless, 6–35 {50} cm tall, hairy along their entire length; from slender taproots.

Leaves: **Basal**; **blades** lance-shaped, widest above the middle, 6–20 {4–27} cm long and 0.7–2.5 {3.1} cm wide, **thin, hairless**, often with purple flecks, toothless or with a few small teeth along the edges; stalks edged with thin, flattened sections (wings) and fringed with hairs.

Flowerheads: Pink in bud and in full flower, with 50–70 5-toothed **ray florets**, each **5–10 mm long** and 1.5 mm wide; florets with both male and female parts; involucral bracts in several overlapping rows, light green with a dark purple central stripe and purple mottling, 11–25 mm long; inner bracts lance-shaped, pointed, with transparent edges; **outer bracts** broader and blunt, **hairy at the base; solitary**; July–August {September}.

Fruits: Rounded, 10-ribbed seed-like fruits (achenes), 6–8 mm long, with a slender, **gradually tapered point** (beak) that is **shorter than the body** (4.2–6.6 mm long), tipped with a tuft of 2 rows of white, hair-like bristles (pappus) 6–12 mm long.

Habitat: Moist subalpine and alpine meadows.

Notes: Other species of false dandelions (*Agoseris* spp.) have orange or yellow flowerheads that can age or dry to a pinkish colour; therefore, care should be taken not to use flower colour as the only differentiating characteristic. The achenes of orange false dandelion (*Agoseris aurantiaca* (Hook.) Greene) have abrupt edges at the tip of the body that form clearly visible stair-steps narrowing from the body to the tip. The leaves of yellow false dandelion (*Agoseris glauca* (Pursh) Raf.) are usually thicker, wider and greyer. • This species is named in honour of Klaus Lackschewitz (1911–95), a Montana botanist who made outstanding contributions to the knowledge of mountain flora in that state.

TALL BLUE LETTUCE

Lactuca biennis (Moench) Fern.
ASTER FAMILY (ASTERACEAE [COMPOSITAE])

Plants: Coarse **annual or biennial** herbs with **milky juice,** somewhat weedy, essentially hairless; stems leafy, 50–200 {250} cm tall, unbranched (except in the flower cluster); from taproots.

Leaves: Alternate, deeply pinnately divided into sharply toothed lobes (sometimes merely toothed), 10–40 cm long, 4–20 cm wide, hairless (sometimes with hairs on the lower side of the veins); stalks winged, more or less clasping the stem.

Flowerheads: Bluish to creamy white (rarely yellowish), **about 5 mm across,** with 13–34 {55} **ray florets;** florets with both male and female parts; involucres narrowly cone-shaped to cylindrical, 10–14 mm high; few to many, in large, fairly narrow, branched clusters (panicles); July–August.

Fruits: Thin, **flattened, many-nerved** seed-like fruits (achenes), 4–5.5 {7} mm long, tipped with a tuft of **light-brown, soft, hair-like bristles** (pappus) at the end of a **short, stout point** (without a slender beak).

Habitat: Moist woods and clearings; elsewhere, in swampy sites and by hot springs.

Notes: This species has also been called *Lactuca spicata* (Lam.) A.S. Hitchc. • **Caution: the milky sap of these plants can cause a skin reaction and internal poisoning.** Some tribes used the sap as a treatment for rashes, pimples and other skin problems. They also applied the leaves to insect stings. The leaf tea was used as a sedative and nerve tonic, and the root tea was taken to treat diarrhea, heart and lung problems, bleeding, nausea, and general aches and pains. • Tall blue lettuce is related to cultivated lettuce (*Lactuca sativa* L.).

WM

WM

Grass-like Plants

Parry's rush

Juncus parryi Engelm.
RUSH FAMILY (JUNCACEAE)

Plants: Perennial herbs; stems slender, round, 10–30 cm tall; densely tufted, sometimes forming mats.

Leaves: **Most** reduced to **brown bladeless sheaths**; **uppermost** leaf usually with a **slender, cylindrical blade** 3–6 cm long.

Flower clusters: Small, irregular, widely branched (cymes), with **1–3 single flowers from** the base of a slender, cylindrical, 2–3 {8} cm long **bract that appears to be a continuation of the stem**; 6 tepals, scale-like, 6–7 mm long, lance-shaped, with dry, translucent edges; the 3 outer tepals slightly longer and more slenderly pointed than the 3 inner tepals; July {August–September}.

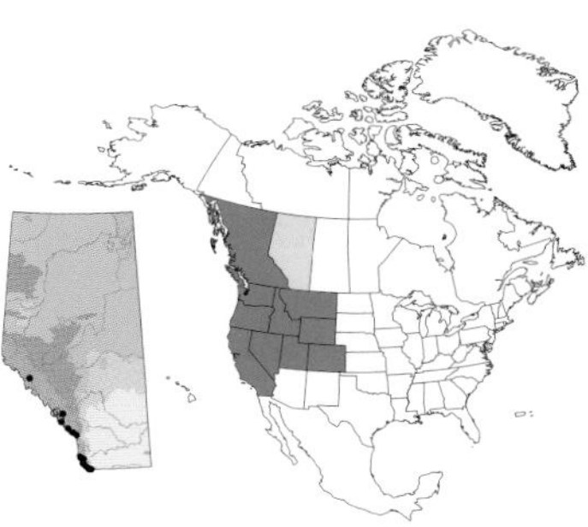

Fruits: Lance-shaped cylindrical capsules, pointed at the tip, equalling or slightly longer than the tepals; **seeds** 0.6 mm long, **with a slender tail at each end** (at least as long as the body).

Habitat: Wet meadows and slopes in the mountains.

Notes: Thread rush (*Juncus filiformis* L.) is a rare species of Alberta fens and marshes, and on lakeshores and streambanks elsewhere. Its flower cluster, which appears in June and July, also seems to be growing from the side of the stem, because the cylindrical bract looks like a continuation of the stem. In thread rush, this bract is at least as long as the stem below, and usually longer. The round, 10–60 cm tall stems are very slender (rarely more than 1 mm wide), with fine, lengthwise grooves, and they grow in rows or small clumps from slender, elongated underground stems (rhizomes). The leaves of thread rush are reduced to tight sheaths, sometimes with tiny, bristle-like blades. The flower clusters are 2–4 cm long and sparingly branched, with 5–15 flowers. Each has 6 small (2.5–4.5 mm long), greenish, lance-shaped tepals, which are slightly longer than the egg-shaped, abruptly sharp-pointed capsules. The tiny (0.4 mm) seeds are pointed but not tailed.

J. filiformis

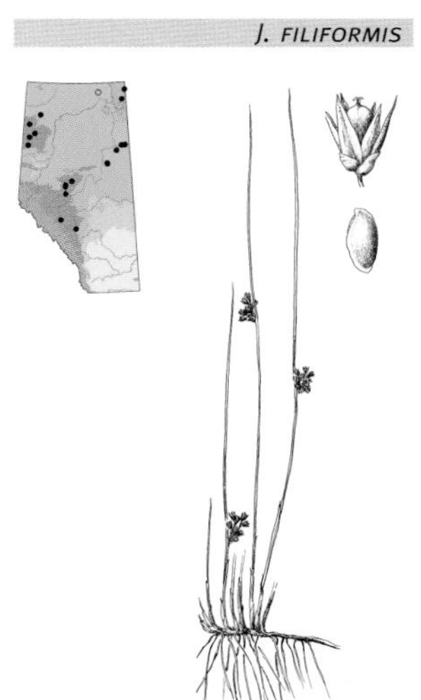

JL

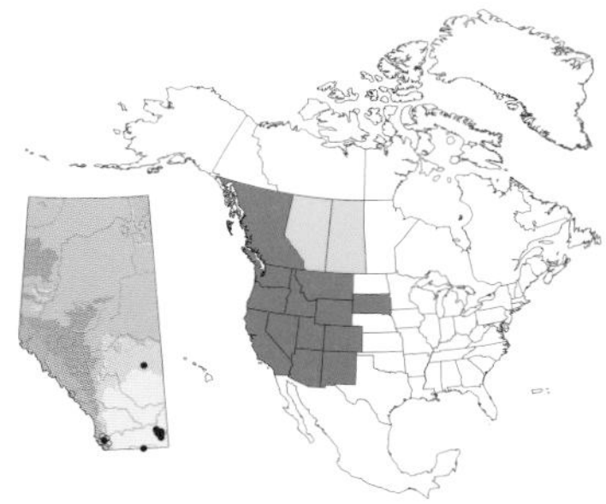

FEW-FLOWERED RUSH

Juncus confusus Coville
RUSH FAMILY (JUNCACEAE)

Plants: Tufted perennial herbs; stems erect, 30–50 cm tall; from dense fibrous roots.

Leaves: On the lower stem; blades **thread-like**, less than 1 mm wide, **with 2 conspicuous, membranous lobes** (auricles) at the base (at the top of the sheath).

Flower clusters: Pale yellowish brown, **0.5–2 cm long, with a few flowers** on unequal, short stalks **at the base of a slender, erect bract several times as long as the cluster;** 6 tepals, 3.5–4 mm long, yellowish with a broad, yellowish green stripe and dry, translucent edges; {June–August}.

Fruits: Egg-shaped cylindrical capsules, 3-sided and notched at the tip, 3–3.5 mm long, slightly shorter than the tepals; **seeds oblong, minutely pointed**, about 0.5–1 mm long.

Habitat: Moist soil in open woods, thickets, and grassland.

Notes: The generic name *Juncus* is the old Latin name for rushes.

Regel's rush

Juncus regelii Buch.
RUSH FAMILY (JUNCACEAE)

Plants: Perennial herbs; stems slightly flattened, 10–60 cm tall, never reaching above the leaves, single or clustered; from stout, elongated underground stems (rhizomes).

Leaves: **Blades flat, grass-like**, 10–15 cm long, 2–4 mm wide, **lacking basal lobes** (auricles) or with lobes less than 1 mm long; sheaths with narrow, membranous edges.

Flower clusters: Small, irregular, widely branched (cymes), with **1–3** {5} **round, chestnut-brown heads** on unequal, 0–8 cm long branches, each head with **10–30 flowers** and 8–20 mm in diameter; **6 tepals**, scale-like, 4–6 mm long, **with a broad, greenish midstripe**, broadly lance-shaped, rough with tiny bumps near tips; the outer 3 tepals with slender-pointed tips; the inner 3 tepals slightly shorter and broader with wide, translucent edges and less pointed tips; basal bract 1–4 cm long; June {July–August}.

Fruits: Egg-shaped cylindrical capsules, rounded at the tip, about the same length as the tepals; **seeds** 1.2–1.8 mm long **with a long tail at each end** (each about as long as the body).

Habitat: Wet montane, subalpine and alpine meadows.

Notes: Long-styled rush (*Juncus longistylis* Torr.) is a much more common species that is similar to Regel's rush, but its leaf blades have 2 prominent rounded lobes at their bases, its flowerheads have 3–8 flowers, its seeds are smaller (0.4–0.5 mm long) and abruptly pointed (without tails), and its capsules are tipped with abrupt, long beaks.

LA

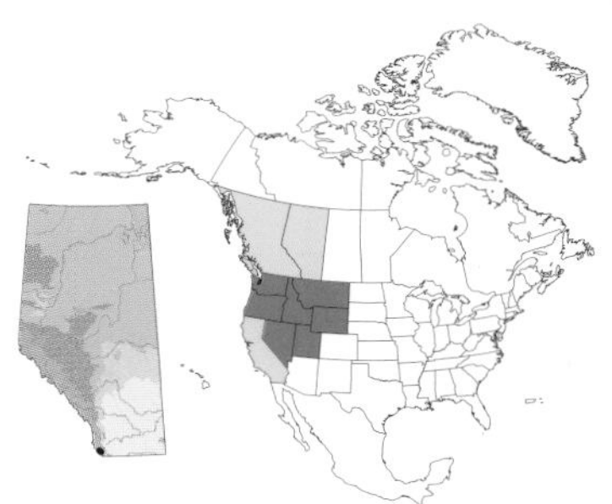

MARSH RUSH

Juncus stygius L. ssp. *americanus* (Buch.) Hult.
RUSH FAMILY (JUNCACEAE)

Plants: Perennial herbs; **stems thread-like, erect, 6–35 cm tall**, single or in small tufts; from slender underground stems (rhizomes).

Leaves: Basal and on the stem, {1} 2 or 3, very slender and **thread-like**, cylindrical.

Flower clusters: Small, **single head** (sometimes 2) **of 1–4 flowers** above a single, erect **bract of equal length** (or slightly longer); 6 tepals, scale-like, 3–6 mm long, lance-shaped to awl-shaped, pale brown with a reddish midvein; August.

Fruits: Light yellowish brown, egg-shaped **capsules**, abruptly sharp-pointed, 6–8.5 mm long, **projecting past the tepals; seeds** 3–3.5 mm long, **with a conspicuous tail at each end.**

Habitat: Fens; elsewhere, in mossy areas around springs and seepages.

Notes: Two-glumed rush (*Juncus biglumis* L.) is rare in moist alpine areas of western Alberta. Its erect stems form loose clumps 2–30 cm high, and its leaves, on the lower stem, are very slender and cylindrical with blades 2–7 cm long. The lowermost bract is leaf-like and extends beyond a solitary flowerhead of 1–4 flowers, with dark brown to blackish, 2.5–4.5 mm long, blunt-tipped tepals. The capsules are egg-shaped with notched tips and dark purplish streaks or mottles, and the seeds are about 1.5 mm long, with a short, white tail at each end. Two-glumed rush flowers in July.

J. BIGLUMIS

LK

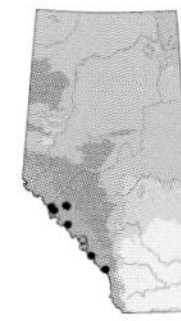

NEVADA RUSH

Juncus nevadensis S. Wats.
RUSH FAMILY (JUNCACEAE)

ES

Plants: Perennial herbs; stems 10–70 cm tall; from slender, elongated underground stems (rhizomes).

Leaves: Blades cylindrical, 5–20 cm long, 1–2 mm thick, divided by cross-partitions, with 2 small (1–3 mm), membranous lobes (auricles) projecting from the base of the blade.

Flower clusters: Light brown to dark purplish brown, open, irregularly branched cymes, 1–12 cm long, with 3–30 few-flowered, 4–10 mm wide heads on unequal branches; **6 tepals, lance-shaped, slenderly pointed**, 3–5.5 mm long, with dry, translucent edges, the outer 3 segments sometimes slightly longer than the inner segments; **lowermost bract much shorter than the flower cluster**; {July–August}.

Fruits: Dark brown, egg-shaped to cylindrical capsules, abruptly narrowed to a short, firm tip, equal to or slightly shorter than the tepals; **seeds 0.4 mm long, minutely pointed**.

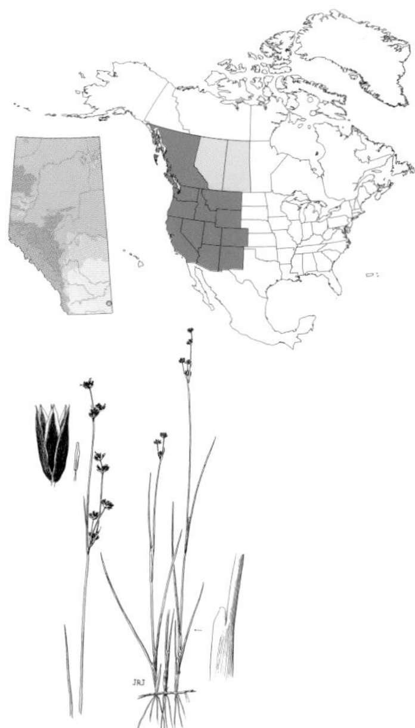

Habitat: Shorelines and other wet sites from lowland to alpine elevations.

Notes: Short-tailed rush (*Juncus brevicaudatus* (Engelm.) Fern.) is also rare in Alberta, but it grows in marshes and on shores in the northeastern corner of the province. It forms tufts of 10–50 {70} cm tall stems, each with 2–4 cylindrical leaves that are divided by cross-partitions. The flower cluster is narrow and 3–12 cm long, with few to many, 2–7-flowered heads. The greenish to light brown or reddish, 2–3 mm long tepals are narrowly lance-shaped with blunt or pointed tips and dry, translucent edges. The reddish brown capsules of short-tailed rush are longer than the tepals, reaching 2.5–4.5 mm in length, with abruptly narrowed, short, firm tips. Unlike Nevada rush, the seeds of short-tailed rush have short appendages (tails) at each end. • Nevada rush provides good to excellent cattle feed, especially early in the year, and later, in hay. It is less palatable to sheep, particularly when dry.

J. BREVICAUDATUS

WJC

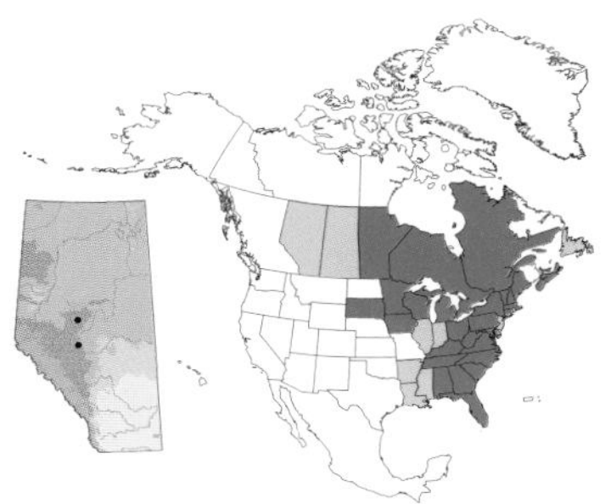

L. RUFESCENS

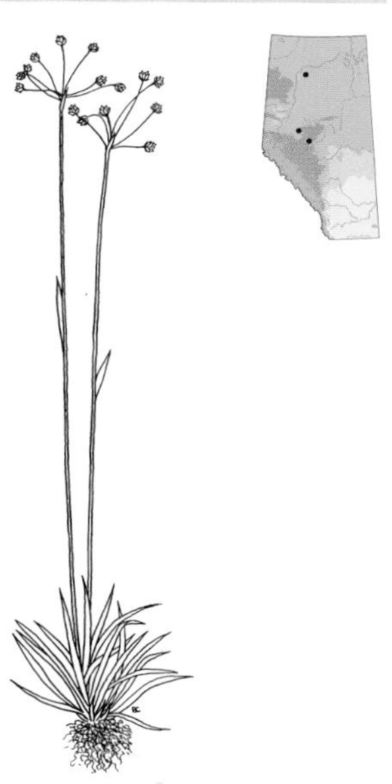

SHARP-POINTED WOOD-RUSH

Luzula acuminata Raf.
RUSH FAMILY (JUNCACEAE)

Plants: Loosely tufted perennial herbs; stems slender, erect, 10–40 cm tall; from fibrous roots.

Leaves: Mainly basal, up to 30 cm long, 3–12 mm wide; stem leaves smaller; sheath forming a closed cylinder (fused down 1 side).

Flower clusters: Open, flat-topped (umbels), with **single flowers** (rarely pairs or small clusters of flowers) on spreading, **unbranched, 3–6 cm long, thread-like stalks**; each flower with 6 scale-like tepals, 2.5–4.5 mm long, reddish brown with thin, translucent edges; {April–May}.

Fruits: Abruptly sharp-pointed capsules, **3–4 mm long, projecting past the tepals**; seeds 1.5–2.5 mm long (including a **conspicuous appendage** (caruncle) almost as long as the body of the seed).

Habitat: Moist woodland, often on disturbed sites; elsewhere, on rocky sites and clearings in hardwood, coniferous and mixedwood forests.

Notes: This species has also been called *Luzula saltuensis* Fern. • Another rare Alberta species, reddish wood-rush (*Luzula rufescens* Fisch. *ex* E. Mey.), is very similar to sharp-pointed wood-rush, but it has narrower (less than 5 mm wide) basal leaves, smaller seeds (about 1.5 mm long), and smaller flowers (up to 3.5 mm long) on shorter (up to 3 cm long) stalks. Reddish wood-rush grows on damp grassy slopes, on the edges of bogs and marshes and on moist sand and gravel bars.

Greenland wood-rush

Luzula groenlandica Bocher
RUSH FAMILY (JUNCACEAE)

Plants: Densely tufted perennial herbs; stems leafy, erect, 10–50 cm tall; from fibrous roots.

Leaves: Basal and alternate, **flat, 3–7 mm wide**, often reddish brown, shorter than the flowering stems, with **blunt, thickened** (callused) **tips**; 2 or 3 stem leaves, short; sheath forming a closed cylinder (fused down 1 side).

Flower clusters: Compact, 3–5 cm long, **head-like**, sometimes with 1 or 2 additional flowerheads on short side branches, above a **conspicuous, thick-tipped, leafy bract** that sticks out at an angle from the main stalk; each flower with 6 scale-like **tepals, 2–2.5 mm long**, reddish brown with broad, translucent edges; inner 3 tepals clearly shorter than the outer 3.

Fruits: Dark brown capsules, 2.5–4 mm long, abruptly sharp-pointed, projecting past the tepals; **seeds 0.8–1.1 mm long** (including the **short appendage** [caruncle]).

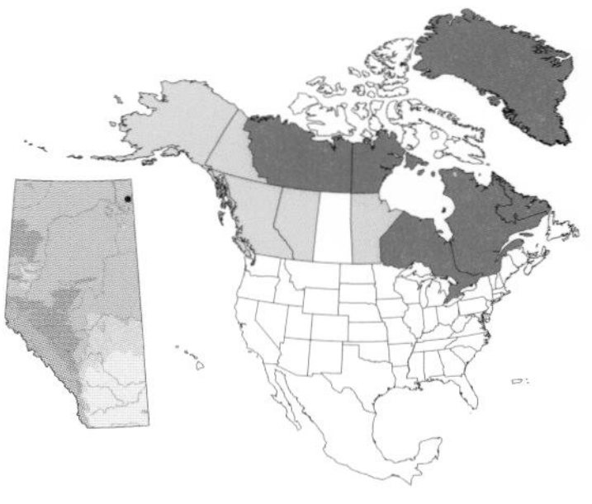

Habitat: Moist, turfy tundra.

Notes: Greenland wood-rush is easily confused with the more common species field wood-rush (*Luzula multiflora* (Retz.) Lej.). Field wood-rush is distinguished by its slightly larger tepals (2.5–3.5 mm long) and larger seeds (1.1–1.4 mm long) with relatively long caruncles.

JL

AWNED NUT-GRASS

Cyperus squarrosus L.
SEDGE FAMILY (CYPERACEAE)

Plants: Sweet-smelling, tufted **annual** herbs; **stems slender, 1–15 cm tall**, 3-sided; from fibrous roots.

Leaves: Mostly basal, 2 or 3 per stem, about as long as the stems; blades 2–10 cm long, 1–2 mm wide.

Flower clusters: Crowded and head-like or more open with 3 {1–5} similar branches (rays) each 3–7 cm long; 2–4 leaf-like bracts at the base, much longer than the flower cluster; spikelets 2–10 mm long, flattened, lance-shaped and widest above the middle, 5–20-flowered, greenish to pale brown; flowers with **1 stamen** and 3 stigmas, **lacking petals and sepals**, borne in 2 vertical rows in the axils of 1–2 mm long, several-nerved, egg-shaped to lance-shaped **scales** that **taper to a slender, outwardly curved point 0.5–1.2 mm long**; {June–July}.

Fruits: Dry, 3-sided seed-like fruits (achenes), egg-shaped and widest above the middle, 1 mm long, brown, shed with the scales; July–August.

Habitat: Moist soil, usually on sandy river flats; elsewhere, on muddy lakeshores.

Notes: This species has also been called *Cyperus aristatus* Rottb. and *Cyperus inflexus* Muhl. • Another rare species, sand nut-grass (*Cyperus schweinitzii* Torr.), has larger (10–70 cm tall), perennial plants, with rough stems bearing hard, corm-like thickenings at the base. Its flowers have 3 stamens and larger (about 3.5 mm long), light-green to light brown scales with short, erect tips, its spikelets are borne on very uneven stalks in irregular clusters and its achenes are 2.5–3.5 mm long, elliptic and pointed at both ends. Sand nut-grass grows on dry sandy soil, including active sand dunes. • The specific epithet *squarrosus* refers to the scales of the spikelets, which have long, curved tips that bend outward at right angles to the main stalk, an unusual characteristic for species of this genus in Canada.

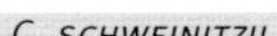
C. SCHWEINITZII

CWa

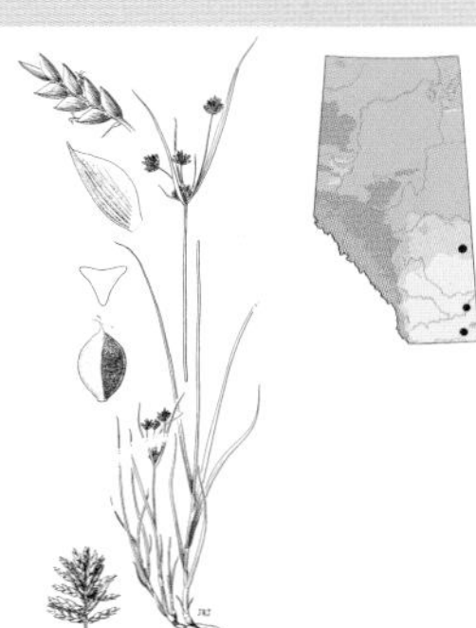

Engelmann's spike-rush

Eleocharis engelmannii Steud.
SEDGE FAMILY (CYPERACEAE)

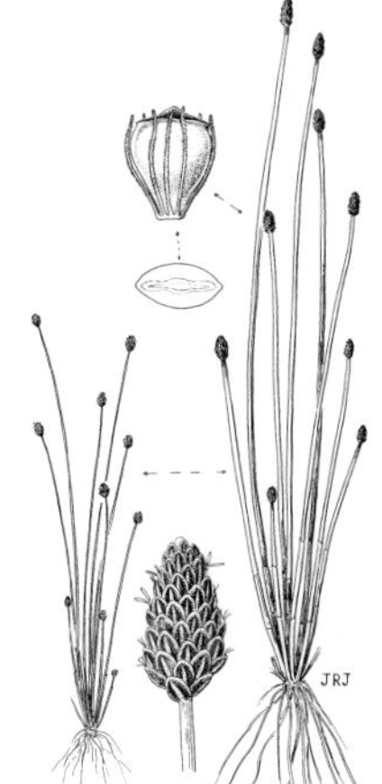

Plants: Tufted **annual** herbs; stems several, ascending, 10–40 {5–50} cm tall, 0.5–2 mm thick, ribbed; from fibrous roots.

Leaves: Reduced to bladeless sheaths; upper sheaths pale brown, tipped with a tiny, tooth-like blade.

Flower clusters: Single, erect spikelets at stem tips, cylindrical to egg-shaped, 5–15 mm long, with many **spirally arranged flowers**; flowers **with 3 stamens and 1 ovary** with a **2** {3}**-pronged style**, borne in the axil of a 1.7–2.5 mm long, brownish scale with translucent edges; {June–September}.

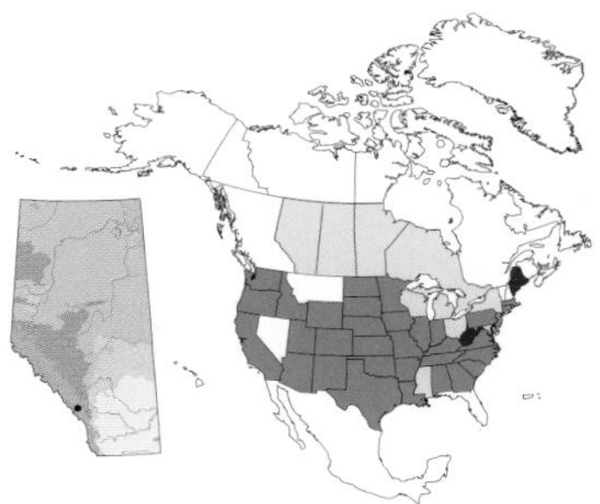

Fruits: Smooth, shining, **lens-shaped** seed-like fruits (achenes), 1–2 mm long, **broadly egg-shaped**, widest above the middle, **abruptly tipped with a low** (about 0.3 mm high), broad, **pyramid-shaped projection** (tubercle) **above a tiny ridge**, also with **5–7 brownish, hair-like bristles** (modified petals and sepals) from the base.

Habitat: Wet places; elsewhere, in moist sandy soils, wet sand, peat, mud and marshes.

Notes: This species has also been called *Eleocharis ovata* (Roth) R. & S. var. *engelmannii* Britt. and *Eleocharis obtusa* (Willd.) Schultes var. *engelmannii* (Steud.) Gilly. • The generic name *Eleocharis* comes from the Greek *helos* (marsh) and *charis* (grace). The specific epithet *engelmannii* honours St. Louis physician and botanist George Engelmann (1809–84).

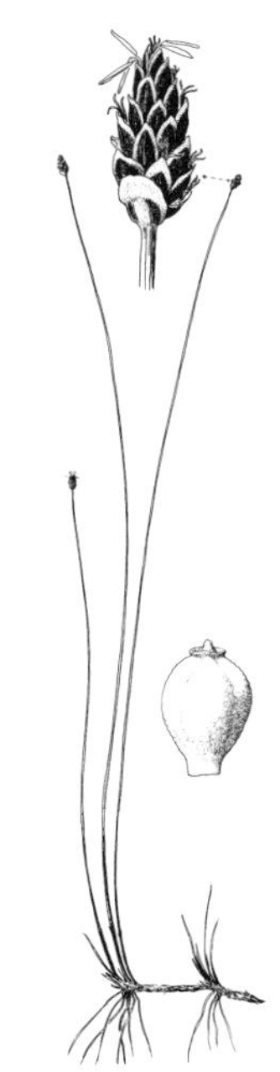

SLENDER SPIKE-RUSH

Eleocharis elliptica Kunth
SEDGE FAMILY (CYPERACEAE)

Plants: Scattered or loosely clustered perennial herbs; **stems 5–40** {90} **cm tall**, very slender, compressed to almost cylindrical, {4} **6–8** {10}**-angled**, with {4} 6–8 vascular bundles; from stout, creeping, **reddish to purplish black underground stems** (rhizomes).

Leaves: Reduced to bladeless sheaths, conspicuously reddish purple near the base.

Flower clusters: Single spikelets, oval to egg-shaped and widest above the middle, {3} **5–12 mm long**, with 10–30 spirally arranged flowers; flowers with 3 stamens and 1 ovary tipped with {2} **3 stigmas**, borne in the axil of an **oval**, 2–3 mm long, **reddish purple to brown or blackish scale** with pale, translucent edges and a notched tip with a small, sharp point in the centre of the notch; {May–August}.

Fruits: Unequally 3-sided seed-like fruits (achenes), 0.6–1 {1.5} mm long, **yellow to dull orange**, with a **honeycomb-netted** surface, tipped with a **short**, pyramid-shaped projection (tubercle) that is **ringed by a tiny ridge**, usually bearing very small, hair-like bristles at the base.

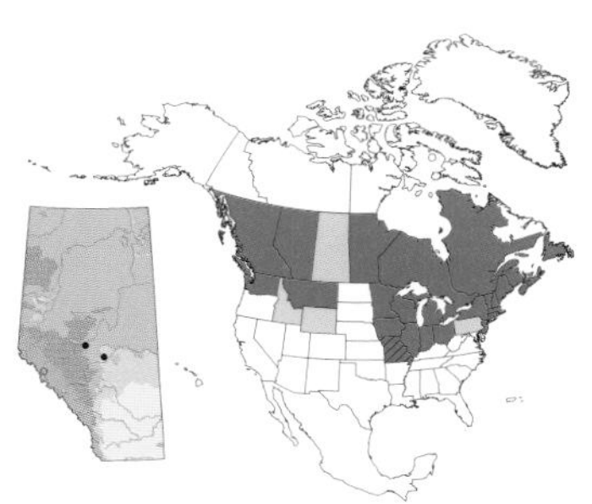

Habitat: Wet places, usually neutral or calcareous conditions.

Notes: This species has also been called *Eleocharis tenuis* (Willd.) Schultes var. *borealis* (Svenson) Gleason and *E. compressa* Sullivant var. *borealis* Drepalik & Mohlenbrock. • Quill spike-rush (*Eleocharis nitida* Fern.) has been reported to occur in Alberta. It is distinguished from slender spike-rush by its achenes, which are minutely wrinkled or roughened, but lack honeycombed ridges. It is also a smaller plant (2–15 cm tall), with few-ribbed, cylindrical stems, and the scales in its spikes have entire (not notched) tips. Quill spike-rush grows in damp, rocky or sandy sites.

E. NITIDA

SLENDER BEAK-RUSH

Rhynchospora capillacea Torr.
SEDGE FAMILY (CYPERACEAE)

Plants: Tufted perennial herbs; stems slender, 10–40 cm tall, 3-sided, solid; from very short underground stems (rhizomes) and fibrous roots; also with long, thin, bulb-like outgrowths (turions) about 1 mm in diameter and 1 cm long, formed at the base of the stem in late summer.

Leaves: Mostly basal with bristle-like blades (at most 0.5 mm wide) rolled inward at the edges, equalling or slightly longer than the stems; **stem leaves** with **bristle-like** blades; sheaths fused in a tube (closed).

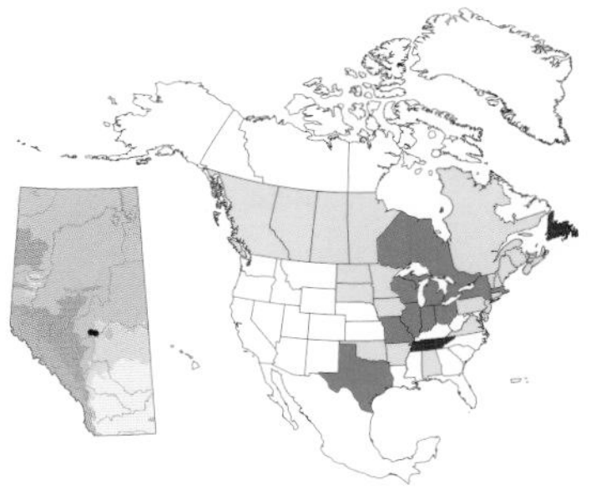

Flower clusters: 1 or 2 rather loose, ascending, ellipsoid heads (glomerules), each **with 1–4** {10} **spikelets**; spikelets ellipsoid, 5–7 mm long, reddish brown, on erect stalks, with spirally arranged scales, the upper 2 or 3 scales enclosing flowers; flowers with **3 stamens** bearing 1–2.5 mm long anthers, a **single ovary** (the upper flowers sometimes with stamens only) and **6** (rarely 9 or 12) **small, hair-like bristles** (modified sepals and petals), borne in the axils of thin, brown, lance-shaped scales with a midrib extending beyond the tip; **the lowermost scale without a flower**; {July}.

Fruits: Granular-textured, oblong to **egg-shaped** seed-like fruits (achenes), widest above the middle, abruptly narrowed at the base, {1.7} 2.5–4.2 mm long, tipped with an egg-shaped to **lance-shaped projection** (tubercle) **about as long as the achene body**, surrounded by **6** {12}, **downward-barbed bristles** from the base.

Habitat: Calcareous fens; elsewhere, in calcareous sites in meadows and swamps and on shores.

Notes: This is the only species of this genus that has been found in Alberta. Another species, white beak-rush (*Rhynchospora alba* (L.) Vahl), has been found very close to the southern and western boundaries of Alberta and may also grow here. It is distinguished by the top-shaped clusters of spikelets, pale brown to whitish scales and more numerous bristles (9–12), which have soft hairs at the base. • The generic name *Rhynchospora* comes from the Greek *rhynchos* (beak) and *spora* (seed), referring to the characteristic projection (tubercle) at the tip of each achene.

R. ALBA

SMB

BEAUTIFUL COTTON-GRASS

Eriophorum callitrix Cham. *ex* C.A. Mey.
SEDGE FAMILY (CYPERACEAE)

Plants: **Tufted** perennial herbs with conspicuous persistent leaf bases; stems slender, **6–25 cm tall**, 1–8 per tuft; from very short underground stems (rhizomes) and fibrous roots.

Leaves: Mostly basal, stiff, linear, 1–2 mm wide; **stem leaves usually single** (sometimes none or 2), attached **below mid-stem**, with conspicuously **inflated sheaths** and **short or absent blades**.

Flower clusters: **Single, erect, egg-shaped spikelets** at the stem tips, fluffy-white when mature, **widest above the middle**, 1.5–2.5 cm long, many-flowered; **flowers with 1–3 stamens** bearing 0.6–1 mm long anthers, **a single ovary** tipped with a 3-pronged style **and many shiny, white bristles** (modified sepals and petals), borne in the axils of **erect, black or greenish black scales**, the **lower 10–15 scales without flowers**; June–July.

Fruits: Dry, 3-sided seed-like fruits (achenes), 1.8–2 mm long, surrounded by a fluffy tuft of 2–3 cm long, white, hair-like bristles; July–August.

Habitat: Wet alpine turf; elsewhere, in calcareous turfy tundra.

Notes: Beautiful cotton-grass has been confused with 2 common species. One is close-sheathed cotton-grass (*Eriophorum brachyantherum* Trautv. & Mey.), which is taller (30–60 cm), with softer, longer basal leaves and with

E. SCHEUCHZERI

LK

stem leaves that lack inflated sheaths and are attached above the middle of the stem. The other is sheathed cotton-grass or dense cotton-grass (*Eriophorum vaginatum* L. ssp. *spissum* (Fern.) Hult.), a species of dry, peaty bogs, which has white-edged scales that bend sharply downward. • Another rare species, one-spike cotton-grass (*Eriophorum scheuchzeri* Hoppe), is not tufted but instead has stems that arise singly or in small groups from creeping stems. It is also distinguished from beautiful cotton-grass by its channelled or triangular basal leaves, its pale-edged scales (of which fewer than 7 of the lower ones are empty) and its beaked achenes, which are tipped with a firm point 0.1–0.2 mm long. One-spike cotton-grass grows on marshy ground in Alberta and on damp tundra and wet peat elsewhere. It is reported to flower from July to August. • The generic name *Eriophorum* comes from the Greek *erion* (wool or cotton) and *phoros* (bearing), in reference to the long, cottony hairs of the seed heads.

DWARF BULRUSH, DWARF CLUB-RUSH

Trichophorum pumilum (Vahl) Schinz & Thellung
SEDGE FAMILY (CYPERACEAE)

CWa

Plants: Perennial herbs, 5–17 {20} cm tall; **stems smooth,** stiff and wiry, **round,** with remains of dead leaves and stems at the base; in loose clumps from short underground stems (rhizomes).

Leaves: Mainly **blackish to brown sheaths**; upper sheaths with a slender **blade 5–15 mm long.**

Flower clusters: Single, egg-shaped spikelets at stem tips, **2–3** {5} **mm long,** 3–5-flowered; **scales chestnut-brown with a green midvein** and translucent edges; **lowermost scale** (bract) **blunt-tipped,** usually less than ½ the length of the spikelet; **no bristles**; 3 stigmas; June {July}.

Fruits: Dry seed-like fruits (achenes), 1–1.5 mm long, **dark brown to blackish,** smooth, with a tiny point at the tip.

Habitat: Calcareous fens.

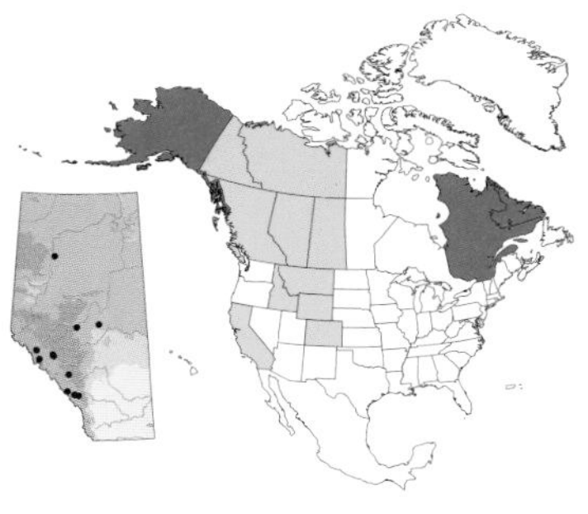

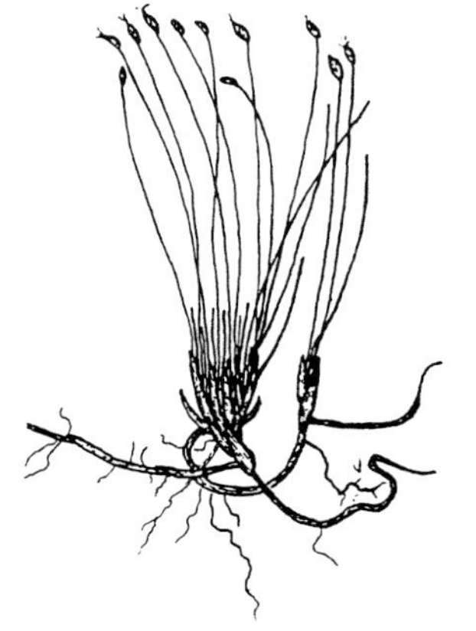

T. CLINTONII

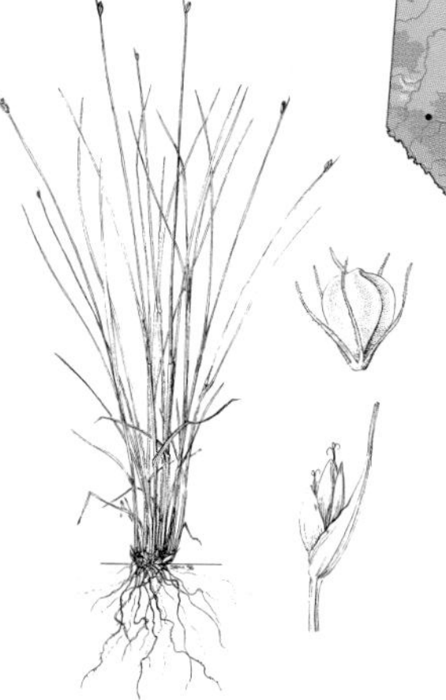

Notes: This species has also been called *Scirpus rollandii* Fern. and *Scirpus pumilus* Vahl ssp. *rollandii* (Fern.) Raymond. • Clinton's club-rush (*Trichophorum clintonii* (A. Gray) S.G. Smith, also called *Scirpus clintonii* A. Gray and Clinton's bulrush) is also rare in Alberta. It also has a single terminal spikelet, but its rough, 3-sided stems are 10–30 cm tall, growing in dense clumps from short rhizomes. Its leaves are flat and much shorter than the stems, and there is a single narrow bract beneath each spikelet. The spikelets are lance-shaped to egg-shaped, 4–5 {3–6} mm long and 4–7-flowered. Their scales are egg-shaped and pale brown, and the lowermost scale has a midvein that is prolonged into a blunt bristle about as long as the spikelet. The achenes are brown, smooth, 3-sided and 1.5–2 mm long, with 3–6, upwardly barbed, 2–3 mm long bristles from the base and 3 stigmas at the tip. Clinton's club-rush is reported to flower from May to June. • Tufted club-rush (*Trichophorum cespitosum* (L.) Hartman, also called tufted bulrush and *Scirpus cespitosus* L.) is a more common species that also has a single spikelet at the stem tip, but it grows in dense clumps (without rhizomes). The spikelets of tufted club-rush are slightly shorter and wider than those of dwarf bulrush, and their lowermost scale is tipped with a bristle at least 1 mm long that sometimes extends past the end of the spikelet. • *Pumilum* is Latin for 'dwarf' or 'small,' in reference to the small stature of dwarf bulrush. The species was originally named for its discoverer, Louis Roland, Frère Rolland-Germain.

RED BULRUSH

Blysmus rufus (Hudson) Link
SEDGE FAMILY (CYPERACEAE)

Plants: Perennial herbs; stems erect, **5–60 cm tall**, smooth and nearly round; growing in **clumps** from extensively creeping underground stems (rhizomes).

Leaves: Mainly basal, lowermost reduced to bladeless sheaths, but upper 1–3 with stiffly erect blades 1–3 mm wide and up to 15 cm long, **blunt-tipped, shorter than the stems.**

Flower clusters: Reddish brown spikes, 1–2 cm long, 5–10 mm wide, with few to several spikelets in 2 vertical rows (ranks) and a single, erect, scale-like or leaf-like bract at the base; **spikelets 2–5-flowered**, 5–10 mm long; scales lance-shaped, shiny brown, lacking stiff bristles (awns) at tips; 2 stigmas; {June} July.

Fruits: Dry seed-like fruits (achenes), 4–5 mm long, 1–1.7 mm wide, pointed at both ends, **light brown** with a **dark, elongated tip**, smooth, **stalked**, with **3–6 fine, upwardly barbed bristles from base,** all shorter than the achene and soon falling off.

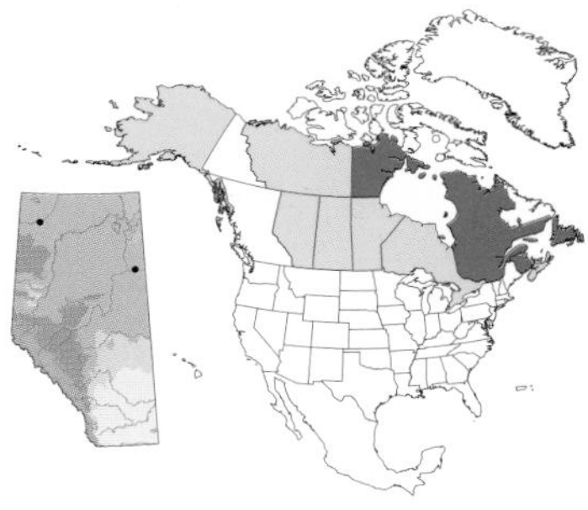

Habitat: Saline marshes.

Notes: This species has also been called *Scirpus rufus* (Huds.) Schrad. • The specific epithet *rufus* is Latin for 'reddish,' referring to the colour of the spikelets.

WJC

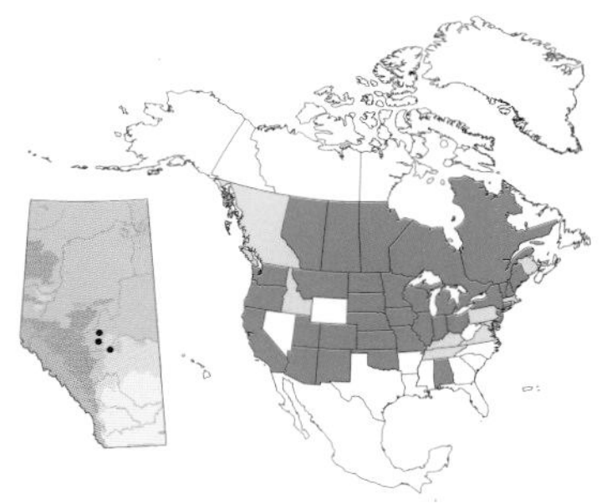

RIVER BULRUSH

Bolboschoenus fluviatilis (Torr.) J. Sojak.
SEDGE FAMILY (CYPERACEAE)

Plants: **Perennial herbs** 50–150 cm tall; **stems stout, 3-sided,** sharply angled, erect, regularly spaced along elongated underground stems (rhizomes) with **fleshy thickenings at the joints.**

Leaves: Mainly on the **middle and upper stem**; long-tapering, flat, with a prominent midvein, 5–15 mm wide, pale green.

Flower clusters: **Flat-topped, with 5–12** often nodding, head-like, **with 1–5 spikelets** on flat, long, unequal stalks **above a whorl of 3–5 leaf-like bracts**; spikelets egg-shaped or broadly cylindrical, 1–4 cm long, 6–10 mm thick; scales brown, tipped with a stiff, curved, 2 mm long bristle (awn); **3 stigmas**; {June–July}.

Fruits: Dry, egg-shaped seed-like fruits (achenes), widest near the pointed tip, **3-sided,** dull grey-brown, 4–5 mm long, with **6 fine, downward-barbed bristles from the base** that are approximately as long as the achene.

Habitat: Margins of ponds, lakes and rivers.

Notes: This species has also been called *Scirpus fluviatilis* (Torr.) A. Gray and *Schoenoplectus fluviatilis* (Torr.) M.T. Strong. • Prairie bulrush (*Bolboschoenus maritimus* (L.) Pallas ssp. *paludosus* (A. Nels.) T. Koyama, also called *Scirpus paludosus* A. Nels.) also has underground rhizomes with swollen joints (nodes), but it is shorter (20–70 cm), with lens-shaped achenes bearing 2 stigmas (rather than 3). • River bulrush is less alkali tolerant than prairie bulrush. It often forms dense colonies in calm water up to 1 m deep. • 'Bulrush' is a corruption of 'pole-rush' or 'pool-rush,' referring to the habit or habitat of these plants. The specific epithet *fluviatilis* is Latin for 'of rivers,' referring to the common habitat of river bulrush.

PALE BULRUSH

Scirpus pallidus (Britt.) Fern.
SEDGE FAMILY (CYPERACEAE)

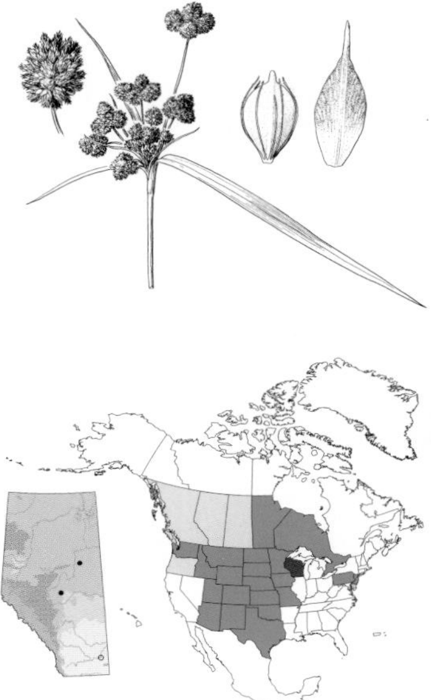

Plants: **Robust perennial** herbs; stems erect, pale green, 30–100 {150} **cm tall**, **3-sided** with blunt edges, loosely clustered; from short, stout underground stems (rhizomes) and runners (stolons).

Leaves: Mostly **on the lower half of the stem**; blades **flat, 5–15 mm wide**; sheaths green, pale brown when dry, not reddish.

Flower clusters: Irregular open, flat-topped (umbels or occasionally compound cymes), with 4–8 dense heads of spikelets on unequal stalks above 3 or 4 short, leaf-like bracts; spikelets greenish brown, 2–8 mm long; scales 2–3 mm long, hairless, pale brown, with a pale midvein extending from the tip as a short bristle (awn) about 0.5 mm long; **3 stigmas**; June–July.

Fruits: Dry seed-like fruits (achenes), pale brown, about 1 mm long, **unequally 3-sided**, pointed at tip, with **6 fine, whitish bristles from base, each downward-barbed above the middle** and almost as long as the achene.

Habitat: In marshes and wet meadows.

Notes: Small-fruited bulrush (*Scirpus microcarpus* C. Presl, also called *Scirpus rubrotinctus* Fern.) is a common species that somewhat resembles pale bulrush, but it has reddish leaf sheaths and lens-shaped achenes with 2 stigmas. • Late in the season, the flower clusters of pale bulrush are often replaced by leafy shoots, and the plants reproduce vegetatively. • When abundant, this species has been used to weave light-duty baskets and to decorate clothing. The leaves were laid over and under food in steaming pits. In the spring, the tender young stems were eaten raw when the shoots were about 20 cm tall. • The small bristles growing from the base of each achene are modified petals and sepals. • *Pallidus* means 'pale' in Latin and refers to the colour of the spikelets.

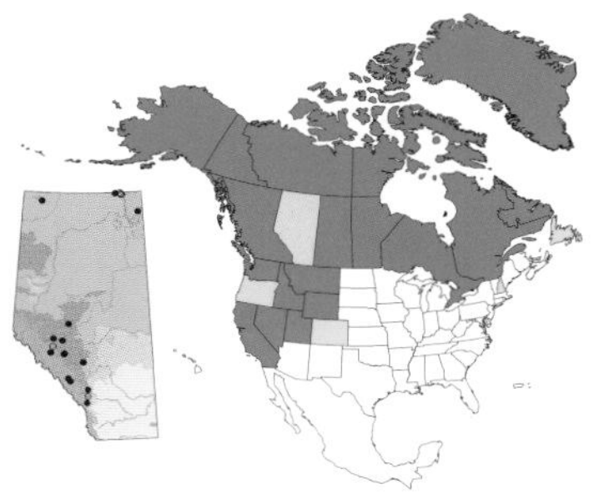

CAPITATE SEDGE

Carex capitata L.
SEDGE FAMILY (CYPERACEAE)

Plants: **Tufted** perennial herbs; stems wiry, 10–30 {60} cm tall; from very short, ascending underground stems (rhizomes).

Leaves: Mainly basal, shorter than stems; blades thread-like, up to 1 mm wide, hairless, with somewhat roughened edges; sheaths chestnut-brown or purplish brown; remains of old leaves persistent (marcescent).

Flower clusters: **Solitary, round to egg-shaped spikes,** {4} **5–10 mm long,** with **male flowers at the tip** and 6–25 **female flowers at the base** (androgynous), bractless; scales of female flowers dark brown to tan, egg-shaped to nearly round, blunt, with broad, translucent edges, much shorter than the perigynia; **2 stigmas**; June–August.

Fruits: **Lens-shaped** seed-like fruits (achenes), 1.5 mm long, 1 mm wide, enclosed in perigynia; **perigynia** pale green or yellowish brown, **spreading, 2–2.5** {3.8} **mm long,** 1–2 mm wide, broadly egg-shaped, abruptly tapered to a slender beak 0.4–0.9 mm long, flattened, with sharp edges, **stalkless, nerveless,** hairless.

Habitat: Wet sites, often in calcareous fens; elsewhere, in moist meadows and shrubby open woods, often above treeline.

Notes: The specific epithet *capitata*, from the Latin *caput* (head), means 'with a head,' in reference to the head-like spikes. No other species closely resembles this distinctive sedge.

SEASIDE SEDGE

Carex incurviformis Mack. var. *incurviformis*
SEDGE FAMILY (CYPERACEAE)

Plants: **Low, creeping perennial herbs; stems solitary,** 2–10 {30} cm tall, erect or curved; **from long, scaly, tough, cord-like underground stems** (rhizomes) and runners (stolons).

Leaves: Tufted near the base, 4–7 per stem, often longer than the stems; blades greyish green, erect or spreading, 2–10 {15} cm long, 1–2 mm wide, usually smooth and with the edges rolled upward and inward; lower sheaths often lacking blades.

Flower clusters: Dense, round or egg-shaped, with **3–5 crowded spikes, appearing like a single spike** 5–15 {20} mm long and 8–15 mm wide, with a small, brown, papery bract at the base; **spikes stalkless, with male flowers at the tip** and female flowers at the base (androgynous); scales of female flowers brownish, with broad, papery, translucent edges, egg-shaped, about 3 mm long and 2 mm wide, shorter than the perigynia; **2 stigmas**; June {July}.

Fruits: **Lens-shaped** seed-like fruits (achenes), about 1.5 mm long, enclosed in perigynia; **perigynia** dark brown, spreading at maturity, 3.5–5 mm long, 1–2 mm wide, broadly egg-shaped, tipped with a slender beak about 1 mm long, faintly to conspicuously nerved, **stalked**, not winged.

Habitat: **Gravelly alpine areas**; elsewhere, in salt marshes and turfy tundra and on sand dunes and river flats.

Notes: This variety has also been called *Carex maritima* Gunn. var. *incurviformis* (Mack.) Boivin. • The spikes of Hood's sedge (*Carex hoodii* Boott) and Hooker's sedge (*Carex hookerana* Dewey) resemble those of seaside sedge, but these species are much larger (15–80 cm tall), their stems are tufted rather than solitary and they grow in drier habitats. Hooker's sedge is also rare in Alberta. It is distinguished by its elongated heads of more widely separated spikes, its well-developed lower bract (at times exceeding the head) and its scales, which are tipped with strong bristles (awns). Hooker's sedge grows on prairies and dry banks, and in open woods at lower elevations; it flowers in June. • When it is abundant, seaside sedge provides a reasonable seed source for small birds.

DJ

C. HOOKERANA

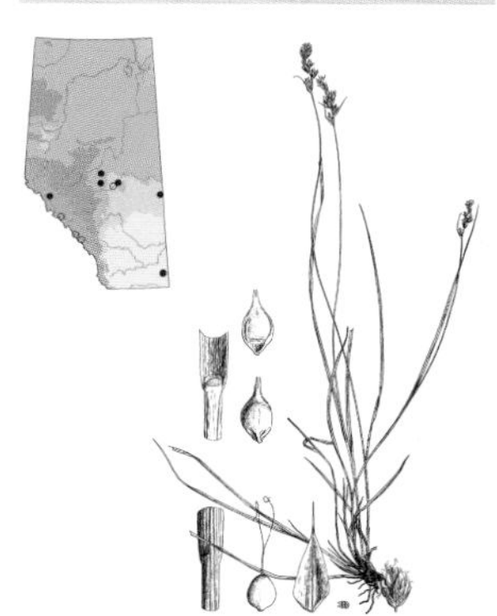

WJC

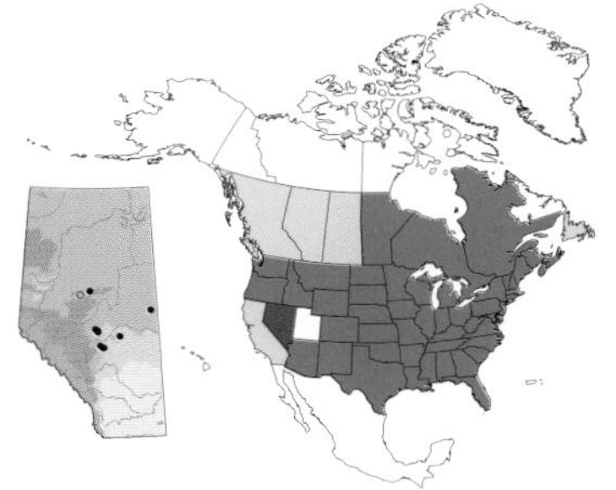

FOX SEDGE

Carex vulpinoidea Michx.
SEDGE FAMILY (CYPERACEAE)

Plants: Densely clumped perennial herbs; stems 20–90 {100} cm tall, stiff, 3-sided with sharp angles, very rough to the touch near the top; from short, tough underground stems (rhizomes).

Leaves: Mostly flat, 4 or 5 per stem, 2–5 {6} mm wide, slender-pointed, usually longer than stems; lowest leaves typically smallest; **sheaths red-dotted, with horizontal wrinkles on the inner side.**

Flower clusters: Dense, greenish to yellowish or dull brown, cylindrical heads, 3–12 {15} cm long, 5–20 mm wide, with **numerous stalkless, often compound, spikes,** sometimes with lower spikes somewhat separate; spikes with inconspicuous **male flowers at the tip and female flowers below** (androgynous); lowermost **bract bristle-like,** up to 5 cm long; **scales** yellowish brown with a green midvein, about as long as but narrower than the perigynia, egg-shaped, tipped **with a long** (1–5 mm) **bristle;** 2 stigmas; {May–July}.

Fruits: Dry, lens-shaped seed-like fruits (achenes) enclosed in perigynia; **perigynia straw-coloured to greenish** (sometimes becoming black), pointed upward to outward, egg-shaped, 2–2.5 {3} mm long, 1–1.8 mm wide, rounded on one side and flat on the other, thick-edged (not winged), tapered to a **flattened beak ½–¾ as long as the body edged with tiny sharp teeth and tipped with 2 distinct teeth.**

Habitat: Swamps and wet meadows; rather exacting in its habitat, requiring non-saline, non-acid soils that are permanently wet but with some drainage.

Notes: This species has also been called *Carex multiflora* Muhl. and *Carex setacea* Dewey. • Awl-fruited sedge (*Carex stipata* Muhl. *ex* Willd.) superficially resembles fox sedge, but its perigynia taper gradually to a beak that is as long as the body, and its scales are tipped with a short bristle. • *Vulpinoidea* is derived from the Latin *vulpes* (fox), because the flower cluster was thought to resemble a fox's tail.

BROWNED SEDGE

Carex adusta Boott
SEDGE FAMILY (CYPERACEAE)

Plants: Clumped perennial herbs; **stems stiffly erect, 20–80 cm tall**, rough to the touch near the top only; from short underground stems (rhizomes).

Leaves: Firm, 4–7 per stem, **shorter than the stems**; blades flat, 2–4 {5} mm wide.

Flower clusters: Stiff, erect, 2–3 {1–4} cm long, **egg-shaped to cylindrical heads** of 4–15 **olive-coloured** spikes; spikes with **male flowers at the base** and female flowers at the tip (gynaecandrous), 6–12 mm long, nearly round; **lowermost bract** broad at the base, prolonged into a **stiff, narrow blade** up to 2.5 cm long; **scales** reddish brown with narrow, white, translucent edges, broadly egg-shaped, **concealing the perigynia**; 2 stigmas; July {May–August}.

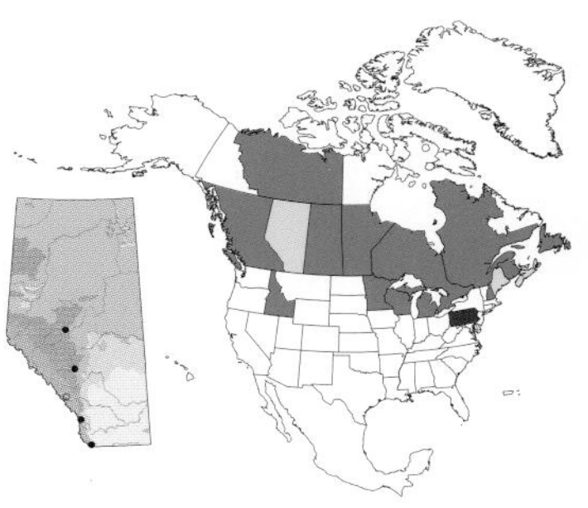

Fruits: Lens-shaped seed-like fruits (achenes), 1.8–2.1 mm broad, enclosed by perigynia; **perigynia** brown, **4–5 mm long**, short-stalked, **shiny**, finely nerved on the back below the middle, edged with a narrow **wing bearing tiny teeth above the middle**, tipped with a **flat, 2-toothed beak**; July {August}.

Habitat: Dry, acidic, usually sandy soil, often under pine trees; generally confined to sandy, disturbed areas in the boreal forest.

Notes: This species has also been called *Carex pinguis* Bailey. • A more common species, white-scaled sedge (*Carex xerantica* Bailey), resembles browned sedge but has narrower, more egg-shaped spikes that are slightly tapered at the base above an inconspicuous lower bract. Its light-coloured perigynia are not shiny, and they remain closely pressed to the spike when mature. White-scaled sedge grows in grasslands on the plains. • The crowded spikes of the widespread wetland species Bebb's sedge (*Carex bebbii* (Bailey) Olney *ex* Fern.) resemble those of browned sedge, but their scales are shorter and narrower and do not conceal the perigynia, and their lowermost bracts are only slightly prolonged (not prominent). • When abundant, browned sedge provides a good source of seeds for small birds. • *Adusta* comes from the Latin word for 'burned' or 'scorched,' probably referring to the colour of the scales covering the perigynia.

ES

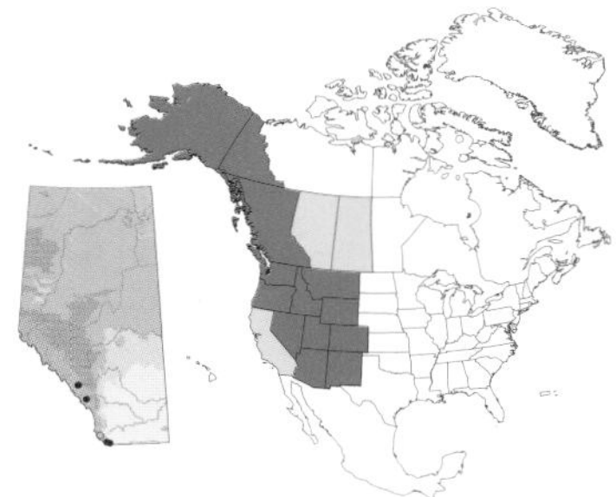

PASTURE SEDGE

Carex petasata Dewey
SEDGE FAMILY (CYPERACEAE)

Plants: Tufted perennial herbs; stems slender, stiff, smooth, 30–80 {90} cm tall, brown at the base; from short, fibrous underground stems (rhizomes).

Leaves: Alternate, 2–5 per stem, clustered near the base, much shorter than the stems; blades firm, flat or nearly so, usually 2–4 mm wide; **dried leaves of previous years persistent and conspicuous** (marcescent).

Flower clusters: Erect, head-like, with **3–6 overlapping spikes**, 2–4 {6} cm long and 1–1.5 cm wide; **spikes with female flowers at the tip** and male flowers at the base (gynaecandrous), **stalkless** (or nearly so), 9–18 mm long; lowermost **bract inconspicuous**, usually scale-like, sometimes tipped with a small bristle; **scales of female flowers reddish brown to brown** or straw-coloured, with broad, translucent edges, broadly egg-shaped, **largely covering the perigynia; 2 stigmas**; {May–July}.

Fruits: Dry, **lens-shaped** seed-like fruits (achenes), 2–3 mm long and about 1.5 mm wide, enclosed in perigynia; **perigynia** ascending, pale when young, brown at maturity, finely ribbed on both sides, flattened to a **narrow, finely toothed wing** along the edges, **oblong to lance-shaped, 6–8 mm long** and about 2 mm wide, tapered to a slender, nearly round beak about 2 mm long.

Habitat: Dry grassland and open woods; elsewhere, in grassland, sagebrush scrub, and dry or even wet meadows, sometimes to timberline.

Notes: Pasture sedge could be confused with 2 common species, meadow sedge (*Carex praticola* Rydb.) and head-like sedge (*Carex phaeocephala* Piper), but both of these sedges have smaller perigynia (3.5–6.5 mm long) that are covered by their scales. Head-like sedge is a smaller (10–30 cm tall) plant that grows in large clumps, usually at higher elevations. It usually has only 3 or 4 spikes, and its perigynia are broader than those of pasture sedge and tend to retain their green colour longer. Meadow sedge is similar to pasture sedge in appearance, but it usually has more numerous (2–7) and more widely spaced spikes.
• Plants growing in shaded situations tend to have much paler scales, without the brownish colour of those from more open areas.

SMALL-HEADED SEDGE

Carex illota Bailey
SEDGE FAMILY (CYPERACEAE)

Plants: Tufted perennial herbs; stems slender, stiff, **10–40 cm tall**, 3-sided, with sharp, rough edges; from short underground stems (rhizomes).

Leaves: Flat, 2–5 per stem, 1–3 mm wide, shorter than the stems.

Flower clusters: Dense, blackish heads of 3–6 stalkless spikes, 6–15 mm long, 5–15 mm wide; spikes with **male flowers at the base** and female flowers at the tip (gynaecandrous), 5–15-flowered, 4–7 mm long; **bracts inconspicuous**, hair-like; scales dark brown to greenish black with narrow, translucent edges, shiny, broadly egg-shaped, blunt, shorter and often narrower than the perigynia; **2 stigmas**; {June} July.

Fruits: Dry, lens-shaped seed-like fruits (achenes), 1.3–1.5 mm long, enclosed in perigynia; **perigynia** blackish brown toward the tip, green to straw-coloured at the spongy thickened base, **pointed outward**, broadly lance-shaped, 2.5–3.2 {3.5} mm long, **flat on the inner side, bulging on the outer side**, sharp-angled but neither flattened nor toothed along the edges, tapered to a beak with 2 teeth.

Habitat: Moist mountain slopes and alpine meadows.

Notes: This species has also been called *Carex bonplandii* var. *minor* Boott and *Carex dieckii* Boeck. • Two other rare Alberta sedges, Presl's sedge (*Carex preslii* Steud.) and Hayden's sedge (*Carex haydeniana* Olney, also called *Carex macloviana* D'Urv. ssp. *haydeniana* (Olney) Taylor & MacBryde), resemble small-headed sedge but are distinguished by their perigynia, which are edged with finely toothed, thin wings and which lack spongy, thickened bases. Presl's sedge is a tufted, 20–80 cm tall species of dry, open slopes in southwestern Alberta. It produces dense, 1–2 cm long heads of 2–8 spikes. Each spike is 6–10 mm wide and has 10–25 flowers. The plump, 3–4.5 mm long, obscurely veined perigynia have dark green tips, and contain rectangular, lens-shaped achenes at least 1.75 mm long. The scales are reddish brown with a green midvein and translucent edges. Presl's sedge flowers in July {June–August}. Hayden's sedge grows in moist, open, subalpine and alpine areas in the mountains. It is distinguished from Presl's

C. PRESLII

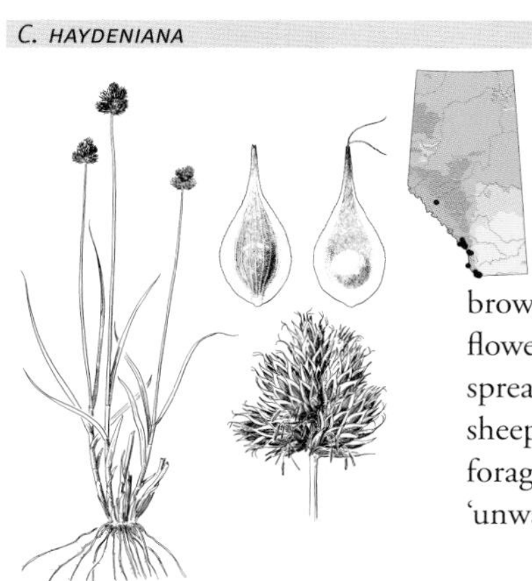

sedge by its larger (4.5–6 mm long), very flat perigynia containing relatively small (1.4–1.7 mm) achenes. • Inland sedge (*Carex interior* Bailey) is a widespread sedge that resembles small-headed sedge, but it grows at lower elevations, its spikes are less crowded, its perigynia are very finely toothed along the upper edges and its scales tend to be brownish. Its upper spike has a very distinct zone of male flowers at the base, and its mature perigynia are widely spreading. • Small-headed sedge is moderately palatable to sheep and cattle and, where abundant, is an important forage plant. • *Illota* is a Latin word meaning 'dirty' or 'unwashed.'

BROOM SEDGE

Carex scoparia Schk. *ex* Willd.
SEDGE FAMILY (CYPERACEAE)

Plants: Densely tufted perennial herbs; stems slender, erect, 20–80 {100} cm tall, 3-sided with sharp edges, rough to the touch near the top; from short underground stems (rhizomes).

Leaves: Firm, 2–6 per stem, 15–90 cm long, 1–3 mm wide, flat or channelled lengthwise, shorter than the stem.

Flower clusters: **Shiny**, often **straw-coloured**, 2–6 cm long, with 3–10 {12} clearly defined, **stalkless spikes**; spikes 4–10-flowered, with **male flowers at the base and female flowers at the tip** (gynaecandrous), egg-shaped, 6–16 mm long; lowermost bract bristle-like or lacking; scales brownish with a green midvein and narrow translucent edges, egg-shaped, pointed, narrower and shorter than the perigynia; 2 stigmas; {June–July}.

Fruits: Brownish, lens-shaped seed-like fruits (achenes) 1.3–1.8 mm long, enclosed in perigynia; **perigynia** straw-coloured to brown, **egg-shaped to lance-shaped, 4–7 mm long**, 1.2–2.6 mm wide, veined on both sides, **flattened, edged with a thin wing** from base to beak, tapered to a flat, finely toothed, 1–2 mm long beak tipped with 2 shallow teeth.

Habitat: Moist to wet sites; elsewhere, moist open woods.

Notes: Tinged sedge (*Carex tincta* (Fern.) Fern., also known as *Carex mirabilis* Dewey var. *tincta* Fern.) is another rare Alberta species that resembles broom sedge, but it has broader, more egg-shaped perigynia (at least half as wide as long) with conspicuous nerves on the outer side, but fine, less visible nerves on the inner side. Tinged sedge has relatively small perigynia that are 3–4.5 {5} mm long and 1.5–2 mm wide. The spikes form oblong heads 1–4 cm long and 1–1.5 cm thick, with light reddish brown scales as long as the perigynia. Tinged sedge is reported to flower from May to July, and grows in meadows and open woodlands in central and southwestern Alberta. • Broad-fruited sedge (*Carex tenera* Dewey) and Bebb's sedge (*Carex bebbii* (Bailey) Olney *ex* Fern.) are more widespread species that resemble both broom sedge and tinged sedge. The spikes of broad-fruited sedge are more widely spaced (like beads on a string), their perigynia have nerves on the outer side only, and their scales are greenish translucent to tawny. Bebb's sedge has smaller perigynia (3–3.5 mm long) that are nerveless or obscurely nerved and brownish at maturity, and its flower clusters are squared (rather than tapered) at the base. • Crawford's sedge (*Carex crawfordii* Fern.) is also similar to broom sedge but has much narrower (lance-shaped to awl-shaped) perigynia on which the flattened edge (wing) almost disappears at the base. • Broom sedge produces abundant seed, but its plants have low nutritional value and are seldom grazed. • The specific epithet *scoparia*, from the Latin *scopa* (a broom), refers to the general broom-like appearance of this sedge.

C. TINCTA

BROAD-SCALED SEDGE

Carex platylepis Mack.
SEDGE FAMILY (CYPERACEAE)

Plants: Tufted perennial herbs; **stems coarse**, 40–70 cm tall; from short underground stems (rhizomes).

Leaves: 3–7 scattered on the lower third of the stem, much shorter than the stems; **blades** 2.5–5 mm wide, **spreading, prominently wrinkled and shallowly pitted on the upper side.**

Flower clusters: 5–8 **spikes** in a head 1.5–3.5 cm long, clustered or the lower ones slightly separate; spikes with female flowers at the tip, male flowers at the base (gynaecandrous); bracts scale-like; scales egg-shaped, dull reddish brown with translucent edges and a green midvein; 2 stigmas; {May–August}.

Fruits: Lens-shaped seed-like fruits (achenes), about 2 mm long and 1 mm wide, enclosed in perigynia; **perigynia** dull green to yellowish brown, appressed-ascending, oblong to lance-shaped, **4–4.5 mm long**, 1.5–2 mm wide, **about as long and wide as the scales**, thin, edged with a wing nearly to base, toothed above the middle, tapered to a beak 1–1.5 mm long.

Habitat: Dry, open coniferous woods.

Notes: Broad-scaled sedge can be confused with several other species. Meadow sedge (*Carex praticola* Rydb.) is distinguished by its coarser growth form, with broader, spreading leaves, leafy stems, clustered spikes and shorter (4 mm long) perigynia. Thick-headed sedge (*Carex pachystachya* Cham.) and small-winged sedge (*Carex microptera* Mack.) have heads of crowded spikes with flatter perigynia containing distinctly smaller achenes. They are also plants of moister habitats. • Another species reported for Alberta, Piper's sedge (*Carex piperi* Mack.), is similar, but its spikes are usually less densely clustered (almost zigzagged), and its perigynia have slender, more rounded beaks and fewer, less conspicuous veins. Piper's sedge has sometimes been included in meadow sedge or broad-scaled sedge, but those species have dull, reddish brown flower scales, without the broad, silvery-white edges found in Piper's sedge, and their flowering heads tend to be shorter, with more densely clustered spikes. Piper's sedge grows in damp meadows.

C. PIPERI

TAPER-FRUIT SHORT-SCALE SEDGE

Carex leptopoda Mack.
SEDGE FAMILY (CYPERACEAE)

Plants: Loosely tufted perennial herbs; stems 20–65 {80} cm tall, sharply triangular; smooth or roughened below the head; from slender, **elongate underground stems** (rhizomes).

Leaves: Light green to yellowish green with a bloom, 2.5–6 mm wide, flat, shorter than the stems.

Flower clusters: Oblong to egg-shaped **heads of 5–7 spikes**, 3.5–4.5 cm long, lower 1–3 spikes usually separate; spikes stalkless or on a short stalk, 9–13 mm long, **13–25-flowered**, usually with female flowers at the tip and male flowers at the base (gynaecandrous); lowest bract 16–26 mm long, with awn 13–23 mm long; scales pointed to short-awned, greenish with white to straw-coloured edges, about as long as the perigynia; 2 stigmas; {May–July}.

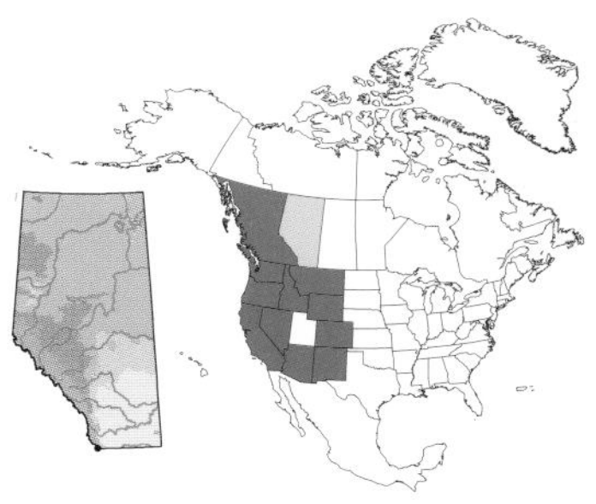

Fruits: Dry, lens-shaped seed-like fruits (achenes) enclosed in a perigynia; **perigynia stalked**, ascending to erect, green to pale brown, **prominently** to weakly **veined**, egg-shaped to narrowly egg-shaped, 3.2–3.9 mm long, 1.1–1.5 mm wide, tapering to a toothed beak 1–1.7 mm long, the tip entire or slightly 2-toothed.

Habitat: Moist woods and thickets in extreme southwestern Alberta.

Notes: This species has also been called *Carex deweyana* Schwein. ssp. *leptopoda* (Mack.) Calder & R.L. Taylor and *C. deweyana* var. *leptopoda* (Mack.) B. Boivin. It can be distinguished from the more common and widespread species in Alberta, Dewey's sedge (*Carex deweyana* Schwein.), in having more spikes per stem (5–7 vs. 2–5), more female flowers in the lowest spike (13–25 vs. 5–12), and short-stalked perigynia with more prominent venation. • The specific epithet *leptopoda* is derived from the Greek *lept* (slender or small) and *pod* (foot), in reference to the stalked perigynia.

LACHENAL'S SEDGE

Carex lachenalii Schk.
SEDGE FAMILY (CYPERACEAE)

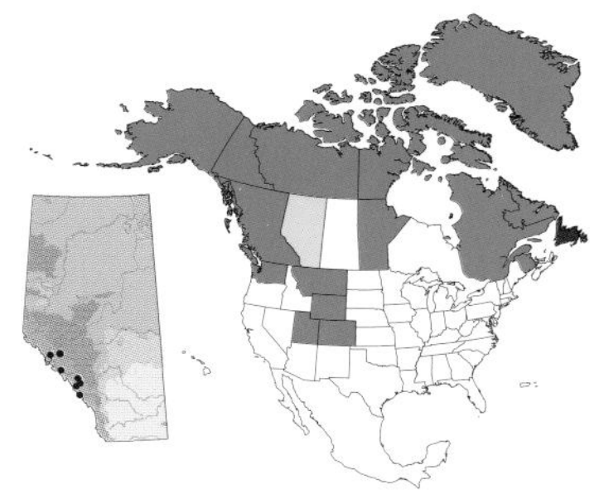

Plants: **Tufted** perennial herbs; stems slender, stiff, **5–30 cm tall**, sometimes a little rough to the touch near the top; often from short underground stems (rhizomes).

Leaves: Basal and on the lower stem, **1–2.5 mm wide, flat with the edges rolled under**, equalling or shorter than stems.

Flower clusters: **Compact heads of 2–4 stalkless spikes, 0.5–2 {3.5} cm long**; spikes with **female flowers at the tip** and male flowers at the base (gynaecandrous) (male flowers sometimes inconspicuous), 5–15 mm long, brownish, 15–30-flowered; bracts inconspicuous; **scales brownish**, sometimes with pale, translucent edges, egg-shaped, **blunt-tipped**, hiding most of the perigynia; 2 stigmas; {July} August.

Fruits: Dry, lens-shaped seed-like fruits (achenes) enclosed in perigynia; **perigynia golden-brown to reddish, densely dotted with tiny pits**, convex on the outer side and flat on the inner, widest at or above the middle, 2–3.5 mm long, 1–1.5 mm wide, tapered to a short, more or less flattened beak with a **translucent tip**.

Habitat: Moist alpine slopes and snow beds; elsewhere, in shallow ponds and open woods, usually in calcareous areas.

Notes: This species has also been called *Carex bipartita* All. (misapplied) and *Carex lagopina* Wahl. • Hudson Bay sedge (*Carex heleonastes* Ehrh. *ex* L.f.) is a rare Alberta species that grows in wet, calcareous sites such as fens and marshes. Its flower clusters resemble those of Lachenal's sedge, with 2–4 crowded spikes, but the perigynia of Hudson Bay sedge are light grey (sometimes turning brown) with short, reddish brown (not translucent) tips, and the upper stems are very rough. • Narrow sedge (*Carex arcta* Boott) is a rare species that grows in moist woods in Alberta and also in

C. ARCTA

wet meadows and on streambanks elsewhere. It is very similar to Hudson Bay sedge and was included in that species at one time, but its perigynia are broadest near the base (rather than at or above the middle) and are tipped with conspicuous, flattened, sharply toothed beaks. Narrow sedge has larger, more compact, head-like flower clusters, with 5–15 crowded spikes. It flowers in July. • The Alberta populations of Lachenal's sedge are widely separated (disjunct) from the main range of this species.

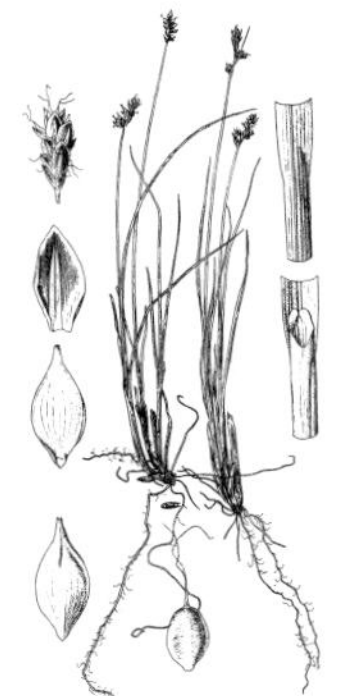

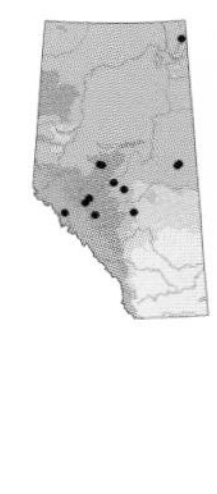

RYE-GRASS SEDGE

Carex loliacea L.
SEDGE FAMILY (CYPERACEAE)

Plants: Loosely tufted perennial herbs; **stems slender, weak, 20–40 {60} cm tall,** rough to the touch near the top, indistinctly 3-sided; from slender creeping stems.

Leaves: Soft, yellowish green, 4–8 per stem, shorter than or as long as stems, 0.5–2 mm wide, flat or with lengthwise grooves, long-pointed.

Flower clusters: Narrow, **1–2.5 {3} cm long heads of 2–5 {8} stalkless spikes**, with the upper spikes touching and the lower ones well separated; **spikes 3–5 mm long**, with **male flowers at the base** and female flowers at the tip (gynaecandrous); lowermost bract bristle-like, 2–8 mm long; **scales white, translucent with a green midvein**, egg-shaped with lengthwise ridge on the back, blunt-tipped, shorter than the perigynia; 2 stigmas; {May–June} July.

Fruits: Dry, brownish, lens-shaped seed-like fruits (achenes) enclosed in perigynia; **perigynia light green**, 3–8 per spike, pointed upward or spreading, widest at or below the middle, **blunt-tipped** (not beaked), {2} 2.5–3 mm long, flat on one side and rounded on the other, spongy, thickened and short-stalked at the base, **distinctly many-ribbed, densely dotted with tiny white pits.**

Habitat: Marshes, moist banks; elsewhere, in sphagnum and wet black spruce bogs.

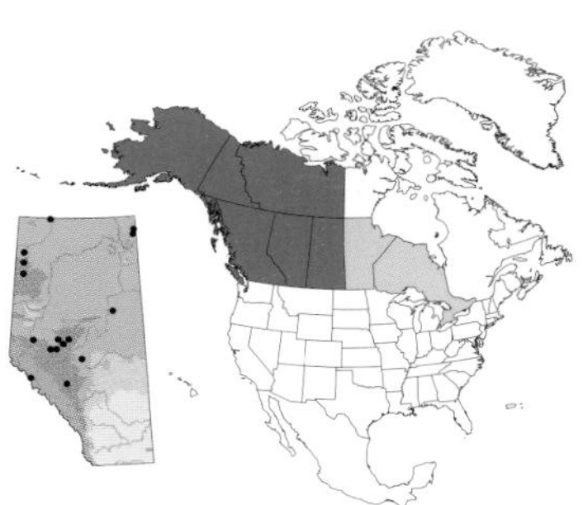

Notes: Three-seeded sedge (*Carex trisperma* Dewey) is a rare species of bogs, swamps and wet woods of central Alberta. It resembles rye-grass sedge, but its flower clusters are longer (3–6 cm long) with widely spaced spikes, its spikes have only 1–5 perigynia, its lowermost bracts are bristle-like and 2–7 cm long (many times longer than the lowest spike), and its greenish brown perigynia are 3–4 mm long. Three-seeded sedge has been reported to flower from May to June. • A similar but more common species, two-seeded sedge (*Carex disperma* Dewey), is easily distinguished from rye-grass sedge and three-seeded sedge by its spikes, which have female flowers at the base and male flowers at the tip (androgynous). • Thin-flowered sedge (*Carex tenuiflora* Wahlenb.) is also similar to, but more common than, rye-grass sedge. It is distinguished by its dense, egg-shaped to rounded heads of spikes, and its larger, whitish silvery, green-centred scales that almost hide the faintly nerved perigynia. • *Loliacea* means 'lolium-like' in Latin. *Lolium* is the scientific name for darnel or rye-grass, a genus of grass that this sedge superficially resembles.

C. TRISPERMA

DJ

WEAK SEDGE

Carex supina Willd. ssp. *spaniocarpa* (Steud.) Hult.
SEDGE FAMILY (CYPERACEAE)

Plants: Loosely tufted perennial herbs; **stems** slender, erect, 5–30 cm tall, 3-sided with sharp, rough edges, **reddish at the base**; from slender, brown underground runners (stolons).

Leaves: Crowded, 0.5–2 mm wide, channelled lengthwise, **shorter than the stems.**

Flower clusters: Compact, **2–3 cm long heads** of 1–4 stalkless spikes; **uppermost spike with male flowers only**, pale, 5–15 mm long, **1–2 mm wide**; **lower spikes** with female flowers only, **rounded**, 5 mm long, 3–6 mm wide; lowermost bract short, with a bristle-like blade; **scales reddish brown** with a light-coloured centre and translucent edges, broadly egg-shaped, pointed, **about as long as the perigynia**; 3 stigmas; {May–June} July.

Fruits: Dry, yellowish brown, 3-sided seed-like fruits (achenes), 2 mm long, enclosed in perigynia; **perigynia 3–5** {10} **per spike, smooth and shiny, rust-coloured, plump**, 2.5–3.5 mm long, 1–1.5 mm wide, tapered to a short beak.

Habitat: Dry, gravelly, eroding slopes and sandy sites.

Notes: This species has also been called *Carex spaniocarpa* Steud. • Glacier sedge (*Carex glacialis* Mack.) is a northern tundra species that is rare in Alberta; disjunct populations have been discovered on dry, calcareous mountain slopes. This small, densely tufted sedge has smooth, wiry stems that are 4–15 cm tall and reddish purple at the base. Its stiff, curved leaves are flat at the base but channelled toward the tip. They are narrow (0.5–1.5 mm wide) and shorter than the stems, and the remains of old leaves persist at the stem base. Each loose, head-like flower cluster is 5–15 mm long, with 2–4 small (2–7 mm long), stalkless (upper) to short-stalked (lower) spikes. The lowermost bract has a short, tubular sheath and a bristle-like blade 5–15 mm long. The uppermost spike is male and the lower spikes are female, with a few (1–6) small (1.5–2.5 mm long), round perigynia that are slightly longer than their scales. The perigynia are greenish at the base, brownish at the tip and faintly veined, with an abrupt, short, cylindrical beak. The broadly egg-shaped scales are reddish brown to purplish black with a pale midvein and broad translucent edges. Glacier sedge is reported to flower from June to July.

DJ

C. GLACIALIS

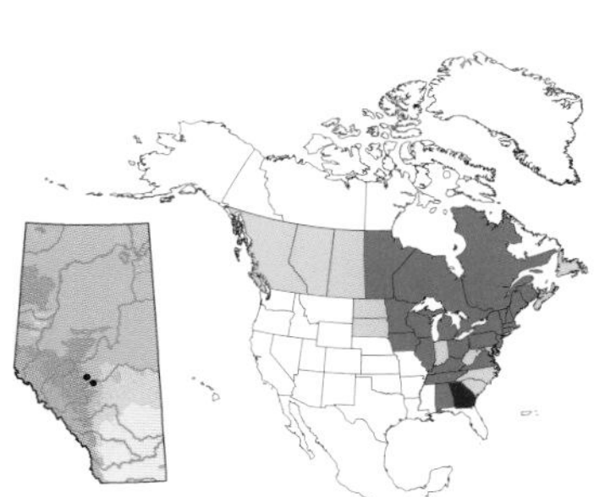

STALKED SEDGE

Carex pedunculata Muhl.
SEDGE FAMILY (CYPERACEAE)

Plants: Tufted, bright green perennial herbs; stems weak, slender, {5} 10–30 cm tall, barely exceeding the leaves, rough to the touch near the top, **strongly purple-tinged at the base**; from short underground stems (rhizomes).

Leaves: Mostly basal, thick, ascending to curved, blades 5–25 cm long, 2–4 {5} mm wide, flat near the base, becoming pleated or with the edges curved upward at the tip, finely toothed on the upper ⅓.

Flower clusters: 4–10 cm long, with 3 or 4 {5} spikes; uppermost spike usually with male flowers only (sometimes with a few female flowers at the base), elliptic, 5–15 mm long; **lower** 2 or 3 {4} **spikes** separate, ascending or spreading, usually with female flowers only, elliptic, 7–10 {30} mm long, 3–8-flowered, **on long, curved, thread-like stalks, some often hidden among the basal leaves; lowermost bract with a short blade**; scales purplish brown, oblong to egg-shaped, with translucent edges and a green **midvein prolonged into a short bristle** (awn), smaller than the perigynia; 3 stigmas; May–June.

Fruits: Brown, 3-sided seed-like fruits (achenes), filling the perigynia; **perigynia** pale green, egg-shaped, 3.5–5 mm long, nerveless, stalked, spongy at the base, **hairless** or slightly hairy above, tipped with a minute, toothless beak.

Habitat: Rich, relatively dry woods, frequently with poplars; elsewhere, also in alder swamps and white spruce and balsam fir forests.

Notes: Stalked sedge is most likely to be confused with the more common beautiful sedge (*Carex concinna* R. Br.), but that species has stalkless lower female spikes, the lowermost bract is bladeless, the scales do not have awns, and the perigynia are more evidently hairy. • Stalked sedge is an eastern species. The Alberta localities are widely disjunct from the nearest records in eastern Saskatchewan.
• *Pedunculata* means 'with peduncles' (the stalk of a cluster of flowers), referring to the long stalks of the female spikes.

BALD SEDGE, SHAVED SEDGE

Carex tonsa (Fern.) Bickn. var. *tonsa*
SEDGE FAMILY (CYPERACEAE)

Plants: Small, densely tufted, **almost stemless** perennial herbs; stems 4–16 cm tall, of unequal lengths, **fertile stems hidden among the basal leaves**; from short, stout, brown to reddish brown underground stems (rhizomes).

Leaves: All basal, **stiff**, flat to channelled, pale green, smooth or slightly roughened above; **blades** 5–15 cm long, **2–4** {5} **mm wide**; old leaves numerous at base of plant.

Flower clusters: Compact, with 3 or 4 {5} stalkless or short-stalked spikes, 10–15 mm long; uppermost spike with male flowers only, 5–8 {4.5–11} mm long on a stalk 0.8–15 mm long; lower 2 or 3 {4} spikes with 5–10 female flowers; lowermost bract small, shorter than the flower cluster; **scales** reddish brown with a green midrib, egg-shaped, pointed, **as long as or longer than the perigynia**; 3 stigmas; {May–June}.

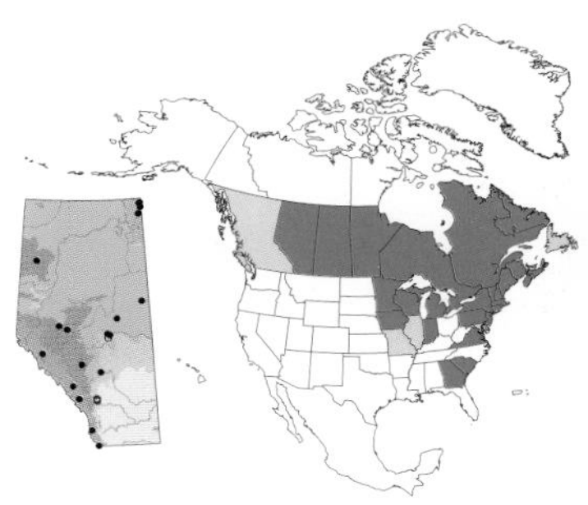

Fruits: Dry, 2-ridged, brown, seed-like fruits (achenes), enclosed in perigynia; **perigynia 2-ribbed, hairless, except for lines of hairs on the ribs along the beak**, 3.5–4 {3.2–4.7} mm long, {1.1} 1.3–1.6 mm wide, abruptly narrowed to a straight, 0.9–1.5 {1.9} mm long beak, tipped with 2 teeth 0.2–0.5 mm long.

Habitat: Open woods (particularly pine) and sandy areas in the boreal forest, especially in disturbed areas.

Notes: This species has also been called *Carex umbellata* Schkuhr *ex* Willd. var. *tonsa* Fern. and *Carex rugosperma* Mack. var. *tonsa* (Fern.) Voss. • Umbellate sedge (*Carex umbellata* Schkuhr *ex* Willd.) is identified by its softer, narrower (1–3 mm wide) leaves and distinctly hairy, smaller (2.2–3.3 mm long) perigynia, with shorter (0.5–1 mm long) beaks. It grows in habitats similar to those of bald sedge, but its distribution extends into the Rocky Mountains. • Two other closely related sedges are more common in Alberta, bent sedge (*Carex deflexa* Hornem.) and Ross' sedge (*Carex rossii* Boott). Both have stalkless male spikes, lowermost bracts longer than the flower clusters and scales shorter than the perigynia. Bent sedge is slender, loosely tufted, with soft, spreading leaves less than 2 mm wide. Its male spikes are 2–5 mm long and its perigynia are 2.5–3 mm long, with short (0.4–0.7 mm long),

C. UMBELLATA

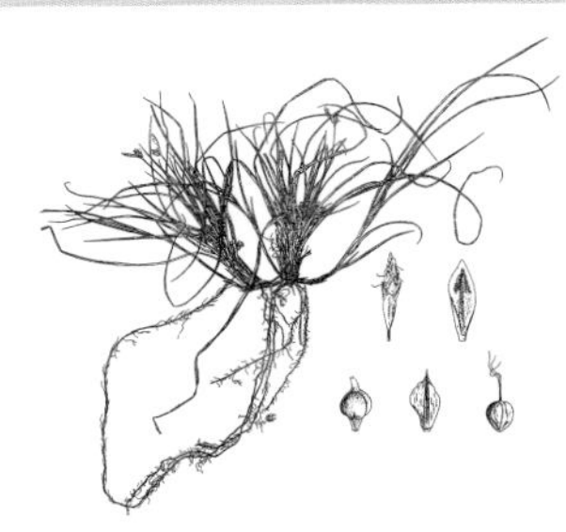

shallowly toothed beaks. Ross' sedge is stout, densely tufted, with stiff, erect leaves more than 2 mm wide. Its male spikes are 12–15 mm long and its perigynia are 3–4.5 mm long, with long (0.8–1.7 mm long), deeply toothed beaks.

PL

Back's sedge

Carex backii Boott
SEDGE FAMILY (CYPERACEAE)

Plants: Small tufted herbs; **stems weak**, narrowly winged, up to 25 cm tall, but much **shorter than the leaves**; forming dense mats.

Leaves: Flat, dark green, 3–6 mm wide.

Flowers: **Single, inconspicuous spikes** hidden among the leaves, each spike **with 2 or 3 inconspicuous male flowers at the tip and 2–5 female flowers at the base; scales long** (**2–7 cm**) **and leaf-like**, concealing the perigynia, sometimes mistaken for bracts (giving individual florets the appearance of separate spikelets); 3 stigmas; {May–July}.

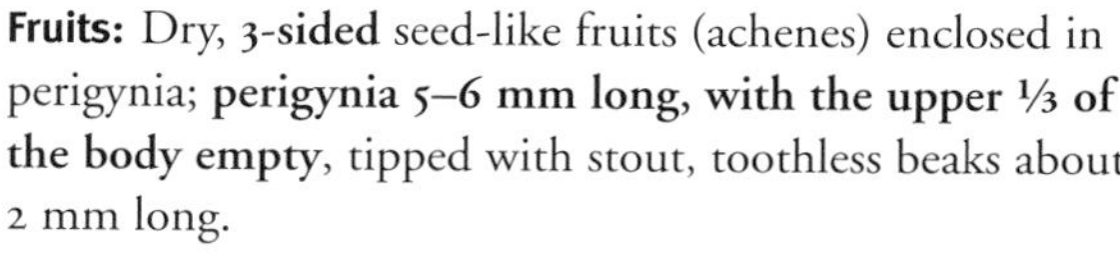

Fruits: Dry, **3-sided** seed-like fruits (achenes) enclosed in perigynia; **perigynia 5–6 mm long, with the upper ⅓ of the body empty**, tipped with stout, toothless beaks about 2 mm long.

Habitat: Dry (to moist), shady woods; elsewhere, in riparian woodland.

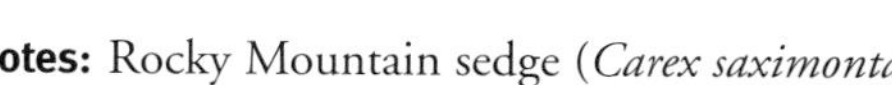

Notes: Rocky Mountain sedge (*Carex saximontana* Mack., also called *Carex backii* Boott var. *saximontana* (Mack.) Boivin) has shiny green leaves with down-curled edges, smaller (4–5 mm long) perigynia in which the achene fills the upper part of the body, and conical, slightly toothed beaks, about 1 mm long. It is reported from the Waterton-Crowsnest area of Alberta; Back's sedge occurs in the northern parkland and southern boreal forest in the central part of the province.

C. SAXIMONTANA

CRAWE'S SEDGE

Carex crawei Dewey
SEDGE FAMILY (CYPERACEAE)

PL

Plants: Perennial herbs; stems slender, stiffly erect, 5–30 {40} **cm tall**, single or in small clumps; from slender, creeping underground stems (rhizomes).

Leaves: Stiff, **pale green**, 6–12, shorter than the stem; blades 5–30 cm long, 1–3 {5} mm wide, flat, usually curved and **spreading; dried leaves** of the previous year **conspicuous** at the stem base.

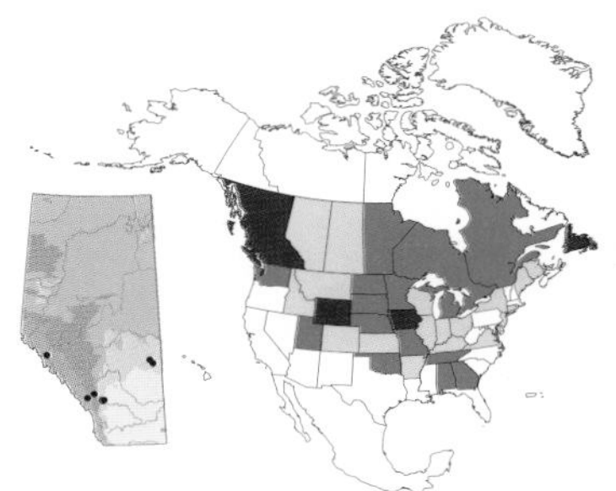

Flower clusters: Elongated, 5–20 cm long, with **2–5 widely spaced, stalked spikes**, with the lowest often borne near the base of the stem; **uppermost spike** with **male** flowers only, very narrow, {5} 10–20 mm long, on a rough, 1–7 cm long stalk; **lower spikes** with **female** flowers only, cylindrical, 10–20 {5–30} mm long, 5–6 mm wide, densely {5} 15–50-flowered, on short (1–3 cm long) stalks or stalkless; **bracts leaf-like with well-developed sheaths,** generally shorter than the flower cluster; **scales light reddish brown** with a pale green midrib and translucent edges, broadly egg-shaped, much shorter and narrower than the perigynia; 3 stigmas; {May} June–July.

Fruits: Dry, 3-sided seed-like fruits (achenes), **enclosed in slightly inflated perigynia**; perigynia **light green to tan, often speckled with tiny, reddish brown, resinous dots,** elliptic, very short-beaked, 2–3.5 {3.8} mm long, 1.2–2 mm wide, hairless, obscurely 15–25-veined.

Habitat: Calcareous meadows; elsewhere, in lime-rich wetlands, on lakeshores and in moist woods.

Notes: This species has also been called *Carex heterostachya* Torr. • Golden sedge (*Carex aurea* Nutt.) is a common sedge that resembles Crawe's sedge, but its styles have 2 stigmas, its perigynia are light green to orange-yellow or brownish, with rounded (not beaked) tips and its spikes are more loosely flowered but are not as widely spaced as those of Crawe's sedge. • Crawe's sedge was named for its discoverer, Ithamar Bingham Crawe (1792–1847).

DJ

NODDING SEDGE

Carex misandra R. Br.
SEDGE FAMILY (CYPERACEAE)

Plants: Tufted perennial herbs; **stems** slender, **erect but often nodding at the tip**, 10–35 cm tall, smooth; from short underground stems (rhizomes).

Leaves: Many, **basal**, thick, shorter than stems, 4–10 cm long, 1–3 mm wide, flat or channelled lengthwise, **often curved**, long-pointed; **dead leaves persisting for several years.**

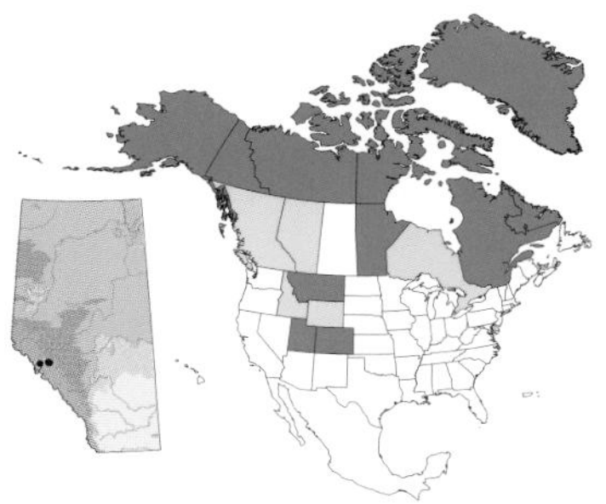

Flower clusters: Loose, elongated, with 2–4 slender-stalked, nodding spikes, each 5–15 {20} mm long, 4–6 mm wide; **uppermost spike club-shaped, with male flowers at the base and female flowers at the tip** (gynaecandrous); **lower spikes** cylindrical, bearing **female flowers only**; lowermost bract inconspicuous, with a long sheath and short blade (sometimes almost bladeless); **scales brownish black** with translucent edges, narrowly egg-shaped, 2.5–3.5 mm long, wider and shorter than the perigynia; 3 stigmas (rarely 2); July {June–August}.

Fruits: Dry, 3-sided seed-like fruits (achenes) with 3 sharp angles, egg-shaped, enclosed in perigynia; **perigynia** purplish black at the tip, greenish to straw-coloured at the base, **narrowly lance-shaped**, 3.5–5 mm long, 1 mm wide, short-stalked, lacking flattened (winged) edges, **gradually tapered to a long, toothed, flattened beak on the upper half.**

Habitat: Dry alpine slopes.

Notes: This species has also been called *Carex fuliginosa* Kuk. var. *misandra* (R. Br.) Lang. • Stone sedge (*Carex petricosa* Dewey) resembles nodding sedge, in that it also has nodding spikes, 3-sided achenes with 3 stigmas, and beaked perigynia tipped with 2 teeth. However, it grows from spreading underground stems and therefore is not tufted like nodding sedge, and its uppermost spikes are tipped with male (rather than female) flowers. Stone sedge grows on dry to moist alpine slopes in southwestern Alberta, and flowers in July. • Nodding sedge and stone sedge are both arctic-alpine taxa with isolated (disjunct) populations in Alberta. • *Misandra* is derived from the Latin *miser* (wretched, unhappy) and *andro* (man), in reference to the inconspicuous male flowers on the uppermost spike.

C. PETRICOSA

PL

Parry's sedge

Carex parryana Dewey var. *parryana*
SEDGE FAMILY (CYPERACEAE)

Plants: Loosely tufted perennial herbs; **stems** slender, **stiffly erect**, 15–40 {60} cm tall, bluntly 3-angled, **reddish-tinged at the base**; from long, creeping, scaly underground stems (rhizomes).

Leaves: Clustered near the base and usually much shorter than the stems, 5–12 per stem; blades 5–15 cm long, 2–4 mm wide, thin, stiff, **hairless**, usually flat with the edges rolled upward; dried **leaves of previous years persistent** and conspicuous.

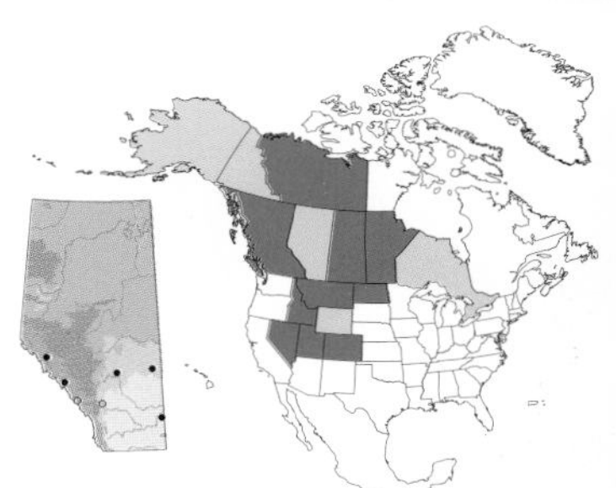

Flower clusters: Elongated, 4–8 cm long, with **3–5 erect, stalkless or stiffly short-stalked spikes**; **uppermost spike** 1.5–3 cm long, **usually with female flowers at the tip** and male flowers at the base (gynaecandrous), but may be male throughout or may have female flowers scattered anywhere along its length; lower spikes 7–20 mm long, 2–3 mm wide, with 7–20 female flowers only, oblong to linear-oblong; **lowermost bract** short, inconspicuous, rarely as long as the flower cluster, reddish-tinged at the base, **essentially sheathless; scales of female flowers nearly round, 2–2.5 mm long, dark reddish brown**, with white, translucent edges and a **prominent midvein**, blunt or short-pointed, 1.5–2.5 mm long, **covering the perigynia**; **3 stigmas**; {May–June} July.

Fruits: Dry, **3-sided** seed-like fruits (achenes), 1.4–1.8 mm long, enclosed in perigynia; **perigynia** straw-coloured (sometimes purplish near the tip), pressed against the main stalk, **hairless, 2-ribbed** (on edges), somewhat flattened, **2–2.3 {3} mm long**, 1–1.5 mm wide, egg-shaped, widest above the middle, **scarcely beaked** but sometimes tipped with 2 tiny (about 0.2 mm long) teeth or **slightly fringed** at the mouth (or both).

Habitat: Moist open meadows, swales and low ground near water, from the plains to moderate elevations in the mountains; elsewhere, on alkaline silt and marl flats.

Notes: Raynolds' sedge (*Carex raynoldsii* Dewey) is similar to Parry's sedge, but differs in that the uppermost spike usually has male flowers only, the scales of the female flower are larger (over 2.5 mm) and purplish black, and the perigynia are longer (3.5–4.5 mm). Raynolds' sedge

C. RAYNOLDSII

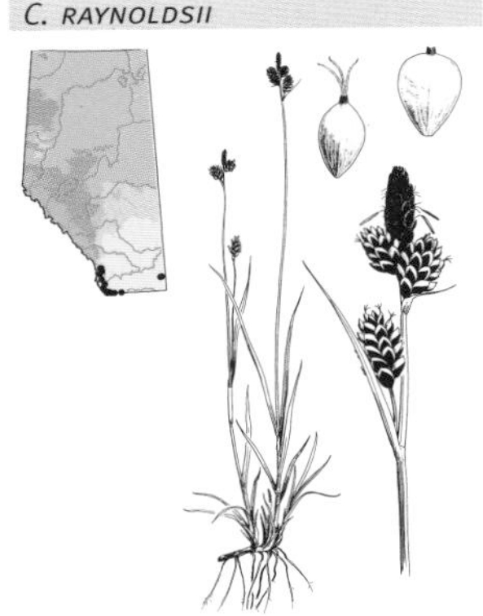

grows on moist open or wooded slopes and is reported to flower from June to August. • Both of these sedges resemble the common species Norway sedge (*Carex norvegica* Retz.). Norway sedge is most similar to Parry's sedge, but its weaker, often arched stems are sharply 3-angled, its scales are 1.5–2.5 mm long and purplish black and its perigynia are slightly larger (2–3.5 mm long) and never fringed at the mouth. • Parry's sedge was named for arctic explorer William Edward Parry (1790–1855).

PL

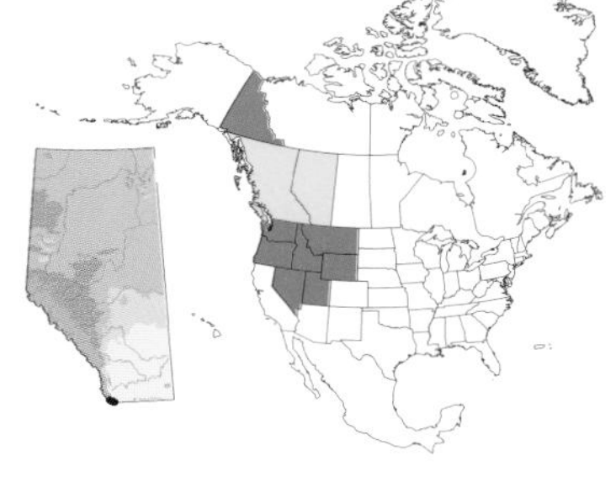

PAYSON'S SEDGE

Carex paysonis Clokey
SEDGE FAMILY (CYPERACEAE)

Plants: Loosely tufted perennial herbs; stems stiffly erect, 15–50 cm tall, 3-sided, with sharp edges, rough to the touch near the top; from tough, densely matted underground stems (rhizomes).

Leaves: **Basal, 8–15 per stem**, 2–6 mm wide, flat with the edges rolled under, shorter than the stems, with **persistent fibrous remains of leaves from previous years**; lowermost leaves largest.

Flower clusters: Compact to slightly open, with 3–8, short-stalked (lower) to stalkless (upper), erect to spreading spikes; **uppermost 1–2 spikes with male flowers only**, cylindrical to club-shaped, 15–35 mm long, 3–4.5 mm wide; lower spikes with female flowers only, cylindrical, 5–25 mm long, 4–6 mm wide, densely 15–40-flowered; lowermost bract leaf-like, sheathless, usually shorter than the flower cluster; scales purplish black with a pale midvein, lance-shaped, narrower than but almost as long as the perigynia; 3 stigmas; July–September.

Fruits: Dry, light brown, 3-sided seed-like fruits (achenes) on short stalks, enclosed in perigynia; **perigynia purple-blotched**, pressed against the spike or pointed upward, 2–4 mm long, 1.5–2 mm wide, egg-shaped to nearly round, **strongly flattened**, abruptly narrowed to a short (0.2 mm) **purple beak**.

Habitat: Mountain meadows.

Notes: Alpine sedge (*Carex podocarpa* R. Br., also called *Carex montanensis* Bailey) and showy sedge (*Carex spectabilis* Dewey) are both very similar to Payson's sedge, but their stems have purplish bases and only 2–5 leaves, of which the lowermost are smallest. They also lack the dried remains of leaves from previous years. Alpine sedge is rare in Alberta, where it grows in alpine meadows, and flowers in June and July. It is distinguished from showy sedge by its nodding (rather than erect) lower spikes and its solid, brownish black scales, which lack the thick, whitish midribs found on the scales of showy sedge. • Payson's sedge is moderately to highly palatable to livestock, and it is an important forage plant when plentiful. It is regularly grazed by sheep, horses and cattle, and is resistant to damage from heavy grazing. In some regions, it is an important stabilizer of exposed soils. • This species was named in honour of Edwin Blake Payson (1893–1927), a professor of botany in Wyoming who studied the mustards (Brassicaceae) and borages (Boraginaceae).

C. PODOCARPA

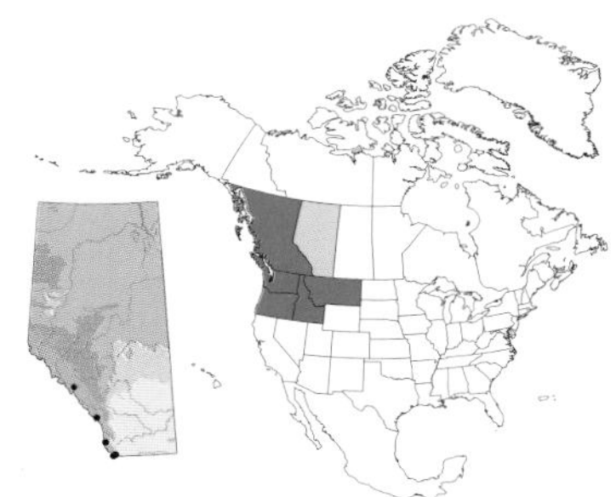

OPEN SEDGE

Carex aperta Boott
SEDGE FAMILY (CYPERACEAE)

Plants: **Loosely clumped** perennial herbs; stems slender, stiff, **30–100 cm tall**, brownish or reddish at base, 3-sided with sharp edges, rough to touch near the top; from **stout, tough underground stems** (rhizomes).

Leaves: **Erect**, 3–5 per stem, **flat**, 2–5 mm wide, **much shorter than the stems.**

Flower clusters: Elongated, with 3 or 4 spikes, 15–20 cm long; **uppermost spike with male flowers only**, 2–3.5 cm long, 3–4 mm wide; **lower spikes** mostly with **female** flowers only, sometimes with male flowers at the tip, 25–75-flowered, **narrowly cylindrical**, 1–5 cm long, 5 mm wide, erect, stalkless or short-stalked; **lowermost bract leaf-like**, about as long as the flower cluster; upper bracts shorter; **scales** purplish black with a light midvein, **lance-shaped, longer and narrower than the perigynia**; 2 stigmas; {April–June} July–August.

Fruits: Dry, lens-shaped seed-like fruits (achenes) **enclosed in inflated perigynia**; perigynia **olive-green to straw-coloured**, somewhat flattened, pointing upward or spreading outward, 2.5–3.5 mm long, 1.5–2 mm wide, **egg-shaped to nearly round**, narrowed abruptly to a short beak.

Habitat: Open, wet ground; elsewhere, on floodplains and marshy lakeshores.

Notes: This species has also been called *Carex turgidula* Bailey. • Water sedge (*Carex aquatilis* Wahlenb. var. *aquatilis*) is a widespread species that is similar to open sedge, but its spikes are all erect (none nodding) on short (less than 3 cm) stalks, its lower leaves are generally larger than its upper leaves and its stems grow from extensive, spreading rhizomes and therefore are not tufted. • Holm's Rocky Mountain sedge (*Carex scopulorum* Holm) also resembles open sedge, but it is easily distinguished by its lowermost bracts, which are always shorter than the flower clusters. • The specific epithet *aperta* comes from the Latin word for 'open' or 'uncovered,' possibly referring to the fact that the spikes are borne well above the leaves, or perhaps to the exposed, spreading perigynia.

BLACKENED SEDGE

Carex heteroneura Boott var. *epapillosa* (Mack.) F.J. Hermann
SEDGE FAMILY (CYPERACEAE)

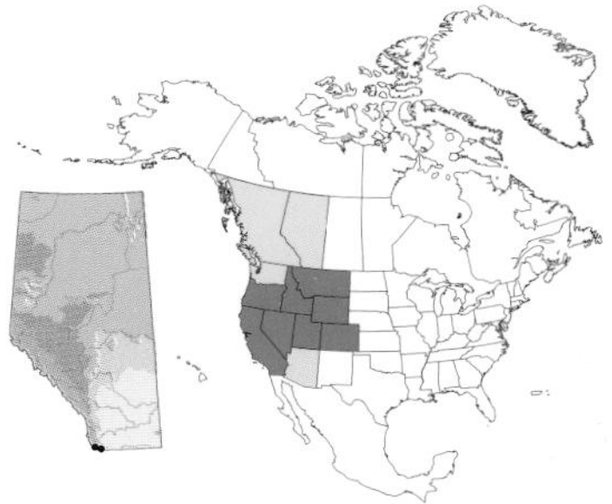

Plants: Densely tufted perennial herbs, with **brown, fibrous remains of old leaves; stems** 15–60 cm tall, **tinged purplish red at the base**; from short underground stems (rhizomes).

Leaves: Stiff, erect, 5–8 on the lower stem, 3–7 {8} mm wide, flat, shorter than the stems.

Flower clusters: Crowded, with 4 or 5 {3–6} spikes; spikes short, cylindrical, 10–25 mm long, 6–8 {10} mm wide, 30–60-flowered, on short, stiffly erect, 3–10 mm long stalks (lower spikes) to nearly stalkless (upper spikes); **uppermost spike with male flowers at the base** and female flowers at the tip (gynaecandrous); lower spikes with female flowers only; lowermost **bract leaf-like, dark red at the base**, shorter than the flower cluster; **scales reddish black with a lighter mid-vein**, lance-shaped, mostly pointed, **as long as the mature perigynia but much narrower**; 3 stigmas; {July–August}.

Fruits: Dry, 3-sided seed-like fruits (achenes), 1.5 mm long, enclosed in flattened perigynia; **perigynia yellowish green** (becoming brownish), pointing upward, widest at or above the middle, 3–4 {4.5} mm long, 1.5–2 {3.3} mm wide, rounded at base and tip, stalkless, dotted with tiny pits, **strongly flattened**, abruptly narrowing to a **reddish purple, 2-toothed beak** about 0.5 mm long.

Habitat: Moist to dry mountain meadows.

Notes: This species has also been called *Carex epapillosa* Mack., *Carex atrata* L. and *Carex hagiana* Kelso. • Purple sedge (*Carex mertensii* Prescott ssp. *mertensii*, also known as *Carex columbiana* Dewey) is also rare in Alberta. It grows in moist montane woods and along streambanks, forming dense, 30–100 cm tall tufts with short, stout rhizomes. Its stout, 3-sided stems are also purplish red at the base, but they have very sharp (winged), rough edges. The leaves of purple sedge are 4–7 mm wide, and their sheaths are often tinged cinnamon-brown. The uppermost spike has male flowers only (or sometimes a few female flowers at the tip), and the lower 4–9 spikes have female flowers only (or sometimes a few male flowers at the base). The numerous, large, clustered, dark-coloured spikes are cylindrical, 1–4 cm long and 7–9 mm wide, with slender,

C. MERTENSII

JP

nodding stalks. The lower 2 or 3 bracts are leaf-like, sheathless, and longer than the flower cluster. The light green to pale brown (often purple-spotted) perigynia are broadly egg-shaped with tiny, purplish beaks. They measure 4–5 mm long and 2.5–3.5 mm wide, and their thin, flattened bodies are finely veined. The egg-shaped to lance-shaped scales are dark purplish brown with a light midvein and narrow, translucent edges; they are much narrower and shorter than the perigynia. Purple sedge is reported to flower from May to July and produces 3-sided achenes with 3 stigmas. • Dark-scaled sedge (*Carex atrosquama* Mack.) is a common species that resembles blackened sedge, but it has rougher perigynia that are scarcely flattened. Its scales are broader than those of blackened sedge and somewhat shorter than their perigynia. • Blackened sedge is eaten by all types of livestock, particularly horses, and is said to be of high value because of its abundant seed. • The specific epithet *epapillosa* means 'without small protuberances,' in reference to the smooth (not bumpy) perigynia.

LENS-FRUITED SEDGE

Carex lenticularis Michx. var. *dolia* (M.E. Jones) L.A. Standley
SEDGE FAMILY (CYPERACEAE)

Plants: Densely tufted perennial herbs; stems slender, erect, **10–60 cm tall**, 3-sided with sharp angles; from short underground stems (rhizomes).

Leaves: Erect, thin, 4–9 per stem, **as long as or longer than stems**, 20–65 cm long, 1–2 {3} mm wide, pleated near the base, flat toward the tip, slender-pointed, pale grey-green.

Flower clusters: Crowded, 5–12 cm long, with 4–6 erect, short-stalked (lower) to stalkless (upper) spikes; **uppermost spike** usually bearing **male** flowers only (sometimes tipped with a few female flowers), 1–3 cm long, 2.5 mm wide; **lowermost spikes** with **female** flowers only but **middle spikes with some male flowers at the base** (gynaecandrous), narrowly cylindrical, 15–40 {45} mm long, 3–4 mm wide; lowermost bract leaf-like with a short sheath, erect, longer than flower cluster; scales purplish or reddish brown with a broad, green, 3-nerved centre and translucent edges, blunt-tipped, smaller than the perigynia; 2 stigmas; {May–July}.

Fruits: Dry, brown, lens-shaped seed-like fruits (achenes) enclosed in perigynia; **perigynia bluish green**, pointed upward, **soon falling off**, dotted with a few yellow glands, **flattened** and sharply 2-edged, lightly 3–7-veined on both sides, short-stalked, **2–3 mm long**, 1–1.5 mm wide, egg-shaped, **abruptly narrowed to a short, toothless beak.**

Habitat: Moist lakeshores and marshes; elsewhere, on river flats and streambanks.

Notes: This species includes *Carex kelloggii* W. Boott *in* Wats., *Carex enanderi* Hult. and *Carex eurystachya* F.J. Herm. • The seeds of lens-fruited sedge are commonly eaten by small birds. • *Lenticularis* comes from the Latin words for 'like a lens' and refers to the shape of the perigynia.

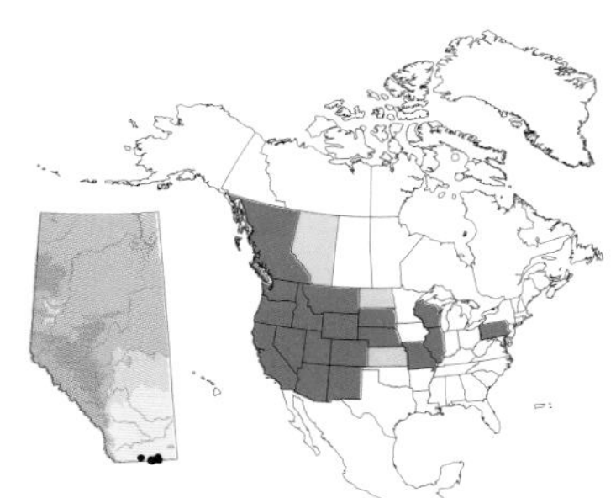

NEBRASKA SEDGE

Carex nebrascensis Dewey
SEDGE FAMILY (CYPERACEAE)

Plants: Tufted perennial herbs, sometimes with single stems; stems 30–100 {20–120} cm tall, stout, 3-sided with sharp edges; from long, spreading, scaly underground stems (rhizomes).

Leaves: Thick, firm, blue-green, 8–15 per stem, 4–8 {3–12} mm wide, flat (sometimes channelled lengthwise), **usually with knobby cross-partitions** (like rungs on a ladder), shorter than or equal to the stems; **dead leaves conspicuous, persisting for several years** (marcescent).

Flower clusters: Open, elongated, with **3–7 erect**, stalked (lower) to stalkless (upper) **spikes**; upper 1 or 2 spikes with male flowers only, 1.5–4 cm long, 3–6 mm wide; **lower spikes** with female flowers only, cylindrical, **1–6** {7} **cm long**, 5–9 mm wide, **30–150-flowered**; lowermost bract leaf-like, sheathless, longer than the flower cluster; scales purplish or brownish black with light-coloured centres, lance-shaped, narrower than but usually equal to or longer than the perigynia; 2 stigmas; May–June {July}.

Fruits: Dry, lens-shaped seed-like fruits (achenes) enclosed in perigynia; **perigynia leathery, strongly 5–10-ribbed, straw-coloured with** tiny, **red dots**, oblong to egg-shaped, 3–3.5 {2.8–3.9} mm long, 2 mm wide, tapered to beaks 0.4–1 mm long tipped with 2 teeth.

Habitat: Marshy ground in the prairies; elsewhere, in seepage areas, often on alkaline ground.

Notes: The name of this species has been misspelled *Carex nebraskensis*. • Nebraska sedge is named after the state of Nebraska, from which it was first described.

SAND SEDGE

Carex houghtoniana Torr.
SEDGE FAMILY (CYPERACEAE)

LK

Plants: Loosely tufted perennial herbs; **stems** rather stout, sharply triangular, **purplish at the base**, 20–60 {15–90} cm tall; from creeping, scaly underground stems (rhizomes).

Leaves: Alternate, 5–7 per stem, as long as the stems; **blades** flat, 10–20 cm long, 2–5 {10} mm wide, slender-pointed, **with rung-like cross-partitions** between the veins, very rough along the edges; sheaths loose and hairless.

Flower clusters: Elongated, 5–15 cm long, with **2–4 spikes**, with a single male spike at the tip (sometimes with a second, smaller one) and 1–3 widely spaced female spikes below; male spike 2–4 cm long; female spikes 1–4.5 cm long, 7–12 mm wide, erect, stalkless or short-stalked; **lowermost bract leaf-like**, 5–10 cm long, about as long as the flower cluster; sheathless or with a very short sheath; scales of female flowers reddish brown, shorter than the perigynia, broadly egg-shaped, pointed or tipped with a bristle (awn), translucent on the edges and green on the midvein; **3 stigmas**; {June–July}.

LK

Fruits: 3-sided seed-like fruits (achenes), enclosed in perigynia; **perigynia** dull brownish green, **strongly many-nerved, short-hairy, flattened**, egg-shaped, **5–7 mm long**, 2–2.5 mm wide, with a {1} 2 mm long beak **tipped with 2 strong teeth**; August–September.

Habitat: Dry, acidic, sandy or gravelly places in the boreal forest, often in pine woods.

Notes: The name of this species has been misspelled *Carex houghtonii* Torr. • Sand sedge could be confused with the common species woolly sedge (*Carex pellita* Muhl. *ex* Willd., also incorrectly called *Carex lanuginosa* Michx.), but woolly sedge has narrower leaves, a more bunched growth form and smaller perigynia (less than 4 mm long) with fainter ribs that are hidden by the hairs. • Sand sedge responds vigorously to disturbance by growing more rhizomes. In natural systems, it would presumably require forest fires for survival.

WJC

WJC

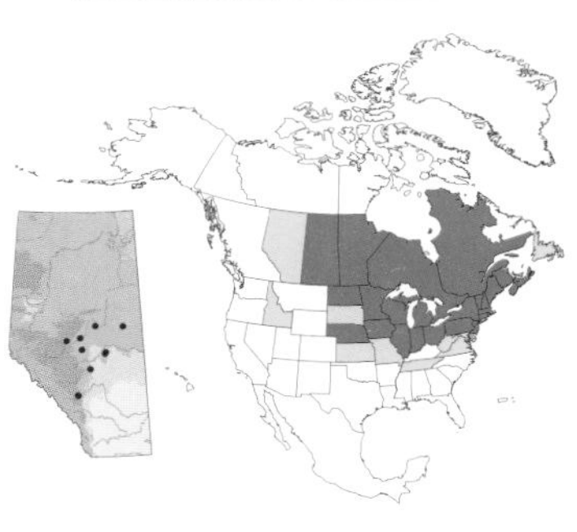

LAKESHORE SEDGE

Carex lacustris Willd.
SEDGE FAMILY (CYPERACEAE)

Plants: Tufted perennial herbs; stems stout, 50–120 {150} cm tall, 3-sided with sharp, rough edges, **conspicuously purplish-tinged at base**; from long underground stems (rhizomes).

Leaves: Usually longer than stems, up to 70 cm long, 5–15 mm wide, greyish blue to dark green with a thin, waxy coat, hairless, rough with **knobby cross-partitions** (like rungs on a ladder), bearing a **conspicuous** membranous collar (ligule) at the junction of sheath and blade; **lower sheaths bladeless, reduced to thread-like fibres with age**.

Flower clusters: Large, elongated, with about 4–6 spikes; upper 2 or 3 {1–5} spikes with male flowers only, very narrow, 1–8 cm long, 3–4 mm wide; **lower 2 or 3** {5} **spikes** with **female** flowers only, thick, cylindrical, 2–10 cm long, 10–15 mm wide, **50–100-flowered**, well separated, short-stalked (upper sometimes stalkless), mostly erect (lower spikes sometimes nodding); lowermost bract leaf-like, with a short sheath, equal to or longer than the flower cluster; scales yellowish brown with a pale green midvein and translucent edges, **about ½ as long as the perigynia**, narrowly egg-shaped, pointed or tipped with a short bristle; 3 stigmas; {May–June} July–August.

Fruits: Dry, 3-sided seed-like fruits (achenes), enclosed in perigynia; **perigynia** olive-green, cylindrical to egg-shaped, 5.5–7 {5–8} mm long, **12–25-veined, leathery**, tapered to a **short**, thick **beak** tipped **with 2 straight or slightly spreading teeth** about 0.5 mm long.

Habitat: Marshes and swampy woods of the boreal forest; elsewhere, on lakeshores.

Notes: This species has also been called *Carex riparia* Curtis var. *lacustris* (Willd.) Kuk. • The scarcity of marshes with a constant water level limits the distribution of lakeshore sedge. • Awned sedge (*Carex atherodes* Spreng.) is a common species that resembles lakeshore sedge, but its leaf sheaths are hairy and the teeth of its perigynia are larger (1.5–3 mm long) and spreading. • Lakeshore sedge is the largest of the native sedges in Alberta. • The specific epithet *lacustris* is Latin for 'of lakes' and refers to the preferred habitat of this species.

PORCUPINE SEDGE

Carex hystericina Muhl. *ex* Willd.
SEDGE FAMILY (CYPERACEAE)

WJC

Plants: Densely tufted perennial herbs; stems slender, erect, **20–70** {100} **cm tall**, sharply 3-sided, rough to the touch near the top, **reddish at the base**; from long, stout, horizontal underground stems (rhizomes).

Leaves: Thin, 3–7 per stem, 30–70 cm long, 3–8 {2–10} mm wide, flat, **often with knobby cross-partitions** (like rungs on a ladder); upper leaves **longer than stems.**

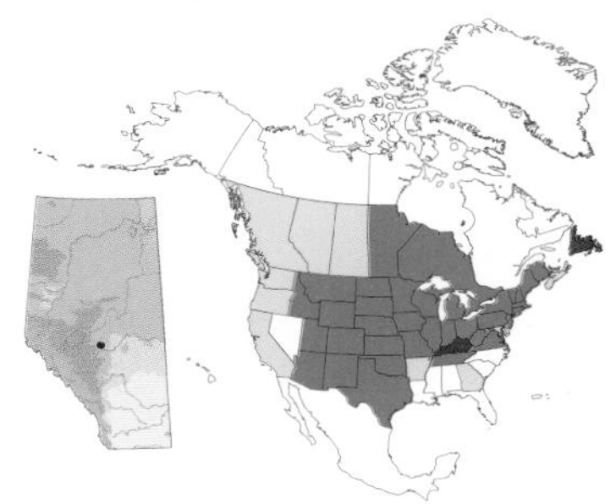

Flower clusters: Elongated, with 2–5 cylindrical spikes; uppermost spike with male flowers only, 1–5 cm long, 2.5–4 mm wide; lower **spikes** with female flowers only, 1–6 cm long, 1–1.5 cm wide, densely 100–200-flowered, **nodding slightly on long stalks** (lower spikes) to stalkless (upper spikes); lowermost bract leaf-like, sheathed, longer than the flower cluster; **scales** with small (1–2 mm), translucent bodies and **green midveins that extend past the tips as large** (2–6 mm), **broad, rough bristles;** 3 stigmas; {May–June}.

Fruits: Dry, 3-sided seed-like fruits (achenes) tipped with persistent, bony, bent or curved styles, enclosed in perigynia; **perigynia** light green, **inflated, pointing upward and slightly outward at maturity, shiny, strongly 15–20-nerved, 5–7 mm long,** 1.5–2 mm wide, narrowly egg-shaped, tapered to a **long, slender beak** tipped with 2 large (2–2.5 mm long), straight teeth; August–September.

Habitat: In heavy shade on mucky soils; elsewhere, sometimes in very open, sunny sites.

Notes: The name of this species has also been misspelled *Carex hystricina.* • Cyperus-like sedge (*Carex pseudocyperus* L., also misspelled *Carex pseudo-cyperus* L.) is a similar sedge that is also rare in swamps and marshes of Alberta. It differs from porcupine sedge most notably in having leathery, rigid perigynia that are only slightly inflated and that bend backward at maturity in 3–6 large (3–8 cm long, 8–20 mm wide) female spikes, some of which often hang on long stalks. It also has conspicuous ligules (much longer than wide) at the base of its leaf blades. Cyperus-like sedge forms large, dense clumps, 30–120 cm tall, from short, stout rhizomes. Its uppermost (male) spike is 2–6 cm long,

C. PSEUDOCYPERUS

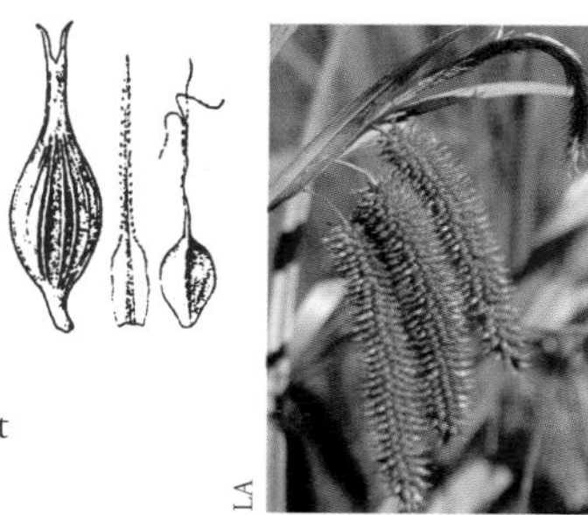
LA

3–4 mm wide and short-stalked. The 3-sided, yellowish brown perigynia are 3.5–5 {3–6} mm long, and they taper to a beak 1–2 mm long, tipped with 2 slender, slightly spreading to straight teeth. Cyperus-like sedge is reported to flower from June to July. It has a more northern distribution than porcupine sedge and is less dependent on heavy shade and mucky soils. To persist, it seems to require habitats that are relatively stable for lengthy periods.

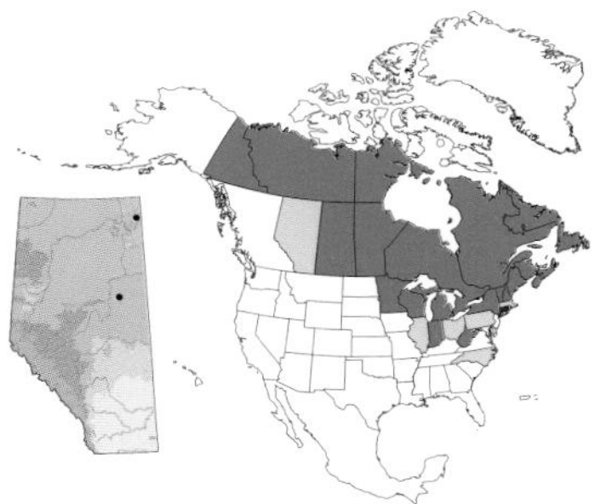

FEW-FRUITED SEDGE

Carex oligosperma Michx.
SEDGE FAMILY (CYPERACEAE)

Plants: Perennial herbs; stems slender, stiffly erect, {20} 40–100 cm tall, 3-sided with sharp, rough edges; scattered along scaly underground stems (rhizomes).

Leaves: Stiff, thread-like, **with edges rolled inward**, 40–80 cm long, about as long as the stems.

Flower clusters: Open, elongated, 6–10 cm long, with 2–4 well-spaced, stalkless (upper) to short-stalked (lower) spikes; **uppermost spike** with **male** flowers only, 1–5 cm long, **very narrow** (about 1 mm wide), erect; **lower spikes** usually with **female** flowers only (upper ones sometimes tipped with male flowers), **round to short-cylindrical**, {7} 10–20 mm long, 5–8 mm wide, **3–15-flowered**; lowermost **bract slender, stiff, longer than the flower cluster**; scales chestnut-brown with a green midvein and translucent edges, broadly egg-shaped, pointed, ½–⅔ as long as the perigynia; 3 stigmas; {June} July.

Fruits: Dry, 3-sided, round to egg-shaped seed-like fruits (achenes) tipped with a persistent **bony style**, enclosed in perigynia; **perigynia 7–10-ribbed**, shiny, yellowish green, **inflated**, pointed upward, **4–7 mm long,** broadest above the middle, narrowed to a short (1–2 mm) beak tipped with 2 short teeth.

Habitat: Wet meadows and bogs.

Notes: This species has also been called *Carex depreauxii* Steud. • Few-fruited sedge is rarely grazed by wildlife, even when abundant. Birds occasionally eat its seeds.

FEW-FLOWERED SEDGE

Carex pauciflora Lightf.
SEDGE FAMILY (CYPERACEAE)

DJ

Plants: Creeping perennial herbs; stems single or a few together, slender, stiff, curved at the base, rough above, 8–25 {40} cm tall; from long, slender underground stems (rhizomes).

Leaves: In clusters of **1–3 near the base of the stem,** shorter than the stem; blades stiff, usually rolled inward, 3–10 {15} cm long, 0.7–2 mm wide, hairless.

Flower clusters: **Narrow, solitary spikes, 7–10 mm long,** with **male flowers at the tip** and **1–6 female flowers at the base** (androgynous), bractless; **scales of female flowers** yellowish brown, with translucent edges and a greenish midvein, lance-shaped, about 5 mm long, shorter than the perigynia, **soon shed; 3 stigmas;** June–July.

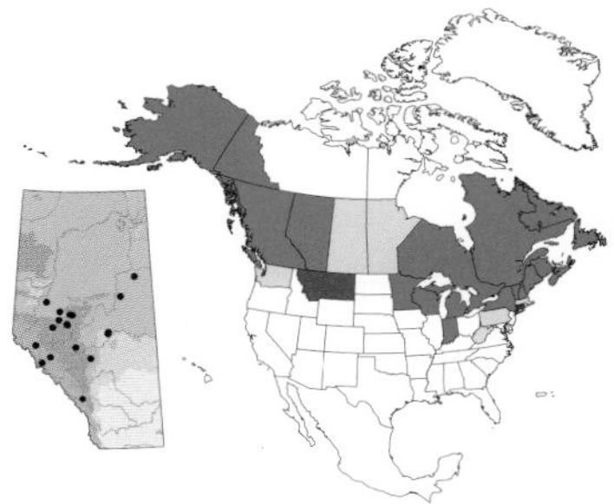

Fruits: Oblong, **3-sided** seed-like fruits (achenes), enclosed in perigynia, tipped with a firm, continuous style; **perigynia straw-coloured,** faintly nerved, the lower 1–2 mm somewhat shrunken and spongy, **short-stalked, spreading or bent backward, 6–7 mm long,** 1–1.5 mm wide, **narrowly lance-shaped, gradually tapered to a long slender beak** not well distinguished from the body.

Habitat: Sphagnum bogs.

Notes: Few-flowered sedge resembles its much commoner relative, short-awned sedge (*Carex microglochin* Wahlenb.), but short-awned sedge has smaller perigynia (4–5 mm long) and more numerous stem leaves (4–8), and its achenes have a small thread-like appendage (rachilla) attached to the base. Short-awned sedge prefers lime-rich habitats, rather than acidic bogs. • Suitable habitat for this species is widespread in the boreal forest, but with so few perigynia per spike, it may just be a slow reproducer that has not yet succeeded in re-occupying its potential range following glacial withdrawal. • The specific epithet *pauciflora*, from the Latin *paucus* (few) and *flos* (flower), means 'few-flowered,' an appropriate name for this often-inconspicuous sedge.

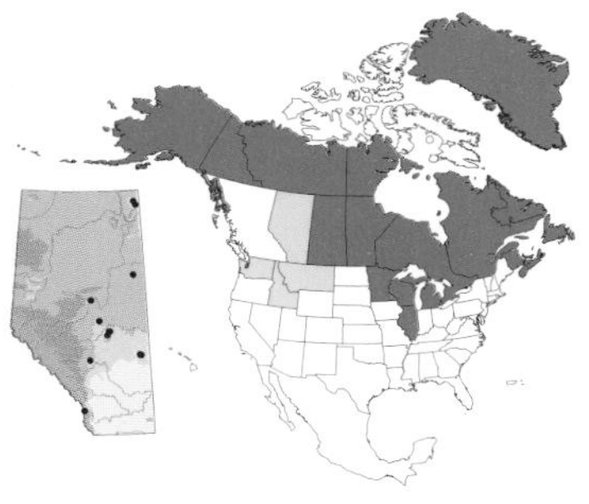

BEAKED SEDGE

Carex rostrata Stokes
SEDGE FAMILY (CYPERACEAE)

Plants: Stout, clumped perennial herbs; stems 50–100 cm tall, with spongy bases; from long, creeping underground stems (rhizomes).

Leaves: **Narrow**, 1.5–4 mm wide, **whitish or bluish with a fine, waxy powder on the upper surface** (bloom), dark green beneath; parallel **veins with thick cross-partitions** (like scattered rungs on a ladder) that appear as tiny warts when viewed under a microscope.

Flower clusters: Elongated, with 4–8 spikes; upper 2–4 spikes with male flowers only, stalked; lower 2–4 spikes with female flowers only, 4–10 cm long, stalkless or short-stalked; scales purplish brown, narrow, pointed and shorter than to slightly longer than the perigynia; 3 stigmas; {May–July} August.

Fruits: Yellowish, 3-sided seed-like fruits (achenes) tipped with bony, persistent, bent styles enclosed in the perigynia; perigynia shiny, pointing outward at maturity, veined, 4–8 mm long, egg-shaped, abruptly narrowed to a 1–2 mm long, 2-toothed beak.

Habitat: Floating fens at the edges of ponds and lakes.

Notes: Beaked sedge resembles bottle sedge (*Carex utriculata* Boott, formerly mistaken for *Carex rostrata* Stokes), but that species has broader (4–10 mm wide) leaves that lack the waxy powder found on beaked sedge plants. The cross-partitions between its veins are also finer and not wart-like. Bottle sedge is one of the most common sedges in Alberta. It grows in shallow water, often with water sedge (*Carex aquatilis* Wahlenb. var. *aquatilis*).

BLISTER SEDGE

Carex vesicaria L. var. *vesicaria*
SEDGE FAMILY (CYPERACEAE)

Plants: Tufted perennial herbs; **stems** erect, **30–100 cm tall**, 3-sided with sharp edges, rough to the touch near the top, **often reddish at the base**; from short, stout underground stems (rhizomes).

Leaves: Flat, 4–10 per stem, shorter than or as long as stems, 20–80 cm long, 2–7 {8} mm wide, **with knobby cross-partitions** (like rungs on a ladder), rough to the touch and rolled under along the edges.

Flower clusters: Elongated, with 3–7 erect, essentially stalkless spikes; upper 2–4 spikes with **male** flowers only, very narrow, 2–7 cm long, 2–4 mm wide, held well above the female spikes; **lower spikes** with **female** flowers only, 1.5–8 cm long, 5–15 mm wide, **30–100-flowered**; lowermost **bract leaf-like**, sheathless, usually **longer than the flower cluster**; scales yellowish to purplish brown with a lighter centre and translucent edges, lance-shaped to egg-shaped, pointed or tipped with a bristle, narrower and shorter than the perigynia; 3 stigmas; {June} July.

Fruits: Yellowish, 3-sided seed-like fruits {achenes) tipped with a **bony, persistent, bent style**, enclosed in perigynia; **perigynia** yellowish green to light brown, **inflated, shiny**, pointed upward at maturity, **7–20-ribbed, lance-shaped to egg-shaped, 4–8** {3–10} **mm long**, 3 mm wide, rounded at the base, gradually tapering to a **smooth, slender,** 2 {3} mm long **beak, tipped with 2 spreading teeth.**

Habitat: Swamps, marshes and shorelines.

Notes: This species has also been called *Carex inflata* Hudson, *Carex monile* Tuckerm. and *Carex raeana* Boott. • Turned sedge (*Carex retrorsa* Schwein.) is also rare in Alberta, where it grows in swampy woods and wet meadows. It is very similar to blister sedge, but its lower bracts are several times longer than their flower clusters (rather than 1–several times longer), and the perigynia at the base of its spikes bend back (downward) at maturity. Turned sedge is reported to flower from May to September. • Blister sedge has little nutritional value for livestock, but when it is abundant, it is grazed by both domestic and wild animals in the late summer and fall. It is a reasonable seed source for small birds.

C. RETRORSA

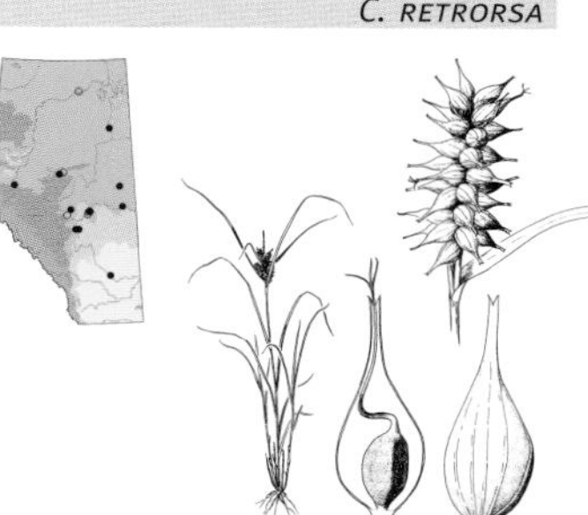

CWa

LITTLE BLUESTEM

Schizachyrium scoparium (Michx.) Nash ssp. *scoparium*
GRASS FAMILY (POACEAE [GRAMINEAE])

Plants: Densely tufted perennial herbs; stems wiry, erect or ascending, 20–60 {150} cm tall, often purplish, branched near the top; forming clumps from short, scaly underground stems (rhizomes).

Leaves: Alternate, light green to blue-green, usually with a whitish bloom; blades **2–5** {8} **mm wide**, flat or folded; ligules 1–1.5 mm long, finely hairy; **sheaths flattened, with a strong vertical ridge** (keel), usually **hairless.**

Flower clusters: Simple or branched (**panicles**), purplish, with **1–few, 2–5** {6} **cm long, arching, spike-like racemes,** on stalks that are often enfolded by the upper leaf; central axis of each raceme (rachis) white-hairy, loosely zigzagged, **breaking apart** above a cupped structure at each joint (node); **spikelets 2-flowered**, borne **in pairs**, each with a **stalkless,** {6} **7–9 mm long, fertile spikelet** and a **stalked, 4–5 mm long, sterile spikelet** with leathery, narrow, 5–10 mm long glumes and small, narrow and leathery lemmas; lemmas of fertile spikelets papery, tipped with a bent, 7–15 mm long bristle (awn) from between 2 small teeth; {July–August}.

Fruits: Grains; mature florets breaking free below the glumes, retaining a small, hairy segment that was part of the main stalk (rachis) of the flower cluster.

Habitat: Prairie grassland; elsewhere, in foothills; usually on calcareous soils.

Notes: This species has also been called *Schizachyrium scoparium* (Michx.) Nash var. *scoparium* and *Andropogon scoparius* Michx. • Little bluestem is an important prairie grass of the true prairie of central North America. In the west, it is usually restricted to areas with high water tables that can provide adequate moisture.

HOT-SPRINGS MILLET, THERMAL MILLET

Panicum acuminatum Swartz
GRASS FAMILY (POACEAE [GRAMINEAE])

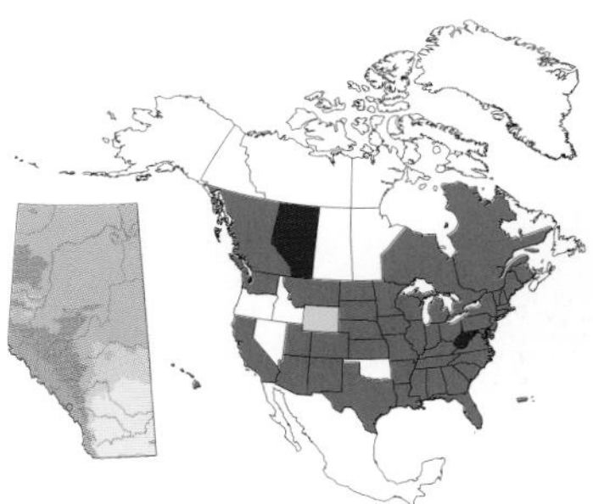

Plants: Densely **tufted or matted, velvety-hairy**, greyish green perennial herbs, with 3 distinct seasonal phases; **winter phase a rosette** of short leaves; spring phase with unbranched stems producing sterile flower clusters; **autumn phase with widely spreading, repeatedly branching stems forming cushions**; stems 10–30 {100} cm tall, ascending or spreading, densely hairy at the joints (nodes); lacking underground stems (rhizomes).

Leaves: Basal and alternate; blades thick, flat, 5–12 mm wide; **ligules** reduced to a ring of **conspicuous hairs, 3 {5} mm long.**

Flower clusters: Open to contracted panicles, 3–6 {16} cm long; autumn panicles usually enfolded in upper leaf sheaths; **spikelets long-stalked, about 2 mm long, 2-flowered**, the **upper flower** with male and female parts (perfect) and the **lower one sterile or** with **male** parts only (staminate); lower glume tiny; **upper glume membranous, hairy**, about equal to the lower lemma; lemmas hairy; **upper lemma small, shiny, tightly rolled inward**; June {July–August}.

Fruits: Grains; mature florets breaking off below the glumes.

Habitat: Marshy places, around hot springs; elsewhere, on moist, sandy soil at woodland edges.

Notes: This species has also been called *Dichanthelium acuminatum* (Swartz) Gould & Clark var. *acuminatum* and *Panicum thermale* Boland (in the first edition of the *Flora of Alberta*).

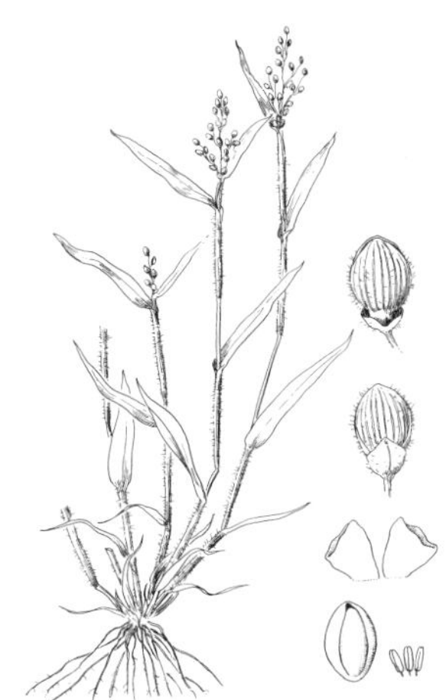

LEIBERG'S MILLET

Panicum leibergii (Vasey) Scribn.
GRASS FAMILY (POACEAE [GRAMINEAE])

Plants: Tufted perennial herbs, with 3 distinct seasonal phases; **winter phase a rosette of short leaves**; spring phase with sterile flower clusters; **autumn phase with a few erect branches from middle and lower joints** (nodes); stems solitary or clustered, erect or ascending, abruptly bent near the base, 30–60 {70} cm tall, silky or rough-hairy.

Leaves: Basal and alternate, **covered with tiny, nipple-shaped bumps and coarse, spreading hairs** (sometimes almost hairless on the upper surface); blades flat, 7–11 cm long, 7–12 {6–15} mm wide; ligules reduced to a ring of hairs scarcely 0.5 mm long; sheaths separate (not overlapping).

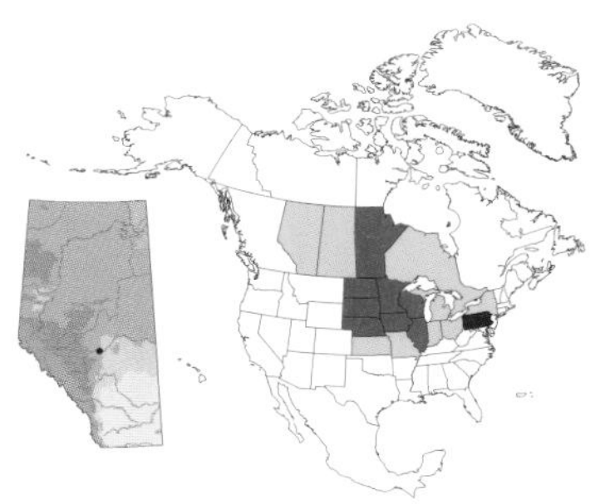

Flower clusters: Contracted panicles, often somewhat enclosed in the upper leaf sheath, 5–10 {15} cm long, with ascending branches; **spikelets 2-flowered, 3–4 mm long**, with long, soft, spreading hairs, the **upper flower with male and female parts** (perfect) and the **lower one sterile or** with **male** parts only (staminate); lower glume 1.6–2.5 mm long; **upper glume membranous, hairy**, about equal to the lower lemma; lemmas hairy; **upper lemma small, shiny, tightly rolled inward**; {June–July}.

Fruits: Grains; mature florets breaking off below the glumes.

Habitat: Dry, sandy soil in grasslands and open woods.

Notes: This species has also been called *Dichanthelium leibergii* (Vasey) Freckman. • Leiberg's millet is also rare in much of Canada and the eastern United States. • Another rare species, sand millet (*Panicum wilcoxianum* Vasey, also called *Dichanthelium wilcoxianum* (Vasey) Freckman, *Panicum oligosanthes* Schultes and *Dichanthelium oligosanthes* (Schultes) Gould var. *wilcoxianum* (Vasey) Gould & Clark), differs from Leiberg's millet in having even smaller lower glumes (up to 1.5 mm long), shorter spikelets (2.7–3 mm long) and shorter flowering stalks (10–35 cm tall) with overlapping leaf sheaths and mostly hidden panicles. Its ligules are longer (1–1.5 mm), and its autumn phase is bushier, with many branches from the nodes and with tufts of overlapping reduced leaves. Sand millet grows in dry, open areas and is reported to produce fertile flowers in June and July.

P. WILCOXIANUM

RED THREE-AWN

Aristida purpurea Nutt. var. *longiseta* (Steud.) Vasey
GRASS FAMILY (POACEAE [GRAMINEAE])

Plants: Tufted perennial herbs, rough with short, stiff hairs; stems stiff, 20–30 {15–40} cm tall; often in large bunches, from fibrous roots.

Leaves: Alternate, mainly near the stem base, strongly rolled inward, 7–25 cm long, up to 1 {2} mm wide, often curved, very rough to touch; ligules membranous, fringed with short hairs, 0.5 mm long.

Flower clusters: **Narrow panicles**, 4–8 {10} cm long, few-flowered, **branches loosely ascending**, turning red {purple} when mature; **spikelets stalked, single-flowered**; glumes unequal, the lower one 8–10 {7–13} mm long, the upper one 16–20 {14–25} mm long; **lemmas hardened**, 10–15 mm long, cylindrical, slightly narrowed at the tip and with **3 similar, spreading bristles** (awns), each 4–8 cm long and rough at the tip; {July}.

Fruits: Grains, **tightly enfolded by hardened lemmas**; mature florets breaking off above the glumes; August–September.

Habitat: Dry, sandy plains.

Notes: This is the only *Aristida* species in Alberta. It has also been called *Aristida longiseta* Steud. • The generic name *Aristida* comes from the Latin *arista* (awn). The specific epithet *longiseta* was taken from the Latin *longus* (long) and *seta* (a stiff hair), in reference to the conspicuous, long bristles (awns). • The rough awns and the sharp points of the lemmas can injure the mouth and nostrils of grazing animals. • Red three-awn is intolerant of temperatures below 10°C at sunrise during the growing season, and therefore it is confined to warm, dry sites.

JL

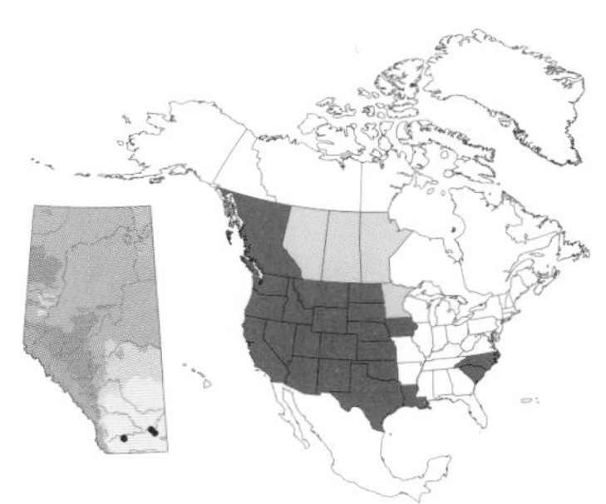

JG

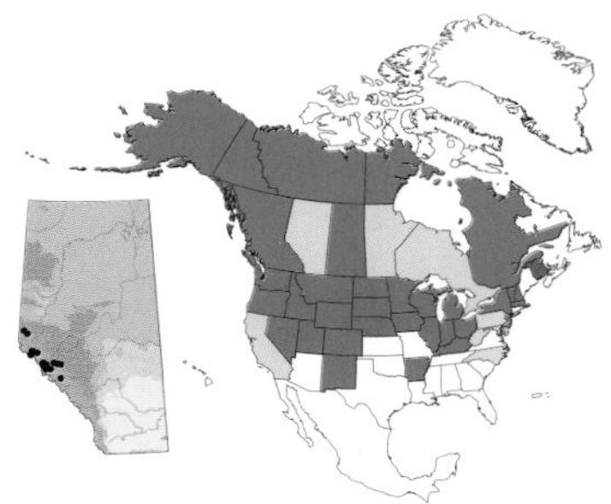

ALPINE SWEETGRASS

Anthoxanthum monticola (Bigelow) Y. Schouten & Veldkamp
GRASS FAMILY (POACEAE [GRAMINEAE])

Plants: Tufted, **sweet-smelling** perennial herbs, with leafy shoots at base; stems 10–40 cm tall, hairless; from short underground stems (rhizomes).

Leaves: Mostly basal, rolled inward, 1–2 mm wide, hairy on the upper (ventral) surface, hairless on the lower (dorsal) surface; stem leaves wider, less than 10 cm long; **ligules less than 1 mm long, ½ consisting of a fringe of hairs**; sheaths purplish, hairless.

Flower clusters: Narrow, bronze-coloured panicles 2–4 {1.5–4.5} cm long with short, ascending branches; **spikelets** tawny, {5} 6–8 mm long, **3-flowered**, with **2 male florets at the base** and a fertile (**male and female**) **floret at the tip; glumes about as long as the florets,** 5–7 {8} mm long, egg-shaped, thin and shiny; fertile lemmas hairy near the tip, pointed; **male lemmas** 5 mm long, hairy along the edges and **tipped with a bristle** (awn) **from between 2 teeth**; awn of the lowest floret straight and 2–4 mm long; awn of the second floret twisted and 5–8 mm long; June–August.

Fruits: Grains; mature florets breaking away above the glumes and between the florets; August.

Habitat: Dry alpine slopes; elsewhere, on dry, acidic peat and rocky tundra and outcrops.

Notes: This species has also been called *Hierochloe alpina* (Swartz *ex* Willd.) Roem. & Schult. • Alpine sweetgrass is similar to the more widespread common sweetgrass or holygrass (*Hierochloe odorata* (L.) Beauv.), but common sweetgrass usually grows at lower elevations, and it has longer ligules (1–2 mm long) which are almost entirely membranous, pyramid-shaped panicles (with spreading branches) and pointed (not awned) lemmas. • Sometimes germination of the seed occurs before the grains are dropped, and small plantlets develop in the panicle. • Common sweetgrass was widely used in ancient religious ceremonies, and it is still used in spiritual rituals by many native peoples in North America.

LITTLE RICE GRASS

Oryzopsis exigua Thurb.
GRASS FAMILY (POACEAE [GRAMINEAE])

Plants: Densely tufted perennial herbs; stems hollow, stiffly erect, 10–30 {35} cm tall, rough to touch; from fibrous roots.

Leaves: Alternate; blades erect, **thread-like, rolled inward,** 5–10 cm long; ligules pointed, 3–4 mm long, with tiny hairs on the outer surface; sheaths smooth or minutely roughened.

Flower clusters: Slender panicles, 3–6 cm long, with stiffly erect **branches pressed to the main stalk; spikelets single-flowered, plump;** glumes similar, about as long as the lemma, 4–6 mm long, broad, pointed (sometimes blunt-tipped), faintly 3–5-nerved; **lemmas firm, curled tightly around the developing grain** and over the palea, **4 mm long, covered with flat-lying hairs,** tipped with a **simple, twisted bristle** (awn) **4–6 mm long** from between 2 small lobes; anthers 1.5–2 mm long; {June–August}.

Fruits: Grains; mature florets breaking away above the glumes and between the florets.

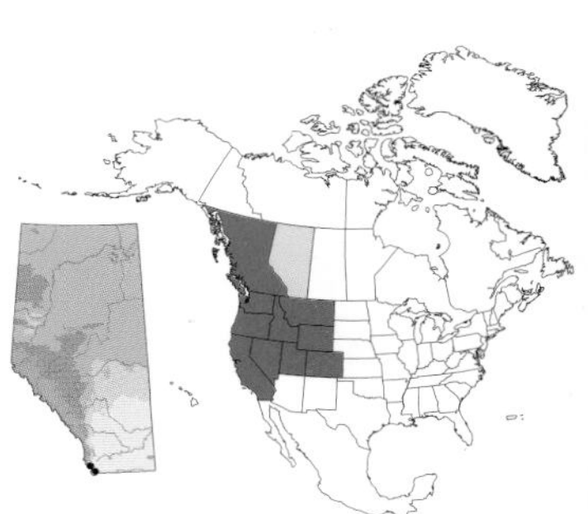

Habitat: Dry subalpine slopes or open woods, usually on sandy and rocky soil.

Notes: Another rare Alberta species, Canadian rice grass (*Oryzopsis canadensis* (Poir.) Torr.), resembles little rice grass but has large (5–10 cm long), more open flower clusters and dark, hairy lemmas with long (6–12 mm) twisted bristles (awns). Canadian rice grass grows in open woods and on hillsides away from the mountains. • Both of these species could be mistaken for their widespread relative, northern rice grass (*Oryzopsis pungens* (Torr.) A.S. Hitchc.), but northern rice grass is usually a taller plant (up to 50 cm tall) and its lemmas have tiny (0.5–2 mm long), inconspicuous bristles (awns) from blunt (not notched) tips. • The specific epithet *exigua* is Latin for 'small, short or meagre,' a reference to the small stature of this species.

O. CANADENSIS

LITTLE-SEED RICE GRASS

Oryzopsis micrantha (Trin. & Rupr.) Thurb.
GRASS FAMILY (POACEAE [GRAMINEAE])

Plants: Densely tufted perennial herbs; stems hollow, erect, 30–80 cm tall, smooth; from fibrous roots.

Leaves: Alternate; blades erect, **thread-like, usually rolled inward**, 1–2 mm wide; ligules squared or shorter in the middle, 0.5–1 mm long, fringed with tiny hairs; sheaths smooth or with fine, short hairs.

Flower clusters: Erect or nodding, rather **open panicles, 5–15** {20} **cm long**, with spreading to erect branches; **spikelets single-flowered, plump**, borne near the branch tips; glumes similar, slightly longer than the lemma, 2–3 {4} mm long, pointed, broad, papery, 5-nerved, hairless or minutely roughened; **lemmas** eventually **curled tightly around the grain** and over the palea, **hairless** (or nearly so), **1.8–2.8 mm long**, tipped with a **simple, straight or weakly twisted bristle** (awn) **4–11 mm long**; anthers barely 1.5 mm long; {June–July}.

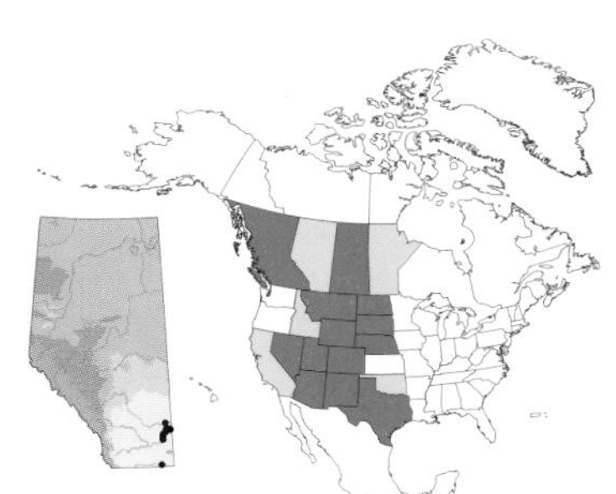

Fruits: Grains; mature florets breaking away above the glumes and between the florets.

Habitat: Dry open slopes, often on rocky ground; elsewhere, in open woods.

Notes: Little-seed rice grass is distinguished from similar species by its hairless lemmas. • The generic name *Oryzopsis*, from the Latin *oryza* (rice) and *opsis* (like), and the common name 'rice grass' both refer to the similarity between these grasses and rice (*Oryza sativa*). The specific epithet *micrantha*, from the Greek *mikros* (small) and *anthos* (flower), refers to the small spikelets of this species.

MARSH MUHLY

Muhlenbergia racemosa (Michx.) BSP.
GRASS FAMILY (POACEAE [GRAMINEAE])

ES

Plants: Perennial herbs; **stems** 30–60 cm tall, slightly flattened, hollow, **hairy at the joints** (nodes) and **smooth and shiny in between**, often branching above; from creeping, scaly, branched underground stems (rhizomes).

Leaves: Alternate on the stem; blades flat, 2–7 mm wide, erect to ascending; **ligules 0.6–1.5** {3} **mm long**, blunt, membranous; **sheaths with a lengthwise ridge on the back** (keel), loose.

Flower clusters: Dense, spike-like panicles, 3–7 {2.5–14} cm long, 5–15 mm wide, with branches tightly pressed against the stem; **spikelets short-stalked, single-flowered**, 5–6 mm long, green (sometimes purplish); **glumes narrow, tipped with long bristles** (awns) equal to or longer than the body, {4} 5–6.5 mm long (including awns); **lemmas hairy on the lower half**, 2.5–3.5 mm long, 3-nerved, gradually **tapered to slender bristles (awns); anthers 0.4–0.8 mm long**; {late July–August}.

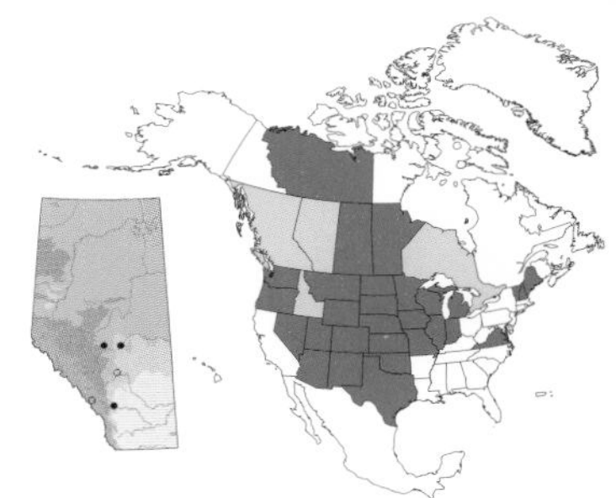

Fruits: Grains; mature florets breaking away above the glumes and between the florets; August–September.

Habitat: Dry sand hills, slopes and eroded banks; elsewhere, in a wide variety of habitats including prairies, meadows, streambanks, edges of woodland, dry rocky slopes and waste ground.

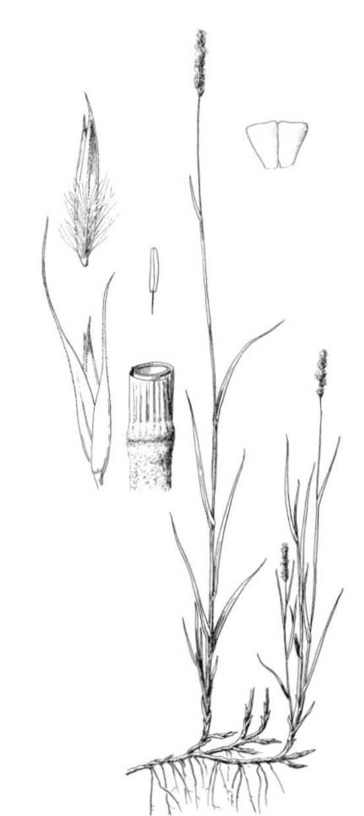

Notes: Marsh muhly is easily confused with the more common bog muhly (*Muhlenbergia glomerata* (Willd.) Trin.), which is usually found in wet sites such as fens and marly shores, but can also grow near ephemeral springs that become dry in summer. However, the stems of bog muhly are hairy and dull between the joints (nodes) and slightly more slender and the leaf sheaths are only slightly ridged. Bog muhly has shorter ligules (0.2–0.6 mm) and longer anthers (0.8–1.5 mm), and its lemmas are hairy almost to the tip. • Another rare species, scratch grass (*Muhlenbergia asperifolia* (Nees & Meyen *ex* Trin.) Parodi), is the only species of the genus in Alberta with open, diffuse panicles (about as long as wide) that break away at maturity. Scratch grass is the main host of the smut fungus *Tilletia asperifolii* Ell. & Ev. When this fungus infects the grass, its spore clusters replace the ovary, eventually releasing a

M. ASPERIFOLIA

JL

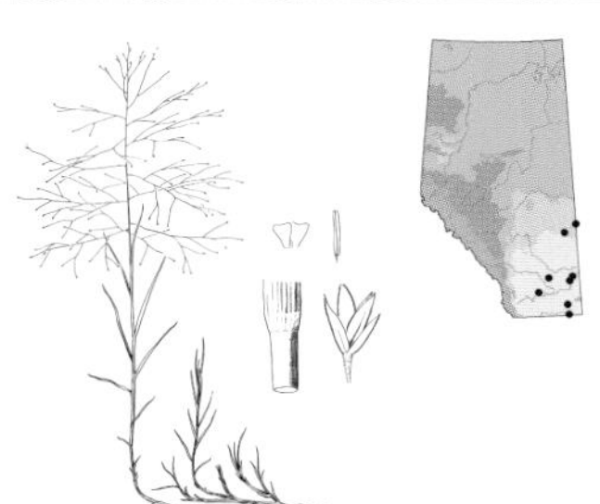

dark-coloured mass of spores. • The muhlys are considered warm-season grasses, growing most rapidly during the warmest part of the year, when many other grasses become senescent.

ES

ALPINE FOXTAIL

Alopecurus alpinus J.E. Smith
GRASS FAMILY (POACEAE [GRAMINEAE])

Plants: Coarse perennial herbs; **stems hairless,** 10–80 cm tall, rather **stiff and erect** (sometimes with bases spreading on the ground); from **slender, creeping underground stems** (rhizomes).

Leaves: Alternate, **few**; blades flat, 3–5 {6} mm wide, rough to touch; ligules squared, 1–3 mm long, irregular or finely torn along the upper edge; **sheaths** often **inflated**, hairless.

Flower clusters: Woolly, often purplish, spike-like panicles, oblong to egg-shaped, **1–4 cm long**, about 1 cm wide, with dense, short-stalked spikelets; **spikelets single-flowered,** flattened; glumes silky to woolly, 3–4 mm long, slightly longer than the lemmas; lemmas 5-nerved, with a **bristle** (awn) **attached on the back near the base and sticking out** about 2–3 mm past the glumes; anthers 0.3–0.4 mm long; June–August.

Fruits: Grains; mature florets breaking free below the glumes.

Habitat: Shores and open woodland; elsewhere, in moist to wet montane, subalpine and alpine areas.

Notes: This species has also been called *Alopecurus occidentalis* Scribn. & Tweedy and *Alopecurus borealis* Trin. • The fuzzy spikelets catch on the fur of passing animals, and in the arctic, plants are often found growing around the burrows of ground squirrels and the dens of foxes and wolves. • The generic name *Alopecurus* was derived from the Greek *alopex* (fox) and *oura* (tail), because the fuzzy flower clusters of some species were likened to the tails of foxes.

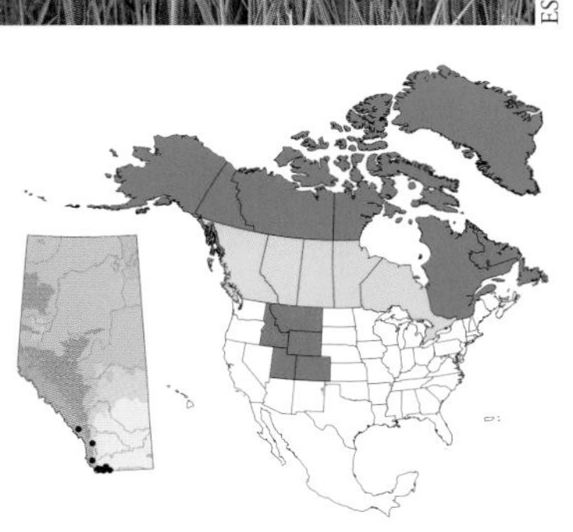

POLAR GRASS

Arctagrostis arundinacea (Trin.) Beal
GRASS FAMILY (POACEAE [GRAMINEAE])

Plants: Coarse perennial herbs; stems 40–100 {25–150} cm tall, single or tufted; from trailing stems (stolons).

Leaves: Alternate; blades 5–20 cm long, 4–10 {2–15} mm wide, flat or rolled inward; ligules prominent.

Flower clusters: Open, pyramidal panicles, 10–20 {25} cm long; **spikelets** purplish (sometimes green to brownish), 3–4 mm long, **single-flowered, stalked**; glumes unequal, shorter than the lemma, pointed; **lemmas awnless**, 3-nerved, densely covered with tiny, bristly hairs; paleas resembling lemmas; anthers 1.3–4 mm long.

Fruits: Grains; mature florets **breaking off below the glumes**.

Habitat: Marshy ground and moist meadows; elsewhere, in damp turfy tundra, heathland and open woodland.

Notes: This species has also been called *Arctagrostis latifolia* (R. Br.) Griseb. ssp. *arundinacea* (Trin.) Griseb. • Because this is a highly variable species, as many as 5 subspecies have been proposed, but comparisons of morphology and chromosome number do not support these separations.

LK

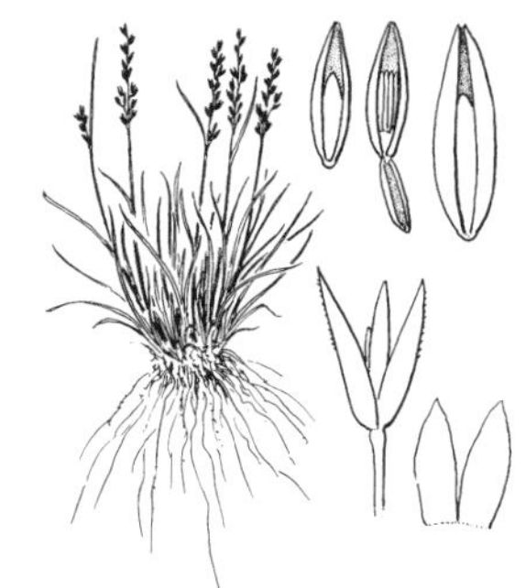

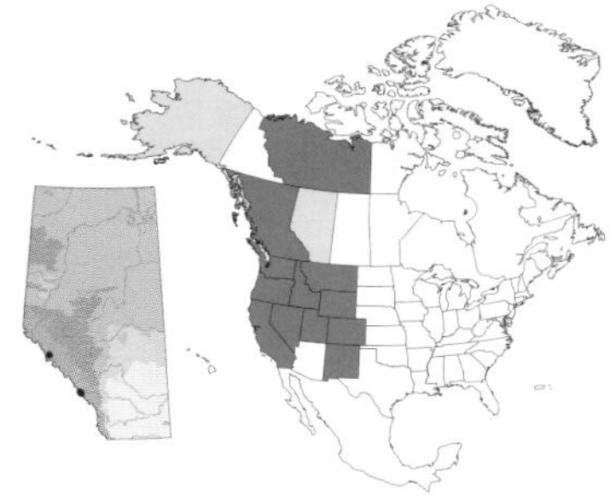

LOW BENT GRASS

Agrostis humilis Vasey
GRASS FAMILY (POACEAE [GRAMINEAE])

Plants: Tufted perennial herbs; **stems 5–15 cm tall; without spreading underground stems** (rhizomes).

Leaves: Crowded at the base, **thread-like**; blades less than 1 mm wide, hairless; **ligules membranous, 0.5–1 mm** long, blunt.

Flower clusters: Narrow panicles, 1–3 cm long and less than 5 mm wide; branches flattened, strongly ascending; **spikelets** deep purple, **stalked, single-flowered, 2–3 mm long; glumes and lemma about equal** in length; **lemmas awnless; palea clearly visible**, ⅔–¾ as long as the lemma; **axis of the spikelet** (rachilla) **not prolonged past the palea or very tiny**; callus hairless; anthers 0.6–0.7 mm long; {July} August–September.

Fruits: Grains; mature florets breaking off above the glumes.

Habitat: Moist meadows and streambanks in alpine areas.

Notes: This species has also been called *Podagrostis humilis* (Vasey) Björkm. • Another rare Alberta species of moist alpine sites, Thurber's bent grass (*Agrostis thurberiana* A.S. Hitch.), differs from low bent grass in that the axis of each spikelet (rachilla) projects from the base of the palea as a tiny (0.1–0.3 mm) bristle. Thurber's bent grass is generally taller (10–40 cm), with longer (5–7 {3–10} cm), looser (often nodding) flower clusters and tufts of flat, relatively wide (about 2 mm) leaves, from short underground stems (rhizomes). It grows in moist alpine areas and flowers in July and August. These species sometimes hybridize. • A small (2–15 cm tall) arctic-alpine grass, frigid phippsia (*Phippsia algida* (Sol.) R. Br.) has also been reported to occur in Alberta. Like low bent grass, frigid phippsia has single-flowered spikelets in small, narrow clusters, but their glumes are tiny and much shorter than the lemmas. Frigid phippsia grows on wet alpine slopes and river flats.

A. THURBERIANA

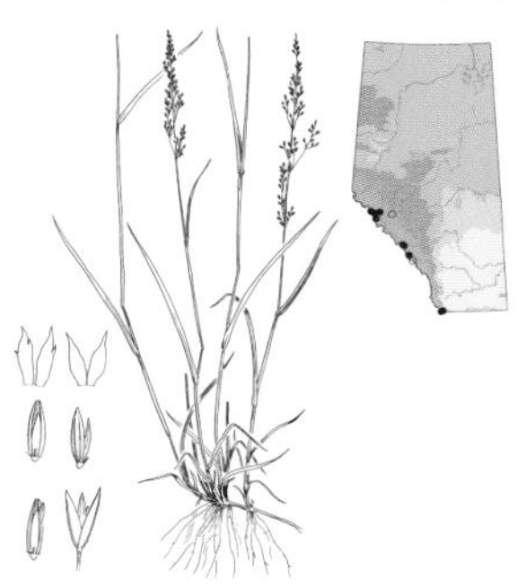

PHIPPSIA ALGIDA

PL

NORTHERN BENT GRASS

Agrostis mertensii Trin.
GRASS FAMILY (POACEAE [GRAMINEAE])

Plants: Densely tufted, dwarf perennial herbs; stems 10–20 {4–40} cm tall; **without underground stems** (rhizomes).

Leaves: Mostly basal; dark green, smooth, erect; blades 0.2–2 {3} mm wide, **usually rolled inward**; ligules 1–2 mm long, blunt, with an irregular edge.

Flower clusters: Open, pyramid-shaped panicles, 1–14 cm long; **spikelets** purplish, 2–3 {4} mm long, single-flowered, **at tips of long, forked, smooth branches** (none at the base); glumes with a rough ridge (keel) on the back, almost equal, slightly longer than the lemma; **lemmas** rough-hairy, **with a bent** or sometimes straight bristle (awn), {1} 3–6 mm long near the middle of the back and sticking out from the spikelet; **paleas inconspicuous or absent**; {July–August}.

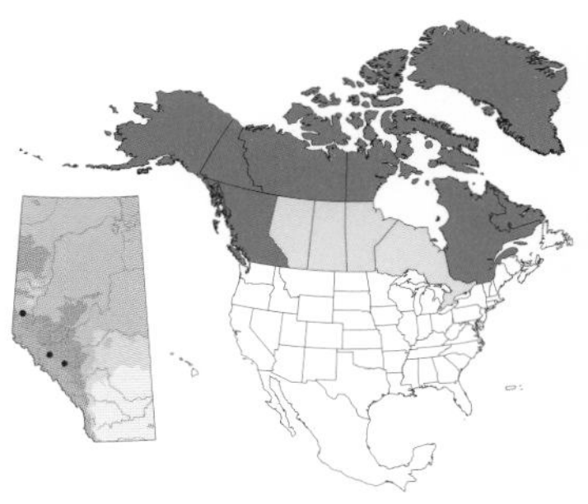

Fruits: Grains; mature florets breaking off above the glumes; August.

Habitat: Moist alpine slopes; usually in areas that hold snow late in the growing season.

Notes: This species has also been called *Agrostis borealis* Hartm. • Another rare species, spike redtop (*Agrostis exarata* Trin.), may be found in habitats similar to those of northern bent grass, but spike redtop is a larger grass (20–100 cm tall) with wider (2–6 mm), flat leaves, longer (2–6 mm) ligules and narrower panicles in which some branches bear spikelets to near their base. It is reported to flower from late June to August.

A. EXARATA

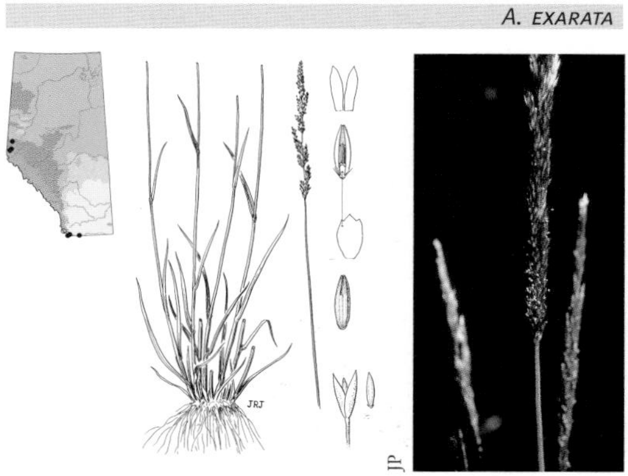

LAPLAND REED GRASS

Calamagrostis lapponica (Wahl.) Hartm.
GRASS FAMILY (POACEAE [GRAMINEAE])

Plants: Loosely tufted perennial herbs; **stems** slender, erect, 30–60 {80} cm tall, **smooth** (sometimes slightly rough just below the panicle), with **2–3 joints** (nodes); from short, thin underground stems (rhizomes).

Leaves: Alternate; blades short, flat or strongly rolled inward, 2–3 {1–4} mm wide, rough to the touch toward the tip; **ligules membranous, 0.5–3 {5} mm long**; sheaths smooth.

Flower clusters: Narrow, soft panicles, often **purplish,** {4} 5–10 (rarely to 15) cm long, 1–2 cm wide, with ascending branches; **spikelets stalked, single-flowered**; glumes purplish, turning bronze, slightly shiny, 4–5.5 mm long; **lemma slightly shorter than the glumes**, 3.5–5 mm long, **with a short, straight bristle** (awn) **from the middle and a conspicuous tuft of white hairs** (callus hairs) **from the base**; callus hairs abundant, of various lengths, the longest **equalling or surpassing the lemma**; August.

Fruits: Grains; mature florets breaking off above the glumes.

Habitat: Moist to dry, gravelly alpine slopes and ridges; elsewhere, on stable dunes and on peaty soil in open heath or muskeg.

Notes: Populations of this species in Alberta are widely separated (disjunct) from more widespread northern populations. • The spikelets of Lapland reed grass resemble those of bluejoint (*Calamagrostis canadensis* (Michx.) Beauv.), but the flower clusters of bluejoint are larger and more open (10–20 cm long and at least 2 cm wide), the callus hairs are fairly equal in length, and the stems are usually taller (60–120 cm) with 5 or 6 joints. • Northern reed grass (*Calamagrostis inexpansa* A. Gray, also called *Calamagrostis stricta* (Timm) Koeler ssp. *inexpansa* (A. Gray) C.W. Greene) and narrow reed grass (*Calamagrostis stricta* (Timm) Koeler) are also very similar, but northern reed grass has very rough stems (sandpapery with stiff hairs) and longer (4–7 mm) ligules, and narrow reed grass has smaller (2–3 mm long) glumes and relatively short callus hairs. • Lapland reed grass is also considered rare in Saskatchewan and Ontario. • The generic name *Calamagrostis* was taken from the Greek *calamus* (reed) and *agrostis* (grass).

SLENDER HAIR GRASS

Deschampsia elongata (Hook.) Munro *ex* Benth.
GRASS FAMILY (POACEAE [GRAMINEAE])

Plants: Densely tufted perennial herbs; stems slender, erect, {10} 30–100 cm tall; from fibrous roots.

Leaves: Mainly basal, a few alternate, soft; blades flat or folded, **1–1.5 mm wide** on the stem, **thread-like** at the base and usually only 2–4 cm long; ligules pointed, 3–9 mm long, finely hairy; sheaths usually hairless, sometimes slightly rough to touch.

Flower clusters: Pale green or purplish, shiny, narrow panicles, {5} 10–30 cm long, with slender, ascending branches; **spikelets 2-flowered, stalked,** pressed to the main branch; **glumes** similar, equal to or **longer than the lemmas,** {3} 4–6 mm long, **thin,** 3-nerved, ridged down the back (keeled), slender-pointed; **lemmas** thin, shiny, squared and torn at the tip, 2–3 mm long **with a straight, 3–5 mm long bristle** (awn) **attached at or below the middle and a tuft of stiff hairs at the base;** {June–July}.

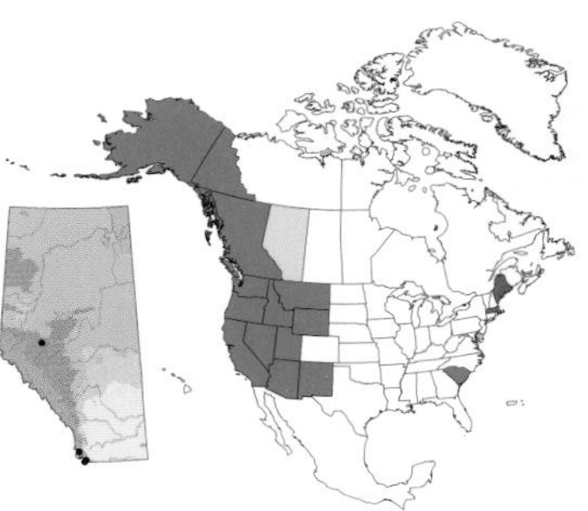

Fruits: Grains; mature florets breaking free above the glumes and between the florets.

Habitat: Meadows and open slopes; elsewhere, on sandy or gravelly slopes by streams and lakes and occasionally in woods.

Notes: This genus was named in honour of L.A. Deschamps, a French botanist who lived 1774–1849. The specific epithet *elongata* refers to the narrow, elongated flower clusters.

NODDING TRISETUM

Trisetum cernuum Trin.
GRASS FAMILY (POACEAE [GRAMINEAE])

Plants: Loosely tufted perennial herbs; stems 50–100 {120} cm tall, hairless, somewhat lax; from fibrous roots.

Leaves: Mostly basal; blades flat, lax, 5–10 {7–12} mm wide, with thin, prominent tips, rough to the touch to soft-hairy; ligules 1.5–3 {4} mm long, irregularly cut; **sheaths split down 1 side** (open), hairy.

Flower clusters: Open, loose panicles, often nodding, 15–25 {10–30} cm long, with slender branches bearing spikelets mainly near the ends; **spikelets 3 {2–5}-flowered,** usually with 3 fertile florets (with both male and female parts) and sometimes with 1 or 2 small, sterile florets above these; **glumes shorter than the lowest floret**, unequal, with a narrow, 1–2 {4} mm long lower glume, and a broader, 3.5–4 {6} mm long upper glume; **lemmas 5–6** {7} **mm long,** faintly 5-nerved, tipped with 2 slender teeth, **bearing a curved or bent, 5–10** {14} **mm long bristle** (awn) **on the upper back** and a tuft of short, **stiff hairs at the base** (bearded) and on the stalk; {May–July}.

Fruits: Grains; mature florets breaking off above the glumes and between the florets.

Habitat: Moist woods; elsewhere, also on banks of lakes and streams.

T. MONTANUM

Notes: This species includes 2 varieties (var. *canescens* (Buckl.) Beal and var. *cernuum*), and it has also been called *Trisetum canescens* Buckl. (in part). • A similar grass, mountain trisetum (*Trisetum montanum* Vasey, sometimes considered a variety of *Trisetum cernuum*), is distinguished by its hairless grains, and its denser flower clusters, with branches bearing spikelets almost to their bases (rather than just near the tips). This rare Alberta species grows in moist, shady sites and flowers from July to August.

Wolf's trisetum

Trisetum wolfii Vasey
GRASS FAMILY (POACEAE [GRAMINEAE])

Plants: Loosely tufted perennial herbs; stems {40} 50–100 cm tall; from fibrous roots, sometimes with short underground stems (rhizomes) also.

Leaves: Mostly basal; blades flat, **2–4** {6} **mm wide**, rough to touch (rarely hairy); ligules 2.5–4 mm long, blunt, irregularly cut, fringed with hairs; sheaths split down 1 side (open), short-hairy to long-hairy.

Flower clusters: Narrow, erect panicles, 8–15 cm long, fairly dense with short, ascending branches; **spikelets 2** {3}**-flowered, green or purplish; glumes usually equalling or longer than the upper florets**, with the lower glume 4–6 {6.5} mm long and the **upper glume 5.5–7 mm long; lemmas 4–5** {6} **mm long**, ridged on the back (keeled), **with a few stiff hairs at the base** and many long hairs on the floret stalk (rachilla), blunt-tipped, **awnless** or with a very small awn (less than 2 mm long) on the upper back hidden by the glumes; anthers 1.5 mm long; {June} July–August.

Fruits: Hairy grains; mature florets breaking away above the glumes.

Habitat: Moist meadows and woodlands in the southern Rocky Mountains; elsewhere, in wet meadows and along streams in the mountains.

Notes: Wolf's trisetum might be mistaken for a depauperate June grass (*Koeleria macrantha* (Ledeb.) J.E. Schultes), but June grass has smaller ligules (usually about 0.5–2 mm long), its florets do not have conspicuous, stiff hairs at their bases and on their stalks, and its glumes reach only to the tip of the lowest lemma. • The generic name *Trisetum* is from the Latin *tres* (three) and *seta* (bristle), in reference to the 3 bristles characteristic of the lemmas of Old World species of this genus.

POVERTY OAT GRASS

Danthonia spicata (L.) Beauv. *ex* R. & S.
GRASS FAMILY (POACEAE [GRAMINEAE])

Plants: Tufted perennial herbs; stems slender, {10} 20–70 cm tall; without underground stems (rhizomes).

Leaves: Mostly basal; blades up to 18 cm long, straight to curled, usually rolled inward, thread-like, hairless to sparsely hairy; **ligules reduced to a ring of hairs**, 0.5 mm long; sheaths with a tuft of long hairs at the throat.

Flower clusters: Panicles 2–5 cm long; branches erect, with 1 or 2 spikelets; **spikelets stalked, 3–8-flowered; glumes 9–12 mm long**, broad, papery, longer than the lower lemmas; **lemmas 3.5–5 mm long, sparsely hairy across the back**, tipped with a **bristle** (awn) **from between 2 slender, pointed teeth**; awns 5–8 {9} mm long, tightly twisted at the base (especially when dry); {June} July.

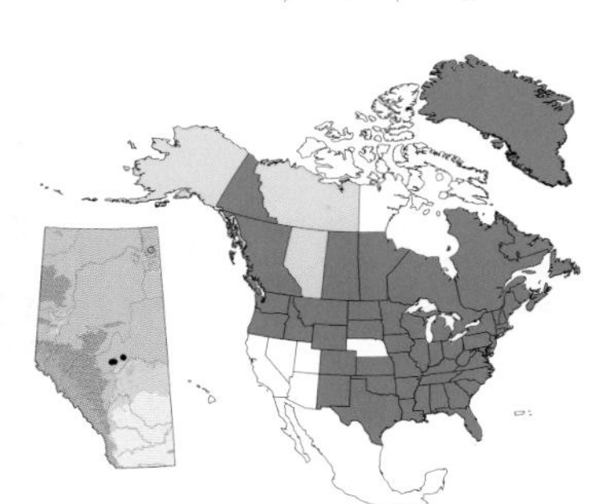

Fruits: Grains; mature spikelets breaking off above the glumes and between the florets; late July–September.

Habitat: Sandy and rocky sites, mostly in dry woods but sometimes in moist meadows; elsewhere, on rock outcrops and dry prairie.

Notes: The name 'poverty oat grass' reflects the ability of this species to grow on nutrient-poor sites and also its resemblance to oats (*Avena* spp.). • Another rare species, one-spike oat grass (*Danthonia unispicata* (Thurb.) Munro *ex* Macoun), differs from poverty oat grass in having a panicle usually consisting of only 1 spikelet and lemmas that are hairless (except on their lower edges). One-spike oat grass grows on open rocky or sandy ground and flowers in June {July}. • California oat grass (*Danthonia californica* Bol.) is also rare in Alberta. It is recognized by its largely hairless lemmas (silky-hairy along the edges and at the base only) and its small, open flower clusters, which usually have 1–4 spikelets on spreading branches. A widespread relative, timber oat grass (*Danthonia intermedia* Vasey), has narrower clusters of 5–10 spikelets, and its leaf sheaths are usually hairless (rather than soft-hairy). California oat grass grows in open, grassy meadows and on rocky ridges. It

D. UNISPICATA

LA

flowers in June and July. • Many oat grasses (*Danthonia* spp.) are often cleistogamous, which means that the florets remain closed at the time of fertilization. Their tiny anthers (often only a fraction of a millimetre long) produce very few pollen grains (perhaps 10–12), which grow pollen tubes through the anther wall and eventually fertilize the ovary. These self-fertilized flowers are usually found on spikelets within the lower leaf sheaths. • The long, bent bristles (awns) of these grasses twist and untwist with changes in humidity. This action may help to drill the seeds into the ground.

D. CALIFORNICA

LA

PRAIRIE CORD GRASS

Spartina pectinata Link
GRASS FAMILY (POACEAE [GRAMINEAE])

Plants: **Coarse perennial** herbs; stems erect, **50–200 cm tall**, hairless; from stout, elongated underground stems (rhizomes).

Leaves: Alternate on the stem; blades fibrous, **5–15 mm wide**, flat or rolled inward, rough with **small, sharp teeth** along the edges; **ligules a fringe of hairs** {1.5} **2–3 mm long**; sheaths distinctly veined, hairy at the collar only.

Flower clusters: Linear, 10–30 cm long, with **10–20 erect, stalkless spikes**, each 4–8 {2–10} cm long; **spikelets single-flowered, stalkless, strongly flattened**, crowded along 1 side of the spike branch **like teeth on a comb; glumes rough to touch**; lower glume 5–6 mm long, bristle-tipped; **upper glume** 8–12 mm long, **longer than the lemma, tipped with a 4–10 mm long bristle** (awn); lemmas 7–9 mm long, rough along the ridge on the back (keel); **paleas conspicuous**, pointed, longer than the lemmas; {late June–July}.

Fruits: Grains; mature florets breaking free below the glumes; August–September.

BH

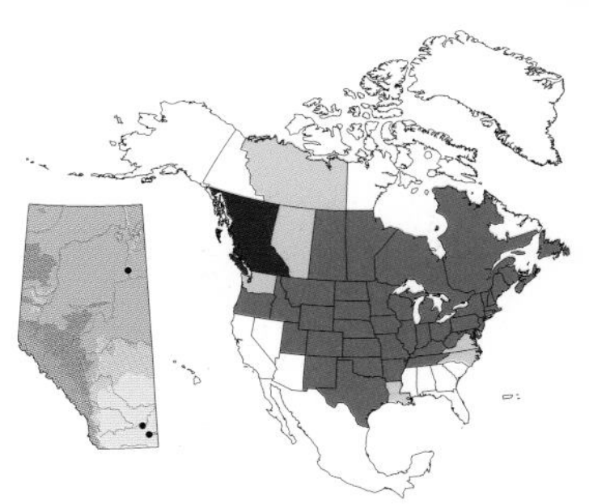

Habitat: Saline shores and marshes; elsewhere, on moist prairie, riverbanks and shores, and in ditches and marshes.

Notes: Prairie cord grass is similar to the more common alkali cord grass (*Spartina gracilis* Trin.). The glumes of alkali cord grass are relatively smooth to the touch and the upper glume does not have a bristle. Alkali cord grass has shorter, less spreading panicle branches, shorter spikes (2–4 cm), shorter ligules (about 1 mm) and smaller, less robust plants, and it appears to be more salt tolerant. • Prairie cord grass is a warm-season grass, meaning that most vegetative growth occurs during the hottest part of the year. • The Omaha Indians used prairie cord grass for thatch on permanent lodges before covering them with earth. Early pioneers used it in a similar manner, as thatching on buildings, haystacks and unroofed granaries. In the southern US, the stems were used for brooms and brushes. • This species provides poor to fair cattle forage when young and soon becomes unpalatable. It does not do well under grazing pressure due to the effects of trampling on the brittle mature stems. • Prairie cord grass is an indicator of native tall-grass prairie. It is unusual to find it as far west as Alberta. Most plants here probably do not set seed. Instead, they increase vegetatively, producing local, concentrated populations. • 'Ripgut' is another common name for prairie cord grass, referring to the sharp teeth along the leaf edges, which **can cut flesh**. • The generic name *Spartina* was derived from the Greek *spartine* (a cord), probably because of its wiry leaves and extensive tough rhizomes. The specific epithet *pectinata* refers to the pectinate (arranged like the teeth on a comb) spikelets.

FALSE BUFFALO GRASS

Munroa squarrosa (Nutt.) Torr.
GRASS FAMILY (POACEAE [GRAMINEAE])

Plants: **Mat-forming annual herbs**, 3–15 cm tall; **stems spreading**, often rooting at the joints (nodes), **branched**, hollow, hairy, rough to touch; from fibrous roots.

Leaves: In **clusters** at stem joints and stem tips; **blades spine-tipped**, stiff, 1–3 cm long, 1–3 mm wide, **with rough, white edges; ligules** consisting of **a ring of hairs**; sheaths crowded, split down 1 side (open), hairy on the edges at the collar.

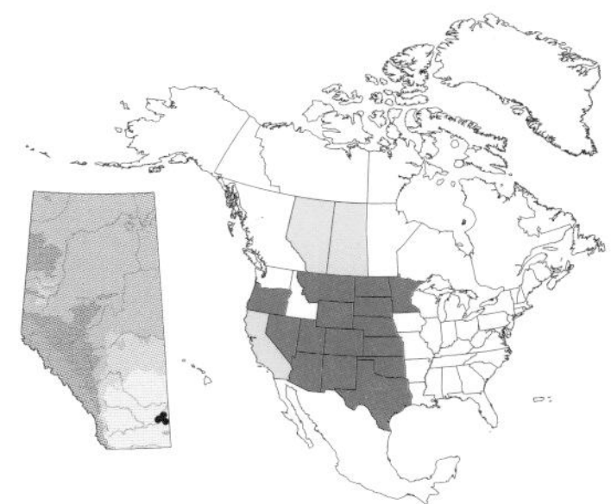

Flower clusters: **Short panicles nestled among the leaves; spikelets crowded in clusters of 2–3**, 6–9 mm long; lower spikelets smaller, 3–4-flowered, with equal, narrow, sharp-pointed, 1-nerved glumes; **upper spikelets larger**, 2–3 flowered, with unequal glumes, the lower glume short or absent; lemmas short-stalked, 3-nerved, tipped with a short bristle (awn) from between 2 lobes, hairy on the edges near mid-length, membranous in upper spikelets, leathery in lower spikelets; anthers 1.5 mm long; {June–August}.

Fruits: Grains; mature florets breaking away above the glumes and between the florets.

Habitat: Dry plains and slopes, often on disturbed ground; elsewhere, on sandy and gravelly soil, on open ground and in old fields.

Notes: The name of this genus has also been misspelled *Monroa*. • This is a very distinctive grass, the only species of its genus in North America, not easily confused with any other grass. It bears superficial resemblance to buffalo grass (*Buchloe dactyloides* (Nutt.) Engelm.) and hence the common name 'false buffalo grass.' • False buffalo grass is a warm-season species, meaning it grows most rapidly during the hottest part of the year. • It is unpalatable to livestock. • The specific epithet *squarrosa* is Latin for 'rough with outward-projecting tips' and describes the spreading leaves and stems of these plants.

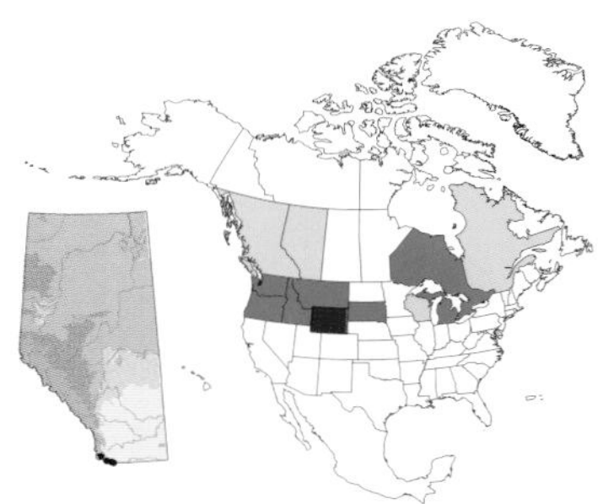

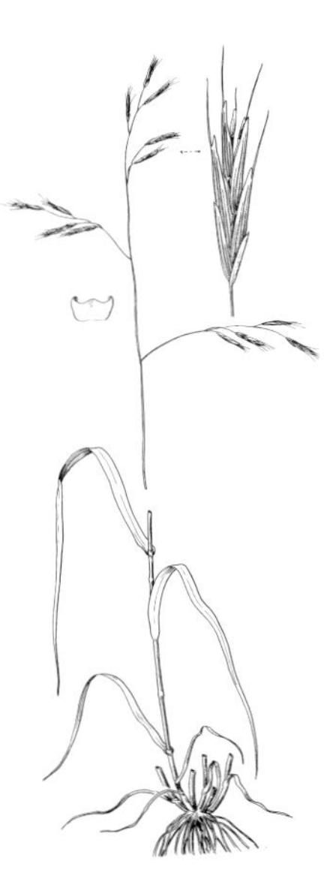

SMITH'S MELIC, MELIC GRASS

Melica smithii (Porter *ex* A. Gray) Vasey
GRASS FAMILY (POACEAE [GRAMINEAE])

Plants: Tufted perennial herbs; stems 50–100 {30–130} cm tall, **usually lacking the bulb-like base** that is typical of this genus; from underground stems (rhizomes).

Leaves: Alternate on the stem; blades flat, {5} 6–12 mm wide, lax, rough to touch, with prominent veins; ligules 3–9 mm long, blunt, irregularly cut; **sheaths** with stiff, downward-pointing hairs, **closed to the top**.

Flower clusters: Loose panicles, 10–25 {30} cm long, with solitary, widely spaced branches eventually spreading or nodding; **spikelets** {3} **4–6-flowered**, {15} 16–20 mm long, often purplish; **lower glume** {3} 4–6 mm long, **faintly 3-nerved; upper glume** {4} 5–8 mm long, **shorter than the lowest lemma**, distinctly {3} 5-nerved; **lemmas about 10 mm long, strongly 7-nerved**, tipped **with a 3–5 mm long bristle** (awn) **from between 2 teeth**; July {June–August}.

Fruits: Grains; mature florets breaking away above the glumes and between the florets.

Habitat: Moist subalpine woodlands; elsewhere, in moist woods.

Notes: This is the only native onion grass (*Melica* spp.) in Alberta that has awned lemmas. • Another rare Alberta species, showy onion grass (*Melica spectabilis* Scribn.), also known as purple onion grass, has fleshy, bulb-like swellings at the base of its flowering stalks. It is distinguished from similar species by its broader, blunt or abruptly pointed, hairless, purplish lemmas, its broad, papery glumes and its solitary stems, which arise from spreading rhizomes. Showy onion grass grows in wet to moderately dry, fairly open sites and flowers in {May–July} August. • The 'bulbs' of onion grasses are edible, with a pleasant, nutty flavour, but they do not seem to have been used by aboriginal peoples.

M. SPECTABILIS

PRAIRIE WEDGE GRASS

Sphenopholis obtusata (Michx.) Scribn.
GRASS FAMILY (POACEAE [GRAMINEAE])

Plants: Slender, densely tufted perennial herbs; stems 20–80 {100} cm tall; from fibrous roots.

Leaves: Alternate; blades **flat, 2–5** {6} **mm wide, rough** to touch on both sides; ligules 1.5–2 {1–4} mm long, irregularly torn, toothed and fringed; sheaths hairless or rough to touch, distinctly veined.

Flower clusters: Erect, lustrous, spike-like panicles 3–10 {2–15} cm long and 5–15 mm wide, with erect branches; **spikelets stalked, 2-flowered** (sometimes with a small, third flower), 2.5–3 mm long; **glumes** very **unequal,** the lower slender, the **upper broadly egg-shaped to almost round**, tapered to a wedge-shaped base and **slightly hooded at the tip; lemmas firm, rough**, covered with tiny bumps (papillose), faintly nerved, 1.5–2.6 mm long, longer than the glumes; {June–July}.

Fruits: Grains; mature florets breaking free below the glumes.

Habitat: Moist sites in meadows and open woods and on shores; elsewhere, on moist to wet prairie.

Notes: A more common species, slender wedge grass (*Sphenopholis intermedia* (Rydb.) Rydb.), can be distinguished by its open, lax panicles and its second glume that is 3 times as long as wide and pointed to rounded (not hooded). • The generic name *Sphenopholis* was derived from the Greek *sphen* (wedge) and *pholis* (scale), in reference to the wedge-shaped upper glumes. The specific epithet *obtusata*, from the Latin *obtusus* (blunt), refers to the broad, rounded tips of the upper glumes.

ES

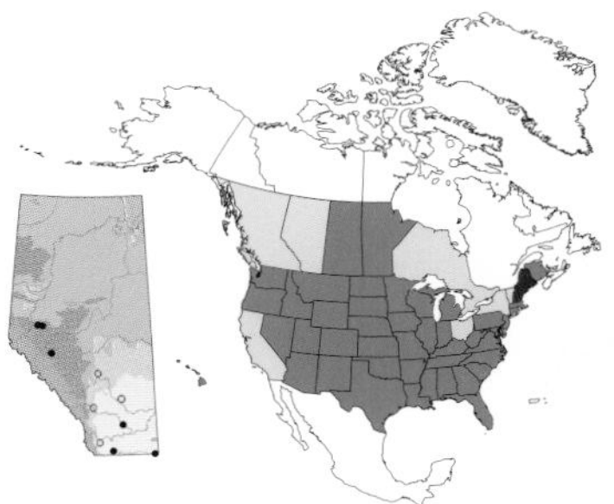

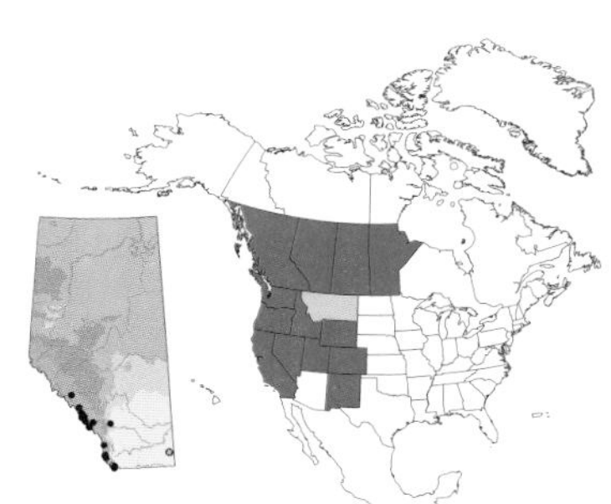

WHEELER'S BLUEGRASS

Poa nervosa (Hook.) Vasey var. *wheeleri* (Vasey) C.L. Hitchc.
GRASS FAMILY (POACEAE [GRAMINEAE])

Plants: Slender perennial herbs; stems rounded, ascending or erect, 30–60 {70} cm tall, hairless; from **long, spreading underground stems** (rhizomes).

Leaves: Mostly basal; blades flat or folded with boat-shaped (keeled) **tips**, 2–4 {5} mm wide; **ligules 1–2 mm long, thickish, short-hairy and fringed with hairs**; sheaths with downward-pointing hairs (sometimes hairless), often purplish near the base.

Flower clusters: Open panicles, 5–10 cm long, with slender, nodding or spreading branches mostly in 2s or 3s, **usually entirely female**, with a few small, non-functioning anthers; **spikelets stalked near branch tips**, {2} **4–7-flowered, 4–6** {8} **mm long**, slightly flattened; **glumes 2–3.5 mm long, shorter than the lowest lemma; lemmas 4–5 {3–6} mm long**, clearly 5-nerved (with nerves converging at the tip), ridged down the back (keeled), sometimes hairy on the lower nerves but never with a tuft of cobwebby hairs at the base; {April–July} August.

Fruits: Grains; mature florets breaking away above the glumes and between the florets.

Habitat: Open woods; elsewhere, on exposed ridges and talus slopes in montane to alpine zones.

Notes: Perhaps the most distinctive characteristic of this species is its peculiarly thickened, hairy and fringed ligules, which are squared at their tips (at least on lower leaves).
• Wheeler's bluegrass resembles early bluegrass (*Poa cusickii* Vasey), but that species lacks rhizomes and has much narrower flower clusters. Its ligules are also thin, sparsely hairy and 2.5 mm long, and it grows in dry, open sites (grasslands, sandhills) at low elevations and on the prairie.

Letterman's bluegrass

Poa lettermanii Vasey
GRASS FAMILY (POACEAE [GRAMINEAE])

Plants: Small, densely tufted perennial herbs; stems {2} **3–12 cm tall; creeping underground stems** (rhizomes) **lacking.**

Leaves: Basal and alternate on the stem; blades lax, mostly **flat,** 1–2 mm wide, with **boat-shaped** (keeled) **tips;** ligules 0.5–2 {3} mm long, blunt, irregularly cut; sheaths split down 1 side (open) for most of their length.

Flower clusters: Narrow panicles, 1–2 {3} **cm long; spikelets 2–5-flowered, flattened** (keeled), purple-tinged, 2.5–4 {4.5} mm long; glumes shorter than the lowest lemma, 2–4 mm long, 3-nerved, rough along the ridged back (keel); **lemmas hairless and smooth, 2–3** {3.5} **mm long,** with **3–5 faint nerves converging toward the rather blunt tip;** anthers about 0.5 mm long; {June–August}.

Fruits: Grains; mature florets breaking away above the glumes and between the florets; July–August.

Habitat: Exposed alpine ridges, in dry, rocky fellfields.

Notes: The range of Letterman's bluegrass overlaps with that of another rare species, bog bluegrass (*Poa leptocoma* Trin.), but bog bluegrass grows along streams and in seepage areas and wet meadows. Bog bluegrass also differs from Letterman's bluegrass in having a tuft of cobwebby hairs at the base of its lemmas, nodding panicles with spreading branches, and longer (3–4 mm) ligules. It is reported to flower from late June to August. • Letterman's bluegrass provides nutritious, palatable forage for mountain goats and bighorn sheep. • This species was named in honour of G.W. Letterman, a botanist who collected the type specimen at Grays Peak, Colorado.

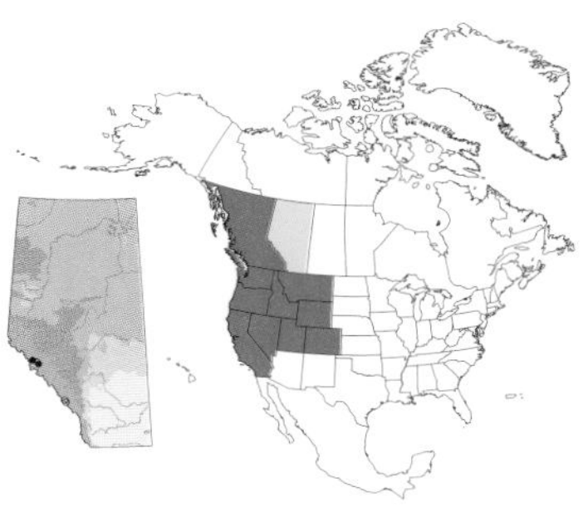

P. LEPTOCOMA

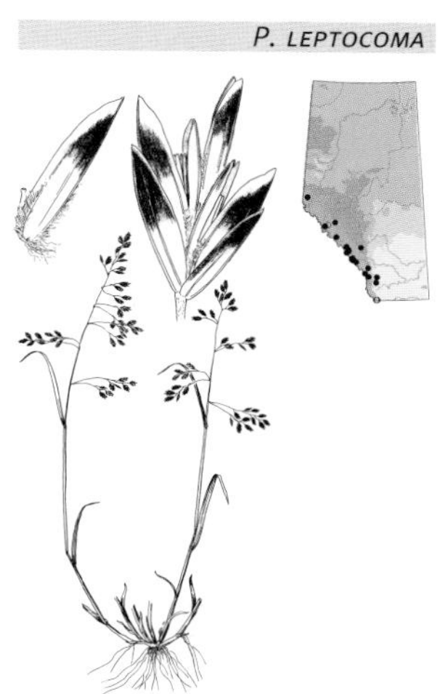

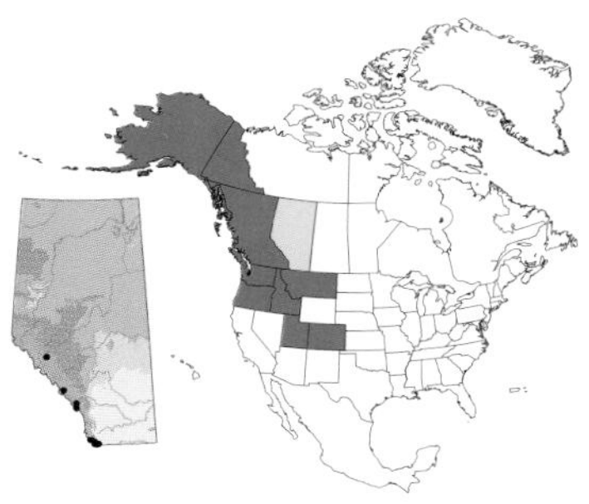

P. LAXA

NARROW-LEAVED BLUEGRASS

Poa stenantha Trin.
GRASS FAMILY (POACEAE [GRAMINEAE])

Plants: Tufted perennial herbs; stems erect, 30–50 {25–60} cm tall; **without creeping underground stems** (rhizomes).

Leaves: Mostly basal, but also a few alternate on the stem; **blades with a boat-shaped tip**, flat or loosely rolled inward, rather soft and lax, 1–2 {2.5} mm wide; **ligules 1.5–3.5** {1–5} **mm long**, finely hairy and rough to touch, pointed and torn at the tip; sheaths hairless, fused into a tube (closed) for about ¼ of their length.

Flower clusters: Nodding, **open panicles**, 5–15 cm long, with spreading to drooping lower branches in 2s and 3s; **spikelets flattened, 3–5-flowered, 6–8** {10} **mm long**; glumes 3-nerved, unequal, 2.7–5.7 mm long, rough to the touch; **lemmas 4–6 mm long, with a clearly defined ridge** (keel) and nerves, hairy on the lower keel and nerves and sparsely hairy between; anthers 1.2–2 mm long; {July} August.

Fruits: Grains; mature florets breaking away above the glumes and between the florets.

Habitat: Open woods at montane elevations; elsewhere, in subalpine meadows and on talus slopes.

Notes: Narrow-leaved bluegrass can be very similar to Sandberg bluegrass (*Poa secunda* J. Presl, which includes *Poa sandbergii* Vasey), a much more common species that grows in similar habitats. However, the lemmas of Sandberg bluegrass are rounded on the back (rather than keeled), and the spikelets are only slightly flattened.
• Wavy bluegrass (*Poa laxa* Haenke ssp. *banffiana* Soreng) is a rare perennial species with soft, slender leaves, similar to those of narrow-leaved bluegrass. It is recognized by its smaller (rarely over 6 cm long), erect panicles with spikelets near the tips of smooth, curved, single or paired branches. Its plants have few, solitary or loosely tufted, thread-like stems. Wavy bluegrass grows on alpine slopes.

TUFTED TALL MANNA GRASS

Glyceria elata (Nash) A.S. Hitchc.
GRASS FAMILY (POACEAE [GRAMINEAE])

Plants: Loosely tufted perennial herbs; stems 60–150 cm tall, fleshy; often in large clumps, from creeping underground stems (rhizomes).

Leaves: Alternate on the stem, dark green; blades lax, flat, 20–40 cm long, 4–10 {12} mm wide; **ligules 3–6 mm long, blunt, with short hairs**; **sheaths fused into a tube** (closed) to near the top, rough to the touch.

Flower clusters: Loose panicles 15–30 cm long, with **spreading branches**, the lower branches often bent downward (reflexed); **spikelets 4–8-flowered**, 3–5 mm long; **glumes 1–2 mm long**, shorter than the lowest lemma, with irregular, fringed edges; **lemmas firm, 2–2.5 mm long, with 7 prominent, parallel veins** and a **blunt, translucent tip**; {May–July}.

Fruits: Grains; mature florets breaking away above the glumes and between the florets.

Habitat: Stream edges and wet meadows in the southern Rocky Mountains.

Notes: The range of tufted tall manna grass overlaps with the ranges of other, more common manna grasses, which it resembles, including common tall manna grass (*Glyceria grandis* S. Wats.) and fowl manna grass (*Glyceria striata* (Lam.) A.S. Hitchc.). Common tall manna grass differs in having hairless ligules, a longer lowest (lower) glume (1.3–2 mm) and lemmas that are purplish rather than greenish. Fowl manna grass has narrower leaves (2–5 mm wide), shorter lower ligules (1.5–3 mm) and shorter lemmas (about 2 mm). • Manna grass is tender and readily eaten by livestock and wildlife when available. • The generic name *Glyceria* comes from the Greek *glykeros* (sweet), presumably in reference to the grains.

FEW-FLOWERED SALT-MEADOW GRASS

Torreyochloa pallida (Torr.) Church var. *pauciflora* (J. Presl) J.I. Davis

GRASS FAMILY (POACEAE [GRAMINEAE])

Plants: Perennial herbs; stems loosely tufted or solitary, 40–100 {15–140} cm tall, often somewhat spreading; from creeping underground stems (rhizomes).

Leaves: Alternate on the stem; blades lax, thin, flat, 8–15 cm long, 4–12 {3–15} mm wide, slightly rough; **ligules 5–6** {3–9} **mm long**, sharp-pointed, usually irregularly cut; **sheaths split down 1 side** (open), sometimes inflated.

Flower clusters: Rather **loose, nodding panicles**, {5} 10–20 cm long, **often purplish**, mostly with 2–4 curved branches per joint (node); **spikelets 4–5** {3–7}**-flowered**, 4–5 mm long, crowded into the upper half of the panicle; **glumes broadly egg-shaped**, {0.8} **1–2 mm long**, irregularly cut along the edges, the lower glume 1-nerved and the **upper glume 3-nerved; lemmas 2–2.5** {1.9–2.9} **mm long**, with **5 conspicuous parallel nerves** (not converging toward the tip) and usually with 2 faint nerves at the edges, short-hairy on the nerves, blunt and broadly translucent at the tip; anthers 0.5–0.7 mm long; {June–August}.

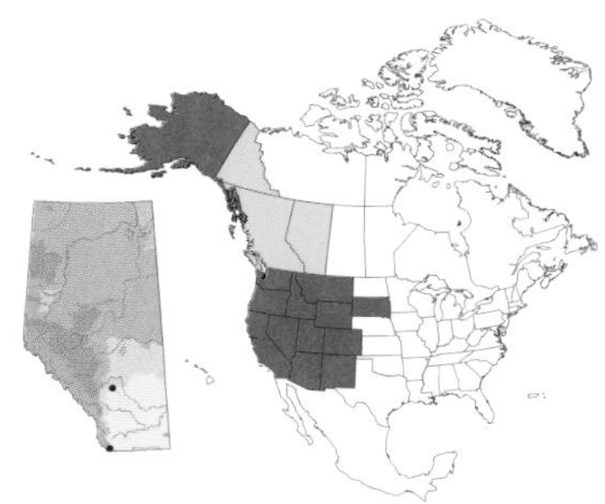

Fruits: Grains; mature florets breaking away above the glumes and between the florets; August.

Habitat: Wet places; elsewhere, in shallow water, wet meadows, woods and thickets.

T. PALLIDA var. *FERNALDII*

Notes: This species has also been called *Puccinellia pauciflora* (J. Presl) Munz var. *holmii* (Beal) C.L. Hitchc., *Torreyochloa pauciflora* (J. Presl) Church and *Glyceria pauciflora* Presl (in the first edition of the *Flora of Alberta*). • Another variety of this species, *Torreyochloa pallida* (Torr.) Church var. *fernaldii* (Hitchc.) Dore, has also been reported to occur in Alberta. It is distinguished by its larger (to 3 mm long), distinctly 7-nerved lemmas. • Conspicuously nerved lemmas are also common in the manna grasses (*Glyceria* spp.), and small-flowered salt-meadow grass was once classified as a species of that genus. Manna grasses are distinguished by their closed sheaths (fused in a tube almost to the top) and their 1-nerved glumes. • The generic name *Torreyochloa* commemorates John Torrey, an American botanist who lived 1796–1873.

TINY-FLOWERED FESCUE

Festuca minutiflora Rydberg
GRASS FAMILY (POACEAE [GRAMINEAE])

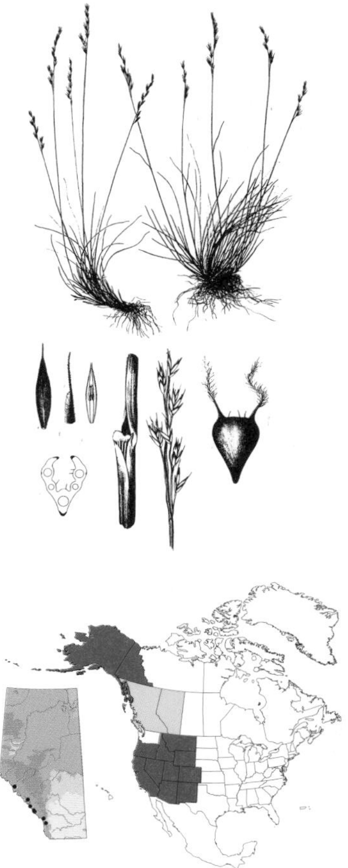

Plants: Delicate, tufted perennial herbs, slightly bluish green; stems 7.5–20 {4–30} cm tall, with the joints (nodes) rarely exposed; old leaf bases not evident.

Leaves: Mostly basal; **blades soft, thread-like**, rolled inward, tipped with a slender bristle (awn); **stem leaves** 0.7–3 cm long; erect, with a **swelling at the base of the blade**; ligules 0.1–0.3 {0.75} mm long, irregularly cut; sheaths split down one side (open), hairless, with a prominent midvein.

Flower clusters: Narrow, somewhat lax panicles, 1–4 {5} cm long, with short branches; **spikelets 3–4** {2–5}**-flowered, 2.5–5 mm long; glumes** unequal, shorter than the lowest lemma, **1.3–3.5 mm long**, short-hairy near the tips; **lemmas 5-nerved**, rounded on the back, **2.2–3.4** {4} **mm long**, abruptly narrowed at the tip to a **0.7–1.5** {0.5–1.7} **mm long awn**; August.

Fruits: Grains; mature florets breaking away above the glumes and between the florets.

Habitat: Alpine tundra and meadows and subalpine openings in the mountains.

Notes: This species has also been included in *Festuca brevifolia* R. Br. var. *endotera* Saint-Yves, *F. brevifolia* var. *utahensis* Saint-Yves and *F. ovina* L. var. *minutiflora* (Rydb.) Howell. • Tiny-flowered fescue is similar to the more common alpine fescue (*Festuca brachyphylla* Schultes & Schultes f.), but alpine fescue has larger spikelets, broadly lance-shaped lemmas, longer awns (1–3 mm) and stiffer, more erect leaves and flower clusters. • *Festuca* is the ancient Latin name for a grass.

PL

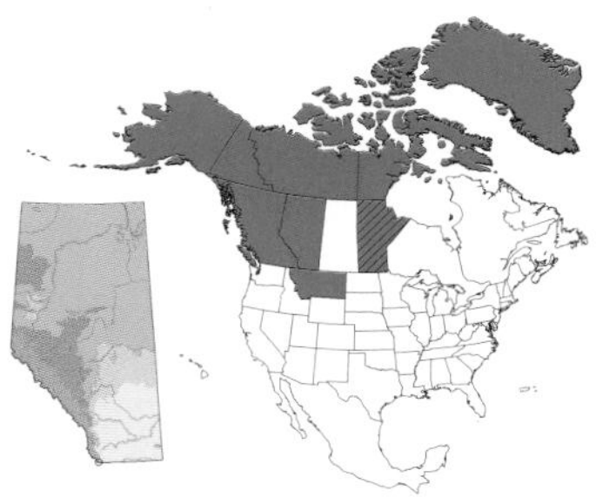

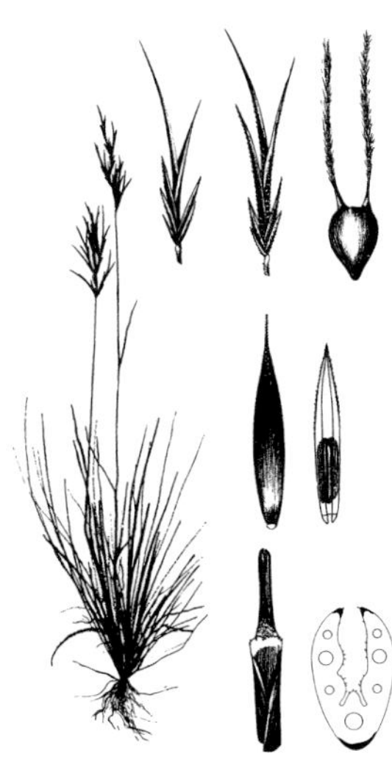

VIVIPAROUS FESCUE

Festuca viviparoidea Krajina *ex* Pavlick ssp. *krajinae* Pavlick
GRASS FAMILY (POACEAE [GRAMINEAE])

Plants: Densely tufted perennial herbs; stems erect, **6–30 cm tall**, rough to touch on the upper part; from fibrous roots.

Leaves: Basal, **½–⅓ as long as the stem**, slender; blades 0.5–1 mm wide, **rolled inward**, hairless, sometimes rough to touch near the tips; sheaths parchment-like, persistent.

Flower clusters: Dense, narrow, almost **spike-like panicles, 1–6 cm long**, with rough, ascending branches; **spikelets few-flowered, upper spikelets with small leaves** projecting from their tips (viviparous); lower spikelets sometimes producing seed; glumes lance-shaped, 2–3 mm long; lemmas purplish, broadly lance-shaped, 2–4 mm long, tapered to a short, firm bristle (awn); anthers 0.3–1 mm long; {July–August}.

Fruits: Grains; mature florets breaking free above the glumes and between the florets.

Habitat: Rocky alpine slopes.

Notes: This species was previously called *Festuca vivipara* (L.) Sm. ssp. *glabra* Frederiksen. It is sometimes considered a viviparous form of alpine fescue (*Festuca brachyphylla* Schultes & Schultes f.) or arctic fescue (*Festuca baffinensis* Polunin). • The flowering spikes of this northern grass are viviparous—that is, small plants develop in the flower clusters, producing leaves and rootlets before falling to the ground. This type of reproduction is often seen in arctic plants, where growing seasons are short, and environmental conditions are harsh. Young plants get a headstart by growing while still protected in the spikelets of the parent plant, and when they fall to the ground, they have a better chance of becoming established and maturing.

WESTERN FESCUE

Festuca occidentalis Hook.
GRASS FAMILY (POACEAE [GRAMINEAE])

Plants: Densely **tufted perennial herbs**; bright green to blue-green; stems slender, 40–80 {25–110} cm tall, with 2 exposed joints (nodes); underground stems (rhizomes) absent.

Leaves: Mostly basal; **blades thread-like**, rolled inward, **soft, hairless**, with an erect swelling at the base; ligules 0.1–0.4 mm long, irregularly cut; **sheaths** hairless, **split** down 1 side to near the base (open), with a prominent midvein.

Flower clusters: Nodding panicles, 5–20 cm long, with the **lower branches** unequal and **strongly bent downward** (reflexed); **spikelets 3–5** {7}**-flowered**, 6–10 mm long, with the florets on slender stalks; **glumes unequal**, shorter than the lowest lemma, **3–4** {2–4.5} **mm long**, usually sharp-pointed, hairless or short-hairy at the tip; **lemmas** oblong to lance-shaped, **5-nerved,** {4} **5–6.5 mm long,** thin and translucent, **with a long, 4–7** {12} **mm bristle** (awn); {late May–July}.

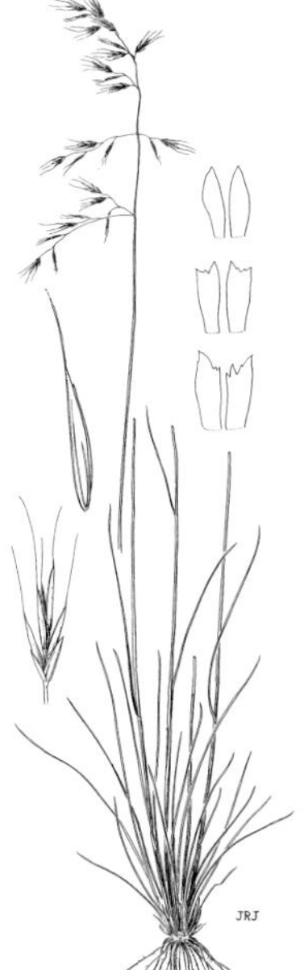

Fruits: Grains; mature florets breaking away above the glumes and between the florets.

Habitat: Dry, rocky, wooded slopes; associated with lodgepole pine and aspen, in the southern Rocky Mountains; elsewhere, in moist woods and along streambanks and lake shores.

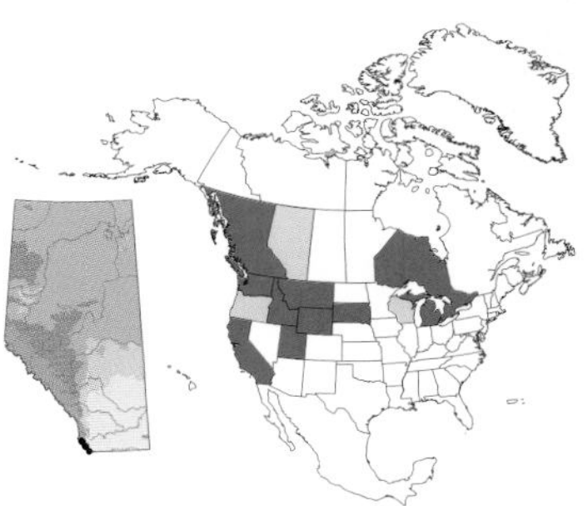

Notes: Immature plants of western fescue may be difficult to distinguish from bluebunch fescue (*Festuca idahoensis* Elmer). • Western fescue's fine leaves and sparse occurrence in shade can make it difficult to detect. • Most native fescues are valuable forage grasses.

BEARDED FESCUE

Festuca subulata Trin.
GRASS FAMILY (POACEAE [GRAMINEAE])

Plants: Loosely tufted perennial herbs; stems 50–100 {130} cm tall, with 2–4 exposed joints (nodes).

Leaves: Alternate on the stem; soft, **flat, 3–10 mm wide, hairless or short-hairy**, deep green; **ligules** 0.2–1 mm long, **fringed with hairs** (ciliate) along the **irregular edge**; sheaths hairless, fused into a tube (closed) for at least ½ their length.

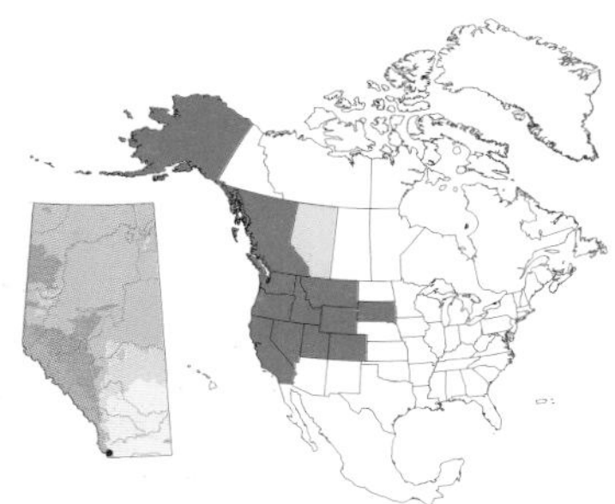

Flower clusters: Open, nodding panicles, {10} 15–40 cm long, with slender branches spreading or bent downward (reflexed); **spikelets 3–5** {2–6}**-flowered**, 7–10 {6–12} mm long, with stalkless florets; glumes unequal, 3.5–5.5 {2–6} mm long, shorter than the lowest lemmas; **lemmas** {4} **5–7 mm long**, usually with a lengthwise ridge on the back (keel), sparsely hairy, with a straight or sometimes kinked **bristle** (awn) **5–10** {20} **mm long**; {May–June} July.

Fruits: Grains; mature florets breaking away above the glumes and between the florets.

Habitat: Moist woods, thickets and shaded banks up to 1,500 m in the southern Rocky Mountains.

Notes: The bristles (awns) of bearded fescue curve or kink on drying. • This species has also been called *Festuca jonesii* Vasey. • Northern rough fescue (*Festuca altaica* Trin. *ex* Ledeb., treated under *Festuca scabrella* Torr. in the *Flora of Alberta*) is a rare grass of boreal and alpine grasslands. Like bearded fescue, it is up to 120 cm tall and has an open, nodding panicle, but it differs in having yellow-green to dark green leaves and purplish spikelets with transparent edges that give a lustrous sheen to the panicle. The leaves of northern rough fescue are less than 2.5 mm wide, the lemmas are rounded (rather than ridged), and the lemma awns are less than 1 mm long. The dead leaf blades of northern rough fescue break off at the collars, leaving entire sheaths that persist for many years. Northern rough fescue flowers in June {July}.

F. ALTAICA

LK

CANADA BROME, HAIRY WOODBROME

Bromus latiglumis (Shear) A.S. Hitchc.
GRASS FAMILY (POACEAE [GRAMINEAE])

Plants: Loosely tufted perennial herbs; **stems** 80–150 cm tall, essentially hairless, **with** {8} **10–20 hairless joints** (nodes); without underground stems (rhizomes).

Leaves: Alternate; blades flat, mostly hairless, **5–15 mm wide**, 20–30 cm long, **with broad lobes at the base extending into small projections** (auricles); ligules blunt, to 1.4 mm long, irregularly cut, fringed with hairs (ciliate); sheaths overlapping, hairless to densely soft-hairy, with woolly collars.

Flower clusters: Spreading panicles, **10–22 cm long; spikelets stalked, 4–9-flowered, 1.5–3 cm long; glumes** hairy, shorter than the lowest lemma, the **lower usually 1-nerved** (rarely 3-nerved) and 4–7 {7.5} mm long, the upper 3-nerved and 6–9 mm long; **lemmas evenly hairy across the back**, 7-nerved, {8} 9–14 mm long, **tipped with a 3–4.5** {7} **mm long bristle** (awn); anthers 2–3 mm long; {late June–August}.

Fruits: Grains; mature florets breaking off above the glumes and between the florets; August–September.

Habitat: Moist streambanks; elsewhere, in meadows and riparian thickets and forests.

Notes: This species has also been called *Bromus altissimus* Pursh, *Bromus incanus* (Shear) A.S. Hitchc., *Bromus purgans* L. var. *incanus* Shear and *Bromus ciliatus* L. var. *latiglumis* Scribn. *ex* Shear. • The generic name *Bromus* comes from the ancient Greek name for the oat, *bromos*. The specific epithet *latiglumis* means 'broad-glumed.'

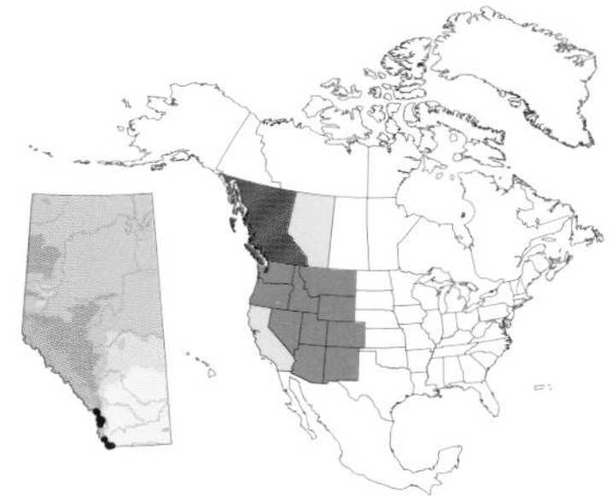

SPREADING WHEAT GRASS, SCRIBNER'S WHEAT GRASS

Elymus scribneri (Vasey) M.E. Jones
GRASS FAMILY (POACEAE [GRAMINEAE])

Plants: Perennial herbs with **a dense, leafy basal tussock; stems spreading, curved to ascending,** 10–40 {60} cm tall; **without underground stems** (rhizomes).

Leaves: Mostly basal, finely hairy; blades flat, 1–3 {4} mm wide, with edges slightly rolled inward; stem leaves less than 5 cm long; ligules barely 0.5 mm long; auricles usually present.

Flower clusters: Dense, **nodding spikes,** 3–7 {12} cm long, breaking into pieces and **separating** from the rest of the stem **at maturity; spikelets stalkless, single** at each joint (node), with 3–5 flowers; glumes 6–8 mm long, tapered to a bristle-tip (awn); **lemmas** {7} **8–10 mm long, essentially hairless,** faintly 5-nerved to the tip, tipped **with a 15–30 mm long, curved, spreading awn; anthers 1.5–2.5 mm long;** {late June–August}.

Fruits: Grains; mature florets breaking off above the glumes and between the florets; August.

Habitat: Dry alpine scree slopes; elsewhere, on montane slopes and in grassland.

Notes: This species has also been called *Agropyron scribneri* Vasey. • Similar species with curving or spreading bristles (awns) in Alberta, awned northern wheat grass (*Agropyron albicans* Scribn. & Smith) and blue-bunch wheat grass (*Elymus spicatus* (Pursh) Gould, also called *Agropyron spicatum* (Pursh) Scribn. & Smith), are normally found in the grassland region or at lower elevations. • Spreading wheat grass hybridizes with a number of species. • The common name 'spreading wheat grass' refers to the curved culms, which 'spread out' from the basal tussock.

SQUIRRELTAIL

Elymus elymoides (Raf.) Swezey
GRASS FAMILY (POACEAE [GRAMINEAE])

GCT

Plants: Tufted perennial herbs; stems stiff, erect or spreading, 10–50 {60} cm tall; from fibrous roots.

Leaves: Alternate, hairless or short-hairy; blades flat, folded or rolled inward, 1–4 mm wide, usually with small (less than 1 mm long) auricles at the base; ligules less than 1 mm long, membranous, fringed with fine hairs (ciliate); **upper sheaths often inflated.**

Flower clusters: Green or purplish spikes, 2–10 {15} cm long and wide (including awns), often partly enveloped by the upper leaf sheath, **breaking apart** at the joints (nodes) when mature; **spikelets stalkless, usually in 2s** (sometimes single or in 3s), **2–6** {1–8}**-flowered**, often with lower lemmas sterile and glume-like; **glumes** more or less **awl shaped**, 1–2-nerved, **tipped with 1 or 2 spreading** (eventually), **5–9 cm long bristles** (awns), sometimes tipped with 2 teeth or with an awn on one side; **lemmas firm**, rounded on the back, 5-nerved, rough to touch or short-hairy, **tipped with 1–3 widely spreading, 2–10 cm long bristles** (awns); {May–June} July.

Fruits: Grains; mature florets breaking free with the glumes and part of the central stalk (rachis).

Habitat: Dry plains and open woods; elsewhere, in dry to moist, often rocky sites from sea level to above treeline.

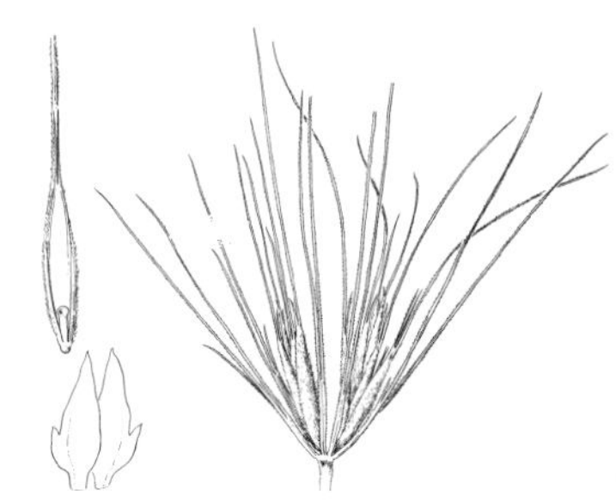

Notes: This species has also been called *Sitanion hystrix* (Nutt.) J.G. Smith. • Squirreltail is a highly variable species, and several varieties have been identified within it, based mainly on differences in hairiness, number of spikelets, number of fertile lemmas and the presence of glume-like florets. It hybridizes readily with smooth wild rye (*Elymus glaucus* Buckley), producing plants that are intermediate between the 2 species, with spikes that break apart at their joints (nodes). Several of these hybrids have been described as species in the past.

LITTLE BARLEY

Hordeum pusillum Nutt.
GRASS FAMILY (POACEAE [GRAMINEAE])

Plants: Tufted, greyish green **annual** herbs; stems 10–40 {60} cm tall, usually abruptly bent at the base, with dark, hairless joints (nodes); from fibrous roots.

Leaves: Alternate on the stem; blades flat, 1–12 cm long, 2–4 {5} mm wide, **without small projections** (auricles) **at the base**; ligules 0.4–0.7 mm long, blunt, irregularly cut, short-hairy; sheaths soft-hairy.

Flower clusters: Erect, **dense spikes**, {2} 3–7 cm long, 10–14 mm wide; **spikelets 1-flowered, 3 per joint** (node), with **2 short-stalked, sterile side spikelets and 1 stalkless, fertile central spikelet**; **glumes** rough to touch, mostly narrowly lance-shaped, {0.5} **0.8–1.8 mm wide** and **tipped with an 8–15 mm long bristle** (awn), but the **lower glumes of the side spikelets bristle-like** (resembling awns); fertile lemma (central spikelet) tapered to a long awn, 10–15 mm long (including awn); sterile lemmas (side spikelets) awn-tipped; {May–June}.

Fruits: Grains; mature florets breaking away above the glumes.

Habitat: Saline prairie, eroded areas, grassland and waste land; elsewhere, alkali flats, roadsides and wetland borders.

Notes: This annual species may be mistaken for the common perennial foxtail barley (*Hordeum jubatum* L.), if foxtail barley is flowering in the first year. However, foxtail barley has slightly nodding spikes, and its glumes are hair-like throughout. • Grains of little barley are common in archaeological digs, suggesting domestication by early peoples prior to the widespread use of corn. • The sharp, rough awns can cause injury to the nose and mouth of grazing animals and can even penetrate hide and flesh.

AMERICAN DUNE GRASS, SEA LYME GRASS

Leymus mollis (Trin.) Pilger ssp. *mollis*
GRASS FAMILY (POACEAE [GRAMINEAE])

JG

Plants: Coarse perennial herbs; stems erect, **60–120** {15–150} **cm tall**, with dense, fine hairs; old withered leaves persisting at the stem base; mat-forming, **with long, thick underground stems** (rhizomes).

Leaves: Basal and alternate on the stem; blades stiff, flat (sometimes rolled), 6–12 {3–15} mm wide, prominently nerved, hairless beneath, rough on the upper surface, **with small, projecting lobes** (auricles) at the base; ligules up to 1 mm long, finely ciliate; sheaths crowded and overlapping.

Flower clusters: Erect spikes, 10–20 {8–30} cm long, 1–2 cm thick; **spikelets** dense, **paired, stalkless** (sometimes short-stalked), on opposite sides of the main stalk (rachis), **4–6-flowered; glumes lance-shaped, flat**, 3–5 {6}-nerved, **hairy**, 12–25 mm long; **lemmas sharp-pointed**, with thin, translucent edges, **soft-hairy**, 10–20 mm long; anthers 5–9 mm long; {June–August}.

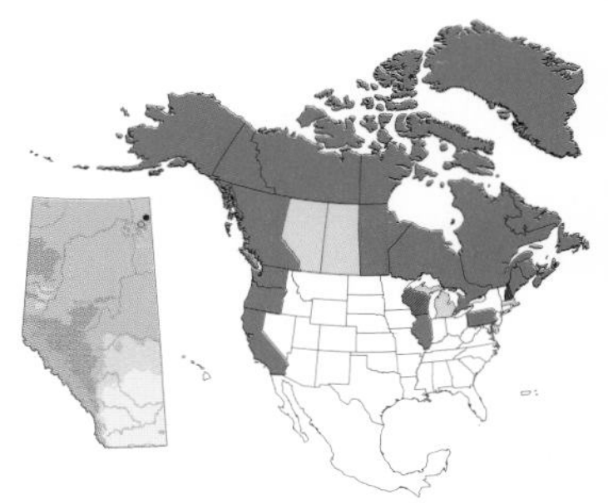

Fruits: Grains; mature florets **breaking away above the glumes** and between the florets.

Habitat: Sand dunes; elsewhere, primarily on coastal sand dunes.

Notes: This species has also been called *Elymus mollis* Trin. and *Elymus arenarius* L. ssp. *mollis* (Trin.) Hult. • In some parts of the arctic, leaves of American dune grass were used for basket weaving and for insulation in boots. • This species forms associations with mycorrhizal fungi. • Virginia wild rye (*Elymus virginicus* L.) is a similar rare grass that grows in open woods and thickets farther south. It is also stout and erect, but it lacks underground stems. Unlike American dune grass, Virginia wild rye has hairless or sparsely hairy lemmas tipped with a bristle (awn), and its glumes curve outward at the base.

ELYMUS VIRGINICUS

Ferns and Fern Allies

BOG CLUB-MOSS

Lycopodiella inundata (L.) Holub
CLUB-MOSS FAMILY (LYCOPODIACEAE)

Plants: **Dwarf perennial herbs**, with prostrate, short-creeping stems 5–10 {3–20} cm long, producing unbranched, ascending to erect fertile branches **3–6** {10} **cm tall**; anchored by many irregular roots on underside of stems.

Leaves: Crowded, in 8–10 vertical rows, **awl-shaped, 4–6** {8} **mm long**, less than 1 mm wide, curved toward the upper side of the stem, broadest near base, tapered to a soft, slender point.

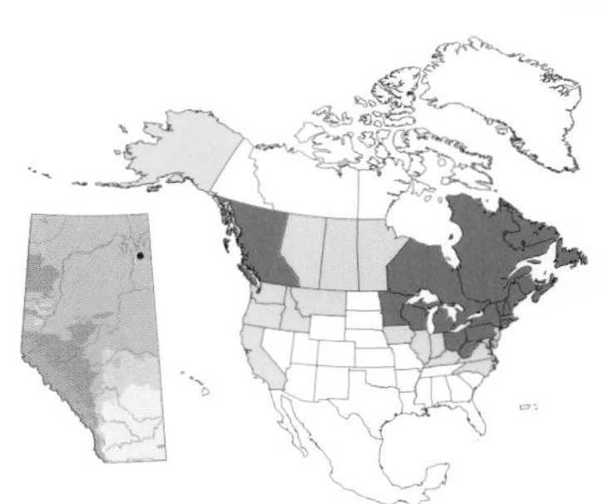

Spore clusters: Round dots (sporangia) about 1 mm wide, in the axils of broad-based, specialized leaves (sporophylls), in stalkless **cones** (strobili) **1–2 cm long** at the tips of fertile branches; spores sulphur-yellow, shed as fine powder through a horizontal opening in the sporangia.

Habitat: Sphagnum bogs; elsewhere, on sandy shores and in marshes and other wet sites.

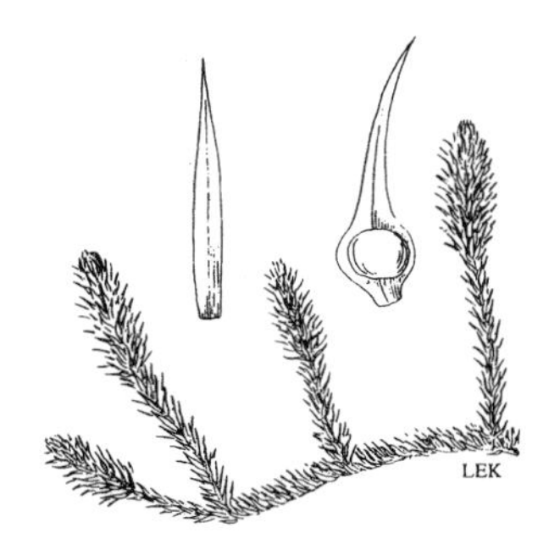

Notes: This species has also been called *Lycopodium inundatum* L. It is also found in scattered boreal regions around the world, including western Europe and Japan. These inconspicuous little plants are easily overlooked. • Another rare Alberta club-moss, ground-fir (*Diphasiastrum sitchense* (Rupr.) Holub, also called *Lycopodium sitchense* Rupr. and *Lycopodium sabinifolium* Willd. var. *sitchense* (Rupr.) Fern., also misspelled *Lycopodium sabinaefolium*), is a low (5–15 {17.5} cm tall) species with small (3–4 {5–6} mm long), broadly lance-shaped leaves in 5 vertical spiralling rows on repeatedly branched stems from creeping underground stems (rhizomes). Its spore clusters are borne in the axils of specialized leaves that are very different from the vegetative leaves, and these are crowded in stalkless or short-stalked strobili at the tips of fertile branches, taller than the sterile branches. Ground-fir grows in open woods and alpine tundra. • The Cree used club-moss spores to determine the fate of sick people. The spores were placed in a container of water, and if they radiated toward the sun, the patient would survive his illness. • Club-mosses produce 2 very different forms of plants: the green, leafy plants (sporophytes) that we call club-mosses and tiny, scale-like plants (gametophytes) that are rarely seen.

DIPHASIASTRUM SITCHENSE

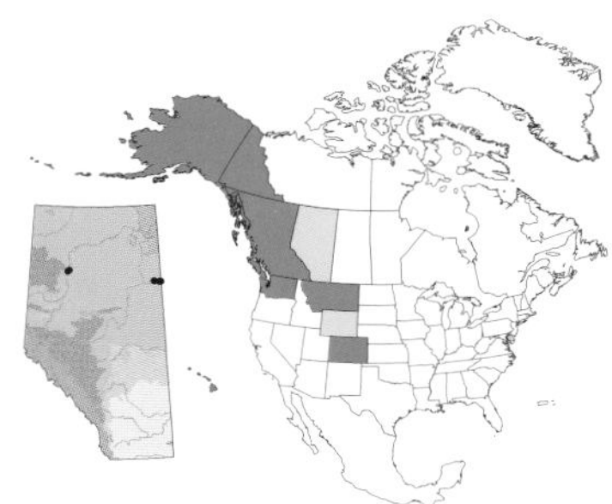

NORTHERN FIR-MOSS, MOUNTAIN CLUB-MOSS

Huperzia selago (L.) Bernh. *ex* Schrank & Mart.
CLUB-MOSS FAMILY (LYCOPODIACEAE)

Plants: **Small, glossy, yellow-green perennial herbs**, with erect, forked, bottle-brush-like stems **5–12** {20} **cm tall**, with **annual rings** as a result of alternating fertile (lower) and sterile (upper) zones which are produced each year, often also producing **small bud-like growths** (gemmae) in the upper leaf axils; from short (mostly 2–5 cm long) creeping stems with roots from among persistent leaves.

Leaves: Densely crowded in 8–10 vertical rows, **broadly awl-shaped, 3–8 mm long**, usually hollow at the base.

Spore clusters: Small round dots (sporangia) about 1 mm wide, **scattered along the stem in the axils of ordinary** (not specialized) **leaves**; spores sulphur-yellow, shed as fine powder through a horizontal opening in the sporangia.

Habitat: Bogs and cold woods in northern Alberta; elsewhere, in moist tundra.

Notes: Another rare species, alpine fir-moss (*Huperzia haleakalae* (Brack.) Holub) grows on damp, mossy ledges in alpine and subalpine zones in southern Alberta. It is distinguished from northern fir-moss by the lack of weak annual constrictions on its bulblet-producing (gemmiferous) branches and by the presence of 1–3 rings (pseudowhorls) of gemmae at the tips of the current year's growth or scattered throughout the mature shoots (rather than in a single ring at the end). • These 2 species are distinguished from other club-mosses in this province by their spore clusters, which are scattered along the stems in the axils of normal leaves, rather than clustered near the stem tips in cone-like clusters or on specialized leaves. Both have been called *Lycopodium selago* L.

H. HALEAKALAE

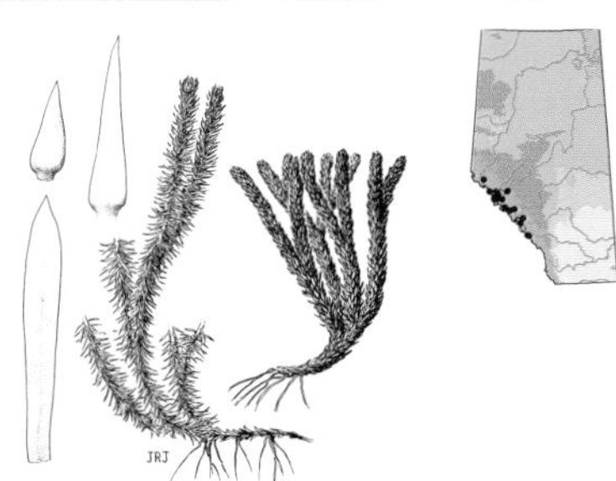

Wallace's little club-moss, Wallace's spike-moss

Selaginella wallacei Hieron.
SPIKE-MOSS FAMILY (SELAGINELLACEAE)

JP

Plants: Pale green to greyish, **moss-like, matted** herbs; main stems slender, trailing, irregularly branched, up to 10–20 cm long; branches ascending, 1–2-forked; producing loose or compact mats with fibrous roots along the stems.

Leaves: Densely **overlapping**, spirally arranged, thick, firm, **needle-like**, 1-nerved, **2–3** {1.5–3.5} **mm long, attached squarely** to the stem, **leaving no conspicuous remnants** when detached, usually hairy and edged with 5–12 stiff hairs, **tipped with a white, 0.2–0.5** {0.9} **mm long bristle.**

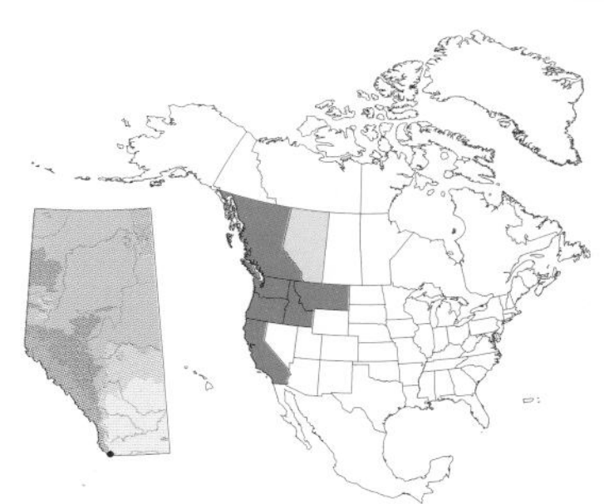

Spore clusters: In the axils of triangular to egg-shaped, specialized leaves (sporophylls) that form sharply **4-angled, 1–3** {9} **cm long cones** (strobili) at the stem tips (often paired); spores bright to pale orange, of 2 kinds (megaspores and microspores) which are borne in separate spore cases (sporangia) in the same cone (usually).

Habitat: Dry, rocky slopes, cliffs and ledges; elsewhere, also on moist, shaded, rocky banks and in meadows.

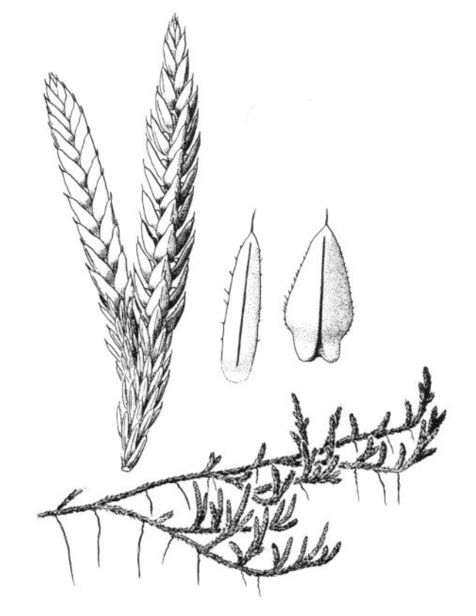

Notes: This small plant resembles and often grows intermingled with prairie spike-moss (*Selaginella densa* Rydb.), also known as prairie selaginella, but that species has smaller, denser mats with shorter, tufted branches. The leaves of prairie selaginella extend down the sides of the stem at their bases, and the lobes remain attached to the stems when the leaves are removed. • The form of Wallace's little club-moss can vary greatly with habitat. In dry, exposed conditions it forms small, compact mats of short stems bearing tightly appressed leaves that narrow abruptly to a bristle at their tip. Plants from moister habitats form loosely creeping mats of longer stems with looser, fleshier leaves that extend down the stem at their bases and taper gradually to a bristle at their tips. • The spores of the spike-mosses produce microscopic plants called prothalli. These are seldom observed, as they usually develop within the walls of the spores. The prothalli are gametophytes, which produce male and female sexual organs. When an egg cell is fertilized, it grows into a green plant that we recognize as a spike-moss. These plants are sporophytes, which produce spores, and thus the cycle begins again.

QUILLWORTS

Isoetes L. spp.
QUILLWORT FAMILY (ISOETACEAE)

(SEE KEY, APPENDIX I, PP. 391)

Plants: Aquatic perennial **herbs**; stems short, **fleshy, corm-like**, 2–3-lobed, nearly round, at the centre of a **dense tuft of onion-like leaves**; from fibrous roots.

Leaves: Basal, several to many, linear with broad spoon-shaped bases, **grass-like**, 2–20 cm long, erect to spreading, straight or curved downward, with **an inconspicuous membrane** (ligule) **up to 2.5 mm long on the inner side** just above the spore cluster.

I. BOLANDERI

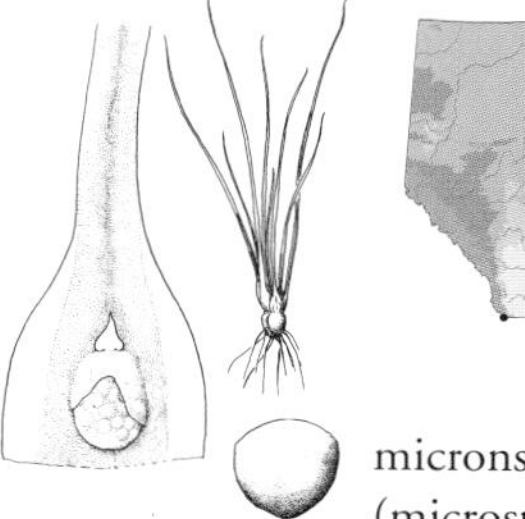

Spore clusters: Single, 4–10 mm long, 2.5–3 mm wide, in a depression **on the inner side of broad, spoon-shaped leaf bases**, covered by a thin membrane (velum); spores of two forms, female (megaspores, 350–700 microns in diameter) and male (microspores, 23–43 microns in diameter), which are borne in separate spore cases (sporangia); variously **ornamented**; late August.

I. MARITIMA

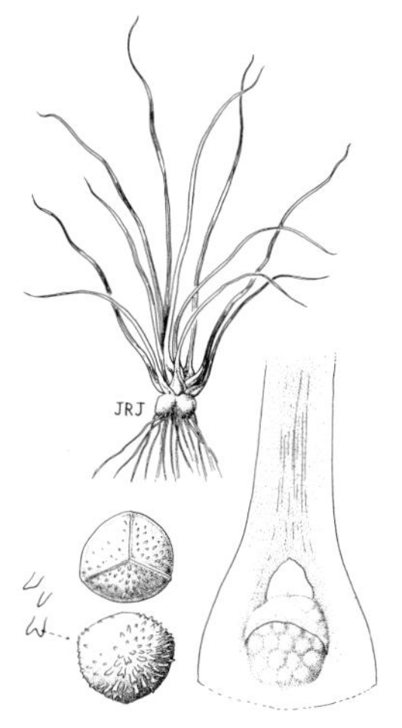

Habitat: The Alberta quillworts are all submerged aquatic species growing in permanent lakes and ponds. Northern quillwort (*Isoetes echinospora* Durieu) and coastal quillwort (*Isoetes maritima* L. Underwood) grow in clear, nutrient-poor, non-calcareous lakes and ponds, in shallow water up to about 1 m deep. Western quillwort (*Isoetes occidentalis* L.F. Henderson) occurs in deep lake water, and Bolander's quillwort (*Isoetes bolanderi* Engelm.) grows in deep water of nutrient-poor alpine or subalpine lakes and ponds in unglaciated areas.

Notes: Western quillwort and coastal quillwort are known only from Jasper National Park. Northern quillwort is known from northern and northeastern Alberta. Bolander's quillwort is known in Canada only from Waterton Lakes National Park. • A fifth species, Howell's quillwort (*Isoetes* *howellii* Engelm.), has not been reported for Alberta but is found within a few hundred metres of the Continental Divide in BC at Akamina Pass. Howell's quillwort is very similar to *I. bolanderi* but is distinguished by its larger (often more than 15 cm) leaves with well-developed peripheral strands and by the larger (over 1 cm long) wing margin above each sporangium. • Quillworts could be mistaken for spike-rushes (*Eleocharis* spp.) at first glance, but quillworts are easily identified by their swollen leaf bases and short, thickened stems (corms). • Hybrids between species are frequent when 2 species grow in the same habitat. Hybrids can be distinguished by their malformed spores. *Isoetes* x *truncata* (A.A. Eaton) Clute, a hybrid between *I. maritima* and *I. occidentalis*, is the only known hybrid in Alberta. • Quillworts are very sensitive to changes in water quality, and the length, colour, shape and rigidity of leaves varies greatly with changes in habitat. • The generic name *Isoetes* was taken from the Greek *isos* (equal) and *etos* (year), in reference to the evergreen leaves of these plants. Two of the specific epithets refer to distribution. *Occidentalis* means 'western' and *maritima* means 'growing by the sea.' *Echinospora*, from the Greek *echinos* (sea urchin) and *spora* (seed), refers to the spiny megaspores, and *bolanderi* commemorates Henry Nicholas Bolander (1831–1897), a botanical collector who worked in the Sierra Nevada with the California State Geological Survey.

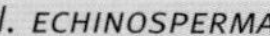

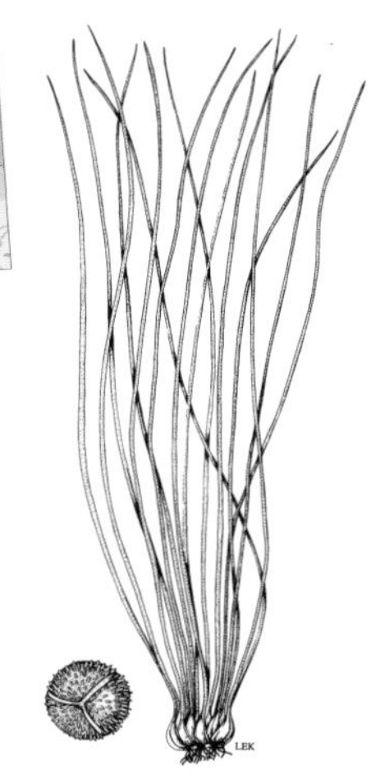

I. OCCIDENTALIS

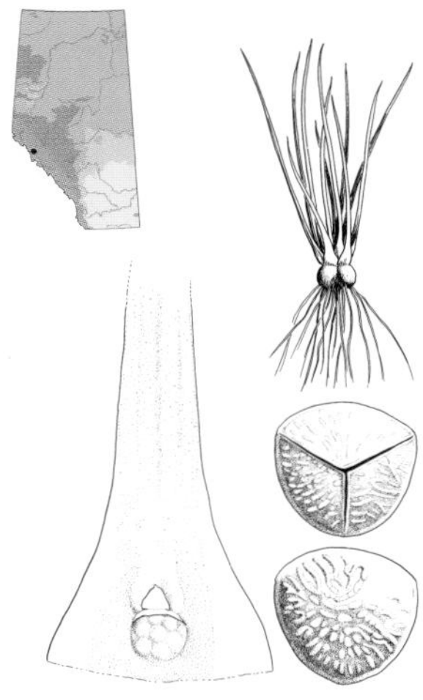

I. HOWELLI

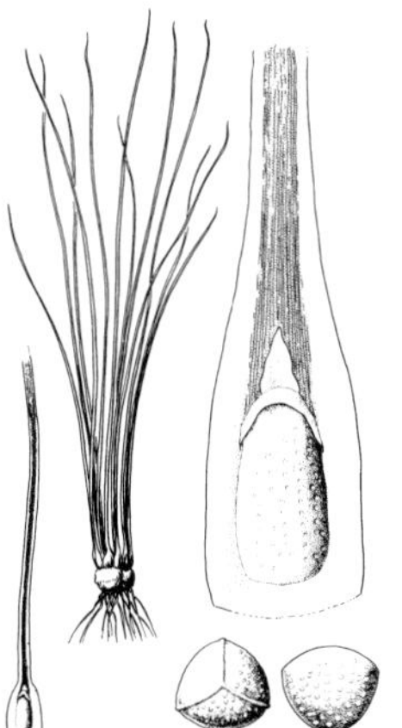

I. x *TRUNCATA*

ELEOCHARIS ENGELMANNII

WW

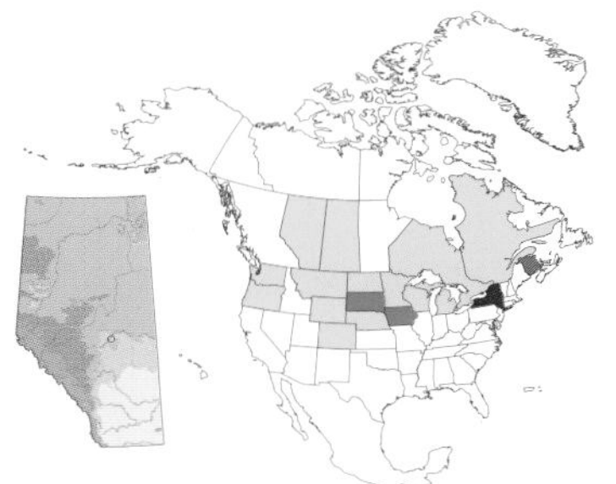

FIELD GRAPE FERN, PRAIRIE MOONWORT

Botrychium campestre W.H. Wagner & D.R. Farrar
ADDER'S-TONGUE FAMILY (OPHIOGLOSSACEAE)

(SEE KEY, APPENDIX 1, PP. 389–90)

Plants: Small, **fleshy** perennial herbs **6–12 cm tall**; common basal stalk usually 5–10 cm tall; from **underground stems with tiny, round bodies** (gemmae) 0.4–0.8 mm in diameter, in grape-like clusters; **appear in early spring** and **usually die by late spring** to early summer before plants of associated moonwort species (occasionally persisting until late summer).

Leaves: Of 2 types, a single short-stalked, sterile blade below a single fertile blade (see description of spore clusters); **sterile blades** fleshy, dull, whitish green, oblong to linear-oblong in outline, commonly widest above the middle, up to 4 cm long and 1.3 cm wide, **folded lengthwise, once-divided** into as many as 5 {9} pairs of segments; segments spreading, usually not overlapping, separated by 1–3 times the segment width and with the basal pair about equal in size, mostly long and narrow to narrowly spatula-shaped, **edged with shallow, rounded or sharp teeth**, usually notched at the tip; veins in a fan-shaped pattern; midribs absent.

Spore clusters: Small, spherical, yellow, stalkless spore sacs (sporangia) borne on specialized, fertile leaf blades; fertile blades **single**, once-divided (rarely twice-divided), **usually stalkless** but sometimes broadly tapered to stalk that is 1–1½ times as long as the sterile blade.

Habitat: Grassy fields and ditches.

Notes: Another rare species, spatulate grape fern (*Botrychium spathulatum* W.H. Wagner), also called spatulate moonwort, has a nearly stalkless, leathery sterile blade that is shiny yellow-green, triangular in outline and divided into as many as 8 pairs of ascending, widely spaced segments. Its fertile blade is once- or twice-divided, and its leaves appear in late spring through summer. Spatulate grape fern grows in fields and grassy openings in the mountains. • Mingan grape fern (*Botrychium minganense* Victorin), also known as Mingan moonwort and *Botrychium lunaria* (L.) Swartz var. *minganense* (Victorin) Dole, is a larger plant, up to 30 cm tall. Its dull yellow-green, linear sterile blade is once-divided into as many as 10 pairs of horizontal to

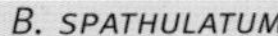
B. SPATHULATUM

WW

spreading segments. The fertile blade is also once-divided (occasionally twice-divided), and the leaves appear in spring through summer. Mingan grape fern is a rare species that grows in a variety of habitats at elevations up to 3,700 m. Many specimens of *B. minganense* have been misidentified as *Botrychium dusenii* (H. Christ) Alston. • Scalloped grape fern (*Botrychium crenulatum* W.H. Wagner), also called dainty moonwort, has a thin, yellow-green sterile blade that is once-divided into as many as 5 pairs of spreading, well-separated segments. Its fertile blade is once- or twice-divided, and its leaves appear in mid to late spring and die in late summer, although they may not appear every year. Scalloped grape fern grows in wet areas and in Alberta is known only from Banff National Park. • Ascending grape fern (*Botrychium ascendens* W.H. Wagner), also called upswept moonwort, has a thin but firm, bright yellow-green sterile blade that is longer than wide (often broadly lance-shaped), up to 6 cm long and 1.5 cm wide and once-divided into as many as 5 pairs of rounded, strongly ascending, well-separated, sharply toothed or shallowly lobed segments. The segments lack midribs, and their veins form a fan-shaped pattern. Some of the basal segments often develop spore clusters (sporangia). The twice-divided, spore-bearing (fertile) blade is $\frac{1}{3}$–$\frac{1}{2}$ again as long as the sterile blade and $1\frac{1}{3}$–2 times as long as the common basal stalk. Ascending grape fern appears in late spring to midsummer in grassy openings in mountain forests. It grows with *Botrychium lunaria*, *B. minganense* and *B. crenulatum*, and hybrids with *B. crenulatum* have been reported. • Common moonwort (*Botrychium lunaria* (L.) Swartz) is a more widespread species of open fields. It has a dark green, once-divided, thick, fleshy sterile blade, with up to 9 pairs of toothless, spreading and mostly overlapping segments, and its fertile blade is once- or twice-divided. Common moonwort appears in spring and dies in the latter half of summer.

B. MINGANENSE

JG

B. CRENULATUM

SW

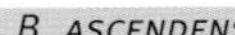

B. ASCENDENS

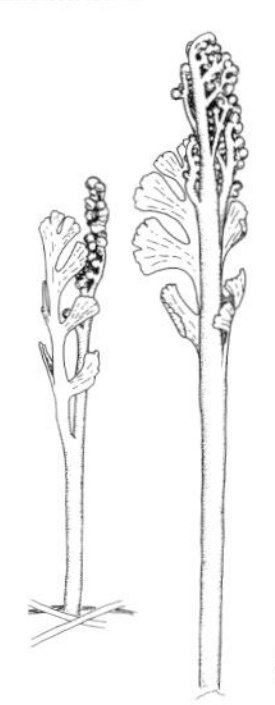

JG

WW

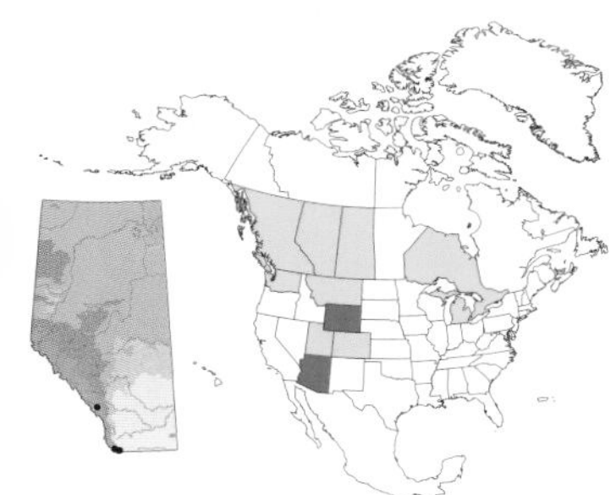

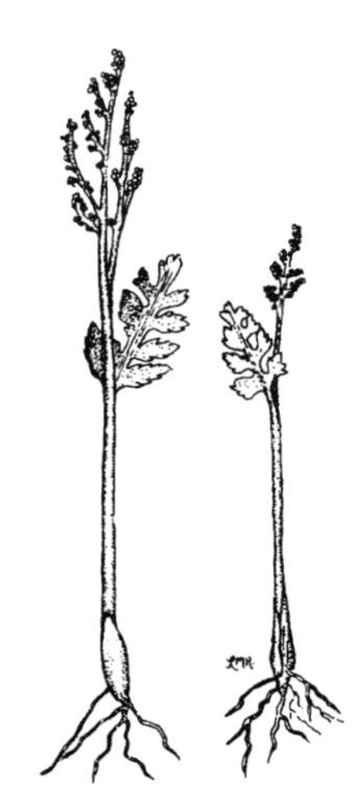

WESTERN GRAPE FERN, WESTERN MOONWORT

Botrychium hesperium (Maxon & R.T. Clausen) W.H. Wagner & Lellinger
ADDER'S-TONGUE FAMILY (OPHIOGLOSSACEAE)

(SEE KEY, APPENDIX 1, PP. 389–90)

Plants: Small perennial herbs {5} 10–20 cm tall; common basal stalk usually 5–10 cm tall; **appear in early spring and die in early fall.**

Leaves: Of 2 types: a single short-stalked, sterile blade below a single fertile blade (see description of spore clusters); **sterile blades oblong-linear to triangular in outline**, up to 6 cm long and 5 cm wide, dull grey-green, **once- or twice-divided,** with up to 6 pairs of ascending, **usually crowded to overlapping segments**; lowest pair of segments commonly much larger and more divided than the others and lobed along the edges; upper segments rounded, smooth-edged to shallowly lobed.

Spore clusters: Small, spherical, yellow, stalkless spore sacs (sporangia) borne on erect, fertile leaves; **fertile blades single,** 1–3 times divided, 2–10 cm long, borne on slender stalks 1–8 cm long.

Habitat: Wooded areas, often with other moonworts, including *Botrychium lanceolatum*, *B. lunaria*, *B. pinnatum*, *B. minganense*, *B. simplex* and *B. paradoxum*.

Notes: This species is also known as *Botrychium matricariifolium* (Döll) W.D.J. Koch ssp. *hesperium* Maxon & R.T. Clausen. • Another rare species, lance-leaved grape fern (*Botrychium lanceolatum* (Gmelin) Angström ssp. *lanceolatum* and ssp. *angustisegmentum* (Pease & A.H. Moore) R.T. Clausen), also called triangle moonwort, grows up to 20 cm in height. It has a green to pale yellow-green, somewhat shiny, triangular sterile blade up to 6 cm long and 10 cm wide, that is once- or twice-divided into as many as 5 pairs of ascending, well-spaced (not overlapping) segments. The leaves appear in late spring to early summer and wither in midsummer. The fertile blade is divided 1–3 times. In Alberta, this rare species has been found only on mountain slopes, but outside of Alberta it grows mainly in open fields and also on peaty slopes, in mountain meadows and in open woods at elevations up to 3,700 m. • Paradoxical grape fern (*Botrychium paradoxum* W.H. Wagner), also called paradox moonwort, does not have sterile blades. Instead, it produces 2 fertile blades (a large blade 7–15 cm long below a smaller blade about ⅔ as long) on a once-divided, 0.5–2 mm wide stalk that reaches up to ½ the total height. Its leaves appear in early summer and disappear in late summer. In Alberta, this rare species grows in grassy openings in mountain forests, but in other areas it is also found in fields and meadows at elevations from 1,500–3,000 m. Paradoxical grape fern does not have a green sterile blade that could provide food through photosynthesis. Instead, it probably acquires nutrients through the fungi associated with its roots (mycorrhizae). The specific epithet *paradoxum* refers to the unique, paradoxical condition of having 2 spore-bearing blades and no sterile leaves. • As its name suggests, stalked grape fern (*Botrychium pedunculosum* W.H. Wagner), also called stalked moonwort, is distinguished by its reddish brown common basal stalk and its long leaf stalks, which approximately equal their blades. The lowest segments of the sterile leaves are relatively wide (egg-shaped to diamond-shaped), and they often develop spore clusters (sporangia). Stalked grape fern grows in brushy, disturbed sites along streams and roads at 300–1,000 m. • Western grape fern apparently hybridizes with paradoxical grape fern in Wateron Lakes National Park to produce the very rare *Botrychium* x *watertonense* W.H. Wagner. This hybrid is distinguished by its broad, sterile blades, which have spore clusters along their edges, rather than on separate fruiting stalks. It grows in grassy openings in coniferous forests in the mountains and is not known from outside of Alberta. The leaves appear in early summer.

B. PEDUNCULOSUM

B. PARADOXUM

B. X WATERTONENSE *B. LANCEOLATUM*

PL

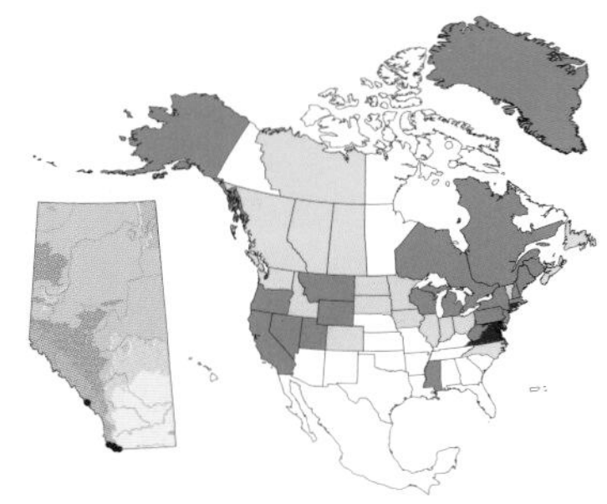

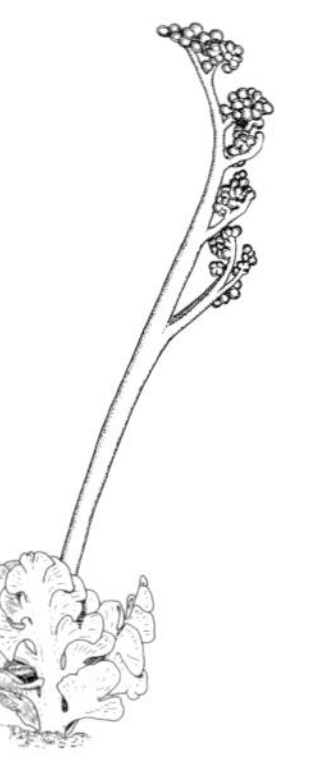

DWARF GRAPE FERN, LEAST MOONWORT

Botrychium simplex E. Hitchc.
ADDER'S-TONGUE FAMILY (OPHIOGLOSSACEAE)

(SEE KEY, APPENDIX I, PP. 389–90)

Plants: Small perennial herbs, 3–15 {25} cm tall; common basal stalk small or absent; appearing from mid spring to early fall.

Leaves: Of 2 types, a single short-stalked, sterile blade below a single fertile blade (see description of spore clusters); **sterile blades thin and herbaceous**, 0.5–4 {6} cm long, dull to bright green or whitish green, linear to triangular in outline, usually **divided** into **3 similar, pinnately divided segments** (pinnae); pinnae with 2–4 {5} pairs of well-developed segments (pinnules), the lowest pair of pinnules usually larger than the others and again divided; stalks of sterile blades 0–3 cm long.

Spore clusters: Small, spherical, yellow, stalkless spore sacs (sporangia) borne on erect, fertile leaf blades; fertile blades single, 3–8 times as long as the sterile blade, mostly once-divided, borne on a stout stalk more than twice as long as the blade.

Habitat: In moist meadows and along the edges of wetlands; elsewhere, also in dry fields and roadside ditches up to 2,200 m.

Notes: This species has also been called *Botrychium tenebrosum* A.A. Eaton. • Another rare species, leather grape fern (*Botrychium multifidum* (S.G. Gmelin) Rupr.), also has the sterile blade attached near the base of the stalk. It is 2–15 {20} cm tall with a shiny, green sterile blade on a stalk 2–15 cm long. The sterile blade can be up to 25 cm long and 35 cm wide, and it is divided 2–3 times, with up to 10 pairs of horizontal or ascending segments. These rather leathery leaves remain green through winter, reappearing in spring. The fertile blade is also 2–3 times divided. In Alberta, leather grape fern has been found in moist sandy areas, but in other areas, it grows mainly in fields.• The generic name *Botrychium*, from the Greek *botryos* (a bunch of grapes), refers to the grape-like clusters of spore sacs on the fertile leaves.

B. MULTIFIDUM

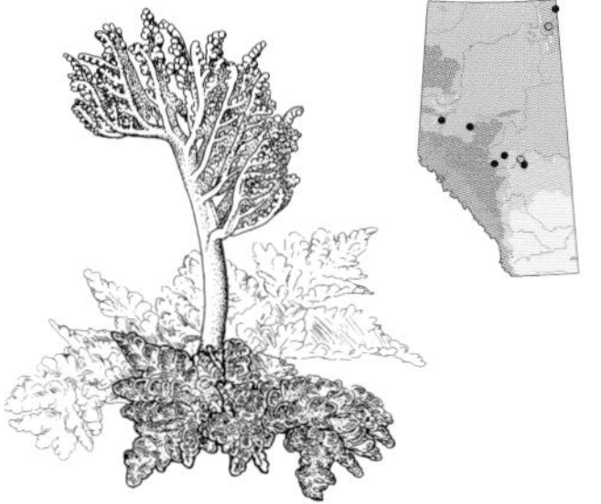

WESTERN MAIDENHAIR FERN

Adiantum aleuticum (Rupr.) Paris
MAIDENHAIR FERN FAMILY (PTERIDIACEAE [POLYPODIACEAE])

DJ

Plants: **Delicate** perennial herbs, with a single to a few **annual leaves** on 10–40 {60} **cm tall stalks**; from stout, short-creeping or slanted underground stems (rhizomes) 2–5 mm thick, with small (3–6 mm long, {0.5} 1–2 mm wide) scales.

Leaves: **With spreading, horizontal blades on erect, wiry, lustrous, reddish brown to purplish black stalks**; blades round to kidney-shaped in outline, 10–40 cm long, **twice-divided, with 6–10 radiating, finger-like branches** (pinnae), each with 15–35 pinnately arranged leaflets (pinnules); **pinnules very thin, greyish green**, with a thin, waxy coating (glaucous), **oblong**, mostly 12–22 mm long, 5–9 mm wide, **spreading** at right angles to the central stalk (rachis), usually deeply and irregularly **cut and rolled under along the upper edge.**

Spore clusters: Oblong to moon-shaped clusters of spore cases (sori) along the upper edge of the pinnules, **covered by the down-rolled leaf edge.**

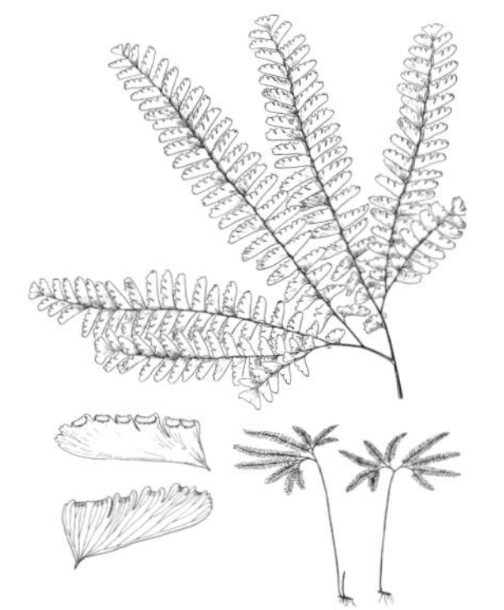

Habitat: Cliffs and boulder-strewn slopes in subalpine areas; elsewhere, in moist woods and seepage areas and on protected creek sides.

Notes: This species has also been called *Adiantum pedatum* L. • This delicate fern requires protection from early or late frost, and is adapted to the wet zones of the western cordillera. In Alberta it is limited climatically by its need for abundant precipitation in conjunction with sheltered rocky habitats. • The generic name *Adiantum* means 'not wetted,' referring to the fact that the leaves shed water. • In the 19th century, maidenhair fern was highly valued as a medicine. It was used in teas and syrups for treating colds, sore throats, flu and asthma. The stems were also used in hair rinses to give hair shine.

TD

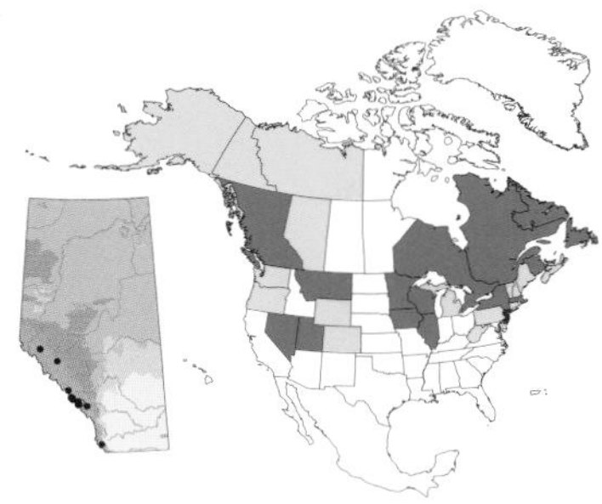

Steller's rock brake

Cryptogramma stelleri (S.G. Gmel.) Prantl
MAIDENHAIR FERN FAMILY (PTERIDIACEAE [POLYPODIACEAE])

Plants: Small, **delicate herbs** with 2 types of leaves (fronds); from **slender** (1–1.5 mm thick), **creeping, few-branched** stems that are succulent and brittle, and that shrivel in the second year.

Leaves: Scattered along stems, delicate, soon shed, of 2 types; sterile leaves, green, 3–15 cm tall, with **blades 5 {3–8} cm long**, broadly lance-shaped in outline, 1–2 times pinnately divided into 9–13 wide, **flat, round-toothed segments**; stalks yellowish green above, reddish brown to purplish and scaly at the base; fertile leaves described under 'spore clusters.'

Spore clusters: Borne on the lower surface of **specialized, fertile leaves**, forming an almost continuous band, covered by **down-rolled leaf edges**, lacking membranous coverings (indusia); fertile leaves stiffly erect, 5–20 cm tall, longer than sterile leaves, with blades shorter than their stalks, 2–3 times pinnately divided into **slender, toothless segments** that are up to 2 cm long.

Habitat: Cool, shaded, **calcareous sites**, on rock or in springs.

Notes: Steller's rock brake is a more or less circumpolar species. • The generic name *Cryptogramma* was derived from the Greek *cryptos* (hidden) and *gramme* (line), referring to the hidden lines of spores clusters under the down-rolled leaf edges.

LACE FERN

Cheilanthes gracillima D.C. Eat.
MAIDENHAIR FERN FAMILY (PTERIDIACEAE [POLYPODIACEAE])

Plants: **Delicate, densely tufted perennial herbs with evergreen leaves,** 8–25 cm tall; from branched crowns or short, scaly underground stems (rhizomes).

Leaves: Erect, linear-oblong, **slender, 4–11 cm long, 1–2 cm wide, 2–3 times pinnately divided** into leaflets (bipinnate to tripinnate), hairless or nearly so on the upper surface, **rusty-woolly beneath and with conspicuous scales on the midribs, central axes** (rachises) **and stalks,** rolled under along the edges; 19–41 leaflets (pinnae), crowded but not overlapping; stalks wiry, 3–12 cm long, chestnut-coloured.

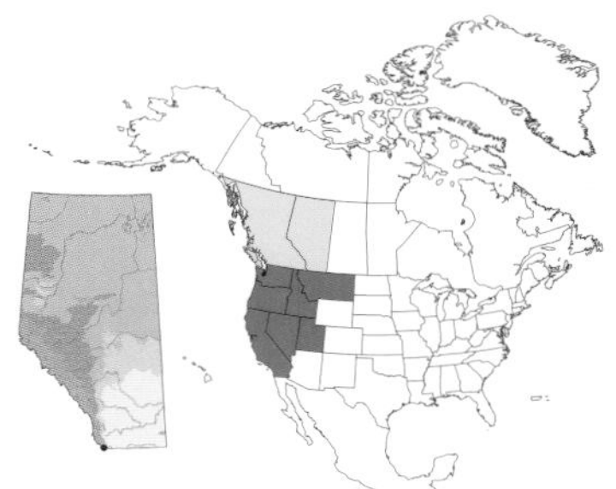

Spore clusters: Protected by and developing **under down-rolled leaf edges,** often appearing to cover the entire lower surface of the leaflet when mature.

Habitat: Ledges and crevices of igneous rocks and shale; elsewhere, in exposed, sunny sites from lower slopes to timberline in mountainous regions.

Notes: Slender lip fern (*Cheilanthes feei* T. Moore) resembles lace fern, but it has wider (1–3.5 cm) leaves without scales, and it grows on calcareous rock. • The generic name *Cheilanthes* was derived from the Greek *cheilos* (lip) and *anthos* (flower), in reference to the down-rolled leaf edges (lips), which overlap the spore clusters. The specific epithet *gracillima* means 'very slender.'

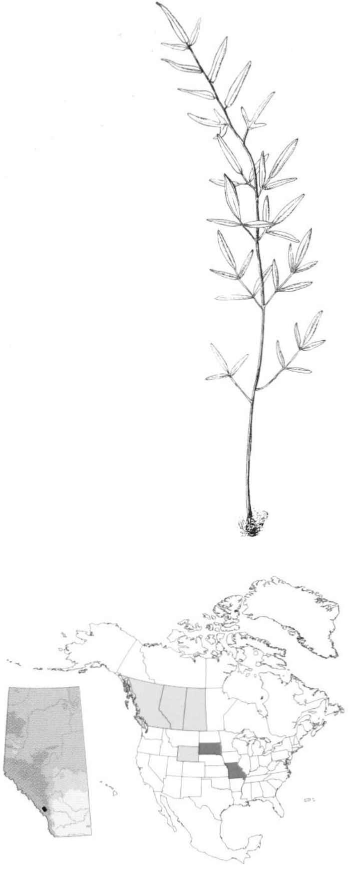

GASTON'S CLIFF BRAKE

Pellaea gastonyi Windham
MAIDENHAIR FERN FAMILY (PTERIDIACEAE [POLYPODIACEAE])

Plants: Delicate, tufted perennial herbs, up to 25 cm tall; from compact, ascending underground stems (rhizomes), 5–10 mm in diameter, covered with thin, reddish brown scales, 0.1–0.3 mm wide.

Leaves: Clumped, 8–25 cm long, of **2 slightly different forms** (dimorphic) with sterile leaves shorter than the fertile leaves; **blades leathery**, elongate-triangular to lance-shaped, 3–6 cm wide, **twice pinnately divided** into widely spreading leaflets (pinnae) with abruptly narrowed **bases that do not extend down the stalk**; leaflets usually divided into 3–7 oblong–lance-shaped, **7–30 mm long leaflets** (pinnules) with blunt or abruptly short-pointed tips; **edges rolled under**; stalks and **main leaf axes** (rachises) reddish **purple to dark brown, lustrous**, rounded on the upper (inner) side, sparsely hairy; young, coiled leaves soft-hairy.

Spore clusters: Long-stalked clusters (sporangia) containing 32 spores, borne on the underside of fertile leaflets in a **band along the edges, protected by down-rolled leaf edges** which cover less than ½ the lower surface; summer and fall.

Habitat: Calcareous cliffs and ledges.

Notes: Gaston's cliff brake originated through repeated hybridization between purple cliff brake (*Pellaea atropurpurea* (L.) Link) and smooth cliff brake (*Pellaea glabella* Mett. *ex* Kuhn), and it always reproduces asexually. It is an apogamous tetraploid. • Gaston's cliff brake is most commonly mistaken for purple cliff brake, but purple cliff brake has densely soft-hairy leaf axes (rachises), large leaflets (pinnules) and smaller spores (averaging less than 62 microns in diameter). Purple cliff brake is an eastern species that is not found in Alberta. • Smooth cliff brake is more common in Alberta. It is distinguished by the hairless lower surface of its leaflets and its nearly hairless stalks (rachises). It also generally has narrower, linear-oblong to lance-shaped leaflets with bases that extend slightly down the main stalk (slightly decurrent).

P. GLABELLA

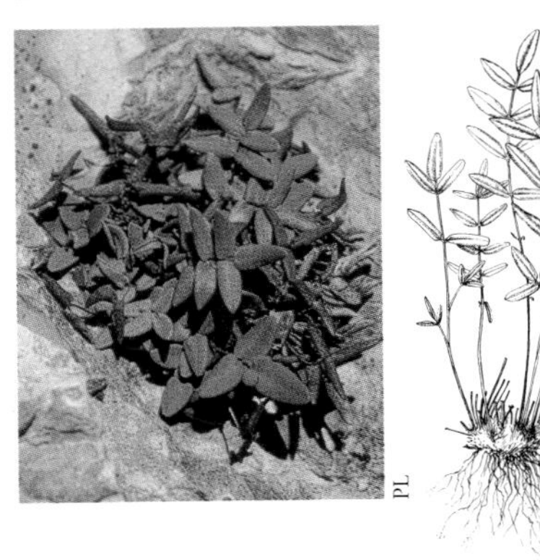

ALPINE SPLEENWORT, AMERICAN ALPINE LADY FERN

Athyrium alpestre (Hoppe) Clairville var. *americanum* Butters
WOODFERN FAMILY (DRYOPTERIDACEAE [POLYPODIACEAE])

TD

Plants: **Tufted** perennial herbs, **20–80 cm tall**, with **annual leaves** (fronds); from short, stout, densely scaly rhizomes covered with the bases of old leaf stalks.

Leaves: Basal, clustered, **feathery**; blades thin, delicate, **obscurely veined**, narrowly elliptic to lance-shaped, 2–3 {4} **times pinnately divided** into slender leaflets; main leaflets (pinnae) in about 20–25 offset pairs, well-spaced, short-stalked, the larger ones 2–8 cm long and with 8–15 offset pairs of deeply toothed or lobed sub-leaflets (pinnules); stalks straw-coloured or red-brown with brown to dark brown, lance-shaped scales at the base, shorter than the blades.

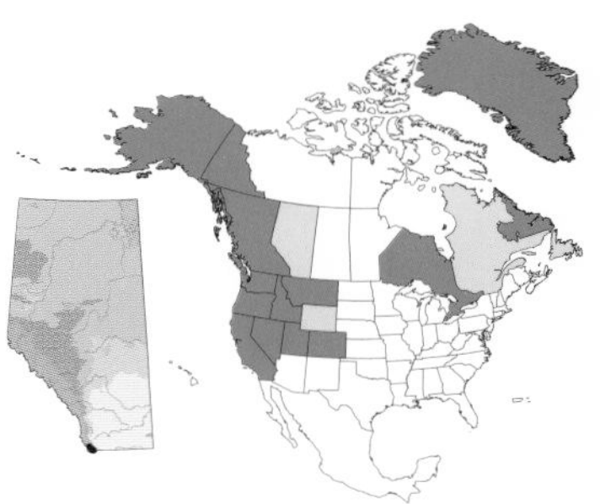

Spore clusters: Round dots (sori) less than 1 mm across, on the lower side of the leaflets, **set in from the edge; indusia completely absent** (sometimes present as tiny scales; independent of season.

Habitat: Rocky alpine slopes and alpine meadows; elsewhere, also along streams, often near timberline.

Notes: This species has also been called *Athyrium americanum* (Butters) Maxon and *Athyrium distentifolium* Tausch *ex* Opiz ssp. *americanum* (Butters) Hult. It is limited in Alberta by its requirement for abundant precipitation in conjunction with rocky habitats. • Alpine spleenwort is very similar to a more widespread species, lady fern (*Athyrium filix-femina* (L.) Mertens), but that fern has longer (40–200 cm), wider leaves, with larger (up to 15 cm long) leaflets. Its crescent-shaped spore clusters have delicate indusia attached along 1 side. Lady fern grows on organic-rich soils in moist woods and thickets. • The fiddleheads of lady fern are sometimes collected for food, but most people consider them 'survival food' only because of their bitterness. • Oil from lady fern rootstocks was used for hundreds of years to expel worms in humans and animals. A single dose was often enough, but too much could cause **muscular weakness, coma and, most frequently, blindness.** • The generic name *Athyrium* was derived from the Greek *athyros* (without a door), in reference to the lack of a protective membrane (indusium) over the spore clusters of some species.

CWa

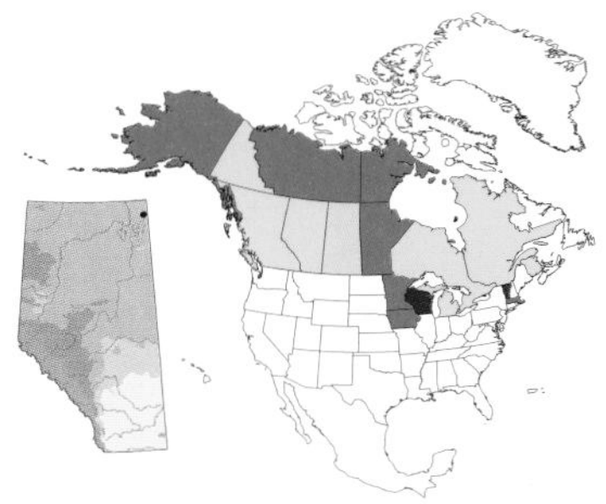

NORTHERN OAK FERN, NAHANNI OAK FERN

Gymnocarpium jessoense (Koidz.) Koidz.
WOODFERN FAMILY (DRYOPTERIDACEAE [POLYPODIACEAE])

Plants: Delicate herbs 5–50 cm tall, with **annual leaves** (fronds) that are **glandular-hairy** on both surfaces; from dark, slender creeping underground stems (rhizomes), 0.5–1.5 mm in diameter.

Leaves: Single, along rhizomes, with blades **triangular** in outline and on long, slender **stalks** (clearly **longer than the blades**); blades 5–14 {3–18} cm long, longer than wide, **firm** and rather stiff or lax and delicate, 2–3 times pinnately divided, with **3 main parts** but the **lower 2 half as long as the upper** one, the smallest leaflets blunt-tipped; **stalks straw-coloured**, dark at the base, **dull and glandular**, 5–25 cm long, with 2–6 mm long scales.

Spore clusters: Round dots (sori) **without protective membranes** (indusia), set in slightly from the leaf edge.

Habitat: Acidic to neutral rock crevices and slopes; elsewhere, on cliffs and in moist woods.

Notes: Northern oak fern is distinguished from its more common relative, common oak fern (*Gymnocarpium dryopteris* (L.) Newm.) by its narrower, firmer leaves. The 3 main leaflets of common oak fern are almost equal in size, and they are also thinner and hairless (not glandular-hairy). • Another species reported for western Alberta, western oak fern (*Gymnocarpium disjunctum* (Ruprecht) Ching), differs from common oak fern in having leaf blades that are about twice as large (8–24 cm vs. 3–14 cm), with the smallest leaflets pointed rather than blunt-tipped. • Northern oak fern could also be confused with another rare species, mountain bladder fern (*Cystopteris montana* (Lam.) Bernh. *ex* Desv., p. 365), but mountain bladder fern has delicate membranes (indusia) cupped over its young spore clusters (these membranes disintegrate with age), and its leaves are usually more finely divided and feathery in appearance. • The generic name *Gymnocarpium* was taken from the Greek *gymnos* (naked) and *karpos* (fruit), in reference to the bare, unprotected spore clusters, which never have indusia.

MOUNTAIN BLADDER FERN

Cystopteris montana (Lam.) Bernh. *ex* Desv.
WOODFERN FAMILY (DRYOPTERIDACEAE [POLYPODIACEAE])

Plants: Delicate, hairless herbs, 4–35 {45} cm tall, with **annual leaves** (fronds); from dark, cord-like, branched underground stems (rhizomes).

Leaves: Single, along rhizomes; blades triangular to egg-shaped in outline, 4–15 cm long and **about as wide as long, 3 {2–4} times pinnately divided** into irregularly toothed leaflets, appearing to have 3 main leaflets but the lower pair very asymmetric and clearly smaller than the upper one; **stalks** 6–20 {30} cm long, **green or straw-coloured** on upper part, dark brown to black at the base, **longer than the blade**, with scattered glands and scales.

Spore clusters: Small, round **dots** (sori) **on veins** on lower side of leaf, partly covered by an inconspicuous, whitish, **hood-like membrane** (indusium) which disintegrates as the spore clusters mature; summer–autumn.

Habitat: Damp, calcareous sites, often by springs or along streams in mixed or coniferous forest.

Notes: Mountain bladder fern might be confused with a much more common species, common oak fern (*Gymnocarpium dryopteris* (L.) Newm.), but oak fern has no indusia on its spore clusters and its leaves are usually less finely divided (less feathery in appearance) with 3 almost equal main leaflets. • The generic name *Cystopteris* was derived from the Greek *kystos* (bladder) and *pteris* (fern), in reference to the hood-like membranes (indusia) that cover the spore clusters. The specific epithet *montana* means 'of the mountains,' although this is not always the case in Alberta.

JP

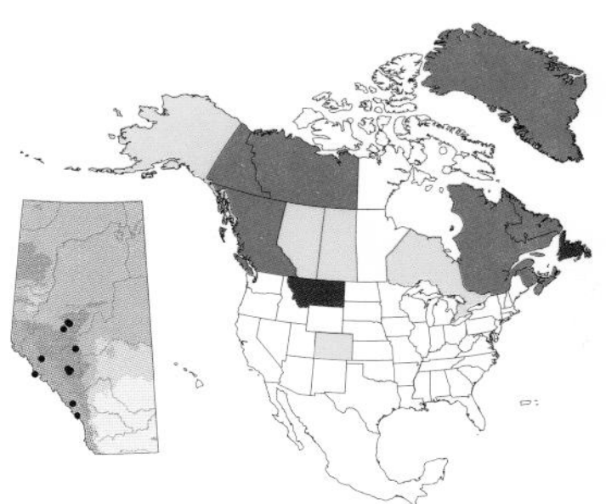

LK

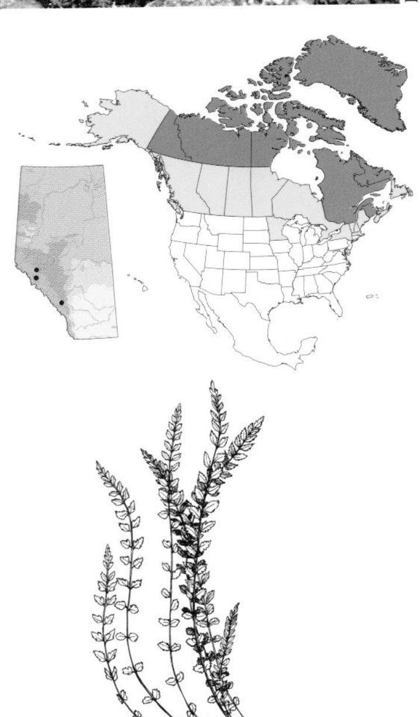

SMOOTH WOODSIA

Woodsia glabella R. Br. *ex* Richardson
WOODFERN FAMILY (DRYOPTERIDACEAE [POLYPODIACEAE])

Plants: Delicate perennial herbs 3–10 cm tall, with annual leaves (fronds); in dense clumps from compact stems covered in brown, finely toothed scales.

Leaves: Pale green, **hairless**; blades linear to linear–lance-shaped, {3.5} **4–16 cm long**, 6–15 mm wide, pinnately divided into **8–15 pairs of egg-shaped to almost round, 3–7-lobed leaflets**, sometimes edged with broad, rounded teeth; **stalks** delicate, hairless, **straw-coloured or greenish** throughout, breaking at a **dark joint near the base** and leaving **persistent brown-scaly bases.**

Spore clusters: Round, borne on the veins; **protective membrane** (indusium) an **inconspicuous disc with 5–8 thread-like segments**, under the spore cluster; summer–early autumn.

Habitat: Moist, shaded, usually calcareous sites, among boulders, on cliff ledges, and in crevices.

Notes: Rusty woodsia (*Woodsia ilvensis* (L.) R. Br.) is also rare in Alberta. It also has jointed leaf stalks, but the stalks are brown, firm, scaly and hairy along their length. The blades are wider than those of smooth woodsia (10–35 mm across), and they are dark green, hairy and scaly. The indusia are more conspicuous, and they have numerous (10–20) dark, thread-like segments. • The genus *Woodsia* was named in honour of Joseph Woods, the English botanist and architect who studied roses (*Rosa* spp.). *Glabella* is from the Latin word for 'smooth,' possibly referring to the relative lack of hairs and scales.

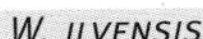

W. ILVENSIS

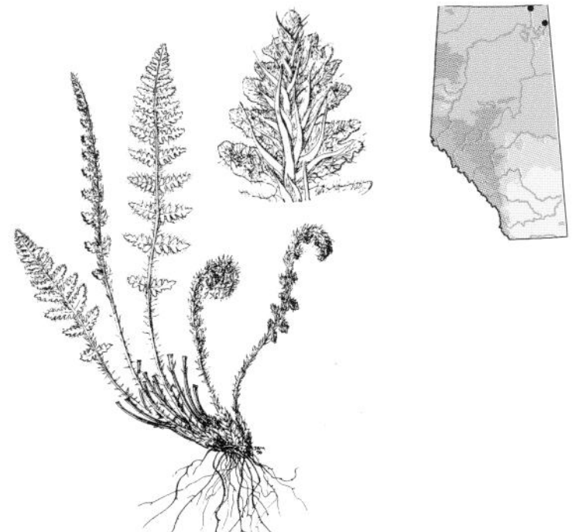

CRESTED SHIELD FERN

Dryopteris cristata (L.) A. Gray
WOODFERN FAMILY (DRYOPTERIDACEAE [POLYPODIACEAE])

DG

Plants: Loosely tufted, **glossy, somewhat leathery herbs, with some leaves persisting** through the winter, **30–80 cm tall**; from short, stout, creeping underground stems (rhizomes) covered with scales and the bases of old leaf stalks.

Leaves: In clusters with **deciduous fertile leaves** and **evergreen sterile leaves**; blades firm, lance-shaped in outline, **twice pinnately divided** into 10–20 pairs of leaflets; leaflets (pinnae) oblong–lance-shaped to broadly egg-shaped (lower leaflets clearly wider than the upper ones), up to 8 {10} cm long, lobed about ⅔–¾ of the way to the middle and edged with spiny teeth, twisted to lie perpendicular to the plane of the blade; sterile leaves spreading and shorter (15–30 cm long) than the erect fertile leaves; **stalks** stout, 10–40 cm long, **¼–⅓ as long as the blades**, with scattered tan scales.

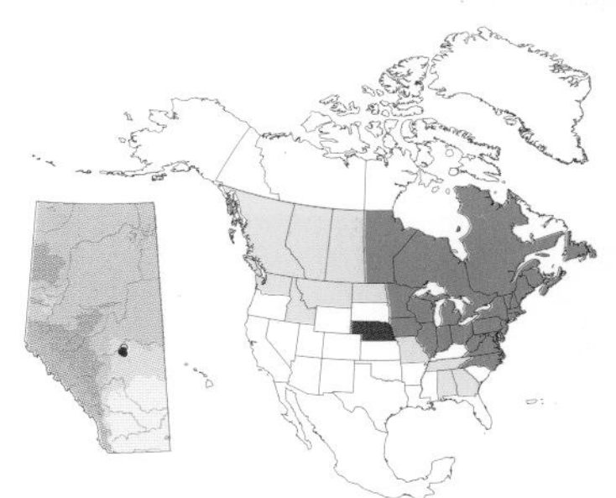

Spore clusters: Round dots (sori) on veins on the lower surface of fertile leaves **halfway between the midvein and the edge**, partly covered by a round to **kidney-shaped membrane** (indusium) **0.7–2 mm wide** and with a deep notch on one side.

Habitat: Marshes, swamps and moist woods and thickets.

Notes: This is the only shield fern (*Dryopteris* spp.) in North America in which the fertile and sterile leaves are clearly different. Because it has evergreen leaves, it can take advantage of high light levels in the fall and spring, when most other plants do not have leaves. The factors controlling its survival in Alberta are not understood, but it is probably important that it have good snow cover to protect its evergreen leaves in cold winters. • Crested shield fern sometimes hybridizes with narrow spinulose shield fern (*Dryopteris carthusiana* (Vill.) H.P. Fuchs), producing ferns with characteristics of both parents. • Another rare Alberta fern, male fern (*Dryopteris filix-mas* (L.) Schott), is very similar to crested shield fern, but its leaflets are narrower (lance-shaped to almost linear), longer (up to 18 cm), more uniform, and more deeply cut

D. FILIX-MAS

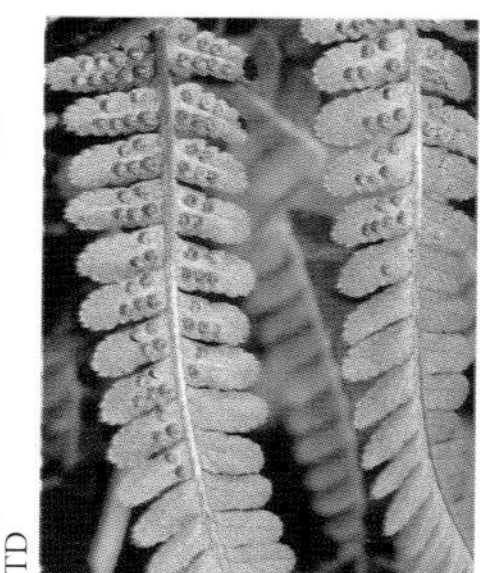
TD

(almost to the midrib). Male fern grows on moist, wooded slopes. It is evidently adapted to a moister climate than Alberta's and is probably limited here by hot, dry conditions in the summer and by lack of protective snow cover in winter. • Both of these rare ferns are sometimes grown in gardens, but neither appears to have escaped from cultivation in Alberta. • The leaves and stalks of male fern contain a chemical that paralyzes the voluntary muscles of the intestinal wall and similar tissues in the tapeworm. This does not kill the worms, but they are easily flushed out of the gut by an active purge.

SS

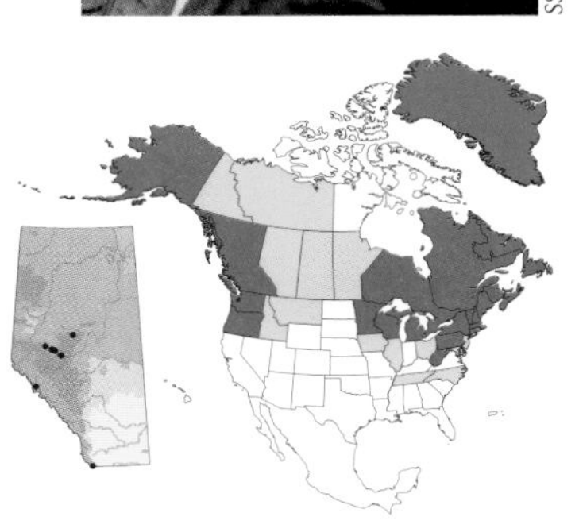

NORTHERN BEECH FERN, LONG BEECH FERN

Phegopteris connectilis (Michx.) Watt
MARSH FERN FAMILY (THELYPTERIDACEAE [POLYPODIACEAE])

Plants: Small but rather coarse herbs, **10–50 cm tall**; from long, slender, creeping underground stems (rhizomes), 1–2 {3} mm in diameter.

Leaves: Single, from rhizomes, erect; blades narrowly triangular in outline, 5–15 {4–25} cm long, 5–15 {4–20} cm wide, **pinnately divided into 10–25 pairs of leaflets** (pinnae), **fringed with hairs** and **also** with conspicuous, **tiny, needle-like hairs** (especially on the lower side of the main axis and veins); leaflets shallowly to deeply cut into rounded teeth or lobes, spreading from the main axis (rachis), but the **lowest pair bent sharply downward**; **stalks hairy**, straw-coloured above, dark and slightly scaly near the base, 5–30 cm long, **1–2 times as long as the blade.**

Spore clusters: Round dots (sori) **near the edges** on the underside of the lower leaflets, **without protective membranes** (indusia).

Habitat: Moist woodlands, on moderately to strongly acidic soil; elsewhere, in moist, shaded rock crevices and on streambanks.

Notes: This species has also been called *Thelypteris phegopteris* (L.) Slosson and *Dryopteris phegopteris* (L.) C. Chr. • The generic name *Phegopteris*, from *fagus* (beech) and *pteris* (fern), means 'beech fern,' perhaps in reference to the habitats of some species.

WESTERN POLYPODY

Polypodium hesperium Maxon
POLYPODY FAMILY (POLYPODIACEAE)

TD

Plants: Evergreen herbs, erect or spreading, usually 5–20 cm tall, **scattered** along thick, creeping, reddish brown, scaly underground stems (rhizomes) up to 6 mm in diameter.

Leaves: Herbaceous to somewhat leathery, oblong to broadly lance-shaped in outline, **4–20** {35} **cm long**, 1–5 {7} cm wide, **once pinnately divided** into 5–18 opposite or slightly offset pairs of **blunt** (sometimes pointed), oblong to linear–lance-shaped **leaflets less than 12 mm wide;** stalks 1–10 {15} cm long, hairless, straw-coloured, shorter than the blades; scales on the lower side linear to lance-shaped, less than 6 cells wide, not toothed.

TD

Spore clusters: Oval (when immature) **dots** (sori) less than 3 mm in diameter on underside of leaflets, **midway between the leaf edge and central veins**; lacking a protective covering (indusium); summer–autumn.

Habitat: Moist, rocky, non-calcareous montane slopes and crevices; rarely on limestone.

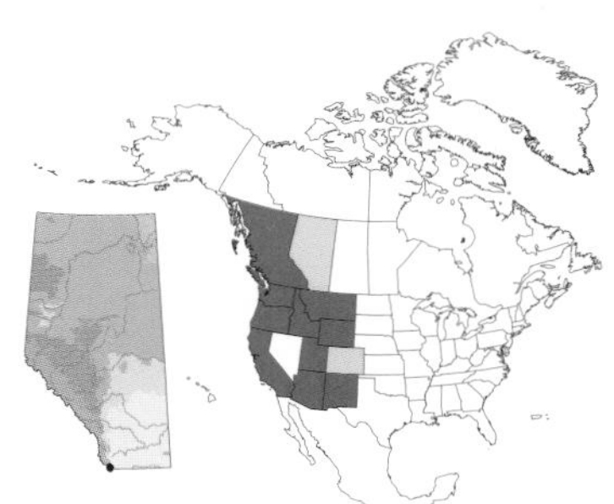

Notes: This species has also been called *Polypodium vulgare* L. var. *columbianum* Gilbert. • Rock polypody (*Polypodium virginianum* L., p. 370) is very similar to western polypody and grows in similar habitats. It is distinguished by its round spore dots (sori), which are located along the leaf edges, and by the scales on its rhizomes, which have dark centres and lighter edges. • The acrid- to sweet-tasting, licorice-flavoured rhizomes of western polypody contain sucrose and fructose, as well as osladin, a compound that is said to be 300 times sweeter than sugar. Although polypody rhizomes have seldom been used as food, they were occasionally used for flavouring, and they were often chewed as an appetizer. However, **all ferns should be used with caution**, as the toxicity of most species is not known. • The generic name *Polypodium* and the common name 'polypody' were derived from the Greek *polys* (many) and *podos* (foot), in reference to the many-branched rhizomes of these ferns.

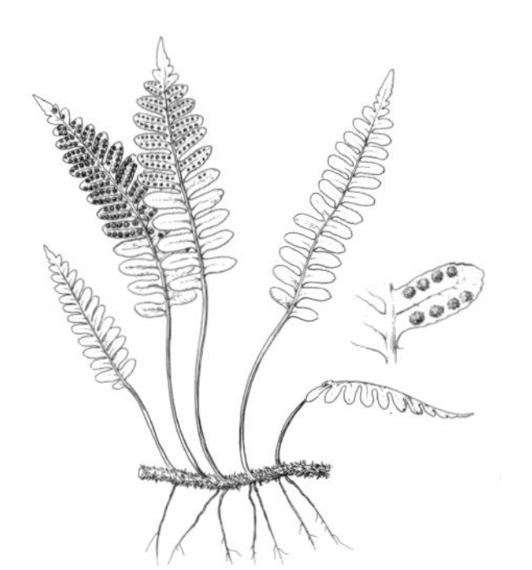

CWa

ROCK POLYPODY

Polypodium virginianum L.
POLYPODY FAMILY (POLYPODIACEAE)

Plants: Evergreen herbs, erect or spreading, usually 10–30 cm tall, **scattered along** thick (up to 6 mm in diameter), creeping, **reddish brown, scaly underground stems** (rhizomes); **scales** weakly **2-coloured** or with a dark central stripe, coarsely toothed along the edges and twisted at the tips.

Leaves: Somewhat leathery, oblong to narrowly lance-shaped in outline, **5–25** {40} **cm long**, 2–7 cm wide, **once pinnately divided** into 10–20 opposite or slightly offset pairs of **blunt** (sometimes broadly pointed), oblong leaflets; leaf axis (rachis) with broadly lance-shaped scales more than 6 cells wide; stalks 5–15 cm long, hairless, shorter than the blade.

Spore clusters: Round dots (sori) less than 3 mm in diameter on underside of leaflets, from halfway between the midvein and the leaf edge to along the leaf edge; lacking a protective covering (indusium) but with glandular-hairy modified spore cases (sporangiasters); **spores more than 52 microns in diameter**; summer–autumn.

Habitat: Moist cliffs and rocky sites in northern Alberta.

Notes: This species was called *Polypodium vulgare* L. var. *virginianum* (L.) Eat. in the first edition of the *Flora of Alberta*. • Western polypody (*Polypodium hesperium* Maxon, p. 369) is distinguished from rock polypody by its oval spore dots, by the uniformly coloured, usually smooth-edged scales on its stems and by the slender (less than 6 cells wide) scales on the underside of its leaf axis (rachis). • Siberian polypody (*Polypodium sibiricum* Siplivinsky, sometimes included in *Polypodium virginianum* L.) is also rare in northern Alberta. It is distinguished from rock polypody by the general lack of gland-tipped hairs on its sporangiasters, by the uniformly dark brown scales on its stems (though these are sometimes obscurely 2-coloured, with lighter edges) and by its smaller (less than 52 microns) spores. Siberian polypody grows on a variety of rocky substrates, including granite and limestone.

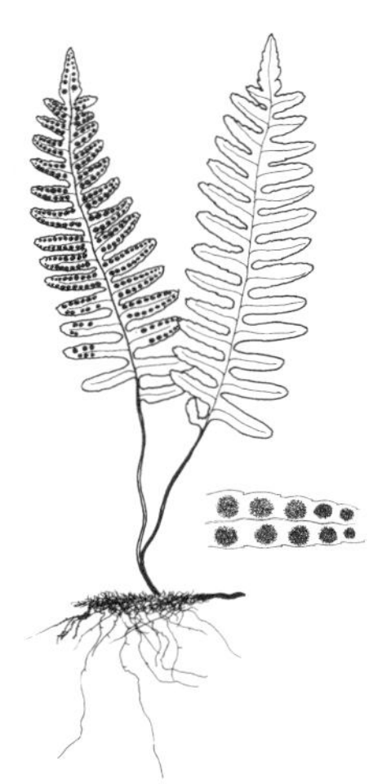

P. SIBIRICUM

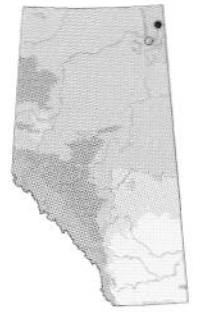

HAIRY PEPPERWORT, WATER FERN, HAIRY WATER-CLOVER

Marsilea vestita Hook. & Grev.
MARSILEA FAMILY (MARSILEACEAE)

JL

Plants: Delicate perennial herbs with aerial or floating leaves, **forming colonies** from thin (0.4–0.6 mm thick), creeping underground stems (rhizomes).

Leaves: Basal, resembling a 4-leaf clover, palmately divided into 4 egg-shaped to spatula-shaped leaflets **5–15** {3–17} **mm long**, with wedge-shaped bases and smooth to wavy tips, somewhat hairy (at least on the lower surface) to hairless, folded upward or spreading on slender stalks 2–10 {20} cm long.

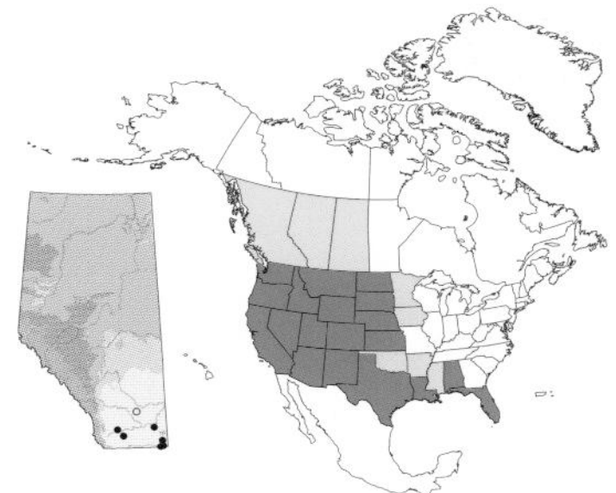

Spore clusters: Bony, bean-shaped cases (sporocarps) **with 2 teeth** near the base (usually), 4–6 {8} mm long and **covered with coarse, flat-lying stiff hairs**, greenish when young, brown when mature, containing about 10–20 spore clusters (sori), each with a cluster of 5–20 large female spores (megaspores) and 2 side clusters of smaller male spores (microspores), splitting in 2 to release spores; few, borne singly on erect, short stalks from leaf axils; late May–August {April–October}.

Habitat: Shallow water of ponds, ditches and depressions, often where ground has dried late in the season; elsewhere, on shores of lakes and streams, often tolerant of alkali.

Notes: This species has also been called *Marsilea mucronata* A. Braun. • Hairy pepperwort is the only species of this genus found in Alberta. • The hard, bony covering of the spore cases helps the spores to survive dry periods. • This genus was named in honour of Count Luigi Marsigli, an Italian mycologist who lived 1656–1730. The specific epithet *vestita* was taken from the Latin *vestitus* (clothed), possibly in reference to the shaggy covering of hairs on the sporocarps.

Addendum

Species New to The Alberta Natural Heritage Information Centre (ANHIC) Tracking List Since 1998

Two field seasons have passed since the original text for this guide was written, and in that time there have been many changes to the Alberta Natural Heritage Information Centre (ANHIC) tracking list. The status of many species in the original manuscript has changed (see Appendix Three). Several other species have been reclassified as rare or have been discovered for the first time in Alberta. This addendum includes descriptions of taxa that have been added to the ANHIC tracking list since 1998.

Two species from the February 2000 tracking list have been excluded. Many taxonomists now include Macoun's cryptanthe (*Cryptantha macounii* (Eastw.) Payson) in the more widespread species *Cryptantha celosioides* (Eastw.) Payson or *Cryptantha interrupta* (Greene) Payson, so this taxon is not described. Similarly, many taxonomists now include northern wormwood (*Artemisia borealis* Pall.) in the more widespread species *Artemisia campestris* L. as ssp. *borealis* (Pall.) H.M. Hall & Clem. var. *borealis*, so it has also been excluded from this addendum.

JG

NORTHERN GRAPE FERN

Botrychium boreale J. Milde
ADDER'S-TONGUE FAMILY (OPHIOGLOSSACEAE)

Plants: Small, **fleshy** perennial herbs **less than 15 cm tall**; appear in July–August.

Leaves: Of 2 types: a single sterile blade below a single fertile blade (see spore clusters below); **sterile blades** fleshy, **shiny** green, **stalkless** or short-stalked, **subdeltoid to deltoid** in outline, up to 6 cm long and about as wide, **twice-divided** into as many as 6 pairs of segments on a single main axis; **segments** ascending, mostly overlapping, with the basal pair usually considerably larger than the adjacent pair, edged with shallow (rarely deeply cut) lobes, **pointed at the tip; veins** pinnate near the leaf base, otherwise **in a fan-like pattern.**

Spore clusters: Small, spherical, yellow, stalkless spore sacs (sporangia) borne on specialized, fertile leaf blades; fertile blades single, once- or twice-divided, about 1–1½ times as long as the sterile blade.

Habitat: Dry meadows on south-facing slopes from Greenland to Eurasia; not well understood in North America.

Notes: This species has also been called boreal moonwort and northern moonwort. • The *Flora of North America* describes northern grape fern as a well-marked species of northern Eurasia (especially Scandinavia) and Greenland. However, this small grape fern has recently been identified in BC and Alberta.

NORTHWESTERN GRAPE FERN

Botrychium pinnatum H. St. John
ADDER'S-TONGUE FAMILY (OPHIOGLOSSACEAE)

Plants: Small, **fleshy** perennial herbs {3.5} **8–15 cm tall**; appear in June–August.

Leaves: Of 2 types: a single sterile blade below a single fertile blade (see spore clusters below); **sterile blades** fleshy, **shiny** bright green, **stalkless** or with a 1–2 mm stalk, **oblong to subdeltoid** in outline, up to 8 cm long and 5 cm wide, **divided 1–2 times** into as many as 7 pairs of segments on a single main axis; **segments at right angles** to the main axis or only slightly ascending, close to overlapping, with the **lowermost pair symmetrical**, edged with deep, regular lobes, squared to somewhat pointed at the tip; **veins pinnately branched**.

Spore clusters: Small, spherical, yellow, stalkless spore sacs (sporangia) borne on specialized, fertile leaf blades; fertile blades single, twice-divided, about 1–2 times as long as the sterile blade.

Habitat: Open, moist to mesic sites in montane, subalpine and alpine zones.

Notes: This species has also been called *Botrychium boreale* J. Milde ssp. *obtusilobum* (Ruprecht) R.T. Clausen and northwestern moonwort. • The range of northwestern grape fern extends from Alaska to the western NWT, and south to California, Nevada, Utah and Colorado.

WOODLAND BROME

Bromus vulgaris (Hook.) Shear
GRASS FAMILY (POACEAE [GRAMINEAE])

Plants: Slender perennial herbs; stems 80–100 {60–120} cm tall, with hairy (sometimes hairless) joints (nodes); **lacking elongated underground stems** (rhizomes).

Leaves: Alternate; blades flat, usually soft-hairy, 5–8 {15} mm wide; **ligules prominent**, {2} **3–5 mm long**, lacking small projections (auricles); sheaths usually soft-hairy.

Flower clusters: Slender panicles, {10–20} cm long; spikelets few, **drooping**, narrow, usually 5–7-flowered and {20–28} cm long; glumes shorter than the lowest lemma, the lower single-nerved, the upper 3-nerved; **lemmas** sparsely hairy to nearly hairless across the back, **hairier at the edges**, narrow; **lower lemmas** 8–10 {13} mm long and **about 2 mm wide**, tipped with a {3} **6–8 mm long bristle** (awn); anthers 3–5 mm long; {late June–August}.

Fruits: Grains; mature florets breaking off above the glumes and between the florets.

Habitat: Open woods; elsewhere, in montane meadows and on rocky slopes.

Notes: This species has also been called Colombian brome. • Woodland brome is found from BC and southwestern Alberta south to California and Wyoming.

PACIFIC BLUEGRASS

Poa gracillima Vasey
GRASS FAMILY (POACEAE [GRAMINEAE])

General: Loosely tufted perennial herbs; stems {10} 30–60 cm tall, frequently spreading at the base; **without creeping underground stems** (rhizomes).

Leaves: Mainly basal; sheaths hairless, closed less than half their length; **blades with a boat-shaped tip** (keeled), lax; **basal leaves hair-like**; stem leaves flat (rarely folded), 0.5–1.5 mm wide; ligules mostly pointed, {0.5} 2–5 mm long.

Flower clusters: Open, pyramid-shaped panicles, 4–10 {15} cm long, **longer than wide**; spikelets **rounded, not compressed,** 4–6 mm long, {2} 3–5-flowered; glumes 2.5–5 mm long, the first usually shorter than the second; **lemmas rounded, with a slight, hairy ridge (keel) on the back, with crisp (not cobwebby) hairs at the base,** about 4 mm long; {May} June–July.

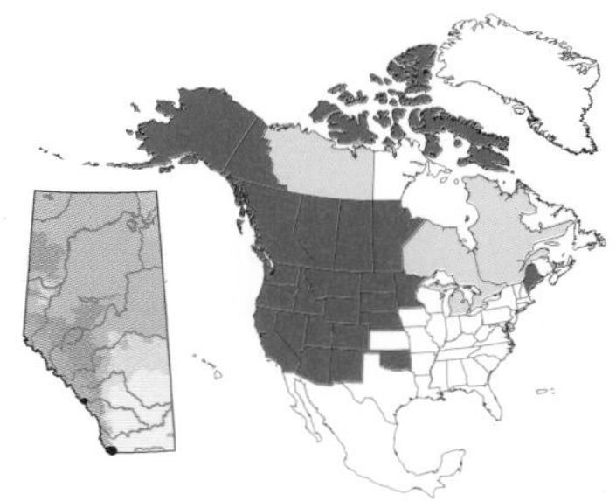

Fruits: Grains; breaking away above the glumes and between the florets; August {September}.

Habitat: Moist montane woods and meadows; elsewhere, on rocky slopes, shaded cliffs, riverbanks and lake shores.

Notes: Pacific bluegrass is found from BC and southwestern Alberta south to California, Utah and Colorado. • Two relatively common species, Canby bluegrass (*Poa canbyi* (Scribn.) Piper) and Sandberg bluegrass (*Poa sandbergii* Vasey), also have non-flattened spikelets and rounded, obscurely ridged, hairy lemmas. However, Canby bluegrass has a narrow, dense panicle and grows in dry to moist grassland. Sandberg bluegrass grows in dry grassland and has crowded, soft, curled basal leaves, very prominent ligules and short panicle branches that are often flattened against the stem.

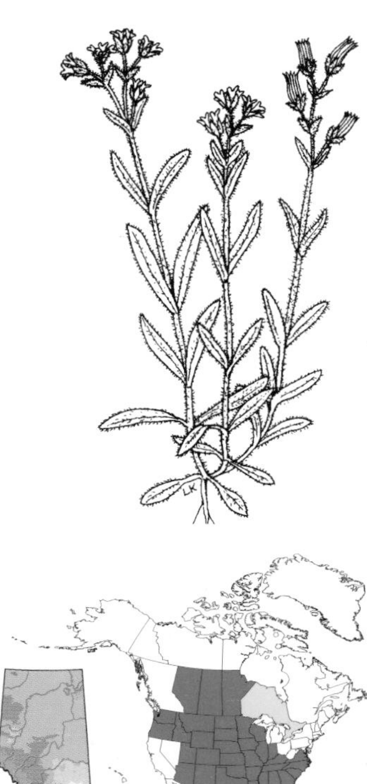

SHORT-STALK MOUSE-EAR CHICKWEED

Cerastium brachypodium (Engelm. *ex* A. Gray) B.L. Robins.
PINK FAMILY (CARYOPHYLLACEAE)

Plants: **Delicate annual** herbs, 5–35 cm tall, with **short, glandular hairs**; stems slender, **erect to ascending**, single or branched from the base; from **shallow taproots.**

Leaves: **Opposite, stalkless**; blades narrowly elliptic to lance-shaped, sometimes widest above mid-leaf, 5–30 mm long, 2–8 mm wide.

Flowers: **Green to whitish**, highly variable, usually with 5 petals and 5 sepals; **petals absent or shorter than to twice as long as the sepals**; sepals 3–4.5 mm long, **with short, glandular hairs** (sometimes hairless), entirely green or with narrow, translucent edges; styles commonly 5; flowers few to many (rarely single), on **stalks ½–1¼ times as long as the sepals, never bent sharply downwards**, forming open, spreading clusters (cymes) above **green bracts**; {April–July}.

Fruits: **Cylindrical capsules**, 6–12 mm long, on straight or slightly up-curved **stalks up to 3 times as long as the calyx**, opening at the tip via 10 small teeth to release rough, grooved, golden-brown seeds.

Habitat: Wet or dry, open sites in grasslands, meadows, open woods and waste places, often on rocky or sandy soil.

Notes: This species has also been called *Cerastium nutans* Raf. var. *brachypodium* Engelm. • Short-stalk mouse-ear chickweed is found across the US, from Washington and Oregon to Virginia and Georgia, and south through Mexico to Central America. In Canada, it is found only in southern Alberta.

ALPINE POPPY

Papaver radicatum Rottbøll ssp. *kluanensis* (D. Löve) D.F. Murray
POPPY FAMILY (PAPAVERACEAE)

DJ

General: **Hairy perennial** herbs with milky sap, loosely tufted, with dull brown, soft, persistent leaf bases; **flowering stems leafless**, stiffly hairy, **6–9 {18} cm tall**; from underground stems (rhizomes).

Leaves: **Basal, grey-green to blue-green** and **hairy** above and below, lance-shaped, 3–7 cm long, pinnately cut into **5 {9} lance-shaped lobes**; stalks to ⅔ of the leaf length.

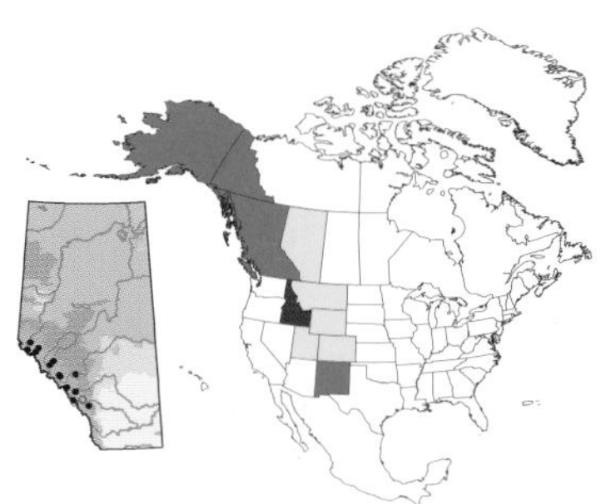

Flowers: **Sulphur-yellow** (drying pale green), rarely pink-tinged to brick-red, **saucer-shaped, up to 2 cm across**, with **4 large, thin petals**; **buds** oval, **erect**, with 2 **dark-hairy** sepals, 8–14 mm long; solitary; June–August.

Fruits: Erect, **stiffly brown-hairy capsules**, usually oblong and broad-tipped (sometimes almost round), 8–12 mm long, tipped with a disc-like stigma with 4–7 rays.

Habitat: Rocky alpine slopes, on shale in Alberta.

Notes: This taxon includes *Papaver kluanensis* D. Löve and *Papaver freedmanianum* D. Löve. • Alpine poppy is a circumpolar species. In North America, it is found from Alaska to the NWT, and its range extends south through the cordillera to Colorado and New Mexico.

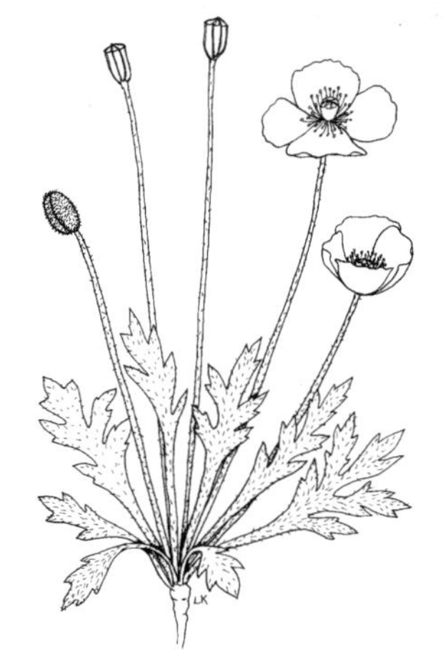

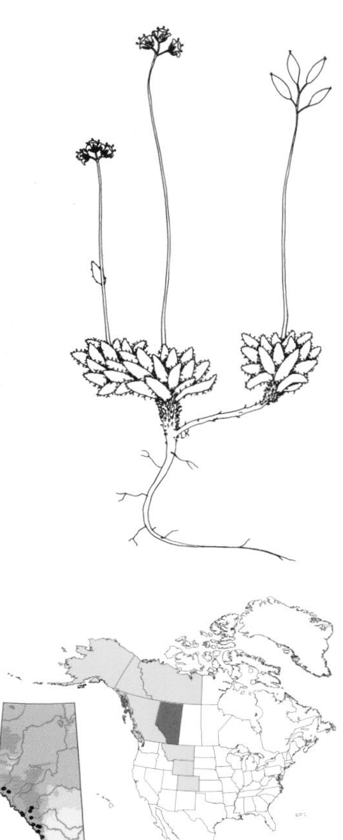

PORSILD'S WHITLOW-GRASS

Draba porsildii G.A. Mulligan
MUSTARD FAMILY (BRASSICACEAE [CRUCIFERAE])

Plants: Small, **tufted** perennial herbs; flowering stems erect, **2–6.5 cm tall**, hairless or sparsely hairy; from taproots.

Leaves: In basal rosettes, lance-shaped and widest towards the tip, **3–12 mm long**, 1.5–2 mm wide, not toothed, **with simple, 2-branched and 4–8-rayed hairs on both surfaces; stem leaves absent or single**.

Flowers: White, about **5 mm across**, with 4 sepals and 4 petals; petals 2–3 mm long; sepals 1.5–2 mm long; styles 0.25 mm long; 2–5 {6} flowers in compact, branched clusters (racemes).

Fruits: Narrowly egg-shaped pods (siliques), widest towards the tip, 4–8 mm long, 2–3 mm wide, **hairless**, splitting in 2 to release 5–9 seeds 1 mm long; **stalks shorter than pods**.

Habitat: Moist, turfy alpine sites; elsewhere, in mesic to dry, rocky subalpine to alpine sites.

Notes: Porsild's whitlow-grass is found in southeastern Alaska, the southern Yukon and western NWT, north-eastern and southeastern BC, and southwestern Alberta.

WOOLLEN-BREECHES

Hydrophyllum capitatum Douglas ex Benth.
WATERLEAF FAMILY (HYDROPHYLLACEAE)

LK

Plants: Small perennial herbs; stems single to few, 10–20 {40} cm tall, hairy; from short rootstocks with slender, fleshy roots.

Leaves: Alternate, mostly **basal, long-stalked**; blades egg-shaped to oval, {10–15} cm long, hairy, **pinnately divided into 5–7** {11} **toothed leaflets.**

Flowers: Purplish blue to white, broadly funnel-shaped, 5–9 mm long, 5-lobed; lobes with slender appendages on their inner surfaces; calyx deeply 5-lobed, covered with long, stiff hairs; styles 2-pronged; **5 stamens, longer than the petals**, hairy at the middle; flowers in **compact, head-like clusters** (cymes) on 1–5 cm stalks, **shorter than the leaves**; {March–July}.

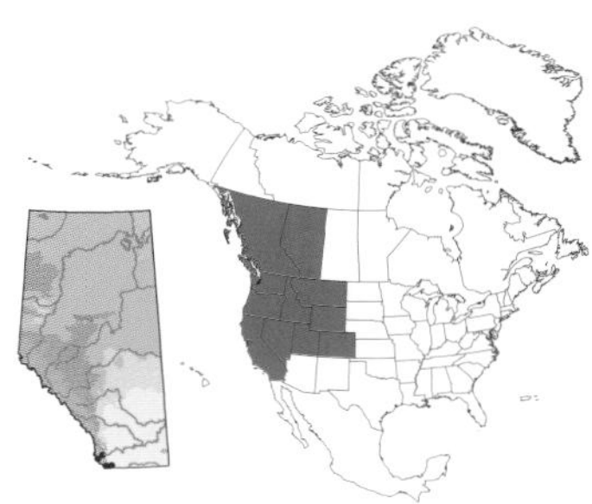

Fruits: Round capsules containing 1–4 seeds.

Habitat: Moist, open or thinly wooded montane slopes; elsewhere, from foothills to well up in the mountains.

Notes: This species has also been called cat's-breeches.
• The range of woollen-breeches extends from southern BC and Alberta to California and Colorado.

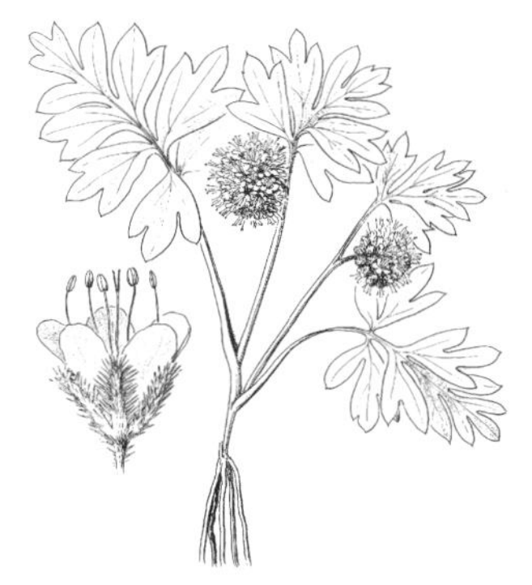

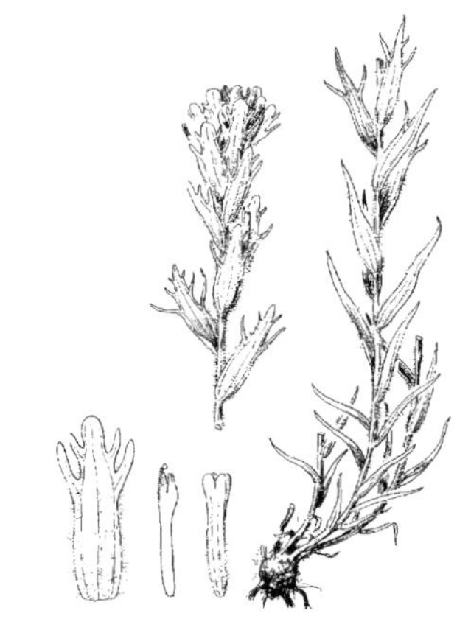

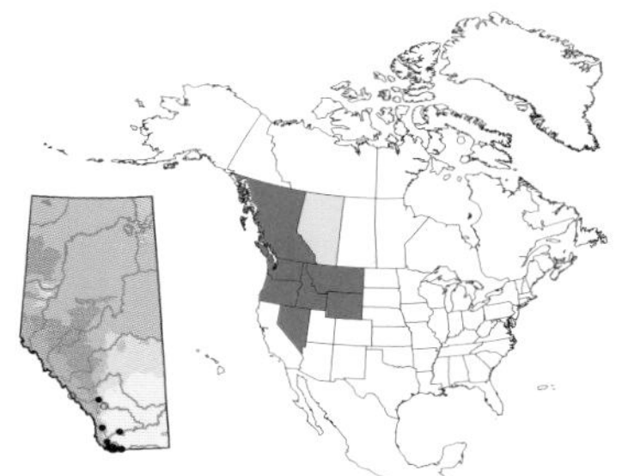

YELLOW PAINTBRUSH

Castilleja cusickii Greenm.
FIGWORT FAMILY (SCROPHULARIACEAE)

Plants: Loosely clumped, **sticky-hairy** perennial herbs; stems simple, erect or ascending, 10–60 cm tall; from root crowns.

Leaves: Alternate, numerous, 2–4 cm long, covered with sticky hairs; lower leaves linear and undivided; upper leaves broader, **tipped with 3–7 slender, ascending lobes.**

Flowers: Sulphur-yellow, densely **glandular-hairy**; corolla shorter than to longer than the calyx, with a **short upper lip** (galea) less than ½ as long as the corolla tube and a prominent lower lip ⅓ as long to almost equal to the galea; calyx tubular, 2–3 cm long, tipped with 4 rounded lobes; **bracts yellow**, oblong, wider than the leaves, with 3–5 slender, ascending lobes, **equalling or longer than the flowers; 4 stamens, enclosed in the upper lip**; styles slender, usually protruding from the tip of the upper lip; numerous, in the axils of bracts in dense spikes that elongate in fruit; {April–August}.

Fruits: Capsules, splitting open lengthwise, containing many seeds with netted veins; May–July {April–August}.

Habitat: Grasslands; elsewhere, in meadows at intermediate elevations.

Notes: This species has also been called *Castilleja lutea* Heller and Cusick's Indian-paintbrush. It was included in *Castilleja septentrionalis* Lindl. in the first edition of the *Flora of Alberta*. • Yellow paintbrush is found from BC and Alberta to Nevada and Wyoming.

CLAMMY HEDGE-HYSSOP

Gratiola neglecta Torr.
FIGWORT FAMILY (SCROPHULARIACEAE)

Plants: **Slender annual** herbs, **clammy with fine glandular hairs** on upper parts; stems more or less erect, 10–30 cm tall, usually diffusely branched; from **fibrous roots.**

Leaves: **Opposite, linear to lance-shaped** and widest above the middle, usually 2–4 {5} cm long, toothless or wavy-toothed, tapered to a narrow **stalkless** base.

Flowers: **Pale yellow to whitish** (lips sometimes purplish), {6} **8–10 mm long, tubular, 2-lipped**, hairy in the throat; calyxes 4–6 {3–7} mm long, with 4 deeply cut lobes immediately above 2 similar, slender bracts; 2 fertile stamens, with a large, flattened disc (connective) bearing 2 parallel pollen sacs; sterile stamens tiny or none; flowers **borne singly on slender, spreading, 1–2 {3} cm long stalks** from upper leaf axils; {June–August}.

Fruits: Broadly egg-shaped, pointed capsules, 3–5 {7} mm long, splitting in 4 to release short-cylindrical seeds about 0.5 mm long.

Habitat: Wet, muddy sites, often in shallow water.

Notes: The range of clammy hedge-hyssop extends east from southern BC to Quebec and Nova Scotia, and south through the US to California, Texas and Georgia.

JG

LK

FLAME-COLOURED LOUSEWORT

Pedicularis flammea L.
FIGWORT FAMILY (SCROPHULARIACEAE)

Plants: Small perennial herbs; stems single to several, reddish purple, **6–10 cm tall, usually hairless, unbranched**, with **1 or 2 leaves**; from spindly roots.

Leaves: Alternate, mainly basal, lance-shaped to linear, 2–6 cm long, edged with **numerous oblong to oval, 3–5 mm, round-toothed lobes.**

Flowers: Yellow, {6–7} 10–20 mm long and about 2 mm wide, 2-lipped, with a **small, yellow, 3-lobed lower lip** and a **deep crimson to purple (usually), arching upper lip** (galea), **style not protruding:** calyxes equal to or slightly longer than the corolla tube, 5-toothed; flowers borne in the axils of short, linear to lance-shaped bracts, forming hairless to woolly, 2–5 cm long, **spike-like clusters** (racemes).

Fruits: Curved, lance-shaped capsules, 2–3 times longer than the calyx.

Habitat: Calcareous alpine meadows; elsewhere, also in moist sites such as snow beds and lake shores.

Notes: This species includes *Pedicularis albertae* Hult. and *Pedicularis oederi* M. Vahl *ex* Hornem. var. *albertae* (Hult.) B. Boivin. It has also been called red-rattle. • Flame-coloured lousewort occurs in Greenland, Iceland and Lapland. In North America it is found in Alberta, scattered across the NWT and Nunavut, around Hudson Bay and James Bay (Manitoba, Ontario and Quebec) and in Labrador and Newfoundland. • Oeder's lousewort (*Pedicularis oederi* M. Vahl) was recently collected from an alpine site in the Willmore Wilderness Park. This is the first verified record of Oeder's lousewort from Alberta. This species is very similar to flame-coloured lousewort, but Oeder's lousewort is distinguished by its larger (over 20 mm long) flowers, with styles protruding from the tips of galeas that are not strongly reddish or purple-coloured. Oeder's lousewort plants are also larger (10–20 cm tall) and usually somewhat hairy, at least in the flower clusters. They may occasionally be hairless except for a fringe of hairs on the floral bracts and sepals. Oeder's lousewort grows in alpine meadows, often on rocky slopes.

PATHFINDER

Adenocaulon bicolor Hook.
ASTER FAMILY (ASTERACEAE [COMPOSITAE])

Plants: Erect perennial herbs; stems essentially hairless to white-woolly, 30–90 {100} cm tall; from short rootstocks with fibrous roots.

Leaves: Alternate, mainly basal; thin, green and essentially hairless above, **densely white-woolly beneath, heart-shaped to triangular** with somewhat notched bases, 3–15 cm wide, usually wavy-toothed or shallow-lobed; stalks long, winged.

Flowerheads: **Whitish**, about **3 mm long**, with **disc florets only**; inner florets functionally male; outer 4–6 {3–7} florets female; **involucres with 4 or 5 egg-shaped, pointed bracts, 2 mm long,** that spread or bend backwards at maturity; flowerheads borne on **sticky, glandular-hairy branches** in open clusters (panicles); {June–September}.

Fruits: Dry seed-like fruits (achenes), **club-shaped,** 5–8 mm long, **lacking bristles** (pappus) but **tipped with stalked glands.**

Habitat: Moist, shady montane woods.

Notes: This species has also been called American trail-plant. • Pathfinder is found from southern Alberta and BC south to California and Wyoming, and also in North and South Dakota, Michigan, Minnesota and Ontario.

LK

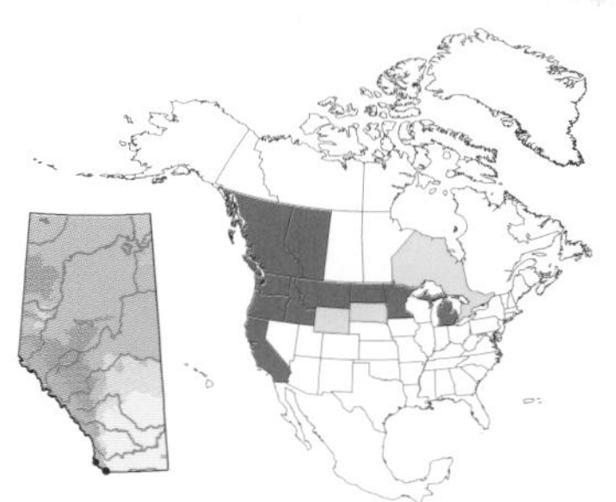

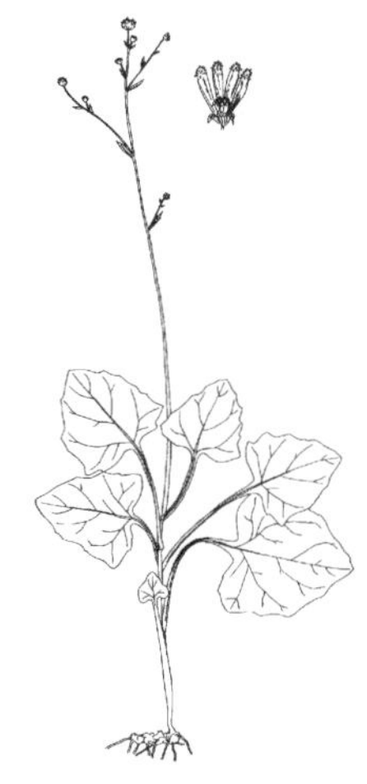

LA

NODDING SCORZONELLA

Microseris nutans (Hook.) Sch.-Bip.
ASTER FAMILY (ASTERACEAE [COMPOSITAE])

Plants: Perennial herbs with **milky juice**, highly variable; **stems usually with a least 1 leaf**, erect or somewhat reclining at the base, 10–50 {60} cm tall, hairless or with minute hairs; **main stem usually with a few branches**; from thick, **fleshy taproots**.

Leaves: Alternate, mainly basal, **linear**, tapered to a slender point, 10–30 cm long; toothless or with slender teeth to spreading lobes.

Flowerheads: Yellow, with **strap-like (ligulate) florets only**, nodding in bud; florets 3–8 mm long, with both male and female parts; involucres 10–20 {8–22} mm high, usually granular, hairless or minutely hairy, with almost **equal, lance-shaped, long-tapered bracts** above a few short bractlets; flowerheads solitary to several, on **long, slender stalks**; {April–July}.

Fruits: Dry seed-like fruits (achenes), {5–8} mm long, **beakless**, tapered to both ends, hairless or finely hairy, tipped with a tuft of 15–20 **feathery-hairy bristles** (pappus) **with scale-like bases**.

Habitat: Grassy slopes and open montane woods.

Notes: This species has also been called nodding silverpuffs. • Nodding scorzonella is found from southern Alberta and BC south to California, Utah and Colorado.

Appendix 1

Keys to rare *Botrychium* and *Isoetes* species found in Alberta

The moonworts and quillworts, as they are commonly known, are complex genera whose species are distinguished by minute diagnostic features. These keys present only species known to occur in Alberta.

A. Key to rare *Botrychium* species

Key adapted from Flora of North America *Vol. 2, pp. 87–90.*

1. Sterile leaf blades triangular, mostly 5–25 cm long; plants mostly over 12 cm tall, commonly sterile, fertile blades absent or misshapen; leaf sheaths open or closed — *Botrychium multifidum*

1. Sterile leaf blades mainly oblong to linear, mostly 2–4 cm long; plants mostly less than 15 cm tall, fertile blades always present; leaf sheaths closed — 2

2. Sterile leaf blades linear to linear-oblong, simple to lobed, lobes rounded to square and angular; stalks usually ⅓–⅔ the length of the sterile blade; plants usually in shaded sites — *Botrychium simplex*

2. Sterile leaf blades oblong–lance-shaped to oblong, pinnate, rarely simple, lobes, if present, of various shapes; stalks usually less than ¼ the length of the sterile blade; plants usually in exposed sites — 3

3. Sterile blades present; basal pinnae fan-shaped to spoon-shaped, with veins like the ribs of a fan, midrib absent — 4

4. Basal pinnae broadly fan-shaped — 5

5. Plants herbaceous; sterile blades mostly less than 4 cm long and 1.5 cm wide; pinnae 2–5 pairs, well separated, margins commonly rounded to toothed; fertile blades 1⅓–3 times the length of the sterile blade; in damp sites — *Botrychium crenulatum*

5. Plants fleshy; sterile blades mostly more than 5 cm long and 2 cm wide; pinnae 4–9 pairs, approximate to overlapping; margins usually entire, rarely toothed; fertile blades ⅘–2 times the length of the sterile blade; in dry sites — *Botrychium lunaria*

4. Basal pinnae narrowly fan-shaped or wedge-shaped to lance-shaped or linear — 6

6. Pinnae strongly ascending; margins conspicuously sharply toothed — *Botrychium ascendens*

6. Pinnae spreading or only moderately ascending; outer margins entire to rounded, rarely toothed — 7

7. Sterile blades folded lengthwise, usually 4 cm long and 1 cm wide; pinnae up to 5 pairs; basal pinnae 2-lobed — *Botrychium campestre*

7. Sterile blades flat or folded only at the base, usually 10 cm long and 2.5 cm wide; pinnae up to 10 pairs; basal pinnae unlobed, or if lobed, not usually 2-cleft — 8

8. Sterile blades narrowly oblong, herbaceous; pinnae nearly round to fan-shaped; margins shallowly lobed; lowest branches of fertile blades 1-pinnate — *Botrychium minganense*

8. Sterile blades narrowly triangular, leathery; pinnae spoon-shaped to narrowly spoon-shaped; margins entire to coarsely and irregularly toothed; lowest branches of fertile blades 2-pinnate — *Botrychium spathulatum*

3. Sterile blades present or replaced by fertile blades; if present, basal pinnae linear to egg-shaped, with pinnate venation, midrib present — 9

9. Sterile blade replaced by a fertile blade, yielding 2 fertile blades — *Botrychium paradoxum*

9. Sterile blade present, distinct from the fertile blade — 10

10. Sterile blades triangular; fertile blades divided at base into several equally long branches — *Botrychium lanceolatum*

10. Sterile blades egg-shaped to oblong; fertile blades with single midrib or 1 dominant midrib and 2 smaller ribs — 11

11. Stalk of sterile blade as long as the blade; blades oblong–egg-shaped to triangular-oblong; basal pinnae rhombic — *Botrychium pedunculosum*

11. Stalk of sterile blade short to nearly absent, up to ¼ the length of the blade; blades oblong–lance-shaped to nearly triangular — 12

12. Sterile blades nearly triangular, basal pinna pair elongate; segments and lobes rounded at tip — *Botrychium hesperium* (This species has been reported falsely from Alberta; the Alberta material is most likely *Botrychium michiganense*.)

12. Sterile blades oblong-triangular to oblong–egg-shaped; basal pinna pair not elongate; segments and lobes with blunt or slightly pointed tips — 13

13. Pinnae of mature sterile blades nearly as wide as long, with slightly pointed tips, veins like ribs of a fan; basal pinnae with shallow, narrow sinuses and 1–3 lobes — *Botrychium boreale*

13. Pinnae of mature sterile blades much longer than wide, with blunt tips, veins mostly pinnate; basal pinnae with deep, wide sinuses and 3–8 lobes — *Botrychium pinnatum*

B. Key to *Isoetes* species

Key adapted from Flora of North America *Vol. 2, pp. 66–68. Characters based on geography, habitat, megaspore ornamentation, and size and shape of the ligule and velum are useful in distinguishing these species, but microscopic examination of the mature megaspores is necessary for positive identification.*

1. Megaspores with spines — 2

   2. Spines long and pointed, not smaller around the middle of the megaspore; microspores spineless or with fine, thread-like spines — *Isoetes echinospora*

   2. Spines blunt-tipped, sometimes joined together to form ridges, notably smaller around the middle of the megaspore; microspores covered with coarse spines — *Isoetes maritima*

1. Megaspores with ridges, not spiny — 3

   3. Megaspores with distinct, roughly or sharply crested, branching ridges; ligules heart-shaped — *Isoetes occidentalis*

   3. Megaspores with low, scattered ridges that often merge together; ligules various — 4

      4. Plants in or out of water; broad, translucent leaf edges (wing margins) extending 1–5 cm above the spore cluster; ligules elongated-triangular — *Isoetes howellii*

      4. Plants underwater; broad, translucent leaf edges (wing margins) not extending more than 1 cm above the spore cluster; ligules heart-shaped — *Isoetes bolanderi*

Appendix 2

Rare vascular plants of Alberta by natural region

Note that not all species in this list are included in the text. See also Addendum, p. 375–88.

Scientific Name	Canadian Shield	Boreal Forest	Rocky Mtn.	Foot-hills	Park-land	Grass-lands	S Rank 1998	S Rank 2000
Adenocaulon bicolor Hook.			•				S3	S2S3
Adiantum aleuticum (Rupr.) Paris			•				S1S2	S2
Agoseris lackschewitzii D. Henderson & R. Moseley			•				S2	S2
Agrostis exarata Trin.			•	•	•	•	S2	S2
Agrostis humilis Vasey			•				S1S2	S1
Agrostis mertensii Trin.			•				S2	S2
Agrostis thurberiana A.S. Hitchc.			•				S2	S2
Allium geyeri S. Wats.			•			•	S2	S2
Alopecurus alpinus J.E. Smith			•		•	•	S2	S2
Amaranthus californicus (Moq.) S. Wats.						•	S1	S1
Ambrosia acanthicarpa Hook.						•	S2	S2
Anagallis minima (L.) Krause						•	S1	S1S2
Anemone quinquefolia L. var. *quinquefolia*				•			S1	S1
Antennaria aromatica Evert			•				S2	S2
Antennaria corymbosa E. Nels.			•			•	S1	S1
Antennaria luzuloides T. & G.			•				S1	S1
Antennaria monocephala D.C. Eaton			•				S2	S2
Anthoxanthum monticola (Bigelow) Y. Schouten & Veldkamp			•				S2	S2
Aquilegia formosa Fisch. *ex* DC. var. *formosa*			•	•			S2	S2
Aquilegia jonesii Parry			•				S2	S2
Arabidopsis salsuginea (Pallas) N. Busch		•					S1	S1
Arabis lemmonii S. Wats.			•				S2	S2
Arctagrostis arundinacea (Trin.) Beal		•	•				S1	S1
Arenaria longipedunculata Hult.			•				S1	S1
Aristida purpurea Nutt. var. *longiseta* (Steud.) Vasey						•	S1	S1
Arnica amplexicaulis Nutt.			•				S2	S2
Arnica longifolia D.C. Eat.			•				S2	S2
Arnica parryi A. Gray			•				S2	S2
Artemisia borealis Pall.			•				S2?	S2
Artemisia furcata Bieb. var. *furcata*			•				S1	S1
Artemisia tilesii Ledeb. ssp. *elatior* (T. & G.) Hult.		•			•		S2	S2

Scientific Name	Canadian Shield	Boreal Forest	Rocky Mtn.	Foot-hills	Park-land	Grass-lands	S Rank 1998	S Rank 2000
Artemisia tridentata Nutt.			•				S2	S2
Asclepias ovalifolia Dcne.		•			•	•	S3	S3
Asclepias viridiflora Raf.						•	S1	S1
Aster campestris Nutt.			•			•	S2	S2
Aster eatonii (A. Gray) J.T. Howell			•		•	•	S2	S2
Aster pauciflorus Nutt.					•		S1	S1
Aster umbellatus Mill.		•			•		S2	S2
Astragalus bodinii Sheldon		•		•			S1	S1
Astragalus kentrophyta A. Gray var. *kentrophyta*						•	S1	S1S2
Astragalus lotiflorus Hook.						•	S2	S2
Astragalus purshii Dougl. *ex* Hook. var. *purshii*						•	S2	S2
Athyrium alpestre (Hoppe) Clairville var.*americanum* Butters			•				S1	S1
Atriplex canescens (Pursh) Nutt.						•	SU	SU
Atriplex powellii S. Wats.						•	S1	S1
Atriplex truncata (Torr.) A. Gray						•	S1	S1
Bacopa rotundifolia (Michx.) Wettst.						•	S1	S1
Barbarea orthoceras Ledeb.	•	•	•	•	•		S2	S2
Bidens frondosa L.						•	S1S2	S1
Blysmus rufus (Hudson) Link		•					S1	S1
Boisduvalia glabella (Nutt.) Walp.						•	S2	S2
Bolboschoenus fluviatilis (Torr.) J. Sojak.		•			•		S1	S1
Boschniakia rossica (Cham. & Schlecht.) Fedtsch.		•					S1	S1
Botrychium ascendens W.H. Wagner			•					S1
Botrychium boreale (Fries) Milde			•				SRF	S1
Botrychium campestre W.H. Wagner & D.R. Farrar					•		S1	S1
Botrychium crenulatum W.H. Wagner			•				S1	S1
Botrychium hesperium (Maxon & R.T. Clausen) W.H. Wagner & Lellinger			•				S1	SRF
Botrychium lanceolatum (Gmelin) Angström ssp. *angustisegmentum* (Pease & A.H. Moore) R.T. Clausen			•				S2	S2

Scientific Name	Canadian Shield	Boreal Forest	Rocky Mtn.	Foot-hills	Park-land	Grass-lands	S Rank 1998	S Rank 2000
Botrychium lanceolatum (Gmelin) Angström ssp. *lanceolatum* (Pease & A.H. Moore) R.T. Clausen			•				S2	S2
Botrychium michiganense			•					S1
Botrychium minganense Victorin		•	•	•			S2	S2S3
Botrychium multifidum (S.G. Gmelin) Rupr.	•	•	•	•	•		S2	S2
Botrychium paradoxum W.H. Wagner			•				S1	S1
Botrychium pedunculosum W.H. Wagner			•				S1	S1
Botrychium pinnatum H. St. John			•					S1
Botrychium simplex E. Hitch.			•				S1S2	S2
Botrychium spathulatum W.H. Wagner			•	•	•		S1S2	S2
Botrychium x *watertonense* W.H. Wagner			•				S1	S1
Boykinia heucheriformis (Rydb.) Rosendahl			•				S2	S2
Brasenia schreberi J.F. Gmelin		•						S1
Braya purpurascens (R. Br.) Bunge *ex* Ledeb.			•				S1	S1
Brickellia grandiflora (Hook.) Nutt.			•				S2	S2
Bromus latiglumis (Shear) A.S. Hitchc.			•		•		S1	S1
Bromus vulgaris (Hook.) Shear			•				S3	S2S3
Calamagrostis lapponica (Wahl.) Hartm.			•	•			S1	S1
Calylophus serrulatus (Nutt.) Raven					•	•	S2	S2
Camassia quamash (Pursh) Greene var. *quamash*			•		•	•	S2	S2
Camissonia andina (Nutt.) Raven						•	S1	S1
Camissonia breviflora (Torr. & Gray) Raven						•	S1	S1
Campanula uniflora L.			•				S2	S2
Cardamine bellidifolia L.			•				S2	S2
Cardamine parviflora L.		•					S1	S1
Cardamine pratensis L.	•	•		•			S1	S1S2
Cardamine umbellata Greene			•	•			S2	S2
Carex adusta Boott		•	•	•	•		S1	S1
Carex aperta Boott			•		•		S2	S1

Scientific Name	Canadian Shield	Boreal Forest	Rocky Mtn.	Foot-hills	Park-land	Grass-lands	S Rank 1998	S Rank 2000
Carex arcta Boott		•	•	•			S1	S1
Carex backii Boott		•	•		•		SU	SU
Carex capitata L.	•	•	•	•			S2	S2
Carex crawei Dewey			•		•	•	S2	S2
Carex franklinii Boott			•				S2	S3
Carex glacialis Mack.			•				S2	S2
Carex haydeniana Olney			•		•		S2	S3
Carex heleonastes Ehrh. *ex* L. f.		•	•	•			S2	S2
Carex heteroneura Boott var. *epapillosa* (Mack.) F.J. Hermann			•				S1	S1
Carex hookerana Dewey		•	•		•		S2	S2
Carex houghtoniana Torr.	•	•		•			S2	S2
Carex hystericina Muhl. *ex* Willd.		•					S1	S1
Carex illota Bailey			•				S1	S1
Carex incurviformis Mack. var. *incurviformis*			•	•			S2	S2
Carex lachenalii Schk.			•				S2	S2
Carex lacustris Willd.		•		•			S2	S2
Carex lenticularis Michx. var. *dolia* (M.E. Jones) L.A. Standley	•		•				S2	S1
Carex leptopoda Mack.			•					S1
Carex loliacea L.		•	•	•			S2	S3
Carex mertensii Prescott ssp. *mertensii*			•	•			S1	S1
Carex misandra R. Br.			•				S1S2	S1S2
Carex nebrascensis Dewey						•	S2	S2
Carex oligosperma Michx.	•	•					S1	S1
Carex parryana Dewey var. *parryana*			•		•	•	S1S2	S1S2
Carex pauciflora Lightf.		•	•	•	•		S3	S3
Carex paysonis Clokey			•	•			S2	S1S2
Carex pedunculata Muhl.		•					S1	S1
Carex petasata Dewey			•				S1S2	S1S2
Carex petricosa Dewey			•				S2	S2
Carex platylepis Mack.			•				S1S2	S1S2
Carex podocarpa R. Br.			•				SU	S2
Carex preslii Steud.			•	•			S2	S2
Carex pseudocyperus L.	•	•			•		S2	S2
Carex raynoldsii Dewey			•	•			S3	S3
Carex retrorsa Schwein.		•			•	•	S2	S2
Carex rostrata Stokes	•	•	•	•	•		S2	S2
Carex saximontana Mack.			•				SU	SU
Carex scoparia Schk. *ex* Willd.			•				S1	S1

Scientific Name	Canadian Shield	Boreal Forest	Rocky Mtn.	Foot-hills	Park-land	Grass-lands	S Rank 1998	S Rank 2000
Carex supina Willd. ssp. *spaniocarpa* (Steud.) Hult.			•				S1	S1
Carex tincta (Fern.) Fern.		•	•				S1	S1
Carex tonsa (Fern.) Bickn. var. *tonsa*	•	•	•	•	•	•	S3	S3
Carex trisperma Dewey		•		•			S3	S3
Carex umbellata Schkuhr *ex* Willd.		•						S1
Carex vesicaria L. var. *vesicaria*			•		•	•	SU	S1
Carex vulpinoidea Michx.		•					S2	S2
Castilleja cusickii Greenm.						•	S3	S2S3
Castilleja lutescens (Greenm.) Rydb.				•	•		S3	S2S3
Castilleja pallida (L.) Spreng. ssp. *caudata* Pennell			•				SU	SU
Castilleja sessiliflora Pursh						•	S1	S1
Cerastium brachypodum (Engelm. *ex* A. Gray) B.L. Rob.						•		S2
Cheilanthes gracillima D.C. Eat.			•				S1	S1
Chenopodium atrovirens Rydb.					•		S1	S1
Chenopodium desiccatum A. Nels.						•	S1S2	S1S2
Chenopodium incanum (S. Wats.) Heller			•				S1	S1
Chenopodium leptophyllum (Nutt. *ex* Moq.) Nutt. *ex* S. Wats.		•			•	•	SU	SU
Chenopodium subglabrum (S. Wats.) A. Nels.						•	S1	S1
Chenopodium watsonii A. Nels.						•	S1	S1
Cirsium scariosum Nutt.			•				SU	SU
Conimitella williamsii (D.C. Eaton) Rydb.			•		•	•	S2	S2
Coptis trifolia (L.) Salisb.		•		•			S3	S3
Coreopsis tinctoria Nutt.						•	S1S2	S2
Crepis atribarba Heller			•			•	S2	S2
Crepis intermedia A. Gray			•		•		S2	S2
Crepis occidentalis Nutt.			•			•	S2	S2
Cryptantha macounii (Eastw.) Payson						•	S3	S2
Cryptantha minima Rydb.						•	S1	S1
Cryptogramma stelleri (S.G. Gmel.) Prantl			•				S2	S2
Cuscuta gronovii Willd.						•	S1	S1
Cynoglossum virginianum L. var. *boreale* (Fern.) Cooperrider					•		S1	S1
Cyperus schweinitzii Torr.					•	•	S2	S2

Scientific Name	Canadian Shield	Boreal Forest	Rocky Mtn.	Foot-hills	Park-land	Grass-lands	S Rank 1998	S Rank 2000
Cyperus squarrosus L.						•	S1	S1
Cypripedium acaule Ait.	•	•					S2	S2
Cypripedium montanum Dougl. *ex* Lindl.			•		•		S2	S2
Cystopteris montana (Lam.) Desv.		•	•	•			S2	S2
Danthonia californica Bol.		•	•	•	•	•	S3	S3
Danthonia spicata (L.) Beauv. *ex* R. & S.	•	•	•		•		S2	S1S2
Danthonia unispicata (Thurb.) Munro *ex* Macoun			•			•	S2	S3
Deschampsia elongata (Hook.) Munro *ex* Benth.			•	•			S1S2	S1
Diphasiastrum sitchense (Rupr.) Holub		•	•	•			S2	S2
Douglasia montana A. Gray			•				S1	S1
Downingia laeta Greene						•	S1S2	S1S2
Draba densifolia Nutt.			•				S1S2	S1S2
Draba fladnizensis Wulfen			•				S1	S1
Draba glabella Pursh			•				S1	S1
Draba kananaskis Mulligan			•				S1	S1
Draba longipes Raup			•				S1S2	S1S2
Draba macounii O.E. Schulz			•				S2	S2
Draba porsildii G.A. Mulligan			•				S2	S2
Draba reptans (Lam.) Fern.						•	S1S2	S1
Draba ventosa A. Gray			•				S2	S2
Drosera anglica Huds.	•	•	•	•	•		S2	S3
Drosera linearis Goldie		•	•	•	•		S2	S2
Dryopteris cristata (L.) A. Gray		•					S1	S1
Dryopteris filix-mas (L.) Schott			•				S1	S1
Elatine triandra Schk.		•				•	S1	S1
Eleocharis elliptica Kunth		•			•		SU	SU
Eleocharis engelmannii Steud.			•				S1?	S1?
Ellisia nyctelea L.					•	•	S2	S2
Elodea bifoliata St. John		•				•	S1S2	S1
Elymus elymoides (Raf.) Swezey			•			•	S3	S3
Elymus scribneri (Vasey) M.E. Jones			•				S2	S2
Elymus virginicus L.			•			•	S1	S1
Epilobium clavatum Trel.			•	•			S2	S2
Epilobium glaberrimum Barbey ssp. *fastigiatum* (Nutt.) Hoch & Raven			•				S1	S1
Epilobium halleanum Hausskn.		•					S1	S1
Epilobium lactiflorum Hausskn.		•	•	•			S2	S2

Scientific Name	Canadian Shield	Boreal Forest	Rocky Mtn.	Foot-hills	Park-land	Grass-lands	S Rank 1998	S Rank 2000
Epilobium leptocarpum Hausskn.			•	•			S1	S1
Epilobium luteum Pursh			•				S1	S1
Epilobium mirabile Trel.			•				SR	S?
Epilobium oreganum Greene			•				SR	SRF
Epilobium saximontanum Hausskn.			•	•			S1S2	S1
Erigeron divergens T. & G.			•				S1	S1
Erigeron flagellaris A. Gray			•		•		S1	S1
Erigeron hyssopifolius Michx.		•					S1	S1
Erigeron lackschewitzii Nesom & Weber			•				S1	S1
Erigeron ochroleucus Nutt. var. *scribneri* (Canby) Cronq.			•				S2?	S2
Erigeron pallens Cronq.			•				S2	S2
Erigeron radicatus Hook.			•	•		•	S2	S2
Erigeron trifidus Hook.			•				S2	S1S2
Eriogonum cernuum Nutt.						•	S2	S2
Eriogonum ovalifolium Nutt. var. *ovalifolium*			•				S2	S3
Eriophorum callitrix Cham. *ex* C.A. Mey			•				S2	S2
Eriophorum scheuchzeri Hoppe			•	•			S3	S3
Erysimum pallasii (Pursh) Fern.			•				S3	S3
Eupatorium maculatum L.		•					S1S2	S1S2
Festuca altaica Trin. *ex* Ledeb.			•				S2	S2
Festuca minutiflora Rydberg			•				S2	S2
Festuca occidentalis Hook.			•				S1	S1
Festuca subulata Trin.			•				S1	S1
Festuca viviparoidea Krajina *ex* Pavlick ssp. *krajinae* Pavlick			•				S1	S1
Galium bifolium S. Wats.			•				S1	S1
Gayophytum racemosum Nutt. *ex* T. & G.			•				S1	S1
Gentiana fremontii Torr.					•		S1	S2S3
Gentiana glauca Pallas			•				S2	S2
Gentianopsis detonsa (Rottb.) Ma spp. *raupii* (Porsild) A. Löve & D. Löve		•					S1	S1
Geranium carolinianum L.		•			•		S1	S1
Geranium erianthum DC.			•				S1	SH
Glyceria elata (Nash) A.S. Hitchc.		•	•	•			S2	S2
Gnaphalium microcephalum Nutt.					•		S1	SH
Gnaphalium viscosum Kunth			•				SH	SH
Gratiola neglecta Torr.					•	•	S3	S2S3

Scientific Name	Canadian Shield	Boreal Forest	Rocky Mtn.	Foot-hills	Park-land	Grass-lands	S Rank 1998	S Rank 2000
Gymnocarpium jessoense (Koidz.) Koidz.	•						S1	S1
Halimolobos virgata (Nutt.) O.E. Schulz						•	S1	S1
Hedyotis longifolia (Gaertn.) Hook.		•			•		S2	S2
Heliotropium curassavicum L.						•	S1	S1
Heuchera glabra Willd. *ex* R. & S.			•				S1	S1
Hieracium cynoglossoides Arv.-Touv. *ex* A. Gray			•		•		S2	S2S3
Hippuris montana Ledeb.			•				S1	S1
Hordeum pusillum Nutt.						•	SH	SH
Huperzia haleakalae (Brack.) Holub			•	•			S2	S2
Huperzia selago (L.) Bernh. *ex* Schrank & Mart.		•		•			S1	S1
Hydrophyllum capitatum Dougl. *ex* Hook.			•				S3	S2S3
Hymenopappus filifolius Hook. var. *polycephalus* (Osterh.) B.L. Turner						•	S2	S2
Hypericum majus (Gray) Britt.	•	•					S2	S2
Hypericum scouleri Hook.			•				S1	S1
Iliamna rivularis (Dougl. *ex* Hook.) Greene			•		•		S2	S2
Iris missouriensis Nutt.					•	•	S1	S1
Isoetes bolanderi Engelm.			•				S1	S1
Isoetes echinospora Durieu	•	•					S1	S1
Isoetes maritima L. Underwood			•				S1	S1
Isoetes occidentalis L.F. Henderson			•				S1	S1
Isoetes x *truncata* (A.A. Eaton) Clute			•				S1	S1
Juncus biglumis L.			•				S2	S2
Juncus brevicaudatus (Engelm.) Fern.	•	•		•			S2	S2
Juncus confusus Coville			•		•	•	S2	S2S3
Juncus filiformis L.	•	•		•			S2S3	S2S3
Juncus nevadensis S. Wats.			•				S1	S1
Juncus parryi Engelm.			•				S2	S2
Juncus regelii Buch.			•				S1	S1
Juncus stygius L. ssp. *americanus* (Buch.) Hult.		•		•			S2	S2
Koenigia islandica L.			•				S1	S1
Lactuca biennis (Moench) Fern.		•		•	•		S2S3	S2
Larix occidentalis Nutt.			•				S2	S2

Scientific Name	Canadian Shield	Boreal Forest	Rocky Mtn.	Foot-hills	Park-land	Grass-lands	S Rank 1998	S Rank 2000
Lesquerella arctica (Wormskj. *ex* Hornem.) S. Wats. var. *purshii* Wats.			•				S2	S2
Lewisia pygmaea (A. Gray) B.L. Robins. ssp. *pygmaea*			•				S2	S2
Lewisia rediviva Pursh			•				S1	S1
Leymus mollis (Trin.) Pilger ssp. *mollis*	•						S1	S1
Lilaea scilloides (Poir.) Hauman			•			•	S1	S1
Linanthus septentrionalis H.L. Mason			•			•	S2	S2
Listera caurina Piper			•				S1S2	S1
Listera convallarioides (Sw.) Nutt.			•				S2	S2
Lithophragma glabrum Nutt.			•				S2	S2
Lithophragma parviflorum (Hook.) Nutt. *ex* T. & G.			•		•		S2	S2
Lobelia dortmanna L.		•					S1	S1
Lobelia spicata Lam.						•	S1	S1
Loiseleuria procumbens (L.) Desv.			•				S1S2	S1S2
Lomatium cous (S. Wats.) Coult. & Rose			•				S1	S1S2
Lomatogonium rotatum (L.) Fries *ex* Nyman		•	•	•	•	•	S2	S2
Lupinus lepidus Dougl. *ex* Lindl.			•				S2	SRF
Lupinus minimus Dougl. *ex* Hook.			•				S2	S1
Lupinus polyphyllus Lindl.			•				S1	S1
Lupinus wyethii S. Wats.			•				S1	S1
Luzula acuminata Raf.		•		•			S1	S1
Luzula groenlandica Bocher	•						S1	S1
Luzula rufescens Fisch. *ex* E. Mey.		•		•			S1	S1
Lycopodiella inundata (L.) Holub	•						S1	S1
Lycopus americanus Muhl. *ex* W.C. Barton					•	•	S2	S2
Lysimachia hybrida Michx.					•	•	S2	S2
Machaeranthera tanacetifolia (Kunth) Nees						•	SR	SX
Malaxis monophylla (L.) Sw. var. *brachypoda* (A. Gray) Morris & Ames		•			•		S2	S2
Malaxis paludosa (L.) Sw.		•			•		S1S2	S1
Marsilea vestita Hook. & Grev.						•	S2	S2
Melica smithii (Porter *ex* A. Gray) Vasey			•		•		S1S2	S1S2
Melica spectabilis Scribn.			•		•		S2	S2

Scientific Name	Canadian Shield	Boreal Forest	Rocky Mtn.	Foot-hills	Park-land	Grass-lands	S Rank 1998	S Rank 2000
Mertensia lanceolata (Pursh) A. DC.			•		•	•	S2	S2
Mertensia longiflora Greene			•		•		S2	S2
Microseris nutans (Hook.) Sch.-Bip.			•				S3	S2S3
Mimulus breweri (Greene) Coville			•				S1	S1
Mimulus floribundus Dougl. *ex* Lindl.			•				S1	S1
Mimulus glabratus Kunth					•		S1	S1
Mimulus guttatus DC.			•		•		SU	SU
Mimulus tilingii Regel			•		•		SU	S1
Minuartia elegans (Cham. & Schlecht.) Schischkin			•				S1	S1
Monotropa hypopithys L.		•	•				S2	S2
Montia linearis (Dougl. *ex* Hook.) Greene			•		•	•	S1S2	S1
Montia parvifolia (Moc. *ex* DC.) Greene			•				S1	S1
Muhlenbergia asperifolia (Nees & Meyen *ex* Trin.) Parodi						•	S2	S2
Muhlenbergia racemosa (Michx.) BSP.		•			•		S1	S1
Munroa squarrosa (Nutt.) Torr.						•	S1	S1
Najas flexilis (Willd.) Rostk. & Schmidt		•			•		S1S2	S1S2
Nemophila breviflora A. Gray			•		•	•	S1S2	S1S2
Nothocalais cuspidata (Pursh) Greene						•	S1	S1
Nuttallanthus canadensis (L.) D.A. Sutton						•	S1	S1
Nymphaea leibergii Morong		•					S1	S1
Nymphaea tetragona Georgi	•	•					S1	S1
Oenothera flava (A. Nels.) Garrett					•	•	S1S2	S2
Onosmodium molle Michx. var. *occidentale* (Mack.) I.M. Johnston					•	•	S2	S2
Oplopanax horridus (Sm.) T. & G. *ex* Miq. var. *horridus*		•	•	•			S3	S3
Orobanche ludoviciana Nutt.						•	S2	S2
Orobanche uniflora L.			•		•		S2	S2
Oryzopsis canadensis (Poir.) Torr.		•			•		S1	S1
Oryzopsis exigua Thurb.			•				S1	S1
Oryzopsis micrantha (Trin. & Rupr.) Thurb.						•	S2	S2

Scientific Name	Canadian Shield	Boreal Forest	Rocky Mtn.	Foot-hills	Park-land	Grass-lands	S Rank 1998	S Rank 2000
Osmorhiza longistylis (Torr.) DC.			•		•	•	S2	S2
Osmorhiza purpurea (Coult. & Rose) Suksd.			•				S2	S2
Oxytropis jordalii Porsild var. *jordalii*			•				S1	SRF
Oxytropis lagopus Nutt. var. *conjugens* Barneby						•	S1	S1
Packera subnuda Trock & Barkley			•				S1	S2
Panicum acuminatum Swartz			•				SX	SU
Panicum leibergii (Vasey) Scribn.					•		S1	S1
Panicum wilcoxianum Vasey					•		S1	S1
Papaver pygmaeum Rydb.			•				S1S2	S2
Papaver radicatum Rottb. ssp. *kluanense* (D. Löve) D.F. Murray			•				S2	S2
Parietaria pensylvanica Muhl. *ex* Willd.			•			•	S2	S2
Parnassia parviflora DC.		•	•	•			S2	S2
Pedicularis capitata J.E. Adams			•				S2	S2
Pedicularis flammea L.			•				S3	S2
Pedicularis lanata Cham. & Schlecht.			•				S2	S2
Pedicularis langsdorfii Fisch. *ex* Stev. ssp. *arctica* (R. Br.) Pennell			•				S2	S2
Pedicularis oederi Vahl *ex* Hornem.			•					S1
Pedicularis racemosa Dougl. *ex* Hook.			•				S1	S1
Pedicularis sudetica Willd. ssp. *interioides* Hult.		•					S1	S1
Pellaea gastonyi Windham			•				S1	S1
Pellaea glabella Mett. *ex* Kuhn ssp. *occidentalis* (E.E. Nelson) Windham					•	•		S1
Pellaea glabella Mett. *ex* Kuhn ssp. *simplex* (Butters) A. Löve & D. Löve		•	•					S2
Penstemon fruticosus (Pursh) Greene var. *scouleri* (Lindl.) Cronq.			•				S2	S2
Phacelia linearis (Pursh) Holzinger			•		•	•	S2	S2
Phacelia lyallii (A. Gray) Rydb.			•				S2	S2
Phegopteris connectilis (Michx.) Watt			•	•			S2	S2

Scientific Name	Canadian Shield	Boreal Forest	Rocky Mtn.	Foot-hills	Park-land	Grass-lands	S Rank 1998	S Rank 2000
Philadelphus lewisii Pursh			•				S1	S1
Phlox gracilis (Hook.) Greene ssp. *gracilis*			•				S1S2	S1
Physocarpus malvaceus (Greene) Kuntze			•				S1	S1
Physostegia ledinghamii (Boivin) Cantino		•			•		S2	S2
Picradeniopsis oppositifolia (Nutt.) Rydb. *ex* Britt.						•	S1	S1
Pinguicula villosa L.	•	•					S1S2	S1
Pinus monticola Dougl. *ex* D. Don.			•				SU	SU
Plantago canescens J.E. Adams		•	•			•	S2	S2
Plantago maritima L.		•					S1	S1
Platanthera stricta Lindl.			•				S2	S2
Poa gracillima Vasey			•				S2	S2
Poa laxa Haenke ssp. *banffiana* Soreng			•				SR	S1
Poa leptocoma Trin.			•	•		•	S3	S3
Poa lettermanii Vasey			•				S1	S1
Poa nervosa (Hook.) Vasey var. *wheeleri* (Vasey) C.L. Hitchc.			•		•	•	S3	S3
Poa stenantha Trin.			•				SU	SU
Polanisia dodecandra (L.) DC. ssp. *trachysperma* (T. & G.) Iltis						•	S1S2	S2
Polygala paucifolia Willd.		•					S1	S1
Polygonum minimum S. Wats.			•		•		S1S2	S2
Polygonum polygaloides Meissn. ssp. *confertiflorum* (Nutt. *ex* Piper) Hickman			•			•	S2	S2
Polypodium hesperium Maxon			•				S1	S1S2
Polypodium sibiricum Siplivinsky	•						S1	S1?
Polypodium virginianum L.	•	•		•			S2	S2?
Populus angustifolia James						•	S2	S3
Potamogeton foliosus Raf.		•	•				S2	S2
Potamogeton natans L.	•	•	•	•	•		S2	S2
Potamogeton obtusifolius Mert. & W.D.J. Koch	•	•					S2	S2
Potamogeton praelongus Wulfen		•		•	•		S2	S2
Potamogeton robbinsii Oakes	•	•					S1	S1
Potamogeton strictifolius A. Bennett		•					S2	S2
Potentilla drummondii Lehm. ssp. *drummondii*			•				S2	S2
Potentilla finitima Kohli & Packer					•		S1	S1

Scientific Name	Canadian Shield	Boreal Forest	Rocky Mtn.	Foot-hills	Park-land	Grass-lands	S Rank 1998	S Rank 2000
Potentilla hookeriana Lehm.	•		•	•			S2	S2
Potentilla macounii Rydb.			•				SI	SI
Potentilla multifida L.	•	•					SI	SI
Potentilla multisecta (S. Wats.) Rydb.			•				SI	S2
Potentilla paradoxa Nutt.						•	S2	S2
Potentilla plattensis Nutt.					•	•	SI?	SI
Potentilla subjuga Rydb.			•				SI	SI
Potentilla villosa Pallas *ex* Pursh			•				S2	S2
Prenanthes alata (Hook.) D. Dietr.				•			SI	SI
Prenanthes sagittata (A. Gray) A. Nels.			•		•		S2	S2
Primula egaliksensis Wormskj.			•	•			S2	S2
Primula stricta Hornem.			•				SIS2	SI
Psilocarphus elatior A. Gray						•	S2	S2
Psoralea argophylla Pursh			•		•	•	S3	S3
Pterospora andromedea Nutt.			•		•		S2	S3
Pyrola grandiflora Radius		•	•				S2	S2
Pyrola picta J.E. Smith			•				SI	SI
Ranunculus gelidus Karel. & Kiril. ssp. *grayi* (Britt.) Hult.			•				S3	S3
Ranunculus glaberrimus Hook.			•			•	S2	S2
Ranunculus nivalis L.			•				SI	SI
Ranunculus occidentalis Nutt. var. *brevistylis* Greene			•				S2	S2
Ranunculus uncinatus D. Don			•	•	•		S2	S2
Rhododendron lapponicum (L.) Wahlenb.			•				S2	S2
Rhynchospora capillacea Torr.		•			•		SI	SI
Ribes laxiflorum Pursh			•				SIS2	S2
Romanzoffia sitchensis Bong.			•				S2	S2
Rorippa curvipes Greene var. *curvipes*			•				SU	SU
Rorippa curvipes Greene var. *truncata* (Jepson) Rollins						•	SI	SI
Rorippa sinuata (Nutt. *ex* T. & G.) A.S. Hitchc.						•	SI	SI
Rorippa tenerrima E. Greene			•			•	SI	SI
Rumex paucifolius Nutt. *ex* Wats.			•				SI	SI
Ruppia cirrhosa (Petagna) Grande		•			•	•	SI	SIS2
Sagina decumbens (Ell.) T. & G.						•	SI	SI
Sagina nivalis (Lindbl.) Fries			•				SU	SU

Scientific Name	Canadian Shield	Boreal Forest	Rocky Mtn.	Foot-hills	Park-land	Grass-lands	S Rank 1998	S Rank 2000
Sagina nodosa (L.) Fenzl ssp. *borealis* Crow	•						S1	S1
Sagittaria latifolia Willd.		•		•		•	S1	S1
Salix alaxensis (Anderss.) Coville ssp. *alaxensis*			•	•			S2	S2
Salix commutata Bebb			•	•			S2	S2
Salix lanata L. ssp. *calcicola* (Fern. & Wieg.) Hult.			•				S1	S1
Salix raupii Argus			•	•			S1	S1
Salix sitchensis Sanson *ex* Bong.		•	•				S1	S1
Salix stolonifera Coville			•				S1	S1
Salix tyrellii Argus		•						S1
Sarracenia purpurea L. ssp. *purpurea*		•					S1S2	S2
Saussurea americana D.C. Eat.			•				S1	S1
Saxifraga ferruginea Graham			•				S2	S2
Saxifraga flagellaris Willd. ssp. *setigera* (Pursh) Tolm.			•				S2	S2
Saxifraga nelsoniana D. Don ssp. *porsildiana* (Calder & Savile) Hult.			•				S2	S2
Saxifraga nivalis L.			•	•			S2	S2
Saxifraga odontoloma Piper			•				S1?	S1
Saxifraga oregana J.T. Howell var. *montanensis* (Small) C.L. Hitchc.			•				SU	SU
Schizachyrium scoparium (Michx.) Nash ssp. *scoparium*			•			•	S3	S3
Scirpus pallidus (Britt.) Fern.		•				•	S1	S1
Sedum divergens S. Wats.			•				S2	S2
Selaginella wallacei Hieron.			•				S1	S1
Senecio megacephalus Nutt.			•				S3	S3
Shinneroseris rostrata (A. Gray) S. Tomb					•	•	S2	S2
Silene involucrata (Cham. & Schlecht.) Bocquet ssp. *involucrata*			•				S1S2	S1S2
Sisyrinchium septentrionale Bicknell			•	•	•	•	S2S3	S2S3
Sparganium fluctuans (Engelm. *ex* Morong) B.L. Robins.		•					S1	S1
Sparganium glomeratum (Beurling *ex* Laest.) L.M. Neuman		•					S1	S1
Sparganium hyperboreum Beurling *ex* Laest.			•	•			S1	S1

Scientific Name	Canadian Shield	Boreal Forest	Rocky Mtn.	Foot-hills	Park-land	Grass-lands	S Rank 1998	S Rank 2000
Spartina pectinata Link		•				•	S1	S1
Spergularia salina J. & K. Presl var. *salina*		•	•		•	•	S2	S2
Sphenopholis obtusata (Michx.) Scribn.				•	•	•	S2	S2
Spiraea splendens Baumann *ex* K. Koch var. *splendens*			•				S1	S1
Spiranthes lacera (Raf.) Raf. var. *lacera*		•					S1	S1
Stellaria americana (Porter *ex* B.L. Robins.) Standl.			•				S1	S1
Stellaria arenicola Raup	•						S1	S1
Stellaria crispa Cham. & Schlecht.		•	•	•			S2	S2
Stellaria obtusa Engelm.			•				S1	S1
Stellaria umbellata Turcz. *ex* Kar. & Kir.			•				S1	S1
Stephanomeria runcinata Nutt.						•	S2	S2
Streptopus roseus Michx.		•		•			S1	S1
Streptopus streptopoides (Ledeb.) Frye & Rigg				•			S1	S1
Suaeda moquinii (Torr.) Greene						•	S2	S2
Suckleya suckleyana (Torr.) Rydb.						•	S1	S1
Suksdorfia ranunculifolia (Hook.) Engl.			•				S1S2	S2
Suksdorfia violacea A. Gray			•				S1	S1
Tanacetum bipinnatum (L.) Schultz-Bip. ssp. *huronense* (Nutt.) Breitung	•						S1	S1
Taxus brevifolia Nutt.			•				S1	S1
Tellima grandiflora (Pursh) Dougl. *ex* Lindl.			•				S1	S1
Thelesperma subnudum A. Gray var. *marginatum* (Rydb.) T.E. Melchert *ex* Cronq.						•	S1	S1
Thuja plicata Donn *ex* D. Don			•				S1S2	S1S2
Torreyochloa pallida (Torr.) Church var. *pauciflora* (J. Presl.) J.I. Davis					•		S1	S1
Townsendia condensata Parry *ex* A. Gray			•				S1	S2
Townsendia exscapa (Richards.) Porter						•	S1S2	S2
Tradescantia occidentalis (Britt.) Smyth var. *occidentalis*						•	S1	S1

Scientific Name	Canadian Shield	Boreal Forest	Rocky Mtn.	Foot-hills	Park-land	Grass-lands	S Rank 1998	S Rank 2000
Triantha occidentalis (S. Wats.) Gates ssp. *brevistyla* (C.L. Hitchc.) Packer			•				S1	S1
Triantha occidentalis (S. Wats.) Gates ssp. *montana* (C.L. Hitchc.) Packer			•				S1	S1
Trichophorum clintonii (A. Gray) S.G. Smith		•		•			S1	S1
Trichophorum pumilum (Vahl) Schinz & Thellung		•	•	•			S2	S2
Trillium ovatum Pursh			•				S1	S1
Tripterocalyx micranthus (Torr.) Hook.						•	S2	S2
Trisetum cernuum Trin. var. *canescens* (Buckl.) Beal			•				S1	S1
Trisetum cernuum Trin. var. *cernuum*			•		•		S2?	S2
Trisetum montanum Vasey			•				S1	S1
Trisetum wolfii Vasey			•		•		S1	S1
Tsuga heterophylla (Raf.) Sarg.			•				S1	S1
Utricularia cornuta Michx.	•	•					S1	S1
Vaccinium ovalifolium J.E. Smith			•				S2	S2
Vaccinium uliginosum L.	•	•					S2	S2
Veronica catenata Pennell						•	S1S2	S1S2
Veronica serpyllifolia L.			•	•	•		S3	S3
Viola pallens (Banks *ex* DC.) Brainerd		•	•				S1S2	S1
Viola pedatifida G. Don					•	•	S2	S2
Viola praemorsa Dougl. *ex* Lindl. var. *linguifolia* (Nutt.) M.S. Baker & J.C. Klausen *ex* M.E. Peck			•				S2	S2
Wolffia columbiana Karsten		•					S2	S2
Woodsia glabella R. Br. *ex* Richardson			•				S1	S1
Yucca glauca Nutt. *ex* Fraser						•	S1	S1
TOTALS: 488	33	114	312	76	101	124		

Appendix 3

Species in this guide that are not found in the *Flora of Alberta* (second edition)

The following list of native vascular plants is new to the flora of Alberta since Moss (1983). The additions are of two types: those representing new discoveries, and others resulting from taxonomic revision to existing groups. This list includes only those taxa that have been documented by specimens and does not include those reported without supporting documentation.

New Discoveries

Agoseris lackschewitzii D. Henderson & R. Moseley
Aruncus dioicus (Walt.) Fern.
Bacopa rotundifolia (Michx.) Wettst.
Botrychium pinnatum H. St. John
Brasenia schreberi J.F. Gmelin
Carex pedunculata Muhl.
Carex supina Willd. *ex* Wahlenb.
Erigeron lackschewitzii Nesom & Weber
Galium bifolium S. Wats.
Isoetes maritima L. Underwood
Isoetes occidentalis L. f. Henderson
Isoetes x *truncata* (A.A. Eaton) Clute
Juncus regelii Buch.
Lewisia rediviva (Gray) B.L. Robins.
Lupinus wyethii S. Wats.
Luzula groenlandica Bocher
Luzula rufescens Fisch. *ex* E. Mey.
Mimulus brewerii (Greene) Coville
Mimulus glabratus Kunth
Nuttallanthus canadensis (L.) D.A. Sutton
Pedicularis oederi Vahl *ex* Hornem.
Poa laxa Haenke ssp. *banffiana* Soreng
Rorippa curvipes Greene var. *truncata* (Jepson) Rollins
Salix raupii Argus
Salix tyrellii Argus
Scirpus rufus (Huds.) Schrad.
Spiranthes lacera (Raf.) Raf. var. *lacera*
Tellima grandiflora (Pursh) Dougl. *ex* Lindl.
Tradescantia occidentalis (Britt.) Smyth var. *occidentalis*
Wolffia borealis (Engelm. *ex* Hegelm.) Landolt *ex* Landolt & Wildi
Wolffia columbiana Karst

Appendix 3

Changes Resulting from Taxonomic Revision

Antennaria aromatica Evert (newly described, Bayer 1989)
Botrychium campestre W.H. Wagner & Farrar *ex* W.J. & F. Wagner (newly described, Wagner and Wagner 1986)
Botrychium crenulatum W.H. Wagner (newly described, Wagner and Wagner 1981)
Botrychium michiganense
Botrychium minganense Victorin (formerly included with description of *B. dusenii*)
Botrychium paradoxum W.H. Wagner (newly described, Wagner and Wagner 1981)
Botrychium pedunculosum W.H. Wagner (newly described, Wagner and Wagner 1986)
Botrychium spathulatum W.H. Wagner (newly described, Wagner and Wagner 1990)
Botrychium x *watertonense* W.H. Wagner (newly described, Wagner et al. 1984)
Carex utriculata Boott (formerly recognized as *C. rostrata* Stokes)
Cerastium brachypodum (Engelm. *ex* A. Gray) B.L. Rob. (a segregate from *C. nutans*)
Festuca hallii (Vasey) Piper (formerly included within *F. scabrella* Trin.)
Festuca minutiflora Rydberg (formerly identified as *F. brachyphylla* Schultes)
Festuca viviparoidea Krajina *ex* Pavlick ssp. *krajinae* Pavlick (formerly *F. vivipara* (L.) Sm. ssp. *glabra* Frederiksen)
Gymnocarpium disjunctum (Ruprecht) Ching (formerly included within *G. dryopteris* (L.) Newman; see *Flora of North America* 1993)
Huperzia haleakalae (Brachenridge) Holub (formerly included within *Lycopodium selago*; see *Flora of North America* 1993)
Mimulus tilingii Regel (formerly included within *M. guttatus*)
Nymphaea tetragona Georgi ssp. *tetragona*
Oxytropis campestris (L.) DC. var *davisii* Welsh
Pellaea gastonyi Windham (formerly included within *P. atropurpurea* (L.) Link; see *Flora of North America* 1993)
Polypodium sibiricum Siplivinsky (formerly included within *P. virginianum* L.; see *Flora of North America* 1993)
Triantha occidentalis (S. Wats.) Gates ssp. *brevistyla* (C.L. Hitchc.) Packer (Packer 1993)
Triantha occidentalis (S. Wats.) Gates ssp. *montana* (C.L. Hitchc.) Packer (Packer 1993)

APPENDIX 4

TAXA PREVIOUSLY REPORTED AS RARE FOR ALBERTA BUT NOT INCLUDED IN THIS BOOK

This list includes taxa that have been considered rare in other publications on Alberta's flora. Many of the taxa are now known to have more than twenty occurrences in the province and large population sizes; they are no longer considered rare. Several other taxa are included on a watch list. These are taxa that have restricted distributions within Alberta but are common within their range. Information is collected to ascertain trends in populations. A taxon may move from the watch list to the tracking list if information suggests that the taxon is in decline. Taxa that are currently on the watch list are indicated with a w.

SCIENTIFIC NAME	SOURCE	COMMENTS
Agoseris grandiflora (Nutt.) Greene	1	lacks documentation
Agropyron violaceum Hornem. Lange ssp. *andinum* (Scribn. & Melderis)	1	
Alopecurus carolinianus Walt.	3	w
Androsace occidentalis Pursh	1, 2	
Angelica dawsonii Wats.	1, 3	w
Antennaria alpina (L.) Gaetn. var. *media* (Greene) Jeps	1	
Antennaria dimorpha (Nutt.) Torr. & Gray	2, 3	
Arnica alpina (L.) Olin ssp. *angustifolia* (M. Vahl) Maguire	1	
Aruncus sylvester Kostel. *ex* Maxim.	2, 3	introduced
Balsamorhiza sagittata (Pursh) Nutt.	1	
Braya humilis (C.A. Mey.) Robins. var. *maccallae* Harris	3	not a published name
Bupleurum americanum C. & R.	1, 2, 3	w
Calochortus apiculatus Baker	1, 3	w
Carex athabascensis F.J. Herm. (*C. scirpoidea* Michx.)	1, 3	
Carex geyeri Boott	2, 3	w
Castilleja hispida Benth.	2, 3	
Ceanothus velutinus Dougl.	1, 2, 3	w
Chrysothamnus nauseosus (Pall.) Britt.	1	
Crataegus douglasii Lindl.	1, 2, 3	w
Disporum hookeri (Torr.) Nichols.	2, 3	w
Disporum oreganum Wats.	1, 2	included within *D. hookeri* (Torr.) Nichols.
Draba verna L.	1	introduced
Dryopteris fragrans (L.) Schott	1, 2, 3	w
Festuca viridula (Vasey)	1	no Alberta records known
Fragaria vesca L. var. *bracteata* (Heller) Davis	1	
Galium palustre L.	1	no Alberta records known
Gaultheria humifusa (Graham) Rydb.	1	
Gentiana calycosa Griseb. var. *obtusiloba* (Rydb.) C.L. Hitchc.	1, 2, 3	w
Habenaria unalaschensis (Spreng.) S. Wats. (*Piperia unalascensis* (Spreng.) Rydb.)	2, 3	

Scientific name	Source	Comments
Haplopappus uniflorus (Hook.) T. & G.	2	w
Hedeoma hispidum Pursh	2, 3	
Ledum glandulosum Nutt.	2, 3	
Lesquerella alpina (Nutt.) Wats.	1	
Lomatium sandbergii C. & R.	1, 2, 3	w
Lonicera utahensis S. Wats.	2, 3	
Luetkea pectinata (Pursh) Kuntze	1	w
Lupinus arbustus Dougl. ssp. *pseudoparviflorus* (Rydb.) Dunn	1	no Alberta records known
Lupinus nootkatensis Donn	1	w
Lupinus pusillus Pursh	2	
Luzula arcuata (Wahl.) Sw.	1	
Luzula hitchcockii L. Hamet-Ahti	2, 3	w
Melica subulata (Griseb.) Scribn.	2, 3	
Minuartia nuttallii (Pax) Briq.	1, 2	w
Mirabilis nyctaginea (Michx.) MacM.	2, 3	introduced
Myosurus aristatus Benth.	1, 3	
Osmorhiza occidentalis (Nutt.) Tor.	1, 3	w
Pachistima myrsinites (Pursh) Raf.	1, 2, 3	w
Pedicularis macrodonta Richards	1	included within *P. parviflora* S. *ex* Rees
Penstemon albertinus Greene	1, 3	w
Penstemon eriantherus Pursh	3	w
Penstemon lyallii Gray	1	w
Phlox alyssifolia Greene	1, 3	
Plantago patagonica Jacq. var. *spinulosa* (Dcne.) Gray	1	
Poa lanata Scribn. & Merr.	1	no Alberta records known
Polemonium viscosum Nutt.	1, 2, 3	
Potamogeton pusillus L. var. *tenuissimus* Mert. & Koch	1	
Potentilla yukonensis Hult. (*P. anserina* L.)	1	
Pteridium aquilinum (L.) Kuhn var. *pubescens* Underw.	1, 2, 3	w
Pyrola bracteata Hook.	1, 2, 3	w
Ribes inerme Rydb.	1, 2, 3	
Ribes viscosissimum Pursh	1, 2, 3	w
Salix boothii Dorn	2, 3	
Saxifraga debilis Engelm. (*S. hyperborea* R. Br.)	1	
Saxifraga mertensiana Bong.	1, 2, 3	w
Schedonnardus paniculatus (Nutt.) Trel.	1, 2, 3	
Scirpus cyperinus (L.) Kunth	2	
Scirpus nevadensis S. Wats.	2, 3	

Scientific name	Source	Comments
Sedum douglasii Hook. (*S. stenopetalum* Pursh)	2	w
Selaginella rupestris (L.) Spring	2, 3	
Senecio conterminus Greenm.	1, 3	w
Senecio hydrophiloides Rydb.	1, 2	
Silene douglasii Hook.	1	lacks documentation
Sorbus sitchensis M. Roemer		
Sporobolus neglectus Nash	3	introduced
Thalictrum dasycarpum Fisch. & Ave-Lall.	2	
Tiarella trifoliata L.	1	w
Tofieldia coccinea Rich.	1	no Alberta records known
Viola glabella Nutt.	2, 3	
Viola selkirkii Pursh	1, 2, 3	
Vulpia octoflora (Walt.) Rydb.	2	
Xerophyllum tenax (Pursh.) Nutt.	2, 3	w

1 Argus, G W. and D.J. White, 1978
2 Packer, J.G. and C.E. Bradley, 1984
3 Federation of Alberta Naturalists, 1992

Appendix 5

Species reported from or expected to occur in Alberta but not yet verified

Several species have been reported from Alberta but lack supporting documentation (i.e., a specimen). Other species occur in close proximity to the province and should be expected to occur here in the appropriate habitat.

Species reported for Alberta but lacking sufficient documentation

Carex piperi Mack.
Carex sitchensis Prescott *ex* Bong. (*Carex aquatilis* Wahlenb. var. *dives* (Holm) Kukenth.)
Cerastium beeringianum Cham. & Schlecht. ssp. *terrae-novae* (Fern. & Wieg.) Hult.
Cornus unalaschkensis Ledeb.
Cryptantha affinis (A. Gray) Greene
Eleocharis nitida Fern.
Elymus vulpinus Rydb.
Erigeron uncialis Blake
Eriogonum pauciflorum Pursh
Festuca lenensis Drob.
Hackelia ciliata (Dougl. *ex* Lehm.) I.M. Johnson
Melica hitchcockii Boivin
Minuartia yukonensis Hulten
Phippsia algida (Phipps) R. Br.
Saxifraga subapetala E. Nels.
Senecio integerrimus Nutt. var. *ochroleucus* (Gray) Cronq.
Stellaria nitens Nutt.
Torreyochloa pallida Church var. *fernaldiii* (Hitchc.) Dore

Species that may occur in Alberta

Achillea millefolium L. var. *megacephala* (Raup) Boivin
Carex bicolor Bellardi *ex* All.
Erigeron ochroleucus Nutt. var. *ochroleucus* Nutt.
Isoetes howellii Engelm.
Minuartia rossii (R. Br.) Graebn.
Ranunculus eschscholtzii Schlecht. var. *suksdorfii* (A. Gray) L.D. Benson
Rhynchospora alba (L.) Vahl

Appendix 6

Alberta taxa classified as nationally rare by Argus and Pryer (1990)

The following taxa are reported to occur in Alberta by Argus and Pryer and were considered to be nationally rare in 1990. These taxa are all considered provincially rare unless otherwise indicated (x). *Many of those that are not considered rare at this time are included on a watch list. These taxa have restricted distributions within Alberta but are common within their range. Information is collected to ascertain trends in populations. A taxon may move from the watch list to the tracking list if information suggests that the taxon is in decline. Taxa that are currently on the watch list are indicated with a* w.

Species Name	*Synonym(s)*	*Notes*
Achillea millefolium L. var. *megacephala* (Raup) Boivin		x
Allium geyeri S. Wats. var. *geyeri*	*Allium rubrum* Osterh., *Allium rydbergii* Macbr.	
Angelica dawsonii S. Wats.		w
Antennaria corymbosa E. Nels.		
Aquilegia jonesii Parry		
Arnica longifolia D.C. Eat.		
Astragalus kentrophyta A. Gray var. *kentrophyta*		
Atriplex canescens (Pursh) Nutt.	*Atriplex aptera* A. Nels.	
Atriplex powellii S. Wats.		
Bacopa rotundifolia (Michx.) Wettst.		
Boisduvalia glabella (Nutt.) Walp.	*Epilobium pygmaeum* (Speg.) P. Hoch & Raven	
Botrychium ascendens Wagner		
Botrychium campestre W.H. Wagner & D.R. Farrar		
Botrychium hesperium (Maxon & R.T. Clausen) W.H. Wagner & Lellinger	*Botrychium matricariifolium* (Döll) W.D.J. Koch ssp. *hesperium* Maxon & R.T. Clausen	
Botrychium paradoxum W.H. Wagner		
Botrychium pedunculosum W.H. Wagner		
Boykinia heucheriformis (Rydb.) Rosendahl	*Telesonix heucheriformis* Rydb., *Telesonix jamesii* (Torr.) Raf.	
Braya humilis (C.A. Mey.) B.L. Robins. var. *maccallae* Harris in ed.	Not a published name	x
Brickellia grandiflora (Hook.) Nutt.		
Calochortus apiculatus Baker		w
Camassia quamash (Pursh) Greene var. *quamash*		
Camissonia andina Nutt. (Raven)	*Oenothera andina* Nutt.	
Camissonia breviflora (Torr. & Gray) Raven	*Oenothera breviflora* T. & G., *Taraxia breviflora* (T. & G.) Nutt.	

Species Name	Synonym(s)	Notes
Carex enanderi Hult.	*Carex lenticularis* Michx. var. *dolia* (M.E. Jones) L.A. Standley	
Carex epapillosa F.J. Herm.	*Carex heteroneura* Boott var. *epapillosa* (Mack.) F.J. Hermann	
Carex geyeri Boott		W
Carex nebrascensis Dewey	*Carex nebraskensis* Dewey, Carex jamesii T. & G.	
Carex paysonis Clokey		
Castilleja cusickii Greenm.		W
Chenopodium leptophyllum (Nutt. *ex* Moq.) S. Wats.		
Chenopodium subglabrum (S. Wats.) A. Nels.		
Chenopodium watsonii A. Nels.		
Cirsium scariosum Nutt.	*Cirsium hookerianum* Nutt., *Cirsium foliosum* (Hook.) DC., *Cnicus scariosus* (Nutt.) A. Gray, *Carduus scariosus* (Nutt.) Heller	
Conimitella williamsii (D.C. Eaton) Rydb.		
Crepis occidentalis Nutt.		
Cryptantha affinis (Gray) Greene		X
Cryptantha kelseyana Greene		X
Cryptantha minima Rydb.		
Dichanthelium wilcoxianum (Vasey) Freckman	*Panicum wilcoxianum* Vasey, *Panicum oligosanthes* Schultes, *Dichanthelium oligosanthes* (Schultes) Gould var. *wilcoxianum* (Vasey) Gould & Clark	
Douglasia montana A. Gray		
Downingia laeta Greene		
Draba densifolia Nutt *ex* T. & G.		
Draba kananaskis Mulligan		
Draba ventosa A. Gray		
Eleocharis engelmannii Steud.	*Eleocharis ovata* (Roth) R. & S. var. *engelmanii* Britt., *Eleocharis obtusa* (Willd.) Schultes var. *engelmanii* (Steud.) Gilly	
Elodea bifoliata St. John	*Elodea longivaginata* St. John	
Epilobium glaberrimum Barbey ssp. *fastigiatum* (Nutt.) Hoch & Raven	*Epilobium platyphyllum* Rydb., *Epilobium fastigiatum* var. *glaberrimum* (Barbey) Piper, *Epilobium affine* Bong. var. *fastigiatum* Nutt.	
Epilobium halleanum Hausskn.	*Epilobium glandulosum* Lehm. var. *macounii* (Trel.) C.L. Hitchc.	

SPECIES NAME	SYNONYM(S)	NOTES
Epilobium mirabile Trel.	*Epilobium clavatum* Trel. var. *glareosum* (G.N. Jones) Munz	
Erigeron ochroleucus Nutt. var. *scribneri* (Canby) Cronq.		
Erigeron radicatus Hook.		
Erigeron trifidus Hook.		
Eriogonum cernuum Nutt.		
Festuca minutiflora Rydberg	*Festuca brevifolia* var. *endotera* Saint-Yves, *Festuca brevifolia* var. *utahensis* Saint-Yves, *Festuca ovina* var. *minutiflora* (Rydberg) Howell	
Galium bifolium S. Wats.		
Gayophytum racemosum T. & G.	*Gayophytum helleri* Rydb. var. *glabrum* Munz	
Gentiana calycosa Griseb.		w
Gymnocarpium jessoense (Koidz.) Koidz.		
Hackelia ciliata (Dougl.) Johnst.		x
Halimolobus virgata (Nutt.) O.E. Schulz		
Haplopappus uniflorus (Hook.) Torr. & Gray ssp. *uniflorus*		w
Hymenopappus filifolius Hook. var. *polycephalus* (Osterh.) B.L. Turner	*Hymenopappus polycephalus* Osterh.	
Hypericum scouleri Hook.	*Hypericum formosum* HBK. var. *scouleri* (Hook.) C.L. Hitchc.	
Iliamna rivularis (Dougl. *ex* Hook.) Greene	*Sphaeralcea rivularis* (Dougl. *ex* Hook.) Torr. *ex* Gray	
Iris missouriensis Nutt.		
Isoetes bolanderi Engelm.		
Juncus nevadensis S. Wats. var. *nevadensis*		
Juncus regelii Buch.		
Lewisia pygmaea (A. Gray) B.L. Robins. ssp. *pygmaea*		
Lilaea scilloides (Poir.) Hauman	*Lilaea subulata* Humb. & Bonpl.	
Lomatium cous (S. Wats.) Coult. & Rose	*Lomatium montanum* Coult. & Rose	
Lomatium sandbergii (Coult. & Rose) Coult. & Rose		w
Lupinus lepidus Dougl. *ex* Lindl.		
Lupinus minimus Dougl. *ex* Hook.		
Lupinus wyethii S. Wats.		
Luzula hitchcockii Hamey-Ahti		w
Machaeranthera tanacetifolia (HBK.) Nees	*Aster tanacetifolius* Kunth	
Malaxis paludosa (L.) Sw.	*Ophrys paludosa* L., *Hammarbya paludosa* (L.) Kuntze	

Species Name	Synonym(s)	Notes
Melica spectabilis Scribn.		
Mimulus breweri (Greene) Rydb.		
Mimulus glabratus HBK.		
Minuartia nuttallii (Pax) Briq.		w
Munroa squarrosa (Nutt.) Torr.	*Monroa squarrosa*	
Nemophila breviflora A. Gray		
Nothocalais cuspidata (Pursh) Greene	*Microseris cuspidata* (Pursh) Schultz-Bip., *Agoseris cuspidata* (Pursh) Raf.	
Osmorhiza occidentalis (Nutt. *ex* Torr. & Gray) Torr.		w
Oxytropis lagopus Nutt. var. *conjugens* Barneby		
Papaver freedmanianum Löve	*Papaver radicatum* Rottboll ssp. *kluanensis* (D. Löve) D.F. Murray	
Papaver pygmaeum Rydb.	*Papaver alpinum* L., *Papaver nudicaule* L. ssp. *radicatum* (Rottb.) Fedde var. *pseudocorydalifolium*, *Papaver radicatum* Rottb. var. *pygmaeum* (Rydb.) S.L. Welsh	
Pellaea gastonyi Windham		
Penstemon albertinus Greene		w
Penstemon eriantherus Pursh var. *eriantherus*		w
Penstemon lyallii (Gray) Gray		w
Phacelia lyallii (A. Gray) Rydb.		
Phlox alyssifolia Greene		x
Physocarpus malvaceus (Greene) Kuntze		
Poa nevadensis Vasey *ex* Scribn.		x
Polygonum douglasii Greene ssp. *austinae* (Greene) E. Murray		x
Polygonum engelmannii Greene	*Polygonum douglasii* Greene ssp. *engelmannii* (Greene) Kartesz & Gandhi	x
Polygonum polygaloides Meissn. ssp. *confertiflorum* (Nutt. *ex* Piper) Hickman	*Polygonum watsonii* Small, *Polygonum imbricatum* Nutt., *Polygonum kelloggii* Greene var. *confertiflorum* (Nutt. *ex* Piper) Dorn, *Polygonum confertiflorum* Nutt. *ex* Piper	
Prenanthes sagittata (A. Gray) A. Nels.		
Psilocarphus elatior A. Gray	*Psilocarphus oregonus* Nutt. var. *elatior* A. Gray	

Species Name	*Synonym(s)*	*Notes*
Puccinellia distans (L.) Parl. ssp. *hauptiana* (Krecz.) W.E. Hughes		
Ranunculus verecundus B.L. Robins.		x
Rorippa tenerrima E. Greene		
Rorippa truncata (Jepson) R. Stuckey	*Rorippa curvipes* Greene var. *truncata* (Jepson) Rollins	
Rumex paucifolius Nutt. *ex* Wats.		
Salix raupii Argus		
Saxifraga oregana Howell		
Senecio conterminus Greenm.		w
Senecio cymbalarioides Buek non Nutt.		
Senecio foetidus T.J. Howell var. *hydrophiloides* (Rydb.) T.M. Barkl. *ex* Cronq.		x
Senecio megacephalus Nutt.		
Sparganium glomeratum Laest.		
Stellaria americana (Porter *ex* B.L. Robins.) Standl.		
Stellaria arenicola Raup		
Stellaria obtusa Engelm.		
Stellaria umbellata Turcz. *ex* Kar. & Kir.		
Stephanomeria runcinata Nutt.		
Suaeda moquinii (Torr.) Greene	*Suaeda intermedia* S. Wats.	
Tanacetum bipinnatum (L.) Schultz-Bip. ssp. *huronense* (Nutt.) Breitung	*Tanacetum huronense* Nutt. var. *bifarium* Fern., *Chrysanthemum bipinnatum* L. var. *huronense* (Nutt.) Hult.	
Thelesperma subnudum A. Gray var. *marginatum* (Rydb.) T.E. Melchert *ex* Cronq.	*Thelesperma marginatum* Rydb. (Rydb.) T.E. Melchert *ex* Cronq.	
Townsendia condensata D.C. Eat.		
Tradescantia occidentalis (Britt.) Smyth		
Trichophorum pumilum (Vahl) Schinz & Thellung	*Scirpus rollandii* Fern., *Scirpus pumilus* Vahl ssp. *rollandii* (Fern.) Raymond	
Tripterocalyx micranthus (Torr.) Hook.	*Abronia micrantha* Torr.	
Trisetum montanum Vasey		
Trisetum wolffii Vasey		
Viola praemorsa Dougl. *ex* Lindl. ssp. *linguifolia* (Nutt.) M.S. Baker & J.C. Klausen *ex* M.E. Peck	*Viola nuttallii* Pursh var. *linguaefolia* (Nutt.) Jepson & J.C. Klausen *ex* M.E. Peck	
Xerophyllum tenax (Pursh) Nutt.		w

APPENDIX 7

RARE NATIVE PLANT REPORT FORM

Please enter all information available to you and attach a detailed sketch or map showing the location of the population.

SCIENTIFIC NAME: ______________________________
COMMON NAME: ______________________________
OBSERVER NAME, ADDRESS AND TELEPHONE NUMBER: ______________________________

____

____

____

OBSERVATION DATE(S): ______________________________
PHOTOGRAPH TAKEN: Y / N
SPECIMEN COLLECTED: Y / N **COLLECTION NUMBER**: ______________
IF YES, NAME HERBARIUM WHERE DEPOSITED: ______________________________

LOCATION INFORMATION:
SITE NAME: ______________________________

____

TOPOGRAPHIC MAP NUMBER: ______________
DIRECTIONS TO POPULATION (*include descriptions of landmarks and distances if possible*):

____

____

____

ELEVATION (*Please do not use elevation from GPS unit*): ______________ ft/m (*circle one*)

(*Complete one of the following and accompany with map or sketch*)
UTM EASTING: ______________ UTM NORTHING: ______________ GRID ZONE: ______________
NORTH AMERICAN DATUM: 27 / 83 (*circle one*)

LEGAL: TWP: ________ RGE: ________ W: ______ M SECTION: ______ LSD: ______________

LATITUDE: ______________ LONGITUDE: ______________
Was the location determined using a GPS? Y / N

POPULATION INFORMATION (*include information on extent in* cm^2/m^2 *(circle one), number of individuals*):

____

____

____

____

PHENOLOGY (*based on average development phase of population--see over*):
____ vegetative; ______ reproductive (*E.G. V6. R7 for a species with leaves fully unfolded and in full bloom*)

____

____

SITE/HABITAT DESCRIPTION (*include information on habitat [alpine, aquatic, cliff, forest, grassland, peatland], plant communities / dominant species / associated species / other rare species / substrate / soils / phenology of dominant species*):

____

____

____

____

ASPECT: ________ SLOPE: ______________ MOISTURE: ______________________________
OWNERSHIP (*if known. Include name/address/phone number*): ______________________________

____

____

CURRENT LAND USE: ______________________________

____

____

HABITAT THREATS/MANAGEMENT CONCERNS: ______________________________

____

____

____

____

Return to: *Alberta Natural Heritage Information Centre, 2nd Floor, 9820 106 Street, Edmonton, AB T5K 2J6 (780) 427-5209. Thank You.*

Appendix 7

Phenology Codes (after Dierschke, 1972)

Deciduous Tree or Shrub (Vegetative)

0 Closed Bud
1 Buds with green tips
2 Green leaf out but not unfolded
3 Leaf unfolding up to 25%
4 Leaf unfolding up to 50%
5 Leaf unfolding up to 75%
6 Full leaf unfolding
7 First leaves turned yellow
8 Leaf yellowing up to 50%
9 Leaf yellowing over 50%
10 Bare

Conifer (Vegetative)

0 Closed Bud
1 Swollen bud
2 Split bud
3 Shoot capped
4 Shoot elongate
5 Shoot full length, lighter green
6 Shoot mature, equally green

Reproductive

0 Without blossom buds
1 Blossom buds recognizable
2 Blossom buds strongly swollen
3 Shortly before flowering
4 Beginning flowering
5 In bloom up to 25%
6 In bloom up to 50%
7 Full bloom
8 Fading
9 Completely faded
10 Bearing green fruit
11 Bearing ripe fruit
12 Bearing overripe fruit
13 Fruit or seed dispersal

Herbs

Vegetative

0 Without shoots above ground
1 Shoots without unfolded leaves
2 First leaf unfolds
3 2 or 3 leaves unfolded
4 Several leaves unfolded
5 Almost all leaves unfolded
6 Plant fully developed
7 Stem and/or first leaves fading
8 Yellowing up to 50%
9 Yellowing over 50%
10 Dead

Reproductive

0 Without blossom buds
1 Blossom buds recognizable
2 Blossom buds strongly swollen
3 Shortly before flowering
4 Beginning bloom
5 Up to 25% in blossom
6 Up to 50% in blossom
7 Full bloom
8 Fading
9 Completely faded
10 Bearing green fruit
11 Bearing ripe fruit
12 Bearing overripe fruit
13 Fruit or seed dispersal

Grasses

Vegetative

0 Without shoots above ground
1 Shoots without unfolded leaves
2 First leaf unfolded
3 2 or 3 leaves unfolded
4 Beginning development of blades of grass
5 Blades partly formed
6 Plant fully developed
7 Blades and/or first leaves turning yellow
8 Yellowing up to 50%
9 Yellowing over 50%
10 Dead

Reproductive

0 Without recognizable inflorescence
1 Inflorescence recognizable, closed
2 Inflorescence partly visible
3 Inflorescence fully visible, not unfolded
4 Inflorescence unfolded
5 First blooms pollenizing
6 Up to 50% pollenized
7 Full bloom
8 Fading
9 Fully faded
10 Bearing fruit
11 Fruit or seed dispersal

Ferns

Vegetative

0 Without shoots above ground
1 Rolled fronds above ground
2 First frond unfolds
3 2 or 3 fronds unfold
4 Several fronds unfolded
5 Almost all fronds unfolded
6 Plant fully developed
7 First fronds fading
8 Yellowing up to 50%
9 Yellowing over 50%
10 Dead

Reproductive

0 sori absent
1 sori green, forming
2 sori mature, darker, drier
3 sori depressing, strobili forming in lycopodium

achene: a small, dry, thin-walled, single-seeded fruit (see Figs. 2, 12, 15, 29)

acrid: bitter and pungent

agamospermous: producing seeds asexually (without fertilization)

apogamous: producing seeds asexually (without fertilization)

alkaloid: a nitrogenous, organic base; many alkaloids have strong physiological effects (e.g., morphine, strychnine)

alternate: attached singly rather than in pairs or whorls (see Figs. 1, 13); cf. opposite, whorled

androgynous: with male flowers at the tip of the spike and female flowers at the base; cf. gynaecandrous (see Fig. 15)

annual ring: the wood laid down in a single year in a tree trunk, visible as a ring when viewed in cross-section because of alternating dense winter wood and less-dense summer wood

annual: completing its life cycle in a single year; cf. biennial, perennial

anther: the pollen-bearing part of a stamen (see Figs. 2, 3, 4, 6, 7, 12, 13, 15, 16)

aquatic: living in water

armed: bearing spines, prickles or thorns

ascending: growing obliquely upwards (see Fig. 26)

auricle: a small, blunt or pointed, ear-like lobe, usually at the base of leaf blade (see Figs. 1, 3, 20)

awn: a slender, bristle-like appendage (see Figs. 16, 23)

axil: the angle between 2 organs, such as between a leaf and stem (see Fig. 1)

axis: the main stem of a plant or the central line of an organ

banner: the upper petal of a 2-lipped flower of the pea family; a standard (see Fig. 6)

beak: a prolonged, more or less slender tip on a thicker organ such as fruit or seed (see Figs. 15, 29)

bearded: conspicuously hairy, usually with long, stiff hairs (see Fig. 8)

berry: a fleshy, single- to many-seeded fruit developed from a single ovary (see Fig. 29)

biennial: living for 2 years, often producing a rosette of leaves the first year and flowering and fruiting the second year; cf. annual, perennial

bilaterally symmetric: divisible into equal halves along 1 line only (see Fig. 8); zygomorphic; cf. radially symmetric

bipinnate: twice pinnately divided (see Fig. 26)

bisexual flower: with both male and female sex organs (see Fig. 15); cf. perfect flower

biternate: twice divided in 3s

blade: the broad, flat part of an organ, usually of a leaf or petal (see Figs. 1, 16, 20, 21)

bloom: a whitish, often waxy powder covering the surface, usually on leaves and fruits

bog: an acidic, nutrient-poor wetland dominated by heath shrubs and *Sphagnum* mosses

bract: a small, specialized leaf or scale below a flower or flower cluster (see Figs. 13, 15, 27)

bracteole or bractlet: a small bract

bulb: a short, vertical underground stem covered with layers of leaves (often fleshy) or leaf-bases (e.g., an onion) (see Fig. 30)

bulblet or bulbil: a small bulb-like structure, often located in a leaf axil or replacing a flower

bur: a fruit or compact cluster of fruits with barbs or bristles that enable it to attach to passing animals (see Fig. 29)

calcareous: calcium-rich; rich in lime

calciphile: a calcium-lover, preferring sites rich in calcium

callosity: a small, grain-like projection on the valve of a dock or sorrel (*Rumex*) flower

callus: a small, hard, thickening, usually at the base of a lemma in grasses

callus hair: the fine hair attached to the callus at the base of a lemma, usually tufted (see Fig. 16)

calyx [calyxes]: the outer ring of the petals and sepals; the sepals collectively (see Figs. 3, 9)

capitate: head-like, forming a dense cluster

capsule: a dry fruit that splits open at maturity and is produced by a compound ovary (see Figs. 13, 14, 29)

carpel: a fertile leaf bearing the undeveloped seed(s) (see Fig. 2); 1 or more fused carpels form a pistil

carpophore: a stalk-like elongation of the receptacle (see Fig. 3)

caruncle: a small appendage at or near the point of attachment of a seed

catkin: a scaly, spike-like cluster of small flowers, usually of a single sex and without petals (see Fig. 13)

caudex: the persistent, thickened stem base of a perennial plant

channelled: marked with at least 1 deep, lengthwise groove (see Figs. 15, 21)

chasmogamous: with flowers that open for normal pollination; cf. cleistogamous

ciliate: fringed with cilia (see Fig. 22)

cilium [cilia]: a tiny, hair-like outgrowth (see Fig. 20)

circumscissile: splitting open along a transverse, circular line, so that the top comes off like a lid (see Fig. 29)

clasping: embracing or surrounding, usually in reference to a leaf base around a stem (see Fig. 1)

claw: the slender, stalk-like base of a petal or sepal (see Figs. 3, 7)

cleft: a hollow between 2 lobes; cut about halfway, or slightly deeper, to the middle or base, deeply lobed, a sinus (see Fig. 1)

cleistogamous: with self-pollinating flowers that do not open; cf. chasmogamous

closed sheath: a sheath that is fused into a cylinder (see Figs. 15, 21); cf. open sheath

collar: the outer side of a grass leaf at the point where the blade and sheath join (see Fig. 20)

column: the prominent central structure of an orchid flower, comprised of the fused stamens, style and stigma

coma: a tuft of soft hairs at the tip of a seed

comose: with a coma

compound: composed of 2 or more smaller parts, such as leaves divided into leaflets and flower clusters consisting of several smaller groups (see Figs. 26, 27); cf. simple

cone: a dense, fruiting or spore-producing structure with overlapping scales or bracts arranged around a central axis, generally woody when bearing seeds and non-woody when bearing spores or pollen (see Figs. 17, 18, 29)

coniferous: bearing cones

corm: a short, thickened, fleshy underground stem without thickened leaves (see Fig. 30)

corolla: the inner ring of the petals and sepals; the petals collectively (see Fig. 9)

corona: the 5-hooded, crown-like structure at the tip of the stamen tube in a milkweed (*Asclepias*) flower (see Fig. 10)

corymb: a flat- or round-topped flower cluster in which the flowers on the outer (lower) branches bloom first (see Fig. 27)

cotyledon: the first leaf (or 1 of the first pair or whorl of leaves) produced by the embryo of a seed plant, developed within the seed; a seed leaf

creeping: growing along (or beneath) the surface of the ground and rooting at intervals, usually at the nodes (see Fig. 17)

crisped: with irregularly curled and rippled edges, like a potato chip (see Fig. 22)

cross-partition: a horizontal line between 2 parallel veins, arranged like an irregular rung on a ladder, often visible towards the base of sedge (*Carex*) leaves; a septum; nodulose septae are thickened cross-partitions (see Fig. 21)

cross-wall: horizontal cell walls separating individual cells in linear series; appearing as thin, purple bands in the hairs of some fleabanes (*Erigeron* spp.)

cyme: a flat- or round-topped flower cluster in which the flowers on the inner (upper) branches bloom first (see Fig. 27)

deciduous: shed after completion of its normal function, usually at the end of the growing season; cf. persistent

decumbent: lying on the ground but with ascending stem tips

decurrent: extending downward; usually describing leaves whose lower edges extend down the stem as 2 ridges or wings (see Fig. 24)

dendritic: branched like a tree (see Fig. 26)

diadelphus: with stamens joined by their filaments into 2, often unequal sets; cf. monadelphous

dichotomous: forked in 2 equal parts, like a Y; cf. trichotomous (see Fig. 26)

dicot: a plant whose seeds have 2 cotyledons or seed leaves; most dicots have net-veined leaves; a dicotyledonous plant; cf. monocot

digitate: finger-like; usually referring to leaflets arranged like fingers on a hand (see Fig. 25)

dimorphic: with 2 forms, as in pteridophytes with sterile and fertile plants or leaves

dioecious: with male and female flowers or cones on separate plants

disc floret: a small tubular flower in a flowerhead of the aster family (Asteraceae) (see Fig. 12)

discoid [in reference to flowerheads in asters (Asteraceae)]: with disc florets only; cf. ligulate, radiate

disjunct: separated; referring to plant or animal populations that are a significant distance from all other populations of the same species

dorsal: on the lower side or outer side (i.e., away from the stem); cf. ventral (see Fig. 1)

drupe: a fleshy or pulpy, single-seeded fruit in which the seed is encased in a hard or stony covering (see Fig. 29)

drupelet: a small drupe, usually borne in clusters (e.g., raspberries) (see Fig. 29)

ecotype: a subspecies or race that is specially adapted to a particular set of environmental conditions

ellipsoid: a 3-dimensional form in which every plane is an ellipse or a circle

entire: smooth-edged, without teeth or lobes (see Figs. 1, 22)

epidermis: the outermost layers of cells

epidermal: of the epidermis

evergreen: always with green leaves

farinose: coated with a mealy powder

fascicle: a compact bundle or cluster (see Fig. 26)

fen: a mineral-rich wetland with slow-moving, often calcareous water with sedge and brown moss (not *Sphagnum*) peat

fertile: capable of producing viable pollen, ovules or spores; cf. sterile

fibrous root: a slender, thread-like root, usually 1 of many in a clump (see Figs. 16, 30)

filament: the stalk of a stamen, bearing an anther at its tip (see Figs. 2, 3, 6, 7, 13)

filiform: thread-like

fleshy: succulent, firm and pulpy; plump and juicy

floret: a small flower in a cluster; usually applied to single flowers of the grass, sedge, or aster family (see Figs. 12, 13, 14, 15, 16)

flowerhead: a dense cluster of florets, often appearing as a single flower in the aster family (see Fig. 12)

follicle: a dry, pod-like fruit that splits open along only 1 side when mature (see Fig. 29)

forbs: broad-leaved herbs

fornix [fornices]: a small appendage in the throat of a flower corolla (e.g., in borages)

frond: a fern leaf (see Fig. 19)

fruit: the ripened, seed-bearing organ of a plant, together with any other structures that join with it as a unit (see Fig. 29)

fusiform: spindle-shaped, slender and gradually tapered at both ends (see Fig. 25)

galea: a hooded upper lip of a 2-lipped flower (see Fig. 9)

gametophyte: the part or phase of a plant that produces sexual reproductive structures, often small and inconspicuous in pteridophytes; cf. sporophyte

gemma [gemmae]: a small, often bud-like body used for vegetative reproduction

gemmiferous: with gemmae

generic name: the first part of the scientific species name, denoting the genus to which the species belongs; cf. specific epithet

germinate: to sprout

gland: a bump, appendage or depression that produces secretions such as nectar or oil

glandular: with glands

glandular-hairy: with hairs bearing glands (usually at their tips)

glaucous: covered with a whitish, waxy powder (bloom) that can usually be scraped or rubbed off

glomerule: a dense, head-like cluster

glume: 1 of 2 chaff-like bracts at the base of a grass spikelet (see Fig. 16)

glycoside: a chemical compound derived from a sugar, in which 1 carbon is replaced by another component, alcohol or phenol

grain: a hard, seed-like fruit or kernel, usually referring to the fruit of a grass

graminoids: narrow-leaved herbs

gynaecandrous: with female flowers at the tip of the spike and male flowers at the base (see Fig. 15); cf. androgynous

herb: a plant without persistent woody parts (at least none above ground), with stems that die back to the ground each year

herbaceous: herb-like, with a leaf-like texture and colour

heteromorphic: with many different forms and sizes

hybrid: the offspring of parents of 2 different kinds (usually a cross between 2 species)

hybridization: the process of creating a hybrid

hypanthium: a ring or cup around the ovary, usually bearing sepals, petals and stamens at its upper edge (see Figs. 5, 29)

hypha [hyphae]: a tiny fungal thread, part of the main body of a fungus

inclined: leaning to 1 side, diverging from vertical

indusium [indusia]: an outgrowth covering and protecting a spore cluster in ferns (see Fig. 19); a protective membrane

inferior ovary: an ovary with the petals, sepals and stamens attached at its top or otherwise above it (see Fig. 7); cf. superior ovary

inflated: hollowed or puffed out (see Fig. 3)

inflorescence: a flower cluster (see Figs. 15, 16, 27)

insectivorous: feeding on insects

internode: the portion of a stem between 2 joints (nodes) (see Figs. 16, 20)

interrupted: discontinuous

introduced: brought in from another region (e.g., Europe)

involucral: of an involucre

involucre: a set of bracts at the base of a flower cluster (as in the carrot family [Apiaceae]) or flowerhead (as in the aster family [Asteraceae]) (see Figs. 12, 27)

irregular flower: a flower in which the members in a series of organs (e.g., the petals or sepals) have different forms or orientations (see Fig. 8); cf. regular flower

joint: a place where 1 part is attached or joined to another; a node (see Figs. 1, 16, 20)

keel: a conspicuous, lengthwise ridge, like the keel of a boat (see Figs. 16, 21); the 2 lower petals of a flower in the pea family (Fabaceae) (see Fig. 6)

lacuna [lacunae]: a small empty space or gap in a tissue

lateral: on the side of (see Figs. 1, 16)

latex: the milky juice of some plants, often containing rubber-like compounds

leaflet: a single part of a compound leaf (see Figs. 19, 25)

lemma: the lower of the 2 bracts immediately enclosing a single grass flower (see Fig. 16); cf. palea

lenticel: a slightly raised, often elongated opening (pore) on the bark of young branches or roots

lenticular: lens-shaped (see Fig. 29)

ligulate [in reference to flowerheads of the aster family (Asteraceae)]: with ligules only; cf. discoid, radiate

ligule: a flat, linear, ray floret in a flowerhead of the aster family (Asteraceae) (see Fig. 12); the thin, membranous projection from the top of a leaf sheath, as in the grass family (Poaceae) (see Fig. 20)

limb: the expanded, often lobed section at the tip of a tubular calyx or corolla (see Figs. 3, 7)

linear: long and narrow with essentially parallel sides (see Fig. 25)

lip: the upper or lower lobe of a 2-lobed (2-lipped) flower, such as an orchid or violet flower (see Figs. 8, 9, 11)

lobe: a rounded division, too large to be called a tooth (see Figs. 1, 3)

locule: a cavity or compartment within an ovary or anther

lyrate: pinnately divided with a large lobe at the tip and gradually smaller lobes towards the base of the leaf (see Fig. 25)

marcescent: with persistent, withered remains

marsh: a nutrient-rich wetland that is periodically inundated by standing or slow-moving water, characterized by emergent vegetation from mineral soil

megaspore: in pteridophytes with 2 types of spores, the larger spores, which develop into female gametophytes; cf. microspore

membranous: in a thin, pliable, usually translucent sheet; like a membrane

mericarp: a single carpel of a schizocarp (see Fig. 29)

mesic: with intermediate moisture levels, neither very wet nor very dry

micron: a thousandth of a millimetre; a millionth of a metre

microspore: in pteridophytes with 2 types of spores, the smaller spores, which develop into male gametophytes; cf. megaspore

midrib: the middle rib of an organ such as a leaf (see Figs. 1, 15, 16)

monadelphous: with stamens joined by their filaments into a single set; cf. diadelphus

monocot: a plant whose seeds have a single cotyledon or seed leaf; most monocots have leaves with parallel veins; a monocotyledonous plant; cf. dicot

monoecious: with male and female parts in separate flowers or cones but on the same plant

mucilaginous: producing sticky or gelatinous secretions

mycorrhiza [mycorrhizae]: the fungal partner in a symbiotic association between certain fungi and seed plants, in which the fungi permeate the roots and assist in nutrient absorption

naked: lacking hairs, scales or other appendages

nectary: a nectar-secreting gland, usually in a flower (see Fig. 13)

nerve: a prominent line or vein in a leaf or other organ (see Fig. 20)

net-veined: with a network of branched veins; reticulate (see Fig. 1); cf. parallel-veined

node: the point of attachment of a leaf or branch; a joint (see Figs. 1, 16, 20)

nut: a dry, thick-walled fruit that does not split open at maturity, usually single-seeded (see Fig. 29)

nutlet: a small nut, distinguished from an achene by its thicker outer covering

obovoid: with a 3-dimensional, egg-shaped form that is broadest above the middle

ochrea [ochreae]: a sheath of fused stipules at the base of a leaf; common in the buckwheat family (Polygonaceae) (see Fig. 24)

open sheath: a sheath that is split down 1 side rather than fused into a cylinder (see Figs. 16, 20); cf. closed sheath

opposite: attached across from each other on an axis (e.g., opposite leaves, see Fig. 1), or directly in front of one another (e.g., staminodia opposite petals, see Fig. 4); cf. alternate, whorled

ovary: the organ containing ovules or young, undeveloped seeds, located at the base of the pistil (see Figs. 3, 4, 6, 7)

ovoid: with a 3-dimensional, egg-shaped form that is broadest below the middle

ovule: an organ that develops into a single seed after fertilization

palea: the upper of the 2 bracts immediately enclosing an individual grass flower; cf. lemma (see Fig. 16)

palmate [leaves]: with 3 or more lobes or leaflets arising from a single point, like fingers of a hand (see Fig. 25); cf. pinnate

panicle: a branched flower cluster, with lower blooms developing first (see Fig. 27)

papilla [papillae]: a tiny, wart-like projection

papillose: with papillae

pappus: the hairs or bristles on the tip of an achene (see Fig. 12, 29)

parallel-veined: with veins running parallel to one another, not branching to form a network (see Fig. 1); cf. net-veined

pectinate: divided into narrow, closely set, parallel parts arranged like teeth on a comb (see Fig. 26)

pedicel: the stalk of a single flower in a flower cluster (see Figs. 3, 11)

peduncle: a main flower stalk, supporting a single flower or flower cluster (see Figs. 2, 8, 12)

perennial: living for 3 or more years

perfect flower: a flower with functional ovaries and stamens; cf. bisexual flower

perianth: the sepals and petals of a flower collectively

perigynium [perigynia]: the sac-like membrane enclosing the achene of a sedge (*Carex* spp.) (see Fig. 15)

persistent: remaining attached after normal function has been completed; cf. deciduous

petal: a member of the inner whorl of the perianth, usually white or brightly coloured (see Figs. 2, 3, 4, 5, 6, 7, 8, 10, 11, 12)

petiole: the stalk of a single leaf (see Figs. 1, 26)

pinna [pinnae]: the main division of a pinnately divided leaf or frond (see Figs. 19, 26)

pinnate: feather-formed; with parts (usually leaflets) arranged on either side of a common axis (see Fig. 26)

pinnatifid: cut at least halfway to the middle in a pinnate pattern (see Fig. 25)

pinnule: a segment of a pinnately divided pinna; the smallest segment of a leaf that is twice pinnately divided (see Figs. 19, 26)

pistil: the female part of a flower, composed of one or more ovaries, styles and stigmas (see Figs. 3, 6, 7); cf. stamen

pistillate: with pistil(s), usually applied to flowers that are functionally female (see Figs. 13, 15); cf. staminate

pith: the soft, spongy centre of a stem or branch

pleated: with parallel folds, like pleats in an accordion

pod: a dry fruit that opens to release its seeds, usually applied to pea-like fruits (see Fig. 29)

pollen: the tiny, powdery grains contained in an anther; the male reproductive units which form pollen tubes and fertilize the ovule

pollen cone: a cone producing pollen; a male cone; cf. seed cone

pollination: the transfer of pollen from anthers to stigmas, leading to fertilization

pollinium [pollinia]: a waxy mass of pollen grains carried as a unit during pollination, as in milkweed and orchid flowers (see Figs. 10, 11)

pome: a fleshy fruit with a core (e.g., an apple) (see Fig. 29)

potherb: a leafy herb that is cooked as a vegetable or thickener

poultice: a moist mass of leaves, bark or other plant material, applied hot or cold to the body to stop bleeding, speed healing, reduce inflammation or relieve pain

prostrate: lying on the ground

prothallus [prothalli]: a small, usually disc-shaped, thallus-like growth resulting from the germination of a spore and producing the sexual organs of the plant

pteridophyte: a member of a division of seedless plants, including the horsetails, club-mosses and ferns

pustule: a small, blister-like swelling

raceme: a flower cluster with an unbranched, elongated central stalk bearing few to many stalked blooms, and with lower flowers developing first (see Fig. 27)

rachilla: the axis of an individual grass or sedge floret (see Fig. 16)

rachis: the main axis of a compound leaf or flower cluster (see Figs. 15, 16, 19)

radially symmetric: with parts arranged like spokes on a wheel (see Fig. 5); a regular flower; cf. bilaterally symmetric

radiate [in reference to flowerheads of the aster family (Asteraceae)]: with strap-like ray florets around a central cluster of disc florets (see Fig. 12); cf. discoid, ligulate

rank: a vertical row, usually referring to leaves on a stem (see Fig. 15)

ray [branch]: 1 of 3 or more branches originating from a common point, as in an umbel or similar flower cluster (see Fig. 27)

ray [floret]: a small, strap-like floret in a flowerhead of the aster family (Asteraceae) (see Fig. 12)

receptacle: the enlarged end of a stem to which the flower parts (in the aster family [Asteraceae] the flowers) are attached (see Figs. 2, 3, 12)

recurved: curved under or downward (see Fig. 26)

reflexed: abruptly bent or turned backward or downward (see Fig. 26)

regular flower: a flower in which the members in a series of organs (e.g., the petals or sepals) have similar forms or orientations; a radially symmetric flower (see Fig. 5); cf. irregular flower

reticula: a mesh-like netting of persistent leaf veins, often covering the bulbs of some members of the lily family (Liliaceae)

reticulate : with a network of branched veins; net-veined

rhizomatous: with rhizomes

rhizome: a somewhat lengthened underground stem; distinguished from a root by the presence of buds or scale-like leaves (see Figs. 15, 18, 19, 30)

rhombic: shaped like a rhombus, a figure with 4 equal, parallel sides and 2 oblique angles; diamond-shaped (see Fig. 25)

rib: a prominent, usually longitudinal vein (see Fig. 15)

rosette: a circular cluster of organs (usually leaves), usually at the base of a plant (see Fig. 1)

runner: an elongated, slender, prostrate branch, rooting at the joints and/or at the tip; a stolon

samara: a dry, winged fruit that does not split open at maturity, usually single-seeded, often borne in pairs, as in maples (*Acer* spp.) (see Fig. 29)

saprophyte: a plant that takes its food from dead organic matter

scale: a small, flat structure, usually thin and membranous (see Figs. 13, 15, 19)

scape: a leafless flower stalk arising from the plant base

schizocarp: a fruit that splits into separate carpels when mature (see Fig. 29); cf. mericarp

scorpioid: rolled lengthwise in bud and uncoiling as the structure develops, like a fiddlehead

scree: rock debris at the foot of a rock wall; talus

scurfy: covered with tiny scales

seed cone: a cone producing seeds, a female cone; cf. pollen cone

sepal: a member of the outermost whorl of the perianth, usually small, green and more or less leaf-like (see Figs. 2, 5, 6, 7, 10, 11)

sexual reproduction: producing offspring from the union of male and female cells, as in the fertilization of the egg cell in an ovule (female) by a cell from a pollen grain (male); cf. vegetative reproduction

sheath: a tubular organ that partly or completely surrounds some part of a plant, as the sheath of a grass leaf surrounds the stem (see Figs. 15, 16, 18, 20, 21)

sheathing: forming a sheath

silique: a pod-like fruit of a member of the mustard family (Brassicaceae) (see Fig. 29)

simple: all in a complete piece, not divided; cf. compound (see Fig. 13)

sinus: a hollow between 2 lobes; a cleft (see Fig. 1)

sobole: a shoot or sucker growing from a rhizome or stem base, usually numerous

sorus [sori]: a cluster of sporangia, often small and dot-like (see Fig. 19)

spadix: a dense spike of small flowers with a thick, fleshy axis (see Figs. 27, 28)

spathe: a large, leaf-like bract enclosing a flower cluster (usually a spadix) (see Fig. 27)

specific epithet: the second part of the species scientific name, distinguishing the species from other members of the same genus; cf. generic name

spike: a more or less elongated flower cluster with essentially stalkless flowers or spikelets (see Figs. 15, 27)

spikelet: a small or secondary spike; the characteristic unit of a flower cluster in the grass family (Poaceae) (see Fig. 16)

spine: a sharp, stiff outgrowth from the stem (e.g., a thorn)

sporangiaster: a modified spore case

sporangium [sporangia]: a spore sac or spore case (see Fig. 19); spore cluster

spore: the tiny, usually single-celled, reproductive body of a non-seed plant (e.g., a fern or horsetail), producing a gametophyte

sporocarp: the firm spore case of some fern allies (e.g., *Marsilea*)

sporophyll: a spore-bearing leaf (see Fig. 17)

sporophyte: the spore-bearing part or phase of a plant, usually leafy (see Figs. 17, 18, 19); cf. gametophyte

spreading: diverging widely from the vertical, approaching horizontal (see Fig. 26)

spur: a hollow extension, usually at the base of a flower, petal or sepal, often containing nectar (see Figs. 8, 11)

stamen: the pollen-bearing (male) organ of a flower, usually consisting of an anther and a filament (see Figs. 2, 3, 5, 6, 7, 13); cf. pistil

staminate: with stamen(s); usually applied to flowers that are functionally male (see Figs. 13, 15); cf. pistillate

staminode, staminodium [staminodia]: a modified sterile stamen (see Fig. 4)

standard: the large upper petal of a flower in the pea family (Fabaceae); a banner (see Fig. 6)

sterile: without viable pollen, ovules or spores; cf. fertile

stigma: the tip of the female organ (pistil) of a flower, where the pollen lands and adheres (see Figs. 6, 7, 12, 13, 14, 15)

stigmatic disc: the broad, flat, round surface of a stigma

stipule: an appendage at the base of a leaf stalk, ranging from slender and awl-shaped to broad and leaf-like (see Figs. 1, 24)

stolon: a trailing, horizontal stem, rooting at nodes and/or tips; a runner

stoloniferous: with stolons

stoma, stomate [stomata]: a tiny pore in the plant epidermis, bounded by 2 guard cells which open and close the pore by changing shape

strobilus [strobili]: a cone-like cluster of sporophylls (see Figs. 17, 18)

style: the middle part of a pistil, connecting the stigma and ovary (see Figs. 3, 6, 7, 13, 15, 29)

stylopodium: a disc-like expansion at the base of a style, as in the carrot family (Apiaceae) (see Fig. 29)

succulent: fleshy, soft and juicy; a plant that stores water in fleshy stems or leaves

sucker: a vertical vegetative shoot arising from the lower part of a plant, typically from the trunk base or from spreading underground stems of trees and shrubs

superior ovary: an ovary with the petals, sepals and stamens attached at its base or otherwise below it (see Fig. 6); cf. inferior ovary

swamp: a wetland that is permanently waterlogged below the surface, and periodically inundated by standing or gently moving water, nutritionally intermediate between a bog and a fen

talus: rocky debris at the foot of a rock wall; scree

taproot: a main root growing vertically downwards (see Fig. 30)

tepal: a sepal or petal, in flowers where these structures are almost identical (see Fig. 14)

terete: round in cross-section, usually referring to cylindrical structures

ternate: divided or arranged in threes (see Fig. 25)

tetragonal: 4-sided

tetraploid: with 4 sets of chromosomes in the cell nucleus

thalloid: like or with a thallus

thallus: the main body of a plant that is not differentiated into stems and leaves (as in *Wolffia* and in pteridophyte gametophytes)

throat: the opening in the middle of a flower, at the centre of a ring of petals or petal-like sepals (see Figs. 8, 9); the opening at the upper edge of a leaf sheath (see Fig. 21)

tomentum: a matted covering of woolly hairs

torulose: cylindrical with alternating swellings and constrictions (see Fig. 29)

trailing: spreading on the ground, but not rooting along the stems

translucent: semi-transparent

trichotomous: branching into 3 equal parts (see Fig. 26); cf. dichotomous

trifoliate: divided into 3 leaflets (see Fig. 25)

tripinnate: 3-times pinnately divided into leaflets (see Fig. 26)

tuber: a short, thick underground branch, usually with several buds or 'eyes' (see Fig. 30)

tubercle: a small, usually rounded, swelling or projection

tuberous: like a tuber

turion: a small bulb-like growth at the base of the stem, often present in some willowherb (*Epilobium*) species

tussock: a compact clump of plants, especially grasses or sedges

umbel: an often flat-topped flower cluster with few to many stalks arising from a common point, like the stays of an umbrella (see Fig. 27)

umbellet: the smaller cluster in a repeatedly branched (compound) umbel (see Fig. 27)

unarmed: without thorns or prickles

unisexual: with 1 sex only, either male or female (see Fig. 15)

utricle: a small single-seeded fruit, thin-walled and somewhat inflated (see Fig. 29)

valve: a section of the wall of a pod or capsule, separating from the other section(s) when the fruit splits open (see Fig. 29); 1 of the enlarged inner sepals that enclose the seed of a dock or sorrel (*Rumex*) flower

vascular: containing vascular tissues (xylem and phloem) that transport water and nutrients within the plant

vascular bundle: a strand of vascular fibers (xylem and phloem) and associated tissues

vegetative reproduction: producing new plants from asexual parts (e.g., rhizomes, leaves, bulbils) rather than from fertilized ovules (usually seeds); cf. sexual reproduction

vein: a thread of conducting tubes (a vascular bundle), especially if visible on the surface of a petal or leaf (see Figs. 1, 16, 20, 21)

velum: a thin, membranous covering, over the spore clusters near the leaf base in *Isoetes* species

ventral: on the upper side or inner side (i.e., closest to the stem) (see Fig. 1); cf. dorsal

viviparous: producing young plants in the flower cluster of the parent plant from sprouting bulbils or germinating seeds

whorl: a circle of 3 or more similar structures (e.g., leaves, flowers) attached at the same node (see Fig. 1)

whorled: arranged in whorls; cf. alternate, opposite

wing: a thin, flattened expansion from the side or tip of an organ (see Fig. 29); 1 of the 2 side petals of a flower (see Figs. 6, 8)

wintergreen: with leaves that remain green through winter but die the following summer

zygomorphic: divisible into 2 equal parts along 1 line only, usually with the upper half unlike the lower and each side a mirror image of the other (see Fig. 8); bilaterally symmetric

FIGURE 1: VASCULAR PLANT PARTS

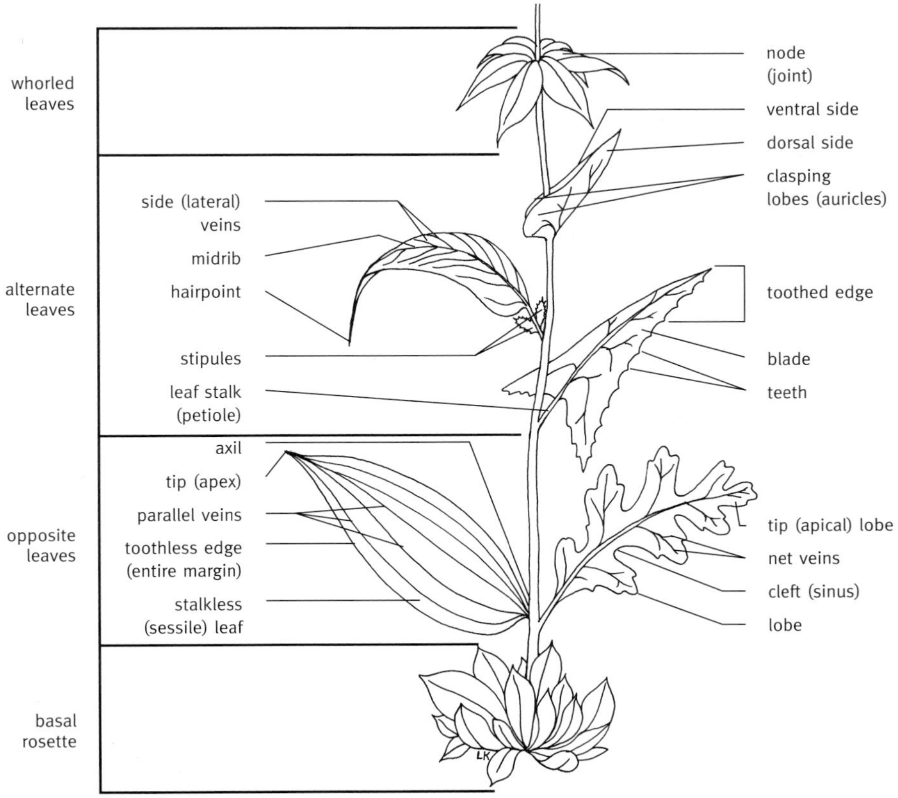

whorled leaves
alternate leaves
opposite leaves
basal rosette
side (lateral) veins
midrib
hairpoint
stipules
leaf stalk (petiole)
axil
tip (apex)
parallel veins
toothless edge (entire margin)
stalkless (sessile) leaf
node (joint)
ventral side
dorsal side
clasping lobes (auricles)
toothed edge
blade
teeth
tip (apical) lobe
net veins
cleft (sinus)
lobe
LK

FIGURE 2: PARTS OF A BUTTERCUP (*RANUNCULUS*) FLOWER

petal
carpels (achenes in fruit)
stamen
anther
filament
receptacle
sepal
flower stalk (peduncle)

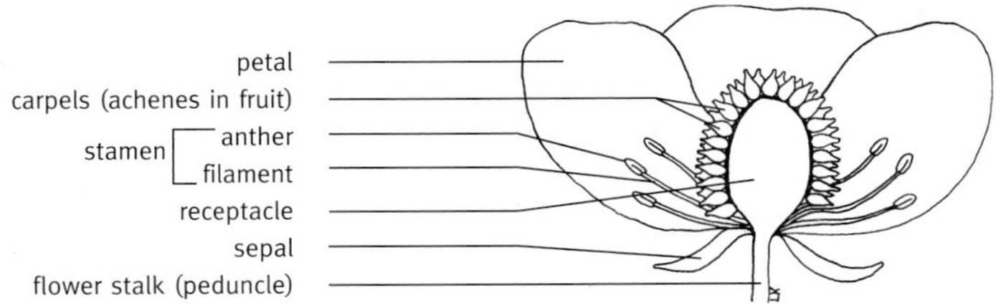

Figure 3: Parts of a bladder campion (*Silene*) flower

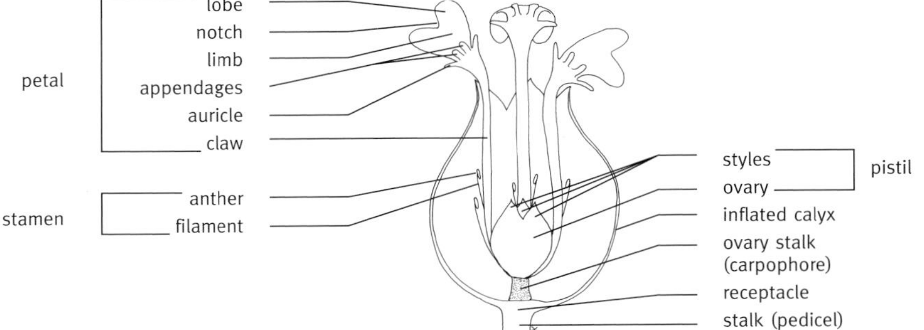

Figure 4: Parts of a grass-of-parnassus (*Parnassia*) flower

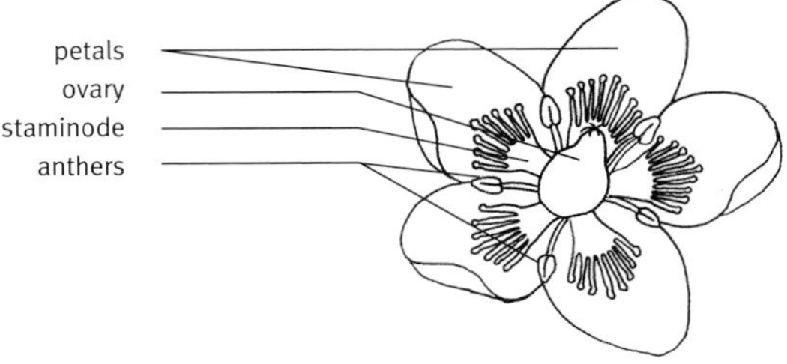

Figure 5: Parts of a rose (*Rosa*) flower (a radially symmetric [regular] flower)

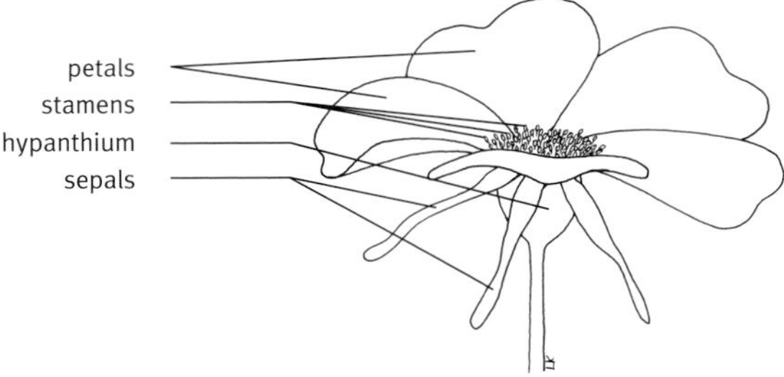

Figure 6: Parts of a pea (Fabaceae) flower

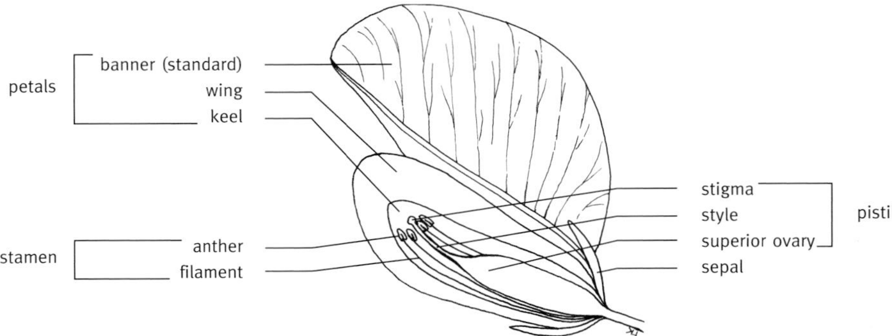

Figure 7: Parts of a willowherb (*Epilobium*) flower

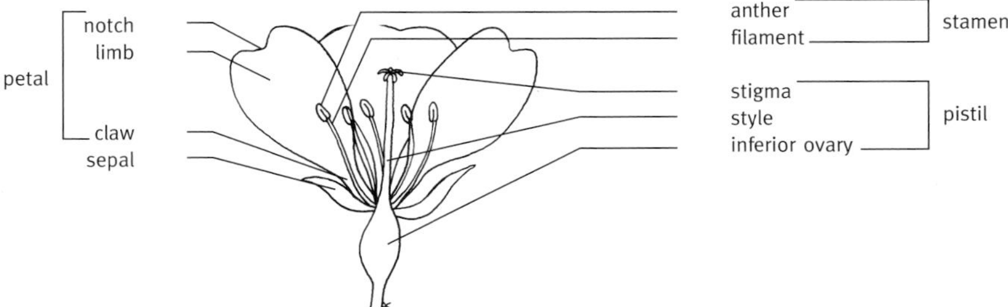

Figure 8: Parts of a violet (*Viola*) flower (a bilterally symmetric [irregular] flower)

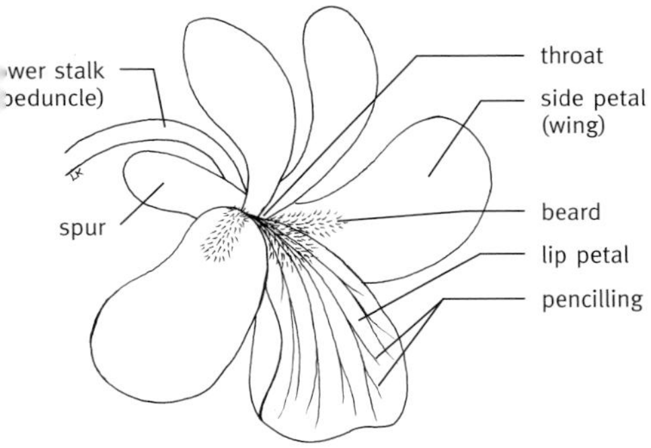

wer stalk
eduncle)
spur
throat
side petal (wing)
beard
lip petal
pencilling

Figure 9: Parts of a lousewort (*Pedicularis*) flower

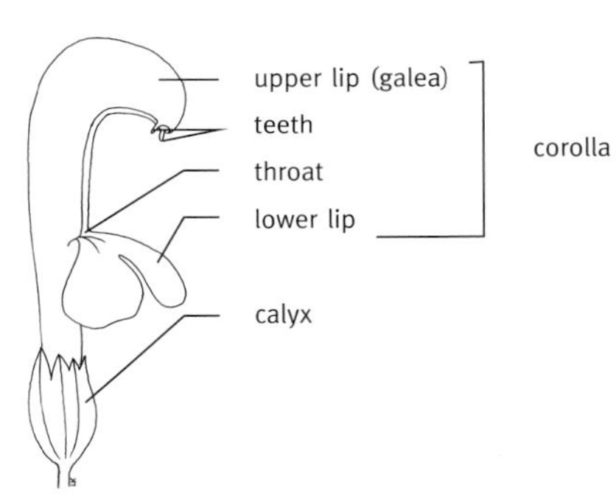

Figure 10: Parts of a milkweed (*Asclepias*) flower

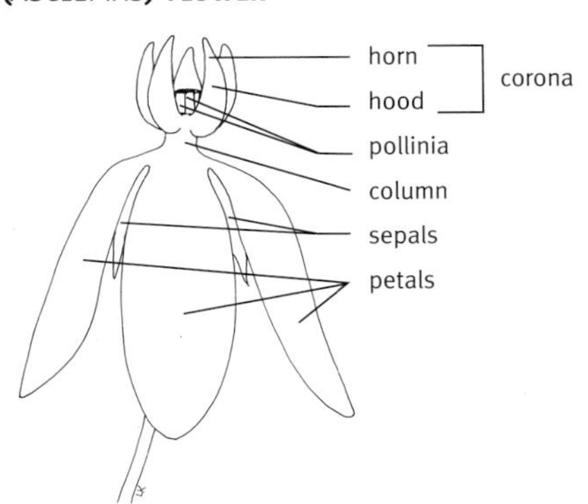

Figure 11: Parts of a bog orchid (*Platanthera*) flower

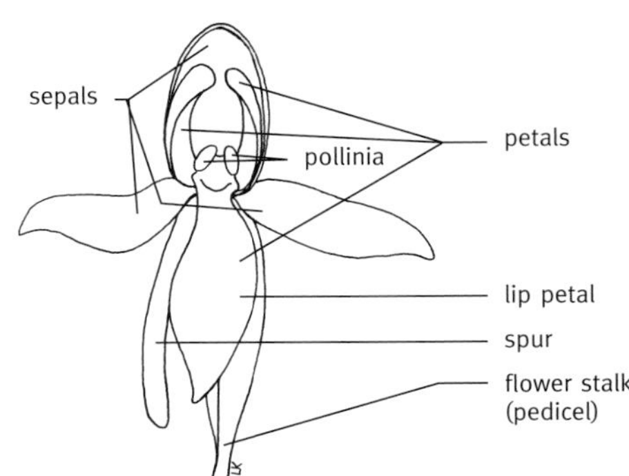

Figure 12: Parts of an aster (Asteraceae) flowerhead

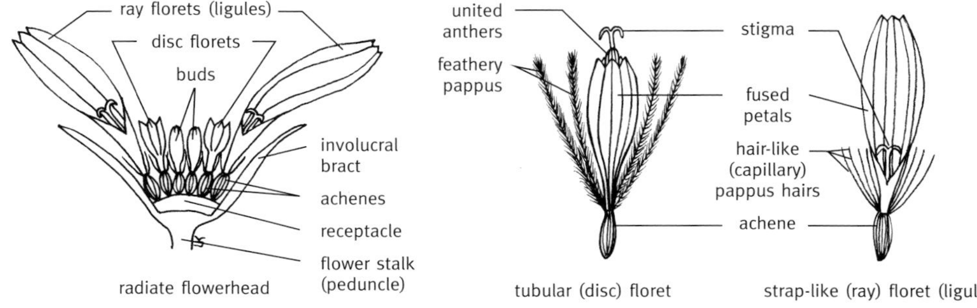

Figure 13: Parts of a willow (*Salix*) shrub

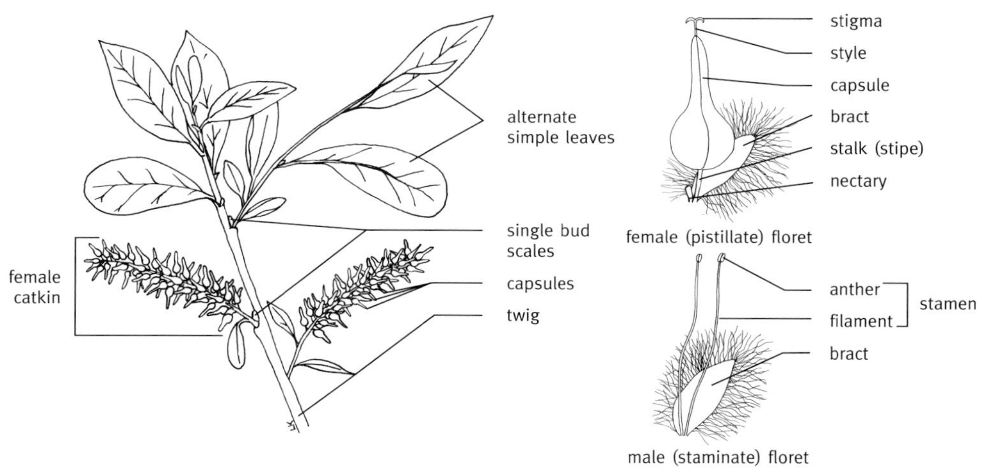

Figure 14: Parts of a rush (*Juncus*) floret

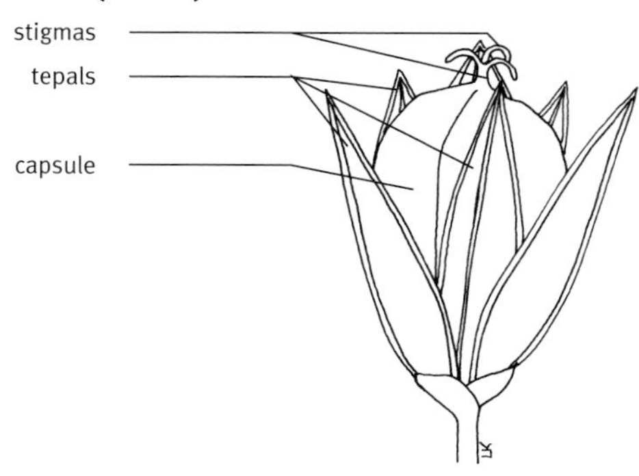

FIGURE 15: PARTS OF A SEDGE (*CAREX*) PLANT

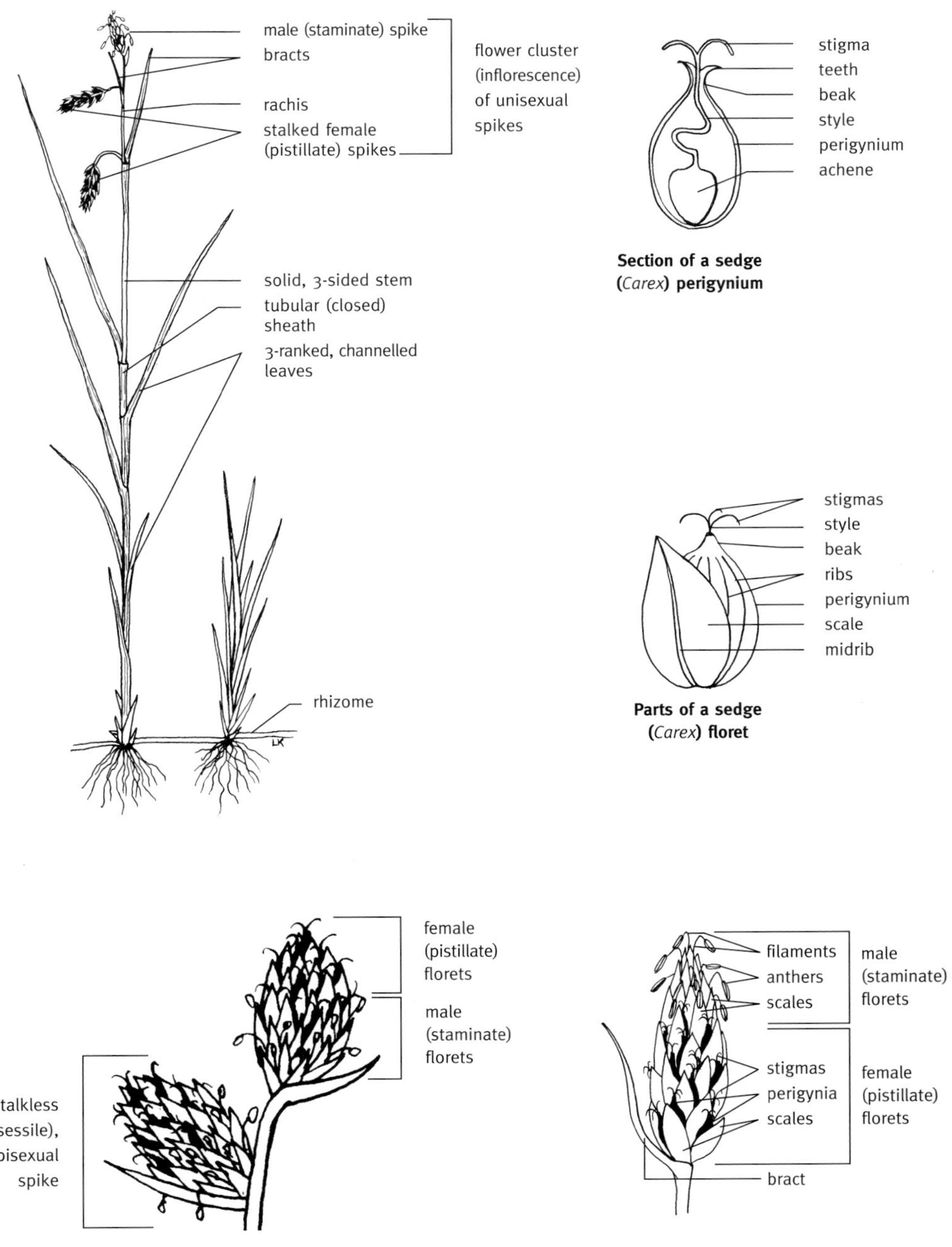

Section of a sedge (*Carex*) perigynium

Parts of a sedge (*Carex*) floret

Inflorescence of gynaecandrous spikes

Inflorescence of a single androgynous spike

Figure 16: Parts of grass (Poaceae) plants

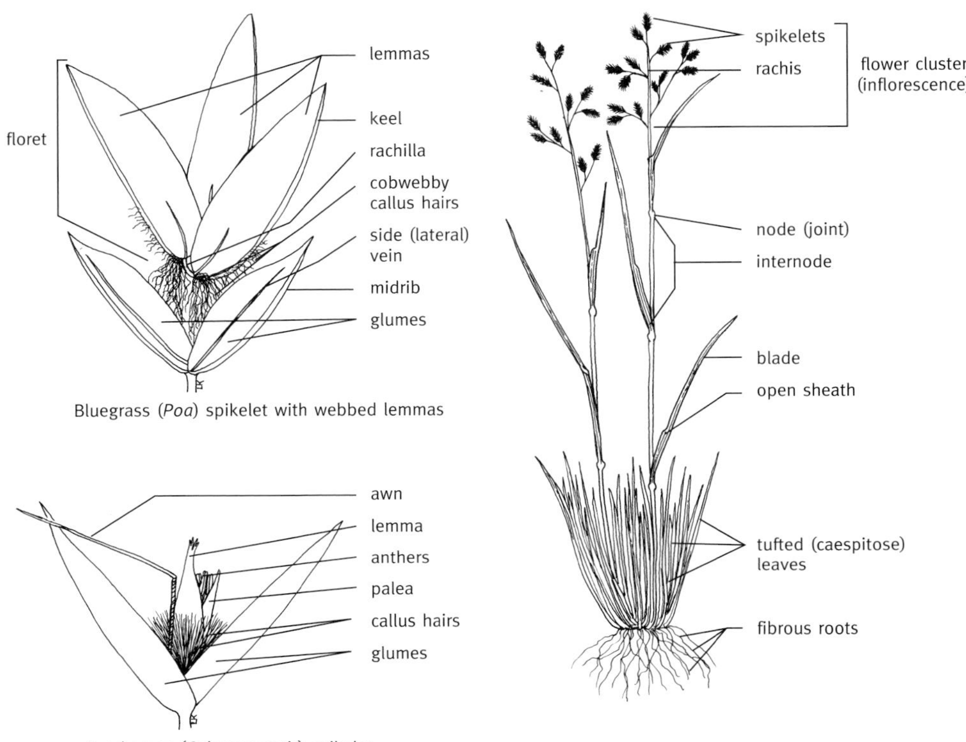

Bluegrass (*Poa*) spikelet with webbed lemmas

Reed grass (*Calamagrostis*) spikelet

Figure 17: Parts of a club-moss (*Lycopodiella*) plant (sporophyte)

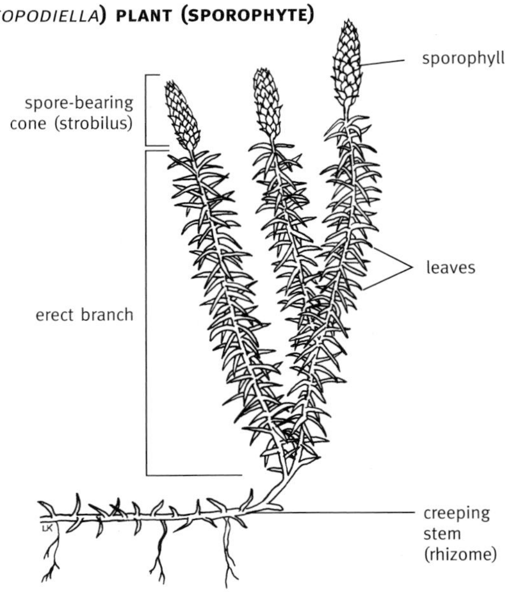

sporophyll

spore-bearing cone (strobilus)

leaves

erect branch

creeping stem (rhizome)

FIGURE 18: PARTS OF A HORSETAIL (*EQUISETUM*) PLANT (SPOROPHYTE)

spore-bearing cone (strobilus)
segmented branches
scale-like leaves
ridged, hollow stem
sheath of fused, scale-like leaves
rhizome

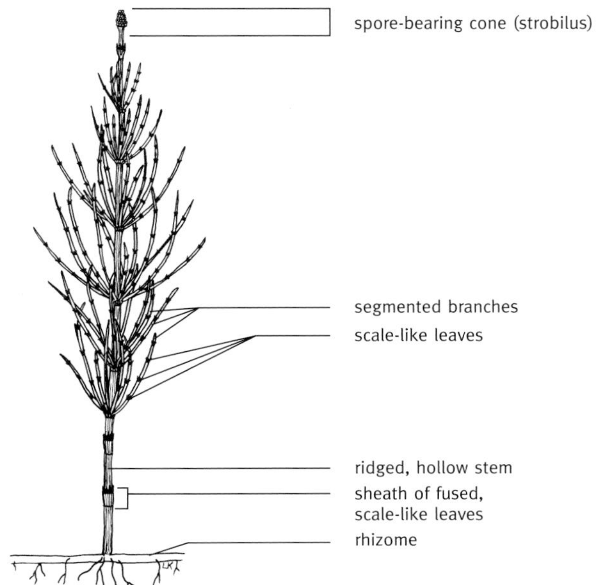

FIGURE 19: PARTS OF A WOOD FERN (*DRYOPTERIS*) PLANT (SPOROPHYTE)

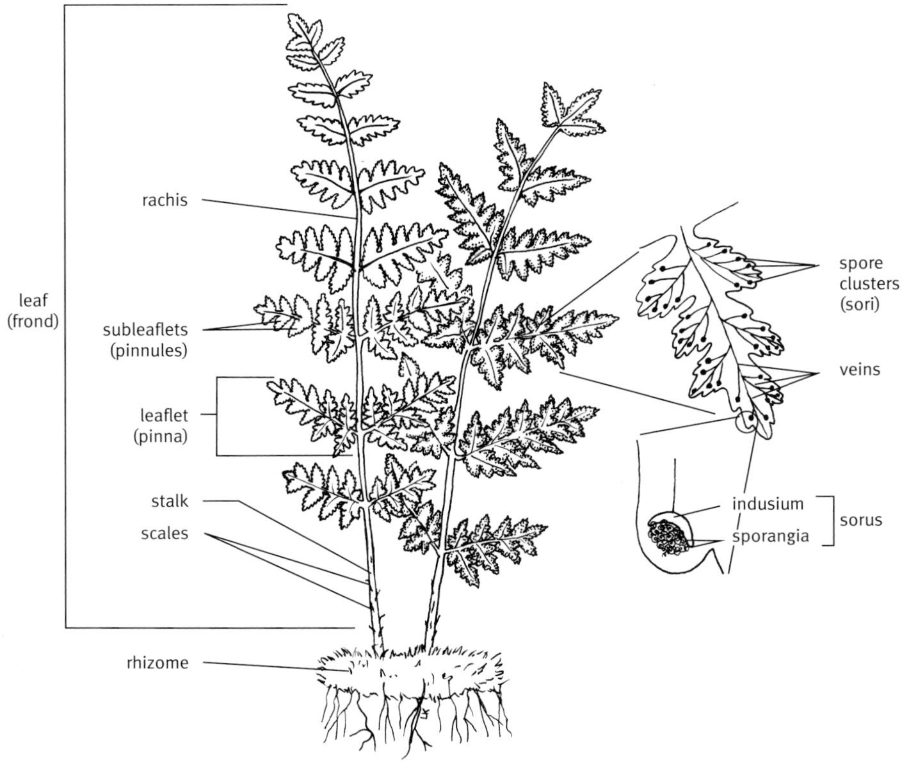

rachis
leaf (frond)
subleaflets (pinnules)
leaflet (pinna)
stalk
scales
rhizome
spore clusters (sori)
veins
indusium
sporangia
sorus

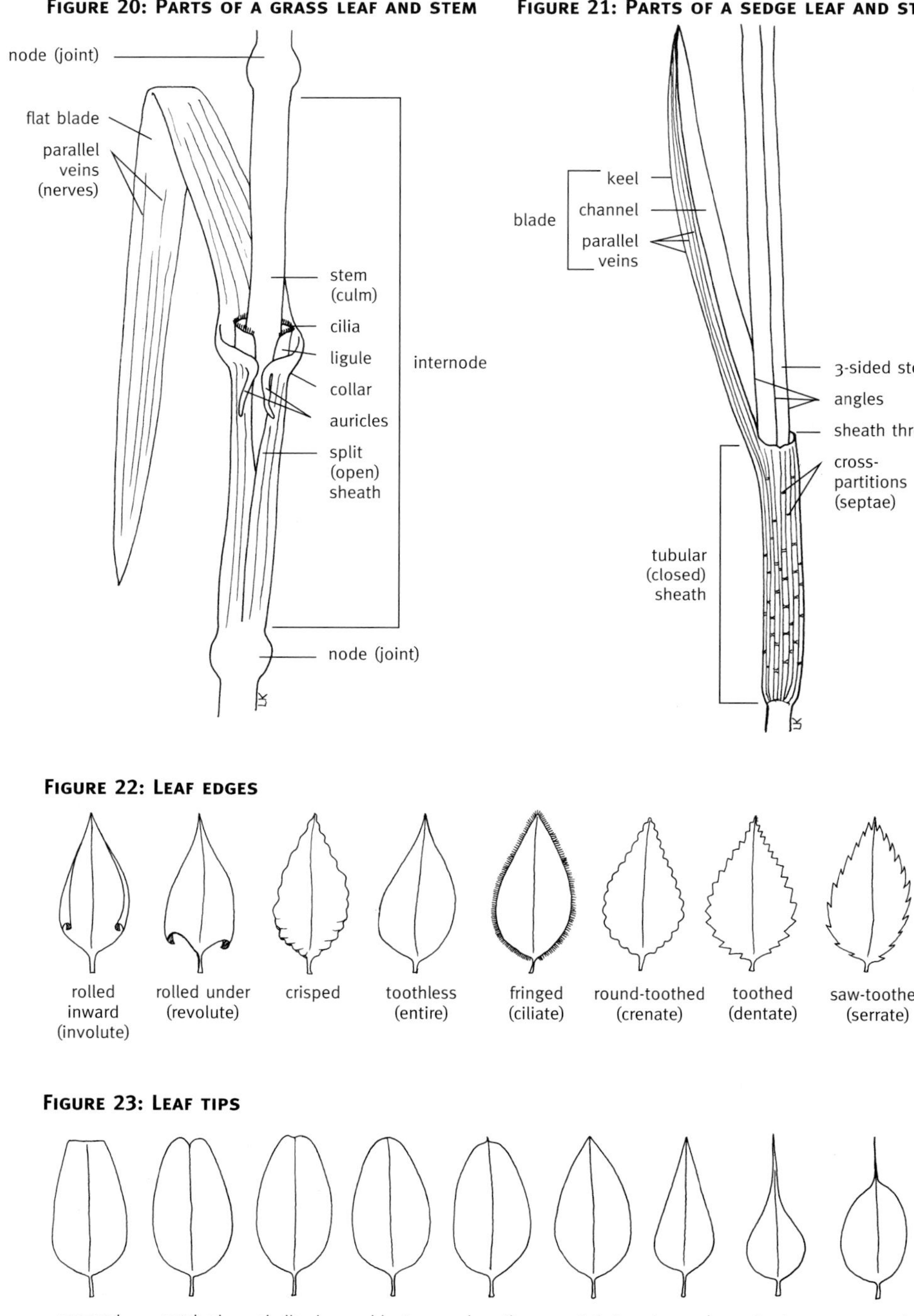
FIGURE 20: PARTS OF A GRASS LEAF AND STEM
node (joint)
flat blade
parallel veins (nerves)
stem (culm)
cilia
ligule
collar
auricles
split (open) sheath
internode
node (joint)
FIGURE 21: PARTS OF A SEDGE LEAF AND STEM
blade
keel
channel
parallel veins
3-sided stem
angles
sheath throat
cross-partitions (septae)
tubular (closed) sheath
FIGURE 22: LEAF EDGES
rolled inward (involute)
rolled under (revolute)
crisped
toothless (entire)
fringed (ciliate)
round-toothed (crenate)
toothed (dentate)
saw-toothed (serrate)
FIGURE 23: LEAF TIPS
squared (truncate)
notched (retuse)
shallowly notched (emarginate)
blunt, rounded (obtuse)
abruptly pointed (cuspidate)
pointed (acute)
tapered (attenuate)
slender-pointed (acuminate)
awned

Figure 24: Leaf bases

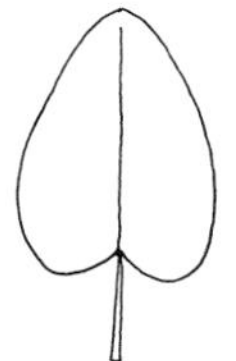

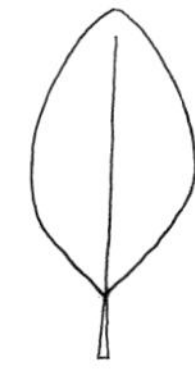

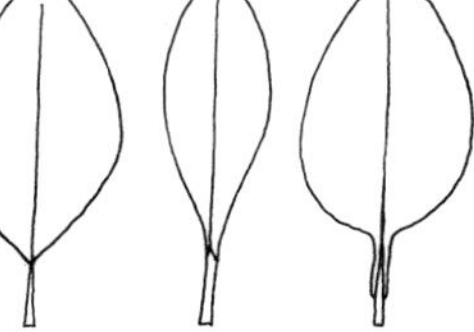

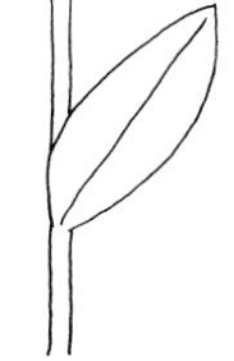

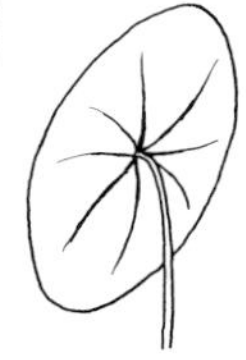

Figure 25: Leaf shapes

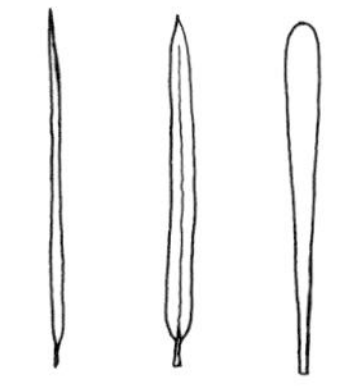

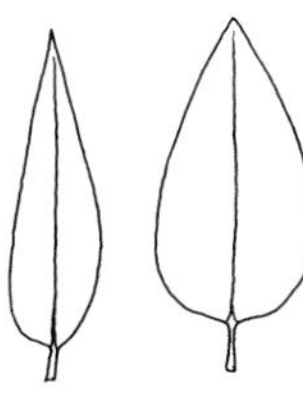

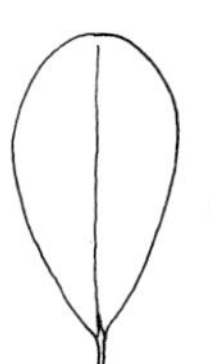

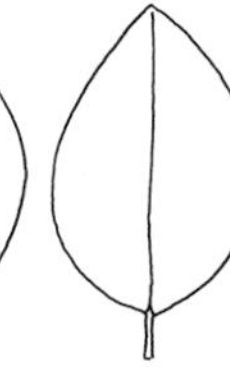

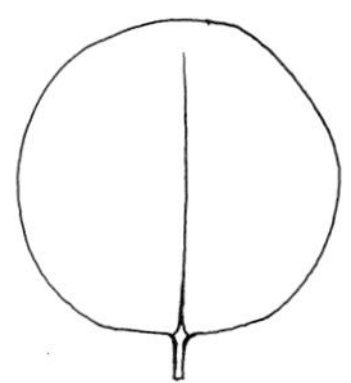

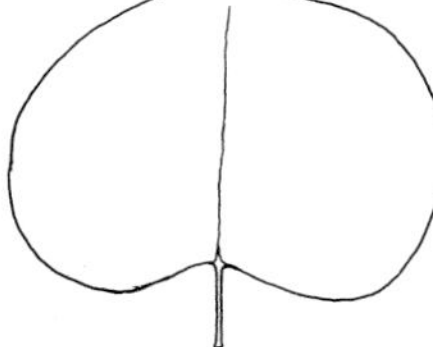

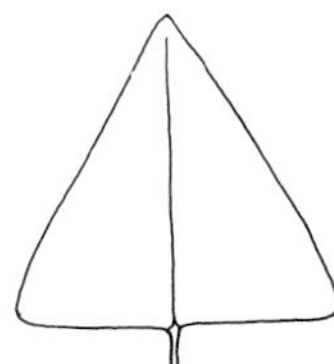

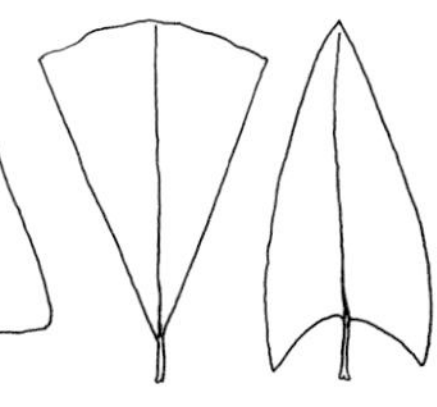

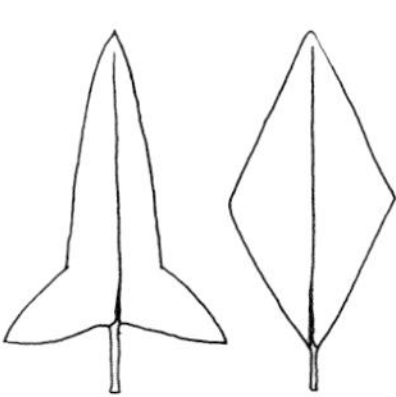

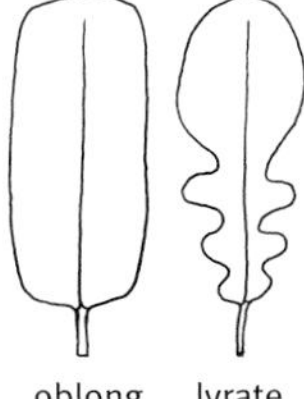

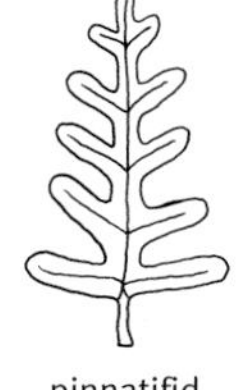

Figure 26: Branching patterns

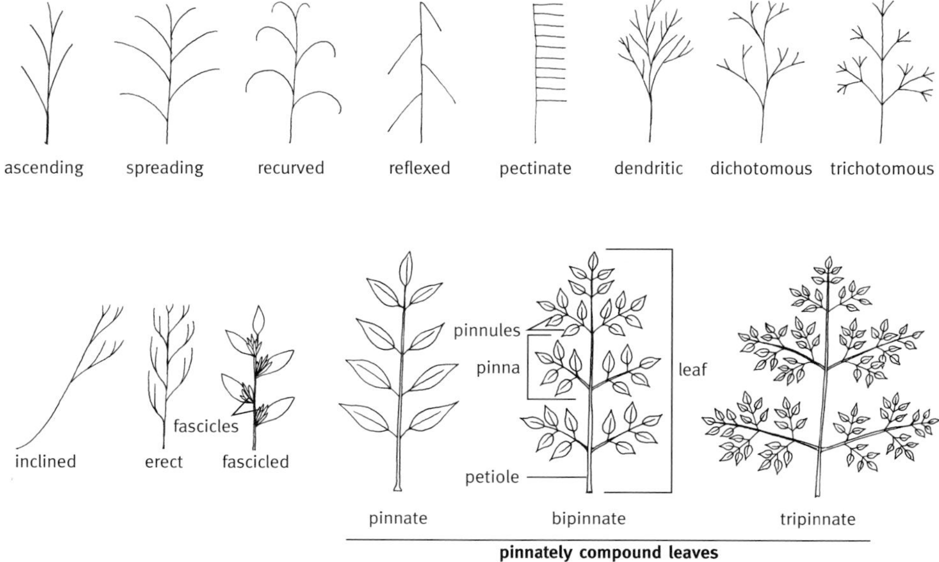

Figure 27: Types of flower clusters (inflorescences)

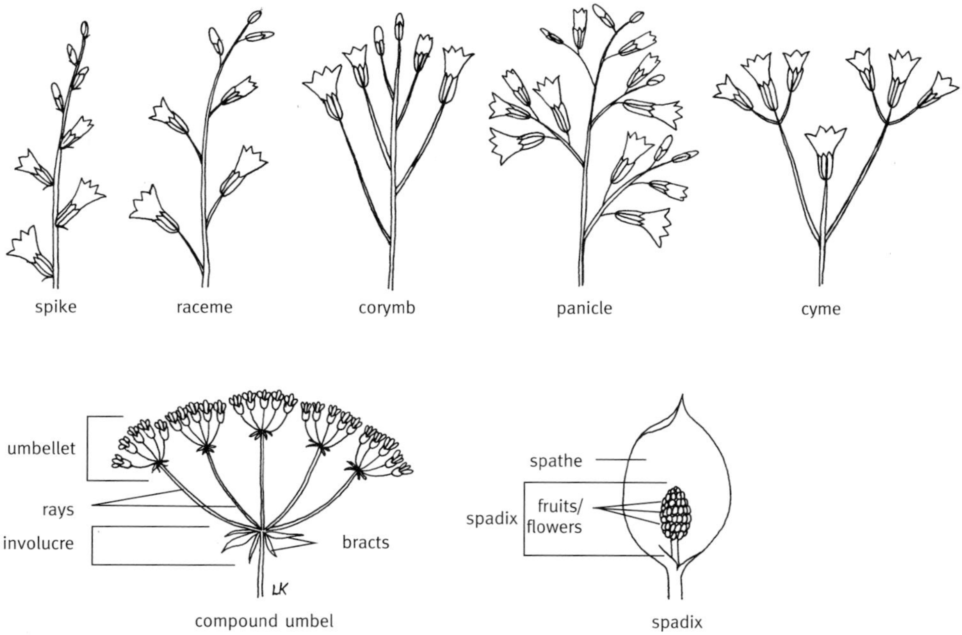

spike
raceme
corymb
panicle
cyme
umbellet
rays
involucre
bracts
LK
compound umbel
spathe
spadix
fruits/ flowers
spadix

FIGURE 28: FLOWER SHAPES

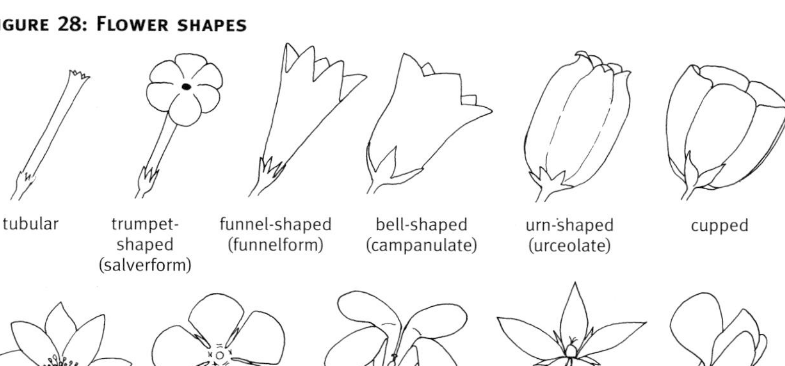

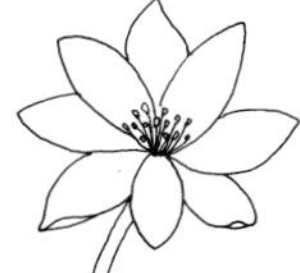

tubular
trumpet-shaped (salverform)
funnel-shaped (funnelform)
bell-shaped (campanulate)
urn-shaped (urceolate)
cupped
saucer-shaped
wheel-shaped (rotate)
cross-shaped (cruciform)
star-shaped (stellate)
pea-like (papilionaceous)
spadix (see Fig. 27)

FIGURE 29: FRUITS

hypanthium
berry
drupe
cluster of drupelets
hip
valves
pores
pome
legume (pod)
capsule
circumscissile capsule
operculate capsule
follicle
beak
feathery style
3-sided (trigonous)
2-sided (lenticular)
pappus
perianth bristles
style
stylopodium
mericarp
torulose silique
siliques
utricle
achenes
schizocarp
wings
samara
bur
cone
nut

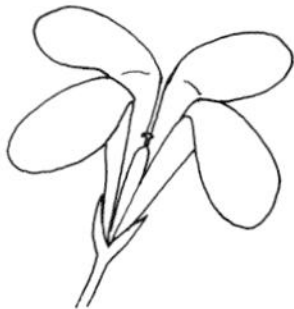

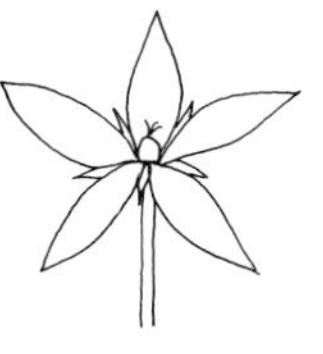

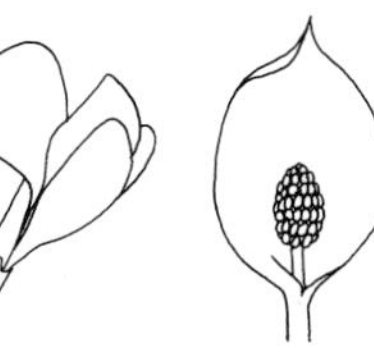

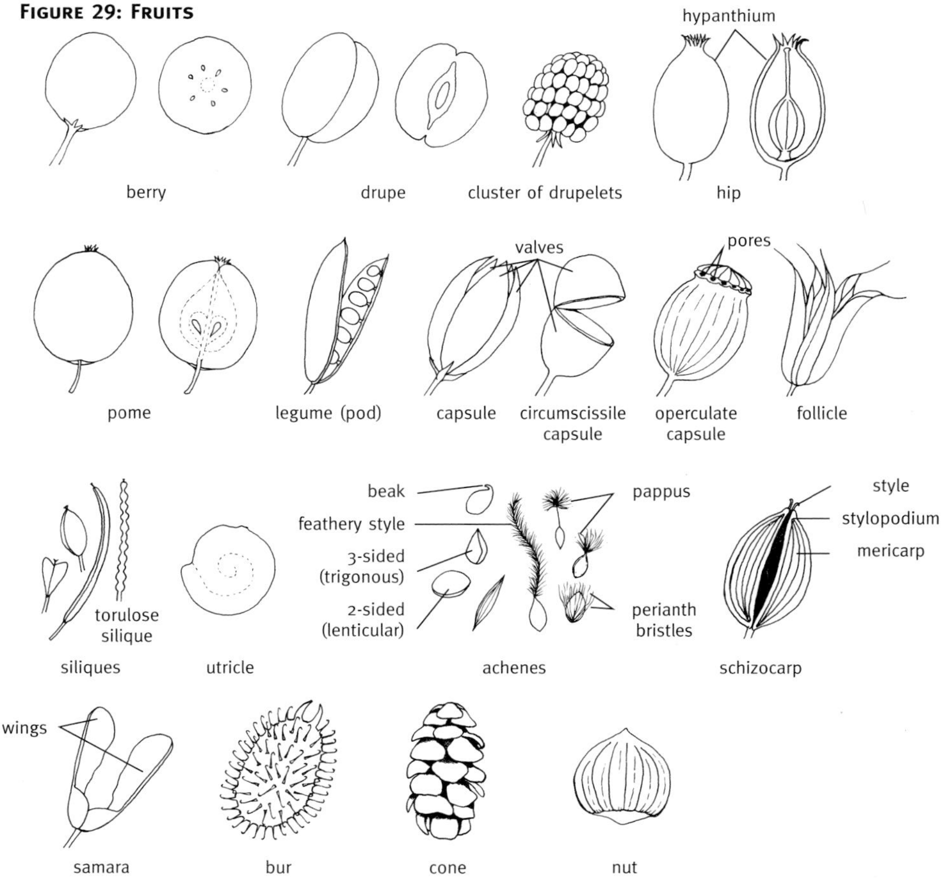

Figure 30: Underground parts

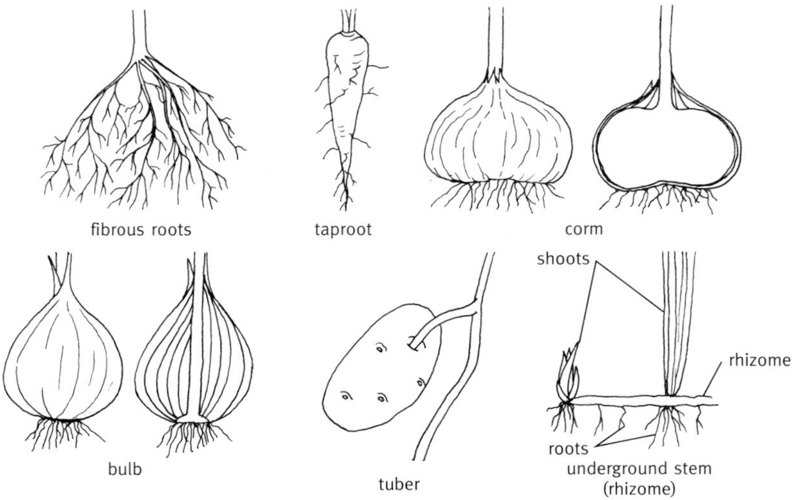

Abrams, L. and R.S. Ferris. 1960. An illustrated flora of the Pacific states: Washington, Oregon and California. 4 volumes. Stanford University Press, Stanford, California.

Achuff, P.L. 1987. Rare vascular plants in the Rocky Mountains of Alberta: summary. Pages 109–10 in G.L. Holroyd et al., eds. Proceedings of the workshop on endangered species in the prairie provinces. Provincial Museum of Alberta, Edmonton, Alberta. Natural History Occasional Paper No. 9.

Achuff, P.L. 1992. Natural regions, subregions and natural history themes of Alberta: a classification for protected areas management. Parks Services, Alberta Environmental Protection, Edmonton, Alberta.

Achuff, P.L. 1996. Status report on the large-flowered *Brickellia* (*Brickellia grandiflora*) in Canada. Committee on the Status of Endangered Wildlife in Canada, Ottawa, Ontario.

Achuff, P.L. and I.G.W. Corns. 1985. Plants new to Alberta from Banff and Jasper national parks. Canadian Field-Naturalist 99:94–98.

Aiken, S.G. and S.J. Darbyshire. 1990. Fescue grasses of Canada. Agriculture Canada, Ottawa, Ontario. Publication no. 1844/E.

Aiken, S.G., L.P. Lefkovitch, S.E. Gardiner and W.W. Mitchell. 1994. Evidence against the existence of varieties in *Arctagrostis latifolia* ssp. *aundinacea* (Poaceae). Canadian Journal of Botany 72:1039–50.

Alberta Forestry, Lands and Wildlife. 1991. Western blue flag. Alberta Forestry, Lands and Wildlife, Alberta Environmental Protection, Edmonton, Alberta. Alberta's threatened wildlife.

Alberta Environmental Protection. 1993. Alberta plants and fungi: master species list and species group checklists. Alberta Environmental Protection, Edmonton, Alberta.

Alberta Forestry, Lands and Wildlife. 1993. Big sagebrush (*Artemisia tridentata* Nutt.). Alberta Environmental Protection, Edmonton, Alberta. Alberta's Rare Plants Fact Sheet No. 6.

Alberta Forestry, Lands and Wildlife. 1993. Dwarf fleabane (*Erigeron radicatus* Hook.). Alberta Environmental Protection, Edmonton, Alberta. Alberta's Rare Plants Fact Sheet No. 8.

Alberta Forestry, Lands and Wildlife. 1993. Geyer's wild onion (*Allium geyeri* S. Wats.). Alberta Environmental Protection, Edmonton, Alberta. Alberta's Rare Plants Fact Sheet No. 4.

Alberta Forestry, Lands and Wildlife. 1993. Hare-footed locoweed (*Oxytropis lagopus* Nutt.). Alberta Environmental Protection, Edmonton, Alberta. Alberta's Rare Plants Fact Sheet No. 9.

Alberta Forestry, Lands and Wildlife. 1993. Mountain ladies'-slipper (*Cypripedium montanum* Dougl. *ex* Lindl.). Alberta Environmental Protection, Edmonton, Alberta. Alberta's Rare Plants Fact Sheet No. 2.

Alberta Forestry, Lands and Wildlife. 1993. Western blue flag (*Iris missouriensis* Nutt.). Alberta Environmental Protection, Edmonton, Alberta. Alberta's Rare Plants Fact Sheet No. 3.

Alberta Forestry, Lands and Wildlife. 1993. Western spiderwort (*Tradescantia occidentalis* (Britt.) Smyth). Alberta Environmental Protection, Edmonton, Alberta. Alberta's Rare Plants Fact Sheet No. 7.

Alberta Forestry, Lands and Wildlife. 1993. What is a rare plant? Alberta Environmental Protection, Edmonton, Alberta. Alberta's Rare Plants Fact Sheet No. 1.

Alberta Forestry, Lands and Wildlife. 1993. Yellow paintbrush (*Castilleja cusickii* Greenm.). Alberta Environmental Protection, Edmonton, Alberta. Alberta's Rare Plants Fact Sheet No. 5.

Alberta Forestry, Lands and Wildlife. 1994. Alpine poppy (*Papaver pygmaeum* Rydb.). Alberta Environmental Protection, Edmonton, Alberta. Alberta's Rare Plants Fact Sheet No. 15.

Alberta Forestry, Lands and Wildlife. 1994. Bog adder's-mouth (*Malaxis paludosa* (L.) Sw.). Alberta Environmental Protection, Edmonton, Alberta. Alberta's Rare Plants Fact Sheet No. 10.

Alberta Forestry, Lands and Wildlife. 1994. Engelmann's spike-rush (*Eleocharis ovata* (Roth) R.& S.). Alberta Environmental Protection, Edmonton, Alberta. Alberta's Rare Plants Fact Sheet No. 13.

Alberta Forestry, Lands and Wildlife. 1994. Jones' columbine (*Aquilegia jonesii* Parry). Alberta Environmental Protection, Edmonton, Alberta. Alberta's Rare Plants Fact Sheet No. 11.

Alberta Forestry, Lands and Wildlife. 1994. Nebraska sedge (*Carex nebraskensis* Dewey). Alberta Environmental Protection, Edmonton, Alberta. Alberta's Rare Plants Fact Sheet No. 12.

Alberta Forestry, Lands and Wildlife. 1994. Smooth boisduvalia (*Boisduvalia glabella* (Nutt.) Walp.). Alberta Environmental Protection, Edmonton, Alberta. Alberta's Rare Plants Fact Sheet No. 14.

Alberta Forestry, Lands and Wildlife. 1994. Upland evening-primrose (*Oenothera andina* Nutt.). Alberta Environmental Protection, Edmonton, Alberta. Alberta's Rare Plants Fact Sheet No. 16.

Alberta Native Plant Council. 1988. Alberta's first rare plant monitoring project: western blue flag (*Iris missouriensis*). Iris 2:3–4.

Alberta Native Plant Council. 1989. Native plant collecting: conservation guidelines. Iris 5:19–20.

Alberta Natural and Protected Areas Program 1991. Threatened plant management plan—A first! Natural Areas Newsletter 15:1.

Alberta Natural Heritage Information Centre. 1998. Rare plant data files. Recreation and Protected Areas, Alberta Environmental Protection, Edmonton, Alberta.

Allen, L.J. 1987. Alberta rare plants. Canadian Plant Conservation Programme Newsletter 2(1):11–12.

Allison, J.L. 1945. *Selenophoma bromigena* leaf spot on *Bromus inermis*. Phytopathology 35: 233–40.

Argus, G.W. 1986. *Salix raupii*, Raup's willow, new to the flora of Alberta and the Northwest Territories. Canadian Field-Naturalist 100:386–388.

Argus, G.W. and C.J. Keddy. 1984. Atlas of the rare vascular plants of Ontario. Botany division, National Museum of Natural Sciences, National Museums of Canada, Ottawa, Ontario.

Argus, G.W. and D.J. White. 1977. The rare vascular plants of Ontario. Botany division, National Museum of Natural Sciences, National Museums of Canada, Ottawa, Ontario.

Argus, G.W. and D.J. White. 1978. The rare vascular plants of Alberta. National Museum of Natural Sciences, Ottawa, Ontario. Syllogeus No. 17.

Argus, G.W. and K.M. Pryer. 1990. Rare vascular plants in Canada: our natural heritage. Canadian Museum of Nature. Ottawa, Ontario.

Babcock, E.B. 1947. The genus *Crepis*. Part 2. Systematic treatment. University of California Publications in Botany 22:199–1030.

Barkley, T.M., ed. 1977. Atlas of the flora of the Great Plains. Iowa State University Press, Ames, Iowa.

Barkworth, M.E. and D.R. Dewey. 1985. Genomically based genera in the perennial Triticeae of North America: identification and membership. American Journal of Botany 72: 767–76.

Barneby, R.C. 1964. Atlas of North American *Astragalus*. Part 2. The Ceridotherix, Hypoglottis, Piptoloboid, Trimeniaeus and Orophaca Astragali. Memoirs of the New York Botanical Garden 13:597–1188.

Bassett, I.J. 1973. The Plantagos of Canada. Canada Department of Agriculture, Ottawa, Ontario.

Bassett, I.J. and C.W. Crompton. 1982. The genus *Chenopodium* in Canada. Canadian Journal of Botany 60:586–610.

Bayer, R.J. 1989. A systematic and phytogeographic study of *Antennaria aromatica* and *A. densifolia* (Asteraceae: Inuleae) in the western North American Cordillera. Madrono 36(4):248–59.

Bayer, R.J. 1993. A synopsis with keys for the genus *Antennaria* (Asteraceae: Inuleae: Gnaphaliinae) of North America. Canadian Journal of Botany 71:1589–1604.

Beaman, J.H. 1957. The systematics and evolution of *Townsendia* (Compositae). Contributions from the Gray Herbarium 183:1–151.

Benson, L. 1962. Plant taxonomy: methods and principles. Ronald Press Co., New York, New York. A Chronica Botanica Publication.

Berch, S.M., S. Gameit and E. Doem. 1987. Mycorrhizal status of some plants in southwestern British Columbia. Canadian Journal of Botany 66: 1924–28.

Bliss, L.C. 1971. Arctic and alpine plant life cycles. Annual Reviews Inc., Palo Alto, California. Annual Review of Ecology and Systematics Vol. 2.

Boivin, B. 1968. Flora of the Prairie Provinces. Phytologia 15:121–59, 329–446; 16:1–47, 219–61, 265–339; 17:58–112; 18:281–93.

Booth, W.E. and J.C. Wright. 1959. Flora of Montana. Part 1. Conifers and monocots. Montana State University, Bozeman, Montana.

Booth, W.E. and J.C. Wright. 1959. Flora of Montana. Part 2. Dicotyledons. Montana State University, Bozeman, Montana.

Borror, D.J. 1960. Dictionary of word roots and combining forms. Mayfield Publishing Co., Mountain View, California.

Bouchard, A., D. Barabe, M. Dumais and S. Hay. 1983. The rare vascular plants of Quebec. National Museum of Natural Sciences, Ottawa, Ontario. Syllogeus No. 48.

Bradley, C. 1987. Disappearing cottonwoods: the social challenge. Pages 119–21 in G.L. Holroyd et al., eds. Proceedings of the Workshop on Endangered Species in the Prairie Provinces. Provincial Museum of Alberta, Edmonton, Alberta. Natural History Occasional Paper No. 9.

Braidwood, B. 1987. A framework for the identification, evaluation, and protection of sites of special interest in Alberta. M.Sc. thesis, Department of Forest Science, University of Alberta, Edmonton, Alberta.

Brayshaw, T.C. 1985. Pondweeds and bur-reeds, and their relatives: aquatic families of monocotyledons in British Columbia. British Columbia Provincial Museum, Victoria, British Columbia. Occasional Paper No. 26.

Brayshaw, T.C. 1989. Buttercups, waterlilies and their relatives in British Columbia. Royal British Columbia Museum, Victoria, British Columbia. Memoir No. 1.

Brayshaw, T.C. 1996. Trees and shrubs of British Columbia. University of British Columbia Press, Vancouver, British Columbia. Royal British Columbia Museum Handbook.

Breitung, A.J. 1954. A botanical survey of the Cypress Hills. Canadian Field-Naturalist 68:55–92.

Breitung, A.J. 1957. Plants of Waterton Lakes National Park, Alberta. Canadian Field-Naturalist 71:39–71.

Britton, D.M. and D.F. Brunton. 1993. *Isoetes* x *truncata*: a newly considered pentaploid hybrid from western North America. Canadian Journal of Botany 71: 1016–25.

Brooke, R.C. and S. Kojima. 1985. An annotated vascular flora of areas adjacent to the Dempster Highway, central Yukon Territory. Volume 2. Dicotyledonae. British Columbia Provincial Museum, Victoria, British Columbia. Contributions to Natural Science No. 4.

Brunton, D.F. 1984. Status of western larch, *Larix occidentalis*, in Alberta. Canadian Field-Naturalist 98:167–70.

Brunton, D.F. 1994. Status report on Bolander's quillwort (*Isoetes bolanderi* Engelm.) in Canada. Committee on the Status of Endangered Wildlife in Canada, Ottawa, Ontario.

Budd, A.C. 1957. Wild plants of the Canadian prairies. Canada Department of Agriculture, Ottawa, Ontario. Publication No. 983.

Burnfield, S.J. and F.D. Johnson. 1990. Cytological, morphological, ecological and phenological support for specific status of *Crataegus suksdorfii*. Madrono 37(4):274–82.

Burt, P. 1991. Barrenland beauties: showy plants of the Arctic coast. Outcrop Ltd., Yellowknife, Northwest Territories.

Calder, J.A. and D.B.O. Savile. 1960. Studies in Saxifragaceae. III. *Saxifraga odontoloma* and *S. lyallii*, and North American subspecies of *S. punctata*. Canadian Journal of Botany 38:409–35.

Case, F.W. Jr. 1987. Orchids of the western Great Lakes region. Cranbrook Institute of Science. Bloomfield Hills, Michigan. Bulletin No. 48.

Catling, P.M. and W. Wojtas. 1986. The waterweeds (*Elodea* and *Egeria*, Hydrocharitaceae) in Canada. Canadian Journal of Botany 64:1525–41.

Catling, P.M. 1991. Morphometrics and phytogeography of the *Eleocharis elliptica* group in Ontario. Canadian Botanical Association, Edmonton, Alberta, and Canadian Society of Plant Physiology, Edmonton, Alberta, Joint Meeting, June 23–27, 1991, Edmonton, Alberta.

Chambers, J.C. and R.C. Sidle. 1991. Fate of heavy metals in an abandoned lead-zinc tailings pond. Part 1. Vegetation. Journal of Environmental Quality 20: 745–51.

Chase, A. 1918. Axillary cleistogenes in some American grasses. American Journal of Botany 5: 254–58.

Chmielewski, J.G. 1993. *Antennaria pulvinata* Greene: the legitimate name for *A. aromatica* Evert (Asteraceae: Inuleae). Rhodora 95:261–76.

Chmielewski, J.G., C.C. Chinnappa and J.C. Semple. 1990. The genus *Antennaria* (Asteraceae: Inuleae) in western North America: morphometric analysis of *Antennaria alborosea*, *A. corymbosa*, *A. marginata*, *A. microphylla*, *A. parvifolia*, *A. rosea*, and *A. umbrinella*. Plant Systematics and Evolution 169:141–75.

Church, G.L. 1949. A cytotaxonomic study of *Glyceria* and *Puccinellia*. American Journal of Botany 36: 155–65.

Clark, L.J. 1975. Lewis Clark's field guide to wild flowers of the mountains in the Pacific Northwest. Gray's Publishing Ltd., Sidney, British Columbia.

Clark, L.J. 1976. Wild Flowers of the Pacific Northwest from Alaska to northern California. Evergreen Press Ltd., Vancouver, British Columbia.

Clausen, R.T. 1975. *Sedum* of North America north of the Mexican plateau. Cornell University Press, Ithaca, New York.

Cody, W.J. 1956. New plant records for northern Alberta and the southern Mackenzie District. Canadian Field-Naturalist 70:101–30.

Cody, W.J. 1971. A phytogeographical study of the floras of the Continental Northwest Territories and Yukon. Naturaliste Canadien 98: 145–58.

Cody, W.J. 1996. Flora of the Yukon Territory. National Research Press, Ottawa, Ontario.

Cody, W.J. and D.M. Britton. 1989. Ferns and fern allies of Canada. Research Branch, Agriculture Canada, Ottawa, Ontario. Publication No. 1829/E.

Cody, W.J. and S.S. Talbot. 1973. The pitcher plant, *Sarracenia purpurea* L., in the northwestern part of its range. Canadian Field-Naturalist 88:229–30.

Cody, W.J., B. Boivin and G.W. Scotter. 1974. *Loisleuria procumbens* (L.) Desv., alpine azalea, in Alberta. Canadian Field-Naturalist 88:229–30.

Coffey, T. 1993. The history and folklore of North American wildflowers. Houghton Mifflin, Boston, Massachusetts.

Colorado Native Plant Society. 1989. Rare plants of Colorado. Colorado Native Plant Society and Rocky Mountain Nature Association, Rocky Mountain National Park, Estes Park, Colorado.

Committee on the Status of Endangered Wildlife in Canada. 1997. Canadian species at risk. Canadian Wildlife Service, Ottawa, Ontario.

Constance, L. and R.H. Shan. 1948. The genus *Osmorhiza* (Umbelliferae): a study in geographic affinities. University of California Publications in Botany 23:111–156.

Constance, L. 1941. The genus *Nemophila* Nutt. University of California Publications in Botany 19:341–345.

Constance, L. 1942. The genus *Hydrophyllum*. American Midland Naturalist 27:710–731.

Coombes, A.J. 1987. Dictionary of plant names. Timber Press, Portland, Oregon.

Coombes, A.J. 1992. The Hamlyn guide to plant names. Hamlyn, London, England.

Cormack, R.G.H. 1948. Orchids of the Cypress Hills. Canadian Field-Naturalist 88:229–30.

Cormack, R.G.H. 1977. Wildflowers of Alberta. Hurtig Publishers, Edmonton, Alberta.

Coupé, R., C.A. Ray, A. Comeau, M.V. Ketcheson and R.M. Annas. 1982. A guide to some common plants of the Skeena area of British Columbia. Province of British Columbia, Ministry of Forestry, Victoria, British Columbia. Land Management Handbook No. 4.

Craighead, J.J., F.C. Craighead, Jr. and R.J. Davis. 1963. Rocky Mountain wildflowers. Houghton Mifflin Company, Boston, Massachusetts.

Crawford, D.J. 1975. Systematic relationships in the narrow-leaved species of *Chenopodium* of the western United States. Brittonia 27:279–88.

Crawford, D.J. and J.F. Reynolds. 1974. A numerical study of the common narrow-leaved taxa of *Chenopodium* occurring in the western United States. Brittonia 26:398–410.

Crow, G. 1978. A taxonomic revision of *Sagina* (Caryophyllaceae) in North America. Rhodora 80:1–91.

Crow, G.E. and C.B. Hellquist. 1985. Aquatic vascular plants of New England. Part 8. Lentibulariaceae. New Hampshire Agricultural Experiment Station, University of New Hampshire, Durham, New Hampshire. Station Bulletin No. 528.

Crum, H. 1988. A focus on peatlands and peat mosses. The University of Michigan Press, Ann Arbor, Michigan.

Daubenmire, R.F. 1970. Steppe vegetation of Washington. Washington Agricultural Experimental Station, Pullman, Washington. Technical Bulletin No. G2.

Davis, J.I. 1991. A note on North American *Torreyochloa* (Poaceae), including a new combination. Phytologia 70: 361–65.

Davis, R.J. 1966. The North American perennial species of *Claytonia*. Brittonia 18:285–303.

de Vries, B. 1966. *Iris missouriensis* Nutt. in southwestern Alberta and in central and northern British Columbia. Canadian Field-Naturalist 80:158–60.

Dewey, D.R. 1963. Natural hybrids of *Agropyron trachycaulum* and *Agropyron scribneri*. Bulletin of the Torrey Botanical Club 90: 111–22.

Dewey, D.R. 1967. Genome relations between *Agropyron scribneri* and *Sitanion hystrix*. Bulletin of the Torrey Botanical Club 94: 395–404.

Dewey, D.R. 1976. Cytogenetics of *Agropyron pringlei* and its hybrids with *A. spicatum*, *A. scribneri*, *A. violaceum*, and *A. dasystachyum*. Botanical Gazette 137: 179–85.

Douglas, G.W. 1982. The sunflower family (Asteraceae) of British Columbia. Volume 1. Senecioneae. Royal British Columbia Museum, Victoria, British Columbia. Occasional Paper No. 23.

Douglas, G.W. 1995. The sunflower family (Asteraceae) of British Columbia. Volume 2. Astereae, Anthemideae, Eupatorieae and Inuleae. Royal British Columbia Museum, Victoria, British Columbia.

Douglas, G.W., G.B. Straley and D. Meidinger. 1989. The vascular plants of British Columbia. Part 1. Gymnosperms and Dicotyledons (Aceraceae through Cucurbitaceae). British Columbia Ministry of Forests, Victoria, British Columbia.

Douglas, G.W., G.B. Straley and D. Meidinger. 1990. The vascular plants of British Columbia. Part 2. Dicotyledons (Diapensiaceae through Portulacaceae). British Columbia Ministry of Forests, Victoria, British Columbia.

Douglas, G.W., G.B. Straley and D. Meidinger. 1991. The vascular plants of British Columbia. Part 3. Dicotyledons (Primulaceae through Zygophyllaceae) and Pteridophytes. British Columbia Ministry of Forests, Victoria, British Columbia.

Douglas, G.W., G.B. Straley and D. Meidinger. 1994. The vascular plants of British Columbia. Part 4. Monocotyledons. British Columbia Ministry of Forests, Victoria, British Columbia.

Douglas, G.W., G.W. Argus, H.L. Dickson and D.F. Brunton. 1981. The rare vascular plants of the Yukon. National Museum of Natural Sciences, Ottawa, Ontario. Syllogeus No. 28.

Dunn, D.B. 1965. The inter-relationships of the Alaskan lupines. Madrono 18:1–17.

Dunn, D.B. and J.M. Gillett. 1966. The lupines of Canada and Alaska. Canada Department of Agriculture, Ottawa, Ontario. Monograph No. 2.

Duran, R. and G.W. Fisher. 1961. The genus *Tilletia*. Washington State University Press, Pullman, Washington.

Eastman, J. 1995. The book of swamp and bog. Stackpole Books, Mechanicsburg, Pennsylvania.

Elisens, W.J. and J.G. Packer. 1980. A contribution to the taxonomy of the *Oxytropis campestris* complex in northwestern North America. Canadian Journal of Botany 58:1820–31.

Ellison, W.L. 1964. A systematic study of the genus *Bahia* (Compositae). Rhodora 66:67–86, 177–215, 281–311.

Elvander, P.E. 1984. The taxonomy of *Saxifraga* (Saxifragaceae) Section *Boraphila* subsection *Integrifolia* in western North America. Systematic Botany Monographs 3:1–44.

Erichsen-Brown, C. 1979. Use of plants for the past 500 years. Breezy Creek Press, Aurora, Ontario.

Evert, E.F. 1984. A new species of *Antennaria* (Asteraceae) from Montana and Wyoming. Madrono 13(2):109–12.

Fairbarns, M.D. 1984. Status report on the soapweed (*Yucca glauca*) in Canada. Committee on the Status of Endangered Wildlife in Canada, Ottawa, Ontario.

Fairbarns, M.D. 1986. Conservation values and management concerns in the Candidate South Castle natural area. Public Lands Division, Alberta Forestry, Lands and Wildlife, Edmonton, Alberta. Technical Report No. T/127.

Fairbarns, M.D. 1989. Bog adder's-mouth orchid (*Malaxis paludosa*) in the Wagner Bog natural area vicinity. Alberta Forestry, Lands and Wildlife, Edmonton, Alberta.

Fairbarns, M., D. Loewen and C. Bradley. 1987. The rare vascular flora of Alberta. Volume 1. A summary of the taxa occurring in the Rocky Mountain natural region. Alberta Forestry, Lands and Wildlife, Edmonton, Alberta. Natural Areas Technical Report No. 29.

Farrar, D.R. and C.L. Johnson-Groh. 1990. Subterranean sporophytic gemmae on moonwort ferns, *Botrychium* subgenus *Botrychium*. American Journal of Botany 77: 1168–75.

Farrar, J.L. 1995. Trees in Canada. Fitzhenry & Whiteside Ltd., Markham, Ontario, and Canadian Forest Service, Ottawa, Ontario.

Federation of Alberta Naturalists. 1992. Potential species for inclusion in the rare vascular flora of Alberta. Alberta Naturalist 22(4), Supplement No. 3:1A–11A.

Fernald, M.L. 1905. The North American species of *Eriophorum*. Rhodora 7:81–92, 129–36.

Fernald, M.L. 1935. Critical plants of the upper Great Lakes region of Ontario and Michigan. Rhodora 37:197–262.

Fernald, M.L. 1950. Gray's manual of botany. Eighth edition. American Book Company, New York, New York.

Fisher, G.W. and M.N. Levine. 1941. Summary of the recorded data on the reaction of wild and cultivated grasses to stem rust (*Puccinia graminis*), leaf rust (*P. rubigo-vera*), stripe rust (*P. glumarum*), and crown rust (*P. coronata*) in the United States and Canada. The Plant Disease Reporter. Supplement No. 130.

Flora of North America Editorial Committee, eds. 1993. Flora of North America, north of Mexico. Volume 2. Pteridophytes and Gymnosperms. Oxford University Press, New York, New York.

Flora of North America Editorial Committee, eds. 1997. Flora of North America, north of Mexico. Volume 3. Magnoliidae and Hamamelidae. Oxford University Press, New York, New York.

Foster, S. and J.A. Duke. 1990. A field guide to medicinal plants of eastern and central North America. Houghton Mifflin Co., Boston, Massachusetts.

Frankton, C. and I.J. Bassett. 1970. The genus *Atriplex* (Chenopodiaceae) in Canada. Part 2. Four native western annuals: *A. argentea*, *A. truncata*, *A. powellii*, and *A. dioica*. Canadian Journal of Botany 48:981–89.

Gale, S. 1944. *Rhynchospora*, section *Eurhynchospora*, in Canada, the United States and the West Indies. Rhodora 46:89–143, 159–97, 207–49, 255–78.

Galloway, L.A. 1975. Systematics of the North American desert species of *Abronia* and *Tripterocalyx* (Nyctaginaceae). Brittonia 27:328–47.

Gerrand, M. and D. Sheppard. 1995. Rare and endangered species of the Castle Wilderness. Castle-Crown Wilderness Coalition, Pincher Creek, Alberta. Special Publication No. 4.

Gill, J.D. and F.L. Pogge. 1974. *Physocarpus maxim*. Ninebark. Seeds of woody plants in the United States. Forest Service, United States Department of Agriculture, Washington, D.C. Handbook No. 450.

Gillet, J. 1979. New combinations in *Hypericum*, *Triandenum*, and *Gentianopsis*. Canadian Journal of Botany 57:185–86.

Gillet, J. and N. Robson. 1981. The St. John's-worts of Canada (Guttiferae). National Museum of Natural Sciences, Ottawa, Ontario. Publications in Botany No. 11.

Gillett, G.W. 1960. A systematic treatment of the *Phacelia franklinii* group. Rhodora 62:205–22.

Gillett, G.W. 1962. Evolutionary relationships of *Phacelia linearis*. Brittonia 14:231–36.

Gillett, J.M. 1957. A revision of the North American species of *Gentianella* Moench. Annals of the Missouri Botanical Garden 44(3):195–269.

Gillett, J.M. 1963. The gentians of Canada, Alaska and Greenland. Canada Department of Agriculture Research Branch, Ottawa, Ontario. Publication No. 1180.

Gillett, J.M. 1968. The milkworts of Canada. Canada Department of Agriculture Research Branch, Ottawa, Ontario. Monograph No. 5.

Gleason, H.A. 1952. The new Britton and Brown illustrated flora of the northeastern United States and adjacent Canada. Hafner Press, New York, New York.

Gleason, H.A. and A. Cronquist. 1963. Manual of vascular plants of northeastern United States and adjacent Canada. Van Nostrand Reinhold Co., Toronto, Ontario.

Gornall, R.J. and B.A. Bohm. 1985. A monograph of *Boykinia*, *Peltoboykinia*, *Bolandra* and *Suksdorfia* (Saxifragaceae). Botanical Journal of the Linnaean Society 90:1–71.

Gould, F.W. and C.A. Clark. 1978. *Dichanthelium* (Poaceae) in the United States and Canada. Annals of the Missouri Botanical Garden 65:1088–1132.

Gould, F.W. and R.B. Shaw. 1983. Grass systematics. Second edition. Texas A&M University Press, College Station, Texas.

Gould, J. 1998. Rare plant conservation in Alberta. J. Thorpe, T.A. Steeves, and M. Gollop, eds. Proceedings of the Fifth Prairie Conservation and Endangered Species Conference, February 1998, Saskaton, Saskatchewan. Provincial Museum of Alberta, Edmonton, Alberta. Natural History Occasional Paper No. 24.

Gould, J. 1996. The status of rare plant conservation in Alberta. W.D. Willms and J.F. Dormaar, eds. Pages 244–46 in Proceedings of the Fourth Prairie Conservation and Endangered Species workshop. Provincial Museum of Alberta, Edmonton, Alberta. Natural History Occasional Paper No. 23.

Gould, J. 1998. Alberta Natural Heritage Information Centre plant species of special concern. Alberta Environment, Edmonton, Alberta.

Gould, J. 2000. Alberta Natural Heritage Information Centre plant species of special concern. Alberta Environment, Edmonton, Alberta.

Great Plains Flora Association. 1977. Flora of the Great Plains. University of Kansas Press, Lawrence, Kansas.

Grieve, M. 1931. A modern herbal. Penguin Books Ltd., Harmondsworth, Middlesex, England.

Griffiths, D.E. and G.C.D. Griffiths. 1990. Further notes on *Wolffia* (Lemnaceae), with the addition of *W. borealis* to the Alberta flora. Alberta Naturalist 20:59–64.

Griffiths, G.C.D. 1988. *Wolffia arrhiza* and *W. columbiana* (Lemnaceae) in Alberta. Alberta Naturalist 18:18–20.

Griffiths, G.C.D. 1989. The true *Carex rostrata* (Cyperaceae) in Alberta. Alberta Naturalist 19(3):105–08.

Guard, B.J. 1995. Wetland plants of Oregon and Washington. Lone Pine Publishing, Edmonton, Alberta.

Gunther, E. 1973. Ethnobotany of western Washington: the knowledge and use of indigenous plants by native Americans. Revised edition. University of Washington Press, Seattle, Washington.

Hafliger, E. and H. Scholz. 1981. Grass weeds. Volume 2. Documenta. Ciba-Geigy Ltd., Basle, Switzerland.

Hallworth, B. and C.C. Chinnappa. 1997. Plants of Kananaskis Country in the Rocky Mountains of Alberta. University of Alberta Press, Edmonton, Alberta, and University of Calgary Press, Calgary, Alberta.

Harms, V.L. 1983. Chenopodiaceae (goosefoot family). W.P. Fraser Herbarium, University of Saskatchewan, Saskatoon, Saskatchewan. Preliminary Saskatchewan Flora Contribution.

Harms, V.L., J.H. Hudson and G.F. Ledingham. 1986. *Rorippa truncata*, the blunt-fruited yellow cress, new for Canada and *R. tenerrima*, the slender yellow cress, in southern Saskatchewan and Alberta. Canadian Field-Naturalist 100(1):45–51.

Harms, V.L., P.A. Ryan and J.A. Haraldson. 1992. The rare and endangered native vascular plants of Saskatchewan. Saskatchewan Natural History Society, Saskatoon, Saskatchewan.

Harrington, H.D. 1967. Edible native plants of the Rocky Mountains. University of New Mexico Press, Albuquerque, New Mexico.

Haufler, C.H. and M.D. Windham. 1991. New species of North American *Cystopteris* and *Polypodium*, with comments on their reticulate relationships. American Fern Journal 81:7–23.

Hermann, F.J. 1970. Manual of the Carices of the Rocky Mountains and Colorado Basin. United States Department of Agriculture Forest Service, Washington, D.C. Agriculture Handbook No. 374.

Hermann, F.J. 1975. Manual of the rushes (*Juncus* spp.) of the Rocky Mountains and Colorado Basin. United States Department of Agriculture Forest Service, Rocky Mountain Forest and Range Experiment Station, Fort Collins, Colorado. General Technical Report No. RM–18.

Hickman, J.C., ed. 1993. The Jepson manual: higher plants of California. University of California Press, Berkeley, California.

Hinds, H.R. 1983. The rare vascular plants of New Brunswick. National Museum of Natural Sciences, Ottawa, Ontario. Syllogeus No. 50.

Hiratsuka, Y. 1987. Forest tree diseases of the prairie provinces. Canadian Forestry Service, Northern Forest Research Centre, Edmonton, Alberta. Information Report No. NOR–X–286.

Hitchcock, A.S. 1950. Manual of the grasses of the United States. Second edition. Government Printing Office, Washington, D.C. United States Department of Agriculture Publication No. 200.

Hitchcock, C.L. and A. Cronquist. 1973. Flora of the Pacific Northwest: an illustrated manual. University of Washington Press, Seattle, Washington.

Hitchcock, C.L., A. Cronquist, M. Ownbey and J.W. Thompson. 1955–69. Vascular plants of the Pacific Northwest. 5 volumes. University of Washington Press, Seattle, Washington.

Holroyd, G.L., W.B. McGillivray, P.H.R. Stepney, D.M. Ealey, G.C. Trottier and K.E. Eberhart, eds. 1987. Proceedings of the Workshop on Endangered Species in the Prairie Provinces. Natural History Section, Provincial Museum of Alberta, Edmonton, Alberta.

Hosie, R.C. 1979. Native trees of Canada. Fitzhenry & Whiteside Ltd., Markham, Ontario.

Hrapko, J.O. 1989. Prairie spiderwort (*Tradescantia occidentalis*) in Alberta. Iris 4:4.

Hrapko, J.O. 1991. Rare and endangered vascular plants. Provincial Museum of Alberta, Edmonton, Alberta. Natural History Reference List No. 209.

Hudson, J.H. 1977. *Carex* in Saskatchewan. Bison Publishing House, Saskatoon, Saskatchewan.

Hudson, J.H. 1978. *Atriplex powellii* at Cabri Lake. Blue Jay 36(3):137–138.

Hulten, E. 1958. The amphi-Atlantic plants and their phytogeographical connections. Kungliga Svenska Vetenskapsakademiens Handlingar 7:1–340.

Hulten, E. 1968. Flora of Alaska and neighboring territories. Stanford University Press, Stanford, California.

Hulten, E. 1971. The circumpolar plants. Volume 2. Dicotyledons. Kungliga Svenska Vetenskapsakademiens Handlingar 13:1–463.

Hunter, A.A. 1992. Utilization of *Hordeum pusillum* (little barley) in the midwest United States: applying Rindos' co-evolutionary model of domestication. Ph.D. thesis, University of Missouri, Columbia, Missouri.

Hurd, E.G., N.L. Shaw, J. Mastrogiuseppe, L.C. Smithman and S. Goodrich. 1998. Field guide to intermountain sedges. United States Department of Agriculture Forest Service, Rocky Mountain Research Station, Ogden, Utah. General Technical Report No. RMRS–GTR–10.

Jackson, L.E. and L.C. Bliss. 1984. Phenology and water relations of three plant life forms (*Penstemon heterodoxus*, *Polygonum minimum*, *Saxifraga aprica*) in a dry tree-line meadow, Washington. Ecology 65:1302–14.

Johnson, D.M. 1986. Systematics of the New World species of *Marsilea* (Marsileaceae). American Society of Plant Taxonomists, Ann Arbor, Michigan. Systematic Botany Monographs Vol. 11.

Johnson, D., L. Kershaw, A. MacKinnon and J. Pojar. 1995. Plants of the western boreal forest and aspen parkland. Lone Pine Publishing, Edmonton, Alberta.

Johnson, H. and B. Hallworth. 1975. Further discoveries of sand verbena in Alberta. Blue Jay 33(1):13–15.

Johnson, J.D. 1989. Uncommon plants from Ram Mountain, Alberta. Alberta Naturalist 19:31–34.

Johnston, A. 1987. Plants and the Blackfoot. Lethbridge Historical Society, Lethbridge, Alberta. Occasional Paper No. 15.

Jones, V.P., D.W. Davis, S.L. Smith and D.B. Allred. 1989. Phenology of apple maggot (Diptera: Tephritidae) associated with cherry and hawthorn in Utah. Journal of Entomology 83(3):788–92.

Kartesz, J.T. 1994. A synonomized checklist of the vascular flora of the United States, Canada and Greenland. Timber Press, Portland, Oregon.

Kartesz, J.T. and K.N. Gandhi. 1990. Nomenclatural notes for the North American flora. Part 2. Phytologia 68:421–27.

Kelly, I.T. 1932. Ethnography of the Surprise Valley Paiutes. University of California Publications in American Archaeology and Ethnography 31: 67–210.

Kerik, J. and S. Fisher. 1982. Living with the land: use of plants by the native people of Alberta. Provincial Museum of Alberta, Edmonton, Alberta.

Kershaw, L.J. 1976. A phytogeographical survey of rare, endangered, and extinct vascular plants in the Canadian Flora. M.Sc. thesis, University of Waterloo, Waterloo, Ontario.

Kershaw, L.J. and J.K. Morton. 1976. Rare and potentially endangered species in the Canadian flora: a preliminary list of vascular plants. Canadian Botanical Association Bulletin 9(2):26–30.

Kershaw, L.J., A. MacKinnon and J. Pojar. 1998. Plants of the Rocky Mountains. Lone Pine Publishing, Edmonton, Alberta.

Kerstetter, T.A. 1994. Taxonomic Investigation of *Erigeron lackschewitzii*. M.Sc. thesis. Montana State University, Bozeman, Montana.

Klinka, K., V.J. Krajina, A. Ceska and A.M. Scagel. 1989. Indicator plants of coastal British Columbia. University of British Columbia Press, Vancouver, British Columbia.

Kott, L. and D.M. Britton. 1983. Spore morphology and taxonomy of *Isoetes* in northeastern North America. Canadian Journal of Botany 61:3140–63.

Krause, D.L. and K.I. Beamish. 1973. Notes on *Saxifraga occidentalis* and closely related species in British Columbia. Syesis 6:105–13.

Krenzer, E.G. Jr., D.N. Moss and R.K. Crookston. 1975. Carbon dioxide compensation points of flowering plants. Plant Physiology 56: 194–206.

Kuijt, J. 1973. New plant records in Waterton Lakes National Park, Alberta. Canadian Field-Naturalist 87:67–69.

Kuijt, J. 1982. A flora of Waterton Lakes National Park. University of Alberta Press, Edmonton, Alberta.

Kuijt, J. and G.R. Michner. 1985. First record of the bitterroot, *Lewisia rediviva*, in Alberta. Canadian Field Naturalist 99:264–66.

Kuijt, J. and J.A. Trofymow. 1975. Range extensions of two rare Alberta shrubs—Rocky Mountain juniper *(Juniperus scopulorum)* and mock orange (*Philadelphus lewisii*). Blue Jay 33:96–98.

Lackschewitz, K. 1991. Vascular plants of west-central Montana: identification guidebook. United States Department of Agriculture Forest Service, Intermountain Research Station, Ogden, Utah. General Technical Report No. INT–277.

Lamanova, T.G. 1991. *Puccinellia* spp. in halophyte phytocenoses in the Karasuk River valley and their nutritive value. Rastitel'nye Resursy 26: 400–09. (in Russian, translated abstract in Biological Abstracts 91 (11), ref. 114185).

Lancaster, J., ed. 1997. Guidelines for rare plant surveys. Alberta Native Plant Council, Edmonton, Alberta.

Larson, G.E. 1993. Aquatic and wetland vascular plants of the northern great plains. United States Department of Agriculture Forest Service, Rocky Mountain Forest and Range Experiment Station, Fort Collins, Colorado. General Technical Report No. RM–238.

Lauriault, J. 1989. Identification guide to the trees of Canada. Fitzhenry & Whiteside Ltd., Markham, Ontario.

Lee, P.G. 1980. *Boschniakia rossica*, northern ground cone, a vascular plant new to Alberta. Canadian Field-Naturalist 94:341.

Legasy, K., S. LaBelle-Beadman and B. Chambers. 1995. Forest plants of northeastern Ontario. Lone Pine Publishing, Edmonton, Alberta.

Lellinger, D.B. 1981. Notes on North American ferns. American Fern Journal 71:90–94.

Lesica, P. 1985. Checklist of the vascular plants of Glacier National Park, Montana, U.S.A. Monograph No. 4. Montana Academy of Sciences. Supplement to the Proceedings Vol. 44.

Lesica, P. and J.S. Shelly. 1991. Sensitive, threatened and endangered vascular plants of Montana. Montana State Library, Helena, Montana. Occasional Publications of the Montana Natural Heritage Program No. 1.

Lesica, P. and K. Ahlenslager. 1994. Demographic monitoring of three species of *Botrychium* (Ophioglossaceae) in Waterton Lakes National Park, Alberta: 1993 progress report. Division of Biological Sciences, University of Montana, Missoula, Montana.

Lewis, H. and J. Szweykowski. 1964. The genus *Gayophytum* (Onagraceae). Brittonia 16:343–91.

Looman, J. 1982. Prairie grasses identified and described by vegetative characters. Agriculture Canada, Ottawa, Ontario. Publication No. 1413.

Looman, J. and K.F. Best. 1979. Budd's flora of the Canadian prairie provinces. Agriculture Canada Research Branch, Ottawa, Ontario. Publication No. 1662.

Löve, D. 1969. *Papaver* at high altitudes in the Rocky Mountains. Brittonia 21:1–10.

Löve, D. and N.J. Freedman. 1956. A plant collection from the southwestern Yukon. Botaniska Notiser 109:153–211.

Luer, C.A. 1975. The native orchids of the United States and Canada excluding Florida. New York Botanical Garden, Ipswich, New York.

Lyons, C.P. and B. Merilees. 1995. Trees, shrubs and flowers to know in British Columbia and Washington. Lone Pine Publishing, Edmonton, Alberta.

Mabey, R. 1977. Plantcraft: a guide to the everyday use of wild plants. Universe Books, New York, New York.

Macdonald, I.D. and B. Smith. 1995. Status report on the Nebraska sedge (*Carex nebrascensis*) in Canada. Committee on the Status of Endangered Wildlife in Canada, Ottawa, Ontario.

Mackenzie, K.K. 1940. North American Cariceae. 2 volumes. New York Botanical Garden, New York, New York.

MacKinnon, A., J. Pojar and J.R. Coup. 1992. Plants of northern British Columbia. Lone Pine Publishing, Edmonton, Alberta.

Maher, R.V., D.L. White, G.-W. Argus and P.A. Keddy. 1978. The rare vascular plants of Nova Scotia. National Museum of Natural Sciences, Ottawa, Ontario. Syllogeus No. 18.

Maher, R.V., G.W. Argus, V.L. Harms and J.H. Hudson. 1979. The rare vascular plants of Saskatchewan. National Museum of Natural Sciences, Ottawa, Ontario. Syllogeus No. 20.

Maquire, B. 1946. Studies in the Caryophyllaceae: II. *Arenaria nuttallii* and *Arenaria filiorum*, section *Alsini*. Madrono 8:258–63.

Mason, H.L. 1941. The taxonomic status of *Microsteris* Greene. Madrono 6:122–27.

McCone, M.J. 1985. Reproductive biology of several bromegrasses (*Bromus*): breeding system, pattern of fruit maturation, and seed set. American Journal of Botany 72:1334–39.

McCone, M.J. 1989. Intraspecific variation on pollen yield in bromegrass (Poaceae: *Bromus*). American Journal of Botany 76:231–37.

McJannet, C.L., G.W. Argus and W.J. Cody. 1995. Rare vascular plants in the Northwest Territories. Canadian Museum of Nature, Ottawa, Ontario. Syllogeus No. 73.

McJannet, C.L., G.W. Argus, S. Edlund and J. Cayouette. 1993. Rare vascular plants in the Canadian Arctic. Canadian Museum of Natural Sciences, Ottawa, Ontario. Syllogeus No. 72.

McNeill, J. 1980. The delimitation of *Arenaria* (Caryophyllaceae) and related genera in North America, with 11 new combinations in *Minuartia*. Rhodora 82:495–502.

Mitchell, W.W. 1962. Variation and relationships in some rhizomatous species of *Muhlenbergia*. Ph.D. thesis, Iowa State University, Ames, Iowa.

Mohlenbrock, R.H., ed. 1976. The illustrated flora of Illinois. Southern Illinois University Press, Carbondale and Edwardsville, Illinois.

Moore, M. 1979. Medicinal plants of the mountain west. Museum of New Mexico Press, Santa Fe, New Mexico.

Moore, R.J. and C. Frankton. 1967. Cytotaxonomy of foliose thistles (*Cirsium* spp. aff. *C. foliosum*) of western North America. Canadian Journal of Botany 45:1733–49.

Morris, M.S., J.E. Schmautz and P.F. Stickney. 1986. Winter field key to the native shrubs of Montana. Montana Forest and Conservation Experiment Station, Montana State University and Intermountain Forest and Range Experiment Station, United States Department of Agriculture Forest Service, Montana. Bulletin No. 23.

Mosquin, T. and C. Suchal, eds. 1977. Canada's threatened species and habitats: proceedings of the symposium on Canada's threatened species and habitats, May 20–24, 1976, Ottawa, Ontario. Canadian Nature Federation, Ottawa, Ontario. Publication No. 6.

Moss, E. 1944. *Lilaea scilloides* in southeastern Alberta. Rhodora 46:205–06.

Moss, E.H. 1959. Flora of Alberta. University of Toronto Press, Toronto, Ontario.

Moss, E.H. 1983. Flora of Alberta. Second edition. University of Toronto Press, Toronto, Ontario.

Moss, E.H. and G. Pegg. 1963. Noteworthy plant species and communities in west central Alberta. Canadian Journal of Botany 48:1431–37.

Mueggler, W. and W. Stewart. 1980. Grassland and shrubland habitat types of western Montana. United States Department of Agriculture Forest Service, Intermountain Forest and Range Experiment Station, Ogden, Utah. General Technical Report No. INT–66.

Muenscher, W.C. 1944. Aquatic plants of the United States. Cornell University Press, Ithaca, New York.

Mulligan, G. A. 1970. A new species of *Draba* in the Kananaskis range of southwestern Alberta. Canadian Journal of Botany 48:1897– 98.

Mulligan, G.A. 1970. Cytotaxonomic studies of *Draba glabella* and its close allies in Canada and Alaska. Canadian Journal of Botany 48(8):1431–37.

Mulligan, G.A. 1971. Cytotaxonomic studies of *Draba* species of Canada and Alaska: *D. ventosa*, *D. ruaxes*, and *D. paysonii*. Canadian Journal of Botany 49:1455–60.

Mulligan, G.A. 1974. Cytotaxonomic studies of *Draba nivalis* and its close allies in Canada and Alaska. Canadian Journal of Botany 52:1793–1801.

Mulligan, G.A. 1976. The genus *Draba* in Canada and Alaska: key and summary. Canadian Journal of Botany 54:1386–93.

Mulligan, G.A. and D.B. Munro. 1990. Poisonous plants of Canada. Biosystematics Research Centre, Agriculture Canada, Ottawa, Ontario. Publication No. 11842/E.

Murray, D.F. 1970. *Carex podocarpa* and its allies in North America. Canadian Journal of Botany 48:313–24.

Nelson, J.R. 1984. Rare plant field survey guidelines. J.P. Smith and R. York, eds. Inventory of rare and endangered vascular plants of California. Third edition. California Native Plant Society, Berkeley, California.

Nelson, J.R. 1986. Rare plant surveys: techniques for impact assessment. Natural Areas Journal 5(3):18–30.

Nelson, J.R. 1987. Rare plant surveys: techniques for impact assessment. Pages 159–66 in T.S. Elias, ed. Conservation and management of rare and endangered plants. California Native Plant Society, Sacramento, California.

Newmaster, S.G., A.G. Harris and L.J. Kershaw. 1997. Wetland plants of Ontario. Lone Pine Publishing, Edmonton, Alberta.

Niehaus, T.F. and C.L. Ripper. 1976. A field guide to the Pacific states wildflowers. Houghton Mifflin Co., New York, New York.

Nilsson, O. 1971. Studies in *Montia* L. and *Claytonia* L. and allied genera. Part 5. The genus *Montiastrum* (Gray) Rydb. Botaniska Notiser 124:119–214.

Ogilvie, R.T. 1962. Notes on plant distribution in the Rocky Mountains. Canadian Journal of Botany. 40:1091–94.

Packer, J.G. 1972. A taxonomic and phytogeographic review of some arctic and alpine *Senecio* species. Canadian Journal of Botany 50:507–18.

Packer, J.G. 1993. Two new combinations in *Triantha* (Liliaceae). Novon 3:278–79.

Packer, J.G. and C.E. Bradley. 1984. A checklist of the rare vascular plants of Alberta. Provincial Museum of Alberta, Edmonton, Alberta. Natural History Occasional Paper No. 5.

Packer, J.G. and M.G. Dumais. 1972. Additions to the flora of Alberta. Canadian Field-Naturalist 86:269–74.

Packer, J.G. and D.H. Vitt. 1974. Mountain Park: a plant refugium in the Canadian Rocky Mountains. Canadian Journal of Botany 52:1393–1409.

Parish, R., R. Coupe and D. Lloyd. 1996. Plants of southern interior British Columbia. Lone Pine Publishing, Edmonton, Alberta.

Pavlik, L. 1995. *Bromus* L. of North America. Royal British Columbia Museum, Victoria, British Columbia.

Peterson, L.A. 1977. A field guide to edible wild plants of eastern and central North America. Houghton Mifflin Co., New York, New York.

Peterson, R.T. and M. McKenny. 1968. Northeastern wildflowers: a fieldguide to wildflowers. Houghton Mifflin Co., New York, New York.

Petrides, G.A. 1992. A fieldguide to western trees, western United States and Canada. Houghton Mifflin Co., New York, New York.

Petrie, W. 1981. Guide to orchids of North America. Hancock House, Vancouver, British Columbia.

Pohl, R.W. 1969. *Muhlenbergia*, subgenus *Muhlenbergia* (Gramineae) in North America. American Midland Naturalist 82:512–42.

Polunin, N. 1959. Circumpolar arctic flora. Clarendon Press, Oxford, England.

Porsild, A.E. 1959. Botanical excursion to Jasper and Banff national parks, Alberta. National Museum of Canada, Ottawa, Ontario.

Porsild, A.E. 1964. Illustrated flora of the Canadian Arctic Archipelago. Second edition. National Museums of Canada, Ottawa, Ontario. Bulletin No. 146.

Porsild, A.E. and W.J. Cody. 1980. Vascular plants of continental Northwest Territories, Canada. National Museum of Natural Sciences, National Museums of Canada, Ottawa, Ontario.

Porsild, A.E. and D.T. Lid. 1979. Rocky Mountain wildflowers. National Museum of Natural Sciences, National Museums of Canada, Ottawa, Ontario.

Potter, M. 1996. Central Rockies wildflowers. Luminous Press, Banff, Alberta.

Primack, R.B. 1980. Phenotypic variation of rare and widespread species of *Plantago*. Rhodora 82:87–95.

Purdy, B.G. and S.E. Macdonald. 1992. Status report on the sand stitchwort (*Stellaria arenicola* Raup.) in Canada. Committee on the Status of Endangered Wildlife in Canada, Ottawa, Ontario.

Purdy, B.G., R.J. Bayer and S.E. MacDonald. 1994. Genetic variation, breeding system evolution, and conservation of the narrow sand dune endemic *Stellaria arenicola* and the widespread *S. longipes* (Caryophyllaceae). American Journal of Botany 81(7):904–11.

Rabinowitz, D. 1981. Seven forms of rarity. The biological aspects of rare plant conservation. H. Synge, ed. John Wiley and Sons Ltd., New York, New York.

Ramaley, F. 1939. Sand hill vegetation of northeastern Colorado. Ecological Monographs 9:1–51.

Raven, P. 1969. A revision of the genus *Camissonia* (Onagraceae). Smithsonian Institute Press, Washington, D.C.

Raven, P. and D. Moore. 1965. A revision of *Boisduvalia* (Onagraceae). Brittonia 17:238–54.

Reddoch, J.M. and A.H. Reddoch. The orchids in the Ottawa district. Canadian Field-Naturalist 111(1):165–67.

Reynolds, D.N. 1984. Alpine annual plants: phenology, germination, photosynthesis, and growth of three Rocky Mountain species (*Koenigia islandica, Polygonum confertiflorum, Polygonum douglasii*). Ecology 65:759–66.

Reynolds, D.N. 1984. Population dynamics of three annual species of alpine plants in the Rocky Mountains (*Koenigia islandica, Polygonum confertiflorum, Polygonum douglasii*). Oecologia 62:250–55.

Ritchie, J.C. 1956. The vegetation of northern Manitoba. Part 1. Studies in the southern spruce forest zone. Canadian Journal of Botany 34:523–61.

Robertson, A. 1984. *Carex* of Newfoundland. Canadian Forestry Service, Newfoundland Forest Research Centre, St. John's, Newfoundland. Information Report No. N–X–219.

Rollins, R.C. 1993. The Cruciferae of continental North America. Stanford University Press, Stanford, California.

Romuld, M.A. 1991. Rare plants of Dinosaur Provincial Park, Alberta. Alberta Naturalist 21:16–22.

Rossbach, R.P. 1940. *Spergularia* in North and South America. Rhodora 42:57–83, 105–43, 158–93, 203–13.

Russell, W.B. 1979. Survey of native trees and shrubs on disturbed lands in the eastern slopes. Alberta Forest Service, Edmonton, Alberta.

Rydberg, P.A. 1932. Flora of the prairies and plains of central North America. Hafner Publishing Co., New York, New York.

Rydberg, P.A. 1969. Flora of the Rocky Mountains and adjacent plains. Second edition. Hafner Publishing Co., New York, New York.

Savile, D.B.O. 1969. Interrelationships of *Ledum* species and their rust parasites in western Canada and Alaska. Canadian Journal of Botany 47:1085–1100.

Savile, D.B.O. 1972. Arctic adaptations in plants. Canada Department of Agriculture Research Branch, Ottawa, Ontario. Monograph No. 6.

Savile, D.B.O. 1975. Evolution and biogeography of Saxifragaceae with guidance from their rust parasites. Annals of the Missouri Botanical Garden 62:354–61.

Schemske, D.W., B.C. Husband, M.H. Ruckelshaus, C. Goodwillie, I.M. Parker and J.G. Bishop. 1994. Evaluation approaches to the conservation of rare and endangered plants. Ecology 75(3):584–606.

Schofield, J.J. 1989. Discovering wild plants: Alaska, western Canada, the Northwest. Alaska Northwest Books, Anchorage, Alaska.

Schofield, W.B. 1959. The salt marsh vegetation of Churchill, Manitoba, and its phytogeographic implications. National Museum of Canada Bulletin 160:107–32.

Scoggan, H.J. 1979. Flora of Canada. 4 volumes. National Museum of Natural Sciences, Ottawa, Ontario. Publications in Botany No. 7.

Scotter, G.W. and H. Flygare. 1986. Wildflowers of the Canadian Rockies. Hurtig Publishers, Edmonton, Alberta.

Scotter, G.W. and J.H. Hudson. 1975. *Carex illota* L.H. Bailey in Alberta. Canadian Field-Naturalist 89:74–75.

Sczawinski, A.F. and N.J. Turner. 1980. Wild green vegetables of Canada. National Museum of Natural Sciences, Ottawa, Ontario.

Shaw, K. 1966. A new species of *Oxytropis* in Alberta. Blue Jay 24:40.

Shaw, P.J. and D. On. 1979. Plants of Waterton–Glacier national parks and the northern Rockies. Mountain Press Publishing Company, Missoula, Montana.

Shay, J.M. 1974. Preliminary list of endangered and rare species in Manitoba. University of Manitoba Botany Department, Winnipeg, Manitoba.

Slack, A. 1979. Carnivorous plants. The MIT Press, Cambridge, Massachusetts.

Smith, B.M. 1992. Status report on the Kananaskis whitlow-cress (*Draba kananaskis*) in Canada. Committee on the Status of Endangered Wildlife in Canada, Ottawa, Ontario.

Smith, B.M. 1992. Status report on the slender mouse-ear-cress (*Halimolobos virgata* (Nutt.) O.E. Schulz) in Canada. Committee on the Status of Endangered Wildlife in Canada, Ottawa, Ontario.

Smith, B.M. 1993. Status report on the little barley (*Hordeum pusillum*) in Canada. Committee on the Status of Endangered Wildlife in Canada, Ottawa, Ontario.

Smith, B.M. 1994. Status report on blue phlox (*Phlox alyssifolia* Greene) in Canada. Committee on the Status of Endangered Wildlife in Canada, Ottawa, Ontario.

Smith, B.M. 1994. Status report on dwarf fleabane *(Erigeron radicatus* Hook.) in Canada. Committee on the Status of Endangered Wildlife in Canada, Ottawa, Ontario.

Smith, B.M. 1995. Status report on the hare-footed locoweed (*Oxytropis lagopus* Nutt.) in Canada. Committee on the Status of Endangered Wildlife in Canada, Ottawa, Ontario.

Smith, B.M. 1996. Status report on the rush pink (*Stephanomeria runcinata*) in Canada. Committee on the Status of Endangered Wildlife in Canada, Ottawa, Ontario.

Smith, B.M. 1997. Status report on tiny cryptanth (*Cryptantha minima*) in Canada. Committee on the Status of Endangered Wildlife in Canada, Ottawa, Ontario.

Smith, B.M. and C. Bradley. 1992. Status report on sand verbena (*Abronia micrantha* Torr.) in Canada. Committee on the Status of Endangered Wildlife in Canada, Ottawa, Ontario.

Smith, B.M. and C. Bradley. 1992. Status report of smooth goosefoot (*Chenopodium subglabrum* (S. Wats.) A. Nels.) in Canada. Committee on the Status of Endangered Wildlife in Canada, Ottawa, Ontario.

Smith, B.M. and C. Bradley. 1992. Status report on the western spiderwort (*Tradescantia occidentalis* (Britt) Smyth) in Canada. Committee on the Status of Endangered Wildlife in Canada, Ottawa, Ontario.

Smith, B.W. 1968. Cytogeography and cytotaxonomic relationships of *Rumex paucifolius*. American Journal of Botany 55:673–83.

Smithsonian Institution. 1975. Report on endangered and threatened plant species of the United States. United States Government Printing Office. Washington, D.C. Serial No. 94–A.

Smreciu, E.A. and R.S. Currah. 1989. A guide to the native orchids of Alberta. University of Alberta Devonian Botanic Garden, Edmonton, Alberta.

Smreciu, E.A., J. Hobden and R. Hermesh. 1992. A checklist of the vascular flora in the vicinity of the Oldman River Dam. Alberta Environmental Centre, Vegreville, Alberta.

Soper, J.H. and M.L. Heimburger. 1982. Shrubs of Ontario. Royal Ontario Museum, Toronto, Ontario.

Soreng, R.J., J.I. Davis and J.J. Doyle. 1990. A phylogenetic analysis of chloroplast DNA restriction site variation in Poaceae subfam. Pooideae. Plant Systematics and Evolution 172:83–97.

Stearn, W.T. 1966. Botanical Latin. Thomas Nelson and Sons (Canada) Ltd., Don Mills, Ontario.

Stearn, W.T. 1983. Botanical Latin: history, grammar, syntax, terminology and vocabulary. Third revised edition. David and Charles, Vermont.

Steyermark, J.A. 1963. Flora of Missouri. Iowa State University Press, Ames, Iowa.

Stoddart, L.A. 1941. The Palouse grassland association in northern Utah. Ecology 22:158–63.

Straley, G.B., R.L. Taylor and G.W. Douglas. 1985. The rare vascular plants of British Columbia. National Museum of Natural Sciences, Ottawa, Ontario. Syllogeus No. 59.

Stubbendieck, J., S.L. Hatch and K.J. Kjar. 1982. North American range plants. Second edition. University of Nebraska Press, Lincoln, Nebraska.

Stuckey, R. 1972. Taxonomy and distribution of the genus *Rorippa* (Cruciferae) in North America. Sida 4:279–428.

Stutz, H.C. and L. Pope. 1973. The origin of spreading wheatgrass (*Agropyron scribneri* Vasey). Proceedings of the Western Grass Breeders Work Planning Conference, Kansas State University, Manhattan, Kansas.

Svenson, H.K. 1957. *Eleocharis*. North American Flora 18(9):509–40.

Szczawinski, A.F. 1975. Orchids of British Columbia. British Columbia Provincial Museum, Victoria, British Columbia.

Tannas, K. 1997. Common plants of the western rangelands. 2 volumes. Lethbridge Community College, Lethbridge, Alberta.

Taylor, R. 1965. The genus *Lithophragma* (Saxifragaceae). University of California Publications in Botany 37:1–122.

Taylor, R.L. and B. MacBride. 1977. Vascular plants of British Columbia: a descriptive resource inventory. University of British Columbia Press, Vancouver, British Columbia.

Taylor, T.M.C. 1970. Pacific Northwest ferns and their allies. University of Toronto Press, Toronto, Ontario, and University of British Columbia Press, Vancouver, British Columbia.

Taylor, T.M.C. 1983. The sedge family of British Columbia. British Columbia Provincial Museum, Victoria, British Columbia. Handbook No. 43.

Tingley, D. 1987. Endangered plants in Alberta: alternatives for legal protection. Pages 115–18 in G.L. Holroyd et al., eds. Proceedings of the Workshop on Endangered Species in the Prairie Provinces. Provincial Museum of Alberta, Edmonton, Alberta. Natural History Occasional Paper No. 9.

Tisdale, E.W. and A.C. Budd. 1948. Range extensions for three grasses in western Canada. Canadian Field-Naturalist 62:173–75.

Turner, B.L. 1956. A cytotaxonomic study of the genus *Hymenopappus* (Compositae). Rhodora 58:208–42.

Turner, N.J. 1978. Food plants of British Columbia Indians. Part 2. Interior Peoples. Royal British Columbia Museum, Victoria, British Columbia.

Uhl, C.H. 1977. Cytogeography of *Sedum lanceolatum* and its relatives. Rhodora 79:95–114.

Uphof, J.C. 1968. Dictionary of economic plants. Verlag Von J. Cramer, New York, New York.

Viereck, L.A. and E.L. Little, Jr. 1972. Alaska trees and shrubs. United States Department of Agriculture, Washington, DC. Agriculture Handbook No. 410.

Vitt, D.H. and R.J. Belland. 1996. Attributes of rarity among Alberta mosses: patterns and prediction of species diversity. The Bryologist 100(1):1–12.

Voss, E.G. 1972. Michigan flora. Part 1. Gymnosperms and monocots. Cranbrook Institute of Science, Bloomfield Hills, Michigan. Bulletin No. 55.

Voss, E.G. 1985. Michigan Flora. Part 2. Dicots (Saururaceae–Cornaceae). Cranbrook Institute of Science, Bloomfield Hills, Michigan. Bulletin No. 59.

Wagner, W.H., Jr. and F.S. Wagner. 1981. Three new species of moonworts, *Botrychium* subg. *Botrychium* (Ophioglossaceae), from North America. American Fern Journal 71:20–30.

Wagner, W.H., Jr. and F.S. Wagner. 1983. Genus communities as a systematic tool in the study of New World *Botrychium* (Ophioglossaceae). Taxon 32:51–63.

Wagner, W.H., Jr. and F.S. Wagner. 1983. Two moonworts of the Rocky Mountains: *Botrychium hesperium* and a new species formerly confused with it. American Fern Journal 73:53–62.

Wagner, W.H., Jr. and F.S. Wagner. 1986. Three new species of moonworts (*Botrychium* subg. *Botrychium*) endemic in western North America. American Fern Journal 76:33–47.

Wagner, W.H., Jr. and F.S. Wagner. 1990. Moonworts (*Botrychium* subg. *Botrychium*) of the upper Great Lakes region, United States and Canada, with descriptions of two new species. Contributions of the University of Michigan Herbarium 17:313–25.

Wagner, W.H., Jr., F.S. Wagner, C.H. Haufler and J.L. Emerson. 1984. A new nothospecies of moonwort (Ophioglossaceae, *Botrychium*). Canadian Journal of Botany 62:629–34.

Wallis, C. 1977. Preliminary lists of the rare flora and fauna of Alberta. Alberta Provincial Parks, Edmonton, Alberta.

Wallis, C. 1987. Critical, threatened and endangered habitats in Alberta. Pages 49–63 in G.L. Holroyd et al., eds. Proceedings of the Workshop on Endangered Species in the Prairie Provinces. Provincial Museum of Alberta, Edmonton, Alberta. Natural History Occasional Paper No. 9.

Wallis, C. 1987. The rare vascular flora of Alberta. Volume 2. A summary of the taxa occurring in the grasslands, parkland and boreal forest. Cottonwood Consultants Ltd., Calgary, Alberta. Alberta Forestry, Lands and Wildlife, Edmonton, Alberta. Publication No. T/164.

Wallis, C. and C. Bradley. 1989. Status report on the western blue flag (*Iris missouriensis* Nutt.). Committee on the Status of Endangered Wildlife in Canada, Ottawa, Ontario.

Wallis, C. and C. Wershler. 1988. Rare wildlife and plant conservation studies in sandhill and sand plain habitats of southern Alberta. Alberta Forestry, Lands and Wildlife, Edmonton, Alberta. Publication No. T/176.

Wallis, C., C. Bradley, M. Fairbarns and V. Loewen. 1987. The rare flora of Alberta. Volume 3. Species summary sheets. Alberta Energy, Forestry, Lands and Wildlife, Edmonton, Alberta. Publication No. T/155.

Wallis, C., M. Fairbarns, V. Loewen and C. Bradley. 1987. The rare flora of Alberta. Volume 4. Bibliography. Alberta Energy, Forestry, Lands and Wildlife, Edmonton, Alberta. Publication No. T/155.

Wallis, C., C. Bradley, M. Fairbarns, J. Packer and C. Wershler. 1986. Pilot rare plant monitoring program in the Oldman regional plan area of southwestern Alberta. Alberta Forestry, Lands and Wildlife, Edmonton, Alberta. Publication No. T/148.

Weber, W.A. 1990. Colorado flora: eastern slope. University Press of Colorado, Niwot, Colorado.

Welsh, S.L. 1974. Anderson's flora of Alaska and adjacent parts of Canada. Brigham Young University Press, Provo, Utah.

White, D.J. and K.L. Johnson. 1980. The rare vascular plants of Manitoba. National Museums of Canada, Ottawa, Ontario. Syllogeus No. 27.

White, H.R. 1979. Endangered—*Cypripedium montanum*. Alberta Naturalist 9, Supplement 1:1.

Whiting, R.E. and P.M. Catling. 1986. Orchids of Ontario. The Canadian Collections Foundation, Ottawa, Ontario.

Whitney, S. 1989. The Audubon Society nature guides. Western forests. Random House of Canada Ltd., Toronto, Ontario.

Wilkinson, K. 1987. The mountain lady's-slipper in Alberta: concerns and recommendations for an endangered plant species. Alberta Forestry, Lands and Wildlife, Edmonton, Alberta. Publication No. T/157.

Wilkinson, K. 1990. Trees and shrubs of Alberta. Lone Pine Publishing, Edmonton, Alberta.

Willard, T. 1992. Edible and medicinal plants of the Rocky Mountains and neighbouring territories. Wild Rose College of Natural Healing, Calgary, Alberta.

Williams, J.G. and A.E. Williams. 1983. Field guide to the orchids of North America. Universe Books, New York, New York.

Willms, W.D. and J.F. Dormaar, eds. 1996. Proceedings of the fourth prairie conservation and endangered species workshop, February 1995 at the University of Lethbridge and Lethbridge Community College, Lethbridge, Alberta. Curatorial Section, Provincial Museum of Alberta, Edmonton, Alberta.

Windham, M.D. 1993. New taxa and nomenclatural changes in the North American fern flora. Contributions of the University of Michigan Herbarium 19:31–61.

Wiseman, E.F. and S.J. Hurst. 1980. Pictures and descriptions of selected seeds not illustrated in Agriculture Handbook 30. Journal of Seed Technology 5(1):1–16.

Wolf, S.J., J.G. Packer and K.E. Denford. 1979. The taxonomy of *Minuartia rossii* (Caryophyllaceae). Canadian Journal of Botany 57:1673–86.

Wong, S.Y., Y. Oshima, J. Pezzuto, H. Fong and N. Farnsworth. 1986. Plant anticancer agents—Triterpenes from *Iris missouriensis*: Iridaceae. Journal of Pharmaceutical Sciences 75(3): 317–20.

Wood, C.E., Jr. 1972. Morphology and phytogeography: the classical approach to the study of disjunctions. Annals of the Missouri Botanical Garden 59:107–24.

All line drawings reproduced in this volume are used by permission of the rights holders.

Pages 337, 338: Aiken, S.G. and S.J. Darbyshire. Fescue grasses of Canada. Biosystematics Research Centre. Research Branch, Agriculture Canada, Ottawa, Ontario. Publication No. 1844/E.

Page 65 (bottom): Bassett, I.J., C.W. Crompton, J. McNeill and P.M. Taschereau. 1983. The genus *Atriplex* (Chenopodiaceae) in Canada. Agriculture Canada, Ottawa, Ontario.

Pages 29 (top), 34: Brayshaw, C.T. 1985. Pondweeds and bur-reeds, and their relatives. British Columbia Provincial Museum, Victoria, BC. Occasional Papers of the British Columbia Museum No. 26.

Pages 11, 15: Brayshaw, C.T. 1996. Catkin-bearing plants of British Columbia. Second edition. British Columbia Provincial Museum, Victoria, BC. Occasional Papers of the British Columbia Museum No. 18.

Pages 77 (bottom), 96 (middle), 118 (middle), 138, 265, 308, 320 (bottom), 354: Cody, W.J. 1996. Flora of the Yukon Territory. NRC Research Press, Ottawa, Ontario.

Page 370: Cody, W.J. and D.M. Britton. 1989. Ferns and fern allies of Canada. Research Branch, Agriculture Canada. Ottawa, Ontario. Publication No. 1829/E.

Pages 231 (bottom), 239: Douglas, G.W. 1995. The sunflower family (Asteraceae) of British Columbia. Volume 2. British Columbia Provincial Museum, Victoria, BC.

Pages 291 (top), 292 (right), 334 (bottom): Douglas, G.W., G.B. Straley and D.V. Meidinger. 1998. Rare Native Vascular Plants of British Columbia. BC Environment, Victoria, BC.

Pages 60 (bottom), 75, 78 (bottom), 356: Douglas, G.W., D. Meidinger and J. Pojar. 1998–2000. Illustrated flora of British Columbia. 5 volumes. BC Ministry of Environment, Lands and Parks and BC Ministry of Forestry, Victoria, BC.

Page 230: Evert, E.F. 1984. A new species of *Antennaria* (Asteraceae) from Montana and Wyoming. Madrono 13(2):109-112.

Pages 33 (top), 54 (top, bottom), 67 (bottom), 77 (middle), 175, 176, 211, 235, 263 (bottom), 272 (bottom), 290: Gleason, H.A. 1952. The Britton & Brown illustrated flora of the northeastern United States and adjacent Canada. Hafner Press, New York, New York.

Page 285: Hermann, F.J. 1970. Manual of the Carices of the Rocky Mountains and Colorado Basin. United States Department of Agriculture Forest Service, Washington, D.C. Agriculture Handbook No. 374.

Pages 5, 6, 7, 8, 9, 24, 31, 32, 33 (bottom), 35, 36, 37, 38, 39, 40 (top, bottom), 41 (top, bottom), 43, 44, 45, 46 (top, bottom), 47, 50, 53 (top, bottom), 55, 259 (top, bottom), 260, 261, 263 (top), 266 (top, bottom), 267, 268 (top), 269, 270 (bottom), 274, 275, 276, 278, 282, 283 (top), 286 (top, bottom), 292 (left), 293, 294 (top), 295, 296, 297 (top), 298, 299, 300, 301, 302, 305 (top), 307, 309 (top, bottom), 310, 311, 312 (top), 313, 314, 315 (top), 316, 317, 318 (top, bottom), 320 (top, middle), 321 (top, bottom), 323, 324 (top), 325, 326 (top, bottom), 327, 328, 329, 330 (left, right), 331, 332, 333 (top, bottom), 334 (top), 335, 336 (top, bottom), 339, 340 (top, bottom), 342, 343, 344, 345 (top, bottom), 349 (bottom), 350 (bottom), 351, 352 (top, bottom), 353 (top right, middle), 359, 360, 361, 363, 365, 367 (top, bottom), 369, 371, 378, 379, 384: Hitchcock, C.L. et al. 1955–69. Vascular plants of the Pacific Northwest. University of Washington Press, Seattle, Washington. Volume 1.

Pages 10, 13 (bottom), 14, 16, 59, 60 (top), 62, 63, 64, 65 (top), 66 (bottom), 67 (top), 68, 69, 71, 73 (top), 74 (top, bottom), 79, 80 (top, bottom), 81 (top, bottom), 82 (top), 83 (top, bottom), 85, 86 (top), 87 (top, bottom), 90, 92, 93, 94, 95 (top, bottom), 97, 101, 102, 103, 104, 105, 108, 109 (bottom), 111, 114: Hitchcock, C.L. et al. 1955–69. Vascular plants of the Pacific Northwest. University of Washington Press, Seattle, Washington. Volume 2.

Pages 17, 18, 20, 21, 116 (bottom), 117, 118 (top, bottom), 120 (top, bottom), 121, 122, 123 (top, bottom), 124, 125, 126 (top, bottom), 128, 129 (top, bottom), 130 (bottom), 131, 132 (top), 133 (top, bottom), 134, 135, 137, 139 (top, bottom), 140, 141, 144, 145 (top, bottom), 146, 147, 148, 151, 152, 153, 154 (top), 154 (bottom), 156 (top, bottom), 157 (top, bottom), 158, 159, 160, 161, 162: Hitchcock, C.L. et al. 1955–69. Vascular plants of the Pacific Northwest. University of Washington Press, Seattle, Washington. Volume 3.

Pages 23 (top, bottom), 164, 168, 169 (bottom), 170, 171, 172 (top), 174, 177 (right), 179, 180, 181, 182, 183, 184, 185 (top), 186, 187 (bottom), 188, 189, 190, 191, 192, 193 (top, bottom), 194, 195, 196 (top, bottom), 197 (top, bottom), 198, 199, 200 (bottom), 202, 205 (top, bottom), 209, 210, 212, 213, 214 (top), 383, 385: Hitchcock, C.L. et al. 1955–69. Vascular plants of the Pacific Northwest. University of Washington Press, Seattle, Washington. Volume 4.

Pages 25, 215, 216, 217 (top), 218 (bottom), 219 (bottom), 220 (top, bottom), 223, 224 (bottom), 227, 228, 233 (top, bottom), 234, 236, 237, 238, 240, 241, 242 (bottom), 244, 245 (top, bottom), 246, 247, 248, 250 (left, right), 251, 252 (top, bottom), 253, 255, 388: Hitchcock, C.L. et al. 1955–69. Vascular plants of the Pacific Northwest. University of Washington Press, Seattle, Washington. Volume 5.

Pages 86 (bottom), 88 (bottom), 107, 155, 268 (bottom), 272 (top): Hultén, E. 1968. Flora of Alaska and neighboring territories. Stanford University Press. Stanford, California.

Page 178: Kujit, J. 1982. The flora of Waterton Lakes National Park. University of Alberta Press, Edmonton, Alberta.

Page 70: Looman, J. and K.F. Best. Budd's Flora of the Canadian prairie provinces. Research Branch, Agriculture Canada, Ottawa, Ontario. Publication No. 1662.

Pages 30, 61, 78 (top), 98, 106, 113, 132 (bottom), 136, 163 (bottom), 167 (bottom), 173, 203, 206, 208, 225 (right), 262, 264: Porsild, A.E. and W.J. Cody. Vascular plants of Northwest Territories, Canada. National Museum of Natural Sciences, National Museums of Canada, Ottawa, Ontario.

Pages 277 (top, bottom), 281 (bottom), 283 (bottom), 284 (top, bottom), 287, 291 (bottom), 294 (bottom), 297 (bottom), 303, 305 (bottom): MacKenzie, Kenneth K. The Cariceae of North America. New York Botanical Garden, Bronx, New York.

Pages 29 (bottom), 130 (top), 312 (bottom), 315 (bottom), 349 (top), 353 (top left): Holmgren, N.H. 1998. Illustrated companion to Gleason and Cronquist's manual of northeastern United States and adjacent Canada. New York Botanical Garden. Bronx, New York.

Pages 376, 377, 380, 381, 382, 386, 387, 439–50: courtesy of Linda Kershaw.

Pages 12, 13 (top), 19, 22, 42, 48, 49, 52, 56, 66 (top), 68 (top), 72, 73 (bottom), 76, 77 (top), 82 (bottom), 84, 89, 91, 96 (bottom), 99, 100 (top, bottom), 109 (top), 110, 112, 115, 116 (top), 119, 127, 142, 143, 150, 165, 166, 167 (top), 169 (top), 172 (bottom), 177 (left), 185 (bottom), 187 (top), 200 (top), 201, 204, 207, 214 (bottom), 217 (bottom), 218 (bottom), 219 (top), 221, 222, 225 (left), 226, 229, 231 (top), 232, 242 (top), 243, 249, 264 (top), 270 (top), 273, 279, 280, 281 (top), 288, 289 (top, bottom), 304, 306, 319, 324 (bottom), 341, 350 (top), 353 (bottom), 362 (top, bottom), 364, 366 (top, bottom), 368: John R. Maywood, courtesy of ANHIC.

Pages 355 (top, middle, bottom), 357 (top, middle, bottom), 358 (top, bottom): courtesy of D. Wagner.

Pages 51, 96 (top), 149, 163 (top), 224 (top), 254, 269 (top), 322: courtesy of Joan Williams.

Photo Credits

All photographs reproduced in this volume are used by permission of the rights holders. Photograph sources are identified by initials running alongside the photograph.

AL	A. Landals
BH	Bonnie Heidel
BM	Bob Moseley
CWa	Cliff Wallis
DG	Dierdrie Griffiths
DJ	Derek Johnson
ES	Kathy Tannas
GCT	G.C. Trottier
JD	Joseph Duft
JG	Joyce Gould
JH	Julie Hrapko
JJ	John Joy
JL	Jane Lancaster
JP	Jim Pojar
JR	John Rintoul
JS	J. Smith
JV	Jim Vanderhorst
LA	Lorna Allen
LK	Linda Kershaw
PA	Peter Achuff
PL	Peter Lesica
PLe	Peter Lee
RB	R. Bird
SM	S. Myers
SMB	Montana Natural Heritage Program
SS	Steve Shelly
SW	Steve Wirt
SZ	S.C. Zoltai
TC	Terry Clayton
TD	Teresa Dolman
TK	Tulli Kerststetter
TT	T.W. Thormin
WJC	W.J. Crins
WLNP	Waterton Lakes National Park
WM	William Merilees
WW	Warren Wagner

Peter Achuff

Lorna Allen

G. Holroyd
Elisabeth Beaubien

Cheryl Bradley

Dana Bush

Patsy Cotterill

Dave Downing

Dave Ealey

Gina Fryer

Graham Griffiths

Coral Grove

Julie Hrapko

Duke Hunter

Ruth Johnson

Kim Krause

Peter Lee

Dan MacIssac

Karen Mann

Heather Mansell

Marge Meijer

Christie Sarafinchin

Arthur (Art) G. Schwarz

Cindy Verbeek

Dragomir Vujnovic

Ksenija Vujnovic

Cliff Wallis

Anne Weerstra

Kathleen Wilkinson

Joan Williams

Bill Richards

LINDA KERSHAW

Linda's interest in rare species began in 1976 with her MSc thesis on rare and endangered Canadian plants. Over the past 25 years, her work has focussed on biophysical inventories in the Yukon, NWT and Alberta. She has authored and contributed to many field guides and papers. Linda now works as a writer and editor when not pursuing her two favourite pastimes: photography and illustration.

JOYCE GOULD

Joyce Gould is currently employed as a biologist with Alberta Environment where she works on protected areas issues and as the botanist with the Alberta Natural Heritage Information Centre (ANHIC). She has conducted plant surveys in Alberta, Ontario, Yukon and Nunavut. Joyce has a BSc in Botany from the University of Alberta and her MSc from the University of Toronto.

DEREK JOHNSON

Derek is a lifetime resident of Alberta. He received his MSc in botany from the University of Calgary. He is currently employed by the Canadian Forest Service in Edmonton where he is a plant taxonomist and ecologist and curates the herbarium at the Northern Forestry Centre. His work has taken him to the arctic, as well as many years studying peatlands in the boreal forest of the prairie provinces.

Ian MacDonald

JANE LANCASTER

An independent consulting botanist, Jane holds a Bsc in plant biology from the University of Calgary. She lives with her husband and family near Cochrane, Alberta.